ROBIN HOOD,
AND THE OUTLAWS OF SHERWOOD FOREST.

ROBIN HOOD AND THE BEGGAR.

INTRODUCTION.

"Come, listen to me, ye gentlemen,
    That be of freeborn blood,
I shall tell you of a good yeoman,
    His name was Robin Hood."—*Old Ballad.*

No country in the world ever produced a hero whose memory has lived through so many ages as that of Sherwood's forester—bold Robin Hood.

Much has been written about his doings, but among the many versions there has been but a slight sprinkling of the true life of this remarkable outlaw.

Endeared to the youth of England by the old songs, quotations, games and proverbs which a few centuries since were made to his remembrance, it is surprising that the modern versions of his life, except in one or two instances, should be so totally at variance with the truth.

The old ballads, it must be admitted, were

No. 1.

rude in composition, and faulty in the sequence of sound, which falls so harmoniously upon the ears.

But they suited our sturdy ancestors, for they expressed in good Saxon language a love of all that is manly and brave, and a contempt for all that is cowardly and mean; thus, they appealed to the hearts of the freeborn, manly youth of England, taught them to aid the oppressed, yet at times soared into the regions of romance, and stamped on every line the most prominent traits of the gallant hero whose life they pourtrayed.

This story of the remarkable outlaw's life claims precedence above the recent versions, upon account of the immense research the writer has had among the ancient manuscripts and pamphlets, some of the latter dating as early as the first introduction of printing in this country.

Among these may be mentioned Wynken de Worde's black letter pamphlets, Ritson's Critical Edition, and the "Lytell Geste" of Robin Hood.

Long and patient has been the study to separate the dross from the metal; but now the task is ended, and the bold yeoman, who has been erroneously termed a robber, will be shown in his true character of one who hated, with a thorough Saxon hate, the Norman oppressors of the English nation; for Robin, when all else bent the knee to a Norman king, betook himself to Sherwood Forest, and kept up an incessant and predatory warfare against the Norman tyrants and enslavers of the people.

With this preface we commend our work, not to the critic, but to the youthful lovers of manly worth and gallant deeds.

CHAPTER I.

ROBIN HOOD, EARL OF HUNTINGDON.

Forth went this gentle knight,
In very rueful case;
The tears out of his eyes did run,
And fell upon his face.

MAY-DAY in the reign of Henry III.—the year one thousand, two hundred, and sixty-five; scene: a massive castle, towering proudly above the scattered dwellings which lay among the trees.

Facing the drawbridge was a broad expanse of level ground, in the centre of this was the May-pole, adorned with alternate stripes of white and black, and festooned with Flora's early productions.

Around this joyous emblem of the coming summer were congregated the villagers, old and young, and among them could be seen scores of men-at-arms, their helmets reflecting back the sun's rays in glittering discs.

The battlemented castle was the stronghold of a Saxon earl, and this merry-making was in keeping with the good old English customs, for opposite the flower-bedecked archway of the castle were a dozen targets, and some fifty yards to the right the prizes which were that day to fall to the most skilful in the use of the goodly yew bow and the cloth yard shaft.

The most noticeable of these was a snow-white cow with gilded horns and a wreath of flowers suspended around its neck; displayed upon an oaken table were prizes of a less value, bows, quivers, arrows, a leathern purse containing three gold pieces, and several good Saxon broadswords, the blades fashioned from the finest steel.

But the prize which excited the greatest attention was an arrow with a golden head, and a shaft of solid silver.

Many a sturdy hand was stretched out to touch the prize, and many an eye wandered from the piece of crimson velvet on which it lay to the butts beyond.

The winner of the silver arrow would, besides the intrinsic value of the prize, be entitled to the much-coveted honour of being crowned king of the May-day revels, and when in the possession of his sovereignty he was at liberty to choose from the maidens present a May Queen.

Thus the prize became an object of more than common interest to the fairer portion of the revellers, and their whispered words to their sturdy companions caused a spirit of emulation among them which bade fair to make the coming contest one of more than ordinary excitement.

The throng began to thicken before the drawbridge, and the musicians, taking their place at the head of the revellers, stood with their eyes fixed upon the archway.

The blast of a trumpet pealing out from one of the towers caused those who were still hovering about the prizes to run across the green and join the expectant throng.

A second flourish from the brazen instrument caused the piper to inflate the bag of his instrument, and the player on the viol to flourish his bow.

A third time the sound was repeated; then issuing from the grim grey arch was a sight which caused the revellers to doff their caps and shout,—

"Long live the Earl of Huntingdon!"

The piper, the player on the viol, and the flutist began a warlike march, and turning about prepared to head the gallant cavalcade.

First came the young earl, a bold, handsome youth of little more than twenty summers, fair almost to a fault, large blue eyes, and masses of long golden hair, which fell in rich profusion upon his shoulders.

He paused when his foot left the drawbridge, and raising his jewelled cap said in English: *

"Welcome, my friends; God send there may be many such sights as this in store for merry England."

"Long live the Earl of Huntingdon!" again shouts the crowd; "long live the Saxon earl!"

A courteous bow, then the cap was replaced, and the musicians, now having a chance to be heard, lost not the opportunity.

Following the young earl was a score of richly-clad gentlemen, neighbours of the Earl, and, like himself, of Saxon blood.

Then came a troop of men-at-arms, and following close upon their heels were the domestics, trundling before them a rundlet of choice Malvoisie.

The Earl halted before the butts, and the competitors in the coming match came forward, many testing the soundness of their bow-strings, others examining the peacocks' feathers

* The language of the Norman oppressors was at this time spoken by the nobles.

ROBIN HOOD

AND

THE OUTLAWS OF SHERWOOD FOREST.

ILLUSTRATED.

LONDON:

TEMPLE PUBLISHING COMPANY, 145, FLEET STREET, E.C.

1869.

upon their arrows. As these examinations had been going forward since the company first came upon the ground it noted the anxiety felt by bowmen that their chance of victory should not be lessened by any failure on the part of the weapons.

Near the Earl stood his henchman, John Gammell, or Little John, as he was named upon account of his gigantic height and immense strength.

Behind the henchman a couple of domestics held the wassail bowl full to the rim with ambrosial wine.

Little John, with the freedom of a favoured follower, leant forward and whispered in his lord's ear:

"Goodly wine, my lord, is waiting; it were a sin when so many thirsty throats are dry, wishing your life may exceed that of——"

"Of what, knave?"

"The accursed Norman oppression, my lord," said the henchman, finding a simile, "by my lady that would be long enough."

The Earl smiled as he said:

"The simile, knave, is but a promise of short duration for my life, for Leicester's good Earl, backed by the people, has stayed this of which thy tongue wags."

"Aye, for a time, my lord; even now dark tidings come from the——"

"Peace, knave! mar not the day with that croaking voice of thine. Come my friends—let the wine be tasted, then to work!"

The stout yeomen, when the Earl's lips had touched the edge of the bowl, passed it to each other, then returned it to Little John.

"Body o' me!" muttered the giant, as he cast his eyes at the empty bowl; "but the carles' throats are as dry as——"

"Thine, John," said a burly yeoman; "to say sooth that is dry enough."

"Or as dry as the cakes made from thy flour, Much," said the henchman; "body o' me! but they are as like unto the mortar between the stones in the old Abbey as aught I know."

"Good for thy jaws," retorted Much the miller, joining in the laughter caused by these sallies; "were it not for this they would rust."

"If that were to happen," said a man-at-arms, "thy pouch, miller, would be without many broad pieces. Give thanks, man, give thanks to Little John, for he——"

"He'd break that back of thine," said the henchman, turning suddenly upon the retainer, "so keep a civil tongue."

The soldier backed out of range, and a movement at that moment among the competitors told the sports were about to begin.

The laughter and merry jests ceased, and the yeomen and maidens crowded around the competitors to watch, as the old chronicler says:—

He that shooteth the best of all,
And fair as an archer should,
At a pair of goodly butts,
Under the merry greenwood;
A right good arrow he shall have,
The shaft of silver white,
The head and feathers of rich red gold—
In England there's not the like.

The twanging of the bow-strings and the whistling of the arrows were the only sounds that broke the silence.

One by one the prizes were carried off, and the victors, as a reward for their skill, were the only archers allowed to shoot for the silver arrow.

There was some judgment in thus selecting the best archers, for the conditions upon which the good people of Huntingdon gave the prize rendered the shooting of an inferior archer a waste of time.

The mark to be hit was a silver coin, placed in the centre of the butt, and unless it was struck by an arrow the precious prize would be returned to those who gave it to be shot for.

To render the shooting more difficult, each archer was allowed but one arrow; thus the contest caused an eager excitement among the friends of the archers, which broke forth in words of encouragement as the eight sturdy yeomen took their places in line with the butt.

One by one the cloth-yard shafts flew onward and were embedded in the target; but, to the dismay of the spectators, the silver coin, clearly conspicuous beneath the sun, remained untouched.

"By the soul of St. Quintain," said Little John, "it were a sad sight to see the arrow leave this part. Come, master of mine, thou hast some skill with the bow; try thy hand."

The young Earl arose from the place where he had been lying during the contest, and taking a bow from one of the discomfited archers laid the arrow on the string.

A steady look at the glittering mark, then the arrow-head was raised to his ear; the twang of the string was followed by a joyful shout, and Little John, tossing his cap in the air, yelled with delight.

It was a marvellous shot; the silver piece was perforated through its centre, and a third of the arrow had gone into the butt.

Amid the uproarious delight which followed this welcome sight the Earl was announced king of the Mayday sports, and a chorus of lusty throats called upon him to select a queen.

The handsome noble's eyes sought but one face among the bevy of fair maidens—that one the fairest of the fair—the loveliest of the lovely—gentle, blue-eyed Maid Marian, old Much the miller's niece.

A few words from the Earl told the blushing girl of her envied fortune, then he led her by the hand to a flower-covered seat near the Maypole.

A hundred hands bedecked the young pair with flowers, then the barrels of old October were broached, the wassail cup refilled, and the lads and maidens joined hands around the Maypole and began the merry dance.

Much, the miller's son, was alone, for although a comely youth, he had joined the revels with his fair cousin, and her election having piqued the remainder of the maidens, they, with wonderful unanimity, refused to become his partner in the dance.

The Earl saw poor Much's troubled face as he was refused, with a haughty toss of the head or a cutting sneer by the maidens, and not wishing to mar the day's happiness by causing one he loved so well to suffer, he called the lonely swain to his side, and bade him take Marian to the dance.

Much's face brightened, and, truth to tell, Marian was as pleased to join in the dance as Much was to take her.

So the sports went on, peals of laughter were mingled with the piercing notes of the pipe, and the monotonous drubbing of the tabor; and young hearts were glad, young feet kept time to the music, and they danced as joyously as though sin, suffering and sorrow were unknown.

The dance was near its end when the Earl chanced to look beyond the tripping circle, and a dark shade passed over his face as he saw two horsemen approach the revellers and pull up their steeds within a dozen yards of the lofty pole.

His inward displeasure was shared by Little John, who still kept close to his lord.

"A fat ecclesiastic," he muttered between his teeth, "and a Norman knight who has helped to give him the substance of our fair land to fatten upon."

The elder of the two horsemen was astride a white palfrey; and, by his dress, a high dignitary of the Norman Church.

His face had but little of that humility which is becoming a man who professed to follow a brighter object than worldly ambition.

He was stern, proud, austere—more befitting a mailed knight than a prelate. Even now, as his eyes wandered over the May-time revellers, an angry flush came to his cheeks, and a cynical, cruel smile played upon his thin lips.

His companion was many years younger—of slight, but sinewy, form. His features, like those of the prelate, were of the Norman type; and would have been handsome, had it not been for the haughty, supercilious expression they bore.

He was armed after the fashion of the times—a coat of link mail, and a closely-fitting steel cap, with a crest of black feathers, showed he had won his spurs upon the battle-field.

A rich baldric supported on the right side an anelace, or long dagger; on the left, a heavy cross-hilted sword.

His black charger—a powerful and swift animal—was caparisoned as though his rider was about to enter the lists, or a field of strife.

The prelate was the first to speak; as, tapping the pummel of his saddle with his right hand, he followed the graceful figure of Maid Marian with his eyes.

"Methinks," he said, "these carles flaunt it bravely—as bravely as though they were masters of the land."

"They deem themselves so, my lord," said the knight; "but, had I my will, every Saxon hind should be driven into the sea."

"The day is not far distant, Geoffrey," was the prophetic reply, "when the Norman sway will be able to do more than even this."

The knight looked at his companion, and, with something of malice in his tone, said:

"Methinks, my lord, you would be one of the last to utter these sentiments."

"Why, Sir Geoffrey?"

"Was it not these Saxons who curtailed the fat revenues of the Church?"

The prelate bit his lips, and his swarthy face crimsoned; but, before he could reply, the knight sprang from his saddle, exclaiming:

"By my halidame, that is the fairest maiden I have yet seen!"

The trained steed remained perfectly still as the mail-clad Norman strode to the very centre of the laughing group—for they had paused in the dance to give their feet and the tired musicians a rest.

The advent of a Norman noble had much the same effect as the appearance of a fox among a flock of geese.

The fairer portion of the sex fled from the path he was pursuing, and clung to such of the sturdy Saxons as had not already ran for their staves and short swords.

There was good cause for this dismay, for the insolence of the Normans was only equalled by their licentiousness, and so much were they feared, that the majority of the English maidens sought the seclusion of a nunnery rather than live in daily fear of being carried off by them.

Marian clings to sturdy Much, and the miller's son, divining the knight's purpose, placed himself before the girl, and said:

"Marry, fair sir; do you not see how you have disturbed our company? Get thee to thy horse's back, lest, perchance, a Saxon arrow may find its way through Norman mail."

The knight heard, and choking back the angry words which came to his lips, answered:

"Fair words, peasant, fair words! I am no hawk, that these doves should flee at my approach. Come, I want but the hand of that fair maid, that I may join the dance."

He advanced closer as he spoke, and Much's Saxon blood getting the better of his prudence, caused him to raise his hand and push the intruder back.

"We want none of thee," he said: "back, or it may be worse for thee——"

The suppressed wrath burst forth at this indignity, and the Norman striking Much a heavy blow upon the chest with his gauntleted hand, said:

"Take that, peasant; stand aside, or my dagger shall slit that wagging tongue."

Much reeled under the blow, and would have fallen had not his father ran forward.

He caught his boy upon his left arm, and flourishing a long oaken staff in front of the knight's face, kept him back, then he placed the good old English weapon in Much's hand, saying:

"Liqour his hide, lad; liqour his hide."

Much grasped the weapon like one who knew its use, and before the Norman could use his sword, the long staff fell upon his shoulders and struck him to the ground.

The Earl of Huntingdon had by this time reached the spot, followed by his henchman, Little John, who quietly remarked:

"Would it had broken his crown, the arrogant knave!"

Marian clung to the young Earl, and he drew her away from the angry Saxons who were now standing in a compact body behind the miller's son, who said, as his adversary regained his feet:—

"We have enough of the accursed meddling of thy race in this fair land; let this teach thee there are English arms yet strong enough to punish Norman insolence."

The prelate had watched this scene with lowering brows, and as the knight regained his feet he dashed towards him, and bending low in the saddle, whispered:

"Mount, Geoffrey, the spearmen are close upon us!"

His companion understood the purport of his words, and jumped into his saddle, the haughty churchman at the same time shaking his clenched fist at the group, said:

"Hinds, you shall remember this day! by the cross you shall!"

He turned his horse as he spoke, and with his companion galloped across the green sward.

As quick as thought Little John fitted an arrow to his bow, and as the shaft whistled through the air, he sung out merrily:

"Keep that, Sir Priest; it will remind you of your promise."

The cloth-yard shaft penetrated the wooden pommel of the prelate's saddle, and despite the efforts of the churchman he could not withdraw it.

His face went pale when first the arrow became fixed in such close proximity to his body, but when he found he was safe he turned to his companion and asked:

"Marked you the knave who discharged this arrow?"

"Aye, my lord, a peasant, a head taller than his fellows."

"He shall be a head shorter," was the fierce rejoinder, "before another hour has passed—ha! here come our fellows."

As he spoke the glitter of a score of spear-points could be seen advancing, and when the troop were within earshot, Geoffrey Lois angrily said:

"A murrain on ye for knaves; while you have been loitering I have been nigh murdered."

He extended his hand towards the villagers as he spoke, and the men at arms wheeling into line, lowered their spears and prepared to avenge the insults their master had received.

The coming of the troop had been seen by the merry-makers, and now the maidens, conjecturing a strife was at hand, fled in a body towards the castle.

There also the retainers had hurried, to arm themselves; and the Earl, drawing his sword, rushed to the front of the archers and called out:

"Lay your arrows—ready my men. Aim at their horses as they advance, then to work with sword and buckler. Hurrah for merrie England, and confusion to the Norman knaves!"

The cry was taken up, and as Geoffrey Lois at the head of the foreign mercenaries who formed his train, came charging upon the Saxons, a flight of arrows brought down a dozen horses.

These animals were in the front; thus those in rear were thrown into confusion, and before they could fill up their broken ranks the incensed villagers were upon them.

The strife was but short. The bowmen closed with their assailants, horses were ripped open by their short swords, and the goodly quarter-staves swept the mail-clad horsemen from their saddles.

Foremost in the fray was the young Earl and his henchman, Little John, the latter wielding a pole, one blow of which felled the war-steed bestrode by Geoffrey Lois.

"Yield thee, ransom or no ransom," said the giant, "or bone o' my body I'll crack thy skull like an eggshell."

He was answered by a fierce thrust from the Norman's sword; then like a flail the stout pole whirled round, driving back those who came to their lord's rescue, and finally settling upon the noble's casque, split the tough metal and rendered the wearer senseless.

The war-cry of the Saxon retainers told the mercenaries a further struggle would be useless, so those who were yet able to manage their steeds turned and galloped from the fight.

The prelate's harsh voice rung out the church's direst curses upon their heads as they dashed past him; but they fell unheard, for the Normans thought more of their lives at that moment than any promised punishments hereafter.

The arrival of the Earl's retainers upon the battle-ground was the signal for the haughty churchman to follow De Lois's spearmen, for the Englishmen would have ducked the ecclesiastic in the horsepond without the least compunction.

Six of the spearmen were slain, and twice that number wounded. The Saxons had escaped without the loss of a life, but many bore ugly marks of the horsemen's long spears.

The Earl, seated upon the floral throne which had been erected for their May King, passed judgment upon the knight.

"For insulting a peaceful gathering," he said, "and drawing a sword upon an unarmed man,—and further, for ordering the armed foreigners to shed English blood, you are sentenced to be stripped of your arms and your steed—these being the lawful trophies of my stout henchman, Little John, who subdued you in fair and open fight; your back to be bared, and for a good English mile you will be flogged with stinging nettles."

The punishment was in accordance with the rough justice of our sturdy forefathers, and when the nettles were found, the sullen captive's face was turned towards the road by which his followers had fled.

Once only he turned when the yeomen were driving him from the green, then he asked in malignant tones—

"I would know the name of him who sat in judgment over me."

"Robin Hood, Earl of Huntingdon," said the Earl; "forget it not; we may meet again."

"We shall."

The words were spoken in vengeful tones; then he started at a swift pace, followed by the noisy crowd.

CHAPTER II.

THE GATHERING OF THE SAXON BOWMEN.

Therefore they called a council of state
To know what was best to be done
For to quell their pride; or else, they replied,
The land would be overrun.

SIMON DE MOUNTFORT, Earl of Leicester, the husband of Eleanor, the king's sister, had, at the head of the rebellious barons, held supreme power over England for nearly three years.

Then came a battle fought near Lewes, in which the weak and irresolute king was taken prisoner, and his army utterly routed by the popular party.

This victory made Leicester sole master of the kingdom; he confiscated the estates of eighteen barons who had fought on the Norman side.

It was when in this position of neither sovereign or subject that Simon de Mountfort laid the foundation of the House of Commons, for he introduced a second order of men to those councils which had hitherto been held by the nobles, who cared but little for the common weal.

Two knights from each shire, and deputies from the boroughs, were ordered to attend and have a share in the government of the State.

A wise and judicious measure, which made him popular with the people, and, as a natural consequence, hated by the most powerful of the barons, and the result was that many of them deserted the confederacy and joined the royalists.

This brief explanation will enable the reader to understand the event which was of such import to the hero of this story—the gallant Saxon Earl of Huntingdon.

It was now the month of July, and upon the drawbridge of Huntingdon Castle the retainers were lounging about enjoying the cool evening breeze.

Although the drawbridge was lowered, the appearance of the men was not as peaceful as upon the opening of the May-day, when the Earl was proclaimed king of the revels.

The men were armed at all points, and upon the battlements could be seen steel-capped sentinels, pausing ever and anon in their walk and looking towards the wood which skirted the roadway.

Besides the host of men-at-arms, there was mingled a goodly number of English yeomen garbed in buff jerkins; these were armed with the stout yew long-bow, and a sheaf of those shafts which had made the archers of England a terror to their mail-clad foes.

Others wore casques and gorgets of iron, and their arms were a short sword and buckler or a long lance.

In those days, every man, according to his degree, was equipped for war, for by an edict issued some time before, every man having a knight's fee was compelled to have a coat of mail, a helmet, a shield, and a lance.

And the same description of accoutrements were provided by all, whether noble or commoner, for whatever number of knight's fees he possessed.

Every free man who had property to the amount of sixteen marks * was compelled to be armed in like manner, and every one that had ten marks, an iron gorget, a cap of iron, and a lance; lastly, all citizens were compelled to have an iron cap, a lance, and a coat quilted with wool.

Thus it will be seen it was an easy matter to raise an effective army in an inconceivably short space of time; and in a few days the Castle of Huntingdon had within its walls all who had sworn allegiance to the Earl's banner.

The demeanour of the men marked this gathering as one far different from that of the May-day.

True all the sturdy yeomen who were present upon the latter occasion were now seen either upon the battlements or upon the level sward before the castle.

The summons had gone forth for the Saxon bowmen to gather under the Earl's banners, for dark tidings came to that peaceful village of the growing power of the Royalists, the Norman oppressors of the people.

Amongst one of the groups who were canvassing the coming events was Little John, and near him Much and his sturdy father the miller.

The henchman had his hands crossed upon

* A coin worth about 13s. 4d.

one end of a long bow, and his loud laugh could be heard as he jested with the yeomen.

"Lewes," said a stout farmer, driving the butt of his lance upon the ground, "should have taught the foreign minions a lesson, and made them fear the Great Earl and the people at his back."

"It should," said Little John; "but the same might be said with the crows you trap when they alight upon your fields; you catch and kill them, but I'd warrant there's plenty to eat the next crop."

"Aye, John, but I am there to prevent them, just as we shall prevent these Normans from devouring our liberties."

"May it be so!" responded little John, in a graver tone than he had hitherto used, "may it be so! I will give my good right hand to see Leicester's Earl master of the county and the Royalists beaten."

"But he is master. Shoulder of St. Hubert, thy speech smellest of more than the tongue utters."

"You are right, Randall—right."

"Come, man," said the franklin, "let us hear thy budget, for thou hast one I'll be sworn."

"Marry but I have. Listen, a messenger came here but yester e'en; he had ridden far; he brought a message to our lord from the Great Earl to this import."

The bowmen gathered closer round the speaker as he continued,

"Prince Edward has escaped, many of the barons have left the league, the Royalists are meeting—that is the substance of his message."

"Substance sufficient," said Much, "to gather the Saxon bowmen—a gathering that will cost the Normans as much as it cost them at Lewes."

"With the saints' blessing, yes," said Little John; "and the sooner we are planting our shafts in the joints of their armour the better for England."

"What delays our lord?" Much asked. "Why does he not lead us to join Leicester?"

"For two reasons, Much," said the henchman; "two goodly reasons—one, he does not know where the Earl is collecting his forces; the second, many of the roads are even now in possession of the Royalists."

"The better for us," said the old miller; "I warrant the Huntingdon spearmen and the bows would make a passage to the Great Earl, even were the whole of the foreign minions who overrun our land to stand in our way."

"See," Little John exclaimed, suddenly, "here comes the messenger!"

A horseman emerged from the wood as he spoke, and when the foam-covered charger came close enough, the crowd on the drawbridge saw on the rider a tabard bearing the arms of Simon de Mountfort, Earl of Leicester.

The tired steed was led to the castle stables, and the messenger shown to the banqueting hall.

Here the knights of the shire were assembled, and, like their leader, the young Earl, they were cased in glittering mail.

Steel casques, ornamented with drooping plumes, were upon the table beside the link gloves, so cunningly fashioned by the armourer as to admit of the free play of every finger.

Against the wall were the long lances and shields, and behind each knight stood an esquire, in close attendance upon their masters.

The board was strewed with brimming goblets of mellow wine, and, indifferent to the coming troubles, the gallant fellows laughed and jested as though the party were one of pleasure in place of being a warlike gathering.

Those were times when featherbed soldiers were unknown, days when kings and emperors led their armies in person, and by their prowess inspired their men to emulate the deeds of those who were ever foremost in the strife.

Bowing low to the Earl the messenger took a folded piece of parchment from beneath his gabardine and said:

"From the Earl of Leicester, my lord?"

The Saxon noble read the few lines the missive contained, then jumping to his feet, said:

"We must to horse, gentlemen;" then turning to his esquire, "Bid the trumpeters sound the call."

As the plumed helmets and mail gloves were being adjusted, the Earl said:

"Prince Edward's forces are gaining strength, and many of the roads are in his power; there is bad tidings from Oxford, but of that anon. England needs her right arm to teach her oppressors that our liberties are not to be trampled under foot by Henry of Winchester's foreign favourites."

He spoke hurriedly, and paced to and fro the great hall, his armed heel ringing angrily upon the stones.

He said England needed her right arm, and by those words he meant the sturdy Saxon bowmen, and well they merited that name; it had been earned on more than one battlefield, where the cloth-yard shaft had done more to decide the fortunes of the day than the mail-clad knights and their army of spearmen.

CHAPTER III.

THE BATTLE OF EVESHAM.

Then Robin he took his noble bow,
And let fly his arrows all amain,
And Robin Hood he began for to smile,
As he went over the plain.

A FORTNIGHT after the day upon which this gallant array left Huntingdon Castle, the Earl joined the forces of Simon de Mountfort.

The anxiety upon the Great Earl's face did not escape the Saxon leader's eyes as the former came forward and said:

"Welcome, Robin; thrice welcome, in this our hour of need."

"You are troubled, my lord. Is it the issue of the coming struggle which causes the gloom upon your brow?"

"Aye, Robin; the scurvy knaves who deserted my banner have ere this joined the Prince, and my gallant army is fearfully outnumbered."

"Did I hear aright?" the young noble asked, "that Gloucester commanded a wing of the royalist force?"

"Too true, Robin. Ha! hither comes one of the advanced guard."

A man-at-arms galloped towards the great leader, and pulling up when within a few feet of him, exclaimed:

"My lord, from yonder hill I saw the banners of the Prince."

"Art sure, knave?—art sure it is not the banners of the barons I expected ere this?"

"Quite sure, my lord. As for the barons, report sayeth they have been met by the prince yester e'en and defeated."

Simon de Mountfort's lips twitched as he heard this news.

"I had expected this," he said, "but let it pass. We have still men enough left to do our devoir as brave men. Let the trumpets sound —to horse, gentlemen, to horse!"

The Earl of Huntingdon sprang upon his black charger's back, and closing his helmet, galloped to the spot where his banner formed a rallying point for the Saxon bowmen.

The confederate host was soon in motion— the Huntingdon archers in the front, headed by the Earl and his gigantic henchman.

So close was the army of Prince Edward that the Earl had but little time to form his men in battle array.

The Royalists as they emerged upon the plain, likewise formed in battle array, and when the great leader beheld the overwhelming numbers which were advancing against him, he made use of these memorable words:

"THE LORD HAVE MERCY ON OUR SOULS, FOR I SEE OUR BODIES ARE PRINCE EDWARD'S —HE HAS LEARNED FROM ME THE ART OF WAR."*

There was a pause as the rival hosts stood face to face, then Leicester placed the old king, who was his prisoner, in front of the confederate lines.

The weak and treacherous old monarch was encased in complete armour, and bestrode a war-horse of magnificent proportions; and much as he wished to escape from the Earl's power, he dared not make the attempt, in consequence of twenty of the Huntingdon archers being placed near him, with orders to use their fatal shafts should it be necessary.

The Earl of Leicester, after these preparations were completed, beckoned for Robin Hood to come to his side.

A few bounds of his splendid charger, and the young noble was beside his leader.

"They outnumber us, Robin," Simon de Mountfort said, "three to one, but the English bowmen may yet give us the day—you understand me?"

"Well, my lord."

"See where the traitors are crowding around Edward's banner; bid your bowmen try their skill upon that point."

The Earl of Huntingdon bowed to his saddle, then turning his horse's head, galloped back to his men.

In spite of the superior force the confederate army had to face, the men were eager to begin the fray.

The knights brought their lances to the rest and drew in the bridle reins, the cross-bowmen placed the bolts in their weapons, and the Saxon archers waited with their feathered shafts placed upon their bowstrings.

The latter had not long to wait for their leader after quitting, Simon de Mountfort dashed to the head of his men, and, pointing to the steel-clad host, said:

"Loose your shafts, men; find the joints in their armour!"

* Vide "Bloomfield's History of the British Empire."

The twang of three hundred bowstrings was followed by a flight of arrows, and the cluster of knights and nobles who were near the Prince was seen to disperse, leaving one-third of their number dead or dying.

"Bravely done!" said Leicester, closing his helmet and sitting himself firmly in the saddle; "may those shafts have found those who turned traitors to their country's cause!"

The battle thus began, and in answer to the discharge of arrows there came a flight of quarrels from the Prince's crossbowmen.

For an hour the air was darkened by the missiles from slings, yew-bows, and cross-bows, then a second line of steel-clad knights advanced with levelled spears upon the Saxon archers.

The latter plied their weapons still faster, and the glittering line was broken as men and horses fell before the deadly shafts.

But the gaps were soon closed, and the very earth trembled under the weight of the charging columns.

At a signal from the Saxon Earl the archers opened their ranks to allow Simon de Mountfort's knights to advance.

The Earl of Huntingdon joined the gallant body; then, spurring their horses, they rode full tilt at the advancing foe.

There was a mighty crash as the two lines met. Men and horses went down as though struck by lightning, then the struggling mass separated, and each seeking an opponent, a general hand-to-hand combat ensued.

The Earl of Huntingdon had selected a Norman knight, whose bearing he remembered as that of the disturber of the May-day revels.

The recognition was mutual, for Geoffrey de Lois called out, savagely:

"The Virgin has heard my prayer—we have met again."

The young Earl made no reply, but as his vindictive enemy strove to drive his lance through the bars of his helmet, he caught the blow upon his shield; his own weapon at the same moment striking the Norman's neck, carried him out of the saddle.

He fell with a crash to the earth, and the victor would have driven his lance-point even through the steel panoply, had not a fresh body of horsemen from either side carried him away.

The contest was fiercely sustained, although one half of De Mountfort's army had fallen.

Still the little band fought to conquer or die upon that fatal plain.

The Earl of Huntingdon's spear was shivered as he rode at the powerful form of Prince Edward, and he would have been slain before he could have loosened his battle-axe, had not a weak voice near him said:

"Spare my life, I am Henry of Winchester, your king."

One of the Prince's army not recognising the old monarch in his armour, had already wounded him, and would have struck the fatal blow had not the Prince left the young Earl, and dashed to his sire's assistance.

The Prince led the old king to a place of safety, then rode to join his troops who were now slowly forcing the confederate army from their position.

The young Earl soon detached his battle axe from the saddle, and his raven plumes were seen where the fight was thickest.

Twice he met the Norman knight, Geoffrey de Lois, but each time they were separated by the charging of fresh bodies of horsemen from the royalist host.

A quarrel from a cross-bow slew the Earl's charger, and before he could disengage himself from under the horse he was surrounded by a score of Gloucester's men-at-arms.

They tore the battle-axe from his grasp, and would have slain him had not Little John seen his lord's peril.

With a huge two-handed sword, the henchman cut a path to the Earl's side; thus mowing down all who came near, he whispered:

"Rise, my lord, the day is lost; the remnant of De Mountfort's army is falling back—our archers alone stand firm—they await your coming—resolved if you are slain not to leave Evesham's red plain while a hand can fit a shaft to a bow."

"The Earl de Mountfort, where is he?".

"Slain, my good lord—slain with others as noble as himself. Come, we have not a minute to lose. See the victors! The foreign minions are revelling in England's best blood."

Little John's words were too true. The foreign mercenaries, enraged at the stubborn defence of the Saxon band, had been slaying the wounded and dying.

The Earl and his henchman fought their way to where the Saxon bowmen still held their ground; then the former, casting away his battle-axe, called for a bow and a quiver of arrows.

Thus armed, he slowly fell back with his unyielding men; and, in answer to the repeated summonses to surrender, he sent a cloth-yard shaft through the hearts of those who made the demand.

Foot by foot the remnants of the gallant band he had led from Huntingdon left the field of slaughter, terrible even in their retreat, keeping at bay the mail-clad knights and their legions of mercenaries, by slaying all who came within range of their terrible arrows.

Defeated but not subdued—his hatred burning still furious against the Norman conquerors—the Earl and his little band of not more than a hundred archers retired from the field of slaughter.

An exultant smile was upon his handsome lips as he brought down the leaders of the host who sought to capture the remnants of the Saxon bowmen.

Until the darkness set in did this little band of heroes elude the advance of the mailed hordes, and when the next day's sun shone upon the plain, all traces of the stubborn Saxons who had survived that fatal day, had departed.

ROBIN HOOD,
AND THE OUTLAWS OF SHERWOOD FOREST.

ROBIN HOOD AND THE EARL MOR OF TIMER.

CHAPTER IV.

ROBIN HOOD THE OUTLAW.

> Some lost legs and some lost arms,
> And some did lose their blood;
> But Robin he took up his noble bow,
> And is gone to the merry greenwood:

EVESHAM's fatal plain spread sorrow and consternation throughout the length and breadth of the land.

Not alone for those who fell upon that fatal

day was this sorrow felt—they had died nobly in their country's defence; but alas! their fall caused the bulwarks of the people's liberty to be trampled down, and left them at the mercy of the foreign minions whom Henry III. openly encouraged in their exultation at the downfall of the people's cause.

The minstrels sang the praises of those who fell on Evesham's plain, but their songs could not restore the dead, or give back to the hapless country the Saxon birthright—liberty.

True, there were many of the Saxon nobility who refused to bend the knee to the Norman court; and leaving their vast possessions to be bestowed upon the mercenary hirelings, they sought a home beyond the seas.

One among the nobles who claimed an English descent laughed the Norman power to scorn; and when all had fled from Henry's vengeance, he drew together the remnants of the bands of Saxon bowmen, and in the fastnesses of the northern forests struck many a blow for the land he loved so well.

This one was Robin Hood, so recently a belted earl, but now an outlaw; his estates confiscated, a price upon his head, houseless—his bed the green sward, his covering heaven's canopy, and nothing to defend him save the good yew bow and the cloth-yard shafts.

A few weeks after the overthrow of the confederate army, and while the Normans were yet rejoicing at their victory, Henry of Winchester caused a grand assembly of the nobles and barons to be held at his Court in London.

It was the last day of the term allowed for the Saxon nobles to make their submission to the king.

Many, to save their estates from being given to the foreign favourites, had already taken the oath of fealty, but a larger number still kept away from the court, despite the mandate which had gone forth, the substance of which was that all who did not make submission to the party in power were to be outlawed by the king, excommunicated by the clergy, and their lands given to the knights of Normandy, who had fought under Prince Edward's banner at Evesham.

It was a goodly sight; the weak and false King seated upon the throne, and wearing a robe of velvet and ermine over his armour, and surrounded by his mail-clad nobles, knights and barons.

The proceedings were opened by the King asking his son whether the whole of the Saxon nobility had made humble submission to their King.

"All, sire," answered the Prince, "save these."

As he spoke, he handed a packet to the King.

The face of Henry became reddened with anger, as he read the list, and when he had finished, he exclaimed angrily:

"So the rebellious varlets would seek an exile in a foreign land sooner then bend the knee to their lawful sovereign."

"It would seem so, sire."

"Well, let it be so; the day of grace has passed, let sentence of outlaw be proclaimed against all who do not attend the Court before the dial marks the hour of noon."

"Your mandate, sire, shall be obeyed."

"Tell me," the King said, "what is the meaning of this mark placed opposite the Earl of Huntingdon's name?"

Prince Edward glanced at the parchment as he replied:

"I know not, sire; unless it is that the Earl has died since the battle."

The packet was about to be given to the scriveners that they might copy the names of the outlawed nobles, when Geoffrey de Lois stepped forward,

"Your pardon, my liege," he said; "but I can tell you the cause of that mark being placed against Huntingdon's name, if I have permission to speak."

The King smiled upon his favourite, whose head was yet swathed in bandages from the effects of the blow he received from the Earl of Huntingdon, and said:

"Speak, De Lois, and freely, for Henry has not a more devoted follower than yourself. How goes the wound? Does it show promise of mending?"

"But slowly, my lord; but for the good steel of which my cap was made, I must have been brained by the blow."

"Well, well; we must see if we cannot find something out of the fat lands of these rebellious knaves to quicken the healing of the wound."

Geoffrey bent low, and his face flushed with joy at hearing this promise, for beyond the suit of mail and his sword, he had but little in the way of wealth.

"May I crave a boon, my liege?" he said, "a boon to elect my choice of the many posts now vacant by the death or flight of the rebellious carles who dared to raise their hands against the Lord's anointed."

"In good time, De Lois, thou mayest, but first tell me the meaning of this mark."

"Its meaning, my liege, my tongue trembles to explain; but, under your favour, I will speak."

"Do so, good De Lois, for my curiosity is excited nearly to womanly feeling; so speak, and fear not."

"Robin Hood, Earl of Huntingdon, my liege, in open contempt for thy gracious proclamation, has publicly made avowal of his defiance to thy power, and now, with the remains of the archers he led to Evesham, has betaken himself to the forest of Barnesdale, from whence he sallies forth at times to rob and slay all who have any connection with thy court or army."

The King heard Geoffrey's emphasised speech with but ill-concealed anger, and when he had concluded, he sprung from his seat, and exclaimed, passionately—

"Is it thus, my lords, you would see my power severed? You have troops of stout men-at-arms under your banner—how is it that I have true swords, and so many weeks have passed since this knave dared to openly defy me?"

Forth from the glittering crowd of mail-clad men stepped fierce William de Valence, Earl of Pembroke.

"My liege," he said, "your barons have not forgot their duty to their sovereign, for twice has an armed party been sent to crush this nest of traitors."

"Well, well, my lord, and the result?"

"Each time, my liege. they have returned with broken crests, their men-at-arms slain, and all that was valuable taken by the outlaws."

"I make here a vow to the Virgin," the King said, fiercely, "that I will crush this gathering. Where is Mortimer?"

"Here, my liege," said the Earl, coming forward, "and ready to do my devoirs as a knight and a noble."

"It is well, Mortimer. Heard you all that has been said?"

"Every word, my liege."

"Know you aught of the matter?"

"I know this, my liege, that Huntingdon's rebellious earl has some seven or eight hundred bowmen with him in the fastnesses of Barnesdale, and their cloth-yard shafts have beaten all who have been sent against them."

"See to it, Mortimer! Take a thousand of your best men and crush this nest of vipers. Hark'ee, my lord; every success gained by them will but swell the dissatisfaction now so rife in the northern counties, and we may have another Evesham, and perchance not the same result."

"I will to horse, my liege," said Mortimer, "and by the hour of sunset the power of this rebellious earl will be nearer its end."

"May the saints grant a favourable result to your journey! Farewell, my lord, when next we meet I trust Huntingdon will be a prisoner."

"A dead one, my liege, for I swear to hang him upon the bough of one of the trees which has afforded him shelter."

The Earl left the audience-chamber, and all who knew his great military skill doubted not the fulfilment of his words.

The King was about to break up the assembly, when his eyes fell upon Geoffrey de Lois, who stood a few paces from the throne.

"Your pardon, De Lois," he said; "I was nigh forgetting you, for this matter troubled me sorely. Come forward, sir knight, and let me know the boon thou wouldest crave."

De Lois bent his knee to the monarch and said:

"My liege, the shrievalty of Nottingham is vacant. May I crave to fulfil the office?"

"It is but a poor one, De Lois," said the King, "after the great work thy strong right arm has done for the State."

"I shall be content, my liege, if you grant at me."

"Be it so, De Lois; your boon is granted. But tell me why you should have chosen this post among the many that are now vacant?"

"My uncle, the Abbot of St. Mary's, will be near the town. It is to receive his goodly counsels I crave the favour you have granted."

"A fitting reason. Thou art a good son of the church and a brave knight, De Lois. Stay —thou wilt require money to keep up a fitting state. To do this I give thee the rents of the lands hitherto held by Robin Hood, of Huntingdon."

The gleam of malignant triumph which came to De Lois's eyes passed away before he took the monarch's hand and humbly kissed it.

"You are too generous, my liege," he said, "and my devotion to you, I hope, will repay such goodness."

"It will, De Lois, it will. Now, my lords, I will retire, for this matter of Barnesdale has moved me much; and in the privacy of my own chamber I may regain somewhat more composure."

Henry left the great council, and his nobles soon after dispersed and went to their homes.

The last to quit the great hall was the newly made Sheriff of Nottingham, and a haughty looking man garbed in priestly robes.

The latter was De Lois's uncle, his companion on the day of the May-time sports, John of Langley, now abbot of the rich monastery of St. Mary's—a magnificent structure situate within a mile of Nottingham town.

"Thy success," the prelate said, as they mounted their steeds, "has been beyond even my anticipations."

A dark smile came to the knight's lips as he answered:

"And mine; but if Roger Mortimer slays this knave, it will be of but little avail."

"Save the fat Huntingdon land," said the Abbot, "methinks that ought to repay the flogging with nettles."

"But in part, good uncle; even were it to balance this matter, there is the broken head he gave me at Evesham."

"This you hope to settle by being Nottingham's sheriff. By the saints I cannot read this, Geoffrey. What hope is there for your vengeance to fall upon a man who tarries in Barnesdale."

"Every hope, good uncle of mine, unless Mortimer's meddling hand baulks me of my vengeance."

"Be plain in thy speech, Geoffrey, or perhaps I shall be tempted to give thee some of that goodly counsel which caused thee to crave thy boon from the King."

The pair laughed heartily at these words; then De Lois said:

"Listen, good uncle of mine, and thou shalt know the weighty reason for my wish to be at Nottingham; from the hour that I received that scourging from the Saxon's hands, I have had a watch kept over the Earl, and when he sought the security of Barnesdale, I bade one of my knaves join his band."

"A good thought, Geoffrey."

"So it has turned out, for the varlet has sent me knowledge of all that passes; and but yesterday he gave me word of the intent of the outlaw to seek a better protection than that he now has in the forest of Sherwood."

"It was for this," said the prelate, "you wished the shrievalty of Nottingham."

"For this only; should they escape Mortimer, I can do the King a service and obtain my vengeance."

"That head of thine," said the Abbot, "is better fitted for a statesman than a soldier."

Geoffrey de Lois smiled at the compliment; then they spurred their horses, and London was soon left far behind.

CHAPTER V.

THE BEGGAR'S BUDGET.

> Robin stood in Barnesdale,
> And leaned him to a tree,
> And by him stood Little John,
> A good yeoman was he;
> And also did good Scathlock
> And Much the miller's son—
> There was no inch of his body
> But it was worth a whole man.

THE wonderful increase of the human species since the time of which we write, has caused a complete change in the aspect of the earth.

The mighty forests then so thickly studded with noble trees, the pleasant dingles and dells where the wild stag, the boar, and the wolf were wont to resort have passed away before the giant strides of civilisation.

Sweet shady glens, where our sturdy forefathers were wont to gather and exhibit their skill in the use of the yew-bow and other free and manly sports are now occupied by populous villages; aye, in some instances, even cities the sites of which cover the verdure-clad dells where the foresters roamed as free and as happy as the sunny air they breathed.

In the densest part of Barnesdale forest the sturdy Saxon bowmen and their gallant leader, Robin Hood, had sought refuge from the tyranny of the victors of Evesham.

The band numbered about a hundred strong-limbed foresters, whose deeds were in high repute among the ill-used people who were compelled to bear the Norman yoke.

The peasant, the artisan, and their wives and daughters already began to venerate the name of Robin Hood and his merry men, for all who lived within the vicinity of the forest had a story to tell of the outlaws' gallant deeds and open hands.

In some instances young girls would relate how they were beset under the greenwood by a Norman knight or baron, and when fleeing from their impertinent attentions, several men clad in Lincoln green suddenly appeared, and gave the Norman and his followers such a drubbing with their quarter-staves, that taught them there were strong and willing hands yet left in England.

In others, the peasant when about to be driven from his cottage, in consequence of not being able to pay the tithes and dues, had been saved by the generous outlaws' ready purses.

True, the rich ecclesiastics, the harsh land-owners, and the Normans who came to reside in the confiscated castles, told a different story when they fell into the hands of the brave foresters, and many a rueful face and empty pouch were evidences of the truth of their words.

In some instances the outlaws were not content with lightening these gentry's purses, but these were particular cases: for example, a rich landlord, who had been one of the first to swear fealty to the tyrants, and sought to ingratiate himself into favour with the Court by his cruelty to the poor upon his estate.

He ventured too far under the green bough, and, being caught, was not only lightened of the rents he had collected, but a stout deer-hide thong was laid upon his back, to teach him to be more merciful in future.

There is no doubt this popularity with the people enabled Robin Hood to forestall all the attempts made to dislodge him from his haunts, for, no matter how secretly the expeditions were planned against him, he was certain to have timely warning to prepare a warm reception for his foes.

It was near the close of a lovely September day that Robin and his followers first heard of the advance of Earl Mortimer, and the confiscation of Huntingdon Castle.

The outlawed Earl's face did not lose its habitual smile when little John gave him an outline of the scenes we have described at the Court of Henry of Winchester.

The appearance of the Saxon archers had undergone a great change since the fatal fight on Evesham plain.

The quilted coats, iron gorgets and helmets, had been thrown aside, and each burly form was clad in a jerkin of Lincoln green, tight-fitting hose, and russet boots with wide tops, so that the wearer, when on foot, could turn the tops down; when mounted, draw them up to the knee.

Their heads were covered by caps of red and blue cloth, ornamented by a drooping feather fastened on the right side.

Their arms were the short Saxon sword, a buckler, a Spanish yew bow, and a baldrick, studded according to the taste of the wearer, was worn across the body, to which was fastened a sheaf of arrows, each a good cloth-yard in length. Drayton, the poet, thus makes mention of this famous chapter in his Poly-olbion:—

"Their arrows finely paired for timber and for feathers,
With birch and hazel pieced to fly in any weather;

*   *   *   *   *   *

And of these Archers brave there was not any one
But could kill a deer his swiftest speed upon."

Thus armed and well versed in forest war-fare, they were more than a match for four times their number of England's choicest troops.

The group under the giant oak consisted of Robin, Little John, and Much, the miller's son, and as the former henchman watched his leader's face, he smote his huge palm upon his thigh and said—

"Body-o-me, master, but the news does not cause thee much concern."

"Why should it John?" said Robin; "we have but thy bare word for it, and that, may-hap, may be influenced by the barrel of Mal-voisie you helped to empty yestere'en."

"Helped to empty!" Little John repeated, "there is some truth in that. I helped, but it was but little assistance the thirsty varlets required when they gathered round the goodly barrel."

"Yet," said Much, with a smile, "they tell how one Little John was seen swaying from side to side as the sun went down, and but for two of the foresters he would have——"

"It's a foul invention, Much," said the giant; "think you I would take more down my throat than my legs could carry? Body-o-me, man, could not the sun have taken effect upon me when we were at the butts yester-day?"

"It could," said Robin, laughingly; "never heed them, John; it was the sun, not the Malvoisie, which made thy legs crook like two bent bows; but come, man, thou hast not told me where thy news was gathered."

"That is soon told, master o'-mine," said Little John; "we have spoken of the sun, and body-o'-me, it made me wondrous athirst to-day."

"The monks," interrupted Much, "will tell thee it was a punishment, John——"

"The monks' words are not worth a groat," said the giant; "thou knowest that right well, or the monk thy fingers lightened of his gold, would have spoken truly, when he said a goodly bough would bear thy body before the week had passed."

"Peace with thy idle prating," said Robin, "Come, thou wast athirst."

"I was, master-o'-mine—I did proceed;

* Another writer, speaking of bold Robin, says:—"In these forests, and with this company, he for many years reigned like an independent sovereign at perpetual war with the King of England and all his subjects, with the exception, however, of the poor and needy, and such as were desolate and oppressed, or stood in need of his protection. When molested by a superior force in one place, he went to another, still defying the power of the law; and making his enemies pay dearly, as well for their open attacks as for their clandestine treachery.

when I felt so wondrously athirst and though I looked well into every rundlet, there was not enough of liquor in any one of them to wet the tip of a finger ; body-o'-me, the thirsty knaves must have drained them last night."

"Mayh ip they did, John, but thy story, man."

"Not mine, master, for when I walked to the edge of the forest, to find the brook, for my thirst had grown prodigious—mayhap the sight of the empty rundlets did this—be that as it may master, when I had drank and drank again, I heard a laugh behind me. No knave shall laugh at Little John, I thought, and getting to my feet, I saw a sturdy beggar leaning upon his staff."

"Thy news, man," said Robin; thou art as long in answering me as a maiden telling her love story."

"Patience, master, patience, as I told the fat friar I caught in the forest; patience, and thou shalt have the story word for word."

Robin stooped to caress one of the large hounds which lay at his feet, and Little John continued :

"Body o' me, when I asked the knave what he had to laugh about, he made answer that brought the quarter-staff I carried upon his pate, and the lusty varlet gave me as good a blow in return. We had a long bout, master, and my hide is sore yet; but the end was we became friends, and he told me all that I have told you; much more, mayhap, for his staff so rang about my ears that it's a wonder I remembered a word."

"Where is the knave ?"

"Where I left him, master, sitting by the brook bathing his pate."

"At the brook through the forest."

"At the brook through the forest, master. I would he had come with me, but as that was not to be done without having a second bout, I left him."

Robin placed his horn to his lips, and blew three clear ringing notes.

"I will see this sturdy beggar," he said, "not only for the news he brings, but to get one so stout to join our merry men."

CHAPTER VI.

ROBIN HOOD AND THE BEGGAR.

He met a beggar on the way,
Who sturdily could gang,
He had a pike staff in his hand,
That was both stiff and strong.

THE mellow notes from Robin's bugle was answered by George-a-Green, who came towards the Outlaw leading a white horse, and the chief as he mounted the beautiful steed, turned to Little John and said:

"Go to the cellarer, John, he will give thee a posset to cure thy bruised hide."

Nothing loth, the thirsty forester, taking Much with him, went towards that part of the forest where the provisions and wine were kept, and Robin galloped through the intricate paths and soon reached the brook.

He found the beggar as Little John had described him, a sturdy, well-built knave, but in place of bathing his head he was seated upon a fallen tree coolly examining divers rents in his cloak.

He affected not to notice the horseman who drew rein within a few feet of the fallen oak, but as he turned over the ragged cloak he soliloquised loud enough for Robin to hear.

"Ten holes has the scurvey rascal made in my cloak, and I did not break his thick skull for it—out upon the cankerly hind, would I had him here now."

"What would'st thou do" Robin asked, amused at the stout built fellow's words, "what would'st thou do, knave."

The beggar rose from the trunk of the tree, and leaning upon his staff, answered:

"Break his thick skull, as I will thine if you do not leave me in peace."

"A murrain on ye for a saucy varlet," said Robin, dismounting, and passing one arm over his steed's neck, "know ye who I am."

"I neither know nor care," said the beggar, "but judging from thy green jerkin thou art one of those fellows who deserve a thrashed hide—by our lady, one of ye had one to-day."

"You are a pert knave," said the Outlaw, "and were it not that other matters require my time I would give thee such a drilling as would make as many holes in thy hide as Little John has left in that clouted cloak of thine."

"Little John !" said the beggar, "callest thou yonder water guzzling carle Little John ?"

"In sooth I do; mayhap thy back can tell more of his quarter-staff than thy tongue his name.

"Ask him, green jacket, ask him whether Allan-a-dale's back felt his staff; out upon thee, there is not a man among ye save one that I would give a pinch of meal for."

"Who is that one then, pert carle ?"

"Robin," answered the beggar, "good Robin Hood, an honest and true man—know you him, young free of speech ?"

"Passing well. I am Robin Hood !"

The name acted like a spell upon Allan-a-Dale; he dropped his pike-staff, and kneeling before the outlaw, said:

"Strike off my head, Robin, with thy good sword, that the tongue which has wagged against thee may speak no more."

"Not so," said the Outlaw; "I would hear it wag of things thou hast heard at the court of him men call England's king—Henry of Winchester."

"Hast not thy fellow told thee, good Robin ?"

"But in part—but in part. Come, man, let me hear all thou knowest."

"All I know, Robin, brings sorrow upon thee. Thy lands are gone, thy name is outlawed, and by the light of to-morrow's sun you will behold Earl Mortimer and nigh a thousand spears entering Barnesdale."

"We will do our devoirs, Allan, let them come."

"Well spoken, bold Robin, wilt thou have Allan's pike staff to help thee, mayhap it will not be the first Norman crown it has cracked ?"

"Right gladly, Allan, but I would not part with thee after we have shown Roger Mortimer the use of the yew bow."

"Thou shalt not, I will stay with thee if there is meat and drink to be found in the merry greenwood."

"There is meat and drink, Allan, aye, more, there is a Lincoln green jacket to replace thy clouted cloak, a good yew bow, a sheaf of

* Patched.

cloth yard shafts, a sword, and a buckler for thy arms, and more, a hundred marks a year as long as you stay with my merry men."

"That will be as long as England has a Robin Hood, and a forest to hold him. I will stay, and thou shalt never regret the bargain."

"I know it—thy hand; there, the bargain is made, and foul fall him who breaks it."

"Amen."

Now, Allan, jump behind me, my steed will carry us to the greenwood."

Robin mounted as he spoke, and Allan, throwing his cloak and the leather bags that hung around his neck, into the brook, jumped lightly upon the horse's croup.

"So my lands are gone," said the Outlaw, as they went through the forest; "dost thou know to whom the false king has given them?"

"Right well I know; Geoffrey de Lois, a Norman beggar, has thy lands."

"Ah! the *disturber* of the May-day sports; there is more in this than mere chance."

"It would seem so, good Robin, for he bears thee no good will."

"Thou knowest much for one of thy calling, Allan."

"My ears are open when men speak; behind the hawthorn I lurked and heard the tramp of horses' hoofs, and when I looked I saw Geoffrey de Lois and a priest riding from the court."

"A priest, Allan? one dark of countenance and sharp of speech."

"The same, Robin, the Abbot of St. Mary's, and uncle to Geoffrey de Lois."

"Did the wind bring their words to thine ear?"

"Marry, but it did, and my ears were sharpened when I heard thy name spoken."

"It was well thou wert near—come, what said the proud Abbot?"

"But little, save in joy that his nephew had been made Sheriff of Nottingham."

"Sheriff of Nottingham!" exclaimed Robin, pulling up his steed, sharply, "by him who died on tree, this smellest of priestcraft more than court favour."

"So thought I," said Allan-a-Dale, "and my thoughts were not wrong, as I knew when Geoffrey de Lois said thou wert going to Shere-wood, if molested at Barnesdale."

"By my knighthode the priestly brain is subtle; well, Allan, didst thou hear how they knew I wert going to Sherewood?"

"I did, good Robin; there's one of Geoffrey de Lois's knaves among your merry men."

"Ah! is it so? that tells how the foreign minion knew so much of our haunts. By our Lady he shall dangle from a good green bough —but go on, good Allan, didst thou hear more?"

"But little, good master, for my breath was nigh gone, running so long behind the hedge-row, but this I heard——"

Robin pressed his steed forward as Allan continued.

"They prayed that Earl Mortimer would fail of his object."

"How so? I can scarcely understand the workings of the priest's crafty brain."

"They prayed he would fail, good Robin, that you might go to Sherewood; then Geoffrey de Lois and the priest would pay off some score they hold against thee."

"A goodly plot! by my knighthode these priests learn some craft in their cloisters! Dost thou know more, Allan?"

"Not one word, good Robin, for I was spent, and when I got strength I came across the country to tell thee all."

"Thou art a good fellow, Allan, and twenty marks shall be thy portion. Where is Morti-mer's band now?"

"On the high road which leads to Barnes-dale. I have been quick, master, for they rode hard to take thine and thy merry men."

"Thou hast, indeed, been quick, and nearly got thy head broken for thy pains."

"Not so, master," Allan answered laughing. "Ask thy long-limbed man whose head was nearly broken."

"I know, I know; and have given Little John a posset to cure the wounds made by thy pike-staff."

"Hadst thou not given him so many on the day before, he would not have so nigh dried the brook. Blade-bone of Saint Peter! how the man sucked the waters down that throat of his, and how my fingers itched to lay my staff across his back as he buried his nose in the water."

"Peace, Allan; here's the greenwood and Robin's men; have a care over that tongue of thine, or there will be some skulls broken before thou hast worn the Lincoln-green many days."

"I will, master, I will. Bone of my body! but this is a goodly sight, five score and more stout archers; there is work here for the Earl Mortimer and his foreign knaves."

"There is, Allan, work enough for him to remember Barnesdale and Robin Hood."

CHAPTER VII.

FOREST WARFARE.

. . . . ! It was a gallant sight
To see them all on a row,
With every man a good broad sword,
And eke a good yew bow.

THE Anglo-Norman troops, led by the Earl of Mortimer, presented a splendid and warlike appearance as they wound in and out of the quiet roads which led to Barnesdale.

The great Earl's banner was in the van; the rich colours with which the arms of his house were embroidered upon the fluttering silk and its mail-clad bearer was a beautiful sight in itself.

The emblazonry upon the shields of the knights who owed allegiance to his house, the glowing colours worked upon the housings of their chargers, and the pourpoints which each knight wore above his mail, and the rainbow-like tints of the scarves which crossed their bodies, the long ends of which fluttering in the autumn air, gave them the appearance of men about to enter a tournament rather than the rude field of battle.

But this illusion, if any of those who saw the Earl and his knights as the little army went on its way through the many towns and villages entertained such, was dispelled when the curvetting war steeds passed onward; and the plainly-clad spearmen passed in close order, their steel caps and the points of their weapons glittering in the sun.

These and the crossbowmen told that other matters than a tournay caused this martial array, for the knights seldom brought their numerous bands of retainers to these meetings, the most ostentatious being generally content with the attendance of a couple of squires, and at the most a half dozen attendants.

Around the stern earl fluttered the gay pennons on the knights' lances, and ever and anon came the blast of a trumpet, calling the men who had fallen out of the line of march to rejoin the ranks.

There was much laughter among the young knights at the object of their long journey, and many wagers were made that the Saxon bowmen would not stay to meet their steel-clad foes.

"A cloth jerkin," said one who rode close beside Earl Mortimer, "will be but a poor check against our lances and spearmen."

"A cloth jerkin," said the Earl, who knew the stubborn Saxon character too well to undervalue the men he had vowed to destroy, "has before this been a match for linkmail."

"Say their arrows, my lord," said the knight; "but, in this instance, I am afraid we shall have had our long ride for nothing."

"We shall see, Sir Raymond. I hope it may be so; it will save us from slaughtering these misguided men. Ha! here is Barnesdale Forest. Sound the halt trumpeter."

A youth, mounted upon a white horse and wearing a surtout richly embroidered with the Earl's bearings, placed his trumpet to his lips and sounded one long, shrill blast upon his brazen instrument.

The small army became motionless, then the Earl, turning to the knight he had addressed as Sir Raymond, said:

"Come, sir knight, push forward with the trumpeter and sound a parley; tell the rebels if they will surrender their leader to our keeping, then quietly disperse, Roger Mortimer will turn back to whence he came."

The young noble would sooner have had the order given to dash into the forest and charge the rebels than do the Earl's bidding, but he dared not disobey.

Fastening a white scarf to the point of his lance, he rode forward with the trumpeter and was absent full twenty minutes.

When they returned, an angry shout came from the soldiers, for both the knight and his companion were shorn of their arms and fastened in the saddle, their faces towards the horses' tails.

Earl Mortimer bit his lips when he saw the manner in which the foresters had answered his messengers, and giving the word for the troops to advance, he entered the forest.

Robin Hood, with Little John, Much, and Allan-a-Dale had met the knight and the trumpeter in one of the fairy-like glades in the great forest.

They seemed to be alone, for not one of the five score archers were visible to the knight, as he drew rein and gave Robin the Earl's message.

"Answer him, Much, and you, John; and Allan, help Much to tell this sweet knight how the Saxon archers fear the Earl's threat."

The three sturdy fellows sprang forward, and before the knight or his companion could turn their horses they were both jerked out of the saddle.

The Outlaw's lieutenant wrenched the half-drawn sword from the knight's hand, then taking him up by the waist as though he were a child, placed him in his saddle with his face towards the horse's tail.

Much and Allan-a-Dale did the same office for the trumpeter, then Robin Hood, laughing aloud at the sight, said:

"Hie thee back, sweet herald, to him who sent thee, and tell how little Robin Hood and his merry men care for big words, although the Earl may have twice five hundred spears and crossbows to back them."

A few stripes from Little John's yew-bow goaded the steeds forward, and the riders, clutching at the hinder part of the saddle, were soon borne through the forest.

"Body o' me!" said Little John, "How the Earl will rave when he sees yon messengers back!"

"Were he only to rave," said the Bold Outlaw, "we need care but little, but peradventure we shall hear more of the whistle of a bolt from a crossbow than Mortimer's gentle words."

"We need care but little for the sound," said Allan, "did not an iron bolt come with it. Ah! look yonder, my masters, and tell me if there is not a morion shining through the green leaves."

"Wondrously like it," said Robin, as he carelessly fitted an arrow to his bow, "but it's a fair mark, Allan, for a feathered shaft to teach the knave to wear a less bright covering for his thick skull."

The arrow whistled through the air as the forester ceased speaking, and the cry which came from the thicket told how well the mark had been hit.

"One knave the less," said Little John, "thou hast slain him, master."

"Not so," said the Outlaw; "see, John, for thyself."

A slight opening between the trees showed one of Mortimer's spearmen running at full speed, his head was bare, the steel casque having been taken off by Robin's arrow.

"One of the foreign thieves in the pay of the Norman," said Little John, "he can take back word that cloth-yard shafts are plentiful in Barnesdale. Body-o'-me, heard ye that!"

The loud fanfare of the Norman trumpets, and the rattle of a species of kettle-drum were heard as Little John spoke.

Robin's lip curled with scorn, when he heard this signal, and looking towards the opening in the forest, said:

"The varlet has told his story, I will answer the Earl's summons to horse."

He placed his bugle to his lips, and wound a shrill defiant call which echoed through the length and breadth of the forest.

"There," laughed Robin; "if the knaves follow that sound, we may lead them to the open glen. Ha! by our Lady, hither they come. To your shelter, John, away! Much and Allan, bid our merry men find the rivets of the Norman armour with their cloth-yard shafts."

They disappeared among the trees. Then Robin, sounding another defiant call upon his bugle, followed.

The force which now began to enter the forest, was three times as great as that of the outlaws.

Their equipment was also better calculated for defence then the foresters' green jerkins, for not only were the men-at-arms and knights cased in armour, but even those who carried arblasts* wore iron gorgets, caps, and defensive armour for their arms and thighs; but there was one weapon they lacked—that, the tough yew-bow and the English shaft.

Riding at the head of his men, Earl Mortimer spurred his war-steed to the little glade, where Robin and his companions had so lately stood.

Not a glimpse of a green jacket was to be seen, and the Earl turning to the knights who crowded round him, said :

"Marry, but 'tis as I said, fair sirs, the sound of the knave's bugle was but the call for his rascals to flee."

"Thou liest! Earl Mortimer," said a voice. "Draw to the ear, my merry men. Saint George for England, and confusion to the Normans."

Upon every side came a flight of arrows, which rattled upon the knights' impenetrable armour, and others finding an undefended part on the less skilfully-made covering worn by the men-at-arms, struck nigh three score of them to the earth.

The attack was so sudden, the shafts so well aimed, that men and horses had fallen dead or dying before a lance could be lowered, or eye had time to mark from whence the arrows came.

The Earl saw he had been led into an ambuscade by the foresters, so spurring his black charger over the bodies of his fallen men, he called out fiercely :

"God and Saint Denis, follow me, all true knights, follow me."

"God and Saint Denis," they repeated, "come forth, Saxon swine, come forth!"

The attempt to penetrate the surrounding thicket was a failure, so the Earl and his lances, after essaying to break through the thick brushwood, drew up their steeds.

The most profound silence had been preserved by the foresters during the time the mail-clad horsemen were endeavouring to force a passage through the bushes, and were it not for the heap of dead and dying who lay in the centre of the glade, with the Saxon shaft driven into their bodies, there would have been nothing to show the forest was tenanted by the Norman troops.

That every movement was closely watched Earl Mortimer soon found, for when he drew up his snorting steed in the midst of the angry knights, a clear voice trolled out merrily from he brushwood :—

> Robin blithely blew his silver call,
> And ere the echoes slept,
> One hundred archers, stout and tall,
> Appeared at right and left.

The Earl struck his gauntletted hand upon his saddle, when the full, rich voice sounded so mockingly upon his ear, and with an oath called upon the arblast men to discharge their missiles into the surrounding bushes.

As the butts of the crossbows came to the men's shoulders, the voice of the Outlaw Chief could be heard shouting :

"St. George and Merry England, draw to the ear, my lusty bowmen, draw to the ear!"

The twang of a hundred bowstrings heralded the coming of a flight of arrows, and the foremost of the arblast men fell to the ground.

Earl Mortimer chafed like an angry lion as he plunged forward to within a yard of the bushes which held the outlaws commanded by Robin Hood.

"The foul fiend take them for lurking dogs!" he cried. "Come out from thy shelter, or——"

A cloth-yard shaft impelled by no ordinary hand struck the Earl's corselet, and checked the completion of his speech.

"Have a care, Lord Mortimer," said the voice that had before spoken, "or the next shaft may find an entrance between the points of thy Spanish harness."

The Earl gnashed his teeth, and backed the sable steed he bestrode from the dangerous points.

Come, sir knights, have none of you heart of grace in this hour, no plan to advise your Earl."

Raymond, the knight of Bayonne, rode to his leader.

"My lord," he said, "he who would crush a nest of hornets must not fear their stings."

"By him who bled for us, I conjure thee to speak more fully, or three score more of our men will follow those who have already fallen."

"It is not meet that I should have spoken before having thy permission, my lord, and your's sir knights. Our men have swords, let them cut a passage to these hinds; also, let the arblast-bolts be sent into the depths of the thicket."

"By my halidome! thou hast spoken well. Fall to, my men; fall to."

The sound of the troopers' swords and axes were accompanied by the hissing quarrells from the crossbows.

A space was soon cleared, and the Earl flourishing his battle-axe, shouted :

"A Mortimer! a Mortimer!"

The cry was taken up by the knights as they couched their lances, and followed the Earl to the glen, which spread to the right and left as clear of timber, and as soft as the richest carpet ever placed by Dame Nature upon the earth.

Then came a sudden check to the advance of the Earl and his knights; the foremost fell to the ground, and those in the rear were struck with confusion by a sudden flight of arrows.

The Earl was the first to disengage himself from his fallen steed; and as he sprang to his feet, he called out :

"Back — back! The hinds have placed stakes for our horses."

The warning cry checked the dense crowd of horsemen, and as they pulled up, there issued from the opposite belt of trees Robin Hood and his Merry Bowmen.

The Earl's angry shout, when he saw the bold outlaws advancing so fearlessly towards the steel-capped host, was aroused by a peal of laughter from their gallant leader.

* Arblast, a crossbow : the missile, an iron quarrell, so called from its shape.

ROBIN HOOD,
AND THE OUTLAWS OF SHERWOOD FOREST.

THE FAT FRIAR DROPS ROBIN HOOD INTO THE BROOK.

CHAPTER VIII.

THE COMBAT BETWEEN ROBIN HOOD AND EARL MORTIMER.

"Their bows they bent, and forth they went,
Shooting in company,
Towards the town of Nottingham,
Outlaws though they be."

THE indomitable leader of the Saxon archers did not permit his lightly-clad men to remain long enough in the open glade to face the line of spears which were levelled when the band issued from their covert.

A single note from his bugle caused them to disappear as suddenly as they appeared before Mortimer's angry host.

The Earl quickly marshalled his followers in line, intending to charge the foresters, and thus at one blow destroy them; but ere the heavy horsemen could strike their rowels into their horses' flanks, the archers had sought the shelter of the trees.

All save their fearless leader had gone, and he, as though loving the danger he had placed himself in, stood leaning upon his drawn sword, regarding the movements of his foes.

"A cloth jerkin," he muttered, "is but a bad shield against a lance head; my merry men are safer behind yon trees than out here. Marry, but the Norman mercenaries like not the fact that a hundred grey-goose shafts are drawn to the ear behind this thicket."

The Earl, checking the advance of his mailed cavalry, seemed uncertain how to act; as Robin had said the knowledge of a hundred unerring shafts being pointed at his followers caused him to act with prudence.

He felt no fear of the issue of a combat in the open ground; here his lances would have scattered the foresters like dust; but as they had gone to the thick cover, he knew as long as a quiver contained an arrow his men would be mere targets for the English bowmen.

While holding a brief consultation with the knights nearest to him, the Earl's attention was called to Robin Hood by Raymond of Bayonne.

"See, my good lord," the knight said, "yonder stands the leader of the outlaws, peradventure it may be to treat with thee for clemency toward his band."

The Earl looked towards Robin, who was now leaning against a tree.

"By our Lady," said the Earl, "thou art right, Raymond; yon Outlaw has done wisely to yield to our clemency, and we'll have speech of the knave; although I may spare his men, he must hang upon the nearest tree."

He went forward as he spoke, then the two leaders were placed about half way between their bands.

The Outlaw smiled quietly when he saw the Earl come towards him, and in reply to a whispered caution which came from the covert behind him, said;

"A malison on thee, John. Keep thine eyes upon the arblast men; leave the Earl to my care."

"But, master," answered the invisible lieutenant, "I pray thee forego this wish to have speech with yonder Earl. Seek the covert, master, and we will give these Normans such a flight of grey-goose shafts as——"

"Peace, knave. Do as I bid thee, or by St. Herman of the Wold thou shalt drink nought but water for the next seven days."

"Body-o'-me!" grumbled the giant, as he drew further into the covert, "body-o'-me! but I shall have but little strength left to bend the bow. Water! for seven long days! Body-o'-me! ugh!"

When the Earl came within speaking distance of the bold Forester, the latter, to show he trusted to Mortimer's honour, sheathed his sword, and, with the hand thus set at liberty, toyed with the rich tassel which hung from the bugle he wore at his hip.

Mortimer, not to be outdone in courtesy, also returned his ponderous sword to its scabbard; then resting the point of his triangular shield upon the ground, he placed his hands lightly upon the upper part, and began the conversation by saying:

"Have I mistaken thy meaning, misguided man, when I come forward to have speech with thee?"

"Thou dost not err, Earl Mortimer," answered the Outlaw. "I sought speech of thee, thinking it were a shame this green sward should be red with the blood of my merry men; and for the matter of that, of thy followers, mercenaries though they be, and enemies to this fair land."

"Thou art right," said the Earl, not doubting but Robin was about to surrender; "it were a shame that blood should be spilt when by a timely yielding of thy body thou mayest pre——"

The ringing laugh which came from the forester's lips checked the Earl's speech, and placing his hand upon the hilt of his sword, was about to draw the weapon.

"Take thy hand from thy sword," said the Outlaw, "for as surely as an inch of the bright blade becomes visible above the scabbard's mouth will a grey goose-shaft pierce thine eye until it reaches the brain; so have a care, my Lord of Mortimer, have a care."

The fame of the wondrous skill possessed by these bowmen had been spread the length and breadth of the land; thus Mortimer's Earl knew the threat was no idle boast, and though a brave man he did not hesitate to remove his hand from the embossed hilt of his weapon.

"The fashion of the Norman Court," Robin said, "is to look upon the Saxon as but a slave to his conquerors—thy brain, Mortimer, has taken up this, or thy words would not have been so wide of the truth."

"In heaven's name, then, disgrace to the spurs thou once wore," said the earl, angrily; "what caused thee to seek this parley, if it were not to yield?"

"A wish to save the shedding of blood, the blood of those who have nought to do with thy mission here. Mistake not my words as those of fear, for at a wave of my hand five-score feathered shafts would be planted among thy followers, who look even now greedily upon the free land which holds England's merry bowmen."

The Earl was growing angrier every moment, and it is probable he would not have patiently heard Robin Hood's words to the end, had he not known that his slightest movement towards his men would have been the signal for a flight of arrows from the copse.

Well skilled in the then rude art of war, he did not wish to bring matters to a crisis while the outlaws had so much the advantage of position.

A position he saw while conversing with the Outlaw Chief, had been rendered still more impassible for his mailed cavalry, by the rows of sharp stakes, which were just visible above the ground, behind which the bold woodsmen stood.

True, he numbered some threescore arblast men in his train, but the weapon being a foreign one, and but lately introduced into England, the men were not so well skilled in its use as he would have wished.

Knowing all this, and hoping yet to draw the foresters from their covert, he repressed his rising passion, also the strong inclination to draw his sword upon the Outlaw.

"My mission here," said the Earl in reply to the forester's words, "is in obedience to the wish of my lawful—aye, and thy lawful—sovereign, Henry of Winchester, King of England."

"Thou liest, Mortimer," said the Outlaw;

"thy coming was prompted by the hate thou hast ever borne to me since my good lance rolled both thee and thy steed in the dust before the whole Court assembled to witness the tournay."

The Earl's brow became as black as night at these words; he too well remembered the tournay of which Robin spoke, and his heart told him it was more in revenge for that defeat which up to the present hour galled his proud spirit, than a wish to save the King, that he had undertaken to subdue or slay the captain of the outlaws.

"The lie back to thy teeth!" he said angrily; "if I went down before thy lance, it was when thou wert a belted Earl, not a leader of thieves and cutpurses; wert thou still a noble, and worthy of my lance, I would even now wipe out the trampling of my crest in that day's tournay."

"Gramercy,"* said the bold Forester, "for thy courteous words, most puissant Earl, although my lands are given to the hungry Norman crew, I am yet as good a man as thou art. Aye, better, for my knee has not yet bent to the foreign yoke, neither has my tongue, with lip-loyalty, saved the possessions of my fathers."

The forester drew the buff gauntlet he wore from his right hand as he spoke, and holding it by the fingers, continued:

"Listen, Earl Mortimer, I will prove I am the better man of the two. Here we stand, in the merry greenwood, my coat but of Lincoln-green cloth, my cap but of felt, and my arms an English sword and buckler; yet, withal this, and despite the Spanish mail which covers thee from crown to heel, I challenge thee to single combat! here, foot to foot and hand to hand, let the issue be with the best man; if thou conquer, my men will yield thee true and lawful——"

"Body-'o-me!" growled a voice in the thicket; "surely, this mad master of mine will not fight that tower of steel. Bones of St. Hubert! but we will not yield while a shaft is left, or a hand to wield a sword."

"Prisoners," he continued, not heeding the interjectional growl of the sturdy lieutenant. "In proof of this, behold my gage."

He flung the leathern glove at the Earl's feet as he spoke, and the latter, trembling with suppressed wrath, stooped and picked it up.

"I accept the combat," he said; "but that men may not say I slew thee in unfair fight thou shalt have the loan of one of yonder knights' armour. Come hither, Raymond of Bayonne," he added, raising his voice; "I would borrow thy——"

"Stay," said Robin Hood, "I will not have even a helmet that has adorned a Norman head. I offer thee combat, and, as the challenger, have a right to my choice of arms—a choice thou wilt accept, unless thy heart has grown weak through mixing with the silken gallants at the court of him thou stylest king."

"Be it so," said the Earl; "I will leave thee for a few moments, that thy peace can be made with heaven; for, as sure as the sun gilds the leaves of yonder tree, thou hast seen thy last day upon earth."

Robin's rejoinder was a light laugh of defiance; and as the Earl walked swiftly to his

* Thanks.

followers, the Outlaw drew his sword and tried the temper of the blade by bending it until the point touched the hilt.

Satisfied that his weapon was to be relied upon, he loosened the straps of his shield and threw it behind him.

There was a dull thud as though the buckler had come in contact with a hard substance.

"Body-o'-me! ten thousand curses upon the buckler," rapped out Little John from his place of concealment; "thou hast well nigh broken my head with that target of thine."

"Keep thy head covered, John."

"Blessed St. Hubert," rejoined the gigantic forester, "would that I had done so. But hearken, master of mine, I was praying to the saints to give thee victory, praying, master, with head all bare, when thy shield came rattling about my ears. But, master."

"What now, knave?"

"Thou must be mad to engage yon steel-cased Earl. Body-o'-me! shall I draw a good shaft ready to aid thee should he get the upper hand?"

"Peace, knave, let thy shafts alone, except yonder host advance. Where are the men?"

"Here, good master, stuck in this copse as thick as flies around a honey pot."

"Listen and keep thy peace till I have done; should the day go against me let no hand move in my cause; they are too strong for us. To save thy carcasses from their spears I will do my devoir with this Earl; should I fall, take my body with thee in thy retreat, and give it a free man's burial. To thee, Little John, rogue as thou art, I give the care of our merry men, see to it, knave, and be less fond of swilling all the wine, whether good or bad, which comes in thy way."

"Body o' me! but I always choose the best, good master; if I am more athirst than my fellows my patron saint is to blame; but here comes thy foe; a grip of thy hand, master; may St. Hubert bring thee safe out of this grievous strait."

Little John's huge hand was protruded through the thick foliage, and Robin gripped it with a force which even brought tears to the giant's eyes.

A rustling among the bushes told that more of the foresters were coming forward to enjoy the honour of a farewell clasp of their leader's hand. So Robin, to prevent this, moved forward to meet the Earl.

"Hast thou," Mortimer asked, "made thy peace with heaven? or does thine heart, even at this moment, fail to second the words——"

"Peace! we lose time," said the Outlaw; "draw thy weapon, man, for the arm which overthrew thee once has lost none of its skill; but stay—ere we begin I must tell thee my mind is changed. My merry men will not yield to thee should I fall."

"The better for yonder knights, who hunger to dim their lance points with Saxon blood. Now have at thee for a false traitor. God and St. Denis!"

Shouting the latter words (the Earl's war-cry), he made a downward stroke at the Outlaw's head, which had it taken effect, would have cleft him to the spine.

The forester's trusty sword caught the blow, as he answered Mortimer's cry, by calling out:

"St. George and Merry England, and confusion to the tyrant's minions."

The combat lasted for some minutes without either party gaining an advantage, and those who watched the play of the trenchant blades, saw that Robin, despite the absence of defensive armour from his body, was by his superior skill and quick eye, quite a match for the Earl.

For some time the Outlaw fought purely on the defensive, and the Earl being armed at all points, and covered by his shield, rained blow after blow upon his adversary.

Every stroke was met with a rapidity and coolness, which caused the fiery Earl to redouble his efforts to slay his antagonist.

Robin smiled when he beheld this; it was all he aimed at. Knowing the heavy armour the Earl wore would soon tire him, the Outlaw kept him at bay until the strong arm began to tire.

Now the forester in turn pressed upon his foe, his blade rang upon the steel armour and the large shield, until the Earl, tired and worn by the weight of his mail, began to retreat.

The hidden foresters could scarce restrain their joy at the sight, and Little John now understood his leader's motive for refusing a suit of mail.

The cumbersome armour though very useful to a mounted combatant, was a decided disadvantage to the wearer when on foot.

Back, step by step, Mortimer went, the Bold Outlaw seeking with his sword point every joint of his adversary's mail.

Back, back, until they were within three feet of the copse where the outlaws were concealed, then the Earl's sword flew from his hand.

He raised his arm to ward off a blow which threatened his head, and quick as thought the forester changed the direction of the weapon, and the point entered the only vulnerable part of the Earl's body.

This was under the arm where the joints of the mail met.

"Yield thee, rescue or no rescue!" said Robin, as the sword point pierced the leathern doublet and began to cut the flesh; "yield thee, or, by St. Herman of the Wold, I will drive this good blade through thy body until the point touches the mail on the opposite side."

"I yield," was the sullen answer; "withdraw thy weapon."

The Outlaw did so; and at the same time made a sign to Little John, who, with Allan-a-Dale, dashed from the copse, and seizing the Earl by the arms hurried him out of sight.

The knights and horsemen had dismounted at the beginning of the combat, and so swift had been their leader's defeat, that ere they could mount their chargers, he had disappeared from view.

Raymond of Bayonne was the first in the saddle, and waving his lance, he dashed his rowels into his charger's flanks, and shouted:

"A rescue! a rescue!"

His companions were not long in following him, and taking up the cry, and the weight of the heavy steeds, as they thundered across the glen, fairly shook the earth.

The spearmen and those armed with the arblast followed as quickly as they cou'd and the horsemen, when within fifty paces of the copse, heard a voice call out:

"St. George and Merry England. Now, my men, now!"

The hiss of an hundred arrows through he air

was followed by the rattle of the steel heads upon the knights' armour, the fall of horses, and such of the riders as were not armed in proof.

Checked, but not subdued, the knight of Bayonne sprung from his horse, and, drawing his sword, called upon the spearmen to follow him; but, when they reached the copse, it was untenanted.

———

CHAPTER IX.

THE EARL'S RANSOM.

In summer time, when leaves and flowers
　On every bough do spring,
It is merry in the gay greenwood,
　And the little birds do sing.
List n to me, ye yeomen all,
　So comely, so courteous, so good:
One of the best that ever bare bow—
　His name was Robin Hood.*

THE mellow tints of the autumn sun flooded Sherwood's fair forest, and the timid deer were leaving their coverts to seek a crystal pond, which lay in the depths of this romantic sylvan retreat.

At the base of a giant oak the ground was strewed with rushes and soft grass, and reclining upon this couch was the handsome and fearless Outlaw, Robin Hood.

His yew-bow and a quiver filled with grey-goose shafts lay near, and his right hand, although his senses were buried in a deep sleep, rested upon the hilt of his sword.

In spite of the price which had been put upon his head, the Outlaw's repose was as little troubled with a thought of danger as though he slept in the stone chamber of the castle which had once been his.

The Forest of Sherwood was, at the time of which we write, little frequented, save by those who were compelled to skirt its margin when travelling; even then, so great was the solitude of its avenues of giant trees and coverts of brushwood, that many an ave or pater-noster were said before venturing upon a journey fraught with so many real and unreal dangers.

Superstition had much to do in preventing even the peasants of the neighbouring hamlets from exploring the forests, for they held a firm belief that nature's solitude was tenanted by woodland fays and nymphs.

The former, they believed, were gifted with the power of cudgelling any daring mortal who should attempt to penetrate the haunts of the deer; and the latter, by their wondrous beauty were supposed to lure men to destruction.

If these causes were not sufficient to keep the forest from being invaded, the knowledge that a band of desperate outlaws had sought refuge in the mystic depths added to the ill repute of the place.

Thus the peasant and swineherd, the farmer and trader, shrank from Sherwood as a place of evil; and those who were compelled to traverse the more open parts did so with sinking

* The ballad from which these verses are taken was given by Ritson to the public at the close of the last century. The original manuscript is preserved in the public library of Cambridge, and it is supposed to have been written during the reign of Henry VI. The above words are modernised.

heart and trembling limbs, starting at the rustle of a leaf, and expecting to behold either a spirit, a nymph, or a forester dart from among the trees.

It will be readily understood that a better place for the outlaws' home could not have been found in the whole length and breadth of the land; add to its repute the nature of the coverts which were impassable for horses, there is little wonder that bold Robin slept so peacefully and soundly in that sweet sylvan glade.

True, no precautions were neglected to prevent a surprise, for the band had many and powerful foes around them.

Upon every point of the forest which could be entered from the high road, there lurked among the brushwood and behind trees lusty green-clad outlaws, who gave timely notice of a foe's approach.

Their signal was certain notes upon the bugle-horns, and so well acquainted were they with the sound of each other's horns that the band could tell exactly where to expect an intruder.

Suddenly the profound silence was broken by a long-winding blast from one of the sentinels, and the Outlaw, springing to his feet, hastily donned his quiver, then as he leant upon the long bow, he passed one hand across his eyes as though to banish the hazy sensation which is felt when one is aroused from a deep sleep.

"That's Allan's blast," he muttered, after listening to the ringing echoes. "He is posted on the high road."

As though the matter was of no more import than the fact of ascertaining from whence the sound came, the Outlaw began to saunter leisurely to and fro beneath the wide-spreading branches of the trysting tree.

He paused when Little John made his appearance at the farther end of the glen, and judging by the lieutenant's face that nothing serious had arisen, he greeted the giant's advance in his usual good-humoured manner.

"What knave," he said, "has dared to make the welkin ring with this rude blast, and disturb the slumbers of Sherwood's King? Is it a fat bishop, who has come this way in all humility to leave us his gold and silver? Speak, John."

"It is both gold and silver, Master-'o-mine," said John, "and a goodly bag, but not brought by a churchman. No, Body-'o-me! they do not, these pious knaves, discard the goodly things of this world so easily, although they let the more sinful portion do so."

"Shorten thy preamble, John," said the Outlaw Chief, "which has been as long as a new-made monk's first prayer, tell thy story man, and a' done with it."

"Body-o-me!" said the giant, for the first time displaying two well-filled bags; "this will tell the story, and in a pleasant way."

He shook the bags until the chink of the metal could be heard—certainly a pleasant sound.

"Mortimer's ransom!" said Robin, laughing, "it is welcome, John, for our royal coffers have been empty of late."

"Bones of St. Hubert!" said John, "but thou sayest true; for nothing but water has passed down my throat this week past. Body-o'-me! I have scarce strength to bend a bow in consequence."

"Shame on thee, John! dost thou forget the good monk they found with a bottle of sack under his gown?"

"I reckon that as nought, good master; it was but a good action."

"How, knave?"

"A good action I did, master. I both drank his sack, and cudgelled his hide, for letting me; but think, good master, the scandal I saved the Church by preventing the holy man getting in a state not seemly for one of his calling."

"Get thee out for a hypocrite," said Robin; "thou carest little for the sins of others when that throat of thine is dry."

"I will not gainsay aught thou sayest, good master; so we'll let the matter stand over until a more fitting time; but concerning these pieces of gold and silver, shall I take them to Much, our steward."

"Do so, John; tell him to have the feast spread at once, that we may give this Earl an insight into our free and merry life; let him spread it in the glen where stands the hollow oak."

Little John's face expressed the delight he felt at the prospect of the banquet, and, humming the refrain of an old ditty, he went towards the covert, but, ere he could pass through the foliage, Robin Hood's voice arrested his steps.

"Stay, Little John," he said, "when the feast is prepared, sound three notes on thy horn, to call in such of our merry men as be out in the forest, for this eve we will trust to the safe keeping of our patron, St. Herman of the Wold; and hark'ee, knave, keep thy itching fingers out of those bags."

Little John cast his eyes upward, and looked the personification of injured innocence.

"Body o' me!" he said, as he went towards the glen, "had I but helped myself to one good piece, I had deserved it for the trouble of carrying."

During the foregoing colloquy between Robin Hood and his lieutenant, the sun had sunk so low that its dusky light was only visible through a slight opening between the trunks of the trees.

The Outlaw Chief, who had resumed his walk after Little John disappeared, paused when he saw the blood-red glow of the setting sun, and folding his arms, attentively regarded the small disc visible from where he stood.

"So," he said, half aloud, "the setting of this day's sun was to be my last hour upon this fair earth, unless I yielded the Lord of Mortimer without ransom. Such was the answer my messenger brought me. But yon blessed orb has seen a different result from the Norman's threats."

"Thanks to thy promise, good master, of wetting the feathers of a goose shaft with the proud Earl's blood."

Robin turned at the interruption, and beheld his stalwart follower, his big face brimming over with good humour as though some recent event had mightily amused him.

"What now, knave?" said Robin," "is it thus you keep my orders?"

"I have kept them, good master, and even now there is a feast being spread that would cause the Norman King to die with envy were he to see it; and body-o'-me! it has all been done without Much looking at even a roast haunch."

"The pursing of thy lips," Robin said, "tells me that something has befallen Much. What is it thou'rt grinning at?"

"But what I expected," said Little John," laughing. "Thou remember'st I spoke of a Curtall* friar I saw yester-e'en hunting a goodly buck?"

"I do, by Saint Herman. I'll teach the shavelings to hunt deer in our preserves. Well, about Much."

"Body-o'-me!" said the Forester, laughing, until his sides shook; "little Much went to teach this holy friar not to hunt our venison; and—ho, ho, ho!—ha, ha, ha!——"

"A malison on thy jaws. Tell thy story without such unseemly mirth."

Little John drew the back of his hand across his eyes to efface the moisture which gathered there during his outburst of laughter.

"Patience, good master, he said, "and thou wilt laugh too, or thou art not merry Robin, the king of good fellows. Well, body-o'-me, when Much bid the friar leave the deer at peace, the holy man laid about him with a stout staff; and though Much fought like a very devil, he has come back so bruised from head to heel, that he can neither sit nor stand. Body-o'-me—ho, ho, ho! The shaveling has trounced the miller's hide—ha, ha, ha!'"

The giant went off in another fit of boisterous laughter, and Robin, in spite of himself was compelled to join in the merriment.

"By Saint Herman of the Wold!" said Robin, when he regained sufficient breath to use his favourite oath, "thou shalt learn better than to laugh at the misfortunes of thy fellows. Here, knave, take thy good oak stave, and seek out this lusty saint, and if thou dost not liquor his hide, not one drop of sack or malvoisie touches that thirsty throat of thine for twice seven days."

Little John's face lengthened at this command, and, well it might, for the expected feasting he had looked forward to was placed out of his reach.

"Body-'o-me! good Master," he ruefully said; "would not to-morrow do as well as to-night? Think thou of the fast I have had so long. I am weak, good Robin, and the holy man's staff would ring upon my carcass like as though it were an empty——"

"To-morrow, be it. Crack the rascal's shaven crown, if thou cans't, and remember, if he beats thee, thy master must e'en try a bout with him.

"Beat me! Shoulder of Saint Hubert! I'll make jelly of the varlet."

Rising clear and ringing above the trees sounded the signal that the feast was ready. Arm-in-arm the outlaws went in the direction of the sound, Little John thinking more of the goodly viands than the trouble which awaited him on the morrow.

Robin left his trusty lieutenant near the glen where the feast was spread.

He went towards a small hut, or rather a cottage, for it was built with blocks of stone, and cemented rudely, but securely together.

Here Robin had kept the proud Earl; it was but a small prison for so great a prisoner.

---

* Stavely, in his "Romish Horseleech," says the Curtall Friars were so called because of the shortness of their gowns. Dr. Stukely avers it was because of the rope they wore round their waists, which is called a "Cordelier," hence the corruption Curtall.

CHAPTER X.

THE OUTLAWS' FEAST.

They washed themselves and wiped themselves
  And down to their dinner sat,
Bread and wine they had enough
  And venison plump and fat;
Hares and pheasants they had full good,
  And river fowl was there,
And there wanted never so little a bird,
  As ever was bred on a briar.

IT was a scene of rare picturesque beauty this feast of the green-clad outlaws; the Chief, conspicuous from his men by the cap of green velvet and jerkin of the same costly material which he now wore in place of the ordinary Lincoln cloth.

There could not be conceived a more beautiful sylvan spot than the place where the long oaken tables were placed—a row of gigantic oaks, in so good a line that it semed the hand of man had planned the acorns which bore such prodigious fruit.

Under the wide-spreading branches of these forest monarchs the feast was held, and so perfect was the covering which nature thus afforded the bold yeomen, that neither sun nor rain could pierce the leafy canopy.

Upwards of a hundred stout foresters were seated at the board, which was covered with the choicest viands the forest, the lake, or the adjoining swamp could furnish.

Upon a huge wooden trencher in the centre of the table, were two smoking haunches of venison, and at each end there was a counterpart of this famous dish.

Upon smaller trenchers were to be seen roasted swans, pheasants, boiled capons, swimming in toothsome sauce, bowls of fresh fish, huge piles of barley cakes.

Nearer the sides of the table were huge flagons of nut brown ale, and beakers of sack, malvoisie, and other choice wines.

Beside each wooden plate was a horn drinking cup; upon the grass near the lower end of the table and supported by large blocks of wood, were several huge barrels, containing a further supply of both good October ale, and the rich juice of the grape; and toward these goodly emblems of joy to a thirsty throat, Little John, from time to time, cast looks of the tenderest regard.

Earl Mortimer was seated upon Robin's right hand, and by the sullen, gloomy expression upon his face it was evident he did not know how soon his captivity would end.

The Outlaw had treated the Earl with knightly courtesy, for although a prisoner held to ransom he wore his sword, and the sable crest upon his helmet floated in the breeze as freely as though he were an invited guest instead of a foe and a captive.

In these warlike days it was the custom to deprive a prisoner of his armour and arms; neither of these had the courteous forester demanded, although the Earl had more than once attempted to escape the vigilance of his guards.

When all were seated, the chief of the sturdy band doffed his cap, an example which was followed by all present; then grace was said, and the business of eating began in earnest.

It was not unfashionable in those days to have an appetite; so the Earl, however much he despised and hated his captors, did as much execution among the viands as the most lusty of the band.

Venison, fowl, and fish, were carved by his dagger, for there were no knives and forks at that period—the dagger which every man wore serving the purpose of a knife with as much readiness as it would find a sheath in an adversary's body.

The feasting was carried on in silence save for a low voiced remark, or jest being spoken by a yeoman to his neighbour.

The fourth part of an hour sufficed to make sad havoc among the edibles; then, at a signal from Robin, a dozen stout fellows jumped to their feet, and carried away the wreck of the feast.

The horn cups were soon passing round, and tongues began to wag under the influence of the nut-brown ale.

"What think you, my lord," Robin asked, "of our forest life? Does not its freedom sit more easily upon our shoulders, than being at the caprice of a false king."

The Earl's temper had been a little improved by the good cheer, and divers horns of wine he had partaken of.

"I will not gainsay your words, Robin," he said, "yet I would not that I were compelled to lead a life fraught with such danger as threatens thee and thy companions, if taken in open outlawry."

"If taken—that was well said, my lord," said the handsome forester; "if taken—that day is far off yet."

"It would seem so," replied the Earl, a touch of anger in his tone, "or I had not been left in captivity so many weeks."

"How now, my lord, has thy captivity been a dungeon or a chain, that thou speakest in such covert bitterness? Saint Herman! thou hast had the forest to roam in, and the best cheer our poverty could afford!"

"Thy cheer," replied the Earl, "has been meet for a king—the forest a bridal chamber; but when the mind is far beyond these, then they are but like a dungeon wall."

"There may be some truth in this, my lord," said Robin. "I did not think thy captivity sat so heavily upon thee as this. I give thee joy, Earl Mortimer; thou art free to depart at any hour."

The Earl's face flushed with joy, and he seemed about to grasp the Outlaw's hand, but he checked the impulse before his companion noticed the half-extended arm.

"Has the good knight Raymond," he asked, "surrounded the forest with his spears, that thy tongue offers me instant freedom?"

"The knight may be among the silken nobles of Henry's court, or at the bottom of the sea for aught I wot," replied Robin; "no, my lord, when my messenger brought word that I should hang when this day's sun set, unless I released thee, I sent them back such answer to their message that soon brought the means of thy liberation."

The Earl's face expressed more than ordinary surprise as he listened to the Outlaw Chief's words. At first an incredulous smile played upon his lips, then, as this faded, he turned his eyes upon the bold forester with an expression in them that told he felt some admiration for the man whose hand had twice conquered him in fair and open fight.

"The means of my liberation!" he repeated; "unless it were a body of good spears; it must be the ransom thy boldness prompted thee to ask; but unless all who owe allegiance to my banner are turned traitors, they would clear this forest of thy band before paying a single mark for my liberty."

"You mistake, my good lord," replied the forester smiling; "for I sent word to all who hold the name of Mortimer as their war-cry, that the sight of a steel helmet or a glittering spear-head being seen by my merry men would be the signal for a grey-goose shaft to pass through thy body."

The Earl started as these words were spoken, and gnawing the ends of his long mustache. he looked as though he would have given much to have plunged the dagger into the Outlaw Chief's heart.

"And would'st thou," he asked savagely, "have kept thy word had the glitter of my spearmen been seen from thy coverts?"

"Would'st thou," said Robin, evading a direct answer, "have hanged me in the forest of Barnesdale, according to thy word plighted to Henry of Winchester, had the chance been thine?"

"By the Blessed Virgin," the Earl angrily answered, "I would, had'st thou ten lives!"

"By Saint Herman of the Wold!" said Robin, "so would I have kept my word, had thou been Henry of Winchester, in place of Roger Mortimer. But come, my lord, a truce to this; you are my guest, and it smacks of scant courtesy to grumble with one who is under our hospitality.

"Thou art right Robin," said the Earl, his passion giving place to a better feeling; "give me thine hand; there, Mortimer is thy friend, for a right good yeoman and true man is Robin Hood."

"Thanks, my lord, there is my hand, one that is always ready to strike a blow for England, and as a true knight thou can'st not gainsay me when I say it is the better for that."

"Men think differently upon these matters, Robin," answered the Earl. "Perhaps ambition guides thy thoughts and deeds, but be that as it may, no matter upon which side we strike, we are friends henceforth, unless we meet in the field of battle, then each must do his devoir for the banner he fights under."

"Be it so, my lord, the day may yet come when this pledge of friendship may serve us both."

The Forester's words were prophetic; for those unsettled times soon brought a change in the mind of the false King, and caused him to banish the very men who placed him upon the throne. But of that, as far as our hero is concerned, anon.

"Come, my merry men," the bold Forester continued, "to your feet, fill your cups to the brim and pledge our guest."

The outlaws obeyed, and Little John to show his good-will to the Earl took up a large beaker of wine.

"Drain off thy goblets, knaves," said Robin, when all were ready. "Drink to Earl Mortimer, and wish he may never meet worse friends than the merry men of Sherwood forest."

The pledge was drank, and so heartily by Little John that he was well-nigh choked by the volume of liquor which ran from the beaker down his capacious throat.

Harm might have befallen the lieutenant, had not Allen-a-Dale snatched up a heavy mallet and began to belabour the giant's back with blows that would have felled an ordinary man.

"Thanks, good Allen," gasped John, "I am better; a murrian on thy cursed mallet, dost want to break my back?"

Allan-a-Dale desisted, and there was a roar of laughter from the foresters at the little scene.

"Silence all of ye," said Robin. "Marry, but thy tongues have quickened full early. Silence, listen to Mortimer's Earl, he would pledge thee in return."

"Body-o'-me!" muttered Little John; "I fear my throat is twisted out of shape too much for me to do honour to my Lord of Mortimer; but I'll try. Let the mallet lie where it is, good Allan," he added, as he saw Allan about to raise the heavy wooden instrument from the ground; "let it lie. It was but my throat had become smaller in consequence of the long fast I've had from good wine——"

"Peace!" cried Robin; "pray heaven, John, to shorten that tongue of thine, for it wags from dawn to sunset without a rest."

"Earl Mortimer was by this time upon his feet, and, holding a brimming goblet of rich wine above his head. The outlaws had also replenished their cups, and Little John possessed himself of a full beaker."

"To ye all, my merry men!" said the Earl; "may ye live here at peace until Roger Mortimer leads a foe to your retreat; for I swear by my knightly word and my oath of chivalry to do no harm to thee by word of mouth or by arms."

He raised the goblet to his lips as he concluded; then, at a signal from Robin, the outlaws again pledged the Earl; this time without Little John requiring the aid of Allan-a-Dale to rescue him from suffocation.

"Have a care, John,'" said Much, who sat near the giant, his hand bandaged and one arm in a sling; "have a care, thou swill-tub, or the fat friar will knock the fumes of that goodly liquor out of thy pate before thy tongue can repeat an ave."

"I care not a groat for the fat friar," replied Little John, "nor thee on his back. Give me but room to wield my staff, Body-o'-me! were he the devil in a curtell gown I would break his pate. A murrain on thee! Have a care, thou thing of a miller's son."

"A malison on thee for a wine-swilling hog," retorted Much; "were not my body sore from the effects of that cursed friar's staff, I would have a bout with thee now. Listen, thou guzzling ox—here, before this fair company, I wager a rundlet of wine against thy best arrow, that yon curtell monk—or devil, for I wot not which—tans thine hide for thee to-morrow."

"A wager—a fair wager!" shouted the foresters; "thou'lt lose thy rundlet, Much, for no forester can bout with John at quarter-staff, much less a shaven monk."

"Peace, my men," Robin said, and in an undertone to Earl Mortimer he added, "these knaves require watching, my lord, for when the wine begins to tell they would as soon fall to and break each other's heads as they would capture and rob a rich churchman."

The Earl smiled, and his face now showed that he enjoyed the scene quite as much as the foresters themselves.

"They are sturdy knaves," he said in reply to Robin's words, "and little wonder we had such stubborn work to win Evesham—now, good Robin, the song thou hast promised."

"The rascals are quiet now," Robin said. "Ho, there, Little John," he added, "if that last sack has not twisted thy gullet out of place, give us thy famous song."

"Thy song, John," chorused the merry foresters, "the song of the Norfolk Turnip."

"Body-o'-me!" said John, clearing his throat, "that song has been trolled so oft that I expect to hear the very trees singing it at dead of night."

A rattling of the horn drinking cups told of the little patience possessed by the foresters, so the giant in a full rich voice trolled out the following humorous ditty :—

Lyttle John's Storie of ye Norfolke Turnippe.*

Some counties vaunt themselves in pies,
  And some in meat excel;
For turnips of enormous size,
  Fair Norfolk bears the bell.

This tale an old nurse told to me,
  Which I relate to you.
And well I wot what nurses say,
  Is sacred all and true.

At midnight how a hardy knight
  Was riding for the lea;
The stars and moon had lost their light,
  And he had lost his way.

The wind full loud and sharp did blow,
  The clouds amain did pour;
And such a night, as stories show,
  Was never seen before.

In vain he sought full half the night,
  No shelter could he spy.
Pity it were, so bold a knight,
  Starved with cold should die.

Now voices strange assail his ear,
  And yet no house was nigh;
Thought he, the devil himself is here;
  Preserve me, God on high.

Then summoned he his courage high,
  And thus aloud did call:
"Fairies, giants, demons, come not nigh,
  For I defy you all!"

When from a hollow turnip near
  Out jumped a living wight;
With friendly voice, and accents clear,
  He thus addressed the knight.

"Sir Knight, no demon dwelleth here,
  No giant keeps this house;
But two poor drovers—good man Veere
  And honest Robin Rouse.

"We two have taken shelter here,
  With oxen, ninety-two;
And if you'll enter, never fear,
  There's room enough for you."

* Much of the quaint humour of this song is lost in rendering the obsolete spelling (as we found it in the Heronshaw manuscript) into a form better suited to the general reader.

ROBIN HOOD,

AND THE OUTLAWS OF SHERWOOD FOREST.

ROBIN HOOD AND THE NORMAN SPY.

CHAPTER XI.

FRIAR TUCK'S CHALLENGE.

THE Earl of Mortimer joined in the uproarious laughter which greeted the close of Little John's story of the wonderful turnip, and the narrator as grave as an owl took no part in the mirth, but looked from one to the other as though angry they should doubt the truth of his statement.

"Body-o-me!" he said, "hand that stoup

over, Allan, for my throat is as dry as though I had swallowed the Norfolk turnip."

"A just punishment," replied Allan, giving the giant the stoup, "for wishing us to swallow it. Holy Saint Dunstan! what's that!"

Allan's exclamation was caused by the stoup, which Little John was in the act of lifting to his mouth being struck from his hand, and to the astonishment of all present an arrow was seen quivering in the oaken table opposite where Little John sat.

The giant's surprise was so great that he kept all his seat while all the others sprang to their feet and seized their weapons.

He was so staggered at the stoup being knocked from his fingers that he could not credit his senses, until he heard the voice of his Captain calling upon him to pluck the arrow from the table.

He did so, and passed it to Robin Hood, who uttered an angry exclamation as he took from just below the feathers a small slip of parchment.

"Stay," he said to the men, who were about to go forth, and discover the daring fellow who had shot an arrow into the very midst of the band; "stay, my merry men, here is a clerkly scrawl upon this parchment. I will read it ere you go.

He did so, aloud, and the writing at once allayed their fears of the forest being filled with King Henry's archers.

"The curse of St. Dunstan upon you for brawling knaves," so ran the billet, *"is it not enough you have come to my land, and robbed me of the deer which otherwise would be mine, but you must scare the few that remain from their coverts. A murrain on that bellowing ox, and his song; by the saints, if I catch him away from the nest of thieves, I'll make him bellow to the tune of a good quarterstaff upon his hide.*

"The devil fly away with the lot. I would not give a pinch of salt for the whole pack.

*"*THE CURTALL FRIAR.*"*

"The Curtall Friar!" repeated Robin. By Saint Herman, he is a bold knave, and he can use a bow as well as the best of us. Heard you the name he gave thee, John?"

"Body-o'-me!" growled the offended giant, tightening his belt; "Blade bone of Saint Hubert! but I did—bellowing ox—a malison upon the shaveling!—my quarterstaff, Allan! —Bone-o'-my-body! but I'll make a jelly of his holy carcass, or my name's not Little John!"

The speaker had, while delivering these words, tested the strength of the stout oaken staff Allan-a-dale had given him. Then, to the amusement of the goodly company, he stalked off towards the thicket from whence the arrow had come.

"Bellowing ox!" he was heard to mutter, as he crossed the glade; "Ashes of Saint Dunstan! make me bellow, will he, the accursed priest! Body-o'-me! I'll break every bone in his skin!"

This incident caused much laughter, and the men again seated themselves at the board, and renewed their application to the good liquor before them.

"What of the rundlet, Much?" Allan asked; "I would not give a groat for thy chance."

"John has not returned yet," replied Much, and when he does, it will not be with so many whole bones as he has taken with him."

"A song, a song," shouted the outlaws at the upper end of the table; silence for our Captain's song."

The Chief, in obedience to this call, tossed off a cup of wine, and, in a remarkably sweet and well-tuned voice, began

ROBIN HOOD'S SONG.*

As blithe as the linnet sings in the greenwood,
  So blithe we'll wake the morn;
And through the wide forest of Merry Sherwood
  We'll wind the bugle horn.

Our hearts they are stout, and our bows they are good,
  As well their masters know;
They're culled in the forest of Merry Sherwood,
  And never will spare a foe.

Our arrows shall drink of the fallow deer's blood;
  We'll hunt them all over the plain.
And through the wide forest of Merry Sherwood
  No shaft shall fly in vain.

Brave Allan and John, who ne'er were subdued,
  Give each his hand so bold.
We'll range through the forest of Merry Sherwood;
  What say ye, my hearts of gold?

"Bravely sung," cried Earl Mortimer, when the clattering of the horn cups and the shouts of the yeomen had subsided; "beshrew me, Robin, but, if I stay with thee and thy gallant company longer, I shall doff the Spanish mail, and take a green jacket and bow."

"You would find good men and true here," said the Outlaw. "That's not the name those bear with whom you are about to mix. But, come, my lord, its growing dark, and I must break up the revel, or there'll be but few sleepless eyes keeping watch to-night."

He arose as he spoke, and taking the arms which had been laid aside at the beginning of the feast, carefully replaced them upon his body.

"To your stations, my merry men," he continued, "and keep good watch, for the Norman sheriff of Nottingham meditates us harm. Come, my lord, don your helmet and sword, and I will see thee safely through the forest."

The Earl complied with the air of one who would as soon have stayed with such good company; but, when he had armed himself, he followed Robin through one of those unknown paths only trod by the outlaws.

CHAPTER XII.

LITTLE JOHN'S RETURN AFTER HIS ENCOUNTER WITH THE FAT FRIAR.

This caused Much loud to laugh.
  He laughed full heartily.
There lives a Curtall friar in fountain's dell,
  Will beat both him and thee.

* * * * * * *

"Take up thy staff," said Little John,
  "Friar, at my bidding be."
"Whose man art thou?" said the Curtall Friar,
  Come here to prate with me?"
"I am Little John, Robin Hood's man;
  Friar, I will not lie."

BRIGHT Sol's rays had scarcely begun to gild the tree tops when the clear ringing notes of the bugle horn called the foresters from their couches.

* This song is not so authentic as the preceding one, for it is taken from a play of "Robin Hood," which was performed at Drury Lane Theatre, in 1751.

The morning gathering took place near the oak where Robin was in the habit of enjoying his afternoon siesta.

Here the band were drawn up in military array, and their arms examined by their leader.

This important duty over, the Chief seated himself under the foliage of the giant tree and heard the reports of those who had kept watch during the night.

"Thou wert at the north side of the forest, Allan," he said, "did ought occur during thy watch worthy of note?"

"An old woman, please you, good Robin," replied the forester, "was all that passed my way."

"An old woman, Allan, had she no gossip about the doings of the town, or was it she was old instead of young that thy tongue spoke not to her?"

"She had lost her way, good master," said Allan, "and while I showed her the broad path her tongue wagged quicker than a dozen magpies could chatter."

"Said she ought of the matter I have spoken about?"

"She did, good Robin, although may be it was but an old woman's gossip—but I will tell thee word for word."

"Thy master," she said, "is a trusty and a good man; he fed my children when they hungered, the Blessed Virgin be good to him."

"I cried amen to this, master."

"Tell good Robin," she said, "that many meetings have of late taken place between the proud Abbot of Saint Mary's and Nottingham's Sheriff."

"Ha!" exclaimed the Outlaw, "proceed, good Allan."

"These meetings," she said, "have borne fruit, for even now the smith is busy casting bolts for crossbows, and the armourers work day and night fashioning steel hauberks too strong for thy arrows to pierce."

The captain laughed at this, and the men joined in the merriment.

"By Saint Herman of the Wold," Robin said, "they will have to fashion such steel as ne'er yet left the hands of an English smith—but go on, good Allan."

"I have told all," replied the forester. "I saw her on to the highroad and gave her a silver mark for her news, but whether true or false we shall see."

"Thou must find this out, Allan," said the Chief; "don thy clouted cloak and go to Nottingham this day, crave alms at the castle gate, and use thine eyes well."

Allan stepped back to the foremost rank of the stalwart foresters, to give place to George-a-Green, who came forward.

"Thou wert on the south side," said Robin. What is thy budget, good George?"

"Not of such import as Allan's," said the forester; "save for this goodly bag of silver which may make up for my scant news."

He gave the Chief a leather bag filled to the mouth with broad pieces, as he spoke.

"Thy watch and ward has borne goodly fruit," Robin said. "What is the name of this good man, who makes us this present?"

"His name I know not," George-a-Green answered; "but he has left his mark upon two of my fellows, who were with me."

"His mark, good George?"

"Aye, master; the pen he used was as good a cudgel as ever grew on tree."

"Thy fellows," the Outlaw said, taking a handful of pieces from the bag, "will want a balsam to heal the marks. Give these to them, good George."

"Grammercy," said the forester; "they will not grumble at this. Shall I speak, master, of the doings of this lusty varlet?"

"Do, good George; it is our custom to hear all that passes in our kingdom, whilst the night birds are abroad."

"It was past the midnight," said the forester, "when we heard the strokes of a horse's hoof coming from the road. I bid the rider stand, or have a cloth-yard shaft through his jerkin. He pulled up, and I saw by the hood he wore over his head he was of a quality to pay the toll which is due from all Normans. Had he been poor, master, and civil of speech, thine orders would have been obeyed, for we touch not the needy and oppressed."

"Such is our rule, good George, and those of my merry men, who break it, I will hang upon the bough of as good a tree as Sherwood boasts."

"A meet punishment," said George-a-Green, "for such as disobey thy lawful will. By the saints! I would be the first to string such a knave to the fair bough above us."

"Spoken like a good yeoman, good George, but thy story, man; thy story, for the sun nigh touches the point when we should be at the butts, to keep up the skill of Sherwood's merry men."

"I bid the carle stand, good master," answered the man; "and, as he threw aside his hood, I saw the face of the Norman villain who holds the lands of the good Saxon franklin, Hedwold, who fell on Evesham's plain."

"I know the varlet," Robin said; "and Nottingham county does not hold one who has a harder hand upon the poor."

"My heart is glad, master, to hear this; for, by the broad pieces, I thought the knave had been collecting the rents of the lands, he has stolen from young Hedwold."

"No doubt of it, George; no doubt of it."

"Well, master, this Norman robber drew a good oak sapling from under his cloak, and, instead of yielding his ill-gotten gains, he laid one of my men at full length upon the earth. Beshrew me! but the knave fought well for his money-bag."

"Quick, good George; see, yonder sun will find us laggards at our post."

"I will hasten, good master, but the story is worth the hearing; for when I saw our poor knave with his crown cracked, I threw the Norman from his saddle."

"The Saints look down upon us, the knave was on his feet, and his cudgel felled another of our men, and he would have escaped had I not given him a tap with my staff to teach him not to do these things."

"That was well done," said the Captain, who took delight in hearing of the recitals of his men, and knowing the emulation this mode of publicly hearing their doings gave his band, he neglected no opportunity of holding meetings like the present; "I hope thou broke his pate for him!"

"I should, master," George-a-Green answered, "had it not been for the steel cap he wore; but, our patron Saint be blessed! the blow laid him beside our fellows."

There was a murmur of approbation at this, for the foresters liked not that any of their band should be punished without the punisher being served the same.

"My hand," continued the forester, "soon found this bag he carried at his belt, and our knaves getting to their feet we hoisted the Norman to his saddle, then, tying his legs, placed a bunch of nettles under the gelding's tail, and away he went—the Norman yelling for help, and his steed kicking as lustily as though he had been possessed by a legion of fiends."

There was a laugh, as the foresters conjured the sight before them; then George-a-Green fell in the ranks, and the leaders of the men, who were out on the other sides of the forest, came forward.

They had no story to tell, therefore, kind reader, we cannot break faith with thee by putting untruths into their mouths and destroying the confidence thou feelest in this veracious narrative.

The first part of the day's duty being over, the signal was given to march, and as the stalwart forms hurried towards the butts the Outlaw Chief, for the first time, missed his faithful follower, Little John.

"Saint Herman keep us from harm!" he said; "where is Little John? speak, my merry men, hast one of thee seen our lieutenant?"

"Mayhap," Allan-a-Dale said, "he has been paying too close attendance upon the good barrels which were broached last night to do honour to Mortimer's Earl."

"Nay, Allan," said the leader walking beside his men; "John never yet slumbered after the first blast of the morning bugle, no matter how deep his potations had been the night before."

The men could not give any reason to account for the giant's absence, although Robin went from the rear to the leading files of his stout yeomen.

"Saint Herman," he exclaimed, when this questioning ended, "now I bethink me, the knave went forth to trounce the curtell friar. Mayhap, being tired after the bout, he has gone to rest in some covert where the sound of our call has not reached his ears."

"Allan," whispered Much, "dost thou think I will lose my rundlet of wine now?"

"Aye, that I do, Much, for as good Robin truly says, John has but gone to rest after the bout, and the deep draughts of sack. Thou knowest, Much, if men sleep over soundly after one of these causes, what must they do after the two?"

"We shall see," Much answered. "We shall see."

They reached an open space, at the end of which the butts (square mounds of earth) were placed.

Here Robin, as was the custom, drew the first bow, and the arrow, although the aim had been a careless one, went true to the mark.

The foresters followed the example thus set them, and with more or less skill hit the small white disc placed in the centre of the mound.

It was good archery, for even those arrows which did not strike the mark, went but a few inches beyond; not one shaft went beyond the butt.

Not more than fifty of the foresters had gone through this pleasant pastime, when those who were lying upon the ground awaiting their turn, gave vent to a roar of laughter.

"What now, my merry men," Robin asked as he turned from the butts. "What now?"

"Look, Master, look," answered Much; "where the ash grove ends, and thou wilt see a sight that it were a pity to see."

It was in truth a pitiful sight to see, for from the ash grove there came a huge forester, his head swathed in bandages, one leg held from the ground as though in pain; under the arm above the wounded leg a portion of a broken quarterstaff was planted, and did goodly service as a crutch, and to finish this mournful sight the forester had his left hand held to his side.

"Little John by Saint Herman, and every saint in the calendar."

"Little John," repeated Much, the miller's son, and several of his companions. "Little John, and as soundly trounced as ever man was."

These words were too true; it was the battered form of Little John, and when he came within hearing it was found he had neither lost his voice or the thirst which habitually beset him.

"Body-o-me!" he roared, and his tones were as sweet as that of an angry bull. "Body-o-me, fetch a stoup of wine, or I die of thirst."

"I've won the arrow," said Much, as he rose and went for a stoup of wine, "and Little John has got a worse trouncing than the friar gave to me."

The angry flush which came to Robin's face passed away when he heard his trusty follower was no worse hurt than the receipt of a good drubbing.

He had feared that matters were more serious, until he heard John's voice; then with the remainder of the foresters, he set up a hearty laugh at the giant's woful plight.

"This friar must be the devil himself under a grey frock," he said, "to thus thrash two of my best men. Saint Herman keep us from such holy men."

"Amen!" said Much, passing at that moment with a huge tankard of wine; "amen, good master; but, if I mistake not, the friar will thrash both thee and thy men before he's done."

"By the saints it will be proved full soon whether Robin can be beaten by a shaveling," the Outlaw said. "Go thy way, Much, and tend John, for he is in a sore plight."

The giant—who, by the way, was over six feet four in height, and had a pair of shoulders as broad as two of the lustiest of the land—stood and leant against a tree, when he saw Much coming with the stoup of wine.

CHAPTER XIII.

ROBIN HOOD AND THE CURTELL FRIAR.

Robin Hood, he took a solemn oath,
  It was by Mary, free,
That he would neither eat nor drink
  Till the friar he did see.

*   *   *   *   *

And coming unto Fountain Del'—
  No further could he ride—
There he was aware of the Curtell Friar
  Sitting by the water side.

THE trial of skill was put an end to by the

appearance of Little John, and the Outlaw Chief and his merry men crowded around the bruised hero to hear how a sham friar had overcome one so stout.

"Thanks, Much, thanks, for that goodly draught," Little John said, after he had received the stoup; "I stand sorely in need of the free juice, sorely in need. Shoulder-blade of Saint Hubert! Much, thy friar has done all he promised."

"And lost thee a good arrow, John."

"Aye, it is so. Seek my quiver, and take the best, Much; and thou mayest as well fill the stoup as thou passest: it will not be out of thy way."

The Outlaw Chief and the band came up at this moment, and it could be seen, by their faces, how great was the difficulty they had to keep from laughing outright at poor John's plight.

"Thou hast met the friar, I see," said Robin; "and the saints be blessed! he has taught thee a little sound religion, John."

"Sound!" said the woful Forester; "Body-o'-me! there isn't a bone left whole in my skin."

"He has a strong arm, this friar, John."

"Friar!" said the giant. "Call him a devil, master—a lusty, roystering, stout and fat-paunched devil—and thou wilt be nearer the truth than calling him a friar. May the evil one roast him with pieces of his own staff, say I."

"Thou hast fared ill, John," said Robin; "if thou hast strength left to speak, tell thy merry companions and thy master, how all this came about?"

"Strength, good Robin, I have no more strength of voice than a linnet. Nay, not so much."

"Yet," Robin said, smiling, "there was something of thy old voice left when thou call'dst out to Much for a stoup of wine."

"It was my throat that spoke, master, for I was wondrously dry, wondrously dry."

"Never mind thy thirst, tell thy story, John. By the blessed Saint Herman, it must be wondrous strange to hear how so stout a forester had his hide tanned by a friar."

"It is a wondrous story, good master," answered Little John, looking over the Outlaw's shoulder to ascertain whether Much was coming with a second supply of wine; a wondrous story, therefore, I will sit me on the green grass, and tell you how it came about."

Suiting the action to the word, the forester seated himself at the foot of the tree, and by the grimace he made, it was plain the posture was not an easy one.

"You must know, my masters," he said, "when the devil's limb, the red-nosed, wine-snivelling monk sent his challenge yester e'en, I took my staff and went through the forest until I came to Fountain Dell.

"There, my masters, I saw a fat monk, who looked more like a barrel with arms, head, and legs, then aught I can compare the knave to.

"He sat near to the waterside, my masters, a good oak staff laid across his knees, and when I saw him, I brought my staff end upon the ground to startle him.

"Body-'o-me! he cared no more for the noise then though it had been a butterfly resting on the grass, but looking up, began to laugh and roll his ungodly paunch about, as though the sight of a forester was a show to be made sport of.

"Body-'o-me! I said, who art thou Sir Saint, that thy sides wag at the sight of a good and true man?

"'True man,' he said, 'and he laughed the more. Who art thou that comes to Fountain Dell so glibe of speech?'

"Robin's man, I said; dost thou know brave Robin Hood, a good and true man?

"'Know him,' laughed the ungodly friar; 'know him, who does not know the arrant thief from Sherwood to Barnesdale.'

"Thou liest, I said, he is no thief, but a good yeoman, so take up thy staff and stand a bout, or by Saint Hubert, I'll crack thy bones, even for the lies thou hast told, in calling my master an arrant thief; would I had cracked his crown then, for I should have escaped my hide being tanned. Body-'o-me, where's Much, the thief has he not come back with the stoup?"

"All in good time, John," Robin said, 'the wine will be here before thy voice gets weaker."

"Saint Hubert be thanked for that. Well, my master, the godly man—the devil's limb, I mean—up and told me he cared not a groat for Robin Hood, and his pack of thieves, and if any came to Fountain Dell, he would baste their hides, as—as——"

"He basted thine," said Allan; "that will do, John; it is a goodly simile."

"Well, my master, and merry men all," said the very much bruised Little John; "I kept from breaking the villain's pate—a malison on my fingers for not doing it when the churl came before me—and the shaven limb of devildom laughed to my face as he balanced his staff on one fat finger, and said—

"'I care not to break thy bones yet awhile, for I want to learn of thee——'

"'Break my bones,' I shouted, for I was getting wroth. Body-o'-me! would I had broken his bare pate before he got to his feet; but it would have been un-yeomanly to have taken advantage—a shame even, would it not? my merry companions; yet I wish now I——"

"Thy story, keep to it closer," said Robin, "or by the patron saint of all true foresters, and that is St. Herman of the Wold, not a drop of the red juice which I see Much bringing this way, shall touch thy lips."

"'Break my bones!' I said, "break my bones!—get to thy feet, man, or by Saint Hubert, I'll rattle this good staff upon thy skull to such a tune as will make thine ears tingle again.'

"Well, my master, the knave did but laugh the louder; and when this was over, he looked up, and asked:—

"'Art thou the knave with a voice like an ox—the knave who plucked my shaft from the oaken table?'"

"'I am Little John,'" I said for I liked not the name he had given me; "'and if thou art not on thy feet in the twinkling of this staff there will be no more fat monks in Fountain Dell in less than——"

"Body-o'-me! when I said this he came to his feet, and, holding his staff in as yeomanlike a manner as any of us merry men, he called out——is Much come with the stoup, master?"

There was a roar of laughter at this, and John, in spite of his bruises, joined most heartily in it.

"I meant not that," he said; for the fat friar called out:

"'Have at thee for a bellowing knave; have at thee—by my patron Saint I'll trounce all the singing out of thy body.'

"Well, my masters, we fell to and fought for three good hours and more, although my skull was cracked and my bones sore; not a rap at the devil's pate did I get!

"Body-o'-me! even then I did not give in, but for nigh another full hour our strokes rang out, and my head had more knocks than the friar had knots in his girdle, and every bone in my body seemed broken.

"So we went on, masters, until my staff broke in keeping off part of his blows; Shoulder of St. Hubert! but his arm was like a smith's, and his staff like a sledge-hammer!

"When my staff broke I got another knock on the pate, and down I went; and, would you believe it, my masters, the knave trounced me the more when I was down, and at every blow called out:

"'Crave a boon, thou thief, or I'll make a jelly of thy carcass.'

"Body-o'-me! I had no breath left to crave a boon, for no matter which way I turned, the accursed staff came down as hard as ever.

"Well, good master-o'-mine, and you, my merry men, the shaven devil trounced me until he could no longer use his arm. Then he gave over and said—bring the stoup, good Much, I am sadly athirst again."

A long pull at the vessel Much handed to him enabled John to finish his story.

"'Send thy master,' he said, 'send thy best men, and I will serve them as I have served thee, and they shall see what it is to interfere with the deer on my domain.'"

"He left me then, my master, and my body was so sore I could not move, but lay there until ye saw me come from the ash grove."

"By the Blessed Mary," said Robin, "I will neither go to the east or the west, neither eat of deer flesh or taste wine until I meet this friar. My oaken staff, George-a-Green; to your care, Allan, I leave our merry men, keep watch upon the Nottingham side. St. Herman of the Wold! trounce Robin Hood will he?"

And with sword and buckler, and carrying his long oaken staff upon his shoulder, the bold Outlaw went to Fountain Dell; and no sooner had he passed through the trees, than he saw the object of his journey sitting quietly at the side of the rippling brook from which the dell took its name, looking as innocent and unconcerned as possible.

———

CHAPTER XIV.

THE CURTELL FRIAR DROPS ROBIN INTO THE BROOK.

Lightly leaped the friar off Robin Hood's back;
  Robin Hood said to him again:
"Carry me over the water, thou Curtell Friar,
  Or it shall breed thee pain."
The friar took Robin on his back again,
  And stepped in to the knee;
Till he came to the middle stream,
  Neither good nor bad spake he.[*]

ROBIN HOOD stood for some moments regarding the friar; and the latter, without once raising his eyes, continued telling his beads, an occupation he was engaged in when the Outlaw first appeared.

There was but little of the ascetic about the monk's appearance, for his face instead of being pale and marked with rugged lines, showing penitence, and a total absence of the good things of this life, was as round and as rosy as an apple.

His body was in keeping with the face above it, for although fat, and as Little John said like unto a barrel, it was evident that there was a wonderful amount of strength in the brawny arms which were but partially concealed by the grey gown he wore.

Had not Robin known so much of the godly man's character, it is possible he would have been deceived by the pious manner in which he told his beads, and by the motion of his lips seemed to be repeating his *Aves*, *Paters*, and *Credos*.

Even had the friar been a stranger, a second look at his eyes and the pursed-up lips, would have told Robin this outward sanctity was but assumed.

Another look would have told him the round face and dark eyes bespoke a fund of good humour and devil-may-care recklessness when there was no distortion, as in this instance, of features which were better suited to a jolly cellarman than to an austere monk.

After these thoughts, which expressed his feelings, had passed through Robin's mind, he bent closer to the holy friar, and touching his buckler lightly with the end of the quarter-staff, attempted to arouse the godly friar from his meditations.

The priest took no notice of this intimation, but continued with increased fervour to whisper his prayers and count his beads.

"Holy man," said Robin at last, "is thy sins so great that thou art compelled to tell thy beads at this hour of the day?"

The friar looked up with the well assumed air of one who had been disturbed in an act of the deepest devotion.

"Sir woodsman," he said, "for so I judge thee by thy jerkin, in heaven's name I pray thee pass on and leave me to my devotion; life is but short, and were I to tell my beads from sunrise to matin song, and from moonrise to sunrise again, there would be but scant time to keep the vow I have made.

The religious zeal with which these words were spoken, the upturned eyes and meekly folded hands for a moment staggered the Outlaw, and he could not believe the godly man

[*] From an old black letter pamphlet, in the collection of Anthony-a-Wood, printed about the year 1610. There is also an earlier copy in the Pepysian Library.

before him, and the lusty player at quarter-staff were one and the same person.

It is not at all unlikely this belief would have gained ground with the Forester had he not observed a smile flit across the monk's face, and seen his eyes furtively regarding the noble form of the Saxon leader.

"Holy father!" said Robin, "far be it from me to interrupt a good man at his devotions; but, having by mischance left my steed in his stable, I would cross the brook, but a vow I have made prevents me from wetting my feet.'

"I will absolve thee from the vow," said the friar, "if thou wilt but pass on, and leave me in peace. Go, my son; *absolutioni pro——*"

"Stay, good father, my vow is not yet told," said Robin, with difficulty keeping from laughing at the part he was playing; "for I swore to Saint Herman that I would not receive absolution; and, further, that any man or animal I found near a brook I would compel to carry me over, or——"

"Thou compel!—at least, I mean, my good son, my patron saint is of more weight than thine; therefore, by him I can absolve thee."

"An absolution I cannot take, holy father; therefore, prepare thyself in all humility to carry me across the stream: or, by the blessed St. Herman! I shall be compelled, according to my vow, to use this carnal weapon upon thy shaven pate."

He held the oaken staff towards the friar as he spoke; and the holy man, losing all sanctity at the moment, rose to his feet.

"A murrain upon thee," he said, "and thy saint. Use thy staff! Blessed Saint Wilfred! had I not foresworn the carnal weapon men call a quarter-staff, I would make thee eat thy words."

"Softly, good father, and prepare to do my bidding, or by all the saints, canonised and uncanonised, I will make thy fleshy carcass as sore that the softest couch will seem a bed of stones."

"Thou do this? thou do this?" roared the friar. "A malison on thy hang-dog face! knowest thou who I am?"

"By report," Robin answered. "A sturdy, roystering knave, who can play a bout with a quarterstaff, empty a flagon, and kill the king's deer with the best woodsman of the forest."

"Repute is a foul calumniator," said the friar. "I am but a poor brother of the Greyfriar's order; but nevertheless, should'st thou try to use thy staff upon me, this goodly fist shall deal thee a buffet which will stop thy prating tongue, as my——"

The friar paused, as though he had said too much; and as Robin gave vent to a merry peal of laughter, he first began to fumble for his beads, which he had put away, as though to prepare for a struggle with the forester.

"As thy staff stopped the moving of my man's limbs," Robin said, finishing the friar's speech; "well, thy confession gladdens me, for I came to make thee do my bidding or pound thy fat carcass to a jelly."

"Ho, ho!" said the friar, putting his rosary out of sight again; "thy man? then thou art the chief of the cut-purses who royster in this forest; art thou? Blessed be St. Wilfred for sending thee here. Ho, ho! thou art the arrant thief, Robin Hood! Art thou?"

"I am, and thou art Friar Tuck, as great a rogue as ever let fly a shaft among a herd of fallow deer. Bless the Saint Herman for sending me to this spot, for now I am more resolved than ever to make thee carry me across, so prepare thy back either for my body, or a taste of this good staff."

"To the devil with thee, and thy staff. Hark'ee, thief, cut-purse that thou art! behind yonder tree there stands as good a cudgel as ever grew; thou shalt feel it!"

He made a sudden rush towards the tree, as he spoke, and would have got possession of the staff, had not Robin stepped nimbly towards him, and tripped him up by the heels.

Placing his foot upon the Curtall Friar's chest, the Outlaw flourished his staff so close above the fallen man's head, that he closed his eyes, as though expecting to feel the weight of the stout stick upon his skull.

"Now," laughed Robin, "my lusty monk, which shall it be, a good trouncing with this cudgel before thou takest me across, or wilt thou take me without the trouncing."

"Without the trouncing," said the friar, with wonderful subservience for his character. "Let me rise, good Robin, and no mule ever carried pack-saddle with better grace than I will carry thee to the opposite side."

The Outlaw allowed the friar to regain his feet, then, setting his face towards the water, Robin leaped lightly on his back.

The Friar bent not beneath the Outlaw's weight, but without a word walked into the stream, and Robin, delighted at his victory over one who had beaten two of his best men, began to troll out the burden of a famous hunting song.

His music came to an abrupt stop when they reached the middle of the stream, for the Friar suddenly parting Robin's hands which had been clasped under his saintly chin, gave a sudden spin round and dropped his burden in the deepest part of the water, and raising his voice blithely sang:

"Choose thee, choose thee, fine fellow,
Whether thou wilt sink or swim."

Taken so completely by surprise, Robin floundered about on his back for a second or two, his face only visible above the water.

But when he regained his feet he dashed through the water after the friar, his trusty blade naked in his hand.

The saintly man stayed not to encounter the Outlaw's wrath, for before Robin's foot touched the bank, the fat friar had broken through the bushes and disappeared from sight.

CHAPTER XV.

ROBIN HOOD AND THE NORMAN SPY.

"He shall not go free," the other replied.
So straight they were seizing him there
To kill him; but Robin Hood cries:
"I pray thee, my men, to forbear."

WHEN the indomitable friar had gone beyond

all hope of being overtaken, the Outlaw Chief shook the glittering drops from his body, and gave vent to a peal of laughter.

"St. Herman," he cried, good humouredly, "yon monk has behaved more like a lusty yeoman than a shaven crown. He has the chance this day, but I swear, by the Blessed Mary, I'll not rest until I have met the lusty varlet foot to foot, oaken staff to oaken staff. Hear my vow, good Saint Herman of the Wold, and foul fall me if it is not kept."

"Having made this vow, the Outlaw took his way through the nearest path to the trysting tree where he knew his merry men would be anxiously awaiting his return.

"Marry," he muttered, "the knaves will laugh when they behold their master in this forlorn plight. A malison upon the cursed friar; he has spoilt my best and newest jacket, for which favour I'll yet thank him with as good a staff as ever yeoman handled."

Muttering thus to himself, he came to within half an arrow's flight of a dense copse, and from the dark foliage, he beheld the glitter of a bright disc, which to his practised eye was no mystery.

"A hauberk, or helm," he said, "and in the very heart of Sherwood. Dolt, that I have been, to leave my good bow under the greenwood tree, but for that, I would put a mark upon yon object, that would spoil its brightness."

The sheltering trunks of the young trees afforded a covert, from which he could, without being seen, watch the movements of him who wore the shining panoply.

"Valour," Robin said in self communion, "would bid me go forward and lay about yon knave with my good sword; but discretion, which is a goodly part of valour, bids me remain where I now stand, and watch for a sign by which I may know how yon varlet came to the heart of merry Sherwood without being seen by my yeomen."

While the Outlaw's thoughts ran thus, the wearer of the steel cap was seen to change his position, and, evidently unsuspicious that he was watched, he left the covert as though with the intention of crossing that part of the forest where Robin Hood stood.

"By Saint Herman," the Outlaw said, "this knave must have more lives than ordinary men, that he flaunts it thus bravely in the greenwood. Ha! blessed Mary, he wears the badge of one I have but little cause to love."

The wearer of the glittering morion was habited in a garb not so rich as that worn by the knights of the period—yet it was richer than the esquires were wont to dress in.

The steel helm has already been mentioned. Except this, he wore no defensive armour. A gaberdine of thick brown cloth was gathered in at the neck, and depended from thence to below the knees.

The cuffs, skirt, and collar were trimmed with rich fur; and embroidered upon the breast was the figure of an eagle, with outstretched pinions and extended claws.

His hose was of the same material as his gaberdine, and his feet were encased in leather boots, the toes without the absurd points then worn by the Norman nobles.

The stranger's arms were a long cross-hilted sword, a dagger, and a spear, such as was used in the chase.

The fellow held an office new to England: he was in the employ of the Sheriff of Nottingham: his duties, to apprehend all who disregarded the law as represented by Geoffrey de Lois.

"So, master," Robin muttered, "thou hast trusted to thy valour too much, if it has brought thee here to take bold Robin or any of his merry men. Ah! whom have we here!"

As this exclamation left his lips, a man entered the glade at the opposite side—a man garbed in Lincoln-green, and armed, as all Robin's followers were armed, with a bow, a quiver of arrows, and a good sword.

The Sheriff's man evidently expected the arrival of him clad in Lincoln-green, for he went forward and greeted them, as one friend would greet another.

"By Saint Herman," muttered the Outlaw, his hand wandering to his sword-hilt, "but this smelleth of treason. Ha! by the holy and true Saint, this is the knave who came to my band after Evesham had been fought; aye, Allan-a-Dale was right—there is a traitor and a spy among my men."

The two, after they had greeted each other, walked [to and fro in open conversation; thus the Outlaw Chief heard every word that passed between them.

"How fares it with thy goodly schemes?" the Sheriff's man asked; "yet I need scarcely ask, for had that arrant thief, thy master, but the faintest suspicion of thy purpose thou would'st not be here."

"True," answered he of the Lincoln green, "I would not, but I have good cause to know he does not suspect I am aught else than a good yeoman of his band."

"Thou hast played thy part well," the Sheriff's man said, "and our good master, the noble Geoffrey, will reward thee according to thy due."

"Unless," thought Robin, "I am first to give thee the reward thy cunning has so well merited."

"I know it," said he of Lincoln-green; "for our master, though somewhat harsh in matters touching his dignity, is good to those who serve him well."

"Which thou has done, good Bayston, and well art thou in the favour of our good lord and the holy prior of St. Mary's Abbey."

"T'is something to be in such——hark! heard'st thou a noise at——hark! there it is again!"

"'Tis but a hare," said the Sheriff's man; "see there—it seeks refuge in yon thicket."

The noise which at first attracted the men's attention was caused by the Outlaw Chief drawing his sword.

"Thy cheek palest," the Sheriff's man continued, "even at the sight of——"

"Not that, De Morley," answered the forester, "not that, it was the thought that mayhap one of Robin's men had passed this way—yet no, that could not be, for I so well arranged that this part of the forest has been left to my charge."

"Then the bird can be taken to-night?" De Morley said, interrogatively; "if the charge of the forest or this part is in thy hands it will be easy for thee to guide us to where the arrant thieves sleep. We can then take the leader and—holy St. Hildebrand defend us——"

ROBIN HOOD,

AND THE OUTLAWS OF SHERWOOD FOREST.

ROBIN HOOD AND THE MONKS OF ST. MARY'S ABBEY.

DE MORLEY'S exclamation was caused by seeing the Outlaw Chief break through the thicket.

The sudden appearance of Robin Hood caused the Sheriff's man to turn from his companion, and flee across the greenwood towards the trees from which the Outlaw had seen him emerge.

"Had I but a good shaft," said Robin, "I would stop thy legs; but it matters not, I shall know the knave again."

The spy seemed at first inclined to follow the example of his companion, but seeing the gallant forester was without his bow and arrows he merely retreated out of reach of the angry chief's arm.

"So," the Outlaw said, "this is thy gratitude, thou who hast eaten at our board and drank our wine, to league thyself with the minions of Geoffrey de Lois. Answer me, knave, what hast thou to plead for this foul work?"

The man retreated still further; and when he had gone between fifty and sixty paces from the Outlaw Chief he fitted an arrow to his bow.

"This," he said, "is my answer. Take it, thou arrant thief!"

Robin's good steel buckler was upon his arm, and as the cloth-yard shaft cleft the air he raised the bright disc before his body.

The arrow-head passed through the steel plate, and before the shaft had ceased to vibrate, the spy again drew his bow-string to his ear.

Warned by the inefficiency of the steel buckler to ward off the arrows, Robin did not raise it in this instance, but with a swift blow with his keen blade he cut the arrow in two.

The shaft was well aimed, for when he cleft the tough wood the point was within a foot of his throat.

"A curse upon thee" said the Spy, "thou art in league with the Evil One, for no woodsman could possess such skill as thou hast this day shown, nevertheless I will try another shaft upon thy carcase."

"If thou dost" said Robin, advancing upon his enemy, "the lowest branch of our trysting-tree shall bear thy body."

"What clemency" the Spy asked, as he drew the third arrow to his ear, "will be given if I yield without sending this shaft at thy carcase."

"None," answered the Outlaw; "thou knowest the laws of our band—a fair trial—death if judged guilty of a deed like this."

"A murrain on thy laws; St. Ulrick send this shaft through thy body."

He discharged the third arrow as he spoke, and the Outlaw, without any apparent effort, cleft it as he had cleft the one before.

The spy's quiver was not empty, and he would have fitted another arrow to his bow, had not the Outlaw run swiftly upon him, and severed the bow-string.

"Yield thee, false knave," said Robin, "or, by St. Herman of the Wold! I will slay thee at my feet."

"I yield," was the sullen answer. "But spare my life, good master, for, had not the Sheriff tempted me with his red gold, I had not been so false to one so good and true as bold Robin Hood."

"Your repentance comes too late," answered the Outlaw; "red gold would not have tempted a good and true man."

"Thou sayest true, master," the spy said, sorrowfully, "yet many men have risked much for the bright, broad pieces."

"Aye, Bayston, and brought themselves to a plight similar to thine."

"Not all, master, not all; some have won: and those who play so high a game, must e'en be content to lose."

"Life is of more value than gold," the Forester said. "Life is the stake you place against a few broad pieces."

"I will not gainsay this, master. Thou art merciful and good; and, although I would have taken thy life but a few minutes since, there is no trace of anger upon thy face. By this sign, I know thy voice will not be silent when the laws of the foresters doom me to death."

"Shall I crave thy life, that thy brain may hatch more mischief against my merry men by so vile a plot as mine ears were open to near Fountain Dale?"

"No, master; I was thy foe, then, a mean-souled traitor; and, although a Saxon, a spy in Norman pay."

"True, by St. Herman! I wonder thy tongue likes the office of telling these things."

"It does not, good Robin, but I must speak the truth. Aye, although the words blister my mouth."

"Quick with thy speech, man, for I see the green jerkins of my merry men at the end of these trees."

Bayston's face went pale when he looked towards the spot where the stalwart bowmen were gathered.

"I have but little to say," he responded; "but little to crave. A few minutes past I was thy foe, and would have driven a cloth-yard shaft through thy breast, until the feathers were dyed with thy noble blood——"

"I need not thy telling to know this."

"True, good master; but it is part of the speech I have craved to make."

"As thou wilt."

"Yes; I was thy foe," he continued, "and when thou hadst conquered me in fair and manly fight, no words of anger came from thy tongue, no expression of vengeance upon thy face; no, thou didst not even bind my hands, but walked beside me, and with fair and gentle speech told me of the great wickedness I had meditated against one so good."

"Hast thou turned priest? for by the saints thy tongue is wondrously glib."

"I have not turned priest, good master; although I may soon stand in sore need of one. Well, thou hast done all this when others would have cleft my skull with their swords."

"It will come to about the same, my poor knave; only in place of a cloven skull thy neck will be stretched."

"Even so, master, it is, but what I deserve although were you to let me live there is not one among thy merry men would serve thee so well, and not one could be of such value to thee and thy band."

"How, knave, how could thy services be above all others of my band?"

"I could tell thee, good master, of the designs of thy proud foe, Geoffrey de Lois."

"How? tell me; surely the arrogant Norman does not hold a knave like thee in his confidence."

"He does, master, as far as the devilry concocted by him and the dark Abbot of St. Mary's Abbey is concerned."

"I begin to understand thy meaning: should thy life be spared thou wilt betray thy Norman master as thou would'st have betrayed me."

"I will tell thee of all the evil they mean; tell in time for thy merry men to prepare for their coming; a knowledge thou couldst not gain unless one of the bowmen were in league with the Sheriff's man."

"Out upon thee for a double-faced traitor—hark ye, knave, Robin Hood and his Saxons would sooner meet their foes foot to foot upon the green turf than have aught of this double dealing."

"When thou goest to do battle with a man," Bayston said, "thou should'st bear the same arms as he bears that there may be no disadvantage on either side; listen, master, in the battle thou wilt have to fight with the subtle Churchman and his kinsmen, thou must use craft against their craft or else they must conquer."

"Ha, there is some truth in this knave's words. Well, if I consent to ask thy life, what surety have I that thou wilt not play me false."

"None other, than my word and vow to the Blessed Mary."

"The oath thou tookest when you joined our band."

"Yes, master, and I would have kept it, but for the Abbot's absolution."

"He gave thee absolution! Saint Herman, but the day will come when I will teach his priest-craft to find others than my men to practise his knavery upon."

"The good Saint Wilfred send the day, master, for I owe neither the Abbot nor his kinsmen much good will."

"Yet, thou wert in their pay?"

"Yes, master; but not a single piece of their money have I fingered, and when I spoke upon the matter, I received but a haughty answer; one not calculated to make me love the masters I served. Thy speech has done more to set my heart against them, than a hundred of their golden crowns would have made me hate thee."

"Peace: I will think this matter over, there may be much truth in thy professions, but there is as much cause to doubt."

They walked side by side until they came within sight of the foresters, and when the latter saw Robin's saturated garments, a shout of laughter greeted his approach."

"Body-'o-me," roared Little John. "Body-'o-me, master-'o-mine, has the fat monk rolled thee in the brook?"

"He has, John," replied Robin good-humouredly; "but he did not trounce my hide."

"That pleasure is to come, Master," "the giant said. "Ho! ho! ho! but this monk is a lusty knave to punish all who come nigh him, as he has punished Little John, Much, and bold Robin—

"Oh, what shall I do, said Robin,
 If the friar he doth see me,
No mercy he'd show unto me, I know,
 And my hide welltanned will be."

"Peace, thou roystering knave," said the Chief; "thy bawling is like the roaring of an ox, 'twould be better wert thou to tell thy beads oftener, and spend less time in singing lying songs."

"Body-o'-me! master," replied the giant, stopping short in his song, "I have but little mind to patter an ave for many weeks to come, for the good friar who baptised thee in the brook absolved me with his saintly staff, and——"

"The fiend take thee and the friar on thy back. Sound a call upon thy bugle to assemble our men; that is, if thou hast recovered as much of thy strength as thou hast the use of thy tongue."

"Good sleep and a draught of malvoisie, master, have done much to heal me, since thou went to take thy baptism in——"

"Peace, knave; sound thy bugle, for we have a matter of some import to bring before Sherwood's merry men."

The duration and pitch of the notes Little John sounded upon his bugle gave unmistakable evidence that his lungs had not received any injury from the trouncing the Curtall Friar had given him.

Long before the echo had died away among the trees, the yeomen came running towards the trysting place.

Under the spreading branches of the giant oak Robin stood, and, as the men came towards him, a wave of the hand directed them to their stations.

They formed a circle before him, leaving a clear space of nearly thirty feet.

It was a goodly sight, this gallant band: their Lincoln-green suits, studded baldrics, the shining hilts of their broad swords, their drooping feathers, and ruddy, honest faces beaming with good humour.

It was a fair and goodly sight; so thought the gallant Outlaw, as he looked at his band.

Close behind Robin stood Allan and Little John, and in the open space before them, Bayston was placed.

An empty quiver hung at his shoulder, a swordless scabbard at his hip, and at his feet an unstrung bow.

His limbs were free, for the Saxons practised not the disgraceful fashion of binding a man's limbs.

The most profound silence reigned during the time the Outlaw Chief related the encounter near Fountain Dale, and the yeomen as they leant upon their long bows, cast many an angry glance towards the culprit.

Bayston stood with folded arms and drooping head anxiously listening to Robin's words, and when the Chief had concluded, he cast a furtive look at the faces of the band.

He saw but little to give him hope, all traces of the habitual good humour expressed upon their countenances had passed away, and given place to sternness.

"You are his judges," Robin said in conclusion; "deal with him as thou wilt."

Little John stepped forward.

"Body-o'-me!" he said; "our master's journey to Fountain Dale has well nigh bred him harm. What think you, my merry companions, should be done to a knave who would thus draw an arrow upon the king of good fellows—bold Robin Hood?"

"He deserves death!"

"Well said, good yeomen; but there must be more voices pronounce the knave's doom than made me answer."

"Raise your right hands," said Allan-a-Dale, "all who wish to see yon carle's neck stretched."

A forest of sturdy green-clad limbs were held aloft.

"Thou seest, good master," Little John said, "the wish of thy bold yeomen. Now it wants but thy consent and our trysting-tree will soon bear bad fruit."

Robin did not answer for some minutes; he was well calculating the effect such a spectacle would have upon his men.

They were enraged now; but when calm reason returned there would not be one among them but would be sorry to behold a fellow-creature suspended by the neck to a branch of that tree, under which their merry meetings were held every eve at sundown.

Another reason for Robin's silence was the aversion his generous nature felt to take away life.

True, the man had most grievously offended; but as it was the first time since the Outlaw's band had been formed, Robin thought he could with safety to himself and his merry men spare the poor wretch's life.

"I must withhold this consent," he replied. "We must be merciful, my merry men, as we hope to meet with mercy ourselves."

There arose a murmur of approbation at these words, and the reprieved culprit came forward and threw himself at the magnanimous Outlaw's feet.

"Rise," Robin said; "it is not meet a freeborn Englishman should bend the knee, except to the Blessed Shrine."

Hugh Bayston arose, and pressed the hem of the Outlaw's jerkin to his lips; then faced the yeomen, who began to close around their leader.

"Hear me, bold hearts," he said; "hear my oath; for I swear by Him who died on tree, to devote the life ye have this day spared to the good of ye and our noble master. If I fail in my oath may perdition seize my soul!"

CHAPTER XVI.

ROBIN HOOD AND THE CELLARER OF ST. MARY'S.

They made the monk himself wash and wipe,.
    And at his dinner sit.
Robin Hood and Little John
    Served him with honour fit.
"Gladly eat," said Robin,
    "Grmercy answer he,
Where's your Abbey when your at home,
    And your patron saint, who is he?"
"Saint Mary's Abbey," said the monk,
    "Though I be simple here,"
"In what office?" said Robin,
    "Sir, the High Cellarer,"

THE man was received again into the fellowship of the stalwart band, a new bow was given to him, also a quiver of arrows.

"Go," the Outlaw said, "take thy post on the Nottingham side of the forest, and keep good watch upon all who leave the town, and you good George-a-Green, go with him, for it is not meet to trust one who has once played us false until we have proved his faith."

"That shall be proved ere long, good master," Hugh answered, "for at matin song I expect the Cellarer of Saint Mary's here with a hundred marks in good silver."

"Are the marks payment for the treachery thou didst meditate."

"No, good Robin; the proud Abbot has a needy relative to whom this Cellarer takes a part of the proceeds of the abbey revenues."

"Is this relative a Norman?"

"He is master, one of the hawks the favour, whom Henry of Winchester, has spread over the fair face of merry England, to fatten upon the labour of her people."

"Saint Herman, but I am right glad I saved thy life, were it only to rob this fat monk of the silver he bears to the lean and hungry Norman. Proceed man, let our merry men hear how much thou art mixed up in the matter."

"I will, master," Bayston answered, "the Abbot knowing my treachery to thee, sent word by his minion De Morley, the knave thou sawest in the forest glade—"

"I know the carle."

"He brought me word to pass the Cellarer in safety through the forest, in order, as he said, good master, those arrant thieves should not despair the good monk."

"Body-o'-me," said Little John, "but I will make this Cellarer say a string of prayers which are not to be found in the missals of Benedictines, Bernardines, or the Grey Monks of Vallambrosa, nay not even among the Cistercians or———"

"Thou wilt keep that prating tongue o' thine quiet," said Robin; "or I will give the monk over to thy keeping; and only those big ears of thine shall hear the good man's, benizons, and——"

"I am quiet, good master," said John, hastily—"as quiet as a chauntry* of monks when the Superior is away. Body-o'-me, I would sooner be cooped up with forty devils than one sleek monk. Quiet, by Saint Hubert! I'll not speak for seven long days."

"Touching the affair in which thou promised to aid," the Outlaw said; "thinkest thou there will be an opportunity of proving thy faith by leading the Sheriff's men to the heart of the forest after nightfall."

"I will, master; although I fear the Sheriff's man has ere this ran with mouth agape to his master, and told of thy appearance; yet he may return; if so, my master, I will lead them to the covert."

"Do this," said Robin, "and by my valour, our oaken staves shall ring a Saxon tune upon the Frenchmen's skulls that will take them long to forget."

The Outlaws were delighted at the prospect of trouncing their foes, and many were the injunctions given to Bayston and George-a-Green as they went to meet the high cellarer of St. Mary's Abbey.

Then the foresters went to their various occupations; not the least important, by the way, were the preparations made for dinner, and the savoury odour which came from a fat buck which was being roasted whole, caused Little John's mouth to water.

There remained now but Much, the miller's son, John, Allan-a-Dale, and bold Robin; and when the giant had regaled himself with several sniffs of the roasting venison, a broad grin came over his features.

"Master," he said, "what name did the saintly man give thee to-day?"

"One akin to that he gave thee, John."

"Body-o'-me! then there's but little chance of either of us forgetting the good priest's services?"

"True, John," laughed Robin; "he has baptized thee and Much with good English oak, I, more lucky, received water for my allowance. There is one here yet who has not seen the meek friar of Fountain Dale. What sayest thou, Allan, to an interview with the shaven devil?"

Allan stroked his long beard, and eyed Little John and Much mischievously.

"I care not," he said, "for any yeoman in England, and would stand a bout with the best among them; but, like Little John and Much, if I were foot to foot with a saintly priest, I fear me I should not let him cudgel me soundly, and not return a blow!"

* Chauntries were chapels used for the singing of masses for the souls of the departed. The jocose forester's simile no doubt inferred that when the Superior was away but few masses were sung by the lazy, over-fat priests.

"Body-'o-me!" said John, "the shaven devil would keep thine arm too much at work to let thee get a fair blow at his shining pate."

"Aye, that he would," said Much; "that he would—take thy staff and try him, Allan."

"Gramercy," said Allan, "for the offer; but I would not cast a doubt upon the statements of three such good foresters, by going for proof of thy words; no, I believe thee as devoutly as though thy words had been sworn upon the book."

"Thy belief," Robin said laughingly, "is most convenient, Allan."

"How so, good master?"

"It saves thy hide, man—it saves thy hide! Ha! that's from the Nottingham side!"

"Aye, master, and George-a-Green's bugle."

When Hugh Bayston and his companion reached the thicket which skirted the high road they plunged into the deepest part, and there remained until the jingle of bells proclaimed the coming of an ecclesiastic, for the pious ascetics loved to bedeck their mules with housings fringed with silver bells.

The ungodly foresters, who cared no more for a mitred bishop than they did for a poor monk of the greyfriars order, were wont to accuse the churchmen with a love of display.

But the good fathers, in that meekness of spirit so characteristic of the sons of the church, scorned the accusation, and averred the silver bells were placed upon the saddle-cloth to remind them of the monastery chimes, so that no matter how deep their meditations were when they travelled, they could not forget the hours of prayer.

"The priest!" said George-a-Green, "and upon a sleek mule, I'll warrant."

"Aye," responded Hugh, "the office of high cellarer and treasurer to such a wealthy abbey as Saint Mary's gives to him who holds it much of the ostentatious display of his Superior."

"He will be in a state as far as worldly goods are concerned, more befitting a monk when he leaves Sherwood than when he entered it."

"By Saint Ulrick he will," Hugh said. "Here he comes; now I think me, George, it will be better for thee to meet him, for were I to do so it would get to the prior's ears, and the good I would do our noble master will be out of the question."

"True," said George-a-Green, "should'st thou lead him to our master all will be known; take my bow, and I will get before the goodly man, so that the meeting may seem one of chance."

The forester passed through the thicket with that silence which proclaimed him a good woodsman, then running towards a line of noble trees he emerged upon the high road.

The Cellarer was a portly jovial monk, just past the prime of manhood.

His rosy cheeks and small eyes, which twinkled good humouredly, told he loved the good things of this life more than the rules of his order, which enforced strict prayer, fasting, and scourging for five out of the seven days.

The mule was as well fed as its rider, and in spite of the thumps which were administered every now and then by the Monk's heels upon the animal's plump sides, he did not move a bit the faster.

No doubt the animal considered a solemn, reverent pace befitting the service into which he had fallen; and, to do him justice, he did not depart from it, no matter how much his rider drubbed away with his heels.

"Unconcerned brute!" muttered the Cellarer, out of breath with his exertions, "had I my will thou should'st fast full and often. A plague take the beast! were it not for my saintly vows, I would cut a goodly switch, and so belabour thy stubborn hide! Get on, thou over-fed dev—beast!"

The mule was proof against this exhortation, and to the Friar's disgust, walked into the centre of the road.

"A murrain on the beast! he has taken me where the sun will take several pounds of good flesh from my poor body. Ah, thou evil one! did'st thou find it too hot that thy carcass seeks the shelter of the good trees—trees—that recalls to my mind the knave I am to meet, and, the saints be praised, here he comes!"

The priest caught a glimpse of George-a-Green's cassock as the forester turned the angle of the road.

"He seems a good youth, for he comes towards me with slow and reverent gait and bowed head. Now let me try and remember the little Latin I once learnt; it will sound well upon this arrant rogue—for rogue he is, although the proud Allatt does receive him in the Locolorium."*

The good monk failed to recall a single sentence of Latin to his memory. So trusting to the forester's ignorance upon the subject, he determined to use a language which should serve to impress the outlaw with profound respect for one so learned.

The Cellarer's mule now condescended to desist from cropping the herbage which grew by the road side. This habit by the way was a source of much discomfort to the good man, for the reins being very short caused the friar to lean over the brute's neck in a way that was not suggestive of ease or grace.

"A fair day, worthy father," said the forester as he came within hearing, the weather is somewhat hot."

"*Benedictine*, my son, *Notus sunus Odryalus meltabus*."

"No doubt, holy father, but being English born I know not the meaning of thy learned words."

"Neither do I," thought the friar; "then aloud, the meaning my son is soon told, I returned thy greeting and said the day was indeed warm."

"It is, holy father, and a day that makes one's throat feel a dryness——"

"True," said the friar, smacking his lips, "true my son; the throat does feel somewhat dry about this hour of the day. Knowest thou of the whereabouts of a clear stream wherein I could slake my thirst?"

"I know of none such about this part of the forest," said George-a-Green, "but my master, who dwells not far from this, has a goodly cask or two of soothing liquor, which, by the brand on the oaken butts, must have come from the Rhine."

The friar turned his eyes piously upward, and played with the bridle of his mule before he made any reply to the forester's words.

"The juice of the wine, my son," he said at length, "is denied to my order; yet, if there

* An apartment in which visitors were received.

is no stream within reasonable distance—for I have but little time to spare—I do not think the saints would be angry if I took a cup of thy master's wine to prevent my dying with thirst; although, understand, my son, I would much prefer a draught from the rippling streamlet."

"I know it, good father, but in this instance thou must be content to drink what comes in thy way. Thou said'st something about having but little time to spare, good father; mayhap, after all——"

"I can find time, my son, to go to the door of thy master's house, for the knave I have to meet will not be here until the noon-day sun is at its zenith.."

"There is plenty of time, then, good father, for it wants a full half-hour of the sun reaching its meridian."

"I am glad thou sayest so; but before we go towards this good master of thine I would know what and who he is."

"The head forest-keeper, holy father."

"And thou?"

"I am a simple woodsman."

"Enough, my son, lead the way; no, it were better for thee to get behind this beast of mine, and, with the good staff I see in thy hand, to belabour him until he moves at a pace that will save his rider from dying with thirst."

George-a-Green complied with this request; and, much to the sleek mule's astonishment, he used the quarter-staff until the brute struck into a sulky trot, which caused the bag of silver under the monk's frock to chink most musically.

The unusual pace shook the portly friar so much, that he called out for George-a-Green to cease belabouring the mule.

The forester did so, but the offended beast disregarded the frantic tugs at the rein, and the voice of the holy man exhorting him to stop.

He had been driven to move at an unaccustomed pace, and, whether from spite, or because he liked it, he would not stop until he carried the friar right into the midst of Robin Hood's merry foresters.

———

CHAPTER XVIII.

FRIAR CUTHBERT BESTOWS A BENIZON UPON THE OUTLAWS.

If thou hast any silver bright,
  I pray thee, let me see.
The monk he swore a full great oath,
  That no silver had he.

* * * * * * *

Who is your master? said the monk.
  Little John, answered Robin Hood.
He is a strong thief, said the monk,
  Of him I never heard good.

THE shout of laughter which greeted the monk upon his arrival among the merry foresters, caused the mule to lower his head and raise his hind quarters, and, at the same time, his hind legs were shot out with such velocity, that they acted like a lever, and the astonished cellarer flew out of his saddle, and lay sprawling within a foot of Little John.

The giant assisted the good man to regain his feet, and with much affected concern smoothed his gown, at the same time bidding him welcome.

"My master greets thee," he said, "and bids thee welcome to a poor forester's dinner, which is now being served."

The friar looked around at the stalwart foresters, then at his traitorous mule, who had made such a show of him before the band. He seemed to form a pretty shrewd guess respecting the company among which he had fallen, for he hugged the bag of silver closer under his arm, and mentally thanked his forethought for having prompted him to fasten it around his body with a stout leathern thong.

"Thy master," he said, "bids me welcome! Pray who is thy master, sir Green-Cassock?"

"Robin Hood," said the giant; "Robin of Sherwood."

"A cutpurse and a robber," said the friar. "Oh, woe is me I came amongst ye."

"Gramercy, Sir Priest," said Robin, coming forward; "is it thus thou givest thanks to an offer of a slice of as fat a buck as ever fed?—is it thus thou repayest the wish we have for thee to drink a cup of good wine with us? Out upon thy courtesy!"

This sounded well—a slice of venison and a cup of wine; and as yet the bag of money was safe.

These thoughts caused the Cellarer to feel more at his ease, and being hungry and thirsty he adopted a more civil mode of speech.

"I crave thy pardon, good Robin, he said; "and would not have spoken so uncourteously had not my mind been filled with sorrow at the unholy behaviour of yonder mule. I give thee thanks for thy offer, and will gladly taste of thy viands, the smell of which comes sweetly to my nostrils."

"Sound a blast, John," said the Outlaw Chief, "and call my men to dinner; for it is not meet that we should keep the good father waiting."

A long and well-sustained note from Little John's bugle called the foresters together, and Robin, leading the friar to where the table was laid, gave him a seat on the right hand.

One of the yeomen handed the monk a long dagger, and the good man was about to attack the smoking joint before him when Robin arrested his hand.

"I crave your pardon," he said, "but it is our custom here in the greenwood to have a blessing said before we eat."

"A goodly practice, my son. Shall I utter the words of grace?"

"Do, good father."

The outlaws uncovered their heads while the friar mumbled out a few words, then the signal was given, and one and all began an attack upon the smoking viands.

The monk was not the worst trencherman present, as he soon proved by the manner he sliced off collop after collop of the rich venison, and when the wine was served he emptied a tankard at a draught.

"I have feasted right royally," he said, folding his hands complacently over his capacious stomach; "and I give ye all thanks for this courtesy, and although the buck may belong to the king, it nevertheless has the true flavour we poor monks so seldom taste."

"The buck, good father," Robin said, "belongs to none save him who slew it. God sent the beast for men's food, not for one man, although he may call himself king, to have the control of the——"

"Stay, my son, my order will not allow me to listen to thy dangerous doctrine respecting the forest laws, so let us have that tankard and we will pledge each other like good and true men,"

"The holy father," struck in George-a-Green, "much prefers water to good red wine. Shall I go to the brook and——"

"Nay, my son, nay, do not disturb thyself upon my account I will for this once drink the same drink as thou drinkest, and if I sin by so doing, I will do penance in my cell."

The foresters laughed at the haste in which these words were spoken, and the eager clutch the friar made at the stoup of wine.

Robin watched the monk as the good liquor gurgled down the saintly throat.

"Drink thy fill," he said, "mayhap the time will come when thou can'st ask me to drink with thee."

"Ask thee! Robin," said the Cellarer, whose head was not quite proof against his libations, "ask thee! by the relics of Saint Ursula, if thou wilt come to Saint Mary's any time after evensong and ask for Father Cuthbert, thou shalt taste of the finest brand in the cellars—what sayest thou?"

"It's a bargain," said Robin; "I will come to-night and join thee and thy brethren after the day's prayers are——"

"Hush, what knowest thou of our jovial meetings in the refectory, surely; but no, thou can'st not know aught, for the poor brothers of our order are compelled to scourge themselves every night, that their bodies may be——"

I will join in the scourging," said Robin, "so be at the gate after nightfall good father."

"I will, here's my hand on't, don't then fail to come."

"I shall not fail. Now good father, that the remains of the feast have been taken away I will ask thee a few questions."

"A thousand; if I can answer them I will."

"What brought thee through the forest to-day, good father."

This question partly sobered the monk, and he closed his arm tighter upon the bag.

"Ah! my son," he said; "'tis a sad and painful story, and I would not bring grief to the hearts of this merry company by talking of my errand."

"We would like well to hear it, good father, for although we dwell in the happy greenwood we have not forgotten there is suffering beyond our kingdom."

"Since it must be, answered Father Cuthbert, "I will speak. Knowest thou a town some three or four arrows' flight beyond the forest?"

"I know a small hamlet of that name.

"Well, town or hamlet, city or village—call it by any name thou likest best. I must tell thee there dwells there a poor man, grievously afflicted in mind and body; 'tis to him I am going, for he seeks the advice and aid of the only true church.

"Poor knave! Art thou going with empty hands upon so sad a journey? Does not the afflicted man need other things beside ghostly comfort?"

"He does, good Robin. A box of salve and a bag of herbs, I have for him under my——

that is, hanging to my saddle, unless that ungodly beast has broken the strap and lost it on the way."

"Is that all thou hast for him?"

"All, my son, all."

"No silver. No money to relieve him in his sore strait?"

"Silver! Blessed be Him who died on a tree! What would a poor monk do with silver?"

"Yet, when thou alighted'st from thy mule, I could have sworn I heard the chink of good broad pieces. Mayhap, I was mistaken."

"Thou wert, my son (a malison on the accursed mule), thou wert, mistaken."

"It gives me pain to hear it," Robin said gravely; "for it is a law among our merry men to make all who have dinner with us to pay for it in bright broad pieces."

Father Cuthbert's face fell when he heard this, but the wine he had drank having given him an artificial courage, he determined to stick to the story he had told.

"Thy custom is a good one," he said, "and no doubt when a rich knight or merchant accepts thy hospitality, it is far better for this good company than a dozen poor churchmen."

"Not so," said Robin: "we have found the fat priests pay better than their lay brothers."

"The saints defend us! Robin, wherever can they get money?"

"Generally from a leather bag, holy father."

"And if, good Robin they have no bag—how then?"

"If they say they have no bag of silver, holy father, we strip them of their garments and flog their hides with nettles."

> "To bid a man to dinner,
> And then him beat and bind,
> It is our old custom, said Robin,
> To leave but little behind."

"Saint Ursula! Saint Dunstan! defend us," growled the monk; "then I must suffer, for no silver have I."

"Thou liest, monk," said Robin; and, for thy lies, thou wilt lose the hundred marks thou art carrying to heal the lame and hungry Norman who awaits thy coming at Blythe."

"Misere Domine pater——"

"Cease thy bewailings, and listen; and, for doing this before this merry company, thou art sentenced to pay me over and above the hundred marks thou hast about thee, twenty gold pieces——"

"Miserere oh——"

"Peace; for these twenty pieces I will call upon thee to-night after evensong; and beware, if they are not ready when I have joined the holy brethren in the refectory—for I will keep that promise also——"

"Twenty devils, thou thief! a murrain on thy hang-dog face!" roared the Monk. "Where dost thou think I can get gold pieces?"

"From under the stone in the buttery; the stone——"

The Friar gave a howl.

"Ten thousand curses!" he cried; "how in the fiend's name knew you where I kept the little savings of——"

"How know I where you kept the pilferings of thy stewardship? I will tell thee, Monk. I saw thee hiding thy gains when I looked through a win——"

"Peace; thou shalt have the twenty crowns; but not a word to anyone of this stone in the buttery floor."

"I am dumb," Robin said. "Now, good father, the hundred marks, then depart in peace."

"Hundred marks! thou art mad, Robin, mad! Where did'st thou ever find a poor monk possessed of so large a sum?"

"This very day!" answered the Outlaw, "as Little John shall prove."

> "Come forth, Little John
> And hearken to what I tell,
> I do not know a yeoman that
> Can search a monk so well."

Little John did search the monk well, and found the bag under his arm.

"Body-o'-me," he said, "but it were a sin for a hungry Norman to finger these good pieces."

"The sin is saved," said Robin. "Now, Sir Monk, mount thy mule and return to the Abbey, and forget not to-night after evensong, or, by Saint Herman, I will remember the stone in the butt——"

"I shall not forget," said the monk, angrily, as he mounted his mule; then as he gathered up the bridle he added to himself, "nor wilt thou if once I have thee inside the Abbey."

> "The monk then beat his mule,
> No longer could he chide,
> Have a parting cup' said Robin,
> Before you farther ride.
> Greet well your Abbot," said Robin,
> And your Prior I you pray,
> And bid him send me such a monk
> To dinner every day."

So sang Little John, but long ere he had finished, the good father was out of hearing. He had had enough of Robin and his merry men for one day; and as he rode through the forest he swore by all the saints he would sooner starve than pay so high for a dinner.

CHAPTER XIX.

ROBIN HOOD VISITS SAINT MARY'S ABBEY.

> The Abbot he rode to the Sheriff,
> With all the haste he could;
> And to him told everything
> Exactly as it stood.

IN a sequestered valley about midway between the confines of the forest and the town of Nottingham, stood the monastery of Saint Mary's.

It was a spacious and noble structure; on one side was the church, which differed but little from the beautiful cathedrals which still exist.

At the southern side of the nave was the great cloister, which had a door at the eastern and western ends of the aisle, so that the great processions could enter and leave the place with that dignity so befitting the splendid rites which took place in the time of which we write.

Over one side of the cloister was the dormitory of the monks, a spacious chamber divided into small cells, each furnished with a bed of rushes, a mat, a rug, and a blanket.

A desk and a stool completed the internal arrangements of these solitary dwellings.

From this apartment a door led into the church, in order that the monks should at all times be near the altar, and ready to attend the summons of the sonorous bell.

At the side of the cloister, and facing the church, was the refectory where the holy brethren took their meals, and near this was the locutorium, an apartment where visitors were received, also where the monks, between the intervals of prayer, sat and conversed.

Beyond this room were the kitchens; adjoining was the buttery.

On the eastern side of the cloister were the chapter-house, the library, and the scriptorium, where the monks employed their leisure in copying and illuminating manuscripts.

On this side also was the treasury where the coffers, the plate, and church ornaments were kept.

The abbot and the chief officers of the abbey had each a separate house: these dwellings stood on the eastern side of the cloister, where, also, were situate the nurses' chamber, the infirmary, and the almonry.

Surrounding these buildings was a high wall, which included within its precincts not only the places referred to, but large gardens, abounding with choice fruits and the rarest plants.

In one place only in the wall was there a means of access to the abbey: this was an embattled gate-house, and within the massive gates a monk was in attendance both day and night.

True, all who knocked at the grim portals did not gain admittance, for, by the means of a sliding panel, defended by a strong iron grating, the monk in attendance was enabled to scrutinise all who stood without.

The soft light from a thousand tapers streamed through the mullioned windows of the cloister, and the clanging of the great bell floating upon the evening breeze told the pious wayfarer who chanced to pass within view of the abbey, that the holy brethren had gone to evening prayer.

Standing upon a knoll which commanded a good view of the abbey and its grounds were three forms, draped from head to heel in long cloaks, which seemed more for concealment than warmth, for the evening was as balmy, as the evenings are wont to be in this fair land.

As the cloaked figures turned from time to time in speaking to each other, the hem of their long garments became displaced, and a glittering object became visible just beneath, which, by its size and the way in which it hung against the leg, could be no other than the steel tip of the long, straight, double-edged sword, then worn by all who could afford to purchase so good a weapon.

The monks' voices rose in full, rich tones as the bell ceased ringing, and before they had reached more than halfway through the chant, the door of the gatehouse opened, and allowed the egress of a man, who, as soon as he saw the portal closed and the light from the monk's taper fade away, ran nimbly towards the knoll where stood the trio.

"Body-'o-me!" said the tallest of the three, as the man from the abbey came within hearing; "hast thou been joining yonder shavelings in their chant?"

"Nay, John," replied the man; "I have but a sorry voice at the best, and one hour with yon full-throated carles would——"

ROBIN HOOD,

AND THE OUTLAWS OF SHERWOOD FOREST.

ROBIN HOOD'S ENCOUNTER WITH FRIAR TUCK.

"Leave this jesting," said another of the cloaked forms, "to another time. Speak, Bayston, of all thou hast heard?"

"But little more than thou suspected, good master," said Bayston; "the Abbot is very wroth at the loss of his hundred marks, and he swears by Saint Dunstan and the devil to hang thee before long."

No. 6.

"Ho! ho!" laughed Little John. "Body-'o-me! but I would——"

"Hold thy tongue, I pray thee," said Robin, "and let us hear more of this Abbot's prating. Go on, good Bayston?"

"I told him, good master, of the Sheriff's intent to bring his men to Sherwood to-night."

"Ah! What said the proud priest?"

"He called for his palfrey to be saddled," Bayston answered; "and told me he would tell the Sheriff of a better plan than taking his men to Sherwood."

"Did he not tell thee so much that thou might'st judge of this new plan?"

"He did not, good master; but I shall know more of it to-morrow at matin-song, for he bid me come to the——"

"And so far," Robin said, "there is nothing to be done save to wait the coming of the Abbot. Dost thou think he will be attended, Bayston?"

"Only by his shaven esquire, friar Elmo—a stout knave he brought from Normandy."

"Gramercy for this," laughed Robin. "Now, John, thou had'st better follow this priest, and take thy opportunity to pull the squire from his mule, then thou canst take his cassock and girdle, and follow the Abbot."

"Body-o'me!" said John, "I like the office well; but, good master of mine, I fear me I shall be sorely tempted to hit the Abbot on the pate before we reach Nottingham town."

"At thy peril! knave, do that. St. Hubert! have I not made a vow to catch this proud Abbot, and bind him to a tree, there to make him sing mass to our merry men? At thy peril crack his crown. By the saints! wert thou to do this, I would send thee to meet the Curtall Friar of Fountain Dell for thy pains."

"Enough, good master; the Abbot's pate is as safe from my staff as though he were my own brother."

"Ah! yonder he rides. Follow him, John."

The Abbot and his esquire emerged from the gate-house as Robin spoke, and little John, gathering up the skirts of his long mantle, ran swiftly from the knoll.

"Now, Allan," Robin said, "we will crave admittance to yon place. Hie thee to the greenwood, Bayston; and, should we not return by midnight hour, bring our merry men hither to give us freedom; for, unless you hear my horn, thou mayest make sure we have been caught in a trap."

"The shavelings may catch thee, good master," answered Bayston, "but we will pull their abbey down, stone by stone, before they shall hold good Allan and thee for long."

"Well spoken, Bayston," Robin said. And as the men went towards the forest, he added: "there may be some good in this fellow, Allan, after all."

"Aye, master, there may be," Allan answered, "for he seems as ready to serve thee as he was to serve the Norman. I like the man well enough, but I like not the sorry manner in which he changes from side to side."

"He is a Saxon, Allan. Peradventure he will be as faithful to us as any of our merry men."

If Our Good Lady wills it so; but, thanks to little Much, this knave will have but scant chance of doing us harm."

"What has Much to do with him, Allan?"

"Only this, master: he has set himself to watch every act of this change-coat, and will do so until he can avow the knave's fidelity."

"A goodly scheme; but, Allan, what is best to be done to gain admittance to yon building?"

"The plan I have advised, master; for it would be but folly to show thyself at the gate in such guise as would make thee known to the wrathful Cellarer."

"Perhaps it is best to follow thy advice, so we will ask admission as two poor brothers of the Franciscan order."

The long cloaks they wore were soon arranged as monkish gowns; the hoods were drawn over their faces; and, bending their stalwart bodies, they leant upon their staves, and went slowly towards the gate.

Neither the first or second summons was answered by the surly porter; therefore Allan beat such a tattoo upon the carved door, that it was heard the farthest end of the building.

The faint gleam of a taper was soon visible under the door, and, when it became stationary, the panel was drawn back violently, and a very red and wrathful face was seen the other side of the grating.

"Saint Mark! St. Ursula! bring a murrain upon thee," said the owner of the angry face. "Dost thou think the house of God is an alehouse? Pass on, whoever thou art, and, for fear of Our Lady's wrath, disturb not the holy men of this abbey with thine unseemly noise."

Having delivered himself of this speech with more acrimony than it is possible to describe, the monk closed the wicket.

"The devil have his shaven crown!" said Allan, "and, were he within reach of the good staff I hold, I would trounce his hide until he needed no more absolution for his sins. Bones of St. Herman! master, what shall we do now?"

"Assail the door, Allan, until the surly churl give us admission. Raise thy staff, and I will help thee."

The din created by the united efforts of the foresters was for some time disregarded; but, as the two warmed with their work, it was evident the porter's wrath could not much longer keep him from resenting the attack upon the sacred edifice.

Robin's arm began to tire, and he was about to rest for a few moments, when the door was flung violently open, and, before either of the foresters could step back, the monk rushed through the open portal.

He was too angry to speak, and, without the least warning, Robin and Allan were felled to the ground by the thick, oaken cudgel the monk had armed himself with.

Full upon their pates they received the knocks, and, as they sat, too much astonished to speak, or attempt to rise, the monk danced around them, flourishing his cudgel.

"The devil palsy thine arms!" vociferated the monk. "Did I not warn thee of the just punishment thou would'st receive for disturbing the abbey at this unseemly hour? Get to thy feet, thou pair of roystering carles, or, by Our Lady! I'll pound thee to a jelly. Get up, I say!"

Both Robin and Allan felt a little dizzy from the knock down, yet the love for a good bout at quarter-staff was so strong a part of their nature, that, had they not a very powerful motive for wishing to gain admittance to the abbey, they would have repaid the monk with large interest and in similar fashion.

But, ruled by the desire before mentioned, they sat perfectly still, save that their right hands were tenderly rubbing their crowns, and assuming as meek a demeanour as was qualified to soothe the monk's just wrath, they waited patiently until the holy man had exhausted his energy by the joint occupations of cursing them, dancing, and twirling his heavy cudgel.

"Holy brother," Robin said meekly, when the monk paused, "hold thy hand, I pray thee, for we meant not to disturb the pious brethren at this——"

"Meant not! meant not to disturb them?" retorted the monk wrathfully; "dost thou think it possible that the devout brothers could say as much as an *ave* with the infernal din thou madest at the door?"

"We crave their pardon," said Robin in great humility; "and thy pardon, good and holy brother; and had not the night been of such blackness we would have wended our way to the shrine of Our Good Lady, and——"

"Our Good Lady!" repeated the monk, lowering his cudgel and stooping to look at the pair; "what art thou, then, that thy tongue pratest so glibly of the blessed patron, whose goodness has raised this humble edifice for her devout sons?"

"We are two poor brothers of the Franciscan order, worshipful sir. We are lately from Palestine, and, being both hungered and athirst and footsore, we came but to crave a few hours' shelter from the storm which is gathering apace."

"Franciscans? I have heard of thy poor order, but I think it would better have become thee to have asked admission in a manner more beseeming thy poverty than like a pair of roystering knaves."

"We would have done so, please you, holy father," said Allan; "but had not time before the wicket was closed in our faces——"

"Get thee to thy feet," said the monk, "I will risk our lord Abbot's wrath for admitting thee; so follow on."

With due respect for their guide, the pair of poor friars kept some distance behind him, and by the shaking of their limbs it seemed they were wondrously agitated at beholding the interior of the sacred edifice.

So thought the monk when he turned and looked at the bent forms of the Franciscans; but could he have seen beneath their cowls he would have beheld a pair of jovial, laughing faces, and the trembling of their limbs he would have found was caused by the difficulty they had in suppressing their laughter. He saw none of this, but inflated by the humble manner in which he had been addressed, he became more communicative as they neared the locotorium.

"The brethren," he said, "are at supper, and, if thou wilt wait my return, I will bring a sufficient portion for thy wants."

"Holy father," Robin said, "it is long since we had the ghostly comfort of sitting in a refectory; and, if the good brethren would not deem it too much for such humble sons of the church as we are, we would most humbly crave admission to this company."

The monk considered for a few moments before he replied to this humble request.

"I will ask the brethren," he said at length. "Meanwhile thou can'st sit here until I return."

The Franciscans bowed low, and the lusty monk took his departure.

"Allan," whispered Robin, "how feelest thy pate?"

"There is a knob on top, master, as big as an apple. How feelest thine?"

"Much the same, Allan. By St. Herman! if I do not raise two on the shaven knave's pate, make a show of me before our merry men."

"I'll break his back," said Allan, spitefully, "or, may I be choked with the string of my good bow."

"We must wait, Allan, until we get him near the greenwood. Hush! here comes the lusty armed thief."

"The holy brethren," said the friar, "have been pleased to listen to the humble request ye have made; therefore, arise, and follow me."

The Franciscans hobbled after their guide, and were by him ushered into the refectory.

"Welcome, my brother," said a fat, jovial monk, who sat at the head of one of the tables; "Welcome, in Our Lady's name, to our poor fare."

Robin mumbled out a few words, which he intended for Latin, and room was made at the centre table for the poor brothers.

"We are English monks," said the fat friar who had welcomed the Franciscans, "therefore, my good brothers, spare your Latin, for we much prefer to hear our mother tongue spoken."

"The saints be praised for that!" thought Robin; "for I feared for this test."

"I'll give a silver piece to the shrine of my patron saint," thought Allan; "for the Latin I feared would betray us ere long."

Considerably at their ease upon this point, the Franciscans accepted a platter of dried peas and roots, which were placed before them, and neither could repress a grimace at the meagre fare.

A goblet of clean water garnished the platter and added much to their discomfort, for they knew that for appearance' sake they must suffer martyrdom by partaking of it.

CHAPTER XX.

THE MONKS' CAROUSAL.

FRIAR JOHN : What is the name of yonder friar,
    With an eye that glows like a coal of fire,
    And such a black mass of tangled hair?
FRIAR PAUL : He who is sitting there,
    With a rollicking
    Devil-may-care
    Free-and-easy look and air,
    As if he were used to such feasting and
    frolicking?
FRIAR JOHN : The same.
FRIAR PAUL : He's a stranger. You'd better ask his name,
    Where he is going, and whence he came.
FRIAR JOHN : Hallo! Sir Friar.
               Longfellow.

THE slow movements of the hungry Franciscans' jaws somewhat belied the story they had told respecting their starving condition.

Allan's grimaces as he masticated the tough supper, were equalled by the wry face Robin made when he took a draught of the cold water.

The jovial-looking monk keenly watched the proceedings of the Franciscans; and by the merry twinkle in his eyes, it was evident he secretly enjoyed the martyrdom the poor brothers were suffering.

"Holy brethren," said the jolly monk, demurely, "your long fasting has rusted your jaws; for the best supper we have had for many long nights stands almost as it did when first it was placed before you."

"Brother," replied Robin, ruefully, "we have fasted long—we have plucked the unripe fruit from the trees in the holy land—we have held a pebble between our teeth for many days to exorcise the pangs of hunger; yet," he added, savagely, "by our dear Lady's shrine, such a supper as this is worse than anything we have yet had."

"Forget not thy vow of humility," responded the Monk; "forget not these roots were the food of our blessed patron saint—this water her drink. Pray, my brethren, for Him who died on tree to bless this food and drink, and ye will be nourished as we are by the simple and wholesome means the Lord has sent us."

"Brethren," said Allan, "your prayers must have some wonderful powers of nourishment in them; for, by the Saints, your bodies are sleeker than those who daily partake of rich wines and fat venison."

"There is much of truth in thy words," the monk answered, complacently folding his hands across his stomach. "We have faith, brother, strong faith. To us the dried roots and green herbs are thankfully eaten, and we praise Him who——"

"Two stoups only of the old oaken butt. A malison on the Abbot for draining the barrel of the rich juice!"

These words were spoken by one of the brotherhood as he entered the refectory, and their effect was to disturb the solemn gravity which the monks had hitherto kept, both in word and look.

The monk placed two tankards of wine upon the table; then, for the first time, became aware of the presence of the poor brothers of the Franciscan Order.

"Greet thee well!" he said, casting one eye upon the platter of roots and the pitcher of water; "greet thee well, holy brethren!"

One of the stoups of wine was placed within reach of Allan's hand, and before the confused friar could take it away again, the forester's fingers had closed round the handle.

"Greet thee well, good brother!" he said, "and gramercy for thy kindness in bringing us this draught of good water. I drink to ye all."

The forester, after he had taken a goodly draught, handed the stoup to Robin.

Our Lady's blessing," said the chief, "upon the well from whence such water as this comes."

The monks looked from one to the other, then at the two Franciscans, who had, by this time nearly drained the wine stoup.

It was evident the jovial brotherhood wished to partake of the good juice; but first they mutely asked each other whether the strangers were to be trusted.

"Good and holy brethren," said the stout monk, who had first given the friars welcome, "in the haste, prompted by your thirst, ye have drank a cordial intended for such of our order as fall sick."

"I crave pardon," said Robin, "but, in the monastery of St. Julian, blessed be the saint, we poor brothers were always sick, and drank but of exactly such a medicine."

"St. Julian," repeated the monk, grinning; "where is the shrine of that good saint?"

"At Walsingham, good brother."

"Walsingham! Thou hast travelled much at home as well as abroad, good brother."

"I have," said Robin, "so has my brother. Tell them, good Allan, thy tongue is given to sweet rhyme; tell the holy brethren of our travels."

The forester looked around at the faces of the monks, as he crossed his hands meekly, and began :—

> "We are strangers, well ye wot,
> And much have travelled, and have viewed
> The Lord's sepulchre and the grot,
> Where he was born of maiden true.
>
> The Shells of Cales, in sign of grace,
> Adorn our heads; and ye may see
> A vernicle,* with his dear face
> Impressed, who died on Calvary.
>
> Upon my cloak Saint Peter's keys
> Were drawn at Rome, with crosses wide,
> And relics from beyond the sea
> We bear, or woe may us betide.
>
> The snow-topped hills of Armony,
> Where Noah's Ark may now be found,
> We've seen—in sooth we do not lie—
> Told o'er our beads and kissed the ground
>
> At Walsingham; our voice we've raised
> At Waltham Eke and Coleraine.
> And to Saint Thomas, we have prayed,
> Who near the Holy Rood was slain.' †

"By Our Lady!" Friar Cuthbert said, "ye have seen much, my poor brothers; but have ye ever seen a fairer abbey than this of Our Lady's?"

"Few fairer," Allan said; "many not as fair. But," he added, with a sly look at the Outlaw Chief, "I never yet saw so fat a body of monks thrive so well upon these dried roots and green herbs, together with the cold water ye gave to us!"

"Ah, brother!" Friar Cuthbert said; "there are many godless men whose evil tongues say we do not thrive upon the simple food the Lord sends us."

"If ye do," Robin said, "ye are the first goodly brotherhood we have met who has done this. Come, holy brother, does not your cupboard hold better comforts than roots and water."

The friar's jovial face became overspread with a smile as he looked at Robin, and meeting the frank, handsome features of the Outlaw Chief, he saw therein that which told him the poor Franciscans loved a good carouse, and would not betray those with whom they joined in this flagrant breach of monastic discipline.

"Brother," he said; "to such as ye who have travelled so far, I will not gainsay but we poor monks do at times—that is, when our surly Abbot is away—enjoy the carnal pleasures of the wine-cup and the table, and if ye will promise, by the vernicle upon your hoods, not to betray us, ye shall join us in such a carouse as

---

* A vernicle—a miniature copy of the picture of Christ, which is supposed to have been miraculously imprinted upon a handkerchief preserved in the Church of St. Peter, at Rome; and those wandering friars who visited the Eternal City usually brought back as a proof of their pilgrimage certain tokens of the places they visited.

† Joseph Strutt is the author of these lines, and the chronicle is headed, "May-day Pageant in the 15th Century."

ye have never before seen in monastery, or any place where the grey-robed brethren are wont to assemble. What say ye?"

"Betray ye!" Robin said, "by the splendour of Our Lady's brow I would scorn so mean an act. Bring forth the contents of thy cupboard, and if ye do not find us as quick with the cup, the song, and the jest, may Our Lady doom us to walk barefoot from here to Mount Armony, our food the dry roots here, and our sandals filled with grey peas."

Further parley was not required, for the fat monks had longed to begin their carouse during the Abbot's absence, and many an unsaintly wish had passed through their minds when they saw the Franciscan's enter the refectory.

"Brother Denis," said Friar Cuthbert, addressing a monk who sat at the end of the table, "I pray thee bring forth the black bottle from yon cupboard, and you brother John, go to the buttery and bring the pasty, and what is left of the noble haunch of the fat buck the saints sent us yestereven."

The two monks obeyed, and while one went to the cupboard and the other to the buttery, a third spread over the table a cloth of the finest linen.

"By Our Lady's beauty," said Robin, when he, in common with the rest of the company, attacked a huge pasty, "the saints selected one of the finest bucks for the good brethren of their order."

"Ours is a good and kind saint," said Friar Cuthbert, who had already partaken of several goblets of wine, "she always tells brother John where to find—I mean she—that——"

"Holy brother," laughed Robin, "seek not to fasten the sin of killing the king's deer upon thy saint; speak like a true man, and acknowledge that brother John has more to do in this than the whole calendar of saints."

"Well, brother Franciscan," said the Friar, "I cannot gainsay thy words: this unholy brother of ours has a fashion of *falling over the wall* at night; and, mind ye, he is fast asleep when he does so."

"I have heard of such things," said Robin; "in Palestine it is common for men to walk about when their eyes are sealed with sleep."

"Such is the case with brother John," the Friar gravely said, "and when in this condition he takes a good yew bow and a sheaf of arrows, and as he wanders through the forest he shoots right and left, and sometimes his arrow will by accident, or by Our Lady's will, find a lodgment in the carcass of the fattest buck. Mark ye this," continued the Friar, "our good brother, although, mind ye, he is asleep, takes the buck across his shoulder and falls over the wall again."

"Does this occur often?"

"It does, brother Franciscan, I may say it occurs whenever we stand in need of a venison pasty, or a good haunch—not oftener than this, good brother."

"Give thanks then to Our Lady," said Robin, "for her mercies in thus giving brother John such wondrous dreams that he goest forth when in full sleep to shoot his arrows right and left. Pass that stoup, Allan, and we'll pledge all good monks who can let fly an arrow so bravely."

They pledged the monks, and the monks pledged the Franciscans in return, and soon the good wine began to loosen the tongues of the saintly men.

Many a lively ballad was trolled out by the friars, and the refrain was taken up by Robin and Allan, who had both good voices.

It was during the uproarious laughter that was caused by one of the monks' songs, the Outlaw Chief's grey robe became unfastened at the throat, and revealed his green cassock and sword-belt beneath.

Friar Cuthbert was the first to notice the Franciscan's under garments, and stopping short in the middle of a chorus, he sat with mouth agape, gazing at the unexpected sight.

"Our Lady preserve us!" he exclaimed at last. "Tell me, brother, do the Franciscans wear green jerkins and long swords under their robes?"

"The order to which we belong," Robin cried readily. "Come, brother, heed not the jerkin; keep up thy song."

The friar, in spite of his heated brain, remembered the admissions he had made respecting the manner in which the monks became possessed of the deer, and thinking Robin was one of the king's forest-keepers, he began to repent most heartily for admitting the pretended Franciscan to the revels.

The majority of the brethren were too far gone to notice the cause of Friar Cuthbert's discomfort, so those who had not fallen from their seats kept up the chorus of the song in thick voices.

"The saints help us!" muttered the friar, "for our grey gowns will not save us since this keeper has learnt——"

Robin leant over to the astounded monk and whispered a few words in his ear.

The effect was magical, for Friar Cuthbert's face changed, and gripping the Outlaw's hand he handed a flagon to him.

"So thou art bold Robin!" he said. "Gramercy for this! But I thought we had a keeper amongst us—a malison upon them! But drink, Robin, drink, king of good fellows, for I wot thou would'st sooner send a grey-goose shaft through a ranger's heart, than tell how the monks of St. Mary's come by their venison."

"Aye, that I would!" said Robin, throwing off his grey robe. "Pledge me, all of ye, pledge Robin of Sherwood!"

Many of the monks arose, and as they swayed from side to side, they pledged the bold Outlaw.

"Robin — hic — Hood — hic — bo — hic — ld — Ro—bin—hic!"

And, having stammered out this, three of the number quietly settled down under the table, and from time to time there could be heard a faint sound of Robin's name, mingled with the chorus of the last song.

More bottles were brought, and soon emptied, more songs were sung; and, as Robin trolled out the following ditty, Friar Cuthbert took the forester's horn, and, blowing upon it, added to the din :—

ROBIN'S SONG.

There lived a vile miser so greedy of pelf,
    That he first robbed his neighbour and then robbed himself;
He starved in the midst of his glittering ore,
    For, though he was rich, yet he made himself poor.

At length, with old age and with sorrow opprest,
  Grim death, with a frown, the vile miser
    addressed—
          Derry down—derry down, &c.

"I've come to demolish you this very day,
  And to bear thee to my warm regions away."
    But the miser replied—
          "Derry down derry down.

"Before I set out, I'm desirous of knowing
  If gold can be got in the place where I'm going?
Because if there's none, here I'm willing to tarry,
  Or, at least, a few bags along with me I'd carry."
          Derry down, derry down!"

To this old grim death answered—
  "Here no longer, thou covetous fool, shalt thou
    stay,
And not one of thy bags shalt thou carry away;
  In the land where thou goest no gold shalt thou
    gain,
And the devil shall plague thee with horrible pain."
          Derry down—derry down!"

To this the miser howled—
  "The devil, I'm certain, will do me no ill,
For he helped me with money my coffers to fill;
  Yet, since where I'm going no gold I can find,
It taxes me sorely to leave it behind."
          Derry down—derry down!" *

Friar Cuthbert wound up the chorus by an extra flourish upon the horn, and deluging the monk who sat next to him with the contents of the bottle he held, he roared out:

"Well sung, Heart of Oak; well sung, Green Jacket. Take thy horn, and I will give thee a roystering stave that will—— Oh! holy saints defend us!"

The refectory door was flung open as this exclamation left the monk's lips, and, to his horror, he beheld the stern Abbot and the High Cellarer standing in the portal.

Robin's hand went to the hilt of his sword, and he looked round for Allan, but the sturdy forester had disappeared. He had left the refectory some time before Robin began his song.

CHAPTER XXI.

ROBIN HOOD AND THE ABBOT.

Said the Abbot, by God and Saint Richard!
  Thou art ever bearding me.
With that, came in a rat-headed monk—
  The High Cellarer was he.
The Abbot and the High Cellarer
  Were standing out full bold,
And the high justice of England
  The Abbot then did hold.

THE Abbot's eyes blazed with fury as he looked from the daring Outlaw to the forms of the monks, who were too far gone to be aware of his presence.

Many of these continued to repeat the chorus of Robin's song, and, from time to time, suck the empty black bottle they so affectionately grasped.

At last the Abbot spoke, and, so great was his rage, that the veins on his forehead stood out like black cords.

"What means this, ye heathen devils?" he said; "is this an ale-house, that ye drink and bawl like so many peasants returned from their

day's labour? Curse ye for a crew of drunken villains. Is it thus the house of God is defiled, if I but leave the abbey? To your cells, all of ye, and scourge yourselves, or, by God's dear Son! I'll have ye flayed alive."

The Abbot and the High Cellarer advanced to the centre of the refectory, and such of the monks as were able to stagger out of the Abbot's sight, slunk away.

"Pour water over these swine," the angry Superior continued, pointing to those who lay about the refectory, "and harkee, Sir Cellarer, let their names be inscribed in the black book: for by Him who made us, I will have as much blood drawn from their shoulders as they have drank of this subtle liquor."

The High Cellarer went upon his errand; then the Abbot turned towards the gallant Outlaw, who kept his seat, and laughed heartily at the sorry appearance the monks made.

"So," he said sternly, "thou above all others art here, and, like Satan, tempting these good men from the path of sobriety and virtue. Answer me, thou arrant thief, and tell me what thou hast to say that I should not have thee hung over the gate-house as a warning to others of thy gang."

Robin laughed aloud at the Abbot's words; and much to the latter's wrath, he helped himself to a stoup of wine before making a reply.

"What I have been doing here, Sir Priest," Robin said, "thou hast evidence before thee. What I have to say against being strung up over the gate-house of this abbey is, thou wilt find the task one of more difficulty than thou thinkest."

A malicious smile played over the Abbot's lips when he heard these words, and stepping back until his hand came within reach of a bell-pull he grasped the silken cord.

"No bird," he said, "ever had less chance of escaping from the fowler's net than thou hast of leaving this Abbey alive; day and night have I waited to have thee in my power, the hour has now come."

"Has it, Sir Shaveling?"

The Outlaw again laughed, and quaffed the red wine from one of the goblets before him.

"Rise, dog," said the Abbot, savagely, "dare thou sit before me—darest thou beard me to my face—rise—go upon thy knees and crave thy life, or by the saints thou wilt never behold another sunrise!"

"Rise, and pay thee respect!" said Robin; "to the devil with thee and thy drunken crew —I care not a groat for ye, although I am, as thou sayest, like a bird in the fowler's net— but have a care, Sir Snarer, I do not cut the fowler's hands with this good blade if he attempt to draw the net closer upon me."

"Knave! caitiff! dog! darest thou threaten the Lord's anointed!—harkee, one pull of this cord and twenty lusty novices who have not yet taken their vows, will be upon thee, so have a care, or I will forestall the Sheriff in his work, by hanging thee from the highest point on the Abbey walls."

"Sacrilege!" laughed Robin, "sacrilege! To rid this fair land of one of the lazy Norman priests who swarm like locusts in merry England, harkee, Sir Shaveling, I would pin thee to yonder wall as I would a noxious reptile, therefore depart and leave me to finish this stoup of good liquor before my patron saint tells me to pollute my sword with thy foul Norman blood."

"Depart! leave thee in peace!" roared the Abbot, beside himself with rage; "a murrain upon thy tongue! may the direst curses of the church——"

"Peace, noisy priest! disturb not a good man over his liquor. Away—leave me. Already my fingers tingle to grip thy throat and beat thy thick skull against yonder wall!"

These words, and the cool, defiant attitude of the speaker maddened the Abbot.

Used as he was to the slavish obedience of the monks, the Outlaw's bold speech and open defiance caused him to forget his saintly character and use language more befitting a man-at-arms than a follower of the cross.

The Outlaw laughed the louder at this.

"By St. Herman!" he said; "the master of this goodly crew pollutes his lips with words that the most ungodly of my merry men would not use. Out upon thy lying hypocrisy, thou Norman thief; doff thy robes—don a buff jerkin, and meet me upon the green sward—blade to blade, foot to foot—for I like not the killing of even such a false reptile as thou art unless thy hand held a good blade——"

The entrance of the High Cellarman caused Robin to pause and throw himself back in his seat and laugh until the tears came from his eyes.

"Ha, ha, ha! sir monk," he laughed; "when wilt thou have dinner with the merry men of Sherwood again? Ha, ha, ha! or dost thou think the charge too high?"

"Aye, laugh," said the Cellarer spitefully; "mayhap thy jaws will not wag so much between this and sunrise."

"Marry, but they will!" Robin said; "and my pouch will be the heavier for the twenty crowns thou owest me. Remember, if they are not paid I must e'en help myself from the place thou knowest of."

The High Cellarer's face paled; he feared these words would cause The Abbot to question him respecting the Outlaw's meaning, and he knew if the proud Norman learned the little secret respecting the stone in the buttery floor there would be a vacancy in the Abbey—this, the officer of high cellarer and treasurer.

Perhaps the most unpleasant part of his thoughts was the knowledge that the late high cellarer would be an inmate of a certain dungeon beneath the abbey, where all who entered abandoned all hope of seeing the outer world again.

"Heed not this arrant thief's prating," he said; "heed it not, noble Abbot, but summon the novices and have him taken to the black dungeon beneath the aisle there; he can tell the rats of the sinful sights he has seen in the abbey—sights, noble Abbot, that will not give to Saint Mary's the odour of sanctity were they told among those who even now malign us with their false tongues."

The Cellarer's suggestion was most acceptable: yes, the dungeon was the best place for one who had seen so much of the godly brotherhood, and to the dungeon he should go.

"Drench these senseless swine," the Abbot said, "and get them to their feet, for I would not for the best golden candlestick we have that the novices should see so shameful a sight; get them to their cells," he added in a whisper,

"then this thief and scoffer at our Order and my authority shall be removed."

The Cellarer had brought with him two large vessels containing water, and in a few moments after the Abbot had thus spoken the former aroused the drunken monks by raising the collars of their gowns and pouring the cold stream down their backs.

They scrambled to their feet, a most uncanonical oath in most cases falling from their lips.

When their blear eyes encountered the Abbot's stern face, they gathered up their wet skirts and reeled from the refectory.

"Ha, ha!" laughed Robin, "what think you of them, Sir Norman? By Saint Hubert, the devil must laugh aloud when he sees such saintly men."

The Abbot made no reply, save by a malignant scowl, and before Robin could cut the bell-pull he gave it a sharp jerk, and the clang of the alarm bell rang out loud and clear in the still night.

The bold Outlaw took no notice of this, but continued to sting the Abbot with his biting sarcasms, making the ecclesiastic bite his lips until the blood came.

He would not reply, although the ill-kept retort caused his frame to shake with anger, until the door which led from the body of the church was thrown open, and a dozen of the novices entered the refectory.

"Seize and bind yon thief," he then said, exultingly, "and convey him to the dungeon beneath the aisle."

The novices were about a dozen in number, and as the foremost of them advanced upon the Outlaw Chief, he sprang to his feet.

A lioness suddenly disturbed by the hunter could not have changed her mien quicker than our gallant hero did his.

The handsome face and lithe form, which had been all repose and good humour, became rigid with anger, and his right hand plucked his sword from its sheath, as his left drew the long dagger which hung at his belt.

The flash of the weapons cowed the boldest of the embryo monks, and they slunk back as the long, straight sword was levelled in a line with their breasts.

"Back, shavelings!" the Outlaw said; "remember, the first who comes within reach of this weapon dies. This I swear by St. Herman!"

The Abbot foamed at the mouth with rage, and he threatened the novices with the direst punishment if they did not advance and seize the gallant forester.

"Show thy dupes the example," said Robin. "Come, sir, first let yours be the task to take Sherwood's king."

The Abbot looked fiercely at the bright blade, and, clenching his hands until the nails cut deeply into the flesh, seemed, for a moment, as though he would have sprung upon the leader of the Saxon archers.

The High Cellarer, who had mighty reasons for wishing the capture of Robin Hood, sidled up close to the Abbot.

"Sir Abbot," he whispered, "when there was a rising expected among the peasants, and they vowed to sack the abbey, thy good friend, the Sheriff, sent thee a score of weapons to be used in case of need. They are now in the buttery, and, as these men have not yet taken the oath to refrain from using carnal weapons, they may serve to aid in overpowering this lusty thief."

"Go, thou, with two of the novices," replied the Abbot, in the same low voice, "and bring sufficient of those weapons to serve our purpose."

The Cellarer left the refectory, making a sign to two of the Neophytes to follow him.

They did so, and Robin who gave a shrewd guess at the purpose of this movement, forced his foes farther back, and, before they could prevent him, he sprang upon the table.

Above where the table stood was an oriel window, and through this the Outlaw turned the bell of his bugle-horn, and sounded three long blasts.

Scarcely had he done this when there came a clatter of arms as the Cellarer and his companions threw the swords and spears they had brought, outside the refectory door.

The three then entered, each armed with a sword, and the remainder of the novices soon possessed themselves of like weapons.

Robin smiled defiantly at the formidable array, and placing his back against the wall awaited their onset.

It would have gone hard with the Outlaw Chief had not his bugle been heard, for the Normans, confident in their numbers, advanced boldly to the attack.

There was a clash of steel as the boldest of the assailants' swords were met by Robin's weapon.

The two foremost of the novices fell back, one with his cheek laid open, the other stabbed through the arm by the anelace.

The Abbot snatched a sword from one of the wounded men, and cursing the neophytes for cowards, rushed upon the forester.

Their swords met, and although the Abbot in common with all of Norman blood, had learnt the use of arms in his youth, he soon had his weapon torn from his hand, and with a howl of rage and pain he staggered back, the blood flowing from a wound in his neck.

In a body the neophytes advanced, and were about to make an attempt to beat down the Outlaw's sword, when a monk, pale and breathless, rushed into the refectory.

"My Lord Abbot," he gasped, "the abbey is besieged by more than four score archers, and their arrows find an entrance through every window and loophole in the abbey."

"Upon him!" shouted the Abbot; "once in the dungeon, I care not if every leaf upon the trees in Sherwood were an outlaw, and every outlaw at our gates."

"My lord," said the monk; "in heaven's name give up this man, before the gate is battered in and the abbey despoiled."

"Battered in! the gate battered in!"

"Aye, my lord; when I fled for the gate-house, the outlaws were endeavouring, with the trunk of a tree, to break down the gate."

As the last word left his lips there was heard a terrific crash, then a shout, as the band, led by sturdy Much, dashed through the gate-house.

Robin took advantage of the confusion this caused, and, striking down all who stood in his path, rushed from the refectory.

"Bar the doors!" said the Abbot; "bar the doors! or the church will be sacked!"

Too late!

The heavy door was hurled back, scattering all who had thrown themselves against it, and Robin, at the head of his men, entered the refectory,

"Seize yon Abbot!" he said; "and ye whose hands are idle trounce well the backs of those accursed monks, who would smite with the sword. Lay on, my men! lay on!"

They wanted no second bidding; and as the Abbot was seized and made prisoner, the tough yew-bows were applied to the neophytes' backs until they yelled with pain.

"It will save ye from scourging your carcasses," the Outlaw grimly said; "now, my merry men, open yon door, and as ye drive these vermin out spare not your blows!"

When the door was opened the novices made a rush, and as a natural consequence there was a crush and the whole body were, for a moment, tightly wedged in the doorway.

It was not pleasant for those in the rear, as their howling testified; and the foresters, warming with this congenial occupation, laid about them with no gentle hand. The refectory was soon cleared.

Among those who received more than their share of the punishment was the High Cellarer, and for many days after his head and body most unpleasantly reminded him of the Outlaw's visit to St. Mary's Abbey.

The foresters would have sacked the church, had not one of the band who had made a circuit of the place returned with the intelligence that all the silver cups had been taken from the altar.

There would have been a search for the costly ornaments, had not their leader taken the archers from the abbey—the Abbot in their midst, his face pale with the probable fate in store for him.

Like most evil minds he judged others by his own standard, for had his and the outlaws' position been changed, he would not have scrupled to have hung their captain upon the first tree they came to when they returned to the forest.

CHAPTER XXII.

ROBIN HOOD'S ENCOUNTER WITH THE CURTALL
FRIAR OF FOUNTAIN DELL.

If thou wilt forsake fair Fountain Dell,
Every Sunday throughout the year,
A noble shall be thy fee;
And every holiday through the year
Changed shall thy garments be,
If thou wilt go to fair Sherwood,
And there rema n with me.
The Curtall Friar had kept Fountain Dell
Seven long years and more;
There was neither knight, lord, nor earl,
Could make him yield before.

THE morning after the events recorded in the last Chapter, Robin Hood, according to his usual custom, assembled his men under the trysting-tree.

He heard the reports of those who had been on watch during the night, but, as there was nothing in them to interest the reader, we will pass on to the buttes where the men were practising their skill with the long bow.

Before this trial of skill was ended, Hugh Bayston came hurriedly towards the Outlaw Chief, his face expressive of matters of more than ordinary import.

ROBIN HOOD,
AND THE OUTLAWS OF SHERWOOD FOREST.

LITTLE JOHN OVERHEARS THE SHERIFF AND THE ABBOT PLOTTING ROBIN HOOD'S CAPTURE.

"Well, Bayston," Robin said, "thy haste heralds news from Nottingham, or I am mistaken."

"Not mistaken, good Robin," said the man; "I do, indeed, bring strange news."

"Thy report, Bayston, for this morning's gathering has been somewhat scant in news."

"Mine will make up for the shortcomings of our merry men," Bayston answered; "for I have much that is strange to tell."

"Let us hear it then, for I see by the faces of thy companions they are more than usually anxious to hear that which thou hast to tell."

"It is of Little John, master."

"Little John! has the giant met the Curtall Friar again?"

"Not so, noble Robin; he is now in the Castle of Nottingham."

"Ha! by my valour, a prisoner?"

"Not so, good Robin. He is there of his own free will."

"St. Herman defend us! What shall we hear next? John in Nottingham castle, and of his own free will!"

"Aye, Master, thou shalt hear his message to thee."

"Speak, man; I am as curious as a woman to hear of this. What says the knave?"

"Thou knowest when he left thee last night to follow the Sheriff?"

"Aye, right well I wot of that?"

"Well, Master, he met a ranger near the town, and wanting the ranger's clothes, he cracked his pate and took them from him."

"The knave! Well?"

"After that he met a serving man and did the same by him."

"What, stripped two men?"

"Not so, Master, for he gave to the first his suit of Lincoln green, and to the second the ranger's clothes; thus he went to the castle in the garb of the serving man."

"By St. Herman, this sounds strangely; but go on."

"Well, master, the Sheriff stood in need of a stout serving man, and Little John took the post."

"The saints defend us, but this is madness."

"Nay, good master——"

"But I tell thee, it is, for John's face is as well known to the Sheriff as it is to me."

"That matters not; Little John has not seen the Sheriff, nor will he, for the serving man was wanted to assist the cook, and by the cook he has been engaged."

"I see the knave's purpose. Tell me his message?"

"It was but this. Tell Robin, he said, I am for a few days the Sheriff's scullion, and when I return to the merry greenwood, I doubt not but I shall bring tidings of all the Sheriff's doings, and mayhap a present for our master."

St. Hubert keep him from harm, for this is somewhat venturesome. Hast thou told me all?"

"All, good master."

"Get thy bow then, and practice at the butts."

Bayston moved away, and Robin again turned to watch the shooting.

He was not long left in peace, for Allan-a-Dale, carrying a large leather bag, came towards him.

"Greet thee well, Allan!" said the Chief; "I am right glad to see thee safe amongst us again."

"Glad I am, Robin, to be here, for I have done heavy penance for leaving the monks' banquet."

"How so? I thought thou had'st left the abbey before the Abbot entered."

"Would to the Saints I had! No matter. When I left thee and the monks it was to visit the buttery and the treasure-room of the abbey."

"And this bag is the result?"

"It is, master; but I'd like to have made the acquaintance of a certain dungeon beneath the aisle of yonder monastery."

"So had I, Allan; but, thanks to the saints, we are free!"

"Aye, master; the saints be praised, we are."

"Let us hear thy adventures, Allan, or the day will be spent before our good archers have shot their arrows."

"Thou shalt hear. Thou rememberest the time I left thee carousing with the monks?"

"I do."

"Well, master, I found my way to the buttery, and I also found the stone where the Cellarer keeps his hoard, and, thinking he mayhap would forget to pay the broad pieces due to thee, I helped myself."

"To how many? the debt was twenty pieces, Allan. I hope thou acted honestly and took no more than our due."

"I was in doubt, master, whether it was twenty or fifty pieces; so I made sure and took the fifty."

"Well," Robin, said smiling; "we owe the honest Cellarer thirty pieces. Remind me, Much, I pay him when he passes this way again."

"I will," said Much; "that is, master, if thou dost not find out some poor peasant's family in sore distress, and empty our coffers to relieve them."

"If so," said Robin," we can still owe the monk the money. Now, Allan, what happened after this?"

"Not content with the fifty pieces," Allan said, "I must needs go to the treasure-room, and being a good son of the Church, I did not touch the candlesticks of silver or the vessels of gold which belonged to the altar, but I found three cups of pure silver. Here they are, master. Thou seest they have the Norman Abbot's bearings, and knowing they were made from the silver collected from the poor Saxon peasants for tithes, I brought them away."

"Thou did'st quite right, Allan."

"Being athirst, after so much trouble in selecting these things, I found my way to the wine vault, and, while tasting of the different brands, in came a drunken friar, to fill the flagons he carried; and I, being too much engaged to notice him, did not know the wine-swilling knave had shut the door after him, until I wanted to come out."

The Outlaw Chief and Much laughed at the rueful face Allan made at the recollection of this mishap.

"Well, master," he continued, "I hammered at the door until I was tired, but no notice was taken, and I thought I must have gone mad when the alarm-bell rang, for I knew you were in danger."

"I was, indeed, sore pressed."

"Well, master, then came the shout of our merry men as they smashed in the door of the Abbey, and rescued thee. After that, I had only to wait until one of the shaven knaves came, and that was not more than an hour since; then one whose throat was parched came and opened the door, and, for fear he should see me, and not let me pass, I waited until he entered the vault, and then I knocked him down with this bag. After being chased like a wolf by a dozen of the shavelings who were in the refectory, I ran through the gate, and came here."

"Thou art welcome," said Much, who, in

his capacity as treasurer to the band, had already relieved Allan of the spoil he brought. "May thy fingers ever fall upon such a goodly haul."

A stalwart forester, who had been appointed the Abbot's guardian, now came towards the Outlaw Chief.

"Well, Clym," Robin said, "what is thy haste?"

"A message, good Robin," Clym answered; a message from St. Mary's Abbot."

"It's import, Clym."

"He craves a boon, master."

"A boon! By St. Herman! the only boon he should crave ought to be——"

"A short rope!" said Much; "and——"

"Peace, Much," laughed the Outlaw Chief. "Although thou art pretty near the truth, I do not think the Priest will crave either a short or long rope, for these churchmen cling to life as strongly as the more sinful portion of the world."

"Aye, they do," said Much, "they do."

"Now, Clym," said Robin, "what is the boon this shaveling would ask?"

"This, good master," Clym responded. "He begs thou wilt, as a man, listen to his prayer. He craves thou wilt let him depart upon payment of such ransom as the poor coffers of the Abbey will pay."

"Poor coffers!" repeated Robin; "by St. Herman! were I to ask as a ransom his weight ten times over in gold, I doubt not but I should get it."

"This Abbot is lean of limb, master," said Much; "would it not be better to have ten times the weight of the fat cellarman."

"Hold thy tongue, thou greedy knave," Robin said; "and you, Clym, return to the Abbot. Tell him we will attend to his ransom to-morrow."

Clym returned to his captive, and the Chief was about to leave the butts, when two bruised and battered foresters came towards him.

"By the saints!" he said, "this is not a comely sight upon so fair a morning. Speak! knaves, if either of ye have a tongue left, and tell how this came about."

One of the bruised archers, a man of powerful frame, and known to be one of the best wrestlers among Sherwood's merry men, tenderly rubbed his bruised pate, and slunk behind his companion.

"Answer me, Tom of Wakefield," said Robin; "and without trying to hide behind thy companion, who is of the two much the sorest?"

Wakefield Tom shuffled to the front again.

"Well, master." he said, "Will Cloudesley and I were keeping watch in Fountain Dell for a fat buck we had long been chasing, when he passed us driven by a shaven friar, who sent a shaft through the deer's side with as sure a hand as the best among us."

"The Curtall knave again, by St. Herman! I'll stop his roaming among the fallow deer; but go on with thy story."

"You must know, master," Tom continued, "Will of Cloudesley had sent a shaft from his bow at the same moment, and it struck the buck within a finger's length of the shaven devil's arrow."

"It were a pity it did not hit the knave's body," said Robin, "a murrain on the lusty thief."

"Would it had, Master, for when we jumped from the bush to claim the deer, the monk turned upon us, and without a word began to liquor our hides with his quarter-staff."

"Aye," said Robin, "and ye had such respect for this son of the Church, that your hands were idle while he thrashed ye."

"Nay, Master," said Will Cloudesley, "shame fall upon us if we were as thou sayest."

"Yet your hides and skulls are beaten by this shaveling as though thou wert two beardless boys in place of being strong limbed foresters."

"Master," said Wakefield Tom, "we laid about us like good and true men, but I take the blessed saints to witness the short frocked friar gave twenty blows to one of ours."

"It is true, dear Master," said young Will of Cloudesley; "no matter how we fought, back hand or short staff, down came the friar's cudgel upon our pates, until he left us so well trounced that we were fain to lie upon the ground until a little of our strength returned."

"Friar, dost thou call him?" Tom of Wakefield said, "by the saints I believe he is one of the devil's lustiest imps, sent to the forest to trounce all who come within reach of his arm."

"Friar, or devil," Robin exclaimed; "I swear by Saint Herman, I'll thrash his saintly carcass before the noonday sun reaches its zenith! Go thou, Will, and bid George-a-Green bring hither my horse."

Retaining only a short sword, such as was then used in the chase, the Chief handed his bow and buckler to one of the foresters, then, jumping upon his horse's back, would have gone thus armed to meet the lusty friar, had not a forester ran towards him with a stout oak staff.

"Tarry one moment, master," he called out, "here is something to absolve the Curtall Friar with."

Robin took the staff, and, bowing his handsome head courteously until his long fair curls were mingled with his charger's silvery mane, he wheeled round and dashed towards the ash grove.

The forester reined in his charger when he came to the Dell, then, placing his horn to his lips, he blew a long winding call.

"St. Herman!" he said laughingly; "if that does not arouse the holy man I know nothing that will."

Robin was not mistaken, the rousing blast did arouse the fat friar; for he became visible at the end of a double row of trees.

The saintly man bestrode a sleek mule, and as the tough animal came nearer to where Robin sat, the latter could scarcely forbear giving vent to a hearty peal of laughter.

The lusty friar, as he rode forward, was looking keenly from side to side among the trees, for the daring intruder; he had a stout quarter-staff tucked under his left arm, his left hand held his rosary, and the fingers of his right were busy telling his beads."

"Ave Maria," he muttered; "blessed be the saints if I catch the knave who has dared to wind his horn in my domain! I'll make a jelly of his carcass! Benedicite! good Saint Wilfred! am I to be disturbed in my devotions by these deer-stealing thieves? The Lord forbid it! ha! it is the Chief of the arrant rogues!"

The forester pressed his horse forward to meet the friar.

"Give thee good day, holy father," he said; "thou art early abroad."

"Early, abroad!" repeated the friar: "it is the hour of morning song; but before I had half told my prayers, the blast of a thief's bugle disturbed my devotions and called me forth to give the rogue a sermon, which will make him remember there is danger in disturbing the Lord's anointed. A malison on the knave! Would he had blown his two eyes out when he sounded that blast!"

"I crave thy pardon, good father," Robin said, "for disturbing thee."

"Oh! it wast thou, wast it! By the saints, I should have thought the ducking I gave thee would'st have taught thee to keep from Fountain Dell."

"Far from it, father," said Robin. "I have brought a staff which has been blessed by the patron saint of all good foresters—the blessed Saint Herman of the Wold; and if it does not leather thy saintly hide, I shall place no more faith in our good patron."

The friar put away his rosary and tightened his girdle.

"Thy patron saint!" he said; "a plague upon both him and thee! Harkee, green jacket, I have a goodly branch here which grew upon the tree planted by Saint Wilfred's own hand. Four of thy thieves has it smote to the earth; and by the blessing of Him whose saint I am, it shall smite thee, or I will leave fair Fountain Dell and become chaplain to thy gang of cut-purses."

"A bargain!" Robin cried, "a bargain! If my good staff fails, I swear by Saint Herman to pay to thee every Sunday throughout the year five silver marks; so get off thy beast, thou thief of a friar."

The priest rolled off his mule, and, twirling the oak staff above his head as though it had been a willow wand, he roared:

"Get off thy beast, thou hang-dog looking cut-purse, get off; or, by St. Wilfred! I'll lay about thee where thou now sittest."

Robin leaped lightly to the ground; and the animals, as though they understood the danger of being too near the long staves, trotted away to a green spot, and began to graze side by side.

"Have at thee, shaven devil!"

"Have at thee, hang-dog cut-purse!"

Exclaimed the combatants, as they stood foot to foot, and raised their weapons.

For a full hour there was nothing heard but the rattling of the oaken staves as the combatants alternately attacked and defended.

It was a rare exhibition of skill. Not in the whole history of the noble game of quarter-staff, is there such an account as the old manuscript details of this long and obstinate battle.

Robin Hood's yeomen excelled in the manly exercises of the day, and their leader was the best and most skilful with bow, sword, or staff; in fact, it is said he could beat any three of his men with the last-named weapon: yet, for a full hour had he tried to crack the Friar's pate, and could not touch him.

The Priest tried his most skilful points with the forester, but failed to get an opening.

Thus they fought until both were utterly exhausted.

"A boon friar," Robin said; "let us rest our arms."

"To the devil with thy boons!" he answered. "Fight on, or yield thee to the power of the good stick which grew upon Saint Wilfred's tree."

"A murrain upon thee and thy saint's tree! Take that for thy shining pate."

Robin's haste caused him to overreach himself, and the friar, catching the blow upon the centre of his staff, brought his hands together, as the forester prepared for another blow or for defence as the case required.

As quick as thought the priest took advantage of Robin's open guard, and making a feint as though to strike his opponent's fingers, he dropped one end of the staff under Robin's guard.

Although the blow was deprived of a considerable amount of force by being delivered so short, it caused the forester to reel backward.

"Yield! yield to St. Wilfred's blessed staff!" shouted the friar, "yield, and forget not the five marks thou hast to pay me every Sunday throughout the year."

Dazed a little by the blow, Robin continued falling back before the friar's vigorous assault, until the latter, feeling certain of his victory, paid less attention to his defence than he had hitherto done.

This was the Outlaw Chief's opportunity. He made a sudden spring forward—beat down his adversary's guard, and the next moment the lusty friar measured his length upon the green sward.

"Blessed be Saint Herman!" Robin said, as he stood over his foe. "Crave a boon, thou lusty thief, or by my valour I'll thrash thy fat carcass until thou art so sore that for forty days thou shalt neither move hand nor foot!"

"I crave thee, hold thine hand," said the friar ruefully. "May the devil fly away with the saint who could not put more virtue in a tree of his own planting, than he has in this."

"Saint Herman! before all thy calendar," the Outlaw said. "Do'st thou yield to him?"

"Since it must be so, I e'en must."

"Get to thy feet, we will return to my merry men, and they will make thee welcome, for we have long wanted such a chaplain as thou wilt make."

The jovial friar grinned at the Outlaw's words, and as they went towards the place where stood the animals, he gave a sly look every now and then at the red mark his staff had made across Robin's cheek.

Judging by the expression of the monk's face, his defeat did not greatly trouble him, possibly he was of opinion that it would be quite as well for him to join the band, as to attempt to hold Fountain Dell against so many strong arms.

Whatever were his opinions about the matter, one thing is very certain, he seemed full of glee as he mounted his mule, and laughed and joked with his conqueror in the most genial manner.

CHAPTER XXIII.

HOW LITTLE JOHN GAINED ADMITTANCE TO NOTTINGHAM CASTLE.

Hearken and listen, ye gentlemen,
All that now be here,
Of Little John, that was Robin's man,
And good mirth ye shall hear.

THE Abbot of Saint Mary's and his companion, the high Cellarer, when they left the monastery were closely followed by Robin Hood's stout lieutenant.

The forester had hoped to have dragged the Cellarer from his mule by disguising himself in the portly churchman's garments, and glean some intelligence of the movements of the Outlaw Chief's enemies.

He was prevented doing this in consequence of the pair riding so closely together, and before he could mature one of the many plans which came into his head, the embattled tower of Nottingham castle frowned above them.

"Gramercy for this long robe!" said the forester; "for by its aid I hope to pass yonder portals unquestioned."

The warder's hoarse challenge was answered by the Abbot, and when the drawbridge was lowered, little John, with matchless effrontery, placed one hand upon the saddle-cloth of the Abbot's palfrey, and boldly followed the pair inside the fortalice.

The armed mercenaries who served under De Lois, bowed their heads and crossed themselves when the Norman priest gave his benediction, and Little John who had by this time released his hold upon the palfrey's trappings drew the cowl of his long cloak over his head, and spreading out his hands right and left seemed to be showering blessings upon the steel-clad foreigners who lined the court-yard.

Here the Abbot and the Cellarer dismounted, and Little John, placing himself before the groom, who advanced to take the priest's palfrey, he boldly caught the bridle and led the animal away.

The Abbot and the Cellarer were too much occupied with the matter which had brought them to the castle to notice the disguised forester, thus Little John was enabled to carry successfully the bold plan he had determined upon following.

At the door of the great hall the Churchmen were met by the major domo of the vast establishment, who greeted his master's visitors; and giving the Cellarer over to the care of the butler, he stalked before the Abbot, flourishing his white wand, much after the fashion of a modern drum-major.

Little John watched this edifying sight from under his cowl, then beckoning the groom to approach he placed the palfrey's bridle in his hands.

"Tend well this beast, my son," he said, "and our saintly Abbot will well reward thee for it."

"I will, holy father."

"In which chamber is the Lord Abbot being shown?" Little John continued, "for my duty compels me to be at his side, wheresoever he may go."

"To the oaken chamber, holy father."

"Thanks, my son; cans't thou do me a favour, by telling me of a nearer way to reach the oaken chamber, than the way by which the Lord Abbot has gone?"

"Aye, good father, I can, a much nearer way, if thou usest thy legs, thou wilt be there a good ten minutes before thy holy master."

"Gramercy, for thy kindness. Remember, if thou should'st ever stand in need of the church's prayers, forget not to come to St. Mary's and ask for Friar John."

"I shall not forget, holy friar, for truth to tell there are some matters I would fain consult one of thy order about——"

"Fear not; but come and open thy lips freely, thy mind shall have ease, and thy pocket be none the lighter. But be quick, my son, with thy directions, for I fear me, the Lord Abbot will reach the oaken chamber first, and his wrath will be great against poor Friar John."

"Follow me, holy father," said the groom, as he gave the steed to the keeping of one of his helpers; "follow me, and if I do not bring thee to the door of the oaken chamber before the pompous major-domo even begins to ascend the large staircase, may I be refused absolution for my many sins."

He led the pretended monk to the great hall, and passing through a door at the side, he reached the corridor by ascending a narrow staircase used only by the domestics.

The groom kept his word, for as Little John pushed open the heavy doors, he heard the major-domo and the Abbot in close conversation as they ascended the grand staircase.

"Thanks, my son," said Little John, turning upon the threshold and spreading out his hands, "receive my blessing and depart."

The man crossed himself, and bowed his head until the forester had finished mumbling a few words, which passed for Latin with the ignorant and superstitious servitor, who, like all his class, felt the greatest fear and reverence for the ruling powers of that dark age.

"Body-o'-me!" muttered the giant as he stood and surveyed the vaulted chamber; "so far has my impudence brought me safely. Will it as safely carry me out of these stone walls?"

While holding this mental debate, he looked about for a place to hide his huge form.

The few articles of furniture which stood in the chamber, although of the most massive make, were so placed that he could not secrete himself behind or at the side of any on e piece

There was not time to alter the arrangement of the winged cupboards or the carved seats, for the Abbot's voice told he was near the top of the staircase.

"Saint Impudence defend me!" said John, as he ran towards the table which stood in the centre of the chamber; "last thought of, but not the least. Gramercy, Master Sheriff, for having such a long covering upon your table."

He had only time to draw his long limbs under him when the Abbot entered the chamber.

"Thy master," he said, looking round, "is not here. Has he been apprised of my presence?"

"He has, most noble Abbot; and he begged thou would'st be seated for a few moments, as he is engaged writing a report of the state of this part of the country to our brave Prince Edward."

The Abbot threw himself into one of the chairs near the table, and Little John had the greatest difficulty in refraining from pinching the saintly leg.

"I hope my noble kinsman," said the Abbot, "has not been angered by the obstinacy of the Saxon churls, who are as thick as weeds in this part of the land."

"Truth to tell, Sir Abbot," replied the garrulous chief servant, "the hinds took it somewhat sore the appointment of forest-keepers, and the issuing of other laws similar to those we have in beautiful Normandy, as thou mightest know, noble Abbot; such laws and ordinances are too good for the government of these boors——"

"Yes, yes—much too good; yet thou sayest they resented their being put into force?"

"They did, my lord Abbot; so much so that our good master of Lois was compelled to hang about a score of the peasants and burn the cottages of about as many more."

"Was their defiance so open, then?"

"It was, Sir Abbot; for the first of the new keepers who went forth upon their duty were found with a cloth-yard shaft driven through their bodies, and but for the example our good master, the Sheriff, made of those I have already spoken about, I do not doubt but the castle would have been attacked."

The Abbot made no answer; and the servitor, well versed in the ways of his master's kinsman, took this silence as a hint for him to retire, which he did with the profoundest bows and his face kept towards the mighty churchman.

"My brother's son," muttered the Abbot, "has a strong head, yet not too strong, for these brats require harsh means to keep them in subjection."

"Do they?" thought the concealed listener. "Take care ye do not go too far, my gentle Norman, for it would be no miracle for a Saxon arrow to pierce thy priestly robe, even wert thou sitting in thine own chamber in the Abbey."

The doors were then opened by a servitor, and Geoffrey de Lois entered the chamber.

"A fair greeting, my lord," he said, extending his hand to the Abbot. "What urgent matter has brought thee to Nottingham?"

"Sit thee down, Geoffrey," replied the Abbot. "Thou shalt hear of matters that will make thy blood tingle unless the air of this island hast changed thee from what thou wert."

"Beshrew me, fair sir," said the Sheriff; "it would not do for a scion of the house of Lois to be changed. Although poor, I may say we have kept the pure blood untainted."

"Aye, aye, I believe thou hast; for, enriching thyself in the land our swords have given us, does our race honour. But it was not of this I came to speak. Draw thy chair closer, and help me to a goblet of wine."

"I will help myself," thought Little John, "when ye have gone. Body-o'-me! it makes me sorely athirst to hear the good juice going down the throats of these Norman knaves."

The Abbot placed the goblet upon the table, much refreshed in body, if not in mind, by imbibing the contents of the rich vessel.

"Knowest thou," the Abbot asked, "of the sore strait our countryman D'Ogremont had placed himself in?"

"I have heard some rumour of a Jew varlet having lent him money."

"Rumour has spoken truly for once," said the Abbot; "for D'Ogremont was in hourly fear of falling into the unbelievers' clutches, when he sent a messenger praying I would advance for his present needs the sum of one hundred marks."

"Which thou did'st, good uncle."

"Assuredly, for our coffers, by chance, were pretty well filled; therefore I sent him the sum by a trusty bearer; but ere he could cross the path which skirts the forest, he was waylaid by the cut-purse gang, and robbed. What thinkest thou of such open insult to our power?"

The sheriff's dark face flushed angrily, and he bit his nether lip until the blood came.

"The curse of my race upon the dogs!" he said wrathfully. "Were this story to get abroad it would give the churlish peasantry heart of grace to again defy me. There is Robin Hood and his band must be destroyed, good uncle."

"I have heard thee use the self-same words many times."

"True! but my vow has lost nothing by keeping, or my hate become the less because every attempt I have made has failed."

"It is strange," the Abbot said,; "thou should'st be so openly defied by these knaves. Stranger still when thou hast a trusty spy in their very midst."

"Not the least strange, good uncle, when it is considered that for the one spy I have, this outlawed thief has fifty."

"How, Geoffrey—beshrew me, this sounds strangely coming from thy lips who should'st be master of this part of the country."

"I hope to be so ere long, but first I must rid the forest of these knaves, and if all goes as well as I have planned, it will not be long before this happens."

"The saints prosper the undertaking, Geoffrey, tell me what mean thy words when thou said'st the cut-purse knave had fifty spies to thy one."

"Had I said five hundred it would have been nearer the truth," De Lois said with bitterness; "do you not know, good uncle, this varlet robs from all of Norman blood, and gives the gold and silver to the poor and sick among the Saxon boors. Thou seest now how it is he has so many eyes watching every movement among my men; by my halidome I do not believe a steel cap glitters beyond the drawbridge but a messenger swift of foot bears him intelligence. Thus it is, good Uncle, I have so often failed."

"This must be altered. St. Hilderband! I will excommunicate from the altar all who touch money that has passed through this knave's hands, I——"

"Anger not thyself, Sir Abbot, neither raise thy voice from the altar steps; none of these will serve our purpose—draw closer, I would not the bare walls even heard the echo of my words."

———

CHAPTER XXIV.

LITTLE JOHN'S NEW SERVICE.

Now is little John the Sheriff's man,
    And well with him does he thrive,
But Little John said, I will pay him out,
    As sure as I am alive.
Now so God me help, said Little John,
    And by my true loyalty,
I shall be the worst servant to him,
    That ever yet had he.

THE Sheriff's plot to entrap Robin was soon told. It was his intention to hold an archery meeting under the Castle walls, and feeling sure the bold outlaw would attend, he resolved to have him slain by a bolt from a crossbowman, who would be placed on the ramparts for that purpose.

"Of the success of thy plot," the Abbot said; "I have no doubt, but should the truth reach the ears of King Henry, I would not give much for thy post as sheriff to this fair county."

"Yet," said Geoffrey, somewhat amazed at the Abbot's words, "our King's favour is all for those who come from Normandy; I have thought he cared not a groat for the lives of the Saxons who yet encumber the land."

"Neither does he, Geoffrey, but to countenance a deed like this, would arouse the discontent of the wealthy Saxon nobles who have bent the knee in homage to him; and thou must remember, there is yet enough of the churls left, were they collected under a good leader, to work even Henry of Winchester and his Norman army mischief."

"There is much of truth and prudence in thy words; yet I would not give up this goodly scheme without I knew another which augured so much success."

"Has thy brain no other?"

"None; for it has been racked month after month with some scheme or other, which has always failed the very moment I felt certain of success."

"Let me aid thee, Geoffrey," said the subtle priest; "although better versed in using bell-book and candle, yet I have no doubt a little of the craft left such as used by those outside the abbey walls."

"Marry, fair uncle, but thou hast; for the solitude of the cloisters seems to wondrously sharpen the inventive powers of those who dwell therein. Speak, fair sir, my soul yearns to hear thy counsel."

"It is this, Geoffrey," said the priest; "hast thou forgotten a certain blue-eyed maiden of surpassing loveliness thou sawest at a certain May-day gathering, before the good King Henry triumphed over his foes."

"Forgotten her!" exclaimed Geoffrey; "by my valour, I fear her face has been more often before me than that of the blessed Mary!"

"That were a sin, nephew," said the ecclesiastic; "nevertheless, I will absolve thee from it, for this maiden is wondrously fair."

"Wondrously! good uncle, she is; but I crave what can the maiden ever be to me?"

"Everything thou could'st wish."

"Ha; dwells she in these parts, that thou art so sure of speech."

"In these parts! hast thou not seen her since she came to Nottingham?"

"Never once, I swear!"

"Yet," said the Abbot, with that slowness of speech which proved he felt a secret pleasure in adding to the feverish eagerness his listener displayed, "she has dwelt within an arrow's flight of the castle ever since thou camest here."

"Impossible, uncle; thou must be mistaken, for, by my knighthood, there is not a maiden's face within five miles of Nottingham but what I have seen."

"Yet," said the Abbot, smiling, "thou hast overlooked the fairest of them all."

"I pray thee tantalise me no further, but tell me where dwells this pearl of loveliness, that I may see her and, Saxon though she be, tell her of the quenchless fire that consumes my heart."

"Thou had'st better do this when alone with her, for she is guarded by one who would as soon crack thy skull as he would a serving man's."

"Nay, good uncle; keep me no longer in suspense——"

"Patience, foolish boy, thou shalt hear. Knowest thou a certain miller, the sails of whose mill thou can'st see even from this window?"

"Aye; I know the varlet right well. It was his lusty arm that beat my men when they went to his mill to gather the tithes I had imposed upon all who dwelt upon the lands near the castle."

"He paid thy dues, then?"

"Aye, by breaking the heads of those of my best men, and beating the hides of as many more."

"Well, Geoffrey, here's a success to thy wooing! for yonder miller is the guardian of the pearl of loveliness—for so thou art pleased to term a woman of earthly mould."

"So much the better. I will have him brought to the castle, and this fair girl shall sue at my feet for his life—that is," Geoffrey added, "if she dwells beneath the carle's roof."

"She does; and by the manner in which she has been kept from thy sight, thou can'st understand how well the miller tends his charge."

"It shall be my care to assist the miller," said Geoffrey; "but thou hast not told me in what manner this girl can aid me in capturing the forest thief."

"Thou wilt be the best judge," said the churchman, "when I tell thee that the pearl of loveliness, as thou namest her, meets the forest cut-purse every eve near St. Ann's well."

The Sheriff sprang from his seat as though he had been suddenly stung by an adder.

"By the mass!" he said, as he hurriedly paced to and fro the chamber, "thou could'st not have told me aught to goad me on to encompass the arrant rascal's death better than this. Rest content, my Lord Abbot, that the insult thou hast received will soon be avenged."

"I knew it would be," said the churchman, "or I would not have left the Abbey after dark to visit even Nottingham's sheriff."

He arose from his seat as he spoke, and was about to leave the room, when Geoffrey de Lois paused in his hurried walk.

"Forgive my scant courtesy," he said, taking his relation's arm; "do me the honour of tasting a cup of burnt sack, which is by this time ready in my chamber."

He drew the Abbot from the oak room as he

spake, and, before the churchman could reply, the hanging-doors closed behind them.

Peering out from beneath the tall cover, Little John made sure he was alone before he drew his long limbs from the cramped position they had been compelled to assume.

"Body-o'-me!" he said, as he seated himself at the table, "I am not much the wiser for the conversation I have heard. Ah! I see a good bottle of canary close to my elbow. I will empty it before I begin to think what is best to be done."

The giant's capacious throat not only swallowed the canary, but the contents of the whole of the remaining bottles.

"St. Hubert be thanked for that!" he said; "it was a goodly draught, and has set my brain in the proper place; and I think unless I find my way to the courtyard, my good master will be a knave the less. Yet," he added, "I would fain have learnt more of this Sheriff's purpose; but I suppose I must e'en make the best of the little news I have gathered."

When he reached the courtyard the warder had just lowered the drawbridge; so Little John, not waiting to rejoin the Abbot and the Cellarer, walked slowly across, devoutly bless-ing such of the men-at-arms as were in his path.

"Safe out of the lion's mouth," he said, when he reached the open space before the castle. "Yet I am loth to go with such a small budget of news; but I——St. Hubert! what knave is this? I would fain know who comes so boldly towards the castle.—Stand friend!"

A few minutes after the forester had crossed the drawbridge the Abbot and his companion descended to the courtyard, and while the groomsmen were bringing the animals from the stable, one of the men-at-arms came to-wards the Cellarer.

"Thy companion," he said "has left the castle, holy father."

"My companion, my son! I came here with the Lord Abbot, none else."

"Was not that tall friar with thee? He came across the drawbridge with his hand upon the Abbot's housings."

"Tall friar," exclaimed the Cellarer, and the Abbot, hearing the words, turned towards his puzzled attendant.

"What is this," the Abbot asked, "that mystifies thee so?"

The Cellarer repeated the statement made by the man-at-arms.

"Thou hast been drinking too freely over thy evening meal," said the Abbot, sternly, "or thine eyes would not have conjured up——"

"Nay, my good lord," said the soldier, "I have been on the ramparts since sunset, and only came to the court-yard as the monk passed over—Ah! by the rood, here he comes to bear out my words."

As the soldier spoke, a tall figure was seen hurriedly coming towards the court-yard, and when he came within a dozen paces of the man-at-arms, the Abbot said:

"Is this the knave?"

"It is, my lord, I would swear to his gown which, as he passed me I thought was made too short for so tall a monk."

"Seize him," said the Abbot, and when the soldiers held the monk firmly, he resumed, "Who art thou to dare, by hanging upon our skirts to gain admittance to this castle."

"Holy father!" roared the man, in a voice which expressed both fear and surprise, "I have never set eyes upon thee——"

"Thou liest!" said the warder, coming forward. "I saw thee both enter and leave the castle."

"A murrain upon thy lying tongue!" roared the man, as he struggled with his captors. "I swear, by the holy rood, I have never before placed foot inside this castle."

The groom came up at this moment with the Abbot's palfrey and the Cellarer's mule, and, hearing from one of the men-at-arms the cause of the disturbance, came to the Abbot, and added his testimony to that which had already been given.

"My Lord Abbot," he said, "I swear, by the cross to this knave. I knew him by the clouts upon his frock. He came in with thee and the High Cellarer, and took thy palfrey when thou did'st please to alight."

"Hearest thou this knave," the Abbot said, sternly. "Surely thou can'st not have heart to deny the words of these men."

"My Lord Abbot," the man said, "I never, until now, saw the——"

"It's a foul lie!" said the groom. "Did'st thou not tell me thou wert of the Abbey of Saint Mary's, and the favoured monk of the Lord Abbot's? Did'st thou not tell me it was thy duty to reach the chamber set apart for his use before him? Deny this, thou false knave, if thou darest."

"I never saw thy hang-dog face before," said the man, sullenly. As for this robe by which thou swearest to me, I have not yet worn long, for, when I came towards the castle, I was met by a lusty varlet who robbed me of my clo——"

"Stop his lying tongue," said the Abbot; "if he will speak with such boldness against the words of these men; "go on with thy questioning," he added, turning to the groom, "that I may hear more of the knave's doings."

"Thou must know, my lord Abbot, "the groom said, "when the knave told me this I took him by a side stair to the oaken chamber, and saw him enter; then, my lord Abbot, I left him and saw not his face until now."

"By the mass!" said the churchman; "the knave has been hidden in the oak chamber during the time I spoke with thy master; run, varlets, run, and fetch the sheriff!"

Geoffrey de Lois came in answer to the Abbot's message, and when the story was told to him he sent a servitor to the oaken chamber to examine the wine-cups.

"For," he said to the Abbot, "if this knave has been there, he could not for his life have passed the wine untouched."

The servitor returned with word that every bottle was drained, and further, by the marks upon the polished floor he could swear a man had been hidden beneath the table.

ROBIN HOOD,

AND THE OUTLAWS OF SHERWOOD FOREST.

ROBIN HOOD TO THE RESCUE.

The Sheriff's brow became as black as a thunder-cloud when he heard this.

"Gaudolin!" he said to a grim-looking soldier, "take this knave, and place him where it will not matter how much his tongue wags of that which he has this day heard."

The unlucky wretch's eyes seemed as though they would burst from their sockets when he heard this order given.

"Mercy, my lord!" he shrieked; "cast me not into a dungeon. I swear by the Blessed Cross, and by Him who bled for us, I have been robbed——"

"Away with the lying knave!" said the Sheriff; "take him hence. Varlets! have I to speak twice?"

Struggling and yelling for mercy, the man was dragged away to the dungeon; then the Abbot and his companion left the castle.

They had not gone many paces from the

drawbridge when they met a tall and stout man wending his way to the castle.

He was humbly garbed, and as humble in manners, for he crossed himself when he saw the holy men, and, bowing his head, said:

"The saints preserve thee, holy fathers; the saints preserve thee from harm!"

"Gramercy, my son, for thy wish," the Abbot said; "here is a piece of money for thee; take it, and our blessing with it."

The man meekly accepted the coin, and bowed in the most abject manner. This so pleased the Abbot that he reined in his palfrey,

"Thou art a good son of the church," he said, "or thou would'st not pay such respect to her followers; what is thy name, and where art thou going?"

"My name, reverend and worshipful sir," the lusty varlet answered, "is Roger Green-law, and I am going to the castle of his high mightiness, the Lord Sheriff, to crave of the chief cook the post of scullion."

"Thou seemest better fit to wear a steel cap, and bestride a war-horse," the Abbot said; "but mayhap thy heart is not in keeping with thy body."

"Reverend father," was the meek answer, "I am but a scullion at heart; although my limbs are somewhat large, my valour is the smallest thou hast ever known; for the whizz of an arrow or the sight of a naked sword causes my knees to totter and my heart to quake; thus thou seest I am but fit to help the noble cook of the Lord Sheriff—the saints be good to him!"

"Thou mayest be all thou hast said, yet thou art a good son of the church, and thy respect for her followers bids me do thee a kindness. Go to the cook, and tell him the Lord Abbot of St. Mary's sends thee, and thou wilt be appointed to the post thou seekest."

This kindness caused the man to bow so lowly that his face was hidden, and while he was in this position the Abbot rode forward.

"Body-o'-me!" laughed the servitor, as he watched the churchman ride away; "little does yon Norman priest know how my fingers longed to pull him from his horse and duck him in the ditch! Ho, ho! by St. Hubert! but this will be a mirthful story to tell good Robin and his merry men! Ho, ho! twice in one night has Little John deceived this cunning knave!"

Laughing until his burly frame shook, the disguised forester reached the castle as the drawbridge was being raised.

After a short parley he was admitted, and conducted by a man-at-arms to the presence of the chief cook, and by that high functionary engaged to chop wood, draw water, and wash the platters.

How he acquitted himself we must leave another chapter to relate.

CHAPTER XXV.

LITTLE JOHN AND THE SHERIFF'S COOK.

The cook was most uncourteous—
There he stood on the floor,
He started to the buttery
And shut fast the door.
Little John gave him such a rap,
His back was nigh bent in two;
And should he a hundred winters live,
He'd be the worse for that blow.

THE interior of the grim fortalice, built by William the Conqueror, was a sorry exchange for the sunny green-sward for Little John.

More than once during the first few days of his dwelling there, the Outlaw's trusty follower felt much inclined to lay a quarter staff about the cook's back, then make his escape; for the cook, like most Jacks in office, was fond of showing his authority over his helpmate.

"Bones of St. Hubert!" growled the forester, as he washed the platters in a dark corner of the kitchen, "would I had not taken the trouble to come here. Body-o'-me! what with scant fare, bad beer, and the prating of this varlet's tongue, I shall be a dead man before I find out anything for my dear master."

"Quick with those platters, thou lazy knave," shouted the cook, "or I'll lay this rolling pin about thy broad back. Dos't thou hear? Is our most noble master to wait his dinner?"

His brawny arms bare to the elbow, the scullion for the nonce came humbly towards his master, a pile of platters held before him.

"A murrain upon thee!" continued the cook, "for a lazy carle. Move thy feet quicker, or, by the—— To the devil with thee! Oh, oh! thou careless thief, thou hast broken my foot!"

Little John, boiling with the anger he did not deem it prudent to show, suddenly, and as though by accident, fell forward, and shot the heavy pile of platters upon the cook's feet.

No monk's face, when kneeling at the shrine he worshipped, could have equalled in penitential expression that of the lusty scullion when he saw the cook dancing about like a hen upon one leg, and yelling with pain.

"Thou awkward fool!" roared the cook; "thou art more fitted to lead swine to the forest than to be here. Out upon thee for a hang-dog thief. Wert thou not so great a coward, I would pound thy hide well."

At the conclusion of this speech the exasperated knight of the kitchen snatched the wet dish-cloth from whence it hung over Little John's arm, and began to strike the scullion over the face, neck, and arms with it.

The cook was a fat, stumpy little man, and John, who affected the most arrant cowardice, ran from the wet dish-cloth, holloaing at the top of his voice:

"Hold thy hand, good master! hold thy hand! Would I had broken my long neck ere I let fall the platters upon thy feet. Hold thy hand, for the love of Him who died for us!"

As nimble in his movements as a deer, the forester led the incensed cook round the kitchen, until the poor little man was thoroughly exhausted, and was fain to sit himself upon a stool, where he puffed and blustered wrathfully, until one of his assistants ran to him with the awful intelligence that the Sheriff was very wrath at his dinner being delayed beyond the usual time.

"A plague upon this thief," said the cook; "this all comes of my goodness in taking a varlet like this into my service. Get out from my sight with thy hang-dog face, or by the blessed Ursula, I'll drive this spit through thy carcass."

Little John retired to the scullery, and while enjoying a hearty but silent laugh, the pompous butler entered the kitchen.

"Gaucher," he said, addressing the cook, "Can'st thou lend me one of thy knaves t aid in moving some beer casks, one that is strong of limb, for I want not a dozen varlets to know the passage to the beer vault?"

"There's a lusty thief in yon corner," Gaucher said, facing round and pointing to John; "take him, in the saints' name, for he is but little good here."

"Come with me, knave," the butler said; "thy master is willing, and I will reward thee with a tankard of beer; but," he mentally added, "it will be from the barrel whose contents went sour after the last thunderstorm. he! he! he! By Our Lady, thou wilt remember it."

"Worshipful sir," John said, cringing before the great man," "I am ready to do thy bidding."

The butler led the way to one of the vaults near the dungeons, and much to Little John's delight, when the door was unlocked, he beheld a row of oaken casks bearing the brand he so much loved.

"Good October," he thought. "By St. Hubert! a brave array. Body-'o-me! but it will be as well to have free entrance to this vault, therefore, I will take this good key into my keeping."

While the butler was busy igniting a torch, the forester noiselessly drew the key from the lock, and concealed it in the breast of his jerkin.

"This way, knave," said the butler. "Art thou strong enough, thinkest thou, to bring yon barrel and place it upon this stand?"

"I will try, worshipful master."

The giant rolled the empty cask away, then with as much ease as though he were handling a bag of meal, he clasped the full one in his arms, and placed it upon the place indicated."

"Bravely done," said the butler; "bravely done; thou hast not even disturbed the sediment, for this, thou shalt have two tankards, if thou likest them."

Little John, as the reader well knows, was always troubled with thirst.

"Gramercy, for thy goodness, worshipful sir," he said, wiping his mouth in satisfaction; "would I had to do thy bidding every day."

"No doubt, knave," said the butler, "but I allow none to enter this vault but myself, for fear the wrong barrel should be drawn from."

"A wise rule, master," said John, smacking his lips and wondering how much longer the butler would be before he filled the black-jack he held, "for it would be a sin for every knave to have access to these good casks."

"Thou art right, knave, and I warrant me there is such liquor in this vault as thou hast never yet seen, much less tasted."

"No doubt, master, for the beer we poor knaves get in the kitchen is but thin stuff."

"Thin stuff!" said the butler, facing round, "how now, knave, would'st thou have flagons of the nut brown ale, brewed in October, and seasoned in wine casks, sent to thy table! Marry, for this insolence I will not give thee the draught I promised."

"I crave pardon, good master," said the forester, humbly, "if by my freedom of speech I have offended; but I swear by the saints I have not this opinion of the good liquor thou sendest to the lower board, it is but the words of the men-at-arms, who grumble the whole time they drink of thy bounty."

This polite speech restored John to the butler's favour, especially the last words, for the butler felt assured the scullion looked upon him as the master of the castle.

"The men-at-arms," he said, "are an idle pack; had I my will they should have nothing but water, for I cannot see of what use they are, except to flaunt with all the women-servants of the castle, and turn their heads with the lying stories they tell of their valour on the plain of Evesham."

"Aye," said Little John; "thou art right, good master; they are, indeed of little use, and it would be as well their tongues were clipped, they cannot say a good word, even of thee."

"I thought this," the butler said; for, like most of his class, he liked his ears tickled with tales of the sayings and doings of those in his master's service; "a plague upon them, but they shall find it will not be the better for them to malign my name; harkee, good fellow, seest thou yonder cask?"

"I do, master."

"It is one of but a poor brewing, at best; but since the last thunderstorm, its contents were turned to as vile an acid as thou hast ever tasted. That cask, knave, shall be the portion of those varlets until every drop be gone. He, he, he! by my faith, if they are not sorely troubled with colic, I am no true man!"

"I shall remember that cask," John thought; then aloud, "a proper drink for the base knaves to speak ill of so good a master."

"Thou art right, knave; I am a good and bounteous master, and, as thy bearing so well pleases me, I will tell thee the virtues of each of these barrels."

He drew a foaming tankard as he spoke, and placing the vessel upon his knee, much to Little John's inward disgust, sipped the bright liquor while detailing the merits of each cask.

"Body-o'-me!" John thought, "has the knave forgotten I have a mouth, and a throat as dry as a new sponge? I would remind the carle; but he may beseem me too bold, and I shall lose the opportunity of learning which of these barrels hold the best liquor. Shoulder of St. Hubert! were I to do that, it would give me much trouble to have to taste them all before I found the best."

"Thou see'st this one," the latter began. "Ah, by the saints! it holds a true and well-flavoured cordial. See," refilling the tankard, "how it sparkles and dances as it flows into this good vessel. Drink! by our Lady, that were a draught to touch the soul. I love this cask, knave, and the one next, and none other lips than mine and the Sheriff's ever quaff their contents."

"There will be another added to the list," thought the tantalised forester. "A curse upon the fellow! his head is of wood, for he has already drank four flagons of the sparkling brew."

"See this cask, knave!" the latter continued, his voice becoming thick, "see how the good ale sparkles as it flows! By my faith, man, it is clearer than the finest wine, and for my part I would sooner have one goodly flagon of this to cheer my heart than all your sack, canary, or malvoisie. What say you, knave?"

"I am of your worship's opinion," Little John answered, "although, truth to tell, my mouth is so dry, I can scarcely speak."

"Ah, I have promised thee a tankard; thou shalt have it."

"Gramercy, good master, would I had to serve thee every day."

The butler staggered from his seat, and Little John, with a rueful face, watched him reel towards the barrel he had set aside for the use of the men-at-arms.

"Ashes of Saint Hubert!" muttered John, "the villain has gone to the sour cask. The foul fiend fly away with him! Does he want to give me the colic?"

"Here, knave," said the butler, reeling forward, "drink this; it will quench thy thirst. I would give thee a better draught, but as thy head is not used to bear even as good a liquor as this, I should be doing wrong. Be quick, and empty the measure, for I must return, and see that my knaves have done their service properly towards the Sheriff."

He handed the tankard to Little John, who, when the butler turned his back to extinguish the torch, poured the ale upon the ground.

"Hast thou drank it?" asked the butler, as he stumbled through the door. "Ah, I see thou hast—and find it good, I'll warant.

"It was good, worshipful sir."

"I told thee so. Come, lend me thine arm. No, stay, I must first lock the door. A plague take it! Where can the key have gone?"

"Is it not among those at thy belt, master?"

"There is one there, but I have two, one not attached to the bunch, for they make such a noise when I have to unlock the door, that all who pass know I am at the vault."

"I can feel no key in the lock, master."

"It matters not; perhaps I did not bring it with me. Take the bunch, thou wilt find the longest of the three large keys will fit."

The forester locked the door, and, as the butler's steps were every moment becoming more unsteady, he was compelled to cling to the strong arm held out for his support.

"Harkee! knave," said the upper servant," "I like thee well, keep in mind all that is said by the varlets about me, and thou shalt guzzle as much of the prime ale thou hast not long since tasted as thou likest. This way, good fellow, this is the buttery."

There was a roguish smile upon the forester's face as he steered the butler to a seat, and when he was about to leave, his companion called him back.

"Harkee!" he said; "I have but little love for that knave, thy master, the fat cook; so if thou can'st contrive to give him a good trouncing, I shall not forget thee."

"But, good master," Little John said, "I shall lose my place, if I do this."

"Fear not fear for that, fear not for that; I will stand thy friend, and none here, except our good lord, the sheriff, has any power in the—— The saints be good to us! here comes thy master, I know well his footstep, he comes to rate me for keeping thee so long; have at him if thou hast a chance; forget not, I will bear thee out."

The buttery door was flung violently open as he ceased speaking, and the cook, armed with a long rolling-pin, or, as it was then termed, a pastry-roller, entered the buttery.

He was very red and very angry, and his eyes glanced first at the butler, then at the scullion.

"How's this, knave," he roared, "that thou hast left thy duty? I did but lend thee to move a cask, and thou hast been gone twice the turning of the glass!"

"I humbly crave——"

"Aye, that is all thy cry! Get thee back to the scullery; get thee back, or I'll quicken thy lazy feet with!"

"Nay, Gaucher," said the butler, adding fuel to the fire; "the poor knave is not to blame, it was I who——"

"Aye, thou; I should have known this when I lent him to thee; no doubt ere long thou wilt have made him as great a beer-swiller as thyself!"

The butler was a younger man than the cook, and had he been able to have kept his legs there would have been a set-to after he had received this insult.

But as it was, and while John was thinking the butler could not have made him a beer swiller upon the contents of the sour cask, the cook flung the wooden roller at his head.

It missed, and terminated its flight against the butler's stomach, who rolled from his seat, and lay gasping to regain the breath which had been so rudely taken from him.

When he could speak he scrambled to his feet, and making a sudden rush upon the cook, caught him by the nose.

"Shut the door," he called out, and John obeyed. "Hold it fast, good fellow, while I baste this varlet's hide."

The cook, nothing loth to vent his long-cherished ill-feeling against the butler, clutched his opponent's hair; for, as in our more civilised days, there was about the same amount of jealousy and ill-feeling in those rude times among the servants of a large household.

Little John, with his back against the door, watched the fight—if fight it could be termed —when one of the combatants held tightly to his opponent's nose, and the other clung by a handful of hair to him who held the most useful and ornamental feature of his face; their right hands being thus engaged, they did not long leave the others unemployed, and to Little John's amusement, the pair struggled and spluttered all over the buttery floor.

"I'll tweak thy nose off, thou greasy varlet," roared the butler; "beer swiller, and I'll teach thee manners."

"I've long waited to baste thee," roared the cook in return, "now thou shalt feel I am thy match."

"Body-o'-me!" thought Little John, "but this is a fair sight."

How long the encounter would have continued it is hard to say, as it came to an abrupt termination through the agency of the stalwart forester.

He had not forgotten the manner in which the cook had belaboured him with the greasy dish-cloth, so when the pair rolled against him he gave his master a blow on the back.

The cook gasped out an unsavoury oath, then fell to the ground doubled up with pain.

So skilfully had the forester put in this blow, that the cook felt assured the butler had taken an unfair advantage of him.

This belief was strengthened by the latter standing over him flourishing the rolling-pin he had picked up, and in the language of the knights, he said:

"Yield thee, ransom or no ransom! or I will slay thee without mercy!"

The cook was unable to reply, so Little John came forward, and taking him in his arms carried him off to the kitchen.

CHAPTER XXVI.

WHAT LITTLE JOHN HEARD WHEN HE WENT TO THE VAULT.

When they had eaten and drunken well,
Their troths together they plight,
That they would both with Robin be,
That very self-same night.
And then unto the treasure-house
Full quickly were they gone.
The locks, that were of very good steel,
They broke them every one ;
Fine silver vessels they took away,
And all that they could get ;
Pixes, and drinking-cups, and spoons—
Not one did they forget.

LEAVING the bruised knight of the spit to the care of his assistants, the forester, with glorious visions of the nut-brown ale floating before his eyes, went towards the vault.

"By Saint Hubert!" he thought, "that rap I gave the knave has served two purposes : it has pleased the butler, and carrying the cook away has pleased him well. Body-o'-me! were I to stay here long, I should have the two fighting which should have me."

When he reached the vault, there was a gleam of light perceptible at the opposite end of the long, gloomy passage.

This sight quickened the forester's movements, yet, before he could unfasten the ponderous lock, the light began to grow larger, and, by the time Little John held the door open, he saw the glare of a torch dancing upon the shining mail shirt of Geoffrey de Lois and the steel caps of two men at arms who were in attendance upon him.

"Body-'o-me!" muttered the outlaw ; "if yon rascally Norman comes to this vault I am lost, and Sherwood will count a knave the less. Ah! they stop! The saints look down upon the poor wretches in these dungeons. I will have a draught of the cask set aside for the butler and his master, then I will try and find out the cause of these knaves' visit to this unsavoury part of the castle."

He had no difficulty in selecting the barrel the butler had pointed out, and by the sound that followed, it was evident the October came pretty near the description set forth by the keeper of the cellar keys.

"Body-'o-me!" said John complacently, "but it is a fair and wholesome drink. I have not tasted better even in the merry greenwood. I shall keep this key, and if there is any truth in that knave Bayston's words, about there being an outlet from beneath the castle to the woods, I will often do my devoirs to these good barrels."

Having made this resolve, the forester left the vault, and after carefully fastening the door, he stole softly towards the dungeon where he had seen the Sheriff enter.

The streak of light which came from the partly closed door told the outlaw that his foe was still inside the dungeon.

Creeping as close as prudence would safely warrant, Little John heard the Sheriff fiercely threatening the wretched captive.

"Darest thou," the Sheriff said, as John came within earshot, "repeat thy lies to my face."

"Sir Sheriff," answered a voice the forester recognised as belonging to the unfortunate man he had stopped near the drawbridge, "I swear by Our Lady I never saw the inside of thy gates until thou gavest the order for me to be seized and brought to this accursed place."

"Dog!" said Geoffrey de Lois, "thinkest thou to escape thy doom by repeating such a sorry tale."

"It is true, by Him who died for us, it is."

"I have told thee," rejoined the Sheriff, angrily, "if thy neck is of value to thee thou had'st better tell who sent thee to spy upon my acts."

"I have spoken only the truth," the man answered, sullenly, "and I leave the issue to the saints who will bear me out of my trouble."

"Thy saints !" the Sheriff said, grimly, "will have to be strong of arm to help thee now, for at sunrise to-morrow thy carcass will swing from the oaken beam across the castle gate."

"Saint Hubert," muttered Little John, "is a good and lusty saint, I will invoke his aid for this poor knave."

The Sheriff and his attendants left the vault as the forester drew back and concealed himself.

"Let the knave have the consolations of our confessor," the Sheriff said ; "and harkee, Berthold, I may require the secret door. Have the tangled brushwood cut away from the exit to the wood."

"I will see to it, my lord."

"It is well. See it is done before to-morrow's noon."

The man-at-arms made a lowly bow.

"After thou hast seen to this matter," the Sheriff continued, "hie thee to a covert near the mill kept by old Much ; thou knowest it, I suppose ?"

"Right well, master," the man said grimly ; "for I was one of those the old thief tanned with his quarter staff."

"Thou wilt be the more eager to aid me," the Sheriff said, "for I shall require thy aid to-morrow."

"To the end of my life, noble sir——"

"Aye, I knew thou would'st, Berthold ; but peace, and pay heed to my words. The old miller goes to the hamlet of Bedford to-morrow, at noon. At that hour bring with thee two steeds, and I will give to thy care the miller's niece, the fair Maid Marian. I wish not to be seen in this matter : therefore, thou wilt bring her to the secret entrance, and lodge her in the chamber overlooking the courtyard. Thou understandest these directions ?"

"Right well, my lord, and they shall be carried out."

"If," thought Little John, "'the good St. Hubert and my master do not interfere."

Geoffrey de Lois and his men left the gloomy passage, and the forester, after watching them ascend the steps, returned to the beer-vault.

"Body-o'-me !" he said : "but it's a great boon to have this good array of beer-casks to amuse me, while I await the coming of the good and pious confessor."

The black-jack was several times filled and emptied before the shuffling of a pair of sandaled feet caused the Outlaw to creep from the vault.

He saw the holy man apply the key to the dungeon door, and, stepping close behind him, John entered the dungeon at the same moment.

The confessor's stout form and flowing robe

concealed the forester's bent form from the hapless captive.

"I give thee greeting, my son," the reverend father said; "thy hours are but few in this world, therefore repent."

"Hold thy prating," said a voice, which caused the prisoner and the friar to start; "hold thy prating, sir priest, this good fellow has more of life in him than either thee o thy master can take away."

The prisoner stood with mouth agape, staring blankly at the man who had robbed him of his clothes; but the friar, recovering from his surprise, turned upon Little John wrathfully.

"Interfere not," he said, "with the offices of holy church; quit this cell, thou rude of speech and hard of heart."

"I will," John said; "and that full soon; come," to the prisoner, "what is thy name? speak man, if thou hast a tongue."

"I am called Will Scarlet by my kith and kin," answered the man; but it can matter little to an arrant thief like thou art what my name and condition is."

"Tie up thy tongue, Will Scarlet," the outlaw said; "I have done thee wrong, but I will now repair it; come, I have a path open for thee to sniff the fresh air again."

"Art thou serious?"

"As serious as the Sheriff is in his intent to hang thee."

"I am with thee, then; lead the way."

"Not so fast," said the priest. "I cannot suffer a prisoner to leave this place. What! ho! without there! a rescue! a res——"

Little John's arm was passed round the priest's throat and tightened until the goodly man was well nigh choked.

When he fell to the ground the forester and his companion left the cell, carefully locking the door after them.

"Come, Will," the forester said; "we will refresh ourselves from a barrel I wot of, then we can bid adieu to the Castle of Nottingham."

"A draught of October," said Will Scarlet, "would be a boon, for I am but under-fed with the bread and water these knaves have given me."

They went to the beer-cellar, and the forester was much gratified when he beheld the manner in which his new companion emptied the tankard.

"Body-o'-me!" he said, "if thou can'st draw a bow and use a quarter-staff as well as thou can'st empty a tankard, thou art fit to be one of our merry men."

"Thy merry men?"

"Aye—Robin Hood's."

"Who art thou to prate of such a good man as bold Robin, the king of good fellows?"

Little John gave a hearty laugh.

"I am Little John," he said: "hast thou ever heard the name before?"

"That have I," answered Will Scarlet; "give me thine hand, good fellow. I forgive thee the vile trick thou hast played me."

They shook hands, or as the old ballad has it, "plighted their troth."

"'I make my vow to God,' said Little John,
    And by my true loyalty,
Thou art one of the best drinkers
    That ever yet I did see.

Coulds't thou shoot as well with a bow,
    To the greenwood thou should'st with me;
And twice in the year thy clothing
    For new should changed be.'"

"What sayest thou?" John asked. "Wilt to the greenwood?"

"Thinkest thou bold Robin would have me in his company?"

"Thou art stout of limbs. Aye, marry, that he will if thou hatest the Norman foe as we do."

"A plague light upon the whole race," Will Scarlet answered. "Would they had but one neck, and that neck in my grasp!"

"Say no more," exclaimed the forester, "thou art one of our own true hearts; come, Will, let us to the greenwood."

"But how, surely the warders will not let us pass?"

"We shall not trouble them," laughed John; "come, let us haste, for I have news for my master, and as we trip merrily to the bonny greenwood, I will tell thee why I borrowed thy clothing."

"It mattereth not, thou hadst a goodly reason, for it is not the fashion for bold Robin's archers to rob a man who has been beggared by the grasping Norman—hark, what is that?"

"The priest," laughed John, "listen to his holy words! I marvel, Will, if he learnt such piety in the monastery wherein he was reared."

Will Scarlet laughed, for the holy man's words coming faintly upon their ears, savoured but little of the order of sanctity.

To speak the truth, he was cursing them with all the vehemence of an ungodly trooper.

"It would be a sin," Will Scarlet remarked, as he passed the tankard to Little John, "for us to leave this Norman stronghold without taking a present for the master."

"By St. Hubert! thou art right, it is a goodly thought, and goes far to show thou art fit to be one of our merry men."

"Hast thou heard since thy stay here the whereabouts of the strong room?"

"I have heard it spoken of by the kitchen knaves as a place filled with cups of the purest silver and pixes* of pure gold."

"A goodly place," said Will Scarlet "and should we find it, bold Robin will be well pleased with the presents we bring him."

"It must be hereabouts," said Little John. "Come, we will make search for it."

They drank to each other, then fastened the cellar door, and began their search for the treasure chamber.

All the doors were examined with care, until they came to one which had a lock of the finest steel.

"This must be it," said the forester; "help me with yon key, Will."

The key was a huge stone, and the pair dashed it against the lock, which flew into fragments, and the Sheriff's treasure lay before them.

Little John made a bag with his jerkin, and it was soon filled; in addition to this, they found two leathern bags filled with money equal to three hundred pounds of our coinage.

"Body-o'-me!" John said with a grin; "the rascally Norman little thought, when he gathered his tithes, we should fall upon it."

* In using this word the author adheres to the old manuscript, although of opinion that by so doing he is open to criticism.

"'Tis a fair punishment," answered Will Scarlet. "Come, John, let us breathe fresh air while we have the chance, for, peradventure, some of the men-at-arms may find their way down here, and we shall change places with yon priest, who clamours and swears more like a caged tapster than a holy man."

"Thou art right, Will; but it grieves me sorely to leave so many good vessels behind; can'st thou not make room for another?"

"Not one, John, not one; I am as well laden as a lazy monk's mule, when the shaven crown goes upon a journey."

Reluctantly, Little John left the treasure-chamber although he staggered under his load; he would have stripped the place, were it possible to have carried all the wealth away.

"If we must e'en leave this," he said, "let us at least have one more draught of humming October to give us strength to bear our load."

Against this Will Scarlet had nothing to say, for his throat was of a kindred nature with Little John's.

CHAPTER XXVII.

MAID MARIAN.

A bonny fine maid, of a noble degree,
With a hey down, down, a down,
Maid Marian called by name;
Did live in the North, of excellent worth,
For she was a gallant dame.
For form, and face, and beauty most rare,
Queen Helen, she did excel;
For Marian then was praised of all men
That did in the country dwell.

THE Abbot's description of Maid Marian did not excel her wondrous loveliness. Formed in the most exquisite proportion, and somewhat above the middle height, the Saxon maiden looked as noble and queenly as the highest lady in the land.

It wanted an hour of noon the day following Little John and Will Scarlet's doings in the treasure-chamber of Nottingham Castle.

Maid Marian was seated near the open casement; the sun, lighting upon her fine tresses, gave her head the appearance of being surrounded by a golden mist.

There was a marked sadness in her large blue eyes, as she looked out upon the green-clad heath, and more than once a deep sigh escaped her lips.

"I would," she mused, "that Robin gave up that strange, wild life. He is nobly born, handsome: so handsome, that when I look into his eyes, I fear me he will see one of nobler blood than myself. Ah, me! should he do so, it will be a dark hour for poor Marian."

There was a suspicious moisture about her eyes as she gave lowly utterance to the fears which beset her heart, and but for the sudden entrance of her uncle, the burly miller, this moisture would have swollen to tears.

"Well, girl," he said, "still pining like a caged linnet. Out upon it! I love not to see one of thy years mope like a maiden whose knight errant has gone to the Holy Land."

"I am not pining, good uncle," she said; "if my face speaks of a saddened heart, it is no truthful guide."

"Nevertheless," said the lusty miller, "it does speak to this effect—What is it, girl? tell thine uncle. A murrain upon all pining and sadness! Such a thing wert never known when England was free. Peradventure it came with the hungry Normans, who fatten upon our substance."

"Not upon thine, uncle," Marian said, smiling, "for thy taxes were paid with thy quarter-staff."

"Aye, girl; thou art right; it was so far a payment that the knaves have not called for their tithes and dues. Tithes and dues—a plague upon the names! Such things were not known in my father's time, but then, girl, England was free!"

"I fear for thee, good uncle," the girl said; "for this proud Sheriff may work thee harm. Confide not too much in his forgetfulness of the manner in which thou visited the exactions of his men. Trust a woman's mind, uncle——"

"Saint Mary, preserve us! Trust a woman's mind! Well, I forgive thee, girl, I forgive thee, for thou art but a timid—— Well, well, I will not chide thee, thou meanest well, but as for this hang-dog-looking Sheriff, I care not this for him."

The miller snapped his fingers as he spoke, then shook his huge fist in the direction of the castle.

"Now gir," he resumed, "tell me what ailed thee when I came here; out with it. Come, hold up thy head, or I shall think thou art not speaking as a maiden should?"

"Well, good uncle," she said; "I was thinking of poor Much, thy son, for one thing——"

"Aye!" said the miller; "I will gage my good right hand, thou wert thinking of another green jerkin at the same time. Thou need'st not blush, girl, it is but natural, for bold Robin, the best and bravest of our Saxon race, is comely enough to win a maiden's heart. As for Much, my sturdy son, I would ten times sooner see him with good Robin, outlaw though he be, than sheriff of this fair county, and he to bend the knee to the Norman tyrant who rules in this fair land. The saints preserve good Robin and his merry men, for of all our race, they alone bid defiance to the French robbers who despoil merry England."

"But the danger they are in, good uncle——"

"Danger, girl!" roared the miller, as though the word tickled his fancy; "Robin and Much in danger, with six score good and true men to draw a bow in their defence? Go to, girl, thou knowest not of what thy tongue pratest!"

"True, uncle, I know but little; but my tongue is guided by my heart."

"As a maiden's speech should. May thy tongue always be thus guided. Now I must away, girl; I came but to say farewell, but thy speech has kept me waiting here; a fair good-day, child—remember, thou keepest within doors, and should any of the silken gallants from the town pass this way, close the casement."

"I will follow thy advice, good uncle."

She kissed the lusty miller's cheek, and he, in return, caressed her golden locks.

"Thou art a comely wench," he said; "indeed thou art; the saints preserve thee until I return."

She watched the burly miller mount his horse and ride towards the road to Radford, then, resting her head upon her hand, she became lost in a deep reverie.

Her mind wandered to the greenwood, and

she saw in fancy the handsome form of her out-lawed lover, as he stood beneath the trysting-tree, and, in her heart, she wished it were her lot to share his joys and sorrows.

Absorbed in these sweet fancies she heard not the door of her chamber open, nor was aware of the presence of a second person, until the ring of an armed heel caused her to look around.

She gave a low cry of affright and started from her seat, then retreated slowly towards the furthest corner of the room.

The intruder was Geoffrey de Lois, he was cased from head to foot in link mail, and above this shining harness he wore a white gaber-dine, emblazoned on the breast with a red cross, as a proof he had fought against the infidels in Palestine.

He stood for some moments dazed by the girl's wondrous beauty, and stood as silent as a statue until she reached the further end of the chamber.

Then he spoke, and his voice told how power-fully his passion for the girl was influenced by being in her presence.

"Marian," he said, "fairest of all the maidens of thy race, why fearest thou me?"

"I fear you not, Sir Knight," she answered with a boldness her pale cheek belied, "yet I would be more at ease if thou would'st leave this chamber where thou hast no right to enter."

"Thou speakest well, maiden," he said; "I have no right here, save the right of one who comes to tell thee how he has sighed and sought to obtain a glimpse of the sweet face which has haunted him from the hour when first we met."

"It is a pity, Sir Knight," she said, with a contemptuous curl of her lip, "thou did'st not choose a time to tell me this more befitting thy knightly vow and my fair name."

"Love waits not for the most fitting time; yet another reason I could urge, fair girl: I saw thy uncle, the good miller, leave this place, and I know the forest abounds with lawless men; therefore, I came to keep thee from their clutches—for, were they to know this place were without thy brave guardian, they would ransack his coffers, and, perad-venture, carry thee off."

"Much, the miller, and his niece have nothing to fear from Sherwood's bold archers," she answered; "therefore, Sir Knight, thy protection is not necessary: and, as I would fain be rid of thy presence, depart as thou camest, or I shall have to summon my uncle's men to teach thee thy duty."

The Knight smiled grimly.

"Thy sweet voice," he said, "would be raised in vain, for the miller's varlets are shut in the stone chamber of the mill, and a dozen of my crossbow men prevent them from leaving; therefore, thou seest thou must listen to my words, no matter how sorely it runs against thy wishes."

The girl's cheeks flushed with anger as she turned her bright eyes towards the speaker. The Saxon beauty was no coward, and had there been a weapon within reach, she would have boldly seized it, and bid defiance to the mail-clad intruder.

She would have done this, although there was not the least doubt respecting the knight's instant victory over her feeble hand.

"Fitting words for one who has sworn to protect the weak and defenceless," she said, scornfully. "Go, Sir Knight, if this is thy Norman chivalry, give me the plain Saxon manners, at which thy class scoff; they, at least, know what is due to a helpless woman."

The girl's words, her defiant yet timid atti-tude sent a thrill of anger through the Nor-man's frame.

He had never before been thus spoken to, and it galled his haughty temper. Folding his arms and frowning angrily, he strode to-wards the maiden.

"Girl," he said, and his cheek alternately flushed and paled, "thy words bespeak thy race. Know that a Norman maiden of thy con-dition would hail with joy the wooing of a free-born knight."

"The manners of the French maidens are not ours," answered Marian, "the saints be praised for it! Take thy wooing to those com-plaisant dames, and learn that a Saxon maiden, however lowly, would sooner listen to the suit of a Saxon swineherd than mate with one of thy accursed race!"

"By the mass," the Sheriff said, stung to the quick by these words; "thou art as bold of speech as thou art fair of face; listen, girl, since it must be open war between us—I came here to woo thee as a knight, to utter my pas-sion in the soft language with which heaven has favoured my race; but thou wilt have none of this, I must therefore tell thee I have deter-mined to make thee mine, and if fair speech will not serve the purpose, I am prepared to use harsher means."

"There speaks thy base nature!" the girl said boldly, although her heart fluttered as she spoke: "but deem me not defenceless, false knight; were I but to raise a cry there would be many and strong hands come to my assist-ance."

"Let them come," exclaimed the Sheriff, clutching the maiden's wrists tightly; "let them come and save thee now.'

She struggled wildly in his grasp, but his hand was like the grip of a vice, and the dove might as well have struggled to free itself from the talons of the hawk as Marian to escape from Geoffrey de Lois.

His passion getting the better of his manhood, he was deaf to her prayers and cries, as he ruth-lessly dragged her towards the door.

"Help, help!" she shrieked; "Arnulf, Arthur, Segwyrd! help, help! haste, knaves, haste and save thy mistress! they hear me not; God of my Fathers; is there none to help me? is there none to save me from this monster?"

There came a mighty voice, rising above the maiden's screams, as the clarion in the field of battle rises above the roar and shouts of the combatants.

"There is!" said the voice, and the chamber window was darkened. "Unhand the maiden, false knight! stain of thy race! false-souled caitiff! Unhand, I say, or by Saint Herman! I will cleave thee to the neck, were thy steel cap forged by the gods instead of mortal hands."

The speaker sprang lightly to the ground while giving utterance to these words, and the flash of a bright blade was seen as he raised his sword to strike down the Sheriff.

ROBIN HOOD,

AND THE OUTLAWS OF SHERWOOD FOREST.

FRIAR TUCK RETURNS FROM PRAYERS.

With a suppressed cry of fury Geoffrey de Lois hurled Marian from him, then drawing his ponderous sword, stood face to face with Robin Hood.

The Norman's dark features flushed with joy as he drew his sword.

"Hast thou made thy peace with heaven?" he said, fiercely lunging at the outlaw's heart;

No. 9.

"if not, thou wilt pass from earth unshriven."

Robin parried the savage thrust with the ease and skill which proclaimed him master of the weapon he wore.

"Thou," he said, "standest in more need of a confessor than I—have at thee, false knight! were thy limbs ten times covered with armour of proof, thy false heart should feel my blade."

"Have at thee, thief!—keep thy boasting, and learn how a true knight can rid the earth of such arrant knaves as thou art."

Their blades crossed as they thus hurled defiance at each other, and the maiden crouching low in the corner of the chamber, prayed that him she loved would be spared.

The mail worn by the Sheriff was forged by a cunning armourer of Milan, and although the gallant forester more than once got beneath the knight's guard, the blade failed to make any impression upon the glittering links.

"Foul fall the hand that forged thy steel jacket!" thought Robin, as he parried the Sheriff's blows, "but for that my sword would long ago have reached the foul traitor's heart."

The Sheriff, confident in attaining an easy victory over the unprotected forester, became maddened with rage when he found every blow turned aside by the Outlaw's skill.

The Norman wielded one of those long-handled blades which could be used with both hands upon an emergency.

This course he adopted, and had one of his heavy downward cuts taken effect, the bold chieftain would have been cleft in two.

The combat was too vengeful to continue much longer, for Robin's arm began to tire in meeting the Sheriff's blows.

There seemed no hope for him; the Sheriff's proof-mail defied his sword, and it seemed Robin must succumb to the odds against him.

His valiant heart felt no fear. He warded off blow after blow; drove the point of his weapon against his foe's impenetrable breast.

In silence they fought, each with his teeth hard set.

Neither spoke as they stood thus, foot to foot and blade to blade, and the poor affrighted girl crouched yet lower—the fierce clatter of the blades ringing upon her ears, and telling that the combat which she dared not raise her eyes to look upon was not yet ended.

———

CHAPTER XXVIII.

LITTLE JOHN'S RETURN TO SHERWOOD.

> God save thee my master dear,
> Said Little John,
> Then answered Robin,
> Welcome may'st thou be,
> And also that fair yeoman,
> Thou bringest there with thee.
> What tidings come from Nottingham?
> Little John tell thou me.

THE lieutenant of the foresters and his companion had not been long in the beer vault when the ring of an armed heel was heard on the stone passage outside.

"Hearest thou that, Will?" said Little John. "Body o' me, but if we are caught here there will be a pair of ornaments for the oaken beam across the gateway."

"It is but one man," Will Scarlet answered, after he had leisurely drained the black jack, "and may be a thirsty soul, who has come this way; if so we'll bid him welcome."

"If not, Will; if he does not turn out to be a man who likes the good dame nature provides, what then, honest Will?"

"We must break his head, John, or choke him, whichever may be most fitting. Fill up the good measure again. Here's to merry Sherwood."

"If we get there," growled Little John. "Nevertheless, we will have another goodly draught—a malison upon the shaven priest, would I had choked him with his own rosary. Heard ye that, Will?"

"Marry, but I did, the holy man hears the knave's footsteps; and our sweet saint bless him, he calls out most lustily to be let out from his cage—pass the measure, John."

"For a Norman brew, Will, this is goodly ale; the saints be good to us, heard ye that, Will?"

"Mine ears would be but little use otherwise—aye, the knave has opened the door and the holy man is loose again."

"Bladebone of St. Hubert!" growled John, "I deserve to be held up for a show."

"What is the matter, John?"

"Aye, thou mayest well ask," Little John ruefully replied. "Strike my thick skull with the black jack, Will, but be careful thou empty it first."

"Strike thee for what, John?"

"For being a dolt, an ass, an idiot, a wittol, a fool, and everything else thou canst think of—ugh!—body-o'-me! I left the key in the door of yon dungeon."

"True, thou didst; well, it cannot now be helped—hush, by St. Gregory, John, they come this way—let us seek refuge behind yon barrels."

"Wittol again art thou, Little John," said the forester, as he filled the black jack preparatory to hiding, "for thou hast left the key in this door."

The red glare of a torch heralded the coming of the priest and his liberator, and when the forester and his companion had concealed themselves, the saintly man, and Berthold the sheriff's warder, entered the vault.

"No doubt, holy father," the warder said, as he entered, "thy throat is somewhat dry after shouting so lustily; and thou mayest well wish a benison upon the butler for leaving the key in the door of this cellar."

"Ugh!" growled Little John, mentally, "I hope the draught ye take will choke the pair."

"It is, indeed, fortunate," said the priest, "for failing the clear water from a spring, good ale is not a bad substitute."

"Shaven-crowned hypocrite!" whispered Little John to Will. "Don't take too long a draught, for we may have to wait some time without getting another taste of the clear-running ale."

Berthold placed his torch in an iron socket which was placed in the wall, then he began to search for a vessel to hold sufficient of the good liquor to appease the churchman's thirst and his own.

"A malison upon the knave!" he said; "there is not even a horn left to taste the contents of this good barrel. Little wonder the rascal left the key here."

"My son," said the priest, "waste not thy words or time. Thou hast a steel cap, and, like unto the fainting soldier upon war's red plain, we will taste of the poor substitute for water. Fill it up, my son; the nearer the liquid is to the brim, the easier it will be for us to drink: we can throw away that which remains."

"Ugh!" whispered Little John, "I should be wondrously athirst before I drank from yon knave's greasy cap; what say ye, Will?"

"It is not over-tempting, John," was the reply, "yet a dry thirst is a sore thing to bear."

The priest and the sheriff's warder seated themselves upon an empty barrel, and, in the most amicable manner, passed the steel cap to and fro, and interlarded their discourse with long draughts from the copious measure.

"I marvel much, Sir Priest," the warder said, "how this mischief befell thee."

"Of which dost thou speak, friend—the confinement in the dungeon, or having to drink of this bitter liquor in place of good, clear water."

"Touching the first, Sir Priest."

"But even as I in part told thee, a lusty knave entered the dungeon, and well-nigh strangled me; then went off with the rascal I was about to shrive."

"It will be unwelcome news to our master," the soldier said; "so for my part I would advise that we appear in ignorance of it, and let those who come to stretch the knave's neck find it out."

"I think thou art right, Berthold," said the holy man; "although falsehood is interdicted by the Church, I am of opinion that in this instance I had better bear the sin of appearing to be ignorant of this matter than deprive our good master of his sleep: for were he to know of it to-night, I feel sure his anger would be so great that he would not rest; therefore, thou seest, good Berthold, it is from a good motive we do this."

"Listen to the cunning priest," muttered Little John. "By the good Saint Hubert, the devil would have but few holidays were his priests to leave off lying."

"The veriest wittol," Berthold answered, "could see your reverence's goodness in thus bearing the sin of falsehood."

"A sin, my son," interrupted the priest, taking the steel cap, and forgetting all about his resolve to throw that which remained away, "that I shall have to answer for by prayer and fasting, and the scourge well laid on my shoulders; for these things I must do when in the solitude of my own chamber."

"There is none more than myself," said the warder, "knows of your true and noble piety; yet, as thou sayest, a falsehood borne from a good motive, I should think, would be less wrong than the telling of lying words by the profane."

"Assuredly, my son," answered the holy man, "not the most learned divine could have placed the matter in a better light. So, good Berthold, as thy cup is now empty, and the close air of this place affects the linings of the throat, we will again taste of the liquor, which, although a poor substitute for water, is not so bad a draught as I had thought."

The warder slipped from the barrel, and while in the act of refilling his steel cap, the sound of coming footsteps was heard.

"Haste, good Berthold," said the alarmed priest; "I would not that we were seen here —at least that I were seen; it would be a lasting scandal upon my name."

The new-comer, as though the sight of the open door, caused him more than ordinary surprise, quickened his pace, and before the warder could rise from his stooping position, the butler entered the vault.

He paused on the threshold, and looking first at the priest, then at the soldier, tried to speak, but rage choking his utterance, he was only able to articulate a confused sound.

When his speech became clearer his wrath burst forth in a torrent.

"A priest," he roared, "and a worthless man-at-arms, and in my cellar. May the foul fiend fly away with ye both for arrant thieves! Thou, Sir Monk, is this thy training, is this thy piety, to sneak like a rat into——"

"Peace, my son," said the priest, "peace, I say; we should not have been here but for a——"

"Peace! dost thou preach to me, thou shaven thief? A pretty priest, forsooth!—a dainty son of the Church. Out upon thee for a smooth-tongued, lying hypocrite——!"

"My son, forbear; invoke not the wrath of the Church upon thy head, by abusing one of its chosen agents. Peace, I command ye!"

"Wrath—the Church—you command me!" spluttered the angry butler. "By our Blessed Lady's favour, thou speakest too boldly for this once; but go—leave this place, if thou canst walk, which I much doubt, by thy red face."

The priest sneaked out, and when safe the other side of the doorway, he turned.

"This profanation," he said, "will be punished by the——"

"To the devil with thee," roared the butler, advancing upon the holy man with clenched hands, "go, or by the mass I will pound thy carcass if thou wert ten times a priest."

The monk, seeing his sacred character would not protect him from the butler's anger, beat an ignominious retreat, and left Berthold to settle the matter.

The latter, seeing there was no escape, seated himself upon the empty barrel, and during the time the butler and the priest were at high words, prepared for the share of abuse due to him, by refreshing himself from the contents of his steel cap.

"So," the enraged knight of the buttery said, as he faced the grinning warder, "thou hast turned thief, hast thou?"

"Hard words, good friend," said the other, coolly, "I found the door open, walked in, and saw a row of goodly barrels, and did as thou would'st have done, tasted——"

"Tasted," roared the butler, his anger rising yet higher at the soldier's coolness, "tasted! beast that thou art; thou hast drank of the barrel which is set apart for our good lord, the sheriff; may the foul fiend take me if I do not tell our master of this."

"Do," said the warder, "and by all the saints I will tell him how well thou keepest thy trust, then I will baste thy fat carcass——"

The butler's endurance was passed; to be insulted in this manner in his own dominion was beyond even the temper of a saint, much less that of the choleric servant.

With a roar like an angry bull he rushed forward to grapple with the soldier, but the latter, knowing the result should he be tumbled off the barrel, sent the contents of his steel cap fair in the butler's face.

The strong ale blinded the butler, and while he gave vent to a string of choice oaths, and struck madly right and left, the warder slid from his perch and left the vault.

Little John and his companion were well nigh suffocated with suppressed mirth, and it was as much as they could do to refrain from giving vent to a hearty peal of laughter.

When the latter found his enemy had beaten a retreat, he wiped his eyes, and thus poured forth his feelings upon the matter.

"A priest and a soldier: a lying, fat hypocrite, the one; the other, a lazy, skulking, lusty thief—both robbers. Would I had twisted that Berthold's neck, for he, of the two, has been the—— Blessed Saint Ursula! what is that? Oh, I know: it is the poor knave, who is to die to-morrow! No wonder he groans! Yet—— Oh! there it is again. I could have sworn the sound came from behind yon barrels, but that cannot be. Fancy the ghost of an empty barrel groan—— Oh!"

The butler stopped abruptly, and his mouth resembled the letter O, for, to a certainty, there came a prodigious groan from the darkest corner of the vault.

The long silence somewhat recovered the servant, and, rising from his knees—for he had assumed the attitude of prayer—he advanced boldly to the door.

"It's that knave Berthold," he said. "He—he—he—the thief, knows the story about the butler I replaced being found dead in this very vault. But, what matters? He has not come back—— Oh! blessed and holy Saint Ursula! be merciful, and drive away the evil spirit."

The hollow groan was repeated, and down went the butler upon his knees. Then came a crash, as Little John hurled the black jack at the torch, and knocked it from its socket.

The flaming brand fell close to where the butler knelt, his hair bristling with fear, and his trembling lips vainly trying to give utterance to the half-forgotten prayers he once knew.

The noise made by the torch—for the flame had fallen in the pool of ale—increased the domestic's fright, and, when it went out, he desisted from praying, and fairly howled with fear.

This was the opportunity of which Little John and his companion availed themselves to leave the vault; and the former, as he passed the howling domestic, placed his large, cold hand over the poor wretch's face.

The butler could bear no more. He gave a prolonged yell, then tumbled face foremost on the ground.

Little John and Will Scarlet debated for a few seconds respecting the propriety of pouring a tankard of cold beer down the prostrate man's back.

They drew the vessel full to the brim for the purpose, but Little John could not find it in his heart to waste so much good liquor, therefore, the well-matched pair drank it between them.

"Now, Will," said the forester, "for the merry greenwood. Follow me, and be careful thou dost not lose any of the good cups of silver or the vessels of gold."

The forester must have had the organ of locality very strongly developed; for although he had only gleaned the position of the door which led to the secret passage from the gestures of the Sheriff when he was in conversation with Berthold, he went straight to it, and

much to the surprise of both, they found it unlocked.

"Body-o'-me!" said Little John, "the Sheriff's warder has been kind to us."

"How so, John?"

"He is preparing the passage for to-morrow—ho, ho! Body of Saint Hubert! but that morrow will tell a different story."

When they neared the outlet the blows of an axe could be heard, and Little John going forward to reconnoitre, saw Berthold busy hewing down the tangled brushwood which grew before the door.

There was a few moments' consultation respecting the best mode of passing the warder. They could easily have done so by using force, but this did not suit the forester.

He wished, if possible, to pass unseen, then the man would have no story to carry to the Sheriff, consequently his suspicions would not be aroused respecting the character of the visitor who had worked so much mischief in the castle.

Chance favoured our adventurers; the soldier paused in his labour, and stood with his back towards the entrance.

There was a torch stuck in the ground; and by its ruddy glare the warder had seen to do his master's bidding.

This torch must be extinguished—but how? Little John soon found the means; picking up a stone he flung it at the light.

His aim was true and the place was in darkness.

"A malison upon the light," growled the soldier, "and a double malison upon my careless fingers for placing the sticks where they could fall upon the torch—marry come up with a wennion."

With this hearty curse, he took up the smouldering torch and began blowing the glowing end to fan it into a flame again.

While he was thus engaged, the forester and Will Scarlet stole quietly past, and despite the heavy loads they laboured under, they started at a quick pace and were soon tracing the high road which skirted the forest.

They had not passed many yards from where the trees began, when two figures sprang out into the centre of the road.

"Stand!" said one of the men, "and pay toll to good Robin."

"I'll break thy back, Much," answered Little John, "if thou dost not stand out of my path; to the evil one with thy *Pawage*."

"Is it thou, giant?" said Much; "we are right glad to hear thy voice again; there has been some talk among our merry men of one Little John, who had turned his sword and bow into a dishclout."

"Aye," answered John, "I'll warrant the tongues of our band have clacked like a flock of geese taking to the water, and their jaws have wagged when they thought of Little John washing the platters—see thee this, thou thief of a miller?"

"Aye, I do right well, and by its sheen should warrant it were made of silver,"

"Right for once, wittol—how thinkest thou I came by them?"

"Found them, mayhap."

"Cudgel thy brains again, Much. No, I'll spare what little thou hast of that article—

* Pawage was the old Saxon expression for toll.

harkee, they are my wages for being scullion to the Sheriff."

"The saints be good," laughed Much, "but the Sheriff pays wondrously well; but tell me, John, who is this lusty yeoman?—he has, I see, also got his wages."

"Yes," answered Little John, grimly, "he has been my helpmate."

"Pass on," said Much. "Thou king of liars! pass on."

"Body-o'-me!" said John; "had I not such presents for our master, I would stay and break thy back."

Much and his companion had by this time returned to the thicket, and, to Little John's amazement, the merry miller's son trolled out the following impromptu verse:

"Some they will talk of bold Robin Hood,
And some of Little John,
But I know how he served the proud sheriff
When he served him as scullion."

"A plague upon thy bawling!" growled John. "This way, Will; but, heed the trees, man, or thou wilt find thyself with a broken pate."

This caution was necessary, for they had entered a part of the forest where the lower boughs of the trees were not more than five feet from the ground.

They had not gone far through this almost impassable path, when a surly voice demanded:

"Thy name, friend; stand! or a clothyard shaft shall pierce thy body!"

"Hold thy prate," answered Little John, "and keep thy shafts for thy foes, most trusty Allan."

"Little John!" exclaimed Allan; "welcome to the greenwood, good scullion, the cooks have many platters for thee to wash."

"The fiend take thee!" said Little John, angrily. "At every turn I am met with like gibes. Come, Will, let us move; and may the saints send a wet night."

Will Scarlet was surprised at the vigilant watch kept by the outlaws, and his desire to become one of the band increased.

"Never mind their gibes, John," he said; "thou hast more to show for thy service than all the scouts who are out to-night."

"Aye," answered the giant, "that is the only balm I have, for these knaves will not forget this scullion business until I crack their pates. Come this way, Will: stoop well thy head, for this path is but used by the deer when they lead their fawns to drink at the stream."

Will Scarlet had good reason to wish the path had been left only for the deer, for his head received many sore bruises before he went far through the tangled path.

"The foresters," he said, not pretending to heed the sore blows he received, "keep good watch, John."

"Ashes of Saint Hubert! yes. Harkee, Will, the forest is some twenty-one miles in length, and seven wide, yet I'll gage my manhood a ferret could not enter among the trees unseen."

"There must be many men in your good company?"

"Some seven score, Will, and every day some good fellow like thyself joins us."

They went on for nearly half a mile, then the forest opened, and they crossed a glade tolerably shut in by the trees.

In the centre of this place stood a square-built stone hut, and Little John went to the door and imitated the cry of an owl.

The signal was understood, for the door was opened by a boy garbed in the finest green velvet trimmed with gold lace.

"Does our master sleep, Aylmer?" said Little John; "if so, I will come in the morn, and tell him strange news."

"Enter, pigmy," cried a voice from within. "Welcome to the greenwood."

Little John and Will entered, and Robin, when he saw the stalwart form beside Little John, smiled.

"What news from Nottingham, John?" he said, "and who is thy lusty companion?"

"Great news, good Robin; my companion is one who would fain join our band."

"What are these vessels of silver and gold, John, which ye both carry?"

"Presents from the Sheriff, master—right royal presents."

"They are welcome. Be seated; I will hear thy news first. But stay, does thy companion know the rules of our band?"

"But in part, good master; but I will warrant he agrees to all if thou wilt take him."

"Upon thy word I will. What is thy name, good fellow?"

"Will Scarlet, please you, bold Robin, Stout Will I am called by my kith and kin."

CHAPTER XXIX.

THE SHERIFF AND THE ABBOT MEET UNDER THE TRYSTING TREE.

Then Robin set his horn to his mouth,
And blew out blasts three,
Then quickly anon there came Little John
And all his company.
"What is your will, master?" said Little John,
"Good master come tell unto me."
"I have conquered the Sheriff of Nottingham,
Therefore I bring him to dine with thee."

THE chamber in which the Chief of the Outlaws was seated, was, for the period of which we write, fitted up in the most luxurious manner, and many of the ornaments, especially the lamps, which hung from the ceiling by silver chains, looked suspiciously like the filagree work lately imported into the country by the Normans.

The couch upon which the Outlaw reclined was covered with leopard skins, and surmounted at each end by lions' heads of solid silver.

Robin Hood's hunting dress was laid aside and in its stead he wore a loose robe of quilted silk trimmed with ermine and fastened by loops of gold thread.

This oriental magnificence contrasted strangely with the rough stone walls of the dwelling, the rush-covered floor and the chinks of the window frames through which the cold night air whistled.

At Robin's feet lay two large deer hounds, whose white fangs gleamed disagreeably when they turned towards Will Scarlet, for the sagacious brutes knew every man of the band, although neither by look or gesture did they show the slightest affection save to their master.

They were powerful, strong-limbed brutes, and well might Robin boast that with his good sword and buckler and his pair of hounds, he feared not twelve ordinary men.

"Now, pigmy," the Outlaw good-humouredly said, "for thy news."

Greatly to Robin Hood's amazement, Little John related his adventures in the castle; but, when he came to the recapitulation of the conversation between the Sheriff and Berthold, the Outlaw Chief's face reddened with anger, and he sprang from his seat, and the watchful dogs, as though they thought Little John was the cause of this display of temper, raised their massive heads, and snarled angrily at the giant.

"Down, Herod! down, Sylman!" Robin said; "have ye no better manners than to show your fangs to your friends?"

The dogs, rebuked, laid their heads upon their paws, and contented themselves by watching the visitors.

Little John continued his story, and, at its close placed the spoil upon the table.

"These presents," Robin said, smiling—for his anger had passed away—"are welcome, John, for our treasury is but poorly supplied."

"Body-o'-me!" the forester said, "I never knew it other than empty. What, in the saint's name, hast thou done with the good coin thou hadst when I left."

"Given it away, John; for I could not hoard up riches and know so many of the poor were suffering through the rapacious locusts who infest our land."

"Thou art ever good," said Little John, "and, were harm to befall thee, the poor would lose a friend."

"And the rich an enemy," said the chief. "Seek thy rest, John, and take with thee this fair yeoman, who seems well able to use a staff or drive an arrow among the fallow deer, or, better still, through a Norman's coat of mail."

"Aye, that he is, master. Now, a fair good night! Come, Will, let us seek a covert for the night, for, to-morrow thou wilt have to prove thy skill in the use of bow, spear, sword, and staff."

The foresters left, and Robin's page, closing the door after them, retired to an inner chamber.

For some time the Outlaw Chief continued to pace to and fro, and by the red flush upon his face alone showing that his mind was disturbed.

"So," he said, as though in answer to his own thoughts, "this priest has set the bloodhound upon the abode of the dove. By my halidome, but he shall hang from the highest branch of our trysting tree if harm befall the gentle girl. What, ho, Aylmer."

The richly dressed page glided to his master's side.

"Hie thee to the place where the abbot is confined," the outlaw said, "and bid his guards bring him hither; be quick, boy, for the matter will not brook delay—rather," he added, when the boy left, "my mind may not long keep in this mood."

The abbot, roused from his slumber by Robin's sudden message, was hurried to the stone building, and brought face to face with the angry outlaw.

The proud Norman first met the forester's gaze with a contemptuous look of defiance—although a prisoner, he deemed himself too powerful to be confined by the chief of the Saxon archers.

"Harkee, sir priest," said Robin sternly, "thy brain hath hatched a plot for the destruction of one who is dear to me—but I swear should harm befall her, I will suspend thy carcass from a green bough—by the holy rood I will! Should ye," he added to the stalwart foresters, who guarded the abbot, "hear three mots from my bugle to-morrow at noonday, stay not for my coming, but hang this priest as ye would hang a rabid dog. Now, away with ye, and forget not three mots from my horn will be the abbot's death-warrant."

The abbot's face went pale, but he retained sufficient composure to walk steadily from the outlaw's presence. Then again Robin threw himself upon the couch, and soon fell into a deep sleep.

When the morning came he inspected his men, heard their reports, and examined them at the butts, and Will Scarlet, who proved himself a good yeoman, was admitted into the band.

As the morning advanced the outlaw's calmness began to leave him, and when the dial showed it was now the hour Geoffrey de Lois had determined to visit the mill, Robin selected a dozen of his best men and left the forest.

When they reached the vicinity of the mill the foresters concealed themselves among the trees, and Robin went forward alone.

He had gone as far as the miller's dwelling when a scream caused him to pluck his sword from his scabbard, and, recking not of the force which might be opposed to his single hand he dashed through the window.

What followed has already been related.

The odds were all in favour of the mail-clad Sheriff, and as he was armed with a much heavier weapon, it was a wonder the lightly-armed Outlaw did not succumb to his foe.

The wondrous skill he possessed alone saved him from being slain, and this skill enabled him to take a sudden leap forward, as his sword blade snapped in two, and before the Sheriff could deal the fatal blow he was seized by the throat.

There was a brief struggle, then a crash of steel, as the Norman was borne to the earth.

Like a flash of light Robin's long hunting-knife leapt from its sheath, and his throat would have been pierced, had not Marian sprang forward, and catching the Outlaw's hand, said—

"Shed not his blood, Robin; let other hands than thine do this."

The blow was arrested, and the Outlaw arose, placed one foot upon his prostrate foe's neck.

"Yield!" he said, "or despite this maiden's prayers I will slay thee."

"I yield," was the sullen answer, "since there is none other to be done; but the day will arrive when I shall meet thee again, foot to foot."

"For that meeting," the Outlaw answered, "I shall be ready; but keep thy boasting until thou art clear of my hands."

The sheriff regained his feet, his swarthy face black with passion, and in spite of his knightly word which he had pledged when he surrendered to the gallant forester, he made an effort to snatch his sword from the ground.

The forester's quick eye anticipated the treacherous movement, and before the Sheriff's hand could touch the hilt the weapon was kicked out of reach.

Geoffrey de Lois scowled savagely, and as though a sudden thought had come to his mind, he placed a silver whistle to his lips and blew a shrill note.

"False caitiff!" said Robin, "is this the way thou regardest thy plighted word? Out upon thee for a recreant! Listen to the answer to thy call."

Robin sounded a blast upon his bugle, then taking up the Norman's long sword he awaited the coming of his men.

"The devil," the Sheriff said triumphantly, for he believed that Robin had come to the mill unattended, "will not save thee; to-morrow shalt thy neck be stretched. Listen, here come those who will bear thee to a dungeon, and this maiden to a chamber, in Nottingham Castle."

As he spoke the door was thrown open, and Berthold, at the head of a dozen retainers armed with sword and buckler, entered the room.

"Seize yon thief!" said the Sheriff. "Ha, ha!—have I not spoken truly, thou cutpurse?"

"Thou hast told a foul lie" answered Robin Hood, as he whirled the two-handed double-edged sword around his head, and kept back the men-at-arms; "judge for thyself."

As the last words left his lips the men-at-arms were hurled aside from the doorway, and Little John, followed by the foresters with bent bows, ran to their leader's assistance, the giant using his clenched fist to clear a path, and the steel-capped retainers going down before it as though a sledge-hammer had been used upon their skulls.

"Make way, knaves!" Little John said, seconding every word with a blow, "or mayhap my fist may batter the iron pots through your skulls. Now, master, what means thy lusty call."

"Only this, John," the Outlaw said: "bind yon Sheriff's arms, then put a rope round——"

"Upon them knaves!" roared the Sheriff. "Use the swords ye hold, and cut these thieves to the earth."

"Ho, ho!" laughed Little John; "large words, master, large words. See, thou, these clothyard shafts. Open thy bawling mouth again, and thy men will be pinned to yon wall."

The men-at-arms drew back, for six of the foresters fitted arrows to their bows, and stood with the strings drawn to their ears.

"Draw to the ear, my merry men," continued Little John, "and if one of the knaves stir hand or foot, send a good yard of birch and hazel through their jerkins."

Three of the outlaws placed their bows against the wall after detaching the strings; these they knotted together; and, seizing the Sheriff, began to tie his arms behind him."

The Norman fought like a tiger, but his strength was as a child's against the stalwart fellows who held him in their grip.

There was not only the disgrace of being thus pinned before his men that galled him, but Robin's unfinished speech left him in doubt as to the use of the bow-string that was to be passed round his neck.

"Now," said Robin, when their prisoner was secured, "pass a loop round his neck, and lead him to our trysting tree; and thou, Much, should he lag on the way, walk behind him and prick his hide with thy sword, if thou canst find a point in his armour for the point to enter."

"His mail," answered the delighted Much, "would have to be forged by the devil if I did not find space enough for the point of this good blade to enter."

"What about these knaves, master," Little John asked, baring his brawny right arm. "I think a good basting with our unstrung bows would be neat punishment for them."

"Thou art right," laughed Robin, "therefore set about it, John."

The hindmost of the retainers, seeing those of the foresters who had not their arrows fitted, busy loosing their bow strings, fell slowly back through the door, and the example, spreading like an infectious disease among the remainder, the whole forty turned tail and left the miller's house.

But quick as they were they did not quite escape, for sturdy old Much riding towards the door and seeing the Sheriff's men upon his domain, struck spurs into his grey gelding's sides, and with the long whip he carried, laid about him right and left.

The old fellow came back chuckling with his victory, and to his astonishment he saw the Sheriff being led out like a convict, and his son, young Much, walking behind the prisoner with a naked sword held in an unpleasantly suggestive manner.

"What now?" demanded the old man, pulling up his steed," art thou going to give the devil a day of merry making by hanging his chosen friend."

"Maybe so, father," answered Much. "but if he goes not on faster than this, I shall let out his black blood long ere we reach the merry greenwood."

"Good boy," said the miller, "by our ancestors this is a goodly sight—string him up, the knave—but where's good Robin, Much?"

"Ask Cousin Marian," answered Much, mischievously; "I saw him holding her by the waist lest she might fall."

"The knave," laughed the lusty old miller, "I'll teach him better manners."

"Do, father—and harkee."

"Well, knave."

"Didst thou grind up flint stones to fill the last flour sacks thou sent to the forest?"

"Out upon thee for a saucy varlet."

The old miller made a cut at his son with the whip, but the latter dodging aside, the thong came smartly across the Sheriff's face, and caused him to use an exclamation not generally used by so mighty a knight.

The foresters laughed and led their prisoner away, and Robin soon after overtook them."

When they reached the trysting tree, Robin Hood whispered a few words to Little John, who when he heard them began to grin and finally bursting out into a hearty laugh, he left the spot, his person swinging to and fro with merriment.

When Little John disappeared, Robin placed his bugle to his mouth, and sounded a long mot for the foresters to assemble.

They came from every part of the forest, and the Sheriff's face, although he would fain have concealed it, expressed the greatest surprise at beholding the many stalwart green clad forms gather around the handsome chief.

When the men were all assembled, the Sheriff's nerves received another shock, for Little John appeared leading the abbot towards the group.

"A friend of thine," said Robin to the Sheriff; "I have brought him here that thou shouldst not be the only one of thy race among the many of Saxon blood."

The abbot started when he saw his nephew, and would have spoken had not astonishment and rage kept him silent.

"Well, John," the chief said, "as we have such good company suppose we go to dinner."

"It would be a sin, master to let the good roast meats be over done. Disperse ye knaves, and spread the board——"

"But, master——"

"Well?"

"Dost thou not think that it would be as well to hang this Sheriff before dinner?"

"Nay, that would be very unyeomanlike—he shall dine first, John, and pay for his dinner, then we can hang the knave."

Not pleasant for the Sheriff this—for he took the foresters' joking for earnest.

The lieutenant set about the arrangement of the board, amusing himself while doing so by singing a ballad of which the following was the refrain :—

> "The Sheriff is welcome here,
> For I know he will honestly pay,
> And I know he has gold if it be but well told,
> Will serve us to drink a whole day."

The verse was soon taken up by the outlaws, and the Sheriff bit his lip with passion at being made such an object of ridicule, among the men he had been wont to despise. Robin, with his back against a tree, listened to his lieutenant's voice, and by the smile upon his lips, it was evident he felt much amused.

CHAPTER XXX.

FRIAR TUCK RETURNS FROM PRAYERS, AND THE ABBOT SINGS A MASS TO THE MERRY FORESTERS.

> "Now let him go," said Robin Hood ;
> Said Little John, "that must not be ;
> For I vow and protest he shall sing us a mass
> Before that he go from me."
> Then Robin Hood took the Abbot
> And bound him fast to a tree,
> And made him sing a mass, God wot,
> To him and his yeomanry."

THE feast spread by the foresters resembled in many particulars the description of that given to do honour to the Earl of Mortimer.

When one of the servers announced everything ready, the chief desired the Sheriff's bonds to be cut, and then invited him to be seated.

However much the haughty Geoffrey and the prelate disliked having to accept the invitation, they had the good sense to hide their feelings, and heartily wishing the first mouthful of venison might choke their entertainers, they sullenly took the seats indicated.

Robin Hood was about to give the word for the ready daggers to fall upon the smoking viands, when looking first up one side then down the other, he missed the rubicund face of the fat friar.

"Hold thy hands," he said, "it is not right we should dine without asking a blessing. Where is our roystering chaplain?"

"I saw him," said the forester, "go towards the north side of the forest before you returned."

"Was it long before?"

"Perhaps an hour, good master."

"To your feet, knaves," said the forester, "and search for our jolly clerk; for I swear not to eat until he's found."

The men were saved this trouble, for at the moment as a score or thereabouts rose to their feet, a lusty and somewhat thick voice could be heard singing—

> "Ye gentlemen and yeomen bold,
> Or whatsoe'er ye are,
> To have a right good story told
> Attention now prepare ;
> It is about bold Robin
> A man much talked upon
> And who was once a man of fame,
> And styled Earl of Huntingdon,
> Bold Robin was his name."

The friar suddenly desisted from his song, then his voice was raised in expostulation to some one near him.

"The foul fiend !—that is, blessed be the saints !—for giving us good liquor. Keep thy feet, men, keep thy feet; for it would be a sinful sight for our master to see ye both in this unseemly state."

These words were uttered in a voice that left but little to be imagined respecting the state of the friar and his companions.

"Our fighting priest," laughed John, "and drunk, or I'm a false prophet."

"Out upon thee for a pair of knaves," the friar was heard to say. "Dost thou not know both feet ye have were given to ye to walk upon, not the hands? Keep upright, or, by all the saints! I will leave ye both without the support of my arm. Come, ye varlets, tune up, and bear me out in a right good stave."

There was a short pause, then the saintly man burst out with the following fragment :—

> "Ah! sweet are the flowers that bloom in May,
> Like wing-gifts dressing the gaily-dressed day,
> And smiling like beauty o'er heart-bending sway ;
> But sweeter than these to the thirsty soul's throat
> Is the——"

"A plague take ye both! thou art drunk; tune up, or, by the saints! I'll split this—— A fair, good day, my merry men and masters all."

It was a strange sight which burst upon the assembled company when the lusty friar uttered this greeting—a sight that caused Little John to roar with laugher.

Emerging from the trees, were seen the lusty friar, and two foresters behind, arm-in-arm, swaying two and fro, as they alternately flashed black bottles over their heads, and took up the last line of Friar Tuck's song, and, with drunken gravity, endeavoured to sing it as a chorus.

"What now, ye roystering knaves?" said Robin; "is it thus ye come before us? Out upon ye. What, drunk! and the sun scarcely beyond noon-time."

ROBIN HOOD,

AND THE OUTLAWS OF SHERWOOD FOREST.

THE COMBAT IN SHERWOOD FOREST.

"Drunk!" hiccupped the friar, reclining on the arms of the foresters; "thou doest us great wrong, master, we have but been to prayers, and feeling athirst after, we drank of Saint Ann's Well, and as thou well knowest the waters are by a miracle of a strength not befitting our poor weak heads."

"Go to, thou knave," Robin said, "here have we kept this company fasting a full hour, through thee. Make thy obeisance to the Lord

Abbot here, then say a fitting race for this goodly feast."

Friar Tuck's companions who had escaped by this time, were seated at the lower end of the board; when the monk found himself thus deserted by his allies, he screwed his face into a comical expression of penitence, and addressing the Abbot said:

"I crave his reverence's pardon for not making my obeisance sooner to one of our cloth, but I wot the Lord Abbot knows full well what it is to drink of the waters of Saint Ann's Well, or maybe waters of similar strength, and his reverence knowing this will pardon my——"

Here the jolly priest, who had been swaying to and fro, suddenly lurched forward, and losing his footing, fell into a huge dish of smoking venison, and sent the hot gravy all over the Sheriff's face.

The latter sprang up with an oath, which was repeated by the Abbot. who chanced to be seated opposite to where the friar fell, and the latter in his efforts to regain his feet, rolled forward and overset the mighty churchman.

The laughter from the foresters was long and loud at this ludicrous scene, and the fat friar, scrambling to his feet, rubbed his shaven crown.

"The saints preserve us," he said, ruefully, "here have I scalded a good knight and upset a reverend head of the church, and it all came about through Saint Ann. Out upon ye for blessing the waters of the well; is it thus ye would serve one who pays the shrine such homage."

The Sheriff, who had by this time cleared his eyes of the hot gravy, smarting under the scalds his face had received, made a rush upon the fat friar.

"Drunken carle," he said, "ungodly desecrator of a priest's robe, I will wring thy neck."

He made a clutch at the friar's robe as he spoke, but the stout priest suddenly ducked his head, and taking the astonished Norman by the waist, held him aloft.

"Now, my master," he cried, "shall I crack this knave's skull or fling him over yon tree?"

The Sheriff's position was not the most enviable in the world, for the strong limbed friar held him with as much ease as though he were a child.

"Come, thou roystering devil," said Robin, "set our guest upon his feet, it will be time if he does not pay for his dinner to crack his skull or throw him over yon tree."

The priest placed the Sheriff upon his feet, and Robin, in the most courteous manner, begged him to be seated.

Geoffrey de Lois complied; he found he was no match for the outlaw's chaplain, and knew it would best serve his purpose to ingratiate himself with the outlaw.

With a forced smile he reseated himself.

"It would be more seeming," he said to the Outlaw Chief, "if this lusty friar of yours would seek the Well he worships less often, and much better for the comfort of thy guests."

"There is much truth in that," answered Robin, "but the knave is deaf to all good advice—come, sir friar, when thou hast done twisting thy face about we shall be glad to hear grace said, for our merry men and the guests here are somewhat tired of waiting so long for their dinner."

Friar Tuck was about to say grace, but 'ere he could begin the Abbot jumped to his feet and sternly said:

"Peace, thou drunken varlet, thinkest thou I will sit here and listen to the Church being profaned by thy words."

The fat friar meekly crossed his hands, and a broad grin overspread his face.

"Far be it," he said, "reverend father, for one like myself to contradict the words of one who draws such fat revenues for wearing our cloth; I am dumb, Sir Abbot, and wait with due humility for thee to perform the office thou willest me unfit to perform."

The Abbot scowled at the fat monk.

"How is this," Robin said; "what, two of a cloth at variance? Come, Sir Abbot, the dinner's cold, and the mouths of my merry men water the more when they see good viands before them, and wait but for the proper words to begin the meal. Come, as thou likest not the grace of the friar say one thyself."

"Use my holy office," exclaimed the indignant churchman, "for the benefit of such cutpurses as ye are! Not a word wilt thou get from my lips; and as for you grinning disgrace to priestcraft, would I had him in my abbey!"

"Ho, ho!" laughed Friar Tuck; "would thou wert safe back there thyself, Sir Abbot; by Our Lady, were it in my power I would make thee use thine office, or flay thee alive!"

"Accursed be such as ye——"

"Stop, Sir Abbot," Robin said; "thou hast used words which are but scant courtesy for all we have done for you. Arise, Allan, and thou, Much."

The foresters obeyed.

"Pass a looped rope over a strong bough of yonder tree."

This order was likewise obeyed, and the proud prelate's face paled.

"Take the Abbot," Robin continued, "and put the loop around his neck, but strangle him not; I want him to have the power of speech."

The Abbot's face went paler, and his legs shook as he was led beneath the dangling noose, and his neck encircled with the cord.

The Sheriff sat aghast, but he moved not, for he saw Little John had unsheathed his heavy sword, and was keenly watching every movement of their foe—Nottingham's treacherous sheriff.

"Now, Sir Priest," said the Chief, "sing us a mass, or, by the splendour of Our Lady's face, thou wilt be a dead man."

"Geoffrey," said the Abbot, "thine arms are free, help me! By Our——"

"If he stirs but an inch," said Little John, "I will cleave him to the chine."

"Now, Sir Priest," said Robin; "sing us a mass, or thou hangest!"

The Abbot made no reply, but his head fell forward as he reflected over the certainty of the fate with which he had been threatened.

Life was sweet to him—very sweet, but to have his pride humbled by the Outlaw was almost as bad as death; yet he thought, "the time may come when I shall be able to avenge this insult."

"I yield to thy demand," he said, raising his head and looking fiercely at the Outlaw Chief; "but, rest content, the wrath of the church will fall upon thy head!"

"When it does, Sir Abbot," said Robin, "I will obtain absolution from our confessor here; wilt thou grant it, fat friar?"

"Aye, right willingly," laughed Friar Tuck, "and as willingly as I grant it to sundry of thy merry men, who come to me in virtue of my holy office."

"Enough," said Robin; "thou hearest, Sir Abbot; now sing us a mass, and in good full voice too, or the stinging nettles I see being gathered shall make acquaintance with thy back; thy kinsman here, the Sheriff, once tasted them, he will tell thee they are far from pleasant."

Geoffrey de Lois darted a look of hatred towards the forester for mentioning the degradation he had undergone when he disturbed the Saxon merry-making.

There was a deep silence during the time the Abbot's voice was raised, and all paid deep attention to his words, save the ungodly Friar Tuck, who rolled his body from side to side, and once or twice disturbed the silence by laughing outright.

When the Abbot had concluded his unwilling office, the noose was taken from his neck, and he was conducted by Allan-a-Dale and Much to his seat.

"Now, my merry men," said Robin, "fall to and show our guests the extent of a forester's appetite."

The men required no second bidding, they fell to with a will that soon made sad havoc with the huge joints.

When the servers brought in the wine, Little John looked at his chief, a mischievous smile upon his good-humoured face.

"Master," he said, "have we not other vessels save those of horn to set before our guests? if not, it were a sin to expect them to enjoy good wine."

"Now I bethink me," Robin answered, "the reserve cups of silver are more befitting the rank of our guests. Go thou, Much, and fetch them hither."

Secretly pleased at this mark of distinction were the Abbot and Sheriff; but when Much returned, laden with the cups Little John and Will Scarlet had brought from the castle, Geoffrey de Lois uttered a cry of rage.

He recognised his property, and ground his teeth in impotent rage, as he saw the grinning Friar Tuck weighing each cup in his hand, as though calculating its worth.

> "The Sheriff was to dinner set,
> And served with silver white,
> But, when his own silver vessels he saw,
> He could have cried for spite.
> Make glad cheer, said Robin Hood,
> Sheriff for charity,
> For this is the way we order our life
> Under the greenwood tree."

"Come, drink, Sir Sheriff," said Robin, "and do honour to my merry men."

The Sheriff could not answer.

He sat like one who had suddenly seen a ghost, and, although his lips moved nervously, no sound came from them.

"This is but scant courtesy, Sir Sheriff," continued Robin; "nevertheless, I will pledge thee in good red Rhenish wine; and thou, Sir Abbot, will I pledge and pray ye are both well kept until our next merry meeting."

He drained the silver cup when he ceased speaking, then held it out to be refilled.

"Master," Little John said, "the cause of our guest's silence is soon told."

"Do thou tell it then, knave."

"That will I. The good Sheriff seems to have forgotten he sent thee these cups of silver as a fair greeting of friendship."

"I!" the Sheriff said in amazement, "I sent these cups! Tell me, knave, how came they here, since it was but yesterday, at matin hour, I saw them safe in my treasure vault?"

"Sayest thou this?" said Little John. "It is most passing strange, for I brought them to our good master yestere'en."

"Thou, thou broughtest them, thief, cutpurse, robber. How camest thou near the castle?"

"The good Abbot there sent me," said Little John, "and bid thy cook tend well so good a son of the church."

The Abbot started, and looked keenly at the forester.

"The knave's voice seems familiar," he thought, "yet I know not where I could have heard it."

"Reverend father," said Little John, using the same words as when he met the Abbot and the Cellarer outside the gates of Nottingham Castle, "I am but a scullion at heart. Although my limbs are somewhat large, my valour is the smallest thou hast ever known, for the whiz of an arrow or the sight of a naked sword causes my knees to totter, and my heart to quake. Thus, thou seest, I am but fit to help the noble cook of the Lord Sheriff. The saints be good to him!"

"Ha!" exclaimed the amazed Abbot, "the very words used by a serving man whom I met when leaving thy castle, Geoffrey."

"Yes, reverend sir," said Little John, "and the very lips which used them, and the very ears that listened to thee when thou wert pleased to call me a good son of the church."

"Ho, ho!" laughed the fat friar; "I will burn six candles at the altar of my patron saint for this. Ho, ho! an abbot outwitted by Little John. Ho, ho, ho!"

The Abbot was amazed at hearing this; and the Sheriff, seeing there was but little chance of regaining his lost treasure, concealed his vexation as well as he could, and, taking up the full cup which had been placed before him, drank in return to Robin Hood's pledge.

CHAPTER XXXI.

HOW THE ABBOT AND THE SHERIFF RODE FROM SHERWOOD FOREST.

> Let me go then, said the Sheriff,
> For Saint Charity,
> And the best friend ever you had,
> I will be to thee.
> Thou shalt swear me an oath, said Robin,
> On my bright brand,
> Thou shalt never waylay me for harm,
> By water or by land.
> And if thou find any of my men,
> By night or by day,
> Upon thine oath thou shalt swear
> To help them that thou may.

THE wine was of the best, and both the Abbot and the Sheriff failed not to do honour to its goodness, and by the time a few flagons had been emptied, the foresters' tongues became loosened, and more than one heart-stirring song was sung.

The Normans began to thaw in their demeanour towards the foresters, and the Abbot so far forgot the humiliation he had suffered, as to address a few civil words to the fat friar, who had by this time paid pretty good court to the juice of the grape, and was quite in a mood either to sing a song or fight a good bout at quarter-staff.

"It is sad," the Abbot said, leaning over towards Friar Tuck, "to see thee, holy brother so forgetful of thy cloth as to appear before thy flock in a state so unseeming for thine office."

"Unseeming," said the Friar, "by Our Lady's favour, Sir Abbot, may I ask if the monks of Saint Mary's never get beyond the state thou seemest to think I have but little right to reach?"

"The monks of Saint Mary's," said the Abbot, "are a holy and zealous brotherhood, who would not taste of the juice of the vine, save in the most extreme case of bodily sickness."

"By the Rood then," said the Friar, "there must be much of sickness in the abbey, for when my master here——"

"Hush," said the Abbot, "believe not the scandal—it is but a lie of thy master's, and one I know so good a priest as thyself wilt not believe."

"But I do," returned Friar Tuck, "and if there is any lies told it is from thy lips, not my master's."

"How now, knave," the Abbot said angrily, "is it thus thou accusest me?"

"Marry, why not?"

"Forgettest thou my rank in the church?"

"Not I; neither do I care though thou wore all the silver mitres in the world."

The churchman's face flushed, and there would soon have been a quarrel between the pair had not Robin interfered.

"Tune up thy voice," he said to the friar, "and give us a good stave, it will be better than quarrelling with the Abbot."

"By the Rood, thou art right, Robin," said the lusty friar. "What wouldst thou have me sing?"

"Give us the 'Maiden and the Knight.'"

"Aye," chorussed the foresters within hearing, "the 'Maiden and the Knight,' Friar, it is the best of thy budget."

There was but little bashfulness about the Friar, so without more ado, and in a good mellow voice, he sang the following characteristic song of the age, when religion and chivalrous vows were so strangely blended.

FRIAR TUCK'S SONG.

"A warrior knelt at the holy shrine
    And he thought of the home he had left behind,
He thought of his love and he blamed the oath
    That called him far from her gentle troth.
'Oh,' he sighed from his inmost heart,
'Light of my bosom, why did we part?'

"A maiden knelt at the sacred tomb,
    Her dark hair shrouded her cheeks of bloom,
And she looked on the knight with a wild amaze,
But he turned aside from a stranger's gaze.
Her love lay calm on her breast of woe,
Like moonbeams on the driven snow,
And the wild tear shone in her eyes of light,
Like the first star of a summer's night.

"The warrior knelt at the shrine again,
    His faith had dispelled his heart's keen pain;
And he prayed aloud that no Pagan hand,
Should again defile the Holy Land.
But a thought of nature gently fell,
To mould a prayer for his Isabel;
'Oh, keep her from all but love's alarms!'
He rose—and his maid was in his arms."

"Well sung, fat priest," said Little John. "Body-o'-me, but it would have served the knight according to his deserts had the maiden stayed at home, instead of following her recreant lover to the Holy Land."

"How so, thou mountain of flesh," asked Friar Tuck; "methinks it was but proper the maid should follow her knight. I wot thou wouldst think so were it thy case."

"Body-o'-me," said John, "it would never be my case, for I should stay with the maiden I loved in merry England, and leave the Pagans to swallow the Holy Land if they liked."

"Out upon thee," laughed the friar, "for an unblushing knave; come, tune thy pipes and give this good company a song."

Little John complied after a few moments reflection, and trolled out the following verse:

In Sherwood lived bold Robin Hood,
    An archer great, none greater,
His bows and shafts were sure and good,
    Yet Cupid's were much better.
Robin could shoot at many a hart and miss;
    Cupid at first could hit a heart of his.

Then hey, Jolly Robin ho! Jolly Robin.
    Hey ho! hey ho! Jolly Robin.

Love finds out me as well as thee,
So follow, so follow, so follow me,
And sing hey, Jolly Robin, ho! Jolly Robin.

"Peace, knave," said Robin Hood, "stun not this good company with thy bawling; come, my merry men, let us show our guests some skill in archery."

The foresters arose, and taking their bows went towards the butts, singing the chorus of Little John's song, the giant and Friar Tuck's voices leading the chorus.

"By my faith," said the Abbot, as he followed the merry foresters, "thou leadest a happy life here, Robin."

"Aye," answered the Outlaw, "we have but little to disturb us; the red deer supplies us with food, and such generous knights as the Sheriff keep us in vessels of gold and silver, and thy high cellarer and others fill our coffers with bright money."

The Sheriff smiled grimly at this allusion to his loss, but he made no remark, his prudence forbade that, and his brain was busy hatching a plan whereby he might recover his lost treasure.

The Normans were astounded at the yeomanry they beheld, for, in a trial of skill between Robin, Little John, and Friar Tuck, three white wands, not thicker than a man's little finger, were set up, and each of these doughty foresters split the mark at the first shot.

Then followed quarter-staff and wrestling; and the lusty Friar, tucking up his long gown, thrashed all who opposed him with the oak staff, and, in the wrestling, he threw more than one stalwart forester over his head.

The evening was now coming upon the earth, and the Outlaw Chief led his guests beneath the greenwood tree, and, surrounded by his band, he named the conditions upon which he would release them.

"Thou," he said to the Abbot, "must send, by one of thy fat, lazy monks, full two hundred marks in bright money."

"Two hundred marks!" repeated the Abbot. "Surely, Robin, thou art joking. Thou oughtest to know full well the poverty of my order."

"Aye, I do, Sir Abbot," laughed the Outlaw. "Nevertheless, if thou dost not pay this sum, I warrant I can keep thee here, and make thee head priest to this worshipful company, and then thou wilt have but our jolly confessor to do battle with for the mastership of the office."

"I will have no other priest here," said Friar Tuck, "unless he can well trounce me with the stout oak staff. If he canst not do this, he will have to be my bondsman, and, if he fail to serve me well, he will be sorry the day ever came that brought him to the world."

"Thou hearest this," said the Outlaw, "and, from what thou hast seen of our curtal friar's arm, methinks it will be better for thee to even melt down the ornaments of the abbey to pay thy ransom than abide with us."

"May the saints send a plague upon thee and thy band of cutpurses!" said the Abbot angrily; "is it not enough that I have been kept in thy power so long, but thy thievish fingers must want to rob me?"

"Choose thee, Sir Abbot," said Robin; "choose thee between paying the ransom I have fixed and being the bondsman of our fighting confessor."

"Has the power of the church fallen so low," the Abbot said, "that I could be left among this pack of thieves without an arm being raised to effect my rescue?"

"Listen, Sir Abbot," said Robin; "the minions of a foreign court have more than once sought to crush Robin Hood and his merry men; but, while there are good English arms left to draw a bow and clothyard shafts to fit to the string, Robin will be King of Sherwood, and all who may be, like thyself, in his power, will be as far from a rescue as though locked in the deepest dungeons of a Norman castle."

The Abbot knew the truth of these words, and with a determination to wring twice the amount of his ransom out of the poor Saxon peasantry, he sullenly agreed to send the money before sundown on the following day.

"I rely upon thy word," said Robin; "but if thou playest me false thou shalt repent of it until thy dying hour. Now, Sir Sheriff," he added, "I will liberate thee upon condition that thou wilt never do aught to molest, or try and capture any of my merry men."

"I will not interfere with thee or thine," the Sheriff said, "if thou wilt let me free."

"I have had proof of thy knightly word," said Robin, drawing his sword; "swear me an oath by thy knightly vow upon the cross hilt of this good sword."

He held the hilt of the sword towards Geoffrey de Lois as he spoke, and the Sheriff kissed the sword, and swore by his vows never to waylay, or cause to be waylaid for good or for evil, any of Robin's band.

"Thou hast sworn," the Outlaw said; "remember thine oath, or by St. Herman-of-the-Wold! I will forget that thou art more than a common peasant, and will punish thee accordingly."

"Fetch the Abbot's palfrey, Much," said Little John, "for it is not meet such proud guests should walk from Sherwood to Nottingham."

The palfrey was brought.

"I seek not any ransom for thee," Robin said to the Sheriff, "for thou hast been generous to us, and we will keep thy cups of silver, and think of the good Norman who for once has been so generous to the Saxon race. Go! I wish thee good speed."

The foresters obeying a signal from Little John, had slowly closed around the group, and when Robin uttered his parting words, some eight or ten stalwart outlaws laid hands upon the Abbot and his kinsman, and before either could divine the motive for this sudden movement, they were lifted from the ground and placed astride the palfrey, their faces towards the animal's tail.

A thin cord secured their feet, then the mischief-loving Much, cut the palfrey across the flanks with his bow, and caused the frightened brute to dart forward among the trees, as much alarmed by the double burden he bore, as by the roars of laughter from the foresters.

As for Friar Tuck, the tears streamed from his eyes, and he rolled about the greenwood well nigh killed by the comical sight.

CHAPTER XXXII.

THE COMBAT IN SHERWOOD FOREST.

There rides a warrior dark and glim,
Through Sherwood's sylvan glade,
And a battle-axe is held by him,
And keen is its polished blade.
And he is cased from top to toe
In panoply of steel;
From the nodding plume, I trow,
To the spur upon his heel.

THE next day the Outlaw Chief mounted his white steed, and armed with sword and buckler, pricked his way through the forest in the direction of the mill.

He went thus fearlessly in the open daylight and alone, for being of a generous nature, he had no suspicion respecting the Sheriff, who he believed having pledged his knightly word, would, as was the usage of the time, scrupulously adhere to the compact he had made, not to interfere with him or his men.

The vast forest was filled with the carolling sweet-voiced birds, and ever and anon a deer would dart from the thicket, disturbed by the heavy hoof strokes of his horse.

It was a fair scene, such a one that is seldom or never met in England now, for bricks and mortar have taken the place of noble trees, and where the red deer were wont to assemble, narrow streets have effaced the sylvan spots.

Robin Hood allowed the reins to fall upon his horse's neck to give free play to the many matters of import which troubled his mind.

First there was the state of England, which, in consequence of the fickleness of the King and the absence of his son, then in the Holy Land, had become the prey of a nest of foreign favourites who thronged around the throne of Henry of Winchester.

There had been several meetings among the Saxon landowners—franklins, as they were termed—of the midland counties, to organise a rising, which should overthrow the power of the oppressors.

At these meetings the bold Outlaw had played a prominent part, for the conspirators were anxious to obtain the aid of one who could command such a warlike body of men.

He was pondering over these matters, and wondering when the oppressed people would take heart of grace and make common cause against the enemy, when he was startled by the heavy hoof-strokes of a war-horse, and the ring of the steel ornaments which depended from the animal's frontlet and housings.

The path he was pursuing was only of sufficient width to allow the passage of his horse, and, as it wound in a serpentine direction, he could not see the new comer, although, from the sounds just mentioned, he knew it could be none other than a knight or a free lance caparisoned for war.

The Outlaw gathered up his reins and loosened his sword in its scabbard, for in those troublesome times no man's life was safe unless he was at all times ready to meet a foe.

Thus it was these precautions were more a matter of habit than any expectation of a coming conflict.

He had not long done this when there came towards him a figure, mounted upon a strong-limbed charger.

The rider was cased from head to foot in armour, and his visor was down, but from between the bars of his helmet Robin caught a glimpse of a pair of dark, restless eyes.

The Forester and the Knight rode forward until their horses heads met, before they exchanged a word.

The mailed rider, no doubt confident in his superior arms, deemed the other ought to yield him place in that narrow path.

And Robin, from the long sovereignty he had held over the greenwood, thought it beneath him to yield, although to a man who was armed at all points.

As there was no possible chance of the horsemen passing each other, they were compelled to come to a standstill, the Knight glaring upon the Forester, and Robin no wise dismayed, scanned the noble proportions of the stranger's steed.

"How now, knave," the Knight demanded, "is not the forest wide enough for thee that thou must come by the very path I have chosen?"

"By Saint Herman!" said Robin, laughingly, "I might ask the same question of thee, for thou thast come by a path which I have chosen to follow."

The Knight, as though disdaining further argument, put forth his hand to where his battle-axe hung by its leathern loop from the saddle.

"Rein thy steed back," he said, haughtily, "or by my valour I will cleave the brute's skull in twain with this axe."

"Far better," Robin said, "to cleave the rider's skull; go to, is it thus a knight makes war upon horses, not men."

"Saint Christopher look down upon me," said the Knight, angrily, "is it thus I am to be mocked by a mere churl?"

"Churl back to thy teeth," retorted Robin, "if my lineage is not better than thine, may the foul fiend claim me for his own; rein thy steed back, Sir Knight, or by Saint Herman I will find a joint in thine armour for the point of my good sword to enter."

The Knight made no reply to this, but, snatching his axe from the pommel of the saddle, he waved the heavy weapon above his head.

"Have at thee, then," Robin said, as he drew his sword, and slipped the loops of his steel buckler over his arm; "have at thee!"

There were a few blows exchanged in the narrow path, and the Knight's war-horse, urged forward by his rider's spurs, slowly forced the fleeter animal Robin bestrode to fall back until they reached the open glade.

Here the combat was continued for some time, the well-trained horses wheeling about like falcons in the air under the impulse of their riders' hands.

The blows delivered by the Knight were borne on Robin's steel buckler, and Robin's sword-strokes were bravely parried by the handle of the battle-axe.

Thus they fought for some time; the Outlaw, by the swift movements of his steed, making up for the other's superior arms.

A fierce blow, delivered by the Knight at Robin's head, was caught upon the Outlaw's shield, but, so great was the power with which it fell, that the buckler was split in two.

The Knight, exulting in his opponent's disaster raised himself in the stirrups, and was about to repeat the stroke, when Robin, by a swift circular cut, severed the plaited handle of the trenchant battle-axe.

The Knight felt for his sword, but, ere he could unsheath it, the Outlaw spurred forward, and, with the remains of the steel buckler, knocked the knight from his saddle.

The dismounted warrior was upon his feet in an instant, and his naked blade flashed in the sunlight as he rushed to meet the bold Forester, who had dismounted when he heard the clatter of armour which announced the fall of the doughty knight.

Foot to foot they fought; but now the fight was in Robin Hood's favour, for his adversary encumbered with heavy armour, could not move with the swiftness of his skilful foe.

The Knight's long spurs, catching in the uncovered portion of the root of a gigantic tree, at the moment Robin Hood was pressing him very hard, caused him to stagger and partly unclose the grip of his sword.

In a second the weapon was wrenched from his hand, and went upward among the branches of the tree with such force, that a perfect shower of leaves descended.

Following this advantage, the Outlaw, with a spring like an angry panther, seized his adversary by the throat, and, dropping his sword, drew his anlace, and, placing the point between the bars of the knight's helmet, he said:

"Yield! or look thy last upon the blessed sun!"

"I yield," answered the Knight, and feel no shame at being vanquished by one so skilled in arms; who art thou, good fellow?"

"Unloose thy helmet," said Robin, "that I may see thy face ere I answer thy request."

The warrior did as he was requested, and Robin saw with much astonishment the fair, handsome face of a young man, who could not have numbered more than twenty summers since he came into the world.

The youth smiled at the Outlaw's astonishment.

"So young!" Robin said, "yet so stout a man-at-arms! Well, Sir Knight, my name is Robin Hood. Hast thou one that can be as boldly spoken?"

It was now the Knight's turn to be surprised, and he sprang forward and seizing the Forester's hand, exclaimed:

"Robin Hood! foul fall my hand for this

day's work, and thanks to Our Lady of Saint Clothilde, my battle-axe has worked thee no harm; it was thou I wast seeking when we met in yon narrow path."

"Thou hast not told me thy name, Sir Knight," the Forester said, releasing his hand from the other's grasp; "when I hear that I may fathom thy purpose in seeking me."

"My name, Sir Outlaw," the young Knight said, "is Walter Henwulf. Hast thine ears ever heard it before?"

"Full oft," said Robin; "has not the minstrel tuned his harp to thy name, and the palmer returning from the Holy Land spoken of thy deeds?"

Walter coloured to the eyes, for he was as modest as he was brave.

"I do not deserve this praise," he replied; "for my arm has done no more in defence of the holy sepulchre then many a man-at-arms."

"Thou wrongest thyself," said Robin; "for the deeds of the gallant Saxon knight are known far and wide, and those who sang them were always sure of a reward, for it has been too much the fashion of late to praise only Norman names and Norman arms, that it came pleasant to Saxon ears to hear some of their oppressed race had equalled the Normans in deeds of arms; but a truce to this, what was thy purpose in coming hither?"

"To bring thee a message, good Robin; a message from one who was once thy foe, but now thy friend."

"I have had many such. What is the name of him who has sent such a brave messenger?"

"My cousin Roger, Earl of Mortimer."

"Ha! has harm befallen the noble earl?"

"Alas! yes. In a council of state where there were none but Henry of Winchester's foreign favourites, Mortimer spoke up boldy for the people, who are every day becoming less, though human beings, by the crowd, who have come from Normandy, to portion and parcel out our fair realm."

"I am glad," Robin said, interrupting the Knight, "to hear Earl Mortimer's stay under the greenwood tree has been of such good, yet sorry he has incurred the anger of the weak and vindictive King; but tell me what fruit bore the planting of this same tree in the midst of such a goodly assembly."

"Thou shalt hear," said the Knight. "There was no mention made by the treacherous King of the offence he had given, but when Mortimer had gone to bed his room was filled with the King's myrmidons, who made him don his mail, and when this was done they left London, and took the road to Nottingham, and the leader of the party had a sealed letter for the Sheriff."

"By Saint Herman," said Robin, "this bodes no good for Mortimer; I know the Sheriff well; he would carry out any order of the King's. Have they lodged Mortimer in the castle yet?"

"About an hour since, for I followed them from London, and had I been in time, I should have tried a rescue."

"Thy single arm would have done but little, yet the motive that prompted thee was good."

"I wish to the saints," the young Knight said, "I had had but the opportunity I would have tried the weight of my battle axe upon the knaves' skulls."

The Outlaw made no reply, he was thinking over the best plan to aid the Earl.

"It is a pity, he said at last, "that I knew not of thy coming; then a score of clothyard shafts would have relieved him. But it matters not; I will rescue him if we have to take Nottingham Castle down stone by stone."

"Generous, noble Outlaw," said the young Knight, "sad it is to see one so good as thyself compelled to hide in a forest because of the cruelty of those who rule with iron hand over our land."

"Nay, Sir Knight," laughed Robin, "be not sorry upon my account, for the life I lead is far easier and merrier than is led by those at court or camp. Come to horse, and I will show thee my band."

They mounted, and the knight sheathed his sword, which Robin handed to him.

Tracing the silent depths of the forest as amicable friends, as they had been but a few minutes before fierce enemies, the Outlaw asked more particulars of the Earl's arrest.

"How knowest thou," he asked, "the letter was given to the leader of the Norman myrmidons if thou wert so far behind the escort?"

"From my page," answered the Knight. "I had sent him to the Earl's lodging, and he saw the whole of the affair."

"Is thy page handsome?"

"He is particularly so: fair of face, and with sunny locks such as many a lady has envied."

"So much the better; where is he now?"

"I left him near the castle, to glean what news he could from the loitering men-at-arms.

Robin smiled. He had thought of a plan by which he could communicate with the Earl, unless he was kept a close prisoner.

"By Saint Herman!" he said, "we shall yet outwit the Norman knaves. Ha! here, Sir Knight, is my band; what think ye of them?"

They had suddenly emerged from a thickly-wooded portion of the forest into a glade where the foresters had assembled.

"A lusty band, truly," said the Knight, in undisguised admiration. "Report has not belied thy fame, Robin."

"It is a miracle, then," said the Outlaw, dismounting, and motioning for one of the foresters to take the Knight's horse, "a wondrous miracle, for report is a common liar."

"It is so," said the Knight, "but in this instance it has spoken truly."

"Come hither, Much," Robin said, "thou art fleet of foot; hie thee to thy fair cousin, and bid her for Our Lady's love, send by thee a kirtle and all garments befitting a maiden to wear."

"Body-o'-me!" said the grinning Little John, "heard ye that, Friar? Our master is about to forsake the Lincoln green for maiden's garb. Ho! ho! ho!"

The fat Friar and Little John were well matched; both were full of quiet humour, both were troubled with thirsty throats, and both could stand a bout at quarter-staff with any three of the band, Robin Hood and Allan-a-Dale excepted.

"Thou'rt jealous, thou fat ox," said the Friar, "because thy body would not go inside anything less than twenty yards of cloth."

"Thou barrel with arms and legs," retorted John, "thinkest thou thy paunch would go in less than a——a murrain on the knave, what's that ?"

One of the foresters who was trying the strength of a new bow a few yards behind the Friar, bent it until the ends met.

The wood was dry, and when thus doubled it split, and one half flew from the man's grasp and struck the fat Friar on his shaven crown.

He jumped to his feet and gathering up his gown started in pursuit of the forester who, as soon as he was aware of the mischief he had done, took to his heels.

"Ho, ho! Body-o'-me!" roared Little John. "Well done, Will; use thy legs, Friar—ho, ho! trounce the knave, I saw him hit thee on purpose."

The latter portion of his speech, as may be supposed, was uttered when the Friar, in spite of his obesity, caught the luckless Will by the collar, and began to shake him.

The forester resented this attack by belabouring his priestly assailant with the broken half of the bow.

The young Knight, in spite of his trouble, could not help joining in the uproarious mirth.

"Come, Sir Priest," said Robin, "thou wilt be set down by our friend as but an ungodly son of the church. I'm sure thy patron saint never used his fists as thou hast done."

"My patron saint," answered the Friar, rubbing the bruise upon his skull, "never had his saintly temper tried as that knave has tried mine. Relics of St. Anthony! but my pate feels as though I had been used for a battering ram."

"Ho, ho, ho!" laughed Little John. "Friar, the bruise on thy skull does not match thy nose."

"How so, thou grinning thief?"

"Because, thy nose is red and the bruise on thy skull is blue."

"I'll give thee one to match."

The Friar snatched a quarter-staff from a heap of these weapons and made a rush at John, who nimbly stepped back, and putting out his foot, upset the priest, and his nose coming in contact with the staff, caused a crimson stream to make its appearance.

"Paint thy skull with it," said Little John, as he took to his heels to escape his companion's threats. "Paint thy pate, fat priest, and it will match thy snout."

The Friar gave chase, but Little John had obtained a good start, and after he had led the fighting priest thrice around the glade, he stopped.

"A truce," he said as the Friar, panting and out of breath, came towards him, "a truce, valiant Friar, and we'll drain a cup of Rhenish to thy reverence."

Next to fighting, Friar Tuck loved drinking, therefore, under the circumstances, as John had cried a truce, he set down the staff.

"A cup of Rhenish," he said, "after that race, to say nothing of the bodily injuries I have received, will not be amiss. Send for it, good John, and mayhap our master here will send for another to pledge this comely Knight, and our sweet self."

"Hie thee to our stores," Robin said laughing; "hie thee, Will Scarlet, but have a care, lest thou art tempted to touch the liquor."

"Not a drop, master," said Will; "unless, mayhap, the tankards may be filled too near the brim, then it would be unfair for me to spill such good liquor in the carrying."

"Now Much, haste to thy fair cousin," Robin said, "and give her the message thou knowest of, unless the bawling of these knaves has driven it from thy head."

"Not a word have I lost," said Much; "thy message shall be taken, and that part thou hast forgotten."

"Go to, knave, go to."

Will Scarlet came up at this moment, and by the appearance of the measures, the sewer had either not well filled them, or Will had prevented the loss in carrying.

"A malison on thy thirsty throat," said John, as he looked into the tankard. "I believe thou wouldst swill at any hour of the day."

"A plague, take thee," said the Friar, when he looked into the measure Will gave him; "were it not that my words would be useless with such an unbelieving knave, I would excommunicate thee with bell, book, and candle. As John sayest, thou wouldst indeed swill at any hour. A shame upon thee, I say."

"I drink to thy reverence," said Little John; "also to thee good Knight and my Master here; I also drink to Little John, the best yeoman here present."

"I drink to thee in return," said the Friar; "I also drink to our master, Bold Robin, and the comely Knight, and better than all, I drink to the saintly Friar Tuck, a true and good son of the church, who, may St. Anthony keep from harm."

The tankards went up to their mouths, and when they left there was not a drop in them.

There was a roar of laughter as the Friar and John looked comically into the measures, then at each other.

"Body-o' me!" said the giant; "thou hast a swallow!"

"A swallow!" retorted the priest; "by the relics of my patron Saint, that were but a draught for a fly! I scarcely felt it."

"By St. Hubert!" said John, "a drop of water on the dry sands of a desert would be as much good as that draught to my thirst! Out upon thee, thou thief, or I will crack thy skull with this measure."

Will Scarlet retreated.

"Come hither, George-a-Green," said Robin; "thou art fleet of foot, hie thee towards Nottingham Castle, and bring with thee a page thou wilt find there."

"Stay, good forester," said the Knight, "and I will give thee a description of the boy. He is slight of build and garbed in green velvet; thou wilt further know him by his long, fair locks, which hang far below his shoulders; haste thee, and a silver mark shall be thy reward."

The forester left, and Robin, with the handsome knight, seated themselves beneath the trysting tree and began to converse of matters which drew their attention from the somewhat rough practical joking of the merry foresters.

They were disturbed in their conversation by the sound of a bugle.

"From Nottingham side," Robin said; "ah! the Abbot's ransom!"

Robin's surmise was correct, for a fat and jolly monk, whom he recognised as having been at the debauch in the refectory, made his appearance, between two of the foresters who had been out on sentry.

ROBIN HOOD,

AND THE OUTLAWS OF SHERWOOD FOREST.

A WINGED MESSENGER.

"Greet thee all," said the monk; "which of this good company is Bold Robin Hood?"

"I am he," said Friar Tuck gravely; "deny it not, sir priest, or I'll flay thy hide!"

"Thou!" said the monk; "then Robin is a show for men to laugh at! I had always heard of him as being comely, and thou art far from being——"

No. 11.

"Reach me that staff, John," said Friar Tuck; "relics of St. Anthony! but I will teach this fellow a due respect for——knowest thou who I am, Father Glib-of-Tongue?"

"Aye, right well, a lusty thief art thou, who——"

"Ashes of the d——, I mean St. Anthony, that staff, I say John——"

"Peace!" said Robin, coming forward. "I am he thou seekest."

"Ah!" muttered the priest; "the very knave who brought such scandal upon our order. So thou art Bold Robin?"

"I am Robin Hood of Sherwood."

"Right gladly do I greet thee," said the priest; "and right glad I am to bear a loving message from my master."

"Unless I mistake much," thought Robin, "this fair speech is but all the shaven rascal has brought; then he added, "the Lord Abbot's message, holy father, I listen."

"He greets thee well," said the priest; "and bid me say the money due from him to thee, surpasses his power to pay: but he will, when the tithes are gathered, send thee it in full, with a fair and just interest for the time thou hast to wait."

"When are these tithes due, holy father?"

"To-morrow at noon," said the unsuspicious priest, "at that hour two of the brethren will go forth to collect them."

"And thy master will pay me then."

"On the noon of the day following, good Robin, for it will take until nightfall for our brethren to collect them."

"Be it so, I will wait until the time thou namest, but mark me, not one hour later; conduct this holy man to the confines of the forest."

"Friar," whispered John to Friar Tuck, "what think ye of waylaying these priests, and taking the tithes."

"A goodly notion," grinned the priest, "I am with thee, John, an' we will baste their hides into the bargain, for I love to thrash a fat monk, John."

"It's a miracle, then," cried Little John, "thou dost not thrash thyself full often."

"I do, John, for do not the rules of my order enjoin scourging, fasting, and severe mortification of spirit."

"Aye," answered the forester; "but dost thou keep to these rules?"

"Ask thyself; last Friday was a day of penitence——"

"Thou knave, I found thee drunk in the ash-grove that very night, and had to carry thee to thy bed!"

"Hear the heathen!" said the friar, lifting his eyes piously upwards; "thou thief, I was overcome by the severe scourging I had given my poor body when you found me."

"Body of St. Hubert!" exclaimed John; "did I not find three black bottles—each had held a quart, I'll warrant?"

"A quart of water, John, for I filled them myself from the well."

"Thou lying hypocrite! I put them to my nose, and they had the true aroma of the wine which they say comes from beyond the Rhine! Out upon thee for a hypocrite! out upon thee, I say!"

"Aye," retorted Friar Tuck, "out upon thee, I say; for hadst thou not thought the bottles yet held enough of the good liquor water, thou wouldst not have stooped to have picked them up."

Little John laughed; the Friar had spoken the truth, for John had fully expected to have found something worth drinking in one out of the three, and so great was his disappointment that he bumped the Friar's head against the branches of the trees, as he bore the saintly man to his hut in the forest.

Next morning, when the friar awoke he had a splitting headache, which he attributed to the strength of the wine, instead of the raps his skull had received, when he lay like a log across Little John's shoulders.

It would have required a very strong wine to have effected either Little John or Friar Tuck's brain, for they were the hardest drinkers in the band, and there were many who could boast of doughty deeds in this respect, for in those days a man who could drink well was esteemed, nay more than a sober self-denying man.

CHAPTER XXXIII.

THE FAIR PAGE.

Robin set his horn to his mouth,
    And blew a blast full good,
That was heard by all his merry men
    Far down within the wood.
I hear my master, said Little John,
    And they ran as they were mad.

WHEN George-a-Green returned he was accompanied by the knight's page, a youth of such handsome features and small limbs, that it was hard at first to believe that he was of the sterner sex.

"Well, boy," Robin said, "art thou disposed to serve thy master in all things?"

"To the death," the page answered, "if he needs it; for my life is Walter Henwulf's."

"The saints forefend," Robin said, "that we should need such a proof of thy devotion. All we shall require now will be a ready tongue, a bold heart, and a watchful eye."

"For the first of these the boy said, "I can warrant I possess, or I would not have so often been termed malapert; for the second, it behoves me not to speak; and for the last, I have eyes that fail not to notice all things that may pass before them."

"I will speak for the boldness of his heart," said the young knight; "for he has followed me with sword and buckler through the Paynims' ranks, and many a haughty Moslem crest has been brought to the dust by yon stripling's hand."

"It needed not thy word, Sir Knight," Robin said, "to speak of this, for there is written in the boy's fearless eye that which tells he will yet make a name, where doughty deeds and strong arms are needed."

The boy blushed at these words.

"Dost thou fear," Robin said, "to enter the castle outside of which thou hast been watching?"

"I fear not to do so, Sir Forester; but I wot there will be little good come of it, for I have been well marked by the crossbowmen on the towers—so well that every knave, I'll warrant, knows the escutcheon embroidered upon my breast as well as they know their greasy buff jerkins."

"This will matter but little," the Outlaw said, "if thou goest as I wish. What thinkest thou of wearing a hood and kirtle?"

"To dress as a maiden, Sir Outlaw?"

"Aye, boy, a skirt and thy fair face will be a passport to the inside of Nottingham Castle."

"I am willing, Sir Outlaw, but the saints

preserve me! how am I to answer the Sheriff should he address me in the words of love?"

"Thy readiness of speech must carry thee out of that," Robin said; "thinkest thou it can?"

"It will go hard with me if it does not."

"Aye," laughed the young knight, "thy tongue will have altered strangely if it has forgotten to help thee from greater difficulties than this."

"It has not forgotten," said the boy. "So my master be not afraid of losing thy page because his tongue hath lost its cunning. Now, Sir Forester, what plan am I to follow?"

"But a simple one, boy," Robin answered. "I will lend thee a palfrey, and one of my merry men shall attend thee as thy servant; and when the evening shadows come upon the earth, hie thee to the castle. Tell the warder thou hast lost thy way; he will admit thee: then thou must try and find out what are the contents of the sealed letter the man-at-arms brought from London with the Earl. Whilst thou art doing this, the man will find out the chamber where the Earl is confined."

"So far," the boy said, "thy plan is of promise; but concerning my leaving the castle, that has not been mentioned."

"Thou wilt leave to-morrow at matin song, and hie to the Greenwood with all thou mayest have learnt."

"Aye," said the page, "if this Sheriff, who, I am told, likes well a comely face, will let me depart."

"If thou art not back by the noon-time, thy safety shall be my care."

"Sufficient," said the page. "I am ready to do thy bidding. Where shall I find the kirtle and hood of which thou just now spoke."

"It will be here anon," Robin said. "Until then, go with this holy friar; he will not only confess thee, but will find a choice nook of venison pasty and a goblet of wine to cheer thy heart."

"Of which dost thou stand most in need," Friar Tuck gravely asked, "the cup of wine and nook of pasty, or the ghostly comfort which mine office permits me to give to such as are weary at heart?"

"Of which of these things dost thou most practise thyself, holy father?"

"Meanest thou the ghostly comfort and the good things of this life?"

"I do, reverend father."

"The ghostly comfort, fasting penalties, and scourgings imposed upon mine order I pass my life in; yea I do these things every hour."

"Thou mayest do so," the page said, "but I, being fonder of the good things of this life, prefer a cup of Rhenish and a nook of pasty before the rigours of thine order."

"Such is the thought of the giddy world," Friar Tuck said, lifting up his hand in pious zeal. "Oh! that it should be so."

They reached a secluded part of the forest, and seating themselves at the base of a large tree, awaited the coming of the man whom the friar had sent for the refreshments.

He soon returned, and much to Friar Tuck's inward disgust, brought only a small goblet of wine with him.

"This fair youth," said the Friar, "is sorely athirst, hie thee back, good forester, and bring another measure of this good liquor."

"Nay," said the page, "this will be more than sufficient for me."

"Thou art wrong, boy," said the fat Friar hurriedly; "thou wilt suffer the thirst of all who eat of venison pasty. It is for thy good I speak."

"Very well; bring the wine, good forester."

Friar Tuck's mouth watered when he saw the boy sipping the rich-juice, and he was cudgelling his brain to invent an excuse to taste the contents of the goblet.

This did not take him long.

"Fair youth," he said, "is that wine of the best, for these foresters have a knack of bringing wine which is not fit for such lips as thine."

"It is of good strength and sweet flavour, reverend father."

"Ah, sweet flavour, I could have sworn it. Reach me the goblet, I will soon tell thee if it is the wine I spoke of."

The boy handed him the cup; and to his surprise the friar emptied it at a draught.

"As I thought," he said; "a plague upon the knaves, they would have poisoned thee. The saints be praised, I am doomed to suffer penalties, thus the drinking of this wine will do me no harm."

"Thanks, reverend father," the page said laughing, for he began to suspect the true character of the friar; "I hope the flagon I see yon knave drinking from behind the tree, is not of the vintage I——"

"Drinking! the knave tasting before he brings thee the cup!" exclaimed the friar. "Ashes of all the saints, but I will stop this scandal."

The priest ran towards the tree, his sandals making so little noise, that he came upon the forester in the very act of tasting the contents of the cup.

"How now, thou knave," he said, "is thy thirst of more consequence than our good name for hospitality.

The man was so astonished that he could not move until the friar snatched the tankard from his hand.

Then as though to avoid a thrashing, he took to his heels and bolted.

The friar looked into the tankard, which was nearly three-parts full.

"It is of the same vintage as the last," he muttered; "it will not do for this fair youth to drink too much, therefore, I must, in spite of all pains of the colic, drink a little of it."

He did drink until there was but only sufficient to cover the bottom of the measure.

This he took to Sir Walter's page.

"This ungodly knave," he said, "has left thee but little of the good liquor; had I not been fleet of foot there would not have been even this left."

"Thanks, reverend father, it is enough."

When the page had refreshed himself he wandered about the forest, and conversed with many of the archers.

He found the sentence of outlawry which was out against them caused their minds but little trouble.

He saw but little of his master during the day, for Sir Walter and Robin Hood were busy in the forest-hut, laying out plans for a general rising throughout the midland counties to throw off the Norman yoke.

When the sun began to disappear beyond

the trees, the handsome page was apparelled, in feminine garb, and mounted upon a pillion left the forest, attended by Allan-a-Dale, who was dressed as a serving man.

Robin Hood and the Knight followed them; but before they left, the Outlaw Chief gave orders to Little John to bring twenty men, and await his return in a wood near the town of Nottingham.

"John," said the fat friar, "my vows prevent me using weapons of steel; but as nothing has been said about a monk amusing himself by shooting arrows, I will go with thee, and should I feel in the mood to shoot, surely I am not responsible if my arrows are cleaving the air, and a Norman knave's body runs against a clothyard shaft."

"Of a surety thou art not," said Little John, "for thy bow is not bent to kill; it is thy pleasure to send a few arrows through the air, and if, as thou sayest, a Norman carcass stops thy shaft, the blame is to the Norman, not to thee."

"My mind is at ease, now, John, for thou knowest I would not do aught to bring disrepute upon my cloth."

"Out upon thee," said John, "for a lusty hypocrite!"

"The words of the scoffer," said Friar Tuck, meekly, "injure not the followers of so good a patron saint as mine."

Robin Hood and Walter Hanwulf had seen the page and Allan challenge the warder, and after a brief parley, they were both admitted.

The Forester and the Knight had been so intensely watching the page that they saw not the approach of the Sheriff and about twenty men-at-arms.

They had been chasing the deer, for a noble buck was being carried to the castle across a strong horse's back.

The Outlaw and his companion were about to move forward and address the Sheriff, but the latter forestalled them by riding forward.

"A fair day, Robin," he said, and a look of intelligence passed between him and the leader of the men-at-arms; "I greet thee well, and would ask what has brought thee from thy forest?"

"But little of harm, Sir Sheriff," the Outlaw answered; "this knight who has but lately returned from the Holy Land, took refuge with me yester-e'en, and to-day he could not leave without looking at the Castle of fair Nottingham."

The Sheriff bent a searching look upon the knight's features, but failed to glean any intelligence from the quiet, handsome face.

"Wouldst thy guest," the Sheriff said, deign to accompany me, he could then see the inside of the place which has so attracted his attention."

"I would gladly do so, Sir Sheriff," the Knight said, bowing; "but an oath I have taken prevents me from entering cottage or castle until I find a maiden who has been lost to me."

Robin Hood had noticed the look of intelligence which passed between the Sheriff and his chief man-at-arms; and he saw that during the preceding conversation the men had gradually closed around the knight and his companions, and now seemed as though awaiting the signal to fall upon them.

The Forester affected not to see this treacher-

ous movement, but he was on his guard, and, as though by mere chance, his right hand toyed with the silver tassel of his bugle.

"Well, Sir Knight," the Sheriff said, "I will not press thee to break thy vow, perchance thou mayest pass fair Nottingham again, then shall I be right well pleased to offer thee such hospitality as befits my station and thy rank."

"Gramercy, Sir Sheriff, for thy kindness!" said the Knight; "I shall not forget."

The Sheriff turned to Robin, and a gleam of malice shone in his eyes.

"I would ask thee to share my hospitality," he said, "for I owe thee many thanks for the good cheer thou gavest me, and the high honour in which thou sawest fit to send me from thy domain; but it would not be meet for an officer so high in the King's favour to ask an outlaw to his castle, but for this, Robin, I would show my courtesy for thy kindness."

"Gramercy," laughed Robin; "how can I express myself at such high honours being conferred upon me?"

"Although I cannot ask thee," the Sheriff said; "yet thou canst accompany us to the castle; my men here can take thee prisoner, and if thou makest thy escape after, it will not be known that I had such friendly feelings towards thee."

"By St. Herman of the Wold," said Robin, there is more in thy speech than its seeming fairness."

"Nay, Robin," said Geoffrey, "thou urgest me, and to prove this I will take thee to the Castle whether thou wilt or not."

He made a sign to his men as he spoke, and they attempted to close around the Outlaw.

Like a flash of lightning, Sir Walter Hanwulf's sword leapt from its sheath as he saw the treacherous Sheriff's intention.

Robin Hood was as quick with his blade, and the pair, standing back to back, checked the advance of the men-at-arms.

"Upon them, knaves," said Geoffrey de Lois, throwing off all concealment, "ten marks for the man who takes the Outlaw, and five for him who takes his companion."

"Not so fast, my masters," said Robin. "Unless thou art tired of life, keep out of reach of this blade, or that held by my friend, this comely knight."

The reward was worth obtaining; and the men-at-arms closed upon the gallant pair, but before a blow could be struck, the Outlaw placed his bugle to his lips and blew a loud blast.

CHAPTER XXXIV.

THE LADY ELFRIDA AND HER SERVING MAN

The first loud blast that he did blow,
He blew, both loud and shrill;
And Little John and Robin's men,
Came running o'er the hill.

"BODY-O'-ME!" said Little John, stopping short in an argument with the curtall friar, "dost thou hear that?"

"Aye," answered the priest, tucking up his gown, "it is our master's horn, and tells he needs our help."

"Follow me," said John, "string your bows, ye knaves, as ye run, and hark'ee, the man who is last will I thwack with as good a twig as ever grew on tree."

The foresters dashed from their covert, headed by the fat friar and Little John, and when they came in sight of their Chief, a most unsaintly oath came from the friar's lips.

He soon outstripped even Little John, and before they reached the men-at-arms, who were by this time pressing hard upon the Knight and Robin, the friar's quarter-staff could be heard ringing upon the soldiers' morions.

"Bones of the blessed Clothilde!" cried the friar, "I will absolve thee—aye, even without confession."

The advent of the fighting friar and Little John's men put quite a different complexion upon the affair, and the Sheriff, spurring his horse forward, made for the castle, followed by his men, and in such haste were they, that the horse with the fat buck across his back, fell into the foresters' hands.

> "Then they looked east, then they looked west,
> For their eyes they were so keen;
> But the sheriff and his company,
> Were no longer to be seen."

Foaming with rage at the failure of his plan, the Sheriff returned to Nottingham Castle.

He was met at the gate by Berthold, who, upon seeing his master's angry face, hung back.

"Well, sirrah," the Sheriff said, "what ails thee, that thou retreatest as though it was a sight to cause thee fear?"

"I crave thy pardon, good master," the man said. "I felt afraid lest I had done wrong during thine absence."

"What hast thou done?"

"Admitted strangers to the castle, good master."

"Ha, by my halidome! but thou shalt suffer——"

"I crave thy——"

"Silence, sirrah; did I not tell thee none were to cross the drawbridge since our prisoner came here?"

"Thou didst, master, but I thought there could be but little harm in giving shelter to a lady and her serving man."

"A lady! is she fair?"

"Of wondrous fairness, good master."

"Her serving man, where is he?"

"In the kitchen, for he is but a Saxon knave, whose breeding is not fit to permit him to sit with thy men-at-arms."

"Send for him hither."

One of the soldiers went for Allan-a-Dale, who approached the Sheriff in a shambling, loutish manner, and stared vacantly about him.

"Well, knave, what brought thee here?" the Sheriff said. "Answer me, and doff thy cap."

Allan looked more stupid than ever, and dragging his cap off, revealed an unkempt mass of red hair.

"My horse brought me here, an' please, your worship," he said, "how came you here?"

"That's not thy affair, fool, said the Sheriff, "so mind thy speech."

"Aye," Allan said, "that's the way; mind thy speech. What does your worship ask me?"

"Hold thy tongue."

"Aye, hold thy tongue, mind thy speech——"

"Fool!"

"Aye, fool. Well, my master, I wot I am a fool, or I would not, even for the love of my dear lady, have come here."

"Thy lady, who is she, knave?"

Allan grinned: fumbled with his cap, and put on such a loutish appearance, that the Sheriff could scarcely refrain from laughing.

"My lady?" he simpered; "that I must not tell thee, for she wants not to be known, and she gave me a silver mark not to tell."

"I will give thee two. So come tell me?"

"Not before all these men-at-arms."

"Thou art right; to the ramparts knaves, and keep good watch, lest the Earl of Mortimer's friends attempt a rescue."

The men-at-arms retired.

"Now knave," the Sheriff said; "here are two marks."

Allan pouched the silver pieces, and the idiotic grin upon his face deepened.

"Good master," he said, "thou wilt not tell the lady what I tell thee, for she is quick of temper, and the whip she carries would soon be placed across my back."

"Not a word, by my knighthood."

"Thy word is given, and I know the Norman knights when they swear by this will be true."

"Come, sirrah; thou art wasting time."

"I had forgotten, good master, that thy race are so impatient; now the Saxon lords and franklins are not so quick of blood——"

"A murrain upon thee and the Saxon dogs! speak only of thy lady, and tell why she has sought the shelter of Nottingham Castle?"

"For two reasons, worshipful sir, which, if thou wilt have patience, thou mayest hear."

"Patience! by my knighthood, thou wouldst try the patience of the blessed St. Ursula."

"Aye, like fire these Norman knights——"

"Wilt thou speak, fool?"

"I am speaking, good master, as fast as my tongue will wag."

"It will not wag much longer, if thou dost not mend thy speech. Come, of what quality is thy lady?"

"Of what quality, sir knight? she is of the purest Saxon blood; although she bid me, if I were asked, say she was but the daughter of a franklin."

"Ah! why this wish to conceal her real state. Dost thou know that?"

"But in part, good master; but in part."

"What is the part thou knowest?"

"I will tell thee; but mind thou must not repeat one word to my lady, for she is quick of temper; and once I can swear when a Knight Templar did utter words of love in her ears, she slit his face with her dagger."

"She must be a haughty dame."

"Thou mayest well say that——"

"To thy promise. Come, tell me all thou knowest."

"It is not much, but thou art welcome to it——"

"A malison upon the fool; am I to hear——"

"Good master, thou dost not give me time; for when the words come to my tongue thy fierce look frightens them away again."

"There, good fellow, I will be of more gentle speech."

"Gramercy for this; for thy looks and words have made me as hot as though I were basting the side of a bullock before the fire."

"I have told thee I will not do this more; now, here is another mark for thee, for thou art a good fellow."

"Eh, I will now tell thee all I know, Sir Knight; for thou art indeed a good and generous noble."

"I listen, good fellow."

"Well, Sir Knight, thou must know my lady, the Lady Elfrida——"

"The Lady Elfrida! yes, good knave."

"The Lady Elfrida is betrothed to a young knight, who has but just come from the Holy Land."

"Ha! but proceed with thy story."

"But she likes him not; for, truth to tell, my lady has more favour for the Norman knights than the highest of the Saxon nobles."

"By the Saints," said the Sheriff; "she has good taste, this lady of thine."

"Of that I wot not; although, truth to tell, there is more of grace in these knights of Normandy than in the best of our Saxon nobles."

"Thou art right; to thy story, good fellow."

"Thou must know, Sir Knight, this Crusader, when he came from doing battle for the sepulchre, he wished to wed my lady, and he sent a messenger to speak of his coming."

"I listen."

"My lady," Allan continued, "heard the man's words; then last night, after all had gone to their chambers, she came to me and bid me saddle her palfrey and my brown horse. I did this, Sir Knight, and, since the moon was in its full have we been in the saddle, and stayed not to eat, drink, or rest until thy warder most courteously gave us admittance to thy castle."

"Return to the kitchen, good knave, and make merry, and if thy lady is as fair as I have heard, thou mayest stay here some weeks."

"Fair!" the serving man repeated, "by the soul of Alfred, she is fairer than a carle's lips like mine could find words to tell."

"It is not fit thy tongue should wag of this matter. Hie thee to the kitchen; I will see with mine own eyes this lady of such great loveliness."

Allan-a-Dale shambled towards the servants' portion of the castle. When his back was turned towards the Sheriff, he stuck his tongue in his cheek.

"By the mass," he thought, "I know not how to keep from laughing outright at the Norman knave. Well, so far all has gone well. Now to find the chamber where the earl is kept."

When the Sheriff left the courtyard, Allan, in place of continuing his way towards the kitchen, turned suddenly and went towards the keep.

"If I am stopped by any knave," he thought, "I shall have but to say I have lost my way."

He shambled up a flight of stone stairs, and found himself in a corridor, from which there opened a number of doors.

"Vastly like prisons," thought Allan. "Ah! here comes a knave who will spoil my travels. I will hide."

One of the recesses enabled the forester to escape the notice of Berthold and two men-at-arms who entered the corridor from a staircase at the other end.

One of the men bore a large platter of eatables, the other, a flagon of ale, or wine—Allan could not see which.

They paused at one of the doors, and Berthold shot back the lock, and gave ingress to his men, who placed the food and flagon upon a rude table, then retired without exchanging a word with the occupant of the chamber.

Although the glimpse the forester obtained of the interior of the chamber was but momentary, he was enabled to discover the form of the proud earl, who, with fettered hands, was striding gloomily to and fro.

Allan watched the men descend the stone stairs, then he stepped cautiously to the door of the earl's prison, and tapped as loud as he dared with the hilt of the hunting knife he had concealed beneath his servitor's jerkin.

The door was of solid oak, and plated with iron both inside and out; thus, if the earl answered his summons he heard it not.

"By the mass," grumbled Allan "this door is thicker than the hides of the knaves who made it. Well, I cannot hold a parley with the good earl, so I must e'en do the best I can. By the Rood! I should like to know what is the best to do."

Looking about him in search of a cue to guide him in the laudable object he had in view, Allan saw a small loophole.

"The very thing," he said; "let me see, there are four doors from this œillet; each room has a place for the admission of light. Now, if I can find a tree, a stone, or aught of like nature opposite this, my task will be easy."

Scrambling up to the loophole, he noticed an object directly in front of the aperture.

It was a blasted tree, of gigantic size, and one Allan well knew.

"By the Rood," he chuckled; "better and better; now let me quite understand, the Earl's prison is four loops from the right of this; ah! but if I stand with my back to the tree it would be four from the left."

He cut a small cross on the back of his left hand.

"I shall not forget now," he said; "the fourth chamber from this cross, when my back is against the trunk of yon tree; now, methinks I had better find my way to the kitchen and court the favour of the fat butler, who, if all Little John and Will Scarlet says is true, keeps a barrel of good October in the cellar for those he loves."

The forester's keen scent led him to the kitchen, for there welled upward from those regions a savoury smell of roast meats and tempting, tantalising stews.

When the supposed lady was conducted by the major domo to the room where the Sheriff was in the habit of receiving his visitors, she watched the pompous servant strut from the chamber.

He no sooner had taken his effulgent person out of hearing, than the page took a most unmaidenlike stride across the room, and quietly shot a small brass bolt into its socket.

"Secure from interruption," the page thought, "unless there are any secret doors behind the tapestry—I'll try."

He did so with the hilt of his dagger, and, satisfied that he should be secure from interruption, the boy began to search among a pile of papers, which were upon a table, and evidently left by the Sheriff not long before the arrival of the knight's page.

A cry of joy came from his lips when he caught sight of a packet, with the Royal seal hanging from it, and quickly folding the document, he concealed it beneath his flowing drapery.

He had only time to do this, when the major domo knocked at the door.

The page quickly slid the bolt back, and the pompous head-servant, followed by two serving men, entered the chamber.

The men brought a huge tray of choice viands and rich wines, and a silver dish of rose-water for the lady to cleanse her fingers after she had partaken of a meal a Sybarite would have envied.

"In the name of my master, the high and puissant Geoffrey-de-Lois, by command of the King sheriff of the shire of Nottingham, I bid thee welcome, fair lady."

He backed out of the chamber after this flourish, and the boy, laughing heartily, attacked the good things before him.

He had only time to finish his meal, when the door opened, and the Sheriff, bowing very low, entered the chamber.

CHAPTER XXXV.

A WINGED MESSENGER.

What wilt thou give me, said the Sheriff,
In ready gold or fee,
To help thee to thy true love fair,
And deliver her unto thee ?

THE boy's graceful inclination of his body, the look of modest confusion, and the partially turned aside head, was a consummate piece of acting, and would have done credit to a modern follower of Thespis.

The Sheriff bent very low in acknowledgement of the lady's presence, and with true Norman gallantry, said—

"Welcome, fair lady to my poor castle, and if thou needest protection, the lance of Geoffrey de Lois is at thy service."

"Thanks, Sir Knight," the lady replied ; "but I would not imperil thy life. I am but a humble maiden, and not of sufficient rank to have a warrior do battle for me."

"Lady," the Sheriff said, "thy beauty would give thee precedence above all the dames, and there are many fair ones at our court."

The lady blushed.

"I flatter thee not," the Sheriff continued. "I speak but as a knight whose vows hold him to aid the weak and oppressed. Speak, lady, wilt thou avail thyself of my good right arm ?"

"Sir Knight," she said, "again I thank thee ; but I dare not avail myself of thy kindness. I sought only the protection of thy castle for a few hours ; grant me this, and I will go on my way to the Abbess of Kirkless Priory, who is a kinswoman of mine."

"To Kirkless, fair maiden—do I read thy intent aright—to seek the cloister ?"

"It is even so. What else can aid me in this my hour of need ?"

"Maiden, I am learned in the world's ways. Canst thou confide to me thy secret, that I mayest guide thee ?"

"I have but little to tell, Sir Knight ; but that little is sufficient to fill my heart with woe."

"So young," the Sheriff said ; "yet so sad. I pray thee conceal nothing, fair maiden ; and thou shalt have my advice as though thou wert my sister."

"Thou must know, then, Sir Knight," she said, "I was betrothed to a youthful warrior who went to the holy land to fight for the blessed sepulchre."

"A fair field, lady, for thy youth to earn his spurs."

"So I am told. But during his absence there came a palmer who reported the knight as slain. I mourned him, and my sire, when my grief had somewhat abated, brought to our dwelling an old noble, who made overtures for my hand."

"Ha and thou ?"

"I hated the man my sire had chosen for me ; and upon the day we were to have been wedded there came a minstrel to my chamber, and from him I heard my true knight yet lived."

"It was sad he did not bring thee word himself."

"Alas, he could not, he was but crossing the seas ; I feigned illness after this, and prayed for the return of my betrothed, but he came not ; and my sire, no longer brooking the delay, bade me prepare for the hateful nuptials."

"Thy sire's heart," the Sheriff said, "must have been of stone."

"He is harsh, Sir Knight, yet I bethink me now, had I told him all he would have relented."

"Thou didst not tell him, then."

"Not one word."

"That was a pity ; yet, peradventure, he had pledged his word to the noble, and could not save thee."

"I fear it was as thou sayest. Well, Sir Knight, the morn came that was to see me a bride, but ere any of the household were astir I aroused my serving man and we left my sire's roof."

"Thou hadst not seen thy true knight, then ?"

"Alas, no."

"Dost thou think he has crossed the seas yet ?"

"Of that I know not."

"Canst thou describe him to me, for I have seen many followers of the cross who have of late returned from doing battle with the Infidels."

The lady drooped her head.

"I fear my poor description," she said, "will not be any great service ; he is fair, Sir Knight, wondrously fair, and bears that look of the true Saxon descent which would single him out from an army of Normans."

"Ha!" thought the Sheriff ; "the very knight I saw with that cut-purse Robin Hood. By the mass! I will soon have an opportunity to repay him for the ready aid he gave the forester."

"Hast thou," she said, "seen aught to resemble my true knight among those who have of late returned from the Holy Land ?"

The Sheriff reflected before he answered.

He did not know for a moment which would be the best course to pursue, whether to answer in the affirmative, and endeavour to persuade her to stay in the castle, or whether to advise her to go on to Kirkless.

He decided upon the latter plan, for he justly argued she would be entirely out of sight when once passed the Priory gates, and as he was a personal friend of the Lady Abbess, he could gain admittance, and work out a plot which had flashed to his brain during the preceding conversation.

"None, lady," he said, "have I met to answer thy description; but as every day beholds fresh arrivals from the Crusade, there is hope yet for thee.,'

"Oh, sayest thou so. My heart fills with joy at thy words."

"May thy heart be a true prophet of the joy in store for thee. Believe me, lady, I will do my devoirs as a true knight to find thy absent love."

"Thanks, Sir Sheriff, thanks; may the saints be good to thee and thine."

"Gramercy, fair lady, for thy wishes," he said. "Now that I have heard thy story, I will, if thou should'st wish, tell thee how I should advise thee to act."

"Whatever thou advisest, I will faithfully follow."

"It is this fair lady. When thou art tired of my poor castle, hie thee to Kirkless Priory, and await the coming of a messenger from me before thou takest of vows which will condemn thee to a life such as one of thy loveliness should'st shun."

"I will follow thy directions. Sir Knight; I will await thy messenger at Kirkless, and I shall watch the sun rise and set with my heart fluttering between hope and fear—hope that thou mayest find my true and brave knight—fear that he may have gone to the bottom of the sea."

"Let hope be thy guiding star, lady. I will soon send thee news of all ships that have brought their burden safely back to England."

"Again, thanks, Sir Knight. Now, as my palfrey has rested, I will leave the castle, for we have a long road to pass over before Kirkless towers are seen over the trees."

"It is not meet, lady, thou shouldst go alone? I will escort thee——"

"Nay, not for worlds, Sir Knight. I shall travel safely with my serving-man, who, though but of little wit, is a good and stout yeoman."

"I yield to thy wish, fair maiden; thy palfrey shall await thee by the time thou hast donned thy hood and cloak."

The Sheriff left the chamber in order that the maiden should resume her travelling garb; and when he was gone, the lady burst into a fit of laughter.

"Hoodwinked," she said; "ha, ha, ha! Most puissant Knight, thou art over-matched by a Saxon page."

The Sheriff, as he descended to the courtyard, thus held converse with himself:

"So this fair beauty loves this knight I have so much reason to dislike. By the Rood! how well my speech suited the occasion; and she deems me the more thoughtful because I bid her seek the priory. Sister Agatha is a comely dame, and not proof against a bribe: this fair one, once in her hands, I can look upon her as mine; by the mass, but she is fair, wondrously fair. A malison upon the knave—her serving man; his speech was either to misdirect me, or the wittol's brains would not give him better knowledge."

He reached the courtyard, and despatched one of the grooms to fetch the horses; another to find the serving man.

Allan-a-Dale appeared; his face flushed, and his gait unsteady, from the close acquaintance he had made with the Sheriff's ale.

"How now, knave," the Sheriff said; "is it thus thou appearest to ride forth with thy lady?"

"Appearest, Sir Knight! By my Saxon ancestors, I appear as a good yeoman should when he has been pledging the health of the lord of this castle. By the saints! it is not often a poor serving man tastes such liquor as thou keepest."

"Go to for a drunken carle; canst thou sit thy horse."

"Sit my horse! aye, Sir Knight, once on his back, the foul fiend himself would find it hard to drag me off."

He climbed into the saddle as he spoke, and made the animal course and prance about the courtyard, much to the danger of the toes of all who stood near.

The Sheriff saw the man was capable of managing his steed, and was about to give him a little advice about his duty to the lovely lady, when the page appeared.

His face was concealed in the silken hood, and the Sheriff went forward and assisted the Lady Elfrida to mount.

"Farewell," he said, kissing the gloved hand held out to him; "be of good cheer; my messenger will soon be at Kirkless Priory with the news thou art waiting for."

"Farewell, Sir Knight, may the saints keep thee from harm. Come, thou knave (this to Allan) the ale thou hast drank has gone to thy face."

The lady and her lusty servant rode over the drawbridge, and when they were upon the green sward the horses quickened their pace, and soon bore them out of sight.

Plunging into the wood, which separated the forest from the castle grounds, mistress and man gave vent to peal after peal of laughter.

The echoes of their merriment brought an answer, in a high, but cheery, voice;

"Body-o'-me!" said the voice: "but thou art merry. Hast brought glad tidings?"

"Aye, John," said Allan; "great tidings. Where is our master?"

"Where every good master should be," the lieutenant said ruefully, "he's at dinner."

"And thou away; shame upon thee, John."

"Away! Bladebone of St. Hubert! our master sent me to look after thee, so hurry in, or not a scrap of meat, or a drop of wine will be left."

Allan and the page trotted through the bridle path, and Little John, anticipating the loss of a dinner, struck through the brushwood and arrived at the glade, where the Chief and his followers were seated, some minutes before Allan and the page made their appearance.

"A place for hungry John," said the fighting friar; "a place, my merry men, or he will eat one of ye."

ROBIN HOOD,

AND THE OUTLAWS OF SHERWOOD FOREST.

THE SHERIFF'S DISCOMFITURE.

"A place!" grumbled the forester, looking savagely on an empty pasty dish which stood before the friar; "a place for what? bare bones and empty platters. A murrain upon thy gormandising, thou fat friar, not to hold me one little nook of as fine a pasty as ever was baked in Sherwood."

"Aye, thou art right," said Friar Tuck folding his hands over his stomach; "aye, and for the matter of that, as fine a pasty as was ever ate beneath the greenwood tree."

"So it would seem, thou fat-paunched thief; but, by the Blade-bone of the——"

The appearance of Allan and the page stayed the forester's speech, and Robin and the knight, jumping to their feet, ran forward to meet the pair.

"What news?" the Outlaw asked; "come, tell unto me."

The boy drew from beneath his dress the royal parchment, and handed it to Robin, who read the clerkly handwriting aloud:

"*HENRY, BY THE GRACE OF GOD KING OF ENGLAND, &c.*

"*To our trusty cousin, Geoffrey de Lois, Sheriff of Nottingham, greeting. By these presents know ye that one Roger, Earl of Mortimer, is an attainted traitor, and, should there be a rising among the malcontents in the shire over which thy rule extendeth, at once bring Roger, Earl of Mortimer, to the block; should the malcontents remain at peace, keep him a close prisoner until thou hearest our Royal will.*

"*Given under our seal, at the Palace of London.*   "HENRY, REX.*"

"So," Robin said; "this is the reward a king would bestow upon one whose good lance set him upon the throne!"

"Aye," said the knight; "such is the gratitude of princes."

"Come hither, Much," Robin said; "hie thee to my hut and fetch me a goose-quill and an ink-horn."

Much ran off upon his errand, and when he returned, Robin cut off a piece of the parchment with his dagger, then, placing it against a tree, wrote a few words.

"Where is Allan?" he asked, when he had done this; "I heard thy voice preaching that thou knowest the chamber where the earl is confined."

"I do, Master."

"Is it beyond an arrow's flight to reach the window?"

"For a Norman cross-bowman it is, good Master, but not for a Saxon archer."

"I am glad thou sayest so; take thy bow and put this packet upon a grey-goose shaft, and send it inside the Earl's chamber; but, harkee, knave, have a care lest thou sendest the arrow through the Earl."

"I will do my best, Master; no man can do more."

Allan-a-Dale took the packet, and selecting a stout bow he left the forest.

"Thou hast chosen a good messenger," the knight said, "and a swift one."

"Thou art right," said Robin, "my winged messengers are sure and trusty, whether they are sent to friend or foe. Now, Sir Walter, let us leave these knaves to roar out their roistering songs, we have matters of more import in hand than to listen to them."

The knight followed the Outlaw Chief to a secluded part of the forest, and for upwards of an hour they walked to and fro in low and earnest conversation.

CHAPTER XXXVI.

THE TWO MENDICANTS.

Stand, holy frir; two mendicants
Crave thy gifts of charity.
'Tis nobler much to give than take,
Then listen as we supplicate,
For two poor beggars we be—
Beggars poor be we.

"BODY-O'-ME!" quoth Little John as he leaned against a tree, "and gramercy, too, but they be long a-coming."

"Thy mouth waters, John, at thoughts of the fat pouches they carry. Is it not so?"

"Hunger and thirst sore press me. By my oath, they shall pay interest for this unseemly tarrying."

"Nay, friend John, thou lackest charity; peradventure they but tarry to rest their burdens."

"I warrant they'll be light enough when I lay my hand upon them."

"Hist!" exclaimed the friar; "dost hear they come to our calling with discreetness?"

The tinkle of bells announced the party as close at hand, on which Little John and his companion trolled out the following ditty:—

Let thy pity loose, good sirs;
Help us! earn our prayers.
Thine alms we crave,
The poor to save.
Thy pity then vouchsafe,
Good sirs, us to relieve;
Help us! earn our prayers.

"Out upon thee! knaves; thy song is like thyselves—of poor account," said the foremost monk as the pair of sturdy mendicants advanced.

"Hunger and thirst leave little room for song. We crave thy help, holy father," answered Friar Tuck.

"By the saints! yon fellow's countenance but ill accords with his condition. Didst ever see such a round paunch as he carries?" And both the monks laughed outright.

"'Twill go ill with thee, an' thou keepest not a discreet tongue in thy head," growled Friar Tuck with bated breath in allusion to the remark of the last speaker.

Little John smothered his laughter as best he could, for he was tickled at his companion's discomfiture.

"We have travelled far, holy fathers, and are sore pressed by want. Bestow on us of thy plenty, but a groat," said the friar.

"Not a stiver. Hark thee, sirrah, trouble us no longer else 'twill go ill with thee," was haughtily answered.

Placing himself in their front, Little John said:

"We have fairly begged, holy fathers, for Charity's sake, and thou refusest to listen. We demand now thy money. Give, else thy plight will be a sorry one."

"The saints defend us! but list to the knave's assurance! Knowest thou our condition, sirrah?"

"But too well, holy father. 'Tis few who know thee better," naively answered Little John.

"Thy conduct is made worse thereby. Go aside, churl, else the church's curse will smite thee sorely."

"A fig for all thy maledictions," answered Friar Tuck, placing himself beside his companion, and snapping his fat fingers as he bawled forth the following ditty:

Let them curse, and they will; 'tis no harm, sirs;
Only cowards and knaves mind hard words, sirs;
For a well filled purse, will lighten any curse,
Make us glad and none the worse.
'Tis no harm, sirs; let them curse, let them curse,
That we came specially to meet thee."

"'Tis well, too, that you should know, holy father——" spake Little John.

But before he could finish, Friar Tuck chimed in with:

"Aye, that it is. As we slept one appeared, telling us to take certain sums of money thou hast in thy possession; which same we mean to do."

The monks' countenances now began to fall most awfully.

It was easy to see that their situation was none of the pleasantest.

Getting down from the mule which he bestrode, one of them said:

"Search and welcome. See I withstand thee not."

"Well said; thou art a jolly fellow after all," said Little John, as he and Friar Tuck proceeded to look closely at the saddle-bags.

To their utter dismay and astonishment, the clatter of hoofs struck upon their ears; and on looking up, they perceived the other monk making off as fast as his beast would carry him.

"'Tis a scurvy trick," exclaimed the friar, as his fat carcass shook with rage; and dealing one blow of his stout sinewy arm to the traitor monk, he jumped on the mule, and hied him off in hot pursuit.

Little John followed with swift strides; but his speed was greatly hampered by fits of laughter.

Friar Tuck sat his mule so unsteadily, and bumped from side to side so comically, that Little John was fain to halt and laugh immoderately, albeit much against his will.

"Oh, for my good bow and a trusty shaft; then would I bring thee to a stand," exclaimed Little John, as the fugitive gained upon him.

Luck favoured the pursuers in their extremity.

Stumbling over some obstruction in its path, the beast threw its rider heavily.

When Friar Tuck came up, he found the monk insensible, from which state he was in no hurry to arouse him.

When Little John arrived, he was rejoiced to find the friar deeply engaged in counting out the contents of one out of several bags of money which lay at his feet.

"'Tis well worth the chase. By my halidom, but 'twill go hard but we pay ourselves for the holy fathers' discourtesies."

"Sawest thou ever such gold pieces? And see how bright the silver crowns are!" exclaimed Friar Tuck in raptures.

"'Twill more than repay the debt due to bold Robin," answered Little John.

"But look you, John, here is something you love right well."

"What mean you?"

"Wine, my little man, that maketh glad the heart of man."

And taking hold of a large leathern bottle, Friar Tuck placed it to his lips, and drank heartily.

"Body-o'-me!" growled Little John, "'twill be precious little of it my parched lips will suck, an' you proceed at that rate."

The portly friar thus admonished, ceased his suction, and handed the bottle over to his companion with a deep sigh, remarking:

"I am ever disappointed in the things I best love."

"Out upon you! for a swilling, round-paunched, hard-pated friar," said Little John, with a merry twinkle in his eye; "my work will soon be done, thanks to your thirst."

"Ah, ah! I never heard better," replied the friar, laughing.

But when he saw that Little John was inclined to suck out the wine to the very dregs of the bottle, his aspect underwent a change. His fingers clutched the air nervously, his lips compressed themselves, and he made sundry gestures of disapprobation, all of which Little John totally disregarded.

"Body-o'-me!" quoth the giant, as he lowered the black jack, "'tis fine. Drank you ever better?"

"'Twas precious little you left for me to pass an opinion upon," growled the friar, as he took up the bottle and applied his lips to it.

With an exclamation of disappointment, he threw it away from him.

"Look, you: you have overlooked this," exclaimed Little John, producing another bottle.

"I cry thee quarter, Master John," said the friar. "Bones of St. Hubert! but 'tis my first drink, I'd have thee know."

"I would fain, see, that it is fit for thy digestion first," said Little John, with a merry twinkle in his eye, and applying the bottle to his mouth.

"Hold, John! Hold! by the mass, you'll burst outright. Think of thy condition, sirrah."

"Ah! that's fine," answered the giant, as he handed the bottle to the expectant friar.

While he drank, Little John sang:

> "Rattle'm, rattle'm rig—
>   A monk, as fat as pig,
>   Got drunk as a lord,
>   Fell into a ford,
>   With his rattle'm, rattle'm rig.
>
> 'Help, ferryman!' the monk cried;
> 'Hie thee quickly to my side;
>   For the river is deep,
>   And I fear its sweep,
>   With my rattle'm, rattle'm rig.'
>
> 'Good monk, thou then may'st lie,
> And in the river deep may tie;
>   For thou art of a sort
>   That's not much worth,
>   With a rattle'm, rattle'm rig.'
>
> 'My curse,' quoth the monk,
> 'Will thee always keep in a funk.
>   No rest shalt be thine
>   To the end of time,
>   With my rattle'm, rattle'm rig.'
>
> So the monk was drowned in the river;
> And the ferryman walketh ever
>   Along its shore;
>   Wailing ever more,
>   With his rattle'm, rattle'm rig."

"Well sung, little man," said the friar.

"Well, let me drink, thou guzzle," answered Little John, as he laid his hand on the bottle. While he drank, the friar sang:

> "Good wine I'll swill,
> And drink my fill.
>   Who cares?
>
> Life is a vapour,
> And goes out like a taper,
>   With cares.

'Tis the merry twinkle
Takes out the wrinkle.
Who cares?

Wine makes us glad ;
Grief makes us mad
With cares.

Let the grape grow ;
Its juice bothers woe.
Who cares?

It makes those who die
In peace to lie,
Free from cares."

"We must be afoot, and that quickly," remarked Little John. "The night draws on apace."

"I'm of opinion, friend John," exclaimed the friar with a rather thick utterance, "that the world's going round."

"'Tis the wine in thy pate, rather," was the humorous reply.

"Out upon thee! By all the bones of the saints, thou blackenest my character past a bearing."

As he spake, the friar tumbled over the figure of the monk, who groaned heavily.

"A murrain seize thee, thou idle lout. Rise up, thou sluggard, and depart."

And suiting the action to the word, the friar seized the monk by the legs and dragged him apace.

"Thou art too rough a nurse, friend," said Little John, laying his arm upon the friar's shoulder.

"Thou errest.   My leechcraft is not at fault.   A rough arousing best suits drowsy folks."

"Nay ; let's try something gentler. Fetch hither the wine ?"

"If I do, may I be compressed into nothing. 'Twould be sheer waste, man."

"Robin would have speech of him, no doubt. 'Twere wise to bring him with us."

"A good thought, John ; a rare bit of philosophy. Ha! ha! thou wag ; thou wantest to find out the secrets of the cellar. Thou can'st not forget the rich juice thy paunch has swilled."

Applying the bottle to the monk's lips, he drank and revived.

"Where am I, good people ; and how camest I hither?"

"By crooked ways and cross purposes, my son," replied the friar with half-drunken gravity."

"I remember. 'Tis plain. The rents. Ah! I'm undone."

"Nay, nay, good friend, thy plight is not such an evil one, an' thou rightly knewest it," said Little John.

"Come, drink, my son," exclaimed Friar Tuck, handing the bottle towards him.

The unsteadiness of his hand caused it to tip, and his poor victim was deluged with wine.

This caused some little merriment, in which, however, the monk did not join.

Saddling the mule, which had not strayed far, the money-bags were carefully slung, and the party commenced its march.

Their coming was joyously hailed by all the band, who quickly thronged about them.

The sight of the money-bags was exhilarating,
and Robin specially commended Little John and the friar.

"But who is he?" the Outlaw asked, pointing to the monk.

"The gracious giver of this bounty," exclaimed Friar Tuck, mockingly pointing to the money-bags.

"Ah! I would have speech of him," exclaimed Robin ; "what ho, there, honest Will, lead hither yon poor woman."

Presently a forlorn-looking wench was led into the presence of the assembled company.

Anything more wretched than her appearance could not be conceived.

She was tattered and torn, dejectedly sad, and withal aged.

"Cast thine eyes upon this fellow of the cowl," said Robin to her, "and say if he is thy persecutor."

"My lord, 'tis he ; this very morn I had a home and comforts ; now am I the most desolate among women."

"Prithee explain, good father," said Robin with knitted brows ; "'tis surely not thine office to despoil the helpless women of their homes and shelter."

"Her rent was overdue. A distraint upon her goods and chattels recovered it."

"To the crown piece, and no more? speak truly, I warn you."

"'Twas ever customary so to act," was the answer, insolently given.

"'Tis false. The church has no such privilege. Extortionate dealings ill become its saintly character."

Then turning to the woman, Robin said, kindly and gently, "What was thy debt?"

"But five crowns when all was told, my lord."

"You sold her out for how much, fellow?" imperiously asked Robin of the monk.

"For what I got."

A sign from Robin brought a quarter-staff down on the saucy monk's shoulders, with a thwack which could be heard far and near.

The force of this strong argument was irresistible. It not only brought him to his knees, but also to his senses.

"Spare me, good sir!" he cried ; "I received twenty crowns for this poor woman's house and chattels.

Turning to Little John, Robin said—

"Pay her," — pointing to the woman — "twenty crowns, and five more for interest."

The money was given into her hand.

Falling on her bended knees she said :—

"May Our Lady protect thee! may the God of the poor befriend thee—keep thine enemies under thee—prosper thy ways, and give thee sanctuary at the last!"

"Amen, amen!" devoutly said several of the bystanders to the simple prayer.

"I thank thee, my good woman," replied Robin ; "thy prayers are too good for such as me."

Turning to Will Scarlet, he said :—

"Give her safe conduct through the forest."

To the monk he said :—

"Harkee, good father. If by any chance you e'er again molest her, thou and thine shalt suffer for it. An' she lacks her rent, I, Robin Hood, will pay for her."

Soon supper was spread on the greensward, and all hastened to do their devoirs by attacking the good thing before them.

But despite their evil repute, they tasted not until Friar Tuck had said grace.

"Sit down, man," said Robin to the monk. "Partake of our homely fare, nor think that the king's deer will mar thy digestion. Thou wilt find it good, I warrant ye."

The invitation was readily accepted, and soon the monk was doing his part of a hungry visitor right well.

The meal had nearly finished when a messenger arrived in haste, desiring audience of Robin.

"Tidings, sir, from Nottingham Castle. The Earl Mortimer dies by the gallows the morn after to-morrow."

"No such ill fate will befall him. Hie thee away and say Robin will be there *in time* Mark you, *in time*."

CHAPTER XXXVII.

THE SHERIFF'S DISCOMFITURE.

I love thee dearly, maiden fair—
I cannot say how dear:
Gorgeous apparel and costly array
Shall be thine. Then say me yea:
For, oh! but I love thee dearly.

But I've a lover other than thee,
And, oh! I love him dear—
His sweetest kisses are all for me,
And his presence is ever near:
For, oh! but he loves me dearly.

"LIST to me, sweet Marian: thou knowest how dearly I love thee. Relent, and be mine."

"'Tis idle, Sir Knight, thus to persecute me. Thou hadst mine answer, long ago."

"If thou knewest how madly I love thee! Night follows day, but to find me with thy sweet name on my lips, thy loved image in my heart!"

"A truce to such idle bantering, Sir Sheriff. Thou can'st ne'er be aught to me but distasteful."

"Methinks one of my degree should'st need not sue so humbly at thy feet."

"Then, why sue at all? Of a truth, thou art not wanted," replied Marian sharply.

"Ever thus haughtily repulsed," muttered the sheriff between his clenched teeth, "it shall not be; but I must dissemble for yet a little time longer."

"Thou art expectant. 'Tis bold Robin, no doubt, whose coming is so greatly solicited," he said with a covert sneer.

"E'en so. 'Tis a name to thy liking, I wot," replied Marian, with a malicious laugh.

"'Tis one derided and contemned by all good men. Thy fair fame receivest a stain therefrom."

A rich, maidenly blush mantled her cheeks: her eyes glanced a furious hate, her fine form upraised itself, as she threw back his scorn in his teeth:

"None but a dastard knight would thus speak to an unprotected maiden. Bethink thee of thine ignoble manner, and begone ere that Robin, thou so much contemnest, arrives to smite thee for thy foul tongue."

"Bravely spoken," said the sheriff, mockingly. "Thou lookest lovelier in thine anger than I before wotted of."

"And thou—— But 'tis idle to waste words on such as thou. Thy chastisement but tarries."

"Nay, fair Marian, be not so coy. Bethink thee we are alone. Robin comes not."

"And thou would'st lay so much as thy littlest finger upon me, thou would'st rue it. Back! I say, base fellow;" and Marian looked queenly in her wrath.

The sheriff was abashed. Virtue conquered vice.

"By my halidom! sweet Marian, thou art a rare wench. I but tried thy temper from mere wantonness. Believe me, thou hast in me too true a lover to harm thee in any wise."

"I fear thee not. Our Good Lady protects those that in her trust."

"Now, hearken, Marian. Robin, whom thou lovest, must be mine some day, and that before long. For thy sweet sake I'll protect him, give me but encouragement to hope."

"Sooner would I see Robin a-dangling from yon tree than buy his ransom at so foul a price."

"God wot thou art hard to please, sweet maid," the sheriff replied testily. "I brook thine insults with but little patience."

"'Tis thine own doing. Thou forcest thy company upon me, knowing full well the disfavour thou art held in."

"Dost know, proud wench, that Earl Mortimer is now my prisoner. How Robin's heart will ache when two morns more will see him die. Thinkest thou of these things when thou bravest my power and despisest my love."

"Earl Mortimer can die like a brave knight, an' it please Our Lady so to will it. Bold Robin knowest full well how to avenge a friend's death; of that no speech of mine need remind thee."

"Be not so cruel, else will my passion o'ermaster my reason."

"I've given thee too much licence of speech already, Sir Sheriff. A good morn to thee."

Marian turned to go.

The sheriff was quickly at her side.

"Unhand me, thou false sworn knight," she indignantly said, as he placed his arm on her shoulder.

"Nay, sweet maid, I shall taste of the nectar of thy sweet lips, and I be shot for it."

The next moment the sheriff was rudely thrown backwards.

George-a-Green stood facing him.

"How now, thou varlet, knowest thou my condition?" asked the sheriff.

"Thou art Nottingham's sheriff, and a bad man to boot."

"S'death, sirrah, thou shalt rue this. I will slit thy malapert tongue an' thou thus address me."

"Thou? thou king's minion," replied George-a-Green contemptuously. "I'll thrash thine hide till it is like unto a well-tanned one. This maiden requires thus much at my hands."

Furious with passion, the sheriff rushed towards him with naked sword and hot vengeance in his eye.

George's quarter-staff flew nimbly about his head for a moment, then descended with force on the sheriff's swordarm.

His weapon dropt.

The next moment he himself lay sprawling at the foot of a tree.

George placed his foot on his prostrate foe, and menaced him with his left hand.

"Robin, darling!"

"Marian, sweet love!"

The lovers were quickly locked in a close embrace.

The noise caused George to turn round unguardedly.

Quick as lightning, the sheriff seized his leg and cleverly upset him. Like an arrow from a bow, he sped away, ere Marian had time to explain the matter to Robin, who had looked on in astonishment.

Regaining his feet, George-a-Green hied him after the sheriff in good style. As he neared him he heard the sheriff utter a peculiar cry. Whinnying with delight came a finely caparisoned, fleet horse.

Mounting its back, the sheriff started off with the speed of the wind, and looking back defiantly at his pursuer, was soon out of sight.

When Robin heard from Marian's lips the story of the sheriff's insults, he ground his teeth with rage, and swore an oath of fearful import that vengeance he would exact from him.

"'Tis for my poor sake thou sufferest these unseemly rudenesses at his hands ; say, dearest, how can I ever repay thee for all this ?"

And Robin looked tenderly and lovingly into her upturned eyes, in which floated a liquid flood of love-light.

"By ceasing to think of them, my sweet Robin. Believe me, thy Marian can endure as well as love."

"True, brave-hearted, noble Marian! Troublesome times are with us. Better days may come ; my rightful patrimony may again be mine. Then, beloved, thou shalt shine as a star, resplendent in beauteous charms, in thy proper sphere !"

"I bemoan not my lot. Thou, Robin, dost ennoble any cause or station. More I crave not than thy love."

"It is thine, dearest ; could'st thou but see into my heart, thy name, sweetest, would there be found deep engraved."

"Thy tell-tale eyes dost this much disclose. 'Tis plain to thy Marian that she bears a place in her Robin's heart."

"But the sheriff—said he aught of Mortimer, my dear friend ?"

"Aye, that did he, and of evil import, too. Could aught of good pass such base lips as his ?"

"His life is imperilled, I wot."

"Of a surety. The third morn from this is not his on earth. So discoursed Nottingham's sheriff."

"'Tis the idle babble of a crazy pate. Fool! Not one hair of brave Mortimer's head will be harmed. Robin's word on that."

"My mind is greatly eased. 'Twere sad were so brave a knight to perish. Ah, me! 'twould be sad—oh, so sad !"

"Even now things are in training to encompass his deliverance. With mine own hand will I strike off his accursed chains, and Mortimer will once again be free."

Robin's handsome face lit up with enthusiasm as he uttered this speech, and his finely-formed head poised itself more firmly on his graceful neck.

"But here comes George-a-Green. What news, my good fellow? Hast he escaped ?"

"I burn with shame to tell it. He has ; and ere this is safely housed in his den. A murrain seize the villain !"

"His luck will not always stand him in such good stead. Mark me, Nottingham's sheriff shall rue this day."

"Put his baseness out of thy memory, Robin dearest," said Marian ; "else will it hamper thy free and generous nature."

"Have no fear, Marian. We crush the poisonous reptile under our heel, and scarce bestow a passing thought on its fate. Geoffrey de Lois is to me as such a one."

The pealing notes of a bugle horn were borne on the breeze.

"Hark! 'tis the signal. Fare thee well, Marian, love! God be with thee, sweetest!"

"One ardent embrace, one impassioned kiss, and Robin hied him off.

George-a-Green waited to attend Maid Marian.

———

CHAPTER XXXVIII.

ROBIN GOES TO THE CASTLE WITH HASTE.

> For I doth thee scorn,
> And all thy craven crew ;
> Such silly imps unable are,
> Bold Mortimer to subdue.

"'Twill but suit the moment for me to do as I have said," remarked Robin to the knight.

"It is a dangerous enterprise to thyself mostly. Consider the watch on the ramparts."

"Bethink thee, though, of the darkness of the night. By my halidom, I am eager for the risk, and deem the hours to go lazily by until it is attempted."

"Nobly said ; I'll be with thee hand and glove."

"Thanks, Walter, thine arm is a trusty one, pledged to hew down Norman swine. By my soul, but it will be something to make all Nottingham ring again, and the sheriff hide his diminished head with very shame."

"Of a verity this is well planned, and I doubt not of its proper execution."

"Doubt! I would as soon doubt myself. But harkee! hither strolls Little John. Beshrew me, but I like his voice ; dost not thou ? List!"

> "I have been in the forest, sir,
>   And a fair sight did I see:
> It was one of the fairest sights
>   That ever met my eye.
>
> Yonder I saw a right fair hart—
>   His colour is of green ;
> And a fine herd of seven score deer
>   Are with him to be seen.
>
> His antlers are so sharp, master,
>   I durst not shoot for dread.
> They've sixty points, or more—and I feared
>   I should be stricken dead.
>
> ' I make mine avow to God,' said the
>   Sheriff,
>   ' That sight I fain would see."
> ' Haste you thitherward, my master, dear,
>   Anon, and go with me."
>
> The Sheriff rode, and Little John,
>   Of foot he was so smart,
> And when they came before Robin—
>   ' Lo, here is the master hart !'
>
> Still stood the proud Sheriff ;
>   A sorrowful man was he.
> ' Woe be to thee, Reynold Greenleaf ;
>   Thou hast now betrayed me.' "

"Well carolled, by my knighthood—a likely ditty," said Robin's companion.

"John, this way; I would have speech of thee."

"I am ever at thy bidding, master," answered Little John.

"Not a trustier friend I wot of; as trusty as my own good sword—as true as my own good bow, John," and Robin laid his hand kindly on his shoulder.

"Thou honourest me too much, master mine, in thy speech. But this I know, for right royal love to thee I trow I can challenge any man."

"Without a doubt, John, man. But list! To-morrow night sees Mortimer free or me a prisoner."

"Body-o'-me! master, the latter may not be."

"I but put it to thee at a venture. I climb the wall; you and a trusty band remain within bowshot to cover our retreat. Let two good steeds be in waiting."

"'Twill be so, master."

"And harkee, John, a file hard as a dungeon door, biting as the north wind, must be mine, and a stout rope to boot."

"Good! by the bones of St. Hubert, all will go merrily!"

"Let twenty trusty men be picked for service under this, my friend (pointing to the knight), to lay away to the right as an ambuscade, in case the sheriff's men are drawn from their cover by your party. Hearest thou?"

"I do, master mine, and this will be the end of it :—

"The Sheriff fled home to Nottingham town—
　　He fled full fast away ;
And so did all the company—
　　Not one behind would stay."

"Ah, ah! friend John ; thou art a soothsayer. 'Twill be even so, and Our Lady will it not otherwise."

At this juncture a messenger came in haste seeking Robin.

"Good news I hope, lad," he asked ; "but say it, quickly."

"'Tis black news, Master. To-morrow at sunrise Earl Mortimer dies."

"How now. What sayest thou?" asked Robin, hastily, "speak again."

"Brave Earl Mortimer at sunrise dies."

"Thou art certified of that?"

"Too surely."

"What unseemly haste. But explain to me an' you can how this has been brought about."

"Berthold doubting the page's appearance, caused him to be watched. His coming hither betrayed him. He hies to the sheriff, and may I be excommunicated an' I ever saw man in such a rage as he."

"Haste, good lad, to the point, to the point."

"The steward suddenly bethought himself of the king's letter, but, lo, it was missing. With rage o'er mad, the sheriff hied him to the earl, and with hard words assailed him, calling him traitor, false knight, and other such unseemly names."

"And the Earl?"

"Struck him to the earth with his iron-girt hands, and e'en forced the breath out of his body almost."

"Brave Mortimer. But what then?"

"But what I've shown. The earl dies at sunrise."

"Thanks for thy despatch, good lad. Thou shalt be rewarded."

Then turning to Little John, he said:

"Sound an assembly. What I just now told you let be done with despatch."

To the knight he said :

"Thou heard'st the foul tidings? But Robin will make them fair ere the light of yon star has dimmed its brightness, or the day dawn. To our purpose, with despatch."

The clear, full notes of Little John's bugle sounded in the still night air.

Instantly all was astir.

Excitement there was, but not confusion.

The foresters marshalled with order and regularity.

In a short space of time all were prepared.

With noiseless tread, the band moved forward to their respective stations.

On their way, two horsemen passed.

A repressed but audible cheer greeted the foremost of them.

It was Robin, the Outlaw, attended by a faithful lad.

Arrived near the castle, Robin dismounted.

"Stay you under yon tree. Come not, but for this signal," and Robin imitated the hoot of the owl three times in succession. "Dost rightly understand thine instructions?"

"Yes, master ; thou shalt not find me tripping."

"Good. But mark me, keep the beasts quiet. Hast provender sufficient?"

"And to spare, good master. They shall not e'en whinney. My word on't."

Facing the castle, and shaking his clenched hand in its direction, Robin said :

"Base sheriff, thou little wottest of my presence here to-night. Thy perfidious designs will be frustrated, and thou, dear Mortimer, ere morning, shalt be free, or I perish."

With silent, but swift steps, Robin sought a dark object to the left.

It was the blasted oak.

"I will pause here till the castle is buried in deep silence," said Robin to himself.

Folding his arms, he leaned his back against the tree, and was soon buried in deep thought.

A hushed silence fell upon all around, unbroken save by the sentinel's tread on the ramparts.

"Now, for my ascent. Our Lady defend me. The risk is not so great?"

Finding that everything he wanted was quite safe, he mounted the oak with the agility of a wild cat, and soon rested amid its scathed boughs.

"'Tis the loophole exactly opposite this tree. Good! now for a trusty messenger."

Taking a blunt arrow out of his sheaf, he strung it to his bow, and fixing to it a piece of parchment, took aim and fired.

Earl Mortimer reclined on his hard couch.

Sleep visited not his eyes.

His thoughts were busy with the past.

The future to him was to be but a short one.

Robin had promised his sure aid.

But the Sheriff had forestalled him by fixing the execution for the morning.

'Twas useless to hope now.

He would nobly meet his fate.

Ah! what was that?

Something had struck the wall, and fallen at his feet.

It was an arrow, having affixed to it a parchment missive.

With eager hands he detached, and read it.

"I am in the old oak over against your cell. Be ready. Signal with your hand."

What joy unspeakable burst over Earl Mortimer's soul at this moment.

Escape was certain; for was not Robin near?

He waved his hand thrice.

A low whistle came in response.

Taking another arrow from his sheaf, Robin affixed thereto a string, to which hung a file.

With unerring aim it entered the loophole.

Mortimer filed, and Robin watched.

Slowly, but surely, the bars were filed.

But it required assistance to remove them from the masonry.

Taking another arrow, Robin attached to it a thin cord.

Again it went with merry aim through the loophole.

The cord was drawn carefully forward by Earl Mortimer.

To its end was attached a stout rope.

It was securely fixed.

Robin descended from the tree.

In a short time he was under the walls.

The rope was in his grasp.

He paused and listened.

CHAPTER XXXIX.

THE BLOODY SPECTRE.

At midnight's hour—so dark—
A figure, bloody and stark,
Haunted the ramparts high.
Its visage was ghastly and wan,
Down its breast the red blood ran,
As the night wind bore its sad sigh.

NOTTINGHAM's sheriff sat in his room quaffing the red wine.

"Ah, ah!" he said; "Earl Mortimer, thy hand, that struck me down like a dog, will be paralysed in death on the morrow's morn!"

After a pause, he cried out:

"What ho! without there! send hither the captain of the guard with quick despatch."

He paced the room hurriedly as he waited.

"And Robin Hood! 'Twill go hard with me, but I so fix him soon, that the gallows will be no longer cheated of its just due. I but bide my time."

The captain of the guard entered, and made a respectful salute.

"Is all in readiness for the morn? are thy men doubly watchful, sentinels alert, the prisoner secured beyond all possibility of escape?"

"Even so; guards within and without—drawbridge and portcullis closely guarded."

"Let a block be placed on the northern tower: let a spike be fixed on high there—the traitor's head shall be uplifted high."

"'Twill be done."

"And mark me, let the headsman bungle not—one sharp, swift stroke. To thy charge I confide these arrangements; see that they are rightly executed. I would be alone."

The captain of the guard, bowing low, departed.

"I will keep the vigils of the night, that the morn find me no laggard."

Filling himself a bumper of wine, he quaffed it at a draught.

"Pshaw!" he said, as if in answer to his own thoughts, "the King will hold me blameless. 'Tis a business once performed cannot be undone. The dead cannot be recalled to life!"

A low, sobbing wail struck upon his ear.

The hour-glass had just run its last grains.

It was midnight.

With a start of horror the sheriff looked about.

Again the same strange noise was heard by him.

"Heavens! what do I see?" he said, as the perspiration stood in big drops upon his pallid brow, and his eyes well nigh started in wild affright from their sockets.

A figure, ghastly and wan, with blood-stained vestments and eyeless sockets, from which blazed a dim, unearthly light, stood with uplifted arm and pointed finger.

The sheriff was terror-stricken.

His parched lips refused to utter a sound.

His frame quivered like an aspen leaf.

His knees knocked together with an audible sound.

Step by step, slowly but surely, advanced the spectre with an inexorable fate.

With a loud cry of terror the sheriff swooned.

Rushing in, his attendants found him thus.

The sentinels trod the ramparts watchfully and in pairs.

The two nearest Earl Mortimer's prison were extremely vigilant.

They conversed with bated breath of the gossip of the day.

"Is bold Robin expected, that we take such precautions?" asked the first sentinel.

"Even so; the outlaw is daring and resolute."

"And kindly hearted, too."

"He is of the Evil One, I opine. 'Tis strangely true, his wonderful deeds. An' he had not some help not of this world he could not do them."

"Right. But hark! heard'st thou not that sound as of a voice calling in deep whisper."

"Nay; but I'll listen."

After a pause the last speaker said:—

"'Tis fancy, I wot. Heard'st thou it again?"

"Nay; it sounded like some ghostly whisper. I wot there are strange things to be seen at midnight's hour within these walls."

"Thou art right. I heard it from Ralph Pleydel but yesternight."

"What heardest thou—aught ghostly?"

"Surely; and in this very spot."

"Nay, thou dost but jest."

"I jest not. Ralph discoursed so sensibly that I was fain to credit him."

"What saw he?"

"Listen, hark! heardest thou not that voice again?" said the other without regarding the question put to him.

"Pshaw! thou dost but tamper with my credulity."

"Prithee spare thy pains."

"I could have sworn to it."

The last speaker leaned over and peered into the black gulph underlying him.

"Nothing can I see," he remarked, "I heard the voice distinctly."

"Calm thy fears, man—but list to that, I heard it that time."

It was a low wail.

"Heavens! 'tis just as Ralph informed me."

ROBIN HOOD,

AND THE OUTLAWS OF SHERWOOD FOREST.

ROBIN CLIMBING TO THE EARL'S WINDOW.

"See, may I be hanged before morning if something comes not this way."

Gliding along came the same ghastly figure that had so scared the sheriff.

Crouching low, the terrified sentinels quivered every limb.

They too had swooned.

When the guard came to relieve them they had recovered.

But they spoke never a word of what they had seen until they reached the guard-room.

"Depend on't the sheriff was scared by it. Heard'st not that he was found insensible in his room."

"'Tis strange; I have oft heard of the

phantom but ne'er seen it. Is it so frightful?"

But never a reply came from the sentinels, save a deep sigh of relief.

Their silence cast a gloom o'er the remainder. The soldiers feared to keep watch, but said not so, except every man to his own heart.

CHAPTER XI.

HOW ROBIN ENCOMPASSED THE EARL'S ESCAPE.

Bold Robin he to the window hied—
Lusty of arm and strong of heart.
'Freedom to Mortimer, or death!' he cried;
'For 'tis nothing shall ever us part.'

NAUGHT but the tramp of the sentinels o'erhead broke the stillness of the night.

"Now, Our Lady prosper me, and I vow to pay at her shrine one hundred golden crowns."

Placing his sword betwixt his teeth, he climbed quickly up the rope, resting himself at times by placing his feet against the castle wall.

His bugle-horn swung to and fro in the night wind, as his sturdy form mounted higher and yet higher.

It was a daring deed.

But bold Robin loved danger, and had braved death too often to fear it under any guise.

The stout rope strained and quivered under his weight, but not a strand started.

His ascent startled the birds that had nestled in the castle walls, and they whirled round the outlaw.

The bats flapped their black wings, and, in their stupid coursing, flew butt against him oft.

He had reached three-fourths of the distance, when the glare of a torch shone o'er the ramparts, and a voice said:

"The outlaw has the daring of the Evil One. It behoves us to be vigilant. Look down. See you aught?"

Robin got as close to the wall as he could, and with bated breath, but a stout, fearless heart, awaited the issue.

"Naught but the deep blackness of the night, and the floating of birds, can I perceive."

"Ah! say you so. There must be cause for their nightly flittings. Hold the torch a little more to the *right*."

Robin gave an inward sigh of relief.

Had the torch been held to the *left*, he must have been discovered.

He listened for the voice of the last speaker.

"I see no cause for the disturbance of these birds. Yet, 'tis strange. Onwards! let our vigils be extended. The safe keeping of our prisoner depends on our watchfulness."

The voices died away in the distance, and soon all was hushed as before.

Robin worked his way upwards, every foot gained giving fresh strength to his energy.

At last he reached the window.

"Mortimer, 'tis Robin," he whispered low.

"Thine hand, brave friend; its pressure makes my heart's blood flow quicker, and sends it curling quick through my veins!"

"How has thy work progressed?"

"Bravely; it requires but thy help to complete it. But thou art in peril of falling."

"Nay, nay, have no fear; 'tis this requires wrenching out of the masonry. Stand aside—my strength is a match for it."

Twining his left hand with an iron grip, round the rope, he pressed his knees against the wall, and with his right hand gave the iron bar a vigorous wrench.

It started from the masonry; but the impetus of his exertion sent Robin swinging a yard or more away. Fearing that evil had befallen him, Mortimer said:

"Speak, Robin, art safe; my God, he has fallen!"

"Have no fear," said Robin cheerily; "I'm safe, thanks to Our Lady. Do thou help me to loosen the bar."

With a united effort they wrenched it from its socket, and it was soon disposed of on the floor. Another was similarly treated, and room sufficient gained for Robin's entrance.

Once in, Earl Mortimer felt relieved of all care about Robin. They were soon locked fast in a friendly embrace.

"What! manacled! By my halidom! they must be removed, and that quickly, else those iron bracelets will retard thy escape."

"Aye, manacled. 'Tis not the greatest indignity I have suffered. But tell me, how hast thou and my friends fared since we last met?"

"Bravely, bravely. Thy condition alone caused us uneasiness. But how came the sheriff to fix thy execution for to-morrow's morn?"

"Beshrew me, I wot not of this matter. He called but yestermorn, and discoursed such hard terms to me that I was fain, manacled though I was, to teach him manners."

"Noble Mortimer! In thee Saxon chivalry finds its paragon. Would that all of Saxon blood were such as thou art."

"Patience, Robin; the day draws apace when the hated Normans shall hide their heads for very shame, and England shall be freed from the hated foreign yoke."

"I agree with thee. Even now the peasantry are rife for a change. Let the King look to it, else will his throne be shaken to its overthrow."

"Hist, Robin, speak low. The night-guard approach. Crouch down under the truckle."

Flinging himself on his hard bed, Earl Mortimer feigned sleep, while Robin was hidden under it.

"Sentinel, is all well?" said the voice of the officer in charge.

"All's well."

"Onwards, march!"

When their retreating footsteps had died away in the distance, Robin came out and sat on the bed.

"I must to work, Mortimer," he said; "thy manacles must be removed."

"I will not say thee nay in this matter, good Robin. To thine office, an' thou wilt, with despatch."

As Robin filed, he and his friend conversed.

"Thou wert observing but just now, Robin, that the country was ripe for a change. Art thou certified of this?"

"My information is reliable. Thousands wait but the watchwords—Liberty! Death to the Norman dogs! to rise."

"'Tis glorious news. Thou shalt hold thine own again."

"I would willingly relinquish all claim to

my just inheritance to see beloved England free."

"Heard'st thou that noise, good Robin?" Mortimer asked, as a dull thud was distinguishable overhead.

"'Tis loud enough, in all conscience. What meaneth it?"

"The soldiers placing the block for my execution."

"A murrain seize the hard-hearted wretch! To treat one of thy degree so. S'death! a dog's death is too good for him."

"Say me. Is it not a refinement of cruelty thus to act? But Nottingham's sheriff little knows Earl Mortimer's heart. It is no craven, I warrant him."

"By Our Lady, no. But 'twill be fine fun to see his outrageous vapourings when the bird is known to have flown."

"Hearest thou not that wailing sound?" asked Mortimer.

"Nay, it struck me not. Thou art nervous, good Mortimer. Imprisonment has shattered thy nerves, and left thee a prey to strange fancies."

"Not so, Robin. Hark! list! heard'st thou it not that time?"

"Certes! I did; a most dismal wail it is. Hast thou a fellow-prisoner hither about?"

"I have no knowledge of such. But the saints forefend us! Look, Robin!"

Standing near was the apparition that had terrified the sheriff and the sentinels.

Mortimer was dumbfounded, and sore dismayed at the sight.

Not so Robin.

He stood erect, gazing on the fearful thing.

"In the name of our Blessed Mary and the saints I adjure thee to speak. Whence comest thou?"

"*'Tis well thou hast spoken. My bones lie mouldering in the nethermost dungeon of this castle. Foully murdered was I.*"

"Thou seekest vengeance on thy murderer! Speak! 'tis whom?"

"*Geoffrey de Lois.*"

"Merciful heavens! the sheriff!"

"Thou wilt avenge me?"

"I swear by high heaven!"

"*'Tis enough. For this thy safety is ensured. Follow me!*"

Robin hesitated; the rope seemed the surest means of escape.

The spectre looked back and beckoned.

Robin and his companion seemed laid under an irresistible spell.

They followed.

The dungeon wall opened, disclosing a secret door to a corridor beyond.

In amazement they followed their ghostly guide.

It led them by an unfrequented way, and after traversing many corridors, they arrived in a certain room.

The spectre vanished through a trap door.

Robin and Mortimer followed.

Down, down, it led them into the lowest dungeons of the castle.

The door of one of these flew open.

In a corner lay a mouldering skeleton.

Robin now understood why the spectre had brought them hither.

It was to give its remains burial.

Seizing an old rusty spade which lay on the dungeon floor, Robin set vigorously to work, and, with Mortimer's assistance, dug a deep grave.

In it they reverently laid the skeleton form. The spectre had vanished.

"We are properly caged," observed Mortimer.

"Nay. My faith in the apparition is strong. We shall be at liberty ere long."

Issuing from the dungeon, Robin turned along a corridor to the left.

They had to use caution, and in places grope their way almost, owing to the black darkness of the place.

"'Tis a mysterious matter, this spectre. What thinkest thou of it, Robin?"

"Rightly judged, 'tis no mystery. 'Tis some young girl entrapped, betrayed, and then foully murdered by the sheriff, to quiet her importunities."

"These dank, dark places, make one shudder. Our Lady, be thanked, I was not here confined."

"'Tis well remarked. In this matter, thou owest him a favour," said Robin laughingly.

"But, hist! there are voices. Caution, an' you value your safety."

It was as Robin said, for a voice gruffly and deep, remarked:

"'Tis nearing daylight. The keys thou'lt find to the right of the door on a nail. Mind, thou openest not the postern to any, save the sheriff, an' he desires you?"

All was quiet again.

"Mark well the footstep, and discreetly follow," whispered Robin to his companion.

A silent pressure of Mortimer's hand, showed he was fully understood.

Cautiously picking their way, they followed the retreating footsteps, guided by the sound merely.

In a short time they emerged through an open door into the morning air, for the first streak of dawn had appeared in the eastern horizon.

Mortimer pointed to it with a significant gesture.

"'Twill all be well, trust me," said Robin.

Tripping lightly across the ground was a young woman bearing a bunch of keys, which she rattled ever and anon.

"The lazy old curmudgeon," said Robin whisperingly, "is having his snooze out. 'Tis all the better for us."

Advancing with boldness, Robin accosted her with, "a good morn, fair dame."

The girl looked round affrighted, and would have screamed had not Robin gently placed his hand on her mouth, saying:

"Nay, my pretty fair one, cry not out, no harm is meant thee."

Seeing from the expression of the girl's face that she was somewhat more reassured, he withdrew his hand.

"Thou seekest exit hereby," she said, "but 'tis denied to all but the sheriff. Who art thou?"

"An' the truth be told we are two roystering squires that were making merry last night in this castle, and losing our way found ourselves here this morning."

"Thou hast not the garb or speech of such," said the girl, shrewdly.

"We beg of you, sweet girl, to let us go before our masters wot of it," said Robin.

And placing his arm round her waist he gave her a hearty kiss.

"Out upon thee for a saucy knave," she replied, trying to catch Robin a smart box on the ear, but he adroitly avoided her.

"Squire, say you," she hurriedly said, "catching sight of his bugle horn. "By the Mass, thou art bold Robin Hood himself. Thy garb is of green."

"Thou hast truly said, wench," he replied, "I am Robin Hood."

"And this is——"

"Earl Mortimer," replied Robin.

"Now the saints and Our Lady be praised," replied the girl, "thou shalt have immediate exit; why said you not your conditions before."

Hurrying to the gate, she unlocked it in haste and held it open.

"Thy name, noble girl," asked Robin.

"Madge Stukely."

"I shall not overlook this thy great kindness, Madge. Thou hast made a friend of Robin."

"And of Earl Mortimer, too," said the earl.

"Quick, quick," the girl replied, struggling from Robin's embrace, "my father comes this way."

"Madge," exclaimed a gruff voice, angrily, "to whom hast thou given exit?"

"To none, father. I but opened the gate to catch the fresh morning breezes."

Robin and Mortimer past out of hearing.

They worked their way round to the spot where the horses were, and passed the scene of the last night's adventure.

The rope dangled from the window, but half its length lay on the ground.

"We both escaped our destruction," remarked Robin, pointing to the rope.

"And such a death!" remarked the Earl with a shudder.

"List!" said Robin; "the castle is alarmed! Thine escape has been perceived. Quick, as you value your life."

The castle was indeed in a commotion. At the dawn the captain of the guard had gone to rouse his prisoner, but, lo! he was gone.

"Escaped! Quick, raise an alarm! to the ramparts! Hie thee to the sheriff, and him acquaint of the matter!" exclaimed the captain in disjointed sentences. He feared for this misadventure the loss of his position, if not his head.

The window soon told the tale, for the rope was fastened there as it was left by Robin. The Earl's manacles lay upon the floor.

"Now a curse on Robin Hood! this is his work!" exclaimed the sheriff, hastily entering the apartment. The storm of passion that he indulged in was indescribable.

The guards were to be executed forthwith, the captain first of all. He was surrounded by traitors and spies, and so forth.

"I would not have had this happen for ten thousand of the best gold pieces in the land!" the sheriff exclaimed : "Now shall I be hooted at for a dolt—a fool—an incompetent! Oh! that I could crush my enemies under my foot! Thus and thus would I do it!" And the sheriff stamped again and again in his impotent rage.

Going to the ramparts, he heard a shout.

"There they go! 'Tis Robin, the outlaw, and Earl Mortimer!"

"Where, where?" said the sheriff.

"'Tis them! 'tis them! a hundred crowns to the man that sends a bolt through their carcasses!"

The cross-bowmen bent their bows.

CHAPTER XLI.

THE FRIAR AND THE STRANGERS.

I seek an outlaw the stranger said :
  Men call him Robin Hood;
Rather I'd meet with that same outlaw
  Than forty pounds so good.

FRIAR TUCK accompanied the party under Little John, and looked gleefully forward to a brush with the sheriff's soldiers.

"My conscience will not be sore troubled, an' I happen to smite one of the Norman dogs. What say'st thou, John?"

"'Twould take more than that to hurt thy sleep, friend. Thou art not of tender years, or conscience either."

"Thou art ever perverse in thy judgment respecting me, a man given unto prayer and fasting."

"Out upon thee, for a hypocrite. E'en now, thou art troubled to digest thy last meal."

"Well, well; I must submit, I suppose, and bear thy slanders, as best I can; but how long tarriest thou here, ere the potting commence?"

"Till morn, belike. 'Twill ill assort with thy slumbers, jolly Tuck, such vigils."

"I must bethink me of some plan to while away the time. I eschew idleness."

"Marry, and thou dost. But we are here."

Disposing of his men to the best advantage, and in accordance with the instructions given by Robin Hood, he threw out skirmishers on either hand, and in both front and rear, to guard against surprises.

Those not on duty, were to idle about without going too far away.

This sort of business was not to the friar's liking, so he took the first opportunity to hie him off to the shade of some wide-spreading tree to sleep, if no better occupation presented itself.

When alone he drew forth from his satchel some venison, oat cakes, and wine.

"'Twas rare luck I fell into, to get me this much. 'Tis scant fare, enough, for a hungry man; but it might be worse."

"I commend the cook for his art. 'Tis a rare art, too. Nature meant me for eating, not for praying. Egad, I unite the two profitably enough."

The wine, too, met with the friar's favour, and he was jolly enough.

"'Twere well to rouse these solitudes; 'tis lonely enough here for a churchyard. Think of friend, Little John; but there was only just enough for one, not two. Besides, that last steak was tough, and would have interfered with his digestion."

In a minute or two he carolled forth :—

"The friar he is a saintly man ;
  He eats betimes and fasts when he can.
Of troubles he has not a few to meet,
  But with scourging and fasting such foes
    he can greet."

"Bones of St. Hubert! how I can remember

penance in my younger days. 'Twas as nauseous to me as a dose of medicine. Ugh!"

"To matins and prayers he gives his days—
Not to mend his own, but other men's ways;
For the fat things of earth he cares not a rush,
Though for all that he likes good wine at a push."

"Ah! things have mightily altered with me, and for the better. Robin is a good superior; not over troublesome. But, Bones of St. Hubert! what is that?"

A rustling noise came from overhead.

"'Tis the wind, no doubt: I'll lay me down and rest—'twill refresh me."

Soon he snored loudly, and it was evident that he was fast locked in sleep's sweet embrace.

The noise caused by the approach of two horsemen failed to arouse him.

They were attracted by his snoring.

"Here is somebody," remarked one of them, who can direct us in our course; I'm afraid we've lost our way."

"Thou canst be well certified of that. Marry! have we not been mouching about these last two hours or more? 'Tis a fact, God wot."

There was a touch of impatience in the last speaker's voice, which was of that soft tone, too, as to proclaim her a woman.

"I'll arouse the slumbering knave; perchance he can direct us."

Placing his mouth to the friar's ear, he shouted with all his might:

"Arouse thee, man! the house is on fire."

This appeal, strong as it was, failed to make any impression on the sleeper.

"Certes, but he sleeps remarkably sound. What ho! thou knave. Dost hear?"

And the speaker gave the sleeping friar several rude shakes.

"And he gave a thwack that broke his back,"

was the friar's dreamy response as he turned over, and snored louder still on the other side.

"Faith, thou deservest to have thy back broken, thou sluggard," said the speaker angrily.

"'Twere best to alight here for a time," said the lady. "'Twill not bring us nearer our goal, an' we ride till morning's dawn."

"Fool that I was to trust ourselves in these places without a guide. But 'tis vain to chide myself now."

The lady dismounted, and tied her horse to a tree, an example which was followed by the gentleman.

"Throw thy cloak about thee, Maria, and sleep, an' thou wilt, whilst I keep vigils till morning."

"Then Robin set his horn to his mouth,
And blew a blast or twain,"

mumbled the friar in his sleep, without, however, interfering with its peacefulness.

"By the Rood! the knave has named the very man we seek. Would that he were not so sleepily conditioned; then would I have speech with him."

"Patience will best serve us," remarked the lady. "I would I were not so faint with thirst."

"'Twere hard to relieve it here," said her companion, "unless this graceless lout has aught by him. I will see to it."

His search was rewarded by finding the remains of the wine and an oaten cake or two.

"I give thee joy, Maria; here have I to eat and drink for thee. Thou canst set to."

Hunger left no room for niceties about the condition of the provender, or the manner of obtaining it, so the lady did as she was bid, sharing with her companion.

"He is not such an ill-conditioned knave, after all; but see, he stirs. I will accost him once more."

Before the speaker could do so, Friar Tuck awoke and groped about for the wine.

Finding it not, he grumbled lustily.

"Two travellers have lost their way, and beseech thine information."

"And I have lost my wine," replied the friar tartly."

"Thou shalt have enough money to buy a pipe of it, if thou dost but inform us of our road."

"Marry! the road is broad enough and straight enough to Nottingham good town. 'Tis only fools can miss it."

"Have a care knave; thou answerest not a civility discreetly."

"I shall crack thy pate, an' thou usest knave to me again. Bones of St. Hubert! thy malapert tongue requires bridling with an oak staff."

"Peace, sirrah, or I'll teach thee good manners."

"Thou! 'Twill be seen full quickly."

Grappling each other they wrestled for full ten minutes or more without an advantage on either side.

At last they were fain to stop for want of breath.

"By my halidom, thou art a sturdy wrestler. None I found could so stand as thou hast done."

"Thou knowest full well the tricks of wrestling, I perceive," answered the friar, "and I fain would serve thee an' I could."

"'Tis easily done; I and my companion seek one Robin Hood."

"Robin Hood! Why man, the trees, the deer, every blade of grass hither about knows him full well:

"Come, listen to me, ye gentlemen
That be of freeborn blood;
I shall tell you of a good yeoman—
His name was Robin Hood.

Robin was a proud outlaw,
Whilst he did walk on ground;
So courteous an outlaw as Robin was,
Was never anywhere found."

"Thanks, friend, for thy ditty. Perchance, thou and bold Robin are acquainted?"

"Full well: full well. Friar Tuck and he are as thick as well-churned butter."

"Thou art one of his merry men, then?"

"Nay," replied the friar gravely, "thou mistakest; I am Robin's chaplain, and must, perforce, renounce merriment for penance."

"Thou knowest well the flavour of good wine," observed the stranger, "for that I drank just now, was good beyond compare."

"'Tis to refresh my inner man, I take it," replied the friar. Thou knowest the old song, perchance:

"Good wine—'tis fine:
Give water to swine.
Never think to drink
Better stuff than wine."

"I would be going, an' it pleasure you, good friar. My companion is tired, and cravest repose."

"Robin Hood's merry-men are near at hand, not two good bowshots off. Follow, an' thou wilt?"

"'Tis Robin I wish to see mightily?"

"He is well employed on good business; but Little John, his lieutenant, can grant thee audience."

Friar Tuck drew Little John aside, and told him how that two persons of condition sought to see Robin.

"Their business. Disclosed they it?"

"Nay; but one is a hugeous fine wrestler. He came well nigh tripping me. Thou canst now guess he is a man of some stuff."

Little John courteously welcomed the strangers, and, without directly soliciting their confidence, intimated that he was acting for Robin Hood, and would gladly assist them, if possible.

"Thanks for thy courtesy, good forester," replied the gentleman; "I would, an' it please you, discourse with you aside."

"I am at your service—say on," said Little John, when he and the stranger had gone apart.

"My name is Richard Wykeham or, Sir Rickard, as folks call me. My patrimony is wrested from me by the contrivances of Nottingham's sheriff, because of the love that Maria Danvers bears me. 'Tis Norman against Saxon—the greedy dogs. My followers were taken at a disadvantage, and I and Maria are here to solicit bold Robin Hood's assistance."

"He ne'er refuses it to the oppressed. But he alone can decide in the matter."

"'Twas in my knowledge that he would do so, else had I not sought him. Can I not have audience with him soon?"

"Pressing matters engage his attention for a time. At Sherwood thou shalt see him."

"Thy counsel is friendly, meanwhile I crave shelter for her who accompanies me. Thine hospitality would much benefit her."

"It is willingly given. Our worthy chaplain, Friar Tuck, will accompany you to our rude home in the forest. On the morrow, accommodation more befitting her condition will be found her."

Calling Friar Tuck to him, he desired him to go with the strangers to Sherwood and see after their comfort.

"'Twill be hard but I make them snug. Adieu, good John, my benison on thee and thine undertaking."

Sir Richard and his lady-love departed, under escort of the friar, who beguiled the way with anecdotes of Robin's prowess, which were eagerly listened to by his auditors.

They were not destined to reach the end of the journey without adventure.

But this must form the subject of another chapter in due course.

CHAPTER XLII.

HOW THE ABBOT CURSED ROBIN AND LITTLE JOHN, BY BELL, BOOK, AND CANDLE.

He cursed him sitting, he cursed him rating;
He cursed him living, he cursed him dying.

WHEN the monks brought the tidings of the loss of the tithes to the abbot of St. Mary's, his rage knew no bounds.

He raved and swore most unsaintly oaths revenged he would be upon Robin.

He summoned his brethren in solemn conclave, and revealed to them the loss to the abbey.

"Curse him by book, bell, and candle!" suggested one of the monks.

"He cares not for such; he leagues with the Evil One," replied the abbot.

"It matters not; he cannot long defy our holy power. Let him be anathema maranatha."

"But let us not lose sight of the power of the arm of flesh in chastising him. He is outlawed, and any man may lawfully slay or maim him without let or hindrance."

"Well said," replied the abbot. "A scheme must be devised against him specially, and next against that renegade Friar Tuck."

"'Twas he who assailed us. Would he were within these walls, that we might question him as to his backslidings."

"'Tis a thing hard of accomplishment, holy brethren," replied the abbot; "but nevertheless our rights must be protected."

"'Tis well said," observed one of the monks. "To me are known two men or more, who, for a consideration, would lend their swords to our holy cause."

"Summon them to our presence; we would have speech with them," replied the abbot, significantly.

A messenger entered at this point to say that one was without desiring speech of the lord abbot.

"Said he 'twere an important matter?" queried the abbot.

"Even so, my lord."

"Admit him to our presence, then."

The attendant bowed low and retired.

Presently there entered a yeoman from the castle.

"The sheriff sends thee greeting, my lord," he said. "Earl Mortimer dies on the second morn from this."

"'Twill be one enemy of Church and State the less," replied the abbot sententiously.

"He is not shriven, and would have some holy man to hear his confession."

"He is excommunicate. His death-agony must not be softened by the Church's holy comfort."

"But the sheriff wots that important confession may be his to make."

"An' even were it so, 'twere not our pleasure to divulge such to any. The secrets of the confessional are inviolable."

"Am I answered in full, my lord?"

"Thou art. Earl Mortimer has consorted with the notorious outlaw, Robin Hood. *That* damns him. My love and duty to your master, and say that the earl will not be shriven by holy monk or friar."

Earl Mortimer had not desired to be shrived. 'Twas the sheriff's art to elicit the abbot's approval indirectly of his death.

When the sheriff's messenger had gone, the abbot ordered a solemn assembly for the morn.

"Let notice be given thereof to all the country round. Let as many as will attend to hear our doom pronounced upon the enemies of our holy church."

That very night three men of ruffianly exterior were closetted with the abbot.

"For twenty marks paid over to each of you, Robin Hood, Little John, or Friar Tuck will cease to further trouble us."

"We swear to execute thy behests," said the leader; and each man laid his hand significantly on the hilt of his sword-dagger.

"Night would best subserve thy purpose. Watch vigilantly, and expose not thy precious lives to these men's taking."

"Thou need'st not admonish us of this. Our contract will be fulfilled, and to thy liking."

"Mark me. Reserve thy weapons for those I named to thee. Once rid of them, the band's dispersal would quickly follow."

"We would have guerdon of thee, for this is a desperate undertaking, of difficult accomplishment and dangerous involvings."

"Art thou distrustful? Thou hast no need."

"We must live. Five marks each would suffice. 'Tis not a large sum."

"Thou art importunate. But, as this is a holy service thou engagest in, take thy needs, and prosper in thy work."

Five crowns each were paid them.

They departed as they came—silently.

On the morrow, the abbot and monks walked in grand procession.

Such magnificence was never before witnessed by many of the simple country folk, who, prompted by curiosity, attended to witness the commination.

The large chapel was draped in black, The candles threw a dim, mysterious light over the place.

The funeral dirge was chanted in solemn tones, which sent the blood rushing back to the hearts of those who never before had heard it.

With stately, measured steps, the procession of monks defiled round the chapel. They knelt devoutly in silent prayer, then uprose, and, with folded hands and bended heads, listened to the abbot.

Robin Hood and Little John were publicly denounced as enemies to the church.

Friar Tuck was not mentioned, the consent of the abbot's spiritual superior being required to such a proceeding being adopted in his case.

Then commenced the commination.

Anathema after anathema poured forth, in clear, uninterrupted tones, from the abbot's lips.

At the end of each curse, the abbot laid his hand, with solemn gesture, on the Bible.

The lighted candle was extinguished.

The bell tolled its solemn toll, and the monks chanted a solemn amen.

It was a deeply awe-inspiring ceremony, and made a great impression upon the minds of the laity present.

The abbot next addressed those present.

Persons sheltering or assisting Robin Hood, or any of his band, would be excommunicated and cut off from all the rights of the church.

The commination was over.

The spectators dispersed.

The monks, with solemn steps, sought their cells.

The chapel was left deserted.

The abbot was alone, mourning over the loss of his money, for a very miser was he.

In thus trying to prejudice the minds of the common people against Robin, the abbot committed a mistake.

True, there were some superstitious enough to be frightened at the anathemas pronounced by the abbot.

Nor was it to be wondered at.

To be excommunicated was in those days a serious matter.

It was to be afflicted with a moral leprosy.

Every person shunned the person under ban.

Food was not allowed to be sold him.

Nor house let to him.

Nor priest to confess or shrive him.

Nor surgeon to attend his ailments.

Nor Christian burial at his death.

The matter was much talked of when the meeting broke up.

There were two men in particular, who, apart from the crowd walked and talked of Robin.

"Dost thou credit that these foreign words have aught of power to hurt bold Robin?"

"'Tis hard to say. But they sounded very dreadful to me."

"Bold Robin cares not for them, nor any of his merry men, either."

Looking cautiously round, he said:

"I join Robin's band to-night. 'Tis free living, and to my liking."

"Nay, Jack, lad, thou art joking, belike?"

Not so. Bold Robin reckons me as one of his band; an' he likes to have me, that's certain sure."

"I should be lonely without thee, Jack. But think of the curse; think of the sheriff's soldiers; think of the gallows, lad."

"Be a man, Dick. It takes not the joining of Robin's band to bring one into queer troubles. Hast not plenty of them now? Where be our bit o' land, our snug little cottage, our poor mother and sister. Thou well knowest. All gone, all! and in the churchyard drear!"

"An' you love me, Jack, no more. It raises a sort of sensation like in my throat to talk of mother. I feel maddened, revengeful, and not the man I should be."

"What thinkest thou of the abbot's curses, now?" said Jack with a quiet sneer.

"I think more of our wrongs. Dick, my hand on't, I hie with thee to Robin the outlaw."

"Meet me under the large oak in Sherwood Forest."

"In Sherwood Forest, under the large oak, I meet thee."

"'Tis well."

CHAPTER XLIII.

HOW FRIAR TUCK AND HIS COMPANY DEFEATED THE ABBOT'S MINIONS.

To see how these together they fought,
    A full hour of a summer's night;
Yet neither of all would yield them aught,
    It was a most cruel sight.

"AND the sheriff say you is in love with Maid Marian?" asked Maria Danvers of the friar.

"Aye, that is he, the ill-conditioned swine. Naught but so bonny a girl as her will suit him."

"And the maid loves Robin dearly sayest thou?"

"Dearer than else in life. For him she lives alone. For his voice is sweet music to his ear. But thou should'st see her for thyself, lady, and thou wilt anon."

"Thou likest a free life, good friar," remarked Sir Richard.

"Truly, truly!"

> " A life in the woods for me,
>   With the fierce wind blowing free."

"Bones of St. Hubert! What's so pleasant as a home under the greenwood tree? Ha, ha! I laugh at the thought of it, and sing—

> " Ha, ha! 'tis well
>   In the forest to dwell,
>   With the green trees sighing o'er you."

"Thou art a jolly companion, good friar, and hast quite made us forget our fatigue. What sayest thou, Maria?"

"A very notably pleasant man, art thou, good friar, and rightly fitted for thine office with the merry men."

"A shrewd remark, lady. Thou hast my liking for its point. Who would not sing and fight for bold Robin?"

"None but a churl, I wot," answered Sir Richard.

"'Tis yet a good pace to your forest home?" queried the lady.

"It is naught, and will soon end. But I am wearying thee with my prating. Thou would'st fain have me silent, fair lady."

"Nay, say on, say on, I pray thee, friar. Thy speech is welcome, and cheereth exceedingly."

"Hast heard of Rob's adventure with Guy of Gisborne," asked the friar.

"But never the proper rights of it," answered Sir Richard.

"Would'st thou hear it? I wot I can give it thee in song right well. Thou must excuse my huskiness, though, for I am very dry:—

> " 'Now tell me thy name, good fellow,' said he,
>   'Under the leaves of bine.'
>   'Nay by my faith,' quoth bold Robin
>   'Till thou hast told me thine.'
>
> 'I dwell by dale and down,,' quoth he,
>   'And Robin to take I've sworn;
>   'And when I m called by my right name,
>   I am Guy of good Gisborne.'
>
> 'My dwelling is in the woods,' says Robin,
>   By thee I set right naught;
>   I am Robin Hood of Barnesdale,
>   Whom thou so long hast sought.'
>
> He that had neither been kith nor kin
>   Might have seen a full fair fight;
>   To see how together those yeomen went,
>   With blades both brown and bright.
>
> Robin was reckless of a root,
>   And stumbled up that tide;
>   And Guy was quick and nimble withal,
>   And hit him upon the side.
>
> 'Ah! dear Lady!" said Robin Hood, 'though
>   Thou art both mother and maid,
>   I think it was never man's destiny
>   To die before his day.'
>
> Robin thought on Our Lady dear,
>   And soon leaped up again;
>   And straight he came with an awkward stroke,—
>   And he Sir Guy hath slain."

"Right well sung, good friar; an' thou pleasest, thou shalt drain a stoup of good wine with me presently."

"'Tis a thing I ne'er refuse. But I finished not all my song. I am hugeous dry, and were I to bawl further, 'twould crack my throttle, I wot."

"Seest thou aught beyond yonder tree?" asked the lady.

"Whither, lady fair? I strain, but see not," answered the friar.

"'Tis but thy fancy, Maria, dear. This old forest hath queer, fantastic shapes for the mind's eye, I take an' but the humour suits one."

"I could have certified to it. A man did appear from thence, and quickly lost himself again."

"'Tis easy to see. Pause, thou, while I go forward."

Forward the friar went.

He had neared the tree, when, with a bound, he was beset by three men.

With nimble quarter-staff, he warded well their blows, shouting out: "St. Hubert to the rescue!"

"Now stay thou here," said Sir Richard to the lady, "I haste to fight."

Dismounting from his horse he drew his sword and was soon ranged by Friar Tuck's side.

Right well and lustily did the friar with his quarter-staff lay about him.

Right well did Sir Richard parry and thrust, and guard and hew.

"An' take that for thy pains, thou knave," said the friar, as he brought his staff down with unerring aim on one of their crowns.

The man dropped as if shot.

"I cry thee quarter," cried he to whom the friar was now in turn opposed.

"Quarter thou shalt have after I have thee well thrashed. Out upon thee, thou cowardly knave. To thy guard and defend thyself."

The friar whirled his staff well and lustily.

Never a blow did he get in return for the many he had given.

With a crack that could be plainly heard for a distance, he soon stretched the second fellow to keep company with the first.

But it fared not so well with Sir Richard.

His foot slipping, his adversary got him at a vantage.

His sword point was at his throat when a stroke from an unexpected quarter, disarmed and badly wounded him.

"Well hit, lady fair, a good stroke. Rise, Sir Richard, thou art not hurt much."

"Not a scratch, good friar; and thou, Maria, hast earned anew my love by saving my life."

"I would that I had holpen sooner. But seeing that thou wast equally matched with thine adversary, I stayed my hand. It was thy mishap brought me to thy side."

Turning to the prisoner who alone of the three could speak, the other two being in sorry plight, thanks to the friar's lusty arm and nimble staff, the friar said:

"Answer me, knave, thy name and condition, quickly as thou valuest sound bones in thy carcass."

"My name is mine own, my condition a soldier."

"Thou hast turned robber, I trow; was this errand of thine own seeking?"

"Nay, and thou trust me I will unfold to thee the name and condition of my employer."

ROBIN HOOD,

AND THE OUTLAWS OF SHERWOOD FOREST.

ESCAPE OF ROBIN HOOD AND EARL MORTIMER.

"Thou art but a sorry knave, and deservest not a boon. But an' thou answerest truly, it shall be thine. Say on."

"The lord abbot of St. Mary's did us employ to thy destruction, and that of Robin Hood and Little John."

"Ah! speakest thou in jest, or truly."

"Of a truth; why else had I sought thee to

No. 14.

thy hurt? Thou art no enemy of mine otherwise."

"By the Rood! this must be seen to. Thou must come with me. No hurt shall befall thee, I swear. Of Robin Hood thou must have audience in this matter."

"My liberty will be imperilled, life even. It will anger thy master, when he heareth of this thing."

"Not so. Thou hast fared the worst in the combat. I am free from scratch, as is my companion also—

> " For a busy man he must be
> To bring Friar Tuck to his knee."

Turning to Sir Richard, the friar asked his advice in the matter.

"Thou hast well advised in this thing, good friar. Let the knave accompany us, that Robin may have his own relating."

"Hearest thou that? So march, fellow, and mind thy conduct."

Leaving the two senseless bravos to recover as best they could, Friar Tuck and his party proceeded onward.

"St. Mary's abbot! By the Rood! but he shall pay for this in gold pieces. He liked not our handling his tithes. Ah, ah! King Robin lets not money pass through his domain without crying snacks."

> " Go now forth, said Robin Hood,
> And bring back unto me,
> All that thou can'st find in money fair,
> All the marks that thou can'st see."

"The abbot has furthermore excommunicated Robin Hood, and cursed him by bell, book, and candle."

The lady crossed herself on hearing this.

Seeing which, the friar said—

"'Tis naught when sin is not at the door. I wot bold Robin will sleep and eat, and laugh and sing, as if my lord abbot had not excommunicated him."

"'Tis a treacherous thing to thus appoint one's death at the hands of an assassin. It behoves not the church's servants thus to act, and one of such high degree, too, as my lord abbot."

Thus spake Sir Richard in dudgeon, for he could ill brook such treachery.

"Let the hare sit," replied the friar; "an' he must be a bold man that would try conclusions with Robin Hood, King of Sherwood's forest.

> " Bold Robin, he cares not a thing,
> For abbot, or earl, or yeoman, or King;
> With his merry men all, and the forest so free,'
> Bold Robin careth naught, not he, not he."

"'Twill go hard with him now he is excommunicate," suggested Maria Danvers.

"Thou hast a befitting reverence, fair lady, for our holy church, an' which thing it pleaseth me to see. But thou wottest not of certain things, else would'st thou not think good Robin hard dealt by."

"He little careth for such things, else hath report much deceived me," replied Sir Richard, laughingly.

"Who approaches, friend or foe?" was the challenge, which rang out clearly upon the night.

"Friends, good archer, friends to Robin Hood and all good men.

"The *word* on your peril."

"Marian."

"Pass on, friends."

"What, Bill, knewest thou not thy friend?" asked the friar.

"Right well. 'Twould be hard to forget thee. But what news from the front?"

"Rare good tidings, rare. But, man, I am hugeous dry. Bones of St. Hubert! but my legs totter from thirst," and the friar seized a flask which hung by the sentinel's side.

"Thy throttle is so large, 'twould not so much as wet its sides such a drop as that, but thou art welcome to it."

The friar quickly drained the wine-flask, and gave a deep sigh of satisfaction.

"The news, man, what of it? Earl Mortimer is——"

"Still in prison, but Robin is with him by this. Our comrades stand prepared for action. All goes well."

"Who are those with thee?" asked the sentinel.

"Two friends of our master; one a foeman beaten, and now a prisoner. Thou need'st to keep sharp vigils. I would acquaint with the commander of the guard."

"Thine advice is welcome, and shalt be well attended to."

The friar and his party passed on, and were soon resting.

Taking his prisoner with him, Friar Tuck sought the commander of the guard, and to him narrated what the reader already knows.

"Speak, sirrah!" he said. "Had'st others with thee in this black affair?"

"None. Three only were of our number; myself, and two others now lying with cracked crowns where they were left."

"Thou must be secured past escape. An' thou art wise, no harm shall befall thee. What ho, there! Guard well this fellow in safe custody."

"There tarriest Sir Richard Wykeham and a fair lady under yonder tree. Little John commends them to thy keeping, until of Robin Hood they have audience."

"I will attend them. Perchance, they need refreshing. Thou, good father, can'st well attend to that," said the commander with a laugh.

"Thou hast well spoken, for :

> " I love to make friends merry,
> And treat them with good wine."

But I waste but my time and they fasting."

Sir Richard and Maria Danvers were soon made comfortable.

Thanks to the friar's promptitude, a good repast was soon spread for them, at which he took good care to preside.

To see him eat and drink, one would have thought that he had fasted for fully a week.

His jollity kept his companions in good humour, and the rich generous wine stirred up his wit and humour, until it bubbled up like a fountain.

The night passed without further adventure.

The garrison at Barnesdale waited news from the front; news of Bold Robin.

That news the morn brought with it.

CHAPTER XLIV

HOW THE SHERIFF AND HIS MEN PURSUED AFTER ROBIN AND EARL MORTIMER.

> Bold Robin and Mortimer hied them away
> From the castle at break of day;
> The sheriff's crossbowmen to slaughter them did vie,
> But their bolts flew harmlessly by.

"SAID I not the Normans spied us out," observed Robin, laughingly, as the bolts from the crossbows came whistling harmlessly by them.

'Twill go hard but we escape them now," replied Mortimer, cheerily.

"Have no fear; but a little further and there await us two steeds, once bestride them and the sheriff may whistle for us, an' it please him."

Thickly the bolts flew past.

The fugitives seemed to bear a charmed existence, for never a bolt harmed them aught.

"Yonder come horsemen to cut off our retreat," remarked Robin, pointing to a score or more mounted men in the distance.

"'Twill be a close race," observed Earl Mortimer, "but Our Lady will befriend us."

"We are arrived. What oh! there, lad; the horses, quick," cried Robin.

Responsive to his call came the youth, but one horse only held he.

"The other beast, knave; speak quickly 'tis where?" said Robin with impatience.

"Even dead. 'Tis but a moment since a bolt smote him and he died."

"A curse on the Norman swine for this misadventure. But we must e'en mount, Mortimer, and ride double."

The knight sprang nimbly up, and Robin vaulted behind him.

Turning to the youth Robin Hood said:

"Hie thee to Little John, and say, Robin is pursued by horsemen and flies northward."

By this time the horsemen headed by the sheriff in person were near at hand—so near, in fact, that the latter could be heard as he shouted:

"Yield thee, Robin Hood and Earl Mortimer, 'tis useless to attempt to escape."

Onward dashed the gallant white charger with its double load.

The preciousness of its burden seemed to animate it to put forth its utmost speed.

Well, right well it breasted its course.

Like a pack of hounds in full cry came the pursuers.

Their foam-covered steeds urged and strained sinew and thew.

"What thinkest thou, Robin," said Mortimer: "gain they on us?"

"Nay, not a foot's pace, Mortimer. Our Lady send that the steed slack not its speed for a little space longer, and all will go well with us."

"Thy life shall not be imperilled by me, Robin," said Mortimer. "Better by far that Mortimer died, than Sherwood's King should the sheriff's captive be."

"Thou art too mindful of me, brave Mortimer. Hie onward, good steed, and soon shall we leave danger far behind."

Looking back, Robin perceived with sadness that their pursuers were gaining on them fast.

"Mortimer," he said.

And the tones of his voice were not so cheery as they had sounded but a few minutes before.

"Speak, Robin. What would'st thou say?"

"The Normans near us. Do thou obey my behests, I conjure thee?"

"An' it imperil not thy safety, thou hast my willing obeisance, Robin."

"Time presses us sore, yon thicket will shelter me. Ride on thou to Little John with tidings of my condition, that aid be quickly forthcoming."

"Never shall it be said that Mortimer thus acted to Robin. 'Tis I that will offer surrender to the sheriff. Ride on thou?"

"'Tis folly, nay madness. Even now the hot breath of their steeds o'ershadow us. 'Twere not well both of us should fall. My woodcraft will stand me in good stead hither about."

With a bound Robin threw himself from the horse.

"Farewell, Mortimer!" cried he. "For my sake, speed onward."

Relieved from his double burden, the white steed bounded forward with redoubled speed, and soon distanced his pursuers.

"Heed not the horseman," cried the sheriff to his followers; "dismount, half a score of ye, and follow yon fellow. 'Tis Robin Hood; a purse of gold to the man who encompasses his capture."

With haste they dismounted, and dived into the thicket after the fugitive.

"Yonder he goes!" cried one.

"Circle out, circle out!" said another; "his capture will thereby be made more certain."

Acting on this advice, they spread so as to draw a sort of half-circle around the outlaw's wake, and so intercept him should he attempt to double upon them.

But Robin, bold woodsman was he!

Not a jot cared he for them pursuing.

He mockingly chevied them on, as, with swingeing pace, he hied him through the thicket.

His heart bounded high and swelled with joyous emotions as the leaves o'erhead rustled to the swaying of the zephyr-like breezes.

He trod a spot he loved to tread, for was not he the forest king?

Anon he had distanced all but three of his pursuers.

"They but tempt their fate," he muttered between his clenched teeth; "think they Robin to capture! 'Twill go hard with me but I teach them that one Saxon is more than equal match for three Normans!"

Actuated by a determination to halt and offer battle to his pursuers, he slackened his pace and rested against a fine old oak.

They saw him thus act with exultant glee.

"Now," they to each other cried, "Robin is ours! The purse will be ours to share. On to the capture!"

Disdaining to use his bow against them, Robin tarried their coming and breathed himself.

"Yield thee, Robin Hood!" cried the foremost; "thou can'st not cope with three."

Robin smiled a grim smile, and his trusty sword leaped from its sheath.

"'Tis what I have long wished for," said the Norman; "now will I test thy swordmanship; have at thee! Comrades, do thou stand by. This is a trial of swordmanship."

"Thou art mad," exclaimed one of his companions; "let us all attack."

"Nay, thou know'st I am affirmed the best swordsman in these parts. I long to try my skill against yon fellow."

"Come on, prithee good fellow," exclaimed Robin. "Thou but wastest time in prating. The *three* an' thou wilt, 'tis not too great odds for Robin Hood."

"Have at thee, thou braggart."

Their swords crossed.

The bright blades clashed as point, guard, and stroke were dealt out skilfully.

"Thou a swordsman!" cried Robin, mockingly, as his antagonist's sword went flying through the air, and he himself received a wound in his sword-arm.

The other two were upon him.

It required a quick eye to catch the movements of Robin's sword.

Soon victory was his.

One of his opponents lay dead.

The other was badly wounded.

Wiping his bloodstained sword on the grass he returned it to its sheath.

With swift steps he swept onward as the remainder of his pursuers came up.

"Ah, ah!" he exultantly cried, "thou Norman swine, Robin bids thee take him an' thou can'st."

The forest echoed this taunt, and his pursuers gnashed their teeth with impotent rage as they saw him go bounding away.

"Not one of those churls but I could send to death," he muttered to himself. "My trusty bow could lay them low in turn. I seek not their hurt, but let them see to't they press me not too hard, else will my forbearance fail me."

Robin halted and debated with himself the best course to pursue.

"'Twill baffle them," he soliloquised, "an' I shape my course back towards the castle. I'll e'en try it. Come, to thy work, Robin, thy merry men await thy coming."

"Yield thee, my prisoner," a voice imperiously said.

Turning Robin confronted the sheriff.

For a moment they stood eyeing each other.

Robin's look was calm and steady, and withal defiant.

The sheriff's glance was full of malignant hatred and supreme satisfaction at the prospect of capturing the daring outlaw.

"Thou hast called on me to yield," said Robin haughtily, "to a Norman, and such as thou, that can never be!"

The sheriff answered slowly and deliberately:

"Threescore men are within call. Thy capture is sure."

"Thou be'st a false sworn knight, insulter of weak and powerless women. Ere Robin yield to thee or thine, his heart's blood will be poured upon the greensward. Defend thyself!"

With a bound Robin Hood was upon him.

Right sore they fought.

"Thy men tarry apace," said Robin contemptuously, as he parried a downward stroke delivered by the sheriff.

"Thou art ill informed on the matter," was the reply, as a straight lunge went at the outlaw's breast.

"Have a care, thou Norman robber," said Robin, coolly parrying it. "Thy carcass will soon dishonour the spot."

"St. Denis, help me!" replied the sheriff as he dexterously guarded his head from a terrific blow aimed at it by his antagonist.

"That to teach thee manners," said Robin, driving his sword through the fleshy part of the sheriff's sword-arm.

But never a pause made he.

He fought him for his life right sturdily, and in his heart cursed the dalliance made by his minions.

Not a scratch got Robin.

His sword seemed a part of himself, so deftly did he wield it.

There was this advantage with Robin in all his encounters—he maintained his coolness, nor let aught o'ermaster his passions.

The sun peeped through the trees at the combatants, and its beams settled now on one then on another with fanciful—nay, playful—effects.

Now they settled on Robin's sword's tip, making it bright with their golden rays. Anon they visited the sheriff, stealing across his face with a slyness, and bringing out into bold relief the workings of his base, passionate nature thereon depicted.

But the swordsmen plied their calling merrily.

Neither had a decided vantage.

The sheriff proved his swordmanship to be of no mean order.

At length, a stroke from Robin disarmed him, but unluckily his sword broke off short in the middle.

"A malison on thy maker, thou traitor steel!" exclaimed Robin, eyeing the broken weapon with unfeigned disgust.

With a bound, the sheriff had regained his weapon, and was upon him, thinking to take him at a disadvantage.

The combat was now a desperate one.

"Half a sword suffices for thy defeat!" exclaimed Robin, as he replied to the sheriff's attack.

"Thou had'st better yield to my mercy. Bethink thee of thy sad condition else!"

"Thou hast the most cause for so considering," answered Robin, beating down the sheriff's guard, and dealing him a blow that staggered him and dented deep his hauberk.

"Now shall the matter end," exclaimed the sheriff, rushing forward with impetuous haste and uplifted weapon.

"Ah, ah!" answered Robin, "thou Norman braggart! what say'st thou to that?"

Springing forward, Robin, with wonderful dexterity, seized the sheriff's sword-arm, and held it aloft with an iron grip.

With a backstroke from the hilt of his broken weapon, Robin dealt him a chest blow that sent him reeling backward.

The sheriff stumbled heavily, and Robin became entangled in his fall.

By a dexterous movement of the sheriff, he got him uppermost.

With vicious grip he seized Robin's throat, and with his arm on his chest, exclaimed exultingly—

"Thou art my prisoner. Yield thee, thou outlaw."

But he little knew Robin's strength.

With a superhuman effort he flung him a yard or more from him.

They rested awhile by mutual consent.

The combat was resumed.

Wrapping his jerkin round his left arm, Robin once again assailed the sheriff, who began to give evidence of weakness.

"Thou art undone, proud sheriff!" exclaimed Robin, as the sheriff defended himself with difficulty, and paced him backwards with uncertain steps.

"I yield not," he exclaimed. Ha! hither hie my men. What, ho! St. Denis to the rescue!"

The noise of approaching footsteps was heard.

Dealing the sheriff a terrific blow that laid him low, as if bereft of life, Robin fled.

His exertions had so weakened him that he was unable to make much headway against his pursuers, who were close upon him.

Robin stood at bay.

With bow in hand, he sought his quiver.

But *three* arrows only there remained.

The remainder had fallen out.

Twang! and one of his advancing foes bit the dust.

The arrow had pierced his brain.

Robin's blood was fully aroused.

He looked like a hunted lion at bay, so terrible his countenance, so noble his attitude.

The fate of their comrade warned them not to advance with temerity.

"'Tis useless to offer further resistance," exclaimed one of them.

"Speakest thou to a slave, thou Norman hind?" exclaimed Robin. "Have a care, else this Saxon arrow will best answer thine arrogance.

"Stand aside," a voice shouted. "This bolt will teach him to desist."

"Say'st thou so," exclaimed Robin.

With aimless aim almost, Robin shot his second arrow.

The promised cross-bolt came not.

The hand that had wielded it had become powerless in death.

"Ah, ah! thou Norman herd," shouted Robin, now thoroughly aroused and excited, "Lettest thou one Saxon defy thee. By my halidom thou art baser than I had e'er given thee credit for."

"S'death, an' thou thus tauntest us, devil or no devil, thou shalt suffer for thy contumaciousness."

A rush in a body, a cry of pain, a prostrate form with a Saxon arrow through his heart, and bold Robin was fearfully outnumbered.

His stout bow he unstrung and plied it like a quarter-staff.

Broken crowns there were, and aching arms, as Robin's blows descended fast and furious.

The very impetuosity of their onslaught defeated their object.

They huddled together so that their efforts to strike Robin down were impeded.

Rightly, merrily fought the bold outlaw.

Not a thought of surrender.

With Marian's name on his lips, and his merry men in his thoughts, he fought desperately and well.

But such odds were overpowering.

With a desperate effort he shook off the grip of two stout fellows who had seized him, and placing his bugle horn to his lips blew thrice clear and loud notes, making the forest resound again.

He was now firmly secured.

His proud fearless heart was not subdued, though fetters held him.

Forward came the sheriff, supported by two of his followers.

"Thou art mine now, Robin Hood, hated outlaw, and who is he that will deliver thee from mine hand!" And the sheriff smiled triumphantly.

"Spare thy taunts and threats, base Norman. That thou would'st do, my speech will not gainsay."

"Thy Marian, what will she say? The roses will fall from her cheeks, her eyes pale, and——"

"Silence! base Norman! pollute not her fair name by thine utterance."

"Ah! ah! by my knightly word, 'tis a thing worth dwelling upon. But hearken, let the maid be mine, and liberty is thine this moment?"

Robin's handsome face became purple with rage.

His whole form swelled with indignation.

With a desperate effort he snapped his cords asunder.

In a moment his hands were upon the sheriff's throat.

Throwing themselves upon him they bore him off his half strangled foe.

"By Our Lady! have a care, proud sheriff, how thou contemnest me again by such base offers, else will I force the breath out of thy dastardly carcass, though a thousand of thy minions guarded thee."

Robin looked kingly in his just wrath.

Gasping for breath, the sheriff ordered him to be well secured and bound to a tree.

"Let him be quickly despatched," he said with furious gestures.

"Fear I death! not I," exclaimed Robin. "I have braved it too often to look on't as an enemy. Thy worst deed, caitiff, shalt find Robin still unsubdued. St. George for merry England! Down with the Norman swine!"

A hushed silence fell on all around.

Robin waited calmly and fearlessly the advent of his merry men or death.

CHAPTER XLV.

HOW LITTLE JOHN AND HIS MERRY MEN BEGUILED THEIR VIGILS.

In the merry greenwood we hide away
From the sunshine so warm and gay;
When the moon's pale light shines o'er the night,
Then we skip it so merry and bright.

"I TELL thee, man, 'tis true. Did not I see them?" said George-a-Green, in an injured tone of voice.

"Thou did'st but dream of this matter, good George, replied Little John.

"Nay, push him not too hard, John," remarked Will Scarlet; "'tis hard to gainsay such sights."

This conversation was the result of a disclosure by George-a-Green of what befel him in the forest the night after he had seen Marian safely home, as narrated in a previous chapter.

Robin's merry men were seated in groups, awaiting the signal for action, and whilst waiting gossipped about all sorts of things.

"Narrate unto us the whole matter, then, George, and let's judge of it in a lump. At present it ill suits my belief to pay credit thereto."

"Nay; I have no wish to tickle any man's ears with goblin stories," grumbled George-a-Green, in reference to Little John's previous disparaging remarks.

"The story—the story!" cried a dozen or more voices.

Reclining in various fashions on the greensward, under the wide-spreading oaks, the foresters listened, while George-a-Green narrated the following:—

"Thou all knowest the Hazel Dell?" he began.

"Right well," chimed in several.

"'Twas there I passed, as the moonbeams shone brightly on my path.

"My mind was not running on any matter in particular, and I tramped lightly along.

"There is a path—a short cut leads down by a running stream—thither I hied me, with intent to reach home in half-an-hour, at least.

"Merry voices I heard carolling forth a sweetly strange ditty.

"The words were so pleasing that my mind has ne'er forgotten them since—

' The night we love, for 'tis then we roam,
    Gathering the dew from leaf and flower;
Hiding 'mid the branches of our forest home,
    Seeking mirth and frolic by the hour.

None to molest or intrude upon our mirth,
    With the moon's pale rays shining clear,
We frolic and gambol as we roam the earth,
    Free from pain, or sadness, or fear.

Join our hands, and sing till the glade
    Re-echo with our blithesome laugh and song;
We'll enjoy what our Creator Great has made:
    Love ourselves, nor work our neighbours any
        wrong.

Then let the forest ring with joyful shouts
    As we dance around the fairy rings so green;
Kiss the moonbeams as they chase us in and out,
    Bathing tree, and shrub, and flower in silv'ry
        sheen.'

"Thou art right, George," observed Little John; 'twas pleasant indeed for thee to listen to such a ditty."

"Ay, man, but proceed. Said they aught to thee?" said Will Scarlet, with a touch of impatience in his voice.

"Thou shalt hear. With curious intent I peered through an opening, and saw a sight not soon to be forgot.

"Hundreds of tiny figures roamed the glade, shouting, singing, and dancing.

"Dreaming I surely thought I was, 'twas so uncommon a thing I beheld.

"Such merry imps I ne'er saw, and of such comely forms withal.

"Lads and lasses were fully bent upon fun.

"Cautiously I crept forward, to more closely look upon so strange a sight.

"'Welcome, George-a-Green! Come forward,' said a score or more of voices.

"I trembled sore at thoughts of going among so strange a company, and held me purposely back.

"'Get thou from behind yon tree, and join our company, else thy case will be an evil one.'"

"Think of that; and what didst thou?" asked Little John.

"I e'en did as I was bid, and hied me among them.

"'Thee shunnest better company than thyself,' said one saucily.

"'Welcome to Sherwood's merry foresters,' said another; and blithely rang out their cheery voices on the night, in welcome to one so unworthy as myself.

"'Twas wondrous strange to look upon what I saw.

"For the space of a good bow-shot these fairies held their merry revels, until thousands could not count out their numbers.

"They were clad in green, and that of the best colour, like to ours.

"The lasses were decked in green kirtles, and their hair was fairly ablaze with jewels, like unto those worn at the King's court.

"Naught could I do but stare with main and might.

"'Drink, George-a-Green,' said one, offering me a tiny horn.

"Fearing to offend so brave and goodly a company, I e'en drank.

"It was but a drain of liquor, but had I drunken a dozen horns of wine, no such fancies would they have worked on me as did it.

"I laughed, sang, and danced, and was as blithesome as the best of them.

"'Ah, ah!' laughed one, 'the forester liketh our wine. Give him of it again to drink, while we sing:—

' Quaff, quaff the wine,
    Fill the horn up to the brim;
Drink it as the moonbeams shine,
    'Twill thee free from ache or whim.

'Twas distilled where violets grow,
    From the choicest flowery sweets;
If the secret thou would'st know,
    Search till the night the morning greets.'

"Suddenly the notes of a bugle horn sounded loud.

"Instantly the fairies hied them off affrightedly, hiding under thicket and brake.

"Rushing in mad career came a herd of deer, with riders to every one.

"The blood within me ran cold, for 'twas a most horrid sight.

"Circling round me came strange-looking fellows.

"Some had deers' heads, with branching antlers: others, heads of swine, dogs, birds, and such like things on a man's body."

"An' thou sawest them plainly?" asked Little John.

"Thou art not more plainly seen of me than were they.

"I stood in their centre, while with horrid glance they looked upon me.

"'George-a-Green! George-a-Green!' said one, that their leader appeared to be, 'long have we waited for thy coming. Thou wilt join our band.'

"My tongue clave to my mouth's roof, my limbs tottered, and helpless was I as a child of tender years.

"In accents harsh and unmelodious they carolled forth in chorus:—

' Hunters merry and free are we,
    Sweeping onwards till break of day;
Nor daunted are we by aught that we see,
    'Tis nothing can bid us our course to stay.

The owl gives out its dismal hoot
    As we ride swiftly and gallantly by,
With arrow keen the red deer to shoot,
    That under the greenwood so closely lie.

Blow a loud note on the bugle horn,
    Shout till the welkins do ring;
Night's shadows give chase to the moon,
    Onward, right forward, and merrily sing!'

"One blew a horn, and instantly the riders fell into rank by pairs, and dashed onwards.

"Last came a solitary rider, holding a deer by a leathern thong.

"An' I had been paid all the gold of the realm,

I could not help going forward and mounting its back.

"With mad and terrible speed did we hie onward.

"Nor brake nor thicket stopped our way, as the hunter's horn sounded loud in our ears.

"Two full mortal hours had we thus ridden ere my senses returned to me fully.

"Our Lady and all the saints forfend me from all harm, I cried aloud.

"'Twas hardly spoken ere the hunters vanished, and I lay on the greensward without life.

"The sun had well risen ere I roused, when I wended my way home, but never a word spake I of this until now."

"Right well told, George," exclaimed Little John. "I would thou would'st lead me thither some moonlit night to see such strange company."

"Thou would'st be befooled for thy pains an' thou did'st," exclaimed Will Scarlet.

"How so?" queried Little John.

"Naught would'st thou see. Only at certain times are they visible to mortal sight."

"Body-o'-me! they be strange folks outright," answered Little John. "They may revel and ride for me. But, Will, believest thou these mysteries?"

"That do I. Strange things have I myself seen ere now."

"The night is long," remarked one of the company, "and need'st enlivening. To thy story then, good Will."

The silence that ensued showed that his auditors were anxious for him to begin his story, which he did as follows:—

"'Twould be hard to find a sweeter spot than Leminton, on Devon's coast.

"I trow I could," exclaimed a forester, starting up. "Where wilt thou find a finer place than St. Michael's, on Cornwall's coast?"

"Nay, I take thee a wager," exclaimed Will Scarlet.

Up started several of the foresters to arbitrate on the contending claims.

"Spare thy breath, merry men all," exclaimed Little John. "Let the story proceed, else will the night run into the morning ere we hear one word of it."

This course was readily agreed to, and Will proceeded, taking care to preface his story with the above challenge again, which was not accepted, thanks to Little John's warning voice.

"Various caves are there to be found if sought after. Fond was I of spending my hours wandering along the sea-shore, and dreamily stretching my length in the warm sun.

"Being thus engaged one day, methought a voice strangely sweet sounded in mine ears:

' Beneath the wave in caverns fair,
  Safe from storms' harsh fury I dwell;
Decked is my couch with seaweed rare,
  Bordered by coral, costly gems, and sea shell.

Sport I merrily 'neath the bright-blue wave;
  Comb I mine hair by help of glass so clear;
Safe I recline when wild tempests do rave;
  Need not have I for anything to fear.

Come, then, with me to my bright sea home;
  Mortal cannot find one so happy and free:
Bid adieu to sorrow, and never more roam;
  Come, love, come, 'neath the waves with me.'

"Rousing, I looked around, and espied a maiden, lovely and fair, reclining on the waves.

"With eager beck and smile so sweet, she drew me near towards her.

"Spell-bound was I, and I could not find speech.

"Right into the sea went I so bravely.

"Her sweet smile so impelled me, that I forgot home, parents, friends, all.

"Giving to me her hand, we sank 'neath the waves, nor feared I the going.

"In a spacious cave I soon reclined with the sea maiden near me.

"Attendants she had in plenty, hieing hither and thither at her beck and call.

"'Twas a sight to see her home 'neath the wave.

"I was e'en fain to close mine eyes, so dazed did its brightness make me.

"Lovelier maiden eyes ne'er rested on, and I was well content to dwell with her for ever.

"But it was not to be.

"My mother's hands had placed round my neck an amulet to charm away evil things.

"This could not the sea maiden resist.

"Furious with passion and hate, she bade her minions seize and bare me aloft.

"I came bereft of life; and on waking, found myself on the shore, with my father bending over me.

"The story I told to all, but was scarcely credited.

"Some said I dreamed, others that the warm sun had impressed my brain with fancies and imaginings.

"One thing none could gainsay. The mark of the maiden's fingers remained on my right wrist, and may still be seen by the curious."

"What thinkest thou of that, Little John?" asked George-a-Green in triumph.

"Body-o'-me! 'tis hard to say. Ne'er have I seen aught that had not flesh and blood like myself. 'Tis strange, so few folks see such."

Morning broke about this time, and the lieutenant marshalled his men in readiness for action.

"Our Lady send brave Robin is safe," he observed. "His bugle hour summons is not yet."

"Hist! heard you not that signal, the owl's hoot. 'Tis tidings of Robin Hood, our master, depend on't?"

Will Scarlet was right.

With hot haste came the lad whom Robin had sent to Little John.

CHAPTER XLVI.

HOW THE ABBOT SERVED HIS FRIENDS.

The abbot he stormed at a furious rate,
  Ye slew not, he cried, my foes I wot.
Slew! cried the fellow, showing his cracked pate,
  By my oath, a good beating from the friar we got.

"SPEAKEST thou truly," asked the lord abbot of an attendant who had just apprised him of the arrival of two out of the three bravos he had hired to assassinate his enemies.

"They wait without, my lord; shall I bid them to thy presence?"

"Now does this matter assume grave import," the abbot soliloquised. "'Tis plain they are apprised of my hand in the matter. Robin Hood's vengeance will follow."

"My lord, the two soldiers wait without."

"A malison on the knaves!" exclaimed the abbot in a rage. "Thrice five crowns have I paid them for failure."

"My message, my lord. Shall I——"

"Peace, sirrah. Desire the knaves to wait without till it be my good pleasure to have audience of them.

The abbot paced the room excitedly.

"All my plans of vengeance are frustrated, and by a rebel in arms against his King and country. I'll to the King and secure his aid against Robin Hood. But first I must have audience of these cowardly louts."

Summoning his attendant, the abbot desired him to show in the men.

They entered with sorrowfully dejected mien.

The friar's lusty arm and stout staff had knocked all sprightliness clean out of them.

"Answer me truly, knaves," said the abbot, fiercely. "Thine undertaking—what of it?"

"Broken pates and bruised bodies, an' it please your lordship," answered one acting as spokesman.

"Thou attacked whom?"

"A lusty friar with oak staff; a malison upon him, he trounced us wofully."

"What, one man, and he a man of peace, to three soldiers!"

"Man of peace!" exclaimed the first speaker jeeringly.

"By my oath his hand is warlike enough, though he be a frocked and shaven priest."

"Ay, that it is. Would that he had kept his stout thwacks for those of his own condition;" and the speaker glanced slily at the abbot.

"Peace, knaves! Thou givest thy tongues too great a license," exclaimed the abbot; "discourse but of the matter on hand."

"Earned we not our money well, my lord? The balance is over due."

"Not a stiver—not a groat! Thou hast had already too much. But what of thy comrade? Speak!"

"We wot not of him. Yon cursed friar's staff knocked our wits clean out of our pates."

"Was he alone," asked the abbot, "when thou fell upon him?"

"Would it had been so; then had we given good account of him."

"Thou did'st sadly bungle in this matter. But thou hast not given answer to my question."

"There was with the friar two others. 'Twas our intention to strike him alone hastily, and in the confusion escape us hither."

"Thinkest thou your fellow is prisonered by the friar?" asked the abbot.

"Thou hast rightly discerned our thoughts, my lord. But we would thou would'st pay us that is our due, and let us depart."

"Said I not but just now, one groat more thou should'st not get from my purse?" said the abbot sharply; "have a care, lest thou fare worse than e'en the friar served thee."

"'Tis better far to buy our silence with money, than force our speech abroad by thy threats," said one of the soldiers boldly.

"Urgest thou such a thing upon my consideration!" exclaimed the abbot angrily.

"Now, by Our Lady, it will be seen, and that soon, that I care little for thy outpourings."

At his summons an attendant entered.

"Call hither the lay brethren to convey these swine to the cell thou wottest of."

The attendant cast a commiserating glance upon the soldiers, and departed on his mission.

"We crave thy pardon, my lord abbot," said he of the bold speech.

"'Tis too late. Thy tongue will have little opportunity to wag abroad."

A significant look passed from one to the other of the soldiers.

With a rush, they were upon the Abbot.

Their daggers struck his side, but harmed him not.

Under his robe was concealed armour of the finest texture.

The next moment they were prisoners.

Despite their resistance they were borne away.

In a cell, dark and drear, they were thrust.

With refinement of cruelty, they were placed in a sort of stocks, chained hard and fast, and joining each other.

Their gaoler brought them food, bread and water, and placed it where their manacled hands could *nearly* reach it.

Struggle as they would, it was past taking.

The abbot had his revenge, ample and full it was, too.

He sat in his room in thought.

With knitted brow and clenched hands, he sought to shape his thoughts.

"On the morrow, I will e'en seek the King and him request to guard my rights from the power of the daring outlaw, Robin Hood."

Touching a secret spring in the wall, there was disclosed to his view a cavity of somewhat large dimensions.

It was filled with gold and silver.

The abbot's eyes glistened with a strange light as he gloated over his hoard.

He saw not another face peer cautiously over his shoulder at the glittering heap.

"All mine!" the lord abbot said. "Not a person within these walls wots of this hiding-place, but myself."

After a pause, he continued:

"He whose cunning fashioned this concealment for me, lives not. His work finished, with it ended his life. 'Twas a cruel necessity," he soliloquised, "but much needed. The dead tell no tales!"

Closing the aperture the abbot seated himself, and regarded himself with complacency in a steel mirror.

"Bold Robin Hood cannot find my treasure, cunning and daring as he is. Did he but know of it, not all the bars and bolts ever forged by man would keep him from it, I trow."

A low chuckle startled the abbot from his unanimity.

He looked fearfully around.

But naught saw he more than himself.

He saw not a figure crouched low under a large oaken table.

Nor dreamed he that Friar Tuck's presence was so near.

How he so mysteriously appeared, must form the details of a separate chapter.

————

ROBIN HOOD,

AND THE OUTLAWS OF SHERWOOD FOREST.

LITTLE JOHN AND THE KNIGHT ARRIVE JUST IN TIME.

CHAPTER XLVII.

ARRIVAL OF THE MESSENGER AND RESCUE OF ROBIN HOOD.

"THY tidings, speak quickly," said Little John to Robin's messenger.

"Robin thy master has hied him northward

whither thou and thy merry men follow with all despatch."

Little John placed his bugle horn to his lips, and blew an assembly.

While his men were forming he plied the messenger with questions.

"Went Earl Mortimer with him?"

"Ay, that did he. The twain sat one horse."

"One horse! Body-o'-me, had they not two?"

"One an unlucky bolt killed dead."

"Ah! pursues them any of the sheriff's men."

"A score or more horsemen, with their master at their head."

"Said Robin aught else to thee; bethink thee ere thou answerest."

"Naught but what I've unfolded."

Scouts came in to report a force of the sheriff's crossbowmen astir and proceeding northward.

"Hie thee to the knight, bid him follow cautiously after them with his party, to act as occasion requireth."

Having delivered this command, Little John turned to the messenger again.

"Seemed the beast at all o'erburdened with its riders twain?"

"'Tis a horse of mettle as thou knowest; and kept its own against those in rear while I looked.'"

"That's good. Bladebone of St. Hubert! my master, Robin, must not fall into the sheriff's sharp claws."

Dismissing the messenger, he turned to his men, saying—

"Robin, our good master, hast hied him northward with the earl, and bids us follow. Brace thyselves to use quick despatch in following. Forward, lads, to the rescue!"

"To the rescue!" was the response shouted by all the band.

With speed they moved onwards, keeping marked silence.

Each one listened to catch the call of Robin's bugle; but it came not.

"What's thy thoughts of this matter, John?" asked Will Scarlet.

"Robin has done his work bravely. Earl Mortimer is with him. Thou heard'st that?"

"I did with great joyfulness. Our Lady send they safe escape the sheriff and his minions."

"Body-o-me!" growled Little John, "an' the base Norman hind but lay so much as his finger on him to his hurt, 'tis his to look to't. His days will be few, and I Little John promise for it."

"Heard'st thou that?" asked Will Scarlet.

Little John listened and replied:—

"'Tis but a bird's note. Robin's bugle hath a clearer sound."

"The friar was of our company a little while back; I saw him but now," said Will.

"He's more congenial work, I reckon."

"How so? He was hot on flying his bow against our Norman foes."

"I sent him with a knight and lady——But heard'st thou not that?" asked Little John, interrupting himself in the thread of his remarks.

The voice of an approaching horseman became plainly audible.

"Our Lady send 'tis Robin," said Will.

"An' it be my master, I vow a pair of silver candlesticks to her shrine; that is, good Will, when I find some fat-pursed fellow to help me to pay for them."

Nearer and nearer came the horseman.

Bounding forward, Little John cried:

"Halt, ye! whoever ye be, at thy peril!"

Earl Mortimer drew rein at Little John's side.

"Our master—what of him?" said Little John excitedly.

"He's in a thicket, a good few steps from here," replied the earl.

"And thou art here!" said Little John, half reproachfully.

"'Tis Robin's own doings, Little John; "my word on't, I'd leave him not otherwise. But advance quickly. I can discourse to thee as we travel."

With quickened pace the foresters moved on.

"Thou must know of Robin's whereabouts," said Little John to the earl, I pray thee move forward at our head."

"'Tis a grand doing," remarked Little John as the earl finished his narration of Robin's daring adventure in the castle.

"Is his equal to be found in this our land?" asked the earl enthusiastically.

"None is before him. Would he were here with our company now. I begin to be fearful for him."

"His speech to me was cheery. He feareth no danger to himself," replied Mortimer.

"Body-o'-me! he never did—never will," answered Little John, as if half amazed at the earl's remark.

"I would have thee bethink thyself too that the sheriff's men are accoutred and ill fitted for a chase through the forest after so good and crafty a woodsman as Robin Hood."

"There is comfort in thy speech," replied Little John, "but the sheriff's crossbowmen are abroad too, knewest thou that?"

"'Twas a thing I lacked knowledge of. But forward, good John, each step advanced is Robin succoured."

"There go some of the Norman hinds," said Little John, pointing to some of the sheriff's men in the distance.

"'Tis even so," replied Will Scarlet, who had by this time joined himself to the earl and Little John's company.

"A flight of arrows would deter their advance," remarked Earl Mortimer.

"Let them get entangled in the wood," replied Little John; "then will our fellows be more than a match for thrice their number."

"Well averred," said Will.

Turning round, Little John addressed the foresters as follows:

"Our master, good Robin, whom Our Good Lady have in her approved keeping, is in yon thicket. Between him and thee are Norman soldiers!"

A defiant shout greeted this harangue.

"Spread thyselves to the right hand and to the left, and teach these Norman clowns good woodcraft."

The cheer that greeted his speech, told Little John that he was well understood.

Unaware of the near proximity of Robin's men in their rear, the sheriff's men went forward.

"'Twill go hard, but Robin be captured this time," remarked their leader.

"Of that I am not well assured. His bugle horn hangs at his side. Its summons gets him instant help; of that thou art acquaint."

"Pish! He's but of mortal mould, and is found at disadvantage as are other men."

"I question not the soundness of thy speech, but it has ever been so, as I to thee have just said."

A flight of arrows in their midst made the Normans look round amazed.

"Advance quickly, one half," exclaimed the commander; "the remainder turn and let fly their cross-bolts rearwards."

This was done, and a shower of bolts went whizzing through the trees.

But each forester had gained the shelter of a friendly tree.

Them the bolts assailed not.

With true aim and swift arrow, Little John's men harassed the foe.

In vain they returned their fire, not a mark to them was visible.

Several Normans had bitten the dust, more were grievously wounded, still they held their ground like hunted deer at bay.

Slowly, but surely, they were being surrounded to their destruction.

Clear and shrill upon the air came three notes of a bugle-horn.

"Forward, my merry men all," shouted Little John. "Robin is at hand, and in sore plight, I ween."

Regardless of the Norman crossbowmen, onwards they dashed with speed.

Each man struggled hard to be first in to the rescue.

Turn we now to the party under Walter the knight. Obedient to Little John's commands, he led them on cautiously in the footsteps of the party of crossbowmen.

By skirting a thicket his manœuvre was unseen by those on the castle ramparts.

With his good sword drawn, and Robin's merry men at his back, the knight kept on.

Little weened the Normans who were tracking Robin to his death, that behind came so many good men and true.

The sun shone out gloriously, and penetrated the forest's gloom, lighting on the helmed heads of the Norman crossbowmen.

'Twere easy for the knight to have annihilated a score or more of them, but prudence forbade one arrow being thrown away.

"They go to Robin," he said in reply to his men's importunities to attack the foe. "'Twill be perilous to stop their advance until we, too, see him whom we seek."

This determination proved a good one.

In due time they arrived at a grove, and, halting his men, the knight reconnoitred.

Three pealing notes from a bugle-horn wakened the forest's echoes.

"'Tis Robin! 'tis Robin!" shouted he, and soon all were dashing forward.

"Little John's men here, too," said the knight joyfully, as they came in sight. "Now is Robin Hood safe; Our Lady be thanked!"

They formed quickly.

Peering cautiously in advance, Little John and the knight saw Robin bound to the tree.

The merry men bent their bows, and waited the signal.

CHAPTER XLVIII.

HOW ROBIN WAS RESCUED BY HIS MERRY MEN.

Draw to the ear my merry men all ;
  True be thine aim, sure thine eye ;
The Norman hinds in scores make to fall,
  Till they and their master be forced to fly.
The merry men drew to the ear so true,
  Each arrow found place in a Norman's breast ;
There fell that day of men not a few,
  Brave Robin and his men to flight put the rest.

"MARK well, those three with bows bent at Robin our master's breast," said Little John, in a suppressed whisper.

The merry men let fly, and the first to fall were the three crossbowmen whom the sheriff had appointed to slay Robin.

There fell also many others, so true did Robin's archers shoot.

With tremendous bounds Little John made for Robin's side.

His keen sword cut his bonds, and soon was his loved master free.

A warm pressure of the hand was all that passed between master and man.

They had other work to do.

"Take this sword, master mine," said Little John to Robin. "Body-o'-me! the Norman hinds must be vanquished quite."

With grim determination Robin rushed forward, dealing his blows right and left.

"Quarter to none!" he cried, as the bright blade he handled cleft in twain a stout Norman soldier's head.

Stoutly did the Normans resist.

Little John found himself hemmed in by a dozen of the sheriff's men.

Right sore they pressed him.

But Robin was at hand, and Will Scarlet too.

The red blood ran from Little John's arm from a slight wound, but for no quarter cried he.

"That for thy pains," he cried, as with terrific stroke he felled the fellow that had wounded him.

Foot by foot he and Robin contested.

Around them the battle raged furiously.

"Ah! ah!" cried Robin. "Thou hast found thy masters, base hinds. True men and free are for slaves a match!"

"St. Denis to the rescue! Hew and slay! give quarter to none!" shouted the sheriff, forcing his way towards where Robin stood.

Armed with a ponderous battle-axe, he struck down not a few of Robin's men.

"'Tis mine, the outlaw to slay!" he said, as with feverish haste he sought a place near his foe.

"Make way for the sheriff," shouted Robin. "Way there, sirrahs, for Nottingham's sheriff!" and a contemptuous laugh rang out clearly upon the air.

Face to face they stood.

The sheriff's battle-axe was lifted high.

It descended not on Robin.

One terrific blow caused the sheriff to reel.

It was dealt him by Little John, and he fell to the ground like a stunned ox.

Fiercer waged the battle o'er the sheriff's prostrate form.

In the *melee* some of his men managed to draw the sheriff away.

"Our Lady be thanked, they fly!" exclaimed Robin. "Pursue! pursue! my merry men all. Let vengeance still be taken upon our foes."

They chased them to the castle gates almost ; and ne'er so bloody a fray was known in these parts for many a day.

The foresters lost not a few, but the sheriff's company lost three to their one.

Right well did Earl Mortimer and Walter the knight ply their weapons.

Each man did his devoir in right gallant style for his master, good Robin.

Saxon bravery was that day well attested, and left its deep impress on Norman hearts.

"Welcome back, good master," exclaimed Little John, seizing Robin's hand. "Body-o'-me! but yon proud sheriff will keep his dastardly knaves far from thee in future, I opine."

Little John's welcome was supplemented by a hearty cheer from the assembled foresters, until the forest re-echoed again with its ring.

"Thanks, a thousand times o'er, my men, good and true," said Robin, in response to the greeting. "This day thou hast more than proved thy devotion to me thy leader.

"Long live Robin! Hurrah! hurrah! hurrah!"

They were the same cheers as have been heard by Britain's enemies many a time since—terrible to such, but inspiriting to friends.

Robin waved his hand and said:

"For this day's work each man will receive ten crowns from the treasury. Those that have fallen their share will be doubled to their friends."

"Each man will share a stoup of the best wine at my expense," said Earl Mortimer; "I publicly thank ye all for your help."

"Long live Robin! Long live brave Earl Mortimer! Confusion to England's enemies! Down with the Norman dogs!" and again went hearty cheers re-echoing through the forest.

"And thee, Robin, my friend and deliverer, what can I say to thee?" exclaimed Earl Mortimer, with emotion.

"Naught of praise deserve I for my friendly action in thy behalf. Thou knowest me as a friend, doubly endeared because of the cause we espouse."

"Thou hast bound thyself with strong cords to my heart, Robin. Perish Mortimer's memory if he should ever unbind them!"

"Ah, my friend," replied Robin, addressing himself in common to all around, "adversity close binds where prosperity ofttimes severs. What mine hand has done for Mortimer, I would do for any of my band. All are alike dear to me, alike true to each other."

Such a noble, disinterested expression of sentiment could receive none other than a warm response.

It was cheered to the full.

Turning to Little John, Robin said:

"Good John, let the dead have sepulture, alike Norman and Saxon; six feet of earth is theirs in common. Let the wounded have tender care; prisoners, if any, strict guard."

"'Twill be so, master. God rest the souls of all alike!"

Many devout "Amens!" followed Little John's charitable wish: for the Saxon foresters carried not their resentment and antipathies beyond death.

A party was soon told off for these offices, and the remainder stood guard against surprises.

A list of the names of the dead and wounded was handed to Robin, and as his eye glanced down it, real sorrow marked his handsome features.

"Will Scarlet is missing, an' it please you," said Little John.

"It cannot be," said Robin. "Will is too stout a Saxon yeoman to yield to Norman fetters. Inform thyself of this matter among the men; they may have knowledge of his whereabouts."

In a short time Little John returned with word that Will had been carried off prisoner by the sheriff's men.

"By my halidom!" exclaimed Robin, "the sheriff had well weigh the matter ere he lays a finger violently upon Will. I hold hostages on which to avenge him."

"Body-o'-me!" growled Little John, "Nottingham Castle will be imperilled, an' the sheriff but hurt a hair of Will's head."

Every member of the band swore an oath to rescue their comrade, who had endeared himself to each one of them by his frank and open nature.

"Let us on now to Sherwood," said Robin. "Our rest this night shall have been earned right well. Onward! march!"

As they went, Earl Mortimer discoursed with Robin about the events of the past day.

"'Tis to me even as a dream," he observed. "Events have so rapidly fashioned themselves, that one's belief is put to the test thereby."

"'Tis nothing, Mortimer," replied Robin. "A life in the forest is as full of events as an egg is full of meat. 'Tis not any one's to say what a day will bring forth."

"'Twill impart such a lesson to the sheriff, this of to-day's, that he will be fain to rest him e'er again he molests us."

"Intrigue and cunning will he next contrive, now that boldness has foiled his plans," said Robin, laughingly; "but he must play his game well to encompass aught of evil against me. Let him consider the reckoning."

"There fell full two score and a half Normans this blessed day," remarked Little John. "It lacks not one of that number, for 'tis mine own counting."

"And of our merry men fell what number?" asked Mortimer.

"Three-fourths of a score to the man," replied Little John, sorrowfully. "Full too many for such an occasion."

"Fought they not well?" said Robin. "I trow I never saw Normans so well conditioned in bravery."

"Their's was a desperate case," replied Mortimer. "Like hunted stags at bay they stood, and in their wild despair gat them the deeds of braver men."

"Well put, Mortimer," exclaimed Robin, who, of all men, liked a well-turned sentence. "But Saxon worth tried the baseness of their metal, and proved it worthless beyond dispute."

"But what of the friar?" asked Robin, suddenly. "His presence I wot is absent from us."

"Sir Richard Wykeham and his lady-love travelled hither seeking your protection," said Little John; "to the friar's keeping I confided them."

"By report he is not to me unknown," replied Robin; "has aught of ill befallen him?"

"Ill! beshrew me! but worse than ill, master mine!" answered Little John.

"Discoursed he to thee of the matter?"

"That did he. 'Tis Nottingham's sheriff is the despoiler of his property. Hast ever known the Norman different?"

"'Twill be mine to offer him means of redress," remarked Robin; "Saxon ne'er craved it of me in vain, and that all men know full well."

"Stand; the password at thy peril!" challenged a sentinel.

"Robin Hood and his merry men!" replied Robin, in quick response.

"Pass; God save ye all!"

Soon were the outlaws resting 'neath their old trysting-places, holding converse of the past day's exploits.

A savoury odour from the foresters' kitchen betokened preparations for a substantial meal, wherewith to allay their hungry cravings.

Robin's first care was to see to the condition of the wounded, who had been borne thither on rude stretchers, formed by the boughs of trees.

Next he had the Norman prisoners brought into his presence.

Addressing himself to the chiefest of them, he said:

"The just doom of ye all would be a short shrift and a long rope; but our warfare is not of such sorts."

"We are prisoners. Thy clemency is well received by us; our thanks are thine."

"'Tis not of this I would discourse," replied Robin; "the sheriff, thy master holdest one right dear to me, and all true men, named Will Scarlet.

"'Tis but one prisoner in return for us all," remarked the Norman.

"'Tis well said. I would out of thy number one be selected to bear my message to the sheriff."

A hurried consultation was held among the prisoners, and one of their number selected for the service.

"Say to the sheriff, I, Robin Hood, certifieth that, unless Will Scarlet be delivered up to me free of harm, within the first twain watch settings, two of those I hold prisoners will pay for it with their lives."

"'Twill be mine to deliver thy words as thou hast given them to me," the messenger replied.

"I further certify that each successive watch setting past the first twain that sees not Will Scarlet in our midst, will prove the last of other prisoners, till the number be expended quite."

"I am certified of thy message."

"I, Robin Hood, have so said, and it shall be done. Mine integrity is well known to the sheriff. Advise him to instant compliance, an' thou lovest thy comrades' safety!"

"Trust me. 'Twill be mine office to so discourse, that my master will be fain to pleasure thee in the matter."

"Depart not yet till thou hast refreshed thy tired condition," said Robin. "Sound to dinner, and that with quick despatch?"

Little John blew an assembly, and soon the foresters were seated at the rude, but plenteous board.

An unwonted silence reigned around.

Respect for the memory of those that had fallen in the strife that day, kept a still tongue in every head.

When the remains of the repast were cleared away, up rose Robin Hood, saying:

"Fill ye to the brim, one and all!"

'Twas done.

"Honour now my toast, I beseech you, my merry men all."

Holding his cup aloft, Robin said with deep feeling:

"To the memory of the brave dead. Full repose to both soul and body, and a resurrection joyful!"

The toast was fully responded to, and the foresters betook them to that rest which they so much needed.

The Norman messenger was conducted to the confines of the forest, and there bid to speed him on his errand with diligence and discretion.

Robin now held discourse with Sir Richard Wykeham and Maria Danvers, and they rested that night with light hearts.

He had promised them succour.

The worth of such promise was too well known to be lightly esteemed.

CHAPTER XLIX.

HOW FRIAR TUCK GAINED UNLOOKED-FOR ENTRANCE TO THE ABBEY.

The friar, he swore with a full round oath,
That to part from such a singer, he was loath.

• • • • • •

WHEN Friar Tuck had finished playing host to the stranger knight and lady, he took himself aside to rest.

But so much had he eaten and drank that sleep visited not his eyes.

"A malison seize the thing! Here am I winking until mine eyes are right sore, and never a nap can I get."

With drunken gravity he staggered up and held a colloquy with himself.

"Friar Tuck, thou art weakening fast through necessity of drink and food. Thy limbs refuse their office. See thou to this matter, ere it be too late, and strengthen thine inner self, that thy limbs may behave themselves more seemly."

He paused, and surveyed his feet, apostrophising them thus:—

"Out upon thee, for lazy fellows! Proceed. Good Robin will ne'er release Mortimer until thou lead'st me to his side."

Whether it was that his feet disliked being rated, certain it is that they slipped from under him, and he rested firm on the broad of his back.

The first blush of dawn was in the eastern horizon, and the birds carolled their matins amid the branches of the forest, as the friar made another desperate attempt to rise, and succeeded.

"'Tis well for my character that that knave Little John is not here, else would he ascribe my present condition to somewhat other than weakness of the limbs. Out upon him for a scandalising tongue!"

"A good man must needs be maligned;
　Fools prate, look wise, shake their heads;
Point as he walks, says he's lightly esteemed:
　Hang them—let them hie them to their beds.

If he drinks but a horn or so of wine,
　Feeling dry, *that* increases by the score.
Why he's a good man still for all they talk so fine:
　Hang them for fools—let them roar, let them roar.

Jolly Friar I am called by foes and friends;
　'Tis a scandal cruel thus me to be-name.
Let them prate, I will use the things that
　nature sends;
Did I not, folks would prate all the same.

After delivering himself of these verses in self-defence of his principle of non-abstinence the friar essayed to walk, and got along pretty well, though very slowly.

"My throat's parched," he said, with a thick utterance; "I will get me to the cellar and drink."

Mistaking the way in his drunken state, he steered an opposite course, and travelled in the direction of St. Mary's Abbey.

A donkey, ragged and hungered, saluted the morn, as the friar passed, in tones so lusty as to make himself heard far and near.

"Greet thee, friend," said the friar, with gravity, "a fine voice hast thou, I would thou would'st troll me a ditty."

As if responsive to the friar's kindly invitation, the donkey lifted up his voice and brayed e'en more lustily than before.

"Thy voice is not of ordinary sort, I wot," remarked the friar. "That quaver thou did'st so well execute tells that in Italy thine education was finished. I would I knew thy name and condition, friend, then would I take thee to my master, Robin Hood, to engage thine help in mass singing, thy voice is so well fitted therefor."

"I would fain hear thy voice again," remarked the friar, after a pause, "and join mine own in sweet concert therewith and thou be so minded."

"Well, an' thou refusest I e'en must show thee the power and compass of my voice. Perchance it will, or will not please thy liking."

Staggering over towards the animal, the friar placed his hand upon his back, and in that attitude commenced his ditty:

" Three jackdaws sat on a convent wall,
   In grave dispute, and sore perplexed,
When a shaven monk, so slim and so tall,
   To all three thus himself addressed:

' Give thee good morrow, sirs, one and all,
   Hast thou aught on thy minds, thou would'st lay bare,
'Tis mine office to hear when sinners do call,
   So confess thyself quickly, without shame or fear.'

The first jackdaw, with air so grave,
   Cleared his throat, wagged his tail, and loudly cawed;
Flapped his wings, hopped about, and looked so brave,
   That his companions did him warmly applaud.

With languishing eye and look demure,
   The jackdaw prepared himself to confess.
Quoth he, ' Holy monk I'm not very sure
   That anything on my conscience doth press.'

The monk looked glum, the monk looked stern,
   Shook his head with grave gesture, and said:
' Unbosom thyself, lest haply thou mourn,
   When too late 'neath the sod thou liest dead.'

Said the second jackdaw, with sad mien:
   ' Our thoughts we care not to disclose.'
Black must they be, then, I very well ween,'
   Quoth the monk, ' thou shalt not have repose.'

''Tis too bad thee to vex, holy Friar,'
   Quoth Jackdaw the third as he sat;
' The fact I'll disclose, and no longer thee tire—
   Our thoughts they dwell on yon cat.'

' He's a rogue, no greater doth live,
   'Cept us three and thou, holy Friar;
To him due penance and stripes quickly give,
   As for us we go mounting up higher.'

In a rage the monk a stone he threw
   At the jackdaws that sat on the wall;
At which they but jeered with caws not a few,
   And mocked when the stone on the Abbot did fall.

Poor monk he got whipped, according to law,
   Stripes not a few on his back fell apace.
Three jackdaws came to his window to caw,
   And jeer him upon his most pitiful case."

"Excel that, and thou can'st," said the friar, on finishing his song.

Whether it was the friar's tones that stirred up the animal to bray, just as cocks do crow when challenged by their kind, does not appear; but a very ancient chronicler has it that the donkey did bray, and that most lustily.

"Well done; thou art well attuned and jolly. But can'st thou do aught at quarter-staff or shoot?" said the friar with gravity.

No answer came to the friar's challenge.

Thou must e'en carry me, fellow, or receive three buffets for thy refusal. Dost hear? Bladebone of St. Hubert! but thou hast a rough hide, though thou art a well-favoured singer.

By dint of great exertions the friar mounted the animal's back; which, left to its own devices, hied it leisurely off towards the Abbey.

The friar slept as he rode, and was borne at last to the Abbey gates.

Looking out through the lattice, the warder espied Friar Tuck seeking admittance.

"Thine errand, father?" he said, on seeing the friar's priestly garb.

A loud snore from the friar was the only response.

"Our Good Lady save us! how he groans," exclaimed the warder; "some holy man doing penance, I wot."

Acting upon this assumption, he opened wide the gate and let the donkey in.

He shook the friar by the arm, but failed to rouse him.

"'Tis a miracle!" remarked the warder; "hither has this ass brought this holy man, and he fast asleep through grievous watchings and fastings!"

He had him carried in bodily, and placed in a dormitory, where the friar slept and snored his fill.

Waking betimes, and feeling a great thirst after his copious libations of the past night, he looked about him for means to quench it.

Seeing a room open of inviting appearance, Friar Tuck made bold to enter, and was fortunate enough to find what he was in quest of.

After satisfying his thirst, he looked about, and was not slow in recognising that he was not in his old haunts at Sherwood.

Though still greatly stupified by his inordinate drinking of the previous night, he was sensible enough to use wariness and discretion in his actions.

Selecting a quiet nook in the room, he coiled his fat person together, and settled himself to finish his slumbers.

When the abbot entered, he awoke, and peering cautiously forth, saw and heard what passed between him and the assassin he had hired, and whom the friar had so signally vanquished the previous night.

"'Twill ill betide me an' I show my face to the abbot. 'Tis quite clear he bears me no love," said the friar to himself as he listened.

Delighted was he to witness the closing scene of the interview as recorded elsewhere.

But more delighted still was he when, peering cautiously over the abbot's shoulder, he saw the glittering treasures of this miserly churchman spread out before him.

So engrossed was the abbot, that he noticed not the friar's presence, although he was close at his elbow.

Taking due note of the position of the secret-spring, the friar stepped back to his hiding-place.

Unfortunately he upset a stool, and the noise attracted the abbot's attention.

He turned round with great haste, but saw not the friar crawling under cover, else had it gone ill with him.

"'Tis strange how nervous I am of late. 'Tis the cares of mine office weigh heavily upon me," said the abbot on failing to see any cause for his fright.

"Mine hands will ease thee of some of thy cares," remarked the friar to himself, "or it will go hard with me."

His hand itched to handle the abbot's gold pieces, and he waited for a fitting opportunity to do so.

Soon this presented itself.

The abbot left.

Cautiously emerging from his hiding-place, the friar pressed the spring, and the abbot's treasure lay opened before him.

His first care was to secure the door from within; that done, he began to hide as many gold pieces about him as he could conveniently carry.

"Now St. Hubert be praised," he said, "but this is fine. Sawest thou ever such gold pieces, Friar Tuck?"

He was in raptures.

"Thou may'st stay here too long, my good fellow," he said, addressing himself, "so e'en get off with despatch.

Laden like a donkey almost, the friar left the abbot's room.

He was met on his way by some of the monks, and had to accept their kind invitation to a repast, although he tried hard to refuse.

He greatly feared detection at the hands of some of the confraternity; especially of those monks, whom he and Little John had eased of the tithes.

Being full of contrivances, however, he lacked not one for the present occasion.

He kept his cowl closely drawn round his face.

"Thy vow, good brother, debars thee from showing thy face to any," queried one of the monks.

"Thou hast rightly conjectured," Friar Tuck replied. "My vow is of such a sort. Nor is my speech to be too long."

"Thy voice hath a familiar sound to mine ears," observed one of the monks that had suffered from the friar's depredations.

"A good man's voice is always familiar to a brother. Goodness makes a bond of brotherhood between such."

After delivering himself of this well turned compliment to his interlocutor, the friar modestly folded his hands across his fat paunch, and eyed the monks sharply from beneath his cowl.

"Thou art not that ungodly man, Friar Tuck?" asked one of the company, rather bluntly.

"But brother of his am I," replied the friar with imperturbable coolness of speech and manner.

"Thou hast a strong likeness to him," remarked his querist. "Our Lady send thou resemble him not in rogues' ways."

Friar Tuck devoutly crossed himself as if the bare mention of such a possibility horrified him.

Inwardly he vowed a vow, mentally registered, to trounce his tormentor's hide the first favourable opportunity.

"Thou hast heard of his malpractices, doubtless," observed the monk.

"'Tis said his sanctity is not highly flavoured with scourgings and fastings," replied the friar; "I will teach him better things, and with mine own hands lay on the stripes thickly."

There was a general laugh at this.

The bare idea of anybody inflicting a scourging on Friar Tuck, strong armed and lusty, was so preposterous that it quite tickled the monks.

"I wish thee well out of thine office," remarked the same monk, laughingly.

"Thou alludest, doubtless, to his strength of arm, and pugnacious condition," replied the friar. "But I, too, can strike a good blow."

Raising his arm he struck his tormentor, who stood near him, a blow which quickly felled him to the floor.

It would be difficult to say whether resentment or astonishment worked strongest in the minds of the monks assembled.

Certain it is that three of them seized the friar.

He was greatly disposed to give them similar treatment, but desisted for fear of consequences.

Assuming an air of innocence, he said—

"Nay, good brothers, be not angered. I but demonstrated my ability to deal with that ne'er-do-well relation of mine. Besides, it was but a gentle blow."

"Gentle!" said the monk who had received it; "gentle, call you it? It was strong, and withal malicious. Hold him fast while I hie to the lord abbot to acquaint him of the matter."

"Nay, nay, good brother, thou mistakest my motive in thus attributing maliciousness as its cause," Friar Tuck said. "I pray thee think no more of it. Here's my hand."

"Let charity prevail," said the monk who had admitted the friar to the abbey; "our good brother was in a sorry plight on his arrival. His weakness was so great as to unfit him to bestride his ass."

"What are these things I feel?" asked one of the monks who held the friar, in allusion to the gold pieces which he had stuffed away about his person in all directions.

"They be part of my penance," replied the friar, quite unconcerned; "stones and gravel have I placed next my person to mortify my body."

"Release him, good brothers, I beseech you," said the friendly monk; "'twould be rank sacrilege to further molest such a holy man."

His intercession prevailed, and Friar Tuck was released.

His proffered hand was not refused by the monk he had so unceremoniously treated.

It was evident, however, that he little relished the warm grip of the friar's hand, which caused tears of pain to spring to his eyes.

He got him as far off as possible from his demonstrative brother, fearing that he would again illustrate some theory with practical force upon his person.

"I shall depart now," said the friar; "my benison I leave with you. Poor I came, poor I depart, to fulfil my vow."

The friar had only been enlightened a few minutes previously as to how he had come to the abbey, which circumstance up to that time was a complete mystery to him.

"Abide yet a little time longer," one of the monks replied; "I will acquaint the lord abbot of your presence."

"Concern not yourself, I pray you," Friar Tuck said. "I am unworthy of having speech of such a holy man."

He added mentally, "I am too well known to him to befool him as I have these."

Turning to the monk who had befriended him, the friar said:

"Let my beast be got ready, good brother. He is but a sorry creature, though well suited to one of my lowly, humble condition."

Friar Tuck stood at the gate bidding adieu to the monks.

He mounted his ass, and was just about to start when a loud outcry was heard.

"Secure him! Hold him fast! 'Tis Friar Tuck."

Before hands could be laid on him, he struck his heels viciously into the beast's sides, and went riding away at a good pace, pursued by the monks.

The friar laughed outright, and urged the ass on to greater speed.

"Bladebone of St. Hubert! wont Little John laugh when I narrate my adventurous stay in yon abbey. Robin Hood, too, will be mightily pleased. 'Twill be a standing joke for our merry men all."

On reaching the forest, the friar was met by a party who had been sent in search of him, headed by Little John in person.

"Body-o'-me!" growled the giant, "thou art troublesome to find. Search have we made high and low for thee. I'm both tired, hungry, and thirsty."

"Ah! ah! ah!" laughingly shouted Friar Tuck. "Chide me not, good John, until thou art acquainted with all particulars of the matter."

"Particulars!" quoth Little John. "Where hast thou been, sirrah?"

"To visit the lord abbot of St. Mary's."

"Thou dost but jest; thy carcass would not be safe within St. Mary's walls."

"Ah! ah! list to this John; list to this! Heard'st thou ever such a merry chink. Gold, too! all gold!" and the friar took out a handful of gold and jinked it up and down.

"Beshrew me! but it sounds of a good sort. Thine absence is ever welcome, an' it bears such interest. Is that——"

"I am in search of my brother, our Friar Tuck," said the friar, laughing uproariously;

> "Saw'st thou aught of brother of mine,
> Sleek of person, and strong of will;
> Tell unto me, good reward shalt be thine,
> If not, I'll go seeking him still."

"Thou discoursest mysteriously. Beshrew me, I like plain speech best. Thy meaning to me disclose."

"Patience, good John; let's proceed. The lord abbot is mightily anxious to find me; I would rather be apart from him."

"Body-o'me!" said Little John; "let but one of his shaven crowns be found by me within Sherwood's forest, an' 'twill go hard with me but that I make his pate ring for him!"

"Heed them not; but of my brother, John; sawest thou him?—

> "Dark is his hair, sturdy his frame,
>   He rideth on beast of good breed;
> Unto thee I cannot disclose his name,
>   Tell to me then, for great is my need."

"Ah! ah! hold me John, or I shall die outright! the matter does so tickle my fancy."

"I care not so long as thou art safe," replied little John; "laugh thy fill; tis a sorry time, though, for merriment"

"How so?" asked the friar, with seemly gravity; "hast aught befallen our master?"

"Our Lady be thanked! he is safe. But others rest them beneath the sod?"

"It grieves me to hear it. But how came it all about. Is the earl safe?"

"I shall discourse thee on the matter at leisure. Meantime, tell me of thine adventures. St. Hubert! but we all gave thee up for lost."

Whereupon the friar told him all.

His arrival was greeted with acclamation by all the band, especially by Robin.

The sight of so many gold pieces was a welcome thing to all, for the treasury was beginning to get very low.

"I'm right glad," said Robin laughing, "that thou hast been so well employed. Sent my lord abbot his love or benison?"

"I stayed not to hear it," replied the friar merrily, "I was too preciously freighted to stay his pleasure."

"Thou may'st seek thy brother, an' thou wilt?" said Robin.

At which there was a general roar of laughter.

"With mine own hand will I scourge his hide," replied the friar; "but, St. Hubert! I am hugeous dry. Hast thou aught good in the cellar?"

"Not a drop," said Little John, with a merry twinkle in his eye. "Of water there is a plentiful supply."

"To the Evil One with thy water. 'Twill go hard with the cellarer, an' he findest me not something good."

"So, so, my lord abbot, thou art well repaid for thy dastardly conduct," exclaimed Robin. "Assassins, too! Thou overreachest the sheriff himself in evil intrigues."

After a pause, he said to Little John:

"Let the prisoner be brought before me. Thou knowest whom. 'Tis the lord abbot's minion, I would see."

In a short time he was brought.

"Thou meritest naught at my hands but death," said Robin sternly, "but I give thee thy life, because Friar Tuck hath promised thee it. See thou offendest not again."

The fellow was conducted to the confines of the forest, and then released.

"Should the sheriff's messenger come during my absence, keep him until I return."

So saying, Robin turned and walked quietly towards St. Ann's Well.

ROBIN HOOD,

AND THE OUTLAWS OF SHERWOOD FOREST.

THE TOURNAMENT AT NOTTINGHAM CASTLE.

CHAPTER L.

Thou art ever welcome, Robin dear,
Thy Marian loves thee past compare.
That thou lovest me, thine eyes show clear,
In my heart thine image I always bear.

"Ah, thou truant," said a sweet musical voice,
as Robin emerged into view.

"Marian sweet! thy chiding is undeserved,
believe me!" exclaimed Robin, as he pressed
the blushing Marian to his heart.

"I did but jest, Robin dear. Thy Marian
knewest what thou wert about, noble Robin."

She looked lovingly into his face, while her's
reflected the happiness that in his shone.

"Stirring times have befallen me since I last

pressed thee to my heart, dear Marian. The earl is free."

"The whole country rings with the account of thy noble exploit; my Robin is the theme of every tongue."

"Unworthy am I of such homage; I but helped a friend. Dastard is he that would not act as did I."

"The strife was sore I heard. But Robin, sweetest, tell me, art thou hurt, and thy Marian know it not?"

"Sweet girl, Our Lady well protects those that in her trust. Thy prayers, too, are they not Robin's? and shelter they not him from danger?"

"Thine—all thine—are they. A present will I offer at Our Lady's shrine, for this her great blessing conferred on thee and me alike."

"Thanks, Marian, darling. But I desire to speak to thee of another matter."

"Say on; I listen."

"With me in Sherwood is a lady — one Maria Danvers."

"Nay, start not, Marian," said Robin, laughingly, nor be jealous."

"Thou merry gipsy; but say on."

"Her would I confide to thy tenderest care."

"Has she no protector?"

"One who values his life as naught in her service."

"She is welcome, dear Robin, for thy sake. Marian will be to her as a sister."

"Thanks; Robin knows not when he has asked aught of thee and been refused."

"I will wait her coming with impatience," said Marian.

"What of thine uncle the miller, Marian; of late I have seen but little of him."

"He is well, but sorely tried by the sheriff's attentions to me."

"He likes not his wooing of thee then?" asked Robin with a roguish smile.

"He threatens to thrash his hide well, an' he shows his Norman visage near the mill again."

"'Tis his meddling is my greatest concern. I would have both thine uncle and thee beware of Nottingham's sheriff."

"Have no fear, Robin; he dreadest thine anger too greatly to do aught unseemly."

"I cannot bear thee out in this. That he fears me is clear; but I opine he would anything brave to get possession of thee."

"Trust to Our Lady, and better times, Robin, dearest."

"Were I other than I am, Marian darling, thou would'st not lack my protection in a nearer, dearer form than now."

"I can wait, dearest. To know thou lovest me, Robin, is to me so sweet that aught else pales before the thought of my happiness."

"Dearest, thou little knowest how I crave for a quieter life. But it cannot be. The land groans under Norman tyranny; our liberties, our dearest, sacred rights are trampled upon; and shall I, Robin Hood, whilome Earl of Huntingdon, shrink from the dangerous task of avenging these wants and injustices."

Robin Hood looked noble in his just anger.

"Never, Robin!" exclaimed Marian with enthusiasm, and hanging by her hand on his shoulder. "Never! Be thine the proud and glorious task to free our land. Then rest."

"Noble, devoted Marian, would that all were actuated by thy spirit, then would the hated Normans be driven from the land, and Saxons have their own again."

"Stay not thine hand, dearest, for thought of me," said Marian. "Bethink thee, that beyond the grave is a happier life where we will ne'er be parted."

"Even so. Here I am hunted, outlawed, condemned by the rulers of the land. But my hand shall make itself felt among them. Then welcome death if needs be."

"Spoken like mine own true-hearted love," said Marian. "But tell me, dearest, how fared my cousin in the fray?"

"He gat him honour on his foes. Much's presence was where danger was most thickly strewn."

"I am glad. But see who comes this way. 'Tis the sheriff and the abbot I wist."

"Truly; let us to cover, perchance they will discourse of things edifying to me."

Screening themselves effectually from observation, Robin and Marian listened.

"Sayest thou the friar thieved thy gold, and thou hadst no redress," asked the sheriff.

"'Tis true," answered the abbot, with an audible groan.

"Now by my halidom this must be stopped."

"But how?" asked the abbot.

"Hie thee to the King; of him ask help; show him thy losses, thine indignities, and the state of the country. I will endorse thy report."

"'Tis well counselled. I myself had so determined, and my coming to thee was on this very matter."

"'Tis a good omen of success I ween. But say, canst thou not counsel me by thine advice how to snare Robin Hood?"

"Of this I have had thought too," said the abbot.

"Ah! of what sort?"

"Of this. Rememberest thou speaking of an archery meeting."

"Yes, yes; but thou did'st not approve it."

"Now I do. Speak fair to Robin Hood, grant him thy protection in speech only. Arrange thy men to encompass his doom."

"Base churchman!" exclaimed Robin between his clenched teeth.

"Hist, Robin; listen!" and Marian laid her hand warningly upon his arm.

"My perception of thy meaning is plain," said the sheriff. "Beshrew me, but it promises well too.

"Be but discreet, and 'twill end well. Thou knowest full well that the King would favour any means for the outlaw's destruction."

"Full well. The outlaw's contumaciousness enrages him beyond endurance."

"Earl Mortimer, too," said the abbot.

"Have no fear. Let Robin Hood but fall, the earl is then undone."

"Thou owest neither any love," said the abbot with a low laugh.

"Nay, but rather dire hatred. But for Robin Hood's cursed interference Mortimer would now be past further mischief."

"'Tis said the country is with he and Robin."

"'Tis said, but requires confirmation. The people are ever for those who successfully rebel. Let but their leaders suffer defeat and they scatter like frightened sheep."

"Of the fray of yesterday. Thou hast not yet spoken of it except sparsely."

"Name it not. 'Twas a bitter defeat. But it shall be avenged. I, Geoffrey de Lois, swear it."

"Believe me, nephew mine, cunning and stratagem oft encompass what force does not. Let my advice counsel thee, and thou wilt yet succeed."

"The archery meeting shall take place. I will e'en commence by granting him a concession."

"How so?"

"I hold one Will Scarlet a prisoner. Him has Robin Hood demanded of my hand."

"Well."

"To hang him I had determined, despite the outlaw's threat to retaliate."

"And now."

"I will surrender him, and be soft of speech in the doing of it withal."

"I perceive thou art rightly proceeding in the matter."

"In a short while I will make advances, profess a friendship for Robin, and invite him to share my hospitalities."

"Have a care how thou proceedest. Robin Hood is shrewd, and is not caught like a foolish bird with chaff."

"Fear not," said the sheriff. "To overthrow him I am bent."

"We will now return," said the abbot.

"When go you to the King?"

"When you have arranged with Robin for the archery match," the abbot replied significantly.

They passed out of sight and hearing.

Emerging from their concealment, Robin Hood and Marian gazed at one another for a few moments in silence.

"Heard'st thou ever such shameless scheming?" asked Robin at last.

"A churchman, too," remarked Marian. "The sheriff I am not surprised at. He, I know full well, is capable of any wickedness."

"Fear not, Marian. This treachery will recoil on their own pates. Mark me in this."

Robin looked stern, and a flush of anger passed over his handsome features.

"Thou wilt not accept the sheriff's treacherous invite to the archery match," queried Marian.

"Will I not rather? 'Tis not fear of danger that will Robin deter."

A look of pain passed over Marian's beautiful features. Love made Robin susceptible of having pained her. She was hurt by his last remark.

He hastened to excuse himself.

"Forgive me, dearest," he said, "I spoke harsh, but not to thee, sweetest. Sooner be tongue of mine cut forth than that it utter one word to cause my Marian pain."

"Say no more, Robin, darling," Marian replied, as she imprinted a tender kiss on his cheek.

"Thus will I repay thee this loving kiss," exclaimed Robin, with tenderness in his voice.

Drawing her fondly to his bosom he kissed her pouting lips and looked into the depths of her love-laden eyes.

"Thou wilt use every precaution, love?" asked Marian.

"Of a surety. The sheriff will not trap me like a wild beast. He will have cause to rue his malicious intriguing against my life."

"Thy trusty followers will attend thee?" asked Marian timidly, as if fearful of arousing her lover's ire.

"Fear not, sweet girl. Hast ever known Robin fail in aught he undertook?"

"Never; for which Our Lady be thanked. But see, hither comes my uncle. Shall we advance to greet him?"

"Even so. I must then leave thee, dearest. Duty claims my strict attention."

Running forward with light and graceful steps, Marian bestowed a caress on her uncle's cheek, saying,

"Greet thee, lovingly, uncle. How art thou to-day? Here is Robin."

The miller grasped Robin's hand with friendly warmth.

"I greet, thee, noble Robin," said Much the Miller. "Thou hast well proved thy Saxon bearing."

"Indifferently, Much, but indifferently. Mortimer, as thou knowest, is safe."

"All the saints be praised for it," replied Much. "But, Robin, whom think'st thou I met but just now? Thou wilt never guess an' thou triest for a year."

"I wager thee twenty crowns against a sack of thy best flour that I tell thee truly," said Robin.

"Wager not, uncle mine," said Marian, laughing, "thou wilt lose."

"Thou seemest to know," said Much, half dubiously, as if debating with himself whether to accept or decline the proffered wager.

"The sheriff and abbot," said Robin Hood, merrily.

"Thou would'st have won, man," the miller replied. "But what think'st thou, they are concocting?"

"Ah! 'tis my turn now to challenge thee to disclose this, Much," exclaimed Robin.

"Nay, thou hast me there. Know'st thou?"

"That do I, and Marian also. We hid and listened to as base a plot as could be planned by man."

"Against thee, I can plainly perceive it was, by thy knitted brows."

"E'en so. But it boots not. The sheriff will be overmatched."

"That will he," replied Much. "He must have a cool head, a brave heart, and steady hand that would plot against thee, Robin."

"Marian will disclose to thee what it is," said Robin; "but I would ask that not a word escape either of thy lips on the subject."

"Thou hast my promise," replied Marian.

"And mine," said the miller.

"Farewell, sweetest," said Robin, turning and pressing Marian to his heart, and imprinting an impassioned kiss on her ruby lips.

"Farewell, Robin, darling; Our Lady forfend thee from all harm."

"To-morrow Maria Danvers will be with you."

Much the Miller looked inquiringly.

"I will explain to thee, uncle," said Marian.

With a friendly parting Robin walked away and was soon lost in the forest.

Marian watched him with loving eyes until his manly form no longer met her admiring gaze.

CHAPTER LI.

ROBIN HOOD HOLDS A COUNCIL, AND RECEIVES
AN INVITATION FROM THE SHERIFF.

So foul a thing I ne'er did hear.
Attend my words, my merry men all,
Bold Robin and thou hast naught to fear,
Though the Sheriff contriveth to make us fall.

"WILL SCARLET has not yet arrived," said Little John to Robin Hood, whom he had gone to meet.

"But shortly will," replied Robin with significant emphasis on his words.

"Body-o'-me!" said John. "Impatience grows apace on me. I would, good master, I had your permit to bring Will away bodily from Nottingham Castle."

"Which thou wilt not," answered Robin with a laugh. "But attend me, I would have speech with you on certain matters of import——"

"And the abbot, he turned him red with rage,
And vowed, with oaths, the friar to cage."

"Friar Tuck, comes this way," remarked Robin, as the lusty tones of the friar's voice reached him.

"What ho, there, chaplain mine!" sang out Robin, "come hither, I much need thy wise counsels."

"Thou hast them at thy command at all times," replied the friar, emerging into view——

" 'Tis ghostly counsel brings comfort and good,
'Tis better than drink, its excellent food."

"Body-o'-me! but *thou* thrivest well on it," said Little John.

"Thou art ever malicious, John," replied the friar. "I vow I am grievously fallen away of late. Fastings and penances, stripes and discomforts——"

"A truce to this badinage, my lieges," said Robin jocularly. "Let's to council."

"I attend you," answered the friar.

Little John looked as grave as an owl, but said naught.

"What I now divulge," remarked Robin, by way of preface, "must remain in your secret keeping until I permit its disclosing."

"Thou art about to confess thyself, my son," said the friar with mock gravity.

"Even so, holy friar," replied Robin with a laugh. "Absolution I crave not; 'tis not my own sins but another's I would disclose."

"Proceed, my ears are itching to hear thy speech."

"And mine arm itches to give thee a buffet for thine interruption," said Little John to the friar.

"Peace; a truce to this bantering," replied Robin. "A short time since I was listener to a plot against our common safety."

"Now Our Lady be thanked!" ejaculated the irrepressible friar.

"Quiet thou prate-pate," said Little John.

"Treachery is engaged to cause our destruction. In friendly guise comes the sheriff to invite us to his festivities."

"Has he a good cellar?" put in the friar.

"Thou never tastedst better than his providing could give thee," replied Little John, smacking his lips at the thoughts of his deep potions in the sheriff's cellar, as related elsewhere.

"Thou wilt accept his graciousness?" said the friar interrogatively.

"Yes, jolly friar, and I would have my merrymen all at my back, but not perceivable," replied Robin.

"Ah, I perceive," remarked Little John; "yon sheriff would hold a tournament."

"Even so, good John, and would us invite to an archery meeting, while the abbot hies him to the king to beseech his aid for our destruction."

"Thine informant, good master?" queried Little John.

"The sheriff and my lord abbot," replied Robin with a bow of mock courtesy.

"Now this is mightily strange," put in the friar. "So tight-fisted are the pair that such imprudent disclosures seemeth not to favour them."

"They recked not I listened, and spoke of their devices freely."

Footsteps were now heard approaching.

The new-comers proved to be none other than Earl Mortimer and Walter the knight.

"Welcome to our councils," said Robin, advancing, and shaking them by the hand warmly.

"I trust nothing of evil import threatens," replied the earl.

"Naught of great import, of a surety, brave Mortimer," answered Robin. "'Tis the sheriff would fain encompass our destruction by stratagem and treachery, when all other means have so signally failed him."

"A base, false-sworn knight," remarked Walter.

"Thou dost truly describe him," replied Robin; "but thou shalt judge for thyself in this matter."

Whereupon Robin related in substance all that he had overheard the sheriff and abbot discourse of.

"Being forewarned," remarked the earl, "thou wilt, of a surety, refuse to peril thy safety by acceptance?"

"Not so, Mortimer. He who would try conclusions with Robin Hood, must perforce be humoured to the full of his bent."

"'Tis as I have always avowed," put in the friar. "'Tis always better to humour one's longing, e'en if it be at the cost of a broken crown."

"So would I treat Nottingham's sheriff," remarked Robin.

"I would that each of you consider well how to circumvent his designs, and inform me of your plans."

"Hist!" said Little John, holding up his finger, his practised ear having detected the noise of advancing footsteps.

The crackling of dried leaves evidenced the necessity of Little John's warning, and soon appeared a party of the sheriff's men, having with them Will Scarlet.

"Thy business," said Robin, advancing.

Then perceiving Will Scarlet, he said, seizing his hand with friendly grasp:

"What! Will, lad, amongst us once again? Now Our Lady be thanked. We owe her much for her goodness to theeward."

"Greet thee, master mine," replied Will, returning Robin's warm-hand pressure. "I am with thee, as thou seest."

"Speak I to Robin Hood?" deferentially asked the leader of the sheriff's party.

"I am he; say on. What is thy master's good pleasure?"

"The good knight, Geoffrey-de-Lois, sheriff of Nottingham, sendeth thee greeting on this wise, in answer to thy message, pertaining to the release of one Will Scarlet, whom I now hold in my keeping."

"Thou holdest," muttered Little John, in high dudgeon, and regarding the speaker menacingly.

"Gramercy!" said the friar aloud and mockingly, "We are mightily beholden to thy master for his tender mercy. Beshrew me——"

"Peace," said Robin. "He but delivers his message to the best of his ability."

Turning to the messenger, he said—

"Say on, and take not offence at aught that has been said. My men are but rude of speech, and lack Norman polish."

It was doubtful whether Robin meant his concluding remark as a compliment or not; certainly his tones had a delicate vein of satire running throughout them.

"Norman roguery," exclaimed Little John aloud.

"Thou art but a Saxon churl," retorted one of the sheriff's party.

"Have at thee, thou foreign knave," said Little John, springing forward.

"St. Hubert! but I am with thee," shouted the excitable friar.

But Robin was too quick for them both.

Hurling Little John back, he said, reprovingly—

"Is it thus thou would'st brawl with friendly messengers."

"I crave pardon of thee, master mine," said Little John, apologetically, "but mine hand itched to trounce the fellow for his presumption. Body-o-me! Saxon churl! An' I but meet thee, Our Lady be witness to the trouncing I'll give thy carcass."

The last part of his speech was delivered in an under tone, audible to none but the friar, who by way of signifying his approval gave him a hearty thwack on the back, for which he was well nigh receiving a sharp return.

"Prithee proceed with thy speech," said Robin to the messenger," and give heed to thy words, for my men are not wont to hear taunt or gibe, without giving fitting retort.

The messenger bowed, but could ill conceal his chagrin, which was evidently shared by his companions.

"My master bade me give over unto thee, Will Scarlet, and receive, as thine own appointing hath put it, those whom thou holdest prisoners."

"I willingly, nay joyfully, receive thee back, Will," said Robin.

To the messenger he said:

"Tarry here; thy men will be forthcoming in a trice. Little John, do thou hie to quarters and bring with thee, free from restraint mind thee, the Norman prisoners, to be forthwith freed."

When Little John had gone, the messenger said to Robin—

"I would, an' it please you, have speech of thee aside."

"Nay, say on; 'tis naught I would have concealed from these I daresay," replied Robin, pointing to his companions.

"I crave thy patience," said the messenger, "but my master bid me deliver my message to thee alone."

"As thou wilt, then," replied Robin offhandedly, at the same time giving his companions a significant look.

When aside the sheriff's man said, speaking low:

"My master sendeth thee excellent greeting and this missive, assuring thee of his great regard for thee personally."

"My indebtedness is great," replied Robin, bowing, but with an ill-concealed sneer on his handsome face.

"He further bade me tell thee that he wishes amity to exist between him and thee in so far as lieth within the scope of his office."

"'Tis a well-put request," replied Robin with a disdainful smile.

"I have finished mine office now, and await thine answer," said the messenger, who, to own the truth, felt ill at ease, and was wishful to be gone.

"Convey to the sheriff my greeting, and acquaint him of my thanks for his proffered friendship. Answer to this he will have anon," said Robin, holding up the missive.

Cutting the silken thread which confined it, Robin read as follows:—

FROM GEOFFREY DE LOIS,
Sheriff of Nottingham,

TO

ROBIN HOOD, whilom Earl of Huntingdon,
With most excellent greeting.

WHEREAS, I, entertaining most friendly intent towards thee, notwithstanding and despite mine office of preserver of the peace of this part of His Majesty's realm, against thee, arrayed in rebellion, am wishful beyond degree to promote a better feeling between thee and me, do hereby specially invite thee, Robin Hood, and thy company to a tournament of games and archery, to be holden contiguous to our Castle of Nottingham, holding thee and thine blameless for the time being for any acts committed against the King's Majesty, in virtue whereof I hereby affix my seal, in token of good faith and amity.

At our Court of Shrievalty, June 23rd, the sixth year of His Most Excellent Majesty's reign.

GEOFFREY DE LOIS,
High Sheriff.

[*Seal.*]

"Ha, ha!" laughed Robin glibly; "by the mass! a well-laid scheme. So, so, sir sheriff, thou essayest to play me false. Have a care, thou art but treading on slippery ground!"

After remaining buried in thought for a time he soliloquised:

"Out of this will I get me both honour and profit. 'Twill go hard with me, indeed, but that thou, proud sheriff, rememberest till thy life's end the said tournament to be holden for my special delectation."

Robin smiled grimly, as he was wont when communing with himself on disagreeable topics.

Strolling leisurely back to the party, he remained in converse with the earl and knight until Little John returned with the Norman prisoners.

Friar Tuck had suddenly disappeared.

The Normans are all before thee," said Little

John, making the customary salutation to Robin.

"'Tis well."

Turning to them, Robin said:

"Thou art free to depart. Take not away embittered feelings to me or mine. We seek not thine hurt nor have ever."

"Our thanks are thine, bold Robin Hood," said one of their number acting as spokesman for his comrades. "Treatment fair and honourable has been ours at thy hands. 'Twill be our duty to represent to our master thine honourable dealing towards us."

Robin bowed and dismissed them with a wave of his hand.

Accompanied by the earl, knight, and Little John, he walked leisurely towards the trysting place.

The party of Norman's meanwhile pursued their way full of glee at their happy release, and full of what they had seen of Robin and his merry men.

Right in their path sat jolly Friar Tuck.

On sighting them he commenced to troll forth the following ditty, as unconcernedly as if such a thing as a Norman was a scarce article in the land:

"Findest thou aught foul or bad,
    Be assured 'tis Norman.
Rogues, liars, cheats, and knaves are they,
    To see such churls quite makes one sad.
Then to my toast, let none say nay—
    Confusion to the Norman."

"Hearest thou that?" remarked one of them angrily. "St. Denis! but he deserves chastisement."

"Heed him not, 'tis the mad-brained friar," remarked one in reply.

"Findest thou aught fair or just,
    Rest quite sure 'tis Saxon,
Good men, and true, and loyal too,
    Base Normans they can never trust.
In wine quite old and goblets new,
    Drink honour to the Saxon."

"By my halidom, 'tis too bad to hear yon shaven pate traduce us in this wise," remarked he who had retorted so fiercely to Little John.

"Thou art at liberty to teach him better manners," answered the leader of the party, "but see that thou doest him no serious hurt."

Lagging behind his companions, the fellow watched them pretty well out of sight ere he approached the friar, who pretended to be unconscious of his presence.

"Thou wert exceedingly merry, just now," he remarked.

The friar looked at him, got up, and shaking himself together, gave a yawn.

The friar's silence nettled him exceedingly.

"Thou must e'en seek my pardon for thy rudeness in song, else will thy priestly office fail to keep thee from chastisement."

The friar began to count his beads, and continued to glance askance at him, but never a word said he.

"Hearest thou not, thou lazy, fat-paunched, shaveling priest?" said the fellow furiously, as he advanced upon the friar to strike him.

"I pray thee excuse my mind's absence, my son," said the friar with imperturbable gravity. "Said'st thou aught to me of confessing thyself?"

The fellow aimed a well-intentioned blow with his fist at the friar's head.

But, marvellous to relate, he soon found himself sprawling on the broad of his back.

"I pray thee rise, my son," said the friar gravely, "'tis unseemly for a Norman to lie thus."

Foaming with rage, his assailant drew his sword and rushed upon him.

With quarter-staff so stout, the friar did him quickly engage.

"My son, thou art but a sorry swordsman," remarked the friar as he beat down the fellow's guard, and dealt him a rap on his pate that sent the sparks flying in countless numbers from his eyes.

Rising, he essayed to fly, but the friar was upon him nimbly, and dealt him sundry thwacks on his back which made him roar lustily.

"Nay, my son," remarked the friar, as he plied his staff, "'tis for thy good I thus scourge thee for thy misdeeds. Thou wilt remember Friar Tuck, I ween, and his absolving, and come not again hurriedly to confess thyself to him."

Leaving him in pitiable plight, the friar turned and walked leisurely homeward, singing,

"With oaken staff
    And arm so stout,
At my foes I laugh
    And put them to rout.

For none care I,
    Naught troubles me long.
'Tis no use to try
    To do me a wrong."

Meeting Little John he appealed to him for a draught of wine to slake his inordinate thirst.

"Bones of St. Hubert but I am hugeous dry," he said. "Ugh! trouncing Norman backs, though pleasant, is hard work."

"Thou hast never bestowed a good thwacking on that scapegrace, hast thou," queried Little John, with a laugh.

"Be certified of it little man to thy great pleasurement. Our Lady! how the fellow roared. Ah, ah!"

"Body-o-me! thou must have a stoup of wine, in which I will join thee," said Little John.

"Gramercy, John, make it two stoups," exclaimed the friar, with lugubrious visage. By the mass I could drink both myself at a single draught."

"Thou shalt have first drink, friend," answered Little John, "so attend me to the cellarer."

The wine was produced, and the friar was deep in the contents of the first stoup, when a messenger arrived summoning Little John in haste to Robin's presence.

He cast a wistful eye on the thirsty friar, but not a sign gave he of leaving the horn which seemed glued to his lips.

"Mind thou forgettest not that I have had naught as yet," said Little John, admonishingly. He then turned round with a huge sigh and grumblings not a few to attend his master.

"'Tis wine that will not keep," said the friar, casting a longing eye on the other stoup which the cellarman had drawn. And it will be a shame to let it spoil."

So saying he seized and drank it at a draught; then hied him off to seek a secure place where to sleep free from Little John's anger.

Little John found Robin with Bayston.

"Hark thee," he said," "this abbot seeks the King, do thou go with him and contrive to learn his business and its ending."

Dismissing him he turned to Little John, saying—

"Let the Lady Maria Danvers be fitly escorted to-morrow to Much, the Miller's. He is acquainted with my intention respecting her."

"Body-o-me!" growled Little John, as he turned from the spot, "this command would have kept; the wine will not, with that thirsty friar near at hand to it."

His prediction was verified, not a drop was left for him.

Giving vent to oaths and growls, and vengeful threats, the giant wrapped his mantle about him, and throwing himself down under the shade of a fine old oak, he was soon wrapped in slumber.

The stillness of the night was unbroken save by the hoot of the owl, and the "All's Well" of the sentinels.

———

CHAPTER LII.

HOW ROBIN AND HIS MEN WENT TO THE TOURNAMENT AND WHAT BEFELL THEM.

Such a brave sight could scarcely be seen,
Gentle and simple, soldiers and yeomen,
Knight and fair ladies, on Nottingham Green,
Did there meet with Robin, the Sheriff's brave
foeman.

Two days after the events recorded in the last chapter, Robin despatched a messenger to the sheriff, conveying his acceptance of the invitation to the archery meeting.

"Let the men be informed," he said to Little John, "to keep themselves ready for instant action, without any index to their suspicions of treachery."

"Body-o'-me!" growled the giant. "Let the sheriff have a fair English fight for it, Saxon against Norman."

"True; but bethink thee, my friend, that hitherto he has been originally worsted in his contentions."

"'Tis any man's case to be beaten once or twice, or even thrice, but let him try on, and it seldom fails that in the end he is victorious."

"The sheriff views it not thus. But fash not thyself about his treacherousness, 'twill receive its deserts, thou hast Robin's word for it."

"Hither comes the sheriff's messenger," said Little John, pointing to him.

"Do thou bring him hither," said Robin. "Doubtless, he brings tidings I burn to know."

"Greet thee, gentle sir," said the messenger in courteous accents. "The sheriff sends thee this," producing a missive.

Cutting the thread, Robin read:

"*The second day from this the tournament will be contested. Thy presence will be greatly welcome and looked for.*
"GEOFFREY DE LOIS."

Dismissing the messenger with courteous thanks, Robin read the missive to Little John.

"*My presence!* think of it, John. Had'st any thought of the sheriff's subtlety being of such high order?"

"Thou knowest well, master mine, that for him I ne'er had aught of love. 'Tis Norman-like, thus to deport himself."

"Give it not a thought, my staunch friend," said Robin, placing his hand familiarly on the giant's shoulder. "But summon our men to target-practice, while I hie me to the butts."

Soon were the merry men engaged in shooting at the butts, when most marvellous shots were made. But none excelled Robin.

His arrow went true to its mark, with never a mischance intervening.

Next in point of excellence came Little John and Friar Tuck, between whom a friendly rivalry existed.

Things gave ample promise of a signal triumph for the foresters at the forthcoming tournament.

Assembling his men together, Robin, with brevity, explained to them his commands.

"Be not enticed or enthralled by Norman subtlety," he said, "and, before all, let not the wine-cup o'ermaster thee."

Hearty Saxon cheers rent the air as Robin concluded.

Could the Sheriff but have heard them, his sense of security in the success of his treacherous scheme would have been shaken to its base.

The auspicious morn arrived at last, and saw Robin and his men up betimes, as was their wont, for no sluggards were they.

In groups of twos and threes, each armed with a *short* bow, dagger, and some with staves, all of which were carefully hidden away, except the latter, the foresters hied them to the tournament, or to certain other positions assigned to them.

Robin, attended by Little John, the friar, the two knights, and Earl Mortimer, sought the abode of Much the Miller.

"Greet thee, Robin dear," said Maid Marian, throwing herself on his breast.

"Thou look'st thy best this morning, love," he said, tenderly and affectionately saluting her blushing cheek.

"'Tis to do honour to my Robin that I tired with carefulness."

"Thou art welcome, brave earl," she said, turning to Mortimer, "and thou, Little John, and likewise thou, holy father (this to Friar Tuck).

"I salute thee, Queen of Beauty," said Earl Mortimer, gallantly dropping on bended knee, and reverently kissing the beautiful hand which Marian extended to him.

"Rise, good knight," said Marian laughingly, and with a deep blush o'erspreading her lovely features, "with knight so true I bid defiance to all competitors."

Robin introduced Sir Richard Wykeham in due course, and Marian hastened to summon Maria Danvers, who had not yet completed her tiring.

After the usual courtesies had taken place, the whole party adjourned to the tournament grounds beneath the castle walls.

The sheriff hastened to welcome Robin, and smiled his blandest on Marian, who returned his courteous salutation with a hauteur bordering on disdain.

"Welcome gallant forester," said the sheriff, "and thou sweet lady. Thy beauteous presence will add to the excellence of the meeting."

"Thanks," answered Robin, bowing low; "thy courtesy doth thee *honour*."

The tone in which these words were uttered, and the emphasis laid on the last word, caused the sheriff to start and look fixedly in Robin's face.

But naught saw he there to fulfil his foreboding that his treachery was known.

Turning away to hide his confusion, he found himself face to face with Earl Mortimer.

They eyed each other defiantly for a moment.

Then bethinking of the part he had to play, the sheriff proffered his hand to Mortimer, which he took but did not press.

To Sir Richard Wykeham he gave a formal bow.

Robin's quick eye noted the presence of the sheriff's men-at-arms disguised as peasants.

Their martial bearing betrayed their identity to one so quick of apprehension as Robin.

A significant glance passed between Little John and his master; both of them having detected the same thing at the same time.

With flourish of trumpets the sheriff's herald proclaimed the conditions of the tournament, and then the lists were pronounced formally opened.

Robin, at the invitation of the sheriff, opened the tournament, and gave a standard of test for the opening of the archery contest.

"Saw you ever so graceful a posture," said a Norman dame who stood a little to the right of Robin as he prepared to shoot.

By his side stood Maid Marian and Little John, the sheriff completing the group.

"St. Denis, a good shot!" exclaimed the sheriff, as Robin's arrow hit a plug of wood in the target and drove it through, passing out at the other side with it transfixed to its point.

"'Twill take no mean archer to better that," was the verdict of many of the bystanders.

Robin laughed within himself at these acclamations, for the shot to him was the easiest his skill could have been tested by.

The contest soon went on apace.

While it progresses, I pray your attention, good reader, to what was passing elsewhere on the ground.

Several burley-framed Norman men-at-arms were drinking freely at a small booth formed of uprights and covered with green boughs.

In their company were several loutish-looking peasants dressed in short cloaks of grey homespun stuff.

Near them loitered Friar Tuck, who pretended to be watching the antics of some merry-andrews who had collected a crowd around them, but who was really listening to the Normans' conversation.

"What think you of to-day's tournament?" asked one of his companions.

"It has no attraction for me, save that of duty," was the reply.

"Here, wench," said one of the company, "fill this flagon with right good ale, and we'll drink confusion to the foresters."

"Have a care," remarked one of his fellows, "thy speech is indiscreet."

"Not so, by my halidom," was the reply, "I scorn the whole lot of those thievish knaves of woodsmen."

"Thou had'st best be mindful of thy speech," remarked one, laughingly; "St. Quintin! saw you not the scowl yon fat-paunched monk gave thee."

Friar Tuck had certainly lowered at the fellow who had spoken disparagingly of his merry companions.

"What, yon shaven befrocked priestling scowl at me! By the Rood! I'll e'en see to it."

Suiting the action to the word, he strode over to where the friar stood, and plucking him by his frock, said:

"Thou did'st scowl at me."

"My son, 'tis unseemly thus to accost one of my condition," said the friar, deprecatingly.

"Avow thyself, fellow; thou art of these foresters, knaves and rogues that they be."

Looking him straight in the face the friar placed his hand quietly on the fellow's arm and gripped it viciously.

"Unloose thy hold," said the fellow, with a lusty roar, "else will I stab thee with my dagger."

"I did but press thee with a friendly grip," replied the friar, in nowise disconcerted.

"Thou art in fault," said the Norman soldiers, gathering around their companion, "and must e'en beg his pardon or get thee buffets not a few."

The friar laughed contemptuously.

"My lineage is Saxon," he said. "Did'st e'en know one of my sort yield to Norman."

"Now, by St. Quintin, thou must pay for thine evil prating," said a great burly fellow, drawing back his arm and striking hard at the friar.

But the blow reached him not.

Raising his left arm the friar warded the blow, and dealt him such a crack with his staff o'er his pate as brought him to the ground.

Drawing their swords the fellow's companions were about to rush upon the friar when the two peasants interfered and kept them off.

"I will fight the best of you at broadsword or staff," said the friar, raising his voice to a shout.

"A ring! a ring!" shouted several bystanders who had seen the whole of the matter.

Attracted by the voice, a dense crowd soon collected.

In the confusion, one of the peasants sidled up to the friar, and said in a low whisper,

"Good Friar Tuck, provoke not a quarrel. 'Tis Allan-a-Dale speaks to thee."

"St. Hubert!" answered the friar, "what, thou! I knew thee not. But these braggart Normans must be chastised. Trust me good Allan, naught ill will befall me."

"Now, thou fat-paunched friar," exclaimed one of the Norman soldiers, whose height over-topped the friar's by a span nearly, "defend thyself, for I vow by St. Denis, to trounce thy hide well, priest or no priest."

"Have at thee," replied the friar with a laugh.

The twain set to right merrily.

The Norman was no mean hand at use of staff.

"That for thy crown!" he exclaimed, aiming a terrific blow at the friar's head.

"'Tis naught my son," replied the friar with ready guard. "That for thy Norman carcass."

ROBIN HOOD,

AND THE OUTLAWS OF SHERWOOD FOREST.

ROBIN HOOD WAYLAYS THE ABBOT.

A heavy blow on the shoulder caused the fellow to reel.

"Well dealt, father," said one in the crowd. "Our Lady be witness, thou art, for a man of peace, a heavy hitter."

The crowd cheered the friar lustily, who warmed to his work.

"Thou did'st receive my compliment with

an ill grace," he said, dealing the Norman another sound rap. "That to keep its fellow company."

Getting off his guard, the Norman dealt his blows wild and furiously.

"Ha! ha!" laughed the friar. "Bones of St. Hubert! thy staff is pliant, but how likest thou that?" dealing his antagonist a blow on his crown, which drew blood freely.

Seeing the discomfiture of their comrade, the other Norman soldiers essayed to attack the friar with their swords.

"Shame, shame!" shouted the crowd, many of whom threw themselves between the friar's assailants, and prevented his being hurt.

"St. Denis! but thou art a jovial friar," said one of the soldiers, getting the better of his temper. "Here is my hand, an' it please thee to press it in friendly mood."

"My refusal would be unseemly, my son," replied the friar, taking the proffered hand, "my ways are of peace."

"Thou must e'en drain a draught with us," exclaimed the friendly soldier.

"Aye, aye!" shouted his fellows, falling in with their comrade's mood. "Let's drink and be friends."

"A cup of good wine will not harm me," answered the friar, as he went in their company to the booth.

"Dost hear, wench? Let's have full horns of thy best wine, and that quickly," said the friendly fellow, as he motioned the friar to a seat beside him.

Nothing loth, the friar joined in the drinking bout; and managed to so ply them with wine and ale in keeping pace with his friendly toasts, that at length the soldiers lost all discretion, and began to prate about the sheriff's designs upon Robin and his party.

These disclosures were listened to eagerly by the friar and the two peasants, to wit, Allan-a-Dale and Dick Withers, who were thus disguised.

"Fifty right good archers, the best in the north country has the sheriff imprest," exclaimed one of the Normans, with drunken elatedness.

"For what purpose, my son?" asked the friar with an innocent mien.

"To slay him, Robin, and his principal men."

The friar exchanged significant glances with his two companions.

"Report has it, that the sheriff has promised him safe conduct," said the friar.

"Believe it not. I vow to thee, that the sheriff, my master, will this day slay Robin Hood."

"'Tis evil to shed blood, my son."

"But that is not all," said the fellow, unheedful of the friar's adverse opinion. "Maid Marian will fall to the sheriff's lot."

"Ah! thy master is a rare contriver."

"A dozen horsemen will hover near, and will suddenly snatch her, and ride away like the wind."

The peasants' eyes were closed, as if they slept.

They listened keenly though withal.

As hoped, the soldiers now began to give evidence of dropping off into a drunken sleep, and the fellow seemed to have exhausted his stock of intelligence. The friar gave a sign to Allan-a-Dale and his comrades.

Rousing themselves as if from slumber, and yawning tremendously, they took leave, the friar alone remaining.

"Fill up again," said the friar, who wanted to see all the Norman soldiers rendered quite incapable of action through drink, being assured that they had been appointed to take a prominent part in the sheriff's treacherous plans against Robin.

"Well put, my jolly cock," answered he who had acted as spokesman for the rest. What ho, there! fill up, fill up with right good liquor. I'll pay."

The friar chuckled to himself at the success of his manœuvre.

"Here, drink, good father," said the soldier, and favour us with a song. Thou art of the right sort to troll one."

"Ay, a song, a song," replied those of his companions who were not too drunk to give utterance to the request.

Willing to gratify their wishes for his own ends, the friar sang

THE SOLDIER.

The soldier he's a notable man,
  Eager for fray and blunt of speech;
He swaggers, struts, drinks, when he can,
  Always ready with sword, some foes to reach.

With smiles greets he each pretty wench,
  Vows that for her he's ready to die.
With wine such vows he's ready to drench,
  Swears by his saint she has a beautiful eye.

True as his good sword, sharp and keen,
  With oath and rush and ready blow,
Seeks he profit! not so I ween,
  The soldier's no knave, I'd have all men know.

Honour to him is dearer than gold,
  For fame and his country he perils his life.
If by foeman o'ercome, he never cries hold,
  But smiles, names her, and falls in the strife.

Charge to the brim, the merry wine cup,
  Shout ye this toast, each true-hearted holder,
Nor bate aught of breath as the red juice ye sup
  Honour, above all, to the warlike brave soldier.

"Honour to thee, thou jovial friar," said the soldiers, one and all.

"'Tis naught; I love the soldier; but false knights I detest," answered the friar, significantly; "an' thou would'st pleasure me," he added, "drink to my toast."

"That will we—the toast?" was the unanimous response.

"*Confusion and destruction to all false-sworn knights!*"

The toast was drunk by all but one with acclamation.

He was not so far gone in drink as to be unmindful of the drift of the friar's toast.

He tried hard to catch its full meaning, but his brains being muddled by the fumes of wine and ale, he failed.

Raising his glass, he drank the toast slowly and deliberately; then turning to the friar, he asked with thick utterance:

"Dost thou mean my master, the sheriff?"

"Of a surety, a false-sworn knight is he," replied the friar in quick response.

"St. Quintin! thou shalt have thine ears slit," replied the fellow, essaying to draw his sword.

"Not by thee, thou Norman swine," replied the friar with a laugh and a push, which sent the fellow reeling to the ground, where he lay, in common with his companions, in a thoroughly helpless condition.

Emerging from the booth, the friar wended his way to the archery butts.

He pushed his way stoutly through the crowd, and gave as good blows as he received while so employed.

"Here comes the friar, master," said Little John to Robin.

"Bring him here," answered Robin; "let him give evidence of his skill, that these archers may see it.

Plucking Robin lightly by the sleeve, Friar Tuck drew Robin aside.

"Saw'st thou Allan-a-Dale?" he asked in a low whisper.

"I did; my merry men are assembling e'en now. Fear nought; but be vigilant."

"Danger is abroad," replied the friar, "and to Marian."

"Have no fear, Robin will be scathless, Marian harmless; but to the butts, and show these braggart Normans thy priestly skill."

"Have at them," said the friar, walking forward with Robin.

CHAPTER LIII.

HOW ROBIN HOOD WON THE SILVER ARROW.

Such an archer as Robin, ne'er was seen,
None did him, in shooting excel.
The silver arrow, with point so riven,
Was giv'n him by her he loved so well.

"A PLACE for our chaplain," cried Robin Hood.

"Cheerfully given," replied Little John.

"Welcome friar," said Much, "your skill is greatly needed to teach these fellows good shooting."

"Ay, that it is," said Gilbert of the White Hand. "With so goodly an archer as thou, friar, 'twill go hard but our victory be rendered even more complete."

"Well shot, Reynold!" remarked Robin Hood, as one of his band slit the wand very cleverly.

"'Tis hardly fair shooting," remarked one of the sheriff's archers.

"How so? Explain," said Robin, turning sharply upon him.

Soon an angry, excited group collected, and the debate threatened to get from words to blows.

"What is it that causes this unseemly strife?" exclaimed the sheriff in loud tones.

"'Tis not fair shooting!" exclaimed half a score of Norman voices in chorus.

"What sayest thou to that?" asked the sheriff of Robin.

"'Tis a foul lie. I am ready to prove 'tis so on the body of any man uttering it."

"Thou art mighty boastful," replied a huge fellow whose height towered far above Robin's.

"Thou mayest try me an' thou wilt," answered Robin. "Peradventure thou wilt find that our excellences are not confined to the bow's use."

"Nay, nay, master mine," said Little John, stepping forward, "demean not thyself in this quarrel. Let my hand deal chastisement to this fellow's presumption. Body-o'-me! 'tis past brooking."

Turning to the Norman, who was surnamed by his fellows Grim Denis, Little John said:

"Thus I challenge thee to mortal combat an' thou wilt, with broadsword, bow, battle-axe, or aught else weapon thou can'st name."

Little John laid his bow with a light stroke on grim Denis's shoulder.

An exultant smile passed o'er the Norman's countenance on hearing this open challenge.

"I accept thy challenge; but as I am loth to shed blood on this festive day "—a malicious twinkle shone in grim Denis's eye—"I, as challenged, choose, in place of the weapons thou hast named, my fist. Blow for blow on each other's body, on chest or back."

His companions looked on Little John ominously.

Well they might.

Grim Denis had killed not a few by a single blow of his ponderous fist.

"Accepted," replied Little John readily. Blow for blow, delivered in manly fashion. Let's about it at once."

"What say'st thou, Robin Hood," asked the sheriff, who, knowing Grim Denis's prowess with his fist, sought to make Robin accessory to the duel by consenting to it.

"I would rather have met him myself in fair fight," said Robin, casting a contemptuous glance on the burly frame and giant proportions of Grim Denis.

"Thou afterwards, an' thou wilt," said the Norman sneeringly.

"'Tis not well to boast ere thy work is done," observed Little John in dudgeon. "Thou wilt not meet any other for a week or more an' I get but one blow at thy Norman carcass."

"Well, well," exclaimed the sheriff, "loth though I be to spoil our merry-making on this wise, thou, Denis, and thou, Little John, hast my permit to do as thou hast agreed in this matter."

"Thou hast *mine*, John, observed Robin. "Fear not, my trusty friend, Robin and thy faithful comrades guard thee."

"Thy meaning?" said the sheriff turning sharply round on Robin.

Drawing himself up to his full height, and with a countenance full of contemptuous anger, Robin answered,

"I hold myself responsible to none for words of mine uttered here or elsewhere. Thou hast mine answer."

The sheriff bit his lip, and could hardly contain the anger that burned within him.

Curbing it with a great effort, he contented himself with saying:

"Thy speech is thine own. I sought not to challenge it to thy detriment. But let's to the ring, else will the day expend itself a full hour or two too soon for the right ending of our merry revels."

Robin made a gesture to Allan-a-Dale and Will Scarlet.

It needed not anything further.

They transmitted their chief's order by signs to his merry men, who stood around in little groups.

It was a curious coincidence that when the ring was formed, Lincoln green jerkins were interposed between the Normans so as to prevent them acting together in concert if meditating treachery.

Marian's faithful body guard attended her everywhere, and now guarded her as she stood a little distance away to the right in company with Maria Danvers.

"Room, more room, sirs!" said Robin as the crowd came surging inwards, curtailing inconveniently the space for the combatants.

"Well put," exclaimed the sheriff. "What ho! back there, I command you."

At length all the preliminaries were settled, and the men stood boldly confronting each other.

What Little John lacked in breadth and height he possessed in suppleness and activity.

"An' thou fallest, John," said Friar Tuck, who had secured a place in the innermost circle, "I'll take thy place. Straight from the shoulder mind thee, fellow" (this to Grim Denis) "or by St. Hubert I'll deal thee a buffet that will——"

"Peace, thou prating shaveling," said a stalwart Norman standing beside him.

"Verily I am a man of peace," replied the friar, with uncommon good-humour.

This only raised a laugh at the fellow's expense, which he hardly relished.

"Thou art more a knave than priest belike," he answered.

He had trespassed too far on the friar's patience, and was now to suffer for so doing.

Turning, the friar caught him by the nape of the neck, and shook him as a terrier does a rat.

Then griping him lower down with his left hand, he lifted him bodily off his feet, swung him to and fro, once, twice, thrice, and sent him flying over the heads of the crowd.

"Knave am I?" panted the friar, after his Herculean feat. "By St. Hubert, thou art a fool, for thy pains, as all can see."

Robin laughed outright; Little John grinned from ear to ear; the Normans looked blank, and the crowd roared mirthfully.

So sudden and unexpected was the affair, that no rescue had been attempted by the Norman soldiers, who now instinctively edged away from the friar, and eyed him askance.

Every eye was soon riveted on Little John and Grim Denis.

"Body-o-me!" grumbled Little John, as his antagonist threw himself into attitude before delivering his blow; "to thy work, man, else will I be sore minded to buffet thee first for thy antics."

The admonition was well merited.

Grim Denis essayed to frighten his opponent by a series of displays.

At length he prepared himself to deliver his blow.

Raising his arm slowly, he drew it back with suddenness.

"Hold," cried Robin Hood, starting forward, "thou art playing foul. In thy clenched fist thou holdest something to aid thy blow."

Grim Denis paled, and then turned red, for it was even as Robin had said.

In his hand he held a smooth round stone to add additional force to his intended blow.

The crowd hissed and hooted him sorely for his unmanliness.

"Deal now thy blow," said Robin; 'tis a man confronts thee."

With savagery in his features, and a brute-like ferocity in his eyes, Grim Denis again raised his arm.

A hushed silence had fallen on the crowd.

With bated breath they awaited the blow.

It fell, and terrifically too, upon Little John's expanded chest.

An exclamation from the crowd, a loud cheer, and Little John was seen standing fearlessly erect, rigid in posture as marble almost.

"St. Hubert be thanked!" exclaimed the friar in fervent tones. "John, dear friend, thou art unhurt."

Robin looked inexpressibly happy; emotion choked his utterance.

Grim Denis's swarthy face paled, the Normans, one and all, exhibited signs of uneasiness, and seemed preparing to rescue their comrade from impending peril.

"The first man who stirs dies," said Robin in a loud voice; "the matter is betwixt man and man. Look to it that ye interfere not with them."

A cheer from the crowd endorsed these sentiments, and aided to enforce neutrality on the part of all present.

Little John's blow was given.

Grim Denis tottered, reeled, and fell heavily to the earth with a loud cry of pain.

Blood flowed from his nostrils.

He was as if dead.

"Room, room, fellows! Back, there!" shouted the friar; "let the man have air."

His true-heartedness made him a friend of the vanquished, and enlisted his sympathy on his behalf.

Kneeling by his side Friar Tuck felt his heart and said—

"Thanks to Our Lady it beats. Here John, man, none so fit as thou to carry him elsewhere."

Between them they bore the fast dying man aside.

The friar remained to shrive him.

Little John returned to his comrades.

On his way he encountered a Norman soldier.

"See to it!" he fiercely exclaimed; "thou hast killed my comrade dear. "My life for thine, but he shall be fittingly avenged."

"Pish," replied Little John. "Thou art no man to so deliver thyself," and he turned from the fellow contemptuously.

Congratulations poured on him from all sides, but he heeded them not, so simple-minded and true was Little John.

Further talk of foul play was there now none. The good name of Robin and his merry men was indisputably established.

One Norman archer pressed Robin's men sore in point of skilful archery.

Slit they the wand?—so did he.

"The friar, where is he?" asked Robin.

"Here, friend Robin," answered a cheery voice as the friar came to the front.

"Take this bow and select thine arrow. Thou can'st cleave yonder wand I wager."

Twang.

The friar's arrow cleft the wand.

"By my halidom," exclaimed the sheriff, "Thou art of a verity a rare priest. Wilt be chaplain of mine?"

"Seest thou my master?" answered the friar, pointing to Robin. "Sooner would I serve him for nought than take service with thee or thy betters even."

"Humph," observed the sheriff. "Thou might'st have framed an answer more courteously."

"Thou hast it, to like or like not at thy pleasure," replied the friar, affixing another arrow to his string and eyeing the sheriff askance.

"Thou art a strange lot," observed the sheriff.

"We are *honourable*, good sir, past all dispute," replied the irrepressible friar as he took aim, the result being that he again split the wand.

The sheriff was dumb; but looked the anger he dared not express in words.

"Fix me a wand full ten yards further away," said Robin.

'Twas done.

Turning to Marian, who stood near him, he whispered in her willing ear:

"Thine eyes, love, inspire me for victory. Thine hand, sweetest. Thou shalt with it present thy Robin with yon arrow; and Marian shall share with me the triumph of the hour."

With grace and ease he took his stand.

Selecting an arrow with care, and trying the temper of his bow, he took a steady look at the mark, and fired.

The wand was slit fair asunder in the middle. Affixing yet another arrow, he said:

"It shall have branches. Look steadily, and soon they will appear.

With consummate skill and ease, Robin fired.

"A miss, a miss!" said several voices, foremost being the sheriff's.

"Thou hast but poor eyes. Observe yet more closely.

Robin fired again.

"'Tis a miss, surely!" exclaimed the sheriff, excitedly.

"Ha, ha!" laughed Robin, merrily; "come with me and be convinced."

The sheriff went, attended by a select party.

"Seest thou that—and that?" said Robin, pointing to the two newly-made slits in the sides of the cloven wand.

"Surely, surely," exclaimed the sheriff; "I hereby adjudge thee the prize, Robin Hood. Choose thou whom thou would'st to present it."

"Marian shall be queen of the tournament," answered Robin.

"A better, worthier choice could not be," said the sheriff, casting an enraptured glance on Marian.

"Worthy in the highest sense," observed Robin; "woe be to the man, be he gentle or simple, that would treat her with aught but esteem."

The eyes of Robin and the sheriff met.

They understood one another perfectly, and were even bitterer enemies than before.

"Attend me," said the sheriff. "Herald, proclaim an assembly in honour of the victor, Robin Hood."

The trumpet gave forth a fanfare inspiriting to hear, and the spectators hastened to where a dais draped with rich stuffs was raised.

Thither the sheriff led Marian, and begged her to be seated.

A splendidly-attired page bore to her side the silver arrow on a massive silver tray, and held it ready to her hand.

The trumpets sounded a triumphant flourish, the people shouted, Marian rose, Robin knelt.

In a musically clear voice, full of sweetness and indescribable tenderness, Marian said,

"Robin Hood, in fair tournament of archery holden in these lists this day, thou hast proved thine incomparable skill as an archer, and art adjudged victor."

Taking the arrow from its resting-place, she continued,

"This is thy trophy of victory; take and prize it dearly."

The trumpets sounded yet another flourish.

In manly tones Robin replied:

"Queen of the lists, incomparably beautiful and matchless, I accept this token, and regard it the more for thy dear sake."

"Hurrah, hurrah, hurrah!" shouted the crowd.

But a change was to come.

CHAPTER LIV.

HOW THE SHERIFF'S TREASONABLE PURPOSES WERE FRUSTRATED BY ROBIN AND HIS MERRY MEN.

> Full many a bow then was bent,
> And arrows they let glide.
> Many a kirtle there was rent,
> And hurt was many a side.

ERE the last flourish had died away, the sounds of bugle horns resounded far and near.

"Seize on Robin Hood and such of his men as thou canst," shouted the sheriff.

"Treason!" exclaimed Robin. "Now woe betide thee, Nottingham's Sheriff. Full well shalt thou rue this."

Placing his bugle horn to his lips, Robin blew three notes, long, loud, and clear.

The crowd hastened to disperse in all directions, and ere long the field was left to Robin and the sheriff's party.

"Yield thee, thou bold outlaw," said the sheriff, "else will I order my men to fall to upon thee and thine."

"Thou false-sworn knight," exclaimed Robin. "Thou traitorous caitiff, ere I or one of my merry men surrender to such as thou, our bodies will rest them on this green sward."

Even as Robin spoke, he and his men retreated slowly and in good order with their faces to their treacherous foes.

"My safe conduct is not for such as thou," answered the sheriff. "Thou art outlawed, and canst be slain or taken by any man at any time or place."

"Draw well to the ear, my merry men all," shouted Robin, as the sheriff's archers bent their bows.

Soon a flight of arrows from Robin's party stretched many a Norman low.

"Robin," said a sweet voice close beside him.

Turning, he beheld Marian, while Norman arrows whistled thick around them, standing as calm and collected, as if the fray had no terrors for her.

"Marian darling!" he exclaimed in agonised tones, "thou here?"

"Surely, Robin," she replied with a smile; "thou in sore danger and thy Marian absent? How could'st thou thus think of me?"

"See—yonder is a safe retreat; hie thee thither, sweet girl; my men will attend you."

"Never, Robin! by thy side I stay. Thou diest, then I too die."

"Noble girl! But time presses, and words must be few. Take thou this bow and throw this quiver across thy shoulder. Thou cans't use it. Be it my office to guard thee. Our Lady forefend thee from harm!"

Pressing his lips to hers in passionate love he turned and viewed the battle, with Marian by his side.

"Little John, how go things?" he asked of his lieutenant.

"Right merrily, master mine. Our shooting

is too strong for the Norman swine. But they follow on apace."

"Seest thou yonder copse?" said Robin, whose quick eye saw that there existed danger of ambush. "Take men, but a few, mind, and skirt it. Belike thou wilt find some *forcign* acorns there."

Little John laughed, saying—

"It shall be done. But body-o'-me! seest thou that? Forestalled are we, master mine."

It was so. Even as Little John spoke a goodly number of Norman foot-soldiers issued forth and took them in the flank.

"St. Denis! Slay and hew the outlaws; three hundred crowns to him who slays Robin Hood!"

"Marian darling, do thou stay with the friar," said Robin, beckoning to him to approach.

"Nay, Robin, I'll with thee."

"And I too will go," said the friar, placing himself by Marian's side.

The Norman soldiers plied their pikes and swords well.

But the merry men were not to be discomfited.

Full sore the fight continued for a space.

"Take that, thou beggarly knave!" said the friar, as he dealt a foeman a hearty thwack for aiming a blow at Marian's defence-less head.

The friar's services were invaluable to Marian.

He shielded her from danger at the risk of his own life, nor tired seemed his arm, although his oaken staff was never still.

Three stalwart Normans pressed Robin sore.

Bound by oath were they to slay or capture him.

His good sword plied he marvellously well.

Strokes rapid and sure dealt he them with it.

Twain of the three were slain by him.

The third had him at a disadvantage.

His Norman sword gleamed aloft in the rays of the evening sun.

"St. Denis!" he cried.

But never a stroke made he. A dagger was in his side.

"Our Lady be thanked, thou art safe," said Marian, her delicately white hand crimsoned with gore.

Her hand had dealt Robin's foe his death blow.

"I owe thee life, darling," said Robin.

"The debt is naught," replied Marian. "Are not our lives bound up together?"

Time for further speech was there not.

Prodigies of valour were performed by each one of Robin's band.

"St. Hubert be praised!" shouted Robin. "Cheer men, cheer! the Normans flee."

Cheer they did, and that only as Saxons could.

Full half a score of men bit the dust in the flight, for Robin's archers were sure of aim and true of eye, and good men all were they.

But the fight went on.

The Norman archers shot them viciously at their foes.

"Body-o'-me! but I am hit!" said Little John, as he sank to the ground.

"Yonder fellow did it," exclaimed the friar, pointing to a Norman nearer at hand than his fellow by ten yards or more.

The fellow shook his hand menacingly, and proceeded to carefully fix an arrow to his bow.

"It is Grim Denis's comrade," remarked Little John in accents of pain. "He keeps his oath 'twould seem."

Robin both heard and saw these things.

An arrow from his bow shot down Little John's assailant just as he was about to fire again.

Maid Marian knelt beside Little John, and with her kerchief tenderly bound up his wound, the arrow from which had but just been extracted by the friar.

"Art much hurt, John?" asked Robin anxiously.

"Grievous enough, master. The knee is hit, and walk I cannot."

"Saw you ever such a company?" said the friar, pointing to the sheriff's party which had just been reinforced by considerable numbers.

"Our Saxon blood is more than a match for such poltroons," replied Robin. "But lean thee on mine arm, John."

"Nay, Robin, that cannot be. I cry thee a boon, master mine; if thou lovest me, grant it."

"Say on, John. Aught of good that Robin can afford is thine. Ask what thou wilt."

Seizing Robin's hand, Little John looked into his handsome, fearless face, and said in solemn accents,

"Thou canst not bear me with thee. Draw, I pray thee, for the sake of Him who once hung upon the tree, and smite off my head; cut deep, sure, and true, that I fall not into yon traitorous sheriff's hands."

Robin cast a look of deep affection upon the upturned face of his friend, and replied with much animation,

"Were the blades of grass, the leaves of the forest, the very earth itself and all its appurtenances, gold, red pure gold, and be all offered me to slay thee, even in friendly guise, I would refuse it as I do thee now."

"Tut, tut, man," said Friar Tuck; "thou art not in such dumps as thou imaginest; my back is broad and strong withal, and at thy service to mount."

Little John shook his head mournfully.

"I will help thee, friar," said Much; "so rise thee, John, else will the sheriff's archers be upon us quickly."

With Robin and Much's assistance, Little John mounted the friar's back.

"I hope yon Norman varlets will not think I turn my back on them," exclaimed the friar jocosely, as he trotted off in fine style, with his heavy, but dear burden.

At this juncture up came Earl Mortimer and the knights.

"Now Our Lady be praised," the former exclaimed; "I see thou art safe, Marian."

"Of a surety," she replied with a smile; "of Norman arrow I am scathless, I trow."

Even as she spoke, an arrow lodged in her Lincoln-green kirtle.

With a laugh she extracted it, saying:

"Thou shalt speed back to thy masters, as a winged messenger, to bear, perchance a token of a maiden's ill-favour to traitorous Normans."

Adjusting it to her bow, she fired.

"Well shot," exclaimed Robin rapturously;

"thou hast unhorsed the sheriff; noble girl, thou shalt have a silver arrow, excelling mine, for thy skill,"

It was even so.

Marian's arrow, aimed not venturously, but designedly, had stretched the sheriff's horse, and brought its rider to the ground.

"The forest will soon be reached," said Will Scarlet, who had just come up, "shall we ambush, master, and teach yon traitor a lesson?"

"Thou may'st, for by my halidom it is a good thought."

"A score of trusty archers will suffice, Will. Let thy design be speedily executed an' thou lovest me."

"What cheer, Little John?" asked Will as he passed the wounded giant.

"Good, Will, lad. Thanks to my sturdy friend who beareth me and my master's good will."

"Thou art but light of weight after all, John," said the friar; "St. Hubert, but thou art not the man I took thee for."

Little John laughed at this fib of the friar's who by uttering it only sought to mislead him as to his being a heavy burden.

"Bravely done, friar," exclaimed Will. "I would give thee help, but that I have pressing business to execute for Robin."

"Nay," said Much, "I am next for John's carrying; come, friar, let me ease thy shoulders."

"Thou canst if thou wilt, Much," replied the friar, "while I arrow those sneaking Normans in good style."

Tenderly and gently they made the exchange, cheered to their work by the acclamations of the entire party, all of whom appreciated the friar's heroism.

"Ambush to the left, Mortimer," said Robin. "Take a dozen archers, the number will suffice, and post among yonder wood. Will Scarlet and party is to the right."

"It shall be done, Robin, but thou exposest thy precious life too freely. And Marian too. I fear for her."

"Thou must to cover Marian," said Robin, casting on her a glance of love and tenderness. "Hie, thee, with Mortimer, an' thou lovest me."

"Nay, Robin; I beseech thee let me stay with thee. Bethink thee of my sore anxiety away from thee."

"Already the sheriff's minions outnumber us. I and a small party will seek to lead them into an ambuscade. It cannot be, Marian."

"Thy side I will not leave, Robin, till I be torn from it," said Marian, casting her arms round him.

"Do thou go, then, Mortimer; Marian stays. Our Lady send her protection."

The ruse was cleverly executed, and succeeded.

Deceived by the small number which remained on the skirts of the forest, and thinking that they alone covered the retreat of their companions, the sheriff ordered his men to advance quickly.

Robin lured them on imperceptibly into the forest, then, by a quick movement, joined Earl Mortimer's party.

The sheriff and his men were like persons bewitched.

They were assailed by flights of arrows from two different quarters, and put to great confusion.

"Charge thy men to the right," he cried in desperation to one of his captains.

They charged, but ineffectually: arrows mowed them down ere they moved a score of paces.

"Ha, ha!" laughed Robin's voice mockingly. "Thou art welcome, Sheriff, to Sherwood."

"A thousand crowns to the man who brings me Robin's head," the sheriff shouted furiously.

In reply came a flight of arrows, and a perfect roar of laughter from all Robin's party.

"A thousand crowns," cried Robin, "I'll give to any man who captures yon sheriff for me alive. He shall hang high, and all of his I this day catch, traitors that they be."

The foresters issued forth, after discharging their arrows.

Fearful of the issue of the combat and of falling into Robin's hands, the sheriff hastily ordered a retreat.

Dire was their flight.

Many fell before the well-directed fire of Robin's men.

Many more were taken prisoners.

Before proceeding onward, Robin called an assembly of his men.

"Bring hither the prisoners," he said.

They stood before him.

Amid a hushed silence, Robin thus spake:

"The sheriff, under base pretence, inveigled myself and my loyal men to a tournament. Basely betraying his promise of safe conduct, he sought our lives, and not a few have this day fallen. This one and all were duly apprised of, and took part in the treachery."

Turning to his men, Robin asked:

"What be these worthy of?"

"Death, one and all!" was the unanimous response.

"Death let it be, then; but not to all. Lots shall be drawn, and the three shortest die 'ere yon sun sinks in the heavens."

The lots were made, drawn, and three were doomed accordingly.

"Will Scarlet," said Robin, in stern accent, "see that they hang one to each of three trees."

There was a wild look of appeal in the doomed wretches' eyes.

"Mercy!" they gasped.

Stern looks, hard as flint, met their gaze; compressed lips denied their cry for that mercy they would have denied to others.

"Allan-a-Dale, take thou the others," said Robin, pointing to the remaining prisoners, "and have their backs well lashed with bowstrings. Rive their clothing and despatch them in ignominious guise to the sheriff, their master."

"Marian, darling, this is no place for thee. Let us go on and see how our friend Little John is."

Attended by his friends, he sought the trysting place, and before taking bite or sup went to Little John's side.

"Well, John, how art thou?" he affectionately asked. "Hast much pain?"

"Naught of consequence. But how can I sufficiently thank thee, master, for thy kindness? But for thee and my friends Friar Tuck and Much, I had ere this been lying low and cold."

"Say naught else, John. Oft has thy life

been perilled for me. I am thy friend, let that suffice thee as it does me."

"John, man, thou must eschew wine," said the friar, looking with concern at his friend.

"I can drink the weak sort," Little John replied. "Under thy hands I put myself."

"Thou art mindful to have a good nurse," said Robin merrily. "Wine will not be lacking for thy use with his command."

The work of the day ended not for some time. Parties were sent out to succour the wounded.

"None but our men, mind thee," said Robin. "Hurt not a wounded Norman, thou cans't e'en refresh him with water an' thou wilt; but bear him not away with thee."

"Marian, darling, thou can'st hardly reach thine uncle's mill to-night," said Robin turning to her.

"I repose here an' thou refusest me not."

"As thou wilt. My poor roof is at thy disposal, and with such faithful hearts to guard thee, thy slumber will be as soft and light as I wish them thee."

CHAPTER LV.

HOW ROBIN AND HIS COMPANY WAYLAID THE ABBOT ON HIS RETURN FROM THE KING.

> The abbot, he looked both left and right,
>   For alarmed was he, and his great company,
> To see Robin not here; 'tis a wonderful sight.
>   But hidden was he 'neath the greenwood tree.

"BLADE-BONE of St. Hubert!" growled Little John, "here am I dying for thirst, and thou deniest me wine. But one stoup have I had this live-long day."

"Patience, little man," answered the friar with a merry twinkle in his eyes; "thy portion has not been lost. Daily I drink it and wish for thy recovery."

"Thou art a thirsty knave, and hast no conscience; thy swillings benefit not me," said Little John, who did not by any means relish the friar's ingenious argument in favour of keeping him on short allowance.

"Ah, 'tis ever so, friend John," replied the friar meekly, folding his hands across his fat paunch. "A good man is sure to be reviled."

"Not for goodness art thou reviled," retorted the giant. "But I'll forgive thee all if thou givest me one flowing horn to drink without let or hindrance."

"'Twould add to thy fever," answered the friar with a grave shake of the head.

"A murrain seize thee! Would I had my staff, then would I catch thee a thwack such as thou hads't not for many a day back."

"Thy wound, man, think of it. Water must thou have for full one month longer, or ill will betide thee."

"'Tis ever in the nature of hurts to demean themselves as thine dost. A leech that was wont to teach me——"

"A fig for thy leechcraft!" roared Little John in high dudgeon. "Here am I unable to stand upright, and thou deniest me proper sustenance."

"Wilful art thou, little man. But I'll e'en indulge thee this once," said the friar, as he moved to where he kept a little store of good wine.

"Ah! thou art my best friend," exclaimed Little John, smacking his lips in anticipation of the forthcoming delightful draught. "Said I not always that thou wert a very prince among friars?"

"This wine," said the friar, unheeding his companion's eulogistic speech, "is from France. 'Tis excellent."

"Ah!" replied Little John, looking wistfully at the jar. "'Tis well preserved, too, remarked the friar."

"But I thirst, give me to drink, good Tuck," said Little John coaxingly.

"I will e'en taste it first, to see it suits thy condition."

Placing the mouth of the jar to his lips, the friar allowed the rich wine to gurgle down his capacious gullet; nor seemed inclined to desist.

"Body-o'-me! but thou wilt finish it quite," roared Little John,

Forgetting his wounded condition, he essayed to move towards his tormentor, and received an ugly twinge of pain in consequence,

"Oh! oh!" he groaned in agonised tones.

"What is it, man?" said the friar, running over to him in real alarm.

To grasp the bottle with one hand and deal the friar a buffet with the other, was but the work of a moment.

"St. Hubert!" exclaimed the friar, rubbing the side of his head, "thou hast yet a deal of strength left. Thy condition is too high. 'Tis water thou requirest."

The giant gave a sigh of delight as he put the empty jar down.

"'Twill soon right me, such draughts as that. An' thou lovest to see me about again, give me abundance of such like wine, and 'twill surprise thee all how soon I walk."

"Hark!" said the friar, putting up his finger. "Heard'st thou ever aught so sweet. 'Tis Marian singing as she comes to greet thee."

Floating sweetly on the evening breeze came Marian's melodious voice, as she sang the following:

> "A pilgrim came to the castle gate,
>   One even' as the sun went down :
> Saying, 'Grant me, I pray thee, within to wait,
>   Sore-footed am I, and too far to yon town.'
>
> "'Get thee gone, thou knave,' the seneschal said,
>   'Thou shalt here no entrance gain.'
> The pilgrim, he sighed, and bent his head,
>   Saying, 'Welcome for me is not here, 'tis plain.'
>
> "'Oh! enter thou pilgrim, weary and wan,
>   Tarry, and rest thee, till morrow's bright dawn.
> None shall deny or bid thee begone,
>   Thou pilgrim that comest with look so forlorn.'
>
> "Thank thee, sweet lady,' the pilgrim, he cried,
>   ' Thy pity doth fill me with joy.
> Blessings from Him who on the tree died,
>   Be thine, may his presence thee ever be nigh.'
>
> "' Now, tell me good pilgrim,' the lady, she said,
>   ' Saw thou aught of my lover so bold ?
> He promised in a year to return, me to wed ;
>   Ah me! I much fear me, his love has grown cold.'
>
> "' Thy lover is here,' cried the pilgrim with joy,
>   As he pressed her in love to his heart.
> Returned is thy Donald, thee to be nigh,
>   ' From thee sweet one never to part.' "

ROBIN HOOD,

AND THE OUTLAWS OF SHERWOOD FOREST.

"THERE FLASHED INTO SIGHT AN UNEARTHLY FIGURE."

"Greet thee, John," said Robin's cheery voice, as he emerged into view, with Marian on his arm.

"Thou art better, John?" asked Marian in softest accents.

"I greatly thank thee, yes. Thou art kind beyond compare."

"He mends apace," put in the friar.

No. 18.

"Water has worked wonders for him, and will do more."

"Will it?" growled Little John with bated breath, and casting a spiteful glance at the friar.

Robin, who understood the matter betwixt John and his nurse, laughed merrily.

"But what think'st thou, John?" he asked.

"Bayston has returned, and with good news."

"Body-o'-me, but 'tis fine hearing. What said he, master mine?"

The lord abbot returns home from the king laden with rich presents and a goodly company.

"Thou wilt despoil him, surely?" asked the friar eagerly.

"Thou hast great love for thy priestly brother, 'tis plain to see," said Robin laughing. "But fear not; my lord abbot shall pay in good coin of the realm for all his evil intents me-ward."

"'Tis fine," said Little John rubbing his hands gleefully, "I will be of your company, master, an' I have to be carried with thee."

"Nay, nay, John," said Robin; "bide thou here till thou art quite healed."

"My presence will go with thee," said the friar.

"Thou art needed to stay beside John," replied Robin with a smile.

"Thou can'st not go, friar," said Little John inwardly chuckling over the thought of serving out his friend.

"I had thoughts of allowancing thee one horn more wine," said the friar looking at him with a merry twinkle; "but thy condition is such as to prevent my intention."

"Thou may'st go without let or hindrance from me; but, master, forget not the wine before thou goest."

Marian laughed heartily at this amusing compact between the friends, and turning, with Robin, left them with kindly greeting in adieu.

Three days' time saw Robin and some of his company hidden in ambush.

"He is sure to come this day?" queried Will Scarlet.

"Bayston leads him. He seeks to avoid my pleasant company," answered Robin with a pleasant chuckle.

"Hist," said Allan-a-Dale; "footsteps approach."

Listening, they heard the voice of the friar, saying, admonishingly,

"Quiet John, else wilt thou topple over and hurt thyself sorely."

"By Our Lady. 'tis the friar, and Little John," exclaimed Robin, as the pair emerged into view.

Seated on the friar's back was Little John, his long legs nigh touching the ground.

The friar perspired at every pore with the weight of his heavy burden.

"St. Hubert," he said, as he came up, "here have I been carrying him for two hours full, being mis-directed. I pray thee some one give me a draught of wine, else will I faint."

Robin handed the friar his flask, observing:—

"We expected thee not."

"Would I had not ventured out," replied the friar, rubbing his back against the tree to get the numbness out of it.

"Thou did'st not but fulfil thy compact," said Little John; "Body-o-me, a child might carry me with ease, and thou grumblest at——"

"Silence," said Robin, with a warning gesture; "they come."

Crouching low in their hiding-place, Robin and his party peered cautiously out.

Coming up the glade was a goodly company of priests and soldiers.

'Twas the lord abbot and his retinue guarded by a goodly number of men-at-arms.

"Thou art sure good Bayston," said the voice of the abbot, who while speaking glanced furtively around. "Thou art sure that this part is free from Robin Hood's presence?"

"He nor his men frequent it not," replied Bayston.

"Now Our Lady be praised, 'tis a goodly sight to see his absence."

Hardly had the abbot spoken, when, with a bound, Robin sprang out, crying in a loud and imperious voice—

"Halt!"

"Who bids us halt," said the commander of the troops. "Aside with thee, fellow, and that quickly, else wilt thou rue this temerity."

"My name is Robin Hood, my lineage Saxon, my position, a free forester of Sherwood."

"Have at thee then, thou arrant knave," exclaimed the rash soldier.

Ere he could reach Robin's side, an arrow from the thicket struck him down.

"Thou hast brought this on thyself. Stir not any on the peril of life. No harm is meant you."

So saying, Robin turned towards the abbot and bade him ride forward.

"Cowards!" shouted the enraged prelate, "would I had a weapon I would strike him dead myself."

"Moderate thy wrath, sir priest," said Robin, with knitted brow, "I have no idle time for dalliance with such as thou. Forward at my bidding."

"Bold, bad man," answered the thoroughly aroused abbot, in view of the probable loss of the riches he carried, "I defy thee. Soldiers, lay on. Fifty crowns——"

The abbot finished not his inflammatory harangue.

An arrow caused his mule to rear and plunge, and fall dead to the ground, carrying him with it.

There was a commotion among the soldiers whether indicative of flight or fight was not plainly discernible.

Robin blew his horn thrice.

From behind each tree, copse, and thicket came green jerkined men, merry foresters, good and true archers.

Spurring their horses, the abbot's mounted soldiers rode swiftly away, none saying them nay.

The abbot was submissive enough now.

Nor threat nor insult passed by his lips, as with affrighted gaze and pale face he stood before Robin.

"Thou haughty, godless priest," said Robin in angry tones, thou well meritest chastisement for thy contumacy."

Never a word said the abbot, nor any priest that stood by.

"Thine errand to the king—confess thee to me, my lord abbot, for the nonce I'll be thy father confessor."

A general titter ran throughout the ranks of assembled outlaws.

"State business, my son, of no importance to thee, took me to the king's presence," answered the abbot, evasively.

"'Tis false. Thou perillest thy safety, and

that of thy followers by thine obstinacy. To the truth, and at once."

Robin's determined look was not to be mistaken.

"My son, thou art hard to move in matters whereunto pertaineth the attainment of aught of interest to thyself," answered the abbot looking Robin full in the face.

"Thine evasiveness will not serve thee," replied Robin; "quick, sir priest, my merry men grow impatient."

"My business to the king was not of thee, but——"

"'Tis false," said Robin sternly interrupting him; "thou art plotting to bring about the joint destruction of myself and followers."

There ran a threatening murmur through the ranks of the assembled outlaws of dangerous import to the abbot and his retinue.

"'Tis but thine own imaginings and suspicions that thus leadest thee to speak," replied the abbot with cool effrontery.

"A truce to this," said Robin excitedly. "Did'st thou not plot under the trees by St. Ann's Well with the sheriff?"

"Ah!" exclaimed the abbot thrown off his guard by the suddenness and truthfulness of Robin's accusation.

Unmindful of the interruption Robin continued—

"What gained thou or he by the treachery executed on us? or what wilt thou gain by thy plottings with the king? They be all known to me."

The abbot changed colour and looked guilty.

"What hast thou to say, sir priest?" asked Robin sternly. "I trow 'tis unseemly conduct for such as thou to meddle in business of a worldly nature."

"Thou hast acted as enemy of mine," remarked the abbot.

"Thou admittest thy guilt, then?" queried Robin.

The abbot spoke not.

"Be it far from me to spill blood wantonly," Robin said; "but thou hast oft tempted thy doom at my hands."

"Slay him! slay him!" exclaimed several of the band in chorus.

Robin raised his hand with an authoritative gesture to restrain the passion of his merry men.

"Enemy of thine thou hast rightly styled me," said Robin; "as of all others who act unseemly towards the poor and oppressed."

"A boon I crave at thy hands," exclaimed the abbot, who perceived that his case was a desperate one, unless he could divert the attention of Robin and his men from his treachery.

"Say on," replied Robin, "what would'st thou?"

"Thou art strong and warlike, I and mine are men of peace."

"And mischief-makers to boot," put in Friar Tuck.

Robin warned him to be silent, and to the abbot said:

"Say on, sir priest."

"A champion would I put forward to do battle for me, with intent that, proving victorious, I be allowed safe passport now and from henceforth, through Sherwood Forest."

"Umph," said Robin, eyeing the abbot curiously, as if to fathom his reasons for the request; "but what if thou art vanquished?"

"Mine be it to suffer at thy hands the pains and penalties befitting such position."

It suited Robin's chivalrous character to never refuse such request.

"Thou wilt grant it," said the friar, sidling up to him.

"Of a surety," replied Robin, with a smile.

The friar rubbed his hands gleefully.

To the abbot, Robin said:

"Thou art accepted in this matter. Appoint thy champion."

Beckoning forward a lusty-looking fellow, robed as a lay brother of the order, the abbot said:

"'Tis my champion. His conditions thou wilt hear from his lips."

"A boon, a boon, master!" cried the friar, kneeling before Robin.

"Rise, chaplain mine," replied Robin, "name thy request, it shall not be denied thee."

"I would be thy champion, as fitting match 'gainst priestly minion," answered the friar.

He was loudly acclaimed by his companions.

"Thou hast forestalled my wish in what thou hast asked," said Robin, "none worthier than thou, jolly friar, to be champion in such a cause."

"Thy conditions, fellow," said Robin, turning to the abbot's champion, whom he eyed critically.

"With oaken staff I'll meet thy man. Three knock down blows to give or take for victory."

"Well spoken," said Robin, admiringly. "Thy name, good fellow?"

"Good-for-Naught Dick," replied he with a grin.

"Acceptest thou the conditions?" asked Robin of the friar.

"Right thankfully; and harkee, Good-for-Naught Dick," said Friar Tuck, "by St. Hubert! thou wilt be good for summat ere I have done with thee, lad."

There was a general laugh at the friar's conceit, and the outlaws began to form themselves into a ring.

"Leave me not outside, fellows," roared Little John, who was seated a little distance off under a tree.

"St. Hubert! thou shalt have a front place, John," said the friar, going over to him, "Mount my back and thou shalt presently see fun of a right good sort."

Much merriment was caused by the friar's carrying John a pick-aback and setting him down carefully in a spot where he could safely witness the coming contest.

Both combatants tried the temper of their staves, and satisfied on this point, took their respective stations.

To it they went right lustily.

Their staves rattled loudly as each endeavoured to overreach the other's guard.

It was evident that Good-for-Naught Dick knew well how to handle his staff.

"Thou art o'er wary," said the friar, aiming a terrific blow at his opponent's head.

"Gramercy, father," quoth Dick, parrying the blow: "thou art pressing in thine attentions."

"Thou art tiring, Dick, thou art tiring," said the friar; "that to help thy sleep," as he caught him a smart rap on his left shoulder.

"'Tis but slight, father," replied Dick, good-humouredly.

"A fair knock-down blow, friar," remarked the abbot, as the friar in guarding himself slipped, and stumbled heavily.

"'Twas not, by St. Hubert! 'twill soon be seen whether thy man can much longer withstand me," exclaimed the friar, nimbly springing to his feet.

Getting within Dick's guard, the friar dealt him a heavy blow on the pate, which brought him to the ground.

"Body-o'-me! that is a leveller. Well hit, friar!" exclaimed Little John in ecstacies.

Dick was not vanquished.

"One to thee, friar," he said, rubbing his crown, with spiteful look.

"Thou hast a hard pate, good Dick," remarked the friar, with a grin; "'twill soften though, anon."

"'Have a care, friar," said Robin; "play not too loosely, man."

The admonition was needed.

Exposing himself for but a moment only to Dick's quick eye, brought his staff down on his pate with force, and the friar stretched his entire length along the ground.

"St. Hubert! but thou art the only man that hast ever brought me down," said the friar uprising, but in nowise disconcerted at his mishap.

To it they went right merrily.

The blow had roused the friar's ire, and Dick was soon to feel its effects.

"Thus perish all Robin's enemies," shouted the friar, as with terrific stroke he broke through his opponent's guard and stretched him lifeless on the ground.

"Hurrah! hurrah! hurrah!" came lustily from Saxon throats.

"Thou art vanquished," said Robin, turning to the abbot.

"Our Lady send thou hast not slain the man," replied the abbot concernedly.

"'Twas thine own seeking," replied Robin.

"Thou art lucky 'tis not thy condition instead of his, my lord," said the friar with a contemptuous sneer.

"I am surety to the king for his safety," exclaimed the abbot, unheedful of what had been said.

"Is he not thy follower, then?" queried Robin.

"'Tis the king's head forester," answered the abbot; "now woe is me, he's dead!"

"Nay, see, he stirs," remarked the friar, "and right glad I am of it. He is a doughty fellow, and knows full well the use of oak staff."

"'Twas said better player existed not in England," remarked the abbot.

"And you hired him with what intent?" asked Robin.

"To get me honour on thee, bold outlaw," replied the abbot.

"Thou hast signally failed; but it recks not now what thine object was," said Robin. I trow thou hast with thee rich booty."

"Nay, by Our Lady," replied the abbot, "thou art misinformed in this matter."

"Thou wilt also sign an agreement to pay further ransom for thy liberty," remarked Robin, unmindful of the abbot's protestations.

The abbot wrung his hands despairingly.

"Thou hast with thee five hundred crowns," observed Robin. "They are forfeit."

"Search, if thou wilt," replied the abbot, "an' thou findest such sum, 'tis thine, and welcome."

"'Twould pleasure me most to receive it quietly at thy hands," Robin replied. "Thou had'st better give it for the asking."

The abbot remained obstinately dumb.

"Seize each priest," said Robin, "and with hunting knife cut——"

"Mercy, mercy!" shouted the affrighted priests in chorus, and looking appealingly from Robin to the abbot.

"Have no fear," said Robin, laughing: "'tis only the skirts of thy frocks the knife will touch."

"'Tis an unseemly thing to do," remonstrated the abbot.

"Thou canst tack them on again," put in the friar with a grin.

With ruthless hand Robin's merry men obeyed his mandate.

Each priest's frock was soon minus its skirt. Sorry figures they made thus denuded of their nethermost attire.

"Search," said Robin, "and it will greatly deceive me but that crowns in plenty will be forthcoming."

The outlaws' search was successful, and as each man poured the crowns he had found in a heap upon the ground, Robin smiled, and the abbot looked glum.

"More remains," said Robin to the abbot; "prithee disclose their whereabouts."

"No more have I to give thee," answered the abbot; "thou hast despoiled me of all."

A signal from Robin brought Will Scarlet and Allan-a-Dale to his side.

"Find me the missing money," he said, pointing significantly to the abbot.

They advanced on him.

Plucking a dagger from his girdle, the abbot brandished it, saying—

"Lay a hand on my person at your peril! Avaunt, ye sacrilegious wretches!"

"Thou art a man of peace, sir abbot," said Will Scarlet, laughing and catching his hand adroitly and with a vigorous twist wrenching the dagger from it.

Seeing the condition of their master, the priests became furious with passion, and rushed to his aid.

But they were easily restrained, one of them in particular.

Friar Tuck seized the opportunity to bestow a good buffeting upon the monk who had annoyed him so grossly when he sojourned for a short time in St. Mary's abbey.

Robin laughed as his two lusty followers caused the abbot to be seated on the greensward in a way which found little favour with him.

Each plucked a shoe from his feet, and slitting the top across, found there silver and gold in abundance.

"Thou had'st much better have given up the money quietly," Robin observed to the abbot, who was beside himself with rage.

"Thou shalt rue this day's work, mark me well," he replied. "Thy course has nearly run."

"I have not done with thee, yet," said Robin. "Have a care how that tongue of thine waggest, else will I mulct thee heavily in coin."

The threat had the desired effect.

Robin and his men returned to his quarters accompanied by the priests and abbot.

Good-for-Naught Dick was accommodated with a seat on the abbot's mule, who had to walk barefooted after his captors, by way of penance.

"Ho! friar," shouted Little John, "Body-o'-me! thou wilt leave me behind man."

"St. Hubert! thou spakest but in time, John," the friar replied. "Mount my back, and I'll run a race with yonder lazy mules for a wager."

The party reached its trysting place in due time.

But the abbot's sufferings ended not.

Summoning Friar Tuck, Robin said—

"Indite me a missive for the abbot's signature."

"With alacrity I attend thee, master mine," replied the friar, coming in haste to his side.

"I sign it not," observed the abbot with a demonstrative gesture significant of dissent.

Unheedful of him Robin said—

"Take thy tablets, chaplain mine, and inscribe the following:—

"*Pay to the bearer, Friar Tuck, (of excellent memory and high reputation) the sum of four hundred marks.*"

The parenthesis was the friar's own addition, and much tickled Robin's fancy when read over to him.

"Attach thy signature to it," said Robin handing the tablets to the abbot.

"Thou refusest? do so at thy peril," said Robin as the abbot turned sullenly away.

He remained obdurate.

"Hark thee, sir abbot," Robin said with knitted brow, "thou shalt stay here, and thy brethren too, until the money be paid, with high interest for each day's delay."

"Thou would'st beggar me quite," said the abbot with vicious mien.

"Thou would'st beggar thyself by thine obstinacy. Bethink thee of my words, else will I measures take to bring thee to fitting sense of what is due to me as thy victor."

"I will sign," said the abbot with a heavy sigh.

Giving the missive to Friar Tuck, Robin said—

"Hie thee to St. Mary's Abbey and bring with thee the sum named."

"Gramercy!" exclaimed the friar; "thou shalt be well served master of mine."

"Mind, not one stiver more or less," observed Robin.

"Thou can'st rely on my precision. St. Hubert! 'twill be grand to hie me on the abbot's mule."

Turning to the abbot, Friar Tuck said with mock humility—

"Thou wilt not object, holy superior, to my bestraddling thy beast?"

"Avaunt thou reprobate!" said the abbot; "pollute not aught of mine by thine ungodly touch."

"Beshrew me! but thou art hard to please," replied the friar; "so I must e'en act without thy consent."

"Would I could go with thee friar," observed Little John in doleful accents.

"Be content, John man, to remain. Thou hast my permit to drink all the wine thou canst't get," exclaimed the friar as he vaulted into the saddle, and rode gallantly off on the abbot's beast.

He arrived in due time at the abbey and knocked loudly at the gate.

"Within there thou lazy knave!" exclaimed he impatiently, as no answer came to his oft-repeated summons.

"Thy business?" asked the voice of the warder at last, and just as the friar's patience was becoming exhausted.

"A message from my lord abbot; open in haste!" and the friar thumped more vigorously than before.

"Thou may'st stay outside until thy manners improve," was the response given by the warder, who little relished the friar's importunings.

"Open, thou empty-pated knave. Keepest thou the lord abbot's messenger waiting thus? St. Hubert! but thou shalt sweat for it."

There is no knowing to what lengths the friar would have proceeded had not the warder acted prudently and opened the gates.

"Can'st thou read?" asked the friar, thrusting the mission under the warder's nose.

"Can'st thou?" was the contemptuous reply.

"Hark, thee, brother," said the friar, in high dudgeon, "wag a civiller tongue, else wilt thou rue it."

"Thy message, what of it?" asked the warder.

"Read for thyself," replied the friar, "and act with despatch."

"'Tis the abbot's signature," observed the astonished warder.

"And 'tis the abbot's money I want," rejoined the friar.

"Four hundred crowns. Nay, but 'tis a large sum. I wot the abbey contains it not."

"Thou know'st not its whereabouts," answered the friar. "The abbot has instructed me where to find the money, which he greatly needs."

"With what intent?" queried the warder.

"Thou need'st not inquire. Lead the way to the abbot's dormitory, else will I get there without thy showing."

Pushing by the astonished warder, Friar Tuck passed hastily to the abbot's room.

Touching the spring, the abbot's riches became disclosed to his view.

"St. Hubert! 'tis a pity Robin so pressingly cautioned precision in the sum to be taken, else would I have enriched him bounteously."

A loud knocking came to the door, which the friar had taken the precaution to effectually barricade against intrusion.

"Ay, knock away till thine arm tirest," he exclaimed. "A pest on thy voice, fellow; thou hast made me miscount."

Still the knocking went on.

"Was it two, or three, hundred I counted?" soliloquised the friar. "St. Hubert! 'twas but two. Ay, knock away till thou tirest, good fellow; 'twill aid thy slumbers."

"'Tis dry work," he remarked as he rested himself and looked around. "I would I had some of the abbot's wine to slake my thirst."

His search for wine was ineffectual, and grumbling sorely he turned to depart.

"St. Hubert!" he exclaimed; "'twill go hard, but I teach these noisy fellows better ways."

Removing the obstructions, he opened the

door suddenly, and with outstretched fist went butt against the warder, who in company with some other monks had been knocking so loudly for some time past.

"Thou hast winded me quite," said the warder, doubling himself together with pain.

"I wot not of it, good brother," exclaimed the friar jocosely, "but thou'lt be better anon. Harkee, I thirst; give me, I pray thee, something to drink."

"Thou can'st have water," said one of the monks that stood by.

"I greatly prefer wine, brother," observed the friar with simplicity; "'tis my lord abbot's order that wine be given me."

"I would see the order thou speakest of," said one of the other monks."

"Read it 'an thou wilt!" exclaimed the friar thrusting it into the fellow's hand.

It was passed from one to the other in wondering astonishment.

"Thou hast the money?" queried one.

"Of a surety," answered the friar, "and must now depart."

"Here is water, brother," said one of the monks putting down a jar at the friar's feet.

"'Tis not to my liking," said the friar giving the jar a kick with his foot and sending the contents running over the floor.

"Thou art Friar Tuck, surely?" said a new comer.

"At thy service, good brother," answered the friar bowing gravely.

"He carries with him four hundred crowns of my lord abbot's money," observed the warder.

"And have the abbot's license for so doing," rejoined Friar Tuck. "Give space there, for my departure."

Pushing them rudely aside, he reached the courtyard, and mounting his beast rode forth unopposed, watched by the monks, who smiled grimly.

"St. Hubert, but 'tis fine!" he exclaimed aloud. "The money is safe, and I hie me homeward with despatch to Robin."

Whereupon he shook his money and sang :—

"Chink, chink, chink, chink!
   'Tis a sound that all love to hear;
   'Tis a sound melodious and dear.
   Naught is there like it this side of the grave.
   'Tis for gold and silver all men crave—
   With its chink, chink, chink!

"Chink, chink, chink, chink!
   Gentle and simple love the sweet sound,
   Sweat and toil till money is found.
   Maiden and knight, soldier and priest,
   Monarch and noble, from greatest to least,
   Love its chink, chink, chink!

"Chink, chink, chink, chink!
   Let the sound go merrily forth,
   Until it circles from south to north.
   Misers hoard gold, fools make it fly,
   For wise men to catch it as it goes by,
   With its chink, chink, chink!"

"Steady, thou reprobate!" said the friar, as his beast stumbled and nearly threw him.

Whizz, went an arrow just over his head and lodged in a tree hard by.

"St. Hubert!" exclaimed the friar, as another arrow came well nigh striking him; "'tis time to dismount."

In his hurry to do so, he stumbled and fell heavily to the ground.

"St. Denis, he is down!" exclaimed a fellow, starting from behind a tree, and running forward, followed by a companion.

Hearing them approach, the friar, with great presence of mind, lay still till they were close upon him, when starting to his feet, he attacked them with his staff.

His first blow levelled one of them outright.

The other fellow drew his sword and set on him courageously.

"Thou art a sorry knave," exclaimed the friar, as his staff descended on the fellow's sword-arm, followed by another on his pate, which well nigh stunned him. "Speak, fellow," said the friar, "whose minion art thou?"

"The abbot's," answered the fellow in great fear and dread.

"Is this his bidding? Speak truly, knave, as thou valuest a sound skin," and the friar brandished his staff ominously.

"We awaited thy return from the Abbey with the money. 'Twas the warder of St. Mary's Abbey directed us."

"Thou can'st return then to tell how thou hast fared," said the friar; "and harkee, bear my word to yon warder, that his evil intentions to me will not be forgot."

Mounting, the friar rode onward, leaving the discomfited knaves to their own cogitations.

"St. Hubert! but 'tis a queer world," soliloquised the friar. "Here am I bearing a simple message and taking home fitting answer, when I am waylaid. Were I common robber they could not worse treat me."

"Greet thee, friar," said a voice close at hand.

"Ah! is it thou, Reynolds," exclaimed the friar, "How fares our good master?"

"Well, quite well. He waits thy coming, fearing that aught of ill would befal thee by the way."

"Gramercy, good master, thou art ever mindful of thy friends," exclaimed the friar delighted that Robin had been concerned about him.

"Welcome, friar," said Robin, advancing to meet him. "Here be I and Little John anxiously watching for thy coming. What hast thou; aught good?"

"List to that," replied the friar, jingling his money; "'tis a sound fit for kingly ears."

"Ay, is it. 'Tis a ransom fairly won, by my halidom. Yonder abbot will think twice ere he again essays to encompass my hurt."

"Let him plot on, he pays liberally," said the friar, "his purse is a long one to my certain knowledge."

The members of the band gathered round the friar, welcoming him heartily.

"Body-o'-me!" growled Little John, "thou wert long gone, I was fain to search for thee almost."

"Hast aught for me to drink, little man?" asked the friar, in reply, "naught but water had they at yon abbey?"

"I have saved thee some," said Little John, handing it to his friend, "thou can'st drink to my speedy recovery."

Summoning the abbot and priests, Robin counted out before them the sum of four hundred silver marks.

"Thou did'st miscount, friar," he observed on finding that there yet remained a hundred or more marks over and above.

"'Tis naught, and not worth speaking of," answered the friar, "there is a fine store of them in the abbot's strong chest."

The abbot looked at him as if to harm him with the glance, so viciously did his eyes gleam.

"Four hundred alone is mine," said Robin.

"By theft alone," retorted the abbot.

"Nay, thou wert fairly vanquished, and art but paying the victor's dues," answered Robin; "above four hundred is thine, take it, and with it safe conduct through the forest."

"An' I meet with no rogues greater than thou," said the abbot, rendered reckless by the sight of his money in Robin's possession.

"Thou art welcome to thy discourteous speeches," Robin replied, "but be discreet withal, else thou wilt suffer more than money's loss."

"Peradventure thou would'st tarry awhile with us," said Friar Tuck, with well feigned humility, "thy presence is desirable beyond measure."

The outlaws laughed loudly at the friar's audacity; the abbot looked furious.

"Thou can'st refresh thyself," said Robin, "and thy followers can do likewise."

"We depart instantly," replied the abbot; "my bitterest curse rest upon thee as my bitterest animosity is thine, proud outlaw."

"Thou art at liberty to depart," calmly answered Robin; "and hark ye, sir abbot, bethink thee well of thy gains and losses, when next thou triest to work harm to Robin Hood and his merry men."

Mounting their beasts, the abbot and his retinue departed in sorry plight, and naught but sadness reigned in St. Mary's abbey for many a day afterwards, owing to its abbot's folly.

"Bayston thou art a true man," said Robin, shaking him heartily by the hand; while his comrades loudly acclaimed him.

"Told I not thee truly, master mine," answered Bayston, "they little recked that I was by when they planned to hide the money."

"Ha, Ha!" laughed Robin, "how ill the abbot bore his misfortune. 'Tis a lesson he ought to profit by."

The bugle summoned them to a bounteous repast, at which the merry laugh and sportive jest went round the festive board.

"Honour me a toast," said Robin.

"A toast, a toast; attention!"

"Honour to our chaplain, Friar Tuck!"

It was drank with acclamation, much to the friar's delight, who loved his companions to demonstrate their love and good feeling for him, after such a hearty fashion.

Toast followed toast, diversified by song and jest, and it was well nigh midnight ere Robin and his merry men sought repose.

CHAPTER LVI.

ROBIN HOOD'S ADVENTURE WITH THE WOOD DEMON.

It fell on a day, as Robin did stray
In the forest in search of fat deer,
That a demon so foul, did him waylay,
But bold Robin for such felt no fear.

NOT long after the adventures recorded in the last chapter, Robin took his bow and wandered alone into the depths of the forest.

"It suits my humour, Marian darling," he said ere starting, "to seek solitude and be alone with nature. Thou wilt not grudge my absence."

"Nay Robin, aught that to thy comfort adds has my sanction, be assured of that."

"Thanks, sweetest; I shall seek out fattest buck from which to prepare thee dainty meat. Adieu! May Our Lady have thee in her safe keeping."

"Adieu! Robin, darling. May all the saints forfend thee from harm, and keep thee free from aught of evil."

One long ardent embrace, and they parted.

Robin went into the greenwood with light heart.

Marian stood and watched his retreating form with loving gaze.

"'Tis thus I love to roam," said Robin half aloud. "Everything is free and untrammelled. Would that my country was so, then would nature seem more beautiful still, and all things partake of joy unspeakable."

Heaving a deep sigh, he went onwards.

He greatly enjoyed the occasion.

It was a grand old forest was that of Sherwood. Gigantic oaks reared their proud heads aloft, their sturdy branches striking out right and left in unrestrained freedom.

Ever and anon the trees assumed fantastic shapes, at times weird and phantom-like; at others, grand and beautiful.

"Fit bower that for knight's lady-love," said Robin, gazing at a cool retreat under the shade of some wide-spreading trees.

His approach startled the deer, which gazed at him for a short time, as if in wonderment at his audacious intrusion, then turning, swept up the glade with a fleet rush.

Rippling, bubbling streamlets crossed his path at turns flowing onward merrily.

The silence of the grand old place was unbroken save by the twittering and carolling of birds, whose tiny, melodious voices seemed lost in the immensity of the stillness reigning around.

In merry mood, Robin awakened the welkin with a song:—

"To the forest, to the forest! to the grand old place,
The bounding red deer so merrily to chase.
Then for king, nor lord, nor peasant care I,
For the twang of my bow makes true arrows fly.

"Wake up the welkin with sound of horn,
Speed on, undaunted by brake or sharp thorn.
Elsewhere is not found such a grand old spot;
Seek'st thou its equal? thou wilt find it not.

"To the forest, to the forest! for is it not grand?
In its coverts, brave Saxons, we can take our stand;
Bid defiance to our foes, and laugh at the strife,
Give me above all things, a merry forest life."

Robin wandered onward, heedless of his course, until he reached a gloomy part of the forest, which had the reputation of being haunted by evil spirits.

"'Tis said that strange forms disport themselves here," said Robin, vainly endeavouring to repress an inward shudder.

"Bah! 'tis folly. With a loud blast of bugle-horn will I rouse these solitudes and its demons, if any there be."

He blew *three* blasts both loud and strong, then listened.

Four answering blasts reverberated through the gloomy place.

"'Tis strange," soliloquised Robin; "four blasts, and stronger far than notes of mine. I will e'en sound again."

Robin blew *four* blasts louder and stronger than before.

Three notes short and defiant came back.

While Robin stood lost in amazement, the place which hitherto (excepting the bugle blasts) had been supernaturally silent, awakened into life; mocking laughter, gibberings and chatterings, and other strange unearthly sounds abounding.

Robin stood his ground firmly and fearlessly.

Nothing met his gaze, although he looked around with eager scrutiny.

"'Tis strange," he muttered; "sounds such as those no mortal lips could utter. I will e'en stay and see the end of this strange adventure."

Barely had he finished speaking, ere a chorus of unearthly voices wildly chanted forth:

"Sounds of wild mirth and revelry make,
　　Ah, ah, ah, ah! ah, ah, ah, ah!
Laugh wild and long, the greenwood to wake,
Wood demons we, whom do we flee?
Summon wild spirits from earth and green tree.
To join in our revels let them haste from afar,
　　Ah, ah, ah, ah! ah, ah, ah, ah!"

Then followed sounds of most devilish laughter, but naught could Robin see.

Suddenly the ground trembled under his feet, a low tremulous noise was heard in the air, increasing in intensity each moment.

Then there flashed into sight an unearthly-looking figure.

Its height towered far above that of Robin.

On its head were branching antlers.

Wild elfin locks hung down its back.

Its face was dark, and carried an expression of fierceness.

Its eyes resembled coals of fire, so fiercely and red glared they.

It was fantastically garbed.

"Thou did'st summon me," it said, "What wouldest thou?"

"I summoned thee not," answered Robin, standing fearlessly erect, and casting a fixed glance upon the monster.

"Ah, ah!" laughed the demon harshly; "thou fearest me."

"I fear thee not," exclaimed Robin boldly. "Why should I?"

"Thy name?" asked the demon.

"An' thou carest to know it, 'tis Robin Hood."

"I can aid thee. Power is mine beyond that of mortal."

"I need it not," answered Robin.

Plucking an arrow from his girdle the wood demon offered it to Robin, saying:—

"'Tis thine on certain conditions."

Robin spoke not.

"Be mine after death, and power, riches, honour, vengeance, all that thou can'st desire, shall be thine. This arrow will render thee invincible as a marksman, make thee king of archers. Say, wilt thou accept it?"

"Avaunt, thou evil spirit," said Robin, devoutly crossing himself, "aid of thine I require not."

"Thou lovest Maid Marian," said the demon abruptly.

Robin was silent.

"She is now in the sheriff's power," and the demon laughed a mocking laugh.

"Thou liest," said Robin fiercely. "Thou but seekest to entrap my soul by falsehoods."

"I would aid thee. Marian is as I have told thee. Would'st see for thyself?"

"Thou art but trifling with my fears," said Robin excitedly.

"'Tis not so, I swear. Of this thou shalt soon have proof."

Waving his arrow thrice, the demon spake certain cabalistic words.

A mist suddenly appeared, and formed a kind of screen.

Gradually it dispersed, disclosing to Robin's view a strange and unwelcome sight.

Marian struggled in the arms of the sheriff's soldiers, as she was being conveyed within the gates of Nottingham Castle.

The picture was so vivid, so real and life-like, that Robin started forward.

"Back!" cried the demon, with voice of thunder. "Thou perilest thy life. Back! I command thee."

Robin stood arrested.

With intense gaze he watched the scene suddenly fade into nothing.

Smiting his forehead in deep anguish, Robin said aloud:

"'Tis an illusion. Marian, darling, thou art safe at Sherwood."

"Thou art still incredulous?" queried the demon.

"Thou but seekest to entrap me," said Robin fiercely.

"Not so," answered the demon; "speak but the word, and Marian will be free. A long life will be thine; 'tis not till after death——"

"Peace, foul fiend, and tempt me not," cried Robin; "else will my trusty sword try thy condition."

"Ah! ah!" derisively laughed the demon. "Thou art rash as well as foolish Robin Hood."

Drawing his sword, Robin attempted to rush forward.

Some invisible power held him back.

Enraged beyond measure, Robin shouted excitedly:

"Devil! demon! hell hound! release thy spell, and quickly will I try thy courage with my trusty sword."

"I would not harm, thee," said the demon pityingly. "Thou art brave, and withal a good archer. Would'st try a bout of archery with me?"

"On fair conditions," said Robin boldly, "I would e'en try thy skill in archery."

"Select thy mark, then," the demon replied.

Robin paused, and casting his eyes about, said:

"I see naught of fitting mark. But I will make thee a proposition."

"Say on," replied the demon.

Picking up an acorn from off the ground, Robin said:

"Hold this loosely between thumb and forefinger, and with mine arrow I will release it. Art thou fearful?"

ROBIN HOOD,

AND THE OUTLAWS OF SHERWOOD FOREST.

"ROBIN, WITH HOOD THROWN BACK, PEERED IN,"

"I accept thy challenge," the demon replied; "do thou name my station."

"One hundred and fifty good strides take thou, then halt."

The demon took his station accordingly.

Affixing an arrow to his bow Robin fired.

The acorn was shot clean away from between the demon's thumb and finger.

No. 19.

"Bravely shot, Robin Hood!" said the demon; "thou wilt not fear now to comply with my conditions?"

"Fear and I have ever been strangers," Robin replied; "name thy want."

"Draw thou further back by paces three-score or more, and place an acorn on thy head."

Robin did so and waited the issue.

Picking up a dead branch from off the ground and quickly stripping off its excrescences with his hunting knife, the demon bent it in the form of a bow. Out of some grass he wove a string, and in an incredibly short space of time he had a bow ready for use.

Placing the arrow he had offered to Robin on the string, he took aim and fired.

Robin stood firm as a rock.

He felt the acorn lifted from off his head.

"'Twas a clever shot," said Robin, turning and lifting the demon's arrow.

His skilled eye saw that the arrow was faultless in shape and beautifully balanced.

"Wilt have it?" asked the demon; "'tis a gift a prince might envy."

"And an honest man decline," rejoined Robin. "No, I want no such aid; my mortal skill sufficeth for all my wants."

"Return it," said the demon with a fierce gesture.

Robin did so; but the arrow clave to his hand, nor could he shake it free.

"Ha, ha!" laughed the demon, mockingly, "thou art mine now. Who of mortal birth grasps this arrow is undone."

Then commenced a terrific struggle.

The demon held fast by the arrow by one end, while the other stuck to Robin's hand with the tenacity of a leech.

The demon tossed Robin too and fro as if he were a mere straw only.

But Robin kept him a brave heart withal.

With clenched fist he aimed a sturdy blow at the demon's body.

With a terrific roar it vanished in smoke and flame, leaving Robin half stunned.

On coming to himself the place was as if such a terrible adventure as had just ended had not occurred.

A peaceful quiet reigned around, and all was hushed in quiet repose.

"I do but dream," said Robin, clasping his brow with his hand, "and yet 'twas too real."

The perspiration stood in large beads upon his forehead, and he shook like an aspen leaf, so terribly prostrating were the effects of the struggle he had just passed through.

"Ah!" he exclaimed on looking at the ring on the little finger of his right hand. "'Tis plain to me now. This holy relic given me by my mother of blessed and pious memory, hath holpen me. Thrice precious art thou now to Robin on such account."

Drinking freely from a rippling streamlet that flowed close by, Robin felt refreshed and hied him homeward.

"The saints send that the demon lied," he said, "else will my strait be sore indeed."

Meeting Will Scarlet he asked anxiously:

"Marian, speak, where is she?"

"A messenger arrived from her uncle shortly after thy leaving. With him she went, in company with Friar Tuck."

"Woe is me, she is undone," exclaimed Robin, in woful accents, "the demon lied not to me."

Will Scarlet heard his master's speech with great perplexity, it seemed so passing strange.

CHAPTER LVII.

HOW THE SHERIFF ENTRAPPED MAID MARIAN.

The sheriff did Marian foully entrap;
Ne'er happened before such a dire mishap.
To Nottingham Castle they bore her away,
Both to her and Robin 'twas a sorrowful day."

BARELY had Robin started on his solitary ramble when a messenger arrived desiring speech of Maid Marian.

"From whom comest thou?" she asked.

"Thine uncle, Much the Miller, sends thee greeting, and informs thee of his sorry condition through sore ailment."

"Our Lady forbid it! Is he much afflicted? and prithee tell to me his true condition," said Marian, imploringly.

"An' thou tarriest long in reaching his side naught but his mortal manes wilt thou behold."

"Oh! say not so, good fellow," exclaimed Marian in piteous accents. "'Tis not so bad with him as thou declarest?"

"'Tis simple truth I to thee convey. E'en take or leave it at thy pleasure."

"I will go with thee," said Friar Tuck, who stood hard by and overheard the conversation. "Peradventure ghostly counsel will prove with him acceptable."

"Thanks, good Friar Tuck," Marian replied, "but would that Robin were here."

"I must e'en return," said the messenger. "What message shall I declare from thee?"

"Thou shalt none convey," replied Marian. "I will convey mine own."

"What say'st thou, Little John?" asked Friar Tuck, in allusion to Marian's projected departure. "Is it seemly or right for Marian to go on faith of such message?"

"'Tis a pressing necessity, friar," answered Little John, "else would I withhold my consent. Thou wilt company her for safety sake."

"Even so, John; and woe be to the man that darest cross her path with harmful intent!" said the friar, in quick response.

"If aught of ill befall her," remarked Little John, "Robin will be sore displeased."

"Pish, man," replied the friar, "thou art like a bird of ill omen to-day."

"Well, well, let her depart an' she will. Bear thou my greetings to friend Much, and say that Little John compassionates his condition."

Marian rode away, accompanied by the friar and the messenger.

"Thou art of friend Much's household?" said the friar to his male companion.

"But lately joined thereto," was the abrupt answer.

"Umph," said the friar, eyeing the fellow critically. "Hast thou aught by thee from thy master to betoken thine identity?"

"Naught but my message. Sufficeth it not?"

"Hast thou any fears of him?" asked Marian of the friar as they contrived to get out of earshot of their companion.

"'Twas but a passing suspicion, dissipated ere thou spakedst."

"'Tis well. My heart is sad. Poor Uncle! Our Lady forfend us. Heard'st thou not that?" asked Marian.

"'Tis treachery, I ween. But 'bide thou close to me, girl," said Friar Tuck, as half a dozen horsemen appeared in sight.

The messenger had suddenly disappeared.

Casting his eyes around, the friar selected a fine old oak for his position, and thither led Marian.

"Have no fear, Marian," he said. "They shall have thee only o'er my dead body."

"'Tis the sheriff's minions," remarked Marian. "'Tis plain this is his doing."

"The odds are not great," the friar said, an' had'st thou but a bow, and I another, we could bid them defiance."

"Greet thee, father! and thee, fair lady!" said one of the approaching horsemen, doffing his hat.

"Greet thee kindly," answered the friar. "Art thou travelling far?"

"We halt here, father," replied the horseman, "to relieve thee of thy fair charge."

"Concern not thyself," answered the friar, "but pass on, my son."

Closer and closer came the horsemen.

"No harm is intended thee," said he who had first acted as spokesman; "'tis the dame we want."

The friar gripped his staff more tightly, but answered not.

"Thou art e'en matched, friar, and wilt best consult thy safety by——"

A sound thwack from the friar's staff caused the animal the speaker bestrode to rear and plunge.

"Have at thee thou shaveling!" said the sheriff's soldiers.

They attacked the friar in a body; but owing to their being mounted they did but confuse themselves in their movements.

"St. Hubert! but thou shalt rue thy knavery," said the friar, dealing his blows lustily and well on all who came within his reach.

Seeing they gained no advantage, owing to their being mounted, three of their number dismounted, and gave their horses to their comrades to hold.

Friar Tuck's eyes glistened joyfully at sight of this.

"Broken pates and trounced hides await thee, thou Norman swine," he muttered. "Marian, girl, keep thou close and fear not."

Standing in front of his fair charge the friar boldly confronted his assailants, who advanced upon him with drawn swords.

Deftly he wielded his staff, and ere many minutes had passed, his antagonists numbered only two; the third lay sprawling on the ground.

At this juncture the friar was startled by a cry from Marian.

The treacherous guide had advanced stealthily, and suddenly pouncing on her bore her away towards the horsemen.

Ere the friar could reach her side one of the horsemen had galloped off with her and was past pursuit.

Taking advantage of the friar's distraction, the remainder of the party, with the exception of the fellow whose pate the friar had cracked, got them clean away.

"Thou art a noisy dame," observed the fellow who bore Marian before him on his saddle, "thy voice must e'en be stopped."

"Base, unmanly knave, unhand me," said Marian, struggling hard to release herself from the fellow's tight grasp.

"Thou wilt find little favour with the sheriff, my master," he replied sneeringly. "Bridle thy tongue, else must I use roughness to that end."

"Nay, nay, gentleness becometh the lady's condition, best," observed the leader of the party, riding up and saluting Marian respectfully.

"An' thou be a true man," she said, looking imploringly towards him, "thou wilt not suffer to see me thus rudely treated."

"'Tis but a soldier's roughness fair dame, and as such is excusable. Believe me no harm is thee intended. I pledge mine honour for it."

"No harm, say'st thou," exclaimed Marian with energy. "What callest thou thy bearing towards me thus far then?"

Marian's eyes sparkled vengefully, and seizing the opportunity when the soldier's grasp was somewhat relaxed she, by a superhuman effort almost, wrenched her right hand free, and plucking a dagger from her girdle, exclaimed, as she raised it aloft—

"Thus and thus will Marian avenge the insult put upon her."

"Thou venomous baggage, furiously exclaimed the fellow, "then will I—"

His hand grappled her throat, and in a few moments Marian would have died, when the leader with a buffet that caused him to reel in his saddle, saved the brave girl's life.

"Thou fool!" he exclaimed angrily. "Can'st thou not take a woman's blow more patiently. Out upon thee for a poltroon."

"Thou shalt answer for this," replied the fellow."

"Silence, and give the lady into my keeping," was the stern rejoinder.

To Marian, with a courteous bow and smile, he said:

"I pray thee to accept of a share of my seat. I can promise thee gentler treatment."

Marian, who saw the uselessness of resistance, and was sadly disappointed that her dagger had not harmed her brutal captors for beneath his buff jerkin he wore a steel cuirass, willingly accepted the offer, and exchanged places.

"Thou wilt give the sheriff courteous greeting," said her companion, as they arrived at the castle gate.

"Thanks for thy courtesy," answered Marian evasively; a Saxon maiden knows full well how to treat her friends."

"'Tis known full well to me that he loveth thee excellently well. Let thy prudence, then, counsel discreetness in thy bearing towards him."

Marian was silent, and her hand fumbled nervously at her girdle.

Breathing an inward prayer for strength and protection, she alighted in the courtyard, where stood the expectant sheriff, radiant with courtly smiles.

"Welcome, lovely Marian, to my poor castle. Thy beauteous presence far eclipseth aught of excellence that within it is contained."

"Thou art a base knight," replied Marian with contemptuous scorn; "thou art brave when danger is absent, and to defenceless women actest treacherously."

"Love useth not discrimination, fair one," replied the sheriff, advancing to take her hand.

"Thus do I proclaim thee coward," exclaimed Marian, as, with open palm, she struck him in the face."

"S'death, thou shalt rue this," exclaimed the sheriff, roused to fury by the insult.

"Would that I had a dagger," said Marian; "then would I smite thee dead, thou poltroon!"

Marian looked queenly in her just wrath, and despite his anger, the sheriff could not but admire her, and this his lcoks plainly told.

Turning to a page, the sheriff said:

"Show the lady to her chamber."

"Thou wilt attend him," he said to Marian, "and wilt do wisely to curb thy temper, and restrain thy hands from unmaidenly acts."

Disdaining answer, she with a glance of ineffable disdain and contempt followed the page with dignified gait and haughty mien.

The sheriff followed her retreating figure with passionate glances, and murmured:

"Proud and haughty thou may'st be, but beautiful beyond compare, art thou, Marian, loveliest among women!"

Rousing himself from pensive mood, he asked:

"Devereux, what hast thou to report? Thou hast well performed thy task, and shalt have fitting reward."

"Naught of resistance sustained we, save from the staff of a fat-paunched friar. St. Quintin, but he struck mighty hard."

"'Twas Friar Tuck! may the Evil One fly away with him," said the sheriff. "Thou did'st give him fitting chastisement, surely?"

"Not so," replied Devereux. "He smote Roderic, who now remains behind, and defied us, spite of our united efforts to o'ermatch him."

"Roderic! said'st thou, Roderic? Now hast thou told a grievous thing; him will Robin Hood slay for Marian's sake."

"Time was pressing," Devereux replied extenuatingly.

"I chide thee, not, Devereux," exclaimed the sheriff; "but I would that brave Roderic had not thus fallen."

After pausing for a time in thought, the sheriff said:

"Despatch a company of horsemen in search, peradventure, he is lying where thou didst leave him." With a low bow, Devereux withdrew to execute the order.

'Twas a spacious, well-appointed chamber into which Marian was shown.

With a deferential bow the page said:

"Hast any commands, lady? gladly will I do aught to pleasure thee."

"Thou can'st leave," Marian gently answered; for her anger was not for the sheriff's minions."

"Shall thy maid attend thee, lady," asked the page; "I will quickly apprise her of thy summons.

Marian heard him not, her thoughts were far away with Robin.

"Greet thee humbly, lady," said a soft voice at her elbow.

Marian started, and looked round. Beside her stood a pretty girl, attired modestly.

"I would that I could serve thee, lady; thou art tired and——"

"Thou hast a woman's heart," said Marian with passionate earnestness, and looking fixedly at her; "wilt thou aid one deeply distressed to escape a fate worse than death?"

The abruptness of the question startled the girl and bereft her of speech.

"So young, and withal so cruel!" said Marian, turning away with choking sobs.

She had construed the girl's silence as betokening a refusal, and the circumstance chilled her heart with despair.

"Nay, lady, thou wrongest me," said the girl with warmth; "Madge Stukely does not possess aught of cruelty in her heart towards thee."

"Madge Stukely!" said Marian hastily; "surely, thou did'st once succour Robin Hood?"

"Hush, lady!" said Madge.

"And wilt succour me—surely thou wilt?" said Marian, throwing herself on her knees before her attendant with clasped hands and streaming eyes.

"Wring not my heart, lady," said Madge, "nor peril thy chance of escape by thus acting. Bethink thee that, should the sheriff overhear you——"

A heavy footstep approached the door.

Checking her speech, Madge motioned piteously to Marian to rise, and hurriedly whispered:

"Courage, I am a friend."

Both listened, fearful that each moment the sheriff would intrude upon them, but the footstep passed to and fro only.

"'Tis a sentinel," said Madge, in a low whisper.

"Better anyone than the traitorous sheriff," replied Marian. "Would that Robin was near, then would I be content."

"Patience, lady," answered Madge, "Robin Hood will not tarry, and thou wilt ere long be free."

"Our Lady grant it," said Marian, fervently, "the hours will go wearily by the while."

"I will acquaint thee of the sheriff's intentions," remarked Madge; "under pretence of serving him, I will get from him his resolves, and 'twill go hard but that between us twain he will outwitted be."

"How can I compensate thee, brave, generous maiden?" exclaimed Marian, seizing Madge's hand and pressing it ardently to her lips.

"By being discreet, dearest lady; all will depend on thy disposition towards the sheriff."

"Thou would'st not have me favour him by aught in word or action," exclaimed Marian, glancing suspiciously at her companion.

"Thou misunderstandest me, lady," replied Madge, "I counsel naught unseemly, prudence only I would advise."

"Forgive me, dear girl," cried Marian, embracing her with warmth, "I will trust thee even with life itself."

"Thy trust will not be misplaced," answered Madge. "But thou art tired, lady, and would perchance hie thee to thy couch."

"I am indeed weary, good Madge," Marian replied, "and will e'en seek repose."

"Our Lady defend and comfort thee," said Madge, before leaving Marian's side.

"Kiss me, Madge—good night."

Marian soon sobbed herself to sleep, and in her dreams was happy.

CHAPTER LVIII.

HOW ROBIN GAINED ACCESS TO NOTTINGHAM CASTLE AND WHAT BEFEL HIM THERE.

"Who art thou fellow?" the sheriff, he said,
"I prithee now tell unto me."
"I am a bold harper," quoth Robin Hood,
"And the best in the north countrie."

FRIAR TUCK gazed wistfully after the retreating party, and muttered oaths not a few.

"Would that the sun had not shined on such a day," he said excitedly; "Would that slain I had been by yon cursed Normans; then had I been past shame."

Leaning on his staff the friar became lost in deep thought.

Turning he beheld the inanimate form of Roderic.

"I have something to show for mine handywork," he exclaimed; "by his garb he is a person of some condition, him will I take to Robin Hood."

Roderic gave signs of returning animation, which the friar aided by fetching him a horn of water from a running stream hard by.

"Stand up, man," said the friar, endeavouring to put him on his feet.

"Devereux, what means this confusion," said the wounded man; "I am faint, oh! this pain," and he groaned piteously.

"St. Hubert! but thou art in bad case," exclaimed the friar as Roderic reeled, and would have fallen heavily had he not caught him in his arms.

"I would that some of Robin's men were here to aid me," exclaimed the friar; "'twill not be long ere some of those Norman swine come to seek him, but budge I will not for the whole herd of them."

Waiting patiently for signs of his prisoner's recovery, and perceiving none, Friar Tuck resolved upon action.

"I will e'en summon assistance by aid of this bugle horn," he said unstringing it from Roderic's person; "I can blow a lusty note if needs be."

Placing it to his lips he blew the foresters' call, then paused and listened.

But save the echo naught else heard he.

"A malison seize the fellows! Fitting call I blew enow, to wake the dead, and yet they come not. I will e'en try again."

Pealing notes he again gave forth, and answeringly came back the welcome notes of the foresters "Advance" call.

"St. Hubert be thanked! they come at last; but I would face the Evil One himself in preference to Robin as bearer of Marian's mishap."

The foresters numbering a dozen emerged into view, headed by Reynolds.

From the opposite direction came a troop of the sheriff's horse, headed by Devereux, in search of Roderic.

"What is thy strait, good friar?" asked Reynolds.

"A right sore one, friend. Marian is borne off by the sheriff, and I, who could not prevent the cruel mishap, am here to tell it. Call'st thou not that a sore strait?"

"Ha!" exclaimed Reynolds, "hither come the sheriff's fellows. Quick, men; use thy bows deftly and strike a blow for Robin and his Marian."

"They seek this wounded knave; but him will they not get. Lend me a bow," said the friar vengefully; "St. Hubert! but I'll arrow them in fitting style."

A horseman came riding forward bearing a white kerchief on his sword's point.

"Hold thine hands friar," said Reynolds; "it must not be that one seeking truce get aught but words. Fitting time for combat will presently arrive; then thou can'st let loose thy spleen an' thou wilt."

"Parley not with such knaves," replied the friar; "they war on defenceless women. Out upon the Norman swine! say I. Confusion to them one and all!"

After delivering himself of this denunciatory speech the friar threw his bow down, and leaning on his staff, gazed in angry mood at the approaching horseman.

Pulling rein, Devereux—for it was he—said—

"I would have speech of the leader of this party."

"Say on," said Reynolds; "but prithee be brief."

"Thou hold'st the body of dear friend of mine, whom may the saints in glory assoilzie! I would ransom it at thy hands."

"It may not be," said Reynolds, "unless thou agreest to ransom for ransom, thy friend for Maid Marian, whom the sheriff has basely entrapped."

"It layeth not to me to declare aye or nay to thy proposal," Devereux replied; "but I will bear it to my master, and bring thee fitting answer speedily."

"Agreed," said Reynolds; "but thou may'st bear thy message to my master Robin Hood, at Sherwood, whither we will bear thy friend, who yet liveth, as thou can'st see."

Roderic had sat him up, and hearing Devereux's voice, essayed to rise to his feet, but could not.

"St. Denis be praised; thou livest Roderic," exclaimed Devereux.

Turning to Reynolds, he said:—

"I will confer with my companions, and——"

"Their decision availeth naught," replied Reynolds, "thou hast mine answer, aught else thou requirest seek of Robin Hood."

"Bravely said, Reynolds, and like a forester true that thou art," observed the friar; "and harkee, fellow," he said, turning to Devereux, "if aught harmful happeneth to but one hair of Marian's head, thy friend will hang high."

Without vouchsafing an answer to the friar's inflammatory speech, Devereux wheeled his horse about and joined his companions.

"Be watchful, Reynolds," said the friar: "yon Normans mean mischief 'tis plain."

"'Twill be their own hurt, then," replied Reynolds.

"Let two bear this fellow to the rear," said the friar, "whilst we face the horsemen with arrow on string."

"Well advised," replied Reynolds; "it shall be even as thou hast said."

"They come!" exclaimed the friar.

Urging their horses to the utmost speed the Normans, headed by Devereux, came thundering onwards shouting:—

"A rescue, a rescue! St. Denis and St. Quintin bestow their aid!"

"Thou wilt want better aid than theirs,"

defiantly shouted the friar. "Aim at their horses, men."

A flight of arrows checked the advance of three of their number, their horses falling under them mortally wounded.

Soon they joined issue, the friar singling out Devereux.

"Have at thee, thou Norman caitiff!" he said, springing forward, staff in hand.

"St. Denis! a rescue! a rescue!" shouted Devereux, rising high in his stirrups as he aimed a terrific blow at the friar's head.

Guarding it deftly, he delivered a tremendous blow with his staff on Devereux's thigh, which well nigh broke it.

"Yield, thee, thou Norman," the friar exclaimed, "else will I trounce the life out of thy carcass."

At this juncture the ears of the combatants were assailed by the sound of a bugle horn.

"'Tis Robin," said Reynolds joyfully. "Lay on my men; St. George, for merry England."

Devereux essayed to turn his horse's head, but the friar was too quick for him.

With the aid of his staff, he vaulted behind him, and grasping him tightly round the body with one hand, he seized the reins with the other, and galloped off with him a prisoner in Robin's direction. Of the remainder of the Normans, those who could, got them away on their horses, while the others yielded themselves prisoner's to Robin's men.

"Greet thee, friar," exclaimed Robin as he drew rein in front of him. "Whom hast thou with thee?"

"He who basely bore off thy Marian."

"Alas!" cried Robin, "'tis true, then!"

"Assailed were we most treacherously," exclaimed the friar; "and though I essayed to prevent it, Marian was carried off bodily before my very eyes."

Reynolds brought his party up, including four prisoners.

"Bind them all," cried Robin, "and carry them straight on to Sherwood to await my pleasure concerning them."

Never a word spake the Normans, for they weened that their strait was a right sore one, and that speech would avail them naught.

"I made a vow to God," said Robin, in hearing of his merry-men, "that I press not bed, nor eat nor sup, till I have entrance gained to Nottingham Castle."

Respecting the poignancy of his grief too much to intrude their speech upon him, the friar and the outlaws stood aside and communed with each o her in under tones.

Beckoning them to him, Robin said, specially to the friar:

"Bear ye this message to Little John. Robin hies him to Nottingham Castle. If in three days from this tidings of him reach you not prepare to seek him; ere that, let none intrude their presence within the castle walls."

"Thy wish shall be obeyed," replied the friar, with dejected mien; "would that I went with thee to share thy perils."

"Nay, nay, good friar, it cannot be," Robin replied; "tarry thou with the rest at Sherwood I would act alone in this matter."

With friendly greetings Robin parted from his merry-men, and took the road to Nottingham Castle.

"Our Lady send that I gain entrance to yon castle soon," murmured Robin; "else will the sheriff encompass his nefarious designs, ere I can prevent him."

Strong in his own ability to accomplish the purpose he had in hand, and buoyed up with the hope of finding Marian scathless, Robin went onwards.

His attention was arrested by the voice of some person sing a roundelay, and he listened thereto with interest:

> "Sing me a song of love, my sweet,
> Melody fit, thy lover to greet;
> Attuned let it be to the love in my heart,
> As smiles from thy love-laden eyes do dart.

> "I sung my lover só sweet a lay,
> That it lived in his heart for many a day;
> I could not deny my love anything,
> He lives in my heart of hearts as a king."

"By my halidom!" said Robin; "'tis just such a person I longed to meet. His minstrel's attire and harp will I take unto me to gain me a passport to yon castle."

"Greet thee, gentle sir," said a cheery voice to Robin.

"Greet thee cheerily, friend," replied Robin; "art thou mindful to travel far?"

"Travel to me is not so rare a thing that I measure the distance of each day's journey," replied the minstrel.

"Thou art a minstrel, I wot," said Robin; "would'st thou earn twenty crowns?"

"Thou jestest, of a surety," replied the minstrel; "such sum hath not pressed my palm for many a day, and folks part not easily with their money."

"See," exclaimed Robin taking the crowns from his gipsire, "they are thine; give me thine apparel and harp; I've great need of them."

"Now, thou art a merry wag, surely!" exclaimed the minstrel laughing; 'tis plain thou hast a mind to play thy merry pranks on me."

"Thou but wasted time," said Robin; "thou wilt do well to pleasure me quickly, else will I have by force that which I would pay thee fairly for."

"Nay, nay, an' thou pratest so finely," replied the minstrel; "thou may'st e'en seek elsewhere for a person to do thy bidding."

"I give the but till I count twenty; bethink thee, saucy minstrel, twenty crowns are better than hard knocks."

"I will e'en try thy mettle, my fine fellow," replied the minstrel plucking his sword from its sheath; "have at thee, bully."

Their swords crossed.

Ere a minute had passed, or they had exchanged but one or two passes, the minstrel's sword went flying from his grasp.

"Thou art the Evil One or Robin Hood," exclaimed the vanquished minstrel, "else would not I, being no mean fencer, be so quickly overcome."

"My name is Robin Hood; hast ought to speak against it."

"Naught save this. Had I known this, I would ne'er have refused thy request. Thou art right welcome to all I have, without payment even."

"Gramercy!" exclaimed Robin, "but doff thy attire quickly, the twenty crowns are thine."

The exchange was speedily effected, and Robin stood habilitated as a minstrel.

"How doth my present guise suit?" asked Robin.

"Seemeth I myself, or would'st thou credit me with another's likeness."

"I have here what will render thy visage altered past knowledge. Mummery is mine office, and I carry with me things which are good aids to such an end."

So saying, the minstrel took from his wallet sundry things, and quickly, by their aid, changed Robin's apparel effectually.

"Thou art no longer bold Robin Hood, whom all men speaketh praisefully of, but a minstrel in very look."

"Looks will not avail fully," replied Robin, "if fitting minstrelsy be wanting. Thou shalt judge of my craft, an' thou wilt while I strike thine harp and troll thee a ditty."

Running his hand skilfully o'er the harp-strings, Robin sang, in a rich, full, musical voice, the following:

"Would'st thou know the name of the maiden I love,"
  Whose voice soundeth softer than cooing of dove;
  Whose lips dis il sweets, whose face is divine,
  Whose smiles are so beaming because they are mine

"'Tis a secret I care not for aught to reveal,
  'Tis a name to whose power fully vanquished I kneel;
  Dost thou seek to know more, 'tis not mine to disclose,
  I have shrined it in love, in my heart to repose."

"Well sung," exclaimed the minstrel; "thou excellest me greatly. Would that I could imitate thee, then would I content be."

"Thou hast made my heart rejoice," exclaimed Robin; "if ever thou requirest friend in need or sore strait, I Robin Hood will stand by thee, hearest thou?"

"Thou puttest too great honour upon me," exclaimed the minstrel; "to serve thee requiteth me fully."

"Adieu, friend," replied Robin; "my time is precious, and I crave thy forbearance."

"Farewell, noble Robin," said the minstrel, seizing his hand and pressing it respectfully to his lips; "Our Lady send thee aid in all thy necessities."

"'Twill surprise me greatly," said Robin to himself, "if I do not outwit yon crafty sheriff. I will seek entrance to the castle without delay."

Arrived at the castle gates, Robin went boldly forward and craved admission, saying:

"Would'st thou hear good minstrelsy, gentle lieges, I crave entrance, and for aught of favours bestowed will tune my song to do thee pleasure."

"Art thou Norman or Saxon," asked the sentinel.

"My lineage is Norman, else would I not seek entrance here," replied Robin.

"Abide thou there then," said the sentinel; "I will ask admittance for thee."

"Thou and thy master will learn my lineage ere long," muttered Robin; "that I am true Saxon will presently appear."

The sentinel returned and bade Robin enter, saying:—

"My comrades are wishful to hear thy minstrelsy, see thou demeanest thyself well, else will I suffer harm for asking thine admission."

"I doubt not but that my craft will please them," exclaimed Robin as he crossed the drawbridge.

"Welcome, welcome, thou minstrel," exclaimed a cheery soldier's voice; "thy presence is most acceptable. Sing us something to beguile our vigils."

"Greet thee all!" exclaimed Robin as he took his seat on a rude bench in the courtyard; "I will to mine office quickly, and crave thy patience while I sing to thee of what is always dear to soldiers' hearts."

"A maid wondrous fair stood by a knight,
  Whose plume waved free o'er helm so bright;
  Sad was her mien, tearful her eye;
  The time for their parting was drawing nigh.

"His war-horse pranced and pawed the ground,
  Near with anxious look stood his favourite hound;
  His warriors were mustering in proud array,
  With eager longings for the coming fray.

"Still the knight he loitered by the maiden fair,
  Stooped her cheek to kiss, stroked her golden hair;
  With murmured vows, and tender clasp of hand,
  Bade her think of him in foreign land.

"Years flew by, and the knight came not,
  His hounds and his hawks had him clean forgot;
  Not so the maiden, who had stood by his side;
  She mourned and grieved and had like to have died.

"'I will seek him,' she said, 'be he living or dead,
  In the land where he went, will my footsteps tread;
  No rest shall be mine, by night or by day,
  Until my weary head on his bosom I lay.'

"She sought and she found him in Palestine's land,
  A prisoner was he, and chained by the hand;
  Brave ransom she paid, her dear lover to free,
  And with Richard, her own love, came back o'er the sea.

"A maid wondrous fair stood by a knight,
  Near God's altar she stood, 'twas a most comely sight;
  No warriors stood by, nor was steel by his side,
  Place had they given to sweet Mabel, his bride."

"Thou art indeed a true minstrel, and shalt stay with us for a long time," rapturously exclaimed one of the soldiers, when Robin had finished his song.

"Is there no gentle lady within these walls whose ears I could gladden with fitting song?" asked Robin.

"There is one of wondrous beauty, but I wot thou can'st not strike the harp for her," was the reply.

"Why so fair, and yet so sad?" asked Robin.

Before fitting reply could be given, the sheriff approached.

"Who art thou, fellow?" he cried.

"A minstrel who wanders o'er the land with harp in hand to sing of the deeds of the noble and brave."

"Can'st thou lighten the heart of its cares by song?" asked the sheriff.

"'Tis mine office so to do. It gives me welcome where'er I go. Am I welcome here, sir knight?"

"Thou art; tarry thou here and refresh thyself; on the morrow I may need use of thy skill."

"Thou wilt be in rare favour," said one of the soldiers, when the sheriff had gone.

"Think'st so? 'Tis honouring to have notice of noble knights," said Robin; "but of this maiden, so wondrously fair, what is her condition?"

"I cannot speak openly to thee on this matter," replied the soldier in low tones; "but an' thou carest to hear more, I will tell it thee anon; 'twould make fitting subject for thy muse."

"But tell me," said Robin; "is there no maiden here of low degree from whose tresses I could gently pluck me a hair to bind up my harp-string. 'Tis of passing excellence for such purpose."

"That there is, good minstrel — Madge Stukely, as pretty a wench as thou could'st see I dare avow she would pleasure thee in this matter."

"Would'st thou summon her, friend?" asked Robin.

"I will; sit thee down meanwhile. I will send thee wine and food, for 'tis plain thou need'st refreshing.

"Madge Stukely," said Robin to himself; "'tis the girl who once served Mortimer and myself so well. Our Lady send that I still find favour in her sight. I will observe prudence in this matter, and bear me patiently the while."

"Madge is tending the maiden I told thee of," remarked the soldier, on returning; "but I will surely send her to thee presently. Do thou eat and drink."

He placed wine and food before Robin, of which he partook but sparingly.

"Here, Madge girl, thou art wanted," said the soldier, calling to her as she came from tending Marian.

"Thou saucepate," she replied, with a saucy toss of her pretty head. "Thinkest thou I heed beck or call of thine?"

"Thou art mistaken," said the soldier with a laugh; "'tis a minstrel seekest thee."

"Nay thou but jestest," she said, stopping in her walk.

"'Tis even so, maiden," said Robin Hood approaching her. "I would crave a boon at thy fair hands."

"I will not say thee nay if 'tis one which a maiden can fairly give," replied Madge, archly.

"I would crave a hair from thy tresses to bind up my harp-string. 'Tis not an unseemly favour I ween for a minstrel to ask of thee, maiden."

"Thou art welcome to it," she said, unbinding one of her luxuriant tresses, and plucking a long hair therefrom she handed it to Robin.

He detained her hand in his grasp, and looking watchfully around to see whether any were within earshot, said whisperingly—

"Hast forgotten Robin Hood, good Madge?"

"Nay, start not so," he said hurriedly, "else wilt thou betray thyself and me too. Cans't thou lead me to Marian?"

"Hist!" said Madge; "converse no more now; we are observed, but meet me at midnight under yonder portico. Till then farewell, brave Robin."

Pressing her hand gratefully he said, aloud:

"Thanks for thy gift dear maiden. I will sing thee on the morrow a love song, and teach thee how to woo thy love in softest accents."

"Thou art welcome, sir minstrel," she replied. "I will not forget thy promise. Adieu."

Robin sang and played for his patrons until they were fain to retire at watch setting.

Refusing the offer of a bed, Robin threw his mantle about him, and casting himself down on one of the rude seats in the banquetting hall feigned to sleep.

Two figures might have been seen at midnight under the portico.

Robin parted from Madge, having fully planned means for Marian's escape.

In vain Robin courted sleep; it visited not his eyes, for momentous issues hung upon the success of his enterprise.

"And thou, proud sheriff," he said, shaking his clenched hand aloft, "shalt find that Robin dares anything when those he loves are in peril."

He paced restlessly to and fro, racked with hopes, doubt, and fears.

"And thou, pale moon, silent witness in the heavens of my resolves, and thou, twinkling stars, resplendent with the celestial glories of other spheres, aid me, I beseech thee; 'tis for the sake of true love I plead."

After delivering this adjuration, Robin threw himself on his hard couch, to seek a repose, which came not.

As daylight broke, he fell into an unquiet slumber, from which he was awakened by the heavy tread of the sheriff's soldiers.

"Thou art a sluggard, friend minstrel," said the cheering voice of the friendly soldier, "peradventure thy dreams have been of lovely maiden."

"'Tis not often I am so taken," replied Robin, sitting up and yawning tremendously. "'Tis broad day, I declare."

"Even so. Thou had'st better betake thee to thine ablutions, and break thy fast, for it may be that the sheriff will require thine attendance presently."

"Gramercy, good fellow; I will e'en do as thou advisest," answered Robin.

He was not ready one whit too soon.

The sheriff summoned him to attend at the door of Marian's chamber.

The sentinel was withdrawn, and the door stood ajar.

Opening it wide with cautiousness, Robin, with hood thrown back, peered in, and shook his hand menacingly at the sheriff, who knelt pleadingly at Marian's feet; while she, with averted looks, showed her contempt and disgust.

She recognised Robin and gave a start, and a half-muttered exclamation of astonishment, although she had been forewarned of his presence within the castle by Madge Stukely.

Noticing her demeanour the sheriff started to his feet and looked round.

But Robin had withdrawn his presence from observation, and stood in the passage brimful of rage.

"'Sdeath!" he muttered between his clenched teeth, "I would e'en rush in and chastise thee thou insolent caitiff. What hindereth me?"

Robin actually gasped for breath, so greatly was he enraged.

ROBIN HOOD,

AND THE OUTLAWS OF SHERWOOD FOREST.

ROBIN DEFIES THE WOOD DEMON IN THE CASTLE DUNGEON.

By a great effort he controlled his passion, and passing his hand skilfully o'er his harp-strings, breathed out in melodious accents the following:—

"Fear not, maiden, thy lover is near,
Dim not the light of thine eye with a tear;
Be patient awhile, and still on him wait,
Be assured that his life is bound up with thy fate.

"When the moon on the earth sheds her light,
He'll hie to thee, sweetest, on wings of the night;
With kiss and caress he'll bear thee away,
In his arms he'll thee hold, with none to say nay.'

"'Tis not such melody I would have thee sing," exclaimed the sheriff angrily. "Thou had'st better confine thy voice to other themes."

"I crave thy pardon," said Robin, bowing low, and casting a reassuring glance at Marian, who returned it with one of love ; "I did but seek to pleasure thee in the matter."

"Sing me merrier strain, or thou shalt speedily quit my presence," peremptorily exclaimed the sheriff.

Bowing his head in semblance of meek submission, Robin sang the following :—

"I will be merry come what may,
    Brief is the span of life's short day ;
Sorrow and grief will come fast enough,
    The pathway of life is always o'er rough.

"Bring me the goblet, fill it with wine,
    Let mirth and sweet smiles on each face shine ;
Cast aside sadness, let it not share ;
    Drive away care, of sorrows beware.

"I drink to thee love, pledge me in return,
    Smile on me sweetest, my heart it doth burn ;
Chide not my wooing, nor deem me too gay,
    Suffer my head on thy bosom to lay."

"Thou shalt have fitting reward for thy lay," said the sheriff, when Robin finished his song ; "'tis well worthy the occasion."

He cast an amorous glance upon Marian, who, now that Robin was near, feared him not.

"Methinks that yon minstrel meant not his song for such as thou," contemptuously exclaimed Marian. "Thou hast ever proven thyself of ignoble condition, despite thy rank and station."

"Nay, sweet Marian, thou can'st e'en gibe or contemn me, an' thou wilt without let or hindrance," replied the sheriff. "Thou art equally lovely in whatsoever mood thou takest to thyself."

"Dost thou forget that there existeth such an one as Robin Hood?" asked Marian defiantly. "'Twould seem thou dost."

"He can be no longer aught to thee," answered the sheriff, gazing at his fair captive with a look of galling effrontery.

"Ah! say'st thou so?" said Robin half aloud, and laying a nervous hand upon the handle of the door.

"I will be plain with thee, thou Sheriff of Nottingham," exclaimed Marian. "Sooner than yield to thy purposes I would e'en smite through my heart with this."

She suddenly withdrew a dagger from her bosom and held it menacingly.

The Sheriff smiled fearlessly.

"'Tis not fitting toy for thy grasp. Thy beauteous hand was formed for love," he said, approaching her gallantly.

"Tempt me not," exclaimed Marian, with a look of fierce determination in her lustrous eyes, as she stepped back, "else wilt thou find when too late that a Saxon maid can hate e'en more passionately than she can love."

"I love to see thy display of spirit," said the sheriff, "it well becomes thy handsome face. Egad it warms my innermost soul to see it."

"Would'st try me?" said Marian, resolutely advancing on him.

The next moment a sharp cry of pain came from Marian's lips.

The sheriff had cruelly grasped her delicate wrist in his iron grasp, exclaiming angrily—

"Thou vixen, I'll e'en teach thee to"——

A vigorous arm hurled him backwards to the ground.

Standing over him was Robin, with menacing attitude.

"S'death, but thou shalt pay dearly for this!" exclaimed the sheriff, struggling to his feet.

Folding his hands across his breast, Robin said :—"Base and ignoble would I be to stand by and see thy rude violence to one so fair and gentle as this maiden. Thou had'st better pause ere doing aught further to compromise thine honour of knighthood."

"Addressest thyself to me, knave?" furiously exclaimed the sheriff. "Thou shalt soon repent thy rashness."

"Stay," said Robin, placing his hand upon the sheriff's arm as he turned to the door to summon assistance.

"Unhand me, fellow," haughtily exclaimed the sheriff, as he strove to shake off the outlaw's grip.

"Bethink thee," said Robin, "of what thou would'st do. Mine office debars thee from using violence towards me. Thou well know'st that a brand of infamy would be set on thee therefor."

The sheriff paused.

Robin's was no idle assertion.

To harm a minstrel honoured as guest was no mean crime, and in those days of romantic chivalry was visited with dire punishment, whether the offender was knight or common yeoman.

Marian gave Robin an imploring glance of silent entreaty to use prudence.

He gave her a reassuring look in return.

"Thou hast not acted a minstrel's part," replied the sheriff. "'Twas naught affair of thine that thou did'st intermeddle with just now."

"Thou errest, sir knight," answered Robin boldly. "'Twould be unseemly to sing of noble deeds and love's honourable dealings to rouse the heart into ennobling action, and stand me by to see innocent maidens maltreated. What think'st thou of the matter ; put it honestly to thy conscience?"

"Cease thy malapert tongue!" exclaimed the sheriff wrathfully ; "'tis not to hear thy prate that I bid thee hither. Hie thee out with despatch."

"Not so, sir knight," Robin answered. "I claim the privilege of my minstrel's calling, and lay an imposition on thee that thou do not further push me disadvantageously in this matter."

"Thou can'st stay, an' thou wilt," answered the sheriff after a pause of some moments, "but not near this lady's bower chamber. Seek thou the courtyard and pleasure my minions, for aught else thou art not fit."

"Thou art rude of speech, sir knight," said Robin rebukingly.

"To such as thou my speech matters not," contemptuously replied the sheriff.

"*Thou* a knight?" said Robin scornfully. "Ha, ha, ha! Methinks the king hast many worthier than thou."

"Thou would'st tempt thy fate then, fellow?" said the sheriff furiously.

"It ill becomes me to bandy words with thee," said Robin.

Then turning, and before the sheriff could interpose, he knelt at Marian's feet, saying, in tender accents, as he kissed her outstretched hand :

"Our Lady befriend thee, lady. 'Tis plain thou hast no friend in Nottingham's sheriff."

"Thanks, good minstrel," replied Marian, warmly grasping his hand. "I salute thee as an honourable man."

Stooping, Marian imprinted a kiss on Robin's cheek, who, whispering, said:

"*To-night, dearest, be ready.*"

So furiously angry was the sheriff as to be bereft of speech almost.

"Thus to be bearded in my own castle, by a poor beggarly minstrel!" he exclaimed at last. "Get thee out, fellow, or this dagger will——"

With a bound, Robin was on his feet, confronting him.

The motion caused a double-edged dagger to fall from his girdle to the floor.

"Ah?" exclaimed the sheriff, "thou carriest arms of a sort unbefitting thy condition. Thou art a spy, and no minstrel, I ween."

"'Tis fine-pointed and keen-edged," said Robin, laughing grimly, as he picked it up. "Would'st read its device?"

Inscribed on the hilt were letters of a rude form, roughly carved.

"I require not to unriddle it," answered the sheriff, with a scornful curl of his lip.

"'Tis this," said Robin, unheeding the sheriff's insult, "*Death before dishonour.* It would ill befit *thine* escutcheon."

"To the door with thee," said the sheriff, imperiously waving his hand. "Thou can'st rest thee to-night. To-morrow get thee gone, else will I put thee forth rudely."

"Unworthy art thou of minstrel's presence."

Turning to Marian, he said:

"I pray thee excuse my departure, fair lady. *Remember!*"

"Remember what?" asked the sheriff quickly.

"*Death before dishonour,*" replied Robin, with significant emphasis, as he strode from the room."

"'Twas an evasion of Robin's; and Marian rightly understood him to mean that she was to be in readiness that night.

In the passage Robin met Madge.

"In a niche to the right side of yon door," said Robin, "I've hidden away a stout cord. Do thou bind it strongly to the window, and at dark let it gently down. Thou wilt hear my song, in the which I will instruct thee and Marian more fully of mine intentions. Adieu!"

"Adieu!" said Madge. "Thy trust of me shall not be betrayed. To-night, when the shadows cast them darkly."

"To-night."

CHAPTER LIX.

HOW ROBIN WAS CAPTURED AND MARIAN ESCAPED.

Away to the dungeon they bore Robin Hood,
They bound him with chains, and swore oaths so rude;
That quickly his life they would take away,
Ere the sun had twice set on another day.

"WELCOME," said the friendly soldier, as Robin descended to the courtyard; "thou hast had a pleasant office, I ween. Did'st see the maiden, and dost not think her wondrous fair?"

"Aye, and pure as fair," replied Robin; "too good is she to mate with yon sheriff."

"Thou art right, there," said the soldier in low tones; "although he be master of mine, yet I must tell thee, that he is too rough in his manner, to woo so fair and gentle a maiden; in good troth he is."

"The exterior mattereth not always in such affairs," remarked Robin; "'tis the heart yon maiden looks to. I opine that not even a king would win her love, if his heart was as foul as your sheriff's."

"Hard words thou speakest, good minstrel," said the soldier good-humouredly; "but thou must be weary and athirst, I have saved a stoup of rare good wine and other dainties. Prithee, come this way."

Robin could not refuse such a friendly invitation, and accordingly repaired to the banquetting hall.

"Room, there! room, comrades, for the minstrel!" shouted Robin's friend to his comrades; "and do some of ye help him to food, while I bring him fitting drink for one of so rare a calling."

Thus admonished, the soldiers vied with each other in doing Robin some favour or another.

He supped right royally, and thanked his friend warmly for his care of him.

"Prithee, name it not," the soldier replied; "thou art our care while thou stayest. I wot thou wilt not depart yet awhile?"

"To-morrow I go; 'tis the sheriff's wish," answered Robin.

"Now a murrain seize all foul tempers, say I," petulantly exclaimed the soldier. "He need not have enjoined thy departure so shortly. We will petition for thy stay."

"Fash not thyself thereanent," said Robin, "'twould be useless."

"Hearest thou, the ill tidings?" exclaimed Robin's friend, addressing his comrades.

"Aye," grumbled one; "'tis always so. Scant pleasure have we, and but as scant wage."

"I will e'en do my utmost to make my short stay welcome to thee," said Robin, seizing his harp and running his fingers over its strings.

The rude soldiers were all attention, as the supposed minstrel carolled the following humorous ditty:

" In Nottingham town of high renown,
    There dwelt a man, sing hey derry down:
 Of stature so high, that it reached well nigh
    Twelve yards or more, right up in the sky.

" This monstrous man was of comely mien,
    His like before never was seen;
 His voice was like a thunder-clap,
    And when he spoke it caused some mishap.

" His very laugh was just like a roar,
    The like of which ne'er was heard before;
 Each step he took was ten yards long,
    He could lift any weight, he was so strong.

" He ate each day fifty loaves of bread,
    When he couldn't get wine he drank beer
      instead;
 Twenty sheep, five bulls (now it was too bad)
    He gobbled each day, till no more could be had.

" The people all began to ask him to go,
    But this monstrous man he only said, 'No;'
 And as day by day he only ate more,
    Soon there began a famine right sore.

"Said the people, 'we'll go and petition the King,'
  'Take my advice,' said a tailor, 'do no such
    thing ;
  I'll make him go, or I'll forfeit my life,
  'How?' askest thou, why I'll get him a wife.

" 'I know of a' wench, a terrible scold,
  She'll just suit, for she's neither too young nor
    too old ;
  She'll have the last word, her tongue's never still,
  It's noise just resembles the clack of a mill.'

" So this monstrous man who away wouldn't go,
  He married the wench, whose stature was low :
  But the noise of her temper made him so mad,
  That he left her in haste, and the people were
    glad.

" The tailor who lived in Nottingham town,
  Was thereafter held in high renown.
  To this day, if a man is the cause of much strife,
  He is quickly wedded to a scolding wife."

"A merrier ditty ne'er was trolled. Here, minstrel, pledge us in wine; thou art of the right sort."

"Thanks, good fellow," said Robin, taking the proffered tankard. "I would propose a toast for thine honouring."

"Call him a churl who refuseth," said Robin's friend. "Comrades, the toast."

Raising his goblet on high, Robin said—
"*Here's safety to her I love !*"
The toast was befittingly honoured.

"May she never prove a scolding wife !" exclaimed one.

Robin joined heartily in the laughter which followed this sally, and in laugh and song, jest and gibe, the time passed merrily enough, although the shades of night cast their dark shadows o'er the earth, and the castle began to give signs of its inmates having for the greater part retired to rest.

Drawing his mantle closely about him, Robin walked with cautious tread across the courtyard to a spot just under Marian's window.

"My song will not attract aught of harm to me or mine undertaking," said Robin half aloud; "I will e'en commence it forthwith; and may Our Lady and all the saints grant me success !"

Striking a few notes on his harp as a prelude, Robin looked up to Marian's window, and beheld a white kerchief fluttering in the wind.

"They are watchful," he said, "and Marian is ready."

In a gentle voice Robin began the following song, every word of which was plainly distinguished by the listeners above :—

"Open thy window, my love, my love,
  To waft me love-sighs soft as cooing of dove ;
  To fall on my soul as doth dews of night,
  To bring to my mind visions so fair and bright.

"Under thy casemate, sweet love, I stand ;
  Let down the cord with gentle hand.
  Wake not the slumbers of night so drear,
  For there is danger abroad I greatly fear."

Robin was so engrossed with the singing of his song that he saw not half a dozen figures crouched near, as if in readiness to spring on him.

"Mine the proud task of freeing thee, love,
  Soon will thy Robin be with thee above ;
  And ere the morn's dawn is awake thou shalt be
  Far away in the forest, free on the lea."

"Seize him ! 'tis Robin Hood !" said the sheriff's voice.

"Ah ! betrayed !" exclaimed Robin. "I shall sell my life dearly."

Plucking his dagger from its sheath he aimed a blow at the sheriff's throat, and, but for the stout intervention of his gorget, it would have proved fatal.

"Bear him to the dungeon," said the sheriff with weak voice; for Robin's blow had not been altogether harmless.

Vainly did Robin struggle.

He was beset from behind, thrown to the ground, and borne off, securely bound, to the dungeon.

"Heard'st thou not that ?" said Madge, wringing her hands; " 'tis the sheriff's voice, and Robin is undone."

"Peace, wench !" said Marian, reprovingly, "else will they hear thy lamentations. 'Tis time for action, not unavailing sorrow."

"What would'st thou do, lady ?" queried Madge, looking admiringly at Marian's animated countenance.

"In the confusion of strife they will not perceive the rope," said Marian, "I will descend by it."

"Risk not thy precious life," exclaimed Madge, in tones of entreaty. "Bethink thee of the perils thou wilt encounter."

"Listen, wench," Marian commanded; "I will escape, bear the news to Sherwood's outlaws, of their master's state, and quickly get him help thereby. Thou wilt aid me ?"

"To the venturing of my life," promptly replied Madge, who, seeing that Marian was determined, sought no longer to persuade her from her purpose.

"Cans't thou conduct me in safety outside these walls, if I once stand in yon courtyard ?" asked Marian.

"That can I, lady," answered Madge; "but if my counsel sound not in thine ears as presumptuous, I would advise thee——"

"What would'st thou advise, wench ?" said Marian with an impatient gesture.

"To don other attire; I have here that which will aid thy escape bravely," replied Madge, producing from a hiding place a suit of man's clothing.

" 'Tis a good thought," exclaimed Marian, "I will e'en shift at once. Do thou guard the door."

The change was quickly made, and Marian stood forth dressed in man's attire.

"What think'st thou of my appearance ?" asked Marian, with a smile.

"Thou wilt pass muster in this light," answered Madge. "What would'st thou next, lady ?"

"I will descend and wait for thee under cover of the wall. Thou wilt come quickly ?"

"That will I, lady," readily replied Madge; "but have a care, I beseech thee, how thou goest."

"Tut, tut, good Madge," replied Marian, chidingly, "be not fearful. I warrant ye that my descent will be safely achieved."

"Our Lady grant it," said Madge, fervently.

Clutching the rope with firm grasp, Marian forced her way through the rather narrow aperture.

"Fear not, Madge, girl," said Marian, before she launched herself forth, "our Lady will forfend me from harm."

The brave girl cast a half shuddering glance into the dark depths underlying her, then with undaunted resolution and settled purpose, commenced her perilous descent.

Madge stood trembling and prayerfully waiting for some token of Marian's safety.

It came at last.

The rope was violently shaken, and one word, "safe!" reached her expectant ears.

"Now, Our Lady be thanked," she exclaimed fervidly, "but I must be cautious lest yon sentinel suspect aught."

Marian was about to leave when she suddenly bethought her of the rope.

"I must not leave thee here," she exclaimed, apostrophising it, "else wilt thou betray the manner of her escape."

Hastily hauling it up, she unfastened, and carefully coiled it round her body, saying:—

"It may be that thou wilt again prove useful."

On gaining the door, Madge, with intent to deceive the sentinel, exclaimed in loud tones:—

"Good-night, fair mistress; may thy slumbers be light, and thy dreams pleasant."

"Greet thee, Madge," said the sentinel to whom she was well known, "thou art late to-night. Late vigils will steal the bloom from thy cheek."

"Gramercy," she saucily replied, "my condition would seem to concern thee greatly; but thou art kindly intentioned, and I thank thee."

"Just one kiss, sweet Madge," said the sentinel, attempting to steal one.

"Oat upon thee, thou saucy knave!" she exclaimed, as she caught him a box on the ear, managing at the same time to elude his grasp.

Speeding down the passages and staircases she soon stood by Marian's side, who was anxiously awaiting her coming.

"Our Lady be thanked! thou art come," said Marian, fervently embracing Madge.

"I am rejoiced beyond measure at thy safety, lady," exclaimed Madge reciprocatingly.

"Did aught detain thee?" asked Marian, in allusion to her delay in joining her.

"A matter of great import, lady," replied Madge; "I have here with me the rope."

"'Twas well conceived," observed Marian. "'Twould have betrayed thee, brave wench, had it remained."

"And hindered my being of service to Robin Hood when thou art in safety," rejoined Madge; "but follow me softly," and Madge held her hand up warningly.

Before they had proceeded far, Madge laid her hand on her companion's arm, saying, in softest whisper:

"Hush! advance not one step further at thy peril?"

The tread of a sentinel was plainly audible quite near at hand.

"While I hold him in converse," said Madge whisperingly, "do thou steal cautiously along yon wall, and wait for my coming. Bide thy time well 'ere thou essayest to move."

Stepping boldly forward, Madge approached the sentinel.

"Stand! the sign!" he exclaimed.

"What! Will, knowest thou me not?" she asked in bantering tones; "beshrew me, lad, but thou hast a short memory of thine own, I wot."

"Is it thou, Madge?" he exclaimed delight-edly; "now am I favoured indeed. Thou hast come to company my vigils."

"Hark at him!" replied Madge coquettishly; "'twould seem that I had naught else to do but attend thee. What next?"

"Why, a kiss to be sure," was the saucy reply, as he stole his hand around her waist and pressed his lips to hers more than once.

Seizing the opportunity, Marian glided quickly by Madge and her companion, and ran swiftly along the wall.

"Did'st thou see aught?" asked the sentinel; "methought something brushed by but a moment since."

"Thou dreamest, Will," replied Madge banteringly; "'twas naught but thine own shadow."

"I could have sworn that it was more than a shadow," he replied; "but it recks not, sweet Madge, so long as thou art by."

"Prithee acquaint me where thou hast gained thy flowery speech from," said Madge laughing.

"Love is a ready teacher," was the prompt reply.

"And thou an apt learner," said Madge; "but I must e'en say good night, Will, else will my father's anger attend mine absence."

"Fash not thyself thereanent," Will replied, "thou would'st not leave me lonely and——"

"Hark! 'tis my father's voice!" said Madge, rudely interrupting his gallant speech, and, darting away from him, with a merry laugh.

"Art thou there, lady?" asked Madge, in a suppressed whisper.

"E'en so, Madge; is all safe?"

"Quite. 'Twill go hard with me now but I quickly place thee in safety; but hush! footsteps approach."

Madge clutched Marian's arm, and drew her back into the shadow of the wall.

"Hast thou any commands respecting Robin Hood, asked a voice; "wilt thou not speedily despatch him."

"Not so," replied the sheriff; "I have a purpose in view; but further, I will not say. My wound gets painful beyond endurance."

The sheriff and his companion brushed so closely by Marian and her companion, that their clothes all but touched.

"Dost not thine heart flutter?" asked Madge of her companion; "mine goes pit-a-pat, and will not cease its busy motion."

"I must confess to feeling anxious," replied Marian; "but I was withal prepared."

"After what fashion," queried Madge.

"It boots not to speak of it now," said Marian; "but I would have thee know that I carry a dagger, and am a Saxon maiden."

"Thou art brave as fair," observed Madge admiringly; "'twas a narrow escape though, was it not?"

"For the sheriff I grant you," replied Marian drily; "but lead on, wench, else will the morn find us still in Nottingham Castle."

"Have no fear, lady, 'ere long thou wilt find the true breeze of the lea fanning thy temple, 'tis but a short step to whither I would lead you."

"'Tis Robin's condition fills me with impatience to be gone," observed Marian; "mine own safety weighs not with me so heavily as does his."

"Thou wilt trust me, lady, to encompass Robin's safety, wilt not?" asked Madge.

"No trustier friend have I found than thou, good Madge," replied Marian gratefully; "it may be that the time will come when I shall fittingly reward thee."

"Nay, lady," answered Madge; "cruel of heart would I be and well deserving of contempt and odium were I to refuse aid to one so good and gentle as thou in so sore strait as thine."

They proceeded silently onward for a time, treading courts and passages with cautious steps.

"It behoves us to observe caution hither about," said Madge in whispered tones; "we approach the postern."

"Will it be difficult of exit?" asked Marian.

"'Twill require more than ordinary prudence," replied Madge.

"I will go forward to the sentinel while thou tarriest here. When thou seest the postern gate open steal through with caution."

"It may be that I have not further speech with thee to-night," said Marian, seizing her companion's hand; "thou wilt henceforth be to Marian as a sister."

Their lips met in a fond embrace, then hands clasped warmly, and Madge went forward full of determination and hope to effect Marian's escape at all hazards.

"Is that you Clement," she asked in soft accents and at a venture, as she fancied that the sentinel's form was not unknown to her.

"'Tis so. Why, Madge girl, thou art about late," observed the sentinel; "art thou ailing?"

"Thou hast rightly guessed, Clement," she answered.

"The heat is most oppressive, would that I had yon postern open to breathe the purer air of night."

"It may not be, Madge," he replied; "strict injunctions have I to open it to none save the sheriff my master."

"The restriction referred not to me I wot," said Madge; "come now, Clement, thou wouldst surely not be cruel in this matter."

"Thou hast a winning tongue, Madge," he replied; "and I must e'en gratify thee I ween."

"Thou wilt thereby earn my gratitude," exclaimed Madge; "haste, thee, then, for I long to taste the fresh air so faint am I."

"Thou wilt not name this matter to anyone," he asked.

"Surely not, dost take me for a simpleton quite."

"There now," he said, "as he cautiously threw back the postern gate, be quick."

Madge stood for a few minutes as if enjoying the night breeze that came uninterruptedly from off the open plain fronting her.

"Hast thou heard aught of Lucy latterly?" she asked at last.

"Naught; hast thou?"

"I had speech of her yesterday, no later," replied Madge.

"Said she aught of me?" he asked eagerly.

"Ay, that did she," replied Madge with a low musical laugh.

"Thou but jestest."

"Surely not. A message have I for thee," answered Madge.

"Prithee name it, I am all impatience to list to thy speech."

"There may be eavesdroppers," said Madge, pretending to look cautiously about.

"Draw aside then, good Madge," said the sentinel, "and I will close the postern the meanwhile."

"Nay, Clement, let it remain, 'twill not harm for a short space."

"Bethink thee of my peril, should it be discovered open," he said in terms of remonstrance.

"Fash not thyself thereanent," she answered, "but come thou here while I tell thee of Lucy."

The bait was too strong to be refused.

Leaving the postern open Clement followed Madge, who drew him some distance aside, and engaged him in deep conversation.

Marian with cautious steps passed forward, and with lightning speed dashed through the open postern unobserved, and was once more free.

She hied not to her uncle's cottage, which stood a short distance away, but with rapid steps took her way to Sherwood.

She arrived there about daybreak, and electrified the outlaws by her presence.

"Robin Hood, what of him?" asked Little John, eagerly.

"He lieth in the sheriff's dungeon," answered Marian sadly. "He was encompassing my escape when the sheriff discovered and arrested him."

"He will not remain prisoner long," remarked Little John, with a determined look upon his manly countenance.

"Thou wilt take steps forthwith, John?" queried Friar Tuck.

Little John nodded.

A few minutes later a council was being held.

Its issues will be for another chapter to disclose.

CHAPTER LX.

HOW ROBIN WAS FREED BY MADGE STUKELY.

"Hist," said Madge, peeping in at the door,
And saw that the sentinel lay still on the floor;
"Fear not, brave Robin, thou shalt soon be free;
And from this vile dungeon go quickly with me."

ROBIN was borne to the lowest dungeon in the castle, the sheriff accompanying him despite his wounded state.

"Thou wilt soon cease to trouble me," the latter maliciously; observed. "My time for vengeance has fully come at last."

"I fear not death," said Robin, contemptuously, "do thy worst, and do it quickly."

"Nay," answered the sheriff, "it pleaseth not my humour to despatch thee quickly; thou shalt tarry my pleasure and time: besides Marian would greet too much for thy loss."

The sheriff laughed mockingly.

Robin ground his teeth with rage, but remained silent.

"Iron him heavily," said the sheriff, "and let a sentinel be stationed in here, close beside him. Let others keep guard near at hand to answer with their lives for his safe keeping."

The officer bowed acquiescently.

"And harkee, let him have bread and water that his proud stomach may be brought low, and furthermore let an hourly report of his safety be made to me in person."

"It shall be as thou commandest," was the reply.

"Adieu, proud outlaw," said the sheriff, "thou hast thrust thine head into the wolf's den to some purpose. I will tell Marian of thy condition."

"Thou shalt yet live to repent these insults," cried Robin; "think'st thou that my death will serve thee aught, while there are others sworn to avenge my fall and thy traitorous conduct?"

"Be it mine to incur all the displeasure that thou boastest of," replied the sheriff; "it will reck not to thee when thou art gone what befalleth me."

"A due reckoning will be exacted from thee," said Robin; "more speech I will not waste on thee."

In obedience to the sheriff's commands, Robin was heavily ironed, and a sentinel placed beside him.

"I would that Marian was safe," muttered Robin, "then welcome death even."

He sank on his rude couch in troubled sleep, and awoke not till the morn was well in form.

Some coarse bread and a jar of water were placed near for his refection; but he touched neither, so intent was he in thought upon Marian's condition.

The dungeon door swung open, and the sheriff entered with furious looks.

"Thou hast accomplices within these walls," he said with hoarse utterance; "disclose their names to me instantly."

"Thou art mistaken in this matter," replied Robin. "None have I but myself, as God is my judge. But why askest thou this question?"

"Marian," said the sheriff, and then checked himself.

"What of her?" asked Robin eagerly.

"She has escaped," said the sheriff. "I had determined to spare thy life for her sake, under certain conditions; but now is it forfeit unless she be returned to me."

"Thinkest thou I would purchase life, or a thousand lives, upon such conditions?" said Robin, indignantly. "Do thy worst now that Marian is in safety."

"Thou shalt hang high ere to-morrow's sun gilds the morning horizon. And mark me, thou once disposed of, Marian shall be mine in spite of fate."

Robin laughed derisively, but said naught.

The sheriff strode from the dungeon, and gave the sentinels outside strict orders to guard well their prisoner.

The day passed wearily for Robin, the only break in the monotony being when the sentinels relieved guard.

The hour of midnight had arrived; all was silent as the grave, except for the sentinels' measured tread, when there arose a loud cry of fear from the guard outside.

The dungeon door was thrown violently back, and there appeared in sight the terrific form of the wood demon.

The sentinel in Robin's immediate vicinity fell prostrate to the earth, and lay as if bereft of life.

"I have come to befriend thee, bold outlaw," said the demon; "thou knowest my con-

ditions. Speak but the word, and thou shalt be instantly safe in Sherwood forest."

Robin stood defiantly upright, confronting his demon visitor, and replied—

"Avaunt, thou spirit of evil. I will have naught to do with thine unholy offers of aid."

"Bethink thee what I offer; safety not only now, but continuously till the hour of death; and then——"

The demon paused.

"And then?" said Robin interrogatively.

"*Thou shalt be mine for ever.*"

"I defy thee and thy power," said Robin, raising his manacled hands, and signing the sign of the cross on his forehead.

"I shall not cease to importune thee," replied the demon, as he vanished in a distant corner of the dungeon, surrounded by a halo of light.

At this juncture, Robin's attention was aroused by a voice calling his name near at hand.

Looking round, there stood Madge Stukely, with finger on lip, and her left arm upraised warningly.

"Thou here, Madge!" exclaimed Robin with astonishment.

"Hist! speak low," said Madge, cautiously treading by the insensible form of the sentinel.

"Why hast thou come?" Robin asked.

"To release thee. I flitted about here since dark until now, and finding the sentinels asleep, gained the dungeon door."

"'Tis useless unless thou hast the key of these," said Robin, holding up the manacles on his hands.

"I bethought me of that," said Madge with sprightliness, "and here it is."

"Bless thee, girl," exclaimed Robin, quite overcome.

"Name it not. Thou know'st of Marian's safety?" Madge queried, as she unlocked Robin's irons.

"I had it from the sheriff's own mouth," replied Robin; "and so angered was he, that he swore to hang me the morrow."

"And meant it too," replied Madge. "A gallows is in course of erection even now, but thou shalt never grace it, I promise thee."

"Thanks, brave girl; twice hast thou befriended me, and furthermore saved her who to me is dearer than myself."

"Thou art now free," said Madge, as the last manacle dropped from Robin's person.

Dropping on his knee, Robin seized her hand and pressed it reverently to his lips as an expression of his gratitude.

In fact, his heart was too full for speech.

"Thou wilt excuse my haste," said Madge, "but time presses, and the guard will be here anon. Come this way."

"Lead on," replied Robin, "I fully commit myself to thy guidance."

With careful steps they took their way along the dark passage, and had barely reached a place of comparative safety, when the measured tread of the relief sounded near.

Placing her hand on his arm, Madge motioned Robin back into a convenient recess, and with bated breath waited for the soldiers to pass.

"Quick!" said Madge, when the soldiers had gone by, "all will be discovered shortly, and thy pursuit commenced."

"They shall not take me alive," exclaimed

Robin, who had taken the precaution to arm himself with the sentinel's sword.

"Every outlet will be guarded," said Madge, unmindful of Robin's declaration. "There is no escape herefrom for thee this night."

"Can I not descend by means of a rope from some unguarded spot?" asked Robin.

"Thou wilt find none such," replied Madge. "I have it. Thou must tarry in my room until fitting opportunity cometh for thy departure."

"Nay," answered Robin; "my presence will endanger thee."

"Name it not," said Madge, "and hark! hearest thou not that thine enemies even now seek thee?"

The noise of many footsteps coming in their direction was plainly heard by them.

Taking Robin's hand, Madge hurriedly said:

"Use thine utmost speed, else will they arrive to intercept our escape."

With fleet steps they rushed down a darksome passage, with pursuing footsteps sounding in their rear.

"This way," said Madge, as she ascended a flight of steps which, but for her, Robin would have passed.

On reaching the top, she motioned to him to halt, saying:

"Listen whether they go past or not."

Nearer and nearer came the footsteps, and then they passed by the staircase.

"Our Lady be thanked," said Madge, drawing a long breath, "they pursue us no longer."

"Thou hast delivered me from them," said Robin, giving her hand a grateful squeeze.

"I would that thou wert safe outside," said Madge, "then would I be glad indeed."

"I have no fear," said Robin. "Let us once baffle their scent, and all will be well."

"Be assured we shall do so," replied Madge. "I wot they will hardly seek thee where thou art going."

"My safety—nay, my life itself—I willingly entrust to thy care," said Robin. "Do thou lead on, brave girl."

"Thou must be silent as the grave," observed Madge as she led the way onwards, "else will my father surely discover thy presence, and all will be lost."

"Trust me," Robin replied; "I will be prudent, and not imperil thee, in any wise."

"'Twas not of that, I had concern," she answered; "but we must now cease our speech, to the utterance of a single sentence even. Thine hiding-place is at hand."

With soft tread she approached a door, and noiselessly lifting the latch entered, followed by Robin Hood.

She took his hand and led him across to a small chamber, which they entered together.

Motioning him to be seated, she listened:

"Is it thou, stirring, Madge?" asked a voice in gruff tones.

"Yes, father," she answered; "I ail somewhat, and cannot rest."

"Get thee to thy couch, girl," her father replied; "'tis not fitting that thou should'st be astir at such a time."

She answered not, and soon the loud snoring of her parent showed that his slumbers had returned.

Motioning to Robin to throw himself on the bed and sleep, she sat herself down near the door to watch.

When the first streak of dawn betokened the approach of morning, she gently roused him, and setting such fare before him as the house afforded, bade him eat.

"Thou must not mind hiding," she observed in whispered tones; "none entereth here usually, but I cannot vouch for freedom from intrusion to-day."

"I will do thy bidding in everything," answered Robin; "fear not to command me in aught thou may'st deem desirable."

"Thanks," she replied; "I will remain near thee all day, by feigning illness. At night, I will lead thee out by a secure way."

"Where wilt thou that I should hide?" asked Robin, looking around the apartment.

"Under the couch," answered Madge with a laugh; "'tis a sorry place for such as thou, I trow, but it will serve thy turn for the present, as well as if it had been better."

"I would e'en creep into a mousehole at thy bidding," Robin gallantly replied, at the same time kneeling down and creeping under the bed.

"Thou cans't spread this under thee," said Madge, handing him a stout rug; "'twill be better than the hard stones to thy ribs."

"Thanks, good Madge," said Robin; "now will I fare me, right well."

"Thou wilt be careful not to stir should any enter to search the room even?" said Madge.

"Rest assured of that," answered Robin; "I will trust to thee entirely."

"Hush!" said Madge warningly; "my father is astir, and is ever watchful of the slightest strange sound."

"Greet thee kindly, father," she said, going out to meet him; "how find'st thou thyself this fair morning?"

"Passing well, child," he answered. "Art thou better?"

"Nay, I am sorry to acquaint thee, that I am not," she replied; "my poor head is like to split with pain."

"Thou must stay within to-day then, Madge," he said concernedly, for he loved her well; "and I will seek an herb that will mend thy condition without fail."

Hardly had he finished speaking, when a loud knocking came to the door.

"Bless me!" cried Madge with well-feigned alarm in her voice and manner. "What means that?"

"Open the door, girl," cried her father. "'Tis some messenger from the sheriff, I wot."

With trembling hands she did as she was bid, and there entered a soldier.

"Give thee, greeting," said old Stukely; "but what meaneth this early visit?"

To which the soldier replied:

"'Tis the sheriff's commands that thou and all others do keep watch to discover whether any strange person loitereth about. Robin Hood has escaped his prison, and is now hidden somewhere in the castle."

"Thou hast declared a strange matter," said Stukely.

"'Tis true, nevertheless. And the sheriff furthermore adds, that a hundred crowns will be his who apprehendeth or killeth the outlaw."

ROBIN HOOD,
AND THE OUTLAWS OF SHERWOOD FOREST.

"ROBIN LEANED ON HIS LEFT ELBOW, WITH RIGHT HAND UPRAISED."

"I would that I had opportunity of earning it," Madge observed; "I would gladly give up Robin Hood."

"Or kill him, if needs be," rejoined her father.

"Nay, I would not deprive him of life," said Madge; "but ah me, 'twill never fall to my lot to earn so much money."

No. 21.

"Be vigilant, and thou may'st," said the messenger, as he departed.

"'Tis passing strange," observed her father, "first goes that chit Marian, whom the sheriff goeth crazy about, and no one knoweth the manner of her going."

"The sheriff was angered beyond measure at

my not preventing it," said Madge, interrupting him.

"'Twas well thou did'st not suffer aught else beside his anger," observed her father.

"Marry come up, father, how thou pratest. There was a sentinel at the door, and yet Marian escaped, how could the sheriff hold me blameful in the matter then?"

"It mattereth not now," said her father, "but as I was just observing until thou did'st interrupt me as is thy wont, thou sauce-box."

"Nay, father," cried Madge, "thou knowest I am dutiful to thee beyond compare," and she threw her arms round his neck and fondly kissed him.

"Well, well, I will not gainsay thee, Madge, girl, but as I was saying, first goes Marian, then this Robin Hood. Surely the Evil One hath holpen them."

"'Twould so appear," Madge answered; "'tis a matter though I mean not to trouble myself about."

"Thou wilt keep indoors, child," said her father, "while I go and gather herbs to brew thee fitting decoction for thy ailment."

"Thou wilt find me here when thou returnest," answered Madge.

"Thou may'st expect my return shortly," he replied, "meanwhile I would that thou would'st make me a nice posset as is thy wont."

"Trust me, father, thou shalt have it," answered Madge, "a safe journey to thee."

Going to her chamber she said to Robin:

"Heard'st thou the sheriff's message?"

"Full well; what think'st thou of it."

"It betokeneth this much—the sheriff is determined to encompass thy capture at all hazards."

"It is as I opine, but disappointment awaiteth him, I ween."

Several dull, heavy thumps on the door sounded through the house.

"Hark to that," said Madge, "keep close else wilt thou be undone."

"Why, Madge girl," said one of the new comers, "what a time thou hast kept us at the door."

"Thou deserved'st to be longer kept," she replied, thy noise hast given me a splitting headache."

"We have come to search thine house by the sheriff's order."

"Father is out," she answered, "thou may'st come when he returns."

"Nay but we must to our search even now," he exclaimed, rudely pushing by her, "do thou stand aside wench."

"Whom seekest thou," she asked, "that thou comest on this wise."

"One Robin Hood—heard'st thou not of the matter?"

"Surely not," she replied, "'twas said he lay a prisoner securely bound."

"He has escaped of a surety, and lies hidden somewhere. Peradventure he hath sought cover hitherabouts."

"'Tis a likely story, surely," said Madge, "thou hast trumped it up for thine own purposes, and to insult a weak defenceless maiden during her sire's absence."

"It mattereth little what thou opinest. 'Tis the sheriff's mandate we fulfil."

"Thou shalt hear more of this anon," said Madge, in pretended anger.

"What room is this?" asked the leader, unheedful of her inuendoes and objections, "it seems of a likely kind for concealment."

"'Tis my bedchamber, sirrah; enter it at thy peril," said Madge, stationing herself in the doorway.

"Stand aside, else will I have to use unseemly violence," was the response to her challenge.

He was on the point of pushing her aside when she seized a pitcher of water which stood near, and dashed its contents full in his face.

This circumstance cooled his ardour, and gave rise to the merriment of his companions at his discomfiture.

"Thou art well served," said one laughing; "it needed not that thou should'st pursue thy search beyond the bounds of modesty."

"I have another in waiting," said Madge menacingly. "Let him who would try my mettle; a maiden's chamber is not fit place for such as thou."

Her determination and vigorous resistance carried the point, and after searching everywhere else save in her chamber, the soldiers retired.

"Thou art safe," she said to Robin; "'twill be some time ere they essay to force entrance here again."

Her laughter resounded through the place, so tickled was she at the remembrance of the sorry spectacle her victim presented drenched with water.

"Thou wilt incur danger thereby?" said Robin! "but thou did'st but serve the fellow right."

"Have no care thereanent," she replied with a hearty peal of laughter; "'twill prove a wholesome caution to the jackanapes in future. Beshrew me, but he looked like a drowned rat."

Madge was as demure as a nun when her father entered, which he did shortly after the scene just narrated.

He applauded her conduct on hearing of the indignity which had been attempted to be put upon her, qualifying his expression of resentment, by saying——

"They are plaguy curious throughout the castle. Thou would'st have thought that I, Zac Stukely, was well known, but beshrew me if they did not stop me at the gate to question and examine me as to my own identity."

"Have they discovered aught?" asked Madge with perfect innocence of manner.

"Naught, save that Robin Hood's presence is nowhere to be found, which thing is surpassing strange, and beyond ordinary comprehension."

"It concerns not us," said Madge: "so 'tis useless to further comment thereon. Thy posset is ready and will spoil, an' thou dost not quickly partake thereof."

Narrowly did Madge watch each new comer during the whole of that eventful day, to see whether aught of suspicion rested upon her or her father of harbouring Robin.

When the darkness of night had fairly set in she summoned Robin forth from his hiding place, and placing refreshments before him bade him eat.

After a hasty meal and a cup of sack, Robin declared himself quite ready to attend her.

"There is a way leading from the castle underground to the lea, by which I mean thee to go," observed Madge.

"'Tis a prudent contrivance," answered Robin; "I have heard of this passage before."

"'Twould be mere rashness to attempt any other outlet," said Madge; "as thou hast heard it declared every place is well guarded."

"May it not be so with the outlet thou hast named," queried Robin.

"Nay, for I hold the key, other than which existeth not," answered Madge; "hence do I know that neither let nor hindrance will there be to our proceeding."

"Thou hast earned my gratitude o'er and o'er," said Robin; "fitting speech have I not to express it."

"Thou shalt talk of thanks when once fairly outside," replied Madge with a bright smile; "till then remain silent thereanent I pray thee."

Having caused Robin to disguise himself in a suit of her father's clothes, and arranged everything necessary for the success of their enterprise, Madge at last bade Robin follow her with caution.

They descended the staircase they had traversed the preceding night, when Madge in a low whisper bade Robin remain while she reconnoitred.

She returned with the intelligence that a sentinel was placed in a spot which they must needs pass to gain their goal.

"What dost thou advise?" asked Robin.

"That we go on," said Madge; "but first remove thy shoes, as will I, lest the noise attract attention."

"A good thought," answered Robin, as he displaced his shoes from off his feet.

"Come now," said Madge; "and above all things keep near me."

"Have no fear," answered Robin; "but stay, suppose the sentinel observeth us, what then."

"Thou hast a dagger," said Madge with pointed significance.

"True; onwards, then, brave girl."

With cautious tread they went forward, and ere long arrived in the sentinel's vicinity.

"Take my hand," whispered Madge, "and edge close into the wall, and let thy breath not exceed the faintest whisper."

Following the course of the wall, they glided by the sentinel in safety some few paces, when one of Madge's shoes fell with a loud thud on the ground.

"Stand! who goes there?" the sentinel challenged.

The fugitives remained motionless as statues.

"'Tis but some animal that hath burrowed hereabout," said the sentinel, in self-explanation of the noise; "I will listen further."

With noiseless motion, Madge stooped and lifted the shoe, then drawing Robin after her, they glided onward without further mishap.

"Our Lady be thanked! we are safe!" said Madge; "my folly was nigh causing our ruin."

"Name it not," said Robin; "'twas a mischance only, and thou art blameless."

"'Tis well 'twas no worse," she replied; "but put down thine hand and feel for an iron ring."

"I have found it," said Robin, after a short search.

"A little to the right thereof thou wilt find a keyhole, to which apply this key."

Robin took the key and did as he was bid.

"Now pull with all thy might at the ring," said Madge.

Putting forth all his strength, Robin gave a vigorous pull, and the door came open.

"There is a flight of steps to go down," observed Madge; "so, with thy permission I will first descend."

"Do thy pleasure," answered Robin, stepping aside to let her pass.

"Now do thou come," said Madge; "my hand will guide thee."

"Wilt thou not lock the door? asked Robin, when he had descended a few steps.

"Pull it down, that will suffice," said Madge; "it is so contrived that it's own weight secures it."

"Mind thy footing," observed Madge, as they started onward; "'Tis not easy walking hitherabout."

"I can find that it is not," said Robin; as he stumbled over some obstruction.

"'Twill be better presently," said Madge; "if thou wilt follow in my footsteps thou wilt not stumble, for every foot of the road is known to me."

"'Tis not much used, I ween," remarked Robin.

"But rarely," answered Madge; "else would it be better kept."

"Did'st thou hear aught," asked Robin, whose well-trained hearing detected a noise.

"Naught," answered Madge; "did'st thou?"

"That did I; hark to it again!" said Robin, as the sound of voices struck upon their hearing.

"I plainly heard it that time," replied Madge; "'tis strange that others than us should be here. But draw aside awhile."

"That voice is known to me," said Robin; "listen for a moment."

"Body-o'-me!" said a grumbling voice; "'tis a strange spot; had I but known it, my footsteps had not hither strayed."

"St. Hubert! but a large thorn has wounded my foot," said some one in reply; "a malison seize upon thee, thou pecksy thing."

"They are friends," said Robin to Madge; "fear not, they are well known to me."

Raising his voice, Robin said:

"What ho, John, and thou, jolly friar!"

"Hearest thou not that?" said Little John, in affrighted tones, which raised Robin's mirth beyond measure.

"Ay, that did I, little man," replied the friar; "'twas just like his voice."

"Be assured on't, 'tis his wraith," observed Little John; "and hearest thou not how it laughs?"

"Dead men laugh not," said Robin; "'tis myself, thy friend, alive and well."

With loud exclamations of delight, the pair rushed forward, and John stumbling, the friar rolled over him in the dark.

"St. Hubert!" said the friar rising, "'twas badly managed, John; I have got of scratches and bruises not a few."

"And thy weight has well nigh bereft me of life," retorted John.

"Never mind," said Robin, who had come up to them in the meantime, "all will soon be right."

"All is right now that thou art here," remarked the friar, stretching forth his hand in the dark to seize Robin's; but took Madge's instead.

"Verily thou hast greatly fallen away, friend Robin," observed the friar. "Thine hand is not half the size it was when thou left us a few days syne."

A burst of laughter from Madge greeted the friar's speech.

"Hast thou any one with thee?" he asked in amazement.

"That I have," said Robin; "one to whom Marian and I owe our lives. But tell me, is Marian at Sherwood?"

"She is, and in good condition," replied Little John.

"I am exceedingly rejoiced thereat," exclaimed Robin, in animated tone. "But we will hie forward; 'tis not fitting place to hold much converse."

"Verily tis not," replied the Friar. "Let thou and John go forward, I will sustain the damsel."

"How know'st thou her sex?" asked Robin with a laugh.

"'Tis easy of discernment," replied the friar. "Thou wilt allow me, fair maiden, to help thee."

"Willingly," replied Madge, with difficulty smothering her laughter.

"Is that thou, friar?" asked Robin, as a dull heavy sound as of a falling body met his ear.

"Aye, that it is," said he, with a groan. "'Twas well I did not bring the maiden with me in my heavy stumble."

"Art hurt?" asked Madge in alarm.

"Nay, have no care thereanent," replied the friar. "My carcass is too hardy to be harmed by such like mishaps."

"Thou wilt let me lead thee?" asked Madge, in winning accents.

"That will I, maiden," said the friar, giving her his fat hand, which she grasped, and then safely piloted him onward.

They emerged into the broad daylight at last, but were so dazed by the sudden transition from darkness to light as to be unable to see aught for a time.

"This is Madge Stukely," said Robin, as he gallantly doffed his bonnet; "twice has she served me, to the saving of my life even."

"She is well known to all of us by report," said Little John, looking at her admiringly. "Body-o'-me! but thou art a brave and comely lass."

"Thou shalt ever be gratefully remembered," said the friar, "and thy name will dwell in the hearts of the merry men of Sherwood."

"Thou overwhelmest me with praises," said Madge, deeply blushing, "the harder to bear because they are undeserved."

"Say not undeserved," replied Robin; "thou shalt have room always in my heart as a sister."

"I am content," answered Madge; "but thou wilt not delay thy going, else wilt thou imperil thy safety."

"Thou shalt have fitting token of my regard," remarked Robin, taking her hand in his, "not in payment of what thou hast done, for naught in this world could do that, but as a souvenir of the noble deeds thou hast wrought for me and Marian."

"Prithee do not think aught of such a kind," replied Madge; "but do thou, brave Robin, hie thee home with thy friends; 'tis but courting danger to longer remain where thou art far from safe."

"The sheriff suspecteth thee not, Madge?" queried Robin.

"Not to my knowledge," she replied: "but an' he did 'twould little matter, for did he but wag so much as his little finger against me with harmful intent, his soldiers would slay him outright."

"'Tis pleasant to hear thee speak so confidently," said Robin; "but I will not distress thee by remaining longer. Adieu, sweet Madge, and may Our Lady bless thee!"

Robin imprinted a kiss on her chaste lips.

Little John looked as if he would like to follow Robin's example, so charming did Madge appear in his sight.

With the freedom of one of his cloth, the friar sidled up to her, saying—

"Accept my benison, daughter, and with it a kiss of peace."

The friar smacked his lips after it, as he would after having partaken of good wine.

"Peradventure thou wilt not refuse a brotherly salutation," said Little John, with a mixture of bashfulness in his tones.

Madge held her cheek to him, but, pretending to stumble, he managed to reach her lips, thereby causing Robin and the friar much merriment, in which Madge and he joined heartily.

"Thou wilt bear my greeting to Marian," said Madge to Robin.

"Assuredly. Adieu! again, sweet maid; in Robin thou wilt always find a devoted friend and brother."

Madge tripped lightly away, and Robin and his companions stayed to gaze after her till she was well out of sight.

As they walked homewards, Robin said:

"How camest thou both in yon darksome place?"

"When Marian returned with news of thy sad condition," replied Little John, "I called me a council, and 'twas decided that myself and the friar should seek entrance to the castle first by yon way, and that to-night the whole band would follow to thy rescue."

"Thanks, good friends," said Robin, with emotion, and grasping each of them by the hand. "Thou art always foremost to my help."

"'Twas much contested, the foremost place in this matter; was it not, friar?" asked Little John.

"St. Hubert! thou art right. The fellows were all mad to proceed to thy help," answered the friar.

"Brave, noble Saxons!" exclaimed Robin with enthusiasm, "what would Robin not dare for thee, or thee for him?"

A party of the outlaws now appeared in sight, and beholding Robin, rushed forward with expressions of delight and great joy.

They escorted him in triumph to Sherwood.

The meeting between Robin and Marian was of the tenderest kind.

Great was the joy of all at his safe return.

———

CHAPTER LXI.

HOW ROBIN AND HIS MERRY MEN HELD MERRY REVELS, AND HUNTED THE RED-DEER IN SHERWOOD FOREST.

Revel and sport my merry men all,
Attend you my summons, come at my call,
To chase the red-deer with loud halloo,
And of noble stags bring down not a few.

"WE shall keep this evening befittingly," said Robin, joyously, "let a banquet be prepared, and harkee, send my commands to the cellarer to bring forth his choicest wines for our drinking."

"Heard'st thou that, little man?" said the friar in ecstatic tone. "St. Hubert! won't it be prime."

"Thou can'st not say me nay any longer," replied Little John. "I will e'en pledge all good men, and drink confusion to our enemies."

"Let there be merry revels to-morrow," said Robin Hood, "Marian will be queen of them."

"If thou wilt be my king," answered Marian, with archness of manner, "I will e'en consent."

"I cannot refuse thee aught, and that thou well know'st, thou merry gipsy," said Robin with a merry laugh.

"I would that thou would'st appoint a hunt for the following day," said Little John, with a somewhat diffident manner.

"Agreed, John," replied Robin. "There will be a right royal hunt, and a fitting prize for him who brings down the finest stag."

"Thanks, good master," answered Little John, "'twill be acceptable to all. Body-o-me! 'tis a long time since we have hunted in full chorus, we'll make the welkin ring again."

"That will we," rejoined the friar. "I wager thee, John, that I bring down my stag first."

"Agreed," replied Little John with animation, "proclaim the wager aloud that all may know its conditions."

"A spick and span new suit of clothes," replied the friar, "an' thou succeedest I will provide fitting attire, otherwise thou must give to me suitable habiliments."

"'Tis a wager," replied Little John, "as all bear witness."

"What of the prisoners?" asked Robin, quickly.

"They are safely bound, master," said Allan-a-Dale. "Would'st thou question them?"

"I will, anon," Robin replied; "thou wilt give them better fare this evening, than their condition or deserts fitteth them to receive. 'Tis a time for rejoicing, and I would that all sharest in it."

This generous sentiment was loudly acclaimed by the assembled outlaws, who loved their chief dearly, because of his noble traits of character.

"Thou wilt not deal harshly with them, for my sake, Robin?" said Marian, laying her hand affectionately on his arm.

"I will deal leniently with them, an' their case deserve it," replied Robin; "thou well knowest, Marian, that treachery must be punished as an ensample to others."

"I know thou wilt deal justly," said Marian; "'tis not in thy nature to do otherwise, but let justice be tempered with mercy, I pray of thee?"

"Well, well, Marian, dearest, thou art accepted in this matter. If they prove not o'er contumacious in their deportment, it will go well with them, for thy sake, beloved."

"I am content," answered Marian with gentle accents; "now will I rest me better in my slumbers on this account."

"I would that thou would'st summon Good-for-Naught Dick hither," said Robin to Allan-a-Dale. "Peradventure, he would elect to be one of us."

"He is of rare good mettle," remarked the friar.

"As thy pate knoweth to its cost," put in Little John with sly humour.

"Thou had'st better try a bout with him, John," merrily retorted the friar.

"Gramercy!" answered Little John with a pleasant smile; "if he dealeth always such blows as thou gottest, I would e'en decline their acceptance."

"If he is sufficiently recovered," remarked Robin, "we will e'en try his mettle on the morrow, friendly wise."

"I wot thou wilt find him a good archer," said Will Scarlet, "he hath the look of it."

"Greet thee, Good-for-Naught Dick," said Robin, as this personage approached under Allan-a-Dale's care. "Thou art better, I trow."

"Even so, master," replied Dick, "I am of hardy stuff, and require a deal of knocking to keep me long off my feet."

"Ah, ah!" laughed Robin, "thou art of the right sort, surely: hast the king thy master aught other of thy like?"

"I cannot say," replied Dick, with an air of modesty that was laughable to behold; "'twould seem thou hast better men nor me."

"Nay," observed Robin, kindly, "'tis not because thou wert once overcome that thou art to be contemned. 'Tis any man's case to suffer such like mishap at times."

"Thanks for thy courteous speech," replied Dick, "I would that those who call themselves by honester name than thou art called, would treat their fellows as thou do'st, 'twould be vastly more to their credit than ranting at a man because of his fondness for liberty."

"Thy compliment I accept," said Robin, "'tis a manly spirit prompted its utterance, and on such account 'tis pleasant to my ears."

"I am of blunt speech, but truthful withal," observed Dick.

"Art thou wishful to return to thy master's service?" asked Robin, "if so thou art free to depart when it suiteth thy humour."

"I bear the king's service no great love," answered Dick, with a grim smile, "'tis hardly free enough for my liking."

"Would'st thou take service under me preferably?" asked Robin; "be mindful though, that no constraint is put upon thee in this matter."

"If thou wilt accept my poor services," answered Dick; "it is my wish to offer them to thee."

"Accepted thou art outright," said Robin; "thou art duly elected one of my band."

"Thou bearest me no malice I ween," said the friar, stepping forward and offering Dick his hand.

"None," replied Dick, taking the proffered hand and shaking it with warmth; "thou lookest not of a sort that one need take umbrage at."

"Thou art a rare good player at quarter staff," observed the friar; "and a true man to boot as thy speech fully showeth."

"These are all thy comrades," said Robin, pointing around to the assembled outlaws; "thou wilt find them of a good sort."

Ere long Dick was busily employed in handshaking and exchanging good wishes with the outlaws, with whom his pert speech and manly bearing had already favoured him.

Drawing Earl Mortimer aside, Robin narrated to him all that had passed since last he saw him.

"Is it not marvellous," asked Robin, when he had finished; "my experience pointeth not to aught like it."

"It is wondrously strange," answered Mortimer; "and I greatly rejoice me that thou and Marian are safe."

"What of Sir Richard Wykham," asked Robin; "sight of him have I not seen since my return?"

"'Tis my forgetfulness that failed to acquaint thee concerning him ere now," Mortimer replied; "but thou must know that during thy absence intelligence of a favourable kind reached him."

"Right glad am I to hear it," said Robin; "was it aught of his possessions?"

"It was. The sheriff had left but a spare garrison; Sir Richard's retainers had assembled and waited his coming to lead them on to victorious possession of their rights."

"This intelligence greatly pleasureth me," said Robin, with beaming countenance; "'twas my resolve to have succoured him an' fitting opportunity presented itself, but thou know'st how busy yon sheriff hath kept me."

"Sir Richard hath counselled me to greatly thank thee for thy generous succour and hospitality. His lady I've will tarry, with thy permission, with Miller Much until such time as he can return for her."

"Surely, surely," answered Robin, "she may stay as becometh her need. And now, brave Mortimer, we will e'en to the banquet, for my hungry stomach doth warn me that the time for food hath arrived."

The bugle sounded the summons to dinner, and all obeyed with alacrity.

Offering his arm to Marian, Robin conducted her to a seat on his left hand, Earl Mortimer being seated to the right, flanked by Little John and the friar.

The latter said grace becomingly, then the outlaws fell to, like hungry men that they were.

It was a fitting repast for a king, and bountifully served without lack or stint for any.

When the viands were removed, the loving cup went round.

Then followed toast and song.

A general call was made on Little John for his famous song of "The Wonderful Pig."

"I will gladly pleasure thee, master and comrades mine," he answered, "though I warn you I am not in fitting condition to do justice to the ditty."

"Tut, man," exclaimed the friar, "thou can'st troll it right well, and we will all help the chorus."

With a few preparatory ahems, and after taking a hearty swig at the wine-skin, Little John sang the song of

THE WONDERFUL PIG.

" There once lived a pig it was said,
That filled folks, young and old, with dread.
What he did and said I'll tell unto thee,
Thou shalt say when I've done, 'tis a famous hist'ry.

" Now this pig grew up from little to big;
Got fat, fought, squealed, and played many a rig,
Prigged acorns in scores, and withal got quite knowing;
His size grew apace, he kept right on growing.

" But sad to tell you, oh yes it's quite true,
For my great, great sire the whole of it knew,
This pig ate his father, and sister and brother,
And, in desperate case, gobbled up his mother.

" Now the loss of his friends made him quite sad;
He grunted, squealed, and got himself bad.
'Cause no more friends were left for him to devour,
He left his old home the country to scour.

" He came to a wood, where lived a hermit,
And settled down there, nor asked any permit.
And in course of time, without reason or rhyme,
This wonderful pig committed this crime:—

" In the noontide heat the hermit he slept,
The pig with soft tread to his side gently crept;
And, oh! to relate it exceedeth all woes,
Ate him right up, not excepting his toes.

" The king he heard of the hermit's fame
And in lowly guise to visit him came;
And in curious mood in the cave took a peep,
Where the wonderful pig was fast asleep.

" On seeing this sight the king was amazed,
And continued to gaze as one does when dazed:
The pig gave a grunt, shook himself and awoke,
When without loss of time the king to him spoke,

" ' Tell me, holy father, what shall I do?
To get rid of my sins, and live chastely too,
How long shall I fast, oh, unto me speak?'
When with look so wise, the pig said, ' a week.'

" The king he went home and shut himself up,
Abhorred meat and drink, shunned the wine cup;
With rods scourged his back and on the ground lied,
In the course of six days why the king he died.

" Before the king died he made him a will,
The writings of which there remaineth still,
With the king's name and seal so big,
'Queathing lands and abbey to the wonderful pig.

" Folks, old and young, came from afar,
Guided, 'twas said, by a wonderful star,
To see this pig, who had grown wondrous tame,
And said ' a-week, a-week,' to all who came.

" He was held by all in fear and awe;
They averred 'twas no pig, but the hermit they saw;
Who for some cause had assumed this guise,
And was chary of talk, because he was wise.

" They built him an abbey, and called him lord,
He had the best food the land could afford;
Nor when he died was his memory despised,
They built him a shrine and him canonised,"

When Little John ended, his song was loudly applauded.

"'Tis exceedingly well sung," said Marian

approvingly; "'tis an odd conceit, though, is it not?"

"'Tis true, every word of it," said Little John, with grave countenance. "I would as lief doubt holy book, as it."

"There's nothing like standing up for one's belief," slyly observed the friar.

"Except *lying* on it," observed Will Scarlet.

"Thou may'st be witty, an' thou wilt," said Little John with dignity; "but for all that, I credit the wonderful pig."

"Thou wert sceptical, John, about the goblins I saw," observed George-a-Green, banteringly. "What say'st thou thereto, now?"

"The same as I before asserted," replied Little John. "Wood demons exist not."

"What say'st thou?" queried Robin.

"That wood demons are not," replied Little John. "Dost thou believe in them, master?"

"That do I," answered Robin; "seeing it would be strange did I say otherwise. Twice has a cursed demon appeared unto me."

"Thou art but jesting, Robin," said Marian, laying her hand playfully on his arm.

"'Tis a truthful assertion, Marian," replied Robin with seriousness. "I would that it were but idle talk I uttered."

"Surely, master, thou did'st not favour him in aught?" asked the friar eagerly; "'tis hard to free one's soul from the grasp of such, when once enthralled."

"Our Lady be thanked, I did not," replied Robin; "but an' thou listen all, I will e'en tell unto thee the whole truth of the matter?"

"We are all attention, master," said Little John. "Body-o'-me! but it appears there are stranger things in this world, than I wotted of."

Amid a deep silence Robin narrated his adventure substantially as the reader has read of it.

The narrative made a deep impression upon all who heard it, but on none more so than upon Marian.

"But thou art free of him, Robin," she asked with a wistful glance at his face, "thou art not bound in compact with him on any wise?"

"Not a hair of my head can he claim," replied Robin, exultantly, "but we will e'en talk of something less ghastly. Fill up to the brim all. I would thine honouring of a toast."

"We are charged, master," said Little John, acting as fugleman to his companions.

"Are the prisoners within earshot?" asked Robin, "if so I would that they were removed."

"Not a syllable can reach them, master," answered Little John.

"I toast the memory of a brave girl, who, next to my Marian, I hold in my heart as a sister. Comrades, here's to Madge Stukely! Health, happiness, and success attend her!"

It was befittingly honoured by all, Marian being enthusiastic in her praise of her.

"As merry men of mine and true," said Robin, "I charge thee one and all to regard Madge as one of us, to be honoured and succoured accordingly."

"Three cheers for Madge Stukely," said the friar; "give her real Saxon cheers."

This call was duly honoured, and from thenceforward the name so befittingly honoured was a dear one to the outlaws.

They broke up at a seasonable hour, and soon all retired to enjoy healthy slumbers, earned by toil.

On the morrow Robin and his followers held merry revels.

The outlaws had been astir early, and under Little John's directions had made fitting preparations for it.

A raised dais or throne had been erected, and tastefully adorned with leaves and flowers.

Thither Robin escorted Marian, and bade her be seated.

"Behold the queen of our goodly revels," exclaimed Robin, bending on knee before her. "To her I do my devoir as her true knight."

"Rise, Robin Hood," said Marian, "and sit thou down on my right hand, as king, to be obeyed by the revellers of this our happy domain."

"Long live Robin Hood and his queen Marian!" cried Little John with stentorian voice.

The salutation was echoed to the full by every one present.

Rising, Robin said:

"Attend you, my lieges all. This our court of revelry is hereby opened unto all. Let harmony and good fellowship be our motto. Strive as friends, be vanquished with good grace, and let a friendly emulation mark all thy contests."

Then commenced a series of manly English sports, games, and pastimes, in which all took a part as occasion offered.

Good-for-Naught Dick's trial proved his worth as an archer, in which art he excelled most of the band.

A goodly repast was spread under the cool shades of the trees, and the revellers sat down to it about mid-day to refresh themselves for their afternoon's exertions.

Much merriment was caused by a race between Little John and jolly Friar Tuck.

"Thou must give me odds, little man," said the friar, "St. Hubert! but thy legs are too long for even distances."

"I will give thee twenty paces," answered Little John; "mind thee, 'tis there and back."

"Nay, John, thou would'st wind one, I perceive," said the friar, with a laugh. "St. Hubert! but my carcass would not have a puff in it did I run half so far as thou proposest."

"I shall toss thee for it," replied Little John, giving the spectators a series of merry winks, "thou can'st not object to that, surely."

"I will not spoil sport," answered the friar, "so let it be as thou proposest. Call thou."

The friar sent a coin twirling up into the air, and Little John shouted, "Rex," meaning king.

"A malison seize the thing," exclaimed the friar with feigned ill-humour, "thou hast won the toss, little man."

"I have to propose a condition," said Little John to Robin, with mock gravity of speech, "let me find favour in thy sight, O king."

"Name it, most trusty and well-beloved cousin," said Robin, humouring the merry conceit to the top of its bent, "thou art accepted in this matter."

"Let him who fails to run the whole distance, drink a flagon of ——"

"Good wine, John man; St. Hubert! but thou art a prime fellow after all," exclaimed the friar, gleefully, interrupting his antagonist ere he could finish his speech.

"A flagon of water," said Little John, with imperturbable gravity.

"Ugh, thou wretch!" exclaimed the friar, "I am inclined to trounce thee for thy pains."

Will Scarlet was the starter.

The signal was, "*One, two, three*, and off!'"

Never had starter greater trouble with restive horses, than had Will with his pair of runners.

First it was the friar who offended; then Little John, with an odd perversity, would mistake one for three, and so on.

But these mistakes were mirth-provoking, and could hardly have been dispensed with.

"Now then," said Will, whose patience was well nigh tired out, "try with might and main to start aright."

The friar and Little John stood ready, expectant for the word.

"Off!"

Away they ran, right merrily.

The friar struggled gallantly on and reached the first goal before his antagonist, which brought down a burst of cheering from the spectators.

But Little John, with tremendous strides, gained on him fast and by the time that half the distance home had been run, passed him by.

"Water!" shouted Little John, as he went by the friar, who was panting and blowing like some monster of the deep.

This allusion to the impending penalty in case of his failing to run the entire distance acted like a refresher on the friar, who, putting on a fresh spurt, gained the goal not far behind his opponent.

"Well done, friar; thou art an excellent runner for thy condition," said Robin; "thou wilt not drink water to-day."

"Not knowingly," gasped the friar; "but I will thank thee for a draught of wine. St. Hubert! but I am wondrous dry."

This soon restored him to his wonted condition, and he seemed rather proud of his exploit than otherwise.

As the revels fast drew to a close, Robin said to Marian—

"What say you to a dance? The earl will join us, as will also Maria Danvers. Art agreed all?"

"I consent," said Marian.

"And I! And I!" came from the others in unanimous response.

"Do thou play fitting melody," said Robin, addressing himself to the harpist of the band, who was no mean performer on his instrument.

The dance commenced, and was gracefully executed.

Plaudits greeted them at its close, for the outlaws, excepting a few of their number, had ne'er before seen such a display.

Then came the distribution of prizes, which were presented by Marian to delighted recipients.

Ere the revels finally closed, Will Scarlet came forward and said:

"Hearken, comrades all. 'Twould ill become us to quit the revels without showing fitting gratitude to our king and queen. What say you, comrades, shall we not crown them?"

"Surely, surely!" was the unanimous response.

Taking two crowns from the hands of an attendant outlaw, Will advanced with deferential mien.

Summoning them to kneel, he first placed a crown on Marian's brow, then did the same by Robin.

Thunders of applause greeted their coronation.

The crowns themselves were skilfully worked with roses and other flowers, and presented an attractive appearance.

Rising, and with Marian's hand clasped lovingly in his, Robin said, in accents tinged with emotion:

"Friends, and comrades all. It hath pleased Our Lady to safely deliver me and Marian from the hands of a cruel and treacherous enemy— to wit, the Sheriff of Nottingham; in commemoration whereof I have holden these revels and festivities, in the which we have all heartily joined. Thou has honoured us by placing on our brows these crowns in token of submission to our will. We thank thee greatly for this thy gracious pledge of loyalty, and bid thee welcome to a banquet prepared for all under the wide-spreading trees of this grand old forest; and on the morrow thou art one and all bidden to a right royal hunt."

The applause at the end of this speech was deafening in the extreme, and prolonged, sending the echoes reverberating grandly through the old forest.

Descending from their throne, Robin and Marian led the way to the banquet, heralded by song and dance.

The repast excelled that of the previous night, and was of a most sumptuous character.

"Pass around the loving cup," said Robin. "Let amity and good fellowship mark our lives throughout."

"Fill to the brim, comrades all," said Little John, "and do honour to this toast."

"Art all charged? Blessings beyond measure attend our king and queen!"

Never was toast more heartily responded to, or so gratefully received.

"'Twould greatly pleasure the company," said Friar Tuck, uprising with a slightly unsteady gait, "if Marian would carol a sweet melody."

"What say'st thou, darling?" queried Robin.

"I will sing one," replied Marian, and without preliminary preparation of any kind, she sang:

"Speech it is golden,
  When by lovers 'tis holden;
  When hearts converse free,
  And sadness doth flee;
  When the soul it unfolds
  The love-secrets it holds.

But speech it is dross,
  'Tis waste, 'tis but loss,
  When by false heart 'tis spoken,
  In pledge of love-token.
  Then maidens be wise,
  'Tis but deceit in disguise."

ROBIN HOOD,

AND THE OUTLAWS OF SHERWOOD FOREST.

DUEL BETWEEN ROBIN HOOD AND DEVEREUX.

"A sweet pretty song," said Earl Mortimer, when Marian's lay was finished.

"And instructive withal," rejoined Little John. "Body-o'-me! but the tongue is not always what it would appear to be."

"Hast thou tested its deceit, John?" asked the friar with a merry twinkle of his roguish eye. "Has fair maiden jilted thee at any time?"

"I would not own an' it were so," said Little John with a laugh. "I doubt much whether any maiden would exchange love now with me."

"Peradventure thou hast not tried one," said Maria Danvers with a merry laugh.

"'Tis hard to assert what experience has not crowned."

"He but argues from his own case," remarked Marian with a mischievous smile. "Convinced that maidens despise him, he despiseth them. Is it not so?"

"Well put, Marian," said Robin. "What answer hast thou to that, John?"

"I will be dumb," replied John, "else will I be worsted in the wordy contest with such fair and ready speakers."

"St. Hubert! but thou turnest a neat compliment," said the friar. "Never despair of getting love of maiden after that."

Thus the evening passed pleasantly, and all retired to rest, well satisfied with the pleasures of the past day.

After a substantial breakfast on the morrow, the outlaws turned out for the hunt.

Robin was fortunate enough to rouse a fine stag at the outset of the chase.

Blowing his bugle-horn, he started off in pursuit, followed by such of the band as could keep up with his fleet running, and accompanied by his deer-hounds.

Soon he distanced them all, and was alone, carried along by the ardour of the chase.

He had twice wounded the stag, which began to evince signs of giving up.

Fixing an arrow to his bow, Robin fired.

The stag was brought to his knees.

Giving a real huntsman's rousing hallo, Robin rushed forward, elated at the thoughts of securing such a fine prize.

But the wounded stag turned at bay.

With lowered antlers, it waited Robin's approach.

In his precipitate haste, his foot slipped, and he fell to the ground.

With unerring instinct the stag saw that the present was fitting opportunity for freeing itself of its tormentor, and thus impelled, rushed forward.

Hastily unsheathing his hunting-knife, Robin leaned on his left elbow, and with right hand upraised, prepared to deal his enemy a finishing blow.

His hounds came up at this juncture, and were bounding onwards preparatory to making a spring.

He caught sight of the animal's infuriated eye, felt its hot breath on his cheek, when it rolled over in the agonies of death, with an arrow through its heart.

The arrow came from Little John's trusty bow.

He had followed on after Robin, catching an occasional view of him, and arrived just in time to save him being viciously attacked, and perhaps slain by the stag.

"Our Lady be thanked thou art safe!" said Little John. "'Tis a noble fellow, though, is it not, master?"

Robin could not at first utter a single word, for emotion kept him silent.

"John," he at last said, "'tis another benefit conferred on me. I would that I could repay thy many services befittingly."

"Let it pass, master," said John, blushing like a maiden almost at Robin's words of praise and gratitude; "I would that I could serve thee better."

"Nay, dear friend," replied Robin laying his hand on his arm, and looking with a manly and affectionate earnestness in his face, "fit-

ting proof have I had of thy devotion to me; would that I had solid gifts for thee; but it matters not, John; we are free, and for Saxons that everything includes."

"'Tis as I like to hear thee speak, master," said Little John, delightedly; "'tis useless fashing oneself about things that have past. It is enough that we have health and strength, plenty of deer for the taking, a home in this grand old forest, and a noble master like thee!"

Little John knelt at Robin's feet, and seizing his hand, pressed it reverently to his lips.

"Rise, John," said Robin; "never was master more fortunate than I; never friend so secure in the love of an honest heart than am I in thine."

At this moment a bounding stag came in view, and passed on close by Robin and his companion.

"Stay thy hand, John," said Robin, as he prepared to send an arrow at the creature; "'tis some one else's sport; let's see who comes."

Even as Robin spoke an arrow whistled through the air, and striking the stag between the left shoulder-blade and the back, brought it down.

"A death, a death!" shouted the friar, rushing forward, and not perceiving Robin or Little John, who were a little distance in the background. "St. Hubert! what will John say to that? John, John, where art thou?"

Plucking out his hunting knife the friar, by sheer strength alone, kept the wounded stag down despite its resolute resistance, and plunged the weapon into its heart.

"'Twas a pity to see thee suffer, poor brute," exclaimed the friar. "St. Hubert! but thou art a noble fellow."

"What hast thou there, friar?" asked Robin, coming forward attended by Little John; "thou hast slain thy stag I perceive."

"That have I master," said the friar without looking up from his work for the moment; "but hast thou seen John? My wager is won, I ween."

"Art rightly assured of that?" asked Little John.

"St. Hubert, how thou affrighted me," exclaimed the friar, looking up with a start. "I did not know of thy presence; but hast thou a stag to show for this? If not thy wager is forfeit I would have thee know."

"That has he," answered Robin, "and a nobler one than thine even."

"What of his own shooting?" asked the friar, quite chapfallen.

"Even so, and in slaying it he succoured me," answered Robin.

"Nay then, John, I am content to lose my wager," said the friar, "inasmuch as thou hast succoured Robin Hood thou deservest it, and much more else."

"I am the forfeiter," said Little John, "'twas Robin's arrow that first brought it to stand. I did but shoot one arrow."

"Did he turn on thee then, master?" asked the friar of Robin.

"That did he, and right viciously. I was in doleful dumps for a certainty had not John shot so opportunely and so well. But come and see his handywork."

"Here, John," said the friar, handing him his flask, "drink man, for thou art a credit to

Sherwood's foresters, and my dear friend withal."

"Gramercy," answered John, "I never refuse good wine, or turn away from a true friend."

"Two finer stags ne'er were seen," observed Robin; "I wot thine is the finest of the twain, friar."

"Nay, master," replied the friar; "mine lacks the stature thine possesseth, and other points of difference existeth; but as thou truly say'st they are twain of a good stock."

"Wilt drain a draught, master, 'twill not harm thee this hot day," said John, as he offered a full horn to Robin.

"That will I, friend John," said Robin; "here's success to our hunt!"

"Hark!" said the friar, "'tis a call for help."

Bounding forward with impetuous haste, followed by his companions, Robin came upon a sight which well nigh curdled his blood with horror.

Hanging to a branch was Marian, and just beneath her stood an infuriated deer, which vainly endeavoured to reach her.

Poor Marian's face was pale with affright, and although she stood the strain on her arms bravely, it was evident to even the most casual observer that she could not much longer endure it.

Had she dropped she must have been impaled on the stag's horns.

"Hold on, darling," shouted Robin, as he nervously fitted an arrow to his bow.

But before he could fire, Friar Tuck had shot with true aim, and the stag dropped lifeless on the greensward.

Hardly had this been accomplished when Marian's grasp relaxed and she fell.

Her fall would have been a heavy one, had it not been that Robin sprang forward and caught her in his strong arms.

"Our Lady be thanked, thou art safe!" said he, as he knelt by her side and chafed her hands.

"Looks she not deathlike," remarked Little John; "'tis sad to see her thus."

"Nay, greet not," replied the friar; "a little water will her revive. I will hie me and fetch some from yonder rippling stream."

"Thanks!" exclaimed Robin; "speed thee on thy way, I beseech thee. Her condition requireth haste and despatch."

Robin tenderly laved her temples with water, and Marian soon showed signs of returning consciousness.

"St. Hubert be thanked!" exclaimed the friar; "this is indeed an overwhelming mercy; art better Marian?"

Robin did nothing but gaze fixedly on her face on which the pallor of death began to give place to a hectic flush, betokening the return of the active principles of life within her system.

"'Twas a brave thing to do," remarked Little John, "for so fair and fragile a maiden to adventure upon such a hunt."

"Thou hast well spoken," replied Robin, in accents in which pride mingled; "a truer maiden exists not. True Saxon is she. But see she has returned to herself."

Gently upraising her, Robin supported her dear head on his manly breast, and caressed her glossy tresses.

Opening her eyes Marian said in feeble accents, "Where am I? 'Twas a horrid dream surely."

"Thou art safe, darling," tenderly exclaimed Robin; "'tis all past, and naught hast thou to fear further."

"Thy voice assures me of it," replied Marian, raising herself and looking fondly into Robin's face; "When thou art near I fear naught."

At this juncture Robin's hounds started off in pursuit of a fawn, noticing which Marian exclaimed in piteous tones:

"Restrain them, I beseech of thee Robin; 'tis my wish to possess the gentle thing, and for it I incurred my past dangers."

Thus besought, Robin quickly called back the hounds, which being well trained and disciplined, obeyed him instantly.

"Down, sirs!" he exclaimed as they came back with slouching gait, "and stir not further but at my command."

Thus admonished, they crouched low at his feet, and kept watchful eye upon his every look.

"If 'twill not distress thee too greatly," said Robin, in gentle accents, "I would fain hear the account of thy misadventure, that is an' thou carest to narrate it."

"Being wishful to share the hunt," said Marian answeringly, "I followed hard after thee, but being less fleet of foot, missed thy presence."

"'Tis naught to thy disadvantage to acknowledge it," remarked Little John. "Few, if any, can keep pace with my master, Robin."

"'Twould seem I am perfection in thine eyes," said Robin, with a laugh; "but to thy narration, Marian darling!"

"I take courage from John's speech," remarked Marian archly; "and will again confess that I was laggard in the chase.

"In wandering onward I got me to a spot where browsed a fawn, such an one as that which thy hounds sought to slay but a few moments past.

"It was withal so young, and of such gentle mien, that I was eager to possess it, and with that intent I gat me from tree to tree to within a short distance of its standpoint.

"With quick movement I sprang upon and captured it, when the tiny darling struggled in mine arms and uttered cries incessantly.

"While bearing it off in triumph, I espied a large stag, the same which here lieth, swiftly approaching, and armed with evil and vengeful intent meward.

"Placing my tiny captive on the greensward, I sought sanctuary, but nowhere could I espy fitting place.

"The enraged animal was but few paces distant, when in the hopelessness of despair, I sprang upwards and caught a bough, the rest thou know'st."

"Of a verity, thou had'st a close shave of death," exclaimed Robin; "thou must not wander alone again, lest evil befall thee."

"There stands the cause of thy mishap," said Little John, pointing to the fawn which stood a short distance off, and looked wistfully toward the party.

"Would'st thou possess it, Marian?" asked Robin; "thou hast but to name thy wish and 'twill be quickly accomplished."

"Is it not a beautiful creature," exclaimed Marian evasively; "'tis a pity to despoil it of its liberty."

"Thou would'st like it; but say so," said John, "and I will get it thee, Marian."

"I will make a proposition thereanent," Marian answered.

"Do thou say on, then," replied Robin; "'twill not be gainsayed."

"I would that no unseemly violence be offered the tiny thing," said Marian, "but let us retire beyond yon tree, and peradventure 'twill stray hither to our band."

"Agreed," replied Robin readily. "Thine hand, Marian love; do thou accompany us, friend John, and thou, jolly friar."

In a short time they were watchfully ensconced behind a large tree.

"Did I not tell thee?" said Marian gleefully. "See, hither it comes with nimble steps to its sire's side."

It was even so, for the fawn ran forward, and was soon at the side of the dead stag.

It sniffed at the blood, and stepped back affrighted. Anon it strove, by dint of cry and caress, to arouse its sire, and failing this, rested by its side.

"I will capture it now," said Marian. "Do thou all remain here while I go forward."

With cautious tread, she left her hiding-place, and ere long the fawn was hers.

"Well done, Marian!" exclaimed Robin; "thou art a clever capturer."

"'Twas well contrived, indeed," replied the friar; "but let a woman alone to accomplish her ends."

"'Tis a blessing they can so succeed, else would I be not here now," remarked Robin; "but hark! hearest thou not that strain? Our Lady, 'tis fine, is't not?"

Borne on wings of the breeze, came the musical chorus of a number of voices, as they sang a hunting refrain.

"Right onward we go, right onward we go,
    With a heep, and a whoop, and a view tally ho!
March on with firm tread, bold front, and bent
        bow,
    The red deer to chase, with a loud tally ho!

CHORUS.—Right on, right on, right on with loud
            shout,
        To startle the forest and bring the deer
            out;
        Forward, then, all, to the horn's merry
            call,
        For this blithesome morn must many
            deer fall.

"Move on, comrades all, with loud shout and song,
    Our view tally ho let the forest prolong;
Be jubilant all, and let deep Saxon hurrah
    Swell forth from our throats, and reach to afar.

CHORUS.—Right on, right on, right on with loud
            shout, &c.

"Right onwards we'll go; see the red deer, he hies,
    He reels, he gasps, he falls, and he dies!
We are in at the death, huzzah, lads, huzzah!
    Tral al la, tral al la, tral al al, al al la!

CHORUS.—Right on, right on, right on with loud
            shout, &c."

The outlaws in merry mood, and bearing with them slung on poles, the carcasses of several fine deer, emerged into view.

Robin and his party cheered them lustily, and going forward, he said in loud voice:—

"Greet thee warmly, my merry men all. I am proud of thy prowess."

"Huzza for Bold Robin our chief!" said Will Scarlet, answeringly, "and Maid Marian, too!"

Forthwith went up deafening cheers, the likes of which had not been heard before in Sherwood's royal forest.

"We have been no laggards either," said Robin pointing to the dead deer which lay around. "Here be three as fine stags as thou could'st find anywhere."

"Not forgetting Marian's captive," remarked the friar. "St. Hubert! but it has been a grand day."

"We will e'en bivouac hereabout," said Robin; "a steak from off one of these fat deer will not be a despicable meal for a hungry man's stomach. What say'st thou thereto, John?"

"That thou art right, master, and soon will we serve up for thee a royal repast. Here, friar, thy help is needed in this matter."

"I attend thee, little man," answered the friar; "but bethink thee that venison steak is but sorry eating without good wine to wash it down."

"'Twill be forthcoming anon," replied Little John; "meanwhile bestir thyself to get things in order."

Soon almost every person was employed in assisting in the culinary arrangements, and all worked with a will, being goaded on by the strongest of incentives, viz., hunger.

In an incredibly short space of time everything was ready, and the outlaws seated themselves around the festive board, which offered to them substantial fare.

"I know not when I have so greatly enjoyed any occasion as I have the present," observed Robin. "My heart is full of joy, and a pleasurable excitement runs throughout me."

"It gives me joy to hear thee so speak," replied Marian, with an affectionate glance; "thou hast had worry enow of late to destroy thy happiness."

"Nay, dearest, 'tis my endeavour to accept without murmuring evil when it comes," said Robin, in reply; "'tis a bitter flavouring to life's cup I grant thee, but nauseous medicine acts beneficially at times."

At this moment one of the band ran towards the party with affrighted looks, exclaiming:—

"Scatter to cover for your lives."

With that thought and ready obedience characteristic of the men, they quickly dispersed and got them in safe positions, wondering what the warning meant.

Their suspense was not of long duration.

Bounding onwards came a majestic-looking stag, the king of the deer, shaping his course right across the open glade where but a few minutes before the outlaws sat carousing.

"Raise not a hand against him!" shouted Robin warningly; "but let him pass unscathed."

The last part of Robin's speech was drowned in a thundering voice, which increased in intensity each moment.

"Keep close for your lives," shouted Robin in tones which were heard above the din.

Sweeping onwards with mad and impetuous speed came a vast herd of deer, presenting to the sight a magnificent but terrifying spectacle.

Nothing could have resisted their close and compact order as they sped onward with whirlpool speed, making the very ground quake beneath the strokes of their hoofs.

And as they swept by what a grand sight the sea of antlered heads presented to the eye of the beholder.

Truly it was grand beyond description.

So entranced were the spectators of this novel and terrible sight that not one among them attempted to shoot an arrow at the horny torrent that had swept past with a lightning flash.

"We would have fared ill but for our timely warning," said Robin, as he emerged from cover. "Naught like it saw I ever before save once, and 'tis many years ago."

"I would not have missed the sight for aught," remarked Marian, "although 'twas a terrifying one withal."

"Mine eyes never rested on nobler stag than yon leader was," said the friar. "St. Hubert! mine hand greatly itched to arrow him, but my heart rebelled against destroying so noble a creature."

"I honour thee for thy speech," replied Robin. "Woodsman though I be, and withal a keen sportsman, yet could I not find it in my heart to slay such a majestic fellow."

"Good-for-Naught Dick deserves fitting reward," said Little John. "'Twas he warned us of their approach."

"Thanks for thy reminder," replied Robin. "I would have speech of him before the whole band, and at once."

"Thou hast done us all good service, Dick," said Robin to him as he came forward with Little John. "How camest thou by the knowledge of the herd's approach?"

"Thou art welcome to the poor service I rendered thee and my comrades," Dick modestly replied; "and as fitting answer to thy question, the matter came about on this wise.

"Being ever a lover of Nature, specially as beholden in such a grand old forest as this, I wandered forth to quietly enjoy her.

"Hardly had I quitted the hearing of thy voices when methought I could distinguish a peculiar sound in the air.

"Judging that it ascended, I gat me on my knees, and placing ear to the ground, listened.

"'Twas then I had an inkling of what was coming, and fearing that the danger would come upon you all unawares, I hied me hither with speed, and, Our Lady be thanked, was in time."

"What say you, comrades," asked Robin, "shall not Good-for-Naught Dick be fittingly rewarded?"

"Surely, surely!" was the unanimous response heartily given.

"Thou shalt wear a silver badge on thy coat," said Robin, addressing himself to Dick, "and twenty crown pieces shall be paid thee out of the treasury."

"Nay, thou overwhelm'st me with benefits," said Dick, deprecatingly.

"And furthermore," said Robin, unheedful of Dick's protest, "I give thee as mine own free gift a goodly bow and quiver of arrows."

The outlaws cheered right lustily, and acclaimed Dick in right good style.

"We will now hie homewards," said Robin,

"but first let the carcasses be properly secured, and be borne with us. 'Twould be unseemly to waste aught."

"A right royal hunt we have had," said Marian, "and escapes most marvellous."

"'Tis an occasion to be long remembered," replied Little John. "Body-o'-me! I shall not soon forget the rush of yon herd; its thunder sounds in mine ears even now."

"'Tis a marvellous old place is this same forest," observed Robin Hood, "and I love it for its associations. 'Twould be hard to find its equal."

Everything being in readiness, the band of outlaws started, headed by Robin, Marian, and his trusty lieutenants.

"Sing us thy marching song, John," said the friar, "'twill help us onward. Prithee do not say nay; in thy hands 'tis easy of accomplishment."

"I crave it at thy hands as a boon," cried Marian. "Thou wilt not surely refuse, John?"

"I will do my best to pleasure thee," answered Little John; and shifting the fawn which he was carrying for Marian from his right to his left arm, he after a few preparatory ahems, commenced

THE MARCHING SONG.

"When the dew is on the greensward,
And the sun hies him eastward,
We'll form our ranks in order,
And we'll march, march to the border.

CHORUS.—Then on, on, march on in haste,
We'll make our foes Saxon steel to taste;
Steady, there, steady, your ranks keep in order,
As we march, march, march to the border.

"When the battle is put in array,
Let none from its front turn away;
March steadily on, prepared for the shock,
March steady there, men, firm as a rock.

CHORUS.—Then on, on, march on in haste, &c.

"Steady, steady, march by the right,
Hurrah, hurrah, the foe is in sight;
Prepare for the charge, level your spear,
Courage, onward, for the land we owe dear.

CHORUS.—Then on, on, march on in haste, &c.

"Archers, march forward, let your bolts fly;
Well aimed, see they drop, see they die:
The battle is over, let victory's shout,
Sound in their ears as our foemen we rout.

CHORUS.—Then on, on, march on in haste," &c.

Little John was heartily cheered for his interesting song, the chorus of which was oft repeated with delight by his comrades.

"Thou art a famous songster, John," observed Marian, "thy melody hath much cheered me."

"Nay," said Little John, "I am but a sorry singer at best."

"Hark to that," cried Robin, "beshrew me but it sounds of a strange sort."

At intervals came a sound which to most, if not nearly all the outlaws, was inexplicable.

"'Tis a combat betwixt two stags," said Good-for-Naught Dick; "and judging by their sounds a most vicious one too."

"Dick is right!" exclaimed the Friar, "'tis well worth witnessing."

"Let us go aside then," said Robin, "'twill amuse us to see the novel combat."

"Thy presence will not scare them," observed Dick: "I have often known them to fight surrounded by spectators. So vicious are they when fully enraged."

"There they are, sure enough!" cried Robin, as the party came in sight of the combatants. "Circle round and daunt them not in any wise."

The stags were both large-proportioned, and therefore possessed of immense strength.

When they came into collision the noise caused by the shock was plainly distinguishable a great distance off, so forcibly did they butt each other.

"Look, look!" cried Marian concernedly, "even now one of them shows signs of weakness. Poor creature, 'tis pitiful to see their deadly strivings."

"They'll fight to the very end," said the friar, "'twould be idle to separate them."

"'Twould be hard to do so, thou meanest," replied Little John, drily, "Body-o-me! they would horn one to death first."

"Be assured I will not essay the task," answered Friar Tuck, with a laugh; "catch me interfering in idle quarrels, 'tis unprofitable work at best."

"Thy prudence is commendable," remarked Robin, smilingly. "Our Lady! saw'st thou that round, 'twas truly a hard fought one?"

"And now one has dropped dead," said Marian, sorrowfully, "and the other is well nigh bereft of life. Ah, me! 'tis sad."

Marian had barely ceased speaking when the victorious stag staggered forth on its knees, and with a hoarse sounding cry rolled quivering on its side and expired.

"Well done, thou antlered knights," said Robin, eulogistically, "thou deserved'st better things than to perish thus in unseemly strife."

"Many perish thus," remarked Good-for-Naught Dick, "'tis seldom that the victor lives."

"What is the cause of such strivings?" asked Marian, "if cause can be assigned therefor."

"Jealousy is at the bottom of it all," answered Little John, with a grin, ere Dick could reply.

"Thou art quite right in thus answering," the latter observed.

"Thou surely jestest," answered Marian, looking in turn from one to the other of the speakers.

"Not so, lady," Dick replied, "'tis true, though strange, as I can avouch."

"I have heard of this before," remarked Robin, "but as the day wanes we must e'en go forward, else will the shades of evening step in to chide our lagging footsteps."

"Thou wilt leave the carcasses?" queried Little John.

"Even so," replied Robin, "were I ever so hungered I would not taste their flesh."

Well pleased with their day's tramping, the outlaws returned to their trysting place bearing with them proofs of their prowess in the chase.

CHAPTER LXII.

HOW ROBIN HOOD FOUGHT A DUEL WITH DEVEREUX.

Their swords crossed and clashed,
Their eyes met and flashed
With deep revenge and dire hate,
And each looked like an avenging fate.

On the morrow a messenger arrived from the sheriff asking audience of Robin.

"Call an assembly," said Robin to Little John, "that all may hear of the matter this fellow would discourse of."

"Now summon him hither," said Robin, when all his men had assembled; "perchance his errand hath reference to our prisoners."

"Thy business with me—of what nature is it?" asked Robin of the sheriff's minion.

"The sheriff, my master, sends thee kindly greeting, and——"

"Thou had'st much better have left thy courtesies behind thee," said Robin sarcastically; "they are not marketable here."

"I but speak as my master hath advised," the messenger replied with humility. "Other words I have not."

"Doth thy master thus insult me with his greetings?" said Robin indignantly, "when in actions he dealeth cruelly and treacherously with me and mine. Let thy message be plainly delivered, else wilt thou have no further audience at my hands."

"I will do mine endeavour to pleasure thee," answered the fellow in abject tones; "the sheriff is wishful to ransom thy prisoners."

"Umph!" said Robin; "and what if I refuse? perchance he will rescue them at the sword's point."

"He is willing to pay thee down fitting ransom in broad pieces, and seeketh information as to thy requirements," said the messenger, unheedful of Robin's remarks.

"Thou can'st go aside," Robin curtly replied. "Fitting answer shalt thou have anon."

When the messenger had been conducted out of earshot, Robin signalled for silence, and thus addressed the assembled outlaws:—

"Listen, comrades all. By base stratagem Nottingham's sheriff inveigled Maid Marian away and gat possession of her person with foul intent."

"The Norman hound!" growled Little John.

With an admonishing gesture to him to preserve silence, Robin continued:

"The prisoners now holden by us were each one concerned in this base unmanly plot against a gentle maiden. These the sheriff now seeketh to ransom, and, as thou hast heard, requireth my terms."

"As thou hast put the matter to the assembly," said the friar, "I would, with thy permission, e'en make a proposal thereon."

"Thou hast my sanction," said Robin. "Say on."

"Let six of our number be selected by lot to appoint the conditions of the ransom, to be approved by the general assembly."

"A sensible proposal hast thou named, friar," answered Robin; "it hath my approval. Hast it thine, comrades all?"

A general assent was given thereto, and six persons were forthwith selected.

They were Little John, the Friar, Allan-a-Dale, Much, Will Scarlet, and Reynolds.

Calling them by name to the front, Robin said:

"Thou hast one and all been chosen by thy comrades to consider this matter of ransom between myself on the one hand and the sheriff on the other. Thou must not forget our honour or interests in thy councilship."

"Wilt thou not preside?" queried Little John.

"Nay; but I will hear thy decision, and consider thereon. To thy task now, and forget not that our honour has been basely and treacherously assailed in this matter."

Drawing aside to some distance from the main body, the six chosen ones prepared at once to confer upon the question proposed to them.

"Friar," said Little John; "thou must guide our deliberations. What say'st thou thereto?"

"Nay, nay, John," he replied, "I would much prefer that thou or some other one of this honourable assembly did assume such office, 'twould be more seemly than for me to hold it, I wot."

Spite of his remonstrances, however, he was duly installed as president of the meeting.

Seating himself on the stump of a tree, and with the others, seated beside him on the green sward, the friar said, with grave mien:

"This meeting hath been convened for the reason thou all well knowest of. The sheriff demandeth our prisoners on ransom, 'tis for us to name conditions."

"Recite to us the particulars of the outrage," said Little John; "'twill refresh our memories."

"Aye, 'tis fitting we should know all," observed Will Scarlet, "and thou, friar, can'st fully acquaint us thereof."

"Listen then. Thou know'st how that a false message came to Marian?"

"True," ejaculated Little John.

"Well, fearful of entrusting one so precious as her to a stranger's hands, I departed with her."

"Thou did'st propose the matter to me, and I assented," said the matter-of-fact Little John.

"Thou art as precise as a book, John," remarked the friar; "but, as I have stated, I went with Marian, and on the way met with a party of the sheriff's soldiers, with whom were Devereux and Roderic, our principal prisoners."

"Yes, and what next?" asked Little John, with impatient gesture.

"St. Hubert, but thou giv'st me no time for gaining breath," observed the friar; "patience John, patience; 'twill all be about presently."

"They impertinently demanded the giving up of my charge," continued the friar, "which I stoutly resisted, and coming to blows dealt that same Roderic a thwack with my staff, which quickly stretched him on the green sward."

"And they returned afterwards," observed Little John.

"Softly, John, softly; thou art as querelous as any housewife," observed the friar grumpily; "thou must know that they bore Marian away by treacherous stratagem, leaving Roderic with me."

"And returned afterwards to his rescue," said Reynolds, aiding the friar's memory.

"Thou art right, Reynolds, lad," said the friar, gratefully, "and now the whole matter is fully known to thee all."

"And a shameful matter it hath been," remarked Allan-a-Dale, "so much so that ransom ought not to be entertained."

"What would'st thou then?" queried the friar.

"That each and all be hanged as a warning to others of their sort," said Allan-a-Dale, decisively.

"And I agree with thee," said Much, "let them pay for it with their lives say I."

"Nay," said Reynolds, "I am for asking a thumping ransom for their misdeeds, their carcasses would but offend our nostrils; but silver crowns would enrich our treasury, and impoverish yonder money-grubbing sheriff."

"Ha! ha!" laughed the friar, and rubbing his hands gleefully. "Well put, Reynolds, I vote with thee."

"And I," said Little John.

"And I agree therewith," said Will Scarlet.

"Four to two," remarked the friar, "'tis decided then that fitting ransom be asked."

"How many prisoners are there in all?" queried Little John.

"Five," replied Will Scarlet.

"But two only are of note though," put in the friar.

"What say you to five hundred crowns each for the two, and one hundred each for the remainder?" asked Little John.

"'Tis not enow by half," grumbled the friar; "say a thousand for each notable, and two hundred for each of the others."

"So let it be," said Will.

"Agreed," cried Reynolds.

"And if it be not forthcoming what then?" asked Allan-a-Dale.

"Why death will and must clear off the score," replied Little John.

"Are we all agreed?" asked the friar.

The answer was in the affirmative.

"We will hie back then, and unfold our determination to Robin Hood."

Having thus spoken, the friar led the way and on rejoining the outlaws, told Robin the result of their conference.

"May it please you, master," he said, "we have agreed to the conditions."

"Name them aloud," Robin replied, "that my merry men may hear."

Placing his arms akimbo, and speaking in loud tones, the friar said:

"Be it known unto thee, Robin Hood, and thou comrades all, that having considered and well weighed this matter of ransom, we opine that the sheriff should pay down in goodly money, a thousand crowns for each of the two notable prisoners, and two hundred for each of the others, and that failing payment of which the said prisoners suffer the penalty of death in their mortal bodies forthwith."

"'Tis for thou, one and all, to assent or dissent thereto," said Robin, addressing his men; "and this shall be the manner of declaration, let each *assenter* drop a stone to the right of yon tree; each *dissenter* to the left."

All the stones were deposited to the *right*.

"Call hither the sheriff's messenger," said Robin.

He came and made a low obeisance, and with folded hands awaited Robin's words.

"Prepare me a missive," said Robin to the friar, "to contain all that thou hast declared, and my men have assented to."

When it was ready, Robin read it to the messenger.

"Bear it to thy master," he said, "and if fitting answer come not thereto in three days' time hence, the prisoners shall hang. Thou art now dismissed."

Without offering a word of any kind in return, the messenger departed in haste.

The third day had half fled when there arrived the sheriff's messenger attended by two servitors, bearing with them sundry bags which gave forth the chink of money.

As before, Robin summoned the outlaws, and when all were assembled, he bade the messenger to deliver his message.

"I have with me five bags of money, each containing the ransom thou hast asked. Thou can'st count their contents if thou wilt."

He laid the bags at Robin's feet.

"Let them be counted," said Robin, motioning forward Little John.

This was done with methodical exactness, and Little John pronounced all to be correct.

"Bring forward the prisoners," said Robin, "and request Maid Marian's attendance."

There was a hushed silence when Robin, with Marian at his side, thus addressed the prisoners:—

"The sheriff of Nottingham, mindful of thy state as prisoners securely held by me, hath sent ransom according to my imposing."

"And we are now freed thereby," said Devereux, haughtily.

"'Tis entirely of our clemency that it is so," answered Robin; "thy crime deserveth no such merciful consideration."

"Crime!" instantly retorted Devereux; "thou art but a common cutthroat and robber, and she standing by thy side but a common woman."

He would have said more, but his voice was drowned by the angry shout which the outlaws gave, as with uplifted daggers they prepared to rush upon him.

"Hold!" cried Robin, imperiously, and beckoning back his excited followers; "the quarrel is mine, and mine alone."

Folding his arms on his breast, and with stern glance cast at Devereux, Robin said with ominous calmness:—

"Thou hast an object in thine insult. What would'st thou?"

"To prove my words on thy body, bold outlaw," Devereux replied defiantly.

"Thou shalt be pleasured," said Robin quickly, "and that instantly. What ho there! men; press back, and give us space."

"Thou wilt not rashly peril thy life," said Marian, urging forward and placing her hand on Robin's arms. "Bethink thee of what thou riskest."

"Marian, darling, stand back, I pray thee," said Robin with gentle sternness. "Poltroon would I be to leave *thine* honour unavenged."

"Choose thou thy weapon," he said to Devereux, "and pray for thy soul's welfare, for, by the saints above, death alone can expiate thine insult!"

"Keep thy vapourings for others," Devereux contemptuously replied, "and look well to thyself; for I swear, by St. Quintan! to rid the land of thy hateful presence."

Devereux tried the temper of many swords ere he finally selected one.

Robin drew his trusty blade, and awaited impatiently for his antagonist to declare his readiness.

Before engaging, Robin, looking around on the faces of his friends, said:

"Thou hast, one and all, my most solemn injunction not to interfere by word, deed, or aught else in this quarrel, on pain of incurring my displeasure. And thou, Marian, quit, I pray thee, this spot."

"Nay, Robin," Marian replied with an imploring glance, "thou wilt let me stay. I will demean myself as a true Saxon maiden, and thy Marian to boot."

"'Tis enough." said Robin; "I am content."

"Hast thou aught to say ere thou commencest?" he asked of Devereux.

"Naught," was the curt reply, as he put himself in attitude.

Their swords crossed amid a silence deep and hushed as that of the grave.

For a time it seemed as if they were equally matched, so well did each wield his weapon.

But it soon became apparent that Robin was only biding his time.

Devereux made a desperate effort to break through the advancing guard.

It was fatal to him, though.

Quick as lightning's flash almost, Robin's sword passed through his body!

The wretched man clutched Robin's weapon, and for a moment held it with an iron grip, while he endeavoured to gather strength to aim a blow that would annihilate him, but the effort proved futile.

His grasp loosened, he cast up his left arm wildly, and with a low moan, and a half-uttered curse fell heavily backwards a corpse.

"'Twas thine own seeking, rash fool," said Robin, as he gazed upon the face of his victim; "and thou hast paid for thy rashness with thy life."

"Our Lady be thanked! thou art safe, darling," said Marian, going over to him, and leaning her head upon his arm, while she covered her face with her hand, to shut out the horror-haunting face of the dead man.

"And thou art avenged, Marian," said Robin proudly, "his foul slander of thee pains me more than could a sword thrust."

"May I crave a boon," said Roderic, coming forward and confronting Robin with lowering brow.

Ere Robin could answer, Roderic drew a sharp-pointed dagger and aimed a treacherous blow at his breast.

"Dastard!" said a stern voice, as a strong arm interposed between Roderic and his intended victim, and dashed him violently to the earth.

"Harm him not, John," said Robin, as Little John knelt on Roderic's prostrate form and pressed his throat till his tongue protruded.

The command came just in time to save the wretched being's life; another moment and Little John's iron grip would have strangled him outright.

ROBIN HOOD,

AND THE OUTLAWS OF SHERWOOD FOREST.

"Thou Norman dog !" exclaimed Little John, uprising and contemptuously spurning with his foot the prostrate form of Roderic.

"Thou had'st better bear him away with thee," said Robin, turning to the sheriff's messenger and pointing to Roderic ; "else will I be unable to protect him from the just wrath of my friends."

Robin's friendly warning was we ll timed, for angry mutterings and threatening glances began to be heard and seen, portending evil to all the Normans then present."

"Give him decent burial," said Robin pointing to the dead man ; "though rash, he was withal brave."

"The cursed Normans," growled Friar

Tuck in Little John's willing ear; "they are as venomous as vipers. I would that I could crush them beneath my heel."

"Body-o'-me!" replied Little John; "'twas ill on Robin's part to hold my hand; another pinch would have sent yon Norman after his comrade."

"And rid the world of a worthless fellow," said the friar; "but ne'er mind, John, there are plenty Normans left to practise thine hand upon."

"Did'st thou not feel the anger at thine heart?" queried Little John, "when yon dead Norman defiled our Marian's name?"

"Aye man, that did I," replied the friar; "and had not Robin dealt with the fellow after his deserts, I would."

"Thou art Saxon to the backbone," said Little John, giving the friar's shoulder a friendly grip; "but we'll e'en eschew such doleful converse, and betake ourselves to the larder."

"Art dry, then, John?" asked the friar, with a sly glance at his companion.

"Art thou?" retorted Little John. "Body-o'-me! thy throat is like parched soil, always gaping for moisture."

"Ha! Ha!" laughed Friar Tuck. "Thou art becoming sententious, little man. But to own to thee the truth, I am hugeous dry."

Fortunately for the pair of thirsty souls, they found ample means for satisfying their craving, for the cellarer, who always stood their friend, did not deny their request on this occasion.

Robin, who with commendable craftiness always sought to efface from the minds of his men aught of a disagreeable nature, held a merry banquet on the evening of this eventful day.

"What hast thou done with thy fawn?" asked the friar of Marian as they sat at dinner; "'twill claim thy attention for some time to come, I wot."

"'Tis doing well," answered Marian smilingly; "and what thinkest thou I've named it?"

"Why, Friar Tuck, of course," replied the friar jocularly.

"St. Hubert forbid it!" said Little John, who overheard the conversation, "else would it turn out a ne'er-do-well like thyself."

"Thou slanderer!" retorted the friar; "but what hast thou named it, Marian? I burn to know."

"Madge! Dost thou not like my choice?"

"I do, if the friar does'nt," replied Robin; "'tis an honoured name in my memory, and shall so continue."

"Thou could'st not have pleasured me better," said the friar. "St. Hubert! but Madge is indeed a bonny and true wench."

"I crave thy pardon," said Will Scarlet, speaking from the other end of the board; "but Good-for-Naught Dick has offered a song; has he thy permission to troll it?"

"Aye, that he has," replied Robin, readily; "'twill be of a good sort too, I trow."

"'Tis about a maiden and her lover, and I hope 'twill pleasure thee all."

THE WOODMAN'S BRIDE.

"There dwelt in the forest in lonely cot,
Rogers the woodman, of humble lot.
He toiled night and day, and his axe he well plied;
He was truthful, honest, and unto none lied.

"Many nobles and gallants rode by his way,
For the road to the hunt by his cottage did lay,
And glances of love came from gallant and knight,
For Mabel his daughter so comely and bright.

"But she only said, 'such are not for me,
Keep thine for ladies of high degree.
Simple maiden am I, and withal so poor,
It never can be that thou'll prove a true wooer.'

"One day Leicester's Earl the cottage rode past,
At the door stood Mabel, and a glance he cast
At her as she stood, and deemed her most fair,
On his heart her image he from that day did bear.

"Leicester's Earl at his castle was not to be found,
They sought him afar, they sought him around;
No trace of him could they anywhere find:
His retainers were sad, for to them he was kind.

"A poor man one day came to Rogers' cot,
To ask him for work, so poor was his lot;
He asked but his food, and wanted no wage,
And Rogers did with him quickly engage.

"His labour was hard, his food was but scant,
He'd to delve, and hew, and water, and plant;
Contented was he, nor shirked any task,
Nor of Rogers did he aught of wages ask.

"With Rogers he'd been near a year and a day,
When to him one day the young man did say:
'I love pretty Mabel, and her I would wed;'
'Thou may'st have her, and welcome,' Rogers, he said.

"They were wed right soon, Mabel and he,
And they left their abode his friends for to see.
The night had set in, it was very late,
When three knocks he gave at a castle gate.

"The seneschal ope'd it with eager hand,
Asked them their business, told them to stand;
He whispered a word; the seneschal bowed,
Stood quickly aside, and their entrance allowed.

"Cried Mabel in haste, 'Whose castle is this?'
He quickly replied, ''Tis Earl Leicester's I wis,
My friends are within, and will give us good cheer,
'Tis late or ere this they would quickly appear.'

"'The earl is so great and we are so poor,
Quickly he'll send us away from his door;
In such a grand place we have not a right,
Let us leave it at once and go out in the night.'

"Mabel thus spake, but he soothed her fears,
Bade her cheer up and dry up her tears,
'There is none in this castle, I unto thee vow,
So welcome to Liecester, sweet Mabel, as thou.'

"The morrow it came, the sun it shone bright,
And gilded all things with a glorious light;
And Mabel sat wondering within stately hall,
Waiting and listening for his loved call.

"'The earl waits thee, lady,' a servitor said,
And with humble gait the way he soon led,
To where were assembled a fair company,
From whose presence Mabel was minded to flee.

"'Look up, sweet Mabel,' the earl quickly said,
'Be not downcast, but hold up thy head,
'Tis I, thy husband, that speaks unto thee,
Dearer than all things thou art unto me.'

"In fond embrace to his heart he did press,
    Sweet Mabel, and her he did gently caress;
    Said to all, 'Behold a true loving wife,
    Guard her as thou would'st guard thine own life.'

"They lived happily for many a year,
    Children she bore him, them he loved dear.
    And many grand folks to the castle hied,
    To see sweet Mabel, the *Woodman's Bride.*"

Vociferous applause greeted Dick on the ending of his song.

"Thou art a good one, Dick," shouted the friar, "beshrew me but thou art, and I pledge thee heartily in red wine."

"Here's to thee, friar," cried Dick in return. "I am well content that my lot is so pleasantly cast. Good fortune and prosperity to all."

"Here's to thee, Dick," cried first one and then the other, until he was loudly acclaimed and toasted by the assembled outlaws.

"What think'st thou of the King, Dick?" asked Robin, when the noise of tongues had abated, "thou hast had speech of him I trow?"

"He hath my liking exceedingly," Dick replied, "he is of rare hot blood though, and would as lief knock one down for a wrong look, as he would laugh at a pleasant saying."

"'Tis said he is a good archer," remarked Little John, "and can bring down his game readily."

"He is all that," Dick answered, "and he's withal a rare one for a good carousal."

"That's a Saxon trait anyhow," said Robin, with a laugh; "but hast naught to tell of the King's doings, Dick?"

"That have I, and if thou carest to hear them I will presently discourse thereof," was Dick's ready response.

"Do so, and earn our thanks," said Robin, "and we will all observe strict attention thereto."

"Thou must know then," said Dick, "that it was just after my joining the King's foresters that I happened to be on guard.

"Watchful was I of the least sound lest any evil-minded body should slay the King's deer."

Dick accompanied this declaration with a significant grin, which set his auditors laughing uproariously.

"Thou art otherwise minded now, Dick," said the friar.

"Surely, surely," replied Dick, with a laugh, "but as I was telling, I kept watchful guard, and presently I espied a fellow, dressed as a comfortable yeoman, approaching.

"'Thy business here? answer quickly, fellow,' I said.

"He gave a contemptuous guffaw in reply, and otherwise heeded not my challenge.

"Presently espying a deer, he up with bow and, with true aim, brought it down.

"My blood fairly boiled at this, and I quickly arrested him in the King's name.

"'I heed not thy behests, or the King's either,' he saucily replied; 'I will shoot at my pleasure for aught thou can'st say or do.'

"'Thou knave, thou had'st better bridle thy malapert tongue,' I angrily replied; 'else will I baste thine hide for thee.'

"'Take that for thy pains,' he answered, as he dealt me a staggering blow, 'thou can'st have more of them if thou art so minded.'

"'That's for thee in ready return,' I cried, catching him a good stroke with my fist; 'how lik'st thou that, thou poaching knave.'

"'Have at thee,' he cried, and at it we went surely.

"We dealt each other buffets not a few, and oft wrestled, but neither gained the vantage of the other.

"'Thou wilt have to come to the guard,' I cried; 'so thou had'st better do so at once.'

"'I trow we have had enow,' he said at last, and thou art a rare good fellow; would that the King had more of thy sort, then would his deer prosper in security.'

"'Thou speakest glibly of the King,' I replied, in great dudgeon, for I was greatly angered by his swaggering gait and talk; 'prithee who art thou?'

"'Ha, ha!' laughed the stranger; 'my name is Hal, and I'm pretty well known in these parts.'

"'Specially for a roystering, poaching thief, no doubt,' I replied; 'but if thou wert the King himself thou must come with me, or else I will take thee per force.'

"Thou should'st have heard him laugh. Heartier chuckling I never heard.

"'I will give thee money,' he said, 'so that thou heed not my doings. None will know of the matter, and more shalt thou have from time to time. What say'st thou?'

"He had barely finished speech when one of my comrades approached."

"'Come hither, Wharton!' I shouted. 'This fellow has been slaying the King's deer, and opposing my authority.'

"To my surprise, Wharton doffed his bonnet and made low obeisance; but the stranger by a gesture restrained his utterance.

"'Hast thou aught worth eating in thy cottage, Wharton?' the stranger familiarly asked.

"'Venison steaks and oaten cakes are at thy service.'

"''Twill do fine. Let us be jogging, man; and thou wilt accompany us, wilt not?' he said, turning to me.

"'Is it all right?' I asked of Wharton.

"'Yes, man,' he testily replied; 'do thou mind thy speech I pray thee.'

"'Nay, nay, Wharton, chide him not,' said the stranger; 'he is a rare good boxer, and an honest man to boot. But let us trot, for I tell thee my stomach is rebelling against its long abstinence.'

"'Surely he did not lay hand on thee,' said Wharton in deprecatory tones.

"'That did he, and I on him. By the Rood! I have not had such boxing for many a day; 'twas give and take and no surrender, as I can avouch.'

"The thoughts of the fray seemed to afford him much merriment, for he chuckled gleefully over them."

"I began to suspicion that he was some notable or other; but I feared not for my conduct, being well assured by my conscience that I had acted right.

"The repast was served, and Wharton brought out some good wine; but he sat not down, and by sign forbade my doing so.

"'Tut, tut, man,' said the stranger, 'seat thyselves and fall to; but first let's say a word of grace as becometh Christians.'

"'Twas the merriest meal I ever had. Quip

and joke and such like came from the stranger's lip ; and when the wine cup had gone a round or two, he began to get right merry, and sang a song which so pleased me, that I got it by heart quite readily, both words and tune."

"Can'st sing it us, now ?" asked Robin.

"Aye can I.　'Tis on this wise."

And Dick trolled out this quaint ditty:

> "Everman,
> 　If he can
> 　　Through life,
> 　　　Takes a wife.
> Or, grows rich,
> 　After which
> He gets fat;
> Failing that,
> He keeps lean,
> 　I well ween.
>
> "All like wine,
> 　When they dine;
> Friends do greet,
> 　When they meet.
> Man is wise,
> 　When he tries
> To be glad,
> Instead of sad ;
> Or to wait
> Upon fate.
>
> "Now my song,
> 　Is not long ;
> But my speech,
> 　It does teach
> Wisdom, laws,
> Just because
> Men should learn
> To them to turn ;
> Or let them be,
> 　Don't you see."

Dick was highly applauded for his song, which greatly pleased the company.

"'Where think you, I first heard that song?' the stranger asked.

"'Why 'tis the favourite song of the court fool, and his own conceit entirely.　'Egad 'tis so sensible in its leanings that it looks elsewhere for fathering than to him.'

"Shortly came several gallants to the cottage, seeking, whom do you think ?

"Why, the King himself, and, may I be addled quite, if the roystering stranger was not he.

"'Tis easy to conceive of my plight thereupon.　I bowed the knee before him, and sought forgiveness for my more than rudeness of speech and action.

"'Rise, good fellow,' he said ; 'thou hast done thy duty well, and I, thy King, will not forget thee.　Here are several crowns, thou can'st take them now without jeopardising thine honesty.

"Turning to Wharton, he said, ' see that thou carest for him well, for such as he are not easily gotten.'

"When the King had departed, I stood like as one in a dream, so strange did the whole matter appear.

"'Ere long I was promoted, and the King thenceforward held me in high esteem.　Such comrades is my story."

"And a right good one 'tis too," said Robin ; "would that the King listened not to evil counsellors, but to those who would defend him and give the land peace and prosperity."

"He oft spake of thee," said Dick, "to the intent that thou would'st forsake the forest and take service with him, both thou and thy merry men."

"It may not be so," said Robin moodily ; "years of oppression are not quickly forgot. No, no, the forest for me where as true Saxon I can withstand all tyrants.　What says't thou comrades all ?"

A ringing cheer came responsive to this appeal, and was prolonged and taken up by the forest in echoing waves, both far and near.

"If the king likes to come here," observed the friar with sly looks, "he can have some of our deer and wine, and pay for his reckoning too like a man."

"He is welcome to come," said Robin, "but I trow he will not trust himself near us. He would as lief thrust his hand into a hornet's nest first."

"Our stings are sharp without doubt," said Little John, "but sharpest of all are they for Norman dogs."

"Right, John," exclaimed Robin approvingly, "but as 'tis late we will e'en retire.　A happy night to you, comrades all."

Ere long the place was locked in slumbering silence, unbroken save by the tread and challenge of the watchful sentinels.

CHAPTER LXIII.

HOW ROBIN HOOD DANCED ON THE GREENSWARD WITH A LADY OF HIGH DEGREE.

> "Art thou Robin Hood ?" asked the lady ;
> "At thy service, Madam," Robin quoth he :
> Then both on the greensward did merrily dance,
> While the lady's retainers eyed them askance.

EARLY on the morrow the pealing notes of a bugle-horn summoned the outlaws to alertness.

"'Twas from the right they came ?" asked Robin.

"Yes, master," answered Little John, "and hark ! there they are again."

"Do thou take a detachment, John, and quickly proceed thence, and let one speed back with news of what has happened."

So saying, Robin busied himself in getting into form, for he liked not to go out anywhere in slovenly guise.

"Little John bid me tell thee, master," said a panting messenger, "that a dame of high degree, attended by armed servitors, has strayed hitherward ; and he desires thy immediate presence."

"Named she her name or lineage ?" asked Robin as he shook back his curly hair and donned his bonnet with care.

"John did not instruct me thereupon, nor did I hear the dame say aught of such a matter myself."

"Friar ! where are thou, friar ?" shouted Robin, "thy presence must not be wanting on this occasion.　And thou, Marian, wilt advise with our cellarer to prepare fitting reception for our high-born visitor."

"Thou shalt find everything as thou would'st have it, on thy return," Marian replied ; "and I fear not but that she will receive gentle and kind treatment at thy hands, Robin darling."

"Trust me, Marian," replied Robin, bestowing upon her an affectionate kiss; "but where tarries that laggard friar? What ho! Friar Tuck!"

"Here I am, master," shouted that personage, as he ran forward with hot haste, wiping his mouth with the back of his huge fist. "What is rife? Naught of evil, I hope?"

"Some high-born dame awaits our coming," Robin answered. "Do thou bring thy musical pipe with thee; egad we'll have some divertment this fine morning."

"A dame of high degree, say'st thou?" queried the friar. "St. Hubert! 'tis more grist to the mill, and will replenish our treasury, and pay for my piping."

"Out upon thee for a grasping wretch!" said Robin laughingly. "Thou would'st not put imposition upon such as her?"

"She is not alone, I wot," replied the friar with a grin, "and let them pay for her, or her for them."

"Forward!" cried Robin to his party; "thou can'st move on more leisurely, else wilt thou have no wind wherewithal to pipe."

Robin was met by Will Scarlet ere he arrived at the spot where his unexpected visitor was to be met.

"How go matters, Will?" Robin asked.

"Well; at first, blows seemed imminent," Will replied, "and would have been stricken too but for the dame."

"The varlets!" exclaimed Robin; "but 'tis well they abstained therefrom, else would they have fittingly suffered for their rash presumption. But of the dame, Will; is she comely?"

"Aye, that she is," answered Will, "eye hath seldom rested on one more comely than her."

"And how taketh she the matter," asked Robin, "in good part I hope."

"Even so," Will replied, "and already she hath struck up an acquaintance with John."

"'Tis well, answered Robin. "for I care not to have dealings with your high spirited dames who treat all not her equal with discourtesy."

Doffing his bonnet in gallant style, Robin, with polished manner, advanced, saying to her—

"Thou art welcome, dame, to the outlaw's domains. Never a thought had I that morning would bring with it such honour for Robin Hood."

"Art thou Robin Hood?" she asked in surprised tones, as she critically surveyed him from head to foot, apparently well satisfied with his appearance.

"At thy service, madam," replied Robin, bowing ceremoniously. "Art journeying far, lady?"

"To the King's court," she replied with gracious manner. "But thou hast a goodly company with thee, Robin Hood. They are thy merry men, I trow."

"Even so, lady," answered Robin, "and loyal and true-hearted each one is."

"I am already acquaint with thy lieutenant, Little John," she observed with a pleasant smile, "but for him my varlets had come to danger I ween."

"There is no need for such thing," replied Robin. "Thou wilt not have cause to regret thy visit to Sherwood, lady, thou hast Robin Hood's word for that."

"Thanks," she replied; then turning to one who was evidently the leader of her armed party, she said, haughtily:—

"Hear'st that, Faulkner. So fash not thyself further, but observe courtesy in return in thy deportment towards these people."

"Rightly put, sweetheart," said one who came forward with easy familiarity of manner, and whose cap and bells betokened his avocation to be that of a fool or jester.

"Cease thy prating, thou jackanapes," said the dame, admonishingly, "thy speech is not required in this matter, sirrah."

"I never hear a good thing said, sweetheart," he replied, "but that I am forthwith constrained to acknowledge it. 'Tis so seldom aught of the kind occurs that it is doubly welcome when it does come."

"'Tis a shrewd speech that," observed Little John, "and betokens wisdom on thy part."

"What! Jasper wise! what an odd conceit!" exclaimed the dame merrily, "not an atom of sense has he in those mischievous brains of his; he is a mass of impertinence from head to foot."

The object of this remark made no reply thereto, for his attention was diverted to the friar, who was seated on the stump of a tree pipe in hand.

"Hilloa, cousin mine, great of flesh," Jasper exclaimed in rollicking tones, "thou lookest on thy perch as wise as an owl; and what hast thou there? egad 'tis a pipe brimful of merry music."

Then turning to his mistress he said with a mirthful leer:—

"What say'st thou, sweetheart, to a dance; yonder minstrel of cassock and cowl will play fitting music."

Hereupon Jasper threw himself into ludicrous attitude, which forced a burst of merry laughter from the assembled outlaws.

On a motion from Robin the friar commenced piping a measured tune with no ordinary skill, his fat cheeks being puffed out to a great extent by his efforts.

"I claim the honour of thy hand for the dance," said Robin, gallantly dropping on his knee, "thou wilt not refuse me, lady?"

"Rise up, fellow," said Faulkner angrily, "thou art forgetful of thy base condition, and need salutary reminder thereon."

"Peace, Faulkner," the dame exclaimed with dignified look and gesture; "thou exceedest all bounds, and need thyself to be reminded of thy lack of prudence."

"Nay, heed him not, lady," said Robin, bestowing a half angry half contemptuous glance upon the officious Faulkner, "'tis ever so with little minds to display a semblance of power, which they possess not a shadow of."

"How likest thou that truth, bully Faulkner?" asked the fool; "but 'tis no use for thy edification I trow, for thy skin is as tough as any well-tanned cowhide."

"Here is my hand, Sir Outlaw," said the dame, as she gave her right hand to Robin, with gracious smile, and cast at Faulkner a defiant glance; "'tis long since I had a dance on the forest green."

"Thou art as gracious as comely," replied Robin, as he gallantly led her forth to the dance amid the plaudits of the assembled company.

"Saw'st thou ever such lithe movements?" asked Little John of Much the Miller's son. "Art not well pleased with our master?"

"As I ever am," was the response; "and the dame, too, doth her part right well. But saw'st thou ever such grim faces as yon Normans wear?"

"St. Hubert be thanked they are not near our cellar!" answered Little John, "else would they surely turn wine sour. Ugh!"

"And markest thou the friar, John?" said Much.

"Body-o'-me!" said John with a grin; "his presence must needs be conspicuous; saw'st thou ever such cheeks?"

Here Little John caught the friar's eye and made such a droll grimace that it well nigh brought the music to a premature ending.

As it was, the instrument gave forth a series of sounds, altogether dissonant with the term musical, caused by the player's attempt to gulp down a strong inclination to indulge in a fit of irrepressible laughter.

"Thanks, fair lady," said Robin, as the dance ended; "thy condescension is only equalled by thy grace and beauty."

"'Tis an enjoyment I little calculated upon, Sir Outlaw, on entering this grand old forest," she replied; "it will dwell in my memory, and the recollection thereof will oft pleasure me."

"Thou wilt surely stay and partake of a refection?" queried Robin; "'tis but a step to our forest home, where all things are in readiness for thy coming."

"I accept thy gracious invitation," she replied, "and will be glad to partake of thy hospitality for myself and attendants. Lead on, Sir Outlaw."

"Nay, my lady," said Faulkner, deprecatingly, "think of the scandal attendant thereon. My lord will be angered thereat beyond measure."

"Tut, tut, cousin Faulkner," rejoined the fool, ere her ladyship could frame fitting answer; "be not so squeamish or high stomached."

And turning to Robin with an air of imperturbable gravity, he continued:—

"Lead on, thou green-jerkined, comely, honourable outlaw, of renown incomparable, dignity unspeakable, honesty irreproachable, and good cheer, come-forth-able. It pleasures me to honour the banquet by my august presence."

"Peace, knave," said the lady with a merry laugh irradiating her comely features, "and do thou, Faulkner" (this with severer mien) "obey my mandate without demurring thereat."

Raising his bonnet on high, and with uplifted voice, Robin said:—

"Three real Saxon cheers, my merry men all, for our gracious and comely lady."

Simultaneously, because fugled by Little John, came hearty cheers responsive to Robin's call.

Hardly had the echoes of the last cheer gone rolling forth along the forest when Little John with stentorian voice, shouted:—

"Three more for our master, Robin Hood."

Then burst forth such rounds of cheers as were scarcely ever heard before in Sherwood's forest.

"And now," said Robin, as he gallantly offered his arm to the dame, "with thy permission, lady, we'll go forward."

She linked her arm in his, and the outlaws formed a guard of honour.

Ere they moved on an outburst of merriment was elicited from all present by the fool's speech to the friar:—

"Knight of the pipe and rounded cheeks, deign to accept my arm in honour of thine incomparable and dulcet strains. Lead on, sweetheart and cousin, thy faithful and round-paunched master attends thee."

"Out upon thee, knave!" said the friar, aiming a blow at the fool's head, which, had he not evaded it, would have left a sore place thereon for many a day; "jingle thy bells for others."

"Marry come up," he replied, "thou art an irascible man of peace; thou requirest lowering."

Before the friar was aware of what was coming, the fool, by agile movement, got cleverly between his legs and gave him as clean an upset as ever he had experienced.

"St. Hubert!" exclaimed the discomfited friar, "'tis unwise I've oft heard to meddle with fools, and now I find its truth."

He cast a threatening glance at Jasper, who with comical grimace peeped at him from behind a secure retreat.

When the temporary disorder caused by this amusing incident was ended, the procession proceeded onward.

Thanks to Marian's superintending exertions everything was ready for the dame's reception.

"'Tis Maid Marian I guess, she said," gazing at our heroine admiringly.

"Thou art right in thy conjecture, lady?" said Robin, as he led Marian forward, who retained her self-possession admirably, "permit her presentment."

"'Tis accepted," replied the dame, as she presented her hand to Marian: "dost like thy forest life, Marian?"

"Freedom and liberty hath ever strong charms for me lady," replied Marian, animatedly; "and I love the free forest breezes."

"As well thou might," the dame replied, seeing that it brings the bloom of health to thy cheeks."

"And happiness and joy to my heart," responded Marian; "but wilt thou not be seated, lady? I will attend thee, seeing thou lackest thy maid's attendance."

"Thanks, Marian!" exclaimed the lady, with a courteous inclination of her stately head; "but I would rather that thou seated thyself at my side."

"Permit me lady," said Robin, "to conduct thee to thy seat; the time passeth and thou art fasting."

"Pardon my curiosity," said the dame in low tones, as Robin led her forward; "but hast thou not with thee one named Earl of Mortimer?"

Robin hesitated ere answering.

"Nay, have no fear, Sir Outlaw," she said apprehensively. "I seek not thy confidence with harmful intent."

"I mistrust thee not," said Robin, pressing her hand assuringly; "but I wotted not that

Mortimer was known to thee, and thereat pondered in thoughtful mood ere answering."

"'Tis well to be cautious," she answered; "but thou can'st trust me, as I know of one who highly esteems Mortimer, and is anxious respecting his welfare."

"Mortimer has gone," Robin said, speaking whisperingly, "to spy out his private affairs, and will be away for some little time. Doubtless *her* you mention will see him; he so intended, for his speech to me betrayed as much ere he departed."

"Thanks, good Robin," she replied with affable familiarity.

Seeing that they were watched by the lynx-eyed Faulkner, they talked no longer in low tones.

Obeying a sign from Robin, Little John, the Friar, Will Scarlet, and several others of the most prominent members of the band contrived to put themselves between Faulkner and the lady at the repast.

She gave Robin a grateful look for this.

As for Jasper, the fool, he gave the friar as wide a berth as possible, and got him into a secure place at the festive board, where he kept his auditors in a state of extreme merriment.

"I can bear a good report of thee to the court, Sir Outlaw," said the dame; "for naught of evil have I seen in thy company, or in thee."

"Thanks, lady," said Robin; "evil repute are we held in, but lovers of our country are we; true Saxons, who scorn to truckle to oppression or tyranny in whatsoever guise it presents itself."

"But our King oppresseth thee not willingly," she answered gently; "he is too well inclined for aught of that."

"We can all, with one accord, and loyally, too, shout 'God save the King!'" Robin fervidly exclaimed.

"Aye, that can we," said Little John uprising; "comrades, honour my toast as true Saxons—'God save the King!'"

Uprose they all, as one man, and with common and well-timed accord, gave forth the loyal wish, "God save the King!"

"But down with Norman tyranny and oppression!" shouted the irrepressible friar.

This inflammatory sentiment acted like fire among stubble.

With uplifted hands the outlaws vigorously acclaimed it, and then ran from lip to lip imprecations and direful mutterings indicative of their detestation and abhorrence of Norman tyranny and oppression.

"Fear not, lady," said Robin as he perceived signs of alarm in her looks, "'tis but an irrepressible outburst of honest manly Saxon feeling that thou hearkenest to. Let tyrants beware of such."

A sign from Robin checked any further ebullition of feeling or temper on the part of the outlaws, and soon the storm subsided into a calm.

Willing to efface from her mind the recollection of what has just transpired, Robin said:

"Would'st thou see our skill in archery lady. Thou hast but to name the wish and soon shall it be gratified."

"Thanks, Sir Outlaw," she answered; "I would witness thy wide-known skill in archery, but first I pray thee let me hear woodman's song."

"Surely, lady, it shall be as thou prayest," answered Robin; "Little John do thou give us of thy best, something in short to gladden the heart and move the fancy."

"Body-o'-me!" responded Little John, "would that thou had'st sought elsewhere for one more fitting than myself for such task, but as thou hast selected me in preference I will e'en do my best."

"Little John's song!" went from mouth to mouth, and soon ensued a strict silence.

"My song," he said, "is called."

THE OWL AND THE MONK.

"List to me, comrades, and I'll tell unto thee,
  Concerning a matter, which in North Countree
  Did happen, as now I will quickly disclose;
  To listen thereto, thyselves straightway dispose.

"There dwelt near an abbey of famed sanctity,
  An owl of rare parts, thus 'twas told unto me,
  That nightly did hoot and disturb the monks' rest,
  And with care and vexation their breasts sore
    opprest."

"His hoot-hoot-hoot did sound in their ears,
  It moved them to wrath. it moved them to tears,
  It preyed on their health, it made them quite lean,
  Did the hoot of this owl, 'twas plain to be seen.

"Said a staid old monk, with shaven crown,
  'This matter is getting the talk of the town,
  And unless we prevent it our credit is gone;'
  At which all his brethren looked very forlorn.

"'Let us all assemble at dead of night,
  And with book and bell and holy rite,
  Curse this owl, lay his dismal hoot,
  And this monstrous scandal quite uproot.'

"Having thus said, this staid old monk,
  Whose brethren all were in a deuce of a funk,
  Held his tongue, clasped his hands, and with looks
    so meek
  Awaited to hear some one else speak.

"From the abbot and downwards they all approved
  What the staid old monk had already moved;
  And in virtue thereof they all looked glad,
  And vowed that this owl in a fix was had.

"The night came in, and the monks moved out,
  With candle and bell they circled about,
  And cursed this owl from head to foot,
  But he followed them close with his dismal hoot.

"They retired to their cells in pitiful case,
  Each looking sad, and with very long face;
  While the hoot of the owl became louder still,
  And in echoing waves the abbey did fill.

"The morning came round and the abbot did call,
  A meeting august of both great and small,
  And declared that they the abbey must leave;
  At which they all did very much grieve.

"Then up spake a monk, and said on this wise,
  While his fellows were wailing and giving forth
    sighs,
  'We have cursed this owl, his power to defy,
  Let now each one begin for himself to try

"'To banish this pest and free our abbey,
  That here we may live, that all men may see
  Our wrath is effective and much to be feared;
  For by wicked devices we're not to be skeared.'

"The monk's wise speech was loudly acclaimed,
  And forthwith resolves were speedily framed;
  Each thought he knew the very best way
  To vanquish this owl that self-same day.

" The abbot scourged himself till the blood
    Ran down his back just like a flood,
    And with grins not a few put on a hair shirt,
    And in various ways sought his body to hurt.

" Some drank ditch water and went without food,
    Their feet cut with flints, and in penitent mood,
    Walked on their knees and abjured their toes,
    And at all earthly things turned up their nose.

" But the monk who had given such good advice,
    Took a sensible plan, as I'll show in a trice ;
    He whipped not himself, but bided his time,
    For his faith was great in the power of bird-lime.

" He knew the spot which the owl did frequent,
    And thither with hasty footstep he went,
    To place the birdlime all about the spot ;
    And in safe hiding place he him quickly got.

" Hoot-hoot-hoot ; ah ! the owl's stuck fast ;
    Said the monk in glee, ' I have caught you at last !
    And birdlime is better than book, bell, or rite ;
    No more shalt thou hoot us to affright.'

" To the abbey he brought this owl so great,
    And forthwith he went on the abbot to wait ;
    But no abbot found he when he got to his cell,
    For the hoot of the owl proved the abbot's death-
        knell.

" And beside, there died of the monks not a few,
    For the owl had scared and put them in a stew—
    So greatly they feared this terrible owl,
    Who cared not for abbot nor priestly cowl.

" Now the sensible monk became abbot next day,
    And for his welfare the monks all did pray ;
    But he told them not how he'd managed the job,
    Lest him of his abbot's dignity they'd rob.

" But this did he, as an emblem of faith,
    He had an owl's phiz cut over the gate ;
    Thus he got to himself most high renown,
    And for many a year wore the abbot's crown."

" Thou hast well sung," said the lady, when Little John's humorous song was ended ; " and as a token of my approbation I give to thee this dagger."

" Thanks, lady," Little John replied with delighted mien ; "'tis too costly a gift for such a poor song."

" St. Hubert !" exclaimed the friar admiringly, " thou art in luck, John. See, 'tis all of silver, and hath a precious jewel in its handle."

It passed from hand to hand, and was greatly admired.

" I will now, if it pleaseth thee," said the dame, " witness thy shooting. I have longed for such a sight, having heard much of thy fame."

" Thou shalt quickly be pleasured in this matter, lady," Robin replied, uprising and waving his hand for his followers to form. " Wilt thou deign to accept of my guidance to the butts ?"

" Right willingly, Sir Outlaw," she replied smilingly, " and thou, Marian, wilt accompany us, surely."

" Of a surety," Marian quickly replied ; " for I love such sights, and were I a man would be a gallant archer above all things."

" Well said, Marian !" exclaimed Robin, approvingly ; " I love to hear thee so speak, as doth also my merry men all."

" Marian for ever !" shouted the friar excitedly ; " may she be the mother of mighty men !"

There came cheers and laughter from the assembled company at the friar's speech, and Marian herself smiled and blushed deeply.

Soon commenced a bout at archery, and each of Sherwood's merry foresters did himself exert thereat.

" I would hold a tourney with thee, Marian," said the lady playfully ; " not that I expect aught but defeat at thy hands."

" I trow thou wilt prove victor," replied Marian ; " but I am nevertheless content to put my scant skill against thine."

" Gallantly spoken both," said Robin ; " and ne'er before have such contest been witnessed in Sherwood forest."

He bade his men to cease firing, and leave a clear arena for the fair competitors in this novel archery contest.

" Choose thou thy bow, lady," said Robin, as he gave her a choice of several ; " and thou wilt find in this quiver arrows of good quality and true make."

" I choose this," she exclaimed gaily ; " and now, fair Marian, I challenge thee, not to mortal combat, but to a fair competition of archery."

" And I do straightway accept the same," exclaimed Marian gleefully ; " Our Lady send me victory !"

" Body-o-me !" said little John, as the dame's arrow struck within the smallest circle of the target ; " 'tis right well aimed."

Marian now took her stand.

Her fine form and full and beautiful bust showed to great advantage in her closely-fitting vest of Lincoln-green.

Her stand might have given heaven-born inspiration, almost, to a sculptor, so full of grace and beauty was it, and withal so natual.

" Well shot, Marian !" exclaimed Robin, as her arrow clave the bull's-eye in splendid style.

" Mercy !" exclaimed the dame, in well-affected tones of astonishment ; " 'tis useless my shooting further, when thou dost put forth such skill at the outset ; but I will e'en try and better my last for love of my own fame in archery."

" St. Hubert ! 'tis well executed," said the friar rapturously as the dame's arrow struck within a space but slightly distant from Marian's.

In fact so near together did they appear that it was difficult to state their exact position unless by going close to them.

Running forward, Robin viewed the arrows carefully, and returned, saying with significant emphasis :

" Room is there, and barely that, for an arrow to pass between the twain. Our Lady ! but 'tis a shot I much covet to make to get me honour in its success.

" Nay," exclaimed the dame playfully, " 'tis betwixt Marian and I, and we must not have a go-between in the matter."

" I am with thee, lady, in what thou say'st," observed Marian ; " 'twill soon appear whether we are not worthy of gaining such honour."

" Bravo, Marian !" exclaimed Robin admiringly, and the assembled company likewise acclaimed her pert speech.

ROBIN HOOD,

AND THE OUTLAWS OF SHERWOOD FOREST.

THE DUCHESS OF LANCASTER AND ROBIN HOOD.

There was a deep silence as Marian drew her bow to its full bent and launched forth her arrow. Cheers rent the air, for so truly aimed was it, that it lodged itself between the other two arrows without disturbing either in the slightest degree.

"Thou art fairly beaten, sweet coz, "observed

Jasper the Fool. 'Twere fitter for thee to have sought my skilful help in thine extremity."

"Thou hast a cup and balls," observed the lady drily.

"Which are thine from henceforth, coz," he answered saucily, "since thou did'st put thv skill against forest maiden. But I wager any one here that I dislodge all their arrows at a venture."

A general laugh followed the fool's sally.

"Thou dislodge them?" said Little John contemptuously.

"Ay, little one," answered Jasper, "wilt wager me?"

"A crown piece will I," replied Little John, ready to humour him. "Here, take this bow, and shoot."

"'Tis a wager, mind thee, as all hearest," rejoined the fool.

"Surely, surely," answered a dozen or more voices almost simultaneously, amid great laughter.

"Shoot, man, shoot," said Little John impatiently. "Art thou fearful of thy crown?"

"I offered not to shoot," answered Jasper with a knowing leer at the company. "All are witness that I did not."

"Body-o'-me! how else wilt thou do it, then?" growled Little John, who little relished the idea of being outwitted by the fool.

"On this wise," replied Jasper, as he took to his heels and ran swiftly in the direction of the target, followed by peals of laughter.

Little John looked on in amazement for a minute or so, and then made an attempt to pursue after him.

"Go not, John," said Robin as he restrained his advance. "There will be good merriment presently."

As Jasper reached the target and with a blow dislodged the arrows, Robin Hood raised his bow and with sure aim pinned one of his lappels to the target with an arrow.

Having won his wager, Jasper sought to retreat, but to his surprise could not.

Shouts of derisive laughter met each futile attempt, and so exasperated him that tugging more violently than before he brought the target down on top of him.

He sprawled and sprawled, and bawled for help, but for a time none put forth a helping hand.

"What of thy wager, sirrah," asked the dame. "Thou art a fine archer surely."

"Naught would content him but to bear away the target as a prize," observed the friar with a merry laugh, and greatly enjoying the fool's predicament.

"Help, sweet mistress," said Jasper imploringly, "and I'll ne'er offend thee any more."

"Release him," she said, "but as for thy promised amendment I rely not on it. 'Tis as often broken as made."

"Here is thy crown piece," said Little John good-humouredly to the discomfited Jasper; "thou deservest it and another to boot for the divertment thou hast made."

"Catch me playing at archery again," said Jasper, with a rueful visage.

"Thou had'st better take back thy cap and bells," said his mistress. "Thou hast fairly earned them this bout."

"Thou art right, sweetheart," he replied; "and I'll wear them henceforth with better grace, knowing full well that I am the rightful owner."

"Well put, Jasper," observed the friar; "and thou shalt not lack a draught of good wine to wash down thy discomfiture."

"The day advances, lady," said Faulkner gravely, "and 'tis time we went our way."

"Nay, be not so impatient man," replied the dame, "I would that thou and thy men display thy skill ere I depart. Pleasure me in this much."

"Ay, do so," observed the friar, "for we would fain see thy Norman expertness."

"'Tis more than a match for Saxon impudence," answered Faulkner, turning sharply on the friar.

"May be, may be," answered the friar laconically; "'tis easy of proving though."

"How meanest thou," asked Faulkner with knitted brow; "think'st that I would exchange blows with such as thou. Thy priestly garb giveth thee license."

"Peace, Faulkner, I command thee," said the dame imperiously: "'tis not well to be so quarrelsome."

"Know'st thou not the old distich, lady?" asked the friar; "'tis this:

"When he could not get to fight with foes,
 He solaced himself by fighting his toes."

"Nay, lady," answered Faulkner with deference; "I did but uphold our honour."

"'Twas unassailed," she replied curtly; "he lacketh sense who umbrage takes at slight offence, and spends his wrath upon trifles."

A murmur of approval followed this rebuff, and the object of it looked rather crestfallen.

"We are ready, lady," said Robin, "for thy delectation and pleasurement to meet thy men in friendly contest. The day owneth many hours of sunshine yet."

"Hearest that, Faulkner?" asked the dame; "hast aught to say thereto?"

"We can throw a spear with here and there a one," he answered.

"I would fain try thy skill then," said Robin, smiling blandly; "take thou thy spear, and I'll meet thy throw with simple buckler."

"Perchance thou mean'st a headless spear," replied Faulkner contemptuously.

"Nay, but thy sharpest," said Robin; "art thou mindful to thus display thy skill."

"Nay, it must not be," said the dame; "thou riskest too much, sir outlaw."

"Nay, fear not for me, lady," said Robin; "I will bear myself harmless in this friendly fray."

"It will take a better than he to harm Robin," answered the friar to Little John; "'tis well to teach these Normans their true worth in Saxon estimation."

"Have a care, Robin," said Marian imploringly and in subdued accents; "thou know'st the price set upon thy death, and yon scowling fellow is a Norman."

"Tut, tut, Marian darling," replied Robin, as he laid his hand caressingly on her shoulder; "have no fear, I shall get me honour on this fellow, and that right quickly."

"Art ready?" exclaimed Robin, turning to Faulkner.

"Quite," was the laconic answer.

"Then I will stand here about, while thou takest thy station at fitting distance away."

"Have a care that thou injure him not, Faulkner," said the dame warningly.

Faulkner answered with a grim smile boding evil to Robin.

"Now throw," said Robin, standing in a defiant attitude, with head thrown back and watchful eye.

And throw Faulkner did with unerring aim and swiftly withal.

But Robin received it on his shield, amid the plaudits of the spectators.

Picking it up he threw it back to Faulkner with such true aim that it alighted at his feet, causing him to give a nervous start.

In vain Faulkner sought to over-reach him ; every throw was well warded, and Robin got to himself enthusiastic applause.

" Now," said Robin, turning gallantly to the dame, " I will with thy permit, sweet lady, display some spearmanship."

By his directions Little John made a white mark, of the circumference of a crown piece, on the trunk of a tree.

Arming himself with a hunting spear, Robin took his station at the tree, and after gazing fixedly at the mark, turned sharply with his back towards it, and ran swiftly forward to a distance of twenty or thirty yards.

Halting suddenly, he turned about swiftly and threw his spear.

It struck with marvellous accuracy the very centre of the white spot.

" St. Dunstan ! well aimed," rapturously exclaimed the dame. " Better spear-thrust have I never witnessed than that."

But Robin had not finished his exploits.

He placed a shield beneath the tree, whose branches came down rather low, and on its centre marked a white spot.

Stationing himself about thirty yards distant, he rushed forward with terrific speed, and when within a yard or more of the shield, delivered his spear thrust, and making an upward bound caught an overhanging bough, and quickly raised himself aloft.

The spear was stuck through the very centre of the mark, and its point protruded through the other side of the thick shield an inch or more.

The plaudits were deafening, and cheer upon cheer rent the air from lusty Saxon throats for their gallant leader Robin.

" 'Twas a strange but well-executed manœuvre," said the dame, " and thou deservest rare praise therefor."

" Nay, sweet lady, thou art too lavish in thy praise of so poor a feat," answered Robin, bowing. " I only once before practised the like, and then 'twas caused by death staring me in the face."

" How so ?" asked the dame. " I would greatly prefer to hear the matter, an' it take not too long narrating."

" I am at thy service, lady, in this as in all other matters," gallantly exclaimed Robin, " and if thou and the company will be seated awhile I will at once narrate it."

Seating themselves upon the greensward they straightway disposed themselves to listen to the story.

" 'Twas many years back," began Robin, " so many in fact that at the time I was but a puny stripling, that the following adventure overtook me.

" Ah ! how it saddens me to think of my state then and now !" exclaimed Robin, with a deep irrepressible sigh ; " but I must not heed such things, and will e'en proceed with my story."

Many a sympathising glance was cast upon Robin, and Marian nestled her head lovingly on his shoulder by way of eloquent though mute sympathy.

" 'Twas, as I said, many years ago that in a forest on my father's estate—may his soul be assoilzied by all the saints !—I wandered wantonly spear in hand eager for sport of any kind, no matter what so long as I gathered therefrom pleasurable excitement.

" I well remember 'twas a lovely summer day, and a delightful breeze fanned my cheeks and gave thereto a healthful glow, while my mind was filled with a deep joy, for naught of care knew I.

" Before long I roused a wild sow and her litter, and after them I went with mad haste, more bent on frolic than harmful intent.

" A long chase they led me, too, as I well remember, and I received not a few falls, but still I persisted, and at length got the lead of them.

" While I was considering whether to spear the sow or not, I heard a loud grunting noise behind me.

" On looking round, I espied an immense boar rushing towards me with furious and evil intent.

" With quick apprehension, I foresaw that to flee along the open glade would be extremely perilous, for the boar would overtake and rive me asunder ere I could get many paces away.

" My quick glance around showed me plainly that there was but one tree which offered me chance of safety.

" But it lay in a direct alignment with the boar's course.

" Quick as thought, I resolved upon my plan.

" Grasping my spear tightly, and bracing my nerves to their utmost tension, I rushed forward with lightning speed.

" I took not mine eye off the ravening beast, which seemed to divine my purpose, and exerted itself to gain the tree before me.

" I had neared sanctuary within a yard or so, and the boar was close advanced on me, when I lifted my spear, and with quick eye and true aim, struck at him.

" Pausing not to note the effect, I sprang upward, and grasped a friendly branch, and with strong arm raised myself to a place of safety.

" On looking down, I espied a welcome sight. There lay the boar transfixed to the earth by my spear.

" Desperation had nerved my arm, and, stripling though I was, lent to it superhuman strength.

" 'Twas the recollection of this that led me to repeat the manœuvre to day for thy pleasure, sweet lady."

" Thou had'st indeed a narrow escape," she replied, with an involuntary shudder, " 'twas a mercy thou did'st escape at all."

" Naught more vengeful is there in creation than a wild boar," observed Little John, " and I would e'en face two men in mortal combat than one such."

" They are noble game though," observed the friar, " and to kill one is an achievement as I can well avouch."

" I would sooner deal with such almost," said Will Scarlet, than with wolves—faugh, they are beasts indeed."

" That they are," quickly rejoined the

dame, "as I well know to my sorrowful cost. 'Twas with me as with thou, sir outlaw. I barely escaped with life."

"Nay, but thou wilt tell us about it, wilt thou not?" said Marian. "Our Lady, how thou must have been distraught with fear!"

"That was I, as thou may'st plainly conceive," she replied, "and the remembrance of that horrible event will haunt me to my grave."

"We are all attention for thy narration," observed Robin, "and eager to hear thy sweet voice."

"I will not detain thee long then," said the dame, with a silvery laugh, "thou hast such a honied tongue, sir outlaw, that one cannot find heart to refuse request of thine."

Looking towards Marian she said coquettishly "Thou art not jealous, I ween, Marian, art thou, for I am fain to steal away thy Robin's heart."

"Not I," exclaimed Marian, humouring the conceit; "Robin is too true to cost his Marian a jealous pang, art thou not, dearest?"

An equal glance replied to this trustful appeal, and Marian was satisfied.

"Well spoken, Marian!" exclaimed the lady; "thou art of my opinion, quite; for I trow that love, to be of worth, must be not guarded by jealous watchfulness."

"'Twas what I said to the steward for chiding me about my love of wine," exclaimed Jasper the fool, who was getting lively again after his recent sad discomfiture. "Marry come up," said I, "true love must not be watched, else will it spoil."

"Thou lovest wine, then," said the friar jocosely. "Egad, thou art not such a fool after all."

"Thou had'st better try me," replied Jasper with a grin; "and I can promise thee that if my wisdom increases in thy estimation according to the capacity of my gullet for wine bibbing, then I will be sworn to be the wisest man in the world: for it takes a hugeous drink to make me cry 'Hold, enough.'"

"I will have thee a bout at wine-bibbing," said the friar.

"Agreed, if thou wilt find the wine," replied the fool.

"Peace, both of you," said Robin, good humouredly, "whilst thou banterest we but lose our story."

"I am dumb, and thou art ditto, brother," said Jasper, turning to the friar, who with his arms akimbo, stood leaning against a tree in a listening attitude, as grave of mien as any judge.

"It is now some four years ago that I had occasion to travel to see a near relation who lay at the point of death.

"My route lay across the country, which was covered with snow as with a garment.

"My haste was such that I took no servitor with me, although the road was desolate enough to make woman's heart fear.

"I rode a graff dapple pony, a strong beast enow, but not o'er swift; and had reached half-way of my journey, or thereabout, when I began to experience for the first time the loneliness of my situation.

"The snow began to fall heavily, and was driven along by a cold, sharp wind, which setting towards me, caused me no little discomfort.

"Not a habitation was visible on any side,

nor saw I a single living thing within reach of my ken.

"I half repented having ventured out alone, and vowed to myself not to attempt such a rash undertaking again.

"I urged my dapple forward, but to my great perplexity and no small share of trepidation he suddenly stopped, and with pricked up ear and distended nostril, quivered from head to foot, while the sweat poured from his sides in a perfect lather.

"I was at a loss to conjecture the cause of this strange conduct on his part, when a distant howl broke to my mind the horrible truth.

"The wolves were on our track, and unless something wonderful occurred to save me I was lost.

"As if impelled forward by some irresistible impulse my dapple started forward with bounding leaps, and withal so unexpectedly that I was near unseated.

"Still the horrid howl sounded in my ear, getting closer and closer each moment.

"I cast a hurried glance behind, and espied a whole pack of these horrid creatures in full career, headed by a wolf of enormous size, which gained on my dapple fast.

"In a perfect agony of despair I cried aloud, beseeching the help of heaven in my dire extremity.

"Behind me came the short snap of the foremost wolf; my senses reeled, I loosened the reins, and was sinking down to the ground, when I felt myself uplifted from my saddle and borne along swiftly.

"Methought too I could catch the reassuring tones of a manly voice, but I trowed not whether all was a dream or not, so bereft of sense was I.

"When I awoke to consciousness I found myself in bed surrounded by familiar faces.

"I knew I was safe, and wept tears of joy.

"Oh, the bliss of that moment, 'tis indescribable.

"It was told me from the lips of my deliverer, that how, having heard my cries, he had dashed forward and rescued me just as the foremost wolf had fastened upon the hinder parts of poor Dapple.

"He is now my husband, and a truer, better man I know not than he has proved to me throughout our wedded life."

"And thou art of noble lineage, I ween," said Robin.

"I am the Duchess of Lancaster," she replied.

"Thou art the more welcome to Sherwood, lady, on that account," said Robin, bending low the knee in respectful homage; "I have heard of thy goodness ere now; and thou art of Saxon lineage too withal."

"Rise, sir outlaw," she exclaimed graciously, "thou art a true patriot and a brave man, whatever thine enemies say of thee. Thou hast my favour and protection too to boot so far as it extendeth."

The outlaws pricked up their ears on hearing that the dame was of such high degree, and forthwith their manner began to get more and more constrained.

"Nay, nay, mind me not, good fellows," she exclaimed with a smile, "but deport thyself as if I was not here in thy midst."

There now appeared bearers of a goodly repast, and soon it was spread on the green-sward.

"'Tis a grateful meal this hot day," the duchess observed, "I like well thy forest life, and in company with my husband would e'en spend some time with thee. What say'st thou, Marian, sweetest, would'st like me for thy sister guest?"

"Aye, that would I, your grace," replied Marian, "but my humble company would ill accord with thine exaltedness."

"Tut, tut," she replied. "station, after all, does not inhumanize me I hope, or make me proud. I long not for homage only, but also for love."

"That thou possessest such from all I truly ween," answered Marian, "for thy gracious-ness exceedeth all I have ever witnessed, and the remembrance of thy presence in Sherwood will always dwell pleasantly in my memory."

"It pleasureth me exceedingly to hear thy declaration," replied the duchess, "and now, sir outlaw, I have a boon to ask of thee ere we part."

"Say on, sweet lady," answered Robin, "and rest assured 'tis granted ere thou speakest even."

"I would that one of thy company do sing me a ballad, for I love to hear such."

"What say'st thou, friar?" queried Robin; "wilt thou pleasure her grace?"

"Ay, that will I right readily," he answered with good-natured alacrity, "and it will be:

THE THREE FRIARS.

"Not far from hence there dwelt three friars,
  Whom most folks said were three great liars;
  But to such foul scandal they paid no heed,
  Being well content a jolly life to lead.

"In a lonely forest these friars they dwelt,
  Nor aught of fear or care they felt;
  They drank good wine, and lived on the best,
  And when they felt tired, laid them down to rest.

"Folks wondered much at the life they led,
  And ere long began these friars to dread.
  Things strange and horrible about them were told,
  Some of which to thee I will quickly unfold.

"'Twas said they held captive a maiden fair,
  Whose cries and shrieks sometimes filled the air;
  And that near their cell were strewn human bones,
  And that many a traveller had heard deep groans.

"'Twas said again that the Evil One
  Kept vigils with them, and approved all they'd done;
  And that many a victim he had flogged with his tail,
  And folks at these friars began for to rail.

"And a man whose heart by fear was undaunted,
  And who to know their secrets very sadly wanted,
  Crept up to their cell in the dead of the night,
  And on peeping in, why he saw this sight.

"Seated were the friars round a rough deal table—
  Dressed in priestly guise, and in cowls quite sable;
  And on the table stood a flaring candle,
  While one of the friars a wine-flask did handle.

"As he listened, he heard one of them say,
  'Drink not too deeply, for this is *his* day;
  He's promised to come—his promise he'll keep;'
  And there ensued then a silence long and deep.

"At last a weary footstep approached the spot,
  And a voice asked for shelter within the friar's cot.
  'I'm a weary traveller, in the forest benighted;
  And great was my joy when this light I sighted.'

"'Come in, thou weary one,' the friars quickly said,
  And within their humble cell the traveller they led.
  'Wash thy feet and rest, and partake of our good cheer,
  While under our poor roof thou hast little to fear.'

"'Thanks, holy fathers,' the traveller he cried,
  As a wallet large and bulky he unslung from his side.
  'It containeth treasures very rich and very rare,
  To thee I entrust it—keep it in thy care.'

"The eldest friar replied, with look quite demure,
  'For riches care we not—we're content to be poor.'
  The other two said naught, but each gave a wicked leer,
  Which had the traveller seen, would have made him feel queer.

"The traveller supped right well, and hied him to his bed,
  On rushes laid his bones, on a billet put his head;
  And soon was fast asleep, nor forgot he to snore,
  Though his pillow was right hard, and his couch naught but the floor.

"In a short space of time another footstep came,
  And soon a knock was heard, and forth came words of blame,
  'Keep me not here all night, quickly open unto me,
  For a long way I've come, I have ridden o'er the lea.'

"'Welcome, sire,' a friar said, in tones of abject dread,
  'Come in, thou'rt welcome, but pray do softly tread,
  A traveller is here,' and he jerked with his thumb.
  'All right, I see,' the fellow said, 'plainly the word is mum.'

"In tones low and whispered, he to them then said,
  'Thou knowest well my business;' the friars were filled with dread.
  'Give us a little longer,' each one cried in haste,
  'I will not, not a minute, you do your breath but waste.'

"'The stranger he has treasure, only think of that,'
  'Let us take it from him.' 'Do you take me for a flat?'
  The fellow said, and laughed, 'No, no, your time's expired,
  So come along with me, for of waiting I am tired.'

"In vain they begged hard, and promised anything,
  The fellow would not listen, though they their hands did wring.
  He whisked his tail about them, and prepared for instant flight,
  To see these friars' faces, it was a piteous sight.

"The traveller got up, saying 'What is the matter?
  'You've startled my sleep with your noise and your clatter.'
  'I'm taking off my friends, in this sweet year of grace,
  Along with me down to a deuced hot place.'

"Thus saying Satan, for know well 'twas he,
  Tightened up his tail, and prepared for to flee.
  But the traveller stepped forth, and shouted out 'Hold!'
  'I will not,' Satan answered, 'they've sold their souls for gold.'

" Then commenced a struggle, for the traveller was
      a saint,
   And the friars were sorely pulled about, till they
      began to faint.
   'They are mine ;' 'no they're not,' first cried
      one and then the other ;
   And this pair of disputants kicked up a pretty
      bother.

" At last the saint he won, and pulled the friars
      away
   From the Evil One, who sought their souls for to
      slay.
   But Satan, in his spite, tore up all the place,
   And of the friar's cell he left not any trace.

" Now all this was seen by him who watched the
      cell,
   And every word's true, my grandsire knew him
      well.
   And furthermore these friars turned out most holy
      men,
   And no more lured traveller into their forest den.

" But with the gold they had they built a monastery,
   And every poor traveller to enter there was free.
   And even to this day children know from their
      sires,
   That that's why the monastery is called 'The
      Three Friars.' "

" Well sung, friar," said the duchess. "It
appears to me that Sherwood is the place for
song."
   "So long as thou art pleased, lady," replied
the friar, " it is sufficient praise for my poor
lay."
   "If 'tis thy grace's pleasure," said Robin,
"I will show thee a display of our forest
warfare."
   "Gladly would I do so, Sir Outlaw," she
replied. "I would e'en witness all that thou
can'st show me at once, for I fear me my time
is short."
   Placing his bugle to his lips, Robin blew a
call.
   Instantly the outlaws sped them in haste to
seek shelter.
   Another blast called forth a peculiar sound.
   'Twas the twanging of bow strings.
   But not an outlaw was to be seen.
   And suddenly there ensued a deep silence.
   Then, in answer to Robin's challenge call,
came first a bugle blast from some near spot,
and then from afar.
   The outlaws now began to show themselves,
but not in numbers; but only in detachments
of twos and threes.
   A summoning blast brought them speedily
together in a body.
   Little John now took the command, and put
the outlaws through a series of military
manœuvres, the performance of which would
have done credit to a trained band of regular
soldiers.
   At the conclusion the whole band marched
forward in ordered ranks and with slow step,
heralding their approach by shrill bugle calls.
   As each company defiled past the duchess,
the outlaws doffed their bonnets and gave a
lusty cheer.
   "'Tis a pleasing sight, Sir Outlaw," said the
Duchess to Robin, who stood by her, "and I
greatly thank thee for the display."
   "Thou hast a welcome here ever," replied
Robin; "and for thy kindly courtesies to us
poor outlaws thou shalt be had in grateful remembrance."

   "I am well content with thy hospitality,
which has been of a kind befitting one of
more exalted rank than mine even," the duchess
replied; "and if ever thou requirest a friend,
good Robin, thou hast one in me, trust me
for it."
   "I will not be laggard in seeking thy good
offices, lady," said Robin, with feelings of deep
emotion. "I am poor and despised, but thou
hast made me forget my condition, and hast
treated the hated outlaw with kindly consideration."
   "For the which I feel truly grateful, gracious
lady," said Marian, kneeling and kissing the
duchess's hand. "I will always think of thee
with heartfelt pleasure, for this is a golden day
in my young life's history."
   "May you never know a sad day," sweet
Marian," the duchess replied; "depend on't I
shall ever hold thee in sweet remembrance."
   A deputation of outlaws now advanced,
headed by Little John.
   "May it please you, master," he said, as he
twirled his bonnet around as if to cover his
confusion of manner, "we have a request to
prefer."
   "Name it, John," answered Robin smilingly,
"and it will be speedily granted, if 'tis in my
power to do so."
   "'Tis not to thee alone, we would prefer it,"
replied Little John, casting a side glance at the
duchess.
   "No, indeed," exclaimed the duchess merrily, "for I can well perceive Little John,
that I'm in some way implicated in the
matter."
   "Thou hast rightly guessed," exclaimed
Little John rapturously, "and hast thereby
relieved me of a load."
   "Well, what may'st it be now?" asked the
duchess with playful manner.
   "Thou wilt not be angered thereat?" said
Little John.
   "Do I look like an ogre, then?" she asked,
with a bright smile beaming on her handsome
open countenance.
   "Nay, thou art an angel surely," Little John
quickly answered.
   "Thou art a flatterer, sirrah," answered the
duchess; "it must be a weighty request thou
would'st prefer, else would'st thou unburden
thyself thereof more quickly."
   "Come, speak up, man," said the friar,
nudging him from behind; "tell the lady
quickly, else will thy courage ooze quickly
out at thy finger ends."
   "Quiet, man," replied Little John, "else
will I forget every word of my speech."
   "Now then, John," said Robin admonishingly, "to thy task, man. Why, I reckon thou
would'st have finished off an adversary long
ere this."
   "Body-o'-me!" said Little John; "not by
speechifying of a surety. But I will e'en try
to acquit myself creditably."
   Kneeling to the duchess, he said in faltering
tones :
   "Gracious lady, incomparably soft——"
   "Tut, you fool, not that," said the friar
from behind.
   Little John gave him an angry backward
glance, and went on :
   "Deign, sweetest lady, to pleasure thy
humble servants with a——with—ahem——"
   Here John stuck fast, greatly to the

duchess's amusement, as well as to that of the bystanders.

"Tell it me," said Jasper the Fool banteringly, "an' I will tell it to my sweetheart. But I know it already, and need not the telling. Wilt wager an' that I do not?"

"What is it?" asked Little John; "for may I be assoilzied if I can put my request in fitting terms."

Throwing himself in a comical attitude, Jasper said, addressing the duchess, his mistress:

"Noble and most potent and ever-gracious lady, deign to look down approvingly on thy devoted servant, and suffer him to lead thee forth to the dance to the dulcet strains of the pipe."

There was a general laugh at the fool's absurd speech, in which the duchess joined heartily.

"Thou art partly right," said Little John, "and partly wrong."

"'Tis with Robin, our master, we would see her dance, not with me, who never yet danced, except when, as a lad, I was fain to do so under the mighty blows of my sire's chastening rod."

"Thou art accepted in this matter," said the duchess, with a merry smile; "but art thou a consenting party thereof, Sir Outlaw?"

Thus addressed, Robin quickly answered:

"I am, gracious lady; and thou art more than kind in thus consenting to listen to the request of my followers."

"'Tis an innocent request enough," she answered, "and if it gives them pleasure to see me dance, it will also pleasure me, for if I can make others happy, then am I thereby rendered happy myself."

"'Tis an axiom but little recognised, though," observed the friar; "were it more discernible and becomingly acted upon, then would our world be rendered happier thereby."

"Thou art called upon to prove its efficacy in thine own person, friar," said Robin Hood playfully, "inasmuch as without thy music we cannot dance."

"True," exclaimed Little John, looking slily at the friar, "and as thou requirest little pressing, e'en begin at once."

"Why not move me with a speech, little man?" asked the friar jocularly. "Thou would'st overcome any person's obstinacy by thy honied speeches."

"A murrain seize thy malapert tongue," growled Little John, as a laugh was raised against him.

Seating himself on a stump of a tree the friar piped away while Robin and the lady danced.

The outlaws acclaimed right heartily, and the enjoyment was at its highest, when whiz came an arrow within an inch of Robin's head.

"Pursue! Pursue!" were the words which issued from a score of throats.

Instant pursuit was commenced by the outlaws, a few only remaining to guard Robin and the duchess.

"'Tis a pity our revels ended so," said Robin to his partner, "but such is forest life, danger lurks about everywhere."

"Our Lady be thanked thou wert not hurt by yon caitiff, whoe'er he was," she replied. "hast thou any conception of his personality?"

"I can make a shrewd guess," replied Robin, "but I will forbear saying aught until I see yon arrow."

Turning to one of his men, he said:

"Hie thee yonder, and fetch the arrow thou seest sticking in yon tree."

"It is as I suspected," said Robin, on examining the arrow. "Roderic, the sheriff's minion, has shot it; see here are his initials."

"Surely it is as thou say'st," replied the duchess, as she glanced at the initials and superscription, and read, "From J. R. to R. H."

"Is he thine enemy, then?" she asked.

"I suppose I must so class him," said Robin, laughing. "Twice has he attempted my life, Our Lady be thanked, with like results."

"The saints grant they capture him," said Marian, looking anxiously at Robin, "else, darling, wilt thou always be in jeopardy at his hands."

"They will be here anon with their report," answered Robin, "but fear not, Marian, sweet, the issues of life and death are not in such base hands as Roderic's. A higher Power than he watches over such things, and appoints them as He willeth."

"True, true," exclaimed the duchess approvingly; "'tis well to have such faith, else would life be one constant scene of fear and worrit. But yonder come some of thy men."

Robin blew three blasts on his bugle horn.

One note only came back in answer.

"They have not captured him," said Robin, "and Roderic is still at large to attempt my life."

Little John now came up, much winded on account of the lengthened chase he had returned from.

"What news, John?" asked Robin carelessly.

"Naught of good," replied Little John. "We saw the back of him only. But whom think you he is?"

"Roderic," was Robin's simple reply.

"Even so," said Little John. "Body-o'-me! how we did run after the swine; but he hied him off on horseback, and so escaped our pursuit."

"But not our arrows," said the friar, who stood by. "I'll be sworn to have given him a taste of Saxon shaft in an unmentionable spot."

"But how got he in unperceived," said Robin sternly. "This thing must be seen to, else will our stronghold be easily assailable by any sneaking cur or dastardly assassin."

"'Tis I'm the innocent cause thereof, I suspect," said the duchess. "Our revels tempted insecurity and laxity of watch."

"It boots not now, fair lady," replied Robin; "but in any case thou art not to blame, be assured thereof in all sincerity."

"See, your grace," said Faulkner, approaching with deferential mien, "already the day is on the wane, and we have some distance to traverse ere nightfall."

"Thanks for thy reminder, good Faulkner," she replied. "We must, indeed, be moving, much as I regret it."

"It pleasureth me exceedingly," said Robin, "to hear thee thus express thyself. Sherwood hath afforded thee pleasure, and we are content; yea, more, are grateful."

"Thou carriest with thee our love," said Marian, "and none shall be so well or so gratefully remembered in our woodland home than Lancaster's duchess."

"Can'st thou not spare Marian for a time?" the duchess asked of Robin; "I will take great care of her for thy sake and her own."

"What say'st thou, Marian?" asked Robin, smilingly; "wilt go?"

"It can't be, lady," said Marian; "I could not endure to be separated long together from Robin. To see him daily and know of his welfare is my sole delight. How, then, could I go with thee, much as I love thee?"

"Thou wilt have sumptuous living, dwell in stately halls, have minions at thy beck and call, and the loving, sisterly care of myself and husband. Bethink thee, Marian, ere deciding fully."

And the duchess looked scrutinisingly into Marian's fair and open countenance.

"Ah, gracious lady," she answered; "what are all these things thou hast named—though excellent in themselves—without contentment? Can stately hall vie with this grand old forest; sumptuous living repay for healthful vigour of mind and body; or attendance of courtly minion for the devoted care and attention of my outlaw friends; and, above all, what could requite me for Robin's love?"

"Well spoken, Marian!" exclaimed the duchess, with evident admiration depicted in her fine countenance; "and I love thee all the better for thy devoted love of friends and home."

"Ah, Marian's worth is beyond compare," exclaimed Robin rapturously; "already hath she renounced dignity and station for my unworthy self."

"Nay, dearest Robin, say not worthless," said Marian with a loving smile; "what would I not relinquish for thy sake?"

"And what would not Marian's friends do for her?" asked the friar; "let ringing cheers best answer the question—cheers from true-hearted Saxons."

Responsively there came bursts of cheering, mingled with acclaiming shouts of "Marian, our forest maiden, for ever!"

"We must now part, sir outlaw," remarked the duchess, "but remember that in me you always have a true friend."

"And wilt thou deign to accept this ring?" said Robin, presenting it to her; "'tis one my sainted mother bequeathed me. If ever thou wantest Robin's help this, on presentment, will bring it thee, backed by scores of strong arms and warm Saxon hearts."

"Thanks, brave Robin Hood," she answered, "and this trifle will gain thee admittance to my presence, when thou showest it."

'Twas an elegant gold medallion engraved with the escutcheon of the princely house of Lancaster.

"I will prize it highly," said Robin gratefully, "nor will I ever abuse the trust thou hast reposed in me, lady."

"Of that I am sure," she replied. "Ere I saw thee and thy trusty followers, I inclined to believe in the idle tales spoken of thy misdeeds, but I am now no longer imposed on by such."

"Ay, 'tis the way of the world," said Robin with a dash of bitterness in his tones; "might is right, and honest manly opposition to tyranny brings but opprobrium."

"Egad thou art right, cousin outlaw," said Jasper the fool with a comical grimace, "and

therefore thou hast might on thy side, as I can avouch according to thine own showing."

"Peace, irreverent knave," said the duchess; "thy quips and pleasantries are not now wanted."

Calling Marian to her, the duchess took from off her own neck a massive gold chain and threw it around Marian's, saying:

"Wear it for my sake, dear Marian, and in token of friendly and sisterly amity."

"That will I, dear lady," exclaimed Marian with deep emotion running through her silvery tones; "it will remind me of thee when absent."

"Thou wilt allow our safe conduct of thee, lady, beyond Sherwood's precincts?" asked Robin.

"And be glad of thine offer," she graciously replied.

Soon all was prepared, and the duchess proceeded on her way, escorted by the whole body of outlaws.

She took a gracious leave of all, and went forward amid the continued cheering of Robin and his men.

Nor quitted they the spot until she and her retinue were well out of sight.

CHAPTER LXIV.

ROBIN HOOD AND THE BUTCHER.

Upon a time it chanced so,
Bold Robin in the forest did spy
A jolly butcher with a bonny fine mare,
With his flesh to the market did hie.

'Good morrow, good fellow,' said jolly Robin,
'What food hast thou? tell unto me;
Thy trade to me tell, and where you dost dwell,
For I like well thy company.'

"I AM going to view about," said Robin to Little John the day following the events recorded in the last chapter, "so do not be alarmed if my absence doth extend itself an unseemly length."

"Good luck attend thee, master mine," replied Little John, "and golden adventures."

"Amen to that," said Robin, with a laugh; "'tis a hint I will not be unmindful of, for I trow our exchequer is getting empty fast."

"Body-o-me! 'tis true," answered Little John, "and something must be done to refill it, master."

"Grieve not thereanent," said Robin blithesomely, "but do thou look after things during my absence, and leave the remainder to me."

Thus saying, he turned away and took his way through the forest, humming snatches of a song to beguile the way.

"Our Lady send me visitors to-day," he said. "And as I live, here comes some one. I will see who it is."

This observation Robin made because of the approaching sounds of a horse's hoofs.

"'Tis a butcher, that's all," exclaimed Robin in disgust as the knight of the cleaver came trotting into sight.

"Beshrew me, but I might get something out of this after all," continued Robin, brightening up; "at least, it promises adventure, and I will e'en stop him."

Advancing into sight, Robin said, loudly:

"Ho, friend, whither goest thou this early morning?"

"To Nottingham, good fellow," the butcher civilly replied.

ROBIN HOOD,

AND THE OUTLAWS OF SHERWOOD FOREST.

"Tell me, I pray thee," said Robin, "what food thou hast with thee, and what is thy trade, also where thou dwellest, for know that I like thy looks and am to thee disposed friendly wise."

"As for the place of my dwelling it matters not," replied the butcher; "as for my trade I am a butcher, bound for Nottingham to sell my flesh."

"What is the price of thy flesh, good fellow," asked Robin, "and furthermore quickly tell unto me the price of thy mare, for I vow that be she ever so dear I have a fancy to buy her."

"I will soon tell thee the price of my flesh, and the price of my bonny mare also," replied the butcher, with a smile illumining his broad jolly-looking features.

"Name it to me then," said Robin, "and it will go hard but we speedily strike a bargain, for thou must know that I greatly long to be a butcher."

"Thou must give me four marks for them, and they are not dear," replied the butcher, looking curiously at Robin, whose freak caused him no little wonderment.

"Four marks then shalt thou have," said Robin, quickly, "so come here and see thy money counted out to thee."

"Thou art a bonny customer," said the delighted butcher, as he pocketed the money, "and here is thy trade stock, and a good mare to boot."

"Thou must change clothes with me, too;" said Robin, "for the which I will give thee a further sum."

"Well, well, I suppose I must e'en humour thee in this matter also," said the butcher with exemplary good humour. "So come along, my roystering buck."

The exchange was soon made, and bidding each other a good morrow, Robin and the butcher each went their separate ways.

Robin stayed awhile on his road to complete his disguise, and was so successful in his object as to defy recognition.

"'Egad," he said with a merry laugh, "I hardly know myself; so hie thee forward, thou jolly knight of the cleaver."

Arrived at Nottingham, Robin went to one of the principal inns, which it so happened the sheriff himself was in the habit of frequenting.

It happened to be a market day, and the place was full to overflowing.

But this in nowise disconcerted Robin, who was rather glad of the circumstance than otherwise, as it offered him a fair chance of selling his stock, and getting some sport thereby as well.

"Greet thee kindly, jolly butcher," said the landlord of the 'Jolly Forester,' by which name the inn was known. "I wish thee a good sale this day."

"We will drink success to ourselves in a cup of good sack," said Robin. "I to thy profit, thou to mine."

"A fair proposition, enough," said the boniface grinning; "so here's at thee in a cup of the best sack the country hereabouts, or, for that matter, that elsewhere can boast of. What ho! there, wench, bring forth sack of thy best, and that quickly."

A goodly concourse were now gathering, and Robin's style and manner got him no small share of public notice and admiration.

The landlord was the first to buy of Robin.

"There's a penn'orth for thee," said Robin, handing him a fine piece of beef; "match it if thou can'st, in the market."

"Thou wilt ruin thyself, friend," said the landlord to Robin in a whisper; "others sell not such quantity for fourpence. 'Tis a friendly warning, I give thee."

"Fear not for me," said Robin jollily. "I can afford to sell at that price, as I will soon show."

Robin went forth into the market, and got for himself a stall beside the fellows of his trade.

"Here's your prime beef!" he shouted out in stentorian tones; "a penny a pound, come and try! What say you, wench, wilt try my fine prime meat; the like of which the market containeth not?"

"Heed him not, good people," said a butcher who stood next him, "'tis rank folly he talks; and his meat is like his talk."

"Prime joints, gallants and ladies all; try before you buy, and if you find aught of fault therewith, pay not at all;" and Robin's customers began to roll in in numbers."

Soon he created quite a panic amongst his fellow butchers, none of whom could sell hardly a penn'orth while Robin's stock kept going off with wonderful celerity.

"Surely he is demented," remarked a stout oily-looking butcher, "else would he not sell at that price."

"Nay, 'tis a freak," exclaimed another; "'tis some mad wag or other bent on fun and adventure."

"'Tis more like to be some prodigal who is running through his money," observed a third; "faith he finds ready customers for his wares."

"Well done, jolly butcher," said one among the crowd. "Would we had more of thy sort."

"Ay, ay," was the response from all sides, "'twould soon learn the butchers manners with their high prices, which are more like to famine prices than aught else I know of."

"I would buy a stone or two of thee," said the sheriff's steward, who stood by. "Can'st thou oblige, or peradventure thou can'st sell me live cattle."

Robin's eyes twinkled mischievously as he heard this demand from the steward, whom he fully recognised.

"I will have speech of thee, anon, fellow," said Robin; "and doubt not but that I can serve thee readily."

"Thou wilt not go yet awhile?" queried the steward. "I would have speech of my master the sheriff, who is now at yonder inn, touching our bargain."

"'Tis there I will go myself presently," answered Robin, "and thou can'st safely expect me."

"'Twill go hard," muttered Robin to himself, "but that I make thee pay for my cheap vending."

By this time his fellow butchers had agreed among themselves to invite Robin to dine with them.

"Come, brother," said one of them, stepping forward as spokesman, "we are all of one trade. Will you go and dine with us?"

"Accursed of his heart," said Robin with a merry laugh, "be he that doth deny a butcher. I will go with you, my brother, as fast as I can."

"Well spoken, bully-boy," said the friendly butcher. "Egad thou hast good points about thee after all."

It was not long ere Robin was able to attend them, and they all adjourned to the Jolly Forester, followed by an admiring crowd, who cheered Robin vociferously.

They all quickly sat down to a bountifully-served dinner, and his followers did Robin the honour to place him at the head of the table.

"Wilt thou say grace an' please thee, master?" said one of the company to Robin.

"That will I," answered Robin with cheerful alacrity.

Amid a profound silence, he said as follows:

"Pray God bless us all, and our meat also. A cup of good sack will nourish our blood, and so do I end my grace."

Robin's grace was loudly acclaimed, and all set to with a good will and hungry appetites on the good things spread out before them.

"Come, come; spare not the wine, good folks," cried Robin, noticing a slackness in the filling of the cups. "Let's be merry while we are together."

"We have not all such deep pockets as thou," observed one of the company.

"Talk not of pockets," said Robin contemptuously. "Bring in more wine, landlord, I will pay the reckoning. Let there be no stint in thy providing as thou valuest my friendship."

"Have no fear on that head," answered the delighted boniface. "I will trust thee to any extent, for thou art one of the right sort."

"Gramercy," said Robin, "let's have the wine in then; and while thou art seeing to this I will sing the company a song."

THE DRINKING SONG.

"Drink, boys drink, push the bowl along,
For mirth and revelry is the burden of my song;
Then drink, boys, drink, fill up the wassail bowl,
And as your cups you chink, let your voices roll.

(CHORUS.) "For it's drink, boys, drink, drive away
    sad care,
    Let not life's ills your souls with woes
    o'erbear;
    So push the bowl along, we'll have
    another bottle,
    And yet another one, to wet our thirsty
    throttle.

"Fill up, spare not the wine, it cheers and glows the
    heart.
Let song and toast go round; be merry ere we part;
Let all with one accord, on high their voices raise,
To greet all absent friends, and our sweethearts to
    be praise.

(CHORUS.) "For its drink, boys, drink, drive away
    sad care," &c.

"'Tis a jolly song, and well sung withal," said the landlord; "and here's some of the best wine I possess to oil thy throttle with."

"Right," said Robin. "Come, fill up, brothers, for though the wine and good cheer be ever so costly, I vow and protest that I will pay the reckoning."

"Here's to our master," said one. "Let's fitly do honour to the toast."

Uprising they clinked horns and drank success to Robin in full bumpers.

"Our Lady," said Robin; "but 'tis fine to see thee, my jolly blades, so fittingly conducting thyselves. Drink, and let's be in no hurry to give over, for before we part I will pay the shot if it costs me five marks or more."

"Is he not a mad blade?" said one to the other; but Robin well knew what he was about all the time, as will presently fully appear.

The sheriff himself was sitting near, having heard from his steward of the mad-brained freak of Robin, out of whom he was minded to make some money.

He said loud enough to be overheard by Robin:—

"It is some prodigal who has disposed of some land for gold and silver, and is now bent upon squandering it all."

"Am I?" muttered Robin to himself; "faith thou wilt be undeceived presently, or my name is not Robin Hood."

Presently the sheriff gat him closer to where Robin sat and asked:—

"Hast thou any horned beasts, good fellow, that thou can'st sell to me?"

Robin gave him a side look unobserved, and with a smile made answer:

"Yes, that have I, good master sheriff. I have two or three hundred, and a hundred acres of good free land, if you will please to see it."

"Yes," said the sheriff, with impatient haste, "and thou would'st dispose of them for what?"

"If you wish to buy," answered Robin, "I will make you as good assurance of it as ever my father made to me."

"I cannot go myself," said the sheriff, "but I will send my steward with thee, and that as soon as thou art minded to start."

"The sale is for cash, mind thee," said Robin, "so let him come prepared, else will he miss a good bargain."

"Let me alone to provide everything that is needful," replied the sheriff; "but when art thou minded to start?"

"As soon as thy minion is ready," answered Robin, "for we have a good distance to ride ere I can show him my land and cattle."

"Wilt pledge me in a cup of sack?" asked the delighted sheriff, who already saw in anticipation a fine money harvest by the transaction.

"It will pleasure me greatly," answered Robin. "Here's to our speedy settlement!"

The sheriff drank the toast heartily, and then retired to settle matters with his steward.

"He will drive a hard bargain with thee," said the friendly landlord when the sheriff had got out of hearing; "be thou careful of him, I warn thee."

"Tut, tut, man," replied Robin with easy indifference of manner, "I will manage the matter all right, as thou shalt afterwards learn."

Soon the steward was at the door ready mounted for the journey.

Taking a warm farewell of his friends, Robin gat him on his mare, and rode onwards with the steward.

"Thou hast the three hundred pounds all

right, and in gold, too." said the sheriff to his steward loud enough for Robin to hear.

"Yes, master," he replied; "and my instructions, too, so have no fear, but safely trust me to strike a good bargain for thee."

Soon Robin and the steward rode side by side, with none other to accompany them.

"What is the news in these parts?" asked Robin carelessly; "I am not acquainted hereabouts myself."

"Heard'st thou not of Robin Hood, then?" asked the steward.

"Who be he?" asked Robin with innocent mien. "Mayhap he is some notable, else would'st thou not have mentioned him on this wise."

"Notable enough," answered the steward with a grim smile; "'tis well he knows not of my treasure, else would he quickly rob me of it. He is an outlaw!"

"This is Sherwood Forest, is it not?" asked Robin, without commenting in any way upon what he had just heard.

"It is," answered the steward in anything but assuring tones; "and may God bless and preserve us both this day from such a man as Robin Hood!"

When they had gone a little way into the forest, a hundred head of good red deer came tripping by them, on seeing which, Robin said to his companion:

"Good sir, do you like my horned cattle; are they not fat and fair to look upon?"

The steward eyed Robin furtively, and muttered loud enough for him to hear:

"I tell thee, good fellow, that I wish I were gone, for I like not thy company."

Without exchanging another word with his companion, Robin put his horn to his mouth and blew three loud blasts.

Little John and all his troop of merry men quickly appeared at the summons.

"What is your goodwill?" said Little John; "tell it me, good master."

"I have brought hither," said Robin, "the sheriff of Nottingham's steward to dine with us to-day."

"Now am I undone," exclaimed the steward with a deep groan; "woe is me that ever I was born!"

"He is welcome to us," said John, unheedful of the steward's wailing, "and I hope he will honestly pay for his good cheer."

"Naught have I, good sirs," protested the steward, in anguished tones; "I pray thee of thy clemency to let me depart."

"Gramercy," exclaimed Little John, with well affected pettishness; "be careful of what thou say'st, for I know that thou hast as much gold, if it be well counted, as will serve us all to drink for a whole day."

They led the steward forward, and Robin beguiled the way by narrating his adventure as a butcher in Nottingham.

"Wished I thee not good luck?" said Little John in a tone of self gratification; "I thought somehow that thou would'st not return empty handed, master mine."

"Nor had he need to," observed the friar, "for the cash is getting pretty low in the exchequer."

A merrier set of fellows ne'er sat round the festive board than was seated in Sherwood Forest on this occasion.

The steward received every courtesy at the hands of Robin his host, and but for the impending dread which was over him would have greatly enjoyed himself.

After the feast was over, Robin took the mantle from off his back, and spreading it on the ground, said to the steward invitingly:

"Come, pour in thy gold here, 'twill contain all thou hast."

"My master forgot to give me the money," said the affrighted steward.

"Dost hear?" said Robin; "pour out and that quickly, else will it fare badly with thee."

The steward looked on the faces of those standing round, and saw naught of compassion marked thereon.

With deep reluctance and many a grievous sigh the steward prepared to do as he was bid.

"Thou art but a laggard," exclaimed Robin with pretended impatience of manner, "and I must needs aid thee in thy task."

Seizing the portmanteau from the steward's hands, Robin proceeded, without further ceremony, to count out the sheriff's gold pieces.

"Just three hundred by right tale," said Robin; "and now, sir steward, as thy host, I will see thee safely out of the forest."

With rueful visage and heavy heart, the steward accompanied Robin to the confines of the forest.

"Have me commended to thy master the sheriff," said Robin with mock courtesy of manner, "and when next thou goest marketing, come not to Sherwood Forest."

Robin watched the retreating figure of the steward as he rode forward, seated on his dapple grey, and then went back to rejoin his fellows, laughing, as he went, at the thoughts of effectually tricking the designing sheriff out of his gold pieces.

"Ho! ho!" said Little John. "I would like to be within hearing when yon steward tells his tale to the sheriff. Body-o'-me! but it would be grand."

The matter afforded a topic for conversation for some time to come, and the outlaws' treasury was well filled again.

CHAPTER LXV.

ROBIN HOOD AND THE TINKER.

As Robin Hood went to Nottingham,
A tinker he did meet,
And seeing him a lusty blade,
He did him kindly greet.

"I AM off to Nottingham again, John," remarked Robin one fine morning. "Do thou keep thine eyes about thee during my absence."

"Surely, master, that will I do," answered Little John readily. "Thou may'st trust me."

"Ay, with everything I hold dearest on earth, John," replied Robin; "for I know full well thy trustiness."

Robin had just entered the town when he met with a tinker.

"St. Hubert!" said Robin to himself; "yon fellow is a lusty blade, and I will e'en accost him kindly to ascertain his craft and other matters."

"Hilloa, my buck," said Robin accosting him, "whither goest and where dwellest thou?"

"Greet thee kindly," said the tinker, taken by Robin's genial manner and handsome form and face; "but why seekest thou to know these things?"

"I hear there is sad news abroad," answered Robin gravely; "and I fear that all is not well."

"Gramercy," answered the tinker; "I am a tinker by trade, and I live in Banbury; but what is the bad news you speak of? Tell me, prithee, without delay."

"As for the news," said Robin with a mischievous smile lurking about the corners of his mouth, and peeping forth from his eyes; "I can only tell thee what I have heard."

"And what may that same be?" replied the tinker testily; "beshrew thee, it takes as much hammering to get aught out of thee as if thou wert a kettle or pot badly bulged."

Robin paused a little while before replying, as if to make what he was going to say the more impressive, and he secretly enjoyed his companion's curious impatience as he stood with open mouth awaiting his communication.

"It is this," said Robin, slowly emphasising each word; "that two tinkers have been set in the stocks for drinking ale and beer."

"If that be all," said the tinker contemptuously; "your news may be all true, and yet not worth a groat. As for drinking good ale and beer, it is what *you* will not lose your part of, I trow."

"No, by my faith," exclaimed Robin, with a boisterous peal of laughter; "for I love it with all my heart."

"And a joke, too," replied the tinker, disarmed by Robin's merry mood.

"But what is the news abroad?" asked Robin; "tell me what thou hast heard? Seeing thou goest from town to town thou can'st not fail of hearing some news."

Looking cautiously around, the tinker said: "All the news I have is far from good."

"Ah," said Robin, "and what might that be?"

"I am in search of a bold outlaw named Robin Hood," replied the tinker.

"What would'st thou with him?" asked Robin, "Perchance, thou seekest his patronage to mend his broken kettles and pans?"

"Kettles and pans!" said the tinker contemptuously. "No, 'tis something of higher import than that, I ween."

"'Tis to borrow money of him then, perhaps?" said Robin facetiously.

"Never a bit of it," answered the tinker; "but I have a warrant from our gracious king to take him wherever I can, and if you can tell me where he is, I can make a man of you."

"Thou delightest me," said Robin, who could scarce conceal his gravity at what he had heard; "but how much expectest thou for the job?"

The king would give me a hundred pounds, if he could but see him," said the tinker; "and if we could but get hold of him, it would be of service to us both."

"Let me see the warrant," said Robin; "and if I can find that it is right, I will do the best I can to help thee to take him this very night."

"That I will not," said the tinker with a grin. "No, no, I will trust no man with that warrant; and if you will not tell me where he is, I must try to take him by myself."

"Cheer up, jolly tinker, thou mender of worn out articles," said Robin, giving him a thumping whack on the back by way of good fellowship. "Cheer up, man, for I know where to find Robin Hood."

"'Egad," said the tinker coughing, "thou hast a thumping arm of thine own, and had'st best keep it for thine enemies, Robin Hood, for instance, for I declare thy whack hath well nigh emptied me of wind."

"Nay, it's nothing," exclaimed Robin laughing heartily; "but come thou with me into the town, and there we shall find bold Robin Hood of Sherwood."

"Saints!" exclaimed the tinker boastingly, "only let me once get sight of him, and he escapes me not. I will baste his hide with this good staff first."

Robin looked at the formidable crab-tree staff with which the tinker was armed, and mentally ejaculated a wish to be kept from knowing its weight from the hands of such a lusty fellow as the tinker.

They entered the town together, and Robin said:

"The day is of the hottest, so what say'st thou to some cool ale or a stoup of wine, ere we go in search of this bold outlaw."

"With all my heart," said the tinker, "for I never refuse so good an offer."

"Thou art of the right sort, I can see," said Robin approvingly, "and we'll have a merry bout of it out of the money thou gettest from the king."

"'Tis a good day's work that I have fell in with thee," exclaimed the delighted tinker; "so come along here be a house that I can recommend."

Robin was glad that it was a house he was not in the habit of frequenting, for he feared detection else.

"They sell good liquors there," said Robin answeringly, "for which they will find we have capacious stomachs, eh! friend? So come in."

"What ho there!" said Robin, calling out lustily and rapping the counter with the hilt of his sword; "what! mine host of the 'Flying Pig,' art thou still asleep, rouse, thee man, and bring hither a gallon of thy best ale for thirsty men."

Boniface now appeared, and was all smiles and apologies, and he lost not a moment in supplying their need.

"'Tis as cheap to sit as stand," observed Robin, "and will e'en ask thee for a room where intruders will not be likely to come."

"I have just the thing," answered the landlord assuringly, "not even the king himself, or Robin Hood for that matter dare enter there without my permission."

"Ah," said Robin, as he strode forward after the landlord, "thou art a rare companion I can see, and withal a stout Norman."

"Norman!" exclaimed the host contemptuously; "none of such am I, but true Saxon."

"Give us thine hand then," said Robin, "and come, thou must e'en drain a horn with us for better acquaintance sake."

"I will be with thee in a minute," said the landlord, "meanwhile do thou go on, nor fear to drink heartily, for the stuff is good as I can well warrant you."

Soon Robin and his companion were drinking heartily, for the heat of the day had made them thirsty.

Robin had an object to gain in plying the tinker with drink, and right well did he bring about its accomplishment.

"Ale is a poor man's drink," exclaimed Robin at last, "so let's have wine, fit for kings, wherewith to make merry. What, ho, there, landlord, bring wine, and of the best, and that quickly."

"Thou art a right sort of blade," said the tinker, with an incipient hiccup observable in his conversation, "and I will e'en sing thee a song."

"Bravo," answered Robin, "let's have thy song by all means."

"I will sing to thee then," said the tinker, "of my own sort, to wit,

THE JOLLY TINKER.

"I am a jolly tinker I'd have you all know,
And of the rightest sort, from my head unto my toe,
My trade I understand, nor fear I any man,
For I work when I will, and drink when I can.

(CHORUS)

"Bring out your pots and pans, I can make old ones new,
All holes I'll quickly stop, whether many or whether few.
I care not aught for dents; now's your time, my gentle dame,
For I'm a jolly tinker of high renown and fame.

"This pot wants a lid, that pan has a leak,
So I mend and patch, 'tis the same from week to week.
I hammer and I tinker, and cheer my toil with song.
'Tis thus I get through life, and merrily trudge along.

(CHORUS)

"Bring out you your pots and pans, I can make old ones new," &c.

"Well sung," said Robin, "here, have another horn, man, 'twill do you good."

"Here's to you," said the tinker, raising his glass aloft, "and confusion to Robin Hood.

A few glasses more made the tinker's head drop on his breast, and soon he was fast asleep.

"Ah, ha, my fine fellow!" said Robin, with a merry chuckle, "thou hast a warrant for my apprehension hast thou? Egad I'm o'er curious to see it."

Barring the door to prevent intrusion, Robin rifled the tinker's pockets and took therefrom the warrant.

"'Tis a good-looking parchment," said Robin, holding it up to the light, and has the King's sign-manual too. Well, well, my blustering tinker, sleep on, thou wilt be a wiser man when thou wakest."

Unbarring the door Robin walked forth, and soon took his way to Sherwood.

Meanwhile the tinker snored on, and in course of time woke up.

Finding Robin absconded and his warrant filched, he called lustily for the landlord, who quickly came.

"What now," said the landlord; "what means this hubbub?"

"I had a warrant from the king," he answered, "that might have been of much service to me."

"Well, what of it?" asked the landlord.

"It was to authorise me to take a bold outlaw that they call Robin Hood; but now my warrant and my money are both gone," said the tinker ruefully, "and I have nothing to pay with; for he that promised to be my friend has run away with the warrant and my money."

"The friend that you speak of," said the landlord, "is none other than Robin Hood, for this much was told me by a friend who saw him as he passed out."

"'Twas not so, surely?" said the bewildered tinker.

"And furthermore, 'tis plain he meant you no good when he first met you," observed the landlord.

"Had I only known that it was he, when I had him here!" exclaimed the tinker, in a tone of vexation and astonishment, "I would have tried my might with him, and one of us should have paid dear for it."

"Robin Hood is not easily overcome," said the landlord; "and it behoves those who try for his capture to be very wary and resolute."

"I will away, I will no longer abide here," said the tinker, indignantly, "but whatever betide me I will go and seek him out, but first I would know what I have to pay."

"The shot is just ten shillings," replied the landlord.

"I would pay it without delay," said the tinker, "if the rascal had not run away with all my money, but I will leave with you my good hammer and my bag of working tools."

"I am content," replied the landlord.

"If I can but light upon the knave I will soon pay you and redeem them."

"Well," said the landlord, "you must not fear him, and the most likely way to find him is to seek him in one of the parks killing the king's deer."

Without any further loss of time, the tinker armed with his formidable crab-tree staff, hied him away to the forest.

He came upon Robin at length as he was chasing the king's deer.

"Who art thou, knave," said Robin, as the tinker approached, "and why comest thou so near me?"

"I am no knave," shouted out the tinker; "no knave, as you shall very soon know, and my crab-tree shall quickly show you which of us has done the other any wrong."

Robin drew his trusty sword and prepared to resist the tinker's impetuous onslaught.

But he laid on him so quickly, and well with his staff that he made Robin reel again with the blows he gave him.

Robin was now fairly roused to anger, and fought most manfully with his sturdy opponent, and the tinker who was getting the worst of it, seemed greatly inclined to run away.

They rested by mutual consent, and then resumed the combat.

In this bout they plied their weapons most vigorously, and the tinker began to get the best of it.

The tinker thrashed Robin's bones so sore, that at last he was fain to yield.

"A boon," cried Robin, "a boon if thou wilt grant it me."

"I would hang thee on this tree, before I would grant it thee," replied the tinker resolutely.

But at this juncture some noise caused him to turn his head to look round.

Seizing the opportunity thus offered him, Robin placed his horn to his lips, and blew three blasts, which quickly brought Little John and Scathelock to his side.

"What is the matter, master?" asked Little John, "that you sit thus on the side of the highway?"

"Here is a tinker standing by," said Robin, "that has tanned my hide soundly."

"As for that tinker," said John, in great dudgeon, "I would fain see whether he would do as much for me."

"Nay, nay," said Robin, "this quarrel must end, for he is a stout-hearted brave fellow, and must not be harmed."

"As thou wilt, master," said Little John; "thou know'st thine own business best."

Turning towards the tinker, Robin said:

"As for thou, jolly tinker, I will give thee a hundred pounds a-year as long as thou livest, if thou wilt become one of our fellowship."

"Hearest thou that, tinker?" said Scathelock.

"For thou art a man of mettle," continued Robin, "as well as a man of metal by trade, and I never thought that any man could have made me so afraid as thou hast. If thou wilt be one of us we will all fare alike, and thou shalt have thy full share of whatever we get."

"Agreed," said the tinker, extending his hand to Robin. "Thou art a jovial fellow, as I can see; so a fig for the king and his warrant, henceforth I will discard pots and pans, and be a merry outlaw."

So he and Robin, together with Little John and Scathelock, joined hands and danced round and round on the greensward.

CHAPTER LXVI.

ROBIN HOOD, LITTLE JOHN, AND WILL SCARLET FIGHT WITH THREE GAMEKEEPERS, AND THEN DRINK THEMSELVES FRIENDS.

They left all their merry men waiting behind
Whilst through the green valleys they passed,
Where they did behold some foresters bold,
Who cried out, "Friends, whither so fast?"

NOT long after the adventure with the tinker Robin Hood, Little John, and Will Scarlet took a walk in Sherwood Forest with a view of meeting with some pastime.

"Our Lady be thanked for such a fine day!" said Robin; "it does one's heart good this weather to roam about in the merry sunshine."

"That does it," answered Will, "and I know of no spot so suited to raise one's spirits as this. Sherwood Forest is indeed a thing of beauty!"

"St. Hubert! but I feel dull rather," said Little John, "and would that some adventure befall us ere long."

"Thou art likely to be pleasured in this wise," observed Robin; "for see, here are three gamekeepers."

"Body-o-me!" laughed Little John, gleefully; "'tis a fine sight for me this fine morning; we will see some sport shortly, or I am greatly mistaken."

Forward came the three gamekeepers of the king, dressed in smart green liveries, with long falchions by their sides, and forest-bills in their hands.

"Stand, ye fellows!" the head keeper shouted peremptorily; "what right hast thou here, fellows, in the royal preserves?"

"Why, who are you," cried Robin, "that speak so boldly here to us?"

"We," replied the keeper, "belong to King Henry, and are keepers of his deer."

"The deuce you are!" exclaimed Robin. "I am sure that it is not so. We are the keepers in this forest, and that you shall soon know to your cost. Come, lay your coats of green upon the ground, and we three will do the same, and take your swords and bucklers, and let us try for the victory."

"We are content," said the keepers. "We are three, and you are the same number. Why, then, should we be afraid of you, for we have never transgressed?"

"Why, if you be three keepers in the forest," said Robin, "we are three good rangers: and before you leave us we will make you know that you have met with bold Robin Hood."

"We are content, then, bold outlaw," said the keepers, "to try our valour with you; and we will make you know before we part, that we will fight before we will fly."

"I like thee for thy pluck," said Little John, who was quite merry at the anticipation of the coming combat.

"Come, then, draw your swords," the keeper continued, "you bold outlaws, and do not stand there prating any longer, but let us try it out with blows, for we hate cowards. Here is one of us for Will Scarlet, and another for Little John, and I myself for thee Robin Hood, because thou art stout and strong."

"Thou never put a better proposition in thy lifetime than this," answered Robin; "so have at thee, thou king's minions, and Our Lady grant us the victory."

They fell to without further parley, and they fought a hard and sore battle from eight o'clock in the morning until past two in the afternoon.

They all showed gallant play, and the three outlaws fought most manfully until all their wind was spent.

Then cried Robin Hood aloud—

"O hold, O hold! I see that you are stout fellows. Let me blow one blast on my horn, and then I will fight with you again."

"That bargain is to make, bold Robin Hood," said the keepers; "therefore we deny it. A blast upon thy bugle horn cannot make us either fight or fly; therefore, fall on, or else begone and yield the day to us. It shall never be said that we are afraid of thee or thy gay yeomen."

"If that be so," cried Robin, "let me know your names, and I will extol your fame throughout the forest of merry Sherwood."

"And what hast thou to do with our names?" asked one of the keepers. "Except thou wilt fight it out, thou shalt not know our names."

"We will fight no more," said Robin; "you are stout men of valour, come to Nottingham with us, and there we will fight it out with a butt of sack; we will bang the wine about to see who wins the day, and you need not doubt but that I have gold enough to pay the cost."

"And we will be brethren as long as we live," put in Little John; "for I love with all my heart, those men that will fight and never flee."

"Agreed," answered the keepers, one and all; "and cursed be he that first breaks the bond of brotherhood now holden between us."

Linked arm in arm, they hied them to Nottingham, and spent three whole days carousing.

Robin behaved himself most nobly, and paid for all that his friends consumed.

When they left for their respective homes, faster friends were there not in the world than Robin, Little John, Will Scarlet and the King's gamekeepers.

CHAPTER LXVII.

ROBIN HOOD RESCUES THE THREE SQUIRES FROM THE GALLOWS.

"What have they done, then," said jolly Robin,
　"Come, tell me most speedily;"
"O, it is for killing the king's fallow deer,
　That they are condemned to die."

"Get you home, get you home," said jolly Robin,
　"Get you home most speedily,
And I will into fair Nottingham go,
　For the sake of the squires all three."

SOME little time afterwards Robin Hood was ranging the forest all round, when he met a lady, who was coming along the high road weeping.

Now Robin was at all times respectful and gallant towards the fair sex, and it grieved him sorely to hear the lady so bitterly weep.

"Why weep you," said he, "why weep you? Weep you for gold or fee?"

"I weep not for gold," replied the lady, "neither do I weep for fee."

"What weep you for then?" said Robin. "Come, I pray thee, tell me what it is?"

"Oh," she said, "I weep for three sons, for they are all condemned to die."

"What church have they robbed," asked Robin, "or what parish priest have they slain?"

"They have robbed no church," replied she, "and they have slain no parish priest."

"What then have they done?" said Robin, "come, tell me speedily."

"Oh," she answered, "it is for killing the King's fallow deer that they are all condemned to die."

"If that's all they have done," answered Robin, "you may get you home speedily; and I will go to Nottingham for the sake of the three squires."

Never was person more overwhelmed with gratitude than was Robin by this sorrowful lady, and she left his presence with secret rejoicing in her heart for the hopes held out to her by him.

Robin's resolution was speedily taken, and he went quickly forward in the direction of Nottingham.

He met a beggar, poor and old, creeping along the highway.

'Twill suit me well," exclaimed Robin, on casting his eyes upon him, "I will change apparel with him, and so gain admittance to the sheriff's presence unsuspected."

"What news?" asked Robin; "What news, thou old beggarman, come tell me what news there is?"

"Oh," replied the beggar, "there is weeping and wailing to-day in the town of Nottingham for the death of the three squires."

Although the coat on the beggar's back was neither green, nor red, nor yellow, but a piece of patchwork of all colours, Robin determined to wear it, and quickly said:—

"Come, pull off thy coat, thou old beggarman, and thou shalt put on mine, and I will give thee forty shillings for the exchange, beside brandy and rum, and ale and beer."

The beggar refused not the liberal offer, and the exchange was quickly effected.

Robin continued his journey and entered the town of Nottingham, where unusual excitement was observable.

He inquired of many the cause of this, and received the same answer every time—"That three squires were condemned to die for slaying the King's deer."

A long way further on he met the sheriff and an escort conducting the three squires to the place of execution.

They were three comely looking gentlemen, and Robin's heart swelled with indignation at the thought that they were condemned for such a paltry act.

"Our Lady bear me witness," he said to himself, "that these three squires die not to-day; for I will encompass their escape even to the endangering of my own life."

Throwing himself on his knees before the sheriff, Robin cried aloud, in tones of supplication:

"One boon; on my knees, I beg of thee one boon; and that is that I may be the hangman for the death of these three squires."

The spectators cast a sorrowful glance on him, but the sheriff was greatly rejoiced, and quickly said:

"It is soon granted unto thee; and all their gay clothing and all their white money shall be thine."

"Oh!" exclaimed Robin; "I will have none of their money; but I will have three blasts on my bugle-horn, that their souls may flee to heaven."

The place of execution was reached, and the culprits ascended the gallows, accompanied by Robin as hangman."

But not a preparation made he; he only blew three blasts on his bugle-horn, at which all were amazed.

One hundred and ten of his bold yeomen were immediately seen marching down the green hill.

"Whose men are those," said the sheriff, anxiously, "tell me whose men are those."

"These are mine," said Robin, "they are none of thine, and they are come for the three squires."

On hearing this, the spectators cheered, and the sheriff, in mortal fear, said:

"Oh, take them, take them; for there is not a man in fair Nottingham that can do what thou canst."

Then were the three squires quickly released from durance, and conducted by Robin and his merry men to Sherwood, where their mother awaited their coming.

Robin's name became greatly extolled throughout the country's side for this charitable deed, and was held in high esteem thereafter.

ROBIN HOOD,

AND THE OUTLAWS OF SHERWOOD FOREST.

GEOFFRY DE LOIS ENTERS THE MILL FORCIBLY.

CHAPTER LXVIII.

ROBIN SEEKS SHELTER IN A TREE FROM SOLDIERS
WHO ARE IN PURSUIT OF HIM.

Then Robin he quickly mounted a tree,
When the sheriff's soldiers he saw on the lea,
Who to take him were bent, but Robin was hidden
Until they from the forest away had ridden.

ROBIN was returning home from Nottingham some days after the event narrated in the previous chapter, and had reached the forest when he espied a short distance away some soldiers advancing.

It was impossible that he could escape them if he continued onwards, so he quickly climbed a tree.

Much to his disgust the soldiers halted under this very tree, and Robin from his lofty position could both see and overhear them as they spoke.

With them was a monk, to whom the leader of the party thus addressed himself.

"We have not yet espied Robin Hood, good father, although we have searched the forest hereabouts well. What say'st thou to this matter?"

"Patience, my son," said the monk; "that he is hereabouts I am well assured. May be he is hidden in one of these trees."

"Thou had'st better climb this one, father," was the reply, "and make good thy words, for we are getting tired of chasing a shadow."

"I could have sworn," said one of the soldiers, "that I heard a rustling overhead, which sounded as if some person was concealed in this tree."

"Methought I heard the same thing, too," said another.

"'Tis but the rustling of the breeze through the branches," replied the leader, who was in an angry mood, and cared not to listen patiently to these idle conjectures.

"Let me ascend," said one. "I was always accounted a good climber, and can soon mount this tree. Have I thy permission, captain?"

"Yes," was the curt answer, "and much good may it do you."

"Have a care, my son," said the monk, for thou hast to deal with the Evil One himself, for this same Robin Hood is one of his children I am truly convinced, and has his aid and counsel to assist him at all times."

"Give me thy blessing then, father," replied the venturous soldier; "or stay, give me rather thy blessing and some holy relic that will forfend me from all harm at the hands of the Evil One."

"Thou hast asked discreetly," answered the monk, "and shalt have them."

Taking off his rosary beads, he gave them him, and pronounced a blessing in Latin, which the soldier understood not, but valued highly.

Raising himself on the shoulder of a comrade, the fellow commenced his ascent and was soon up the tree.

Meanwhile Robin had crept out cautiously on one of the branches, where the foliage was so dense as to effectually screen him from observation.

Moreover he held his good sword firmly between his teeth, and held his bow ready for action if necessary.

"Can'st thou see aught?" asked the soldier's comrades.

"Naught yet, save the horns of a large owl; but I get me forth forward."

He looked around, but failed to perceive anything but the top of Robin's hat feathers, which he took for the horns of an owl.

"Search the branches," said the voice of the leader; "thou may'st as well conclude thy quest properly, now that thou art up there."

Thus commanded, the fellow crept out on the very branch on which Robin was seated.

He must inevitably have discovered him had not a fortunate incident occurred to bar his further progress.

A large wood-snake reared its head suddenly, and prepared to strike.

It had lain concealed among the branches, and was disturbed by the soldier's approach.

Uttering a cry of terror the soldier lost his presence of mind, and releasing his hold, came crashing through the branches, and fell heavily to the ground.

"Saints forfend us from all harm!" said the terrified soldiers, as their comrade came into their presence so unexpectedly.

"He is dead," said the leader; "and this comes of your idle fancies."

"Nay, he is but in a swoon," replied the monk, as he knelt down by the soldier's side. "Hie some of thee for water. Thou wilt find plenty hereabouts."

They undid his clothes, and sprinkled his face with water, and soon the fellow revived sufficiently to give a succint account of his adventure.

"What caused thy mishap?" asked the monk.

"The Evil One himself stood before me," he replied; "in the form of a monstrous snake he withstood me; his eyes were large as drinking horns, the scales on his back were immense, and he had the mane of a horse."

"I had my suspicions," remarked one of his comrades, "when thou did'st name the owl's horns, for such birds are always found attending evil spirits."

"It behoves us to leave this place immediately," said the discomfited soldier, "else will the monster pounce down on one of us and bear us off."

"Fear not," said the leader; "the presence of our good father secures us from harm."

"I am not so certain that I could overcome such a monster as him," said the monk in dubious tones, "and would therefore counsel a prudent retreat."

"'Tis sound advice, and we had better take it. Saints forfend us! heard'st thou not that rustling, and that strange noise?" said one of the soldiers.

Robin availing himself of their fears, had commenced to shake the branches, and utter deep groans.

The first to fly was the monk, and after him quickly sped the soldiers, all eager to place as great a distance as possible between themselves and the threatened danger.

Robin descended and enjoyed a hearty laugh at the ludicrous scence he had just witnessed.

But he was not so safe as he imagined.

The leader of the soldiers, suspecting something, hid behind a tree near at hand, and saw Robin descend.

Issuing forth from his hiding place, he called upon him to stand.

"Who art thou," said Robin, "that callest on me to stand in Sherwood's forest? Have a care, bold sir, else will I quickly speed an arrow through thy arrogant carcass."

CHAPTER LXIX.

THE ABBOT AND THE MONKS OF ST. MARY'S ABBEY HOLD A CONFERENCE.

'Twas in St. Mary's Abbey the abbot and his friar—
They held a conference long, I trow, concerning of the shire;
The tithes they wanted to be raised, the coffers low, forsooth—
The gold had been transplanted by the hand of Robin Hood.

"Come hither, brother John," said the abbot, motioning to a friar who was in the act of leaving the refectory. "Come hither; I would have speech with thee, for of counsel such as thine I stand much in need."

"Holy father, I am at thy bidding," said the friar, slipping a flask beneath his skirt, then muttering to himself, added, "a malison on thee for thy favours on those who little need them. Marry! if thy nose is half so keen as thou hast proved thine eyes, thou wilt soon discover that this flask contains not such liquor as is stilled in yon purling brook."

"Now, John," said the abbot, impatiently, "get thee seated. Thou movest as though thy life was more than man's allotted span, and thou wast sparing all thy energy for a future day."

The monk seated his huge body, and having secured the flask between his knees, smoothed his ruffled brow, and was all attention to the abbot's words.

"My lord, the sheriff, is sorely vexed at the doings of Robin Hood and his cut-purse band. They have drained the treasury, and it will ill fare with us if we do not something to replenish it."

"Hast thou decided upon any plan?" asked Friar Cuthbert.

"By our Lady, as yet, no! 'Tis to ask of thy counsel I came hither. St. Mary! what has to be done must be done quickly."

"The Saints guide us!" muttered brother John. "Cannot our brother Denis give us advice?"

"Ay, troth can I," answered the monk addressed. "Does not our Lady need an offering at her shrine? and when next we meet at mass "——

"That will not do," interrupted the abbot. "For the jokes these knaves have played us we must levy a tax. The miller has great wealth, and he has raised the sheriff's wrath. On him we must be hard, and others that I have on record. Go thou," he added, to Friar Cuthbert, "and fetch the tablet thou wilt find on my escritoire. Stay!" he ejacu-

lated, after a moment's thought—"I will hie myself thither. Thou mayest disturb that which thou needst not."

He rose from the bench as he spoke, and, to the great delight of brother John, hastened from the refectory.

No sooner had he gone, than the monk drew the flask of liquor from its concealment, and gulped down its contents.

"Confound thy thirsty throat!" said Friar Cuthbert, placing his hand on the empty flask. "A malison on thy ungodly manners! By our Lady! thou mightest have held thy hand fore this!"

"Saints protect us! But I had forgotten thee, quite!" said the monk, with a penitent look. "A fever, I fear, is settling on my brain."

"A fever has settled in thy throat!" said the other, testily; "thy guzzling will bring thee to a sorry end at last."

"I fear thy words are too true, brother. It was for that reason I forsook the water of our Lady's well, but I hope by fasting and heavy penance to "——

The entrance of the abbot interrupted his speech, and they resumed their former consultation.

The scroll of parchment he had obtained from his escritoire contained a lengthy list of names, which was carefully read by the monks, and Friar Cuthbert, under the dictation of the abbot, affixed a sum to each of the names.

It was late when they had finished, and it was a relief to the shrivelings when the abbot retired to his cabinet.

"Beshrew me! but this will cause some stir in Nottingham," observed Brother John; "and I fear we shall have to press hardly on some to get this money."

"Marry, and by our Lady, I fear thou speakest true. What thinkest thou of this matter, Brother Denis?"

"Holy Mother! thou askest me of that I wotest not. Thou, Friar Cuthbert, knowest more of these ungodly sinners than I; but I opine the Screffe will be sore displeased if we lack in success."

"Thou sayest true; but the miller, I know, will not yield him easily. He is a stubborn dog, and that he has proven fore this."

"And his son, Much, is as stubborn as he. By the rode, he is a stubborn knave, and holds well to that good-for-naught, Robin Hood."

"A murrain on the fellow, say I, and all his outlawed band, though, in troth, he is a jolly fellow."

"As thou hast proved," said Brother John, with a knavish smile. "I dare vow, by our Lady, that the scars on thy back hast not yet healed from the scourging thou had to inflict on thy saintly carcass when he paid us his last visit."

Friar Cuthbert rewarded his compliment with a bitter scowl.

"Talk not of the past," he said, reprovingly. "We shared in the pleasure, if not in the pain. 'Twas thy craftiness alone shielded thee."

Friar Cuthbert was in high dudgeon, and there is no knowing how far matters would have gone had not the cellarer made his appearance.

It was the hour for the evening meal, and he began to lay the scanty repast on the table when Brother John said—

"Holy Mother! have you nothing better than this to set before us hungry souls? We are a parch with thirst, and our bodies are growing weak."

"Saints preserve us!" replied the cellarer. "What can I give thee more? Thou knowest 'tis full a week thou had the misfortune to fall over the wall."

"Holy brother, be not too rash in thy speech. Thou hast sins enough to confess without adding more thereto. If I have to shrive thee, thy confessions will be great."

Brother John rose as he spoke, and the cellarman looked at him indignantly.

"What meanest thou by "——

"Simply this, thou man of trouble. Hast thou searched the buttery?"

"Marry! have I not?"

"Well, lookest thou in the little nook, and thou wilt find such a buck as thou hast not seen these many a day. 'Twas by accident 'twere killed, 'twas by accident I found it, and by the same Divine Providence it camest where thou wilt assuredly find it."

The head cellarer and Brother John left, and at an hour when the monks were supposed to be in prayer and scourging themselves for their sins, the four saintly men were doing penance over a flagon of good sack and a haunch of as prime a deer as ever grazed in Sherwood.

Here they cracked their jokes and gave utterance to many remarks that would have shocked their ears had they been in other company, and would assuredly have brought down the vengeance of the church upon them, and subjected them to six weeks' scourging and penance.

CHAPTER LXX.

CONFLICT BETWEEN ROBIN HOOD AND THE SOL-
DIER—THE KNIGHTS FIGHT A DUEL IN THE
GLEN.

Beyond compare were the knights disguised as they
    fought in the leafy dell,
Nor dreamt that two intrusive eyes by chance had
    on them fell;
But Robin Hood and George-a-Green to well-
    screened covert hied,
And watched the raining sparks that fell from
    blows on either side.

THE leader of the soldiers that so suddenly confronted Robin Hood was a man of no common stature—a giant, in fact; and when he stood before the bold outlaw, he seemed capable of overpowering two of the size of Robin.

"Yield, proud catiff!" said the soldier, arrogantly. "We have long sought for thee, and the search has not been in vain. Yield thee at once, while it may be well with thee."

"Saint Hubert! but thou hast a willing tongue," replied Robin boldly. "Thy followers are far from thee ere this; what sayest thou if I make thee prisoner instead?"

"Saxon hound! thou wilt find tough work if thou goest against the law. My master, the sheriff, has sworn to have thee hanged, for the trick thou playest on him of late, and he charged me to bring thee to him, be thou living or dead."

"Confound thy insolence and thy master's too!" said Robin Hood. "Body o' mine, but he has soon forgotten that I am king of merry Sherwood. Dost thou know that one blast of this horn would bring my gallant archers to this spot, and thou wouldst have more luck than brains if thou escapest the shower of cloth-yard shafts that would whistle round thy head?"

"Thou liest, dog! and for thy speech I swear thou shalt not leave this spot alive. Yield thee at once, ere I cleave thee to the waist."

Robin Hood gave a defiant laugh.

He longed to have a bout with the Norman giant.

Leaning his bow against a tree, he unslung his buckler, and drew his sword, saying—

"Lay to, Norman hind! and if thy arm is not as stout as it looks, thou wilt soon have more than thou hast bargained for, and just cause to remember thy meeting with Robin Hood."

"Cease thine idle prattling," said the soldier, fiercely. "'Tis not to bandy words we have thus met. Saint Denis and the Virgin! thou shalt soon find how true I speaketh!"

As the soldier spoke, he took two strides up to Robin, and dealt him a furious blow.

It was caught on his trusty blade, and did no harm further than letting Robin know that he had no weakling to contend against; in fact, it required all the outlaw's strength to keep his guard.

"One to thee," said Robin, returning a swift blow on the giant's left shoulder, that dented his mail and made him wince with pain.

"Have at thee, Saxon hound!" cried the exasperated soldier; and his eyes flashed fiercely as he bent savagely to the attack.

Blows and thrusts were now given with lightning rapidity and as quickly guarded, and the grass was trampled down in a regular circle where the soldier walked round Robin Hood, who stood firmly in the centre.

The soldier was not quite so good a swordsman as Robin Hood, but this deficiency was made up in his wondrous amount of strength.

To one who had not known Robin Hood, it would have seemed that he must soon yield to his powerful foe, whose body was encased in proof steel; but Robin was confident in himself, and was watching an opportunity to thrust his sword's point between the joints of the mail.

The soldier, having received several desperate thrusts that almost pierced his breast-plate, became aware o Robin's intention, and exercised more care, parrying each thrust with admirable skill, and heeding less the feint blows made at his body.

"Blade-bone of Saint Hubert!" said Robin, tauntingly, "thou art a long time fulfilling thy promise. Were I the giant and you the pigmy, I would have eaten thee ere this."

These words inflamed the soldier.

"Insolent knave!" he yelled, savagely, "I will eat thee ere I have done, and grind thy bones to powder. Take that for thy insolent speech!"

"And that for thy boasting!" said Robin, with a smile, as he turned aside the soldier's blow, and thrust the point of his sword between the chinks of his armour, just sufficient to draw blood.

"A murrain seize thee!" said the soldier, smarting under the pain. "Thou hast spilt a good man's blood. Saint Denis! thou shalt rue this sorely."

Grasping his sword with both hands, he rushed furiously on Robin, and cut and slashed in such a manner as to compel the outlaw to use all his strength to prevent his being hit.

The soldier still kept moving swiftly round, in the hopes that his adversary would turn giddy, and his hopes were realized at length, for Robin slipped on the trampled grass, and fell backwards on his left arm.

"Saint Denis and the saints protect thee!" said the soldier, viciously, "for marry! I will grant thee none."

With that he made a terrible downward sweep at his prostrate foe; but his foot slipping, as did Robin's, he missed his blow, staggered forward, and his sword buried itself so firmly in the ground, that it resisted his efforts, which were by no means weak, to withdraw it.

Robin was on his feet in an instant.

"Now, thou Norman dog! what say ye if I treat ye with the just resentment thou so richly deserve?" said he.

"Thou hast certainly gained the better o' me," replied the soldier, sullenly; "but it's no fault of mine, as thou knowest. Had not the evil one caused my foot to slip, ere this my sword would have cloven thy Saxon carcase."

"Saint Hubert and Saint Ulrick, is it thus ye beard me when thy life is in my hands?" said Robin, sternly.

"Bold Robin," said the soldier, deprecatingly, "I have heard enough of thee to know thou wouldst not take my life unfairly. A boon I crave."

"On thy knee be it then. Ah! Will Scarlett, what bringst thee here?"

"My legs, as thou seest, and they are in woeful plight."

They were, indeed, in woeful plight, and blood poured from more than one wound, whilst his dress was studded with thorns and brambles.

"Body-o'-me!" said Robin, eyeing him ruefully, "let us hear what has befallen thee;

it's something more than brambles that hast torn thy lusty limbs in such a fashion."

"Blade-bone of Saint Hubert! but thou speakest right," said Will Scarlett, wiping the sweat from his reeking brow.

"Say on; I am burning to hear of this wondrous thing."

Will Scarlett looked down at his wounded leg, then went on—

"Fearing some harm had befallen thee as thou didst not return to thy word, I strayed through the forest, and, having walked apace, I got me wondrous dry, when I suddenly bethought me of a stream in the warlock's dell. My bow and trusty staff I laid against a tree, and gat me down to cool my burning tongue, when I felt me caught a sore grip from behind."

"Ah! 'twas a wolf," interposed Robin; "the place is swarmed with them."

"So I found to my grief, for two or three came boldly up, and, before I could gain my staff, body-o'-me! they attacked me sore as ever I was attacked in all my life. They howled and I shouted until the welkin rang again, and my oaken staff rattled on their pates right merrily."

"By our Lady! thou hast escaped narrowly."

"Gramercy! yes. But I see thou hast a *friend* here, and I must be short of speech. Having cracked the pates of a dozen or so, I found I should have to fight the whole pack, so I battled my way through the scrub, and then took to my heels, leaving them to feast on their dead comrades; and thus you see me."

"Thou bearest proof of having a sharp tussle; but seest thou this minion? He is one of a pack of Norman wolves that have trespassed on our lands; the rest have fled; and, as the saints have delivered him into our hands, it is but meet we take him to our court. What say ye?"

"As thou sayest, so say I," replied Will, and seeing the sword buried in the ground, he gave it a blow that snapped it close, adding, "Thus would I serve every treacherous blade that strikes against the cause of freedom!"

As they travelled through the forest, they heard a lusty voice singing:

You may talk about the solitudes of cloisters,
But give to me the freedom of the woods;
Though they call them a set of noisy roysters,
Ne'er lived such merry men as Robin Hood's.

"Well done, Friar Tuck," said Robin, as the portly form of the saintly rogue appeared through the foliage. "What, doing penance again?"

"Ay, good master," replied the friar, taking a bottle from his lips; "'tis for thy sins, not mine, I suffer."

"'Tis sore trials thou hast to bear," said Will Scarlett, eyeing the bottle affectionately. "Let me assist thee in thy arduous task, for I see thou canst scarcely rise with thy over-oppressed burden."

"Nay, good brother. It is mine to bear,

and I do it cheerfully. The saints will aid me should I break down."

"Good Saint Hermin! I fear thou bearest too much already," said Will, making a clutch at the bottle, which the friar hastily thrust behind him, which drew forth a laugh of merriment even from the stern soldier.

"Peace, man," said the friar, in mock solemnity; "thou wilt incur our Lady's displeasure if thou disturbest me in my devotions. Hie thee, and get thee gone!"

"Heaven forbid I should do anything wrong," said Will, gravely; "but my throat is hugous dry, and thou hast therewith to moisten it. Give me, good father, but one consoling draught."

The friar could not resist this appeal, and he handed the bottle to Will, who glued his lips to it, and did not remove them till a fly could have walked dry-footed over the bottom.

Friar John glanced ruefully down the neck of the empty vessel, but made no remark, as Robin Hood warned them it was time for the evening meal.

The shadows began to lengthen, and a cool, refreshing breeze swept down the glade, rustling the branches of the stately trees, and making the young saplings bend gracefully before it.

As the party moved on in silence, the sound of voices in a neighbouring glade assailed their ears.

"Ah! who have we here?" said Robin Hood. "Go you forward, and I will turn aside and see."

Suiting the action to the word, Robin darted into the dense foliage, and was soon lost to view.

With every inch of the ground he was well acquainted, so that it did not take him long to find the speakers.

They were two men, disguised in such a manner as to excite Robin Hood's curiosity; and he ensconced himself in a thick bush to watch their proceedings.

From their conversation he gleaned that they were rivals both contending for the affection of a young and handsome lady. Of their birth and estate he could form not the least idea, though, from their bearing, it was evident they were of no mean order.

At a signal from one of them a monk appeared from the opposite side of the glade, and then Robin Hood, for the first time, discovered several horses grazing between the trees.

After confessing them both, he left by the way he came, and two men, disguised similar to the former, appeared on the scene, each bearing in his hand a sword.

This convinced Robin Hood that a duel was to be fought, and that the last comers were to act as seconds, though they retired to some distance when the duellists crossed swords.

Such a fight then ensued as Robin Hood had rarely witnessed, and he stood fascinated, as it were, delighted at what he called his good fortune.

As one or the other gained the advantage or put in a skilful thrust, he could scarcely restrain an exclamation, and his excitement was so great that it was with difficulty he resisted the inclination of rushing from his concealment.

At length the victory was decided in favour of the youngest of the two, who was a stout, powerful young fellow, who had won the admiration of Robin Hood by his almost matchless skill in using his rapier.

Three sharp thrusts and passes had been given with lightning rapidity, when the elder combatant, losing sight of his adversary's eye, received his sword through his breast.

With a groan and a dull thud he fell to the earth, and the seconds closed in upon the scene.

The confessor, who added leechcraft to priestcraft, examined the wound, and pronounced it mortal, and then fulfilled the duties of his priestly office by giving him absolution.

The dying man spoke but very few words, and Robin, from his concealment, could hear they were anything but favourable to his successful rival.

The proceedings had evidently been carried on with great secrecy, and to render it more complete, one of them took a shovel from his saddle-pack, and speedily dug a hole in which to deposit the body.

"Peace to his soul!" said the priest, as he watched the filling in of the grave; "and now, Sir Duke, 'tis my advice that you get thee gone to Leicester."

"By my Halidame!" thou speakest truthfully, Sir Friar, and thou wilt not forget to offer up mass for him that's gone. Thou shalt have of nobellys* a full score for thy holy work; and thou, Dunstan," he added, to one of the others, "shall not fall short in thy reward; but, hark ye, not a word must thou breathe of that thou hast seen. Meet me here at this spot a week hence this very day, and we will humble the proud dame that hath caused this bloody strife."

So saying they all leapt on their horses, and dashed off at full speed, taking different roads, leaving Robin Hood rooted to the spot.

The sound of the horses' hoofs had almost died away in the distance when he recovered himself, and he walked to the spot to see if any trace of the lineage of the dead man or his more successful opponent had been left behind.

His search was fruitless, and as he turned away and was making for the road, he struck something with his foot that jinked.

He looked down, and, to his surprise, beheld a miniature portrait of a fair and lovely girl.

"Saint Hubert! this will I keep," he muttered; "it may aid me in frustrating the designs of those villains. Gramercy! how lovely are those eyes! A week hence they meet again. Aha! I will startle them. That

---

* Gold coin, value 6s. 8d.

varlet duke, as he was called, had a steel shirt beneath his disguise. I saw it, and that is proof of his treachery."

Thus musing, Robin Hood sauntered on until he was disturbed in his reverie by loud shouts and peals of boisterous laughter.

They proceeded from his men, and he soon found himself in their midst.

"Where is thy prisoner?" was the first question he asked of Will Scarlett.

"Marry, come up! but he is safe. Master o' mine, the rogue has not had such cheer for many a long day.

Robin looked around, and under a huge bench lay the Norman soldier, his sturdy legs outstretched, and Friar Tuck seated beside him, as though giving him absolution.

"Good Friar Tuck, thou appearest well employed," said Robin, approaching the priest, in whose hand he could see the glitter of several crown-pieces. "Art thou giving him shrift and cleansing him from all worldly lucre at the same time?"

"Saints forbid! Unless I misinterpret thy words," said Friar Tuck, "I am but taking care of it, as he is incapable of doing so himself."

"Holy man, thy goodness is beyond compare," said Robin, laughing. "Thy duties are heavy in this world. Saints preserve thee if they are not lighter in the next!"

Friar Tuck turned up his eyes in a sanctified look, and replied—

"'Tis but meet I should bear it meekly, even as he who died on the rode; though, by our Lady, it is but little my poor weak frame can bear."

Robin Hood could not restrain his laughter when he compared the friar's speech with his portly form, for his waist would have stood measurement with some of the trunks of the old oak trees around. The sound of a horn, however, diverted his attention.

"Hold! Cease thy babbling tongues!" cried Robin, sternly, to some of the party who were still laughing loudly at some practical joke they had played on one of their number.

"George-a-Green, get thee to the right, and see who visits Sherwood at this hour."

The forester obeyed without hesitation, and was soon out of sight in the intricacies of the forest.

A savory smell now began to mingle with the air, and assail the noses of the hungry woodmen, who had been anxiously waiting their chief's return.

Friar Tuck having rolled the huge carcase of the giant over so as to make room for the feet of those who were to occupy the bench, gat himself together, so as to be ready at the signal to fall to.

Little John was not far behind, and Allan-a-Dale seated himself by the friar's side.

Whether it was the sharpness of Robin's speech or the smell of the smoking viands quickened Will's pace, it is hard to say; certain it was he soon returned.

"What news bring ye?" asked Robin.

"A messenger from Nottingham; Gilbert of the White Hand is leading him hither."

"Is he from the sheriff, think ye?"

"Of that I did not stay to spear," replied Will, confusedly.

Robin Hood said no more, but turned away, and fixed his eyes across the glade in moody silence.

Gilbert of the White Hand soon made his appearance from the other side, bringing with him the messenger, a man clad in rustic garb, and of stalwart build.

"What seek ye, my man?" said Robin, in cheerful tones, seeing the rustic was abashed.

"One Robin Hood, King of the Forest," was the meek reply.

"I am he. Say on what thou hast to say."

"'Tis of the sheriff of Nottingham and the monks of Saint Mary's Abbey, that I would have speech, but "——

"Speak boldly; none but friends have we here," said Robin, seeing the man hesitate. "What is thy grievance?"

"Ashes of Saint Dustan! my hurt is great. The abbot has levied on me a tax, the which I am unable to pay, and "——

"What sum? Name ye it."

"Fifty marks, good sir; and should I sell all I have, I could but get me twenty."

"And what said he if thou didst not pay?"

"He would sell me out, stick and stone."

"Fash not thyself thereanent," said Robin. "A malison on the scurvy knaves! Get thee to thy home; I will settle thy account with the abbot."

"Good master mine, thou hast not yet heard all."

"Art thou sorely in need of something for thy present use? I forgot me; perhaps thou art sorely famished, and the odour of our kitchen has set thy bowels yearning."

"Nay, good Robin; thou knowest not that my wife is sick unto death even. Now she may be gone, and the monks will not give her shrift until every mark is paid."

"Holy Saint Hildebrack! if thou sayest true, I would send their ungodly souls to a warmer region, and hasten their passage with a cloth-yard shaft."

"'Tis even as I say; and as I have heard of one, a goodly priest of thy company, I came hither to crave a boon at thy hands."

"Thou wouldst have thy wife shrift by our good friar?" said Robin, divining the man's thoughts.

"Ay, would I. Good Friar Tuck, as I have heard him called in the town."

"A wine-swilling rascal," muttered Robin, as he faced towards the board where the saintly man was keeping his companions in a roar of laughter.

"What ho, Friar Tuck!" cried Robin Hood: "a poor woman stands in need of thy shrift, and thou must needs be speedy, as she is at death's door; so hie thee away at once, if thou hast eaten thy fill."

Little John gave a grin as the friar looked up with rueful face.

"Body o' me, thou hast a sore life of it, friar," said Little John; "'tis no wonder that, with all the wine thou guzzlest, thy temper is still sour."

"Neither is it a miracle that, spite of all the good things thou eatest, thy thick skull sounds so hollow," retorted the friar, bringing the stoup he had just drained down on the head of his tormentor with such force as to make it ring again.

Will Scarlett burst out in a laugh.

"Bone o' mine, Little John, 'tis hard to tell which sounds most hollow, the stoup or thy head."

"It matters little, brother," said the friar, assuming his former gaiety; "they are both empty."

This brought a laugh from all those seated at the bench; and Little John, at whose expense the laugh had been raised, was determined to cry quits with him before long.

In the meantime the rustic had seated himself at one of the benches, and was doing justice to a platter of juicy venison such as he had not tasted in the whole of his life, while the friar lifted his gorgeous carcass, and crawled slowly away in search of his mule.

When he was gone, Little John hied him to the cellarer, and prevailed on him to let him have a bottle of the sourest beer and another of his choicest wine.

By this time the voice of Robin Hood was heard, shouting—

"Friar Tuck, wert art thou, thou slothful knave?"

Robin Hood knew that it was not in accordance with the friar's habits for him to journey far after the evening meal; he usually sought the solitude of some lonely spot where he could rest his weary frame, and moisten his throttle at will, though it was a secret only known to a few; as he gave it out that prayer and fasting was his sole occupation in his absence.

"Surely," thought Robin, "the fat-paunched knave has not forgotten my instructions, and laid his portly self down; if so, I will lay my staff on —— Ho, here he comes."

"Come along, thou irksome jade," he could hear the friar say, as he tried to urge his mule at a faster speed than suited her liking. "Saint Peter! it would weary the patience of Job had he such a beast as thee."

Little John assisted him to mount, and holding up the wine, said—

"Let good fellowship exist between us, good Friar Tuck; seest thou I have not forgotten thee quite. Here is a good supply of that which thou likest, and payest more attention to than all thy devotions."

"Now, may our Lady's blessing rest on ye," said the friar, placing the wine to his lips just to taste its flavour; then, returning the bottle to Little John, he added, "Thou hast a thong of hide I see; afix this firmly to my girdle behind so that it may not spill, and I will ever bless thee for thy favours."

This was just what Little John expected;

and, substituting the sour beer for the wine, he bade the friar a good journey, and hied him away to the shelter of the trees, where he could watch the friar and give vent to his laughter, which was almost choking him.

Under guidance of the rustic, the twain left the friar pouring a blessing on the head of his generous friend, Little John, and the more delighted at his good success.

<hr>

CHAPTER L.

SCENE IN NOTTINGHAM CASTLE—LITTLE JOHN
PLAYS A PRANK ON FRIAR TUCK.

The sheriff swore and got him wrath, when he the
    news did hear;
The abbot prayed, himself he cross'd, and trem-
    bled much with fear.
"A murrain seize their worthless souls," the sheriff
    loud did bawl—
"Come hither, knaves, I've work for ye;" the
    soldiers 'beyed his call.

GEOFFRY DE LOIS, the sheriff, and John of Langley, his uncle, sat in the oaken chamber, the same in which Little John had had such an adventure a short time before; they were alone, and, from the manner in which they spoke, it was evident the subject of their conversation was of great import.

"Dost thou say, good uncle," burst out the sheriff, "that the miller rebelled against my order?"

"Marry! thou hast heard aright; and he is but one of a score that not only laughs at my words, but openly defies your power."

"A malison on the knave! His doings must be seen to. His lands are broad, and the trade of his mill thrives well. Saint Quentin! but he shall find I am not to be laughed at."

"Thou wilt have some trouble to convince him of that, I fear, Sir Sheriff. He is strangely fast to that robber of the forest."

"Robin Hood! Marry, but his wings soon will I clip. 'Tis sore vexing the king is so busy at court."

"But the prince?"

"By my halidame! thou dost well to name him," said Geoffry, smiling bitterly. "He takest not after the king. His aid I would not peril to seek. He would not countenance such doings as we have in Nottingham; and if he should chance go to Barnesdale and meet with this forest outlaw, he might espouse his cause, restore him to his earldom, and thrust out the sheriff of Nottingham."

"Dost thou think it probable?"

"Marry, come up! 'Tis not at all unlikely."

"Saint Mary! Then, 'tis but need we keep such doings to ourselves?"

Geoffry remained thoughtful.

The name of Prince Edward seemed to have awakened unpleasant memories in his mind.

The abbot broke the silence.

"Canst thou not think of some means by which we could rid ourselves of this pest—this sacrilegious scum that makes as free with

ROBIN HOOD,

AND THE OUTLAWS OF SHERWOOD FOREST.

"THE HORSE DASHED ON, SNORTING WITH PAIN."

our coffers as though he held their lawful right, and keeps us in a constant fear and dread?"

"Faith, do I not! Half the wealth I possess would I give to know of such means."

It was the abbot's turn now to be thoughtful. Presently he said—

"Hast thou forgotten the Baron de Breante? He was once a staunch friend of thine."

"Saints forfend I should have forgotten him!" replied Geoffry, with vehemence. "I was once his friend, thou shouldst have said. He would willingly assist in rooting out this pest; but Robin Hood once conquered, and De Breante acquainted with Nottingham and its wealth, he would turn upon us, drive us from hence, and take possession of all we now hold."

Such was Geoffry's sentiments, and they were true. The staunch friend the abbot had named, though Geoffry de Lois, when in humbler circumstances, had assisted him in wresting the land from others, would have turned round had he the chance, and have served him likewise.

The king had no power over this. The Norman barons held sway over the land, and his time was too much taken up with other matters at court to attend to every grievance, thus accounting in some way for Robin Hood and his merry foresters holding possession of Sherwood Forest so long without being routed. Edward, the king's son, espoused the cause of the people; but in those turbulent times little could be done in the way of justice.

During this digression many different plans had been discussed; but the only project they could hit upon was the one the abbot had previously devised, and had been already put in force by the inmates of Saint Mary's Abbey."

Before leaving, the abbot handed the sheriff a scroll of parchment, on which was inscribed the names of those on whom the tax had been levied—a mark to each, indicating whether it was accepted cheerfully or renounced with disdain.

The sheriff's brow clouded ominously as he read the names of the defaulters, and he threw down the scrip with a terrible oath.

He stamped and raved in such a manner that even the sheriff trembled.

"What ho! without there!" he thundered at the pitch of his voice.

A page entered, and, seeing the passion depicted in his master's features, he withdrew, fearing he might come to harm.

Geoffry recalled him.

"Come hither, varlet! Saint Hubert! 'tis time thou learnt thy duty; a hundred lashes with the bow-string would teach thee better manners!"

The page approached, trembling in every limb. He, doubtless, thought his master would put his threat into execution.

"Groveling hound!" cried Geoffry, fixing his gaze on the boy's pale face, "thou heardst my words, and well mayst thou tremble thereanent! Hie thee to the captain of the guard—bid him haste hither at once, and prepare thine own back for as good a scourging, as e'er had priest or friar."

The boy disappeared on the instant, and the captain of the guard soon made his appearance.

The sheriff eyed the soldier narrowly, but he could not see the least sign of fear in his face. He was too much accustomed to such scenes to heed them much.

Being satisfied that his looks made no impression on the man, Geoffry said, in his severest tone—

"Get thee a body of thy stoutest men, and all those whose name you find inscribed thereon. Use no violence, if thou canst avoid it; but come not without them, or thou mayst as well return without thy head."

He accompanied the words with a significant gesture, which the soldier sufficiently understood, so that he did not stay for its interpretation.

Geoffry seated himself with a horrid oath, and gazed full in the eyes of the abbot.

"Hast anything else to opine?" asked he, with the air of a man who was perfectly satisfied with himself.

"Saint Dunstan!—no. Marry! methinks thou dost well."

Truth was, the sheriff was afraid to suggest further; the wrath of his nephew was anything but pleasing.

"Kinsman of mine," said the sheriff, "it pleasureth me to hear ye speak thus. A stoop of wine, I am sure, cannot hurt thee, after so much fatigue."

The abbot's eyes began to twinkle, and his composure began to return. He knew his nephew was reputed for having the choicest wine, and beer of the best brewing of any round that part.

When the wine had been pretty freely discussed, the Abbot's heart began to warm, and his tongue to relax.

"We have much trouble had with this knavish miller," he said, "and the more so since his farm was sold to pay the fine for the release of that rebellious son of his."

"Saint Quinton! Much, you mean," said the sheriff, grinding his teeth. "A murrain on the knave! for much am I in his debt. He thwarted me with his proud cousin."

"Marian?"

"Ay. She is a saucy ronyon; but her charms resist I cannot. Saint Herman! she prefers the outlaw to me—a Saxon cur of his condition. Hark! what noise is that?"

Shouting was heard in the corridor without, and a scuffling of many feet.

A loud rap was heard at the chamber door.

"Who knocks without?" cried Geoffry, half in anger, half alarm.

"'Tis me—Maulac," replied a voice.

"Enter Maulac," said the sheriff, standing aside.

"Saints forfend me! now may our Holy Lady, whose shrine I do worship, protect me from harm, and this sad disgrace."

As the abbot gave utterance to these words, he glanced despairingly at the tankards on the table, and as it would take too long to remove them, he cast his eyes anxiously round in search of a place of concealment.

As was the case with Little John, no such place met his view, so, like him, he thrust himself under the table.

He had scarcely ensconced himself when the door opened, and Friar Tuck, and the man whose wife he had been to give shrift to, were led in between two soldiers.

The holy friar did not observe the look of consternation on the sheriff's countenance; his whole thoughts were absorbed in the tankards and their contents.

His companion looked woefully crestfallen.

"Who have ye here, Maulac?" asked the sheriff, of the captain of the guard.

"This man," replied the soldier, "is named on the scrip as owing fifty marks, and the black cross is on his house; so that none dare cross the threshold until he pays, and our holy father the abbot gives him absolution."

"And this friar? Saint Hubert! go on," said the sheriff, impatiently.

"We found him in his house."

"Ugh! what of that?"

"He was giving shrift to his wife, who is since dead."

"Gramercy! 'tis well thou found the arrogant knave! Saint Quintin! but we shall have the castle razed about our ears if this continues."

A dead silence followed his words, which was broken, however, by a strange sound on the floor.

The abbot, in addition to a shirt of mail, always carried a dagger concealed beneath his gown, and it was this falling on the oaken floor that disturbed them.

Of a natural consequence all eyes were instantly turned under the table.

"Saints forfend us!" exclaimed Friar Tuck, crossing himself devoutly, and casting his eyes upwards in well-feigned horror; "the Evil One himself has taken sanctuary beneath the table."

Burning with rage, and wishing the Evil One had taken the dagger, Friar Tuck, and all into his sanctuary before they had discovered him, he drew himself out from under the table.

Abashed and hurt at being discovered in his disgraceful position, the abbot slunk out of the room, darting an angry look at all who met his gaze.

When he had gone, the sheriff said—

"Lodge these fellows in the deepest dungeon, Murdock; and hark'ee, let them be forthcoming when I need them, or dread the consequences, for if they escape, thy head shall top the loftiest battlement of Nottingham Castle!"

With this he left the chamber, and the captain of the guard summoning his men from without, escorted the prisoners to their future abode.

In the interval Friar Tuck managed to possess himself of a bottle of good malvoise, and in the few seconds the captain was summoning the guard, he sampled the tankard of sack, which had not yet been tasted by the sheriff and his companion.

The soldier gave an angry growl on seeing him linger at the table, and his own lips longed to taste of the sparkling beverage, but fear of the sheriff's wrath overcame the temptation.

Through various gloomy passages, and down many a flight of steps, they took their way, until the dampness and fœtid smell announced they had arrived beneath the moat.

"Saints forfend us!" exclaimed the friar, as the soldier turned the key in the rusty lock of a studded door. "The curse of the Virgin rest upon thy head, if ye leavest us in such a place as this!"

"Marry! 'tis but our master's will we obey," said the soldier, who was greatly superstitious.

"By He who died on the cross, the sin will lay heavy on thee," said the friar, placing his crucifix to his lips with one hand; with the other he had to sustain the bottle.

"Get thee forward with the light," cried the captain to him who held the torch. "I fear me I have mistaken the door!"

"Ashes of St. Dunstan! I trust thou mayest so," said the friar, glancing in at the open door, for the ruddy glow fell on the dripping walls and pools of stagnant water that lay in the hollows of the floor. "Saint Mary! I will absolve thee from all blame in this matter if thou wilt but find us better accommodation."

The sanctified mien of the priest and the sight of the crucifix had its effect on the captain, and the rest of the soldiers, four in number, shared in his sentiments.

Locking the door, they retraced their way up several flights of steps, and turned down a dark gloomy passage.

The walls on each side were studded with doors, and at one of these the leader stopped.

It was a much more comfortable apartment than they had been first shown into, though it was anything but cheerful.

The walls were black and cheerless, and a huge stone served as a couch, a wooden bench substituted a table, and a three-legged stool concluded the furniture.

"Ashes of the Saints watch over thee, and may'st thou rest in peace," said the priest, crossing himself devoutly, and placing his hand on the captain's bared head. "My son, no evil shall befall thee for thy piety.

A few words of Latin, which might have been Arabic for aught the soldier knew, completed the ceremony, and Friar Tuck and his fellow prisoner were alone.

Hugh Garston (the man's name), was a saddler by trade, and had served in that capacity to the Earl of Huntingdon, but since the castle had changed hands, business had failed wonderfully with him.

The castle, therefore, was not entirely unknown to him, and with many of its intricate windings he was familiar. He marked well each passage they had traversed, and could tell even on which side of the castle the prison lay.

Leaving them to discuss the merits of the bottle of wine the friar had purloined, we will explain how the twain got in their unfortunate position.

As it was growing dark, and the man naturally felt anxious about his spouse, the friar urged on his mule as fast as the obstinate beast would go, nor did he halt until they were within the precincts of Nottingham town.

It was here the friar disburdened his mind of that which had sorely oppressed him all the journey.

"By our Lady! this night travelling makes one hugeous dry. I am sorely athirst, and my throat is parched to cracking."

"Sorry am I, good father," said the man, "that I have not therewith to ease thy sufferings."

"Trouble not thyself thereanent," replied the friar. "Loose thee that bottle from my girdle; it contains a balm that will soothe my bodily ailment, else could I not travel an inch farther. Gramercy! thanks be to our Lady, from whose well this pure water was drawn," said the priest, with due reverence; "without it, we poor mortals could not exist."

"Amen," said the man, making a sign of the cross, and the friar raised the vessel to his mouth.

Being, as he had expressed it, hugeous dry, the friar took a hugeous draught.

It had scarce entered the channel, however, through which it had to pass before arriving at its destination, when it was returned with a gulp, and the friar gave a most dismal groan, accompanied by an expression which it is needless to repeat.

"A murrian seize the ungodly knave!" he burst out, as soon as he had relieved himself of the treacherous draught. "Saint Peter! had I him here, I would pound his long carcase to a jelly! Saints preserve me! but the rascal has poisoned me quite."

The man, as well he might, stared in wonder at this strange outbreak.

"What ails thee, good father?" he asked.

"Ashes of Dunstan! thou may'st well ask," replied the friar. "That ungodly rascal has given me sour beer, instead of the good water of St. Ann's Well; and I will put him under sore penance for that which he hath done. How much further have we to go?"

"Not far from yon inn where thou seest the red light."

"Gramercy! 'tis well; for had we far to go I wouldst surely die.

The sight of the inn revived the friar, and he urged his beast up the steep hill at a pace that was far from the animal's liking.

The door of the rude hut was opened by an old dame, who seemed to carry her weight of years with much difficulty, and the friar was soon ushered into the humble dwelling, and seated beside the couch of the dying woman.

The friar had some skill in these matters, and it needed but a glance to tell him that the end of the sufferer was fast approaching, and that what he had to do must be done quickly.

It was late when the friar had completed his holy duties—too late, in fact, for him to return home, so that it was arranged that he should stay there for the night.

This was not what Friar Tuck would have wished. He liked not being separated from the band of merry foresters; but he was compelled to yield to circumstances.

Suddenly he bethought of the inn, and as he was about to lay himself down, he uttered a deep moan.

"Saint Herman! but thou seem'st wondrous bad," said the man attracted to the friar's side by the lamentable sound. "Sorry am I, good priest, that I have nothing to give thee to stay thy malady."

"Have no care thereanent, my son," replied the friar, and, handing him a gold piece, he added, "hie thee at once, I pray, and get me its value in wine; for, spite of my saintly vows, I must have something to ease my malady."

"Thou shalt, and that quickly," said the man, placing an earthern pitcher under his arm. "Boddikins! I wilt serve thee, reverend sir."

As the man entered the inn, a man-at-arms stood in his way, but made room for him to pass, and drew himself in the shade.

"Beshrew me! but thou art a crafty knave!" said the innkeeper, as the man threw down the coin and called for the liquor; "'twas but to-day thou wast as poor as any pedlar, now thou art calling for liquor such as would do grace to the table of our lord of Nottingham, and payest for it with money that wouldst go far in paying thy debts. Boddikins! thou must have some goodly company, else thy saint hath blessed thee wondrously."

"Peace, knave!" said the man; "thy impudence is beyond compare. Serve me if thou art so minded, else will I seek my wants elsewhere."

"Friend, thou art at liberty to do so, if it pleasure ye; but whither thou goest, ye will have to give good account of that thou hast."

The landlord spoke this in a cringing tone, and seemed not at all willing to part with the gold, which he had safely deposited.

"Wilt return me my money, or serve me the liquor?" demanded the man, whose patience began to tire. "Dost take me for a rogue, that thou disputest my honesty?"

"Nay; Saint Hubert forbid I should judge ill of thee; but thou hadst not one mark this morning, and thy condition is well known to me."

"Peace, babbler! 'Twere best thou meddlest with thine own affairs. 'Tis hard a man's honesty should be judged by one of thy calling."

"Get thee hence, then, and let thy face be

seen no more," said the indignant landlord, placing the wine on the board. "'Tis of charity I restrain my will to pound thee to a jelly. Get thee gone; or, by Saint Denis, thou shalt rue it sore!"

Taking the pitcher, and darting a vengeful look at the landlord, the man left.

The soldier, from his hiding-place, heard all that passed, and, being curious to know how the man had been so suddenly possessed of so much money as to lavish it in wine, he followed him at a distance to his cot.

Through the chinks of the shutters it was not difficult for the soldier to see what was passing within. He saw the fat friar, and well knowing the edict of the abbot, he hied him to the castle at once, and informed Maulac of what he had seen.

Thus it was that the benevolent friar found himself an inmate of Nottingham Castle.

CHAPTER LI.

ROBIN HOOD, DISGUISED AS A PALMER, HAS SOME DIVERSION.

Disguised as a palmer he to Nottingham did hie.
A Norman on his capture bent, thereabouts did
    him spy;
Though he wotted not 'twas Robin Hood who sat
    so meek and still,
He knew'st him to his heart's content before he
    left the mill.

ALTHOUGH the arrest of Friar Tuck and the saddler had been made as secret as possible, it was soon known to Robin and his men, and they one and all swore to release them at the peril of their own lives.

Well knowing the vindictive nature of De Lois, and not certain to what extremes his vicious kinsman might urge him, Robin deemed it expedient to set about the work of liberation at once.

The men concurred in this, and Little John, who inwardly accused himself as being the cause of the friar's arrest, offered to make another trial at entering the castle.

"Have a care, my long friend," said Robin Hood; "'twill not be so easy to escape from the lion's den as 'twas heretofore."

"Good master o' mine, have no fear there-anent. Beshrew me! wer't the devil's den, I would find my way out!"

"Of thy valour I have little doubt, but thou knowest the sheriff hast been sorely bit of late, and I wot me he will have the castle well watched."

"Saint Hubert! I will not gainsay thy speech; 'tis reported every loop-hole is well watched, and soldiers hath been stationed in the abbey."

"Then I wot me there will be stirring work in Nottingham," said Robin Hood, "and I will gat me amongst them with all speed. I would not that any harm befel our saintly friar, for he is a good fellow, and withal jolly, though I opine he is more worldly than godly!"

"Beshrew me, but thou art turned sooth-sayer, fair master o' mine," said Little John,

with a smile; "though I opine he will find more spiritual than worldly comfort in the dungeons of Nottingham!"

"Thou art a shrewd fellow," interposed Will Scarlet; "but bethink thee, John, of the beer-cellar; they may have lodged him there in mistake."

"Saints forbid! if they have we shall find him not alive. He will stretch his sacred skin until it burst!"

Little John was about to give vent to a hearty laugh, but he checked himself, and turned pale when he thought of the trick he had played the friar, and the barrel of sour beer he himself had partaken of in the vaults.

"Body o' mine, what ails thee?" asked Will, in alarm. "Hast thou been taken with a spasm?"

"Gramercy, no!"

"What then?"

"Thou rememberest the barrel of sour?"

"Aye, well do I."

"And the feeling that camest over thee when thou puttest it to thy lips?"

"Boddikins, yes!"

"Well, bethink thee of the bottle of sack thou help'st me to drain last eve, and the bottle of sour I gave to Friar Tuck."

"Body o' mine! I had quite forgotten it."

"Well, 'tis to this I put the capture of the friar. His bowels have been drawn into little knots, and his arms have failed to use his staff."

"Saints protect us! well may'st thou turn pale. Body o' me! I would not be in thy shoes for a trifle when he gets free again!"

"Boddikins, no! I wot me I shall have to crack his shaven crown, or"——

"He will beat thee to a mummy. Ha! ha! thou had'st better see thy confessor before thou meet'st, or I trow me thou wilt go to heaven without shrift!"

Here the foresters burst into a hearty laugh, much to the chagrin of Little John.

The appearance of Robin Hood put an end to the mirth.

He was disguised as a palmer; a long white beard depended from his chin, and hung half way down his breast, and a stout oaken staff, held in his brawny hand, supported his tottering steps.

"Now, hie thy ways, my merry men all; and you, John, get thy pigmy carcase cased in yonder carrion's suit. 'Twill fit thy form well, and I fear me not thou wilt make as fine a soldier as any to be found cased in Norman mail."

It was towards even when Robin arrived at the miller's house, and he gat him sad when he found the huge fabric was at rest, though a stiff wind was blowing over the lea.

Marian answered to his summons.

Her face was pale and wan.

Tears dimmed her lustrous eyes.

"What ails thee, my love?" asked Robin, in alarm. "Saints forfend that any hurt has befallen thy uncle! Speak, Marian; let me hear."

"Our Lady be praised! no such hurt as

thou opinest has befallen him, but a grief of which thou wottest not hath fallen on our house."

"Saint Herman of the Wold! speak, lass, that I may'st know all," said Robin, with intense excitement, and grasping her hand impulsively.

"Nay, good Robin," replied Marian, pensively, "'tis a sore trouble, but it concerns thee not. Already I see thou hast dangerous work in hand; but have a care, good Robin; there are many seeking thy life, and they may see through thy disguise, as I have done, spite of thy palmer's cloak and stooping gait."

"Fash thee not thereanent. 'Tis thy love, dear Marian, that makes thine eyes so keen. Where'st thy uncle, that I may have speech of him concerning this sad matter?"

"He has hied him to Sherwood, and is now in quest of thee. He little dreams thou hast ventured thus rashly under the very eyes of thine enemies."

"Fie! let not that trouble ye. But let me hear of this sad grievance that lies so heavily at thine heart, that I may set thee right."

"Our Lady bless thee, Robin. Thou'st heard, I s'pose, of the new levy?"

"A tax again!" ejaculated Robin, fiercely. "Hast the Norman cur dared to oppress thy kinsman again? By my halidame, but he shall sorely rue this oppression. Canst name the sum thy uncle hath to pay?"

"That can I not. 'Tis heavy though, I ween, for I heard him say that, unless thou couldst assist him, the mill must be sold."

"And thy uncle turned out houseless to pleasure the caprice of our Norman oppressor? Saint Herman! thou dost well to tell me of this. I will pay the debt with the tyrant's own coin."

Robin pressed her to his breast and imprinted a warm kiss on her cheek.

"Fear thee not, sweet Marian, that thou or thine shall come to harm. I must hence, and shouldst thy uncle return 'fore I, repeat what I have said."

Marian hung on his neck, loth to part from him.

Tears welled from her eyes, and coursed down her delicate cheeks.

Her endearments brought the moisture even to the eyes of the stern outlaw, and he made a gentle effort to withdraw himself from her embrace.

She clung to him more closely, and gave full vent to her feelings; then, as a sound caught her ear, she raised her eyes, and resumed a calmness that struck Robin with admiration.

It was the rising of the latch that caused her to start so, and she whispered to Robin—

"A spy. By Our Lady, the house is surrounded with them."

"What brings him hither?"

"Forsooth, I ken not, unless he saw you enter."

"Saint Hubert! he shall feel me ere I leave," muttered the outlaw, fiercely. And, as he spoke, he strode to the door.

Carefully drawing the bolt, he grasped his staff, and reseated himself.

According to his expectations the door opened, and a stalwart fellow entered.

He glared around, and looked crestfallen, as though he had been disappointed.

"What seek ye?" demanded Marian.

"One whom thou hast concealed here, or rumour whispers falsely," answered the intruder, with sarcasm.

"Then thou wilt find whom thou seekest, and depart an it please ye," replied Marian, with arrogance.

The man cast a savage look at her.

A deadly gleam glittered in his eye.

"Marry, and I will do as thou sayest, ronyon," he said, turning to the door.

Motioning to someone outside, he added—

"Keep thine eyes about thee, Gourdin, and shouldst thou see anyone try to escape, speed a quarrel through his carcase. A Norman bolt is fittest meat for a Saxon dog."

"Saint Denis, thou mayest trust to me. I will cut as clean a hole in his jerkin as e'er tailor cut for button," replied a voice.

"Thou wilt not be troubled, I wager me," muttered the man, half-aloud; "my stout sword shall feel the thickness of his cloth ere long, or"——

"Where seek ye first?" asked Marian, interrupting him.

"I choose my own pleasure." answered the man, baring the blade of a stout two-edged sword as he spoke, and striding towards a couch.

The clothes he quickly overturned, and examined well beneath; then searched a closet which was used as a larder.

He swore bitterly at not meeting with success, and scowling round at Marian and the disguised Robin, cursed them both in turn.

Robin, though burning with indignation, kept down his rising wrath, and trembled, as though in fear.

This trepidation was not wholly assumed. He feared the villain would lay hands on Marian, and the violent effort he had to make in repressing his temper caused his agitation.

"I have not yet done, though thou mayest think so," said the man, insolently. "There is the room above yet; he may be there; but first, I must have a kiss from those pouting lips."

He grasped Marian rudely by the waist, and ere she could offer any resistance to his vile proposal, or he could effect his object, a blow from the palmer's staff stretched him full length on the floor.

The soldier, for such he was, sprang to his feet, and picking up the sword that had fallen from his grasp, said, hoarsely—

"Holy palmer, or whatever thou beest, thy pilgrimage to Palestine hath rendered thy arm powerful for one of thy years; but though thou hast made thy journey to the Holy Land in safety, thou shalt not leave this place alive."

Robin gave a derisive laugh.

This incensed the already enraged soldier all the more, and, blind with fury, he made a desperate rush at Robin Hood.

But the outlaw was too quick for him.

A blow from the palmer's staff sent the sword flying, and a blow on the shoulder almost dislocated the joint.

The soldier gave a yell of mingled pain and anger.

"A murrian on thee, thou Saxon hound!" he cried, fiercely, picking up a stool, and hurling it full at Robin.

The outlaw stooped and it passed over his head, dashing itself to fragments against the stone wall, beyond, and fell strewing with pieces the floor.

"Have at thee, Norman cur!" cried Robin, springing to renew the attack, but before he was aware of the soldier's intention, he sprang up the ladder leading to the room above, and drew it up after him.

Here Robin was baffled.

His means of pursuit were cut off.

"Norman hind!" he ejaculated, giving full vent to his wrath, "thou shalt stay there now, till I think fit to release thee."

"He canst not escape, Marian?" he asked.

"By our Lady, no! unless he can force his body through a loophole."

"Saint Hubert! I canst not stand this," said Robin, chafing as he heard the man's footsteps overhead. "I will have at him at all hazards."

So saying, he dragged the heavy table under the hole, and, piling one stool above another on the top of it, he clutched his staff and began to ascend.

But even now he could not get through the hole, as his chin was only clear of the floor, and, having no foothold, he could not climb up.

The soldier, on seeing Robin's head, rushed to clutch him by the hair, and before Robin could bring his staff up through the hole, the fellow succeeded in his object.

A curse escaped him, however, when it came off in his hand, and revealed the fair locks of the very man of whom he had come in search.

A blow from Robin's staff staggered him, though, in a literal sense, not more than his recent discovery, for it seemed to him like an apparition.

Robin Hood could not reach his body from his position, but he could just reach his shins, and by the application of sundry sharp, and by no means sparing blows from the end of the long staff, he kept him dancing pretty lively, until the fellow, smarting with pain and sweating at every pore, started off at a run.

The sacks of flour had recently been removed, and as the pedestrian went round and round, his footmarks described a neat circle on the whitened floor.

As the wretch's exertions were renewed to keep pace with, if not ahead of, the swiftly gyrating cudgel, Robin's laughter increased, until his merriment, causing him to lose his balance, brought him on to the table, thus giving the howling Norman a respite, and an opportunity to rub his bruised and burning shins.

"Gramercy! I am not hurt, nor have I done with you, howling cur!" cried Robin, springing to his feet, as Marian rushed in terror towards him.

"Good Robin, thou hast given it full well," said Marian, as soon as her fears were silenced. "Our Lady! he will not forget thee, I trow."

Robin set up the stools in a trice, and his head again appeared through the trap to the no small mortification of the soldier, who, taking advantage of the respite, was trying to force his burly frame through one of the loopholes.

This, of course, was no easy matter under any circumstances, as the aperture narrowed outwards; but fear did that which cool determination would never have accomplished, for when Robin appeared, his legs and the after part of his body were on the outside.

On seeing this, Robin feared he would escape.

"Mayst thou smash thy ugly carcase in thy fall!" he exclaimed, as he made a vain effort to spring up through the trap, which, owing to the unstable perch on which he stood, almost brought him to grief. "Thou Norman dog!" he added, with vehemence, "thou shalt have yet more before Robin Hood and thee part."

To gain the upper room seemed an utter impossibility, as the fellow had placed the ladder in one corner out of Robin's reach, and there were no more stools at hand.

But Robin was equal to the emergency.

Placing his staff crosswise through the hole, he performed an evolution, only capable of being performed by one of great strength, and landed on the floor above.

Simultaneously to his springing to his feet, a whizz was heard, and then a sharp cry, and the soldier fell in on the floor, howling piteously, and rolling about in great pain.

The outlaw fully understood the cause.

The fellow without had fully carried out his intentions.

Hearing the noise from within, and calculating that his comrade had been successful in his search, and was belabouring the fellow before taking him to the castle, he kept his eye curiously fixed on the door instead of the loopholes, for he never dreamt of seeing anyone appear through them.

He was deceived, however, for his quick eye saw something move, and waiting patiently until a good butt presented itself, so that he might take better aim, he let the bolt fly just as the after part of the soldier came to his view.

Robin, in spite of the grudge he owed the soldier, could not but pity him in his present state, and having relieved him of his new appendage, he placed him in as comfortable a position as possible.

Robin was not yet done, as he informed

Marian through the trap, as he replaced the ladder.

In an instant he was by her side.

A kiss she unresistingly received on her cheek.

"Now, fair one, it is thy turn to act," he said, smilingly. "Call yon fellow in as if he were required. Now, Marian, show thyself good in this matter."

Marian did as she was desired, and Robin Hood drew behind the door until the fellow walked in.

No sooner had he done so than Robin snatched the crossbow from his hand, drew his sword from its sheath, and the fellow was harmless.

Once he essayed to use his skein, but Robin checked him by giving him a blow on the arm that almost broke it.

"Greet ye," said Robin, in a voice slightly sarcastic, that sent the hot blood mantling in the soldier's cheek; "greet ye, good friend Gourdin. If thou seekest Robin Hood, he is here, but before thou takest him, I would see thy skill in leechcraft, and if it is as clever as thy skill in archery, thou wilt earn the prayers of thy wounded friend."

Gourdin was as mystified at the manner of his captor as he was at his speech, but a sudden thought flashing across his mind made him suddenly aware of the truth.

Robin pointed for him to mount the ladder, giving him an unpleasant intimation of his impatience by an insertion of the point of his sword.

Having invoked the anger of all the saints on Robin's devoted head, and consigned his soul to the unfathomable regions of the damned, the man obeyed.

"Idiot!" was the first salute his friend gave him as he appeared up the ladder; "perish thy soul for a crow-scare, for thou art fitted for nothing else! Thy carrion carcase would disgrace a muck hill."

"Gramercy! good cousin," replied Gourdin, chafing under his comrade's sarcasm, but concealing his anger, "thy recommendation would earn me favour at court, especially as thou speakest from experience."

"What mean'st thou, devil's imp?" asked the soldier, with a scowl.

"That thou'st proven my crow-scaring, and as I am to be thy leech and father confessor, I would'st have thee mind thy speech, or thou may'st find thyself condemned to eternal purgatory."

"A malison on thee, thou prating knave! I would give thee advice. Have a care, good sir; thou hast passed a *quarrel* between thee and me, and thou may'st find me *quarrelsome*."

"Thou would'st have been, I little doubt," retorted Gourdin, with a sneer, "had not a friendly hand rid thee of it. But as it lays between thee and me whether thou hast thy wants attended, I bid thee select thy words."

The wounded man made no reply, but darted a fiendish look at his companion, who set about dressing his wound.

"Hast done?" asked Robin, as the man rose from his knees.

"Gramercy! yes."

"Then take the fellow on thy back, and bear him hence. Thou can'st show thy master thy handicraft, and bear Robin Hood's compliments with thee."

Gourdin was about to make some stinging remark, but prudence forbade him, and Robin having seen them safe into the lower room, assisted the wounded man on to Gourdin's back, and passing a thong swiftly round the two, bound the arms of one and the legs of the other so firmly together, that it was an impossibility for the wounded man to dismount without assistance.

Having enjoyed a hearty laugh, which made the walls ring again with the sound, Robin led them forth, and set them on their way anything but rejoicing.

Marian was in high glee at this achievement, and Robin seating himself by her side, shared her merriment.

But her joy was suddenly changed to sadness when she thought of Robin's danger, which was now increased, as they knew of a surety he was sojourning at the mill, and she said, plaintively—

"Dearest Robin, hie thee at once to Sherwood. There thou art safe; here danger encompasses thee."

"Fear not, love," said the outlaw; "what is danger to ye, is pleasure to me. Ah! did'st hear that?"

"Too surely did I," replied Marian, in alarm. "Thou wilt not heed my warning, though thou hast reason to believe my speech."

The blast of a trumpet at that moment burst on their ears, accompanied by the heavy tramp of horses' feet.

CHAPTER LII.

THE STRANGE DOINGS OF NOTTINGHAM'S SHERIFF.

From London town a gallant knight did wend his
    lonely way;
He neared the forest of Sherwood with spirits
    blythe and gay.
One hundred pieces in bright gold he had beneath
    his seat—
Before he came to Nottingham he Robin's men did
    meet.

THE abbot did not leave the castle at the time he shuffled out of the room; but hied him into another apartment, where he was soon joined by the sheriff.

"We shall not long want for a goodly company," was the sheriff's remark as he entered. "Why bringest thou that shaveling here?"

"'Tis but right," replied the abbot. "All those who will not yield to thy will and submit to the dictates of the church, must suffer for it."

"Saint Quentin! but thou art free of speech, my saintly kinsman. 'Twill go hard with me, I trow, if these doings reach the king's ear."

ROBIN HOOD,

AND THE OUTLAWS OF SHERWOOD FOREST.

ROBIN VISITS THE PRINCESS.

"Ugh! thou art afraid. I see not e'en the foreshadow of danger."

"Thou art bold for a shriveling; but thy saintly robes shield thee from all harm; though I much fear thou wouldst have good chance of excommunication if you shaveling priest, who caused you so much trouble, should escape, and reveal to his brethren the vision he just now saw."

"Saint Benedict curse the knave!" ejaculated the abbot, "and all such prying locusts. He is in one of the lower dungeons, said you not?"

"Beneath the moat!"

"There let him rot; he is not fit to go at large. A murrain seize upon his ungodly carcase, and the devil upon his soul!"

"Of a surety, thou needst not fear he will live long under my hands; but I have one thing to tell thee I have just heard."

"Patron Saint! my ears are at thy service!"

"Harkee: this miller, whose skill is beyond compare, has insulted our ears by sending his man to ask payment for the last score sacks of flour supplied to our good cellarer. What sayst thou, doth he not grind for thee for nought?"

"Marry! I trow not. Doth he not have spiritual comfort and absolutions out of number? Relics of Saint Anthony, call you this nought?"

"Quotha! thou art a devout sinner!" said the sheriff, with a ghastly grin. "Nature hath formed thee for thy office, and moulded thee aright. Thou shirkest the miller's pay, and my coffers hath to refund the whole."

"Man of flesh, thou wotteat not of that thou speakest. Thou hast no need to pay unless thou likest."

"By my halidom, thou speakest in riddles. How can I avoid payment?"

"Thou canst tax him sorely until he canst not pay; the mill thou canst then claim for thy debts, and thy serfs can work it at thy will."

There was a cunning leer in the abbot's eye that Geoffrey did not fail to notice; but as the plan was to his liking, and likely to prove beneficial, he made no remark.

The page at this moment announced the arrival of a messenger from the king.

"Conduct him hither," said the sheriff, aside to the abbot; "he brings news of some import, I durst wager!"

The messenger, a knight of no mean distinction, entered, the clank of his spurs heralding his approach.

"Greet thee well, cousin, from the court?" said Geoffrey, in well-feigned sauvity. "Thou hast ridden hard, an' I judge of thy appearance!"

"Odds Boddikins! yes; more so than I like."

"Marry! what mean ye? Hast thy horse taken fright?"

"Saint Hubert! thou mayst well say the rider was afright. Our Lady! but I ne'er was so skeerd in all my life!"

"Didst come through the forest?"

"Beshrew me! yes; but I wager my sword against thy falchion, I travel not that road again!"

"Ah! thou hast seen Robin Hood. Is't not so?"

"Saint Denis! I saw fifty at least!"

"His men?"

"Adzooks! I trow not. Clad in green were they, and like unto devils more than men. I count myself of swordsmen one of the best; but my arm was but as a reed to theirs. Gramercy! 'tis a wonder I gat'st here alive!"

"Ashes of my patron saint! 'tis as you say; the robbers hold the country in their hands, and life to them is but as naught. Marry! 'tis time thy master the king looked to such matters as these. Lost thou aught?"

"Troth did I! one hundred gold pieces, a present to thyself from his gracious majesty."

Geoffrey, bit his lips, till the blood flowed from them.

"One hundred gold pieces," he repeated to himself.

"A kingly fortune for us, at this present good abbot," he added. "What sayest thou?"

The abbot was too deeply engaged with his own thoughts to reply; and Geoffrey repeated the question.

"Ashes of our patron saint, the good St. Mary! defend us from the hands of these robbers; they meritest the just resentment of the church. I will curse them by the holy rood, and condemn them to everlasting purgatory," replied the abbot.

Then he relapsed again into the same state of dreamy thought, calculating in his mind how much of the lost money would have fallen to his share to keep up the abbey and its sanctity, and to supply the good things of his cellar.

Sadly depressed, and vowing eternal vengeance against Robin Hood and his merry followers, the abbot left the castle gate.

Not far had he proceeded when he met a great crowd.

They were hooting and hallooing, and intersecting the noise with shouts of laughter.

"Use thy spurs, lout!"

"Thy beast stands in good need of water."

"Tighten thy saddle girth!"

These were among the various shouts that assailed the ears of the good confessor, as he drew rein to inquire of one who was looking on agape as to the cause of the uproar.

"I wot not, good father," replied the man, reverently bowing, as his hand rested on the ecclesiastical robes of his questioner; "but I will get me forward, an' it please thee, to inquire."

"My blessing on thee if thou dost, and bring me true account."

"Marry will I, good father."

And with this the man mingled with the crowd.

The abbot from his elevation could see that two soldiers, one bearing the other, was the occasion of the sport; but from the crowd around he could not see they were bound.

Presently the man returned.

"What news?" demanded the abbot.

"Good father, an' it please ye, said the man bowing, "two soldiers have been in search of Robin Hood, and the twain have returned sorely beaten and bound."

The abbot muttered something in Latin which, in a more comprehensive language, would have greatly shocked the ear of his devout listener, and shambled off in the direction of the abbey.

If his rage was increased against the brave outlaw before, it was now doubly so, and he reached the gates of the abbey in less time than he had supposed, his thoughts were so utterly confounded.

The sheriff, as may be supposed, was in no better mood.

When the news reached him he stamped and swore most vehemently.

His retainers—even those who were compelled to be near him—gave him as wide a berth as possible.

The butler had a tureen emptied over his head, and, scalding hot as it was, was compelled to wear it as a casque.

The cellarman had the ale he so richly prized dashed in his face; and the knight, who had so lately arrived, shared in the general *melée*, by having one of the massive oak chairs bumped on his toe, the seat of an enormous carbuncle.

The knight, acting on the hint, wisely took his leave of the room at the first opportunity, and, without so much as delivering the message with which he had been entrusted, left the castle that night.

Stukely, the head-warder, was not neglected.

He was threatened with a horrible lingering death, by incarceration in the White Tower, the very name of which, owing to the horrors associated with it, was sufficient to make the blood of the hearer run cold.

This tower was the loftiest, and the walls were covered with a white chalky substance, from which it derived its name.

The interior was a room twenty feet square, fitted with racks, and hung about with instruments of torture of every description.

There was the holy chair under which was a plate that could be heated at pleasure; whilst an iron band could be placed round the stomach of the occupants, and drawn so tightly as to cause the most horrible torture.

In one corner stood an infernal device, known as the Mother of Mercy.

It was a curious shaped hollowed contrivance, into which the delinquent was placed, and by means of screws and levers, another hollow piece of iron was brought down, and so firmly compressed, that the body was squeezed out of all human shape, and the unfortunate victim died shrieking and howling in the greatest of agony.

But of this anon, we must leave it till its proper time, and commence another chapter.

CHAPTER LXXIII.

THE ATTACK ON THE MILLER'S HOUSE—GEOFFREY IN A FIX.

And Much the miller's son lay there, for he was wounded sore,
A heavy noise was heard without, and crash came in the door.

THE tramp of horses that Robin had heard ceased a few yards from the mill-door, and Robin, peeping through a small chink, discovered a score of soldiers well mounted.

Robin, in the few moments that elapsed since we left them, had undergone a wonderful metamorphosis.

He had doffed his palmer's suit, and donned that of a miller. His ringlets were clustered up and thrust into a rude hat, and a profusion of flour-dust covered him from head to heel.

So complete was his disguise, that Marian would have failed to have recognised him had she not possessed a previous knowledge of the manner of his disguise.

The leader of the party dismounted, and knocked loudly for admission, which summons Marian did not immediately answer.

This aroused the soldier's ire, and he battered the stout oak planks with his sword hilt until he was tired.

In the meantime, Robin had taken his position up aloft, having used the same precaution as its late occupant, to haul up the ladder.

"Now, proud dame," said the leader, staggering in as the door was thrown open; "we have proofs good and many that the famous outlaw, Robin Hood, is concealed hereabouts; and, as it suits not our taste to be played with like our fellows, we take either one or both."

"Both!" echoed Marian.

"Ay; ar't deaf?"

"Marry, no! But thou seemest sore uncivil.'

"Ugh!" growled the leader, "and thou art smooth of speech; but I care not for thy glib tongue. Robin or thou must hie with us to the castle. Dost hear?" shouted the fellow, as he thrust Marian aside and pushed his way into the room.

"Right well," answered Robin, and scarce had the man thrust Marian aside, when he fell with a cloth-yard shaft through his heart.

Marian, with an alacrity that well became her, closed the door instantly, and shot the heavy bolts.

Robin posted himself overhead at the principal loophole.

Here he could command a view of the front part of the house, and cover any of the soldiers that dared overstep the bounds.

The soldiers waited impatiently the return of their leader, and as time wore on apace they began to grow uneasy.

A conference was held among them at length, and three of the party dismounting, made towards the door.

It was now time for Robin to commence operations.

He had armed himself with the miller's

bow and a quiver of good arrows, and he let fly one amongst them that set the horses rearing, and the whole host in confusion.

Before they could recover, a second shaft whizzed on its way, intended for him who undertook the lead.

Fortunately for him he escaped, through having to stoop to extricate his sword; but the arrow, passing over him, pierced the mail of his comrade, and sank deeply into his breast.

"Sawest thou from whence yon missile came?" asked he, who now took upon himself the command.

"Ay, did I," said the third one, who had dismounted; and, as he spoke, he fitted a bolt to his crossbow.

He did not use it; for a cloth-yard shaft struck him down on the instant, and another almost immediately lodged in the chest of one of the horses.

In its agony the noble beast pawed up the ground, and reared and plunged in such a manner that the rider had much difficulty to keep his seat; then, turning about, gallopped off in the direction it had come.

The rest of the soldiers, whose horses had become unmanageable, swore horribly at this, and the leader, taking his horse by the bridle, led his party to the shelter of a thicket.

Robin's arrows followed them until they were completely hidden, and their oaths and imprecations told how well they were harassed.

The bold outlaw kept vigilant watch, and a quarrel striking the stonework within an inch of the loophole, where he was stationed, apprized him of the discovery of his ambuscade.

"Saint Denis protect thee!" he muttered, as his eye caught sight of a steel cap glistening between the foliage, and he sped an arrow to the spot with unerring aim.

The cap and its wearer disappeared; but another object claimed Robin's attention.

It was the form of a man creeping under the hedgerow towards the mill.

Robin drew his bow to the ear, and prepared to give the new comer a check as soon as he appeared in the open; but he slackened the string as he recognised the well-known form of Much, the miller's son.

He had with him a female, Grace, the foster-sister of Marian, and they were quickly ushered within the stone walls, a shower of bolts striking the door as it closed behind them.

"Marry! but thou hast had a narrow escape, good Much," said Robin, as he grasped him by the hand. "Now will we show those Norman dogs what Saxon arms can do."

"I trow they are already enlightened on that point," replied Much. "An' I am not mistaken, thou hast settled a few already."

"Saint Hubert! stone walls are wondrous things; but get thee fettled at once, Marian will take care of Grace, and thou must bear me company."

The soldiers, thinking the foe had slacked in vigilance as he was sparing of his shafts, ventured closer, taking care, however, to keep well in shelter of the brushwood, and when they were within fifty yards they let fly such a shower of bolts, that it was a miracle Robin was not hit.

"Ugh! Now will we rout them, good Much," he said. "The knaves have dismounted, and crept to yonder copse. Let fly!"

The arrow shot into the thicket, but, contrary to Robin's expectations, the soldiers sprang out from a neighbouring copse, and made for the door, shouting their war-cry.

The cloth-yard shafts were no longer of avail.

The soldiers were battering at the door with their falchions.

"A malison on the knaves!" cried Robin, at finding himself outwitted. "They must not enter, Much, or they will terrify the women."

"'Twill not be the door will keep them out, good Robin; for though 'tis of stoutest oak, it is but old, and the fastenings are the worse for wear."

"An' be it, we must fight them hand to hand. I fear me not but we shall do them yet. See'st thou the rascals have sent for more aid?"

"Gramercy! we must e'en look about us as well. Canst climb, Robin?"

"Saint Hubert! needst thou ask? But what ails thee? Saint Herman! thou look'st pale as ash!"

"Fash not thyself thereanent, but get thee on my shoulder. Thou wilt find a hole leading to the roof."

"Thou forgettest the ladder."

"'Tis no use. Thou must climb quick, or yon varlets will be upon us."

Robin did as he was desired, and then it was he discovered that his companion was wounded in the shoulder.

The din at the door was now terrific, and they could hear the ring of an axe, like some one felling a tree.

"Harkee, they are making a ram to batter in the door. Quick! good Robin, on thy stout arm must we now depend."

Robin needed no other incentive.

Drawing himself through the hole, he was soon on the roof and creating sad havoc among the besiegers, who, finding it too hot for them, beat a precipitate retreat.

Their number was greatly thinned, so that it needed but small space to hold them, and they consulted each other as to how they should next proceed.

Some proposed that the battering-ram should be abandoned, but the leader protested against this, and stripping the belts from the bodies of their dead comrades, that they had contrived to draw under cover, he formed them into slings.

Robin had laid himself down under shelter

of the rough coping, and through a chink he watched their movements.

The tree was felled and stripped, and eight stalwart fellows bore it between them, their comrades covering their advance with their cross-bows.

The exigence of the moment caused Robin to be quick and decisive in his movements; and his first act was to bring down the leader of the party.

On seeing their leader fall, the discontented soldiers became unruly. They threw down their slings, and quarrelled with the others.

Robin settled the dispute by giving them a shaft or two, not with the intention of hitting any of them, for he was already sick at heart with the slaughter he had done, but to scare them away, in hopes they would not have the courage to return.

Those who were against using the ram availed themselves of the opportunity, urging, as their excuse, the fall of the two leaders, and the folly of throwing away their lives in an attempt which would not result in their success.

Robin was not sorry when he saw them mount and depart; but he gave them a shaft just to acquaint them with the fact that they were not yet out of danger.

Much's wound was more serious than Robin had expected. He had lain him on a couch, and subjected himself to the careful hands of Grace, who, as soon as the soldiers were far enough away, ventured out, and gathered some herbs to dress the wound.

"How gat'st thou that?" asked Robin; "I trow me 'twas not in the room above."

Much pointed to the door.

There was a hole in it where a bolt had entered.

"Seest thou that?" he asked.

"Beshrew me! I do; but thou didst not speak of it at the time."

"Marry! thou wouldst not give me time for speech an' I had a mind; but 'tis nought now those dogs are driven hence."

"Saint Dunstan! they went sorry enough, I wot me; but it grieves me to see thee laying there."

"Trouble not; I shall soon be well. A stoop of good wine and Grace's skill will soon get me round. But thou art a-thirst; I, ill-mannerly knave, have forgotten to order thee refection. Marian!" he added, "thou knowest the marks on my father's favourite butt?"

"Beshrew me! yes. Thou meanest the good stuff he uses to clear his throat of dust?"

"Thou hast guess'd; now get thee gone, for thy Robin stands much in need of it."

The moon that had lighted them during the sanguinary fray still shone in all it's splendour. It was at its full, and shed a light almost equal to that of day.

Not forgetting the mission that had brought him from the forest, Robin, having refreshed himself and given Marian a parting kiss, left the mill.

Scarce had he been gone one half-hour, when a loud knock was heard at the door.

Grace was tending Much, and Marian was fulfilling some household duty, when they were disturbed.

"'Tis thy father," said Marian, going towards the door.

"Take thy time," said Much, raising on his elbow; "for aught we know, it may be some of the soldiers returned for the body of that fellow Robin has thrown out."

"Perchance he has brought more fellows with him," suggested Grace.

The knocking was repeated.

"How now, roisterer! who is there?" demanded Much.

"One that will teach thee thy manners if thou dost not open quick."

"Marry! but thou must wait until thy tongue is smoother of speech; thou art not at the Squeaking Pig nor the Scottish Piper."

"Saint Herman! thou art an impudent knave whoever thou beest, so open at once that I may teach thee manners."

"Get thee hence, man, and break not the peace of an honest man's house; an' we meet perchance we get to blows, so take an honest man's word and get thee gone at once, or thy crown may suffer for thy impudence. A malison on the knave," he muttered to himself. "If I could rise I would make him feel my staff."

"Saint Quentin!" cried the voice, in an angry tone, "thou dost refuse admittance to one who bears thee no ill. A murrain on thee. Thou shalt eat every word thou hast said."

With that a loud bang was heard at the door.

A few hasty orders mingled with oaths were given.

Another bang, and the door crashed open, sending the bolts flying across the room, and a man, hideous with rage, stepped in, grasping in his hand a sword.

"Goeffrey de Lois!" exclaimed Marian, as soon as she could recover breath.

"Ay, 'tis me! Stand aside, minx; let me chastise that knave that has so long kept me without."

"Nay, thou shall not hurt a wounded man," cried Marian, fiercely. "What brings thee here at this hour and in this disguise?"

"Minion! am I to be questioned by thee? Stand aside, or thy sex will not spare thee."

"Monster! although thou art the sheriff, this insult shall not be forgotten. Dearly shalt thou rue the hour that brought thee here."

"By my halidom! thou speakest glibly for thy sex," said the sheriff, almost bursting with rage. "I have heard of thy doings; and that varlet Robin Hood, who laughs me to scorn, him will I hang upon a gibbet, and thee will I take to cheer me in my lonely hours. Ha! ha! and thy uncle, I will have him racked."

"Wilt thou, forsooth? Thou mayst find thyself mistaken, Norman Sir," said the miller, stepping between him and Marian sword in hand.

Geoffry drew back, astounded.

"Thou here, varlet? Me thoughtest thou wert in the dungeon of the Keep."

"Thou thoughtest wrong for once, as thou seest, unless thine eyes are false as thy tongue, and thou canst not believe them."

"Arrogant knave! Thine insolence shalt not go unpunished. Ho! without there!"

"Ha! ha!" laughed the miller; "thou mayest shout. Boddikins! thy men are safe ere this."

"What meanest thou, knave?" demanded Geoffrey, fiercely.

"That, like thine own, their sting is powerless."

The sheriff could not contain his passion longer.

He uttered a fierce oath, and made a desperate thrust at the miller.

But his arms were seized from behind with a stout grip, and the voice of Robin Hood whispered in his ear—

"Thou art wrong this time, good friend. Thou hast erred in coming here; so put by thy babbling toy, and let's be friends."

"Carrion!" thundered the outwitted sheriff; "thou addest insult to thy braggadocia. Gramercy! it shall not be long ere thou cravest a boon at my hands."

"And thou wilt grant it," retorted Robin, with a light laugh. "Thou wouldst not refuse such a friend as I? We have supped together, ridden in each other's company, and now we meet again quite unexpected."

The miller had politely disencumbered the sheriff of his sword, so Robin loosed his hold, and courteously offered him a seat.

"Well mayest thou laugh, bold outlaw!" exclaimed the sheriff, almost afoam. "Not long shalt thou enjoy the privilege. Thou art an arrant rogue, and thy end shall well become thee."

"Ugh!—give such prating to the wind. It becomes the Lord of Nottingham to demean himself according to his rank when visiting his *friends*."

Robin placed such stress on the last word that it went to the sheriff's very vitals.

He would not have borne it so meekly, but unarmed, he could not contend against two such men; and, besides, he could see the forms of several foresters about the door.

Robin gave the miller a hint that time was on the wing, and that the sheriff must needs be hungry from his journey. "Besides," he added, "he has yet to go to Sherwood."

The sheriff looked aghast; but it was no good saying nay, so he had to swallow his wrath.

CHAPTER LXXIV.

MADGE STUKELY'S STRATAGEM.

The friar bent his shaven head,
And played his part so well;
What passed between the lass and him,
None but themselves could tell.

THE warder of Nottingham Castle had suffi-cient faith in his master to believe he would keep his promise of punishment even if he failed in fulfilling many others, so he took especial care to keep the keys in his own possession, and to honour the prisoners with a glimpse of his portly person each time they were visited by the jailer.

This was serious annoyance to his daughter.

Madge was not exempt from the natural laws of her sex. She was touched with the mania curiosity; and if any strange man came into the castle—whether lord, knight, squire, or peasant—Madge was never the last to see him.

But this time she seemed totally baffled.

What rendered it worse was, she was more curious than ever to view the new inmates.

She had heard that one was a jolly old fat monk, with rubicund face, and merry laughing eye, so she was resolved to see this new wonder.

Every means known to her she tried, even to the borrowing of the key by stealth; but since his last disaster, old Stukely slept with them under his head.

From rumours circulated abroad it was thought necessary to post double sentries around the castle and on the ramparts, and as parties were constantly being dispatched about the town, it often happened that the cell was left unguarded.

When such was the case Madge was sure to know it, and she would creep to the door of the cell, and listen to the singing of Friar Tuck.

He had a clear voice, and not wanting in melody, so that it is not to be wondered Maria was smitten with him before even seeing him.

"Beshrew me, father!" she said, one evening, after racking her brain for some invention for the accomplishment of her wish, "thou keepst the keys pretty close; hast thy confessor given thee orders to carry them as a rosary in punishment for thy many sins?"

"Gramercy! 'tis no business of thine! An't please me to wear thee affixed to my girdle, thou durst not gainsay it."

"Marry! but thou getst funny in thine old days, father; one would think thy head was crack'd a bit."

"Crack'd a bit or no, 'tis much better than to lose it altogether; heardst thou not what the sheriff said?"

"Ay, did I; but I heed not his posh."

"Thou mayst have reason to do so ere long," said the father, reprovingly. "In these days it is needful to look well after thy speech. Marry! did thy words but reach the sheriff's ears, he would not treat them lightly."

Madge bent her head, and assumed a well-feigned look of contrition.

"Father," she said, in a penitent tone, "I crave thy pardon for my rashness; sorry am I that I have offended thee."

"And how long will thy sorrow last?" asked her father, sternly.

"For ever, an' it please ye; thou knowest I am ever ready to atone for my misdeeds."

"Ay, and good reasons hast thou for doing so," said the warder, sternly. "Thou art always straying from the paths of rectitude; though, as our good Lady can bear witness, I pray often for thy soul."

"Heigh ho!" sighed the wily girl. "Mercy me! never shall I be better, I fear, until our good father giveth me absolution."

"Gramercy! I would have ye to him at once, an' it were possible, for my mind is sorely troubled about thee."

"If it please thee, I will hie to the monastery at once," said Madge, wiping her tearless eyes.

"No, no!" cried her anxious parent. "Not for the world—nay, more, not for all the wealth it contains, would I let you leave the castle after dusk hour. Thou art a good girl in some things, and I care not that thou shouldst fall into the hands of the rude soldiery that swarms the town."

"But they would not dare to insult me, father," she said.

"I have said, and that is enough," replied Stukely, "so set thyself at rest on that score; so get thee to thy devotions, while I make my rounds and see that all the gates are secure."

Madge Stukely had no wish to visit the Abbey of St. Mary's, but had her father given her permission to leave the castle, she would have hied her to the mill, where she usually spent her time when an opportunity offered.

To leave the castle at night without his consent or some well-framed excuse, would bring down upon her her father's just resentment, and as he was rather severe at times, and punished her by confining her to her chamber, it was most essential, under present circumstances, that she should avoid incurring his wrath.

The warder prepared to don his steel cap and buckle on his sword (his usual custom of a night), when the sound of heavy footsteps in the corridor caused him to quicken his movements.

"The guard is already on the way," he said, as he strode to the door. "Thy chatter, girl, hadst like to cause me trouble. Get thee to thy room."

Madge Stukely rose to follow him, but her father pressed her back.

"Nay, nay," he replied, in answer to her appeal to accompany him. "Rumours enough have reached the sheriff's ears of thy doings with the prisoners."

"Father, you wrong me," replied Madge, in a tone of injured innocence, which she knew well how to assume.

The warder gazed on her with an eye of pity.

His stern nature for a moment relaxed.

"Far be it from my will to wrong thee, lass," he said, stroking her head affectionately. "Calumny is abroad, and not only thy reputation but mine is at stake."

"Let me accompany you this once," she said, glancing appealingly in his face. "If thou art distrustful of thy daughter, it is but meet others should be. Forbidding me to take the prisoners food, as was my wont, is enough to prove thy distrust and raise the finger of suspicion against me."

"And what makes thee so desirous of visiting the dungeons, the very name of which ought to awake thy maiden fears?"

There was nothing promising in her father's voice, and he stared at her as though he would pierce her through.

Seeing that his suspicions were aroused, she replied, quickly—

"Fear, father! Thou knowest that, like thyself, I am a stranger to it. Did a Stukely ever fear aught but dishonour?"

This had the effect Madge desired.

The warder was proud of his unsullied name, and doted on the girl who bore a strong liking to one he had fondly idolized.

"'Tis thy mother's words, girl," he said, half choking as a cherished memory flitted to his mind. "Thou shalt accompany me if thou canst give fitting reason for thy wish to do so."

"To please thee in all things is ever my wish, dear father," she said, affecting to sob.

"My wish, girl! What is it to do with this whim of thine?"

"All. Thou wishest me to have absolution, and yet canst not trust me to the abbey."

"Well?"

"There is a holy man confined within the castle, and as his time is short "——

"Ay, to-morrow he'll grace the scaffold."

"This last act of piety, then, will weigh well in his favour when he arrives in the "——

"Tut, tut, girl. He is an outcast, a wandering, good-for-nought sinner, that "——

"Father, father!" cried Madge, interrupting him, "this is scrilege."

Stukely was not proof against the superstitions of the age, and he paled a little as he started from his daughter's grasp.

"Madge, he said, hoarsely, "thou shalt go according to my promise, but I will keep an eye on thy doings."

"Thou mayst so and welcome," thought Madge, as she hurried along the corridor after him.

In the guard-room the soldiers were already waiting him.

The captain of the guard made some jocular remark about his not being punctual, but as Stukely was in no very pleasant humour he made no reply.

There were other prisoners in the castle, and these were first visited, so that the man who carried a large pitcher of water and a basket of little brown loaves had lightened his load before reaching the cell containing the friar and his companions.

"Gramercy! may the blessings of our lady rest upon thee," said the friar, as his eyes fell on the pitcher. "I feared you had forgotten us, and that we should have died of thirst."

"Let not that trouble thee," said the soldier,

with a sneer. "Thou canst have as much water as would drown a man of any other condition than thine, for 'tis said he that is born for the noose, water will not harm."

"By the rood, thou art an ungodly rascal," said the friar, chafing inwardly. "Thy weight of sins would not suffer thee to float long, I trow."

"Thou art right, good friar," said Madge; "had they craved thy blessing, it would have more befitted them. For my part, I think it hard we have no confessor in the castle, and as my father will not let me go to St. Mary's, I must needs ask to be confessed of thee."

Friar Tuck, short as his imprisonment had been, had suffered much from bodily infirmities.

The prison diet was not such as to suit his priestly palate; so that, after he had swallowed the contents of the bottle he had purloined, he spent his time in prayer and fasting.

Turning his eyes from the coarse food the soldier had placed on the bench in loathing, he gazed rapturously on the face of his fair penitent, in whose eyes, spite of her efforts to the contrary, a merry twinkle was discernible.

"Come on," said the captain, seeing she lingered. "Thou art mighty fond of priestly company, I trow?"

Her father stood near the door, and hearing the soldier's remark, he became nettled.

"I will see to her," he said, rather tartly. "Get thee to thy bed. Thy comrades are waiting to relieve thee, an' I am not mistaken."

The soldier scowled, but made no reply: and, ordering his men to fall in, they marched back to the guard-room.

The priest and his penitent had retired so far out of hearing as the limits of the cell would allow of, and Madge—as her father supposed—was making known the sins of which she wished to be forgiven to the saintly rogue, who was listening with great attention to her words.

As the warder leaned against the wall with his arms folded, a footstep, hurrying along the passage, startled him.

"A malison on the knave, who ever he be!" he growled, as it sounded near the cell. "He wants me, whomsoever it is, and 'tis plain he must not come here."

He passed out of the door, and closed it after him.

"Who comes?" he demanded.

"Is that Stukely?" asked a voice.

"Marry, an' it is. What bringest thou here at this hour?"

"Thou hast the keys of the portal, and one, bearing message from the sheriff, seeks admittance."

"I will be there as soon as thou; so haste thee back, and prepare to lower the drawbridge."

The man growled an assent, and hurried from the spot.

When he turned the passage, the warder re-entered the cell, and glanced impatiently towards the friar, who seemed to be engaged in deep and earnest prayer.

"A murrain seize thee all!" muttered the warder, perplexed. "I must e'en leave them to their devotions, or I may get into such disgrace as not even the prayers of the Pope would exclude me from."

Turning viciously from the cell, he locked the door, and hurried away in no pleasant humour.

It was a relief to all when he had gone.

Madge breathed more freely, and the friar suddenly ceased his prayer.

"Confound the old simpleton!" he said, as the footsteps of the warder died away. "I must needs have a kiss in memory of our good success. Not one have I had since last we "——

"Silence—not a word of it; already strange whisperings are agait, and my father more than suspects me. As I supposed, thou art the jolly friar of Robin Hood's, and I will do all I can to release thee and thy friend here."

"My benison on thee, good lass!" exclaimed the friar; "but bringest thou aught with thee to eat? for my inward man has suffered sorely of late, as thou seest I am falling away apace."

"Indeed, I have not," replied Madge, "so thou must e'en wait until thou reachest merry Sherwood; there thou canst feast, as thou hast done before, on the king's venison."

"Saint Dunstan! I would that I were there now," replied the friar, mournfully; "but thou speakest of escape—how is it possible, think ye?"

"When Madge says so, I have never failed me yet."

He was about to question her as to how it was to be affected, when the dungeon door opened, and Stukely, heated and flushed, stepped in.

"How now, good father," he said, in a voice that grated harshly; "hast completed thy holy task?"

"Gramercy! yes," answered the friar; "and if thou, my son, desirest absolution, I will give it thee."

"Matters of more import trouble me now," growled the warder; "would that thy master, Robin Hood, were in thy place, then might I have both peace of mind and rest of body."

"If my prayers can aid thee in thy wish, thou canst have them, my son," said the friar, deferentially; "my time is but short here, as thou sayest I am to go the way of all flesh in a few short hours, therefore I would have thee avail thyself of the offer at once."

"Nay, good father," replied the warder, struck with solemnity by the friar's words; "I have matters on hand that demand my immediate attention."

"I trow me thou hast enough to do," replied the friar, "even to the hanging of us in the morning; would I could acquit thee of this task."

ROBIN HOOD,

AND THE OUTLAWS OF SHERWOOD FOREST.

THE FRIAR AND THE WOUNDED KNIGHT.

There was a kind of irony in the friar's tone that Stukely did not fail to perceive, and he retorted—

"Would that no harder task came to my share; I would hang thee a hundred times were it needed, and think it a pleasure."

"I doubt thee not, my son, thy wickedness is beyond compare ; but thou mayst alter thy views ere the morning dawns."

"We shall see," growled the warder, as he took his daughter's hand and led her away. "We shall see."

CHAPTER LXXV.

THE SPECTRE IN THE GLEN.

A rough hewn lance the weapon was
He at the rider hurled.
It struck the horse—it reared and plunged.
Then through the forest whirled.

FAIR shone the moon, lighting up the glades, and shedding an halo of brightness on the green waving leaves, as they sported in the gently wafting gale.

Save the noise of their rustling, not a sound was to be heard ; all seemed as silent as the grave, and gave the forest an awe-inspiring aspect.

An owl or a bat, as it flitted from the branch of one tree to another, was the only visible sign of life, until two figures emerged from a thickly-wooded knoll, and entered the open forest.

They were both enveloped in a thick cloak, and, as they walked, the jink of spurs was plainly audible.

"'Tis somewhere hereabouts," said the tallest of the two, "and yet I wot me not exactly, though I marked the tree with the point of my dagger."

"Ah, Dunstan," replied the other, "like myself, thou art not an over-good forester. I trow me, Robin Hood would not have such difficulty to find a spot he had marked."

"Odds boddikins ! thou art right ; but look thee about for a tree with a cross upon it."

"Thanks to thee, thou hast set me a task not easy to fulfil ; all night might we hunt about, and not find the one we seek."

"Spread thee out abit," said Dunstan ; "'tis hereabouts, I can take my oath."

The other did as he was desired, and after searching about for some time, he exclaimed—

"By my halidame ! I have found it at last !"

Not hearing a reply, he looked around, and found he had wandered some distance from his friend, and, placing his sword in the ground, so as to mark the spot, he went in search of him.

After searching about for some time without success, he was about to call out, when it occurred to him that some of the foresters might be prowling about, and their visit might be discovered.

In this dilemma he walked about, scarce knowing how to act, when a sound met his ears, and following the direction, he came upon his companion, who was digging lustily at the ground beneath a huge oak.

"St. Hilderbrack ! what art thou doing ?" he exclaimed.

"Thou shalt see presently," answered Dunstan, wiping his reeking brow. "Dost see this mark ?"

"Ay, marry. And I have seen its fellow." Dunstan looked aghast.

"What ?" he exclaimed.

"I have seen its fellow."

"Thou art joking."

"Truth, am I not ! Come, see for thyself, and be convinced."

Dunstan accompanied him to where he had placed his sword, but on reaching the tree, the sword was nowhere to be found.

What seemed more strange, the earth had not been disturbed, at least so far as they could see.

"Witchcraft, by Saint Mary !" said Dunstan. "I swear I marked but the one tree, and this must be the third we have discovered. What say you, Sir John ; do you think Daverill Duke has been here ?"

"Saint Hubert ! there is no telling. An' thou art not playing me false, it must even be so."

"Gramercy ! Sir John, but thou art lavish in thy praise. Dost thou think I would bring thee here to deceive ye ?"

"Of that I little wot, but I trow me some meddling hand has interfered with our arrangement. My sword concerns me most. I would not take for it two hundred marks !"

"Ye prize it dearly, dost thou not ?"

"Marry ! do I ; and I will seek until I find it. Thou canst go on with thy labour an' thou choosest."

With that he glanced around, and saw another tree similar to the one under which they stood.

He strode towards it, and to his horror, found it marked like the one he had just left.

"Of a surety the place is haunted !" he muttered to himself. "Fain am I to leave this job for another time."

He joined his companion, and was about to communicate his thoughts to him, when he found he was gazing at something that rooted him to the spot.

He looked about but could see nothing, and striking Dunstan hard upon the shoulder, he asked—

"What ails thee, man ; art thou bewitched also ?"

Dunstan started, and turning, fixed his eyes, which were swollen and bloodshot, on his friend.

"I have seen a spectre," he said, hoarsely ; "a vision I would not see again for the benison of a priest !"

"Thou art dreaming, surely," said Sir John, trying to assume an indifferent tone. "The solitude of this place has weakened nerves."

"Would it were as thou sayest !" replied Dunstan, in a thick, husky voice. "By the Virgin ! I swear it was"——

"Whom ? Speak ! Let me know, good Dunstan."

"The Lady Eleanor."

"Impossible ! Thy imagination is heated."

"Of a troth ! my brain is all a-glow, but mine eyes have not lost their perception."

"Then 'tis wondrous strange, unless our secret has been told to her by some crafty knave, and she hath followed us here. I cannot account for it."

"I agree with thy opinion; but I swear me, Sir John, she looked not mortal."

"When sawest thou her?"

"Between the open leading to yon glade. Seest yon ash?"

"Ay, do I."

"I was beneath its branches. She stood; and I saw her eyes fixed on me, and a kind of green light flashing from them."

"Ha! ha! Now am I the more convinced thou hast been deceived," cried Sir John, with an affected laugh. "Come, aid my search for the sword, and if thou findst it, thou shalt not want for reward. But first tell me—what didst thou get for thy share in that night's work?"

"Not a mark."

"Thou hast forgotten, surely?"

"Troth, have I not! Good cause have I to remember; Sir Daverill Duke pays only with promises, else would you not have seen me here."

"'Tis well. Thy tale is plausible and strengthens thee in my favour. Hadst thou given other excuse I should have thought thou wert playing me false. The miniature my brother always carries with him I would fain possess, and we had been successful, it would have been fortunate for thee; as it is, I see not the least chance since some mysterious hand hath imitated thy mark."

"Even so; and were it not, I would not stay, having seen that vision."

"Fool! idiot!" cried Sir John, trying to look bold; "some squeamish fancy hath seized upon thy brain. Thou didst not flinch thy duty on the night of my brother's murder."

"Saint Hubert! load me not with taunts, Sir Knight," cried the trembling ruffian. "I had no hand in his death more than thou."

"Liar! Away, ere I spurn thee with my foot!" thundered Sir John. "Thou knowest more than thou wilt reveal of this affair. Thou hast e'en played me a trick this very night, the which thou shalt dearly rue."

Dunstan bit his lip.

His rage was beyond all control.

"Sire!" he hissed between his clenched teeth, "beware of that thou dost, for I am desperate."

He half drew his sword as he spoke, and Sir John saw sufficient in his eye to confirm his words.

"Dunstan," he said, in a slightly authoritative tone, "hast thou forgotten the difference between our positions?"

"Nay, Sir Knight; I have told thee before that my memory is not so slight as thou wouldst aver. I have not forgotten the difference betwixt thee and me; but if thou thinkest to treat me as a dog, thou wilt find me no cur."

Sir John, in the absence of his sword, felt himself at his enemy's mercy; therefore, he softened down in his tone, and spoke more socially.

Pleased at having humbled the proud knight, Dunstan put up his sword, and extended his hand, saying—

"We come as friends, Sir John, and 'tis need we leave as such. What sayest thou—shall we take our way back?"

"If thou art in a hurry; if not, I will find my sword first."

Dunstan gave a startled cry, and the knight, on following the direction of his eyes, beheld a figure dressed in white, standing so that the moon fell upon her; but, before he could recognise form or feature, the moon was overshadowed by a dense cloud, and ere it had passed, the figure had vanished.

"Strange!—most wondrous strange!" muttered Sir John, who felt like one who had seen something and was not certain of the fact. Aloud he said, "What Lady Eleanor is this of whom thou speakest? I saw but little of her, and know much less."

"Hast not heard of Eleanor of Castile?"

"Edward's wife?"

"The same. Thy sojourn in Palestine hath made thee a stranger in thine own land."

"Odds Boddikins, thou art right. I have heard but little of court affairs lately. I was told she was at the court of France."

"Thou wert rightly informed, Sir Knight; she hath but returned a few weeks, and was staying at Leicester with her lord the prince when we left for here."

"Thou knowest her then?"

"By sight only. I was present at the passage-at-arms given at the palace when Sir Daverill Duke was so shamefully disgraced."

"Saint Denis! I have heard somewhat of this. Thou wert his esquire, wert thou not?"

"Even so; and that caused the quarrel with thy brother and him. The Lady Agnes stood thy brother's favourite, and"——

"Daverill slew him?"

"Ay! But as I told thee before, it was in fair fight."

Sir John fixed his eye on his companion's face, and watched his countenance narrowly.

He had a strong presentiment that his brother had met with foul play.

The other stood his scrutiny well, and never once changed feature, until the sound of a horse on the road startled them both.

As they crept into a thicket that skirted the road, to watch, the glitter of something which caught the eye of Sir John, and rushing towards it, he discovered it to be his lost sword, which he eagerly clutched, for he prized it dearly, as it had carried him through the whole of the crusade.

Anxiously they listened to the sound of the horse's feet, until it died away, and they were once more left in silence and solitude.

With the recovery of his sword, Sir John's courage returned, and he said in a resolute tone to his companion, "I have not yet told thee, Dunstan, the motive which prompted me to seek the portrait of Lady Agnes, even at the peril of disturbing my poor brother's remains. Can I trust thee with the secret?"

Dunstan was rather taken aback by the

knight's sudden change of manner, but he got himself together and replied—

"Thou hast trusted me so far, hast any reason to repent thy confidence?"

"Marry! have I not; saving I have gained naught by it."

"Is there naught else I can serve thee into prove my fealty to thee?" asked Dunstan, stroking his beard with an impetuosity that spoke the state of his mind.

"Yes!" answered the knight, after a moment's reflections, "there is one thing."

"Name it."

"Swear by the cross-hilt of my sword that thou wilt do my bidding, even to the taking of a life so long as we remain in the forest."

"Nay, thou wouldst not stay here till Sir Daverill comes to keep his appointment," said the hireling, tremblingly, as an unpleasant thought flashed to his mind."

"I have not said so. Thou askest my pleasure, I have told it thee."

"And I refuse?" queried Dunstan, gathering courage.

"I will force thee to comply," was the knight's stern answer, "or leave thy carrion carcase a prey to the hungry wolves."

Dunstan eyed the half drawn-sword in silence; he was meditating in his mind what he should do; he knew the knights superior skill in the use of the sword, and though he would not have hesitated to thrust a dagger in the heart of an unsuspecting foe, he had not the courage to meet his equal in fair fight.

"I yield?" he said, at length.

Sir John gave a sarcastic grin, as the humbled ruffian knelt down and kissed the jewelled hilt held to his lips.

"Rise!" he said, and I will tell that which I have promised. Thou rememberest the great tournament given by the king before the sad affair at Lewes?"

"I do, my liege?"

"'Twas there I first saw Agnes Avelyn, and I became enamoured of her; but her smiles grew colder, and I little knew the cause until my brother, wounded almost to death at the battle of Lewes, confessed his attachment to her. He showed me her image which he wore next his heart, and assured me that a friend at court had advanced his attachment. And that friend, from what I have since heard, is well known to thee.

"From that hour I resolved me not to be a stumbling-block in the way of my brother's choice—the brother I so fondly loved, yet unconsciously hated—and I hied me at once to Palestine, heedless whether I won a diadem or found a soldier's grave; this brought on me the displeasure of the king and his few faithful adherents, who accused me of deserting his cause."

"Troth, well do I remember it," said Dunstan, interrupting him. "It enhanced thy brother's favour in the eyes of his lady love, who accompanied her fair mistress to France. My master, Sir Daverill Duke, grew jealous of him, but at the palace royal he un-

horsed him, and broke his lance. This led to the late quarrel, and you know its result."

"Ay, do I, and sorry enough I feel that it should be so; but Daverill Duke shall not triumph over me. Agnes shall be mine; and this Eleanor that thou speakest of shall stand in my way no longer."

"How now? St. Mary! thou wouldst not raise thy hand against "——

"Assuredly not. Thinkest thou I am daft? Murrain on thee for thy presumptive speech. Hast not sworn to serve me?"

Dunstan looked aghast, and stood like one petrified.

"Speak, Sir Knight. What mean thy words? Let me learn the worst."

Sir John fixed him firmly with his gaze, and a cruel smile contracted his lips, as he replied—

"Unless thy tongue wags falsely, Eleanor of Castille, the woman that has so contaminated my name, is in this forest, and she must not leave it alive."

"Spare me this!" cried Dunstan, sinking on his knee. "For love of Him who died on the Cross, grant me yet another boon!"

"Name it; an' I seem it fit, I will."

"Spare Eleanor, and on Sir Daverill let thy vengeance fall. Cheerfully, then, will I acquit me of my task—my oath. Nay, more; I will be thy slave."

"Babbling fool!" replied Sir John, as he spat on the kneeling man. "Rise, and let me brand thee as a coward—a wretch fitted not to live. But thou shalt do as suits my pleasure; so get thee up, and hie thee to thy task ere morning breaks upon us."

"Saints forfend!" gasped the scrupulous villain. "I have left a bad master, and got me a worse. I tell thee, I cannot do this thing; so let me depart."

"Thou departest not till thou fulfil my bidding. Thou hast heard my words; and if thou prayest for a whole season thou wilt never alter my decision."

Eleanor of Castile, the bride of the future king, was a general favourite with the people; and, as Henry of Winchester grew more unpopular every day, the down-trodden and oppressed populace looked anxiously forward to the time when Edward would occupy his throne.

Many of the nobles who had forsaken the cause of the king and suffered by the usurpation of their lands would have flocked to the court had Edward been king, as he did all in his power to suppress the outrages of the Norman barons, that had spread themselves over the country like so many locusts.

Thoughts of this, and a dread of the punishment he would suffer if he failed or was discovered, was the cause of Dunstan's reluctance. He had no horror of committing the foul deed.

A light purse and a heavy heart rendered him callous and indifferent to what he did, for beside his sword, he possessed no riches. His late master, Sir Daverill Duke, from whose service he had withdrawn himself through a quarrel, took heed not to pay him too well, so as to keep him subservient to his will, and treated him as a slave.

But like most people, who hold other ones' lives as naught, and buy and sell it at a price, he valued his own dearly, and he would shudder when the thought occurred to him that he must one day give it up.

This it was that nerved him on the present occasion ; and, seeing Sir John turn his head for a moment, he drew his sword and made a deadly thrust at him.

The rattle of the scabbard, however, caused the knight to turn ; and, meeting the blow on his sword, he closed with his opponent.

"Have at thee, knave!" thundered the knight, exasperated at the cowardly advantage taken by his companion. "Twice hast thou proved thy treachery, and now will I chastise ye as thou deservest."

"We shall see," replied Dunstan, foaming with rage ; "thou hast not yet proved thyself equal to the task."

The knight scowled and bent himself vigorously to the task ; but Dunstan, with his natural instinct of self-preservation, and rendered desperate by his position, defended himself with great difficulty from the swift blows of his assailant.

Sir John, angered beyond bounds, lost his wonted coolness, and cut and thrust more like a madman, thus prolonging the fight, and exposing himself in such a manner that, if he had been matched with one more skilled in the art than Dunstan, his life would have paid the cost.

Dunstan's arm, however, began to flag.

The swift blows his opponent had kept in full play, and a sharp parry and skilful turn of the wrist, sent Dunstan's sword flying some paces away.

Sir John was upon him in an instant ; and, clutching him by the throat and holding his sword to his breast, he cried—

"Now, hound, what sayest thou ? Have I idly boasted ?"

"My liege, thou hast not," gasped the outwitted ruffian.

"What sayest thou, then, if I have my dues of thee ?"

"I throw me entirely on thy mercy. I scarce dare crave of thee a boon."

"Thou art right. Thy life is fairly forfeited ; though I would fain thou fulfillest thy promise."

A cloud darkened the ruffian's brow as he heard these words.

He was entirely at his enemy's mercy.

"Quick, I await thy answer!" thundered Sir John. "Hast courage to do me the service thou would freely do for others—or am I to stretch thee a corpse?"

"I will serve ye," growled Dunstan, sullenly, "and thou shalt have no cause to complain."

"Let thy actions prove the truth of thy words," said the knight, "and if thou only dost thy work well, one hundred marks will I give thee on the spot, besides the reward I promised thee yesternoon."

Dunstan's eye brightened at this.

"How sayest thou we can accomplish it ?" he asked.

"Leave that to time, I will instruct thee. First we must find what manner of retinue she hath with her."

"A goodly staff of nobles, I trow "——

"Unless she hath come by stealth," said Sir John. "I wot me the prince knows not of her coming. He would not trust her in this forest with Robin Hood."

"Saint Hubert ! no ; though I durst wager the hundred marks thou hast promised me, that she would be more safe with him than with the fawning nobles at court."

"'Tis possible ; though 'tis no business of ours to fash ourselves thereanent. Keep thou thine eyes and ears open, and heed that thou exposest not thyself to meddling eyes."

So saying the twain left the glade, and skirting along the grass that lined the road, looked well about them for anything they might discover of the royal party.

They were not long ; for as they came to a break in the foliage, which was unusually dense in this part of the forest, they beheld on a clear space a lady surrounded by a score of horsemen.

In their midst was a monk, and Dunstan, at that distance even, could recognise in his features those of the confessor that attended them at the duel.

This explained who had been the traitor, and it was evident they had come to visit the grave, and they were lost as to the precise locality of the spot.

The monk appeared to be giving the knights, who were mounted and clad in mail, directions where to institute their search, though it was plain to Dunstan he knew but little of it himself.

Presently they turned their horse's heads and galloped off, leaving the princess and the monk to themselves.

The princess was clad in a gorgeous dress of spotless white, which contrasted well with the glossy hair that she wore, floating in wavy abandonment from beneath her costly tiara.

She sat her horse, a coal black steed, with that grace and ease that well became her queenly dignity, and walked it gently across the sward while she held conversation with the monk.

The twain watched her eagerly, and noted every movement, and drew themselves closer into the covert for fear of being seen.

As they did so they came upon the carcase of a boar, with a javelin sticking in its flank ; it had evidently escaped from its pursuers and fallen dead on the spot.

Sir John took charge of the spear, and retreated from the carcase, which emitted no fragrant odour, and, having found a tree that was easy to ascend, he climbed up into its branches, and Dunstan followed.

From their elevated position they could see

all that passed, and even command a distant view of the forest as a wide avenue opened on the opposite side of the plain, and the trees were but thinly clustered.

Not a word indicated the return of the horsemen, and Eleanor began to grow impatient, and seemed to be rating the monk rather smartly for not taking greater heed.

Glad of any excuse to sneak off, the monk started his mule into a brisk trot, as though he had suddenly recollected something that he had forgotten, and the princess exercised her horse over the whole circle of the plain.

So near did she venture to the tree in which Sir John and Dunstan were in ambush, that they could hear her muttering her complaints.

"A malison on thee!" growled Sir John; "why didst thou not give her thy sword point; thou couldst have reached her from thy perch."

"Marry could I; but "——

"No 'buts'; thou couldst have done it, and thou art to blame."

Dunstan gave a groan.

"I—I could not!" he stammered.

"Well, lookest thou well to thy next chance, or maybe thou mayst find me not so lenient with thee!"

This admonition had its effect.

As the horse sauntered by on its next circuit, the javelin Sir John placed in Dunstan's hand was hurled at Eleanor's breast.

The trepidity of the ruffian saved her life, however. The dart that was to have proved fatal to her missed its mark, and buried itself in the horse's side.

For a moment the proud beast kept on its way, then reeled as though stricken by a thunderbolt; then gathering itself from the sudden shock, it reared and tossed in a manner threatening to overthrow its rider.

Eleanor never for a moment lost her presence of mind, but with a courage, wonderful for one of her sex, she brought the staggering beast up from his knees, and looked around to discover from whence the shot had come.

She failed in this, and only had time to fix herself firmly in the saddle when the horse dashed on, snorting with pain.

Owing to the dense growth of the underwood, horse and rider disappeared from view, leaving Sir John and his companion in a dilemma, from which it was not easy to extricate themselves.

CHAPTER LXXVI.

RESCUED FROM DEATH.

"How many men hath Robin Hood?"
She asked; "I trow a score."
Said George-a-Green, "thou'rt wrong forsooth;
He hath four times as many more."

A MALIGNANT smile played on the sheriff's features when he saw the rich wine the miller poured into the stoup, and he needed but little pressing to test its flavour.

He had not tasted anything like it since his visit to Sherwood; for, in truth, it was of scarce vintage, and had been presented to the miller by Robin Hood.

"Don't like it, Sir Sheriff?" asked Robin, seeing him smack his lips. "I trow me, thy cellars could not produce its equal."

"Thou'rt right. 'Tis a shame such liquor should fall to the share of such worthless rascals as thee."

"Ha! ha!" laughed Robin; "a life in the forest would acquaint thee with many good things that thou knowest not of, even in the castle."

The sheriff scowled, and bit his lip. There was truth in the outlaw's words.

"Ye are right, and maketh good use of the things that fall into thy thieving hands; and well mayest thou do so, for, I wot me, thy doings will be cut short "——

"Tut, tut!—let us not get to words that overset fellowship. Thou art here, and 'tis but meet that we treat according to thy rank. Thou wouldst not have us set before thee sour beer such as thy Norman soldiers swill like unto swine?"

"Saint Quentin! heed thy speech, Master Robin. Thou art the craftiest knave I wot of in all these parts; but thy cunning will cause thee to outwit thyself, an' thou mindest not what thou doest."

"Let not that trouble thee, good sheriff," Robin replied, in a well-mimicked tone. "Thou wilt have nothing to answer for but thine own sins, which, I wot me, are many, and quite enough for thee to look after."

"Arrogant knave! have a care, or I will smite thee down!" cried the exasperated sheriff.

"Do so, an' thou wilt," retorted Robin; "though, forsooth, thou ill repayest the hospitality thou hast received by such words as thine."

The sheriff's rage would not allow him to hear more.

Rising from the table, he seized an empty stoup, and dealt a heavy blow on the head of his tormentor.

Robin returned it in good full.

With a well-directed blow of the fist he stretched De Lois full-length on the floor, and spurned him with his foot.

"Caitiff! thou shalt rue this insult!" he said, hoarsely; "thou shalt have good cause to remember raising thy hand to Geoffrey de Lois."

"And thou shalt not soon forget Robin Hood!" cried the bold outlaw; "so get thee to thy feet, and place thyself under the protection of my merry men; they will see that no harm befals thee on thy journey through the forest."

The sheriff had not time to speak ere he was seized by two sturdy foresters, who, spite of his struggles, led him from the mill.

The parting between Robin and Marian was affecting. She clung to his neck, and besought, with kisses, to take heed lest the sheriff might harm him.

"Have no fear," said the bold outlaw;

"thy Robin is safe whilst twenty arms in Sherwood can bend a bow; and as to thine own sweet self, no harm shall befal thee."

"'Tis not for myself so much as for thee, that I fear," replied Marian. "Thou knowest the sheriff's venomous nature, and he will try his best to do thee harm."

"Ha! ha!" laughed Robin, lightly; "thou art like all thy sex. But fare-thee-well; look well after Much, and I will leave thee and Grace in care of the miller for a while."

The arrival of the sheriff and a score of his men-at-arms prisoners was received with a loud cheer from the foresters assembled around the trysting-tree, and they asked many questions of their comrades as to where they had lighted on such a nest of Norman cut-throats?

The blast of a horn, borne on the morning breeze, put an end to their discourse, and the prisoners were conveyed out of sight, and placed in security, whilst George-a-Green and Allen proceeded in the direction of the sound to reconnoitre.

They had not gone far when the clatter of horses' feet met their ears, and they saw the goaded beast on which the Princess Eleanor rode dash into sight from beneath a cluster of trees.

It was going at such speed that, though George-a-Green tried all his efforts to stay it, it broke from his grasp, and the sturdy forester was hurled to the ground.

Allan-a-Dale, who was swift of foot, tried hard to clutch at the leathern thongs of its bridle, but failed, and, throwing away his sword, he gave chase with all the speed he could command.

The chase was a desperate one, for the horse took its way heedless of brambles and briars, and had not the princess been well-skilled in horsemanship, and bowed her head as it passed beneath the branches, she would have met with instant death.

Allan still kept up the pursuit, though it seemed an hopeless one, until the horse reached a stream over which it swam with its rider, the pain of the wound causing it to use such exertion as it at other times would have been unable to do.

On the other side was a herd of deer, into which it charged furiously, and the horns of one of the startled animals caught the dress of the now terrified lady.

Unable to extricate herself from the antlers of the deer, the poor beast was drawn along in a manner unsuitable to its taste, and turning obstreperous, it made frantic efforts to free itself—so much so, in fact, that the princess was unhorsed, and fell heavily on the sward.

The deer still struggled desperately to free itself of its trammels, and turned upon the unfortunate cause of its entanglement with a fury that no human being could long withstand, and would soon have gored the princess to death.

Fortunately Allan, who had forded the stream, came up at this juncture, and with a well-aimed blow, buried his skeath in the deer's breast that sent it reeling.

Another blow, equally well dealt, laid it lifeless, and Allan's attention was soon directed to the wounded and terrified lady.

"St. Herman! she hath fainted!" he said to George-a-Green, who, at that moment, joined him. "Get thee a little water from the stream."

While George-a-Green departed to get the water, Allen chafed the lady's snowy hand, and he had good opportunity to scan the features of the sufferer, and meditate on the delicate and beautiful proportions of her bare throat and shoulders.

"I wot not of her condition, but I trow me she is of high lineage," said he to George, when he returned.

"Marry! and I think thou art right, comrade. We must bear her gently. I trow me not what Robin will think when he learns there are such fair visitors to Sherwood."

Allan knelt him down and bathed the lady's fair brow and moistened her lips, but it was some time ere she gave forth the least signs of returning life.

"I would we had a stoop of Robin's good wine," said George-a-Green; "I wot me it would bring her to an' she was dead!"

"What sayst thou?" asked the lady; "didst name Robin Hood?"

"Ay, did I. Know'st thou aught of him?"

"By hearsay only. Art thou of his band of merry men?"

"Marry! are we; and as soon as thou art able to walk, we will lead thee to him, an' it please ye."

"Naught would please me so much; but is't far from here?"

"St. Hubert! an arrow shot twice from Robin's bow would reach it."

"I will accompany thee thereto, and as this mishap has shaken much my nerves, a few hours' rest may regain me somewhat more composure."

"Adzooks! thou wilt be most welcome I assure ye, noble lady, for thou seemest such," said George-a-Green, offering her his arm; "and I promise thee thou wilt find as good cheer in Sherwood as at the court of Henry himself."

"Thou speakest bold, young man, for one of thy condition. I take thee to be a forester only, and yet thou speakest as lightly of the court as though thou wert well acquainted there."

"Gramercy! the reproof is needed, though I speak me of that which I have oft heard. I trow me they have no richer trappings, nor no purer, freer air to breathe than we."

The lady smiled as she looked around at the luxuriant foliage, and seemed rather surprised when she saw Allan shouldering the deer he had slain.

"Thou makest free with the king's property as it were thine own," she said; "hadst no fears of the keepers of the forest?"

"An' it please ye, my lady," answered George-a-Green, "the king hath no better keepers than Robin Hood and his merry men. I trow thee, no Norman hind would dare draw bow in sight of a green jerkin."

"Thou art unjust," said the lady. "Thou takest the deer thyself, and yet will not allow others to do so ; dost know that thy neck is endangered by so doing ?"

"An' it please ye, we have no fear thereanent. What we take is but small recompense for our services. Thou seest how well we keep watch, or thou mightest have laid and died."

"Marry! thou art right, young man, after all. But what men do I see through yonder open ?"

"They are Robin's !"

"Gramercy! how many such hath he ? A goodly score, I trow."

"Five times that number, good lady. But here comes Robin ; he will answer best for himself."

"Greet ye, lady," said Robin, bowing. "What chance honours us with the visit of one so fair to this our forest court ?"

As he spoke he took her hand, kissed it, and then led to the trysting tree.

CHAPTER LXXVII.

THE WARDER OUTWITTED.

The warder stout of Nottingham,
He laid him down to sleep.
His quiet was disturbed I ween,
By page from outer keep.

MADGE STUKELY retired to her room, but not to sleep ; she watched her father as anxious as ever cat watched mouse, and noted his every movement.

The jink of the keys would cause her to start, and the sound of his foot would bring her to the door of her chamber that led to the kitchen and sitting-room, where she would peep and mentally pray that he might give himself up to sleep.

The prayers were at length answered ; the warder rubbed his eyes, yawned, and then laid himself drowsily on the bench.

"When will they want me again ?" he muttered. "When will they disturb me, I wonder ? 'Tis well I am of easy temperament, or I trow me I should get wrath with the knaves."

Then he stretched himself out, yawned again, and at last settled himself down to rest.

He had lain him on the bare boards, with nought but a pillow for his head, and under this pillow he deposited the keys that were quite a load for anyone to carry about.

Scarce had he got himself comfortably lain, when a page entered, and announced the arrival of a monk from the abbey.

"A malison on the priestly dog !" growled Stukely. "Why could he not have waited till morning ?"

"Boddikins ! thou knowest why full well. Hast forgotten thy work for to-morrow morning ?"

"Marry ! and I have not ; but what need

has a monk for a confessor ? He does penance and such like, does he not, in atonement for his sins ?"

"Saint Mary ! I wot not, neither care I to meddle with these things."

"Then why put thyself in such a sweat when thou knowest his sins must be so small that they need no forgiveness, or so great, that it is impossible they can be forgiven."

"Boddikins ! I will stay to hear no more. Thou wilt not only get thyself into trouble, but me also, if thou wags thy jaws so fast ;" so saying, the page hurried away, and his laugh made the passage ring again, as he made towards the keep.

The warder followed him, and, as Madge had hoped, forgot in his hurry to take the keys ; in fact, he was determined to open the doors to no one, if possible, that night.

On reaching the wicket, the porter, in his half-drowsed, sleepy state, was holding deep altercation with some one who wanted admittance.

"Hallo, hallo ! who's there ?" growled Stukely, pulling the porter back. "Who demands admittance at this hour ?"

"A monk from St. Mary's," replied the porter, surlily. "Mary ! and he will not be said him nay."

"Thou art a fool to bandy words with such a one. Thou hadst my orders that none but the sheriff be admitted. Come, let me see which of the brethren it be," he added, at the same time he approached the small grated window over the gate.

Above the wall on the other side of the moat, for the drawbridge was raised, he could see the rubicund visage of brother Denis, who, as soon as he caught sight of the warder's face, shouted—

"How now, thou lazy varlet ! Dost not get enough sleep ? Come, rouse up, and open the gate ; this cold wind ill accordeth with my thin garments, and, besides, I am fatigued with my journey."

"Sorry am I for thee, good father, but thou wilt have to travel back ; thy services, I find, will not be needed."

"Saint Mary !" growled the monk, testily, "I must e'en stay here to-night. Thou knowest the abbey gates are closed at vespers."

"What know I of such matters ?" answered Stukely ; "I have enough to do to busy my head with that which concerneth me. But thou hast a companion with thee ; dost he, too, desire entrance to the castle ? "

"Thou hast guessed it, and if thou hast the least regard for thyself, thou wilt admit him at once."

"Whom may he be ? "

"One that beareth news from the sheriff."

"Marry ! I heard the sheriff was at Sherwood. How can he bring news ?"

"Saint Dunstan ! thou art a fool ! Dost not see he is one of thine own soldiers escaped ? I met him on my way here, and he informeth me that he is charged with the office of executioner."

ROBIN HOOD,

AND THE OUTLAWS OF SHERWOOD FOREST.

THE ATTACK ON THE SAXON KNIGHT.

"What token hath he of his good faith? His face is unknown to me, and it behoveth one to be cautious in these times."

"Saint Mary! thou art a stubborn knave, and thy insolence shall meet with its reward!" cried the angered priest. "Thou art prone to unbelief, and if thou alterest not shortly, thou wilt find another more fitted in thy place."

This threat had its effect on the warder, inasmuch as he said to the soldier on guard in that part—

"Get thee to my room, and thou wilt find the keys on the long settle. But, stay," he added, thoughtfully, "I will e'en go myself, for I have vowed not to let them go from my keeping."

He was not gone long, and when the priest was admitted, he gave him so sound a rating that Stukely trembled.

"See here," he cried, "thou unbelieving sinner! Dost know thy master's signet ring? If not, it is time thou learnest, and thy duty too, at the same time."

"Do you of a surety say thou hast seen our good master, Geoffry de Lois, at the foresters' court at Sherwood?" asked Stukely, of the tall mail-clad soldier, eyeing him at the same time with distrust.

"Marry come up!" replied the soldier. "Hast not proof sufficient without further questioning? What could I gain by giving thee a lie?"

"Thou speakest fair words, and I must e'en believe too, for this ring, I trow, the sheriff would not entrust to one whom he did not know, though, for my part, I have no knowledge of thy features."

"Well mayst thou not know me," answered the soldier, indifferently. "Six months have I been a prisoner in the forest, and no chance of escape had I until this very even, when I got me away secretly, and bring you this news."

This somewhat assured Stukely that the man's mission was genuine, though in his own mind he could not help thinking that all was not as right as it should be.

He gave the priest, however, over to the page, with strict orders to see him well tended, and the soldier he took with him to his own room, determined to keep his eye on him, and not let him mingle with the rest of the soldiery.

"Art there, Madge?" he cried, on entering his room.

"Ay, father," Madge replied. She had been listening at the door, and hearing the strange footsteps, she wondered who her father's companion could be.

On seeing it was a soldier, she drew back, and, with a disdainful toss of the head, was about to retire again, when her father stopped her by saying—

"See what thou hast in the way of eating, lass, for this poor fellow hath escaped from the varlet Robin Hood, and his journey must have fatigued him sorely, though he has not fared bad during his captivity, if what I hear of the daring outlaws is true."

"Gramercy! have I not!" said the soldier, casting a sly glance at the smiling girl; "though I trow me it is not pleasant to be mated with a set of outlaws. Yet, I must own, I ne'er had jollier times than since I last left the castle."

Madge gave a slight laugh, and bounded away to examine the contents of the buttery, her father in the meantime resuming his place on the long settle, taking care, however, this time, not to remove the keys from his girdle, so as to make sure of their safety.

When Madge returned she was well loaded, for the opportunity was one she had been anxiously looking for. She had a basket of venison pasties, and a flagon of nut-brown ale, and a small flask that contained something of a richer flavour.

"Thou canst now fall to and appease thy hunger, good sir," she said, as she spread a cloth on the rude oak table, and placed the viands before the soldier; "but how camest thou here?" she asked, in a whisper.

"Dost know me, then?" queried the soldier.

"Marry! and I do. Thy harness doth not alter thy face. It needs but such eyes as mine to see that the forester, sculleryman, and soldier are one."

The soldier started.

"You will not betray me, Madge?" he asked.

"Boddikins! no; for thy master's sake, if for naught else, I would keep thy secret. But, heardst thou of Friar Tuck and his dilemma?"

"'Twas concerning that brought me here. Thinkest thou there is any chance of his escaping?"

"That do I, and if thou hadst not come, he would have come to no harm. I have got the key of his cell, though I fear me if we dally too long, my father will discover his loss."

"Then we will "——

"Hist! he moves; he is not yet sound asleep. I have something I gat from the wise woman when my teeth were sorely apain; it will make him slumber more soundly."

Madge glided into her room, and when she returned, she placed a small phial beneath her father's nostrils, then when he had drawn two or three breaths, she secured the stopper, and placed the phial in her breast.

"Dost often do that?" asked Little John; for it was he who had personated the tall soldier.

"Nay, never before thought I of it; but in future it may do me good service."

Stukely was soon fast enough asleep, and snored loud enough to have given one an idea of a litter of pigs snorting; then Madge, after several preliminary arrangements, bade Little John follow her as quietly as possible.

Little John needed not this precaution, as, during the few moments Madge had been occupied in her room, he had encased his feet in a wrapper of cloth, and thus was enabled to walk without the least noise.

Madge had taken with her a taper and tinder-box, for she was afraid to carry a light through the passage, which led to that part of the castle where the dungeons lay, for fear of discovery.

This was a good precaution, as they had to pass the posts of several grim-looking sentinels, whose forms were revealed to them as they paced the battlements or guarded the various doors, for the moon shone brightly, and when they were not in the shade of a portico or buttress, their steel caps and bright falchions glittered like silver in the moon's rays.

Keeping close to his guide, who passed on swiftly, John, little dreaming of danger, at least in that quarter, got several nasty blows from the arched roof, for his extraordinary height would not permit him to stand erect in some of the passages.

This, however, did not affect him much, though he was glad when the dungeon door was reached.

"Saint Herman! I thought me thou hadst forgotten us quite," said the friar, who had been anxiously watching for the appearance of Madge; then jocosely added, "Thou wilt not earn my benison, if thou doest not better than this."

"A plague on thy blustering tongue, sir priest!" answered the girl, smiling, as she placed the flask in his great fat hand. "Wet thy throat with that, and see if thou canst not find softer words, for I have brought thee a visitor."

The friar placed the vessel to his lips, and allowed the contents to gurgle down his rapacious throat before he made any reply.

"A visitor! Thou hast been well set to work," he said, so soon as he could recover his breath. "Pray whom may he be?"

"One who hath kindly offered his services as executioner, and thy friend, the abbot, has so far honoured the memory of thy visit to him as to send one of his head monks to lighten thee of thy sins, and pass thee on thy journey with a conscience less burdened than it is now."

"Saint Herman! but thou art a thoughtful lass to let me have converse with the man that is to squeeze out my wind," said the friar, in a tone not the most pleasant, for he could just discern through the gloom the tall figure clad in mail that leant against the door. "Hast brought my confessor as well?"

"Indeed have I not; I feared to give offence, as I thought thou mightest be able to manage such matters thyself; but as the hangman could not well be dispensed with, I brought him at once, and I will show him to thee, lest thou should go off without knowing to whom thou owest this especial kindness."

Madge gave a merry grin as the friar mumbled some unintelligible sentence, and lit the taper.

Friar Tuck did not even venture a look at the man who was to fulfil the detestable office of hangman, but directed his whole attention to the basket of pastry, on which the famished saddler had already commenced operations, and wetted his thirsty throttle with the good old ale that Madge had brought.

"Gramercy, lass! thou hast judged our palates rightly; though 'tis no pleasant remembrance thou hast brought to remind us that we shall soon fall short of the good things of this world."

"Thou hast feasted long enough, and hadst thou but fasted as well, and devoted more time to thy prayers, thou wouldst go on thy journey more cheerful."

The fat-paunched friar dropped the pastry he was eating, and gazed at the speaker in astonishment.

"Saint Benedict! I could have taken an oath I knew that voice," he said.

"Whose voice tookest thou it to be?"

"That of one of the veriest knaves I ever knew," replied the friar. "A little man in form, like thee, though I trust, my son, thou art better in other ways."

Little John laughed right out; he could not help it; and the friar, fixing his eye, recognised him instantly.

"Now, by the rood, this is a wonderment great. Hast thou come to fill up my last cup of bitterness with another bottle of sour? or what other mischief has tempted thy long legs to carry thee hither?"

"Thou hast heard already, so it needs no repeating. To-morrow, at daybreak, I will give thee proof of that which brings me hither. It will be a goodly action to rid the world of a sinful priest like you. Ha! ha! I will also act as your confessor."

Little John burst into a hearty fit of laughter, in which they all merrily joined.

CHAPTER LXXVIII.

ROBIN HOOD MAKES A FRIEND AT COURT.

Bold Robin, as it was his wont,
 He gave his guests a treat,
And ere the sports were broken up
 Performed he many a feat.

"To whom are we indebted for the honour of this visit?" asked Robin, as he handed the princess a seat. "One whose rank and sex demands our greatest respect, I ween."

"Nay, Robin, if thou art he, thou hast underrated thy favours. It is for me to return thanks, not thou," said the lady, with a smile.

"About that we will not dispute. Thou hast arrived most opportunely. We have another guest beside thee."

"Indeed! May I beg the favour of his name?"

"Geoffry de Lois, the Sheriff of Nottingham."

"Is he thy guest?"

"Marry! thou wilt find him here, good lady, to eat and sup with thee."

Eleanor gave a start as the outlaw uttered these words.

She was not a stranger to the ill-will the sheriff bore Robin Hood, for complaints about the bold forester were occasionally reaching the king's court.

The princess viewed with wonderment the grand preparations that were being made for the banquet, the more so as she had not named her noble descent, and had it not been that she felt sure she was not recognised by Robin or any of his men, she would have thought he had known her.

It was a source of great comfort to her

when she found De Lois did not recognise her, and she took her seat with comfort at the board.

The sheriff was altogether as uneasy; his brow was sullen and clouded, and he burned to revenge the insult of the bold outlaw.

The keen morning air had freshened the appetites of the party, which was augmented by the savoury odour proceeding from the kitchen, and when the cloth was laid they fell-to with vigour.

Robin Hood glanced over the various groups, and his heart felt heavy when he saw the vacant seats of his two faithful followers, the friar and Little John.

"A truce there, my merry men all!" cried Robin Hood; "let every man fill his stoup, and drink the health of our noble guests."

Loud acclamations greeted his proposal, for the foresters were naturally a thirsty set of dogs; and as the first cravings of their appetites had been appeased, they ceased the onslaught they had commenced on the smoking viands.

"It is but meet that we toast our lady friend the first," said Robin Hood, rising, an example which all the men followed. "Here's to her health and future happiness, and may she always meet with as true friends as those she has met in Sherwood!"

The toast was drank and loudly cheered, after which the princess, who was delighted, addressed them with a short speech, taking care, however, not to let a word drop that might lead to her identity.

Another ringing cheer, which was taken up by the echo of the woods, followed this, and then Robin proposed the health of De Lois, who was chafing within himself like a caged tiger.

"Here's to our illustrious guest, the Sheriff of Nottingham!" he shouted, at the top of his voice, so that all his men might hear; "may he often honour us with his presence, and may we always have as good cheer as the present to greet him with."

Loud and prolonged shouts greeted this, much to the annoyance of De Lois, in whose ears the shouting had somewhat the resemblance of a pack of howling wolves.

"Curse them!" he muttered, savagely; "I would their hated words stuck in their hideous throats, then would I be happy; Odds boddikins—a malison on the knaves!"

Eleanor did not fail to notice his discomfiture, and she could not but loathe him when she compared his dark, frowning, and horribly distorted features to those of the frank, honest, and open-hearted countenance of Robin Hood.

There was something in him that she could not account for, that seemed to impel her towards him, and she could not repress a sigh when she compared the free-and-easy life of the forest to that of her own regal home.

According to his custom, Robin Hood, as soon as the banquet was finished, passed the word for the men to prepare their sports.

The butts were fixed; and Eleanor was not only delighted, but surprised at the skill displayed by the well-practised archers.

She had seen the extraordinary skill displayed by the renowned Kentish bowmen, but the shooting of Robin Hood, George-a-Green, and Will Scarlett exceeded even her most sanguine expectations.

One of the feats performed by Robin Hood was to send a shaft perpendicularly into the air, and catch it as it descended; then stringing it on the instant, he let fly at a bird that was scarcely descernible in the sun's glare; and a second shaft from his hand pinned the wounded bird in its descent to the branch of a tree, ere it reached the ground.

"Well done, Robin!" exclaimed the princess in ecstasy. "I trow me it would be a task of difficulty to find thy equal at the bow."

"Marry! and thou art right, fair lady; in such matter I yield me the preference to none, though I wot me if thou hast travelled as far as Kent, thou hast seen some excellent archery."

"None to equal this, fair Robin, though they are strong of arm, and boast much of their skill. Truth, they are men of sturdy frames and sinewy arms, and practice well with the cloth-yard shaft, but I trow 'tis but few of their number can draw to the ear like my merry men. For skill I grant ye the preference."

"And ease," added Robin. "Seest thou? 'Tis no more to us than a lady spreading her fan. I am sorry my Marian is not here to give thee some diversion."

"Thy Marian!" exclaimed the princess, in surprise. "And dost thou enlist females in thy service?"

"Thou shalt see if ye mean to prolong thy stay among us; though I would not press thee to stay longer than thou thinkest fit; but one more thing I have to show thee before thou goest hence."

Robin Hood beckoned to Will Scarlett and George-a-Green to approach him, and whispered something in their ears.

The two foresters, without waiting to reply, walked away in opposite directions, to the right and left of Robin Hood.

At about forty paces they stopped and turned a half-face to each other, and, like Robin Hood, selected an arrow from their quivers.

A moment's pause ensued, during which Robin Hood glanced at his followers to see if they were ready.

"Fly!" he shouted when he saw their arrows strung, and the three bows twanged together—at least so it seemed, though Robin's was a little behind the others, yet so close upon them, that the keenest eye would have failed to detect it, and the arrows met at an angle, and fell shivered to the ground within two paces of one of the butts.

This feat was loudly acclaimed by the foresters, and even the Norman soldiers, who had been allowed to witness the feat under a strong guard.

Geoffry de Lois, in the impulse of the moment, joined in the shout, but suddenly recollecting his position, and the hatred he bore Robin Hood, he became silent again, and mentally cursed himself for his momentary forgetfulness.

Robin Hood took no apparent heed of this, though he must have been blind not to have noticed it; but bowing an acknowledgement of the lady's lavishing praise, he took her by the hand, and led her to the butt.

Here the pieces lay scattered, and, upon examination, it was found that Robin's arrow had cut those of George-a-Green and Will Scarlett completely in twain, and broken itself by the shock; but the barb, with a portion of about three inches of the shaft, had fixed itself firmly in the centre of the target.

Eleanor was about to express her surprise, when Robin checked her by saying—

"I will yet show thee another feat which is most useful in archery. Seest thou a small white spot amongst the leaves of yonder tree?"

Robin pointed to a tree at some distance, and when Robin had sufficiently directed her gaze so that she could discern the white mark, it vanished.

This was what he expected, and while Eleanor was gazing at the tree and wondering why he had called her attention to it, something dropped from the branches, which, from the distance, it was difficult for her to determine whether it was a man or some bird.

Whatever it was, it sprang instantly from the ground, and made a dash behind the tree, and Eleanor saw a small white mark against the dark trunk as the figure swung round behind it.

Rapid as was the figure's movements, Robin had time to let fly a shaft, and the sharp whizz of the goose-quill was followed by a terrible howl.

"He's hit!" cried Robin, addressing himself to Will. "Go fetch him here; let us see what carrion has taken possession of our merry greenwood."

Will Scarlett set off at a run, and soon appeared, leading a man who was writhing with pain, and roaring something after the fashion of a wild beast.

"What, Dunstan! how came you here?" was just upon the lips of the princess, but she checked her speech, and turned her head in the hope of not being recognised by the ruffian.

Robin noticed this, but attributed it to another cause. He ordered Will to take the fellow away and extract the arrow which had fixed him to the tree from his hand, adding—

"Such sights are not fitted for a lady's eyes; neither is such music concordant to her ears; the howl of a pack of wolves would be more agreeable, I am sure, and the grin of a hyæna more pleasant than the look of his villanous features."

Eleanor breathed more freely when the man had gone away, and, as she was fearful of discovery, as her visit to the forest was a clandestine one, and she did not wish it to come to the knowledge of her husband, she intimated her intention of leaving shortly.

Robin had in some measure expected this, and was therefore prepared for the announcement, and as a drizzling rain put an end to the sports, he asked the lady to accompany him to his residence.

"Now, lady," he said, as he handed her to a seat of the softest furs, "I entreat of thee to tell me where thou art going, that I may give thee fitting escort through the forest, which is, at the best of times, not safe for a lady to travel alone."

"Gramercy! Robin," replied the lady, "from what I have seen of thy men there is nought to apprehend of danger; though I may say I have experienced great danger"—and her cheek flushed as the recollection of the cowardly attempt on her life flashed to her mind—"in coming hither."

"It is as well to be cautious," replied Robin; "danger, as thou sawst just now, lurks in every tree. The Norman hounds, that serve to swell the numbers of the forest beasts, lurk about in expectation of their prey; and I trow me yon fellow I caught seated in the branches was one of them, and 'tis more than likely he or some of his fellows caused thee thy almost fatal accident."

A flush mantled the brow of the princess as he uttered these words.

It appeared to her, as he said, more than probable that Dunstan had had a hand in the affair, though for what reason she was at a loss to conjecture.

She now remembered seeing two men prowling about the forest when she was in search of the knight's grave, and the monk's strong denial to name the rest of the participators in the affair when she urged him to do so on the commencement of their journey thither.

As these thoughts flashed vividly to her mind, and she began to reflect on the different incidents of that night, it occurred to her that a foul act of treachery had been meditated, and only frustrated by the hand of Providence, and this fully determined her to avail herself of the protection offered by Robin Hood.

The few moments occupied by these reflections had been taken advantage of by Robin Hood in taking a good survey of his lady visitor.

Her noble deportment and stately figure had won his admiration, and the more he gazed on her the more fully convinced he became that something more than ordinary was the reason for her keeping her name and condition a secret.

He was too sensitive, however, to urge her against her will to disclose it, but he could not master the inclination he felt to know something more of her.

"Pardon me, lady," he said, breaking the painful silence maintained on both sides for the last few moments; "but you could not have been so courageous to near the borders of the forest without some attendance ?"

"Saints forbid I should act so indiscreetly ! A dozen staunch friends had I ere I lost them in the forest."

"And thy horse, too, deserted thee ?"

"Gramercy ! it could do no other ; the poor beast was so goaded, as thy men could tell the ; but thou canst provide me another an I pay thee ?"

"I will lend thee one which thou canst return at pleasure," replied Robin Hood, colouring at the mention of payment. "Robin Hood is not so poor but that he can grant thee this trivial boon."

"Nay, thou must receive some recompense, as I have bethought me to accept thy offer of protection ; thou must name a sum to see me safe to Leicester Castle."

Robin Hood glanced at her as though he would search her through.

"Art thou staying at Leicester ?" he asked.

"Ay, with the widow of the late Earl de Mountford."

"The king's sister ?"

"The same ; and now I have told thee so much, I pray thee ask me no more."

"I had but one other question to ask," said Robin, eyeing the ring upon her finger, "and that I can answer of myself, from what I have seen."

Eleanor blushed, and removed the ring from his gaze. But too late ; Robin Hood had seen the armorial bearings of Prince Edward graven upon it.

"'Tis as well thou hast assumed a disguise," he said, as he noted the princess's trepidation. "Of my own knowledge I can avow that Edward is no favourite with the Normans. Had his father acted like him, he would not have had to ask the aid of those Norman curs ; stout English arms would have flocked to his banner, and struck terror to his foes. But, there, who can foretel the future ?—who can recal the errors of the past ?"

Eleanor had a favourable opinion of the honest outlaw before, but she now looked upon him as a man who had been persecuted and foully culumniated.

"Robin Hood," she said, "I would I could see thee reinstated in thy earldom. Oh ! that the king were not so blinded by his flattering courtiers, that he could see into the hearts of his false knights, who, with bended knee and subtle tongue, pour poison into his ear; then would he be surrounded by strong arms and faithful hearts, such as his own ! Gladly would I intercede in thy favour, but "——

"I need it not, Eleanor of Castile—for as such I recognise thee, though for reasons of thine own thou may'st deny it. I am happy as a king, for here I reign supreme ; the forest is to me more than a kingdom, and my trusty men are more faithful than the fawnlings that surround his Majesty. Besides, thy words confirm thy visit to these parts to be a secret one, and it would but lay thee

open to slander were it known thou had visited the outlaw."

"Fash not thyself thereanent, though, by our Lady ! I must confess thee right ; Edward does not bear thee the malice thou presumest, though thy arms have been borne against the king. Beshrew me ! but he wishes thee well, Robin, though I wot me he hath enough whispered in his ear through thy friend, the sheriff, to poison his mind against thee."

"Pshaw ! let not the name of so vile a reptile contaminate thy lips. Geoffry de Lois is at present a favourite with the king, but should aught cross him, or his possessions be more limited, he will at once turn against the king ; but I trow me thou art anxious for thy journey, so I will hie me at once and prepare for thy departure."

Robin was not long in making arrangements for the disposal of his men during his absence, for he was anxious to see the princess safely on her way himself, the more so after what had transpired, and he knew the dangers that menaced her.

Horses were soon brought, and having refreshed themselves, and completed their toilet, for Robin was particular on the point, especially on an occasion like the present, they set off on their journey towards Leicester.

Robin, however, took the precaution to have an escort of his favourite bowmen, a wise precaution on his part, as future events will show.

CHAPTER LXXIX.

A NIGHT IN THE VAULTS.

The friar sat in his cell,
Bewailing his sad fate,
When Little John he entered
With helmet on his pate.

THE head warder slept soundly under the effects of the drug administered to him by the fumes he had inhaled from the phial, and while he slept a strange scene was enacted in the dungeon appropriated to the express use of Friar Tuck and the saddler.

The former had resumed his usual gaiety since his bodily wants had been administered to, and the latter had had a great weight removed from his mind by Little John informing him that his wife's body had received decent interment by the hands of the foresters.

As the time drew near for the guard to go their customary round, Madge slipped out of the hall, and was about to close the door, when Little John caught her by the shoulder.

"Begone ! fash me not with thy foolery !" she said, tartly, "lest thou would have the guard down upon thee."

"Marry ! 'tis concerning of that I would have speech with thee. Where goest thou in such haste ?"

"Trouble thee not with my affairs. I must begone ; so long as thou art quiet, thou hast nought to fear."

"But thou wilt surely not lock the door?" said Little John.

"Of a surety I will," replied Madge; "why askest thou such a question?"

"It concerns me much, or I should not have done so," replied Little John, evincing some alarm. "Saint Herman! shouldst they find me here"——

"They will not—thou will be quite safe. I shall have the key."

"But should thy uncle awake?" suggested Little John, drawing her within the cell. "How canst thou answer for my absence?"

"Trouble not thyself thereanent, man," said Madge, laughing; "thou art safer here in company with our good friar than with me; besides, my father, should he wake, and catch thine unruly eyes fixed on me, he could at once imagine thou hadst come purposely to rob him of his treasure."

"Saint Herman of the Wold! thou reckonest me up sorely," said Little John, giving her an amorous glance. "Now, had mine eyes the roguish expression of our friend's here, I might have given thee credit for thy speech."

"Vile slanderer!" cried Friar Tuck, with a merry twinkle in his eyes. "Had I my good staff here I would pound thy long carcase to a jelly, and teach ye to be more guarded of thy tongue. What saw ye ever in me to justify such an assertion?"

"Enough to satisfy me that I am in the right."

"St. Mary! but thou art an arrogant knave, and may sorely rue this speech. Wait till I get thee"——

"On the turret. Ha, ha!" interposed Little John, laughing. "There will I sweat thee when the hempen neckcloth is adjusted."

Friar Tuck could not help laughing, in spite of the terrible meaning those words conveyed; for though it had been arranged for him to be hung at daylight, he had such implicit faith in the warder's daughter, that it was treated as a joke.

"And then you think of having her to thyself?" he added, continuing the badinage. "Ah me! I wot not what she can see in thy hang-dog face to possess thee in her favour. She must have a strange liking for an executioner."

"Strange liking or not, it is but meet she should prefer the executioner to the culprit. Gramercy! it would ill-requite her to waste her affections on a dead man; and thou mayst consider thyself such already, for thy paunch will ensure thee a speedy death."

The friar glanced down at the part mentioned, and seemed satisfied to find it had not fallen away so much as he had expected, for there was the seat of his only comfort; prayer and fasting did not agree with him, but prayer and feasting were his very life.

Madge saw at once that if she did not interfere, they would keep on talking until something serious resulted from it, so she reminded them again of their folly in detaining her.

"Ay, 'tis for our good she speaketh," said Friar Tuck. "Saints forfend that we shall do aught to bring her to harm! Go, lass; but first take my benison to protect thee on the way."

As he spoke the crafty friar sidled up to her, and placing his arm round her neck, pressed his fat lips to hers, and gave a smack that might have been heard in the passage without.

Little John was about to do the same, but Madge, guessing his intention, rushed out of the cell, slammed the door, and turned the key.

She listened at the key-hole to the friar's merry laugh; then turning on her heel, with a face radiant with smiles, she hurried to her room.

She had scarce got in and ruffled her bed as though she had been sleeping on it, when the tramp of armed men was heard in the corridor.

"What ho! there Stukely!" shouted the captain of the guard.

No answer came, so he called again.

"A murrain on the fellow! he sleeps as sound as a trooper," he said to one of his men.

"A trooper's horse, captain," said the man addressed, for he concluded the hint was for him, as he was a sound sleeper; "I trow me, that's what you mean."

The parry was as good as the thrust, so the captain deigned no reply, but hammered at the door with his sword-hilt.

"Now, Stukely!" he shouted again, "rouse up. I trow me, thou art bottling off a little sleep this time."

"Odds boddikins! what art thou about, man?" cried Madge, dashing open the door, and affecting to be startled from her sleep. "By our Lady! one would think thou hadst come to jeopardize our ear-drums. Hast gone past thyself, man, or have you made acquaintance with the cellarer?"

"It matters not to thee, jade. Where is thy father?"

"Where thou wilt have to seek him, if thou art not civil."

"Methinks thou art in thy pets, lass. What say you?" asked the soldier, gruffly.

"And thou hast exceeded thy duty," replied Madge, with a disdainful toss of the head.

This was the only retort she found to be of any avail, and having studied its effect, she used it both to officers and men alike.

It had its effect this time.

"Now, now, Madge," said the officer, smoothing down; "keep thy temper, I pray. Sorry am I at having disturbed thee; but wake thy father, girl; we don't want to stay here all night."

"You are are at liberty to go."

"Ay, but thy father?"

"He sleeps, and to wake him is more than I durst."

"But thou must, I tell ye," cried the

soldier, his temper beginning to ruffle. "It is of his own choosing, not mine."

"Then thou had better do it, if you will be obstinate ; and the Virgin protect ye if he is in no better mood than when he laid him down !"

Madge stepped aside for them to pass, and the soldier stepped boldly in.

Stukely was snoring aloud, and though the officer tried to wake him, he could get nothing from him but a grunt.

"Saint Quintin ! but he sleeps soundly," cried the soldier, turning red in the face. "Give me the keys, lass, for I trow me there is no such thing as waking him."

"I told thee so at first, but thou art so prone to unbelief that my words are wasted. Get thee gone, and let me hie to my couch."

"The key ! the key !" shouted the captain in despair, and stamping his foot to give vehemence to his words. "Give me the key, lass, or "——

Madge did not wait for him to finish the sentence.

With a pouting lip, and a disdainful toss of the head, she said—

"Take what seemest thee fit ; I will have no further speech with thee, so I bid ye a pleasant night."

So saying, she drew-to the cloak she had hastily thrown over her, and entered her own room, slamming the door after her.

The soldier gave vent to sundry rapid oaths, and having made one more fruitless effort to wake the warder, ordered his men to fall in, and hurried on his rounds.

Madge Stukely listened to their retreating footsteps with delight, and when they had gone too far to return, she entered the room where her father slept.

He still snored heavily, and to make sure of his not waking, she passed the phial across his nostrils again.

Some few minutes were thus occupied in making arrangements, and having completed these, she made her way to the dungeon again.

This time she carried no light, as she had left the taper in the cell, and just as she had got within a few feet of the door, she came full butt upon some one.

"Who's there?" cried the soldier, who had been suddenly aroused from his sleep. "Stand, or forfeit thy life !"

His sword rattled as he loosed it from its sheath, and had not Madge adroitly dodged aside, it would have run her through.

The impetus caused by the force with which the soldier delivered the blow sent him reeling forward, and his head came heavily in contact with the opposite wall, and the soldier fell to the floor stunned.

With a presence of mind which was really astounding, Madge recovered herself, and getting accustomed to the gloomy light that came through the loophole in the wall, she saw the man laying bleeding and stunned.

"Gramercy ! 'tis well he did not recognise me," she muttered. "The spirits can well answer for this, and as he is well versed in spiritual lore, he will doubtless be able to give his comrades a description of the ghost in the morning."

As she muttered this she knelt down, and got a sufficient glance of the man's face to recognise him, and then she used the phial, which she had used to her father, to his nostrils.

A groan burst from the chest of the wounded soldier as the drug took effect and passed through his lungs, and then he lay as one dead.

When Madge entered the dungeon, she found the trio anxiously awaiting her. Little John especially, for he had been listening at the door, and heard the clang of the soldier's sword as it dropped from his grasp to the stone floor as he fell.

"Good Madge, has any harm befallen thee ?" he asked with bated breath.

"Our Lady be praised ! I have escaped all harm, though how it would be more than I could tell thee."

"Ah ! then I trow thou wert in danger ?"

"Assuredly, yes ; but I floored the sentinel that stood in my way, and you see I have arrived safe."

"Have they placed a sentry on the door, then ?" asked Little John, scratching his head.

"Marry have they ! But the saints protect me ! 'twas through my own folly."

"Foolish girl ! you have committed some rashness, and placed yourself in danger for our sakes."

"Yes, I must own it is as thou sayest ; foolish enough have I been. Had I given up the key of this dungeon, you would not have had a sentry over you."

Little John noticed the arch smile that played on her lip, and was about to make some reply, when Friar Tuck checked him by stepping boldly up to Madge, and saying—

"'Twas my benison, my daughter, that helped thee out of thy peril. I will give thee another to shield ye from future harm."

He seized Madge as he did before, by placing his arm round her neck ; but before he could accomplish his purpose, she gave him such a smack on the cheek as made his face glow again.

It was Little John's turn to laugh now, and he did so right lustily, much to the annoyance of the friar, who had to submit, as it were, to double punishment.

"Saint Benedict ! thou art rightly served," said Little John ; "thou deserved all thy punishment for thy greed. Had thou received thy proper deserts, thine other cheek would have shared likewise."

"Saints forfend that we should have to suffer thus for having of a liberal disposition !" said the friar, trying but vainly to elongate his fat, chubby face. "Saint Mary ! it is worse than doing penance."

"You will have to do penance much worse, I fear me, if thou alterest not thy ways

ROBIN HOOD,

AND THE OUTLAWS OF SHERWOOD FOREST.

THE SCENE IN THE WHITE TOWER.

soon," said Madge, throwing as much irony into her voice as possible. "Dost feel inclined to stay here altogether?"

"Stop here! I would sooner go to the dev——heaven, than stay in such a place as this," Friar Tuck replied. "But then all good men have to bear with much persecution."

"And ye are one amongst them, I presume, or thou wouldst not sound thy trump so loudly; but while we wait here time is on the wing, and such an opportunity as this, once lost, is never to be recovered again."

"Thou art right, my daughter; I agree with thee in that," said the jolly friar, trying to look serious—a part in which his rubicund visage would not assist him. "Lead on, my daughter; we will follow in thy steps."

"Silence! raise not thy voice above a whisper, lest it reaches other ears than thou intend it for; our path is one of danger, but if thou but follow my directions, all will be well."

They left the cell, and Madge carefully locked the door, a circumstance which the trio noticed with as much interest, and still greater pleasure, than when last she performed that office.

Madge carried a light, which she shielded beneath her cloak for fear of it being seen by any of the sentinels, whose heavy tread was wafted in from the battlements by the chill morning air.

Their way lay past the sentinel, and Madge stooped down to ascertain if he still slept.

He looked pale and ghastly by the flickering light, his brow speckled with blood, and his bosom heaving so gently as to give him the appearance of death.

"'Tis well," muttered Madge, rising from her knee and hurrying onward. "Come on; I hear footsteps approaching."

Her quick ear detected the sound long before the others were aware of it, but they soon heard the hasty tread of a soldier approaching towards where the sentinel lay, and they could hear the clank of his scabbard as it caught against the wall in his hurried walk.

"Stay here," she said at length, after the end of a long passage was reached; "I will replace the key for fear my father wakes."

She was scarcely a moment gone, but it seemed an hour to the men; for the soldier had by this time discovered the sentinel on the floor.

He had stumbled against his foot, which threw him off his legs; and he scrambled up, swearing most lustily.

"A malison on thee, thou sleeping dog," they could hear him say as he tried to rouse the fellow. "By saint Denis! thou art ever sleeping on thy post; but I trow me a scourge of nettles will awake thee in the morning."

"'Tis the captain of the guard; I recognise his voice," whispered Madge; "we must be quick, or the guard will be down upon us."

Scarce had she uttered the words when the voice of the captain was heard shouting at the top of his voice—

"What ho! there! the guard! A light! a light!"

The tramping of heavy feet was now heard, and the glare of a torch was visible at the other end of the corridor.

"On, on!" whispered Madge, "or, by our Lady, we shall be discovered! The alarm bell will be rung, and the whole garrison will rush to arms!"

"Let them come!" cried Friar Tuck, grasping a staff he had picked up on the way, with a look of fierce determination. "Had I possessed such a treasure as this when they pounced upon me, I should not be here now."

Little John drew a short sword from its concealment, and waved it above his head.

"Lead on, Madge," he whispered. "I am desperate now, and with this I could cut my way, if needed, through a host of the Norman swine!"

"Come on, then," with caution whispered the girl. "Keep hold of each other, that neither of us miss the way."

They needed no second telling to do this, for the weaver, who was of a nervous disposition, held on to the friar's vestment in front, and Little John's hand in the rear.

It was now evident the garrison had been roused; lights appeared hither and thither, and the clank of mailed feet rang on the stone floor of the passages.

"Stukely! Stukely!" was the cry that next assailed their ears. "Stukely! Stukely! where are the keys?"

The fellow who was shouting added to the din by hammering the cross hilt of his dagger against the oaken door of the warder's room.

"Stukely! Stukely!" he still halloed. "A malison on thee, thou lazy knave!"

Suddenly his voice ceased, as though he had entered the warder's room, and then a jingling of keys was heard as he rushed back along the passages.

It was the captain of the guard that caused such a stir in the castle. As Madge did not give him the key, he placed a sentry on the door, so as to ensure the safety of the prisoners.

The soldier he put on guard chanced to be the one to whom he had made the allusion about his sound sleeping, and the captain very justly, as we have seen, suspecting he would fall into his old habit, paid him a visit to see how he kept his watch.

Then was it he found him stretched apparently lifeless on the floor.

The blood on his face led him to suspect that violence had been used, and that something wrong had happened.

A fearful malediction burst from him when, on opening the cell, he found the prisoners were gone, and the man who was to have served as executioner missing.

"Search the castle from turret to keep, and from the battlements to the lowest dungeon! What ho there, De Lancey! see every outlet guarded, and let not a soul leave the walls!"

The man addressed turned on his heel and hurried to obey his command.

A party of soldiers, who had hurried from the guard-room at the first alarm with drawn swords and flaming torches, followed the captain through the gloomy passages, searching every room that was not locked in their way.

"Saint Quintin! but they have the heels of us," said the captain of the guard, savagely. "That confounded rascal must have been asleep when they attacked him."

None of the soldiers ventured a reply, but muttered bitter curses to themselves; for the captain was so furious they feared to raise his further ire.

More like one mad, he rushed from chamber to chamber, and turned aside the heavy furniture, and thrust his sword into the recesses to make sure there was none hidden there.

In the meantime another party, headed by De Lancey, searched the upper part of the castle, and the sentries were ordered to keep a good look-out from the battlements to see whether anyone entered the forest hard by.

It chanced to be that the captain hit upon the right road the fugitives had taken; and, as Madge was not provided with a light, they had to make their way very cautiously, for the queer architecture of the place formed so many out-juttings that Little John had to feel his way and guard his head with his hand.

"Saint Benedict save us! and let us out of this place without a broken crown," muttered the tall forester, as in saving himself from running full but againstt a pillar, he struck his head against the vaulted roof. "By our Lady! such travelling as this ill suits my taste."

"Grumble not, my son," said the friar, giving an inward chuckle as Little John's head every now and then bumped like a mallet against some projection. "Thou must learn to endure with patience that which thou canst not avoid."

"Body o' me! I have endured enough already to my thinking," growled Little John; "I should like to see thy fat paunch jammed between these pillars. Saint Hubert! but thou deservest it richly."

"Holy Mother forgive thee for thy speech," said the friar, with mock solemnity; "thou wilt have to save up all thy marks to bribe the monks of Saint Mary's to offer up mass for thee. By the rood! thou will not find them so ready in confessing thee as I have been."

"A fig for thy confessions and thy benisons too; thine own sins will employ thee sufficiently, so fash not thyself with me."

"Thou will have other matters to fash thee an ye move not faster than this," said Madge, in an undertone; "see you that?"

The men turned, and at the further end of the passage behind them they could see the red glare of a torch.

Suddenly four men, clad in mail from head to heel, turned an angle, and hurried towards them, searching well each nook as they came.

"The captain of the guard is with them," said Madge, slightly trembling. "Heaven send they do not overtake us."

"Have we far to go?" asked Little John.

"Marry have we! We must make our way to the passages under the moat, which is on the other side of the castle."

"Can'st not reach it by some other way than by these passages?" inquired the friar,

perspiring freely with his exertions and the close air of the place.

Madge had no time to reply, but seizing the friar by the shoulders, she pushed him into a small opening in the wall, and entered herself, bidding Little John and the saddler to follow.

Closing a door behind them, she listened, and heard the captain of the guard urge his men to push forward, accompanying the order with a round oath or two.

The passage they had entered was a much narrower one than that they had left, and was more difficult to navigate, for the friar had scarcely width for his rapacious carcase, and Little John had to stoop so much as to cause him great inconvenience.

Impelled forward by a sense of fear, the party made much better progress than might have been expected; but they had scarce traversed half the passage when the soldiers were heard at the door by which they had entered.

"Holy Mother protect us!" said the friar, who was in advance of the party; "we shall surely die in this place if they do not overtake us, which I trow me they will; we shall all die of thirst."

Little John had been thinking of the same thing, and when the friar broached the subject he expressed his opinion freely.

"Body o' me! holy man, I opine with thee, for my legs grow weak, and my throat is as dry as a miller's sack. Canst not prevail on thy saint us to help out of this?"

"Nay, my son, none but the Evil One can assist us here. An evil purpose brought thy long shanks hither, and an evil spirit will have to get thee out, and if thou never more seest light of day, thou will but poorly atone for thy sin in offering to put the rope about the neck of a holy man."

"It will be some comfort to know that we all share alike," said Little John, with a quiet grin. "We shall go to heaven in good company, and that is a comfort."

"Heaven, thou rascal! Thinkest thou it was made for such rogues as thee? Thou wilt find a hotter place ready for thy reception."

"I wot me it can be little worse than this," replied the tall forester, who, from the position he had to assume and the close atmosphere, was suffering greatly; "but I trow me, yon knaves will have that door down very soon, an' it is not strong."

"Fear not thereanent. I did not forget me to bolt it well, and it is of good thickness. Naught but a ram could break it from its fastenings," said Madge; "but get thee on, Friar Tuck; thou barrest the way with thy unwieldy proportions, and if aught should happen to the door, it will fare ill with us in this place."

"But the outlet. Thinkest thou the soldiers will forestall us?"

"Gramercy, no! We are safe from that, for they would have to pass the haunted dungeons of the moat, and I trow me, they would not venture upon that, and besides "——

Her speech was interrupted by the friar's fat carcase barring the way, and Little John, forgetful of the holy man's presence, rapped out an invective.

"Blade bone of Saint Hubert!" he cried, rubbing his pate, which the sudden collision had caused him to hit against the roof, "thine ungodly carcase will be the ruin of us all. Get thee on, man. Dost not hear the fellows hammering at the door?"

"By the rode, thou mayst well say get on!" replied the friar, panting. "I trow me, this passage was made only for such skeletons as thee. I can get me not another inch forward."

"Saint Denis! how is that?"

"'Tis too narrow."

"And thou art too fat. A month's fasting would do thee some good. I trow me, thou art robbing me of the flesh I stand so much in need, and hast my share as well as thine own.

"Thou mayst take thy share, then," growled the friar, wiping the beads from his brow. "Ye are welcome to it an' ye take it at once; if not, I may not so readily consent to part with it anon."

"Keep it, then, thou glutton," said Little John, laughing; "I trow me, I would not carry thy iniquitous burden, for I would sell it to good Robin to feed the hounds. But hie thee on, or by my halidom we shall stay here and rot!"

"I wot me not how it is to be done. I am as far as I can get. Odds Boddikins! but the place ought to have fallen on the fellow's head who made it!"

The saddler trembled on hearing these words, for he was in the rear, and as the soldiers woke the echoes of the subterraneous vaults with their exertions to break open the door, he expected every moment to hear it come down with a crash.

"Body o' me! but this is a fix," he said to Madge, who was next him. "Knowest thou of any remedy?"

"One only; but I fear me it will not avail us any good."

"Name it," said Little John. "Mother, it will never do to stay here!"

"There is another door hereabouts, but I fear me we shall fail to find it in the dark. It is so built as to represent the masonry, that 'tis hard to detect it with a light."

"And whither does it lead?" asked Little John, anxiously.

"Towards the buttery; but it has been so long in disuse that I fear me it would be hard to open an' we found it."

"We will try. 'Tis of no use staying here; 'twill not do to stick in this den; I am almost stifled already."

Madge squeezed herself with difficulty past the saddler and retraced her way back along the passage, feeling the wall on both sides as she went.

Little John followed her example, almost squeezing the life out of the saddler in his effort to pass him.

"On which side is the door?" queried Little John, as he joined Madge in her search.

"The right as thou standest. 'Tis of oak, thy dagger point may find it."

Little John acted on this suggestion and tapped the wall as he went along, but nothing but hard granite met the point of the steel.

Madge still continued her way listening to the click click of the dagger, for all was now silent, as the soldiers, wearied with their exertions, had either paused to recover breath, or abandoned their task in despair.

The death-like stillness, which was rendered more solemn by the click of the steel, which, in the gloomy vault, sounded not unlike the death-watch in a sick chamber, was, however, suddenly broke by a deep moan, that fell with a sepulchral sound on the ears of those attentive listeners.

"Saint Mary! what is that?" asked the saddler in terror, clinging to the wall for support.

The moan was again repeated, and the forester, bold of heart as he was, could not help sharing the saddler's alarm, for the noisome atmosphere of the place had served to weaken the nerves of all but Madge, who was much more accustomed to it.

"I trow me, 'tis our good friend the friar," she said, as the thought struck her that the friar had fainted; "hie thee back, man, as thou art rearmost."

The saddler obeyed though not without some reluctance, for his knees trembled so violently, and his head so ached, that he could scarcely totter.

At length he reached the place where the friar's obese form stopped the passage, and, to his terror, he found he was either swooning or dead.

He passed his hand over his forehead, which, like his own, was bathed in a cold, clammy sweat, and he almost fainted himself, when he thought of the impossibility of procuring a drop of water.

The man soon hastened back and imparted the horrible news, which was received with anything but a feeling of pleasure by the others.

"Holy Saint Hildebrand! what can we do?" Little John burst out, suddenly; "he will lay there and die, and we canst not assist him. Saint Herman! but this comes of his over-gorging; an' he had been like any of us we might have got on safely. Ah! didst hear that?"

The cause of this expression was a dull thud, and Madge ran her hand hastily over the surface of the wall in search of a secret spring.

It was the door they had found, and the thud was caused by Little John's dagger piercing the oak, and scarcely was the expression clear of his lips when Madge shouted—

"Found at last!"

"Saints be prayed!" responded Little

John, as, placing his shoulder against the door and his foot against the opposite wall, he made the door move on its rusty hinges, and let a cool current of air into the place.

This not only revived them but allowed them to pass each other without the risk of staving in each other's ribs, and Little John, without waiting to examine the place, rushed to the assistance of the groaning friar.

In his efforts to try and force himself through the narrow portion of the passage, which widened again after a few feet, he had become so firmly fixed that the efforts of the powerful forester were useless in trying to extricate him.

As he had fainted and his body sank down, it acted like a wedge; and, though Little John tried to raise him, he was unable to, owing to the narrowness of the place and his own inability to use his strength to any advantage.

"Blade-bone of Saint Hubert! but this beats all. Saints protect him! for, I trow me, earthly aid can avail him naught."

"Sorry am I that this hath happened," said Madge, sighing; "but now the soldiers seem to have gone, thinkest thou we can venture a light?"

"Marry, and I see no reason to fear aught of danger from that now. We must risk it. I trow me, it would not do for me to return to Sherwood without good Tuck."

"Neither wouldst thou feel comfortable; but try thy hand at this, for I cannot strike a light for trembling."

The sudden revulsion from heat to cold—for the passage that had been hot almost as an oven had become like unto an ice well since the door had been found—sent a cold shiver through her delicate frame, and what with having no sleep all night and the great exertions she had undergone, Madge was almost done.

The light was a great assistance to Little John, insomuch that he was enabled to see the formation of the wall, and use his judgment, and to which way the fat body of the friar wanted moving.

It was like moving a bag of sand; but the forester succeeded at last in pulling it out a few inches, though it was at the risk of the friar's arms being dislocated, and Little John had the satisfaction at length of being rewarded for his exertions.

With one hand clenched on the friar's fat shoulder and the other fixed on the rope or cordon round his waist, he pulled and tugged till the friar's huge form fell at his feet with a force that threatened to deprive the holy man of what little breath remained in him.

The fall, however, did him good, and Little John having dragged him to the door of the newly-found passage, had the satisfaction to see him open his eyes.

This passage was some six feet wide, so that they had plenty of room, and the cool air that swept through it soon brought the friar round.

Madge was busied in wiping the perspiration from his face, and Little John was gazing on in silence, when a crash was heard that made the arched vaults ring again.

The soldiers had renewed their attack on the door, and had been successful, for the clang of mailed feet and the clash of weapons followed the din of the breaking in of the door.

"The Virgin be praised! we are safe here from pursuit!" said Madge, as she sprang to the door they had just entered, and secured it firmly. "They will pass us, for none knowest this passage but my father, and he doubtless is still asleep."

But she was mistaken; a circumstance of which she became aware by hearing the stern voice of the warder shouting—

"Look thee about, men. They have entered somewhere here. I saw them through the hole in the door but a minute since."

"Try thy blades on the walls. There is an oaken door here about that leads to the dungeons under the west wing!" he added, fiercely. "Lay about thee, men, with lusty arm, or our search will be baulked."

"Have you seen to the secret outlet?" asked one of the soldiers, in an undertone.

"Ay, there is nought to fear in that direction."

"Haste, haste! hie thee hence at once," said Madge, who had become alarmed on hearing her father's voice. "If ye tarry here, I would not give a fig for your safety."

"But the friar? we caust not leave him here."

"Nay, Little John, neither would I wish it; the black dungeon would be his portion, which is worse than ten thousand deaths!"

"The black dungeon! and what of it?"

"Saint Mary! ask me no further about it, my blood already curdles when I think of it. Haste thee; caust thou not carry the friar?"

Under other circumstances Little John would not have hesitated to say yes, but to carry the friar in his present state was next to an impossibility.

In the first place, the ceiling of the vault was no higher than the one they had left; and in the second place, the friar was too heavy for Little John, who, with the additional weight of armour, could scarcely carry himself.

"Come here, friend," he said to the saddler. "Take thou one of his arms, and I will take the other; betwixt the two of us, I trow me, he will walk."

"Come on, then; I trow me, it shall not be my blame if he do not; but let us haste, or the carrions will be upon us."

Madge gave a look of rebuke, for it included her father as well as the rest, and a natural love of her parent did not allow her to hear him thus talked of with impunity.

The saddler coloured and blustered some excuse, but nothing further was noticed of it. They had matters of greater import to occupy their minds.

The soldiers had discovered the secret door,

and Stukely had sent some of them for the ram they had used on the other door, though it was evident it would not do much, owing to the narrow state of the passage.

However, it was tried, and did more execution at one blow than the soldiers could have otherwise done in an hour.

"Steady, man, steady!" cried Little John, as they supported the friar, and led him between them. "'Tis a pity thou wert not supplied with four feet, for thou likest to drag thy paunch along the ground."

"And what likest thou, thou son of Satan?" mumbled the friar, suddenly recovering the use of his tongue.

"I would like to get out of this place with a sound pate and a whole skin," replied Little John.

"Which I fear thou wilt not," interposed the saddler. "I wot me, there is not an eye, save the friar's, winking in the castle."

"And dost thou dare presume that I wink?" growled the friar, scarcely able to articulate a word for the dryness of his throat. "Thou art mad, man! and had I not given thee shrift, I should say thou wert possessed of a devil."

"Rest thy tongue, and use thy legs a little more," said the forester petulently. "Thou graceless rogue, I would thou hadst some nettles in thy shoes."

"And what, think thee, should be thy portion?"

"A stoup of good sack, and a trencher of pasties."

"Ha! ha! now thou hast brought me to life again, since thou talkest of these things," said Hilderbrant. "What would I not give to join thee in such penance?"

"Well, keep thy legs, man, or thou wilt breakfast with me on the turret. Thou hast not forgotten the purpose for which we came to Nottingham?"

Friar Tuck looked about him in surprise. All that had passed during his stay in the castle seemed to him like a dream.

"What noise is that?" he asked, as the blows of the ram thundered against the door. "Saints protect us from an earthquake, say I!"

"And thy soul from perdition!" chimed in Madge, "for thou art sinful enough to go there. Now, what sayest thou to staying behind?"

"Saints forbid, my pretty lass! I trow me, though, thou would stay and bear me company."

Friar Tuck said this in his usual joyous tone; but for all that, Madge's words had their effect on him.

He quickened his pace, and tried to keep up with Little John and the saddler, who were almost dragging him along.

Bang! bang! still echoed through the vaults. Bang! bang! crash! Then came a shout as loud and deafening as though a legion of fiends had broken from their chains, and the hurried clattering of feet and the jink of mail added to the din.

"Now need we thy prayers, Friar Tuck," said Madge, in a tone of less alarm than might have been supposed; "thou must hide somewhere until I can find some means of getting thee past the walls, for thou heardest that that outlet was locked, and, I trow me, well guarded."

Unpleasant as were the words, Little John knew them to be truth, and he began to look about him for some hiding-place.

"Didst not say the buttery was hereabouts?" he asked, as a thought of bygone days flashed to his mind.

"Thou hast guessed it," replied Madge, in her usual gay tone; "but why speakest thou of butteries when, in a few moments hence, thy masticating faculties may be placed out of order?"

"No matter—'tis as well to die on a full stomach as an empty one; for, seest thou, 'tis the only good thing of this world we can take with us."

"A truce with this badinage, sirs," said Madge, as the footsteps rapidly gained on them. "I must leave you soon, or if it be known to the sheriff that I, Madge Stukely, the head-warder's daughter, assisted one of the followers of Robin Hood, and he could get proof sufficient, my head would not be worth the scrapings of a porridge-pot when the sheriff returns."

"Dost think he will ever return, lass?"

"Odds boddikins! I cried a truce, and thou offerest me not a single boon. Hast no fear of danger?"

"Saint Hubert! for myself I care but little; they press hard upon us though. In truth, I think they will not find the way we have just now come."

Madge had taken them a zig-zag route after leaving the passage; and, as the voices died away at times, she fancied their pursuers had taken another direction.

The sudden glare of a torch, however, dispelled this hope, and Madge fairly trembled.

"Quick—quick in here," she cried, huskily; and, dashing open a door which was only partly closed, she bade them enter, and, turning the key, which fortunately happened to be in the lock, she fled like the wind along one of the dark passages, taking the key with her.

Light as was her footstep, the quick ear of one of the men detected it; and Stukely, with the whole of the guard at his heel, followed in her track.

CHAPTER LXXX.

THE PLOT FAILS.

Beside the lady Robin Hood did ride upon his steed,
The night was drawing on apace, which made him haste his speed;
A troop of horsemen clad in mail did hie them from the dell:
The knight received a lusty blow, and from his horse he fell.

THE day had been one of continued showers, and as evening drew on apace the sky lowered, and gave tokens of an approaching storm.

Wild, heavy gusts blew through the trees, and still heavier showers fell at intervals, threatening destruction to the myriads of insects that had been enticed from their burrows during a few days drought, and wetting the traveller to the skin.

Such was the evening when Robin Hood and the Princess Eleanor neared the borders of the forest, and Robin smoothed the roughness of the journey by conversing on topics in which the princess seemed the most interested.

He had taken care to provide her with a large cloak made of skins, which completely covered her, and when the showers came on she drew the hood or cowl over her head, and Robin courteously led her horse.

It was after one of those showers, and when Robin had resigned the charger to the guidance of its fair rider, that a party of horsemen were seen to emerge from the shelter of a thickly-wooded dell, and espying Robin and the strange figure—for the princess did look strange in her new attire—that rode beside him, the knight who commanded the horsemen rode up to them.

"Greet ye, stranger," said the knight in an arrogant tone. "Greet ye; whither are ye bound?"

"Where thinkest thou? Have thy choice, an' if thou guess but truly I will tell thee."

"Saint Quintin!" said the knight, "thou art free of thy speech, Mr. Glib-of-Tongue. S'pose I make thee accompany me."

"If thou art capable of doing so, I commend thee for thy actions; but if not, I count thee as a vile braggart."

"Thou shalt judge of that for thyself," resumed the knight. "Who have you for a companion?"

"That thou must see of thyself, for I am not one who carries information for the pleasure of every meddling fool. First tell me thy name?"

"That will I; and then I will expect thy answer as truthful."

"Thou shalt have it; an' then tell me truly, an' thou liest I shall"——

"What?" demanded the knight, imperatively.

"Tilt thee on thy back."

"Gramercy! 'tis well to find one who boasts so rarely. I am De Bossel. Knowest aught of my name?"

"Never before did I hear it, and I wot me thou hast never before spoken it."

"What! callest thou me a liar?"

"To thy teeth, sirrah! Thou hast lied deeply."

"Saint Hilderbrack!" cried the knight, colouring. "Thou hast spoken freely for one in thy condition, especially when 'tis considered I have a score of trusty fellows at my back, lusty, stout of arm, and each one an equal for thy friend and ye."

"Had thou double the number it would fash me but little, base knave! Stand aside. Make room for me and my friend."

"It is thy place to give way for me. Get thee on to the grass, or by my halidame, I will teach thee manners to thy betters!"

"Thou braggart," Robin Hood replied, "make way, or by Saint Dunstan, thou shalt rue it!"

"Have at thee!" cried the knight, aiming a terrible blow at Robin's head, and the men at arms spurring on their horses, immediately surrounded the princess.

This was sufficient to satisfy Robin Hood that an ambush had been planned, and that the knight well knew the lineage of his charge, as no hand was raised against her, only the soldiers tried to cut her off.

Between Robin and the knight the fight was a strongly contested one, and their horses seemed to take the whole of the road, as they obeyed the rein, and wheeled and charged with untiring energy.

"What ho! there, my merrymen!" shouted Robin, as he saw the soldiers' intention to carry off the princess. "What ho, there! George-a-Green to the rescue!"

The blast of a bugle was heard, and the foresters who had followed under shelter of the forest, dashed into the road, and formed a cordon round the princess.

"Charge!" cried the leader of the troopers. "Cut the rascals down!" he vociferated, fiercely. But this was no easy matter to perform.

A phalanx of arrows, well strung and drawn to the ear, made the troopers recoil a pace or two.

The knight was too hotly pressed to observe all that was passing, for the sword of Robin Hood fell with such swift and rapid blows on the knight's mail, that his armour was dented in several places, and had it not been made of the toughest steel, his life would soon have been forfeited.

Robin's skill was now put to its greatest test, for being clad only in his jerkin, he was open to the blows of his opponent, but he parried the thrusts, and guarded the blows with such admirable skill, that the knight could not so much as inflict a scratch upon him.

The leader of the troop would have brought some of his men to his assistance, only that the foresters kept them in play, for having fired their shafts they grasped their staves, and attacked the mounted men with great fury.

Crash! crash! came down the heavy poles on the heads and arms of the horsemen, who tried vainly to reach their assailants with their swords.

Will Scarlett played his quarter-staff right merrily, and many an iron casque gave way beneath his blows, and as the blood began to trickle down their faces, several of the soldiers dismounted.

Foot to foot, hand to hand, and sword to sword the foresters then met them, and the ground was soon strewed with the bodies of the wounded or slain.

George-a-Green was hotly engaged with

the leader, who still kept his horse, and tried to cut a road towards the princess.

In this he failed, for the foresters never allowed the soldiers to break through them. If they gained any advantage, they drove them back again in a manner deserving of great credit.

In the meantime Robin had managed to unhorse the knight by lunging well at him, and dealing him a blow on the sword-arm, that cut through the mail, and nearly cut through the wrist.

"A boon! a boon!" cried the knight, as Robin wheeled his steed, and stooping in his saddle, placed his sword to his throat. "A boon I crave, if thou art Robin Hood."

"Whom else tookest thou me for?" asked Robin, sternly.

The knight was dumb. He would have iven Robin the lie, but the fierce tone of the utlaw caused him to change his mind.

"And who are ye?" asked the outlaw, judging the cause of the knight's silence. "Speak, caitiff, or thy life shall answer for thee."

The knight thus urged looked sullen and crest-fallen, for he saw at a glance that he need not expect assistance from any of his party.

"Dost grant me the boon I crave?" he asked, after a pause.

"Saint Herman of the Wold! thou shalt have it if thou deservest it. Much depends on thy manner of answering."

"Gramercy! I am John of Linden!" exclaimed the knight. "Now grantest thou my boon?"

"Name it."

"Let me depart without further questioning."

"Thy boon is hard to grant, for I see thou hast plotted this work full well; but rise ye, and let us hear who sent thee on this mission."

"Thy promise—dost forget it?"

"I have made none yet, so loosen thy tongue," said the bold outlaw. "Remember, thy life is still at my disposing."

"Then thou refusest to grant me a boon?" said the knight, rising from the damp earth and replacing his sword with his left hand, for his right was quite disabled; "thou makest me doubt thy word that thou art Robin Hood."

"Thou shalt have full proof of that if thou require it," said Robin, with a smile. "Dost know that Robin Hood is King of Sherwood, and that all who trespass on his grounds doth pay a tribute? Thou hast laid thyself open to this, and I fine thee one hundred marks."

"Extortion!" cried the knight, with a frown. "I have heard thee spoken of as a daring robber, and had I not been wounded I would not yield me to thee."

"Saint Hilderbrack! I would it was as thou sayest, for I like not the taking of thy life, knave as thou art, in cold blood; the tax thou wilt have to pay and thy boon, I will leave to an after consideration."

Leaving the knight in the hands of Will Scarlett and another of the foresters, Robin went to the side of the princess, who still wore the cloak of furs, though the rain for a time had ceased.

"Gramercy! 'tis well I did accompany thee," he said, lightly grasping the small white fingers extended towards him. "This is proof sufficient that a design of mischief has been worked against thee. I will not leave thee after this till I see thee safely within the castle gates."

"May the blessings of our Lady rest upon thee, Robin bold, for this thou hast done. Hast seen yon traitor's casque yet raised?"

"Nay, fair lady; and, I fear me, he gives not his name aright. Knowest thou aught of John of Linden?"

Eleanor turned pale.

"Of his brother I have heard somewhat," she said, concealing her emotion.

Seeing that his questions gave her pain, and that she gave not her answers readily, Robin desisted from further inquiry, and resigning the rein of her steed to one of his men, he got forward to see after the rest.

The fight had been a short but decisive one, as the bodies strewn around bore proof of, and resulted in the victory of the foresters, only one of whom was wounded to any extent.

He had received a sword thrust through the muscle of his arm, and a blow from a falchion had gashed his skull; but he had received good attention, and been placed on one of the riderless horses that had not joined the soldiers in their flight.

Robin looked around on the field of battle, which had occupied nearly a quarter of a mile of the road, and counted ten of the soldiers lying within that space.

Four of them were already dead, two were wounded past recovery, and the rest were so battered about the head and face as to be scarcely recognisable.

They had been taught the weight of an oaken staff when wielded by the arm of a forester, and the oaths that came from some of them confirmed their disapproval of such warfare.

George-a-Green was soon engaged in collecting the wounded soldiers together, and assisted the foresters to bind up the wounds and bathe the huge bruises, that had taken a variety of hues; then he proceeded to Robin, to get from him further orders.

"Hast seen to all their wants?" asked Robin, as George-a-Green approached.

"Ay, good master, and I have given them all the wine we could spare."

Thou hast done well, and deservest reward for thy services, which thou shalt have, never fear. The knight, whose treachery hath caused us so much trouble, shall well repay thee all."

Sir John, who was within hearing, winced more at these words than from the pain of his wound, and he would have made some reply, but was afraid of criminating himself further, for he had seen Dunstan fall into the

ROBIN HOOD,

AND THE OUTLAWS OF SHERWOOD FOREST.

THE CONSPIRACY IN THE WOODS.

hands of Robin Hood, and he did not know what excuse Dunstan had made for his being found there.

Not wishing to betray himself, he did not make any effort—which would, at all events, have been fruitless—to free the ruffian; but having secured his horse, which he had left at a woodman's cot, he rode hard to the hostel where his retainers were staying, and led them to the dell, where they laid in ambush, intending to pounce upon the princess as she passed, when he would carry her off to a distant part of the forest and murder her, hoping that when the body was found suspicion would be raised against Robin Hood or his men.

This crafty plot might have succeeded had not Robin Hood taken such necessary precautions as he did; for if he had sent a couple of his men as an escort, they would have been slain, their bodies hidden, and portions of their clothing been laid beside the body of the murdered princess, to give a colouring to Robin's guilt; and a bow or a quiver of arrows would have brought the murder clear home to the foresters under circumstantial evidence; for no men but Robin's about that part could use such bows or arrows as they did.

"Well, hast found thy purse yet?" said Robin, narrowly eyeing the knight. "'Twill be dark ere long, and I have tarried only for thy pleasure."

"Gramercy! thy kindness hath not its equal," replied Sir John, in a slightly sarcastic tone. "Far be it from my pleasure to hinder thee of thy journey."

"Caitiff! cease thy lying speech ere thou tempt me to tear out thy lying tongue. Thou hast failed in thine evil design, and now, by my faith, thou shalt pay for it!"

Sir John darted a fiery glance through the bars of his visor, and haughtily replied—

"Take my sword—'tis all I possess; ye have rendered it useless to me. It may at some time do thee service."

Robin laughed outright, though his passion was slightly raised; and he said—

"Search him, George-a-Green; thou knowest well where to find these caitiff's hoards. See what he hath, and leave him not a mark for his insolence."

The forester was not long in his search, for, as he had imagined, the knight had not set out with such a retinue unprovided with cash, and he soon spread out before the chief a goodly store of gold and silver.

"Just two hundred and fifty marks," said the forester as he finished counting. "Dost think that is the whole?"

"Nay, search again," said Robin, carelessly folding his arms.

A further search proved his surmise right, for another hundred marks were found sewn in the knight's saddle; and as the darkness began to grow intense, Robin leapt across his steed, leaving Sir John to brood over his discomfiture.

A heavy shower of rain, that lasted the remainder of the journey, caused the party to set off at a brisk pace; and it was with joy that Robin at length beheld the lofty towers looming in the darkness.

At the first hail the drawbridge was lowered and the gates thrown open, and Robin Hood entered the castle, leaving his men under shelter in the courtyard.

Leaving Robin in a sumptuously furnished apartment, the princess retired to change her dress, leaving the bold outlaw to enjoy his meditations the while.

Presently a page entered, and Robin was shown to another room, still more superbly furnished, where a refection was spread, and the princess now joined him, magnificently robed.

"This part of the castle has been kindly appropriated to my use," she said. "What thinkest thou of it, Robin? Dost envy me my home?"

"I envy thee of nothing," said the bold outlaw. "I am happy only in my greenwood home. But I dare presume thy castle at Windsor far outvies this in splendour."

"And thy forest home is equal to it, surrounded by nature, and excels it in happiness, for thou hast brave hearts on whom thou canst rely. I have few, if any, in whom I can place much faith. Even Scipio, who attends me here, has the looks of a traitor."

"Ah! 'twas him I saw as I entered the hall. I saw he eyed me distrustfully. Dost think he is an eavesdropper?"

"I opine he is; but he knows not the nature of my journey to the forest; did he, I would bind him to secresy by an oath."

Robin made no reply, for a rustling of the drapery at the door made him suspect they were watched.

"Some prying eye," he whispered, glancing towards the door. "Be cautious, I pray thee."

Eleanor nodded an assent, and when Robin was about to take his leave, Scipio was standing in the outer hall.

There was a fierce frown on his visage, and his eyes seemed to read every word of the whispered conversation.

Robin did not fail to detect the cunning in his leering eye, and as he gently pressed the hand of the princess when he bade her good-bye, he whispered to her—

"If thou art at any time in danger, and need my assistance, thou knowest where I am to be found."

Sir John watched the bold forester and his merry men depart with a look of bitter hatred stamped on his features, and many a burst of rage and withering malediction fell from his lips as their forms sank from view in the darkness.

The foresters had placed the wounded soldiers under shelter of the trees, so that they hurt but little from the rain; but as this was no fit place for them to pass the night, Sir John set him about to find some more suitable spot.

But whither could he wend his way? He knew of no habitation in that part of the forest, and he strode him about upon the greensward in a state of mind inconceivable.

Presently the glimmering light from a casement caught his eye between the trees, and having formed a sling for his wounded arm, he hied him with all haste towards the light.

He was deceived in the distance, for it took him near half an hour to reach the door of a small hovel built in the side of a rock, and which he afterwards remembered as being talked of as the cell of the hermit of Woodland Dell.

As he neared the spot the light vanished, and he saw the venerable occupant of the cell emerge from the door.

His head, white as the driven snow, was bared, as were also his feet; a rosary hung from his girdle, and his left hand leant heavily on his staff.

At that moment the moon peeped forth from behind a cloud of blackness, and as the bright mail caught the gaze of the holy man he started.

"Holy Mother! what brings thee to my door, my son? If thou seekest aid, I have none to give thee," he said, eyeing the knight distrustfully.

"Thou canst surely give me shelter from the storm," said Sir John, with a rueful look. "Dost not see that I am wounded?"

"Thou art a man of war and tribulation, and I am a lover of peace. I sought the solitude of this dell so that I might trouble and be troubled by no man, for which reason I left the Abbey of Saint Mary and became a hermit."

"But, good father, thou canst not deny me so small a boon as to refuse me shelter for the night. Dost not see that the storm hath not abated? Thou wilt not close thy door against me on such a pitiless night."

"My son," replied the friar, "when thou hast braved the storm as oft as I have thou wilt not fear it so much; e'en now I am going on my pilgrimage to the shrine of Saint Mary's Well, and thou knowest 'tis some miles from here, yet do I journey thither thrice a week; but thou canst stay if thou likest in my humble hut till I return. Thou wilt find such humble fare as my scant means allow of, and thou canst rest thee on my humble couch."

CHAPTER LXXXI.

ROBIN'S RETURN IS WELCOMED WITH ILL NEWS.

When Robin left fair Leicester
He straight to Sherwood came,
On his way he met a forester,
Roderick by name.

ROBIN HOOD'S return to the forest was hailed with pleasure by the foresters, as events had occurred that required the presence of their chief.

"How now, Roderick?" asked Robin, as the forester stepped from a covert into the road; "hast kept good watch over the prisoners in my absence?"

"Marry have we, good master mine; but withal one of them has managed to escape."

"How canst thou have kept good watch, then?" asked Robin, displeased.

"'Twas not to our blame, good master. Thou knowest yon rogue ye pinned to the tree?"

"Well?"

"Through him was it the prisoner escaped."

"How so? Loose thy tongue, man."

"Marry will I, if thou givest me breath. Thou knowest Allan-a-Dale is well skilled in leechcraft; but the rogue would not let him touch him, and we put him in the cave, where he howled so that 'twas feared a blood-vessel would burst."

"It would have been well had it done so; but go on, what then?"

"It rained so that our men could not keep above ground, and all but the woodwards, who were on picket, got them to the cave and laid upon their furs to sleep; but the howling of the brute kept them awake, and 'twas proposed to lay him on a bench beneath the trysting tree."

"Well, well, speed thee in thy story," cried Robin, impatiently.

"He still lay shouting and groaning with pain, for thy arrow was through his hand, when De Lois offered to try his skill at surgery, in which he is quite an expert, and whilst we were busied with some other matters they both took to their heels."

"Saint Hilderbrack! and they escaped?"

"Nay, the man we caught; but De Lois we could nowhere find, though we spread out and laid about the bushes with our quarter-staves."

"Herman of the Wold! thou wast a lazy set of rogues; there wast enough of thee to keep guard. I wot me, but thou shalt not forget this sore neglect. An' I had left Will Scathelock to look after thee, this would not have happened."

"Good master mine, it grieveth us sore that such should happen; but Gilbert of the White Hand thou hast most to blame."

"Gilbert of the White Hand," quoth Robin; "dost thou want to shift the blame from off thy shoulders, Roderick? Thou hadst the prisoners in thy keeping, and had thou been a good Saxon this Norman dog would not have escaped."

"Marry, and thou wilt have it so I must needs hold my speech; though I trow 'tis but fair that others share my blame."

"Thou wilt learn more of that anon; but what didst thou with the varlet when thou caught him?"

"Placed him in the inner cave; and, as he would not keep his prate, we silenced him."

"How?"

"We scourged his back with nettles, and I trow me, his howling soon ceased. An' we had not done so he would have held on till now."

"Thou didst well in this. But seest thou yon thing moving among yon trees? Is't a man, think ye?"

"I wot me not; but I soon will see."

"Ay, get thee forward, and let thy speed be such as to make up for thy neglect."

Roderick darted off like a fawn, keeping well under shelter of the trees; and, as Robin's way lay to the right, he was soon lost to view.

The foresters who accompanied Robin to Leicester Castle were no little pleased to return ; for their clothes were drenched, and their green jerkins and leathern shirts fitted tightly to their skin.

Many and anxious were the questions asked of them by their companions as to how they fared on their journey, and then with woeful face they recounted in their turn the escape of Geoffrey De Lois.

"Marry, and I would not stand in thy shoes for an earldom," said George-a-Green ; "I trow me, Robin will not forget thee for this."

"Odds boddikins ! an't could not be helped ! That howling thief was the cause of it."

"Gramercy ! 'tis well thou hast him to blame ; though, I trow me, Robin deals too lightly with such rogues."

"Ay, a long rope and a short shrift is best for them ; for, by our Lady ! they give us trouble enow, and bring no grist to the mill. The sheriff would have paid us handsomely an' we had kept him."

"But thou hast lost him ; and now tell me what news thou hast heard of Friar Tuck and Little John."

"Saints protect them from all harm, for we have heard naught as yet of them ; but I trow me, Robin will not long stay idle since Geoffrey has escaped."

Their conversation was disturbed by the note of a bugle horn sounding through the forest, and a messenger was despatched to see who it could be.

CHAPTER LXXXII.

LITTLE JOHN, FRIAR TUCK, AND THE SADDLER MAKE MERRY AT THE SHERIFF'S EXPENSE.

When down in the cellar
Little John bold,
With the Friar and Saddler,
Made merry, we're told.

HAD Madge Stukely searched the castle through no better hiding-place could she have found than the one that had offered itself so accidentally, though Little John and his companions did not think so when they heard her turn the key.

"Saint Herman ! we are in a pretty fix," said the forester to Friar Tuck, when the sound of the soldiers' feet had died away. "I trow me, Sherwood Forest will not see much of our company again."

"How so ?" asked the friar, in a tone that bespoke one ill at ease. "Dost think the lass will not find her way back ?"

"Body o' me, but she may not have the chance, if old Stukely or any of those Norman swine get hold of her. I trow me, they will keep her in close quarters."

"Saints forfend her from such harm, for our sakes as well as her own ! Marry ! it will go hard with us if she be not forthcoming with the key !"

"'Tis to thee all blame will be attached if aught ill befalls her," said Little John, trying to stifle the unpleasant feelings his position had called forth, by increasing the friar's fears. "Marry ! 'tis but right thou should offer up mass for her safe deliverance, as upon her safety depends thine own."

"And thine ! What of it ?"

"Blade-bone of Saint Hubert ! it troubles me not, so that thy ungodly carcase first yields its breath, for should I die first, I fear me thy gluttonous nature would tempt thee to feast upon my poor half-famished carcase ; and though 'tis said to be good to die in company with a priest, I opine it would ill suit my taste to be buried inside one, be he ever so good and holy, which I fear me you are not."

"Get thee to with thy banter, unholy knave !" replied the friar, whose spirits seemed to have lost their natural buoyance. "An' I am not mistaken, thou wilt need something yet at my hands, if matters take not a different turn !"

"Fortunately they have," replied Little John, in a much mellower tone than he had hitherto assumed. "I can dispense with thy services now, good Friar Tuck, so leave me, or at once hold thy peace."

Friar Tuck was about to retort pretty freely, when a strange sound met his ears.

His ready instinct at once assured him it was the sound of liquor running from a tap.

"Where have you got to, my son ?" he asked. "You have hit upon a treasure ; and if my nose is not deceitful as thy tongue, it is a discovery that will do us all good."

Little John could not answer until he had drained the measure of ale he held to his lips, and then he said—

"Fortune, indeed, hath befriended us ; 'tis the beer-cellar that hath given us shelter, and we may make ourself merry at the sheriff's expense. Here, put this within thy hugeous carcase, and then let our friend slake his thirst."

The poor saddler, who had shrunk despairingly into a corner, recovered his spirits a little when he had emptied the measure twice, and Friar Tuck conversed in a more exhilarating tone.

A footstep in the stone passage interfered with their carousal, and brought the song Friar Tuck was singing to an abrupt termination, and made them all listen in breathless suspense, as the footsteps ceased at the door.

"Odds boddikins !" they could hear the fellow say in a drowsy voice ; "methought I left the key in the door. Confound my sleepy head ! it will prove my ruin some day."

"It is the head cellarman," whispered Little John, as he recognised the voice ; "a stuck-up knave he is too. Marry ! I would not give a fig for our safety if he discovers us."

"Saint Mary ! it would go hard with him if he came in here to spoil our diversion," answered the friar, who had imbibed so freely of the nut-brown ale as to look indifferently on the affair. "I'd crack his brainless pate," he added, " if it were necessary to our safety ; but listen, the rogue—what says he ?"

The man, having paused for a moment, as though to collect his thoughts, then broke out again.

" A pest on the thing ! where could I have laid it ? Who would have thought that Sir Geoffrey would have come home at this time ? I would rather he had stayed in Sherwood a month than this had happened."

The sound of some one approaching broke his reverie, and it being unusual for any one to be prowling about that part of the vaults, he hid to see whom it might be.

" What, ho ! De Lancy, what brings ye here ?" he asked, as that personage appeared. " Hast taken to night-walking or spirit hunting—which ?"

" Ah ! those eyes tell me you have had little to do with the affair of last night. Have you not heard of the escape ?"

" I heard that De Lois had returned, and that alone concerns me," growled the cellarman ; " but if you have been prowling about, one of thy gluttonous rogues hath stolen the key of this door, and I advise ye, if thou wouldst escape trouble, to have it restored at once."

" My men are not thieves," replied De Lancy, indignantly ; " a soldier values his honour too much to commit such a paltry act, though I am sorry for thy loss, as it precludes the possibility of my thirst being ameliorated."

The cellarman had suffered much from the pranks of the soldiery, and believing that De Lancy was the leader of the plotters, he turned from him with a scowl, and hurried from the vaults in no pleasant humour.

De Lancy went on his way swearing vengeance against the head cellarman, and vowing bitterly to make him repent his words ; when, as he turned the sharp angle of one of the passages, a female stepped from a dark recess, and proceeded swiftly in the direction he had come.

This was Madge, and gladly was she received by the three prisoners, who were somewhat startled by the grating of the key in the lock.

" Silence—not a word," she uttered, sternly, as Friar Tuck began to loose his tongue. " My father is arrested for this night's affair, so get thee clear of the castle with all speed ; and if you have aught of respect for me, do thy best in saving him from an ignominious death, which otherwise will assuredly be his portion."

The trio were struck completely dumb by this announcement, and they followed Madge in silence, for they were too overpowered to speak.

Through several intricate passages she led them until they came to the secret door, which, owing to the vigilance of Stukely, was guarded by a soldier on the outer side.

" Keep out of sight all of ye," said Madge, taking a huge key from her waistband, with which she quickly opened the door.

" Who comes ?" shouted the sentinel, whose quick ear was alert to every sound. " Ah ! you, Madge ! " he exclaimed, as her smiling face appeared in the outlet.

" It is me, William," was her reply ; " they have not chosen thee a pleasant spot ; you must be dull, I ween, in this lonesome place."

" Marry come up ! you have guessed it, lass ; but, I trow, it is more lonely for thee to travel about these dark passages without a companion. What brings thee here, lass ? Has your father made you messenger ?"

" Partly so ; though, in truth, I came here of my own free will to acquaint you with the news ; for, I trow me, you have not heard of thy master's return."

" De Lois—has he returned ?"

" He has, and a fine rage he is in at losing the sight he anticipated ; for he hurried home purposely to see the hanging of the prisoners. Get ye to the right of yonder buttress, and see if the beam is raised on the northern turret, for I wish not to be seen by the sentinels on the ramparts, for it would give them great pleasure to report my being here with you."

This bit of flattery on the part of Madge served her purpose ; for the soldier, believing she held him in some esteem, obeyed at once, glancing down at his tall, straight limbs as he paced along.

" Now fly, and forget not what I told ye," she said, having beckoned her companions to her side. " Hie thee at once to bold Robin, and tell him of my father's condition."

Scarce had the words left her lips than the noise of a sword being loosed from its scabbard startled them.

" Stand ! you are my prisoners !   Attempt to move, and I cut ye down !" cried a hoarse voice.

The voice sounded in a thicket a few paces from the door, and a soldier instantly sprang therefrom, and placed himself before Little John and his party, who were pushing on towards the forest.

" Yield !" thundered the soldier, brandishing his sword ; " further attempt at escape will be useless. I have a party of men at hand."

Scowling horribly at Little John, whom, owing to his suit of Norman mail, he took to be one of the soldiers, he added—

" Saint Denis ! you will find yourself a head shorter for this treachery. You have learnt the secret of the *black postern*, and a fatal knowledge it shall be to ye."

Little John's reply was a swift blow of his sword upon the soldier's mail that made the sparks fly from it, and before the forester could repeat the blow, he found himself surrounded by four armed men, who prepared to attack him with their naked swords.

CHAPTER LXXXIII.

ELEANOR'S PRESENT TO MARIAN.

The Saxon Knight he strode his steed,
    And gaily did he trot it;
The Normans quickly stopped his speed
    When he did little wot it.

In one of the apartments set apart for the use of the Princess Eleanor during her temporary residence in Leicester Castle, two persons were in deep conversation long after the rest of the inmates, the sentinels excepted, had sought repose.

They were Eleanor of Castile and a Saxon knight, the only courtier in whom the princess could place implicit reliance.

How long they had been closeted it would have been impossible to determine, and it would have been as difficult to form a guess of the subject of their discussion before the princess raised her voice in making a reply.

"Well, do as thy judgment seemeth fit," she said, falling back in her seat; "to your discretion I yield entirely."

"And I promise thee my deeds shall merit thy good faith, an' I do not fall into the hands of some of the followers of this bold outlaw."

"Trouble not thereanent; you have only to fear meeting with the sheriffs' men, who, according to report, have taken to robbing on the highway to satisfy their masters' greed and vanity."

"I will take with me a trusty follower, if you think it prudent?"

"No, thy journey must be alone; and when thou arrivest at Much the miller's house, if Marian is not there hie thee back with speed; above all, keep thy journey a secret; and if any curious body should question thee as to thy destination, make them believe you are going to St. Mary's Abbey to pay thy devotion and crave the abbot's blessing."

The princess walked across the apartment and drawing aside the folds of a curtain, she took from the recess beyond a heavy canvas bag.

"This," she said, handing it to the knight, "is all I can send her at present; but mind ye breathe not a word from whom it comes, neither mention the name of Robin Hood; and above all, reveal not your own name and lineage, for thy journey teems with dangers."

It yet wanted a few hours to day when the knight set forth on his journey; and after leaving the town some distance behind him, he redoubled his speed.

Little did the knight imagine that the Moor had listened to their plans, and that he had sent a swift messenger on before him to Nottingham.

Nothing of any consequence occurred to him on the way until he sighted the mill, and then a party of Norman soldiers, that were laying in ambush, made their appearance.

Guessing their intentions, the knight un-slung his heavy battle-axe, and wielding it above his head, shouted them to come on.

"We are with thee," cried the leader of the party, "for at our peril we must not let ye pass. You will have to accompany us to our master, the lord of Nottingham."

"Invoke the aid of thy patron saint, then," shouted the knight, "for know ye, I will not accompany you alive to Nottingham. Stand aside, varlets, lest I cleave thee to the waist."

The Norman leader made a sign to his followers, and they all closed in upon the knight, but at the first stroke of his axe a soldier fell.

Their number was strong, but the Saxon knight, confident of his prowess, reined his horse with such admirable skill, that none of the soldier's could get near the prancing animal.

Still the terrible axe did its work, and thinned the number of the knight's opponents, though they narrowly watched his movements, and made several attempts to take him in the rear.

The Norman leader had been informed of the exact amount the Saxon carried, and this gave him more courage than he would otherwise have possessed, for the crafty Moor had started on a fleeter steed than the heavy war-horse, and was hurrying towards Nottingham Castle when, luckily for him, he met a party of the sheriff's soldiers going towards the mill, for Geoffrey had dispatched them as soon as he returned home in search of Much, the miller's son.

The leader had craftily formed his men into two parties, one party being marched up close to the mill-house, the other party was planted in a copse a little distance away to act as a reserve in the event of any of the foresters being about, a circumstance which would have rendered their services necessary.

Finding himself worsted and likely to be beaten, the Norman leader gave the signal for the reserve force to come forward, which signal was answered by the blast of a horn a little to the left in the forest.

This was the opposite direction to that in which the soldiers lay in ambush, and it gave the leader of the soldiers some uneasiness, which, however, was allayed for the time by the heavy tramp of the soldiery.

In the moment's cessation caused by this, the knight was enabled to gather fresh strength, and the soldiers had time to see how their comrades had fared.

As the steel caps of the reserved force came into view, the leader resumed his former arrogant mien, and in an insulting tone he cried to the knight—

"Now, Saxon churl, you must yield or perish, for, by the Virgin, while one of us lives we will not own thee as "——

A cloth-yard shaft piercing his neck prevented him finishing the sentence, and the next moment a score of foresters, with Robin at their head, emerged from the greenwood.

"How now, Sir Knight? What chance has thrown thee in the midst of this nest of devils, for I see by thy crest that thou art of Saxon blood, and I trow me it is a godly sight to see these vermin licking the dust."

"And who may you be?" asked the knight, raising his visor. "I like not answering questions to those with whose name I am unacquainted, though I opine ye are a Saxon, and I mistake not thy tongue."

"A true Saxon am I," replied the outlaw, "and my name is Robin Hood. Now thou canst judge whether we meet as friend or foe. True, there are few in the king's service who owe me any goodwill, for I despise the gaudy moths that flitter about the throne."

"Sorry am I we have met, but as it is so, I will dismount and have further speech of you. I see your men have scattered the Norman swine to the winds."

"Ay, and as many more would have followed their example had they been here; but you look faint, thy task has been no mean one; you used that heavy axe with no niggard hand, I trow. Get you along with me to the building on the hill, and I will procure you refreshments."

It was the mill that Robin alluded to, and as that was the knight's destination, he did not hesitate in going there.

"Robin, I am so glad to see you," said Marian, as she caught sight of the forester's form. "I have so longed to know how it fared with thee at Sherwood."

"Ah, sorry am I we had not your company," said Robin, embracing her: "whom think ye we had for our guest in your absence? Canst guess?"

"Nay. How can I answer you, good Robin," said Marian, smiling in his face; "you have such strange visitors at your court, that it would ill repay me to guess."

Robin whispered in her ear, and Marian started.

"An' thou wert given to lying, I would not believe ye," she said; "you have been deceived, dear. It could not have been "——

"Hush! By Saint Herman! mention not the name; it might bring destruction on the head of England's brightest gem; not for the world would I have any harm befal her at my hands."

The knight, who had watched with interest the meeting between the loving pair, now ventured to speak.

"Good sir," he said, "I would crave one moment's speech with your fair companion, an' it please ye."

"Welcome thou art," Robin replied, "and if thy business is private, I will leave you for a time. Where is Much, good Grace; has his wound yet healed?"

Robin followed Grace into the inner chamber, and Much, on hearing his voice, rose from his seat.

"Greet ye, good Robin; hast seen aught of Little John," said the miller's son.

"Troth have I not, but word reached me of one who needs our help. Stukely has raised the sheriff's anger against him, and "——

"You intend succouring him? I thought as much, for, by our Lady, it would not have done to let De Lois carry out his intentions against the friar. For myself I fear they will take me or distrain the mill if my father fails in raising the paltry sum they have imposed upon us."

"Fear not for that," exclaimed Marian, who had overheard the last part of his speech as she entered; "seest thou here what Providence hath sent us."

"How came ye by this?" said Robin, taking the money Marian offered him in his hand; "has yon knight turned out to be thy banker?"

"Nay, 'tis a present from the noble lady you just mentioned. She sends this as a token of respect for the manner in which you entertained her, and your gallantry in escorting to the castle."

"Under present circumstances, I accept it," said Robin, "although it was to you it was sent; this will clear the miller's debt, and replenish our funds, which, by-the-bye, are at present at a low ebb. Now for the business that brought me here.

"Little John and the friar I think you said were safe, and Stukely must soon be out of danger; for his daughter's sake, I would not leave him to his fate; I must try what effect my argument will have on the sheriff, and if we fail in coming to terms, I must use force."

"No better time than this could you put such a project into execution, for the garrison is so weakened, and the people in such a rebellious state, that De Lois will have to use all his means to keep them down, which will prevent him doing much in the way of strengthening the castle."

It was late when Robin and the knight left the mill, and they parted on the border of the forest.

CHAPTER LXXXIV.

THE SHERIFF'S TYRANNY.

Thy daughter holds a secret,
And from her I will wring
The words that shall denounce thee
An accessory to this thing.

WHEN De Lancy reported the escape of Friar Tuck and the saddler to Geoffrey de Lois, he raved and stormed in such a manner as to make the soldier tremble for his own safety.

All his fierce passions seemed to be suddenly developed, for it galled him to think that Robin Hood and his followers should thus openly defy him, and he bit his lips, and paced the oaken floor like a tiger walks the limits of its iron cage.

"Foiled! foiled!" he muttered hoarsely, "but there will yet be a day when he shall feel my sting. I will despatch the abbot once more to London to make a last appeal to the king for his aid in crushing this infamous outlaw, the fiend in human form that mars my prospects, and foils me at every point: and Stukely—ha! ha!—he also shall suffer."

He laughed, and a satanic grin settled on his features as some horrible project occurred to him, and then turning fiercely on De Lancy, who stood at the door ready to fly if need be, he hissed rather than spoke—

"Where is Stukely?"

"Confined in the White Tower."

"Let him be brought here at once; he must need a change of air," said Geoffrey with a sarcastic grin. "And his daughter Madge, what of her?" he asked.

"She is in her own chamber, under a strong guard."

"The baggage! It is to her cleverness I attribute the failure of my plans; she's a vixen, and I'll teach her not to meddle with the affairs of Geoffrey de Lois."

De Lancy did not wait for him to finish, but disappeared at the first intimation; and when he was gone, De Lois ordered the trembling page to summon the cellarman into his presence.

With bowed head and sheepish mien the head cellarman entered the august presence of his master, and though there was that in his appearance which spoke of a muddled brain, it was more from fear than any other cause.

Sadly lowered in dignity was the once pompous butler, as he stood in the presence of his frowning master, who, after gazing at him a few moments as a wild beast might be supposed to eye its prey, he soundly rated him.

"Saint Dunstan! hast forgotten thy duty entirely, that thou hast thrice to be reminded that the table is not laid? How is it that an hour has passed, and no signs of either meat or drink maketh its appearance?"

"My lord," whimpered the butler, "'tis no fault of mine, I assure thee. Gaudin the cook hath prepared nought for thee, and some thievish knave hath taken the key of the vault.

"A murrain seize thee for a fool or a liar, I wot not which. Dost take no better heed of the things in thy charge than to let the whole garrison have access to the cellars? I will make thee more mindful of thy duty by giving thee short allowance, and filling up the vacancy with blows. Get thee gone from my sight, or, by the mass, nothing will save ye from having thy hulking carcase pounded to a mash!"

The butler waited to hear no more, but sidled out of the room with the velocity of an eel, and in the passage he met Stukely, being led between two soldiers.

Fully prepared to meet his fate the stern warder seemed to be, for he quailed not beneath the withering gaze of his angered master, who eyed him with the deadly ferocity of a serpent.

"Well, what account bring ye of the prisoners I left in thy charge?" asked De Lois. "You have them all right, I suppose?" he added, with a sneer.

"Faith, have I not, though 'tis not to my blame," replied Stukely, with either real or assumed indifference. "The fellow you sent to perform the duty of executioner can tell thee more about them than I."

"Go to with thy insolence!" vociferated the sheriff. "What man thinkest thou I sent to do thy work? I engaged thee as warder and headsman, and if thou hast never performed the latter it is no reason I should humour you to it always. What knave was it that deceived thee so? Let him be brought here, and answer the charge against him."

"Saint Dunstan! that is impossible, my lord."

"How so?" thundered De Lois.

"Inasmuch as he did not stay behind, but aided the prisoners to escape. Marry! 'twas his arm that cut down five of thy staunchest men-at-arms, while the friar and the other rogue, armed with a couple of saplings that the friar plucked up by the roots, kept those who flew to the rescue at bay, giving them many a bruise from the blows their sturdy arms dealt.

Geoffrey's face went through a series of contortions and assumed a variety of hues, whilst his whole body seemed to writhe as though in agony.

"The curse of Saint Anthony rest upon the knaves! May their souls wither and the lightning's flash blast them! It is the varlet Little John that hath deceived thee," he added, to Stukely, "and thou must suffer in his stead. As to thy ronion of a daughter, I will have her tortured until she confess all."

Stukely turned pale and his whole form trembled.

With all her faults he loved his daughter, for his iron nature was not proof against a parent's feelings.

"Sir Geoffrey," he said, trying to assume a firmness he did not feel, "what hath my daughter done that your anger should be raised against her? Is it not enough to torture the parent without using cruelty to his child?"

"Child—ha! ha! Thou art a good nomenclator," said De Lois, as he watched with delight the torture his words inflicted on his hearer. "You fellows can find a name for anything that may exculpate ye from blame. That girl knows a secret I would fain possess, and thy duty shall it be to put her to the rack until she discloses it."

Like the violent tremblings that announce the shock of an earthquake, so did the warder's iron frame shake as the words of De Lois fell on his ears.

But it was only for a moment the qualm lasted; and then, like the ocean when the fierce storm is past, his bosom rose and fell with a regular motion.

"Geoffrey De Lois," he said, in a voice the very calmness of which made the sheriff start, "fate hath made thee my master in some things, but not in all; nature bids me rebel against thy stern edict. I have suffered enough from thy tyranny and borne with it

ROBIN HOOD,

AND THE OUTLAWS OF SHERWOOD FOREST.

MARIAN AND THE KING.

but this monstrosity has made me an altered man. I defy you now, and set all thy threats at defiance; do with me what you will, I scorn you."

The sheriff sat during this speech like one utterly deprived of all power to move ; and then, starting suddenly to his feet, he cried, imperatively—

"To the dungeon with him, De Laucy, and see that he is securely ironed and chained to the floor ; and, mark me, if he be not forthcoming at my will, thou shalt swing in the *infant's cradle*."

This threat was sufficient to guarantee the fulfilment of the order to the letter, for the horrible contrivance named was such as to make the stoutest heart quail.

It was an iron box of coffin shape, and slung in the form of a cot, and when the victim was placed within it, and the cot swung to and fro, some horrible machinery connected with it being put in motion caused the sides and ends to gradually collapse, so that the occupant found himself being crushed to death at each pendular motion.

There was a gleam of satisfaction in the sheriff's eye as he watched them depart ; and, pacing the room as he had done before, he fell into a deep reverie, from which he was startled by the voice of the page announcing the arrival of his uncle the abbot.

"Greet ye, kinsman mine," said the abbot, entering. "Allow me to commend thee for thy dexterity or craft in escaping from the den of that king of robbers."

"Incarnate devil you should have called him," said De Lois, savagely. "Can we devise no means by which to rid ourselves of him ? It is for that I have summoned thee hither."

"By he who died on the rode, I have thought of no means yet ; and, though I have sent a letter to the king, I "——

"Ah ! hast thou done so ?"

"Even so. As soon as I heard of your defeat at the mill I sent Cuthbert away at once, but no answer have I yet received."

"Dost know where the king is at this time ?" asked De Lois.

"At St. James's I heard ; but a short time ago a godly man, whose pilgrimage brought him this way, gave me such information."

"Then thou mayst consider him too busy to attend to thy missive. Cuthbert will have his journey for naught, and "——

"Fash not thyself thereanent, good kinsman mine ; than Cuthbert no man of my knowledge hath freer tongue ; fear not that he will leave London without making his speech heard."

"Well, I leave it to thee as you are cool of head and wise of judgment, but how gettest thou on with the tithes ?"

"Poorly—very poorly, and I am sorry to say that the people grow more averse to the late levy."

"Indeed—that must be seen to."

"And readily, for it is not improbable that matters may turn out worse ; for old Gamwell of the Grange has taken much interest in it, and consequently raised himself in popular favour. But what of the miller ?"

"I have sent a party of picked men to seize both him and his son, and take possession of the mill ; and, to ensure success, I gave fifty of my best men to the expedition."

"Fifty's enough to storm a tower," muttered the abbot. "Success is certain—but hark !" he muttered to De Lois, "didst hear that ?"

'Twas the sound of a bugle at the outer gate, and, in answer to their expectations, the grating of the drawbridge followed, and a body of soldiers passed over into the court-yard.

"Ah ! 'tis the party returned from the mill," said De Lois, in ecstacy. "'Tis well thou didst wait, good abbot, so that thine ears may hear the good news as soon as mine own ; and when the obdurate miller and his son is brought before thee, you can give him the sound rating he so richly deserveth."

"Show him hither," replied De Lois, in answer to the page's announcement that a soldier waited at the door. "Well, what news have ye ?" he asked, in the same breath.

"Unfavourable," answered the man hesitating.

"What, hast killed the miller in the fray ?"

"Nay, my liege ; not so much as seen him have we. On nearing the mill, a mounted Saxon attacked us, and Robin and his men put us to the route."

Geoffrey did not wait for him to complete the sentence, but made him start to the door by shouting, "Away, minion !" and made him hasten his flight by hurling a stone ewer at his head, and the abbot, taking the hint, silently withdrew also.

CHAPTER LXXXV.

THE MEETING IN SHERWOOD FOREST.

The winged shaft sped on its way, the deer struck in
    its side,
One groan it gave of agony—one gasp, and then it
    died.
The king he urged his charger on, 'twas at its greatest
    speed,
And gleefully he turned his eyes to where the stag did
    bleed.
The nobles followed closely on, the hounds did loudly
    bay :
"Gramercy ! 'tis a noble stag," the king was heard
    to say.
"To Nottingham let it be borne, the sheriff will you
    greet,
"And bid him to prepare himself our royal self to
    meet."
Then Robin he stepped forward, and said in voice
    aloud—
"Back, back, good king, thou canst not see—thine eyes
    are in a cloud."
"Odds boddikins ! what mean you, knave ?" Robin
    answered without fear—
"Back, royal king, I thee command, 'twas I who killed
    the deer."

THE mild summer weather that prevailed when King Henry left his court to start on his journey to Nottingham changed suddenly, and was succeeded by cold, bleak winds, and heavy showers of rain, that rendered the journey not only tedious but laborious.

The king's retinue consisted of several knights and their esquires, besides which he had an escort of fifty men, all mounted and armed to the teeth, to be ready in case of an emergency.

This rendered the journey less comfortable, for as the road-side inns in those days were few and far between, a long day's journey had to be performed before rest or refreshment could be obtained, and then it frequently happened that many of the soldiers, with their horses, had to lay in the fields, which, in such weather, was not very refreshing.

It was no wonder, then, that the king and his nobles wished their journey at an end, and gazed with longing eyes at the herds of fattened deer that crossed their path when they entered the forest of Sherwood.

"What thinkest thou of that, D'Anville?" asked the king turning in his saddle to the noble that rode nearest him. "Is it not a glorious sight, one that does thine eyesight good, eh, my cousin?"

"Saint Benedict!" I know not whether your majesty is joking or in earnest. Such a herd doth pleasure mine eyes to a certainty, but I opine the haunch of one of those noble beasts, if well dressed, would pleasure my stomach much more."

"Thou art in nowise a fool," said the king to his favourite; "and in troth in such matters few of my subjects are : for instance, there is Robin Hood, who, I am told, infests this forest, plunders the wayfarer, and if all the crimes accredited to him are true, he is guilty of fifty others ; he lives on such fare as ye saw every day, and here am I, the king, obliged to make shift with anything I can get."

"Robin Hood," said the duke, meditatively, "is it he who was once called the Earl of Huntington—he who dealt me such a blow at the battle of Eavesham?"

"One would think thy forest-keepers would look more to your rights," said a noble who rode on the other side of the king. "'Tis sorry time when an outlaw shoots with impunity the king's deer ; an' I were a forester, I would trounce him well. Hark ! some one is at the chase, even now ; I can hear the hounds, if I mistake not."

"Ay, 'tis Wharton my head-keeper," replied the king, glancing in the direction of the sound, which was borne to them on the breeze ; "he is coming down yon glade. A trusty follow is Wharton, and stout of limb."

"We may have some sport then, my liege, if he hath his bow and quiver with him ; and I trow me, a slice of good venison will be acceptable to us all."

"By my halidame, thou shalt have it," said the king ; "the first red deer we see shall serve our table. Here comes the man, let us hear what he saith."

"Rise, good fellow ; I would have thy advice," he said to Wharton, who stopped several paces from the king, and bent his knee. Canst fetch down a deer that we may eat, for the keen air hath sharpened our appetites ? Hast thou a bow ?"

Wharton placed a whistle to his lips and blew a shrill call.

In a few moments, a boy laden with a bow, a bill-hook, and quiver of arrows, appeared through the foliage, and stepped into the road ; but at the sight of the royal train he drew back.

"Thy henchman lacks courage, forsooth," said the king, with a smile ; "he is not used to such company, I presume ?"

"He is bashful only. Come hither, boy ; show the king a little of thy skill."

Wharton had some difficulty in restraining the hounds that had scented a herd of antlers ; and walking to an opening in the trees he said to the boy—

"Fetch down the finest of the herd, boy, and gain the favour of the king."

"A good shot—the deer is hit," said the king, as the animal staggered and fell on its side ; "lead us to an opening that we may get through."

The road at this part was lined on both sides with a dense thicket, the branches of the trees making it almost impenetrable, for they were only a few feet from the ground, so that it was necessary to ride round to reach the glade where lay the wounded deer.

"Gramercy ! 'tis a noble stag," said the king, as they entered a break in the thicket, and came in view of the animal, which was at its last gasp. "Get thee some of thy followers, Wharton, and have it borne to Nottingham, whither we are journeying ; the sheriff will see that it is fittingly dressed, and tell him to speed with his culinary arrangements."

The forester bowed his knee, and was about to send the boy for assistance, when a cracking of the branches betokened the approach of some one, and three persons emerged suddenly into sight.

The king started in surprise on being the intruders, and the nobles frowned indignantly as they approached to where they had suddenly drew rein.

"Back, back, good king ! A merry day to you, nobles all !" said Robin Hood, who, with Much, the miller's son, and Marian, formed the trio. "'Tis a pity that thine eyesight so sorely deceives ye."

"Odds boddikins! what mean you, knave?" cried the king, with a frown. "Who is it that dares speak thus in our royal presence ? A murrain on thy ugly carcase and a halter round thy neck, if thou makest so bold again."

The king grasped his spear, and spurring on his horse, was about to fell the bold outlaw with his lance, when Robin, raising his hand, waved him back, and cried fearlessly—

"Back, royal king, I command ye ! 'Tis I slew the deer, as the shaft will prove."

"Minion ! who art thou to beard the king in this fashion ? Answer me ; and if you make not fit apology for your speech, you shall suffer, even as the stag."

"There is no king here save me," cried Robin, gently relieving himself of Marian's embrace. "ROBIN HOOD is king of Sherwood Forest, and I defy even ye to dispute his rights."

"Out on ye, knave! seize the caitiff!" cried the king, in anger. "Bear him away to Nottingham Castle. His head shall grace the highest tower ere sun sets this even."

The Duke d'Anville spurred on his charger, and snatched his sword from its sheath; but before he reached Robin's side the outlaw blew three loud blasts from his horn, and in an instant every tree seemed to produce a man.

The king was astounded as the green forms came from behind the trees, and rose up from the hollows in the grass, and, as superstition was rife in those days, he and his followers had a suspicion that the glade was enchanted.

Henry glanced around at the impenetrable barrier the archers formed, as, in a half-circle, they stood with bows drawn to the ear, and the terrible cloth-yard shafts pointed at the royal train.

The momentary fear that this sudden apparition, as it were, caused in the minds of the king and his nobles was soon dispelled by Henry himself dismounting and walking up to the outlaw.

"Robin Hood," he said, "reports of ye and your doings have reached our royal ears at court, and as you have openly defied the power I have sent against thee, beat and plundered everyone that hath need to pass this way, and even now hath insulted me to my teeth, I am determined to put a stop to your doings and punish ye with mine own hand."

"Saint Herman! I would rather you set one of your fawning servitors to do this, as I would not willingly raise my hand against you," said Robin, boldly facing the king. "I am no mean braggart, as you may think me; and if I crack your royal pate, I fear thou wilt wear thy crown uneasily."

"Go to, fellow, and get ye a couple of staves that I may trounce thee as thy malapert tongue deserves. Saint Hilderbrack! I'll soon teach you who is king!"

One of the outlaws brought forth a couple of quarter-staffs, and Henry of Winchester and the outlawed chief set-to briskly.

"One to me!" said Robin, as his staff came down with a thwack, shattering the diadem that adorned the king's brow; "another such, I trow, will satisfy thy wants."

"Have at thee, caitiff," cried the king, losing his temper and hurling a fearful blow at the outlaw, who nimbly stepped aside, and as the king fell forward, the outlaw's staff was laid flat on his back from neck to buttock.

The blow was a terrific one, and stretched the king on the sward, where he lay for some time gasping for breath.

The Duke d'Anville, who was a favourite of the king, slipped from his saddle as the king fell, and picking up the fallen staff, cried—

"Thou forest minion, I will punish thee, and revenge the insult on our king. Take that for thy pains."

"And that for thine!" replied Robin, guarding the duke's blow, and hitting him on the leg in such a manner as to draw from him a cry of pain.

By this time the king had recovered sufficiently to renew the bout, and a fierce one it was, for it lasted over three hours, neither yielding until they could not strike a blow, so utterly exhausted were they.

"Thy hand, Robin Hood," said the king, when the bout was over. "You are a brave fellow, and have shown such play to-day as I have not before witnessed. Marry! thy skill would give us much diversion in the lists. I must now acknowledge thy right as king of Sherwood, for none can equal thee in valour or tame your proud spirit."

"Thanks for thy courteous speech, good king," said Robin, bowing. "Now, if it pleasureth thee, we will heal our bruises with the best our forest home affords."

"Gramercy! 'tis little that our hungry stomachs will refuse," replied the king; "so lead on, Robin, and we will see what kind of food the deer will make."

CHAPTER LXXXVI.
THE TWO DOCUMENTS.

First came a letter from the king,
  That puzzled him full sore;
Another came from Edward,
  And plagued him more and more.

THE high sheriff having despatched a message to his chief counsellor, the lord abbot, he paced his room in a state of feverish excitement, waiting his arrival.

A faint gleam of satisfaction was visible on his visage when his kinsman entered the chamber, and took his seat at the table.

"Good uncle mine," said De Lois, affecting a respect for the holy man he did not feel, "matters have come to a sore pass at last, and thy allwise head must form a project to relieve us in our dilemma."

The priest looked glum, and tried to clear off the abstracted air that seemed to enshroud him, by taking a copious draught of the liquor, which by this time had been supplied.

"Now, by our lady, you have perplexed me sore," he said, after he had given his lips a smack. "How can I, a man of peace, give thee counsel in such matters? You have already done a foolish trick in allowing that prating priest to escape. You promised me that he should never more see the light of day, and had you kept to your word, not only the outlaws but many in the town would have to seek spiritual comfort from the abbey, whereas, through that ungodly thief escaping, he will rob us of our dues, and hold us up to ridicule."

"But I have arrested the head warder and his clatter-tongued daughter; from her we may find out who is in fault, and who to punish."

"That will be but little use unless we have

the power of doing so.   While Robin Hood lives we shall have no peace.   I opine it would be our best plan to rid ourselves of him at once."

" But how ?"

" Can you not bribe some one to poison him ?"

" A good thought if we could carry it out ; but you know how the fools you last hired failed."

" That is no reason why another trial should not succeed.   Come, De Lois, is there not one out of all your retainers you can trust with this "——

" Murder," added the sheriff, interrupting him. " There are many who would undertake it for a goodly sum, but few who could accomplish it.   It would be safer and easier to enter the tiger's lair and steal a cub, than to rob the outlaws of their chief."

" True, the knaves hold him in high esteem, and have such confidence in themselves, as to set both church and state at defiance. But hast heard aught of the king ?"

" Boddikins ! no.   Hast thou ?"

" Of a surety I have.   A palmer that knocked at the abbey gate as I left, spoke of having seen him on his way hither."

" Saint Quintin ! this is a strange matter. He sent not word that he was coming. Good uncle, we must look well to our concerns. 'Fore God ! I hope he will not interfere with our doings."

" Let not that fash thee, good kinsman, but have a tale ready for him about the foresters and their doings. I wot me, he will not meddle with aught else, least of all our doings in the town."

The sheriff continued to pace the floor again, and after a short silence, he asked—

" What of the miller ? "

" Saint Mary ! he is like the rest. He says he cannot pay, and when I threatened to distrain on the mill, he gave me but ill words for my answer, and his minx of a niece banged the door in my face."

" A malison on the knaves ! Why did you not curse them ? "

" It is of no use. That fat-paunched Friar Tuck, as they call him, gives them absolution, so of what good is my speech? Saints forfend us ! if they go on as they have done, they will consign the abbey and all in it to perdition before many months have turned."

" Who's there ? " demanded the sheriff, as a knock sounded at the door.

The voice of the page answered, and De Lois drew back the bolt, and admitted him.

The page handed him a sealed packet, and having informed him that the bearer had departed in haste, he left the room.

" By our Lady ! 'tis from the king. It is sealed with the royal seal."

" Open it, then, good nephew, and let us hear the news, for I vow by my staff and cowl, that 'tis a treat to receive a dispatch from court ! "

" In these days ; but see here what an

epistle. Read it, as thy skill in such matters is far before mine."

The abbot took the scroll, and having run his eye over it, remarked—

" 'Tis of a surety from the king, but I see not that it bodes us any good."

" What sayest it, then ? "

" That he and his train will be here tomorrow morning, and to prepare well for his reception.   The hungry wolves! they will devour all before them, and our cellars will be emptied without the least remuneration."

" By the foul fiend ! what thou sayest is true, and he hath fifty men-at-arms in his train.   I wot me, they will make sad havoc with our buttery; but there, he may have come purposely to rid the forest of the outlaws, and if so, it will well repay us."

" A good thought, De Lois.   Now set the cellarnian to work, for I trow me, the king is a hearty eater, and his drink is accordingly."

" Ay, he hath a hugeous dry throttle and an endless paunch, which, by-the-bye, proclaims him to have been intended for one of thy holy calling."

" Bridle thy tongue, Sir Sheriff, unless thou canst give good explanations of thy words," said the abbot, scowling from beneath his hood ; " your sins are already enough to bear ye down."

" And thy sins would topple thee over, had you not such a food receiver to balance them. Saint Denis ! it is all a load for thee to bear."

The page entering a second time put an end to the argument, and the sheriff opened his eyes in surprise when he beheld Prince Edward's seal.

His cheek paled and his hand trembled as he opened the packet.

The abbot eyed him in silence, and in turn his cheek blanched as the sheriff's agitation increased.

Having fortified himself with a stoup of Burgundy, he ventured to ask—

" Hast ill news, man, that thou shakest so ? Holy Virgin! thou seemest to be suffering of a palsy."

" Read for thyself, and when thou hast done so maybe thy nerves will slacken also."

The sheriff refreshed himself with a stoup of wine while the abbot read, occasionally muttering as though to impress certain paragraphs on his mind.

The epistle ran thus—

" Prepare the torture chamber of the White Tower for the reception of a prisoner who is on his way under a strong escort to your castle, and will arrive in the course of a few days from the receipt of this.

" P.S. His coming is a secret, and I would have thee keep it from my father the king, inasmuch as it is an affair of my own, and I wish him not to know it."

" What can this mean ? And what purpose can he have in doing this ?" said the priest, in an awe-inspiring tone. " Saint Mary ! 'tis unfortunate the king should happen to come at this time."

"Saint Quintin! 'tis as thou sayest. Did this reach the king's ears I would not give a fig for our conditions, and to offend the prince would be equally as bad."

"In either case it bodes us no good. I would we had kept our grumblings to ourselves, then the king would not have paid a visit to this part of the country. Now I advise thee to do what thou intendest with the warder, even to the hanging of him if it seem thee fit."

"Indeed, good uncle of mine, thou art hasty in thy counsel. Hast forgotten what I told you that I should like further proofs? then might I find out who aided that good-for-naught rogue, Robin Hood, and that pert minx, Marian, to leave the strong walls of the castle; and more, that varlet the Earl Mortimer."

"And what will you gain by it? Thou mayst strike off a dozen heads at least without fear. 'Tis only by a terrible warning, as I can vouch, that you need hope to stop such doings."

The sheriff gulped down another goblet of the sparkling juice, and the abbot followed his example, moaning as he did so—

"It is a sin that the Lord's anointed should be debarred the luxuries which you sinful knaves revel in with impunity. 'Tis hard, indeed, that we should have to sneak out of sight of the public eye to get a draught of the juicy grape. By our patron saint, I would gladly change conditions with thee, Geoffrey."

"Out upon thy grumbling, man; thy ruby nose and rounded face belies thy words. Wert thou the high sheriff and I the lord abbot, thy earthly pilgrimage would soon be at an end."

"And what would become of thee?"

"I would pray hourly for the bier to rest my legs of its hugeous load; for, I trow, 'twould be easier for me to carry a knight's mail than to be hampered with such a carcase as thine."

The abbot burst into a laugh.

"Would I could persuade thee to take the cowl, and have thy head shaven; by our Lady, thou wouldst often have to do penance. And when thou hadst done six weeks' prayer and fasting, thou wouldst pray for the beer to strengthen thy inward man, instead of the bier to rest thy lusty limbs."

"Go to for a malapert knave, as thou art. I am tired of thy whimperings. Saint Hilderbrack! thou deservest a severe scourging for thy impudence."

"With stinging nettles, such as the Saxons use on a May day," retorted the abbot, with a malicious smile.

Geoffrey de Lois coloured at the allusion to his degradation, and he turned livid with rage.

With a look, fierce as a tiger's, he turned upon his kinsman, and muttered hoarsely—

"John of Langley, if you are not tired of my friendship, never utter such words again, for, by the Virgin, if you do, we shall for evermore be foes, as deadly as we are now sworn friends."

The abbot of St. Mary's felt the rebuke, and the cold glitter in the eyes of his kinsman made him repent his words.

Not another word was spoken by either.

A wide breach that time alone could heal was made in their friendship, and the abbot, summoning his followers, left the castle in dejected mien.

"Adzooks! 'tis more than I can bear, even from him," muttered the sheriff when he had gone; "had he been other than my uncle I would have trounced his hide; but there, 'tis as well we parted only in words."

With such thoughts as these the sheriff paced the floor all that night, and when the gray dawn began to creep through the barred casement, he breathed a sigh of relief.

CHAPTER LXXXVII.

THE FORESTERS' FETE.

The king he made him jolly,
For he was full of fun;
He stuffed his hide with venison steaks,
And so did every one.

"Zounds! by our Lady! the rogues make pretty free with our deer, my cousins!" exclaimed the king, as parties of foresters began to troop in from all sides loaded with game. Saint Hubert! the knaves know how to choose the best deer."

"'Tis a knowledge we all boast of," replied Little John, who chanced to stand by the king's elbow. "Body o' me! it would not do to eat the lean and withered, while a good fat juicy buck is to be had for the seeking."

"Out upon thee, for an infamous knave! Dost know I am the king, and that thy dishonest fingers rob me when thy bowstring twangs?"

"Blade-bone of Saint Hubert! of that I never thought me. But surely thou dost not mean to say there are two kings in Sherwood?"

"Graceless scamp! have I not told thee that I alone am king?"

"Good master, ye did; but I am so given to unbelief, that I took no heed of thy words. Robin Hood is the only king we acknowledge in the greenwood."

There was a mischievous smile in the forester's eye as he spoke, but which the king failed to notice.

Of a hasty disposition, and unused to such bold discourse, it was no wonder his temper got the better of his prudence, and, forgetful of the tanning Robin had given him, he seized a staff that lay on one of the benches, and rushing at Little John, who was leaning quietly on an oaken pole, he shouted—

"Thou long-legged imp, I will trounce thee till thy lank carcase writhes like a dying snake! Take that, for thy insolence, and in future put a guard upon thy malapert tongue!"

So saying, he made a terrific blow at the

tall forester, who, springing to his full height, dealt his adversary such a ringer on his pate that made the blood to flow.

"Well done, little man!" exclaimed the friar, who was resting his huge carcase against a tree, and refreshing his spirits with a bottle of good sack. Try thy luck again; perchance the king will knight thee for thy handiwork."

Henry of Winchester darted an angry look at the speaker, and then returned to the fray.

"Hold!" cried Little John; "I bet thee all I have, five marks, against all thou hast, that thou canst not draw blood on me in one half-hour, even if thou exerted all thy skill."

"Done!" cried the king; "and this fat paunched rogue, who appears to pay more heed to his worldly comforts than his spiritual wants, shall be stakeholder. Here, man, spread thy kirtle for the money."

Friar Tuck placed the bottle once more to his lips to ascertain whether it was dry before he laid it from his hand, and then he did as the king desired.

"Saint Mary! thou hast fallen into luck's way, good friar," he muttered to himself. "An' I were so inclined, I might withdraw with this; but if Little John wins, I shall not go short, I ween."

The battle was strongly contested by both parties, and though Little John gave the king sundry hard raps, yet could he not get one blow at the tall forester.

"A malison on the knave!" cried Henry, excited with pain and anger. "I trow me, I have got into a pretty nest of devils. Saint Dunstan! the fellow works on springs."

It certainly did seem so, for Little John, owing to his lank arms, could overreach the king's guard; and, as every opening was watched by the forester's quick eye, it is needless to say that he got many nasty knocks.

For more than half-an-hour Little John kept him in this play, and then, getting tired of it, especially as the odour from the kitchen assailed his nose, he gave the king such a stinger on the ear that felled him like an ox.

"Body o' me, thou hast killed him quite!" said the friar, transferring the coin into his own pocket. "Stand aside there, idiot, or thou wilt get thyself into sore trouble."

"It matters not much, so that we win," said the forester, carelessly; "but as thou hast the stakes, and I have fairly won them, I propose we have a flagon of the best."

Friar Tuck, of course, did not object to this, and leaving the king in the hands of his nobles to strap up his wounds and so forth, they slunk away into a quiet corner.

There they enjoyed themselves to the devotion of Bacchus, which the two penitents gulped down with evident gusto."

"Thou wouldst, then, like another such a bout, friend John?" asked the friar.

"If the payment was equal I would not care," replied the outlaw.

"Thou shalt have both diversion and money to," cried a voice, hoarsely; and, on looking up, Little John beheld a knight who was gazing at him with flashing eyes.

"Body o' me! thou mayst find out thy mistake, Sir Knight," Little John answered, arrogantly; "for my part, I would crack every one of your Norman crowns; but look to thyself, man, and thou wilt find enough to do."

It was with more than usual spirit the twain fell to, and in less than five minutes the staves of both were broken off short.

In the heat of the moment, the knight drew his sword, and made a lunge at Little John, but ere his purpose could be accomplished, Friar Tuck seized him in his lusty arms and hurled him to the earth.

The horn sounding for the foresters to assemble put an end to the fray, and the brazen notes of the trumpet called the soldiers together.

"How fares it with us surrounded by such an host?" said Little John, approaching Robin's side; "dost think it prudent to trust to such men as these?"

"We have had the king's word for it that he intends us no harm, and for the present I dare trust him. Get thee forward and see that the soldiers are well dispersed among our own men, so that if they mean treachery we may be ready for them."

"There are the soldiers of De Lois. What of them?"

"They must remain in the cave, and their sojourn among us must be kept a secret. Hast seen well to their wants?"

"Allan-a-Dale is tending them, and they seem well satisfied with his arrangements. Marry! I dare wager there is not a man among them but would rather join us than return to Nottingham."

"'Tis not my pleasure that they remain here longer than is necessary," replied Robin. "'Tis well they stay here till Stukely is at large."

Little John went away to arrange the soldiers, who were pretty cheerful, and were in great expectation of the promised feast, the fumes of which now began to scent the grove.

Robin repaired to the bench under the trysting tree to do honour to his guest, whose tongue began to loosen as the fumes of the wine worked up in his head.

"Ye have a good company, Robin, and a merry spot to boot," said the king. "'Tis no wonder you cling so to a forest life when surrounded with such good things."

"Ay, 'tis a life you well might envy, though we are hunted like the forest deer. Here's to thy health, Henry of Winchester; so let us fall to, and a fig for dull care or thought of the morrow."

It was a merry sight to see the steel caps of the soldiers and the glitter of their warlike dresses as they intermingled with the green jerkins of Robin's men, and loud and clamourous was the uproar as they set to with right good will.

The soldiers, whose food had chiefly consisted of dry bread and salt during their heavy march, made the venison suffer greatly, and the jokes passed freely, and were loudly acclaimed by the hilt of their daggers striking the table.

Marian kept up the king's spirits by her lively discourse, and when the bench was cleared of all but the wine flagons, the king, addressing Maid Marian, said—

"I had not thought to find such company as thine in Sherwood's Forest. Thou hast pleasured us greatly; now, I pray thee, favour us with a song."

"An' it is your majesty's pleasure I will do so; but you must not expect to find such melody in the forest as thou hast in thy regal palace," said Marian, modestly.

"An' it please thee we will judge of its merit for ourselves," the king answered. "Silence there, varlets! Dost think thou art in the guard-room of the Tower?" he shouted to his men

The soldiers and the outlaws were, indeed, uproarious in their mirth, and Little John, the friar, and several others of the foresters did all they could to keep them so, for they wished them to leave with a favourable impression on their minds.

"Now, Marian darling, give us thy ditty. I know thou canst oblige us," said Robin Hood, chucking her playfully under the chin.

Thus importuned, Marian could not refuse, and she sang the following stanza to her lover :—

> In Sherwood lived stout Robin Hood,
>   An archer great, none greater;
> His bow and shafts were sure and good,
>   But Cupid's were much better.
> Robin could shoot at many a hart and miss—
> Cupid at first could hit a heart of his.
> Chorus.—Hey, jolly Robin! ho, jolly Robin! hey, jolly
>   Robin Hood!
>
> A noble thief was Robin Hood,
>   Wise man was he could deceive him;
> Yet Marian, in his bravest mood,
>   Could of his heart bereave him.
> No greater thief lies hidden under skies
> Than beauty closely lodged in woman's eyes.
>   Hey, jolly Robin! etc.
>
> An outlaw was this Robin Hood,
>   His life free and unruly;
> Yet to fair Marian bound he stood,
>   And love's debt paid her duly.
> Whom curb of strictest law could not hold in;
> Love with obedience and a wink could win.
>   Hey, jolly Robin! etc.
>
> Now wend we home, stout Robin Hood,
>   Leave we the woods behind us;
> Love-passions must not be withstood,
>   Love everywhere will find us.
> I lived in field and town, and so did he,
> I got me to the woods, love followed me.
>   Hey, jolly Robin! etc.

The chorus was repeated again and again, in which the king heartily joined, for the good cheer he had met with gladdened his heart.

Cheer after cheer followed this, and the forest echoed with peals of merry laughter, for never before had Sherwood's trysting tree such company beneath its spreading boughs.

"Now, Much, it is thy turn," said Marian, blushing with maiden modesty at the praises lavished on her by the enraptured king. "Let us hear thy old ditty which so often I have heard at the mill."

"Fair cousin of mine, I must e'en comply if ye wish it," answered Much, and in a clear, melodious voice he began—

> Now wend we together, my merry men all,
>   Unto the forest side,
> And there to strike a buck or a doe
>   Let our cunning all be tried.
> Then go we merrily, merrily on
>   To the greenwood to take up our stand,
> Where we will lie in wait for our game,
>   With our bows all in our hands.
> What life is there like to bold Robin Hood's?
>   It is so pleasant a thing;
> In merry Sherwood he spends his days
>   As pleasantly as a king.
> No man may compare with bold Robin Hood,
>   With Robin, Scathelock, and John,
> Their like was never, and never will be,
>   If in case that they were gone.
> They will not away from merry Sherwood
>   In any place else to dwell,
> For there is neither city nor town
>   That likes them half so well.
> Our lives are wholly given to hunt
>   And haunt the merry greenwood,
> Where our best service is daily spent
>   For our master, Robin Hood.

"Huzza! huzza! for Much's song!" shouted the friar, as Much finished the last line. "Three cheers for Robin Hood and his high-born guest."

Such shouts as seldom had been heard made the welkin ring again, the soldiers gladly joining in, much to the edification of the king and the chagrin of several of the nobles.

The Duke d'Anville was one of the dissatisfied ones, but Robin, though he saw his disaffection, and read his thoughts in his sinister looks, took no apparent heed of it.

This made the other noble sorely vexed, and determined not to be beaten, he struck up a song which, in other company, might have ended fatally to him.

> A rogue at heart is Robin Hood,
>   And so are all his men;
> I would not give a single groat
>   For all the lot, I ken.
> He is a tyrant to us all—
>   A traitor to his king;
> I'd like to break his bones right small,
>   And make him loudly sing.

"Hold thy peace, man!" cried a knight beside him. "No place to speak thy thoughts is this, I ween. Save thy speech for a better time."

Excited with wine, and inflamed with jealousy, the duke heeded not his words, and was about to continue in the same strain, but the fierce glances of the knights assembled at the board restrained him.

The king waxed wrath at his behaviour, but as it was no time to bandy words, he said, to divert their attention from his conduct, which, had it been allowed to continue, would have brought the just resentment of the foresters upon him, "I have heard of thy skill in archery. Let us hie to the butts, it will serve to revive us a little."

"Right willingly I comply," said Robin. "Get thee the butts in order; I trow me, we must have such sport as becomes our noble company."

ROBIN HOOD,

AND THE OUTLAWS OF SHERWOOD FOREST.

"HOLD!" CRIED ROBIN; "STAY THY HAND."

The butts were soon fixed and all in readiness for the commencement of the sports, when Robin, arm in arm with the king, proceeded thither.

Some good shooting was carried on; but Robin had given orders that nothing extraordinary was to be done until the knights were emboldened to bet upon their skill, for

Robin meant not to let them go until he had fleeced them of every coin as a remuneration for their fare.

It was his plan to make every one who could afford it pay well for their dinner; and, as the nobles were generally supplied with coin when travelling, he was determined they should not leave without paying the piper.

"Thou art a good marksman, I trow," said Robin to the king, as he tried the distance of the butts with a shaft. "Marry! there are few of us can beat thee, if any can equal thee."

The king was fond of flattery and this speech suited him, so he tried another shaft and struck the butt.

"Now, see if you can shoot an arrow as straight and at such a distance," said Henry; "I wot me, there are few of thy followers whose arm can equal mine for strength."

Robin humoured him and let his arrow fall full twenty paces short of the butt, which raised the laugh of the nobles sorely against him.

"Now let our friend of the hyena breed try his skill; if his archery is aught in comparison to his grinning he will beat us all."

The knight winced under the severe rebuke, and took the proffered bow from the hand of the outlaw with anything but a graceful mien.

It was Robin's own bow that had been offered him, and it required no mean strength to bend it; a fact that the knight discovered to his disgust, for he could not draw it to half the length of the shaft.

As might have been expected, the arrow fell sadly short of the mark; and, as this was the true specimen of his shooting, as Robin could see at a single glance, he put him down as a victim.

Several other knights tried their skill with like success, amongst whom was a leader of the Kentish bowmen; but whether it was inefficiency of skill, or fear of out-shooting the king, Robin could not fully determine.

"Now, D'Anville, I will lay thee fifty crowns that I shoot as far in once as ye shall shoot in twice. What sayest thou to that?"

"That you are a scurvy knave and a glutton, for not being satisfied with what you have."

"Marry come up! nature hath furnished you with a wise head; 'tis well you encase it in steel, for, though it may be made of the best of stuff, I trow me it is but soft."

"Wrong art thou, good master mine," said Little John, just loud enough for the duke to hear; "his head is thick and wooden, and consequently hard as an iron pot; were it not, being empty, it would collapse."

A laugh came from the bystanders, in which even the king joined.

D'Anville bit his lip and walked away, muttering as he went—

"Marry come up! with a wennion on ye all! St. Peter! ye shall rue this."

When he had gone, another took the field. A tall, well-built fellow was he; stepping up to Little John, who appeared his own height, he said—

"You seem much to favour me in bulk and size; what say you if we tell our strength?"

"Agreed; and I leave ye to thine own choosing as to how it shall be."

"The bow," was the soldier's reply.

Little John bowed, and gave his opponent the preference of the first shot, which hit the butt, and glanced off.

"Try thy hand again, man. I'll bet thee aught thou likest that you hit not the target at a distance of five paces more."

"I will bet you fifty marks to your ten I can hit it," said the knight, producing a handful of money that made Little John's eyes sparkle again as it consisted mostly of angels.*

This time the target was not hit, and in his turn the knight bet on Little John's skill.

"If you can hit it as you boast," he said, tartly, "I will give you one hundred marks; if not, you will return me my money."

Little John aimed recklessly at the butt, and struck it in the same place as the knight had at first, and this was at the extra five paces; Little John was looked upon by the soldiers as no mean marksman.

The king even looked favourably upon him, and the rest of the knights, profiting by what they had seen, took heed not to bet their money against him.

"Now, Marian, show thy skill," said Robin, leading her forward. "The king will have something to tell on his return to court of the shooting. I opine we can give him such sights as he hath not seen for many a day. Seest thou yon bird taking flight?"

Marian glanced in the direction his hand pointed, and, as by a miracle, the bird fell.

The king uttered an exclamation of surprise, and blushed at his own doings, for it was a feat that few could have performed.

The foresters in turn showed their skill, each having some peculiarity of his own, some sending an arrow straight in the air, and catching it as it descended; others placing their cap a few paces from them, and firing upwards, allowing the arrow to fall and pin it to the earth; but the last and greatest feat was that performed by the outlaw himself, and which, owing to its danger, was only practised on particular occasions.

Selecting two apples, one large and one small, he placed Marian in front of one of the butts, and putting the small apple on her bare head, he placed the larger one on top; then walking to a distance, he took aim; and the small apple was carried away on the point of the arrow, leaving the one that had been placed on the top, resting on Marian's head.

This was a test of firmness and courage he did not often subject her to, for the least motion might have caused her her life, and

---

* A gold piece, worth 10s.

had her frame trembled in the slightest, the apple must have rolled off.

The spectators held their breath during the performance; and as the second arrow split the remaining apple in twain, a shout of applause burst from them.

This concluded the sport, for it was plain to all that another trial of skill on the part of the nobles would only add to their disgrace, so they returned to the board where the wine was ruddily sparkling.

"A malison on thy thirsty throat," said Little John, as he looked into the flagon they had left, and found it empty. "Thou hast been paying thy devours to the tankard, while I have been labouring at the butts."

"What better employment could I choose, Sir Knight of the Rueful Countenance?" said the friar, smiling. "It was not meet that one of my profession should test his skill at ms."

"I will make you test your skill at legs, if you hie not to the cellarer, and get this filled," said Little John, bringing the empty flagon rather heavily on the friar's shaven crown. "Get thee gone, ungrateful knave; a run will do your fat carcase good."

"And you, long shanks, would harm but little were you to accompany me," retorted the friar, rubbing his bruised pate. "And I would remind ye that—

"'Tis naught to give a friend advice,
Though hard it be to take it;
And when you crack my crown again,
Take heed you do not break it."

"Ha! ha!" laughed Little John; "'tis split, an' I may judge by the ring of it."

"I disagree with thee," said Will Scarlett, interposing. "If I am a judge of *sounds*, it is more hollow than cracked."

"Your opinion was not wanted," growled the friar, who did not relish having to leave the comfortable seat he had provided for his huge frame. "An' thou wert a Christian, you would have pity on one of my years, and perform this office for me."

"No! no! Go thyself, thou lazy lout. It is little thou dost, save eat and drink; and I trow thou canst do thy share of both, and more so of the latter; so get ye gone, for I'm hugeous dry, and my tongue is swollen wondrously."

The friar raised his huge carcase, and shuffled off in the direction of the cellar; but in returning he mistook his way, and ensconced himself in the shade of an overspreading bush.

"Now, perchance, I may get a few moment's comfort," he reasoned to himself; "and Little John, well knowing my weakness and my inability to walk far, will have only himself to blame for my having to drop down here. Zounds! won't he roar when he finds the liquor not forthcoming."

He was right; Little John did not forget to growl and heap sundry expletives on the head of the friar for his long absence, which he attributed to anything but the right cause.

"Confound the glutton! He has gorged so that he has fell asleep in the cellar, or else the cellarer has refused to serve him, seeing he has had enough, and he is afraid to return. Saint Denis! my limbs are stiff; but I will go in search of him, and I will trounce the rascal if I find him asleep."

Little John had not the opportunity of doing the latter, for the friar had chosen a spot but little frequented, and though the tall forester laid about the bushes with his staff, and hallaoed at the top of his voice, the echoes alone answered them.

This left the forester no other alternative than to get the liquor for himself or go without, the former of which two he hastily decided upon.

As he made his way to the cellar, however, venting his rage on the friar, a voice was heard shouting his name, and Allan-a-Dale, out of breath, ran to his side.

"Our master desireth speech of thee at once," said Allan-a-Dale, puffing lustily; "he hath been seeking thee some time past. Come on, man; thou must not delay."

"By the rood, this is too bad! Hast seen aught of Friar Tuck?" mumbled Little John.

"No; and I opine it would be better for thee if thou saw him less often, for he is a guzzling varlet, and will bring trouble on ye some day."

"Not worse than he has at present, I ween, for the knave has hidden his shaven pate in some hole where I cannot find him, and, what is worse, he has taken a flagon of the best malvoisie to keep him company."

"Little John," said Robin, as the tall forester entered the outlaw's apartment, "the king hies him to Nottingham at once; take fitting escort with thee, and show him by a near way through the forest, and call thou at the mill on thy way back, and learn the news."

The king parted warmly from Robin Hood, and sorely pressed him to accompany him to Nottingham; but Robin had seen sufficient in the manner of the nobles to teach him to be wary, for he had noticed the duke in whispered conversation with several of the knights, and after that they treated the outlaw with much coolness.

Therefore, he prudently declined accompanying the king; but gave him escort well befitting his station.

CHAPTER LXXXVIII.

THE KING AND GEOFFREY DE LOIS.

When he arrived in Nottingham,
The king was grieved full sore,
To listen to the words the sheriff
In his ears did pour.

You are mistaken in the man—
The minion, he's no good;
There's not another man, I ween,
So false as Robin Hood.

THE expected arrival of the king caused some commotion in Nottingham Castle, insomuch as apartments had to be provided for his numerous train.

For many years part of the castle had remained in disuse, either from its reputation of being haunted or from want of occupants, as the men-at-arms were the only ones that required much room for their garrison.

Rumours were not long in reaching the town, for the castle, like most places, had its tale-bearers and wondermongers, so that the curiosity and excitement of the people were raised to their highest pitch.

At every inn and hostel it was the chief topic, and the soldiers of De Lois were questioned and cross-questioned pretty closely by the innkeepers concerning the preparations being made within the castle, as it was an object of great importance to them to learn whether they might expect the soldiers to be picketed upon them.

"You appear anxious about his majesty," remarked a stout yeoman, who was enjoying a flask of ale; "one would think that the king had taken lodgings of you."

"Odds boddikins! there is no such luck. An' he were to come well paid might I be; but a troop of hungry horsemen is no trifle for an honest man to keep. Saint Mary! they devour all before them like a field of locusts."

"You have tried them, then?"

"Zounds! yes; and enough of them had I, I assure you. My dame can vouch for their appetites, for she tended them."

"Didst feed them well?" asked the yeoman, finishing his ale.

"'Gad, an' we did! and they departed lazily enough, though they had more respect for our company than we had for theirs."

"Then you may make sure they will come here again if there is the least chance; soldiers are but weak mortals, as I can avouch, and like not seeking strange places when"——

"Hist, man, hist!" said the alarmed innkeeper; "let not the dame hear you say so, or she will want me to sell out stick and stone. Saint Anthony! she hath more horror of these fellows than I even, and fore 'Gad, that is enough."

"What are you prating at there?" squeaked a voice in the back ground; "hast lost thy tongue and found a crow-clapper, man, that thou giveth gab to every one that enters?"

"Peace, dame! Thou knowest naught of our conversation. Didst do so, thou would be less angry."

Dame Smith was not one to be so easily put off; she nagged well at her spouse, and even gave the yeoman a specimen of her vocal abilities, so that he was glad to sidle out.

It was late in the day when Henry and his train arrived at the castle gate.

The drawbridge was already lowered, and the portcullis raised, for the sentries on the battlements had reported the approach of the royal retinue, as it emerged from the shelter of the forest.

In the courtyard Geoffrey met the king, and assisted him to dismount, and personally escorted him to the oaken chamber, which had been fitted up in what was considered a gorgeous manner for the period.

"Greet ye, my cousin," said the king, who spoke not until they were closeted; "I find thou hast comfortable quarters even in these secluded parts."

"And yet it is not so comfortable as we would wish it," said De Lois, with feigned meekness. "There is one of whom I have made complaint that causes us sore uneasiness."

"Who may that be, De Lois, that can give thee any trouble when protected by such stout walls, and defended by such sturdy men-at-arms as I just now saw?"

"One Robin Hood, the most daring robber hereabout. Little heed pays he to laws or rights, and he seizeth on everything that comes to his hand as though it were his rightful property."

The king looked glum, and sank back in his seat in deep perplexity.

De Lois narrowly watched the monarch's changing features, and as he sat his evil mind conceived a tale suitable to his purpose.

"And this robber keepeth you in hourly terror?" resumed the king, after some moments' silence; "hast no means of bringing him to subjection?"

"None, my liege, unless"——

Geoffrey paused; but only to assume a modesty he did not feel.

"Well?" said the king, giving him an assurance to go on.

"Pardon, my liege, if I make too bold a presumption; unless you grant us some aid."

"As to that, De Lois, it is almost impossible," said the king, for Robin Hood had won himself into his favour by his manner of reception, and the king could not but notice the contrast between the servitor cringing at his feet and the bold outlaw that had confronted him so boldly. "Thou hast doubtless heard of the serious turn matters have taken at court?"

"Indeed, have I not, my liege; and I assure you it is as much as I can do to keep things in order here. The people are in open rebellion through Robin Hood, and they even set the church at defiance."

"Why do you not alter it? What use is it of me giving you power if you fail to use it? You have plenty of rich lands, and by this time, I ween, your coffers are well stored."

Geoffrey de Lois turned pale.

"You have calculated wrong, my liege; I am poor. This land yields me barely a living."

"And yet you chose it."

"It was previous to my knowledge of it; I assure you this place is not an enviable one."

"I cannot see how that is; but I stand in need of some refection if ye are not too poor to supply us therewith."

"My liege, thou art welcome to all I possess," said the sheriff, cringingly. "Saints forfend that I should neglect to provide for thy wants, though little time indeed was allowed me for so doing."

The king watched him depart, and a smirk played on his lip as he leaned his elbow on the table and placed his head thoughtfully in his hand.

"This is the high sheriff of Nottingham," cogitated the king. "Well, 'tis a visit not thrown away, for a monarch can never know his subjects too well. This wealthy Norman requires a week to provide a dinner, whereas Robin Hood, who lives on other's means, provides a banquet fitting for a royal court at an hour's notice. There is the lord abbot yet, I trow," continued the king; "him, too, must I visit, for I will not believe but that he hath well fledged his nest."

The meal that was served in the banqueting hall far exceeded the king's expectations, and though roast beef was served in profusion, the quantity of venison that was supplied in huge smoking joints, impressed him with the conviction that in spite of the number of foresters he employed to look after the game, his deer was none the safer for it.

The knights formed a goodly company, and as the abbot had been invited, the huge oaken bench was well occupied.

Having partaken sufficient of the luxurious viands to assuage the keenness of their appetites, the knights began conversing with each other, and the king, who as yet had not broken silence, fancied his quick ear could detect the name of the outlaw being mentioned in not very favourable terms.

"What say, D'Anville?" he asked, catching at the duke's speech. "Art talking of that caitiff, Robin Hood?"

"An' it please ye, my liege, I but mentioned his name."

"Speak out; let us all hear what thou sayest of him."

"I merely passed an opinion."

"It may be good for us to hear it. What opinion hast thou of him?"

"That he is a scurvy knave."

"You proved him as such, I presume?"

"Ay, and that long follower of his that they called Little John, forsooth! not much of a little one was he."

"Such was my opinion; but his size does not constitute him a rascal nevertheless."

"No, my liege, but his actions do. Dost remember how soon he filched thee of thy gold!"

"It was truly earned. The fellow fought like a lion. Saint Denis! had we a few such followers, little need we fear."

"But as enemies, my liege, they are dangerous," broke in De Lois; "had you to deal with them as I, soon would you find it so."

"No doubt; but I ascribe half thy woe to want of energy. Now, I guess me thy uncle, the abbot of Saint Mary's, could advise thee in this matter."

"'Tis hard, my liege, to deal with such knaves," replied the abbot, with becoming modesty. "They defy both church and state,

and poison the minds of others who have hitherto been loyal subjects. Something must be done, and that speedily, to rid the country of such pests, or the shrievalty of Nottingham will soon be of little worth."

A glance passed between the abbot and the sheriff, and De Lois gave a ghastly smile.

"What do you propose should be done?" asked the king, draining his goblet.

"'Tis hard to advise, my liege, unless you drive him out of his stronghold by force; even now he hath over a score of my best men in his hands."

"How came they there?"

"Treachery, my liege. They were waylaid, and, being unarmed, were unable to make any resistance."

The abbot screwed up his mouth into a grin at this; but owing to his cowl it was not perceivable.

"If such be his doings," said the king, waxing wrath, "an end must be put to them. He and his band must be routed, and for that purpose I will hie me back quickly to London, and procure the necessary force. To do this, I must borrow of you at least two thousand angels.

Geoffrey de Lois sank back in his chair like one stunned, and the abbot shuffled uneasily in his seat.

The king did not fail to notice the effect of his words, and out of sheer disgust, he said—

"Thou mayest make it four thousand, for our treasury is low, and as the taxes will soon again become due, thou canst easily spare it."

"Good king," said De Lois, with difficulty mustering courage, "I fear me it will puzzle us to find a hundred gold pieces between us," meaning himself and the abbot. "We have many debts that it is impossible to collect in so short a time."

"Dost know of no Jew hereabouts," queried the king, "whose hoarded coffers you might squeeze?" and as he spoke, he glanced significantly towards the abbot.

"Marry! and we do not, my liege," replied Geoffrey, trembling.

"None that we could borrow of for a time? for if thou speakest true, when we rout the robbers from Sherwood we shall have plenty wherewith to pay our debts."

"Alas! none that I know of, my liege."

"And thou, good father, hath no sinner confided to thy sacred ear the name of his secret hiding-place?"

"Saint Mary! the people about here are too poor to amass much wealth," said the abbot, craftily; "indeed, they are little less than beggars, and my time is wholly spent in giving free absolutions and distributing alms, so that the tithes scarce reach my hands ere they are distributed again."

The king listened to this in sullen silence, but made no comment; he only yawned, and intimated his wish to retire.

The page lighted him to the bed-chamber

prepared for him, and as the page retired, D'Anville slunk into the royal chamber.

Till a late hour they were closely closeted, and when the duke slunk out again with a smirking gait, Henry of Winchester flung himself on the bed, and tried to sleep.

His thoughts, however, were not such as to let him repose. The incidents of the past day haunted his mind, and he tossed restlessly on the sumptuous bed that had been prepared for his royal person.

D'Anville had been gone some hours; and the old tower bell had long since tolled the hour of the midnight watch, when a slight rustling awoke him from his reverie.

At first he took no heed of it.

"It was but the wind," he thought; but the shaking of the tapestry that surrounded the bed caused him to look up.

A startled cry rose to his lips, but he suppressed it as he beheld the figure of a female, clad in white, standing by his bed-side.

His first impulse was to clutch at it, and ascertain whether it was real or otherwise, but a kind of superstition held him in its thrawl, and he was unable to do so.

The flickering light of the miserable oil lamp shed a sombre gloom over the apartment, and a kind of fascination kept his eyes fixed on the shaded face of the figure, whose features he tried vainly to discern.

"Speak," he at length gasped, with a desperate effort. "Be thou living, or an inhabitant of another world, speak! What brings thee here, to trouble our royal presence?"

"Injustice and a foul wrong," replied a sweet, musical voice, that sounded angelic in the spacious chamber. "An' thou art the king, thou wilt surely look to this matter."

"Name it; 'fore God, I swear to do all in my power."

"Be not too rash of speech, mortal, for thou art not proof against the evil machinations of the world, e'en though encased in royal robes. Thou art but mortal, but yet may do much."

"In what way? Speak, I conjure you, and end my suspense."

"Procuring the pardon of one Stukely, the late head-warder," replied the apparition. "The tyranny of De Lois has consigned him to a dungeon, the most horrible and "——

"Stukely!" cried the king, rising on his elbow, and passing his hand over his clammy brow. "Was't he who once saved my life?"

"The same, and now he lays in a dungeon suffering unutterable torture. Say thou wilt promise to release him, and I will trouble thee no more."

"'Fore heaven, I promise thee!" gasped the king, his whole frame bathed in sweat; and when he wiped the moisture from his brow and looked again, he saw the figure disappear through the wall at the other end of the apartment.

"Strange!" he muttered, clasping his heated brow. This is some trick by those who know my weakness, or is it a visitation from the spiritual world? I heard that parts of the castle are haunted, but be it mortal or spiritual, I will know the truth."

With this he sprang from his bed, and hammered at the wall with the hilt of his sword, but it gave back no hollow sound; it was solid to all appearance as a rock.

For nearly an hour the king paced the chamber, a prey to the most horrible thoughts, for he had given his word he would release the warder, and yet he knew of no means of doing it.

He might order De Lois to set him at large, but if Geoffrey had an object in confining the man, which it was certain he must have, he might deny all knowledge of him, and remove him secretly to some part of the castle which would preclude all possibility of the king finding him.

Morning was breaking through the casement, and the king could hear the measured tread of the sentinels on the battlements without, when he once more threw himself on his couch.

CHAPTER LXXXIX.

THE DUNGEON OF SKULLS.

Encased in heavy irons
The prisoner did moan,
The ghastly heads about the walls
Would freeze the blood to stone.

WHILST the transactions described in our last chapter were taking place, Stukely, the ex-warder, was shut up a close prisoner in one of the most horrible dungeons the castle contained.

He was heavily manacled, and huge pieces of iron were fixed to a band at his waist, whilst chains of intolerable thickness were fastened to his legs.

This of itself would have been sufficient to have borne down the aged man, but Geoffrey's malicious nature was not such as to meet things half way; so, to complete his cruelty, he had an iron cradle formed of pieces of iron placed perpendicularly and banded strongly together, the sharp points being upwards, and only two inches apart, which reached the armpits of the prisoner, and forced him to stand upright to prevent them piercing his flesh.

To an ordinary mind, this torture would have seemed complete, but to such a man as De Lois it was insufficient. He had the walls, which were blackened by time, hung about with grim and ghastly skulls, whose eyeless sockets were constantly filled with slimy toads and other reptiles that abounded in the fœtid place, and gave the grinning skulls, with their fleshless gums and glistening teeth, an aspect horrible to look upon.

Such was the fearful contrivance Geoffrey had employed to compass his selfish ends; and when we consider the torture inflicted by the knowledge that his daughter was in the power of such a fiend, without a soul to protect her, it is easier to imagine than describe the sufferings, mental and bodily, of the persecuted warder.

It was on the night, as we previously stated, that Geoffrey was entertaining the king, that one of the mailed knights, affecting indisposition, arose from the feast, and quitted the banqueting-hall.

"Who comes?" cried the sentinel, who had been placed on guard without the door, as a mark of respect to the king.

"One of the royal train," was the reply, and the man, lowering his halberd, said—

"Pass on, Sir Knight."

"Of the jovial countenance," he might have added, had he seen the grin on the noble's face, as he passed along the various passages towards the room until lately occupied by the warder.

It was dark, but he made his way with comparative speed, as though trusting to a previous knowledge of the place, but when within a few paces of the warder's door, he came to a stop, by running full butt against a sleepy sentinel.

"Out, knave! what do you mean by this?" muttered the knight, grasping the soldier by the throat. "Asleep on thy post—eh? Dearly shall you pay for this."

"Saint Mary! do not betray me whoever thou beest," said the soldier, trembling in the iron grasp, and wondering who his captor could be.

"Betray you, hound! Did I hang you on the spot I would but be doing my duty; an' it were not for turning executioner, I would do so too. Tell me thy name, knave, that I may report thee or let thee off which seemest me fit."

"And who art thou, pray, to question me thus?" said the man, suddenly recollecting that the voice was not familiar to him as that of one of his officers.

"One who would hang thee at a word, insolent varlet," was the reply, in a deep, sonorous tone. "I have given thee a chance of liberty; dost refuse it?"

A shake, such as satisfied the man that the speaker was one of no mean strength, followed these words, and brought him with a cry of pain to his knee.

"Thy name, minion, ere you tempt me to squeeze out your vile breath on the spot? Your name, ere I execute my threat!"

"Will of Dowley," answered the man, almost choking. "Now wilt thou leave me to my post?"

"One word first. Where is Stukely?"

"In the Dungeon of Skulls."

"Where is that?"

"At the foot of the White Tower."

"Lead me thither, and I will reward ye."

"I dare not. My life would be in peril."

"I will pay thee handsomely."

"And then betray me. "No, I will not leave my post. If you have a right to visit the dungeon you must know its locality."

"Again I warn ye," uttered the knight, fiercely. "Lead the way, or, by my halidame, to-morrow's sunset shall not find thee in the land of the living."

The soldier felt for his sword, but it was gone; he did not notice in the confusion that it had been extricated from its sheath.

Finding himself unarmed, and feeling the point of his adversary's sword at his throat, he said, sullenly—

"Follow me; I will lead the way."

"'Tis well thy wisdom has returned; an' you had refused, thy life would have been worthless ere this."

Through several dark corridors and along a number of dark passages, upwards and downwards, the knight followed his guide, keeping good note of the road they traversed, and counting the steps as they ascended or descended till the man halted, and in a husky voice said—

"I must leave you here; there is another sentry at the end of this passage, and if you want admittance to the cell, he alone can aid thy wish."

"Here, take this for thy trouble, Will of Dowley; you can now return."

CHAPTER LXL.
ROBIN HOOD HAS A STRANGE ADVENTURE.

Upon the narrow bridge
They met and argued long,
And then to quarter-staff they went,
With lusty arm and strong.

HAVING parted with the king, Robin Hood called those of his foresters together who were about the stronghold, and held a council, which led to an examination of the prisoners.

They mustered a good number, and as they showed an unwillingness to leave the good cheer of the forest and a life of idleness, for the drudgery and hard fare of the castle, Robin Hood agreed that they should remain under a promise of doing something in return for their food.

The bold outlaw had many reasons for not parting with them at present.

Firstly, as he expected Geoffrey de Lois would urge the king to attack the stronghold, it was as well to lessen the sheriff's force as much as possible. Secondly, he did not mean to part with the soldiers unless they became too troublesome, until he was enabled to demand of the sheriff fitting ransom for them.

Thus resolved, Robin Hood addressed his followers.

"What say you, merry men all—dost think we need fear treachery?"

"'Tis as well to guard against it, good Robin," replied George-a-Green. "'Tis easier prevented than mended, I trow."

There was a scowl of anger on the brows of several of the Norman soldiers at the forester's speech, and they would, doubtless, have made some hostile movement, had not the presence of a strong guard of bowmen restrained them.

Robin noticed it, and he at once pointed them out, and ordered them to be taken from the rest and confined in the strongest cave.

This produced a good effect on the others.

All disaffection seemed for a time at an end; so fixing his eye sternly on the Norman soldiers, Robin said—

" Since it pleaseth thee to remain with us in the forest glade, it is but meet that ye lighten the labour of my merry men ; and to this end, if it be agreeable, you will assist them in felling timber ; but mark me, in consequence of the undying enmity that exists between the Norman and Saxon race, a strict watch will be kept on your actions"

He paused, and gazed on the stern visages of the soldiers, expecting a reply.

Nothing but an unintelligible muttering, which Robin immediately recognised as one of disapprobation, came from the most of them, which assured him that nothing but the strictest discipline would keep them in subjection.

For a few moments he regarded them with the strictest scrutiny, and then without relaxing a muscle of his stern features he added—

" My proposition appeareth not to meet with your approval ; say, is it so ?"

" We will not submit to be thy slaves," answered a tall soldier, striding forward.

" Slaves ?" ejaculated Robin ; " a set of skulking hounds are ye ! Thou wouldst feast on our good cellarage, and yet not sweat thee a hair. Ye have misjudged my leniency for tyranny, and now I will make thee work, and measure thy stomach accordingly."

" A tyrant indeed hast thou turned," replied the soldier, haughtily.

" Tyrant !" repeated Robin, calming his voice, " it hath pleased thee to make me so, so blame but your own folly. Had I given you your deserts, a stout thong and the branch of a stout oak, would have been your portion long since."

The frown on the soldiers' features grew still darker, and they glanced fiercely round at the stern faces of the outlaws, as with bow and arrow in hand, they stood ready to quell any disturbances.

Robin again spoke.

" Think not that fear of thy proud master hath made me deal thus leniently with thee up to this, for I promise ye that the first who shows signs of rebellion shall suffer death, and it shall be meted out to ye in the full measure of a cloth-yard shaft."

He waved his hand and the guard fell in and marched the prisoners away, leaving Robin deeply immersed in thought.

Soon after he was surrounded by a score of his followers, who seated themselves around the bench beneath the trysting tree.

" Now will I tell ye," he said, " what I will do with these scurvy knaves, the Normans. A malison on the whole of them ! They shall cut stakes sufficient to enclose our stronghold ; for, I wot me, though the king puts a good face on us, the craft of De Lois will turn his mind against us, and before long we shall find ourselves besieged."

The outlaws listened in silence ; but their brows were knitted, and angry glances were darted in the direction of Nottingham Castle.

" It is against this I would have you prepare yourselves," continued Robin ; " and when ye work with the soldiers show no sign of distrust, but keep well on your guard, and have good bowmen in ambush ready about you ; with the rest leave me to deal. Now I leave you for a while, and trust to your faithful obeyance."

Having refreshed himself with a stoup of wine and a few mouthfuls of food, Robin selected a stout staff, and hied him towards Nottingham.

Absorbed in thought, he did not notice that he had taken a road which led to Fountain Dell, which, since his set-to with the friar, he scarcely visited.

The late rains had very much swollen the brook, so for convenience the foresters had felled a huge tree across it, forming a bridge from bank to bank.

Robin Hood, with eyes bent on the ground in deep meditation, reached the bridge much sooner than he was aware, and had taken one pace along the trunk before he noticed that a passenger had already started on the other end.

A full voice warbling the following was the first to apprize him of the fact.

Who cares a fig for Robin Hood ?
　　　Hey down, ho down !
He may have archers strong and good,
　　　Hey down, derry down !
Whilst I have a lusty bough,
　　　Hey down, ho down !
I'd like to meet the rascal now,
　　　Hey down, derry down !

" Saint Hubert ! thou shalt not long be in want of thy wish," Robin said, raising his eyes, and meeting the lusty singer full in the face ; " if thou valuest thy crown I would advise thee to return, for thou seest there is but room for one to pass."

" And that one ?"

" Me ; unless thou offerest strong reason against it."

The man gripped his staff, and took a searching look at Robin, whom he mistook for a royal forest-keeper, and curling his lip in disdain, he replied arrogantly—

" I dispute thy right to the preference. Thou shalt get thee back, or I will crush thy head to a meal if thou dost not obey."

" Marry ! your words are large. One would think thou wert Robin himself," said the outlaw ; " but as you are but an empty braggart I challenge you to a bout."

" Agreed ; and when I have pounded thee well thou wilt own I am Robin Hood's equal ; so have at thee, knave, and no more idle boasting."

Foot to foot the combatants stood on the narrow bridge, and dealt each other lusty blows, not a few that made the dell echo back the sounds.

" Zounds ! thou art a tough one," muttered the man, as he began to pant with his exertions. " Saint Denis ! thou hast some knowledge of the sport."

" As you shall find," returned Robin, at the same time whisking his staff under the fellow's ear, and sending him sloush into the

ROBIN HOOD,
AND THE OUTLAWS OF SHERWOOD FOREST.

"THERE! THERE!" SHRIEKED THE FRENZIED MAN.

brook. "Dost think Robin Hood himself could deal you such a blow?"

The man picked himself up, and scrambled to the bank, sadly damped both in ardour and apparel.

Shaking the water from his hair and

bushy beard in no pleasant mood, the man retorted—

"An' thou wert Robin himself, I would have at thee again. So lay to, for I mean to repay thee all with good interest."

"Ye are welcome, friend, so long as my staff and my arm holds out," replied Robin, "and as ye hold such good opinion of yourself, I will make you a promise."

"What of ?"

"Twenty marks if you give me the first three blows."

"Count that as one," cried the man, making a feint at Robin's cheek, and hitting him on the leg. "Thou art a crafty fox to deal with, be thou a keeper of the king's deer or no."

"You will learn who I am soon enough," replied the outlaw, as he struck the man a blow on his right leg that made him wince, guarded off his adversary's staff, and brought down his stout oaken bough on the head of his foe.

"Count that two."

Robin spoke this with a tone of irony in his voice, for he felt vexed within himself at not being able to settle with his man sooner.

However, at it again they went, and fortune played on both sides for a time, but at length settled in favour of the man, who shouted boastfully—

"Two, th "—

He could not finish the word, which was to have pronounced him victorious, for Robin, by a dexterous parry, sent his staff whirling from his hand, and dealt him a thwack that stretched him at full-length on the sward.

"I meant not to hit thee so hard," said Robin, as he gazed reflectively on the pale, upturned face of his vanquished foe. "Thou hast proved thyself one of sinew, and I will make thee all recompense in my power."

So saying, he took a flagon from beneath his girdle, and held it to the bloodless lips, then procuring some cool water from the brook, he bathed the man's temples.

This soon brought him to, and another application of the flask recovered him sufficiently to stand on his legs.

"I yield thee conqueror whoever thou mayst be," said the man, as soon as he could speak. "Tell me thy name, that I may know thee in future."

"It is needless. More than once have you had it on your tongue within this last half-hour. Bethink you awhile; you may guess it."

The man, pale as he was, turned even paler.

"St. Mary forefend that it be Robin Hood!" he suddenly exclaimed. "Say, is it so, that I may make fit reparation?"

"Fash not thyself about that. I am Robin, and one, judging of thy former speech, that you have wished to have a bout with. Say, is it not so, good fellow?"

"Indeed, and 'twas my ambition once, but that blow you landed on my pate has dis-missed that ambitious desire. Gramercy! 'tis a wonder my skull-pan did withstand it."

"It is useless now regretting. Let us mend our wounds with a stoup of good wine, and as we jog along you can enlighten me of much."

"In what way ?"

"By stating thy name and condition, and the purpose that brought you this way."

"Marry, will I ; but first I must be assured thou art bold Robin."

"My word on that, and if it suffice not, I will again try my skill for twenty marks."

"Twenty devils ! I would not have such another blow for twice twenty marks. Come, let us haste to the inn, for my throat is sorely adry."

Yet would he not believe he was talking to Robin Hood.

In lively chat the time was passed until they reached the inn, and the man imparted much valuable information to Robin during that time.

"Give us of thy best, good Father Redcap," said Robin, as the host, with deferential mien, inquired their wants.

"Malvoisie or sparkling hock ?" asked the host, adjusting his red woollen cap. "To such as my cellar affords ye are right welcome."

"Malvoisie let it be then, that I may drink our friend's health here, though as yet I know not his name."

"Quotha ! you may know that for the asking ; it is no strange one in these parts. Hast ever heard of Darby Dillon ?"

"Marry ! have I, if thou meanest the brewer, and sorry am I that I have not met thee before. I trow me, a few barrels of thy choicest brewing would be very acceptable."

The host entered with the wine, and Robin poured out a measure and handed it to the brewer, who smacked his lips at the delightful beverage. He had not been accustomed to the like.

"Holy mother ! such stuff would not harm even the dainty palate of a monk," said the brewer, smacking his lips. "On such like could I live the rest of my days."

"I trow me, 'tis a relish after guzzling so much ale. 'Tis but a poor drink to confine one's self to, but nevertheless 'tis good by way of a change."

"Saint Denis ! didst thou but once taste of my brewing, thou wouldst patronize it often, for I make no idle boast when I say there is no such to be had for twenty miles round."

Robin listened with patience to the brewer's self-praise, and pushed the wine round freely. Then he said—

"Good fellow, I believe thy words, and if it is thy beer that makes thee so stout of arm and lithe of limb, I envy thee of it, and as I have a few fellows hewing timber in the forest, such drink would well befit them."

"Thou hast hit upon it, and glad would I be to serve ye. We can come to a fair price, and I will allow thee a little to boot if thou hast a quantity."

"You can bring as many barrels as you like, and I will meet you at any time you name in the dell, where we met to-day."

"Thy name, friend," cried the brewer, starting from his seat in delight, "thy name. I wot me from this time we shall be henceforth friends."

"You will know my name soon enough," replied Robin, laughing. "You have surely seen enough of me to know me again. Some one will be there to meet you, and you need only ask for the Lord of Sherwood."

The brewer slightly coloured, and seemed for a moment uneasy.

The mention of the Lord of Sherwood brought to his memory an unpleasant recollection of the outlaws.

"Art thou one of Robin Hood's foresters?" he asked, surreptitiously.

"I, gramercy, no!" replied the outlaw, boldly. "What induced thee to think so? Dost think I look like one of his followers? Out upon thee, man! Drink, and perchance the good liquor will help to clear thine eyes."

This importunity was not easily resisted, and Robin soon saw that the ripe juice was taking effect upon the brewer, which was just as he desired.

"Holy—hic—Mother—hic. This strong stuff takes me off my legs," said the brewer, as he tried to rise, but sank again in his seat. "Hurrah! hic, for the good malvoisie—hic—and the nut-brown English ale."

He flourished the goblet above his head, and then drained its contents, after which he essayed once more to rise, but failed.

"A malison on the stuff! After all—hic—it is no good," he said, eyeing Robin, who was laughing heartily, with a dull, stupid air. "How am I to cross the forest—hic—in this state?"

"I will assist thee, man, an' my company is not troublesome. Get thee on thy feet, and try what thou canst do."

Although Robin had plied the man with drink until he was incapable of taking care of himself, it was not his intention to leave him in his helpless condition. Besides, he had noticed a leathern bag stowed beneath the man's jerkin, and he longed to know what it contained.

His 'cute judgment led him to surmise what might probably be the contents, and he was doubtless not very far out.

Having settled the score, and bid the landlord good-day, Robin took the brewer by the arm, and led him out of the inn, and struck into a by-path leading through the forest, where he soon eased him of his bag, and laughed boisterously at the fun.

"So-ho! what roystering knave is this, that makes the welkin ring with his ungodly mirth?" cried a loud voice, and at the same moment the bulky carcase of Friar Tuck essayed from a clump of bushes.

At the sight of Robin he softened his voice.

"Greet ye, good sir," he said. "I wot me

thou hast a troublesome companion. So overburdened is he with sin, that I fear me he will need absolution."

"Not at thy hands, good father," said Robin, laughing." Already have I eased him of his troublesome load, but if thou hast assistance at hand, thou mayest see him safely to his home. He is a brewer, and will doubtless in some way recompense thee for thy trouble."

The friar interpreted Robin's meaning, and with a kind of half smile, he turned towards the bushes and shouted—

"Where art thou, long of limb and slow of gait? Uncoil thy ugly carcase, and hie thee hither."

Presently Little John made his appearance, rubbing his eyes, and growling most woefully at having been disturbed.

Robin instructed them what to do, and taking the brewer between them, they led him away, Robin watching them till they were out of sight, when he indulged in another fit of hearty laughter.

CHAPTER LXLI.
THE CAPTIVE JEW.

The soldiers did dismount
Then followed such a din,
And with a ringing shout
The door was battered in.

FIERCE blew the blast, and a cold, drizzling sleet fell on the moor, as a party of soldiers urged their jaded steeds over the crisp, springy grass, which crunched beneath their heavy hoofs, and formed a relief to the deathly silence of the calvacade.

There were twenty of them in all, and in their midst rode a figure muffled in a dark cloak, so that nought, even of his face, could be seen.

The horse bearing this strange figure was led by one of the soldiers, two of whom rode on either side, and in the front rode a single horseman of monstrous height and majestic figure, who looked a very colossus as he sat immovable and erect in his saddle.

Neither of the horsemen were deficient in height or proportions; but the solitary rider was conspicuous among them all, and when at length he broke the silence, his voice sounded like that of a stentor.

"Halt!"

The party came to a sudden stand, and at another word from the tall rider one of the horsemen fell out, and galloped to his side.

"Maulac."

"My liege."

"Knowest thou aught of this part of the country?"

"Indeed do I; few know it better."

"Dost remember an hostel hereabout?"

"The King's Arms; but 'tis but poor lodgings for your"——

"Enough, so long as it gives us shelter for a while; this forced march hath tried us sorely. Our horses stand much in need of an hour's rest."

Maulac bowed, and wheeling his horse to the right, charged up a steep slope, where he drew rein, and took a survey through the murky darkness.

"It is but a mile," he said, as he cantered back. "A few minutes will take us to the spot, though, as I said before, you will find but sorry fare."

"I have said, and that is enough. Lead on, good Maulac."

Maulac now took the lead, and the cavalcade was once more in motion.

At a rude, dilapidated building they halted, and Maulac, dismounting, rapped heavily at the stout oaken door.

The growl of a fierce mastiff answered his summons, and the repeated knocking at length aroused the drowsy host.

"Who knocks without?" he shouted, with the ill-humour of one just awakened from a sound sleep. "Begone at once, for I know 'tis no good brings you from home at this hour."

"Open at once, thou prince of knaves!" cried Maulac, beating the pommel of his sword against the door. "Open, I tell thee, or we will force our way in."

"Thou art a braggart, and saucy withal! therefore I bid thee go thy ways, for I will not admit thee till a proper hour," shouted the innkeeper, growing more ill-tempered.

"Dismount," cried the tall horseman, "and teach this fellow manners. Saint Quinten! an' we hang him by the ears to the door-post, it will humble him a little."

Six of the soldiers that formed the rearguard dropped from their horses, and, placing the reins in the hands of their comrades, made a desperate assault on the door of the inn with their broad shoulders.

The massive door resisted for a time their desperate efforts to force it, but yielded at length, and as the barrier gave way, the dog flew out and seized a soldier by the throat.

A blow from a falcihon made him relax his hold and roll over with a cry of pain, which so far dismayed his master, as to cause him to fly for his life.

Maulac strode in after him, and caught sight of him rushing up the rickety stairs, and he followed him at lightning speed.

By this time the whole household was alarmed.

The screams of women and children mingled with the oaths and curses of the men.

With unsparing hand the soldiers cleared away the fragments of the door, and having procured a light, they took a hasty survey of the place.

On the basement were two large rooms, and one of them they hastily converted into a stable, the other was taken possession of by the men.

The upper part of the house was also divided into three parts, the room over the tap being appropriated to the use of the host and his corpulent spouse; the second was occupied by a number of men working on a neighbouring farm; and the third was devoted to travellers; but at present it was only occupied by a solitary knight.

Maulac, having ascertained all this during his pursuit of the host, who had baffled him in the darkness, soon completed his arrangements, by bundling the men into the room occupied by the landlord and his wife, and quietly intimating to the knight that it would be best for him to seek some other quarters.

There was a ghastly grin on the knight's features as he rose on his elbow, and fixed his eye on the face of the intruder.

"Saint Hilderbrack!" he growled, "it is hard times when a wounded soldier has to turn out of his warm bed for a set of scurvy knaves who go about pillaging the country, and robbing the honest of their hard earnings."

"Thou two-faced hypocrite!" cried Maulac, sternly, "well mayst thou prate, for thy honesty is of long standing. Saint Benedict! how long is it since thou cut a throat?"

"Maulac, this from you is too much! What I did was more at thy instigation than mine own liking; but you can have your say out; I cannot resent it; my arm is weak."

"Ha! ha!" laughed the soldier, in bitter derision, "Sir John has, maybe, been up to his old tricks. Well, I have often told you how it would end."

"Taunted me, would be a more fitting comparison."

"Go to with thy comparisons, and get thee out of this; for, by my faith, if thou movest not of thine own good will, I will get thee assistance."

The knight fixed his eye on him with the cold glitter of a serpent.

"Maulac," he said, "time was when you would not have dared to use such words to John of Linden."

"Time, as the wind, changes; and I, bad as I own myself to be, cannot look upon you but with disgust. I will give thee time to rise, and if thou movest not quickly I will call my fellows to your aid."

This threat was accompanied by a stride towards the door, and the knight, fearing the consequences, rose without further argument.

A strong body of men then ascended the stairs, and the figure muffled in the cloak was led in.

Pale and ghastly was the face the removal of the cloak revealed; and, as the captive glanced round at the stern visages of the soldiers, a shudder passed through his frame.

"Got of Abraham!" he muttered, unconsciously aloud, "vhen vill the oppression of thy chosen people cease?"

"When such ugly wretches as you cease to exist," said the tall figure, striding in. "By our Lady, the obstinacy of your race will be shaken before long."

"Mine Got! your cruelty must soon cease. It cannot last for ever. Your thirst for monish vill von day be satisfied."

"Not till thy avarice allows thee to disgorge thy hoarded wealth; for I have sworn to wring from thee a confession of thy secret hoard. Thou and thy brethren drain the country of its strength, and though fair offers have been made to thee, yet do ye remain obdurate."

"Edward, prince though you are, I do not fear your threats. It ish not such as you as vill make me forget my duty to my bredren."

"Peace, fool! Away with thee, and prepare thyself for the tortures you justly merit. Let him be well guarded, Maulac; he can rest his bones on the softest plank he can find."

The Jew was about to reply; but Maulac, seizing him by the rope that pinioned his arms, thrust him to the other end of the room, and stationed an armed sentinel over him.

The prince strode haughtily to the room he had chosen for himself and Maulac, where the latter soon joined him.

Spread upon a board was a repast the best the house could afford, and the prince, whose appetite was sharpened by his long ride, set to with as much gusto as did his favourite follower.

Thus the remainder of the night was passed, and when in the morning the trembling host informed the prince that the king and his retinue had passed that way only a few days before on his way to Nottingham, he decided upon staying there until the departure of the king, a decision anything but pleasant to the worthy host.

CHAPTER LXLII.

THE KING'S ANGER.

The king was vexed and sorely wrath,
He thought the sheriff lied;
He for the warder loudly called,
And to the dungeons hied.

GEOFFREY DE LOIS was astir as soon as the king; for, like himself, he had passed a restless night, and when morning awoke, refreshed from the arms of night, it found the sheriff standing, with bleared and sleepless eye, gazing out on to the black waters of the moat, which might have been well comparisoned with his own guilty mind.

At that moment the bugle sounded, summoning the drowsy soldiers from their sleep, and soon after a knock was heard at the chamber door.

Not wishing to be found in this predicament, De Lois slipped into bed, and pulled the clothes well about him; then pulling a thong that was attached to the bolt of his chamber door, he shouted for the page to enter.

The page approached him tremblingly; for at first glance, he missed his master's mail from their wonted place, and in a faltering tone said—

"The king wishes to see you, my lord, at your earliest convenience."

"Did he give you no other message?"

"None, my lord."

"Conduct him to the oaken chamber; I will join him there in a few moments."

The page withdrew, and Geoffrey sprang from the bed, and made a hasty toilet, then hastened to join his royal hostage.

Geoffrey de Lois gave a perceptible shudder as he gazed on the pale cheeks and quivering lips of the king.

He could see by his clouded brow that something was amiss.

"All hail to your majesty!" he said, bowing deferentially. "By the virgin! you look like one unwell. Has aught in the castle disagreed with thee?"

"You have guessed aright," replied the king, eyeing him sternly. "I hear strange doings are enacted in the castle."

"An' it please your majesty to name them, I will endeavour to explain as much as lay in my power," said Geoffrey, trying to assume a firmness he did not feel. "Probably a mistake has in some way arisen."

"I trust it may be so; though I fear it otherwise," replied the king. "Have you a prisoner in the castle?"

"None, my liege."

"On your oath?"

"On the word and honour of a loyal subject, which is more."

"Bethink thee; thou mayst have forgotten."

De Lois made a cringing bow, and, falling on his knee at the feet of his sovereign, replied—

"My duty to thee, my liege, would quicken my memory."

Henry regarded him for a moment in silence, and then turned away and paced the room with rapid strides, whilst his fingers twitched nervously in his beard.

"De Lois," he said, suddenly halting and confronting the still-kneeling villain, "I doubt the truth of your words. Send hither the warder, that I may question him."

Geoffrey summoned the page and gave him some instructions in an undertone.

Presently a soldier, with a bunch of keys hanging from his waist by a chain, entered, and bowed to the king.

"Art thou the head-warder?" demanded Henry.

"I am, your majesty, and at your service."

"You name?"

"Walter Hind."

The words were scarcely clear of the man's lips, when the king turned fiercely upon the sheriff.

"Where is Stukely?" he demanded in a voice of thunder.

"He has left my service long since, your highness. He was old and unfit for the office."

"Indeed!" sneered the king, "then we will see for ourselves, and have our own judgment on this matter. Lead on to the dungeons."

De Lois took the lead by a tortuous route, the torch-bearer following closely on his heels, the warder next, the king following in the rear.

At the door of each cell Geoffrey stopped, the warder opened the massive door, and the king, taking the torch in his own hand, minutely examined each dungeon.

In their course several rooms were visited, Geoffrey taking scrupulous care not to go near the apartme't where Madge Stukely was confined, and also reminding the king that the dungeons of the White Tower were wholly set aside for prisoners of state and special purposes of the king.

This had its effect so far as to limit the king's visit to only a few of the dungeons, those which his majesty thought the most likely to have been used, so that he returned to the oaken chamber with the impression that he had been deceived by his midnight visitation.

At an early hour the castle was visited by the abbot, who had made an effort to disgorge some of his treasure, and never did he perform the journey between the abbey and the castle with a heavier heart.

Bitterly did he bewail his fate, and call upon the name of all the saints he could think of to bear witness of his martyrdom, as with his load he ascended the stone stairs.

Geoffrey seemed suddenly to revive, as, panting from his exertion, the fat abbot entered the chamber.

The sight of the holy man's load wrought this change on him; for, though he did not like parting with his ill-gotten gold himself, he secretly rejoiced at the rich coffers of the abbey being squeezed, and he parted more willingly with the little sum he had himself scraped together.

That evening the king left greatly displeased with his visit; but not without a lingering presentiment that Robin and his followers ought to be exterminated.

The abbot had not failed to pour the poison into his ears, and Geoffrey backed him up with his argument, which had great weight with the fickle king.

Geoffrey watched his departure in nervous anxiety, and it was not till they were no longer in view from the battlements that he felt he could breathe freely.

"Saints be praised that he hath gone!" he muttered, aloud. "May he never return, unless it be to scatter that band of outlaws, and bring their leader in chains to be hanged."

"By our Lady, thou hast just uttered my thoughts!" exclaimed the abbot, who chanced to be at his elbow, "only that I do not like him departing with my gold. He has beggared the church, and, I fear me, I shall not be able to keep my promise with our patron saint."

"What promise?" demanded De Lois, gruffly.

"The offering I vowed to make to the shrine of the blessed Mary; two dozen candles, and "——

"A feast to thine own ungodly carcase."

"Saints forgive thee for thy sins! an' thou turnest not from thy worldly ways thou wilt have to do long penance in purgatory."

"I shall have to pay a visit to the buttery first; for, believe me, good uncle, I have not relished my food since Henry first arrived. I had hoped that his visit might have boded us good to our lands, which, in a measure, is now worthless."

Their discourse was interrupted by the page bearing a missive.

"From Edward!" gasped De Lois, running his eye over the superscription.

Geoffrey and the abbot then retired to read the contents, and consult as to the best manner of receiving him.

They were closely closeted for some time, and then the abbot left, a malicious grin being concealed by his cowl as he drove out of the castle gate.

Once more alone Geoffrey fell into a deep reverie, and paced the floor, muttering incoherently.

Suddenly he started, and taking a huge key from a shelf, he exclaimed—

"Now is my time; the work must be done speedily. That chattering jade shall be placed on the rack, and Stukely, with his own hands, shall work the screws that must draw from her the confession. This will be revenge," he added, bitterly. "How delightful to watch his agonized features as he listens to his daughter's groans. Ha! ha! This will in part repay me for the loss of my hated enemy, Robin Hood, who defies me—ay! and holds me up to scorn."

With these and a thousand other thoughts that flashed to his heated imagination, Geoffrey pursued his way up the flights of steps and along the gloomy passages, until he reached the door of Madge's chamber.

"Is your prisoner safe?" he demanded of the man who mounted guard.

The man replied with some trepidation in his voice; for though he had seen her safe an hour previously, and he was certain no one had entered or left since then, yet after the mysterious disappearances of late, and with which she was supposed to be connected, he could not truthfully assert she was still there.

"Wretch! answer me. Is she still there?" thundered De Lois, his eyes flashing fire. "How long have you been on this post?"

"Since sundown, my lord," stammered the man.

"'Tis well. Have you the key?"

The man fidgeted about under his doublet for some time, and Geoffrey, impatient at his delay, raised his fist, and dealt him a fearful blow.

The soldier staggered and fell, a stream of blood gushing from his nose and mouth.

"Idiot! I'll brain you!" thundered De Lois, hoarse with passion. "Rise, minion, or I'll draw your teeth with "——

Rage would not permit him to finish the threat, but a stamp of his iron heel upon the flags brought the soldier to a sense of his danger, and he scrambled to his feet.

"Varlet! I have a mind to choke thee!" hissed De Lois, as the man still continued to fumble for the key. "If she hath escaped through thy agency, thou mayest dread the consequence."

"My lord, if such be the case, I wot it not. Faithfully have I fulfilled my duty. Here is the key."

Geoffrey snatched it from his hand, and thrusting it into the lock, sent the door crashing open with his foot.

With the glare of a tiger he glanced around, and on the bed he saw what he supposed to be the girl's figure.

"Ah! she sleeps," he muttered. "Terrible shall be her waking. Now for the father. I will prepare him for his fate."

Locking the door, and taking with him the key to prevent her escaping in his absence—for his brutality to the man had inspired him with a feeling of dread that he might retaliate—he hurried in the direction of the White Tower.

"Who comes?" cried the sentinel, whose quick ear was alert to the slightest sound, and the clank of a scabbard accompanied the challenge.

"Thy master, idiot!" was the reply. "Canst not see? I wot me it would quicken thy sight did I poke out thine eyes with my anclace!"

The soldier lowered his sword, and allowed him to pass on to the dungeon door.

With a soul full of mischief and malignant hate, De Lois rushed to the door and opened it, but before entering, he snatched the link from its niche in the wall, and held it as far in as his arm would reach.

One cursory glance he took at the horrid, grinning skulls, which seemed to wag their fleshless jaws as though in very mockery of him, and then he fixed his eye on the cradle, as the horrid machine was called, but the iron bars were empty, and the pointed spikes were minus of the arms that were intended to rest upon them.

With a growl such as might be supposed to come from a wild beast when goaded into madness, he rushed forward, and thrust his hand between the bars to ascertain the truth, for he scarcely believed his vision.

"Gone! gone!" he gasped, and the words seemed to come up in gulps. "Foiled, by the powers of infernal darkness! The chain broken, and all my hopes of revenge vanished. Grin on, you goblin heads! Well may you mock me," he continued, as his eyeballs glared viciously round. "By all the saints in Christendom, I will have restitution for this! A score of heads shall roll off before to-morrow's light, and Madge Stukely's shall be the first!"

Snatching his anclace from its jewelled sheath, he rushed madly from the dungeon, and made a blow at the sentry, who had watched him from the door.

Fortunately for the man, he divined his intentions, and had time enough to ward off the deadly thrust, that must otherwise have proved fatal, and Geoffrey staggered forward from the impetus of the blow.

He soon regained his feet, but by that time the man had fled far enough in the darkness to baffle him, and with a horrid grin, and a sweeping malediction, De Lois made for the chamber of Madge.

"Saint Quintin! I will not this time be foiled!" he hissed between his teeth. "This shall square accounts between us."

He clutched his weapon in his hand, and hurled the sentry aside, and then entered the room.

With a bound he reached the side of the bed, and raising the weapon to the full length of his arm, brought it down with all his force on the prostrate body.

Horrible was the cry that came from his lips, and deathly was the aspect of his features when he found that the supposed body was but a bundle of clothes, made to resemble a woman, and which had been so artfully contrived as to deceive even the careful sentinel.

Driven to the height of madness, De Lois even raised his weapon against himself, and would have succeeded, had not the soldier rushed up to him and caught his hand at the nick of time.

———

CHAPTER LXLIII.

THE BUTLER'S REVENGE.

He filled the foaming tankard,
And gave it to the man,
Who little ken'd what it contained,
As along the vaults he ran.

IT was with anything but a feeling of rejoicing that the arrival of Prince Edward was hailed in the castle.

With the departure of the king all love of royalty had died out, for his visit had imposed upon the soldiers extra work and double duty, and they expected the visit of the prince would impose upon them the same.

Night had set in when they reached the gates, and their entrance was conducted with all secrecy.

De Lois personally inspected the lowering and raising of the drawbridge; for recent events had taught him to place but little reliance in his men, and this precaution did not wholly ease his mind.

Arrived in the court-yard, Edward dismounted, and strode haughtily to the sheriff's side, then whispered something in his ear.

"Most noble prince," said De Lois, bowing meekly, "everything is arranged as your missive desired. Shall I order the prisoner to be led to the White Tower?"

"An' thou wilt do so at once, it will give me much pleasure; and then, if thou hast aught good, I will do honour to thy board."

"Of that which this poor shrievalty affords your highness shall have the best."

"Quick, then, be it; for matters of great import depend upon this night's work. What has to be done, must be done speedily and with caution though there is less danger to apprehend in this quiet town than in London, where the populace are already incensed against the king."

Geoffrey made no reply, but hung his head.

"Dost apprehend any danger?" asked the prince, eyeing him searchingly.

"Than Nottingham no place hath keener eyes and sharper ears," replied De Lois; "and even the hounds that are in my pay and keeping would not scruple at eaves-dropping."

"Keep strict watch upon them, De Lois, and show to me the delinquent. "By our Lady! it shall be his last offence."

"But you will not need their services, will you?"

"Not in this private business, I trow me. I am not so unwise. I have, in my escort, some half-dozen fellows well trained in this work—gold refiners—you understand me; they separate the pure *metal* from the *dross*. Ha! ha! they will thoroughly purge the rascal of a Jew."

De Lois breathed more freely.

He feared that even the threat of death would not deter his men from whispering the news abroad, especially when boasting of their deeds and chivalrous actions over a flagon of ale.

Amongst those who suffered most, or rather growled the most, by the visit of the prince, were the butler and the cook. Many a tiff they had on that eventful night; for, as is often the case on such occasions, everything appeared to go wrong.

According to their own assertions, which were proclaimed in no decorus manner, neither were in fault, and yet they tried to lay blame to each other; and the messenger, whose face appeared at the door at regular intervals—for he dare venture no further on the hostile ground—had a good share of the abuse.

The chief cause of all this, had it been known, was attributable to the butler, who, for some slight offence on the part of his inveterate enemy, the cook, had sworn to be revenged—a vow which he most righteously kept.

In his office as cook, Gaucher naturally perspired very freely, and being a corpulent man, it required some extra stimulants to keep him on his legs, for which reason he was allowed what beer he could drink, which was no inconsiderate quantity.

A large flagon was kept in the kitchen for this purpose, and it was through the demand to have this replenished at a time which was the most inconvenient to the butler—namely, when he was indulging in a chat with a pretty blue-eyed lass, who had visited the castle on business—that the morning's disagreement had occurred.

The cook was justified in his demand, and the butler was bound, by the rules of the castle, to comply; for all this the butler felt hurt at the lowering of his dignity, and he hit upon a terrible revenge.

Sending the sculleryman on with the pitcher, the butler entered his own room under pretence of getting the key, but which was really to further his diabolical scheme.

In one corner was a cupboard used for storing various herbs and compounds; and from the numerous jars he selected one which contained a kind of powder or bruised root of a brownish colour, a handful of which he placed in a stone mortar, and mixed it with a little beer, which mixture he emptied into a drinking horn, and, with a quiet smile of satisfaction, he placed it under his doublet, and hurried to the cellar where the sculleryman awaited him.

"Saint Ursula! what ails the man?" asked the butler, as, when the pitcher was about half full, he emptied the mixture he had brought with him into it unperceived. "Why, thou look'st as lean and haggard as a wood faggot. Doth thy master starve thee?"

The sculleryman, who was as long and thin as the master was short and podgy, started at his voice, for they were the only words of commiseration he had heard since his employment at the castle, then glanced ruefully down his lank form, which was as flat as a board, and sighed.

The crafty butler bestowed on him a look of pity, and placing the horn, which still contained a little of the brown mixture, under one of the barrels, he filled it with ale, saying—

"Here, good fellow; 'tis of such as this thou standeth in need. Did thy master share the contents of the flagon equally with thee it would alter thy condition."

The man accepted the liquor with a profusion of thanks, and chuckled within himself at having found favour in the eyes of so great a man, for his former visits to the cellar had been rewarded by a cuff or a growl from the irritable butler.

"Now go thy way, and see if ye can keep thy meagre lips from the pitcher; for, in sooth, I do not wish to keep running to and fro all day attending on that thirsty master of thine."

The man returned the empty horn, and, raising the flagon in his arms, departed with the words of the butler ringing in his ears.

But the temptation of testing the quality of the ale was too strong to be resisted, especially as he found he was not followed, for the butler had purposely stayed behind to allow him this indulgence.

"Saints forgive me if I am doing wrong!" he muttered, as he rested the pitcher in a niche of the wall, and allowed the foaming beverage to gurgle down his throat. "Saint Hilderbrack, that is good! 'Tis of a rare cask. I must e'en have another draught. Such like I have never before tasted."

The ale was all afoam with the motion of his carrying it, and having taken another draught of about a pint, he measured with his finger to see how far it was below the rim, for his master allowed him a little for *spilling*—a circumstance that invariably occurred, unless when the butler followed closely on his heels.

"So you have got it, and I have conquered!" exclaimed the cook, in triumph, placing his fat hands on his broad hips. "Ah!

ROBIN HOOD,

AND THE OUTLAWS OF SHERWOOD FOREST.

ROBIN HOOD MEETS THE PRINCESS IN THE GARDEN.

soon will I humble that proud fellow; and, as they say in the guard-room, lay him in the dust. Ha! ha!" he laughed, as the thought occurred to him, "lay him in the dust, and choke him; then may he cry for wine, but I will not give him water." He paused to take a draught of the ale, and then, rubbing his fat stomach, continued—"Capital stuff! I have frightened the rascal at last. He finds that Gaucher is a lion when roused —a very Tartar, and this knowledge has made him fill my pitcher from the sheriff's best barrel—the very best. Oh, it's delightful!"

He wiped the perspiration from his brow, and then took another good swig; then, placing the pitcher in a sly corner, he turned threateningly to his man, and shouted—

"You thieving rascal, let me catch you smelling it, let alone tasting it, and I'll flog you within an inch of your life. Such stuff is valuable, and not fitted to such palates as——Ugh!"

Simultaneous with the cry his hands went to his sides, his eyes rolled up, and then his body bent double; at least, as far as his obesity would allow.

"Saint Quintin! that is a stinger," he ejaculated, as the spasm passed and allowed him once more to assume his perpendicular; "Holy Mother preserve us from many such."

A cry from the other end of the room caused him to turn his eyes in that direction, where his man was similarly situated.

"A malison on the knave! he his mocking me," he cried, savagely; and, to vent his spleen, he took a ladle from one of the dishes and hurled it at the sculleryman's head.

Fortunately a sharp nip caused him to bend his head lower; so the missile failed its inten ledmark, and the next moment Gaucher was rolling on the floor groaning with pain.

The butler, who had been watching through the chink of the door, now entered.

"How now, master cook?—what ails you?" he asked, with well-feigned commisseration.

"It would puzzle me to tell you," replied Gaucher, scrambling to his feet with a horrible grimace. "I can only say I was never in all my life so bad."

"Ah! 'tis as I have often told you, good Gaucher; you were never intended for a cook; those great fires will be the death of you—you have not pith enough to stand it. Now, were I in your place, I could stand it like a "——

"Devil, as you are! Go away; do you not see I am in pain?"

"Well, thou art a poor one to bear it. I pity thee from my heart; for I wot me, thy pain will in no way appease the appetite of our master, who hath given me orders to prepare for a noble guest; and here come the knaves with the meat."

Four lusty fellows entered bearing huge joints between them slung on poles, which they rested on the floor.

"Holy Mother, help me out of this trouble," raved the distracted cook; "how thinkest thou, man, I can cook all this and suffer such pain?"

"Indeed I know not," replied the butler, with a malicious grin; "thou wilt surely have to get some one in thy place; for thy man here seems to be no better than thee; over-feeding hath given him the bile, no doubt. But I will leave thee to it, as I cannot idle my time in talking."

The butler strode out of the room and retired to the solitude of the buttery, where he could indulge in his mirth without fear of interruption.

Gaucher was not sorry when the butler was gone, for his taunts increased his agony, which seemed to grow worse at each draught he took of his favourite beverage, and the huge fires began to blaze more fierce.

The sculleryman of the two was not so bad, though his lank form continued to imitate the opening and closing of a carpenter's rule; but the fearful invectives heaped upon him at intervals by the groaning Gaucher, served in some way to alleviate his pain—at least it helped to move him brisker than he would otherwise have done.

The tantalizing butler gloried in the mischief he had caused, and made frequent visits to the kitchen from which Gaucher or his man was invariably missing.

Geoffrey de Lois suffered internal anguish in consequence of the delay, but he was forced to control his passion in the presence of his guest.

When the smoking viands did appear they fell-to in such a manner that showed their appetites had not lost by the delay, and many a good bottle they emptied in washing it down.

CHAPTER XCIV.

THE SCENE IN THE CHAMBER OF THE WHITE TOWER.

Fierce grew the fire, the flames arose,
   And shrieks came from the Jew,
The White Tower was the place to make
   Him reveal all he knew.

THE last sound of the curfew bell had long since rolled away, and nought save the tread of the heavily-armed sentinels as they kept their lonely watch on battlement and tower awoke the stillness of the moonless night.

In the town the lights had gradually dwindled out, and all in the castle save one had yielded to the darkness.

That one faint glimmer came from the loophole of a lofty turret, which, from its height and ignorance of its real name, the townspeople designated the Eagle's Nest, for even on a fine day its summit seemed towering up into the clouds.

This loophole, from which the light so dimly shone, was the only ingress of air or light to the chamber of the White Tower, with which was associated such horrors as none but those who had witnessed them could ever imagine.

The soldier on sentry on the battlements beneath crossed himself devoutly when his eye caught the light, and muttered an Ave Maria.

The sound of voices startled him, and directly after two figures emerged from the shadow of a buttress.

The soldier gave the challenge, and the password was given by the two cloaked figures, who passed on to the White Tower.

They were Prince Edward and the sheriff; and as soon as they entered the massive door, it was closed and barred behind them.

The sight that met their gaze on entering was enough to make the blood of anyone with the least humanity run cold.

The executioners were already assembled, and their prisoner was prepared for the torture, though apparently he was suffering quite enough already.

His long flowing beard had been shaven, or rather torn off, by some jagged instrument, which left his face and chin torn and bleeding, yet for all this he showed not the least sign of fear, but eyed his tormentors with a look of stubborn resolution.

When the prince was seated he ordered him to be brought before him, and in a stern voice, he said—

"Azevedo, it hath come to our knowledge that thou hast accumulated much wealth, and thereby impoverished the state, which stands much in need of that same; and furthermore, that thou art in league with others of thy race who hath similar hoards: disclose what thou knowest of this, and thou mayest depart in peace; refuse, and thy punishment shall be such as mortal cannot bear."

"Mein Gott! I swear I know noting of dis. I am but a poor man—I am ruined!"

"Idiot, wag not thy false tongue so fast; thou knowest all that we wish to learn."

"I swear, good prince, I do not."

"Where have you hidden your treasures?" demanded Edward, sternly.

"Mein Gott! I had none to hide; your soldiers took de little monish I did have to keep me from starving, and dat vash de savings of many years' hard vork—hard vork!"

"Lying hypocrite!" thundered the prince, eyeing the cringing Jew with a look that seemed almost to pierce him through; "hast forgotten the thousand pounds you received from Mordecai—the two thousand doubloons transmitted to you from Spain?"

"'Tis false! I swear I had no such monish! I swear, by de Got of Abraham, I had not so much in my life."

The Jew trembled and wrung his hands despairingly; but the prince remained unshaken in his belief, and laughed to scorn his protestations of innocence.

"Wretch!" he exclaimed, "you are as false in your speech as in your dealings, but I will wring from you the truth, though it be at the cost of your life. Dost know one Don Alvesey, the richest Spaniard of thy creed?"

"I do not."

"And yet he is a countryman of thine."

"That I will not deny, most noble prince; but you cannot expect me to know all men of my country."

"Have I not said he is a Jew—an amasser of wealth?"

Edward began to lose his temper at the stubborn answers of the Jew, for Azevedo showed not the least sign of yielding to his wish.

"Look you here," he said, in a voice slightly hoarse with rage; "one chance more I give you, and then you need expect no mercy; 'fore heaven! I swear I will not spare you one pang."

"May de Got of Abraham soften your hard heart!" exclaimed the Jew, raising his clasped hands as in supplication to heaven, and rolling his eyes sanctimoniously upwards.

"Prayers will avail thee little. Unbind thy tongue in fitting manner, or prepare thyself for tortures of which thou little dreameth."

The prince still continued to eye him narrowly; and, as his features changed with the fierce struggle working within him, he nourished a hope that the Jew would confess without the necessity of further torture.

He was deceived, however.

In the momentary struggle he had gathered fresh nerve, and hoped by maintaining a firmness to deceive the prince and thus save his hoarded treasure, which was to him dearer than life.

The prince was too schooled in the ways of the world to be thus easily hoodwinked.

"What think you, De Lois, of this Jewish dog?" he asked, turning to the sheriff. "I would that I had your opinion on this matter."

"By the saints! I can hardly give your majesty advice, unless it be to roast the carl, for he is evidently of much cunning, and endowed with as lying a propensity as any I wot of."

"Then thou wouldst"——

"Place him in the chair; it is a safe and speedy remedy for such complaints."

"Even as thou sayest will I do, good De Lois."

As he spoke he motioned to the soldiers who stood beside the prisoner, and instantly he was seized by them. Then he was thrust with brutal force into a large chair, and an iron band passed round his waist, which, being worked by a screw, drew it tight across his chest, and prevented him from rising.

One herculean fellow, with bared, brawny arms, worked the screw, while Moulac watched the signals of the prince, who viewed with wrapped attention its effect upon the prisoner.

A deathly silence, broken only by the screech of the rusty screw as it worked in its grove, fell upon the witnesses of this horrible scene, until the hoarse breathing of the Jew proclaimed the band sufficiently tight, and then the prince cried—

"Hold!"

Then all relapsed into painful silence again, the deep breathing of the Jew alone being audible.

"Now, what sayest thou, Azevedo; do you remember aught now of thy treasures?"

"Naught, by de Got of Israel, I swear!" gasped the Jew.

Edward made a sign for the man to loosen the band a little to allow the Jew to speak; but he said no more, only wiped the sweat of agony from his brow.

"A malison on thee and all thy race! I will make thee bark, thou Jewish dog!" cried the prince, unable to control his passion. "De Lois, thou knowest what to do."

Geoffrey bowed; he felt flattered by the compliment; and, taking a torch from the hand of one of the men, he thrust it under the chair, and set fire to a pile of resiny wood that had been previously placed there.

The inflammable matter was soon in a blaze, and a cloud of black smoke almost stifled the Jew; but he stood it with perfect firmness, and gave a kind of hysterical laugh.

But the worst was yet to come.

The chair was so constructed as to be hollow, and was composed of sheets of iron riveted together, so that as the flames rose they filled the cavities with tremendous heat.

As the fire took hold more fuel was applied, and then the soldiers withdrew to a respectful distance, for the heat soon become unbearable.

Azevedo groaned, clenched his hands, and ground his teeth most horribly, as the iron began to grow hot.

Fearful, indeed, was the torture, yet his greed of gold enabled him to bear it, whilst the soldiers gazed on in silence and in wonder.

As the flames increased and diffused the heat, his courage, however, gave way; and, with a spasmodic effort, he tried to free himself.

This was, of course, useless; and a groan burst from him which was followed by a heart-rending cry of agony that echoed fearfully through the massive chamber; and, flinging up his arms he cried to be released.

His persecutors, enraged at his former obstinacy, paid no heed to his appeal.

They listened unmoved to his unearthly and horrible cries.

As the flames quickened, and the heat increased, the cries of the sufferer grew more and more appalling; and then at the instigation of De Lois, the prince consented to his release.

Shrieking with pain, for the heat had contracted his muscles, and his limbs were drawn up to his body, the sufferer was laid on a hard bench; and as he gave signs of becoming unconscious, a strong stimulant was poured down his throat, which revived him, and made him become more sensitive to the pain.

The horrible expedient had its effect, and between the groans of agony the Jew divulged all he knew, imparting more information than the prince had actually believed him capable of.

One hour later, the prince, in company with De Lois, left the White Tower; and soon after, the soldiers who had acted in the atrocious affair sallied forth bearing in their midst the lifeless body of the Jew, who had fallen a victim to the torture, and died at the close of his confession.

CHAPTER XCV.

THE MEETING IN SHERWOOD FOREST.

To merry Sherwood then they hied,
And held their meetings three;
They did agree the sheriff for
To hang upon a tree.

In spite of the strict precautions of the sheriff to keep the visit of the prince a secret, the news by some means worked its way into the town, and aroused the indignation of the people.

Even the death of the Jew became known to them; and though in those days the life of a Jew was considered of little or no value, yet the occurrence served to remind them that they who were possessed of money might share a similar fate.

Among these was a wealthy farmer named Hugh Middleton, who was an intimate friend of the miller's, and who, like himself, had suffered greatly from the sheriff's oppression.

On his land he employed many men; besides which, he had great influence in the town, so that he was enabled to take up the matter with warmth, and with more likelihood of success than many others.

One evening he called at the mill, and held a long discourse with the miller and his son, who entered freely into his opinion, and advised him how to arrange matters.

Acting on this advice, he dispersed his men over the town and the little villages around, giving them money to enable them to enter the various inns and public places, where they might hear the different discussions and gain an insight into the thoughts of the people.

In this manner he sounded and found that the people were adverse to the tyranny of the sheriff, and were willing to resent it providing they had a leader and some one to organize them.

This soon reached the ears of Robin Hood, who was delighted with the scheme, and promised at once to give it his support.

Roaming leisurely one evening in the forest glade with Marian on his arm, he chanced to meet the farmer, who saluted him with—

"A good day to you, bold Robin, and to your graceful Marian; it is many a day since I had been pleasured with the sight of either of you."

"Ay, friend Middleton; it was last at the May-day festival, an' I mistake not."

"You cannot mistake it if you bethink of the glorious flogging we gave to the Norman that day?"

The farmer pointed towards Nottingham as he spoke; and his broad sun-burnt face wrinkled into a smile.

"Thou hast not forgotten the sheriff's discomfiture, then? Neither hath he, I trow. St. Herman! how the nettles made him run! wot me no rogue ever used his legs faster."

"Nor wagged his tongue more freely. Ha! ha! it did one's ears good to hear him strain his lusty lungs."

"It was indeed a good sight to a true Saxon; and in like manner would I serve every Norman dog that treads on the neck of the free sons of this soil. By St. Herman, I would like to sweep the whole of them from the face of this earth!"

"I'm with thee in that, Robin," said the farmer; "and since we have met, I will e'en tell thee of a design to lower the proud dignity of Nottingham's sheriff."

"I have heard somewhat of it, and like it much."

"Wilt aid me?"

"To the best of my power."

"Marry, 'tis well. I thought as much; but how far am I to rely on thee?"

"You can have my whole support, and count upon my own arm as well; fourscore good bowmen can follow you at once if needed."

"I must first calculate my own strength," said the farmer, "and for this I must borrow of thy council; thinkest thou it would be prudent to hold a meeting in the forest?"

"A score if it is needed; what need you fear?"

"A sudden attack from the sheriff."

"Bah! set thyself at rest on that point. Geoffrey hath matters of greater import to keep him at home; but to prevent such an occurrence, which, as you say, might happen, we will guard against it."

"Thou art a true friend of the oppressed, good Robin," exclaimed the farmer, shaking him heartily by the hand; "but seest thou we have sighted the mill? What sayst thou if we enter?"

"Marry! an' it please thee, we will. Know you whether Much, the miller's son, is within?"

"He was, an' it may be an hour since, for I called as I passed that way."

At that moment the flutter of a dress in the neighbouring copse caught Marian's eye, and, with the fleetness of a fawn, she released her hold of Robin's arm, and flew forward.

"Grace! Grace!" she called, waking the echoes with her melodious voice.

"Where art thou, my sister?" replied a voice in the thicket. "Hie! this way, Marian, lass."

"Here am I, good Grace," she replied, stepping between two bushes; "but who hast thou with thee?"

She drew back as she spoke, for Grace's companion hid herself in the foliage, as though not wishing to be seen.

"I hope I have not intruded?" she added, modestly.

"Not in the least; though thou hast arrived in time to learn a secret. Nay, do not blush, it is one thou mayst know."

"Have you a man here dressed in maiden attire, then?" asked Marian, with a laugh.

"Get thee to, lass, for thy unruly speech! Did thy cousin, Much, hear thee, he might make *much* harm of thy words; and thou mightst incur my displeasure. Saw ye ever a man with such a lovely face as this?"

She threw back the hood from her companion's face, and disclosed the merry features of Madge Stukely.

Marian uttered a cry of joy, and fell into her arms, and the twain lovingly embraced.

"Thou art out for an airing, to get a breath of the greenwood air, I presume?" said Marian when her joy had ceased. "When wilt thou come and visit us at Sherwood?"

"Any time it seemeth you fit," replied Grace. "You cannot have heard that she has left the castle?"

"Marry! and I have not. By our Lady! how did this happen?"

"Did not thy Robin tell thee?" asked Madge.

"In truth he did not. He keeps most matters to himself of late. Come, tell me how this happened. I feel most anxious to hear."

"She eloped with a gallant knight," replied Grace, mischievously. "Do you not think she had good courage to descend from the window by a rope?"

"A rope! By our Lady! I was prepared to hear it was by a silken ladder. A rope indeed! Thy lover was very ungallant."

"You would not have said so, I opine, had you seen him raise the sentry that opposed us in his arms and drop him into the moat.

By our Lady! that deed alone ought to have won for him a maiden's heart."

"Ha! ha! then 'twas for this thou loved him?"

"Partly; though heaven forbid I should throw away my heart on any of the faithless sex."

"'Tis a pity thou hast a heart at all to dispose of," said a voice in the thicket, that startled them. "Body o' me! it was ill-disposed of when assorted to thee."

"What mean you, knave? Come forth and answer!" cried Madge recognising the voice.

Little John's tall figure emerged from the bush, and he stepped before them with a graceful bow.

"Now what have you to say concerning the disposal of hearts?" demanded Madge.

"Nought, saving that every lady should have two," said the forester, with a merry twinkle in his eye.

"And what of the men, pray?" asked Madge, tossing her head.

"They should have none."

"Indeed, thou art hard upon thy sex," replied Marian. "What reason do you assign for their not having two also?"

"Their inability to keep them. At present one is more than they can guard against. The shafts of Cupid are not to be resisted."

"I trow he could not bend a bow with thee," said Grace, "nor let fly an arrow more true to its mark than thy wicked eyes, if the accounts I have heard of the quantity of hearts thou hast smitten in the town be true."

Madge cast on him a reproving look, and Little John hung his head as though abashed.

Stepping up to her side, he was about to imprint a kiss on her cherry lips, when a hand caught him by the shoulder.

"How now?" cried a gruff voice. "What mean you by this, bold forester?"

Little John turned and found himself face to face with her father.

There was an angry frown on the warder's face, and he trembled slightly with passion.

"Speak up; what mean you by this?" he cried again.

The tall forester stood astounded. He did not expect such words from the man he had rescued from death, and it was some time ere he could answer.

"I see no harm in taking a simple kiss, good sir. I have not offended in aught else that I am aware."

"Thou art a knave and a rascal!" cried Stukely. "She is my daughter, and thou must not e'en steal a kiss without permission of mine."

"Bladebone of Saint Hubert! I know not what to make of you, Sir Warder. You are a hard-hearted sire; but if kissing your daughter offends you, I will do so no more."

"'Tis well; this time I forgive thee; but mind how thy promise is kept; for, by the rood, I will not spare you if I catch you at such like again."

So saying, he caught hold of his daughter's arm, and drew her away from the group.

It was a few nights after the interview between Robin Hood and the farmer that a gathering of the townsfolk of Nottingham took place in the forest of merry Sherwood.

The sky was clear, and the moon shone with a radiance almost equal to daylight, which enabled the men to recognise one another, and assure themselves that no traitors lurked in their midst.

The miller, and Much, his son, held a council apart from the rest on a rude seat formed for the accommodation of travellers and others.

It was the trunk of a felled tree that had been rolled under the branches of a stout oak, which formed a good shelter from either rain or sun, and here they sat, free from observation of the immense crowd that mustered in the open glade.

Robin Hood took upon himself to address the meeting, and he was listened to with great eagerness and attention; for the populace looked upon him as their only friend and defender of their rights; therefore, his sentiments met with a ready approval, and the oath he administered was freely taken.

Whilst the bold outlaw was thus engaged, the farmer joined the meeting under the tree, where the miller was endeavouring to impress upon the mind of his son the many disadvantages they laboured under.

"Saint Mary!" he exclaimed, after listening for a few moments in silence, "thou hast the head of a lawyer, good miller, and once did my mind entertain such a thought as thou hast just hinted at."

"What, the impossibility of knowing each other?"

"Ay! for 'tis impossible to recognise every face. We must have a password. But here comes bold Robin; he will help us out of this difficulty."

The meeting had broken up, and the men were dispersing in various directions when Robin Hood bent his way to the tree.

There was a smile on his brow that proclaimed his satisfaction at the proceedings, and he greeted the farmer with a cordial shake of the hand.

"How seemeth matters now?" asked the miller, as Robin greeted him in turn. "Think you the men have any courage?"

"Courage!—ay, and strong hopes. Gramercy! I wish not to speak with better fellows. True Saxons, pith and sinew."

"Then Geoffrey will have cause to shake," quoth the farmer, clutching his staff. "'Tis time we gave the Norman dogs something to howl at."

"And the abbot?—him you will not let off scot free, I opine?" chimed in Much. "He is as big a rogue as any, though he hides his villany beneath his saintly robes; but the question, father, do not forget that."

"Fear not thereanent, my son; than I no one wishes our success more heartily."

"What trouble is this?" asked Robin. "Is it aught that needs my advice?"

"'Tis this," replied the miller. "We have raised a goodly number of men, and by our next meeting it may be doubled. Geoffrey de Lois is crafty, and may set some of his curs to watch about, and learn, if possible, our plans. He will disguise them; therefore i will be necessary to provide a means to detec the wolves from the sheep."   t

"An' thou hast read my thoughts thou couldst not have divined them better," replied Robin. 'Twas but now, as I walked hither, I thought of this, and I at first hit upon a plan of marking each man by a coloured ribbon worn on the arm; but I argued within myself that this might be worn by the enemy, so I dismissed that idea, and thought of a better one."

"Did I not tell thee Robin would assist us?" cried the farmer, rubbing his hands in glee. "I long to hear of thy scheme, good sir, for I opine it is a good one."

"And as simple as it is good," said the bold outlaw, grasping the farmer by the hand, and giving it a peculiar grip. "Didst notice aught particular?" he asked, looking round at each.

"Marry! I saw nought worth noting no more than we see every day," replied the miller, surprised at the question.

"Then I have met with success. That which is known to everyone is no secret. This is simple, and will baffle all our enemies."

Robin then took the hand of each in turn, and explained to them how the peculiar grip was to be given.

It gave satisfaction, and was highly approved of both by the farmer and the miller and his son, and then they discussed matters equally important.

It was some hours ere their conversation ended, and then they parted, each taking the nearest road leading to their homes.

CHAPTER XCVI.

HOW LITTLE JOHN AND THE FRIAR MADE THEIR JOURNEY TO THE BREWER'S.

John gave the friar a push—
'Twas not with an ill-will;
He fell upon his back, and then
Went rolling down the hill.

"Body o' me! but our master hath given us no easy task!" growled Little John, as he strove desperately to keep the brewer, who had become perfectly helpless, on his feet. "An' it were not for the prospect of testing the quality of his brewery, I would fain leave the knave under shelter of one of the trees, to get home as best he might."

"And thy master's displeasure, thou may'st add," remarked the friar; "for I trow me, he could not look over thy disobedience, an' it came to his ears."

"Unless I were to tell him of your laziness you shaven rogue! Did he not send you to assist, and here I have both you and him to drag up the steep? But I murmur not, for when I reach the brow of the hill I will roll you both down."

"And precipitate thyself head foremost," replied the friar, laughing. "By our Lady! it would take thee a month to roll down, for thy fleshless bones would stop at every blade of grass. Ho! ho! I should not like to have to wait at the bottom for thee."

"Insolent knave!" gasped Little John, panting from his exertions. "Were it not for the trouble of getting this fellow again on his feet, I would lay him down, and soundly trounce your hide. But I will not trouble myself with thee any more. I will speak to the Lord Abbot, and see if he cannot impose a penance upon you, so as to keep your huge paunch within limits, for I wot me thy dimensions are equal to that of an ox, and soon will you need as many legs."

It was not without just cause that Little John complained, for the pathway over the hill was so steep that he had much difficulty to keep himself from falling back, added to which he was burdened with the fat brewer, to whom the friar, instead of giving assistance, clung for his own support.

Little John, spite of his difficulties, could not help laughing at his own suggestion of the friar walking on four legs.

It seemed something so funny to him as in fancy he pictured the corpulent friar wending his way up the steep on all-fours.

Friar Tuck heard his laugh, and judging himself to be the cause of John's merriment, his red visage became purple, and he darted an angry look at the forester from his little fiery eyes.

"How now, thou long, unshaven imp!" he exclaimed, savagely, for the ascent was painful to him, and made him perspire pretty freely. "What is it that tickles thy ungodly fancy so?"

"Get you out, man! it is not your business!" retorted Little John, giving the friar a push with his long arm.

The friar, thinking Little John was about to strike him, raised both his hands to defend himself, and in so doing he lost his hold of the brewer, and thus lost his support.

For a moment he stood erect, tottering, his face contracted into a look of horror, and then losing his balance, he fell backwards, and rolled down the hill.

The forester burst into a loud laugh as the friar's fat carcase went to the earth with a dull thud that almost deprived him of the little breath that remained to him, and his merriment increased as he saw him gyrate slowly down the hill.

The friar tried vainly to stay himself.

He clutched at the grass, but it gave way in his fat hand, and matters bid fair for seeing him speedily at the foot of the ascent.

Little John could not restrain his laughter, and he was compelled to lay down his load, for it rendered him helpless, and seating himself on the grass, he watched the friar's progress in great glee.

Fortunately for the friar, a large stone, which, however, bruised him, and failed to check his course, turned his body in another direction, and his carcase came in contact with a bush.

To this he tenaciously clung, and lay as one dead till he recovered sufficient breath to rise on his knees and look around.

Ruefully he turned his gaze up the slope where Little John and his burden were reclining, and his heart fairly sank as he calculated the distance he had lost.

To rise on his feet was more than he dare again risk, and to stay where he then was was quite out of the question, for the brewer's house was not far distant, and it was the only place thereabouts where it was at all likely he could quench his burning thirst.

Sticking his toes firmly in the ground, and settling his knees so that he might not slip, he ventured at last to release his hold of the bush, and mutter an Ave Maria, which devout act he was compelled to perform with the laugh of the forester ringing in his ears.

Thus fortified and strengthened, with a look little short of despair he again turned his eyes up the hill, and in a fit of sheer desperation commenced the ascent on all-fours.

This, owing to his corpulence, was not only tedious, but painful, and he wheezed and groaned, and groaned and wheezed, in a manner that was truly pitiable.

Even the heart of the forester began to relent, but it was not till he had let him drag his tortuous way over twenty yards of the steep ascent that he went to his assistance.

"Bladebone of Saint Hubert! thou wilt e'en keep us waiting here all night, good father, if thou dost not mind thy pace," said John, in feigned commiseration. "Body o' me! but thou crawlest on thy belly like a snake."

"And you stand laughing like a king's fool," retorted the friar, darting at him a vicious look.

"Saint Herman! I did but think thou wert joking; an' thou makest thy way to heaven no quicker, I trow me, I shall get there first."

Little John gave a quiet grin, for he secretly delighted at the friar's torture, and he gave a hearty laugh when he assisted him to rise, and their eyes both met.

Friar Tuck only darted an angry look at his tormentor, but said nothing; he was till at the mercy of the forester, so prudence bade him hold his tongue.

When they reached the brow of the hill, however, he gave full vent to his thoughts, and he soundly rated his companion, and in the heat of his passion he recommended Little John to the full anger of all the saints he in the moment of his wrath could call to mind.

Little John affected repentance, and promised to make all the atonement in his power, and then returned to the assistance of the brewer, who was snoring lustily.

Putting forth his huge strength, the forester

raised him on his shoulder, and carried him like a child up the hill, where the friar was seated, wiping his bald pate, which was bathed in sweat.

"Now, good father, let us again try our luck," said Little John, after pausing to recover breath. "I wager you can beat me down the hill."

"By the mass! it were easier to do that than beat thee at thy tongue ; never before did I come across thy equal ; thou art gifted with the gab, and no mistake."

"And you with the power of rolling. Ha! ha! could our good friend here but have seen you, he might have made you a good offer for your carcase."

"What for ?" growled the friar.

"A brewing vat, or perchance a beer butt—'tis roomy enough ; and did he prop you up, your short fat legs would serve well for a stand."

"And, thou most excellent tormentor, to what use could he put thy long unsightly carcase ?"

"Nought, unless it were as taster and watcher, forsooth, for you would need watching, or you might topple over and roll as you did "——

Little John would have finished the sentence, but was prevented by the friar putting his fat hand over his mouth, a movement which proved fatal to the holy man.

In stepping forward the toe of his sandal caught a large stone, which caused him to fall forward, and in his endeavours to save himself he fell on his side, when, curled up like a ball, he rolled down the hill.

"Beshrew me! thou art a lucky fellow," cried Little John, as with a laugh he hitched his load well on his shoulder, and followed the friar's whirling form at a speed detrimental to his safety.

Friar Tuck bore up with this second calamity with more fortitude than he had been led to expect, for when he rose to his feet his face bore the trace of a smile.

"Now, sinner, try thy hand at this, and see if thou canst beat me," he said, in a tone of triumph.

"An' I were to, I should lose, good father, unless "——

"What ?"

"You agree to take the brewer."

Friar Tuck looked at the giant in dismay.

"No, no," he said, " it is thy bargain, and thou mayest keep to it. By the mass! 'tis but dry work ; I am dying of thirst."

"Then push you on, and let us see what a journey brings forth, for, like thyself, I am hugeous dry and hungry withal. Get you forward, man, and prepare his friends for his reception."

This was good advice, and worth acting upon, insomuch as it exonerated the friar from his share of trouble in assisting the brewer, so he trudged on as fast as his obesity would allow.

Little John kept pace with him, and soon they had the satisfaction of seeing the brewer's house.

They were met on the threshold by the brewer's wife, a stout old dame, who, as soon as she saw the state of her spouse, began to wag her tongue most furiously.

The sight of the friar, however, kept her under certain restraint, and after seeing to the safe disposal of her lord and master, she invited Little John and the friar to sup.

Gladly her offer was accepted, and the pair fell-to in a manner that astonished their hostess, who was greatly relieved when they left.

It was not till a late hour, and even then she had some difficulty, for they had fallen in love with the brewer's ale, and the friar had some tendency towards the brewer's wife, who laughed and chatted with them freely, and gave them a sample of her best wishes on leaving to help them on their way.

CHAPTER XCVII.
THE ABDUCTION OF MAID MARIAN.

He hovered round the hill
  'Till Marian he spied,
He seized her—threw her 'cross his horse,
  Then to the forest hied.

When Henry of Winchester left Nottingham Castle his mind was sorely perplexed.

D'Anville rode next him, and whenever an opportunity offered he made some remark such as only served to incense the king the more, and remind him of the failure of his visit.

"My liege," said D'Anville, after a longer pause than usual, "it seems to me that as no one has money hereabouts, and there is no great commerce for them to speculate in, they must have some way of getting rid of it."

"Of that I am already aware," growled the king ; "have you turned jester in the absence of Golinbert ?"

"I crave your majesty's pardon," continued the duke, " 'twas in no jest I spoke. I merely wished to remark that as they all complain of being robbed by Robin Hood, there must be some truth in it."

"Umph!" growled the king testily; "what consolation does this knowledge bring with it?"

D'Anville winced under this second rebuke, but as he had broached the subject he was determined to follow it up.

"It brings no consolation, my liege," replied he, " but it gives us a slight inkling of the princely sum the outlaw must amass in one year. Father Absalom's coffers—and they are considered of no mean importance—could scarce be compared with his."

There was a long silence.

At length the king spoke.

"By our Lady, D'Anville, I see some truth in thy words; the outlaw must have amassed much wealth, and a little of it would do us some good in our present need."

D'Anville's sallow features lit with a ghastly smile.

ROBIN HOOD,

AND THE OUTLAWS OF SHERWOOD FOREST.

MAID MARIAN AND THE KING'S PAGE.

"My liege," he said, "who is to dispute your right to it? It is evident the robber is draining the country of its revenue, and, as De Lois says, bringing the shrievalty of Nottingham to ruin."

"'Tis as thou sayest, good cousin," replied

the king, warming with the subject; "he is not only a robber, but a traitor; 'tis no wonder he could deal with us so liberally."

"And feast us on your majesty's deer," chimed in the duke.

This was sufficient for the weak-minded king.

The mention of the deer brought to his remembrance the insolence of Robin Hood.

"By the mass his doings must be seen to," he exclaimed; "it behoves us to look about us when traitors treat us with open defiance, and shoot our deer as if it were their own. Make thee a note of this, and remind me of it when we reach our royal court."

D'Anville bowed, and the king rode on in deep reverie.

But the duke was too crafty to let the subject rest; he knew the king's changeable temperament, and as he owed Robin Hood a grudge, he was determined to compass his ruin while he had a chance of doing so.

"Would it not be best, my liege, to take strict and speedy measures?" he said, bowing. "The sooner we begin the easier it will be to accomplish."

"Ay, and I commend thee for the thought; but at present it would not be prudent to commence open warfare with him, for you see he is bound up in the forest, and his men, I trow, are true and staunch as oak. Couldst thou not devise some means of settling with him quietly? I know thou hast an inventive brain, D'Anville."

"My liege, already have I a plan to propose. Thou canst invite him to a tournament on Finsbury Fields; once in the archery ground, he can easily be arrested. I would undertake the duty an' thou givest me permission."

"Do you think Robin Hood would be fool enough to travel so far for our pleasure?"

"Marry, he durst hardly refuse; but if that plan suits not, I have another."

"Name it."

"There is the maid Marian."

"Ah! what of her?"

"He doats on her, and I durst venture to assert he would travel to London in search of her were she thereabouts."

The king's eye brightened.

The suggestion suited him well for more reasons than one.

During his short stay at Sherwood his eyes had not been wholly closed to the beauty of the miller's daughter, and when he gazed upon her lovely features and well-knit form, he could not but envy Robin of his choice.

Such a combination of beauty, ease, and grace he had not thought to meet with in the deep recess of the forest, and even in the short space of his acquaintance with her he had half resolved to carry her off.

Now more than ever he longed to do so; but he concealed his true sentiments from D'Anville, and said—

"Of what use would Marian be to us? She is the outlaw's treasure, certainly, but of little value to us. She does not carry his gold about with her."

The duke winced, and bit his lip in vexation at the supposed blindness of the king.

"My liege," he said, after a moment's pause, "once possessed of her, you will have a talisman that Robin Hood, with all his skill and cunning, cannot withstand. On discovering his loss, he will, of course, seek her. A whispered rumour in Nottingham town will bring him to London. He can be seized; his force will be weakened by his absence, and then what is to hinder us from routing his band and taking possession of his wealth?"

This explanation was all the king needed, and he promised D'Anville that he should head the expedition, as he was so clever in concocting it.

The duke was in raptures.

He would have cut the throat of a dying man, or strangled an infant at its mother's breast, to win the favour of the king.

"If it so please your majesty," he said, "I would rather go on this mission at once. There is not so much danger attending it now as there will be if we delay it."

"I cannot spare you a force sufficient," was the king's reply. "How many men will you need?"

"Four trusty fellows only. The less the better, as our movements will be less easier watched."

"There is judgment in thy words which giveth us pleasure. I will endow thee with full powers at once, so choose thee the four men thou wouldst take."

D'Anville gave another cringing bow, and bringing the party to a halt, commanded four of the men to fall out.

They were four of the stoutest of the party, and, after a little more ceremony, D'Anville wheeled them round, and retraced the way they had come, leaving the king and his party to pursue their journey.

This part of their way lay up-hill, and the duke led the way but slowly, so as not to blow their horses, which were heavily caparisoned; but as soon as they reached the level road, he spared neither rein nor spur, and the party set off at a brisk trot.

Than D'Anville no better man could the king have chosen for such a mean task. He was endowed with the low cunning of a fox, and his propensity for thieving was equally as good as that animal's.

At some distance from Sherwood Forest he halted his men, and secured their trappings so that they might not jingle, and, ordering the soldiers to make as little show as possible of their armour, he drew his own cloak around him, and again took the lead.

After another sharp ride he again halted, and planted his men in ambush, where they were to remain until he gave the signal.

He left them there, and proceeded alone, taking by mere chance the road leading to the mill.

As he wandered along, letting his horse

take its own pace, and wondering within himself how he should act, the rustling of a bush startled him from his reverie.

He looked up, and, to his surprise, beheld Marian eyeing him curiously through the bushes.

"Sweet lady," he said, drawing rein, and making a most graceful bow, "may I ask of you how far it is to the nearest cottage ?"

"A mile perhaps, perchance it may be more. Art thou a stranger in these parts ?"

The duke urged his steed nearer to her, and concealed his face, fearing she might discover him, and replied—

"Good lady, it is my misfortune to be so, and with shame I own it."

"Shame! for why? Hast thou committed thyself in some way ?"

"Only in not knowing of the abode of beauty sooner."

"Sire! what mean you ?" demanded Marian, giving her head a disdainful toss "Go thy way, and give less freedom to thy tongue, or, marry, thou wilt meet with fit chastisement."

"Stay, lady; a thousand pardons do I crave !" cried D'Anville as she turned to depart. "You named not the road I must take to the cottage."

Marian paused, and pointed with her lily hand, and then turned to leave.

The duke saw that this opportunity, if not at once seized, would be a good opportunity lost, and one perhaps that might never occur again.

Urging his horse suddenly forward, he brought it to the side of the astonised Marian, and seizing her by the waist, he raised her bodily on his arm, and placed her before him on the horse.

"Help! help !" shrieked Marian, as soon as she could recover sufficiently to understand her position.

"Saint Dunstan! if thou makest that noise," growled the duke, "I will put an end to thy croaking, so be quiet, and no harm need ye fear."

At a signal his men came from their ambush, and a minute later they were galloping back the way they came.

CHAPTER XCVIII.
THE KING'S INTERVIEW WITH MAID MARIAN.

Upon a gorgeous seat she sat,
  Her heart with anguish torn ;
I love you, Marian, said the king,
  To that I will be sworn.

On, on sped the little party, the tramp of their heavy war-steeds echoing on the hard road, sending a chill to the heart of the half-conscious Marian, as she gradually recovered from her fright.

"Where—where am I ?"

Such was her exclamation as she recovered with a start from her reverie ; for full half an hour she had been like one dead.

"With friends, so it please ye; with foes, an' it suits ye better."

It was a gruff voice that gave the reply, and on turning her head Marian recognised the features of D'Anville.

"Sirrah," she demanded haughtily, as she strove to free herself from his embrace, "what means this insult. Do not think I will bear it tamely. Unhand me, sir, and let me dismount."

"Not yet; our journey is not completed. Make thyself comfortable. By the mass, I intend you no harm."

"Harm!" iterated Marian; "don't call this no harm—this outrage. You will dearly repent of this, sirrah, so I warn ye, and demand my instant release."

"'Tis more than I dare to do, fair lady," replied the duke, trying to smile ; my life depends upon your safety."

"To whom do I owe this insult, then ? Surely not to the king ?"

"Thou hast rightly guessed; 'tis no less a personage than his majesty, I assure you. But raise thy garments, fair one; see, the water from the hills has raised the stream, and we must ford it."

"Must ! is there no other way ?"

"None that we choose to take. See, yon fellow's horse is up to the saddle-girths, so prepare thyself."

One of the soldiers had ridden forward, and the water was some inches above his knee, therefore Marian prepared herself for a wetting, as she would not expose her limbs to the soldiers' rude gaze.

D'Anville's horse, owing to its heavy trappings and extra burden, had some difficulty in crossing the stream, which ran rather rapidly, and more than once the gallant beast lost its footing ; but D'Anville, with spur and bridle, recovered it again, and at length it got firm footing on the other side.

Marian, as was the duke, was wet to the skin, for the waves leapt over the horse's back, and she shivered as her cold wet garments clung to her.

Once more on the road, D'Anville gave the word to advance, and the horses, freshened by their immersion, galloped on at a brisk pace.

Seeing that protestations were useless, Marian bore her fate with calmness, and after a few hours' silent ride, the party again drew rein.

One of the soldiers assisted Marian to dismount, and D'Anville led her through the gates of the large stone building where they had halted, and from the conversation between the duke and an armed knight, Marian learnt that the king had only departed from there a few hours before.

"We expected ye, though not so soon, good lady," replied an ancient dame, as she tottered up to the side of Marian. "Good mercy me ! you are wet; but thank the Virgin I have some dry raiment for ye, so hie with me to the queen's chamber and arrange thy toilet."

"The queen's chamber ! Holy Virgin ! for

what purpose have I been brought here? Good woman, canst thou enlighten me any?"

"Not at present; I daresay the king will tell you, if so be he has not already," answered the dame, drawing her parchment visage into a smile.

The tone and manner in which this was spoken, instead of allaying, served to increase Marian's curiosity, and inspired her with a kind of fear.

"Does the king live here?" she ventured to ask after a pause in which she had taken a cursory view of the apartment.

"At times," replied the dame, "but 'tis mostly when the queen offends his majesty; he comes here for solitude, solace, and comfort. But you forget, lady, your wet garments are doing you harm."

As she spoke she handed Marian a sumptuous robe, and when Marian glanced at it and thought of the woman's words, a fearful truth flashed to her mind.

"Would I could get a messenger to acquaint Robin of my destination," she thought. "Oh, how gladly would he fly to free me from this horrid place!"

"Horrid place!" exclaimed the woman in surprise, as she caught the last words, which Marian had unconsciously uttered loud enough for her to hear. "Horrid place, indeed! Fair lady, thou hast forgotten this is the Tower of Love."

Marian shuddered.

The very name acquainted her with the nature of the place.

She had heard it spoken of by Robin Hood as the place where the king carried on his secret amours, and where he lavished his time and money on his favourite mistresses.

"Holy Mother! protect me from insult and violence," she muttered, fervently, as she changed her dripping garments for the dry gorgeous robes, and secreted the little dagger she always carried in her breast.

Worn out with fatigue and worry, she then laid herself down on a sumptuous couch, and unconsciously wept herself to sleep.

How long she lay she knew not, but when she awoke, she found the woman, sitting half hid by a screen drawn across a recess, watching her.

On seeing her eyes open, the woman approached, curtseying.

"Good lady," she said, "nought since thou hast been here hath passed thy lips. Say, is there aught thou could wish for? Say but the word—thou shalt have it."

"Liberty is all I crave," replied Marian, giving utterance to her thoughts. "'Tis far preferable in my eyes than all this mocking splendour."

The woman bestowed on her an angry glance. She was disappointed, but determined not to be beaten; she touched a small silver bell, and a handsome page entered, bearing on a dish of burnished gold a supply of the most tasty viands.

Struck with the beauty of the page, and the thought that he one day might be of service to her, Marian followed with her eyes his graceful form as he left the apartment.

"You seem taken with the beauty of the boy," remarked the woman. "He is handsome, is he not?"

"Truly so," replied Marian, confused; and then remembering that she would require strength to carry out her design, if it were at all possible to do so, she yielded to the woman's persuasion to partake of the food.

The woman modestly withdrew to the other end of the room whilst Marian, silent, and thoughtful, partook of the refection, and when she had finished her meal the bell summoned the page.

"His majesty the king has arrived, and wishes to see her ladyship as soon as she is disposed to visit him, in the antechamber," said the page, bowing to the female attendant, and then he modestly withdrew.

It required a great deal of persuasion to get Marian to leave the room, but at length she consented to obey the king's summons.

She found him busied in poring over some Scriptural lore, but he turned as the curtains were drawn aside to admit her, and he handed her to a seat.

At first a feeling of awe crept over her on finding herself in the presence of the king, but she soon mastered this, and recovered her composure.

"Fair one," said the king, addressing her, "it hath pleased us to look favourably upon thee, and though the manner in which we have brought you here may appear unseemly in thine eyes, yet our future kindness ye need not fear."

Marian, who had sat with her eyes drooped to the floor, now raised them.

"Pray, may I ask," she said, "for what purpose you ordered me to be brought here?"

"Respect for thee, my fair one. We could not brook to see one so lovely as thyself passing thy young life in a forest amongst a band of outlaws, whilst we have room for thee at our court. Thanks to the blessed Virgin, we have passed the age of barbarism. Thou shalt be one of us—ay, even the bosom companion of our royal self. Sleeping or waking, we will watch over thee as a flower of tenderest form."

"Sir!" cried Marian, her eyes flashing with scorn—"sir! I cannot call you king, or thou would have spared the blush of maiden modesty that thy words have caused to mantle my cheek. Away! leave me untarnished as I am, or return me to the greenwood as you found me, a simple flower, where, under the care and nurture of him thou callest an outlaw, I may grow up free from the vile contamination of royalty."

"Woman!" thundered the king, startled by her bold reply, "thou hast surely forgotten that thou art in the august presence of England's king!"

Marian started from her seat, and eyed him from head to foot.

"England's king!" she iterated scornfully. "Say, rather, oppressor. If this be a specimen of thy kingship, 'tis no wonder the true Saxons disown thee as a ruler. For the nonce I despise you, neither do I fear your power."

" 'Tis no more than I might have expected from this wild, uncultivated child of nature," muttered the king. "She has been brought up in rebellion, the associate of outlaws; but she may be reclaimed—at least, I will give her a trial, for in beauty there is none can excel her."

He touched a gong, and the woman answered the summons, and the king having whispered a few words in her ear, strode angrily out of the antechamber.

CHAPTER XCIX.

STUKELY HAS A NARROW ESCAPE OF HIS LIFE.

> They met old Stukely on the hill,
>   He for mercy loud did cry;
> Much grasped him by the throat,
>   And swore that he should die.

THE rebellious infection spread rapidly, and the townsfolk of Nottingham were emboldened by Robin Hood taking the lead, so that in a very short time a considerable little army was formed, and a bold front was shown at the next meeting (where they were put through a kind of drill) that was at once imposing and formidable.

Armed with a short cross-handled sword and a stout quarterstaff, the bold Saxons only waited the hour when they were to attack their Norman oppressors.

Robin had taken great care in forming the men into companies, and placing a leader to the head of each, whilst active spies watched the movements of De Lois, and brought him faithful accounts.

Thus it was that the bold chief became aware that a traitor lurked amongst them, for the sheriff began to place his castle in a state of defence, and gave his men additional drill in the courtyard of the castle.

Robin Hood, on hearing of this, at once set about to discover whom it might be that had thus warned the sheriff, and it was not long before he made the discovery.

The grip of the hand betrayed the culprit, who was no other than Stukely, the ex-warder of the castle.

Robin had suspected him from the time he refused to take the oath and become one of them; but he kept his suspicions to himself, for he did not wish to harm him so long as he remained neutral, on account of the services Madge had rendered to the band.

From the time when Stukely chided his daughter for encouraging the suit of Little John, nothing was known of the whereabouts of either the warder or of Madge. It was supposed they had sought shelter in some cave, as Stukely was sometimes observed strolling in the forest, and then would suddenly disappear.

He had also been observed at the meetings, but the men, thinking that after the behaviour of De Lois, he would turn against him, viewed him not with distrust.

"Now, good master mine, what think you of the knave?" queried Little John, after the test had been applied; for no man who had not taken the oath had been initiated into the mystery of the grip of the hand. "Do you not think he deserves a knave's reward?"

"He certainly does, John; the more so from the fact of you saving his life; but for another's sake I would not "——

He paused, and Little John, understanding the cause, heaved a sigh.

The forester had formed an affection for the warder's daughter, and for her sake he would have looked over the faults of her father, but in duty to the rest of the band he said—

"It is certainly hard, good master, to give him his deserts, for Madge's sake; but still it is necessary to put him under some restraint; for my part, I would willingly advocate his freedom, but for our mutual interest it is necessary to "——

"Hang him!" interposed a voice, and Much the miller soon stepped from behind a tree.

Little John gripped his staff, and had not the moon peeped forth at that moment, and discovered his features, the giant's arm would have brought the staff down on his pate.

"Body o' me! you may bless the saints for your preservation," said the giant. "An' it were not for the moon, you would have paid dearly for your eavesdropping."

"Call it by some other name," replied Much, indignantly. "There should be no secrets kept from us. Are we not one? and do we not all work for the same cause?"

"Marry do we!" said Robin; "and far be it from my wish to do aught contrary to the wishes of the band; but in this case, which I hold exceptional, I should like to "——

"Intercede for the traitor," interrupted Much, "which is contradictory to rules."

The cheeks of the outlaw flushed, for there was truth in the bold assertion of the miller's son. His brow lowered as he replied—

"Leave this matter to me; it concerns thee not. There shall be justice done, never fear."

Robin turned away, and hurried homeward with a quick step, leaving Little John and Much to talk the matter over with themselves.

When he was gone they held a long dispute, for Much argued truly that Stukely ought to be hung in accordance with their rules, whilst Little John pleaded in the warder's favour.

They were interrupted by the appearance of the miller, who was sauntering along the glade, humming a song.

He stopped short, with an exclamation, on beholding Little John and his son.

"Hallo! Master Much, how is it you have not sought your couch? When I left you an hour hence, you were going home. Both Marian and Grace will be uneasy at your delay. Ha! ha! a pretty fellow, indeed, are you to act as guardian to the fair sex. Ha! ha! come along, boy—come along."

" Nay, be not so hasty, good master miller ; Much needs some advice in regard to the sex you name. He does not appear to hold them in high esteem."

" For to-night, at least, we will let this dispute rest," said Much. " Good-night, John. I shall meet thee to-morrow."

Thus they parted, but not far had they gone when they beheld a burly figure in the path before them.

Much recognised it to be the form of Stukely, booted and spurred as though he had come from a long journey.

" Who is that, boy ?" asked the miller of his son ; " my eyes grow fearful weak of nights. Adzooks ! it would be hard for me to send a shaft true to its mark after dusk hour."

" I should like to send a shaft—ay, to the full length of a yard through yon varlet's carcase," replied Much, in anger.

" How so, lad ? Give thy reasons."

" 'Tis he that hath proved the traitor ; his wily tongue hath made Geoffrey aware of the rising."

" How know you so ?"

" Marry ! 'tis known of a truth. But hasten ; let us overtake him, and I will explain the meanwhile."

The miller quickened his pace, and Much informed him of what he had overheard, to which the old man listened in deep silence.

" Thou art right, lad," he said, after a pause ; " he must be brought to judgment and suffer according to our oath. As to Madge, she will be well provided for."

By this time they had got within hearing of the warder, who, startled by their footsteps, turned.

" How now, good fellows !" cried Stukely, loosening his sword, for he feared mischief. " Ho ! 'tis thee, miller."

" Ay, 'tis me, as thou seest. Thou seemest to have come from a journey. Has aught ill befallen thy daughter ?"

" Nay, friend ; and to prove thou art mistaken, I have but just thought of starting on a journey."

" A long one, I presume," suggested Much, eyeing him closely, " for thou art booted and spurred, and moreover thou hast harnessed thyself in thy best ?"

" To Nottingham only," replied the warder, evasively.

" As I thought. By the mass ! thou art a good courier."

" What mean you, lad ?"

" That you serve your master well to travel in such haste by night."

" Master ! Ha ! ha ! I have none now. I have quarrelled with De Lois, and now I am free."

" You would fain have us believe so, but we know you are still hankering to regain thy place as warder, so be careful, for thou art suspected of more than one treacherous act."

" Liar !" thundered Stukely, and being a powerful man he wrenched the short staff from the hand of Much, and would have laid it freely about his head, had not the miller's son prevented him.

Strong and active as a deer was Much, and with a lightning movement he avoided the blow aimed at him, and seized Stukely by the throat before the miller could interfere.

" Traitor ! I will take upon myself to be thy executioner !" vociferated the enraged youth, but ere he could execute his threat the sound of horses' hoofs broke on their ears, and the outlaw chief dashed up the road mounted on his fiery steed.

" Hold !" cried Robin ; " stay thy hand !" Then, as he reined in his spirited horse, he added—

" Unhand him, Much, lest I forget the tie that links us together even as thou hast forgotten to obey the mandate of thy chief."

Much released his hold, and looked at Robin with a bitter scowl.

" I obey you," he said, sarcastically ; " but for all that I swear I will be revenged. Stukely has proved himself an enemy, and even your interference will not save him when next we meet."

" Go to, lad," cried his father, who bowed humbly to the outlaw's decision in all things ; " hast forgotten the rank of him to whom thou speakest ? Marry ! it would but serve thee right did the earl well trounce thy stubborn hide."

" 'Twould be better did he trounce the hide of him that needs it. Ha ! where has the varlet gone ?"

Much looked round in surprise as he uttered this exclamation.

Stukely, in obedience to a sign from Robin, had taken advantage of the moment and slipped unseen into the bushes.

Much was about to follow, but the miller caught him by the arm, and whispered a few words in his ear.

This calmed him, at least to all outward appearance, though he muttered some threat to himself.

" Where goest thou, good Robin ? " asked the miller, seeing him mounted, " an' it be not too rude to ask."

" To the mill. It has been reported by the watchers that a party of soldiers have been seen near your house ; the purpose that brought them there has yet to be discovered."

" Who told thee of this ?"

" A stupid lout, who, instead of watching them, brought the news to Sherwood."

" Were they the sheriff's men ?"

" I wot not ; I have told thee all I know."

" Zounds ! I hope nought has happened to the girls."

" Saint Herman ! do not name it ; had one of my own men told me of this I might have heard more ; but we waste time here ; get thee up behind me. Much can walk."

Much assisted his father to mount, and the prancing steed set off at a good trot with its double burden.

———

CHAPTER C.

ROBIN HOOD HEARS NEWS OF MARIAN.

The news struck Robin to the heart—
He fell down on the grass;
His actions and his troubled mind
Showed he perplexed was.

ALTHOUGH Much the miller's son travelled on foot, he arrived at the mill long before Robin Hood and his companion.

A near cut across the forest had shortened the distance of his journey by a mile; and the news of the soldiers being seen in the vicinity of the mill-house made him speed his journey much quicker.

When Robin arrived, he found him pacing to and fro on the sward in front of the house, and his manner caused Robin to dismount without ceremony, bringing the miller with him to the ground at the same time.

"Has aught befallen thee or thine?" asked Robin, breathless; though the answer might have been plainly read in Much's face. "Speak man! keep me no longer in suspense."

"My cousin Marian is gone!" replied the distracted youth.

Robin; Hood staggered, the news overpowed him.

"Gone!" he vociferated, "and no one knows whither. Now by all the saints, I swear I will not rest till I find her."

"You need not travel far, for I opine," said Much, his lip quivering with excitement, "that knave you forbade me to chastise knows more of it than you are aware."

"Stukely?"

"Ay, he is a villain at heart, and had I him here, I would squeeze the life out of him but he should tell me where is my fair cousin!"

Robin was almost afraid to speak, the words of the miller's son were so prophetic, and at the same time brought with them a reproof.

"And Stukely you believe to be the cause of this?" he said musing.

"Such is my opinion, though by the saints, it would grieve me sore to judge ill of him wrongly."

"'Tis enough. Knowest thou aught of where this Stukely is to be found?"

"Marry! I do not, neither know I any who can give thee any such information; of late nought of him has been known."

"By my halidame, we will see to that at once; I will to Nottingham; perchance I may glean some news."

Hadst not better change thy garbage?" queried the miller; "thou wilt have better chance of speech with the soldiery."

"Marry, I do not like thy proposal well; a buff jerkin and peasant hose will favour my plans."

The bold outlaw soon doffed his gay costume of scarlet and green, and habited himself in a leathern doublet and hose, such as were worn by the civilians at the time; and then mounting his steed, whose costly trappings had been changed for a humbler suit by the miller's son, rode in the direction of the town.

He stopped on reaching the door of the principal inn, which was but a sorry place in comparison with the inns of these days, and giving his horse in charge of the rustic who acted as stableman, Robin strode into the public room.

As he had anticipated, the company was composed of soldiers who were discussing amongst themselves the late events that had transpired in the castle, and moistening their lips at frequent intervals from a jug of ale that stood on the bench before them.

One of the soldiers, a dark, swarthy looking fellow, who appeared to take the lead in the discussion, and who, judging from his manner, appeared brimful of news, nodded to Robin Hood as he entered; and the daring chief having called for a tankard of ale, sat himself down by his side.

"Welcome, friend," said the officious soldier. "You are a stranger in these parts, I trow? If you have travelled far, you may perhaps give us some fresh news?"

"Marry, 'tis but little I can tell thee," Robin replied; "I have journeyed far, but scarce a soul have I met on the road. Drink, man, and pass it to thy comrades; perchance they can amuse us with the news of Nottingham."

The soldier raised the flagon to his lips, and took a futive glance at Robin, to whose open countenance he took a great liking.

"Good master," he said, "I see you are not of a warlike disposition, so I fear our news will but ill suit you; however, if it be no offence, such news as we wot of you shall hear."

"Nothing would better please me. I have heard strange stories of the old castle; but never did I have the pleasure of hearing aught concerning it from the lips of one such as yourself, who must of course be better acquainted with the truth."

Thus flattered, the soldier, who chanced to be Will of Dowley, imparted to Robin all he knew concerning the visit of the king, and also of Prince Edward, and the various rumours which were about concerning the Jew, not forgetting his own encounter with the tall knight, which, by-the-bye, was highly coloured.

Robin listened attentively to his narrative, a great part of which was already known to him, but learnt sufficient to assure him that Marian had not been conveyed thither.

As the flagon was emptied, Robin took care to have it replenished, which much pleased the company, and they whispered in his ear secrets that would have cost them their heads had it come to the sheriff's knowledge.

The conversation was broken up by the entrance of a pedlar, who took his seat amongst them, and seeing the soldiers were the worse for liquor, spread out before them his wares.

"Put up thy trash, man," said Will, annoyed at his interference; "a soldier has little to spend on such trash."

The Jew, in his turn, became annoyed, and, as he gathered his glittering baubles into his pack, he remarked—

"Ah! mein Gott! monish is alvays scarce, 'specially vid me. Is dere not von blue-eyed lass you would like to make a present of von crucifix?"

"Ha! ha!" laughed the soldier; "a crucifix, eh? What damsel would not prefer the hilt of a broken sword? No, no, Master Moses; a tress of hair would be valued by a soldier's sweetheart more than all your trinkets."

"Ah me! dat is de vay of all you. Christians; you like not to part vid your monish, and yet you steal all de ladies' heart s I saw sufficient to convince me of dat as I came here. By Gott! if dey vill not give you deir hearts, you run avay vid dem soul and bodish."

"What do you mean, knave?" cried the soldier, rising in anger. "Dare you aver we court them dishonourably?"

"Mein Gott! no," exclaimed the trembling Jew. "I speak only vot I saw."

Robin stayed the soldier's arm that was raised to strike the Jew, and when order was restored he demanded of the pedlar an explanation.

"God forbid I should tell von lie. It was as I came down de road I heard de sound of horses, and vhen I looked up, I saw von party of soldiers riding hard towards me, and fearing they might rob—run me down, I mean—I stepped into de hedge."

The soldiers glanced angrily at him as he incautiously hinted his fear of being robbed, but Robin Hood, who was interested in the narration, pacified them by passing the ale along.

"Go on with thy story, good Moses," said Robin. "Did they see thee?"

"Dey did not, but I watched dem, and as dey passed I see von of dem vith a lady in his arms, and she was calling on him to stop. I tink I before see de lady at de old mill on de hill-side.

The cheek of the outlaw crimsoned, and his eye lit angrily as he asked—

"Which road took they?"

"To London, me tink; for dey vere de king's men."

"How know you that?"

"By de arms on deir breastplates. Mine Got! should I not know, ven I travel so much?"

"Think you they went to Leicester?"

"No, I feel positive dey go to London. Mine Got! de devil vould not deceive Moses."

Robin did not wait long after hearing this; he settled his score, called for his horse, and soon reached the door of the mill-house.

The miller and Much were astounded at the news; they would rather she had been inside the walls of Nottingham Castle than in the power of the king; for, as he had so many different places, it was hard for them to determine where to seek for her with anything like success.

"A malison on the knave!" cried the enraged outlaw, as he paced to and fro the stone floor of the room. "By the mass! I will seek her; and not only will I find her, but punish the villain who has dared to commit such an outrage. King or devil, he shall feel my resentment! Much," he added, after a moment's thought, "hie thou with me to the stronghold; we must devise some means to raise sufficient money to carry me on my way. Those Norman hinds have impoverished us with their keep, and it is not yet time to make their master pay for it."

CHAPTER CI.

LITTLE JOHN AND THE BREWER.

A murrain on the knave!
His beer is watered well;
The reason of it being so,
Himself self shall quicky tell.

As may be supposed, when the brewer recovered from the effects of the wine, he had but little recollection of his promise to Robin Hood, and it was entirely to the kindness of his spouse, he was indebted for the knowledge of the manner in which he came home.

She watched with feverish anxiety his return to consciousness, and then she did not fail to let him have a full specimen of her oratory powers, which, if it failed to cure his aching head, served to dispel the mist from his muddled brain.

"Silence, dame, or thou wilt drive me mad!" he exclaimed, having borne it till he could no longer. "Did the fellow you name leave no message with you?"

"By the mass! I had not forgotten it. An' I remember rightly, they hinted at an order for some beer. Holy father! what a fool thou hast made of thyself. Thou hast perchance lost a good customer."

"Be thrifty of your words," said the brewer, as some recollection of the transaction began to dawn on his mind. "Darby Dillon is no fool, as you shall see. I have a customer to deal with that requires some cunning. You say my bag was missing when I arrived home?"

"Gad! 'tis too true. I, thine own lawful wife, would not tell thee a lie."

The brewer leant back on his seat, and thrusting his hands into his pockets, relapsed into deep thought.

"I have it," at length he exclaimed, starting from his seat, and hurrying into the yard, where his men where at work.

He then pointed out several empty barrels, which he ordered to be placed in a kind of dray, and which were then filled with water. A small barrel of ale was then placed on behind, and taking his leathern whip, he started on his journey, taking with him one of his men.

His wife watched his strange proceedings from the window, and as he did not previously inform her of his intentions, she wondered what he could be about. But she comforted herself with the remark that he was certainly going mad.

ROBIN HOOD,

AND THE OUTLAWS OF SHERWOOD FOREST.

MAID MARIAN'S VISIT TO THE DUNGEON.

The jumbling car, after jolting for some hours over the stony road, arrived at the place appointed by Robin Hood, where it was met by Little John, who had been sent there to keep watch.

Long before it arrived in sight, Little John

heard the rumbling of the wheels, and he roused the friar, who had accompanied him out of friendship, it was presumed, but in truth only in the hope of getting a good draught of the liquor.

"Body o' mine! you have kept us waiting here long enough," growled the giant, "and now, I fear, your horse will not be able to cross the stream. We will come over and lighten your load a little, for waiting here so many hours in the broiling sun makes one fearfully dry."

Suiting the action to the word, Little John crossed the bridge on which the brewer and Robin Hood had had their encounter, and the friar lazily followed.

"Bladebone of Saint Hubert! such stuff is rare," exclaimed the forester, licking his lips, after emptying the measure the brewer had filled from the small cask. "Come hither, good Friar Tuck; open thy broad shoulders and take in thy fill, for I opine we shall have small chance of doing so when those Norman fiends once taste it."

Friar Tuck acted on his advice, and the brewer got tired of filling the measure long before they got tired of emptying it.

"Adzooks!" exclaimed Darby, "never before saw I such gluttons. Saint Denis! I might as well try to fill the brook as to attempt quenching thy thirst. By the mass! were all the folks in Nottingham such thirsty souls, I would soon make a fortune."

"You will as it is," replied Little John, laughing; "but we have yet got to get them across."

"And I have yet to be paid," said the brewer, with a knowing shake of the head.

"Of that you need not fear; so come on, good brewer, and try the strength of your steed."

The brewer looked at the speaker, and then at the stream.

The prospect made him scratch his head, for the banks of the stream were so steep that the horse, if he got to the middle of the stream in safety, would never reach the opposite side.

Little John knew this, and had already calculated upon it.

"Now, sir," he said, "you see your difficulty; and it is now my turn to strike a bargain."

"So long as it gets us out of this difficulty, I do not mind," replied the brewer, "so name it at once."

"It is evident the barrels must be carried over, and as neither your horse nor your man are able to do so, I will undertake the job providing you pay me?"

"What do you require?" asked the brewer again scratching his head.

"The small barrel."

"Holy Virgin! you know not how to value your services," exclaimed Dillon; "by the mass, that will take off all the profit."

"That matters not to me, thou canst take them back if it seem ye fit; I trow me 'tis

but reasonable payment. Say but the word, are we to return to our master with this?"

Little John jinked a bag of gold, and the sound set the brewer thinking.

The cask Little John demanded was the only one that contained the genuine beverage, and that had been sorely shaken of its contents, therefore the brewer would have to part with his beer for nothing, and only get paid for the water.

To this he consented at length, however; and Little John bent to the task, taking care, however, to carry his own barrel over first.

Friar Tuck accompanied this cask, and well he did so, for as Little John was making his journey across the bridge with his last load, the tree bent so under the weight, that it snapped and let both him and the barrel into the water.

The barrel being well-filled sank, and Little John scrambled to the other side, much to the merriment of the friar and the discomfiture of the brewer, who had been grinning from ear to ear at seeing the giant stagger across the bridge with the casks of water, but as the last one disappeared, of course, all his hopes of payment vanished with it.

It was now Little John's turn to laugh. The stream coursed between Darby Dillon and him, and as the brewer was afraid to venture out of his depth, and Little John was not inclined to cross and recross again, they were unable to come to any settlement.

Little John did not let this trouble him, as it was his intention to settle the debt with his quarter-staff; but rolling the barrels under a shady tree, he and the friar made themselves merry with the liquor Little John had so truly earned.

The brewer viewed them from his position in mingled disgust and despair; he called loudly upon the forester to throw the bag over to him, but Little John urged his inability to do so as an excuse, and then set to ravenously on the venison pasties Friar Tuck had taken care to provide.

"Body o' me! friar," exclaimed Little John, as the thought occurred to him, "it will not do to drink all this good stuff at once, and two such thirsty throats as ours will soon drain the cask. What say you if we take a little from each of the others?"

"Dishonesty, John, is a bad example to set before one of my humble profession," replied the friar, trying to look grave. "St. Mary! I could not countenance such an act; but if so be thou art bent upon this evil, I will e'en turn my back."

"You are an accommodating sinner," rejoined the forester. Body o' me! you deserve an indulgence from the Pope. Turn your head, man, and then thou needst not see what I drink."

"Thou canst hand the measure round here, my son," said the friar, meekly; "it matters not then whether thou drawest it from the barrel or dip it from the stream."

"There is more truth in your words than

you imagine," muttered Little John, as he discovered the brewer's deception, and was about to vent his spleen on the brewer, but to his surprise he was gone.

Turning to the friar, he said—

"I fear this ale will be too strong for your humble palate ; it is of a different brewing, and I would not for the world have it disagree with you."

"Saints forbid it should do so, my son ; but I will forgive thee if it should be so," said the friar turning round, contrary to his promise, in his eagerness to obtain it.

An expression, such as never ought to have left his lips, escaped him as he took the measure and tasted; and after heaping a host of expletives on the head of Darby Dillon, they both laughed heartily at the joke.

CHAPTER CII.

LITTLE JOHN HAS A STRANGE ADVENTURE.

He sought the hermit's cave
'Twas fraught with horrors rife,
But when the gold he saw
It much did please his sight.

ROBIN HOOD, on his return to the stronghold, made hasty preparations for his departure to London, and surveyed with evident satisfaction the work that had been hastily carried on.

The timber that had been hewn and sawn by the Norman soldiers had been formed into a strong barricade, with loopholes here and there for the outlaws to use their bows in case of an attack.

This was protected by a deep trench which the foresters had themselves dug, and formed mounds with the earth, and which would have enabled them to carry on a fierce war with their assailants, as the trenches could be approached from within the barricade by means of holes dug deep in the earth.

This arrangement was concealed from the knowledge of the soldiers ; a wise precaution on the part of the foresters as events will show.

Having viewed what was done, and given orders for further improvements, Robin Hood summoned his chief followers and divided them into two classes, woodwards and rangers ; the former were to keep the outposts and guard the forest from intruders, the latter were to look after more important matters, and to see to the safety of the prisoners.

Much the miller's son and George-a-Green were constituted chief rangers, and Allen-a-Dale and Will Gammell were made chief woodwards.

Robin chose for his own party Little John, Will Scarlett, and a dozen bowmen ; but they were not to travel in a body, as it was considered imprudent, but they were to travel in pairs.

Before reaching the outskirts of the forest they separated, each with an understanding where to meet ; and Robin proceeded alone as he was mounted, and had to go a little out of his way to the smithy, his horse having cast a shoe.

Little John and Will Scarlett went together, but by some means they got separated in the wood, and the sudden outburst of a storm that had threatened them at starting, caused Little John to seek shelter.

The part of the forest he was in was not such as to afford much shelter ; the trees were stunted and bare, though the underwood was of dense growth.

As he was trying to shield his lank body from the rain, which was falling like a deluge, beneath a friendly bush, he was startled by a herd of deer ; and, as he was aware that the instinctive animals were making for a better shelter, he followed them.

They entered a densely wooded dell ; and, after Little John had ensconced himself beneath a thick foliaged tree and recovered his breath, which the run had deprived him of, he looked around him and fancied the place looked familiar to him.

" Body o' me !" he muttered, shrugging his huge shoulders ; " this is poor shelter for man or beast ; I must beat about for some better place to pass the night. Gramercy ! 'tis well I think on't ; somewhere here abouts dwells the hermit of woodland dell."

He glanced his eye around and saw what he took to be a beaten path.

" Ugh ! 'tis cold," he muttered, as the wind whistled round his ears, and the damp struck through his clothes from the ground on which he was seated. " Bladebone of Saint Hubert ! such weather will kill a body, but it can't last long at this rate, however."

He felt for his flask and drained it, and then another troublesome thought occurred to him.

The hermit was poor ; and, even did he succeed in finding him, he could not take the food of the aged man without making him some recompense, which was totally out of his power, as Will Scarlett carried his pouch.

However, as the rain slackened according to his expectations, he determined to seek the hermitage and crave shelter for the night ; and, after pursuing the path for some distance, he came in sight of the hovel.

It was but a wretched place, though to outward appearance strong ; it had been built partly of stone and partly of boughs of trees, which were rotting from the water that ran down the rocks when it rained heavily.

Little John did not stay to think of this.

The door yielded to his touch and he entered.

" Empty," he muttered, as no object met his glance when he gazed round the gloomy interior, so he strode fearlessly in.

He was, however, wrong in his conjecture.

A slight rustling met his ear, and a gaunt, emaciated figure rose up on the wretched pallet that filled a recess at the further extremity.

Little John, whose eyes had now become reconciled to the gloom, started in horror at the sight he saw, and was about to flee, when the voice of the strange figure arrested him.

"Stay, whomsoever ye be. If thou art he whom I takest thee for, thou wilt not close thine ears to a dying man's wish."

"Body o' me! if thou art mortal I will not; but if you are what you seem, I must hence at once."

"My son," replied the hermit, "if thine heart is steeled against pity, go; but if thou hast the humanity and courage of a Christian, stay."

The forester looked at the strange figure, whose bones seemed to pierce through his ragged garments, and he debated within himself whether he should go or stay.

There was a look so melancholy on the parchment visage of the recluse that it struck pity to the heart of Little John, and, though he fain would have left, he hesitated undecided.

"Be not afraid," said the hermit; "thou art strong and lusty, and need fear no harm from one borne down by age and infirmities. Say, wilt thou grant me one boon, and I will reward thee with my choicest blessings."

"Good father, I can scarce deny you," replied John, summoning courage; "the storm without increases, and, though this hut is but poor shelter, I must e'en be grateful for it."

"Then listen," cried the hermit, his sunken eyes lighting with a gleam of satisfaction. "I have been wronged, deeply injured, and I wish to be revenged."

"On whom?"

"One thou doubtless knowest well; but first I must tell thee who and what I am. My father was a wealthy clothworker, and when he died he left his hoarded treasure to me and my sisters, of which there were two, Lydia and Jane. The former entered the priory of Kirkless, taking with her her share of the money, whilst Jane married a young and worthless scamp, who not only squandered her portion, but craved for mine also. Freely would I have shared it with him had he asked it, but the wretch resorted to baser means; he placed poison in my cup, but the skill of a leech saved me. A mock burial deceived my would-be murderer, and the stout coffin that was supposed to contain my body bore away the prize he coveted, my riches, so that he believed he had committed the crime without reaping any benefit. The men I secretly employed little dreamed of the deception, attributing the weight to the lead which they supposed lined the coffin, whilst the sum of two hundred marks sealed the lips of the monks who admitted me into the abbey of Saint Mary's. None but myself knew of the wealth the coffin contained, and careful was I to conceal from the abbot the place of its consignment, though when I was less weak I made frequent stolen visits to the spot, scraped away the earth, and distributed the gold freely among the poor. Rumours of this reached the ears of the monks, and the abbot imposed severe penance upon me for not disclosing the source from whence I obtained the money; and

thus goaded, I left the haunts of men and sought shelter in this dell. This place was raised by the peasants I had assisted, and here I have lived, nursing the secret until it is no longer of use to me, for I feel that my pilgrimage on earth will soon be brought to a close."

He paused, and wiped the clammy dews from his brow, and Little John, who had listened to him in wrapped attention, drew a deep breath.

"My son," continued the hermit, fixing his dim eyes on the forester, whilst his claw-like fingers played in his long matted beard, "thou hast opportunely arrived. First, thou must promise to give my body Christian burial; and secondly, thou must revenge me by informing Stukely that thou hast seen my ghost. Do not start, my son; 'tis the guilty conscience of the murderer and wrong-doer that conjures up such sights in the horrible imaginations of their heated brain; but thou canst say to him nevertheless of a truth that thou hast seen one whom he supposes dead, and that my troubled spirit has vowed to haunt him to the death!"

Little John shuddered.

He stood speechless, gazing fixedly on the spectre-like form of the holy man, who, viewed in the gloomy light, looked more like a spectre than an inhabitant of the earth.

The sepulchral voice of the dying man once more resounded through the dismal place, and fell in hollow tones on the ears of his listener.

"Beneath thy feet," he said, pointing with his long gaunt fingers, "lies the treasure I would have thee seek. One portion thou must give to my niece Madge Stukely, a portion thou mayest keep thyself, and the rest thou must take to bold Robin Hood, the rightful Earl of Huntingdon, the true friend of the poor and the oppressed. All this thou must swear upon thy bended knee, for I see by thine equipage thou art a man of war," he added, impressively. "By the virgin! thou must swear on thy hope of salvation."

"You can e'en take my word without this, good father," replied Little John, awed by the speaker's solemn manner. "Sorry am I that it lays not in my power to give you shrift."

"I need it not, my son; my life hath been passed in prayer and atonement. Swear but to do as asked. The coffin that was prepared for my murdered body will now serve to hold my remains; the spade which has served to dig roots for my worldly wants will now serve the double purpose of providing a last resting-place for my body, and repay thee for thy pains."

The hermit raised his long gaunt arms to heaven, and, with the name of the virgin on his lips, sank back on the pallet.

Darkness grew on apace, and the situation of the forester, bold as he was, was not a very agreeable one.

After a search he found a small lamp and

lit it, and cast his eyes on the occupant of the miserable bed.

He lay stiff and rigid as a corpse; his eyes open and fixed with a stony gaze on the roof; his bony fingers clasped and raised heavenwards, the crucifix of his rosary pressed to his bloodless lips.

A silence painful to the forester now reigned through the venerable pile, and nought but his own deep breathing, save when the blast shrieked fiercer through the trees, awoke the deathly stillness of the place.

Little John approached the couch and placed his hand on the pallid brow to make sure the hermit slept the sleep of death, and a cold, icy chill struck through his frame.

"Gone, gone," he muttered; "and, as I cannot sleep, I will commence my task; 'tis a cheerless one, but nevertheless from it I will not shirk."

So saying, he took the spade and commenced digging up the earth; and, when he had got to a great depth and met with nought but the soil, he turned weary, and sat himself down on the heap of earth he had thrown out, to rest and consider whether he should carry on what appeared to him a fruitless task.

By chance his eyes wandered to the bed, and to his horror he beheld the hermit's ghastly form sitting bolt upright; his sunken orbs fixed steadily upon him, and his bony fingers pointing towards the hole.

"Thy promise, my son, remember thy vow," he uttered, in a solemn tone, and once more resumed his recumbent position, leaving Little John in a state not easily to be described.

"Of witches and warlocks I have heard much," thought the giant, "but of such like as this, never before did I hear. Holy Mother! aid me to keep my vow, and deliver me safe from this horrid place."

With this muttered prayer he again set himself to his task, and soon had the satisfaction of hearing the spade strike against something that gave back a hollow sound.

This restored the giant's wonted strength, and he soon brought to the surface the coffin, released the lid, and feasted his eyes on the glittering gold.

Having taken sufficient for his present wants he dug a hole and buried the rest, then placed the corpse in the coffin and buried it in the trench.

By this time day was beginning to dawn, and, having patted the earth well down, he left the hermitage and carefully closed the door.

CHAPTER CIII.

A BOLD ADVENTURE.

The stronghold Stukely entered
In well befitting guise;
And though the outlaws saw him,
He baffled their keen eyes.

It was not love for the sheriff that made Stukely act so treacherously to the outlaws; in his heart he hated De Lois, but, from motives of his own, he kept his true sentiments to himself.

His father had been a wealthy merchant in the city of London, and had had considerable dealings with the clothworker mentioned in the previous chapter, hence it was that Stukely became acquainted with Jane, the mother of Madge.

Mixed up with politics—which in those turbulent times proved the overthrow of many—he soon found himself in difficulties, and lastly in prison, which terminated in his death, and reduced his wife and one son to beggary; which broke the mother's heart, and threw the child upon the world.

Left to his own resources Stukely soon worked his way into society, choosing the gay and thoughtless for his companions, though his resources were limited to his own inventive mind and crafty disposition.

Profiting by the lesson taught by his father, he carefully avoided political broils; and though of a proud spirit, he was often compelled by his poverty to stoop to the basest meanness.

Often would he lighten the gay roysterer when, under the mask of friendship, he assisted him to his home; and when his fingers clutched the yellow dross, he would anxiously long for more.

As he grew up to manhood, his avarice increased; and when he married the clothworker's daughter, he hoarded her money away bit by bit, until he had secured it all, giving her to believe that he had spent it.

He had a purpose in this; he had an eye to the wealth of his brother-in-law; and could he have obtained it, he would have fled to the continent with his wife, and have enjoyed it in retirement.

But fate ordained it otherwise; his wife died, and his plot failed, as the hermit's words verified.

From that time Stukely became an altered man; the death of his wife, whom in heart he secretly loved, made him thoughtful, and cling with an ardent affection to his child.

He got employed at the castle, where he by his assiduous manners worked his way up to chief warder, and carefully placed his little earnings with the rest, which he had hidden in a secure place in the castle.

Often in his leisure he would repair to his secret hiding-place, and count over the glittering coin, which he intended as a dowry for his daughter, whom he wished to see married to one of high estate.

In his hasty escape from the castle, he had not been able to carry this with him; but he hoped, by fawning and deceit, to worm his way once more into the sheriff's favour; and once possessed of the keys to remove his wealth, and leave that part of the country for ever.

Not far from Nottingham were the remains of a castle, that had been laid almost in ruins in one of the civil wars, and which was shunned by the people, as it was reported by the monks to be the abode of evil spirits.

Brave, and not over superstitious, Stukely took up his abode in the only part that was habitable, and with his daughter, who like himself was void of fear, lived in solitude.

His previous knowledge of the place and the country round enabled him to leave and enter at his will without being seen or suspected; and as the old chests furnished him with disguises, he was enabled to carry out his plans favourably.

A friend in the town conveyed his communications to De Lois, so that he had little to fear until the countersign betrayed him, and he fell into the hands of Much.

This made him alter his plans; instead of prowling about the forest, and stealing interviews with the prisoner Duncan as he had done before, he disguised himself in a deerskin, which disguise was so effectual, as to deceive even the noble animals he imitated for a time. And a few hours after he had escaped from the hands of the miller's son, he was creeping round the forester's stronghold in this disguise.

He was noticed by the woodwards, but they being deceived by the darkness, and too intent upon other matters to observe his awkward gait, took no heed of him, and little dreaming of such a deception, they imagined him to be the favourite deer Marian had tamed and brought up by her own hand, and which had perfect range of the place.

Duncan had put him up to this, and emboldened with success, Stukely even ventured to pass the sentinels, and enter the cave.

In doing so, he had to pass a bench, at which Will Gammell and George-a-Green were seated; but he took heed to keep as far out of observation as possible, and crept along the dark passage and entered the cave.

Stealthily as were his movements, however, the foresters' keen hearing detected the sound, and peering into the gloom, Will Gammell remarked—

"Marry, 'tis no wonder, comrade, that we feel sad at Robin's departure, when the poor fawn cannot rest even."

"Ay, but 'tis her mistress's absence she feels; she misses her caressing hand, especially when it's feeding time; 'twas but yesterday I noticed how sad the poor thing looked."

Stukely heard this with delight, and enjoyed a laugh in secret; for in truth he looked a very sprightly imitation of the brisk animal he represented.

On through the cave he went, however, and entered that occupied by the prisoners, most of whom worn out by their day's toil, lay fast asleep upon the skins which, spread upon the floor, served for beds.

A few, however, were still awake, and holding a whispered conversation; amongst these was Duncan, and Stukely crawled to him, and nestled down by his side, where he remained for some time.

Their plans were then discussed, after which Stukely departed with the same caution, and was clear of the stronghold before it was light.

CHAPTER CIV.

THE REWARD OF GUILT.

"There, there, I see him now!"
The guilty wretch did cry,
As starting from the bed whereon
In agony he lie.

AWARE of his danger if discovered by any of the band, for Much, the miller's son, had made his treachery known, Stukely hastened with all speed to get clear of the forest.

He had a long way to go. Daylight was fast approaching, and what was worse, his disguise restricted him to a limited pace.

He would gladly have thrown off the skin and abandoned it, but had he done so his discovery would have been certain, for in his way he saw many of the foresters pacing up and down, their quick ears alert to the least sound, and their bows clasped in their hands ready to string an arrow at the instant.

It required his utmost caution to avoid coming right upon them, so that he was compelled to make his way through the underwood, and keep in the track frequented by the deer.

In coming he had passed many of the antlered tribe, and they had fled at his approach, and he hoped they would do so again or else not notice him, but he was doomed to disappointment.

Having come to a place where two roads branched off, in either of which he could see the tall form of a forester standing beneath a tree, he was compelled to take the wood between, which he found was tenanted by a herd of well-grown stags.

To make a passage through them he knew would be attended with great danger, but he was compelled to do so, and he boldly set forward.

As he passed the outer ones, who served as a kind of picket, without causing any alarm, he considered his danger passed, but, alas! he was mistaken.

A huge buck, king of the herd, rose up his head, and began sniffing the air, meanwhile watching the strange object that had startled him with wonderful instinct and distrust.

Having given another long sniff to assure himself that he was right, he startled his companions by giving a long protracted whine, and then darted full butt at Stukely, who was knocked over and almost crushed to death by the many feet that galloped over him, and left him for dead.

More than one pair of antlers had been thrust against him, and would have probed him had it not been for the skin, but nevertheless he was so sore and bruised that he could scarcely move when they had gone.

So sudden and unexpected had been the attack, that he was unable to offer resistance or use his knife, and it was fortunate for him they did not return to the attack, or it must have ended in his death.

With bitter groans and mental curses, he made his escape from the spot, and under shelter of the trees dragged his bruised limbs to the border of the forest, where he threw off his disguise and endeavoured to reach his home.

Madge was not only surprised but shocked when she saw him enter bruised and bleeding. She had been anxiously waiting his return.

To her anxious inquiries as to how it had occurred he gave an evasive reply, for he was too cunning to let her into the secret of his villainy, but she tended him well, dressed his wounds, and got him into bed.

Tortured with agony, both of mind and body, Stukely rolled and tossed on his bed all that day, his daughter even fearing to go near him, so terrible were his mutterings.

Towards night he was seized with delirium; his eyes rolled about wildly, and his mutterings grew more fierce and abstracted.

Madge was bewildered what to do for the best.

She would have got the assistance of a leech, but she knew that would add to their peril, for their hiding-place would become known, and De Lois might easily capture her father in his present helpless state.

Thus night drew on, the very night on which the hermit had expired, and when the bell in the town proclaimed the midnight hour, and the owls and bats began to fly about the ruins with their horrid croaking voice, Stukely awoke from a troubled sleep.

But what a change the last few hours had wrought in the appearance of the man!

His stout, portly form had become emaciated and thin.

His arms became long and gaunt; his features cadaverous and unearthly.

Large drops of sweat hung in beads on his brow, and his eyes, which were sunken, glittered red and wolfish.

Madge recoiled from him in horror.

She could scarcely recognise her parent's voice in the hollow, sepulchral tones that came from his throat.

A few moments' reflection, however, sufficed to enable her to gather courage, and she listened to his ravings with stoical calmness.

"Away, fiends! quit my sight. Thou canst not want me yet," he raved; "'twas not I who murdered him—I did not take his old. Away! away! Leave me, or I shall go mad. Ha! ha! again he haunts me. There—there," cried the frenzied man, "I see him now! Take him away, fiends; 'twas not I put the poison in the cup. Go! let me die in peace."

Madge gazed in horror and abstraction at the wall to which he pointed with his long gaunt arms, and a bright halo seemed to spread over the dark surface, and in its midst she could discover the figure of a man half bent with age, his white flowing beard covering his chest; in one hand he held a rosary, and in the other a silver cup, which was of dazzling brightness.

Raising the cup to his lips as though drain-ing its contents to the very dregs, the strange figure raised it heavenward, and then moved his lips as though in the act of prayer.

The figure then vanished, the halo melted away, and the gloomy rushlight was all that illuminated the room.

"Father! father!" shrieked Madge, as she sank upon the bed; "what horrible crime have you committed to cause that strange spirit to haunt you?"

"None, none, my child," replied Stukely, trembling; "it was not I did the deed. 'Fore heaven, I am innocent!"

"Holy Mother, grant it may be so; but I cannot hold you guiltless after hearing such words as you have uttered."

"Silence, lass, unless you would have me curse you. Dost think I would turn mur"——

The word choked him.

He could not finish the sentence, but fell back on the bed pale and rigid as a corpse.

Madge bathed his brow and moistened his lips with wine, and used her utmost endeavours to bring him to.

She herself felt ill; the worry and excitement were too much even for her strong nerve.

Anxiously she watched for his recovery, and ardently she longed to learn the truth; but morning found her in the same predicament—her father had evidently gone mad.

CHAPTER CV.

ROBIN HOOD VISITS FAIR LONDON TOWN.

Some cunning knave the words did hear,
　And speedily did hie
To tell the captain of the guard
　Where Robin Hood did lie.
*　　　*　　　*

They reached the house, St. Dunstan's Head,
　And battered at the door,
As soon as it was opened
　The soldiers in did pour.

ROBIN soon made his journey to London, where the court was assembled, and was soon joined by his merry men.

It was a house in the vicinity of Fleet Street where they met, and as it was kept by one Pengarth, who had known the earl in his prosperous days, he met him with cordial greeting.

"How now, Robin?" cried the bluff old host; "what wonderment brings you from your greenwood home, where report has it you reign supreme, feasting at pleasure on the king's deer, and washing thy throttle with the best of wine at the abbot's expense?"

"Ha! ha! that much thou knowest, then," cried Robin, laughing heartily; "thou hast been well informed, good Pengarth, and hath a good knowledge of things; the lion leaves not his lair without a purpose."

"And that is"——

"Stay, stay, be not so impatient; both I and my men have travelled far, the dust hangs like cobwebs in our throat, and I trow me, we are all ready to do our devoirs to anything thou hast in shape of meat and drink."

"Body o' me! thou art right, good master," cried Little John, who had visited every inn on his way. "Saint Herman! the stuff is so thin and watery that 'tis impossible to quench ones thirst."

"Good fellow, thou shall have no cause to complain when I have served you," said the host, eyeing the enormous dimensions of the giant; "few leave here without satisfaction. Saint Dunstan, whose head swings on the board without, can bear witness of that same."

"By Saint Mary — ever blessed be her memory!—you would do well to offer up mass, but for a vintner I fear you are ill capacitated. Body o' me! my throat is parching, and my whole body is drying up for want of nourishment."

Pengarth took the hint and disappeared, but soon returned from the cellar accompanied by a trencherman, who soon spread before them a repast.

This somewhat soothed the giant's ailment, and the party, whose appetites were freshened, soon did justice to the huge joints set before them.

"Now I will tell thee the purpose of my visit," said Robin, when his hunger was appeased; and he informed Pengarth of the strange abduction of Marian.

"Quotha, I would not have your task if she is in the king's keeping; of late his temper is such that few who offend him escape with their heads. Only a few days hath he been in town, and the Tower hath seen more than one victim."

"Herman of the Wold! thinkest thou I fear him? Gramercy, no; tell me where he is likely to be found, and I will beard the tyrant in his den."

Robin uttered these words in a tone of firmness, and struck his hand vehemently on the table.

"Peace, Robin, I pray thee; guard thy tongue; thy words will involve both thee and me in danger too; many prying ears are ever ready to listen and carry such news to the king."

"Zounds! I fear them not," cried Robin, in disdain; "but canst thou tell me the cause of yon bowmen hieing eastward as I came hither?"

"Forsooth, I wot not exactly; report speaks of a grand archery fete to be held in Finsbury Fields."

"Saint Hubert! sayst thou so? Then they go to practice at the butts?"

"Ay, and a grand banquet is to be held at the palace. 'Tis said the king will not appear in person, but Prince Edward and the gracious Eleanor will do the honours in his stead."

Robin rose from his seat and paced the floor in thoughtful mood.

"Marry! I will be there," he muttered. "I will get fitting guise. Pengarth," he added, to the host, "you must learn more of this; it concerns me greatly."

"Troth, will I, all in my power. Stay you here to-night?"

"I am not certain."

Robin had a reason for not giving him a decided answer.

Pengarth's own words had made him cautious; not that he suspected his host would behave treacherously towards him, but it was as well to be careful.

He did not stay there that night; he sought another lodging, and disposed of his men separately, and it was as well for him he did so.

Soon after the houses were closed, and the citizens had retired quietly their beds, those living in the vicinity of Pengarth's house were awakened by the tramp of a body of armed men.

They stopped at the door of the hostel and loudly demanded admittance, accompanying their demand with a thundering knocking at the door with their sword-hilts.

"Open, in the king's name!" shouted the leader.

"What for?" demanded the host.

"Your roof shelters a traitor!" was the stern reply.

"Thy informant hath deceived thee; albeit I will open and let ye judge for yourselves."

"Do so quickly, or by the saint whose holy visage thou hast dishonoured by placing it over thy door-post, I will break open the door."

"No violence is needed," rejoined Pengarth, opening the door; "a good and true citizen ought not to be molested at this hour of the night. Saint Dunstan! it is worse than sacrilege."

"Peace, fool! show the light. Did thy head grace the temple gates, the king would have one traitor the less to fear. Boddikins! I would give my own halberd in the absence of a pikestaff to set thy effigy on."

Pengarth would have resented this rude speech but he thought of the words of the sage, "A still tongue maketh a wise head," so he remained silent.

The leader dashed into the house, followed by half-a-dozen of his blustering crew, the rest remaining outside to guard against escape.

Every room, cupboard, and cellar was then searched, and even the bed-chamber of mine host and his spouse was not held sacred; Mrs. Pengarth was pulled from her bed, and even her frilled nightcap was torn from her head to satisfy the enraged leader that it was not the person he sought in disguise.

Having completed their fruitless search, and tested each barrel to ascertain its contents, the soldiers left, swearing bitterly at the hoax played upon them, and hurried back to their quarters.

"A malison on the knaves!" growled the indignant host, as he thrust his night-capped head out of the window and watched their departure; marry! it is not even safe to lie in one's bed. Marry come up, with a wennion on them all! say I. Thank heaven Robin was not here."

ROBIN HOOD,
AND THE OUTLAWS OF SHERWOOD FOREST.

THE RECOVERY OF THE STOLEN CROWN.

Having relieved his outraged feelings thus, and poured a heap of the bitterest invectives he could imagine on their heads, the host withdrew, closed the window, and once more joined his spouse, who was venting her indignation in a manner well worthy of her size and volubility of tongue.

CHAPTER CVI.

THE MEETING BETWEEN ROBIN HOOD AND THE PRINCESS.

Bold Robin the outlaw to London did hie,
To hear news of his loved Marian.
When he told the princess of his terrible loss,
The tears down her cheeks fast they ran.

IT was a grand day in the great city ; it was the twenty-second day of June, and consequently Prince Edward's birthday ; and as he was an especial favourite with the people, they made it a holiday.

The bells of the various churches gave forth their merry peals ; and the houses of the principal money lenders, settled in what is now called Lombard-street, had their houses decorated with flags and ribbons ; and all the principal houses in line with Temple-bar shared in the great demonstration.

The road between Temple-bar and the then village of Westminster were lined with throngs of citizens gaily dressed, and proud knights in glittering mail, accompanied by their esquires, were seen galloping in all directions.

Then might be seen a party of monks, headed by the Abbot of Westminster, accompanied by the Poet Laureate, on their way from St. Paul's to the Abbey, and forming a beautiful view on this glorious summer morning.

Among the busy throng might be seen a trio of gaily-dressed pedestrians eyeing the different crests emblazoned on the breastplates and equipages of the knights and earls as they cantered past on their spirited steeds.

They were Robin Hood and his trusty followers, Little John and Will Scarlett.

On an open space a party of men were making preparations for a fair, and as they stood watching them the crowd that had collected seemed to be seized with a sudden commotion.

"The king's favourite !" remarked a smartly dressed citizen to his companion ; and turning in the direction of the object that had caused so much stir, Robin Hood recognised the features of D'Anville.

The duke was magnificently equipped, and as he sat majestically in his saddle, he glanced haughtily at the crowd of faces turned towards him.

As his eye caught that of Robin Hood, his features suddenly changed, his brow knitted, and his face assumed a troubled look.

"Odds boddikins !" he muttered, "methinks I know that face, though at present I cannot call it to mind."

"Gaspar !" he added to his page, as he slackened his pace to let the page come up with him, " saw you you fellow in the crowd, glaring like one possessed of an evil eye ?"

"Marry did I, master mine ; his look was one meant for an insult."

"Didst mark him well ? Think you you would know him again ?"

"I' faith would I ; the look he gave thee I shall never forget ; I took heed of him the more as he did not doff his cap."

" 'Tis well ; I would have you watch him ; it will be a gold piece in your purse if you find out his name."

The page bowed, and dropping from his saddle, gave the reins to one of the soldiers who formed the party, and hastened back on foot.

He soon reached the spot where Robin and his men had stood, but, to his disappointment, he had gone, and though the page wandered about among the throng, he was compelled to give up his search in despair.

In the meantime, Robin Hood mingled with the gay revellers, who became more boisterous as the day advanced, and by listening to their conversation, learnt that which assisted him in his plans.

A grand banquet was held at St. James's ; and the knights and barons who had been favoured with an invitation flocked thither at the hour appointed.

Conspicuous amongst them was a tall, masculine figure, clothed from head to heel in a suit of burnished mail ; his visor was drawn closely down, and a sword such as was worn by the crusaders hung by his side ; he was attended by two equerries, and they rode boldly up to the barrier that guarded the palace gates.

A murmur of disappointment passed through the crowd of spectators at not being able to see his face ; and the men-at-arms that were placed to throw open the barrier to those who gave the countersign, eyed him with a look bordering on suspicion.

Though it was understood that the king could not be present, the utmost caution was observed to allow no one that was opposed to the king's views to enter the palace, for he secretly feared some treachery on the part of the dissatisfied barons.

Within the barriers the courtyard was lined on either side with soldiers of the guard, and when the challenge was given and not replied to, the sentry stepped before the horse of the silent rider.

"Back, fool !" cried the unknown ; and digging his spurs into his horse's flanks, he cleared the bar, followed by his equerries.

"Treason !" thundered the astonished soldier, recovering from the violence of the shock, by which he had been thrown down. "Seize the traitor !"

The captain of the guard sprang like a tiger at the rein of the first rider's horse, but a blow, dealt deftly by the unknown, laid him on his back.

On seeing their captain's danger, several of the guard flew to his rescue, whilst the others, armed with their long pikes, closed round the other horsemen.

"Yield thee, traitor, whoever thou art !" cried the captain of the guard, as he sprang to his feet and drew his sword.

"Minion, stand aside !" cried the unknown ; " call off your hounds, or by my halidame you shall rue this insult !"

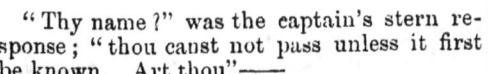

"Thy name?" was the captain's stern response; "thou canst not pass unless it first be known. Art thou"——

"A friend of the king's," cried the horseman, "and a true knight, as you shall find if you delay me longer."

He spurred on his horse as he spoke, and the captain, who had a narrow escape of being trodden under foot, aimed a terrific blow at the unknown's head, but the horseman's sword flew from its sheath, and the captain's weapon went spinning through the air.

The soldiers drew back clear of the horses' feet, and one of the equerries rode up to the side of the mysterious knight, and whispered in his ear—

"'Tis best to settle this dispute, Sir Robin, for I see other eyes are upon us."

The unknown glanced around, and seemed to have thought well of the advice.

Fixing his keen eyes on the discomfited captain, he said—

"Pick up your sword, Sir Knave; I will report this conduct to the king." Then, producing a ring, he added, "See you this?"

The soldier started.

His flushed cheek turned of an ashy paleness.

"I crave your pardon, Sir Knight," he faltered; "'twas the strictness of my orders caused me so to act."

"'Twas thine insolence, fool; but I forgive thee, and yonder busysides who hath caused all this, as well. Send hither someone to look after our steeds."

Awed by the speaker's austere manner and imperative tone, the captain turned vengefully on his men, and said to them, loud enough for the stranger to hear—

"Marry come up, with a wennion on ye all! Into sore trouble have I gotten through ye. Odds fish! ye shall share with me the punishment. Go; some of ye take charge of the nobles' horses, and see that ye take great care of them; and—do ye hear me?—try by all means to win back the good opinions we have lost through this folly."

This speech assured Robin Hood (for it was he that played the knight's part) that he would have no further trouble; and, as the soldiers showed him great courtesy, he rewarded each with a gold piece, and strode into the banqueting hall.

The gorgeous scene of revelry was already commenced, and knights and nobles lined the boards that seemed to groan under the weight of the huge smoking joints, and the massive tankards of wine that seemed ready to bear them down.

Beneath a canopy hung with crimson and gold, upon a raised dais, sat Prince Edward, conversing with the Princess Eleanor, who appeared cheerful, and smiled occasionally as the conversation went on.

Amidst the confusion and noisy ribaldry, the entrance of our hero and his brave foresters was not noticed, so they doffed their helmets, and seated themselves at a table in a remote part of the hall, where they could see all that passed and yet not be exposed to the observations of others.

As they sat thus, noting all and conversing in low whispers, they were startled by the tinkling of bells, and to their surprise the king's jester made his appearance from beneath the board at which they sat.

"A merry time to ye, gentleman all," exclaimed the fool, rubbing his eyes. "I forgive ye for disturbing me in my sleep."

"Sleep!" replied Robin, trying to hide his vexation; "you must have had a troubled one. Did you dream at all?"

"Marry did I! and a queer dream it was, my cousin. I dreamed"——

He hesitated, and cast his eyes around to observe if they were alone.

"What did you dream?" demanded Robin, angrily.

"That you were vexed with me," replied the jester.

"And thy dream is fulfilled," said Robin; "and didst thou hear any strange sounds in thy *sleep?*"

"I did; but I will tell ye my dream as it appeared to me. Methought I was wandering in a wood, and got me so tired that I lay me down to sleep; when, lo and behold you! I was startled by the winding of a horn; I listened, and heard voices approaching; and, looking up, I beheld *three foresters.*"

Robin's heart beat against his ribs as he listened to the jester's story, but he allowed not the least sign to betray his thoughts.

"Who were they?" he asked, with well-assumed calmness.

"They were Robin Hood, Scathelock, and Little John," was the jester's reply.

"How knew you them?"

"By their voices; though, I trow me, they were well disguised. Their hair and eyebrows had turned much darker, and, had I not known them of yore, I should have taken them for Normans instead of Saxons."

Robin's brow grew thoughtful.

"Betrayed," he muttered; "the varlet has listened to our discourse; a malison on this devil's imp, for his eavesdropping!"

He was about to add something to the jester, but Golinbert had gone as mysteriously as he came, and Robin noticed that they had become the object of observation of some of the guests.

A moment after he observed the fool at the back of the royal throne.

"Saint Herman! that fellow knows our secret and means to betray us," whispered Robin Hood to his followers; "look well to your weapons; it may yet come to blows, for if they offer to lay hands on us we shall have a sharp tussle."

"Body o' me! thou art right, master," replied Little John; "'twill not be like fighting in the greenwood; there with our good yew bows we might soon riddle their harness, but steel to steel requires hard hitting."

"Zounds! we should stand but a poor

chance among so many, though, I wot me, they would have a sample of our skill before they mastered us, and then our merry archers could cover our retreat."

"Herman of the Wold ! I am not so sure of that,' replied Robin ; "these walls are thick, and our bodies might be made small hash of ere the ring of steel met our companions' ears. But see," he added, "the jester converses with the prince."

"Ay, by the mass ! and the princess too," remarked Little John. "Now I wish I had given the rascal a sly poke ; had we known he had lain under the table we might have given him a prick that would have settled him."

"Pshaw ! it hath not come to that yet ; the prince will not molest us in the presence of Eleanor ; I have faith in her."

"You may put your faith in the Virgin if that jackanapes whispers your name about," said John, with a shrug ; " Eleanor will have but little power over the prince in this crowded assembly ; more than one enemy's face I can recognise at the upper end of the hall."

" D'Anville, for one," Robin remarked, "and the fellow we thrashed, John of Linden, is another."

"Body o' mine ! I can count a score of knights we crossed swords with at the battle of Eavesham," said Little John ; " but I e'en will not forget to freshen my inward man with a bumper of wine, for fear matters turn out awry."

"Hist ! thou ungodly sinner," said a voice, and Golinbert made is appearance as before ; " more need have ye of the councils of a priest, for, by our Lady ! a hempen neckcloth will soon grace thy neck if ye commit murders as coolly as ye plan them."

Little John was completely taken aback by this speech.

"Now do I truly believe the fellow is a devil's imp, if he be not the devil himself," he thought, "else how could he hear our words when at the other end of the hall."

Golinbert seemed to divine his thoughts, for he said—

"It may seem strange to ye that a fool should know so well of your thoughts and actions, but 'tis explained when I tell ye I have had another *dream*."

"Go to, with thy dreams, incarnate devil !" growled the discomfited giant ; " thou art a witch or a sorcerer, an' I opine rightly. Saint Hubert ! thou wouldst make a fine trade in frightening old women."

" I' faith, but I fear I should do but little with such unbelievers as you, for I have told you the truth, yet you will not believe it."

"A malison on thee and thy truths too ! What lie did I see ye whisper to the prince ?"

" By the cross of Saint George, and a thousand dragons !" exclaimed the fool, affecting to be surprised, "it is my turn now to denounce you as a practiser of the black art. How knew you that I whispered a lie to the prince ?"

" It hath left its mark on thy lips," replied Little John, smiling good humouredly, as

much from the effects of the wine as his timely joke. "Know ye all men by their works, saith the prophet ; therefore I christen thee liar, and opine from thy manner of dress that thou art a prince of devils."

"And I christen ye the prince of thieves !" retorted the jester ; "for he that stealeth from the king stealeth from the people, and he that stealeth from the church taketh the hard earnings of the poor ; yet, for all this, I take you to be a good fellow ; for, though you have killed many a fat buck and helped yourself from the treasury of the church, your master, Robin Hood, hath been generous to the poor and needy, so I will e'en drain a cup to the merry foresters of Sherwood !"

"Treason, by the mass !" replied Robin, his features rendered fierce and despotic by the dye he had used for his disguise. " I would advise ye, Master Jester, to be mindful of your words, and be careful how you drink to the health of a band of outlaws in the presence of the king's guests."

"If it offends thee, and makes ye jealous, I will e'en drink to thee, Sir Knight of the Crooked Antlers," said the fool. " I am wondrous dry, so here's to the lord of Sherwood !"

Robin now saw that disguise was no longer needed, but he was perplexed as to Golinbert's real intentions.

If he was draining the cup of deceit, he was doing it openly, he thought ; but if his mind was as frank and open as his words, he might be most useful to him.

He would have questioned him and sounded him, but the jester darted away and mingled with the throng, the tinkle of his bells sounding through the hall long after he was lost to view.

"Holy Virgin ! this fellow puzzleth me sorely. I cannot imagine his motives for making so free with us, though I should think he can mean us little harm. Ah ! see, again he speaks with the princess."

Little John turned his eyes in the direction of the throne, but Golinbert had gone before he did so, and D'Anville was conversing with Prince Edward.

"Quotha ! the knave is a mystery ; he puzzles me more and more, but I will fathom him, and"——

" Find thyself mastered, good Robin," interposed the jester, stepping suddenly before them. "The well is deeper than thou dost imagine."

"And that supplies your wit," said Robin Hood, scarce knowing whether to smile or frown ; "the sooner it runs dry the better, and a spring of purer speech taketh its place."

"Marry come up ! good master, sobersides," said the fool ; "one would not take thee for the chief of Sherwood's merry men. Perchance some ill hath befallen good Friar Tuck, and thou hast filled his post as chaplain ?"

"A truce with such bandinage. Knowest aught of the names you have mentioned ?" said Robin, tartly.

"Of a truth I do. In journeying to Nottingham on business for our gracious princess, I chanced to fall in with this Robin, and he rendered me a service that made me indebted to him for my life."

"Ah! now I remember ye," cried Robin, starting from his seat as the jester lifted his cap from his brow. "Thou wert harnessed as a knight, and visited the mill."

"I did; for, though it is not publicly known, I often throw aside my cap and bells, and sally forth on dangerous missions, armed."

"Then for this favour thou owest me, as ye treat danger so light, it may not perhaps be asking too much of thee to render me a service in return?"

"Name it. I cannot in duty refuse."

"Take this, then," said Robin, handing him a ring; "give it to the princess, and tell her 'tis from one who would have speech of her."

Golinbert glanced at the glittering bauble, and without saying a word darted away on his mission, leaving Robin in perplexity as to whether he would execute his mission or not.

His suspense was of short duration, for Golinbert returned in the same mysterious manner as before, and said—

"Her highness will be pleased to see you in the grounds. There is to be a masquerade, for which I will find you fitting costume."

"Thanks, Golinbert; but how shall I know her?"

"Fash not thereanent. I shall be there; but to prevent mishaps, I will explain that she will be attired in plain costume, and masked. So farewell! Make thyself merry, and easy withal, until we meet again."

But Robin's nature was not such as to allow him to remain inactive.

A party of nobles had gathered round the prince, evidently discussing some topic of interest, and he longed to learn its purport.

To do this he would have to change his position, which he did, boldly walking to the upper end of the hall, and seating himself where he could overhear them.

It was about this time that Prince Edward entertained an idea of visiting the Holy Land, the sixth crusade, that of St. Louis, and for this purpose he was trying to raise funds unknown to the king, his father, who was draining the country of its wealth, and squandering it in other ways more frivolous and less satisfactory to the people.

Inheriting from his father an inveterate hatred to the Jews, he extorted large sums of money from them, wherewith to furnish the means to carry out his projects, and the horrible means he resorted to to obtain this end were only in part atoned for by his distinguished bravery afterwards, and the heroic devotion of his wife.

Robin Hood was not long in gleaning sufficient from the conversation to acquaint him with the nature of the meeting.

"Thou knowest, D'Anville, where this dog is to be found," said one of the knights. "By the rood! 'tis easy to detect the Jewish rascals a mile off; I can hunt them to earth by their smell."

"Marry, your nose might be envied by an alchemist," returned D'Anville. "if it has such a keen scent of gold. St. Dunstan! but I will hunt the rascal out if he is to be found."

"And where thinkest thou we had better take him?" asked the prince.

"To Nottingham; it will not do to take him to Windsor, my liege; and the Tower will be no safe place."

"Thou art right; I think well of thy speech," said Edward. "To Nottingham with him; there we can keep our secret from the king, for De Lois is too great a coward to breathe a word to mortal soul when I forbid him."

This arranged, the prince returned to the side of Eleanor. And D'Anville, with John of Linden, withdrew to a retired spot, where they supposed they could converse without fear of being overheard.

Robin did not appear to heed them, but his quick ear was strained to catch every word.

"I give thee great commendation for the manner in which you performed your exploit," said Sir John; and envy you of the favour you have won from the king."

"Ay, well you might," rejoined D'Anville, boasting; "for knight-errantry, methinks I claim precedence; and for gallantry, I dare aver there is not my equal."

"So I think; and as I have a matter on hand, an affair that will just suit your taste, I have no fear in asking you to aid me."

"Out with it, and name thy conditions? If 'tis an affair of gallantry, I can do it cheap."

"Know you one Daverill Duke?"

"I do."

"And the Lady Agnes?"

"Yes!"

"And my brother, than whom, it was supposed, no better swordsman existed?"

"Marry do I; once only did I cross blades with him, and it was enough to satisfy me."

"'Tis well," muttered Sir John; then aloud he added—

"My brother, as you know, once aspired to the hand of the fair Agnes, but was thwarted by Daverill, who beguiled him into the woods and treacherously slew him; he now thinks himself secure; but I have sworn to thwart him; the Lady Agnes shall never be his bride."

"'Sdeath! then what do you propose—an elopement?"

"Something of the kind; we must bear her to the shores of Bretagne."

"How is this to be effected? Where stays she now?"

"At Whitby."

"Ah! say you so? then by my troth we shall have some work; 'twill be dangerous, but I like it the more for that."

"Be not too rash, good D'Anville; I like your courage, but we must avoid useless danger. The walls of the castle are strong; though 'tis not yet certain whether she stays there or at the abbey."

"In either case we need not fear. I give you my promise to aid you."

"And I will not fail in rewarding you."

"'Tis agreed. I must leave you now; I have an appointment. Farewell."

"Zounds!" muttered Robin half aloud as he watched the departing forms; "by the mass! you will have an appointment you little wot of." So saying, he returned to the board where he had left Little John and Will Scarlett.

Golinbert was there awaiting him; and he beckoned him to follow him when he approached.

Touching a spring, a panel opened like a door; and on passing through, Robin observed a passage leading to the right, and to the left a flight of stone stairs leading upwards and downwards.

The jester having closed the door, led the way upwards, and entered a small room.

"Now thou canst cast thy shell, and don what attire thou mayest choose; here are plenty," said the fool.

Robin threw aside his mail and took a survey of the various articles before him; then, picking up an instrument that lay in the corner, he said—

"Since thou art so fond of trite sayings, I will e'en assume the garb of Triton; see, here is my trident, Master Jester, so fit me up accordingly."

"That will I, to the best of my poor abilities. No one will deem you a forester in such guise."

Robin's toilet was soon complete, and the jester led him out into the grounds.

As they passed along the terraces lined with the gay masqueraders, the outlaw was surprised to see the Moor, Scipio, whom he had seen at Leicester Castle; he was in attendance on the princess, who motioned him to retire as Robin approached, and, taking the arm of Eleanor's head lady-in-waiting, he led her from the spot.

"There sits her highness," said Golinbert, pointing to a female seated on the brink of a marble fountain; "I will leave you now, and return to your followers and try to 'liven them with my merry jests."

Robin approached the princess with a deferential air, and bowed courteously as he stopped before her.

With his thick black beard and uncouth attire, Robin had no fear of detection, and Eleanor was some time ere she could believe the rude figure before her was the bold, handsome outlaw she had seen in the forest.

"I crave pardon for appearing before"—— began Robin, but the princess interrupted him, and bade him dispense with all ceremony.

"Something more than curiosity," she said, "has tempted you to risk so much danger in coming here; were you discovered, the axe or the gibbet would be your portion,

for the fawning servitors that profess so much love for the king would be only too glad to sweep from their path one whose good deeds are so much boasted of as thine."

"I thank thee for thy compliments, and must admit that it was no trifle brought me hither. My Marian, the dearest treasure my heart can know, has been torn from me by some vile caitiff, and I have come hither to seek her."

"Marian," exclaimed the princess; "accursed be the hand that hath culled so fair a flower. Dost think she hath been brought to our court to bloom for a time, and then wither like a crushed rose?"

"Marry! I know not, but I have strong doubts of the king having a finger in this matter."

"Impossible!"

"I would it were so, but my suspicions are well founded. I have almost heard a confession from one reptile's lips, and had I him only in my grasp I would wring a confession from him."

"Who is this you suspect?"

"D'Anville."

"Holy Mother!" said the princess, sighing; "I fear your suspicions are well founded, but I may assist you if you will aid me in return, should I require it."

"Too glad will I be to do aught in my power; but in what way think you you can help me?"

"It matters not so long as I promise you; do not fear I will fail to keep my word; but see you, the eyes of yon crafty Moor is upon us; leave me, and quit the castle as soon and as quietly as possible. Golinbert will instruct you how to act."

Robin glanced sideways to where the Moor stood, and he saw him gazing attentively upon him; so he walked away and darted into the shrubbery, where he relapsed into a kind of dreamy thought.

The voice of the jester aroused him from his reverie, and Golinbert led him by a secret way into the palace, where he changed his attire from that of the fierce Triton to that of a gallant knight.

Robin and the jester remained closeted till a late hour of the night, then Golinbert ordered the horses, and conducted the foresters clear of the palace gates.

CHAPTER CVII.

MAID MARIAN AND THE DISGUISED PAGE.

The passages she ran along
Devoided were of light;
Yet, heedless of the darkness,
She sped with all her might.

IMPRISONED in the lonely tower, Marian, though surrounded with splendour, pined for freedom.

The ruddy glow of health faded from her cheek, her spirits became depressed, and she ofttimes refused to partake of her food.

The aged dame, who served as her companion and jailer, noted this with feverish anxiety, for she knew not how to account to the impetuous king for the strange behaviour of her charge.

She hinted to Marian that if kindness had not the effect of reconciling her to her fate, severer means would be resorted to, and Marian, feeling herself totally helpless and at their mercy, assumed an air of gaiety she did not feel, and affected to be indifferent to her position.

Thrown off her guard by this deception, the old woman became less stringent in her watchfulness, which afforded Marian an opportunity of conversing with the page.

A fine handsome youth to all appearance was the page, but Marian soon saw through the deception: she was a female, and like herself a prisoner, so she could converse freely and commiserate with her.

In the silent hour of night, when the old woman thought Marian slept, she held her stolen interviews with the page, who recounted to her her perils and adventures, the many fruitless attempts she had made to leave the castle, and her utter hopelessness of ever doing so alive.

"Despair not, good sister," Marian would say, in the hope of cheering her. "There may be a time yet when together we shall tread the mazes of the greenwood."

"Nay, do not raise in my breast a hope that is doomed to be crushed. I have a presentiment that I shall never more breathe the air of freedom."

"Hope on, my sister. Since I have been acquainted with thee, I see a ray of hope gleaming in the dark prospects of the future. We may yet find some means to escape from this horrible den."

"Never. You know less of the king than I do; he is base and treacherous, and as remorseless as he is vile."

"I have already learnt that, and therefore place no reliance in him. Have you no friend, no one to whom you could trust a message?"

"None," replied the page, sorrowfully. "And yet I bethink me of one who might serve us," she added, "were it possible to have speech with him."

"Who and what is he?"

"Like myself, a page, but he is never permitted to enter this tower; his duties lay at the farther end of the castle."

"Is it impossible to reach him?" asked Marian, dejectedly.

"I fear so, my lady; to risk it would be risking death. This tower is set aside for purposes that the king hath good cause to keep a secret, therefore it is guarded well; every passage and door hath a sentry, and even the dungeons beneath it have no communication with the others."

"This is in truth, then, an infernal region; and now you have told me so much, I feel I could brave any danger to escape from it. This page I will myself seek, if you direct me."

"Saints forbid you should expose yourself to so much danger! Of a surety I feel it would prove your death. You have not the password, and even if you had, and succeeded in finding the boy, he would not listen to you, for in this place each one holds his fellow as a spy."

"Your words bode little good, but nevertheless they embolden me to try; only point out to me the passages I have to pass through, and I will chance the danger."

"Nay, by the Virgin! thou shalt not!" exclaimed the page, emulated by her words and resolute manner. "My duty shall it be to brave danger, which is lessened by my knowledge of the place. Give me thy message, and if 'tis possible it shall speed safely on its way."

Marian replied with a look of heartfelt gratitude—the heroic devotion of the page deprived her of all speech.

At length she took a relic from the gold chain round her neck, and giving it into the hands of the page, she said—

"Let him hie with this to the forest of Sherwood, place it in the hands of one Robin Hood, and tell him to haste to the rescue of his Marian, who is in danger, and in the power of the king."

"Had we not better forbear mentioning the king?" asked the page, thoughtfully.

"Why?" demanded Marian.

"He may fear the king's power, and thus will not venture an attempt of thy rescue."

"Fear not for that. Let this message but reach him, and we are free; bolts, bars, and even stone walls will not deter him."

"Then I will venture," said the page; "and may the Virgin aid me in my task."

"Hist! Away!" whispered Marian; "here comes the old hag."

Scarcely time to pass out into the passage had the page, when the old woman appeared from an inner room.

There was a frown on her wrinkled visage, and she eyed Marian with distrust.

"To whom were you speaking?" she asked, in a hoarse, croaking voice.

"Marry! I know not that I have spoken to any but yourself; nought have I heard save the wind whistling past the casement," replied Marian, in well-feigned astonishment.

"Thou liest! but, old as I am, I can see through thy deceit. As I sat telling my beads I heard voices in this room, and I feel confident some one must be hidden here."

"Then you had better search and satisfy yourself whether it be true or not," said Marian, with dignity; "beside ourselves, no one is here to my knowledge."

The old woman bit her withered lip, and instituted a strict search, which proved as Marian had said, and the old woman retired, scowling horribly, to her bed.

In the meantime the page repaired to her apartment, armed herself with a long dagger, and sallied forth on her dreary and perilous journey.

At the end of a long stone passage, which

was totally dark, she descended a steep flight of steps and traversed another long passage, at the end of which stood a grim sentinel leaning against a strong iron door.

"Who comes ?" shouted the man-at-arms, placing his hand on his sword ; his quick ear had caught the sound of her footsteps, and he took the pine torch from its niche and glared into the darkness.

"'Tis I, good Hubert," replied the page, who knew the soldier well.

"Ah ! Emelie," cried the soldier, starting ; "what brings ye about disturbing the bats in their midnight gambols? Has aught happened to the lady—the king's new mistress, I mean ?"

"Boddikins ! yes ; she hath been taken sick, and there is no leech in the tower, so Deborah hath sent me with a message to the page of the outer keep, to ride to the abbey and procure the assistance of Father Absalom."

"Body o' mine! why did she not come with you ?"

"She could not leave the sick lady."

"Then I fear I cannot let you pass."

"You must; 'tis a matter of life and death. The king will be angered if aught ill occurs through thy folly," said the page, who was fully prepared for the emergency.

"Troth ! and well do I know it," replied the soldier, shrugging his shoulders ; "if another prisoner escapes I shall need a priest myself ; a dungeon beneath the keep would be my portion, and the rats would soon clear my bones of what little flesh remains on them."

"Escape, Hubert ! Surely you must be dreaming, for 'tis a matter too serious to joke upon. Give me the key, and then you can swear you did not open the door."

"Ah ! neither will I, so hie thee back to Deborah and get the signet ring."

"And by that time the lady's malady will have increased, so much so perhaps as to render her past recovery ; and then, mind you, I will exculpate you from no blame—but there," added the page, "this is the usual reward of kindness ; this is how you repay me for bringing you food and wine when you were confined for sleeping at your post. You would have died had it not been for me, and I should have been hung up by the thumbs had I been discovered."

This reproof struck home to the soldier's heart, and, unable to resist the appeal, he opened the massive door and allowed her to pass on.

"One barrier passed," muttered the page ; "may the blessed Virgin grant me like success throughout my journey," and she crossed herself devoutly as she muttered her feeble prayer.

Keeping her hands outstretched between the walls so as to guide her way, she hurried onward ; but by some means she missed her way, and came full butt against a wall, then rebounding with the shock, she fell sideways down a steep flight of steps, overthrowing some one in her fall.

It was a soldier on guard, and he muttered a fierce oath as he sprang to his feet.

"What, ho ! there —a light," he shouted, in a voice that made the vaulted passage ring ; "quick there, man, or the minion will escape."

Fortunately the page was unhurt, and as soon as she recovered from the shock, and became aware of her mistake, she slipped off her shoes, and, pressing herself closely against the wall, she slid past the man, guided by his voice, and passed within an inch of the point of his sword.

As she slipped round the angle of the wall a red glare burst into the passage in an opposite direction, and a party of armed men rushed into view.

Emilie—such was the name by which the page was known—was partly concealed by the shadow of a buttress, and as the soldier whom she had disturbed in his sleep was guarding the spot where he expected his foe was laid, she had a good opportunity to escape.

Taking advantage of this, as she had some distance to go before coming upon another sentry, she bounded fleetly forward until the end of that passage was reached, and then she stopped to listen.

The boisterous mirth and ribaldry that assailed her ears told her that the men whom the sentry had summoned put no faith in their comrade's words, and believed themselves to be the victims of a hoax ; for they chaffed him pretty freely, and used some very strong expletives.

The page did not stay to hear more, but proceeded with more caution, as the abutments of the masonry obliged her to use great care.

For all this, however, she suffered more than once by striking her shins against the stonework, but at length she reached a large chamber, which served as a chapel.

Before the altar burned a small silver lamp, which served to render the place more gloomy, and made the row of pillars that supported the arched roof look like so many grim spectres.

Emilie took a good survey around.

She knew that the entrance to the chapel, which led into a small courtyard which separated the tower from the keep, was always guarded, and to pass it was one of her greatest dangers.

Creeping stealthily on under shade of the pillars, she suddenly came upon a figure kneeling at his devotions ; it was the guard she so dreaded to meet, and she crept silently past him.

As she crossed the paved yard the moon suddenly peeped forth, and she discovered the warder of the keep giving instructions to one of the men.

"'Tis no matter," she heard him say, as though in argument ; "not a soul is to enter or leave the gates to-night. I have strict orders from the king to this effect ; so heed well my words, and mind you obey them."

Both the men's faces were turned from her, so they could not see her, and she slid behind a buttress to watch and listen.

ROBIN HOOD,

AND THE OUTLAWS OF SHERWOOD FOREST.

THE COTTAGE ON THE HEATH,

"And what of Hal?" demanded the man; "it is no use saying him nay; if he takes a fit in his head to visit the armourer's daughter, there is nought but a tether will keep the hot-headed scapegrace within the walls."

"You have heard my orders; not a soul is to leave or enter, or on thy head be the blame if such does occur. As to Hal, dub the rascal with the flat of thy blade if he dares to go against the order."

The warder strode away, leaving the soldier who had to guard the postern in no pleasant humour; but he tried to hum a tune, and walked leisurely to and fro.

Taking advantage when his back was turned, Emilie crept from buttress to buttress, and at length entered the keep unobserved.

Assured that Hal was not asleep by having seen a light at the loophole of his room, she crept stealthily up to his door and knocked.

"Who comes at this hour?" growled the sleepy page, opening the door. "Ah! by my faith!" he exclaimed, as the light fell on Emilie's face; "you here?—one would think you possessed a thousand lives instead of one, to risk it in this manner."

"The emergency is equal to the risk," replied Emilie, gliding in and closing the door; "but you are sleepy, Hal; have you passed the evening over the armourer's forge?"

"I have but just returned from there, but I should have stayed till to-morrow's sun had not Lockley issued strict orders to the contrary."

"Then I fear you would not venture with a message from me?"

"To whom."

"Robin Hood, the late Earl of Huntingdon."

"For thee I would, as ye granted me a boon I once craved. You remember it, do you not?"

"When I saved the armourer's daughter from the insults of the soldiers on their return from being defeated at the battle of Lewes?"

"Just so; and ever will it be remembered by me. I may say, I am indebted to you not only for her honour, but her life; therefore, I cannot do too much for you in return."

"Then hie thee as speedily as possible with this, and deliver it into the hands of Robin Hood—you will find him either at Barnesdale or Sherwood—and tell him his Marian is a prisoner in this castle."

"Saint Dunstan! I have made my promise rashly. I shall run a double risk of losing my life, if the outlaws do not spit me on a cloth-yard shaft. I shall be imprisoned, if not hanged, on my return for being so long absent."

"Zounds! do not go if thou art a coward," said Emilie, in disdain.

"I must; Hal breaks not his word with friend or foe. Trust the missive to me; I will be answerable for its success."

With this they parted; Hal to prepare himself for the journey, and Emilie to make her way back—a task unavoidably full of danger.

She crossed the courtyard and passed through the chapel, however, free from observation, but she feared it would not be so easy to pass the sentinel whom she had knocked down on the stairs.

She was right.

The fellow had learnt to use more caution, and he paced with heavy tread the gloomy passage, which was now lighted by a glimmering lamp.

When his face was towards the page, she could see that he was angered, for his brow was knitted, and his dark eyes flashed with a revengeful light.

As she approached him, keeping under the shadow that had before assisted her, she could hear him heaping the bitterest oaths on the heads of his companions, who vowed that he had been frightened by the shadow of an owl or the wings of a bat, many of which, startled by the glare of the torch, flapped lazily about, and then with a dismal croaking noise disappeared in the holes in the roof.

Pass him she must; and nerving herself for the occasion, she waited till the soldier turned to walk away from her, and then, fleet as a deer, she bounded towards the steps.

Alas! with all her care, she was doomed to misfortune; her toe caught one of the steps, and threw her violently on her knees.

The man-at-arms leapt round as the sound startled him.

His sword leapt from its sheath and clashed on the stones as Emilie with desperation got to her feet and bounded up the stairs.

"By my halidame, I will not this time be foiled," muttered the soldier, fiercely. "A malison on the knave! he flies like the wind; but he cannot go far, and when I catch him I'll prick him for his pains."

On through the darkness flew the pursuer and pursued, and Emilie had near gained the post of Hubert, when she stumbled; and the soldier, who was close upon her, falling over her as she fell, buried his sword deep in her side.

Emilie gave a stifled cry, and then became insensible, her head having come in contact with the flags.

The noise caused by this and the clatter of the soldier's mail aroused Hubert, who, snatching his torch from the wall, opened the door and rushed to the spot.

A deathly pallor came over him on seeing the condition of the page, and he repented bitterly his folly in allowing her to pass.

"So-ho! what means all this?" demanded Hubert, as soon as he could speak. "Rise, comrade, and let us see if the lad is much hurt."

"A thousand curses on him! I hope I have settled him," growled the man-at-arms as he rose to his feet. "He nigh broke my neck an hour since, and now, I fear, he has quite broken my leg."

"You can stand on it, at all events," replied Hubert. "But see, the boy bleeds. Fool you must have been to wound him!"

"Neither man nor devil do I allow to play pranks with me when on duty," said the soldier, raising the page in his brawny arms. "Saint Dunstan! 'tis the king's page. Well, I owe him a grudge."

"What for?"

"No matter; 'tis well that I remember it. He thought himself a big man, no doubt, when he struck me for kissing the amourer's daughter."

"Is that the only spite you owe him?"

"Ay—and enough, is it not?"

"To my fancy, no—which I am certain is contrary to your opinion," said Hubert, glancing maliciously at his fellow-soldier.

"That matters not, I tell ye; 'tis time now for me to be avenged. What ho, there!—the guard! Aha! now will my revenge be satisfied."

He laughed a hollow, fiendish laugh as the thought occurred to him, and he fixed his satanic glance on the page's pale features.

"A malison on the whole of his Saxon race," continued the soldier, malignantly, as the footsteps of the guard were heard hurrying towards them. "I am of true Norman blood, and never will I forgive an insult from the hands of a Saxon cur."

"How know you he is a Saxon?" cried Hubert, waxing wroth. "He may be a countryman of mine; but no matter for that —he is true and steadfast in his friendship."

"Hallo! what have we here? Found the goblin at last? Ho! ho! Gainsay it who can, when I aver this is a night of adventures."

"So I should say," growled Hubert, with a huskiness in his tone; "such a night of adventures as you will have reason to remember."

Hubert had stanched the blood, and though he could not leave his post, he followed them as far as his eye could reach as they bore the apparently lifeless form of the page to the guard-room.

CHAPTER CVIII.

IN THE DUNGEON OF THE KEEP.

Upon the pallet she did lay,
　Her fair brow bathed in dew
In Marian she found a friend
　With heart both kind and true.

In one of the lowest dungeons of the fortress, far removed from the haunts of man, lay the lovely page, a prisoner, doomed to suffer the most horrible of deaths.

Added to the dank, fœtid smells that arose from the wet, slimy floor, and oozed from the dripping walls, was the horrid fact that the place was literally swarming with noxious, slimy reptiles—such as toads, worms, and other loathsome creeping things, that gave forth a fearful hissing sound, and added to the slow "drip, drip" of the water as it fell from the roof and formed in puddles on the floor.

As she rolled in agony upon her hard couch, and tried to pierce the inky darkness, a thrill of horror shot through her frame, for at her feet she fancied she could see a small spot of light, not much larger than the top of her finger.

"What can it be?" she wondered, as her dim eyes remained fixed upon it. "Is it a token of good or evil? Has this anything to do with my fate?"

"Methinks it is," she muttered. "Ah, 'tis gone!" And her heart sank within her as the bright spot disappeared, and all was again blackness. "It is, then, an omen of evil. Thus shall I perish, and my memory become void. Thank the Virgin, I have sent the message, and Marian may be saved, though I am lost; for no earthly being would venture into this horrid place, even were the fortress razed to the ground."

Thus mused the page, and murmured a fervent prayer, when the bright spot again met her eye.

Then a footstep caught her ear, and she heard a sound as of the drawing of a rusty bolt.

Presently the door opened, and a flood of light, that dazzled her eyes so much that she could not see, burst into the gloomy cell.

"Holy Mother! has the wretch a heart hard enough to assign one so fair and noble to such a fate as this?" said a voice. "Open thine eyes, good Emilie, and assure me that the noisome vapours have not wrought upon you their deadly effects."

Emilie opened her eyes on recognising the voice of Marian, and gazed in superstitious awe on the features of the speaker.

"Is it true, or do mine eyes deceive me?" asked the wounded page. "Art thou in the flesh, or is this some trick of the crafty monks whom I have often seen practising their deceitful arts?"

"Fear not; I am your friend, and have come to save you," said Marian. "'Twas through me you incurred the governor's anger by breaking his stringent laws, and now I will not desert thee in the hour of need."

"Thanks!—a thousand thanks!" murmured the feeble girl. "I see it all now; it was the light of your lamp I saw shining through the door. But how came you to find me, or even know of the place of my confinement?"

"I heard from Deborah that you were discovered and wounded, and that you were suspected of planning my escape; and scarce an hour since she told me you were to be imprisoned alive and starved to death."

"Deborah told you of this?"

"Ay; and it gave her much pleasure; and I vowed within myself that I would release you if you still lived, or perish in the attempt."

"But she will miss you, and then we both shall be lost," said Emilie, in alarm.

" Let not that trouble thee. I found a drug among the bottles of medicine that would bring on sleep without any injurious effects. I poured some in her wine, and she is now like one dead."

" Saints be praised! Yet I see not how ye can aid me. I am so weak, I cannot stand; and when I move, my wound bleeds afresh."

" I have come fully prepared for that. A soldier named Hubert, who puts himself forward as thy friend, accompanied me hither, or I should not have found you; he stands in the passage without, and will carry thee if need be."

" Thanks, dear lady; let him enter at once, for I feel that if I stay longer in this place I shall die without even the aid of a confessor. Already has the cold hand of death fallen upon me, and "——

She swooned; and Marian, alarmed, summoned the soldier, who placed a flask of wine, which he purposely brought with him, to Emilie's lips.

This revived her greatly, and restored her to consciousness, so that after a while she was able to be removed.

Taking her fair form in his brawny arms, the soldier gazed upon the pale but lovely features, and a suspicion of the truth flashed vividly to his mind.

" Quotha!" he muttered to himself, "such features Eleanor herself might envy; oft have I thought the page was not a boy, and now, on close inspection, that thought is strengthened."

He made no further remark, but left the dungeon followed by Marian, who bolted the door behind them.

Hubert led the way through several passages, and up a steep flight of steps that brought them into the armoury; then resting the page on the floor, he walked up to a suit of mail that seemed like a sentry among the others, and touching a spring it moved, and disclosed a door.

This also opened by a spring, and the soldier made a sign for Marian to approach it with the light.

She did so, and beheld a long gloomy passage, similar in shape to those she had traversed, but dry and hung about with cobwebs.

" Once through here," whispered the soldier, "we are safe. Few if any besides myself know of this place; here Emilie will be safe, and my wife and yourself can tend *him*."

He laid peculiar stress upon the last word, but Marian was too agitated to notice it; she knew if the page was missed from the dungeon, or herself found absent from the room, that an alarm would be given, and the castle searched.

Having resumed his burden, the soldier again led the way; and to the surprise of Marian he brought her to a small but neatly furnished room; it was like a cave in appearance, and though gloomy on first entering, a few moments' survey assured her it was a palace compared to the dungeon they had just left.

The page had lain like one dead during the passage hither, but now she began to revive; her wound was much easier; and Marian gave her another draught of wine to sleep her.

" Now rest thee and make thyself easy," said the rough but honest soldier; "we must leave you; but my wife, who is a kind soul, will soon attend you."

" Heaven reward you for this kindness, Hubert; 'tis more than I dared to expect from you; but if it ever lays in my power to render you a service, you may rely upon—— Ah! what is that?"

" The alarm-bell!" replied the soldier.

" Then away!" cried the page; "quick or you will be lost! and both of you will suffer for the kindness you have done."

The bell still continued to toll, and each moment seemed to grow louder, which caused the soldier some uneasiness.

" You must leave the light," he said to Marian, "we must travel in the dark; but fear not to trust yourself with me; I meant to have pointed out the way to you on our return, but now we shall have hard work to get back unseen."

Marian placed the light in a nook, and laid the refreshments Hubert had brought within Emilia's reach, then put herself under the soldier's guidance.

On reaching the armoury, Marian noticed, although it was dark, that they did not leave it by the way they had first entered; but as Hubert had forbidden her to speak, she made no comment, but followed him with one hand grasping his sword-belt to guide her.

" Ah! heard you that?" whispered Hubert, stopping suddenly short; "the guard is out, we must be cautious in our movements."

The sound of voices and heavy footsteps that had startled the soldier's quick ears now became audible to Marian, and she trembled lest they might be discovered.

It was not of herself she thought so much, for she had fully made up her mind to risk her life in the attempt to escape, but she feared for the safety of her guide, whose life would assuredly be forfeited if he was found in her company; and then the page must either die of her wound or suffer a lingering death of starvation.

Nearer and nearer the sounds approached, and Marian fancied she could hear Hubert's name mentioned.

" Had we not better return?" she asked of Hubert, in a whisper. "I fear me, I have got you into sore trouble."

" Hist! all depends on our silence. It is most likely they will not seek us here, they are in a passage that runs parallel to this, and only divided by a few oak slabs; this passage is seldom used, and then only by the monks, when they visit the vaults, which is not often."

"To the vaults, did you say?" whispered Marian, in alarm.

"Ay, but I did wrong in telling thee; 'tis a subject ill-fitted to a lady's ears, but situated as we are at present, we must not be too particular. I hear Olinbert's voice, and he is a cruel tyrant; from him we need expect no pity."

Marian shuddered, but recovering herself, she was about to make some reply, when Hubert clutched her by the arm and drew her to him; at the same moment the red glare of a torch lighted the passage, and a party of armed men hastened towards where they stood.

CHAPTER CIX.

THE KING'S FETE.

"Come hither, Tepus," said the king,
"Bow-bearer, after me;
Measure me out with this line
How long our mark must be."

ROBIN HOOD did not leave London at once, as Eleanor had supposed he would do. The thought of his Marian made him ripe for any daring adventure.

Disguised, he and his followers, day after day, visited the archery practice, and there he learnt by chance that the king had sent a messenger to Sherwood, with an invitation to himself to attend a grand joust and tournament.

"Ha! ha! he shall find me there to time," laughed the bold outlaw; "but I wot me, Henry has some meaning for this condescension. I must be wary, and this job may turn out a good one."

It was on a Wednesday the tournament was held, and a goodly number of knights and nobles attended it. A grand stand was fitted up for the ladies, and Robin observed that both the queen and the princess were present.

Robin rode on a splendid charger, and was clad from head to heel in a suit of burnished mail. He kept his visor closed, and save his fiery charger and costly suit of mail, he was only distinguished from the rest of the knights by a small green plume.

This fluttered gracefully in the wind, and made him distinguishable to his followers from the rest who entered the lists for the tournament.

Robin took no part in the sham battle, but took up a position where he could get a good view of it, and he soon found that he caused some sensation amongst the spectators, who wondered whom he could be, as he entered his name as the Forlorn Knight.

When the joust was ended the tournament commenced, and Robin selected for his opponent D'Anville, whom he recognised by his crest.

At the first tilt, the duke's lance was shivered against Robin's mail, and D'Anville fell from his horse badly wounded.

In the next bout Robin was again success-ful, and before one half-hour had elapsed he had unhorsed five of the knights without himself receiving a scratch.

Loud were the acclamations in favour of the unknown but valorous knight, and Edward himself, who was fond of the sport, and envied the showers of applause heaped upon Robin, took up the victor's gauntlet, which Robin had thrown down as a challenge open to all.

Edward was of noble figure, and rode his horse majestically, and those who were acquainted with his deeds of valour withdrew their smiles from Robin, who, they felt certain, would this time be robbed of his laurels.

Robin Hood, however, did not allow this to daunt him.

His quick eye took in the gigantic proportions of both horse and rider, and he calculated at once the odds that were against him.

Fixing himself in his saddle, and firmly grasping his lance, he met the prince's heavy charge with a firmness that drew a shout of applause from the spectators.

Every one had been watching in breathless expectation to see both horse and rider borne down by Edward's massive steed, but Robin disappointed them. He turned aside the deadly lance as he would a reed, and the prince's horse staggered back on its haunches, as the breast-plate of Robin's horse struck it full in the breast.

No shout followed this.

Save the gasping of the wounded steed, that had received its death-blow, all was hushed into silence.

All eyes were mechanically turned on the princess, who sat pale and rigid as a statue, but allowed no sound to escape her.

"Gramercy! 'tis well you are not hurt!" said Robin, as the prince, by the aid of several nobles, who had flown at once to his assistance, was raised to his feet. "'Fore heaven I swear I will tilt with you no more."

"By our lady! thou art a sturdy knight, whoever thou may be, and well hast thou earned the prize. I would fain crave of thee a boon if I thought thou wouldst grant it," said the prince.

"I must first hear it before I promise," was Robin Hood's reply.

"Raise thy visor, and let us look upon the face of one so stout of arm. Marry! the king hath just cause to be proud of so staunch a follower."

"That boon I cannot grant," replied Robin. "I am under a vow, and dare not break it."

"In that case I will not press thee, though I feel sorely disappointed. See—the queen beckons thee, so attend her at once."

Robin took the hint, and rode up to the royal box, where the queen waited to bestow the prize.

It was a silver dagger with a gold hilt set in diamonds, and she delivered it to him with fitting address.

To reach it, Robin had to go near the princess, and, as their eyes met, she recognised him in spite of his disguise.

"I will make sure," she thought; "I may be mistaken, though 'tis like his rashness. By his voice, I would tell him from a thousand."

"Brave knight," she said; "though we have not the pleasure of seeing thy face, we commend thee for thy skill, and congratulate ye on your success. 'Tis a prize worthy of one so chivalrous, and I hope its blade may be as true as steel when used against the king's enemies."

"Gracious and most noble princess," Robin replied, "your words shall be ever cherished in my memory. I hope you will pardon my rudeness in wearing my visor closed in the august presence of yourself and our gracious queen. I am in mourning for the loss of my lady love, and am under a vow to hide my face for a number of days"——

"Name it not," said the princess, who saw that the queen's eyes were upon her, and feared lest an unconscious word might escape her own lips or those of the outlaw. "See—the sports have again commenced."

Robin glanced around, and saw two men ready to play at quarter staves, and one of them he recognised as Little John, though he was not attired as a forester.

The man with whom Little John was matched was of gigantic proportions like himself, though clumsier built, but, to look at, possessed of superior strength.

He was no mean player either, and dealt his blows so vigorously that Little John, with all his tact, had a hard matter to save his crown.

Little John had a stout oak bough which he had brought with him from the woods, and this was often splintered in fending off the blows that made the air ring again, and brought forth the shouts of the spectators.

For full ten minutes Little John only acted on the defensive; but when that period had elapsed he found his man was losing breath, and the forester began in right good earnest.

Three successive blows, head, leg, and arm, he dealt upon his adversary, who, had it not been for shame, would have roared with the pain, for the blood, trickling from the man's head, told how deftly Little John had dealt his blows.

It was now the man's turn to defend himself—a task which he found impossible, for Little John kept him dancing round with an incessant muttering of curses.

"Yield thee!" cried the forester, whose arm began to tire of hitting, "or I will give thee such a blow as will take thee a full month to recover."

"When one of us is beaten I will give in, and not till then," was the sullen reply. "I will yet give thee a drubbing."

"Have at thee then, and learn thy folly!" cried Little John, as, whirling his staff sharply round, he brought it down with

terrific force on the man's head, and stretched him bleeding and senseless on the sward.

No sooner was the man down than his place was filled by another of about the same size and sinew; he was a blacksmith, and had on his apron, and had his sleeves rolled up to the elbow, displaying a muscle better fitting to an ox.

"I will have a bout with thee when thou art at leisure," he said, in a bullying tone.

"Nought will so pleasure me. I am ready; let us at it at once. Say whether thou wouldst choose a broken leg or a cracked pate?"

"Both, if you can accommodate me," was the blacksmith's reply; "but, I trow me, thou wilt be a little deceived, for no man hath been able to tan my hide for the last five years past."

"Then I will promise to do it for you in less than five minutes," said Little John, "so make thyself ready for a sound beating."

The blacksmith laughed, and stood his ground with a look of defiance; but the first bout brought him to his senses, and before the time Little John had named had expired, he was stretched helpless on the grass.

It was Will Scarlett's turn now, and he gave a specimen of some excellent play, and soundly basted the hides of those who were bold enough to face him.

One of these chanced to be Maulac, and after receiving his dressing with a good grace, he shook hands with Will, and vowed he would stand his friend.

Several others also tried their skill, and then, as the time was fleeting rapidly, quarter staff was dropped, and the bowmen took their places at the butts.

In the meantime Robin had changed his suit, and appeared in his suit of Lincoln Green as did John and Will Scarlett, the rest of the foresters retaining their disguise as citizens, mingling with the throng.

The king's best archers had been chosen for the occasion—the pick of the Kentish bowmen. Each man, tall in stature and strong of limb, armed with a good yew bow and a quiver of arrows within an inch of the length of those used by Robin Hood and his followers.

The Kentish bowmen deemed themselves proficient in the skill of archery, and boasted that no one could draw an arrow to the head with any of them, for their arrows were of a clothyard long, though not according to the measurement of the forester of Sherwood.

The butts were already fixed, and the distance was soon measured off, and then some admirable skill was displayed by the men of Kent.

"By the wars!" said the king to Eleanor, as an arrow struck the plug in the centre of one of the butts, and carried it out the other side; "'twas a strong arm fired that. By my halidame! it pleaseth me to see such fellows round us. I trow there is not such to be found throughout the land."

"One would think so; but I have heard

the foresters of Sherwood are much better skilled."

" 'Tis but hearsay," replied the king, trying to conceal his anger; " but your words remind me of a remark I just now heard. It was something alluding to a party of foresters having been seen hereabouts."

" I would that Robin Hood was amongst them," said Eleanor. " I have heard so much of his fame that it would do our eyes good to see him."

" And so you shall, for I see him now," said the king, pointing to a distant group. " By Jove! they are holding a dispute about the shots."

Eleanor did much like the manner and look of the king.

The way in which he made mention of Robin Hood, made her suspect it boded the forester no good.

Following him with her eyes, as he walked away, she saw him approach one of the knights, and whisper in his ear.

" Holy mother protect him from harm !" she muttered. " He hath acted rashly in coming here; but outlaw though he be, I would not like to see him come to harm."

" And whom may it be, pray, that makes you so interested in his fate ?" asked the queen.

She had been absent for a few moments, and Marian had not noticed her return, thus enabling her to overhear her mutterings.

Marian started at the sound of the queen's voice.

" He of whom I speak," she replied, " is one richly deserving of my favour—a bold archer, whose equal I never yet beheld."

" Keep us no longer in ignorance of his name then. Marry ! 'tis strange the king did not acquaint me of this."

" Perchance he has some motive for keeping it secret. Have you made a wager with him ?"

" Indeed I have, and a good one ; so if this archer be of such skill, I would fain enter him in my lists against the king."

" If you do you may depend upon success. See you yon handsome fellow clothed in Lincoln green ?"

" Ay, I took him for a king's archer. He is a forest-keeper, I suppose ?"

" You may call him as such, but he considers himself Lord of Sherwood."

" Ah ! is it, then, Robin Hood ?"

" It is. Have you seen him before ?"

" No ; but I heard he was invited. We will speak with him. I have heard of his doings with the bow, but I credit not such stories."

" I commend your majesty's wisdom, but I assure you, when once you have seen Robin Hood send a shaft, you will have no further doubt of his skill. Ah ! heard you that ?"

The twang of a bowstring struck on their ears, and they saw Robin standing at the mark. He had just discharged an arrow.

" 'Twas no weakling that sent that shaft !" exclaimed the queen. " A dozen such, and I might stand good for the king's wager ; but we waste time ; let us set about it at once."

Eleanor called to her page, and bade him tell Robin to attend her at his leisure.

Robin did so as soon as he could excuse himself from the butts, and the queen made an agreement with him.

After the first prizes were won—all of which were carried off by Robin's men in disguise—the grand shooting commenced.

As the queen had remarked, the stake was a heavy one—three hundred tuns of beer for the soldiers, a supply of wine for the knights and nobles, and a present for the archers who might win.

Tepus, the king's bow-bearer, measured the distance, and the archers who were to compete on both sides were brought forward.

At the first set off, the shooting went in favour of the king, and many of the ladies began to despair that the queen would lose.

She, however, appeared not the least troubled, and when the king made some allusion to the sport, she merely remarked that it was in jest.

" Jesting or not," said the king, " the game is hard against thee ; as yet, thou hast not one mark."

" Marry, I care not. I dare bet you one hundred marks the game will yet be mine."

The king smiled, and walked away.

To do him justice, he did not know Robin had taken part with the queen ; the bold outlaw had disappeared suddenly from the scene, and now he stood by, clad in scarlet instead of green, so that the king did not recognise him.

" Now, Sir Richard," said the queen, addressing a knight who stood by, noting well all that passed, " you are given to sport. What will you bet that my archers lose ?"

" Saints forbid I should be so discourteous as to bet against thee," replied the knight. " Here is our worthy bishop ; he is a man of spirit, and perchance hath more at present than I to bet. What say you, father ?"

" By the rood ! not one penny will I bet against her majesty. Did she require spiritual comfort, I would freely give it ; or did any but the queen challenge me, I would wager with them."

" Zounds ! I will take ye !" cried Robin, stepping forward.

" And my money !" retorted the priest.

" If I win, which at the present seems doubtful ; the king hath his own chosen men, and here are we strangers every one. Boddikins ! not yet have we made so much as a mark."

" I will bet thee," said the bishop, meditatively, " even to the last penny in my purse."

" How much in all ?" asked Robin.

" Fifteen score nobles."

" Near an hundred pound," muttered Robin ; then added aloud, " Agreed, good priest ; here is my bag ; let it lay with thine on the sward."

Will Scarlett and Little John, who had

been listening, exchanged a sly glance with each other.

"Body o' mine! it does one's eyes good to see a priest so easily taken in. Quotha! the Bishop of Hereford is not so close as St. Mary's abbot."

Little John whispered this in Will's ear as they walked to the butts, where the shooting had again commenced.

At this juncture things took a turn in favour of the queen.

Little John and Will brought the marks even, and Robin, with affected carelessness, settled the bet.

Scarce deigning to look at the wand he let fly and cleft in twain, which so took the king by surprise that he would not have it fair.

"Have an eye to him," he muttered to the knight he had before spoken to; "I will swear he is no other than Robin Hood. Let him shoot again, and I shall know him."

"An' I opine rightly, the bet is fairly won," said Robin, angered at the king's imputation; "but, if it be needed, I will try again. Pick ye your best bowman, and I will let him choose his own mark."

"And I will beat ye!" interposed a rude, blustering fellow, pushing to the front. "What say you to another score?"

"Two, if need be," replied Robin.

"One will more than cure thee of thy bragging," replied the man. "Tepus, measure us another score."

Tepus measured the score, and the braggart bowman let fly at the butt, but came not near the wand.

Robin smiled.

"Tepus," he said, "an' it be not too much trouble, put thy line to another score; I cannot shoot at so short a distance."

The archer gave a bitter smile.

Robin's derisive tone stung him to the quick; but a certain amount of confidence in himself, and a feeling almost amounting to certainty that Robin would lose, buoyed him up.

The bold outlaw turned his face from the butt, and walked the other twenty paces Tepus had measured, and then, turning round without seeming to take aim, he let fly.

A loud whizz was heard as the gray goose-quill cleft the air, and then a cry was raised by the breathless bystanders.

"'Tis hit! 'tis hit! the queen hath won!"

The king watched Robin, and he saw by his manner of drawing the bow that it was he, and said so in the hearing of the bishop.

The holy man then became wrath.

"Had I known it to be that robber, I would not have bet one penny," he said. "He robbed me one night on the way to our good brother the abbot. He promised he would pay me again, but not one penny have I seen."

"Ay, and thou didst say mass to my merry men," said Robin, laughing heartily. "Well, for that I will fain return thee half of thy gold again."

"Nay, nay," said Little John. "We are strangers; but as we had a share in the work, let us have a share of the money. What say you, Master Loath of Speech?" he added to Will Scarlett.

"I hold with thee," was the reply, and Robin Hood did according to their wish.

CHAPTER CX.

AN AWKWARD PREDICAMENT.

The soldier's wife was jealous,
    Of that there was no doubt;
For she said unto Hubert—
    "Now I have found you out."

MAID MARIAN felt in the folds of her robe for her dagger when she saw the men approaching her, and she made up her mind to resist being taken, even if it resulted in her death.

Hubert had drawn her into a small nook, and tried to shield her as much as possible with his own body in the hope of shielding her light dress from the glare of the torch-light.

In doing this he forgot that he was exposing his own breast-plate and iron helmet, which was more dangerous by far, but a shout from one of the soldiers apprised him of the fact when too late.

"On, lads! quick!" shouted the warder, who was foremost of them all. "A sound flogging ye shall have if they escape us now."

The soldiers made a rush, but the warder in his hurry stumbled, the torch fell from his hand, and the whole party fell upon him, putting out the light, and leaving them all in darkness.

There was a succession of oaths as the soldiers scrambled to their feet, and the warder, grumbling to himself, had to scramble about for his keys.

In the meantime Hubert was not idle.

The momentary glare of the torch had showed him a door, which he knew existed thereabouts, but which it would have been impossible for him to find in the dark.

As soon as all was darkness he crept towards it, thrust it open, and passed through, leading Marian after him.

They were now in a long corridor, studded here and there with loop-holes, that afforded them a glimmer sufficient to enable them to see their way.

"Haste, lady," said the soldier; "there is a door at the end of this passage that leads to the ramparts. If we gain it before those fellows get a light, we may yet reach our rooms in safety. If not, we must seek safety in one of these cells, and trust to the strength of bars and bolts, which will not be much to depend upon, as they are rusted with age."

"What place is this?" asked Marian, with a shudder, as she observed that the walls on either side were studded with small iron doors.

"It was once the abode of monks and

ROBIN HOOD,

AND THE OUTLAWS OF SHERWOOD FOREST.

THE NORMAN SPY.

friars, and these doors you see lead to the cells beneath our feet. It is now the haunt of rats and poisonous reptiles, and the receptacle of bones of human skeletons."

It was a relief to the poor girl when the passage was traversed, but her troubles was not yet over. The door leading to the ramparts was guarded by a stout man-at-arms.

His measured tread was audible to Marian and her guide long before they reached the outlet, which was a low arch, guarded by a strong door.

"A malison on it ! 'tis locked," muttered Hubert ; "ah ! and guarded by David the Black. Body o' me ! this is unfortunate."

"Is this the only outlet ?" asked Marian, alarmed at the manner of his speech.

"The only one I know of," Hubert replied ; "the door I could soon force, but it would alarm the fellow outside."

"Could you bribe him, think you ?"

"Ay, with a foot of steel, could I reach him," said Hubert, with a bitter smile ; "he is the most treacherous knave in the whole stronghold—none like him, yet all fear him, for he seems to hold the lives of us all in his hands. For myself I have no fear of him, but to betray you would be his greatest pleasure."

"Then fly and leave me ; 'tis better for me to perish than to jeopardize the lives of us both ; see to your own safety ; you have a wife depending on you."

"And have you no one to mourn your loss ?" asked the warm-hearted soldier.

"Indeed I have," replied Marian, with a sigh.

"Then I will not leave you to a fate so terrible, for if you escaped the searchers you would only wander about these dismal passages and vaults until hunger preyed upon you, and starvation and misery resulted in your death. No, no," he added, with vehemence ; "I will not leave you, I will take my chance with you whatever it be."

"Death then to thee both !" cried a voice ; the door was dashed open, and David the Black stood like a demoniac statue in the opening.

As his tall form stood up in bold relief between them and the gray sky beyond, he looked like some giant risen from the pit of darkness ; his eyes seemed to flash in the gloom, and his sword gleamed in the uncertain light.

"Ha ! ha !" he laughed, as he viciously glared at the form of Marian ; "'tis a glorious sight to see the king's mistress in company of a common soldier, in such a spot, and at such an hour. Zounds ! this discovery will be a good feather in my cap."

"A thorn in your heart," cried Hubert, sternly ; "it will impose upon me the task of ridding the world of such a wretch as you."

"Softly with thy words," hissed David ; "the alarm-bell has been sounded, and if I put an end to ye on the spot I should be fully justified in so doing."

"You will first have to do it," said Hubert, clutching his sword ; "make way and let us pass, or I will open the breach which your carcase has filled up."

"A true soldier never leaves his post," was the taunting reply. "David was never yet known to flinch from his duty. Ha ! ha ! 'tis not likely he will do so now."

Hubert waited to hear no more.

He drew his weapon, and, reckless of the consequences, closed with the taunter.

Marian trembled when the blades met with a crash, for she feared the noise would bring the soldiers to the spot.

It was this fear that caused Hubert to hold his hand so long ; but, now he had commenced, he set-to in good earnest.

"Yield thee, caitiff !" cried David, on finding himself hard pressed ; "yield, and I'll grant thee a boon."

"Thyself will most need it," replied Hubert, laying on more fiercely ; "my blade is ever ready to drink a tyrant's blood."

These words angered David ; and, seeing that nought but hard fighting could avail him, he set-to with all his vigour.

Hubert was bleeding from a wound in the shoulder ; which rendered him weak, and necessitated him bringing the fight to as speedy a termination as possible.

David had backed him into a corner where he could scarce use his sword ; and, seeing the danger of his position, Hubert made a lunge forward and sent his sword with such violence into the giant's chest, as to force the point out at his back.

"Out on thee for a fiend !" gasped the giant, as he staggered to the wall, then fell his length on the stone floor ; "the evil one has aided thee in this. Curse you—a thousand curses on you !"

These were his last words.

He fixed his glittering eyes with a savage gleam on his conqueror, then rolled over dead.

"One barrier removed," muttered Hubert ; "but he will be missed, and if the relief come and find his dead body here I shall be suspected more than ever."

"And punished, of course, though it was in fair fight."

"Punished, ay, tortured in a manner less preferable than a thousand deaths ; he is the favourite minion of the governor of the Tower, and his loss will deeply affect him ; I must bury him, and then fly these walls for ever."

"Bury him where ?" asked Marian, glancing meaningly at the flags.

"In the moat. I know the steps leading to the water-gate ; there is usually a boat moored there ; if we reach it in safety we may escape."

"It would be worth the venture even should we fail," said Marian, shivering, for the chill morning air began to tell upon her.

Hubert stood for a moment gazing on the stark features of the dead soldier, wondering in his mind whether it be best to carry the body with him or let it remain.

To carry it away and throw it into the moat seemed to him the safest ; so, throwing off the unpleasant feeling his disagreeable task created, he raised the body in his arms, and hurried along the ramparts.

Marian followed him with palpitating heart, for she could see the dark forms of the sentinels above them, and she feared they might detect their movements.

What added to her alarm was the fact that

one of them had stopped, and was leaning over the battlements just above where they had to pass.

Fortunately her fears were unfounded.

The man, wearied with watching, had leant on the battlement to rest himself, and had fallen asleep—a circumstance that Hubert pointed out as soon as Marian hinted her fears to him.

"It is fortunate for us he sleeps," said Hubert, stopping before a grated door. "This is the water-gate; 'tis not locked, you see, so I will descend while you keep watch. Should any one come, tap three times with your heel on this stone."

The door seemed to have been unused for years, and the steps that led down to the moat was thickly matted with slime and grass.

Hubert had to descend with care for fear of slipping, his danger being heightened by the extra weight of the dead body.

On reaching the stone platform at the bottom, he looked around for the boat, but it was gone. It had probably drifted away and sunk, for a portion of the rope that had held it was still fastened to the iron ring in the wall.

Vexed at this discovery—for Hubert had intended to leave the castle had the boat been there, and send a message to his wife; but now it was impossible to do so.

Carefully dropping the body into the inky water so as to make no noise, Hubert looked around to see if any prying eye was watching him; he could see none, so he returned to Marian.

"Not the least chance of escape have we now," he said to Marian, who saw despair marked in his very looks. "We must trust to Providence to aid us."

"Marry! it will not do to give it up so easily," replied Marian. "Can we not return to the page, and hide ourselves for a time?"

"We can," replied the soldier; "but how long can we live without food."

"I thought not of that; and as I can suggest nothing to remedy our condition, I will leave everything entirely to you."

Hubert stood in the shade of the buttress, under which they had taken shelter for some moments, with his eyes bent meditatively on the ground.

The sound of a footstep startled him.

His hand flew like lightning to his sword, and his eyes glared viciously round.

"Stand back for your life, good lady!" he said to Marian; "we are watched. See you yon figure crouching along the wall; it is a spy; but he shall dearly pay for his meddling."

As the figure drew closer, Hubert clutched his sword, and held it ready to deal a fatal blow.

"Put back thy weapon, it is not needed," cried a voice, the silvery cadence of which made Marian start, and Hubert to spring forward, exclaiming—

"My wife! by the saints! How came you here, Rebecca?"

"Fear for your safety," she replied; and as she threw off her disguise, and caught sight of Marian, she, in her turn, also started.

"Hubert," she said, her dark eyes flashing with jealousy, "how is it I find you in company with this lady? Thrice hath the captain of the guard been to ask for you, and here you are flirting with—with "——

She could say no more. Her feelings choked her utterance, and a flood of tears came to her relief.

"Peace, woman!—calm yourself!" said the soldier, deeply affected by the scene. "Let us quit the sight of prying eyes, and then I will explain."

"It needs no explanation. It answers of itself. Ah, me! glad would I have been to have remained in ignorance."

She burst into a fresh flood of tears, and sobbed bitterly.

Marian, as soon as she was able to speak, tried to sooth her; but the woman was too deeply afflicted to hearken to her.

Hubert then tried to bring her to a true understanding of the case; but she was deaf to all reason, and hysterically laughed and cried by turns.

The few moments she remained in this delirium seemed an age to the soldier, for he loved his wife, and her accusation of infidelity cut him to the quick.

"Rebecca," he said, when she so far recovered as to listen to him, "I swear on the honour of a soldier that I have not wronged you. This lady is a prisoner in the tower. In aiding her, or, rather in serving the page you hold in such high estimation, I have brought trouble on us all. I have been missed, and "——

"Hist! 'Tis enough!" exclaimed Rebecca, drying her tears. "I knew they were searching for you, though for what purpose I could not tell, and, fearing some harm had befallen you, I muffled myself, and had been searching a full hour before Providence led me hither."

"Were you seen coming hither?" asked Hubert, anxiously.

"No."

"Then we may venture to our room without fear."

"Yes, by the skeleton staircase."

The skeleton staircase was sufficient in name to inspire a female with dread, but in appearance it was more so.

The oldest part of the tower had in former days served as a monastery, and the room now occupied by Hubert and his wife had been what the abbot called a penance chamber.

It was in the highest part of the building, and was reached from below by a ladder, supposed to have been formed from the bones of departed saints.

Up the centre of the wall tall trees had been placed endways on each other until they reached the top, and into this one end of the bone was fastened, the other end being fixed in the wall, and forming a kind of circular staircase or ladder.

Up this the monks barefooted had to wend their way, and to scourge themselves in the penance-chamber, the number of times of ascending and descending depending upon the enormity of the crime.

Those whose crimes were very heavy had to kiss certain skulls that hung at intervals on the walls, each bearing the name of some saint, and this was a penance of all others that the monks detested.

Up this staircase, however, Marian had to ascend, and though time had divested it of some of its horrors by letting the ghastly skulls fall from their pegs, yet it was still horrible enough to render the ascent disagreeable.

The staircase was shut off from the room by a strong oaken door curiously carved and thickly studded with iron nails, which had formerly been kept bright, but were now covered with a thick coating of rust.

The interior of the room had been divested of its monastic decorations with the exception of an altar that was hidden by a screen, and Marian found it much more comfortable than she had expected it would be.

Seeing that she was faint and weary the soldier's wife prepared some food, and when they sat down to partake of it, Hubert, faithful to his promise, told his wife all that had happened to him during his absence.

"And now, I trust, we may be safe until we find some means to leave the tower," he added, in conclusion. "In the meantime, however, you must not neglect the page."

"I will see to her at once," replied Rebecca. "None dare molest me in my journey thither, and I may learn how far suspicion implicates you in this affair, and whether Deborah has missed her charge."

When Rebecca had made her necessary arrangements (such as concealing beneath her dress a portion of food, a flask of wine, and a small bundle of herbs) she left, and Hubert began to pace the room in deep thought.

"They will come, I have no doubt," Marian heard him mutter; "but it is not for my own safety I fear. No; 'tis of Rebecca. I think her fate will be too terrible for her to bear. Love for her has made me bear the humiliation of being ranked as a common soldier after passing my days from boy to man within these walls a faithful servitor of the king. The time is past for me to assert my rights; but I will"——

He paused suddenly in his walk, and listened.

A slight sound at the door, by which his wife had left, startled him.

"Impossible!" he thought. "She cannot have returned so soon. Ah! I will see who it can be."

Snatching up his sword, he strode to the door, and cautiously opened it.

No one was there; but he fancied he saw a shadow glide away in the darkness, and when he closed the door, and returned to the room, Marian saw that his face wore a ghastly smile.

"A spy!" he muttered, unconsciously, loud enough for her to hear. "Let him come again, and I will—no matter. 'Twas a secret I learnt by watching the monks at night from my chamber window. I have been ever fearful of trying its effects; but under present circumstances it may be of some use to me."

After fumbling awhile in his doublet, he produced a small key; then, drawing aside the screen from before the altar, he opened what appeared to be a cupboard, and took therefrom an iron-bound casket.

Marian watched him in fear and trembling, for he handled it like one who had some powerful engine in his grasp, and yet fears to use it, lest it do mischief to himself.

Unmindful that Marian was watching him, he took the casket to the further end of the room, and unlocked it with the key he had used for the cupboard, then cautiously inserted his hand.

From his manner Marian expected to see him bring forth some horrible instrument; but, to her surprise, when he withdrew his hand, it only contained what appeared to her a mixture of coarsely-powdered earth, or as she described it, when speaking of it afterward to Robin Hood, "a mixture of dark green (such as she had seen used at the pottery) dried in the sun and crumbled into powder."

This, after carefully running it through his hand, as though to ascertain whether it were damp, he carefully replaced, then sat down and waited anxiously the return of his wife.

She was not long absent, and as he threw open the door to admit her, he saw that her cheek was as pale as marble.

"Saint Denis! what ails thee?" he exclaimed, gazing anxiously into her face. "Is the page worse? or has any of the villains dared to"——

"No, no! I have heard ill news. We must fly from here. The governor has signed a warrant for your arrest; for you were seen to throw the body of David into the moat."

"A malison on the knave's prying eyes! whoever he be," exclaimed Hubert. "We cannot fly: we must seek safety in the vaults."

"Nay, we must leave the tower, and quit this part altogether," replied Rebecca; "and the sooner we set about it the better, for even now the guard may be making their way hither to arrest you."

"Impossible; we have not wings to take us across the moat."

"But I have the key of the sallyport, leading from the passage under the moat to the outer ditch, which is dry. I saw it hang in the warder's room as I passed, and I took it."

"Then we may count ourselves as safe; but what of the page?"

"Trouble not about her; let us look to ourselves. Hark! do you not hear the guard approaching?"

The clatter of armed feet ascending the

steps at the end of the passage was now plainly audible, and gave them to understand that they had wasted valuable time in argument.

" Fly by the secret door !" gasped Hubert, hoarsely. " Leave me to settle with them," and while Marian and Rebecca were snatching up some apparel, and making for the staircase they had so recently ascended, Hubert emptied the contents of the casket at the foot of the door, where the soldiers were expected to enter.

By the time he had done this, and possessed himself of a small bag of gold (the savings of many years), the iron tramp reached the door. The glare of a torch shone through the chinks, and a gruff voice was heard demanding admittance in the name of the king.

As no answer was given, the demand was followed by a battering against the door, which began to yield as Hubert closed the door of the secret staircase after him.

Before the stout blows of the enraged soldiers the door was compelled to give way, and it fell from its fastenings with a crash, precipitating the soldiers into the room.

A fearful oath broke from the leader's lips on finding the room empty.

He glared around, and stamped his foot with rage.

" A murrain seize them ! they are gone, and we are baffled," he shouted. " Yet," he added reflectively, " they are within the precincts of the tower, and we will find them, or raze the walls about their ears."

Then again his rage broke out.

He stamped his iron heel on the oaken floor, and foamed at the mouth and nostrils.

" Come hither," he shouted to the torch bearer, who remained in the passage without ; " look well about, sirrah, and make sure that they are not hidden."

The man tremblingly obeyed.

Every nook, corner, and cupboard he searched, and even looked behind the altar, but not a vestige of anything human could he see hidden ; so he struck his torch against the wall to freshen it, preparatory to taking their journey back.

In doing this, some of the sparks fell among the dust on the floor, which had been trodden to a powder under foot. A bright flame shot up, followed by a loud noise, and a dense cloud of smoke.

The walls shook with the shock, and the roof of the room fell in, burying the charred and blackened bodies of the soldiers beneath the ruins.

CHAPTER CXI.

THE KING'S TREACHEROUS ATTEMPT AT CAPTURING BOLD ROBIN.

For Robin nobly stood his ground,
So did his merry men.
And every blow the soldiers gave
They got them back again.

VEXED at his defeat, and chafing inwardly at the deception played upon him by Robin Hood, the king was now determined more than ever to wreak his vengeance on the daring outlaw.

Amongst the knights assembled round Henry's royal person D'Anville was the most conspicuous.

He looked exceedingly pale, and his wounded arm was bandaged, and in a sling.

" Now is your majesty satisfied with the baseness of his treachery ?" asked the duke, pushing his sallow face forward. " Did I."—

" Did you what ?" thundered the king, interrupting him, for he was in one of his ill humours, and glad to quarrel with any one ; then added, tauntingly, " Did you beat him at the tournament ?"

" I did not, my liege," replied D'Anville, quailing beneath the king's steady gaze ; " but had the herald announced him as the outlaw Robin Hood, I would have proved my loyalty by slaying him before your eyes."

" Go to with thine idle prating ! " said the king in anger. " I trow we have had enough of this of late. Had Robin Hood been in thy place and thou in his, the king would have one traitor the less to care for."

" Marry, 'tis hard for one so loyal as myself to be judged thus harshly by his sovereign," said D'Anville, bowing meekly before the king ; " wounded as I am, I would yet make an effort to"——

" Enough !" cried the king ; " we have other matters on hand now without listening to your prayers ! " then, turning to one of the knights, he added, " You have my instructions, see if you can carry them out without further bungling ; and if you do so, in addition to the reward promised you, I will permit you to keep all the money and other valuables found on the rebel chief or his followers."

The knight bowed and withdrew, and the king walked away, muttering to himself.

Robin Hood and his men did not stay to share in the revelry of the soldiers, but took their way across Moorfields towards the city.

Little John and Will Scarlett walked with Robin, and though they were frequently pointed to by the citizens who were journeying the same way, yet they appeared to take no heed of any one, but chatted to each other, and made the air ring again with their boisterous laughter.

Not wishing to let every one see what part of the city they were about to enter, Robin Hood branched off into a less-frequented path, and soon the trio found themselves travelling alone.

Little John and Will had been imbibing pretty freely all the afternoon, and now they began to be merry, and took it in turns to sing a song, and thus it was they did not hear a party of horsemen galloping after them at good speed.

Robin's quick ear, however, caught the sound, and, though it was growing too dark for him to recognise the riders at any distance, he suspected they were up to no good, as none of the horses were allowed to travel on the gravelled path, but were reined on either side on to the grass.

This the outlaw presumed at once was to deaden the sound of their hoofs, and allow them to come upon them unawares, which they would have done had not Robin's experienced ear detected them.

"Keep up your roystering," said Robin, as his companions left off in the midst of a refrain to ascertain the cause of his looking back; "have your bows ready if needed, and keep a tight grip on your staves, for I opine we have an ugly set of jackals bearing down upon us."

This ruse on the part of the foresters had its effect, for as the singing was continued the horsemen did not dream that they were discovered.

At a distance of only a few yards ahead of them, Robin noticed a clump of trees and an old post that formed a junction to several cross roads, and he hastened his men forward so as to gain their shelter before the horses came up with them; but, as they found this could not be accomplished by walking, they took to their heels and ran.

But this precaution was taken too late.

The leader of the mounted party, guessing their intention, spurred on his charger, and ordered his men to swoop out and intercept the foresters at every point.

The trio now found themselves hemmed in, not one of them being able to gain a shelter, and the leader of the party (whom it may be as well to state was the knight the king had so recently given instructions to, and promised so great a reward if he proved successful), after assuring them of their helpless condition, commanded them to surrender.

"To whom, and for what?" demanded Robin, in turn.

"A knight in the service of the king," replied the leader. "As to your offence," he added, carelessly, "if your memory is so weak, his majesty will no doubt remind you of it."

"Humph! indeed. And did his majesty order our arrest?"

Robin folded his arms as he put this question as though he was going to hold a parley, though in truth it was only to loosen his sword and place his bugle ready to his hand.

"By what other authority think you I dare make an arrest on the king's highway?" said the leader, haughtily, for he considered the foresters as already captured, and he wanted to hasten back to receive the king's praise for his admirable skill and expedition.

"And if we refuse to submit?" said Robin, coolly.

"Then I will take you by force."

"Dead or alive, I presume?"

"Ay, you may depend on't. You see we are no weaklings, and have the advantage of you by many."

"So it seems," replied Robin, musingly, as he cast his eye round at the horsemen ranged in a circle; "twenty ruffians to us three honest men; well, I see there is little chance

for us, and, as we shall soon exchange this pure air for the stifling atmosphere of a dungeon, I must e'en blow a blast on my horn to clear my throat and prepare myself for the change."

As there was nothing extraordinary in this request the leader made no effort to oppose it; but when Robin blew three distinct notes so loud as to make the horses start, even accustomed as they were to the blast of the war trumpet, he began to suspect he had done wrong.

"Dismount!" he shouted to the soldiers nearest him; "secure the prisoners and bind them."

But the soldiers found this a difficult task.

As they reached the ground the foresters' long staves laid them sprawling, so the leader, flourishing his sword, ordered his men to lay on without mercy.

The outlaws were prepared for this and would have held out to the very last, which would probably not have been long, as the soldiers took heed to cut off their retreat to the trees; but a party on foot suddenly appearing from the grass in the back ground, gave a different aspect to affairs.

These were Robin's men; and, as soon as they saw how matters stood, they let fly a shower of arrows that proved fatal to more than one of the horsemen.

Then commenced a fearful hand to hand combat.

The foresters gripped their tough oak boughs and belaboured the soldiers so soundly, that they found their stout swords and long pikes were of little use against the outlaws' heavy staves.

"Lay on right well, my merry men," shouted Robin in glee, as saddle after saddle became vacant, and the riderless horses took fright at the din. "Batter their iron harness, and crack their worthless crowns; give them just cause to remember the scurvy part they have played."

As yet the knight had managed to keep his seat, and, in fact, had kept his person from harm.

It was not, however, through any wondrous valour of his own; it was partly because his armour was of better metal than the soldiers, and partly because he kept as far as possible from the thick of the fight.

Robin Hood, however, singled him out, and they set-to in right good earnest.

"Yield thee, caitiff!" thundered the enraged leader; "I would deal mercifully with thee, spare thy life, and even grant thee a boon, if thou wert not so headstrong and "——

A blow in the face from Robin's staff smashed his visor and made the blood gush from his face.

As he reeled in his saddle Robin caught him in his muscular arms and laid him on the grass.

This brought the fight to a close.

The few soldiers that remained seeing their leader prostrate, their comrades stretched around bleeding and groaning from their wounds, and themselves getting the worst of the battle, threw down their arms, and cried for quarter.

To such an appeal the bold foresters were ever ready to listen, and some of them took the iron caps of the soldiers, and, lading water from a brook hard by, gave drink to the wounded, and bathed the wounds of those who were badly hurt.

The close proximity of the soldiers to succour made Robin fear at first that he would have to break through his established rule of not binding his prisoners ; but the jaded appearance of those who surrendered, and their frequent protestations of having had punishment enough, made him abandon such a design.

With his own hand he attended to the wounded knight, and also took from his breast a packet sealed with the royal seal ; and, having raised him on his horse and lashed him with his saddle girth, he gave him in charge of one of the soldiers, and ordered him to walk the horse gently back to the place where they had started from and inform the king of what had happened.

Anxious to learn the contents of the packet Robin ordered his men to mount on the horses that had not taken to flight, and, mounting one himself, he left the soldiers to look after their wounded comrades, and then rode rapidly on.

At a turn of the road they halted, and Robin gave his men instructions how to act, as he chose to travel as before in company of Little John and Will.

That night they did not stay in London, for from the contents of the packet Robin felt that his presence was required at Sherwood ; and, as he relied on Eleanor sending him what information she could concerning Marian, he started at once for home.

Having learnt sufficient from the king's treachery to assure him that any means would be resorted to to effect his capture, he determined to be wary, so that he took a circuitous route and joined his followers at a wayside inn.

The host was at first surprised to see such a goodly company, and was afraid he could not accommodate them as they pretended to be strangers to each other ; but, as they promised to put up with any shift rather than travel farther, he promised to do what he could for them.

CHAPTER CXII.

THE RECOVERY OF THE STOLEN CROWN.

Henry born at Winchester,
  At Gloucester he was crowned,
With gold wire (the regalia being lost)
  They bound his head around.

WHILST the king was engaged in deceiving Robin Hood, Prince Edward was as treacherously employed with moneyed Jews.

The confession wrung from Azavedo

afforded him great facility for this, and Edward was not the man to let such a golden harvest as the Jews promised, slip through his fingers when it needed but an effort of his own to grasp it.

A party of his own trusty servitors, many of whom would have sold themselves to the evil one to retain the prince's favour, had been actively employed in searching out those of the unfortunate race whom ill will or envy caused to be pointed out as the amassers of wealth.

Inducements in the shape of a promised reward were often held out for such discoveries, but they were rarely fulfilled, it generally resulting in an appointment to some office, which frequently cost the holder his life after a few months of what is erroneously termed enjoyment, but which in truth was no better than misery and anxiety.

The secret league, as Edward's emissaries were termed, and which seldom consisted of the same parties twice, with the exception of the principal confidants, for to ensure secrecy the menial members of the league were sent abroad, or got rid of by some means, and other ones employed, or forced to do the work under a promise of a reward which was invariably given to them, even if it were taken from them again.

It was Edward's mode of doing business, when he had anything of this kind on foot, to send a summons to the party informed against, demanding him to appear at one of the courts of justice under a penalty of death, to answer an imaginary charge preferred against him, and which he had never before heard or thought of.

In the meantime every precaution was taken to prevent escape ; and as the house of the richest of the Jews was in general the most rickety, though defended by the strongest doors and a superfluity of bars and bolts, an entrance had often to be effected by the roof.

Such had been the employment of the secret league for the last few days ; and in the dead of night the gates of Nottingham Castle closed upon twelve of the most abject and pitiable wretches to look upon that the earth could produce.

De Lois received the prince with the same cringing courtesy as before, though in truth he wished him far away ; strange things had transpired of late in the town, that Geoffrey wished to keep from the knowledge of the prince.

That night, however, the sheriff had little of Edward's company, he had travelled far, and needed rest ; but in the morning the mock trials commenced.

The first six of the culprits were arraigned on the charge of damaging the coin, by scraping and chipping it, to which charge they all pleaded not guilty ; but the stern judge would not listen to this, his decree was that they must either give up all the gold and valuables in their possession, or forfeit their lives.

It was hard to determine which of the two was the most valuable to the Jews ; without riches, they might as well be dead, and without life their riches were no good.

Therefore it required time for them to arrive at a decision, and Edward gave them till night, in a cold damp cell, to consider of it.

Five others were then brought in, and accused of aiding the Saracens, by advancing them money, to which they pleaded not guilty ; but as evidence was not considered necessary to criminate them, Edward passed upon them the same sentence as the others.

The twelfth, an aged and reverential-looking Jew, was accused of the more ignoble offence of treason to the crown, and holding negotiations with the French, who were waging perpetual war with England.

This was a serious charge, but like the rest met with a denial ; and Edward, who wore a mock suit, and was otherwise disguised, to render the farce more imposing, fairly lost his temper at this.

"Son of Baliol !" cried the prince, scarce knowing what he said in the moment of his wrath. "Is it thus you stand and boldly give us the lie ? Recall those words, or you may repent when it is too late !"

"Do vith me vot you pleash, you can hurt de bodish, but not de soul. I care not vot you do. I speak de truth, and care for no vonsh."

Edward grew more enraged at this.

His eyes became bloodshot, and his lips grew livid.

"Hence !" he shouted to his assistants, "away with him ! find a berth in the lowest dungeon ; and feed him upon swine's flesh until his lying heart recants !"

The executioners gathered round, and was about to execute the order, when the Jew, thinking more of the swine's flesh than of the imprisonment, fell on his knees before the prince.

Edward waved his myrmidons back, and they obeyed with a grunt of dissatisfaction.

"Save me—save me ! Spare me from dis !" implored the Jew. "Mine Got! let me not lose my salvation !"

Edward's brow darkened.

He was angry, for when he ordered the executioners to fall back, it was in the hope that the Jew was about to reveal something, but finding himself disappointed, he ordered the men to seize him.

This seemed to rouse the Jew to a true sense of his danger.

He sprang to his feet, and ere a hand could reach him, he took from beneath his robe a crown.

Edward eagerly snatched it up, for he fancied he recognised it, but he could not have sworn to it had it not been for a letter engraved on the inside, for the diamonds and jewels had been extracted.

"Caitiff !" cried the prince, "how came you by this ?"

"Honest, I assure you," replied the Jew. "I bought it."

"Of whom ?"

The prince glanced meaningly at the scribe, who was noting everything down.

The Jew answered less readily than he had hitherto done, and he wavered as though preparing a lie.

Edward noticed this, and he put the question again.

"One merchant," replied the Jew, at length.

"His name ?"

"Mine Got ! I know not ; my memory ish very, very bad."

"Ay, and so are thine actions," replied Edward. Then motioning to his attendants, he added, "Search him ; there may yet be other things about him that he hath forgotten."

The Jew fairly groaned when he heard these words.

He made an attempt to struggle, but strong arms held him fast, and willing hands soon found in the folds of his garment two other crowns similar in size, but of different shape, and less costly material.

Edward stared as they were brought to light.

"Minion !" he said, his eyes glowing fiercely, "'tis no wonder that royalty comes to the throne without a crown (alluding to his father, who, in consequence of the regalia being lost, was crowned with a round of gold wire), when such dogs as ye have three at one time in your possession. Where got ye them? for 'tis plain ye came by them through no honest means."

"Dis von," said the Jew, trembling, "I got from one Frenchman, Debriseau. 'Tis very fine gold, and I gave him plenty for it."

"How much ?"

"My all ; every penny I possessed."

"And what did you think of doing with it ?"

"I vosh taking it to de—de bishop, to see if he could find out who it belonged to, for I knew it must belong to somepody."

"Very kind and generous of you, certainly," remarked the prince, with sarcasm. "So you purchased the whole lot, spent your last farthing to do this good thing ?"

"Yesh."

"Liar !" muttered the prince to himself ; then added, with feigned commiseration—

"'Tis a wondrous tale you have told, and none but an unbeliever can doubt it ; and as it is the first generous act I have heard of being performed by a Jew, 'tis but meet that you have just reward."

The Jew's eyes sparkled.

He had entertained a fear that his tale would not have been believed, and now that he had, as he supposed, laid the foundation, he made up his mind to build upon it.

"Got be merciful to you, good prince," he said, bowing before the throne, "may you live long to rule de nation, and be a blessing to de people. Vhen my brederen scoff and

ROBIN HOOD,

AND THE OUTLAWS OF SHERWOOD FOREST.

DOINGS OF THE SECRET BAND.

revile you, and call you cruel, I always say you are humane, and now can I not say so, | when you reward me for vhat I have done?" "Even so," replied the prince, affecting to humour him, "and thy reward shall be doubled when thou answerest truly the questions I put to thee."

"Name them, good prince; I am thy servant."

"Where hid you the jewels?"

The Jew's jaw dropped.

He rolled his eyes up to the features of the prince, then drooped them beneath Edward's searching gaze.

"Speak out," cried Edward, suddenly changing his tone, "or by the saints I will find a means of uncaging thy tongue."

The Jew still hesitated, but the sight of a pair of thumbscrews in the hands of one of the men aroused him from his lethargy.

He then commenced a long rambling statement, which the prince did not believe. In fact, from the very manner of the Jew, it was evident he meant to deceive him, so he ordered the thumbscrews to be at once applied.

The sharp pang of agony that accompanied the first turn of the screw was more than the Jew's nerves could bear, and he shrieked, and implored for them to be taken off.

As Edward had not resorted to these means out of wanton cruelty, he ordered the torture to be suspended, and the Jew, still smarting under the pain, expressed a willingness to answer any question.

CHAPTER CXII.

THE FIRST STEP TO LIBERTY.

Lithe of limb and strong of nerve
Was valiant Marian;
And few with her could draw a bow,
Deny it those who can.

THE secret which Hubert had learnt (or, at least, partly so) through watching the monks at night when practising their mysterious rites and searching their mystic lore, had near proved a fatal discovery to him, for not only was his own room laid in ruins by the shock, but the whole of the secret staircase came to the ground, through the upright pole giving way.

Fortunately for him at that moment he had reached a spot where the masonry was broken, and to this he frantically clung as the stairs gave way beneath his feet.

There he found himself clinging when the thunder-like roar had died away, and he lowered himself down by the jagged stonework until he reached the pile of bones.

His first thought then was to look for his wife, whom he little doubted was laying a mangled corpse beneath the heap of ruins; and, in the desperation of the moment, he began tearing away at the rubbish with his hands.

The voice of Marian, however, arrested him.

"Good Hubert," she said, "fear not; thy Rebecca is safe; she has gone to look after the page, and will join us at the sally port."

"If we reach it, which is doubtful," replied Hubert, wiping the perspiration from his brow. "See you not that the garrison is in arms?"

"With courage we may yet baffle them," said Marian, as she glanced up at the battlements, and saw the men-at-arms hastening to and fro.

Hubert made no reply. He saw a pair of eyes watching them from a loophole opposite where they stood.

Drawing Marian into the shadow of a buttress, he bade her stay there out of sight, and then, crawling stealthily along the wall, disappeared in a low doorway.

When he returned he brought with him a cross-bow, and a handful of bolts, one of which be fitted on reaching the cover of the buttress.

"A malison on the thing!" he muttered. "'Tis so long since I have sent a shaft, I fear me I shall not strike the mark."

'Tis thine hand trembles," said Marian, as she noticed that the soldier shook with excitement.

"Ay, my whole frame seems unnerved. I fear me I shall not be able to hit the mark I aim for."

"Pray, what mark have you in view?"

"The head of a skulking knave, to whom I owe more than one grudge, and whose inquisitive eyes I blame for watching me throw David into the moat. He is watching us now, and as soon as he finds what way we take, he will set the guard upon our track."

"Marry! let me have a shot at him, then," said Marian; "my hand is steadier than thine."

"And weaker," rejoined Hubert. "Thy nerves may be strong, but the jerk of the bow would break thy delicate arm."

"Fash not thereanent," replied Marian, laughing. "A life in the greenwoods hath given strength to my sinews. Give me the bow, show me the mark, and I pledge my word to hit it."

The soldier stood for a moment, uncertain how to act.

He felt abashed at his own weakness when he heard the words, and gazed at the form of the speaker.

After a moment's reflection, however, he consented to yield up the crossbow to Marian, and he showed her the place where the upper portion of the man's face was still visible.

Marian eyed the place for a moment, and then dropping down on one knee, and shielding as much of her form with the buttress as she possibly could, she took aim and fired.

Hubert stood watching her with a feeling bordering upon fear, and when the bow twanged, he expected to hear the bolt strike the stonework.

He was deceived. The iron shaft entered the loop-hole, a stifled groan was heard, and the face disappeared.

"Bravely done!" gasped Hubert, with an effort to recover his breath. "You have closed his eyes for ever, and now I would have you try another shot."

"Willingly," was the response.

Hubert led her out upon the ramparts, and pointing to a distant figure, leaning on his halberd, with his back towards them, he said—

"See you yon fellow? He guards the passage through which we must pass. Heed him well, and make sure your aim, or we are lost."

Marian kept her eyes steadily fixed on the object, and fitted another bolt.

Resting the bow on the edge of the parapet she let fly, and the man fell. At the same moment, a fearful shriek rent the air.

CHAPTER CXIII.
ROBIN HOOD HAS SOME DIVERSION WITH THE KING'S BOWMEN.

And when the news they came to hear,
  Their minds on mischief quick did turn;
To rob and thrash bold Robin's men,
  Their itching fingers hot did burn.

ROBIN HOOD and his merry men soon made themselves at home at the roadside inn. They called for wine, toasted each other, and sang songs till a late hour of the night.

The host, a particular man in his way, though grateful for their custom, did not approve of so much noise; for though there was but one cottage within half-a-mile of his house, he feared, he said, that he might annoy his neighbours.

Robin laughed heartily at this when it was told him, and ordered the landlord to supply them with more liquor, hinting, at the same time, his intention of sitting up all night.

This proposition was of course seconded by Little John, who wished for no better sport, and was loudly acclaimed by the rest.

Sorely annoyed, but unable to help himself, the landlord was forced to comply, and he retired to the outer room in no very cheerful spirits.

As he stood listening to the shouts and merry laughter of his guests, and mentally cursing them, he was disturbed by a knock at the door, and on opening it, a tall soldier entered.

He was clad in a buff jerkin, girded round the waist by a leathern belt, russet boots, a slouched hat with a feather in it, and on his left hand he wore a leathern glove.

"Ah!" muttered the landlord, "one of the king's bowmen;" then he added aloud to the man, "Late travelling, is it not? and rather a strange circumstance to see you alone."

"My comrades are not far off," replied the man. "I left them down the hill whilst I came in search of this house. We want a lodging for the night."

"Saint Mary! you will not get that here," replied the host, in alarm. "How many do you muster?"

"A dozen besides the captain, which is myself; of course you will not reckon him in."

"I shall certainly not let him in," answered the host, savagely. "I have no room. Quotha! the house is full."

"Of roistering knaves, I opine, from the noise I heard coming down the road. Who are they? Do you know them?"

"Marry! I do not."

"Strangers, then?" remarked the soldier.

"To me they are, though they seem to make themselves at home. I shall be glad to get rid of them, for I am wearied of their noise, and tired withal, and wish to get to sleep."

"Ugh!" muttered the soldier. "Can I see the fellows?"

"You cannot; they have taken the liberty to bolt the door to prevent me interrupting them."

"Bodikins! they set you at defiance, then?"

"Ay. And I am afraid to say aught, for fear of a quarrel."

"Ah, for fear of your pate, you mean? Well, it does not do for a man of your years to risk a broken crown; but I will tell you what I will do"——

"Nothing rash, I hope?" interrupted the host, trembling.

"Quotha! no. I will bring up my men—turn out these noisy dogs, and if they go not away quietly, we will give them a taste of our bow-strings."

The landlord liked this idea, especially after being so insulted; but he objected to the noise that must necessarily ensue.

"I like your proposal very well," he said; "but I cannot have my neighbours disturbed at this hour of the night."

"Ha! ha! we shall make no noise. We will just give them a quiet ejectment; and if they offer to kick up a row, why, we'll give them something to howl for."

"No, no; it will not do."

"Why not?"

"It may end in bloodshed, and, and"——

"Trouble not for that; I will bring up my men before this storm bursts. The rain began to fall as I hastened hither. Draw me a jug of ale," he added, "before I go."

The landlord drew him the ale, and he tossed it off at a gulp; and then, with a knowing shake of the head, he left.

Boniface took great care to close the door after him; for in his own mind he was glad he was gone; but when the noise of the foresters, which had hushed almost to silence, began again, he began to swear most lustily, and longed for the soldier's return.

Little did he think, however, that his words had been heard by his guests, who quietly removed a board from the top of the door, and saw and heard all that passed.

The soldier had little difficulty in persuading his comrades to enter into his plans, as the rain began to fall heavily, and a sharp, biting wind swept the lonely road; so they returned with him, their minds fully bent on mischief.

The host met them at the door, and strictly enjoined them to silence, urging his opinion that a sudden and unexpected assault would be far better than an open one.

Whilst the soldiers were refreshing themselves with a barrel of good ale, the host collected his small force, which consisted of an old man, who filled the office of brewer, woodchopper, etc., and a stout lad who served as stable-boy.

These, with the host, made the soldier party equal in number to that of the guests, and when they had drank sufficient to render them pot valiant, it was considered time to commence operations.

A glance, obtained through the chink of the door, enabled the leader to survey the men he was about to eject, and then he recognised the parties that had so shamefully beaten them at the butts, and this was enough to excite the soldier to anything.

" By the rood !" he said to his men in an undertone, " Our Lady has been good enough to lead us to the very place we so much desired, and hath placed within our reach the vengeance we so much covet ; so prepare yourselves for a scuffle, that shall win back the honours we have lost."

The soldiers listened in astonishment to his speech.

" Marry ! what mean you, captain !" asked one bolder than the rest.

" Mean ! that we are beneath the same roof as the scurvy knaves that have robbed us, cheated us of our just renown as the most expert of archers, and taken from us the favour of the king."

The men heard his speech with evident pleasure, and some of them made towards the door of the room to wreak a speedy vengeance on their successful rivals, but their leader held them back.

" Be not too hasty," he said, in the same suppressed tone. " they have with them the money of which they cheated the bishop, and that must be ours. If we mind not how we act, we shall apprise them of our intentions too soon, and the purse-bearer, with the other trophies, will make his escape."

" We must surround the house," he added ; " so go you," he pointed to those nearest the door, " keep good watch, and spare not your shafts if they attempt to leave by the window."

The bowmen, thus ordered, withdrew to keep guard without, taking with them the old man and the boy to point out the principal places of egress.

The landlord then closed the door, and barred and bolted it.

This done, it was necessary for him to look out a place of safety for himself, and, with an adroitness that did him credit, he squeezed his burly form between two upturned casks.

The leader of the bowmen waited until he had snugly ensconsed himself, and then he knocked at the door of the room where the foresters were still keeping up their noisy mirth.

" Who's there ?" demanded a voice within.

" Me. Open it once, you noisy roisterers," replied the leader, mimicing the landlord's voice.

" Well, if it's you, I opine we must," was the growled response, and the bolt was drawn, and the soldier entered.

The foresters were seated round the board, and appeared to be far in their cups, which the leader noticing he motioned his men to follow him.

" Drink, comrades," said Robin, staggering from his chair, with a cup of sack in each hand. " Drink to the good yew bow ; for by my faith, I see ye are archers like ourselves."

" Ay, good men and true," interposed Little John, rising, and reeling to the door, which he closed as if by accident, and then shot the bolt.

The leader and the half-a-dozen men who had followed him were prisoners, but they were not aware of it ; Little John had acted his part so well.

" Here's to your healths, gentlemen all," said the leader, draining one of the cups of wine. " I trow me you are a set of jolly good fellows, and know how to choose good wine. Methinks I have seen some of ye before."

" Marry ! is it so ?" asked Robin, in affected surprise, steadying himself by the table. " Odds bodikins ! mine eyes grow dim ; 'tis the confounded ale we have been drinking as a foundation to the wine. Drink again ; let us have another bumper ; and then, perchance, 'twill clear this mist from our eyes."

This was a treat the bowmen seldom enjoyed, so they accepted the invitation ; but whether it was the strength of the wine to which they were unaccustomed, or whether the wine had been tampered with, it so happened that at the third draught they found themselves gradually overpowered.

Robin did not appear to notice this, but kept up his tone of gaiety, observing—

" Marry ! now I come to look at ye, methinks I saw ye at the sports. Wert thou not the archer that carried off the prize ?"

This had the effect of rousing the leader to his senses.

" Zounds !" he cried, glancing fiercely at Robin, " it was I who won it fairly ; but one of thy scurvy companions did rob me of it. Saint Denis ! had it not been for the presence of the king I would have soundly trounced the knave on the spot."

" Ay, and well he deserveth it, if he hath cheated you," said Robin. " Point him out if you can, and I will assist you even now to cudgel his hide."

" That I can do of mine own accord," replied the soldier, glancing fiercely round. " Yon red-headed scamp," he added, pointing to Will Scarlett, " is the minion. By the mass, he shall crave my pardon, or I'll smash every bone in his skin."

" Ay, and throw his carcase to the wolves," rejoined Robin, with a smirk. " Hark how the wind howls and shakes the casement. By the rood, one would imagine that the house was surrounded."

This was meant as a hint in allusion to the men without; but the leader of the bowmen did not take it. He was too deeply engrossed in meditating revenge.

That he had recognised Robin was plainly to be seen, though he tried as much as possible to conceal that fact; and Robin Hood, on the other hand, was also as cautious in keeping his suspicious secret.

"If not surrounded by wolves, it is certainly infested with jackals," remarked Will Scarlett, returning the leader's look of hatred. "I could well afford to break my quarter-staff over the shoulders of some of them."

"To whom do ye allude?" demanded the bowman, haughtily.

"Any who may think my words worthy of notice," was the cool reply.

"Take that, then, as the harbinger of your fate; 'twill, maybe, teach you how to respect those in service of the king."

As he spoke, the leader grasped his bow, and dealt what was intended for a heavy blow, but Will swept it aside with his arm, and sent the leader reeling back with a blow in the chest.

Enraged at their leader's humiliation, the soldiers in the room drew their swords and prepared to resent the insult; but after a short scuffle that proved harmless to all but themselves, they found themselves pinioned hands and feet with their own bowstrings.

All this had been so quietly arranged, that the host, though he listened in trembling expectation for the sounds of conflict, was as ignorant of what had occurred as the men without, and when Robin opened the door and took a look round, the landlord was perfectly amazed.

"Holy Virgin! where has the old sinner gone?" muttered Robin, glancing at the barred door. "Surely the knave has not retired and left us to help ourselves? By the mass! if he has he may keep the doors closed to-morrow, for we will empty every barrel."

Such was not to be the case, however; for the host, on hearing the words, thrust out his nightcapped head, and afterwards crawled from his concealment.

"Forsooth, you have chosen a strange place to nap in," said Robin, affecting not to notice the confusion of his host; "one would imagine you bore not the least humanity, to let those poor fellows stay without in the pitiless storm. Summon them in, for, by my halidame, 'tis not fit weather to keep a watch-dog out of his kennel."

"But," began the astonished landlord, surprised at the strange turn of events, "but"—

"We have had enough of the buts for one day," said Robin, interrupting him, "and desire a change, in the form of an ale barrel. Call in the men at once, or their buff jerkins will be turned into wash leather. In the meantime, I will take the key of the wine cellar, and help myself to a jug of sack,

which, by the way, I must highly commend for its quality."

The landlord would have remonstrated, but finding it was useless, he unbarred the outer door, and Robin took the key from the wall.

Glad enough were the soldiers to accept the invitation to enter, for they were nearly drenched, and withal tired of watching; but they were taken by surprise when, on entering the room, they were seized and bound like the rest of their companions.

The lad and the old man, after pointing out the various posts that needed watching, crept in at the backway, and slunk up to the garret, where they listened to the rain pelting on the thatched roof until sleep overpowered them.

The twelve bowmen, however, made a ludicrous show, as, bound and gagged, they were ranged in a row on a bench at the further end of the room, with the landlord seated in a chair before them.

Little John took upon himself the duty of cellarman, and also acted as cupbearer, taking care to taste of every flagon of wine before filling the cups for the others.

"Now, good fellows all," said Robin, with a smile, "I think it is time we toasted the health of our worthy host, and return him thanks for the kind and hospitable manner in which he has treated us."

The toast was drank, and loudly acclaimed by the foresters, who battered their cups on the oak table, and laughed heartily at the pain and uneasiness the host and the others were suffering.

When the tumult ceased, Robin ordered the gags to be removed, and a jug of ale to be given to the bowmen, on the condition that they drank to the health of Robin Hood and his merry men.

To this they were forced to comply, and afterwards compelled to sing, much to their annoyance and the amusement of the foresters, who kept up the carousal till daylight made its appearance.

CHAPTER CXIV.

ESCAPE FROM THE TOWER.—REBECCA IS WOUNDED.

The ditch without the sally-port
Was dry and grown with grass,
The sentinel on the battlements
Did watch and see them pass.

"Onward for your lives!" whispered Hubert, hoarsely, as the party descended a flight of stone steps, and he closed the stone slab over the hole or trap-door that he had opened to admit them.

"Hist!" muttered his wife; "let us keep our mouths closed and our ears open, we know not who may be lurking about. Let me lead the way."

Rebecca was a woman of strong nerve, and it was to her love of danger and adventure that she owed her knowledge of the vaults and subterraneous passages beneath the tower.

Often, when a girl, she had made her way alone to the sally-port, and now, even in the dark, she felt no fear of being able to do so again.

But many months had passed since her last visit, and many changes had been wrought in that time; a portion of the crumbling masonry had fallen down, and she only discovered this by stumbling over a large stone and fearfully bruising her face.

This brought the whole party to a stand; but Hubert pushed forward to ascertain the cause, and soon learnt the danger of their position.

"Holy Virgin!" he said, in a tone calculated to inspire his hearers with dread, "the passage is blocked; we must return, or"——

"Or what?" demanded Rebecca, observing him pause.

"Try the passage of the black swamp."

"Better that than stay here," replied his heroic wife. "I have been through it more than once, and never came to harm."

"Ay, and so have I; but never in the dark. It is full of pitfalls, and the water is so filthy that the least disturbance causes it to give forth an effluvia that may prove fatal to our delicate companions."

"For my part," said Marian, who was assisting the page, "I have no fear, and I am ready to venture; but Emile, I fear, will not be able to bear it."

"If she can bear the smell I will carry her," said Hubert; "what think you of that? Rebecca can lead us clear of the holes, which have been sunk to prevent prisoners escaping from the dungeons of the keep."

This suggestion they all readily assented to; and they groped their way back to the steps where they had entered, at the foot of which Hubert opened a strong iron door.

It was bolted on that side, evidently to prevent any one entering the passage by it, and went down a step into the passage, which was found to be knee deep with water and mud.

"Holy mother! what would I not give for a light?" whispered Hubert. "If we fall into one of the holes we shall soon be eaten by the rats. Close the door, Rebecca, and trust to providence to guide our steps."

Marian offered up a humble prayer, and then they set forward on their perilous journey, which, after many narrow escapes of death, they managed to perform.

After wading through the slush and mire for near half an hour, they entered a long passage, dry and lighted by gratings in the roof; and then Rebecca told Marian that they had passed under the moat, and would soon breathe the air of freedom."

It was a relief to all parties when they reached a low, grated door, and felt the fresh air gush in upon them; but they felt their joy suddenly checked when the door was found to be locked and the key gone.

"Trapped, by the saints!" exclaimed Hubert, as he eyed the niche where the key was usually kept, with a look of utter despair. "After all, we have periled our lives for naught."

"Marry, have we?" Marian replied; "but 'tis of no use despairing. Through me you have had all this trouble, and now I would freely give my life to save"——

"Pshaw! let not that trouble ye," said the heroic Rebecca; "we have arms and strength; let us use them. The door may be forced; it is old and weak."

Hubert started like one aroused from a lethargy, his wife's words had inspired him with fresh hope; yet he looked sad, and seemed to be uneasy.

Rebecca's suggestion was tried, however, though it at first seemed hopeless; but the door eventually gave way, and they found themselves in the dry ditch, which was overgrown with grass.

The sally-port, owing to its importance, was a point necessary to be well guarded even in times of peace, and sentries were so placed on the battlements that they could watch if anyone approached it; and also, to enable them, in times of war, to cover the sallying party with their cross-bows.

This Hubert knew; but he had hoped that the confusion in the tower would have drawn the men away to other parts—which hope, alas! was doomed too soon to whither.

Places were cut in the opposite side of the ditch to allow anyone to ascend; and as the party made their way thither, they were startled by a shower of bolts flying about their ears.

"On, quick!" gasped Hubert, as his cap went flying on the point of an arrow. "If we gain the trees, we may yet escape to the woods."

Another shower of arrows and bolts now darkened the air, but did no harm to the fugitives; and, before the bowmen could again fix their shafts, the party gained the parapet of earthwork that ran round the edge of the ditch.

As the next shower came, they threw themselves down under the parapet, and might have remained there safe from the barbed missiles, had it not been for the certainty of being pursued.

The news that they were seen, spread through the tower like wildfire. Parties were sent hither and thither to intercept them, whilst the governor himself, with a body of armed men, started at once in pursuit.

Between the ditch and the wood was an open space, and across this the fugitives had to go, exposed to the shots of the bowmen, who let fly so thickly that it was a wonder any of the party escaped with life.

Rebecca, however, was the only victim. She fell with a quarrel in her side, and Hubert instantly flew to her assistance.

With a wail of bitter grief, he raised her in his arms, and carried her to a clump of trees, where the others had sought safety;

then carefully extracting the barbed missile, he tore open the dress and bound up the wound.

"Thanks!" she faintly gasped. "Now all I want is a draught of water, then fly for your life and leave me; my life is not worth much now."

"Say not so, dearest!" exclaimed her loving husband, as he held to her lips the cold water that Marian had dipped from a purling stream. "You must live, dearest, if only for my sake."

"It cannot be, my time is come. Fly, that I may die with the pleasure of knowing that you, at least, have escaped."

"Never!" vociferated Hubert. "Death alone shall part us; whilst there is life there is hope."

"Alas! there is but little hope for me," replied Rebecca, mournfully. "I feel I am sinking fast. You have still health and strength; use it while you yet have a chance of escape, and I will endeavour to drag my way to the abbey, where Father Absolom will give me shrift."

"Nay, thou shall not go alone, neither will I leave thee here," cried Hubert, determinedly. "A good wife hast thou been to me; where I go thou goest, where you die there will I die also."

Marian did all she could to alleviate the pain of the sufferer, and then Hubert raised her in his arms, and hurried towards a dense part of the forest, as though he did not feel his burden.

Emilie stood in need of Marian's assistance to enable her to follow, and when they reached the thicket they could hear the soldiers shouting to each other in the wood.

At times the voices sounded quite near, and it seemed each moment as though their hiding-place must be discovered; but Marian silenced their fears, as with her ear, experienced as it was to forest life, she marked the movements of the soldiers.

"Now we are safe," she said, as she took her ear from the ground, and rose from her knees; "they have gone to the right, and the abbey, you say, is to the left."

"Just so," replied Hubert; "but we dare not go there."

"For why?"

"For more reasons than one. In the first place, the monks visit the tower."

"But they would not betray you, surely?"

"I would not trust them."

"Indeed, you judge them harshly."

"Ay," replied Hubert, bitterly; "they are poor, and I, unfortunately, am the same."

"One would think that would bind you firmer together, and serve as a reason for their assisting you."

"Not so, I assure you. A handful of crowns would make them betray me, even were they bound by oath not to do so. But we must on, for my wife grows weaker. I know of a path not more than two miles from here, and thither will I take her."

Marian damped the lips of the wounded woman, and then the party once more resumed their journey in the same manner as before.

―――――

CHAPTER CXV.

MALCOLM OFFERS TO BETRAY ROBIN HOOD.

The Abbot and the Sheriff did loud their voices raise,
De Lois he lost his temper, and gat him pale with rage.
The Abbot soon did calm him by whispering in his ear
A word or two that made the Sheriff tremble much with rage.

UNDER the careful nursing of his daughter Madge, Stukely made rapid strides towards recovery; and, as he lay in his bed, weakened by the fever, his subtle brain was ever plotting mischief.

So soon as he was able to get about, he paid a visit to his friend, through whom he carried on a private intercourse with De Lois.

The sheriff was galled when he heard that Robin Hood had quitted the forest on his visit to London, as Prince Edward's protracted stay at the castle prevented him making an attack on the outlaw's stronghold.

The threatened assault on the castle, which De Lois had been daily expecting, now seemed to have been entirely abandoned. The people were quiet, and appeared to listen to the abbot's advice, attending regularly at mass, and apparently yielding without a murmur to the sheriff's tyranny and oppression.

But the fire of discontent was only slumbering for a while, waiting Robin Hood's return to awaken it.

Geoffrey De Lois did not dream of this— the deception was so real; and now he looked upon the outlaw as his only enemy —an enemy that he must get rid of at any price.

The same night as Edward left Nottingham, De Lois and his uncle, the lord abbot, met in the oaken chamber to consult the best plan of attacking the foresters before Robin's return.

"I wot me it must be done quickly," Geoffrey suddenly broke out in the midst of their whisperings. "Success is sure to attend us; and if thou art afeard to face the anger of a few of the townsfolks, I am not."

"Neither am I, good nephew mine," answered the saintly man; "an' it please ye, I will throw aside my gown and kirtle, and don the harness of a knight, and follow thee to the battle."

"Battle!" repeated De Lois, with a sneer. "Why I could spit a dozen of the rascals on my own sword. Battle! Ha, ha! This shows you have had but little experience in the art of war. But there, you are to be pitied."

"And you to be blamed," retorted the abbot, with provoking calmness.

"In what way? name it."

"Allowing yourself to be beaten and duped by such a knave. By the mass! had I only had him once in my power as you have done often, he would now be as powerless as the Jew whose throat you squeezed with the bowstring last even."

"Enough; let us have no more of that. Marry! 'tis not a subject to be broached."

"We are alone?"

"Ay; but yet such matters should be breathed by neither. We must forget it: treat it but as a dream."

"Indeed! 'tis a terrible one then, and one I shall never forget. Thou wilt need much at the hands of thy confessor, I opine, if such is to be thy regular work."

Geoffrey de Lois bit his lip.

There was truth in his kinsman's words; and, although it was but a taunt, it almost choked him with rage.

"We quarrel without cause," he said, at length hiding his wrath; "I needed your presence as counsellor, not as judge. What think you of that fellow Stukely?"

"He is not to be trusted, but treated with caution. I never liked the fellow's looks. Even now he may be deceiving you."

"He can do no harm, however. If his words are not worth a dump, 'tis as well to hear them."

"And how will you reward him?"

"According to my promise," replied De Lois, with a bitter smile. "I promised him a swing from the oaken beam, and he shall have it. Saint Quintain! 'tis but his just desert."

The abbot gave a ghastly grin.

"De Lois," he said, "thou hast a good way of arranging matters. In what way do you intend rewarding my services?"

"One-third of the spoil shall be yours, if I am successful."

"If my prayers can aid thee, thou shalt not fail. Make preparations at early morn, and steal upon the varlets when the sun is rising. I will perchance aid you more than you imagine, for I have learnt through Stukely, a means of entering the outlaws' stronghold, without exciting suspicion."

"You have!" gasped De Lois, seizing the abbot by the shoulder, as he moved towards the door, "St. Quintain, let me into the secret, also."

"Wait patiently the time; I dare not at present disclose it. Good night; may success attend us all."

The abbot strode away, leaving De Lois in a state almost amounting to fever.

His brain seemed in a whirl, and after standing for some moments trying to imagine what his kinsman could mean, he cursed him bitterly for his closeness, and then sank into his seat.

A hasty footstep approaching the door aroused him from his reverie.

"A stranger knocketh at the gate, and demands admission," said the page, on entering; "he hath business of import with thee, and will take no denial."

"A stranger; gave he no name?"

"Sir Henry Malcolm."

"Lead him hither."

"A tall, dark man soon appeared, and after taking a cautious survey of the room, he seated himself, without being asked to do so, at the table.

"Well, Malcolm, what brings you here?" demanded Geoffrey of his guest, as soon as he could recover from his surprise. "Hast repented of the quarrel we had a few days since?"

"Forsooth, I have not; but if you have a grain of sense you will forbear taunting me. We can render each other a service."

"Aha! I thought you preferred the good abbot's friendship to mine; you have soon grown tired of each other, I ween."

"Ay," replied Malcolm, with a bitter smile. "I trusted him, and"——

"He deceived ye. Well, well; I knew it would be so."

"Would I had known it sooner. I have made him my confidant, and now I have to rue it. But to the point. I stand in need of money. You can assist me, and I will give you that in return that shall fully recompense you."

"First let me know of this wondrous thing, then name thine own conditions," answered Geoffrey, a gleam of cunning lighting his visage.

"I will deliver Robin Hood into your hands, on condition that you pay me well."

"Impossible; it cannot be done."

"Say not so, until you have first heard me out. I have just heard news of the outlaw; he is on his journey from London, and I know the spot where he can be waylaid and easily taken."

"By the mass, such news is too good to be true. I will give thee one hundred marks, if you but effect his capture."

"Ugh! Double it; consider the risk."

"On my part only. If you have such faith in the belief of what you can do, how is it you could not come to terms with the lord abbot?"

"Because he has failed to keep the promise made between us; not a penny can I squeeze out of his tight-closed purse. Then, again, I have a boon to crave, that he would be powerless to grant."

"Name it."

"The pardon of Stukely and his daughter. Let him return to his former office, and then you will have it to say that you have done a just act, and accomplished a long-coveted revenge.

Geoffrey scowled.

The name of Stukely was like poison in his ears.

After a moment's consideration, however, he pretended to yield; not that he meant to pardon Stukely, but in the hope of learning the secret spoken of by the abbot, of outwitting his self-conceited uncle, and capturing Robin Hood.

Concealing his evil thoughts behind a forced smile, De Lois ordered wine to be brought, and then talked over their arrangements, Malcolm talking over his deeply-laid schemes, and Geoffrey making promises he never intended to keep.

ROBIN HOOD,

AND THE OUTLAWS OF SHERWOOD FOREST.

DEATH OF THE OLD WOMAN ON THE HEATH.

CHAPTER CXVI.

A BRACE OF VILLAINS DEFEATED.

In Hollow-oak Dell, a-down, a-down,
　The ambush laid in wait,
When Robin, Scathelock, and Little John
　Came on with steady gait.
* * * * * *
The foresters clutched their oaken staves,
　And stood them back to back ;
Their blows fell on the Norman crowns
　With many a woeful thwack.

Long before the sun tipped the hills and gilded the lofty turrets of Nottingham Castle, the brazen trump sounded to horse, and troopers and bowmen assembled in the court-yard.

Amongst those who assembled was De Lois ; and, as the faint light revealed his features, the dark frown upon them contrasted strangely with the glitter of his burnished mail, which encased him from head to foot.

Seemingly unmindful of the noise occasioned by the clatter of horses' hoofs and so many armed feet bustling about the paved yard, he glided amongst the men and gave his orders to the different leaders, then disappeared in the shadow of an arched portico, where Malcolm awaited him.

"Your party awaits you," said the Sheriff ; "a dozen of my staunchest horsemen and a like number of bowmen. Place yourself at their head, and may success attend you."

As he spoke he pointed to a party of men, mounted and on foot, drawn up in close order at the foot of the drawbridge.

"I am satisfied, and feel confident of success," replied Malcolm, eyeing the stout body of men. "I hope to bring the rebel back with me ere the sun sets again. Farewell ! May success attend us both."

So saying, he strode away and mounted his horse, which awaited him, and led the way across the drawbridge, followed closely by the sheriff and his party.

Silently they glided along the road until they got clear of the town, for fear of disturbing the inhabitants, and then they took different roads, and pushed on as fast as the men on foot could march.

Scarcely had the sound of the sheriff's party died away in the distance than Malcolm's quick ear caught the sound of horses' hoofs upon the road in front of him.

"Zounds !" he said to the leader of the soldiers, " this is unfortunate. We must hide ourselves. It will not do to be seen journeying in company at this hour in the morning. Whom, think you, can it be coming to meet us ?"

"Marry, some knight, perhaps, and his esquire, with a message to the castle. I will draw my men in the shelter of yon thicket, and leave you to challenge the strangers, whoever they may be, if you think it advisable."

Malcolm consented to this, and rode forward to hasten his meeting with the horse-men, whose forms he could now see through the trees.

At a sharp turn in the road they met, and he was surprised to see Stukely and a villanous-looking ruffian, both armed to the teeth.

"How now ?" he demanded. "Hast caught scent of the fox that thou hast come to meet me ? Quick ! tell me thy news, be it good or ill."

"Saint Benedict !" growled Stukely ; "you kept me waiting a sore time at the cross-roads. This fellow here brings us some news of our game."

"Of Robin ?"

"Ay. He took shelter for the night at the Jolly Ploughman. 'Tis some miles from here ; and, as he will not start till day has well set in, we may gain the shelter of Hollow-oak Dell, and waylay him as he passes."

"But he has some of his men with him, and we shall need more help," interposed the ruffian.

"I have plenty of help at hand," rejoined Malcolm. "Yo, ho, there ! Yo, ho !"

At this moment the soldiers came from their concealment, and Stukely gave a grin of satisfaction as he recognised the leader, from whose observation he concealed his own features by closing the bars of his helmet.

Malcolm, Stukely, and the ruffian rode on, a head abreast of each other, the two former holding a whispered conversation until they arrived at the place where they proposed laying in ambush.

Hollow-oak Dell was thickly wooded, and bordered on each side by a dense forest, through which the dell made a short cut, making the journey shorter by several miles than by the road.

No place could have been better adapted for a sudden surprise : a dense underwood on either side formed an ambush for the cross-bow men, and a glade sheltered by trees served as a hiding place for the horsemen, where they could remain within call, and sally forth at any moment.

Malcolm soon arranged his force, and stationed the ruffian in the hollow oak at the foot of the dell, where he could command a good view of the road, and then Malcolm and Stukely seated themselves at the foot of the tree and regaled themselves with a flagon of wine.

At intervals Stukely broke the conversation which they had resumed by shouting to the man in the tree, whom he addressed as Brownley, asking him if he could see aught along the road, and exhorting him to be vigilant in his look-out.

Brownley was a hired ruffian, and had been promised good pay for his services, and therefore did his work well, and the first appearance of a man in the road was noted by his keen eye at once.

Stukely started to his feet as soon as the man announced what he saw, and climbed up beside him, when he readily recognised Robin Hood, Little John, and Will Scarlett.

They were walking arm-in-arm down the

road, trolling a song, and were evidently unconscious of the danger that awaited them.

With the cunning of an Indian, Stukely watched their approach, and it caused him some uneasiness when they came to a sudden halt, and seemed inclined to pursue their way along the road instead of turning into the dell.

To his joy, however, they did not ; and he slid cautiously down and concealed himself, a vicious gleam lighting his visage as their voices heralded their approach.

He did not hear the low, owl-like hoot, however, that had been given and answered when the foresters first stopped ; and when he counted on his force and the few that were to oppose him, he chuckled inwardly with delight.

"Stand ready for a spring ; surround them at once," he whispered to the bowmen near him ; "take them alive, and use no unnecessary violence."

"Now, now !" he added, and he gave the signal to the others, who rushed from their concealment at the sound of his voice, and completely surrounded the astonished foresters.

"Stand off, an' you prize your lives !" cried Robin, as the trio clutched their quarterstaves and placed themselves back to back. "By the mass ! matters have taken a queer turn, when we are to be assailed by robbers on the highway."

"Robbers ! aha !" replied Stukely, with a sardonic grin. "It will perchance remind thee that we have met before, when I tell thee thou art arrested in the king's name."

"And it will doubtless remind you that I defy the king's power, and dispute his authority, when I tell you that I will not surrender ; and, more, that I will trounce your hide for your insolence, if you are not off at once."

"Quotha ! the man is mad !" broke in Malcolm. "See you not, sir outlaw, that you are in our power ? We number seven to your one. Marry, I trow, 'tis but little, save a broken crown, you can gain by fighting."

"A true man reckons not on odds," retorted Robin, gathering up his staff ; "but I leave it to your choice whether you let us pass or whether we make you."

This brought a grin from the soldiers, who treated the matter only as a jest ; and, so confident did they feel in themselves, that they did not even draw their swords.

This insult, however, angered Little John, and with one swoop of his staff he laid two of the brawny bowmen bleeding on the grass, and then looked round with a fierce glance to see who else would dare the same thing again.

It was now time for the leader of the soldiers to get angered.

Seeing his men thus handled, he did not wait to consult Malcolm, but ordered his men to draw and lay on.

With fearful oaths, the Norman soldiers obeyed ; but the tough staves sent some of their swords flying back splintered in the faces of those who used them, and many a thick crown proved its weakness ere many minutes had elapsed.

"Odds bodikins ! lay on, you knaves !" cried Malcolm, as he strove vainly to force his way through the compact body that hemmed the foresters in like a wall. "Zounds ! cut the rascals down, since they have chosen their own fate."

Thus emulated, and burning with rage at the heroism of their Saxon opponents, the soldiers trampled on the bodies of their wounded comrades, and strove to get within the huge circle described by the long oak poles that acted like scythes, and mowed down a Norman bowman at each gyration.

Stukely fairly foamed with rage, and called upon the horsemen to dismount and assist their comrades with their long falchions ; but ere they could obey, Robin blew his horn, and a party of foresters rushed from between the trees, and with their staves commenced an assault upon the mounted men.

Many of the soldiers had already disengaged one foot from the stirrup, and were dropping to the ground when the unexpected attack commenced, and thus, taken at a disadvantage, they were unable to resist the crashing blows that fell upon their iron-cased heads.

The others, taking warning by this, reseated themselves in their saddles as hastily as possible, and prepared to defend themselves as well as they could ; for they could do little in the way of fighting, owing to the narrowness of the place and the rushing to and fro of the riderless horses, that became wild on feeling the reins loosed about their necks.

In this manner the foresters soon reduced their opponents to equal numbers, and took the strain off the hands of Robin and his two hard-pressed companions, and a fight, such as Hollow-oak Dell had never before witnessed, was speedily brought to a close.

Both Malcolm and Stukely, on seeing the turn matters had taken, jumped into an empty saddle and galloped off, leaving the beaten soldiers in the hands of their victors, and the ruffian Brownley, who had never ventured to quit his post, safely concealed in the tree.

Heedless of the shrieks and cries of the fallen soldiers, who were unable to rise, Malcolm and Stukely spurred on their horses over the helpless men, trampling them under foot, and thinking only of their own safety.

Curses and imprecations they heaped upon each other on gaining the road, and mentally cursed themselves for the manner in which they had acted.

But Little John did not care to see them get off so scot free.

When he had settled the leader, with whom he had been engaged, he and his companions darted away through the dell, and gained a bend in the road, which hid them from view.

They had had sufficient time to get some distance, and Little John even doubted his own ability to hit them ; but, stringing an arrow on the instant, he let fly, and had the satisfaction to see the foremost horse and its rider roll over in the road.

The horse was just turning the bend when the arrow struck it, and the hindermost rider being unable to check his steed in its headlong course, stumbled over the fallen carcase, and threw its rider into the opposite ditch.

This double catastrophe happened so momentary that Little John had not time to prepare a second arrow, and when the second horse fell he started towards it with his utmost speed.

Stukely was just scrambling from the ditch when he arrived, and Little John seized him by the neck and hauled him out of the slime, then dragged him to the spot where Malcolm lay groaning.

Malcolm was too much hurt to rise.

His horse had fallen upon him, and injured him so much internally that he was past all human aid.

Little John made Stukely fetch him some water, and give him all the aid in his power; but he never recovered his speech, and died a few minutes afterwards, a victim to his own treachery.

"Now, varlet, what hast thou to say for thyself, that thy fate should not be like his?" demanded Little John, of Stukely. "Thou art a vile traitor, and thy cunning hath proved too much for thee. What sayst thou, if I stretch ye lifeless beside yon carrion cur?"

Stukely's cheek paled, and he shrank from the honest gaze of the stern outlaw, yet his spirit would not allow him to crave for pardon.

"Do with me as you think fit," he replied, with desperate firmness. "I am in your power, and yet will I not crave a boon."

This reply did more in his favour than if he had fallen on his knees and begged for mercy.

It recorded well with the giant's bold spirit, and made his heart warm towards him although he was his enemy.

Perhaps it was because he saw in the parent the same undaunted pride that he had so admired in the daughter—the same look of resolute defiance that Madge assumed when anyone chided her for a fault, and the same heedlessness of danger that made her bring her father to his present state.

As Little John loved Madge in spite of Stukely's aversion to it, it was no wonder he viewed his fault so lightly, and doubtless it was this prevented him putting his threat of death into execution.

"He is a villain, there is no doubt," Little John thought to himself "but still I cannot find it in my heart to hurt him. I will frighten him, however, and that may serve as a caution to him in future."

"Is it pride or a knowledge of your guilt that prevents you asking a boon?" said Little John, sternly. "Have you so many crimes on your guilty conscience that you deem your punishment just?"

"Nay, those whose hands are free from all crimes and evil doings need crave no pity, neither is it meet that they should beg for mercy from those whose heart is too hard to give it."

Stukely had now gained his wonted firmness; the weakness which the love for his daughter instilled into him had been mastered, and he looked without quailing into the face of the tall forester.

Little John eyed him with a glance that seemed to fathom his inmost thought, and, in a tone of deep solemnity, he asked—

"What sayst thou of the murder of thy wife's brother? Was that not a crime? Dost think the flames of purgatory will ever cleanse thee of it?"

"Peace! What mean you?" gasped the guilt-stricken wretch, his limbs trembling as though he had been seized with palsy, and his cheeks and lips turning of a livid hue. "What fiend has put this in your head?"

"Fiend! Ha! ha! When the spirits of the departed visit the earth, and cannot find rest in the grave, do you call them fiends? If such be the case, then surely have I seen a"——

"Hold! I prythee!" cried Stukely interrupting him. "You have not seen"——

"The spirit of thy wife's injured brother—murdered—poisoned by thy hand; robbed of life to appease thine accursed thirst for gold."

Had Little John pierced him with his skean, he could not have wounded him more than he did with these words.

Stukely clasped his hands to his brow in agony, and the sweat poured from him in streams.

"Holy Mother!" he half shrieked, "I call upon thy aid. Save me, I pray, my brain is burning—my heart-strings are ready to burst. Forgive me, Holy Virgin, or I shall go mad!"

Tears gushed from the eyes of the agonised man, and he sank on his knees on the grass, and offered up a prayer.

Moved at the sight, Little John felt his own strong nerves give way, and he repented having carried out his promise to the hermit so far.

"Rise," he said; "and if thy repentance is as sincere as thou wouldst make me believe, get thee to some retired spot, and spend thy days in prayer and repentance; go," he added, authoritatively, "live a life of atonement, and let thy latter days be as pure of sin as thy younger days have been free from virtue."

So saying, the forester turned away, leaving Stukely still kneeling on the grass, weeping like a child.

CHAPTER CXVII.

MADGE STUKELY PAYS A VISIT TO THE OLD WOMAN ON THE HEATH.

For at her father's absence
  Her heart was troubled sore,
She sought the cottage on the heath
  And knocked at the door.

The old witch sat beside the hearth,
  Where on the embers bright,
She was preparing of a charm
  For her to work that night.

"It is not my father, and yet methought I heard a footstep. Where can he be? Two days has he been gone, and I wot not what called him from home so hurriedly. I fear he has come to harm. Saints forbid that he should have again fallen into the hands of the sheriff!"

Thus mused Madge Stukely, as for the twentieth time since daylight had dawned she closed the lattice that overlooked the rugged and ruinous path that led to the entrance of her lonesome abode.

Two restless days and sleepless nights had she passed since her father left her, promising to return shortly; and every sound that she heard she fancied was his footsteps returning. But when she looked forth upon the dreary path, amid the waste of ruins, and saw him not, her heart sank and her mind was filled with fearful imaginations.

The rooms they inhabited, though old, were comfortably fitted up but cheerless, and especially so the once light-hearted girl, who, as we have seen, had been used to the gay ribaldry of the soldiers of the castle, and now sighed for the mirth and jollity that she had always been used to.

Since Stukely had taken her from the mill-house and made her abide in the ruins, she had known no companionship but that of her stern, despotic father, and now, in her present lonely state, she even sighed for that.

Had she known that his absence would have been so long she would have paid a visit to the mill, even at the risk of incurring his displeasure, for he had forbidden her to leave the place, he himself procuring the food for them, which was but little they needed, for, unsettled in mind and body, they neither of them ate much.

"Ah, me!" sighed Madge, as she laid down her rosary, and then took another survey from the casement, "this life will kill me. I can endure it no longer; my father, I feel certain, has fallen into some mischief. There is old Dame Morton, who lives in the cottage on the heath, she is a kind old dame. I have heard she is gifted with second sight; she told old Michael the blacksmith true enough when she said he would not live to see bold Robin Hood restored to his estates, and cured—she cured the armourer's daughter when she was bewitched by the beggar-man for not giving him alms, and why should she not tell me of my father?"

As she stood musing thus, a young fawn came out from among the ruins, and, uttering a plaintive cry, entered a thicket, making the welkin ring again with its sorrowful notes.

"Poor thing, it has lost its parent," she muttered to herself. "It is searching for its mother." And then, as the thought struck her, she added, "Why should I not seek for my father?"

The thought was both sudden and strange; but nevertheless it had its effect upon her. Taking a basket in her arm, as though she was going to gather sticks, she left her ruined home and closed the door after her.

Dame Morton, or the wise woman of the heath, as she was called, lived two miles distant from any other house, in the midst of a lonely heath, where she made a scanty livelihood by working on the minds of the credulous, and settling the disputes of foolish lovers.

Not only the poor, but the rich often sought her; for superstition was rife in those days, and the minds of the people were constantly kept in a ferment by the black arts practised by the monks.

Madge hurried on with all speed till she reached the cottage, and the old woman kept her some time knocking at the door, as she was doing something that she did not wish prying eyes to see, but when she opened the door, and saw Madge, whom she knew, she apologised for keeping her so long waiting.

"And now, my canny bairn, what brings thee to the heath?" asked the shrivelled old dame, her parchment visage wrinkling into what she meant for a smile. "Hast been crossed in love, or hast thou married against thy father's will?"

"Neither," replied Madge, mournfully. "I come to ask your advice. You have no doubt heard that we have left the castle?"

"Ay, so thou hast, my canny one," whined the old hag; "it had slipped my memory, quite. Grammercy! now I think on it, I heard you had left this part of the country."

"I would that we had; it would be better for us. But I have come to talk of other matters. Can you tell me ought of my father? These two days I have not seen him."

"Wot ye where he is gone?"

"Of a truth I do not."

"Said he nothing that would enable thee to form an opinion?"

"Nay."

"Thinkest thou he has any enemies?"

"Many, I fear me."

"Know ye of their names?"

"Geoffrey de Lois is one. I cannot mention any others."

"Humph!" grunted the old woman, and she fixed her eyes on the burning embers, as though she could read in them the answer she was planning in her mind.

"The Sheriff De Lois," she added, after a pause of some seconds. "Is he at Nottingham?"

"I know not. He owes my father no good will, and I fear he has fallen into his hands."

"Umph!" growled the old woman, again, and fixed her eyes once more on the burning embers. "Let me look at thy hand," she presently added.

Madge held out her hand, and the old woman uttered a deep growl.

"There is much trouble there," she said, "war, and bloodshed. Has thy father taken into his head to meddle with the affairs of Robin Hood?"

"Alas! I cannot say. I hope not. Yet, I fear"——

"Then thou mayest rest assured it is so. Thy father has meddled with that which he ought to have left alone. Depend on it, he has brought upon himself some trouble. Go home, and make thyself as comfortable as thou canst. To-night I will work the potent spell; and in the morning, if he does not return before, come hither again."

"Madge burst into tears at these words. She firmly believed the old woman saw the trouble she spoke of marked on her hands. But the old woman only spoke from facts that she knew, as Stukely had called upon her only a few days before, to procure a charm which was to fortify his life against all danger.

To this charm, Stukely, in his ignorance, had attributed the saving of his life, and the cause of his absence will be seen in future events.

Had Little John have known what injury he was doing to his beloved master, in allowing Stukely to go free, he would have slain him on the spot; but he did not, and the mischief was done unwittingly by him.

When Madge's grief had somewhat subsided, and she had dried her tears, she was about to return home, but the old woman bade her stay.

"Thou art in love, my canny lass," she said. "Nay, it is no good denying it to me; I can see it in thy face, and read it in that sigh. Take heed what thou dost, for by the Virgin! if thou marryest him thou lovest, though he may be true to thee, thy life will be a cup of bitterness. Hear me, lass," she added, impressively—

"The owl may nestle with the dove;
One loves, one fears the light.
You cannot alter night to day,
Nor change the day to night;
And thus with our opinions,
One's dark, the other's light;
And when two different minds do meet,
We call them day and night."

Madge was at a loss to understand the magic words. She was about to inquire their meaning, but the old crone waved her away, and, with a heavy heart, she left the cottage.

CHAPTER CXVIII.

GEOFFREY DE LOIS GETS DEFEATED.

The friar and the abbot met,
And sorely they did tussle;
Tuck threw him down upon the ground,
And then his jaws did muzzle.

GEOFFREY DE LOIS on entering the forest proceeded with caution, and sent on a-head an advance-guard of six mounted men to see the way clear, and give notice of the appearance of anything like danger.

He had with him all the available force he could spare, without leaving the castle unprotected—about two hundred men in all, horse and foot.

Besides those, he had ten men whom he called sharp-shooters. They had a kind of instrument invented by the monks of Saint Mary's. It was a kind of iron tube fastened on to a stick with wire, and it would by means of a wire spring, project a missile (a piece of iron about four inches long, and about the size round of the little finger) twenty yards with deadly effect.

These men were trained to lay upon the grass and shoot, and they were to crawl as close to the enemy as possible, and harass them fearfully, without letting them know from whence the dangerous shafts came.

With this novel improvement in the mode of warfare then practised, Geoffrey looked forward to a decisive and easy victory, which opinion he was the more confirmed in when he thought of the aid the abbot had promised him.

As we have observed, Geoffrey had been well informed of the foresters' movements, such as the strict watch kept by the woodwards, and he expected every moment to hear of the advance-guard coming upon one of the watchers; but as they did not, he looked upon this as a sign of the outlaw's carelessness.

As he was thinking of this, he beheld a figure emerge from a clump of trees, and thinking it was one of Robin's men, he put spurs to his horse, and galloped forward to strike the fellow down before he could give an alarm.

He was surprised, however, to hear the voice of his uncle challenge him.

The abbot was so well disguised, that before he challenged him, Geoffrey did not recognise him; but he was pleased when he found out who it was.

"By the saints! you have arranged matters well," said the abbot. "I did not think thee capable of such good generalship. By the rood, thou deserveth success, if but for this alone."

Geoffrey bowed a stiff acknowledgment, and made a sign for his men to halt whilst he spoke to the abbot, who gave him great praise for the precaution of sending in the scouts.

"Look ye here, kinsman mine," said De Lois, pleased with the flattery, "I have vowed to rout the rascals to-night at any cost. Perform thy promise well, and success is certain."

"Ay, that will I; and I hope that in the hour of victory you will not forget your duty to the Church."

"Zounds!" replied De Lois, in well-feigned surprise, "do you take me for such an ungrateful sinner? Saint Dunstan forbid that I should rob thee of thy share. Come, thy blessing, good abbot, and bethink thee of some sacred relic thou has stowed away upon thee somewhere."

With this assurance of a share in the spoil, the abbot placed his hand beneath his robe and took from his breast a small sealed packet.

Presenting it to De Lois, he said,

"Take this, nephew mine. 'Tis a relic that will shield thee from all harm; it contains a hair from the head of our patron saint, the Holy Virgin; guard it as thou wouldst thy life, and thy life shall as surely be guarded by it."

Geoffrey took the sacred relic, kissed it, and placed it in security, and when the abbot had given the soldiers his blessing, the sheriff gave the word to move on.

The abbot turned slowly away, and entered a narrow path on the right, which led by a shorter route to the outlaw's stronghold, and before he had proceeded far, he was joined by a man clad in soldier-like attire.

"Ah, Dunstan! you are here betimes," said the abbot, addressing the new comer. "How fares matters with thee?"

"Good, sir abbot; no better could I wish them. The rascals have withdrawn the outposts, and are making merry on the strength of the good news they have heard."

The abbot gave a quiet grin.

"What news is that, my son?" he asked.

"That Robin is returning from London, laden with the trophies of victory. He is expected soon, and they are having a last carousal before his return."

"Then we can easily surprise them."

"Ay, and capture every one. The prisoners are tired of their captivity, though, if they had acted as I have done, they might be free."

"Ha! ha! made friends with the wine-swilling Friar Tuck. Well, had it not been for the money I smuggled to you, you would not have been able to do so; but I hope you will make good amends for that, and earn your reward and my benison."

"Good father, thou needst not fear for that. I will show you the entrance to the stronghold. Hast brought with thee the soldiers?"

"They are on the way, let us haste to meet them. If nought happens them they will halt within bow-shot of the outlaw's stronghold. In the meantime, as we trudge on, thou canst tell me all thou knowest."

As Dunstan had said, they had little reason to fear being molested in the forest; not a soul did they meet to challenge them, and they arrived at the place where they intended to halt without the sight of a single green jerkin.

Dunstan, armed with a sword that the sheriff had brought purposely with him, took the lead, and showed them the weakest point of the stronghold, and De Lois halted his men and formed them into lines.

De Lancy had charge of one division, and he led the attack by leaping from his horse and making an attempt to scale the palisade.

In this he failed; but as day began to break through the heavens, he saw that the place had been more strongly built than either he or Dunstan had imagined, and he held a council apart with De Lois and several of the oldest warriors.

It was then decided that artifice must be used.

Tall trees were hewn down and made into poles, which were thrown across from the outer edge of the ditch to the top of the palisading; and the bowmen then crawled along them, thus attacking the stronghold at several points at once, leaving the horsemen to form a cordon round the place to prevent any of the foresters escaping.

This ruse, of course (had matters been as they supposed), must have been successful. But, contrary to their expectations, the foresters were prepared for them. Showers of arrows came from the loopholes at the poles, and the scaling party fell thick and fast, wounded or dead, into the trench.

Never had De Lois been so thoroughly deceived before.

He cursed, and swore, and stamped about in a violent passion, shouting to his men, who had thrown themselves down behind the mounds of earth for shelter, to fill up the places of their fallen comrades.

On the other hand, the foresters maintained the strictest silence—the twang of a bow or the flight of an arrow being the only sign that the enclosure was inhabited.

The abbot, who, at the first onset, under the assurance of subduing the foresters without their being able to strike a blow, had put himself in the midst of the men, now thought it prudent to retire; but, as he was slinking away beneath the trees, a strong hand gripped him by the neck.

"Be not so hasty, good father, I beseech thee," said a well-known voice in his ear. "'Tis long since you paid us poor mortals a visit in the forest, and we stand much in need of thy goodly counsel."

His eyes lit with a malicious gleam as he turned and fixed his astonished gaze on Friar Tuck, and he muttered, hoarsely,

"Curse you, for a son of Beelzebub! Release me, ere the hand of heaven punishes you for molesting one of the true followers of the cross."

Friar Tuck gave a laugh that made his fat sides shake.

"A true follower of the Evil One art thou," he said; "and I mean not to part with thee until thou confessest all thy crimes. Let us hasten from the sounds of strife, for which are not fitted such ears as ours, and, in the solitude of some quiet dell, thou canst confess thy manifold sins, and I will give thee that absolution thou so much needest."

The abbot bit his lips, and with a voice hoarse with rage, replied—

"Ungodly sinner! Your insolence is beyond all compare. I will punish you as you deserve. By the rood, you shall atone for this with your life."

So saying, the abbot took from beneath his skirt a short-handled sword, and brandished it in the air; but before he could use it, the friar wrenched it from his grasp.

"Treacherous hound!" said the friar, with a smile that showed how little he feared the abbot's anger; "thou hast acted the part of an ass, and, therefore, deserve to be treated as one. I have a good bow-string with me, which I use to tan the hides of unbelievers, and also to scourge myself with when necessity needs it. It is long—very long since I had a use for it, and now I think it may do me some service."

The abbot was naturally a coward, and had he not been, it was enough to make him tremble when he found himself seized in the friar's powerful grasp, thrown down on his hands and knees, a thong fastened to his neck, and the friar dragging him along.

This humiliation was too great for him to bear, however.

In spite of the friar's threats, he made an effort, and sprang to his feet; but the friar felled him again with a single blow.

"Help! help! De Lois! De Lois!" thundered the abbot, at the top of his voice. "Help! murder!—help! he"——

"Odds bodikins!" muttered the friar; "thou hast chosen thyself for an ass; and as you bray as one, I will not let thee open thy mouth. Not that I fear for De Lois—he has too much to attend to, without troubling with thee. I will show thee that Friar Tuck is no fool, and that treachery to bold Robin, my master, is sure to meet with its reward."

As he spoke, he took the rope or scourge from round the abbot's waist, and tied it across his mouth in the form of a gag, and then led him onwards again on all fours.

Presently the friar heard a noise somewhat like a groan, and on looking about, he saw a figure leaning against the trunk of a tree.

Seeing that the fellow was wounded, Friar Tuck led his prisoner up to the spot, and then found that it was Dunstan—a discovery which afforded the friar much delight.

"Well, my friend," he said, eyeing the traitor's rueful countenance; "what ails thee? How is it that you are not leading the *brave* Normans into the stronghold? Hast brought them so far, and then left them?"

The traitor replied with another deep groan, and pointed to his breast, which the friar had not noticed was bleeding.

In the struggle he had been wounded accidentally by one of the sharp-shooters, who, on seeing him crawl away, and taking him for one of the foresters escaping, had shot one of the bolts at him, and hit him.

The blunt instrument had entered his breast below the left nipple about an inch, and the pain was so excruciating that he could not speak; and he could hardly stand, even with the support of the tree.

Friar Tuck hated the fellow for the treacherous part he had played; for he had wound himself into the friar's favour by feigning penitence and giving the friar all the money he possessed to grant him absolution, and obtaining his freedom to walk about the stronghold with less restriction than the rest of the prisoners.

The friar, however, was not so blind as not to see through the ruse.

He knew perfectly well at the time he took the money that it had been secretly conveyed to him from St. Mary's Abbey, and that Dunstan was playing the part of a Judas.

This knowledge he also imparted to George-a-Green, who enjoyed many a hearty laugh over the flagons of wine purchased with the money, and a strict but secret watch was kept over Dunstan's actions, and thus they were prepared for the sheriff's attack.

Yet, for all this, the jolly friar could not bear to see the man suffer without giving him some help.

He soon stripped him of his doublet, extricated the bolt, and bound up the wound, and then moistened the wounded man's lips with the wine from the black jack that was the friar's constant companion and only solace in the absence of Little John.

But one of the main arteries had been severed, and it was impossible to stay the flow of blood; so the man slowly sank, and died while the friar was giving him shrift.

The death of his accomplice, or tool in crime, had no effect upon the callous heart of the abbot, who only wished that the friar had died in his stead; but it galled him greatly when Friar Tuck told him how he had been sworn.

"A malison on thee for a heretic and a wizard!" the abbot burst out savagely; "'tis to thee, then, that we owe this partial defeat of our plans. By the mass! you shall suffer for this, though at present it may seem that all goes well with you, and the accursed band with which you are in league."

"Give thy prating to the winds, for I want none on't," replied the friar, with a hearty laugh.

"I will conduct thee to a spot where the noise of strife shall not affront thy saintly ears, and where thou canst offer up thy heartfelt prayers without a fear of being disturbed."

He had allowed the abbot to rise to his feet, for he found it tardy work in leading him on all fours, and he conducted him to a secluded spot, which, for its solitude, he had chosen as his own place of resort when he wished to be alone, and enjoy an hour's peaceful sleep.

ROBIN HOOD,

AND THE OUTLAWS OF SHERWOOD FOREST.

THE WOUNDED BUCK.

Here he bound the abbot firmly to a tree, and, having loosed the gag to allow him to breathe freely, he left him to his own reflections, and then crept through the thick underwood to obtain a glimpse of what was going on at the stronghold.

By this time, De Lois and his leaders had tried many ingenious contrivances, such as rams to batter down the fence, and archers stationed in the trees to fire over the enclosure; but when they tried they could not meet with success.

An hour of such warfare had been carried on, and a score of the sheriff's soldiers had fallen beneath the outlaws' unerring shafts, when a bugle, thrice sounded, rang on the morning air.

It was impossible for any one who had once heard Robin wind his horn not to recognise its sound in those loud ringing blasts, and De Lois looked like one stricken to stone when they fell on his ear.

"Saint Quinton!" he muttered, savagely to De Lancey, "'tis Robin Hood himself! By the mass! how is it he hath escaped?"

"Marry! 'tis hard to say, Sir Sheriff. By the mass! 'tis true what report saith, that he is a devil incarnate."

"Not only a devil, but a prince of devils!" exclaimed the exasperated sheriff. "His men are a legion of fiends, but I fear them not. I have the blessing of our good lord the abbot, and a hair of the blessed Virgin's head, which is enough to protect us against the machinations of a thousand fiends, even were they fresh from the bottomless pit."

He took the packet from his breast, and kissed the consecrated wafer with which it was sealed, and then held it to the lips of De Lancey.

The soldier kissed it with fervour, then devoutly crossed himself, whilst his men who were near enough, looked upon them both with reverential awe.

"To horse!" shouted De Lois to those of his followers who had dismounted. "To horse! Follow me!"

He dug the spikes on his iron heel deep into the flanks of his fiery charger, and dashed through an opening in the trees in the direction of the bugle sound, followed closely by his mounted men-at-arms.

The clash of steel, snorting of steeds, and trampling of feet as the horses tore up the ground with their hind hoofs when bounding forward, had scarcely subsided, when the notes of the bugle again winded through the forest.

"On, on!" shouted De Lois, wild with excitement. "One hundred marks to the man who takes the traitor alive!"

He had scarcely uttered the word, when Robin Hood himself made his appearance through the foliage, and stepped into the glade, followed by Little John and Will Scarlett.

The sight of the array of armed men, formidable as it looked in the morning sun, which reddened the spear points and glittering armour of the soldiers, seemed to have no effect on the daring outlaws, who stood with arms folded, watching the cavalcade approaching them.

This boldness, though it seemed to place them in the sheriff's power, annoyed him sorely. He goaded his steed until the blood gushed from its wounded sides, and shouted with bitter oaths to his men to quicken their speed.

The troops thundered on, making the very earth seem to tremble under their iron hoofs, and though they were but a minute, as it were, flying over the quarter of a mile of ground that separated them from the daring outlaws, it seemed to Geoffrey an age.

Snatching his sword from its sheath, so as to be ready to cut Robin down if he attempted to fly, he raised it threateningly above his head; but just as he was performing this act, the ground trembled beneath the horses' feet, and horses and riders suddenly disappeared.

Simultaneously as they fell into the trap prepared for them—which was a platform of thin slabs placed temporarily over a hole and covered with earth a party of foresters sprang up from the grass beneath the trees, and made for the spot.

On nearing the edge of the pit, a scene of confusion impossible to describe met their gaze.

Horses and riders were struggling to free themselves from the entangled mass, in which struggle neither arms nor heads were spared.

Broken limbs, battered brains, and dying horses, lay mingled in a heap, and Geoffrey De Lois was seen crawling out of the confused mass, apparently unhurt.

On seeing him, Robin Hood flew to his assistance, and helped him out of the hole, and the rest of the foresters set to work in rescuing the others.

Little John made good use of his prowess in this.

The soldiers, for their own safety, had turned their swords and pikes upon the horses, to stay their frantic kicking, though a great many of the powerful war steeds had broken their necks in the fall.

When Geoffrey found himself safe from the death that had threatened him, and saw himself in the outlaw's hands, he fairly foamed with rage, and he drew his dagger and made a thrust at Robin's breast.

In this he failed, however; and the next moment he found himself stretched helpless on the sward.

But his actions stimulated his men to make a blow for freedom, and many who might have been rescued, fell victims to their own folly in doing so.

De Lancey would have been one of these, had not Little John saved his life by snatching his sword from his hand when he was about to give battle to Will Scarlett, and De Lancey, with the rest of the prisoners, were bound hand and foot, and placed under the outspreading boughs of an enormous oak.

CHAPTER CXIX.

FRIAR TUCK RESCUES THE LORD ABBOT FROM A DISAGREEABLE SITUATION.

As night came on with deepening shade,
The wolves they left their den,
To seek for food, as was their wont,
In the abodes of men.

FRIAR TUCK, from his position, could obtain a good view of the fight, and when De Lois gallopped off with his men, he felt anxious to know how those who were left behind were going to act.

Stealing cautiously from his concealment, he saw a party of crossbow-men gathering dry sticks and leaves, which they handed to their comrades in the trench, who placed them against the palisade, and set fire to them.

These operations were going on in a different part to that where the fighting was being carried on, therefore the foresters did not notice it, as their attention was otherwise directed.

Another ruse they tried was to thrust stakes into the loopholes, which they rendered immoveable by fixing one end in the ground, and which acted so effectually as to preclude the possibility of an arrow being shot through them by either party.

Friar Tuck, however, no sooner saw this than he made a signal, which was understood by George-a-Green, and before the bowmen preparing the fire could get ready for defence, a party of foresters burst through the artfully contrived holes in the sides of the trench and fell upon them with their quarter staves in a manner that was anything but desirable.

In like manner another party surprised those who were still endeavouring to scale the wall, and then a terrible hand-to-hand encounter commenced.

This was raging fiercely when Robin appeared upon the scene, and the followers he brought with him joining in the fray, soon put an end to the fight.

The foresters, according to their usual custom, set about at once in attending to the wounded on both sides; and the loss on the side of the outlaws was found to be ten, but of the soldiers, there were near one hundred killed and wounded.

The prisoners on this occasion, owing to their great number, were all firmly bound, and placed beneath the trees under a strong guard. De Lois, however, in the confusion, contrived by some means to escape.

While these matters were being settled, Little John and Will Scarlett strolled into the wood in search of game, and they soon afterwards returned, each with a good buck on their shoulders.

George-a-Green, Allan-a-Dale, and two or three others followed their example; and the cooking preparations were carried on with great vigour.

Friar Tuck met Little John as he returned from the chase, and the pair shook hands heartily, and expressed their pleasure at seeing each other after so long an absence.

"Body o' mine!" exclaimed the long forester clutching the friar's fat hand, "what hast thou for my bodily comfort, after so long an absence? By the saints, I have often thought of ye and the wine stoup which I trow hath been your boon companion in my absence."

"Heaven forgive you your wickedness, you unshriven rogue," replied the friar. "You are of a gluttonous nature, and take all men to be so; but you are wrong, I have passed my time during your absence in fast and prayer. Now you have come, I must, for friendship sake, throw aside all saintly vows, and drink a stoup to your health in like manner to such rascals as yourself."

Little John rolled up his eyes in well feigned sanctity, and crossed himself like a devout Christian, and replied—

"Body o' mine! good father, let me not tempt thee to sin. Defile not thyself with wine for my sake. I would not, for the best barrel of rich juice that ever came from Burgundy, have it on my conscience that I caused thee to sin against thy will."

Friar Tuck found himself in a fix.

Little John had fairly beaten him with his own weapons; but the friar, with his natural cuteness, soon found a hole to creep out of.

Putting his mouth to Little John's ear he said in a tone of deep solemnity—

"Listen, my son, and thou mayst hear that which none but myself can tell thee."

"Well, well."

"Thou hast heard of the treachery of Duncan, and his villany in trying to put an end to us all by poisoning the wine."

"What!" gasped Little John opening his mouth to its full extent.

"Why, he poisoned the wine!" replied the friar, scarcely able to contain his composure.

"The dev— the deuce, he did! Then he deserves a thousand deaths. Marry come up with wennion on the rogue for spoiling such good stuff. But how came you to find this out?"

"I watched the rogue, of course. How did I find out his treachery, think you?"

"Zounds, 'twas fortunate."

"Indeed it was; and what was more fortunate, I understood the qualities of the drug he used. I knew its antidote, and not one of the whole band would venture to drain a stoup unless I first tasted of the flagon."

"Body o' me! most wonderous strange is this," said the giant, a suspicion of the truth flashing vividly to his mind. "By the blade bone of our patron saint! had I not heard it from thine own lips, I should have considered it a lie; but as it cometh from thee, I cannot dispute its veracity."

After settling matters thus, the worthy pair hied them to the cellarman and freely indulged in the potent liquor which they highly praised, each pretending to have tasted none so rare for so long a time.

The friar's eyes glistened when he saw Little John's well-filled pouch, and he questioned him closely as to how he became possessed of so much money; but for the present the giant would give him no satisfactory reply.

"'Twas from one of the cloth I got it," he said; "but when, where, or how, I am under an oath not to reveal. But thou canst rest assured it was not from thy friend the abbot. By the mass! 'tis a long time now, since we squeezed his tight-drawn purse."

Friar Tuck burst into a laugh.

The mention of the Lord Abbot reminded him of the predicament he had left him in.

"By my faith!" he exclaimed, "'tis well you have made that remark, for I left him in a strange predicament some hours since we met; and as he was not in the best of humours, I left him to compose himself."

"Where?" exclaimed the astonished Little John.

"In a little nook thou wottest not of; but I will hie thither, and if it seem thee fit thou canst accompany me."

"Marry, will I," replied the giant; and they hurried off to the place named.

Before reaching the shaded dell, where the abbot was bound to the tree, their ears were assailed with a horrid howling and a succession of angry growls, which assured them that the wolves were making a repast on the unburied dead. Little did they imagine, however, that the abbot was one they had selected for their prey, and their surprise may be easier imagined than described when they beheld the saintly man battling furiously with the hungry wolves.

Fortunately he had got one hand free; and, in the absence of a more efficient weapon, he was defending himself as lustily as he could with a crucifix he had taken from his neck, and which proved a formidable weapon in the hands of a desperate man.

The tree formed a protection for him behind, or he would soon have fallen a victim, of which the torn and tattered state of his clothing, which hung in shreds, bore testimony.

Several of the most ravenous were busied in devouring the carcase of their companions which the abbot had struck senseless to the earth, and this rid him of a few of his foes; but the others seemed bent upon dining on the abbot's fat carcase. At the approach of Little John and the friar, the wolves showed their anger at being disturbed, and with hideous growls turned upon the new comers, and they had some difficulty in keeping them off, as they were completely surrounded by them.

Friar Tuck tore down a bough, and Little John did the same, and they laid about them in such a manner that the wolves were glad to desist, and slink off in the direction of the others, who were feasting upon the dead carcases of the horses in the pit.

The abbot was then released; and never before was he so pleased at the sight of a forester as he was then.

CHAPTER CXX.

MAID MARIAN STRIKES A BLOW.—DEATH OF REBECCA.

They listened in the deep green woods,
Where angry words were rife,
And then a noise assailed their ears,
Of men engaged in strife.

As Hubert and his little party neared the heart of the dense forest that stretched on either side of them for some miles, they were startled by the sound of voices near them.

The soldier whispered for them to halt, and they stood in a clump of trees to listen.

The voices proceeded from several persons, and Hubert recognized some of the speakers.

"If you have no evil intent, why are you absent from the Keep," asked a gruff voice sternly. "I believe you have aided the prisoners to escape, so I shall take you back, and you can plead your innocence to the governor, if you think he'll believe you."

"Plead my innocence!" replied a voice which they recognised as Hal's. "Never! my tongue is not given to lying, neither do I practice fawning at the feet of those who blame me without cause."

"Aha! your bullying will not save you," said the first speaker, ironically.

"I do not wish it," replied Hal with scorn. "Take me before the governor if you think it meet, or let me go, and I will return of my own accord."

"No, no," growled another, "you gave us some trouble in catching you, and a quiet walk back with you will allow us to get breath, and show the governor that we have not been idle."

"Quotha! thou art right, comrade," remarked he with the gruff voice; "and a stretch on the rack may make the young pertface disclose the hiding place of the others."

When Marian heard to what conclusion they had arrived at, her cheek flushed, and clutching her dagger, she crept from the bush where she had been listening with strained ears, and made towards the speakers.

As she gained a spot where she could obtain a view of them, she saw that a desperate struggle was going on.

The two burly soldiers were endeavouring to bind the spirited youth, and he was trying to prevent them.

Bold as he was, and lithe and supple as were his limbs, his endeavours were useless against such unequal odds, he was thrown on his back, and the pair falling on him began to pass thongs around his limbs.

Marian's blood was now fairly up.

The sight seemed to nerve her with a courage that even astounded herself, and springing lightly behind one of the kneeling men she buried the dagger in his shoulder.

With a cry of pain the man started to his feet and turned round upon Marian, but a sudden faintness seized him, and he fell backwards on the sward.

By this time Hal had released himself from the other man and dashed him to the earth, and he then flew to the assistance of his deliverer.

He had only time to entwine her with his arm ere she fainted, the excitement had been too much for her, the thought of having taken a human life filled her with horror.

Neither of the fellows, however, was seriously hurt.

One of them sprang to his feet; and, drawing his short, heavy sword, aimed a deadly blow at the head of the defenceless boy.

Hal saw the blow coming, but was unable to parry it; yet, with an impulsive movement, he stepped aside, and the fellow staggered forward.

As he did so, Hal tripped him with his foot, and threw him heavily on the ground, where he lay for a moment stunned and senseless.

Quick as lightning Hal raised Marian in his arms, and, stooping, seized the prostrate soldier's sword; but the man, recovering his senses, seized the blade, and in the struggle that ensued the sword pierced his left breast.

Hal had scarcely rid himself of his opponent when the man who had been wounded in the shoulder renewed the attack.

The brave youth cut him down with one swift blow, and then carried his charge to the thicket, where Hubert and the page were listening, in silent dread, to the noise of the conflict.

Rebecca was much worse, her life seemed to be ebbing fast; and, as it was her wish to be taken to the abbey, that she might enjoy the comforting words of a priest, Hubert determined to take her there at all hazards.

As they had some distance to journey through the forest, they did not arrive at the abbey till late, and the strains of music swelled from the sacred edifice, for the monks were at their evening vespers.

Hal waited until the sounds ceased ere he knocked at the heavy door.

A wizened priest answered the summons, and growled lustily at having been disturbed.

"What ho! who knocks at eventimes?" he asked, angrily.

"A poor man who has lost his way,"

replied Hal, meekly. "For the love of Him who died on the tree, do not refuse to open."

The saintly man thrust his face close to the small grated hole in the door, and tried to pierce the gloom to see whom it might be, but his sight was too feeble, so he opened the portal.

As he did so, he caught sight of so many figures that he started back in alarm.

"Saints defend us!" he shouted; "I have opened to one sinner, and lo! a host appeareth. Hie thee home, ungrateful dogs, I will not admit thee!"

He banged the door to, and tried to close it, but Hal was too quick for him; he thrust in his foot, and pressed the door back upon the monk.

"Avast, Hal!" exclaimed Hubert, alarmed at his companion's manner. "Calm yourself; you are excited. We shall bring upon us the wrath of the abbot, and that is what we most wish to avoid."

Hal was so incensed at the conduct of the priest, in attempting to close the door, that in the heat of the moment he paid no heed to Hubert's warning, but pressed the door so violently back as to almost deprive the priest of breath.

At that moment another monk appeared in the long corridor leading to the hall, and Hubert on seeing him entered the hall, and drew the party in after him.

The new comer happened to be Father Absalom, and Hubert knew him well, and in as few words as possible he explained how it was that the monk in charge of the door was found in such a predicament.

"My son," said Father Absalom, eyeing the soldier sternly, "I know not how to forgive ye for this desecration of the house of God, and such barbarous treatment of a true follower of the cross; and, moreover, I should like to know what brings thee to the abbey at this hour?"

"We came to crave a few hours shelter, good father, and also to ask thy blessing for one who stands in need of it," Hubert replied.

"Thou shalt not ask in vain, then," said the holy man, concealing the dark scowl on his features from Hubert's gaze. "Say, who is it that needeth shrift?"

Hubert uncovered the pale face of his wife, and, as the priest gazed upon her, she slowly opened her eyes.

By this time Hal had released the priest; and, as his temper cooled, he craved the good man's pardon for what he had done.

"My son, thou art forgiven," replied the priest. "May thy sins be as easily forgiven thee also; but I fear thou wilt have to undergo much penance before"——

Father Absalom held up his hand to enjoin silence.

Then, in a clear voice, he said, "Lead them to the refectory that those who are hungry may eat of such as our hospitality will allow,

then let each be brought separately to the confessional."

The priest led Hal, Marian, and the page away, but Hubert remained standing, with Rebecca leaning on his arm.

Then Absalom touched a small silver gong, and two novices appeared, bearing between them a litter.

Hubert placed Rebecca in it, and she was silently borne away, Father Absalom taking the lead, muttering a prayer in Latin and crossing himself devoutly.

In this manner they proceeded along several passages until they entered the chapel, which was nearly darkened.

Two candles burnt dimly on the altar, and a small wax taper burnt before the picture of their patron saint (St. Benedict) which hung upon one of the walls.

Before the altar the monk stopped and turned, and the novices rested their load at a signal given by him.

Rebecca was now almost too far gone to speak; but the monk poured the contents of a small phial down her throat, and the stimulant revived her a little.

Hubert stood for a moment with uncovered head, gazing speechless on the pale face before him, and then his manly strength gave way to a childish weakness, and he fell upon the litter and madly imprinted a kiss on the clay cold lips of his dying wife.

"Don't weep," said Rebecca, feebly; "my days in this world are numbered, grieving cannot restore to me the health I have lost. Dry up thy tears, dearest, and let me die in peace."

Father Absalom waited until the soldier had expended his strong grief, and then he gently raised him from the litter.

Then followed a mournful scene.

The priest stood by the side of the dying woman and whispered comfort in her ear, whilst one of the novices lit the incense and waved it to and fro, until its fumes scented the whole of the chapel.

Some minutes were spent in these acts of devotion, and Hubert seemed like a man bereft of reason; he stood rocking his body to and fro, and large tear-drops rolled down his cheeks.

At length the priest placed the crucifix to Rebecca's lips, and she kissed it, and this seemed to arouse the soldier from his deep abstracted grief, and he gazed calmly upon the white, upturned face of his wife.

Then another prayer muttered by the priest awoke the stillness of the chapel, and ere it was concluded, Hubert found himself gazing upon a corpse.

CHAPTER CXXI.

MAID MARIAN BRAVES THE FURY OF THE PER-
FIDIOUS FRIAR—FATHER ABSALOM'S REVENGE.

> The crafty monk to Marian
> Did make an overture ;
> Had it not been for treachery
> His death would have been sure.

SCARCELY had the breath departed from the body of the soldier's wife, than the priest ordered the chapel to be deserted by every living soul. Hubert was not even allowed to remain ; and a solitary taper was alone left to burn upon the altar.

Father Absalom, although affecting so much piety, was a crafty knave at heart.

The slight glance he had caught of Marian's features sufficed to convince him of her beauty, and this was enough to awaken the evil passions in his breast.

In his visits to the tower he had learnt that the king had chosen a fresh mistress, and though he had not been able so see her during those visits, the fact of her being in company with the king's page, and Hubert and Hal, whom he knew well, assured him that Marian was the newly imported treasure that the king so closely guarded.

That they had escaped, and been pursued, he readily conjectured, and though Rebecca had not stated correctly how she was wounded, he was not long in guessing the truth.

"By the mass ! " he muttered to himself as he walked along the gloomy corridor, " 'tis strange how circumstances throw temptations in one's way. She shall be mine ! Aha ! If she refuse—never mind, we shall see ! "

At the end of the passage he stopped, and was joined by the two novices, who appeared to be his satellites.

"Send each of those sinners, who seek to have their souls purely cleansed, to my sanctum," he said. "I would see the men first, as thou knowest. Now, haste thee ; for if thou lackest speed, a scourging will assuredly be thy portion."

The novices obeyed, and walked like mutes towards the room where the visitors were seated holding converse with each other in whispers.

He was some time closeted with the men, of which party Emilie formed one, and then Marian was summoned.

"One would little think," said the crafty churchman, "that one so graciously blessed with the worlds gifts could have so many sins stamped on so fair a brow as thine is. Yet 'tis well thou hast repented in time, that I mayest render thee as spotless and pure as thou oughtest to be."

Marian was a little confounded at these words.

She scarce knew how to interpret them, especially when he said that she was blessed with the world's gifts.

"Alas, good father, you have been deceived if you think I am endowed with any worldly riches," she said. "I am indeed poor ; the clothes that I wear even belong to another."

"I am aware of that, my child," replied the crafty priest, ogling her ; "but she whom you borrowed them of is dead."

"That is no reason that I should count them mine."

"Certainly not, my child ; but I did not speak of them as the good things thou inherited. Thou hast assuredly forgotten thy good looks."

Marian immediately divined his meaning.

Rising herself proudly erect, she said,

"Sire, I deem this as an insult."

"Thou hast deemed it wrongly, then. Few of thy years would look upon flattery as an insult."

"'Tis no matter, so long as I do," was her curt reply.

"Ah, then, thou art certainly unmindful of the great gift nature has bestowed upon thee. Come, whisper in mine ear ; is it not so ?"

Marian could scarcely contain her rage.

She felt inclined to turn her anger upon the priest, but the sanctity of the place restrained her.

Father Absalom, who had studied nature, and could almost read anyone's mind in their looks, on seeing the turn matters had taken, now tried his art at wheedling, and even went so far as to tell her that his heart was overflowing with love for her.

Marian scarcely heard what he said ; when she found out the actual meaning of what he said she turned a deaf ear to him.

But Absalom was not to be so easily put off.

First he tried promises : life, wealth, happiness, and a life within the cloisters ; then he resorted to threats.

"Fool," he muttered hoarsely in her ear ; "'twill be best for thee to accept my offer, for if you still persist in thy obstinacy to refuse it, 'twill be better for thee that thou wert not born."

"Fiend !" retorted Marian. "Is it thus you disgrace the holy order under which you pretend to serve ? Let me depart from this horrid place at once."

Father Absalom gave a quiet grin, such as a hyena might be supposed to give, then replied in a whisper hoarse with concentrated rage and disappointment—

"Ye may say what ye like, but thou wilt have to choose between me and the king. Accept my proposals, and I will give thee shelter ; refuse, and I will have thee taken back to the place from whence thou hast come."

Marian was perfectly startled at this villanous proposal.

She found that she was in the power of man, less merciful than a she-wolf would be when robbed of her young, and, what was worse, she saw not the least chance of extricating herself.

Never before did she so much feel the loss of her dear Robin as at the present time.

Not even while in the power of the king did she feel herself so helpless.

Her emotion at first was so strong that she felt absolutely powerless, and she had to clasp the oakwork to prevent herself from falling.

Taking advantage of her momentary weakness, the priest once more ventured to whisper his fiendish threats in her ear, and even went so far as to place his arm round her waist. But she shrank from his touch as though he were an adder, and a sudden reaction in her frame changed her weakness to the strength of a young lioness.

"Hence, fiend!" she shouted, making an effort to shake off his hold; but the subtle villain clung the firmer to her, and, wrought to a pitch of desperation, she dealt him a stinging blow on the ear that sent him feeling.

Astounded at this unlooked-for assault, Absalom was some time ere he could speak; and during this interval his face alternately changed from black to white, and then settled down to a kind of greenish yellow.

But Marian did not fear him now.

She had stricken a blow, and was fully prepared to follow it up with others, if so needed.

Not so with the priest.

The blow had cowed him, and the more so as a bright dagger glittered in the hand of Maid Marian.

"Ay, coward, you may quail," she said, in her clear, silvery voice. "Do not stand and tremble there like a stag bayed by the hounds, and with a dozen arrows strung ready to take its life, as is the fashion of your royalty when they hunt. Speak but another word, let your foul lips but pollute mine ears with another word, and I will send you to that account for which you are so little prepared."

If Father Absalom was not cowed before, he was completely cowed after these words, and he stood ghastly and grim leaning against the wainscoting.

Then by degrees he shuffled along by the wall, and pressed his finger on what appeared to be the brass head of a nail.

The door of the confessional was then thrown suddenly open, and the novices, like two statues, stood in the opening, awaiting the orders of their chief.

At a gesture from him, they both stepped suddenly forward, and, before Marian could become thoroughly aware of her danger, so as to offer resistance, the pair pounced upon her, the weapon dashed from her hand, and she stood helpless, a prisoner in the hands of her two lusty jailers.

Absalom gave a loud, mocking laugh, when her capture was securely effected, and, with a bitter smile of triumph on his lips, he cried, "Away with her to the cells! Let her be bound to the cross, and when solitude, misery, and hunger have tamed her spirit fittingly, to become a follower of Him who bore His trials patiently, I will visit her."

The novices turned away in silence, and was about to lead her from the confessional when the voice of the priest arrested them, saying—

"Stay. Let the others be confined also; they are turbulent spirits, and need taming as well. Hence, quick! Let my orders be obeyed at once."

The novices obeyed, and the friar was left alone to hatch his villanous plans.

CHAPTER CXXII.

THE LORD ABBOT GETS INTO FURTHER TROUBLE.

They pelted him, they hissed him,
And loudly they did hoot.
He had not a whole rag on his back,
Nor on his feet a boot.

WHEN Little John and Friar Tuck led the lord abbot into the midst of the assembled foresters, his forlorn plight and half-nude condition caused them much merriment.

Many were the broad hints thrown out in Saxon that were galling to the ears of the Norman abbot, and he even wished that they had left him to take his chance with the wolves, rather than have brought him there, where the butts and jeers came thick and fast from every side, and he was unable to return them.

This was not permitted to continue long, however; for Robin, though delighted at seeing the abbot suffer, would not allow his men to carry the joke too far, for they would soon have stripped the worthy churchman of every rag; and as he had only a few tatters on him, he would soon have been reduced to a state of nudity.

After the word was given for the foresters to desist, there was not one of the band that dared or even would have disobeyed Robin Hood's orders.

Being a portly man, the abbot was soon attired in the worn-out vestments of Friar Tuck, which vestments fitted him very well, considering all things, and the lord abbot looked as spruce as a dog on a fair-day, at least so the foresters described him.

As the sheriff had escaped, and there were a great many of the Norman prisoners, Robin Hood deemed it prudent to hold fast to the lord abbot, as he made sure of obtaining a good ransom for him, even if some of the others chanced to slip away.

This was not at all improbable, especially as the night shadows were deepening fast, so a meeting was held between the chief members of the band to arrange what measures to adopt.

At such a time this was no easy matter, especially as the sheriff and the high cellarer of the abbey had been played so many tricks, and were well up to every move, therefore a little controversy ensued.

Little John, however, offered to arrange the matter, and his offer was readily accepted.

"Now, sir abbot," Little John said, "I have a question to ask of you, and it depends greatly on the manner in which you answer whether you ever reach the abbey again alive."

"A malison on thee for an impertinent knave," replied the abbot, colouring with rage. "Hast forgotten, varlet, who I am?"

"Not at all, good father. Respect for the Church has taught us to know you full well; and, therefore, we wish to treat you with all the deference due to one filling so high and profitable an office."

"Cease thy bickering, pert caitiff!" exclaimed the exasperated churchman. "Let me hear the question thou hast to put, and if it seem me fit, I will answer it."

"'Tis this," Little John replied. "In what condition didst thou leave the coffers of the abbey?"

"By the mass, thine insolence is beyond all compare. Dost think I have nought to do but boast of wealth? Marry, 'tis enough for me to attend to the souls of my unruly flock, the bad example ye and your companions have set the people have made them as uncontrollable as the wild deer that bound in the forest and "——

"Good father," Little John said, interrupting him, and assuming a tone of mock reverence, "we know you have much to do, and have many difficulties to encounter; but, at the same time, we know that in thy zeal for the Church you not only purge the soul but clear the pockets of those who visit the shrine of St. Mary; and, therefore, we should like a little of the precious metal to devote to our own private use."

The abbot groaned bitterly on hearing this, and he cast his eyes anxiously round, as though meditating a run; but Little John gave him a hint that the palisade was too high for him to drag his burly carcase over.

The outlet, though not closed, was too well guarded for the abbot to entertain an idea of escaping that way, and the groups of foresters that laid around upon the grass convinced him that an attempt to run would be perfectly fruitless.

The lord abbot was, however, a powerful fellow, and the thought of his gold being in danger added to his strength, and nerved him to make an effort to regain his freedom.

The fact of the sheriff escaping and leaving him behind was sufficient to goad him to any desperate act, and as he was an expert in the quarterstaff, he determined to have a bout with Little John.

He did not tell him so, however, for he meant to have the play all to himself, and as a pole lay within his reach, he seized it, and rushed upon the astounded forester.

Little John, though taken by surprise, was not to be so easily overcome.

The blow that he was compelled to receive did not strike him on the head as it was intended to do, but glanced down his cheek and caught him on the left shoulder, and, as the abbot raised the staff ready to strike again, Little John's giant grip was fixed upon the pole.

Smarting from the pain of the blow, and vexed at the abbot's boldness, the forester wrenched the staff from the churchman's hands and laid it soundly about the abbot's back.

This made the holy man roar lustily, and caused no little mirth for the foresters, who laughed heartily at seeing the abbot dance upon the green sward.

"Now, what think you of your treachery?" said the outlaw, when his breath compelled him to cease his cudgelling. "Dost think you will want another sample of the like?"

The abbot gave a demoniac grin.

Not only did he smart with pain, but the degradation galled him sorely.

"You shall suffer for this," he hissed savagely. "There will be a day of reckoning between us."

"Ay, and a day of settling accounts. Body o' me! 'tis wasting time to talk to one of thy obstinate nature; 'tis as well to acquaint thee at once with our master Robin Hood's intentions."

"There is no need of it; I want not to hear of it," cried the abbot. "He is a base robber, and I know full well what to expect from such a thief as he."

"Oho!" laughed Friar Tuck, who, tired of watching the scene from a distance, now came up to get a closer view of the abbot's angry visage.

"Oho! good saint! you forget there is a greater thief than Robin Hood. Were I asked my opinion I should give thee and thy rogueish kinsman the preference. But what art thou going to do with him?" he asked of Little John.

"Hang him, perhaps; his neck is well fitted for the halter. I would shoot him, but I cannot afford to waste a good clothyard shaft on such a crow."

The abbot hardly knew how to treat this threat.

There was a spice of banter in Little John's tone; but he seemed to have some meaning in his actions, for he produced a long strip of hide from beneath his doublet, and made one end of it into a running noose.

This he slipped dexterously over the abbot's head, and drew it tight.

He then dragged the terrified abbot under the outspreading boughs of the trysting tree, and, throwing one end of the thong over a bough, he pulled down on it until it was tight.

This Little John placed in the hands of two stout foresters, who he beckoned towards him, and then the farce began.

Having whispered a few words in the ears of Friar Tuck, Little John shouldered a huge billet of wood, and placed it on its end at the abbot's feet whilst the friar disappeared in one of the caves.

In a few minutes he returned, bearing in his hand the articles necessary for writing, and these he placed on the rude table Little John had so readily made.

The giant placed the pen in the hand of the

ROBIN HOOD,

AND THE OUTLAWS OF SHERWOOD FOREST.

THE MAGICIAN.

abbot, and then made a sign to the men to loose the thong; then Little John, with a threatening gesture, ordered the abbot to write down what Little John dictated to him.

The abbot was astounded at the forester's audacity, for the words dictated were to the effect that the abbot having been seriously hurt in escaping from the outlaws' strong hold, had been compelled to seek shelter in a woodman's hut; that there, by chance, he met with a kind friar, who not only dressed his wounds but also instructed the woodman as to how he might easily put an end to Robin Hood's life.

Little John having fully impressed on the abbot's mind the words he wanted written, then allowed him a few seconds to vent his wrath and calm down, after which he said to the abbot sternly—

"Now, forsooth, put thy pen to the parchment and commence, for by the blade-bone of my patron saint I swear, if thou wilt not do it thou shalt not live to see another sun rise."

The abbot still persisted in his obstinacy, but a sharp tug at the thong made him change his mind, and he wrote the required words and flung it at the tall outlaw.

Little John handed it to the friar for inspection, and when he pronounced it correct, the giant placed it before the abbot again and further dictated to him.

This paragraph purported that the bearer of the note had kindly undertaken the journey to the abbey, that he was to be provided with all he asked, as he had been instructed how to act, this precaution having been taken to prevent the outlaws making use of the letter in case of it falling into their hands, and lastly adding that one of the monks was to hasten to Nottingham to acquaint the sheriff of the abbot's escape, and also to borrow of him the sum of two hundred marks.

This having been written and duly signed was sealed and stamped with the abbot's signet ring, after which the abbot was compelled to disclose the places where the principal part of his treasure was hoarded.

"Now, good father, we will seek you good lodging for the night," said the outlaw; "for you must tarry with us until the missive is answered."

The abbot gave a sigh that seemed to come from the very bottom of his chest, and followed the outlaw to the cave, where he was left under the guardianship of the two foresters who had followed him there.

CHAPTER CXXIII.

THE TALL FRIAR.

As Friar Tuck and Little John
Their way along did wend,
They met a jolly mountebank
Whom they did much offend.

At early dawn Friar Tuck and Little John, dressed as Franciscan friars, left the stronghold and proceeded by a by path through Sherwood Forest towards St. Mary's Abbey. As the pair trudged on, chuckling with delight at the trick they had played the abbot, they came upon a man seated beneath a tree.

"Greet ye, good fathers," said the man, clearing his eyes with his knuckles, for he had evidently just awakened from a sound sleep. "Can ye assist a poor soul in trouble?"

"An' we can, we will," replied Little John, eyeing the stranger narrowly from beneath his cowl. "Our early walk has disturbed you I fear."

"It matters not, good father, for I must get me on my way. By the help of your blessing and a little directing, I may find out which way I need to go."

"Holy Virgin! thou hast only to say, and thy wants we will supply."

"Canst tell me, then, what forest this is? Last night I strayed hither, not knowing my way, and being tired, laid me down to rest, and I slept until your voices awakened me."

"My son, thou art on the borders of the king's royal forest of Sherwood, and I wonder how thou durst trust thyself to sleep here. 'Tis well thou hast not become acquainted with the members of the daring band which infests the forest. Marry! and had they have seen you, you would not have had a whole bone left."

"Gramercy, father, you must take me for a weakling. Quotha, 'twould take a bold fellow to give me my fill of cudgelling. 'Tis part of the profession of one that travels through the country as I do, to know how to handle a staff."

"My son, thou wouldst know far better how to handle a good slip of venison, didst thou have it in thy way," retorted Little John. "Thou art a coward, I opine, and a Norman to boot. Thou art as much used to cudgelling as your Bruin there, and he takes all thy blows, I ween, and returns none."

As the forester spoke he pointed to a young bear that lay on the grass, muzzled and chained to the trunk of a tree.

The man was sorely hurt at his being compared with his beast, and gave himself an air of offended pride.

"Hush, my son," said Little John, "what I have said you will find quite true. Which way do you journey?"

"Towards Nottingham."

"'Tis fortunate for thee that thou art going that way, for you need have no fear of meeting Robin Hood's men in that direction."

"Robin Hood!" ejaculated the man, in surprise.

"Ay, thou hast heard of him, maybe, an' thou art straight from London?"

Little John noticed how the man started at Robin's name being mentioned, and he fancied he had seen the man's face before, but where was at present a mystery to him.

The man hesitated before replying, and seemed evidently lost for an answer.

"I have certainly heard of him," he said, at length; "but 'twas in Kent. The tales of his marvellous skill have set me longing to have a bout with one of the rascals," he said at length. "Zounds! I should like to give them just one turn, such as would make them stare."

The fingers both of Little John and the

friar were itching to give the fellow a sound dressing.

Little John in particular could scarce keep his hands off the man; but his holy vestments, and a hint that the fellow might be a spy from the friar, made him check the impulse that seized him on hearing the man's braggadocia.

To end further argument, however, and give the man an opportunity of having his wish fulfilled, Little John said—

"My son, ye appear sorely hungered. Get thee on thy way, and if you pass a small house on thy way, knock at the door, and thou wilt find such requirements as thy body needeth there. So take with thee my blessing."

The man bowed devoutly, and Little John muttered a few words that were as unmeaning even to himself as to his listener; and the friars once more went on their way.

The man, as soon as they were gone, took from his pocket a piece of stick, in which he cut two deep notches, and, placing it in his pocket, commenced his frugal repast.

CHAPTER CXXIV.

THE SOLDIERS VISIT THE ABBEY.

"Come tell me," said the friar,
"The meaning of this din:
The soldiers in their ire
Will dash the portals in."

INTO one of the deepest dungeons of the old abbey Maid Marian was thrust by her ruthless conductors, and to render her position the more painful, they had bound her firmly to a large wooden cross that stood in the centre of the dingy vault, and then left her in darkness to her fate.

This room or vault was the punishment cell for refractory novices; there they expiated their crimes by suffering unheard of torture, and Marian was doomed to share in the horrors of that place.

Well knowing that in neglecting to carry out the friar's orders they would bring punishment on themselves, the novices did as Absalom had desired them; in fact, they had in a manner crucified their fair victim.

Her body was bound to the upright post, so that her feet was clear of the ground, then her ancles were tied, and her arms outstretched and bound by the wrists to the arms of the cross, and in this manner she was suspended.

The agony she endured it would be impossible to describe.

The stiff cords cut into her tender flesh, and though she could have shrieked with pain, yet she bore it with devoted heroism.

Her companions were subjected to tortures somewhat similar; their limbs were screwed into large wooden frames, and so tightly compressed as to prevent the blood circulating freely, and in addition to this the close air of the cell threw them into a violent perspiration which brought on a maddening thirst.

Having accomplished their fiendish work the assistants returned to the friar to receive further instructions.

Father Absalom was seated with his back to the door when they obeyed his summons to enter, therefore they could not see how rage-distorted were his features, for when he turned to them he had assumed his usual treacherous smile.

"Ezra," he said to one of the novices, "hie thee at once to the tower, and make it appear as though thy visit were accidental. Keep thine ears open and thy mouth closed, and learn whether 'tis suspected the fugitives have taken shelter here.

Ezra was about to turn away, when the gate-porter rushed along the corridor, pale with fear and breathless with the exertion.

Without waiting to be announced, he hurried into the chamber where sat Father Absalom, and gasped out—

"I pray you hasten to the gate, good father; a party of armed men demand admittance and will not be refused."

"A curse upon them!" cried the friar, springing to his feet. "What want they, I wonder?"

"They demand the delivery of the fugitives into their hands, and will hear of no excuse."

"But surely you did not say they were here."

"Assuredly no. I denied all knowledge of them; but they will not believe it. The governor of the tower is the leader of the party, and he threatens to burst the gate if we do not open it to him."

"Sacrilege by all that's good. We must teach him better manners. Let the governor be admitted, but his men must stay without."

The governor was too prudent a man to enter the abbey alone. He prevailed on the porter to allow two of his men to accompany him, and the rest he ordered to fall back from the entrance of the sacred pile.

Father Absalom had time to compose himself before the governor was ushered into his presence, and seemed deeply engrossed in poring over the contents of a large book that lay open before him.

"Well, and what brings you here?" demanded the friar, raising his eyes from the book and fixing them searchingly upon the soldier. "Have you come here to disturb the sanctity of this holy place?"

"Nay, good father, but I must tell thee that the king hath been smitten with the charms of some fair beauty, and he brought her to the tower. She scorned his addresses, and he vowed he would keep her until she looked favourably upon him. To me he entrusted her safe keeping; but by some treachery she hath escaped, and my head will be forfeited if I restore her not."

"My son, ye have done a wrong thing in coming here. Do you suspect that the monks of this peaceful abbey have a hand in this treachery ?"

"Marry, I know not; yet I have good cause to believe that this roof at present shelters them."

"Say you so ? then I presume, when I say they are not here, you will banish that belief."

"Not till I am thoroughly assured."

"You doubt me, then ?"

"I must; at present it is a matter of life and death with me."

The crafty priest was about to make some evasive reply, when the porter once more appeared, and informed Absalom that the soldiers were still clamouring at the gate, and demanding, in insolent language, to be admitted.

"Dost hear that ?" demanded the friar. "Such insolence will not be tolerated. Go at once and order your men to desist."

On arriving at the gate the governor found matters as the porter had stated—the soldiers were in a state of great excitement, and he at once began to remonstrate with them. But the men would listen to no reason; they had found the dead bodies of their comrades, and they demanded the perpetrators of the foul deed to be given up to justice, as they conjectured that they had sought sanctity in the church. On hearing this the governor with his own hand undid the massive fastenings of the gate, and threw it open to his men.

They entered with a rush, and the clank of mailed feet, and the clatter of steel echoed with a din through the corridors, and the men bore the stiff bodies of their comrades into the chapel, muttering fierce oaths of vengeance.

Father Absalom was crafty enough to have the body of Rebecca removed to a place of security, and the doors leading to the vaults where the prisoners were confined locked and the keys hidden, thus obliterating all traces of the fugitives having entered the abbey.

The monks, terrified at the noise, and fearing the rudeness of the soldiers, bolted themselves in their cells, thus removing every obstacle in the way of the soldiers' search.

Father Absalom tried to make his voice heard, and appealed to the governor for his aid in quelling the soldiers' fury; but he might as well have tried to tame a savage. The soldiers, regardless of all honour due to the reverend father, and forgetful of the sanctity of the place, spread about through the building, and searched everywhere where it was likely a human being could be hid.

At length, after an hour's fruitless search, they left, and Absalom was thankful when the massive gate was closed after them.

They, however, took the dead bodies of their comrades with them, though the friar tried to persuade them to leave the bodies with him that they might have proper interment.

"My curse go with them!" muttered Absalom, as from the window over the gate he watched the soldiers move off in a body. "I will be revenged on them for this; those they have sought they shall never find whilst the walls of the abbey stand, and then nought but a heap of bones shall mark were they have been entombed.

CHAPTER CXXV.

THE OLD CRONE AND THE MILLER'S SON.

"Stay! stay!" she cried, "ye know him not,
  He is a Norman hound;
After no good is he, I ween,
  Of that I will be bound."

A SWIFT messenger soon bore to the king the news of Marian's escape, and when he heard of it he stamped with rage, and swore by all the saints he could think of that he would again get her into his power.

Calling to his side one of his favourite knights, in whom he placed great confidence, he ordered him to send scouts to all the villages that lay on the road between the town and Nottingham.

These men were to be disguised, and were to hang about the villages and watch who passed through them, and to forward their information to certain points, where messengers, provided with swift steeds, would convey the news to head-quarters.

One of these spies was the man we have before noticed with the bear, and in his disguise he had good opportunities of learning what was passing.

But being a stranger to those parts he did not acquire so much information as might have been expected, for he did not seek such places as one well acquainted with the country would have done.

Thus it was he was found on the borders of Sherwood forest, though in truth it is hard to say that he would have ventured to trust himself in the heart of the forest, even had he known that it was there he might have heard much.

The mention of the mill-house, which was one of the places he was desired principally to watch, gave him some hope of being on the right track, and when he had finished his scanty meal he prepared to journey thither.

As he was about to rise and fulfil his bent, he caught a sound as of someone singing.

He listened, and a clear voice, singing the following strain rewarded his pains—

The morning air dispels our care,
  When the red deer bounds so gay;
With good yew bow away we go,
  To hunt in the forest away.

We make a good mark with clothyard shaft,
  For no marksman do we care,
With the eye of a hawk we bend to the sport,
  And the goose-quill flies through the air.

The startled deer the whizz does hear,
  As the bowstring's echoing twang;
But ere he turns his head it lies him dead,
  And we to his side have sprang.

"Well done, Wharton! After that I think

thy throttle needs moistening. Come, take a pull at the flask."

"Ay, that will I, friend George-a-Green," replied another voice ; and then there burst forth a hearty laugh."

"Ha! ha! well I did not think it so near empty," said Wharton. "By my faith! I did not expect when I gave it to that hungry giant that he would have swallowed the whole."

"I will learn the better next time, I ween. Hallo! what have we here ?"

As George-a-Green gave utterance to this exclamation, the two foresters appeared at a turn in the road, and caught sight of the mountebank preparing for his journey.

"Ods boddikins, friend! You seem to have fallen across strange game in the forest."

"Marry! where did you hit upon this animal ?"

"Not in this country, I ween."

"So I should say ; and I trow you would not care to part with him ?"

"At what price ?"

"Well, one of the fattest deer that you can point out in yonder glade, and a few silver marks thrown into the bargain."

"Zounds! Dost take me for a thief—a poacher ?"

"Why ?"

"To accept of the king's deer as payment for a noble beast like this. Look ye, I would not part with this animal for all the deer that run wild in the forest. He is my faithful friend and companion, and though I whip him sometimes to make him dance, yet I love him as a child."

"A strange affection," replied George-a-Green ; and then both the foresters burst into a hearty laugh.

"Quotha, it may appear strange to you," said the man, concealing the anger which the laugh of the foresters had aroused within him, "but you forget that I solely depend on him for my living. But as we have met, you can perhaps guide me to some house where I may procure him some meal, for I have wandered many miles, and have not so much as seen the thatch of a cotter's hut."

"Marry, that could we do with pleasure, had we time. But here comes jolly Much, he will most likely pleasure you so far."

Wharton explained to the miller's son the man's wants, and then with George-a-green hurried on, leaving Much and the mountebank in deep discourse.

After the man had answered a number of questions put to him by Much, the miller's son said,

"Saint Herman! I will not see ye lost for the sake of my going a few minutes' walk out of my way. Come, jog with me, and I will endeavour to get ye what you want."

As it was not in his way to go to the mill, Much took the man to a cottage, and there he was supplied with a jug of ale, and a bag of meal for the bear.

Just previous to their arrival, an old crone had been begging, and she was crouching down stowing away her wares, and also the things she had begged, and she eyed the man curiously enough.

The man evidently did not notice her, for he had so many questions to ask concerning the state of the country, the number of the inhabitants about that part, and also as to whether the king or any of his court ever came that way.

Much did not greatly approve of the man's inquisitiveness, for he asked many questions that seemed not at all to concern one of his profession, but too much of other business to occupy his mind to take particular note of the man.

They both left soon after, the man taking his way to Nottingham, and striking into a path across a ploughed field.

As Much walked on slowly, in deep thought, he felt a hand laid lightly on his shoulder, and on turning, he found the old crone standing by his side.

"Woman!" he said, angrily, for he was annoyed at her interruption of his thoughts. "Woman! what want ye with me ?"

"Know you that man ?" she asked, not appearing to heed the sharpness of his speech.

"No ; neither do I want. Saint Herman! I should have enough to do did I heed the looks and names of everyone I meet."

"But on this occasion it was perhaps as well you did so."

"For why ?"

The old crone whispered in his ear.

"Out, woman! get thee to—thou art dreaming."

"Ay, so you may think ; but 'tis a vision real. Think you my old eyes have been deceived. No, no ; they still do me good service."

Much scarcely knew how to answer the woman.

He felt annoyed at her delaying him, and yet he was interested in her words.

"An,' I felt certain the fellow acts the spy," he said, "I would follow him and wring his neck, as I would an adder's."

"The simile is good," replied the old woman. "The fellow means mischief ; his presence here is an omen of evil. Ah, you may laugh, but old Dame Norton is not easily deceived."

"Get the to, woman, I am tired of thy prating ; thy words may serve to please the silly rustics and their simple swains, but to ears of a follower of bold Robin Hood they are as idle as the wind."

The forester turned away, but the old dame clutched him, and in a hoarse voice, croaked, "Could I tell you of your cousin Marian, would you listen ?"

Much started, the mention of his cousin and the possibility of hearing of her, opened his ears to anything.

"Speak," he said. "If thou knowest ought of her tell it me ; but beware, old hag, how you trifle with one who has it in his power to punish you."

The old hag gave a ghastly grin.

"Listen," she said, in a clearer voice than before. "On my head be it if my tongue offend you."

Much was about to give his consent, when the shrill blast of a horn rang through the forest, and turning on his heel, he dashed into a thicket and disappeared from the view of the old crone, who stood gazing after him in mute astonishment and chagrin.

CHAPTER CXXVI.

THE PROPHECY OF THE OLD WOMAN OF THE HEATH.

She poured such wondrous tidings
In Madge's listening ear,
That made her blood to curdle,
And filled her heart with fear.

WHEN Much had gone, and the old hag had somewhat recovered from surprise, she hobbled away in the direction of the heath, but a rustling in the bushes caused her to halt, and on looking round she beheld Madge Stukely.

"Ah, my pretty lass," she exclaimed, "and where, if I may be so bold to ask, are you going so early?"

"To the mill," was Madge's reply.

"Marry you are? And what seek you there?"

"My father has again left, and I wish to seek the advice and assistance of a friend."

The old dame gave an hysterical laugh.

"Friend," she said; "and in whom do you expect to find one, think ye?"

"Maid Marian," Madge replied.

"Maid Marian," repeated the old woman. "Then if such is the case, you need trouble yourself no further. She is in as great, if not greater, need of assistance herself than you are at this present moment."

"Holy Virgin! you are in jest, are you not? Say, is she again in the sheriff's power?"

"Worse."

"She cannot be."

"'Tis true. Have you not heard that she has been missing for weeks? Robin himself has sought her without success: and, what is worse, I fear he *never* will."

Madge eyed the old woman with distrust. She had some faith in her power as a soothsayer; but now she fancied she was deceiving her.

"Name your reasons for so thinking," she said, "if you have any."

"I have too many. But stay not here to talk. Hie with me to my humble cot; there I will tell you a secret that I would not breathe to other mortal's ears."

Madge obeyed reluctantly, and when the old woman had seated herself by the fire, she began—

"As I sat dosing over my scanty fire last night, I had a vision, and methought I was back again in the crowded village, where I once used to live, and that the sound of wheels rumbling by caused me to look out at the door.

"I looked down the long and densely-populated streets; the light of the clear moon, falling in showers on the road, afforded a brilliant light, but not a form met my view, or sound greeted my ear.

"All was still and silent as the grave—the pulseless grave. Can it be, thought I, that all the vast congregation that usually throng this populous city are gathered to repose, save, perchance, some night-watcher, like myself, or fevered, restless mortal, whose step is upon the brink of eternity, and whose eye has already pierced the mysteries of that 'undiscovered bourne,' yet trammelled still by some frail tie to earth?

'The spirit, struggling, sways from sphere to sphere.'

"And then, again, I thought what a strange power has the vengeful night; what a gleaner of the annals of the past; how she gathers together the vague nothings which haunt our uneasy pillows, to set them in skeleton array before us; the innocent, the guilty, the highest, the lowest, the meanest, the best, have all felt this influence, and their spirits have bowed beneath the spell, even as the brave spirits of old have bowed beneath the spell of the sorceress.

"Starting from thoughts like these, I turned my eyes to the mirror—the one you now see covered with the mystic cloth, where the slanting rays of the moonbeams were shining steadily.

"Just then the shrill cry of a watchman broke the solemn stillness. For a moment the street echoed with the sound; then came the hoarse murmur of a distant voice in answer, and all was then silent as before.

"Again I looked towards the mirror. I passed my hands before my eyes, for I thought fatigue had made me giddy, or that my sight deceived me; but no! slowly, yet steadily, the old frame grew and expanded, while the plate seemed to swell and dilate in the same manner, until it covered one side of the apartment.

"I sat almost breathless, regarding this singular object with a fixed and earnest gaze. Suddenly it paused, and, for a moment, the moonbeams glittered and danced upon the polished surface like a troop of silver spirits, then glided softly towards the frame, where they rested, flinging a pale, golden light distinctly around. I stood motionless, for, in the middle of the plate, but seemingly far in the background, there slowly towered an ancient castle, with battlements and turrets, moat and drawbridge, all of which, faint in outline at first, gradually assumed a firm and tangible shape.

"'Ah, child, you may shudder,' she said, as Madge began to show some signs of fear, 'but 'tis true. 'Tis a terrible thing to look into the dark future.'

"Soft green lawns spread out in front, and dark thick forests reared them at the side. A little village nestled in the vale beneath the castle, just near enough to form a portion of the landscape, while at a little distance stood the ivy-grown chapel, with its pleasant yard, dotted with green mound and lofty monument, where the humble and proud were sleeping together.

"Faintly and plainly the picture spread itself to view. I saw the drawbridge lowered, and a gay and gallant party upon steeds of gentle blood rode forth; there were ladies and knights, hound and hawk, and the time was morning, for the sunbeams were gilding the noble old forests, and, as the party rode gallantly by, I thought I saw the dew-drops sparkle upon their coursers' hoofs, as they crushed the tender grass beneath their heavy tread.

"They had all come forth, as I thought, when suddenly from the gateway two riders issued. The one was a fair and gentle maiden; the other, by his mien and lineaments, her sire, and apparently the owner of this stately domain, for he hastily gave some directions to the crowd of attendants who stood in the castle yard. I could hear no words nor sounds of any kind, but the looks and manner explained all. On, on they sped, and were soon lost to my sight in the windings of the forest. Yet still I gazed, and presently there crept from out the shadow of the bridge, with light and stealthy steps, a dark and slightly-formed girl. Her eye was black, fierce, and reckless, while her dress and face betrayed her origin at once, for the red gipsy mantle hung gracefully from her shoulder, and her cheek had browned beneath warmer skies than those which glowed above her then.

"Gliding and springing along from shadow to shadow, she gained a narrow bridle-path, which led to the village, and there, under a white blossoming thorn, she sat down. Not long did she remain alone; a young horseman retraced his steps, sprung from his steed, threw the bridle over its neck, and hurriedly entered the little path where the young lady reposed.

"She sat apparently abstracted, feigning ignorance of his approach, until he laid his hand upon her shoulder—then, with a quick, joyous motion, she sprang suddenly into his arms, and leaned her head upon his bosom.

"The cavalier looked earnestly around, as if to mark if they were observed; then, putting her from him, he seemed to pour forth words in a rapid manner. I could but conjecture, from the violent gesture and gleaming eye of the girl, that, whatever he might be saying, it was displeasing to her.

"He pointed frequently toward the castle. and, at length, at what I conceived to be an impatient demand on her part, he drew from his richly-embroidered vest a miniature—the miniature of the lovely maiden I had seen ride forth but a little while before.

"Eagerly did she snatch and fix her gaze upon it; then, with a contemptuous smile, she gathered her mantle around her, and fled toward the village. The young nobleman— for such he evidently was—stood looking

after her a few minutes, then mounted his steed, and rode quickly away.

"A faint mist now fell upon the mirror; the moonbeams waved and flickered over its surface with a pale, restless light, then returned to their station on the frame, while the mist parted like a rent veil, and again the picture was there. Then again a party rode forth, but the hounds and the hawks were no longer there; yet there was a fair and happy bride, with a merry bridegroom; the white robes and veils of the blushing bridesmaids floated out lightly on the breeze to the old abbey, where the bell loudly pealed.

"I even fancied I heard their low, silvery laugh, as the bridesmen, with their hands upon their bridle reins, whispered some gay jests slily in their ears. Merrily they sped along.

"The shriven priest laid his hand upon the young couple as they knelt before him, and his quivering lips moved in prayer. Then the young wife rose up, and fell sobbing into the arms of her sire, while the happy bridegroom proudly received the congratulations of those around. They turned and rode back to the castle, but not before a light form stole out from the chancel, and cast one look at the bride. I saw each gothic window of that old castle blaze with light; the bonfires gleamed wildly on every little hill and knoll between it and the village, while softly the pale moon looked down upon that scene of joyance, filling every nook and corner of that wide domain with her radiant sheen, and shining full upon the form of the young girl, as she stood, with folded arms, beneath the white blossoming thorn.

"The mist swept across the mirror for an instant, shrouding it from my gaze; and when I looked again there was hurrying to and fro in the castle. Men came out, and, speedily mounting, rode away; while pacing the lofty hall with quick, irregular steps was the young nobleman whom I beheld first by the gipsy's side, then at the altar with the beautiful maiden.

"As I gazed long and wistfully at him, his face became suddenly familiar to me, and when I went to move to obtain a better look of him, I started from my reverie."

"And pray what did you see in all this?" asked Madge, once more breathing freely.

"More than you expect; but to make sure that I was not deceived in what I anticipated, I worked a mystic charm."

"And then?" exclaimed Madge, scarce knowing what she uttered.

"I found that my surmises were correct. Dame Morton is seldom deceived.

"But, pray explain what you saw," said Madge impressively, for I long to hear of this wondrous thing."

"'Tis easily told. The fair damsel and the noble I saw leave the castle first were Marian and the king; the second pair that were wedded, was John of Linden and Lady Agnes, but the ladies were no consenting parties in these acts, mind. Treachery was at work—treachery base and foul, and it would not surprise me did we hear of some terrible slaughter occurring through this."

"Saints forfend us from such a calamity! Already is the country in enough commotion and alarm. But how do you account for Marian being in the company of the king?"

"Did I not say, lass, that treachery was at work. Depend upon it, Marian is in Henry's power, and also that the Lady Agnes is being made the dupe of some foul plot."

"Then 'tis time that Robin was made acquainted with this. Did he but know Marian was being subjected to his insults, Robin Hood would not spare him an inch, although Henry is clothed in his royal pomp."

"Ha! ha! thou art right, lass. 'Twas to speak to him that took me out this very morn. Robin shall know of it, and Marian shall be once more free from the toils of her proud oppressor."

The old hag then settled down, with her chin resting on her hands, and gazing into the fire seemed to be gathering an amount of wisdom from the shapes formed by the burning embers.

Soon after, Madge left; but the old woman still occupied the same position, simply rocking backwards and forwards as her feelings agitated her.

How far the old woman's surmise was right, we must now leave to a future chapter.

CHAPTER CXXVII.

WHAT BEFEL LITTLE JOHN AND THE FRIAR ON THEIR WAY TO THE ABBEY.

'Twas in a shady dell
They sat them down to rest,
And to them befel
It was a merry jest.

FRIAR Tuck and Little John, on leaving the mountebank, made all speed towards the abbey; but, as the sun began to gain power, and the roads were very dusty, the throats of the sanctified pair began to get dry.

"Body o' me, friar, this is sore travelling," said Little John. "I am sorely athirst. How fares it with thee? How far is it from here to Saint Mary's well?"

"Good brother," replied the friar, "ye have suffered nought as yet. If ye take up the cross ye must bear it. You forget that we are on a pilgrimage, and that, as true penitents, we must submit to a little hardship."

Although Friar Tuck made this devout speech he was none the less tired of the journey himself than was Little John.

The heat and the exertion he had to make to keep up with the giant strides of his companion made the perspiration pour from his corpulent form, and he longed to have a rest and moisten his lips with a draught from the black jack Little John had provided him with at starting.

Thump—thump—he could feel it beat against his hip as he shuffled along, and more than once he felt inclined to turn aside, and in some shady nook take a pull at its contents unknown to the forester.

But this was impossible.

Little John gave him not the least chance to gratify his wish; he seemed to hang to him like a leech.

To take the bottle out before him he knew would be tantamount to asking him to drink, and if he did so he was well aware that there would be little left for himself.

Besides, he did not know how they might fare at the abbey, neither did he know whether his companion had provided himself with a bottle also.

While he was thus ruminating, Little John gave another groan.

"By the mass, brother, I am almost choking. I shall not be sorry when I get me rid of this sanctified robe. I like it not, dangling about my legs. What say you to us turning into yon covert, and having a rest?"

"By all means; I like thy proposal much. There is a brook there, too, where thou canst slake thy thirst. I know thou must be dry, for ye supped too much wine overnight."

"Ay, and now thou seest I have to suffer for it; but now I have turned friar, I do as you do, water shall be my only beverage."

The giant gave a grin, and nudged his companion just where the bottle hung, much to the annoyance of the friar.

"Zounds!" exclaimed Little John, as his hand came in contact with the hard substance. "I forgot me, thou hadst a bottle; here is a quiet spot, we can sit and rest ourselves, and, moreover, partake of some refreshment."

A cluster of trees shaded the bank from the sun, and the ripple of water sounded close by.

The place was refreshing enough, and our weary travellers seated themselves very comfortably under the outspreading boughs.

Little John took out his wallet and shared its contents with the friar, and Tuck wondered how it was that Little John was so patient in not asking after the bottle; but as he hoped he had forgotten it, he did not offer to bring it forth.

He was almost parched, however, and felt half inclined to pay a visit to the brook, but his aversion to water was so great that he forbore to do so.

To his astonishment Little John rose.

"'Tis sorely against my will," he said, "but I must wash down the pasty with that horrid stuff."

"What horrid stuff?" demanded the friar, fearful that he was making an allusion to the concealed bottle; but Little John's reply was only to point to the stream, and silently walked away.

He did not go down on his knees and drink in the friar's sight, but turned aside, and, when he was completely hid from the friar's view, he took from beneath his vestment a black jack, which he placed to his lips until it was nearly empty.

ROBIN HOOD,

AND THE OUTLAWS OF SHERWOOD FOREST.

THE WANDERER.

In the meantime, Friar Tuck was not idle. He chuckled with delight when Little John walked by the side of the brook.

"Thanks to thee, my long friend; may the saints bestow on thee their blessings for this charitable act!"

So saying, the crafty rogue took from his curtle the flask Little John had provided him with, and, raising his eyes heavenward, he placed the neck of the bottle to his thick, fat lips.

He took a good swig, and kept his eyes fixed on the sky, as much for his own convenience, as it allowed the fluid to gurgle down his throat.

He remained in this position some seconds, and then, with a convulsive start, he took the bottle from his lips and gave a horrid grin.

Little John had began his pilgrimage like a good Christian, and had filled the friar's bottle with water.

The surprise more than the water almost choked him ; and, as he ejected a mouthful, he gave vent to an ejaculation that was any.thing but in keeping with his saintly office.

He did not see the dark pair of eyes peering at him through the bushes, nor the grinning visage that was scarlet with suppressed laughter ; and this was one comfort, though certainly a poor one in comparison to what he had suffered.

"A malison on the treacherous knave!" he said bitterly. "He thinks of making this a sport ; but I will be even with him, and, moreover, he shall have one gratification the less."

"He shall not see that I have been bitten," he added. "I will pretend to act submissively; and then, when he least expects it, then I will have my revenge."

Emptying the flask of the remainder of the water, so as to lighten his load, he returned the flask to its concealment, and smoothed his ruffled features, so that anyone would have thought that nothing had disturbed his equanimity.

At this moment, Little John made his appearance, and walked towards him with apparent innocence, and the pair of rogues chuckling within themselves at the trick they had played on each other, went on their way."

CHAPTER CXXVIII.

THE PRIEST'S VISIT TO MARIAN.

As through the vault he went,
And softly trod the stones,
He did not see a living man
Crouched amongst the bones.

AFTER the visit of the soldiers, Father Absalom was more than ever prejudiced against the unfortunate beings he had imprisoned.

He paced his room in an angry mood, gave vent to several unsaintly and unbecoming expletives, and gazed at the walls as though they were the cause of his uneasiness.

Presently he halted before a large painting of one of the saints, and, touching a spring, caused it to fly open like a door, and disclosed behind it a large dark cavity.

"Shall I," he muttered, "or shall I not ?" He paused meditatively.

His right hand clutched something in the breast of his robe, and he seemed half-inclined to draw it forth as he stood with one foot in the opening, and glared into the darkness beyond.

"I cannot," he muttered on, "and yet I feel that I must be revenged. This double insult I cannot bear. Many a soul have I sent to its last account for less than this ; but never before did I feel so much repugnance as I do in meditating this act."

He glared around the chamber as though seeking for some object to inspire his soul with courage ; but no such object met his gaze until he took his hand from his breast and held before his eyes a dagger.

His eyes glittered wildly as he gazed upon the dazzling sheen of the burnished blade, and he made several feint stabs with it as though trying the power of his arm.

"There is yet sufficient strength left," he said, half aloud. "The old man is still no weakling. Courage alone is what I now want, and then I can "——

A footstep at the door startled him.

Pressing the picture back into its place, he turned to see who it was had trespassed on his privacy.

"Enter," he said, in answer to a low tap, and the shaven head of a monk appeared between the folds of the hangings that screened the door.

"Art thou alone, good Father Absalom ?" asked the monk.

"You see I am," answered Absalom, pettishly. Then, in a canting tone, he added, "Saving the presence of Him whom mortal eye cannot see, there is no one here. Why seek ye me at this hour ?"

"To inform thee of the sins of one of our brethren."

"Ah ! what is it he has done ?"

"He hath partaken too freely of wine, and is now making an inglorious noise in his cell, and "——

"From whence did he obtain it ?"

"I know not. I could swear, by the relics of our patron saint, that he has not left the abbey for this last month ; but where he could obtain it without is past my comprehension."

Absalom looked at the monk as though he would pierce him through with his glance, and then said—

"Let this matter be seen to at once, good Matthew. By Our Lady, matters have come to a sore pass, if it be not found out whence he got the unholy water. It shall be told in the ears of the bishop, and he will recommend the whole of ye a sound scourging and a long fast, which will make thee pay less heed to carnal matters, and attend more devoutly to thy spiritual rites."

The monk hastily withdrew, and Absalom, once more left to his own reflections, began to think of his horrid schemes.

The secret panel again opened to his touch.

He clutched the dagger in his breast.

Then, with trembling hand, he seized a

small lamp, and cautiously descended a steep flight of stone steps.

Hurrying along a dark passage, he soon found himself in a large vaulted chamber.

In the middle of the room he stopped, and began examining the floor with his fingers, until he found a ring buried in the stone slab.

By the aid of this he raised the slab, and again descended until he reached another vault similar to the first, but more horrible in appearance.

Around the walls were skeletons—the remains of human beings that had been imprisoned; and, feeble as was the light, it was sufficient to reveal that they were secured to the walls by heavy rusty chains.

Absalom only took one glance at the hideous objects.

They reminded him of deeds long done, but not forgotten, and, with a shudder he hastened to a door in the wall, opened it, and passed through.

He was now in the corridor where the cells were situated, and a few moments sufficed for him to find the one in which Marian was confined.

A ghastly grin overspread his features as he opened the door with a key, which he took from a bunch at his girdle, and peered in.

"Well, how fares it with thee now?" he said, jeeringly, eyeing the girl's pale features with demoniac triumph.

Marian made no reply.

Her lips were compressed with agony.

She could have shrieked, but she would not, but bore the torture which was indeed excruciating.

"You will not answer me," said the friar, wrathfully? Please thyself an' ye will, and then we will see whose power is strongest."

Still Marian did not answer, and Father Absalom bit his lips.

At that moment he was suffering greatly himself.

His rage at being thus defied almost amounted to madness, and, with a fearful invective, he slammed to the door, and hurried back the way he came.

As he passed through the chamber where the skeletons were chained, he did not stay to look around, though he took the precaution to turn the key in the lock and take the key with him.

Had he done so, he would have seen that the palace was not only inhabited by the dead, but that a living soul beside his own breathed the fetid air of the vault.

CHAPTER CXXIX.

HAL HAS A STRANGE ADVENTURE.

The priest, he muttered savagely,
  As Hal saw him go by,
The shriven rogue said, "by my hand
  Maid Marian shall die."

As Father Absalom ascended the steps leading from the vault a light form stepped from the shadow of the wall and fol-

lowed him with his eyes as long as he remained in sight.

This strange figure was Hal.

He had escaped by some means from the dungeon where he had been confined, and was groping about for Marian's cell at the very moment the friar entered it.

In groping about in the darknesss, he came by chance upon the door of the vault.

Finding that it yielded to his touch, he entered, and felt carefully around; but as nothing but human bones met his touch he made an effort to regain the door.

In the darkness this was no easy task, for the skeletons were so numerous, that turn which way he might he was sure to come upon one of them.

This added to his perplexity, and filled him with vague superstitions, which in spite of his endeavours he could not shake off, and although he frequently crossed himself, and muttered the virgin's name, the cold, clammy bones seemed still to haunt him.

In the midst of his perplexity, and when the cold beads of perspiration were bathing his brow, a faint light caught his eye, and a footstep, accompanied by the sound of mutterings, caught his ear.

Anxiously he strained his eyes, and eagerly strained his ears, and to his dismay, or rather astonishment, the light and the sounds grew plainer.

In an agony of suspense, and a dread of what he might expect to behold, he crouched down silently by the side of one of the skeletons, and tremblingly awaited the appearance of he knew not what.

At length, however, the light burst into the vault, and the form of Friar Absalom appeared in the doorway.

Hal was not a timid youth, but when the priest turned the key, and he heard the harsh grating of the lock, his courage fairly gave way, and he gave an inward groan, and crouched still lower even until his cheek rested against the bones of his fleshless companion, so fearful was he of being seen.

"I could have murdered her with a blow," he heard the friar mutter as he passed; "but no, that would not be revenge. I will keep her, torture her; she shall consent to be mine, and then it will be time to talk of killing her."

Hal at once conjectured that she of whom he spoke was Marian, and his fears at that moment vanished.

He felt inclined to spring forward and clutch the friar by the throat; but the sight of a dagger hanging loosely in his girdle restrained him.

"No, I will not;" he said thoughtfully to himself. "I may get wounded, and then all chance of escape will be for ever gone. What I do must be done carefully. I am free so far, and, if I can but free the rest, we may then in a body escape."

By this time Father Absalom had passed out of sight, and Hal, stringing his nerves, began to consider which plan to adopt.

In the few moments the friar had occupied passing through, Hal had taken the opportunity to survey the door, so that he knew exactly how to walk to it in the darkness.

But, as he had feared, it was fastened.

The lock was a massive one, and by the feel of it seemed too strong for him to easily break.

He placed his broad back against the door, however, and gave it a blow that made it shake, and this circumstance bade him hope that he might yet force it.

Another blow assured him that it was not so strong as he had imagined, and a third prize with his shoulders caused the rusty fastenings of the lock to give way.

Then the door yielded with a crash, and he felt a stream of cold air waft his cheek; and he staggered into the corridor overcome with his exertions.

Bewildered and scarce knowing how next to proceed, he leant against the wall for support, when he fancied he heard a slight groan.

He listened, and it was again repeated; and, convinced that he was not deceived, he made his way along the wall in the direction from whence it proceeded.

For some distance the wall was smooth and unbroken by anything; but at length he felt what appeared to be a door, thickly studded with nails.

To this he placed his ear, and a stifled moan seemed to come from within; and he placed his mouth close to the door and whispered as loud as the fear of discovery would allow him.

"Who is it within? speak, I am a friend. For the love of the Virgin, keep me not in this suspense!"

Marian, for it was the poor, tortured girl that had given utterance to the moans, immediately recognised the voice, low as it was, and she replied—

"'Tis I, Marian, good Hal; but I fear you cannot aid me, the door is locked, and withal strong, so go, save thyself, and tell good Robin Hood the fate that hath befallen his Marian.

"Never! I will not leave you in this den," vociferated Hal; and with that he gave the door a cracking blow with his foot; but he made no impression on it, saving making it send a hollow noise through the corridor.

CHAPTER CXXX.

THE FEAST OF ST. NICHOLAS.

In the Abbey of St. Mary's
  The monks so hale and stout,
  Did homage to the viands good,
  And pushed the wine about.
    *   *   *   *   *
Little John, he sat, with visage very long,
Whilst Friar Tuck so merrily, carolled out a song.

LITTLE JOHN and the friar proceeded in silence until they reached the abbey, where they received a cordial greeting, for they were so well disguised, that the monks failed to recognise them.

Brother Cuthbert took the missive, and read it.

"By the mass!" he said aside to Brother John, "we may consider our mirthful jollity at an end. The Lord Abbot is not a prisoner in the outlaws' stronghold, as report speaketh. He will be here soon, so we must make the most of what little time remains to us."

"And what of these knaves? It will not do to let them know of our doings in the abbot's absence?"

"Saints forfend that we should! good brother. We must keep them in the lower room. By my soul! I would not that they caught a smell of the venison haunch, much less pollute their lips with tasting it."

"Another question, brother. Who can we send to the abbey?"

"Our worthy Brother Thomas.

"Canst trust him, think ye?"

"In this matter only he is a shrewd knave and withal a good churchman. We dare not open his eyes to our doings, or his glib tongue would wag in the abbot's ears; but in this matter he is the safest one to send."

"'Twill rid us of him, at least," said John, meditatively. "Were he a staunch friend, we might give him a stoup of wine to strengthen him on his way; but "——

"Saint Dunstan! thou art mad, John! I opine we can find room for all the good liquor we get. No, no. Let him slake his thirst and refresh his limbs at the holy well. Saint Mary, of ever blessed memory, will see to his wants, and heed well that nothing ill befalls him on the way."

"But, sayest thou of a truth that the abbot is coming back?" asked the monk, thoughtfully.

"Read for thyself, man."

The monk took the packet, and was about to open it, when the opening of the door startled him, and the high cellarer appeared.

There was an angry flush on his visage as he beheld the two thus engaged, and, as a lawful right, he demanded to know the contents of the packet, and also from whence it came.

"From our reverend father, the Lord Abbot," replied Friar Cuthbert, in a tone of deference.

"And why didst thou not give it me?" demanded the high cellarer.

"I knew not of thy return."

"Neither did you care. Couldst thou not have asked, is thy tongue cloven to the roof of thy mouth?"

"Marry, is it not; neither did I think there was harm in my not asking. Saints forbid that I should do ought contrary to the rules of our order."

The high cellarer was too angered to answer.

He snatched the missive, the seal of which was broken, and tore it open.

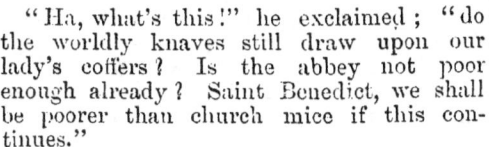

"Ha, what's this!" he exclaimed; "do the worldly knaves still draw upon our lady's coffers? Is the abbey not poor enough already? Saint Benedict, we shall be poorer than church mice if this continues."

The high cellarman was speaking feelingly for himself.

While the coffers of the abbey were well stocked he could appropriate a little to his own use, but when they began to run low, he had to be careful, for fear of being missed by the abbot.

We have previously seen that he had a secret hoard for his own private use, and that the outlaws helped themselves therefrom, to the great discomfiture of the high cellarer.

To replace his loss it had taken him some time, and required a great deal of screwing and scheming, but he had accomplished it at last and added somewhat to it, a circumstance that made him the more uneasy now.

Having finished reading the note, he folded it up carefully, and placed it in his breast, remarking as he did so—

"'Tis strange the abbot should send for money, and moreover employ strangers for his messengers. Where are the good men?" he added. "Let me have speech of them."

Friar Cuthbert pointed to a dark corner of the room, where the friar and Little John stood watching all that passed.

They did not appear to hear the remark, for they moved not from their seclusion, in truth they were both afraid that the high cellarman would recognise them.

The high cellarman moved towards them.

"And so you have come straight from our father the abbot," he said.

"The missive we brought with us implies as much, and we wish that you would make haste and give us what we need, that we may hasten back, for in truth the abbot will look anxiously for our return."

Little John acted as spokesman, and he imitated such a sanctified air that easily deceived the high cellarer.

"And are you not afraid to trust yourselves with this sum?"

"Why need we be afraid?" asked Little John.

"Why? Marry! thou must know that the roads are infested with robbers. Did no one molest thee coming here?"

"Holy Mother! what could they gain by waylaying two poor priests? Marry! we started on the road without food or water; 'twould have been a charity had they taken us in and given us to eat."

"Then thou must be famished. Here, Brother John, take our poor brothers to the refectory, and give them wherewith to appease their hunger. By the rood! they have borne their part like good Christians, or they would have asked for refreshment ere this."

Then, to Friar Cuthbert, he added—

"I will myself go to the sheriff, and, in the meantime, look well after the poor wayfarers, that they may render a good account of the treatment they receive during the abbot's absence."

A few minutes later, the high cellarer mounted on a mule, left the abbey gates, and sauntered along the road in the direction of Nottingham.

Little John and the Friar were ushered into a room where the novices sat to partake of their meals, and soon a humble repast was set before them.

Neither of them, however, could relish the coarse meal. In passing the door of the high cellarer's chamber a smell had assailed their noses, that made their stomachs long for something more delicate.

What they smelt was the haunch of venison Friar Cuthbert had alluded to, and though the stout door was closed, and the chinks stopped up to prevent the smell escaping, yet it did not serve to conceal the delicious odour from the keen scent of the foresters.

The novices had finished their meal, and they left to pursue their studies, and Little John and the Friar were left by themselves to finish their repast.

"Saint Thomas! this is playing the priest in earnest!" quoth Little John, after feasting his eyes for some time on the goblet of clear, cold water placed before him. "Body o' me! we have entered on our pilgrimage in pure saintly style."

"Ay, now thou knowest, and, mayhap, will be convinced that a priest's life is not one of feasting and sleeping as thou wouldst have it. Thou seest now that the deception lies with thyself, but for all this, I see no difference in thy condition; thou art as fat and sleek as ever."

Little John darted a vicious look at the friar when he uttered this retort.

"Marry, I would not for the world blow myself out as thou dost with water. However, I do not grumble at this sort of fare, though, by the blade-bone of our patron saint, 'tis but sorry living for a good forester."

In this jangling manner they passed a full half-hour, and then Little John began to tire of it.

He fancied the water began to gripe him, and, as he knew that the monks of St. Mary's were anything but abstainers from the good things which the Lord had provided for the wants of man, he was determined on making a search.

Leaving Friar Tuck to console himself in solitude, and to finish, if he wished it, the coarse meal which they had scarcely tasted, Little John rambled about the labyrinth of passages until he reached the door of the refectory, where the principal monks took their meals.

Friar Cuthbert was in the act of raising a goblet of malvoisie to his lips when Little John opened the door and thrust in his head.

The friar's back was towards the door, so that he did not see the cowled head, but brother Denis, who sat opposite, and was about to help himself to a slice of steaming venison, saw him, and he dropped the carver, as though an arrow had pierced him.

This act attracted the attention of the other monks, who were enjoying, with much gusto, the sumptuous repast, and when they saw the strange head and the dark, gleaming eyes gazing upon them, they shared in Brother Denis's alarm.

Friar Cuthbert was the most collected of them all.

He had freely partaken of the potent draught, and he was in a fit state of eloquence to make an excuse for being found in company with such things as were forbidden by the Church.

He rose, and was about to speak, but Little John interrupted him by saying—

"Let not my presence disturb ye, good brethren. I would not have intruded on thy privacy had I known thou wast at thy devotions ; but, now I am here, I may as well inform thee of my mission."

Friar Cuthbert was willing to listen to anything, for he now saw that it was impossible to hoodwink the supposed friar, and he was afraid that he would return to the abbot with a mouthful of news concerning what he saw.

There was but one way that he could see of settling the matter quietly, and that was to invite the intruder to sit down and partake with them ; and even in doing this he was incurring great risk.

"Good brother," he said, "what is thy malady ? Hath the sober diet, which our good abbot imposes upon us for our good, disagreed with thee ? "

"In good sooth, friar, thou hast rightly guessed. I must tell thee that certain brethren of the abbey, to which me and my companion belong, have an indulgence from the bishop to keep up the feast of our good Saint Anthony, and it falleth upon this very day, and it grieves us that we have not been able to keep it in befitting manner, and "——

"By the mass! thou art situated exactly the same as we are. Call thy brother, and with us thou canst sit down and eat. 'Tis passing strange that this thing should occur to us both on the same day. Make thyself at home. But one thing I must desire of thee, and that is that ye make no mention of it either to the abbot on thy return, neither to the high cellarer, for the rules of St. Mary's are so strict that a month's penance would not be sufficient atonement were it known."

"Good St. Anthony forbid that we should act treacherously to thee ! We are good churchmen, and our promise, once given, is never broken. So fear not there anent. Thy secret is safe in our keeping."

Friar Cuthbert chuckled inwardly at his good success ; and when Little John was gone the rest of the monks commended the friar greatly for his ruse.

In like manner also did Little John rejoice, but when he told Friar Tuck of the run of luck he had had he would not believe him.

"Come, see for thyself, then," said the giant ; "thou art at the best but an unbelieving rogue, and deservest not to share in the feast of our good saint ; but for all that, I have reason to believe that thou wilt be convinced."

Friar Tuck conducted himself in befitting manner when he entered the room, and seated himself at the board, where he proved himself as good a trencherman as the rest.

Little John, as Friar Cuthbert had desired him, made himself at home, and, throwing aside the priestly mien he had assumed, made himself as free as though he were amongst his forest companions.

His company just suited the monks, who thought more of their present temporal than of their future salvation, and they joined right lustily in the chorus of his songs, and vowed him one of the jolliest friars they had ever seen.

Friar Tuck was no less mirthful when the wine began to flow in his veins ; but he spoke but little until his enormous appetite was appeased, then he sang the following—

Why shouldn't we friars be jolly? I ask—
Why shouldn't we monks be gay?
When the red deer boundeth in the woods
There's a hand ever ready to slay.

Then why shouldn't we have a glorious feed
Off a venison haunch so prime—
Why shouldn't we drown our sorrows? I ask
In a flagon of rich red wine?

There's a stout lusty robber they call Robin Hood,
An outlaw he is so bold ;
And he never scruples at killing a deer,
E'en in the king's presence, I'm told.

Then why should we, who have greater right
To the produce and fat of the land,
Go to bed fasting and praying each night
When there's plenty good things at our hand?

When Friar Tuck had finished he was loudly acclaimed, and the jolly old monks gulped down the wine, and, reckless of all consequences, called for another song.

CHAPTER CXXXI.

THE HIGH CELLARMAN AND THE SHERIFF OF NOTTINGHAM.

De Lois was filled with anger
And paced his chamber floor,
Thinking of his losses,
When a knock came at the door.

FLUSHED with wine and heated with passion, Geoffrey de Lois paced his chamber, deploring his misfortune, and vowing fresh vengeance on the authors.

"Marry come up, with a wennion on them all!" he muttered savagely. "They are a nest of demons, and those who proffered to assist are as bad."

"And that ass of a Malcolm to fail!" he added, bitterly. "He said his success was certain, or I would not have trusted him; and then, again, my kinsman, the all-wise abbot, to think of him being foiled, is of itself enough to drive me mad."

"But I will have no more of him and his priestcraft," he broke out aloud. "Henceforth, I will trust to no one but myself; but there, I forget that my men are in captivity, and my garrison is so weakened that I could not even protect the castle from an assault, much less muster a force in the field."

"Who's there?" he demanded, gruffly, as a knock sounded at the door.

"A messenger from the lord abbot wishes to see you," answered the page, entering.

"Lead him hither," said De Lois, in the same surly tone.

"A messenger from the abbot," he thought to himself, as the door closed behind the page. "Where can he be, then? Not in the hands of the outlaws, I opine?"

He had not time to reflect further, when the high cellarer entered.

"So you have a message from the lord abbot," he said, testily.

"An' it please ye, I have," replied the functionary, not at all pleased with the tone and manner of the sheriff.

"Out with it at once, then; let us have no bickering. Has my uncle escaped, or is he still in the hands of that robber?"

"I bear a missive from him; 'twas brought to the abbey by two friars, who are waiting anxiously to return with the answer, and"—

"Money, I suppose? Curse them, that is all they think about."

The high cellarer crossed himself devoutly, and handed the missive to De Lois; but he could not decipher the strange characters, so the high cellarer read the contents to him.

Geoffrey listened in feverish anxiety, until he came to the end of the scroll, and then he burst into a violent fit of passion.

"The idiot!" he ejaculated, fiercely. "Where does he think I can get such a sum from? This last failure has ruined me. A malison on his stupid pate, to think I can spare so much!"

He wound up his speech with an expletive that made the high cellarer shudder, and then continued to pace the room with long, hurried strides.

The shriveling eyed him meditatively, and heartily wished he had not taken upon himself the task of messenger; but his repentance came too late, and he was forced to listen patiently to the sheriff's incoherent mutterings.

After pacing the floor for some moments, the sheriff came to a sudden stand, and facing round to the high cellarer, said—

"I must trouble you once more to read that accursed scroll. By the saints! the contents are too much for my memory to contain."

The high cellarer obeyed, and De Lois, without speaking a word, strode out of the room.

When he returned, he held in his hand a small bag, and chinking it so that the high cellarer might hear that it contained money, he handed it to him, saying—

"Take this to thy master, and may his wounds soon heal; and, moreover, tell him to heed well how he arranges his plans, for, by the bones of the dead, if he does not succeed after what he has promised, the friendship between us will for ever cease."

The chink of the pieces rattling against each other, was music to the ears of the churchman, so much so that he scarcely noticed the last of the sheriff's speech.

Placing the bag in a place of security, beneath his sombre robe, he slunk out of the chamber, and blessing the soldiers he met on his way to the portal, he mounted his mule, and, heedless of the great crowd mustered in the great space before the castle, he urged his steed as fast as possible towards the abbey.

There was a large concourse of people assembled in the market-place; but his mind was too intent upon other matters to heed them, or inquire what they were about, and he pushed on, scarcely deigning to glance around.

But what were his thoughts?

What was it that so occupied his mind?

Not the words of De Lois, certainly, for they did not concern him. No; it was the money; he could feel it jerk against his hip, and whenever the mule stumbled, he fancied he could hear it jink. It was the money he thought of, and he felt a secret hankering to possess it.

To lighten the bag of a few silver pieces, he thought, could be no harm; but then he might be found out; for when the sheriff and the lord abbot met, the latter would be sure to inform his uncle of the shortcomings of the specified amount.

"I will have the whole," he muttered, determinedly. "'Tis but a risk, and 'tis well worth that. I have risked greater danger for less gain, and have been successful. Why should I not be successful now?"

"But what tale can I invent?" he mused. "A good one it must be, I trow, or"——Ah, I have it! I will return to the abbey with disordered dress, vow I have been robbed, and throw suspicion on the band of outlaws that are leagued with that notorious robber, Robin Hood."

He liked the scheme much, and laughed heartily to himself at the idea of his cunning being equal to the emergency. How he succeeded, we shall see.

————

CHAPTER CXXXII.

HOW LITTLE JOHN MADE THE HIGH CELLAR-
MAN DISGORGE HIS HOARDED TREASURE.

Tne money he divided into portions ten.
And hid them 'neath his raiment where he thought no
　　one would ken;
Then on his mule he mounted, and sat himself astride,
　And round about him looked to see that no lurking
　　robber him eyed.

THE high cellarer rode on, planning his villany ; and to further aid his scheme, and give colour to the lie he had invented, he turned his mule into a by path that was but little used.

So deeply engrossed was he in thought, and so intent upon his scheme that he did not notice a figure clad in Lincoln green crouching behind a pile of timber.

Neither did he observe the pair of eyes watching him, or he would doubtless have pursued a different course to that which he meditated.

Having made up his mind to appropriate the money to his own use, his next thought was how he might best secure it from observation on entering the abbey, for the least chink of the precious metal, either in dismounting, or walking was sure to betray him.

Turning his mule into a thick clump of trees, he assured himself as far as he was able that no one had seen him leave the road. He then took out the bags and divided the money into several lots, which he wrapped up in a portion of his garment he had torn off, and then secured it beneath his under raiment next to his skin.

He next tore his robe into shreds, and bedaubed his face with mire to make it appear as though he had been roughly handled, and had had his clothes torn in the struggle ; then, remounting his mule, he started forward on his journey.

A pair of keen eyes, however, had narrowly watched his movements ; and, before he had gone many yards, he heard a voice shouting after him along the road.

He felt a little alarmed at the first sound of the voice, and turned to see who it could be ; but his fears soon vanished, when he saw an aged pilgrim tottering along the road, apparently tired and footsore.

He was leaning heavily on his staff, and appeared to have exhausted his strength in shouting ; but the worthy churchman was in no humour to heed him, so he dug his heels into the poor beasts ribs and endeavoured to urge him forward more quickly.

The mule, thus goaded, quickened his speed ; but, for all this, the pilgrim was resolved not to be left behind, and he moved after the high cellarer with long but steady strides.

On finding that the man gained instead of losing ground, the high cellarer began to get enraged ; and he showered his blows with vigour upon the poor beast, and also heaped his maledictions on the head of the poor pilgrim.

"Stay—stay, good father, I am faint," shouted the traveller, in a weak voice ; "do not leave me, or I shall die by the roadside."

"Die then, curse you! and trouble me not," muttered the angry churchman. "By the mass ! I would have given a silver piece rather than have seen thy visage."

By this time the man came up to him, and laid his hand on the trappings of the mule, and puffed and blowed as though he was out of breath.

"I pray you begone," said the high cellarer, concealing his wrath, but speaking sharply to the man ; "see you not that my beast is jaded, and that I am but in a sorry plight myself."

"Marry do I, good father ; but thy condition is far preferable to mine. I have travelled many a long weary mile, and I can scarce drag my weary limbs along, and yet have I many a long mile to travel."

"May I ask to what place you are journeying ?"

"The shrine of Saint Mary's, there to lay down my head, and rest my weary bones in peace. This, I hope, will be my last pilgrimage ; and, I trust, if you are journeying my way you will assist me in getting there."

"Good fellow, were it in my power I would do so ; but how can I assist you ? You see I have been waylaid by a set of ruffians, and sorely beaten. I stand in much need of assistance myself ; so, take my blessing, and make the best of your journey as best you can."

The head cellarer then urged on his mule, and tried to shake off the man's hold of the trappings, but he only clung the faster, and the beast was thus doubly burthened.

"For the love of him who died for us, do not leave me to perish," said the old man, piteously. "Give me thine aid, I pray, as far as it lays in your power."

"I cannot assist you," exclaimed the baffled rogue. "Go thy way in peace ere you anger me to deeds of violence."

The old man fixed his flashing eyes on the speaker, and clutched him with both arms round the waist, and, in a determined voice, said—

"Nay, thou shalt not go. I am resolved to share the mule with thee. Let me ride but one mile, and I will be satisfied."

"Not an inch," replied the head cellarer, delivering a smack with the flat of his hand full in the face of the man ; but the next moment he found himself dragged from his saddle, and laid sprawling in the middle of the path.

In an instant he was on his feet, and grappled with the man whom he took for an aged and feeble pilgrim, but whom he found was a young and stalwart forester ; for in the struggle the travel-stained robes of the stranger were torn off, and disclosed the stalwart limbs of Little John.

Never was the high cellarer more astounded

ROBIN HOOD,

AND THE OUTLAWS OF SHERWOOD FOREST.

BOB BLAND'S REWARD.

in his life than he was on making this discovery.

The deception had been so complete ; the
height of the forester having been hidden in

his stooping gait and his rough, manly voice being softened with his mimicry.

No sooner, however, did he find out the deceit than he assumed his dignity, and began to rate Little John smartly.

"Insolent knave! How dare you assault me in this manner on the king's highway? Was there no other "——

"Peace, good father. I mistook thee for a rogue in disguise, but now I recognise you, and see my mistake. Thou art the high cellarer of St. Mary's Abbey, if I judge aright."

"You have rightly guessed, and shall soundly sweat for this act of deceit and treachery; but thy disguise proves that some motive has induced you to do this robbery, perchance, for 'tis well known that your itching figures are ever ready to rob even the poor and needy."

Little John burst into a hearty laugh.

"I will not deny that I have a motive in disguising myself, and if thou wilt be my confessor I will breathe into thine ear the truth."

"Do so, then, 'tis the only recompense you can make for the bruises you have inflicted on my body."

"You must know, then, Little John began, "that my master, Robin Hood, has a strange liking for gold, and cares not in what way he obtains it, so long as it is by honest means, and therefore he levies a toll on all who may think fit to pass through this forest, which he has taken into his keeping for the king."

The high cellarer bit his lips with excitement as he listened to these words.

"Insolent carl!" he said, "is this the explanation you promised me? Stand from my path, or, by the mass, I will have you denounced from the altar, and, moreover, disgraced with a good flogging in the market-place."

"That your heart is good to do so, I have no doubt," replied Little John; "but as to your harming us further than by threats, I apprehend but little danger."

"Ah! you shall see. Do not imagine that the church is to be insulted with impunity. You have escaped thus far with impunity; but remember there is a day of retribution at hand, when you will have to settle accounts, and then you will have to answer for all this."

"For that I am prepared; and I hope you are as fit to pay your debts. In the first place you are now trespassing on my master's grounds, and must pay the toll he demands."

The high cellarer looked aghast.

"Do you still insist in this daring insult?" he said. "Think you I carry a purse unless on a visit to the sick? And even did I do so, I would not part with a fraction to such a robber."

"Then it will be my duty to take it by force. You are a cunning rogue, but you will not deceive me; so turn out the bag I saw you so carefully stow away."

"Wh—a—t b—a—g?" gasped the high cellarer.

"That which you brought from Nottingham—the sweating of the poor, and the rental of the broad lands that are by right the lawful possessions of my master, Robin Hood, Earl of Huntingdon."

"Liar! I have no such money, neither has your vile master the least pretensions to the name he so vilely usurps. Beware what you say; and, moreover, what you do, or the king's ears may be open to your scandal."

"Body o' me, I fear that but little. But as I came not to bandy words with you, or hold an idle parley, I desire that you give up the money, so that we may both part quietly."

Little John gripped his staff with one hand, and held out his other hand to receive the money; but the priest hesitated, and did not seem at all inclined to part with it.

The giant waited, until his patience was fairly tired, and then he administered a sharp blow across the high cellarer's shoulders, which caused the saintly man to howl with pain, and he made a desperate effort to regain his seat on the back of the mule.

"Not yet, good father," exclaimed Little John, clutching him by the arm, and looking him full in the face. "Not yet; you leave not this spot until you produce the money. Mind, I am in earnest, and if you have the least doubt of my sincerity, I will give you sufficient proof thereof."

At this moment, they were startled by a deer bounding across the path, and then an arrow whizzed through the air, and struck it in its side.

"Blade bone of Saint Hubert! What knave is it chasing my master's deer?" shouted the forester. "Marry! 'twill go hard with the rascal, if I catch him poaching, whoever it be."

"Hist, cease thy prating!" said a voice he soon recognised, and Much, the miller, stepped out from the cover of the trees.

Little John was about to greet him, but Much interrupted him by exclaiming—

"Ho! ho! who have you here, my modest shriveling? You seem to be mightily taken up with the saintly company of priests. I trow me, you will have free shrift and a passport to speed you straight to heaven."

The high cellarer glared viciously at the speaker, and then waited to hear what Little John would answer.

The giant was in a merry mood.

He drew his sombre cloak about him, and, putting his cowl down over his face so as to leave only his eyes visible, he replied—

"Unholy sinner—guzzler of wine, and destroyer of the king's deer, have you come here to mock me? or are your eyes so blind, as not to be able to see that I am giving this ungodly varlet shrift—that I am his confessor, that I am attending to his spiritual wants, and that he, as a recompense, is about to give that which will provide for my bodily comforts, and release him from a great responsibility?"

So saying, he administered another thwack

across the broad shoulders of the priest, and gave him to understand that, if he did not produce the money he had concealed about him, he would pound him to a jelly.

Thus admonished, the high cellarer pulled a long face and began to expostulate; but the giant was in no mood for further parlance, so he caught him in his brawny arms and quickly denuded him of his vestments.

Much was not prepared for the sight he was about to witness, and, when the little coins dropped one by one on the ground with a chink, he opened his eyes in amazement.

"Saint Herman of the Wold!" he exclaimed; "thou art a lucky fellow, Little John, to find such a booty. Thou hast done well in thine office as confessor, and I have a mind to don the cloak and cowl and follow in thy footsteps."

Little John gave a quiet grin, and made a sign to Much to assist him in picking up the neatly folded parcels (of which there were ten), and the twain quickly disposed of them about their own persons.

They then held a consultation as to whether they should take the mule with them or allow the high cellarer to mount, and it was finally agreed that, as he was now eased of his load and had only his own carcase to carry, that he should walk.

The priest demurred slightly at this; but, thinking it the most prudent course to make his escape in a whole skin, he shuffled off, vowing vengeance and heaping curses upon the foresters and their leader, Robin Hood, as long as he was within hearing.

Little John and Much stood laughing at the joke, and watching the high cellarman until he was out of sight, and then they set off in the direction of the stronghold, and the giant amused the miller's son by narrating his adventure in the abbey.

"Marry, I know not how you found courage to leave such comfortable quarters," said Much. "For my part, I would have stayed there as long as the good things lasted."

"Quotha! 'twas a hard struggle, you may depend; but the thought entered my head, and as we were likely to be discovered, I thought it best to act as I have done."

"But the friar—what of him? How came you to leave Tuck behind?"

"Let the shriveling answer for himself. He is all right, you may depend. Do you not see him on yonder rise?"

The forester pointed through the trees to a grassy slope, on the side of which was a thick clump of trees, and seated comfortably beneath them they could see Friar Tuck wiping the perspiration from his bald crown.

The foresters made towards him, and when the friar caught sight of them, and beheld the mule Much was leading, he burst forth into an expression of delight.

"My benison on ye, my children!" he exclaimed. "'Tis a treat I little expected to see and enjoy. 'Tis a comfort, at least, to know that one kind soul bestows some pity on the sufferings of a free follower of the cross."

"Name it not, good father," replied Little John, with mock deference. "It is but our duty to aid thee, if it lay in our power; but what hast thou in thy poke—anything wherewith to heal our sufferings?"

"First tell me thy malady, and then I will answer. Art hungered or athirst?"

"Both."

"Then I can supply thy wants. Here, help thyself, and then I will trouble thee to assist me, for I feel sorely faint, and am borne down with exhaustion."

Much took the poke, and soon emptied it of its contents, which was very acceptable to the hungry pair.

There was a thick chunk of venison and a number of small oaten cakes, and a large jar of good Rhenish wine, which the trio soon set to demolishing, and then the friar told his tale as to the manner in which he left the abbey.

"When you were gone," he said, "and I found your departure excited no suspicion, I sat down again and made the monks, who were regular topers, guzzle so much of the wine that they knew not what they were doing, and quite forgot all about the return of the high cellarer.

"Then I hunted about till I found the closet where the leech of the abbey kept his medicines and drugs, and finding a jar containing powder, the qualities of which I knew, I took a portion and dropped a pinch into each of the horns from which the monks were drinking.

"This sent them to sleep; and when I found all safe, I made another search for the place where the tithes were hidden, and I filled this leathern bag with as much as it would hold, and throwing it over my shoulder to try its weight, I found it was almost as much as I could carry.

"But thinking of the long way I had to travel, and the support my body would need to enable me to carry so great a load, I filled this poke, and, tying the two together, I slung them over my shoulder and walked quietly from the Abbey."

"But did you meet with no resistance at the gate?" asked Little John.

"Faith, I did not! The warder looked at me rather suspiciously; but as he had no idea of what the bags contained, and as it was no business of his to ask, he made no remark; besides, your leaving the abbey before me, to return, as they supposed, to the lord abbot, so completely lulled all suspicions, that he never so much as noticed that neither Friar Cuthbert nor Brother John accompanied me to the gate.

"'Tis a mercy for thee, then, that the fellow was so stupid, or, by my halidame, they would have administered a sore castigation to thy hide had they found out thy deceit; but thou art safe. Let us drink to the health of the jolly friars, and also to his holiness the high cellarman, to whose credulity we owe our present good fortune and success."

This was agreed to, and loudly acclaimed by the others, and the three took a copious libation and drank to the health of the high cellarer in the wine that the friar had abstracted from the high cellarman's own private store.

In the midst of their rejoicing and conviviality, they were disturbed by the winding of a horn, and a party of foresters—a dozen or more in number—made their appearance over the brow of the slope.

Amongst these were Will Scarlett, George-a-Green, and Bayston, and, as soon as they saw the jovial trio, they made all speed towards them.

CHAPTER CXXXIII.

THE AWFUL FATE OF FRIAR ABSALOM.

There seemed a strange fatality
Settled on this race.
The blood poured from his mouth and ears,
And nostrils, down his face.

FATHER ABSALOM, on returning to his room after his visit to the vault, was in anything but a pleasant humour.

He seated himself on his hard wooden bench, and dropping his head in his hands, gave vent to his passion in a series of groans and horrible gnashings of his teeth.

"Revenge! revenge!" was the only articulate sentence he uttered, and even this could only have been heard by the ear of an attentive listener.

For some moments he sat thus, brooding over his imaginary wrongs, when he was startled from his reverie by a strange sound, and he raised his bleared eyes with a kind of fear and trembling, and looked around the ill-lighted apartment.

At first he could see nothing to occasion him any alarm; but after a moment's scrutiny, he beheld a large rat nibbling at a piece of candle he had unconsciously thrown away.

That this was one of the inhabitants of the vault he readily conjectured, and he felt assured that the vermin had entered his chamber by the secret door; but for all this, he did not feel satisfied with its presence, and he shook and groaned as he eyed it, as though he was in the presence of some huge beast of the forest.

But what was the cause of his doing so? The rat, to all appearance, intended no injury to him: besides, he had wherewith to slay it on the instant, if he wished.

A few words will explain the cause of his fear.

It was a superstition in his family that a rat, however bold, would not venture into the room in which any member of the family slept, unless some fearful calamity was about to fall upon that especial member, and for several generations this superstition had been verified; and whenever a rat (a black one, it was the case generally) ventured into the room, that member had shortly after met with some horrible and violent death.

His great-grandfather had been killed by a flash of lightning while reading the midnight mass in an old chapel over the tomb of a knight slain in one of the civil wars.

His grandfather was slain by the hand of an assassin, in mistake for a priest who had offered some insult to the daughter of one of the Saxon nobles, and his own father had died before the altar in a fit.

This strange fatality was looked upon by those who knew of it as a judgment from heaven for their wickedness in breaking the laws of the church, which prohibited them from marrying, and which law they secretly violated; for each of them, with the exception of Absalom, married, and had one son, a boy; and, as we have seen, Father Absalom, instead of profiting by the warning given him would have made Marian his wife by force.

No wonder that he trembled at the sight of the animal, which had evidently come to warn him of his fate; neither is it surprising that his eye-balls started from his head, and that he was filled with silent horror.

A footstep, however, came to his relief and broke the spell, and the rat, alarmed at the sound, disappeared without finishing his meal.

The footstep was that of one of the novices, who, as we have seen, were constantly at his service, and, as the shriveling entered, the friar fixed his keen eye upon him, and remarked—

"Hath Ezra returned?"

"Not yet, good father," was the reply.

"He has not yet had time to perform the journey there and back on foot."

"Then I will teach him to move smarter," hissed the priest. "Less food and additional penance may, perchance, do much towards this, and I will try its effects."

"By the mass, we have enough of that already," replied the young man, angered at the remark, for he knew that it pertained to himself as well as to his companion. "By the Virgin! if scourging and fasting will fill our souls for eternal bliss, we are well prepared to make the journey heavenward already."

Father Absalom was not used to be answered in this manner, and, what with the liberty of the novice's speech and the tumult of his feelings previously, the friar seemed changed suddenly into a madman.

It was near a minute ere he spoke, but when he did it was in a voice of thunder, and his eyes flashed like living coals.

"Minion! hound of Lucifer!" he shouted fiercely, "is it thus you dare to taunt me? Hence, quit my sight, ere I am tempted to chastise you!"

The young man was a powerfully-built fellow, and these words stung him to the quick. His proud spirit was raised, and, in the moment of his anger, he retorted—

"Blasphemer! I fear you not! but warn you to be cautious in laying hands on me; for, by all the saints, if you do, I will resent it to the death."

This boldness wrought the friar's anger to its greatest height, and, springing forward, he aimed a blow at the speaker's head that must have telled him had it struck him; but he stepped adroitly aside, and the priest staggered forward with the impetus of the blow.

In doing so the toes of his sandal caught something, and tripped him, and he fell with all his weight, the violence of the increased force against the wall almost crashing in his skull.

The novice—alarmed at this, and fearful of the consequences, if anything serious should result from it, for he felt certain that he would be blamed—raised him instantly; but he could do nothing for him, as the blood was pouring copiously from the mouth, ears, and nostrils of the priest.

In this state he raised him in his arms, and lifted him into the small bed in the wall, and finding that he was fast dying, he closed the curtains and prepared to make good his own escape before the terrible calamity was discovered.

Reaching a bunch of keys that hung on the wall, he hurried from the chamber of death, and proceeded to the vaults, resolved upon releasing Marian from her captivity, and, as an atonement for the injury he had done her (in acting according to the priest's orders), to place her in safety beyond the abbey walls.

He was surprised, however, on searching the cell in which he had left her, to find it empty; and it puzzled him greatly to imagine how she could have released herself, as there was no trace of any violence having been used.

That she must have had someone to assist her he felt certain, from the fact of his having left her securely bound; but who it could have been he could not imagine, as Ezra was away from the abbey, and he was the only one beside the friar who knew of her place of confinement.

After some moments quiet reflection, however, he noticed that which had before escaped his observation, and that was that the door had been forced open, and this determined him upon making a further search.

His first thought was to visit the cells of the other prisoners, but they were likewise gone, and he was fairly puzzled to account for it.

But he was a man of strong mind, and not easily to be baulked in his projects, and, as he possessed an amount of cunning as well as a clear, calculating brain, he set his wits to work to solve the mystery.

Placing the feeble light he carried close to the ground, he carefully examined sundry marks that had been made in the damp and dust that had settled on the floor.

These were the impression of footmarks, and he traced them for some distance along the corridor, where he found that they terminated, and he then retraced them back again past the door of the furthermost cell, and

along a narrow, vaulted passage that led to a secret outlet.

As he proceeded to where the dirt was less trampled, he distinctly marked the footsteps of three different persons, and these he immediately guessed were those of Hubert, the page, and Hal.

Following them up carefully until he came to a place where three distinct passages branched off, he found that the party had separated, and in his uncertainty of knowing which passage to take, he followed the footsteps that had followed the straight course.

For some distance he diligently pursued his way, carefully watching the ground, and buried in deep thought, when suddenly he was startled by someone pouncing upon him.

A powerful hand then grasped him by the throat, and a voice hissed huskily in his ear—

"Silence, or this moment is your last!"

This strange and unlooked-for proceeding brought him to an upright position, and looking up hastily, he beheld himself face to face with the soldier Hubert.

"A malison on thee, knave that thou art!" exclaimed the astonished youth. "Loose thy hold, or by the saints I will brain you like an ox!"

"Ah! 'Twill be no easy matter as you will find," replied Hubert tightening his grasp. "'Tis a task much more easily boasted of than done; but since you are in my power I will take no mean advantage of you, but simply grant you a boon, providing you answer my questions correctly."

"First, you must answer me a question," replied the young man resolutely.

"Where is the lady whom I left a prisoner in yonder cell?"

"With me, and under my protection. What want you of her?"

"Nothing. I would release her from this place, and"——

"Place her in better security, I opine?"

"Not so. You are mistaken."

"'Tis fortunate I am; but still I have a suspicion."

"You can dispense with it at once then, and listen to me. Father Absalom, your oppressor, is dead, and if you will listen to me, and trust yourself in my care, I will lead you to life and liberty. Refuse me, and you can wander about these gloomy vaults until death claims you."

Hubert bit his lip.

"Dost think thy wily tongue will make me loose my hold?" he asked, peremptorily.

"I care not. Your fate rests entirely with yourself. If you would wish to stay here, *murder* me; if not, release me, and I will set you free."

"False wretch! it is not in your power. You are but the slave of that base wretch who wears the cloak of righteousness to conceal his villany. You would deceive me; but look you here, I would think no more of crushing out your life than I would were you a toad."

"By our Blessed Lady, I swear what I assert is true. I have before said that I came not to harm you. Why not trust to my word, and "——

"Fall into the snare. No, no. I have you and will keep you fast."

The young man gave utterance to an oath, and made a desperate but feeble effort to free himself; and then, in a fit of desperation, he thrust his hand into his bosom, and pulled forth a long two-edged dagger.

This at once convinced Hubert that it was no use of his further persisting, and it was now his turn to listen to the threats of the other.

"Now, where is the woman?" demanded the novice, fiercely, for the dagger and the sudden change in the appearance of the soldier, gave him additional courage.

Hubert did not reply, but slunk back to the wall out of the way of the point of the glittering weapon.

At that moment the eye of the novice caught sight of a figure at the further end of the passage, and he rushed forward in the direction, and soon stood face to face with Maid Marian.

Marian naturally shrank back on seeing him.

She remembered his visage, and recognised it at once as the face of the man who had assisted in binding her to the cross.

For a second or two they stood regarding each other—the one with loathing, and the other wrapped in wonderment and admiration at her beauty.

"Good lady," he said, "fear no harm from me; I would not injure you. And as to your friend there, of such hasty temper, I forgive him, and consider he knows not a word of what he says."

"And what proof have we of your sincerity?"

"Simply this," and he held up a key; then added, "This is the talisman that can open for you a road to liberty; now, what say you? Are you satisfied?"

"I shall be, if you explain what miracle has changed your mind in our favour; but till then we shall remain enemies to each other."

The novice exhibited signs of anger at this, and he was about to make some hasty reply, when they were startled by a loud crash.

CHAPTER CXXXIV.

DEATH OF THE OLD WOMAN ON THE HEATH.

Madge to the cottage hied,
And found her wan and pale.
Then drawing to her side,
She heard her wondrous tale.

A spell she had been working,
The fumes got down her throat,
And deadly were the drugs she used,
To make the antidote.

WHEN Madge Stukely returned to her cheerless home, and found that her father was still absent, she threw herself into a seat and wept bitterly.

How long she sat in this manner she knew not, but she was suddenly aroused by a low hoot, and, on looking up, she beheld through the gloom an owl perched on the window sill.

"Blessed Virgin!" she exclaimed, starting to her feet, and making the sign of the cross. "What means this harbinger of evil? Am I to have still further trouble? Is my father dead, or "——

The owl flapped its wings, and giving another dismal hoot, flew away; and as Madge stood gazing in wonderment after it, a thought suddenly occurred to her.

"I will to the old dame at once," she muttered. "How foolish it was of me not to mention the subject while I was there. She can at least tell me whether my father is living."

With this she snatched up her cloak and hood, and left the ruins; and after a sharp walk, she reached the cottage of Dame Morton.

She knocked loudly at the door; but as her summons was not answered, she began to fear that the old dame was out, or that something serious had happened to her, for the dame was far advanced in years, and frequently complained of a twittering at her heart.

Madge knocked again, however; and still receiving no answer, she began to be apprehensive, and wishing to learn the truth, she raised the latch, and as the door was unbarred, she entered.

The sight that there met her gaze fairly startled her.

There was no light, save the faint glimmer of the fire; but this was sufficient to enable her to look round the apartment, and view its contents.

In one corner lay what appeared to be a corpse, covered over with a white sheet, and in the bed, apparently at her last gasp, lay the old woman of the heath.

She raised her head slightly and smiled, when she found it was Madge that had entered, and whispered something too inarticulate for Madge to hear.

Madge Stukely, though still possessing some of her former courage, which had been sorely tried during her heavy affliction, could not help feeling awed as she gazed around.

Seeing that the old dame still exhibited signs of life, she approached the bedside and said—

"What is the meaning of all this, I see? How is it that trouble has come upon you so suddenly? Who's body is that I see outstretched yonder?"

"See for yourself," replied the old woman, feebly, "then tell me whether you see any likeness between that corpse and Robin Hood."

Madge gave a start of surprise; but, recovering herself, she approached the sheet and raised it.

There was a face apparently of a dead man, and it was cold to the touch; and, moreover, resembling the features of the outlawed Robin Hood.

Madge stood for some moments with her gaze riveted on the pale features, when it suddenly struck her that the face was not human, and, pulling back the sheet to examine the hands, she found that what she supposed to be a dead body was only an effigy.

The face had been carefully moulded in wax, and the lower extremities were formed of bunches of heather.

On making this discovery, Madge at once questioned the old dame closely concerning this strange proceeding, and thus she explained to her fully the reason of her employing her time in this manner.

"I have had a vision," she said, "and in it I saw bold Robin being poisoned by one of your own kin. Your aunt, though perhaps you know her not, and I made the effigy, and tried my skill to the utmost to work an antidote upon it; but I failed, and the deadly drugs I had to use have taken effect upon myself, and now I am past all recovery."

Upon the table a book lay open, and its pages were filled with mystic figures that Madge could not understand, and several bottles containing various drugs with which the old woman had evidently tried to work the charm that had so signally failed.

Madge procured a cup of water, and gave it to the old dame to moisten her lips, in the hope that she would recover speech, and be able to give her further information.

This served to revive her a little, and then she asked Madge to raise her head as her breathing was difficult, and she thought that by raising her head it would ease her of her pain.

Madge took a piece of furniture and a bag of wool, and made her a soft pillow, and then she was enabled to speak more freely.

"Madge Stukely," said the old woman, "thy race is for ever accursed. Your father has plotted deeply against Huntingdon's lawful earl, and it is decreed that, by the hand of one of thy blood, bold Robin shall be slain."

"No! no! do not say that!" shrieked Madge, half frenzied. "Speak! Does my father still live?"

"He does; and better for him would it be were he dead already as his soul is overloaded with crime, and yet his hand will be stained with fresh blood of his fellowman."

"Mercy! mercy!" shrieked Madge. "It cannot be as you say. Dame Morton, you must be mad."

"It may please ye to think so; but, for all that, I am as sure as yourself. Many think that Dame Morton, the wise woman of the Heath, is wandering, but it is only to soothe their own conscience, and to "——

She paused suddenly in her speech.

Something in her throat choked her utterance, and Madge flew to her assistance immediately.

From that moment the old dame never more spoke.

Her eyes became glassy and fixed.

Her head sank back on the pillow, and her lower jaw dropped.

Then Madge felt her pulse, and found that its pulsation had ceased, and that the old dame had ceased to exist.

CHAPTER CXXXV.

THE KNIGHT'S CONSPIRACY.

At silent hour in dead of night,
   They in the forest met,
And 'ranged their plans of villany,
   Then slily homeward crept.

WHILST the incidents related in the last few chapters were passing, a scene no less striking was being enacted at the castle of Windsor, the residence of Prince Edward and the Princess Eleanor.

A grand banquet and tournament were to be held in honour of a party of brave knights that had returned, battered and maimed from the Holy Land, and it was publicly announced that the prince and princess would honour the festival with their presence.

One night previous to the sports coming off, a party, the same as we before noticed at the palace, met in the park adjoining the palace, and held a long conference. The party was composed of Sir John of Linden, the Duke D'Anville, and several knights, who wore their crests upon their helm and breast-plates, and bore other tokens of nobility.

"He must die, and I care not how," said Sir John, speaking huskily. "He is a traitor, and as such he shall feel my just resentment."

"But have you considered what danger you will incur if found out in this? Do you know that Daverill Duke is an especial favourite with the king? Have you heard that he saved his majesty's life while hunting in the royal park?"

"I have heard as much, but report, as you know, confines itself not always to the truth."

"In this case it has. 'Tis a fact of which I am well known; and, more, I can vouch that he sat last evening near the king."

Sir John's eyes flashed with fury and hate.

"I have heard of that even, and believe it not; but if true, it adds one more reason why I should hate him the more."

"But a lady is more the cause of your quarrel than this, is it not?" asked one of the knights.

"Ay, the Lady Agnes," replied D'Anville. "She is proud and beautiful, and slights him, not so much as deigning him a look when he dons his casque to her."

"But she is in the north, if I am not mistaken."

"At present she is; but how long she will remain there I know not. But as that has nothing to do with our presence here, let us confine ourselves to more important business."

"Rightly spoken, D'Anville," chimed in Sir John. "We have met to discuss the best means of ridding ourselves of this royal favourite. You all hate him the same as I do, and I know he stands in the way of us all. What say you, how shall we dispose of him ?"

"A foot of cold steel, driven home with a strong and willing hand, would settle the business," suggested one of the knights.

"Nay, that will not do," said another. "Such a course would involve us in danger. In the first place, there is a risk in bribing an assassin, and in the next place there is danger of his denouncing us to add to his gain."

"Your words are indeed truthful," said D'Anville, "and now I bethink me there is a way more safe open to us. The coming tournament may offer you a chance of revenge."

"Ay, but even then we run a risk."

"Pooh! it can be easily done. You can enter the lists against him, unhorse him, and drive your dagger home to his heart."

"But should I fail, or, if successful, be suspected, what then ?"

"We shall be near you, and our words will go far in your favour," argued D'Anville.

Sir John did not much like the proposal, and he hesitated before replying.

After a moment's thought, he said—

"Well, if you promise me your support, I will e'en consent. 'Tis but a paltry stake if I lose. My life while he exists is not worth caring for."

"Well done, friend—your hand!" exclaimed D'Anville, his dark eyes gleaming with devilish cunning. "'Tis well we have settled this meeting so amicably. Now let us separate, and make our way to our respective quarters as quietly as we can, and, if possible, unseen."

Then each shook hands and parted, each taking a different route, under shadow of the trees.

But how different were the thoughts of the Duke D'Anville and his dupe, Sir John !

The former was gloating over the victory he was about to obtain over Sir John, whom he, in his heart, detested ; for the duke had himself fallen in love with the description of the Lady Agnes, whom all the knights who had ever seen her face looked upon and worshipped as the loveliest of beings.

Sir John of Linden, on the other hand, was picturing in his mind the degradation he would heap upon his rival's head, and in the heated excitement of his brain he imagined to himself his enemy laying prostrate before him, and the red stream oozing from his side.

In fancy he could hear the faint moan of the wounded man, and his cry of agony was drowned in the loud clamouring and shouts of the spectators, and he laughed silently to himself—a fiendish kind of laugh, as he slunk along beneath the overhanging boughs with long and rapid strides.

CHAPTER CXXXVI.

THE TREACHEROUS ACT OF THE MASKED ESQUIRE.

The knights they boldly met,
    And fired with hate and rage
With prancing steed and quivering lance,
    They fiercely did engage.

SINCE the meeting of the knights a week had rolled around, and the day of the opening festivities had arrived. Conspicuous among the tents that lined the lists were those of the rivals, Daverill Duke and John of Linden. Several combats had already taken place between different parties, but slight interest was manifested, as they were fought with "weapons of courtesy," or the lance without the steel head.

But at length a single horseman entered the arena, and was announced by the herald as Sir Daverill Duke, and his appearance was greeted by a tumultuous shout, followed by a low murmur of approval, as he slowly rode around the barrier, bowing gracefully to the ladies, and removing his visor entirely as he paused before the elevated throne, upon which were seated the king and his royal consort. There, upon the queen's left hand, was seated the lovely and radiant Eleanor.

Sir Daverill Duke, the king's favourite, having completed the circuit, paused before the entrance of Sir John's tent, where hung his well-burnished buckler and stood his lance, as well as two-handed sword and battle-axe.

As he reined his powerful charger, Sir Daverill raised his well-tempered lance, and flung it against the shield with such power that the weapon pierced it through and through, while the tough ashen staff was shivered into fragments.

A loud murmur of astonishment ran through the assembly at this unusual act, and had hardly died away when the tall, massive form of Sir John appeared in the open entrance, and seeing who was the challenger, a slight sneering smile curled his lip as he spoke—

"So, my young tiger, thou bravest thy death, dost thou ? By the bones of my murdered brother ! it shall not long await thee ! I had almost despaired thy coming, but as the wise men say, 'Better late than never,' and thou wilt find to thy cost that thou art early enough !" laughed the challenged knight.

"And, I mistake not, thou wilt find I am, before the hour is over ! But I am not in the mood for bandying words with thee ; sharp and keen weapons suit my fancy better. Roland, another lance, man ! dost thou hear me ?" And as the trusty weapon was placed in his hand, he backed his charger to the opposite end of the list and awaited the coming of his foe.

It was now Sir John's turn to shout—

"What ho ! thou knave, a fresh buckler. Perdition seize thee ! Where art thou, thou scurvy villain ?" and the choleric knight looked round for his esquire.

"Here, master," spoke a man, dressed in

ROBIN HOOD,

AND THE OUTLAWS OF SHERWOOD FOREST.

THE DISCOVERY OF THE HERMIT'S TREASURE.

the knight's livery and wearing a mask. "Thine esquire was taken very suddenly ill, and begged me to take his place for the nonce."

"Who art thou that speakest so brave? What canst thou do?"

"I am a soldier, good sir; and I"——

"Enough, varlet—out of my way!" replied the knight as he received the buckler and vaulted into the saddle, causing his fiery charger to curvet and prance as he rode around the lists.

A brave and true knight he appeared as he bestrode his war-horse, and his dark, handsome face caused many a fair maiden's cheek to flush, and her heart to throb as he cast an admiring glance toward them.

It was well-known to most of the nobility assembled that the two knights bore each other ill-will on account of the fair Lady Agnes, but of what nature the dispute was that brought the present challenge about they were not aware.

A dead silence reigned for many minutes;

scarce a form moved or an eyelid quivered as the two knights confronted each other, looking the defiance they scorned to utter.

For an instant they remained thus; then, as with one accord, they settled themselves more securely in their saddles, and took a firmer grip upon their lances.

Then came the clear, shrill note of the herald's trumpet, as it sounded the onset; a quick tramping of hoofs; a loud crash, as the opposing knights met in the centre of the arena; one shrill neigh, then the confusion subsided, and when the cloud of dust slowly rose upon the air, the result of the tilt was perceivable.

Sir John was still seated in his saddle, although his target was transfixed by his adversary's lance.

On the other side, Daverill was standing by the side of his dying charger, upon whose forehead could be seen the print of Sir John's spear.

A low murmur ran through the assembly, and, as if in obedience to it, Sir John vaulted from his charger, and drawing his huge two-handed sword, advanced to meet his antagonist, who was similarly armed.

Slowly they circled around each other, each narrowly watching for an unguarded moment on the part of his adversary that might present a favourable chance for a deadly thrust or furious blow.

As if tired of dallying, Daverill opened the fray by levelling a stroke that would have ended the contest then and there, had not Sir John parried it with his massive weapon.

Then the blow was returned, closely followed by deadly thrusts and strokes, until the air seemed fairly alive with gleaming weapons.

It seemed almost a miracle that the knights could so long live amidst such a storm of steel, sharp and keen, guided and driven by strong arms moved with hate and rivalry.

A puff of wind dispersed the cloud of dust that enveloped the two combatants, and as they appeared in full view, the weighty brand of Sir John whistled through the air and alighted full upon the helmet of Daverill.

Loud and clear rang the thirsty steel, and for a moment the knight staggered under the force of that dreadful blow.

Fortunately for him the brand glanced, cutting its way through helmet, morion, and neck-plate, when its force was stayed.

A shout of wonder, mingled with applause, rent the air as the full effect of this wonderful blow was manifest.

Rallying, Sir Daverill, before his exultant foe had regained his guard, stung with rage at his momentary defeat, levelled an irresistible stroke that alighted just at the junction of the neck and body.

Deep sank the blood-stained steel into the quivering flesh, and with one last despairing cry the gallant form of Sir John of Linden tottered and fell, to rise no more of its own free will.

The battle was over, the victory won, and, stooping, Sir Daverill plucked from the dust-stained helm of his vanquished foe the plume that surmounted it.

During the combat, the masked esquire of Sir John stood with clasped hands and deathly pale features, gazing as if spell-bound upon the prostrate form of his master.

At the fatal termination he glided forward, and throwing himself upon the prostrate form, strove with trembling fingers to unclasp the helmet from his brow.

The heralds and men-at-arms now advanced, and seeing that the fallen knight was beyond the aid of human hands, told the esquire thus much.

Sir Daverill stood by watching this, and, as he leant upon the pole of a broken spear, the page noticed that he was wounded, and seeing him stagger and about to fall, he ran to his assistance.

He caught him in his arms, and went through the motions with one hand, as if he was trying to loose the knight's mail; but, instead of doing so, he whipped his dagger from its sheath and buried it in the knight's bosom.

CHAPTER CXXXVII.

THE RELEASE OF THE LORD ABBOT.

"Go, Little John," said Robin Hood,
    "The abbot now release;
Likewise free the soldiers, and
    Let them depart in peace."

WHEN Little John and the friar returned to Sherwood, and it was made known to the foresters the rich booty they had brought with them, the outlaws made the forest ring with their cheers, and in their excessive glee, gathered round the giant and the portly friar, and raising them on their shoulders, the foresters carried them thrice round the enclosure, and then rested them at the foot of the trysting tree.

This ceremony was performed in view of the Norman soldiers who were still captives, and though they tried to return the smiling glances of the foresters with a look of stern indifference, yet they could not help laughing within themselves at the ludicrous figures Friar Tuck and Little John looked.

As soon as Little John could, he tore himself away from the excited crowd, and visited the quarters occupied by the chief, and he found Robin Hood seated on his couch, in anything but a pleasant mood.

He started as the giant entered, and gazed at him inquiringly.

"Well, what news have ye?"

Little John stared at him in amazement.

There was something in his tone and manner he did not like.

"What ails thee, good master?" he asked. "Hath aught ill befallen thee? Body o mine! thy cheeks are as pale as any moon-beam, and thy eyes are as wild as though thou hadst been scared by some horrible vision!"

"Get thee to, with thine idle gossip!" replied Robin Hood. "Tell me how thou hast fared. Speak out, be it ill or well?"

"Marry! good master mine, what news I have to tell you is good. Myself and good Friar Tuck hath both returned laden."

"By Saint Herman! that is well!" exclaimed the outlaw, his eye brightening as he spoke; "we need it much at present. Didst see Will Scarlett on thy way hither?"

"I did; he is without now, guarding the money-bags."

"Call him hither. I have pressing business for him to do."

Little John withdrew, and when he returned with Will Scarlett, they both bore a heavy sack, and each of them emptied the contents of their sack at the feet of the outlaw chief.

Robin Hood took up a handful of silver pieces, and gave them to Will Scarlett, saying—

"Hie thee at once to the cottage on the heath, and there you will find the body of Dame Morton. I have promised to give it decent burial, and wherever Madge Stukely desires ye to lay it, there dig a grave. Take with thee a few stout fellows, and when the body is decently interred, raze the house, every stick and stone, mind ye, to the ground."

Will Scarlett departed, wondering in his mind the cause of this strange proceeding, and when they were again alone, Little John asked of Robin Hood what had befallen the old woman.

"Sit you down," Robin Hood replied, and his brow again assumed that troubled look. "I must tell you that I have had a dream—a visitation; a something that seems to haunt me wherever I go."

"Pshaw! 'tis but fancy, good Robin."

"Not so, John. I thought so at first; but since that I have had a proof that my apprehensions were well founded."

"Indeed! but you do not mean to say that you have given yourself over to these strange fantasies? Perchance you have only been the victim of a disordered imagination."

"I would that I could say so, good John; but you know not what matters of import have occurred to me these last few days."

"Truth, do I not, good master, and fain would I be to hear of such."

"And I would fain tell thee, for few, if any of my band, saving thyself, know aught of my pedigree. You know that Madge Stukely is related to me in some manner."

"Ay, I remember hearing as much; but in what manner, saving by blood, I know not that she is a kinswoman of thine."

"'Tis as well that ye know no more; though, in truth, I would that I had one friend to whom I might divulge this secret. But the hour grows late, and we have much to do. The loss of Marian presses heavily on my mind, and Much, the miller's son, hath told me that which will not let me rest until I have found her."

Little John would fain have asked Robin what he had heard and seen, but he did not like to while the chief was in his present mood, so he amused himself with gathering up the treasures that lay on the floor, and then deposited them in the place where such things were kept.

While he was thus engaged, Robin Hood sat watching him, and when he had done, Robin said—

"Go ye, Little John, and see that the lord abbot is released, and likewise free the soldiers, who have suffered enough in their defeat and humiliation, and send a strong guard with them to see that none lurk in the forest."

Little John listened in astonishment to these words.

He could scarcely believe his ears.

"Marry come up, good master!" he said. "Surely, you will not"——

Robin made a sign for him to be silent, and the giant, unwilling to obey, left the presence of the chief.

When left alone, Robin Hood again relapsed into deep thought, and was some moments so wrapped in meditation that he did not hear the ringing notes of a horn sounding through the woods.

A footstep disturbed him, and on looking up he saw the tall form of his sturdy trenchman standing in the doorway.

"A messenger wishes to see you," said Little John, in answer to Robin's inquiring glance. "His condition is of one that has travelled far, and he is in great haste."

"In haste, say you? Did he name his employer?"

"Body o' mine! he did not; and I forgot to ask. Yet, methinks, he wears a face I have seen before."

"Where do you suppose?"

"St. Dunstan! It puzzles me sorely to say. Yet, when I bethink me, 'tis the jester, Gondibert."

"Ah!" exclaimed Robin, starting to his feet, "Show him hither at once; he may bear news of Marian, or"——

He checked himself suddenly, and made an impatient gesture for Little John to depart.

When the messenger entered, although well disguised, Robin's quick eye soon recognised him.

"Come you from the princess?" Robin asked.

The jester paused before replying, and cast an uneasy glance around.

"Are we alone?" he asked.

"Saving the presence of my faithful hounds, no one is here but ourselves," Robin replied.

"Pardon me, good sir; but where such sharp eyes are found, there may we expect to meet with ears as keen. Therefore, as my mission is secret, and of much consequence, I like to use caution."

"I praise, rather than blame ye for so doing," said Robin Hood. "But tell me what errand brings you to Sherwood? Quick, good Gondibert, my anxiety is great."

The jester bowed, and, taking a packet from the folds of his doublet, handed it to Robin Hood.

The outlaw took it, but as he was unable to read the characters on the parchment, he sounded a low note on his horn, and Friar Tuck answered the summons.

Robin handed the missive to the friar, without saying a word, and the latter, well knowing what to do, opened and read.

Robin's brow gradually knitted, as the friar read on, and when the friar had finished, Robin remarked—

"Is that all? Gave she no account of my Marian?"

"None," replied the friar. "I have given you word for word. It speaks of nought but the Lady Agnes's danger, and reminds you of the promise you made to protect her."

Robin Hood beat his brow in agony.

Never before had the friar seen him take anything so much to heart, and he almost wished that he had not read the missive so truly.

After a short struggle with his feelings, the outlaw recovered his composure a little, and then muttered, half aloud—

"I have promised her, and though it will inconvenience me, I will keep my faith." Then aloud he asked, "Gave she no other message to you than this, good Gondibert?"

"None, saving that I was to bear to you her best wishes," replied the jester.

Robin bit his lip, to conceal his vexation, and then ordered the dinner, which was waiting, to be served, and the horn sounded the assembly.

CHAPTER CXXXVIII.

THE JOURNEY THROUGH THE FOREST.

Through swamp and marsh, and wooded dell,
  Maid Marian she hied;
Hubert in woodcraft was not skilled,
  She had to be his guide.

*   *   *   *   *   *

They ate a steak, and quenched their thirst,
  Then a river tried to cross:
But she saw no more of Hubert;
  He was for ever lost.

CRASH!—crash!—came down the masonry, and the vaults were instantly filled with dust, and the passages echoed back the din.

A huge opening appeared in the arched roof of the vault in which Marian and the two men stood; but fortunately none of the falling mass had injured them, though all were stricken with fear.

Even Hubert, the brave soldier, shared in the alarm, and, though he was assured of his own and Marian's safety, yet he trembled when he thought of the probable fate of the page and Hal.

As he stood with one arm supporting the form of Marian and the other arm resting against the wall, a bright, red flash for an instant lit up the vault, and a heavy peal of thunder, that seemed to shake the ground beneath their feet, assailed his ears.

Hubert, as we have seen, though greatly terrified, had not lost his reason, and in that momentary gleam of light, he saw sufficient to convince him that what had been done was caused through the violence of a storm.

Of this he felt the more certain, as flash after flash lit up the vault, and peal after peal deadened his ears, and there he stood, rooted to the spot, with his eyes staring and fixed, awaiting he knew not what.

The novice had totally disappeared, and in the place where he stood was a pile of stones, breast high, and which filled the passage from side to side.

When Hubert recovered himself sufficiently to understand his position, he turned his head, and awaited the next flash to see where the passage led, when he saw that it only went a few yards, and terminated in an iron door.

The key of this he supposed to be the key that the novice had in his possession, and deeming it awful to remain longer in that situation, he laid Marian down, and then began a search for some way of escape.

This seemed only possible by the roof, and as no more of the *debris* appeared to fall, he climbed on to the pile of stones, and standing with head up through the broken roof, awaited the next flash of light to reveal to him the nature of his position.

But what a sight did that vivid glare disclose!

His head reached through the aperture, and was above the broken masonry, and on a level with the floor of a large and spacious cavern, and as he shifted the direction of his gaze, and waited each succeeding flash, which came at irregular intervals, he could see that one part of the roof was completely crushed in, and there was the dark canopy of the heavens beyond it.

From what he could see at each cursory glance, he was not long in conjecturing what had happened; for, within a few yards of the opening through which he had thrust his head, laid a huge bell shattered into a thousand fragments, and around lay broken pillars, and other evidences of some part of the abbey having been struck by the lightning, and he muttered an Ave Maria when he thought of the miracle that had saved him from being crushed to death.

By this time every particle of dust was settled, though it had left a parching dryness in his throat, and, fearing for the safety of Marian, he descended as cautiously as the darkness would permit him, and raising her inanimate form in his stalwart arms, he contrived, after a great deal of exertion and sundry slips, that threatened destruction to them both, to land on the broken floor above, and then he contrived to drag his own weary body up through the hole.

This last effort almost overpowered him.

Panting for breath and almost choking for a drink of water, he sat down to recover breath.

By making good use of his eyes whenever the lightning lit up the vast cavern, he discovered a flight of steps at one end, let into the wall, and apparently leading to the ground above.

Towards these steps, as soon as he was able, he made his way, and cautiously ascended; but before he had counted twenty steps, he found himself in a low arched passage in which he had to stoop. Determined not to give in, he groped his way painfully along it.

For some distance he counted his steps, so that he might the better find his way back; but he got tired of this, and when he was about to despair of finding any outlet, he stumbled against another flight of steps.

Hoping these were the last, and being enabled to stand erect, he mounted them nimbly; but, to his surprise, he found his head come suddenly in contact with some hard substance above him, and, with a half-stifled groan, he clutched at the wall to prevent his falling.

This act, though, in itself, simple and natural enough, was the cause of discovering that which on any other occasion he might have sought for in vain, for his hand came in contact with a nail in the wall, which was evidently connected with a spring, and a door flew open, and he fell forward in the aperture,

The fall partly stunned him, but when he recovered, the thought occurred to him that it was only his body kept the door from closing again—a surmise that was partly verified by the fact of it pressing hard against him.

While he was thinking of this, and wondering what he could do to prevent it shutting, a luminous glare lit up the place, and he found that beyond where he was was a cave, and the opening, through which the lightning came, was the entrance, and beyond it seemed to be a dense forest.

Almost within reach of his hand he saw a piece of wood, and with it he propped open the door, and then began to search about for some means of procuring a light.

By means of a stone and a piece of old rusty blade, he soon set light to a portion of his garments, and with this he ignited a few dry sticks, and afterwards made himself a pine torch.

With this it was easy enough for Hubert to retrace his way, and he was not long in bringing Marian to the cave, where he laid her before the fire, for the night was cold, and the chill had stricken into her frame.

Provided with the torch, he was enabled to take a good survey of the place, and to his surprise, he discovered that it was not only stocked with fuel, but that it was also provided with food, for in a corner a small stream of water oozed out of the rock, and in a nook he found several hard-baked cakes, which were in good condition, though they appeared to have lain there some weeks.

There was also an earthen bowl, and this he soon filled with water, and he poured a little of the cool beverage down Marian's throat and moistened her parched lips, which so far revived her as to enable her to speak.

The cave had been used at one time by the monks of the abbey, but had gradually grown into disuse, and since that time a band of robbers had inhabited it, and it would seem that they had very recently deserted it; for, in addition to what we have already named, Hubert found a bag of meal, a small iron pot, and a bundle of deer-skins.

With these Marian made a very comfortable bed; and, after she had rested awhile, she made some porridge, and this greatly revived the pair of them.

When morning came the storm was still raging furiously, and Hubert, on venturing forth a few yards from the mouth of the cave, saw several trees scorched with the lightning, or torn up by the roots with the fierce wind.

For several days the storm remained unabated, and then it suddenly ceased, much to the joy of Marian and her staunch adherent; and, as their food was all gone, they started off in search of some hospitable cottage.

But the dangers they had to encounter in travelling was far above their expectations, for the paths were blocked up with heaps of fallen leaves and uprooted trees, and the brooks were swollen into rivers by the heavy rains.

They had started on what they supposed the most beaten path, in the hope that it would lead them to some village; but in fording the streams they lost all trace of the beaten track, and found themselves wandering in the midst of a wild, intricate forest.

Darkness seemed to creep upon them unawares, and as it was useless as well as dangerous for them to venture further, they looked about them for a shaded spot where they might rest for the night.

Hubert, though a good soldier, was little versed in the art of woodcraft, so that he had to trust more to the guidance of Marian, who was now thoroughly exhausted, and threw herself down on the damp ground beneath an outspreading yew tree, and tried to compose herself to sleep.

Hubert kept watch over her as long as he could, and then sleep overcame him, and it was morning when he awoke again.

Hunger was now the chief misery from which they suffered; but they bore it without a murmur and again pursued their way.

As the sun rose, it gradually gained strength, and towards noon the heat became so excessive, and the vapour from the damp earth became so strong that they completely lost their strength, and were compelled to sit down by the side of the brook to rest and quench their thirst.

While there they were startled by a sound which was familiar to Marian's accustomed ear; and, springing to her feet, she glanced in the direction whence the sound came, and through the trees she beheld a herd of fine fat deer basking in the sun.

With an expression of delight she pointed this out to Hubert; but he gazed at them mournfully and only shook his head, for he saw no means by which he could get even the leanest of them into his power.

"Fash not thyself thereanent," replied Marian, in answer to a remark that he made; "I will show thee what I have learnt by living in the greenwood."

So saying, she took the rusty blade that Hubert had brought with him, and, selecting one of the tough bows of the yew tree, she quickly fashioned it into a bow, and then made a bowstring of the bark of a young saplin, which she twisted in the form of a rope.

Another tree, which she soon found, supplied her with arrows; and, in the absence of a grey goose quill, she used leaves to guide the arrow on its way.

Hubert was completely astounded at the skill and dexterity she employed in doing this; for, though he had been used to the cross-bow, he was useless in either making or using the long-bow; and, when she took aim at a distant tree to try her weapon, he was astounded at the strength and precision of her aim.

The next arrow she fired gave greater proof of her skill; for a red deer fell, and, in less than an hour, they were enjoying a frugal meal.

It was only a steak griddled over a wood fire, but it appeased their hunger; and, having slaked their thirst at a stream, they again set forward.

They were still uncertain as to the road they were travelling; and, having crossed the glade, they again dived into the underwood; and, after travelling for an hour, found themselves on the bank of a broad river, and on their right they could just see the tops of a range of lofty mountains.

At a glance, it was sufficient to see that an attempt to cross the river would be attended with great danger, but Hubert was determined to try it at all risks; for, on the opposite side, he fancied he could hear the ring of a woodman's axe in the distance.

Marian was equally resolved.

She armed herself with a stout bough and followed him in; but a sudden rush of water swept them off their feet, and they were carried swiftly down the stream.

Marian soon became unconscious, but her fingers instinctively clutched the bough, and

to this, probably, she was indebted for her life; for when she came to herself she was lying upon the bank, her clothes partly dried by the sun, and the branch still in her grasp.

As soon as she was able she looked around in search of Hubert, but he was nowhere to be seen. He had been thrown ashore in some other part; or, more probably, had gone down in the stream.

As soon as her stiffened limbs would allow her she crawled away; and, in the distance, a cottage broke upon her view. She struggled hard to reach it but was unable, and sank down exhausted by the roadside.

As she sat wondering what she should do the sound of voices aroused her; and, on looking round, she beheld several persons approaching her.

They were, to all appearance, of gentle blood; and, after closely questioning her and ascertaining her condition, they assisted her to the cottage of a goatherd.

CHAPTER CXXXIX.

THE BURIAL OF SIR HENRY MALCOLM.

With glaring eyes and anxious looks
He glanced the chapel around;
But Stukely, whom with gaze he sought,
Was nowhere to be found.

STUKELY, the ex-warder of Nottingham Castle, though defeated, was of a spirit too proud to be subdued, when Little John left him his thoughts of repentance changed to those of hate, and he gathered himself up slowly from the ground, and, with a bitter vow of vengeance, he took a hasty glance at the forester's retreating form, and then hurried away in an opposite direction.

Too cautious to expose himself to further danger by keeping along the road, Stukely, when he had gone far enough, as he supposed to escape observation, turned into the thicket, and was soon out of sight.

Once under cover his progress was less speedy, for the tangled underwood checked his course a little, and beside, he was unsettled in his mind as to which road he should take, for though he had left the body of Malcolm on the road, he intended to return and give it decent burial.

His first thought was to hasten to St. Mary's Abbey, and get assistance from the monk; but when he thought of his defeat, and the anger he would incur, not only from the abbot but Geoffrey de Lois, he banished the idea, and made up his mind to pay a visit to Kirkless Priory.

It was some distance, but he did not mind that, and then he remembered that on the road there was a small friary and a chapel, and thither he resolved to go and seek assistance.

*　　*　　*　　*　　*

The monk that answered Stukely's summons was not like the generality of monks. He was a thin man, with sharp features, tall as a soldier in stature, and though evidently well-stricken in years, he seemed to bear the elasticity of youth.

He eyed Stukely from head to foot before questioning him, but failing to gain any information from his scrutiny, he taxed him pretty closely.

Stukely gave him all the satisfaction in his power as to who he was, with the exception of revealing to him his real name (which, by the by, was not Stukely), and then he informed him of Malcolm's disaster.

At the mention of Robin Hood's name, the monk, who had good cause to remember the outlaws, having been compelled on one occasion to visit the stronghold against his wish, readily consented to lend Stukely the required aid.

Six sturdy friars were dispatched with a litter to bear the dead body to the chapel, and the next day preparations were made for the interment of the body, with all the respect due to one who had fallen in so holy a cause as the capture of the sinful outlaw.

Sir Henry Malcolm was a knight of no mean condition, though, at the time he offered his services to Geoffrey de Lois he was in difficulties, and, moreover, greatly in want of money; but when his friends learnt his fate, they hastened to the chapel to see that his remains were decently interred.

A rich uncle paid a good sum for the mass to be read over him a certain number of nights, which ceremony was indispensable, owing to his dying without shrift.

The chapel was draped in black, and tapers were burning on the altar when the mourners assembled, and then the music swelled out its mournful strains, aided by the voices of the nuns.

Stukely drew himself behind one of the pillars to survey the solemn ceremony, for a kind of awe crept over him, and made him tremble; and when the priests chanted the prayer for the repose of the dead a sad recollection of his own sinful career flashed upon his mind.

Upon the coffin lid rested the knight's helmet and plume, and when the melody ceased, and the night wind disturbed the plume, it rustled wildly against the silken pall, and made those who heard it shudder.

Stukely gazed minutely upon the bier that supported the coffin, richly adorned with the knight's escutcheon, and which stood between himself and the altar, and a profound gloom settled on his dark, arched eyebrows.

Then again the music struck up, and the chanting continued until the time was come for depositing the coffin in the earth, and then the music ceased, and a profound and awful silence reigned in the chapel, only broken by the sobbing of the mourners, who had thrown themselves on their knees. Four

of the nuns now approached the bier, and raising the coffin, in silence bore it towards the open grave.

Stukeley had fallen into a deep reverie, from which even the heavy tread of the departing friars failed to arouse him.

The coffin was lowered gently into the grave, it disappeared, and the friars were about to cover it with a marble slab, when one of the mourners gave a loud shriek, rushed forward and seized the arm of one of the friars who held the stone, and with gestures wild as a maniac's, and with a voice, which was the very accent of despair, he shouted—

"Not yet! not yet! He was one of the boldest of our race. Let not his bones be covered until every member present who is the slightest akin to him by blood, has sworn to avenge his death."

With involuntary horror the spectators started back, and stood gazing motionless and in silence on the strange figure of the speaker.

His stature was colossal, and as a gust of wind blew aside his funeral cloak it revealed his form clothed in burnished steel. His countenance was also awful to look upon, for his eyes blazed, his lips foamed, and his hands twined in his coal black hair, which hung in dank masses, of which he tore out handfuls and strewed them on the coffin as it laid in the unclosed grave.

"No—no!" he cried, while his thundering voice shook the vaulted roof, and while he stamped upon the hallowed earth with fury. "Not yet shall the marble close over his mouldering bones! Not yet shall the marble hide him from our view; not till all concerned have sworn to devote to the demons of darkness the murderer and all his accursed band!"

Then his bloodshot eyes wandered from one to the other of the pale, ghastly faces turned towards him, and he pointed to the lady superior of Kirkless Priory, who had presided over the duties of the nuns.

"One," he ejaculated; and then his gaze wandered round as though in search of an object difficult to find, and then abandoning his object in despair, he snatched his dagger from its sheath and held its cross hilt to his lips.

Then, lowering his voice, he added, impressively—"Hear me, all of ye, and bear witness to my oath, for by the Virgin I swear that I will not rest until I have avenged Sir Henry's death, and may my withering curse rest on those who are akin to him, and do not strike boldly in his cause."

Stukely who, as we have said, had ensconced himself behind one of the columns, could bear to hear no more.

His brain whirled, his sight grew dim, and a faintness caused his limbs to totter, and he sank prostrate and lifeless upon the cold stonefloor.

Yet as his eyes closed, and before his senses

quite forsook him, he fancied he could see the form of the hermit, and hear him faintly whisper, "And my death let it also be avenged in like manner as my cousin Malcolm's."

CHAPTER CXL.

STUKELY IN THE MONK'S CELL.

The monk, good Father Peter,
    Did give him wine and food,
And then sat down and told a tale,
    Which was for Stukely's good.

WHEN Stukely recovered himself, the chapel was vacant, and the lamps and torches all extinguished. The total darkness which surrounded him added to the confusion of his ideas ; and a considerable time elapsed before he could recollect himself sufficiently to arrange in their proper order the dreadful circumstances which had occurred. The image of his murdered brother-in-law haunted his imagination, and resisted all his efforts to chase it away.

Bewildered, irresolute, daring scarcely to admit the possibility of his having witnessed what he had, determined to quit the gallery, and pursue his way to the great entrance of the chapel.

The darkness was profound, and he reached the gates with some difficulty ; but here he found his intention of departure completely frustrated.

During his swoon the doors had been carefully locked and barred, and though his strength was great, it was still insufficient to enable him to force them open.

Exhausted with his fruitless efforts, he abandoned the attempt, and made up his mind to return to the gallery, and remain there quietly till morning should enable him to regain his liberty ; when he recollected having seen at the further extremity of the aisle a cell, which generally was tenanted by one of the brethren, whose office it was to keep the chapel in order, and by whose care probably the doors had been secured.

Thither he bent his way, hoping to obtain his freedom by the friar's assistance, and at least certain of finding a less damp and unwholesome shelter for the night.

Feeling his way from pillar to pillar, he proceeded slowly and cautiously ; it was not long before a ray of light at some distance guided his steps, and a low murmuring voice assured him that the cell was inhabited.

He pushed the door gently open ; a lamp, which was placed in the nook of a narrow gothic window, threw its light full upon the pale face and grey locks of the friar, who was kneeling before a crucifix, with an immense rosary in his hand, and his eyes fixed devoutly upon the Redeemer's countenance. Stukely was both too unwell and too impatient to wait for the conclusion of his prayer ; he stepped into the cell, and the sound of his heavy tread roused the monk from his devotions.

He started up, and looked around, amazed at so unusual an intrusion. But no sooner did he cast his eyes upon the visitor, than he fell prostrate upon the earth before him, loaded him with benedictions, and poured forth a profusion of thanks to heaven, which had thought the meanest of its servants worthy of so unusual and distinguished an honour.

In the moment of his strange infatuation, the monk had believed that the pale face of Stukely was that of an angel, which had come to visit him on earth, and he began repeating his paternoster, when Stukely dissipated his illusion by saying—

"Rise, good father ! I am a mortal like yourself, and what is more, am a mortal, who greatly needs your assistance. During the late mournful ceremony, a sudden illness overpowered me : I became insensible ; no one observed me, and I found myself, on my recovery, alone, in darkness, and inclosed within the chapel. Doubtless, you possess the means of opening the gate, and can restore me to liberty."

"Truly I can, my son, answered the monk ; "and it is but just that I should be the person to let you out, as I was the person who locked you in so carefully. Mercy on me, poor old man ! I little thought that I was locking in anything but the dead, and myself.

"But oh ! all ye blessed spirits ! you must have been ill indeed, sir, for the poor corpse as it lay in its shroud, did not look paler than *you* do at this moment. Nay, in truth, it was your paleness which made me so sure of your being a spirit, when I first looked on you ; for I thought that no living thing could have had a countenance so bloodless.

"But how I stand here talking, when I ought to be doing somewhat to assist you ! Here, sir," he continued, at the same time hastening to a small walnut tree cupboard, and spreading his whole store of provisions before the stranger ; "here is some refreshment, here is bread, and fruit, and hard eggs, and here is even some venison for you ; for, alas the day ! I am old and weak, and our abbot has forbidden my fasting and keeping the spare holy diet which I used, and which I *ought* to keep.

"Ah ! I shall never have the good fortune to be a saint, nor even a martyr, heaven help me ; but I will not murmur at Providence, sinner that I am for saying so !

"Now, good sir, eat, and refresh yourself, for it makes my heart bleed to see you look so pale. And see ! I protest, I had like to have forgotten the best of all ; here is a small bottle of a most rare cordial ; it was given me by Sister Lydia, the fat prioress of Kirkless, and she assured me that its virtue was sovereign, and I would now ask thy opine."

Stukely, faint as he was, and though he would have been glad to taste the wine, was reluctant in doing so as his purse was not in fitting condition for him to reward the

ROBIN HOOD,
AND THE OUTLAWS OF SHERWOOD FOREST.

THE DISCLOSURE.

monk for his kindness; therefore he hesitated and appeared to be lost in thought.

But it was not of the wine he was then thinking. He was thinking of the Prioress of Kirkless mentioned by the monk, and the strange vow taken by the mysterious mourner.

The monk, seeing him hesitate, and supposing it was caused by a feeling of delicacy, again urged him to drink, saying—

"Now taste it, good son, I beseech you; I am sure it will do you service; not that I ever tried its good qualities myself, but Sister Lydia has, and she is a devout person, who, I warrant you, knows what is good. Now taste it, good sir, in the name of St. Ursula and the eleven thousand virgins—rest their souls, though nobody ever was lucky enough to find their blessed bodies!—I beseech you, now, taste it!"

The benevolent manner of the old man was irresistible. Stukely partook of the cordial, and the warmth which immediately diffused itself through his chilled veins, and the glow which it produced upon his cheeks, sufficiently testified that Sister Lydia had not said too much in favour of her present.

Brother Peter now pressed him to partake of the viands placed before him; and Stukely, finding that his person was totally unknown to the monk, thought that by engaging him in conversation he might most easily and expeditiously learn whether his suspicions concerning the prioress were true.

Accordingly, he took some of the refreshments which his host presented to him, and found no difficulty in leading the conversation to the funeral and its cause; while, on the other hand, Father Peter, believing his discourse to be directed to a stranger, whom curiosity alone had led to ask such a question, and who had no personal motive in doing so, felt no hesitation in answering the questions put to him, without disguise, and in their fullest extent.

"You shall hear all that I know, sir," said the old man; "and I believe I know more of the matter than most people. Indeed, you'll marvel, perhaps, how I came to know so much, when I tell you that her history is mixed up with a murder as foul as it was heartless."

Stukely gulped down a horn of wine, and tried to listen with as much composure as he could assume, and the monk continued—

"You must know, sir, that some twenty years ago, there was an old clothworker, by name Malcolm, who left his large domains"——

"Nay, pr'ythee, my good father," interrupted Stukely, impatiently, "proceed to the murder at once, and leave out the bequest of the old man."

"Leave out the bequest!" cried Brother Peter. "Heaven help us! You might as well bid me tell you the story of the Fall of Man, and leave out the apple! Why that bequest has made the whole mischief; and into the bargain, sir, I must tell my own story my own way, or I shall not be able to tell it at all.

"This clothworker had three children, to whom he left all his wealth, and one of the daughters, for there were two, took the veil and devoted her life to prayer for the forgiveness of her own sins and those of her father; and whilst the other daughter, a sprightly damsel, full of life, married a worthless scamp, who soon brought her to ruin and ultimately to the grave, and also took the life of the brother to enrich himself with his supposed wealth."

"Haste with thy story, good father," said Stukely, unable to conceal his emotion. "Did he die, then?"

"Ay, and was buried; but his money was not so plentiful as was supposed, it barely purchased candles and payed for a dozen masses. But it was sufficient that he was murdered, and"——

"But the murderer, what became of him?"

"'Twas never properly known. He left the country, it was supposed; but I have never heard that he has been seen since—and how is it possible I should, when I scarcely leave the threshold of this venerable pile."

"Marry, thou art right; but 'tis passing strange that you should know as much as thou dost."

"By the saints! 'tis not so strange as you would deem it. I was one of those who bore the coffin, and my hand it was that closed in the grave."

"Zounds! Then thou knowest where he was buried."

"I do, and could take you to the spot."

"Was it in the chapel he was buried?"

"By the mass, no, 'twas on the borders of the forest, and though I argued that his spirit would haunt the earth until the body was buried in consecrated ground. Yet the abbot of St. Mary's would not hear of it, and Sister Lydia has often spoken to me on the subject as to whether it would not be better to disinter the body and bring it hither."

"A good thought, and I wonder one of thy judgment did not act up to it, for I have often heard of such things as thou speakest. Marry, I would not for a handful of marks visit the spot where they buried him."

"And you are right; thy wisdom is discreet. How can the soul rest when the body is disturbed by the sounds of mortal feet treading above it, and probably often disturbed by the sound of sinful voices. St. Ursula, the matter speaks for itself; and, now I bethink me, I will just speak to good Sister Lydia again concerning this matter."

Stukely was so interested in the discourse that he did not notice how the time had flown by, until the daylight began to creep through the grated window into the cell, and then a cold chill went through him, as a puff of cold air fanned his heated cheek.

Having thanked the friar for his information, and disposed of another horn of wine, Stukely then left the chapel, promising the monk that he would pay him another visit at no distant period, and then hurried away in deep thought.

CHAPTER CXLI.

THE ADVENTURE AT THE VILLAGE HOTEL.

'Twas but a wretched wayside inn
Where Marian did rest;
From what befel her in that place
Her mind was sore oppressed.

MAID MARIAN received every attention at the hands of the cotter's wife, who, so far as her humble abilities would allow, administered to her wants.

Owing to her utterly exhausted condition, Marian was several days before she could leave her bed, and during that time she learnt that she had been journeying in a direction contrary to that which she had supposed; therefore she resolved as soon as her strength would permit her, to start in the direction of Nottingham.

On the evening before the day of her intended departure she gave to the dame a small jewel of great value, as a recompense for her kindness; and, in the morning, the goatherd offered his services to accompany her some distance on the road, an offer which Marian readily accepted, and the pair accordingly set forward.

Fortunately for Marian, she still possessed a few jewels, which she had secured about her, and which, fortunately, had escaped the observation of Father Absalom; and with these in her possession, though she had no knowledge of the road, she hoped to be enabled to perform the journey in safety.

That night they reached an hostel in a small village, and having ascertained that Marian could obtain accommodation there for the night, the goatherd left her to return home, as his duties would not permit of his longer absence.

Marian, fatigued with her journey, having partaken of a little refreshment, retired to her room, and threw herself on the couch, where she lay for some time ruminating on her position, and wondering in her mind whether she should have the pleasure of beholding her beloved Robin Hood again.

A loud hammering at the outer door startled her from her reverie, and then she heard the host's gruff voice demanding who was there.

What answer was given she could not hear, but she concluded it was satisfactory as the wooden bar was removed and the door was opened; and then another voice complained of the host's delay in admitting the travellers, for there were two, a fact which she ascertained by the clank of their feet on the stone floor of the outer room.

"Pardon me, Sir Knight," she could hear the host reply, apologetically. "An' I expected such customers, I would not have stayed to inquire who knocked; but in these times it behoves one to be careful, as there are many rogues about, who would not scruple to rob an honest man, and knock out his brains afterwards."

"What!" cried the other man, who had not before spoken. "Do you dare insult our dignity by even presuming that we were such? Minion, I warn thee to heed thy speech, for had ye have chosen to put out thine ugly head from the loop-hole above, thou wouldst have seen that we were knights of good condition."

"Marry! I meant no insult to you!" said the half-frightened host; "but I must tell thee what befel me a few nights since. I put out my head as you say, to ascertain who it might be that knocked at so unreasonable an hour, and I discovered him to be a drunken roisterer returning home from the sports at Windsor, where he boasted of having cracked a score of crowns, and, as a sample of his skill he dealt me such a stinging thwack upon my pate, that has made it ring ever since, and of which you can see I still bear the mark in the size and form of an egg."

The host uncovered his bald head as he spoke, and disclosed a large discoloured bump, which was, if anything, larger than the size he named, and the sight somewhat dispelled the anger of the knights, for they burst into a roar of hearty laughter.

"Ha! ha! It served thee right, Master Slothful; he should have given thee another such, and then it would have prevented thee sleeping so soundly. By my halidame! my fingers itch to give it thee myself; for I trow me we shall stand here talking all night, and be none the better for our visit."

"Body o' me! I hope you are but jesting," replied the discomfited host, replacing his cap, and shuffling towards a small closet. "By the cross of St. Andrew, I swear that thou art welcome to the best my house can afford."

"And what of our steeds? Hast provender and shelter for them?" asked one of the knights.

"Marry! have I, though 'tis but a sorry place—a small thatched hovel, where the monks of St. Barnabas put up their mules, when they come to gather the tythes. It is at your service, if you like to accept of it; and here also is a rundlet of such wine as will do you good, and which I keep expressly for the sainted lips of the lord abbot."

At this stage of the conversation, Marian's curiosity was so far aroused as to awaken in her a desire to see the faces of the speakers.

A thin partition of boards only separated her apartment from the common room, and as the boards had been badly put together, or were shrunk, the light streamed through the crevices, and to one of these chinks she crept quietly and peeped through.

From this position, she was enabled to see all that passed, and as the knights had doffed their casques, which they had placed on a bench, and were standing with their faces towards her, she had a good opportunity of scanning their features.

The face of one was totally unknown to her; but the face of the other she instantly recognised as that of D'Anville's. She remembered seeing him at Sherwood, and also remembered him as the villain that had stolen her from her greenwood home.

Many a woman similarly situated would have fainted, but Marian, as we have seen, was very courageous for one of her sex, and this discovery had quite an opposite effect upon her.

As soon as she had sufficiently satisfied herself that it was the duke, she commenced a search to ascertain if there existed any other outlet besides the door she had entered by, and, aided by the light through the chinks, she found that there was a window secured by a strong shutter, which was held in its place by a heavy cross-bar.

To remove this without making a noise, even if her strength would permit her, seemed an utter impossibility. But having ascertained so much, she returned to the hole to watch, and learn, if possible, the intentions of the visitors.

"Adzooks! D'Anville," said the other, thumping his empty goblet on the table. "Here we are drinking and making merry whilst our poor beasts and our esquires are shivering with the cold. What say you if we house them and then return to our good cheer?"

"A malison on them," growled the duke; "let them cool; they have had a warming with the long ride, and now, I opine, that the rest will do them good."

As he spoke he glanced towards the host' who fairly trembled as their gaze met, and, fearing that his laxity of duty would bring upon him its just punishment, he ascended by a ladder to an upper floor as fast as his obesity would permit him, and shouted out loudly—

"Jack! Jack! were art thou, lad? Come, rouse up, you numskull, or, by the mass! I will give ye such a pounding as will frighten ye out of a year's growth."

But neither the shout nor the threat disturbed the sound sleep of the lad, who was worn out with his hard day's labour, but a hard blow from a cudgel, dealt by the host's in no wise puny arm, aroused him to consciousness.

D'Anville went with the lad to door, and pointed down the road to a clump of trees, where the esquires and the horses were resting, and Jack soon bounded off, and conducted them to the hovel before-mentioned, and having seen to the horses' wants, and supplied the famished esquires with food and a pitcher of good ale, he returned to his bed.

His master would gladly have followed his example; but his duty would not permit him, for his visitors, having made a good meal off a round of beef, commenced washing it down with copious draughts of wine.

The host stared in astonishment at the manner in which D'Anville poured the rich juice down his throat, and, as flagon after flagon was filled, and almost as quickly emptied, he began to wonder whether his guests were in a position to settle the enormous score they were running up, for the wine was of the best quality, and he had learned from former experience that it was not always the most gaudily-equipped knight who carried the best-filled purse.

He was leaning, with arms folded, against the wall, turning this over in his mind, when a remark from D'Anville startled him and filled his mind with further perplexity.

"Zounds! we have fallen into good luck, Sir Arthur," said the duke. "I did not think of meeting such good cheer on our first starting. If we fare as well throughout our journey northward, and are successful with the fair Lady Alice, I will make a fitting present to the church on our arrival in Bretagne."

"Aha!" laughed Sir Arthur, "I opine you will give the priest that marries you a rare present, a silver crucifix, or a golden chalice. Ha, ha!" and then he intimated by a gesture to D'Anville to be wary of what he said, as the host began to prick up his ears.

The duke was far gone in wine, but not so far as to be heedless of the caution, and, without the least sign of embarrassment, he said—

"I wot me he shall have no just cause of complaint, Sir Arthur; but see we are keeping our host from his bed, and it is getting near morning. Perchance he has some quiet spot where we can lay down and snatch an hour's sleep."

"Gramercy! 'tis a good thought on thy part, D'Anville; for myself I can answer that I stand in need of rest. What say you, good Boniface, can you oblige us?"

"Good sirs," replied the astonished host. "Sorry am I that I cannot. I have "——

"St. Dunstan!" cried D'Anville, interrupting. "We will take no excuse; a bed we will have, if it be even thine own. 'Tis wondrous strange that an hostel like this, where we can meet with such good cheer, has not a spare room!"

"It would not have been so, had I been aware of your coming," said the host, scarce knowing how to reply, for he feared to let them know that Marian was in the next apartment, for fear that in their excited state they might offer her some rudeness. "Had I known," he continued, "that we should have been honoured with your presence, I would have prepared a reception for you fitting to your condition."

"Get thee to with thy parlance," said D'Anville, ironically, rising at the same time, and approaching the door that led into

Marian's room; and pressing it firmly with his hand, he tried to open it.

It resisted his pressure, as Marian had bolted it on the other side, and the duke, turning sharply upon the host, demanded angrily—

"What have you concealed here, knave? Open the door, or, by my halidame, a blow of my heel shall save thee the trouble."

The man hesitated.

He knew not how to act.

The duke, however, settled his uncertainty by catching him by the throat and holding him firmly against the wall; at the same time whispering hoarsely in his ear—

"Open it, varlet, or I will squeeze out your vile breath ere you have time to utter a prayer for your sin-laden soul."

It was evident the threat was given in earnest, for the eyes of D'Anville flashed with a fierce light, and he prepared to tighten his grip on the fat throat of the host, when the host consented to open the door, and implored in piteous tones to be released.

But the promise was easier given than performed.

Although the fat host used all his endeavours, and expended his breath in hurling his fat carcase against the door with a force that seemed sufficient to bring down the partition, the door did not yield.

The duke and Sir Arthur watched his panting exertions with a quiet kind of smile, and when it was seen that the blows took no effect upon the door, Sir Arthur said—

"I opine there is some mystery in this. How comes it that the door is fast on the inside? Have you the abbot sleeping within, or have you given shelter to a wretch of a pedlar, who has secured the door to prevent his being robbed of his paltry trinkets?"

"Marry, I have given shelter to neither," replied the trembling host, wiping the beads of sweat from his broad forehead. "An' I must tell ye the truth, some poor woman hath sought shelter under my roof for the night."

The duke exchanged a meaning glance with his companion as the man stammered out these words:

"Do you hear that, Sir Arthur?" the duke asked. "Now, what think you the minion deserves for keeping us these hours in this cold, cheerless room with no company but our own, when we might have been enjoying the society of some beauteous damsel, and moreover, have passed the time away in some lively chat? Marry come up! but I have a mind to skin the knave."

"Ay, by St. Paul, the caitiff deserves to be hung up by the heels and soundly whipped with a saddle girth," said Sir Arthur; "and he shall have it too unless he produces something quickly to open the door."

Trembling in every limb at the fearful threat, the host took the bar of oak that he used as a fastening to the outer door, and with it he battered down the door of the room, and effected an entrance.

Taking the lamp in his hands, he was about to call upon Marian, whom he supposed to be inside; but D'Anville snatched the lamp from his hand, and thrusting him aside, stepped through the battered door.

A fearful oath broke from his lips as his amorous gaze wandered round the deserted room, for, instead of the trembling and half-nude form of a female as he expected to see, he found the room vacant, and the shutter and bar laying beside the open window plainly showed the way by which the fair occupant had quitted the room.

With another fierce oath, the duke flew to the window, and looked out in the hope of seeing the fugitive flying away across the fields, and determined in his own mind to follow in pursuit at all hazards; but he was disappointed; although the grey dawn was fast breaking, not a vestige of any living soul was to be seen as far as the eye could reach.

CHAPTER CXLII.

HOW D'ANVILLE PAID THE LANDLORD OF THE HOSTEL.

And then he told the tale,
    As they did ride along,
How Daverill Duke the king's life saved,
    With his good arm so strong.

Two days had elapsed since the incidents recorded in the preceding chapter had taken place, when the duke and his companions, having drunk themselves tipsy with wine, and then having drunk themselves sober again with beer, began to think of taking their departure from the hostel.

During their stay they and their esquires had made an open house of the inn, and had invited all who passed by to enter and drink to the health of the corpulent host, and the country swains did not forget to drink deeply in the much-praised rich brown ale, good evidence of which was to be seen in the quantity of empty barrels that strewed the floor of the cellar.

But the day which the host had ardently looked for—the day of reckoning—was come, and whilst the horses were being equipped the old dame even honoured the guests with her presence, and the host seemed to be in the best of humours, and laughed and chatted right merrily.

But neither the host nor his wife had the least inkling of the manner in which the debt was to be settled, or they would not have been so joyful.

D'Anville was preparing to pay them off in a different coin to that which they expected.

When the horses were harnessed, and the knights had donned their mail, the duke summoned the host, and bade him bring the stirrup-cup in which the health of all present, not forgetting the king, was toasted.

The shouts and merriment were kept up until the wine disappeared, and then a scene of a different nature was enacted.

The duke's own horse was led to the door of the inn, and the paunchy host was compelled to stand erect upon its back, while D'Anville mounted behind him, and, provided with a stout thong, he lashed the landlord to the iron stanchion (from which he had removed the signboad) by passing the thong over the iron support and under the armpits of the host, and by this means, when the horse was moved, the plump carcase of the terrified innkeeper was suspended in mid air, and he occupied the same post as his signboard had previously done.

As may be supposed, the host did not suffer all this to be done quietly; he kicked and flung his legs about in the most furious manner he was capable of; but as this did him no good, and only exhausted him, and added to his pain, he became less obstreperous in that part, but let loose his tongue upon his tormentors pretty freely.

His entreaties, threats, and curses, however, were of no avail in obtaining his release; for the loud cries of the assembled villagers drowned every sound of his voice, and the younger portion of the crowd, who looked upon his affliction merely as an opportunity given to them to indulge in sport, pelted him with all sorts of missiles.

The infuriated hostess would have resented this last outrage on her spouse, both tooth and nail, had not some of the labourers of the village, who had not yet recovered from the previous day's libations, have kept her in fear; and so the unfortunate host was compelled to submit his huge carcase to the boys as a target, at which they pelted with all their might, rotten eggs, apples, and even horse chestnuts.

Sir Arthur and the duke enjoyed the fun mightily, and when they had rendered their sides sore with laughter, they scattered a few small coins among the crowd and rode away.

When their mirth had a little subsided, the haughty pair began to discuss matters that more seriously concerned them, and in the course of their conversation the name of Sir Daverill Duke was mentioned.

"But how came he to creep so quickly in favour of the king?" asked Sir Arthur. "Marry, 'tis a thing so strange that I scarce can credit it! Once thou wert in Henry's favour, and how you came to lose it also puzzles me."

"Ay, and well it may. You know but little of king's favouritism. You have not long been a visitor at Court; when your experience is as old as mine your wondering will cease."

There was a tone of bitterness in his speech that Sir Arthur did not fail to notice, and this made him the more anxious to hear how it was that his companion had lost his place at the king's elbow, and also how it was that Daverill Duke had so artfully crept into his place.

This knowledge to a young aspirant like himself was most invaluable; but as he did not wish to appear too anxious to gain the information, he put the question in as indirect a form as possible.

The duke, thrown off his guard by his apparent simplicity, entered fully into the details, and, without reserve, explained all.

"I will tell you," he said, "as we have entered upon this expedition as friends; but mind, Sir Arthur, you do not breathe it again to mortal ear. If I succeed in what we have undertaken, I shall ever more be at enmity with his majesty; but if I fail I may yet stand in need of his friendship."

"Fear not, D'Anville; you can place explicit faith in me, and a more fitting opportunity of whispering it in my ear, without fear of being overheard, may never again present itself."

"Truly; and now I must explain that the Lady Agnes, of whom we are now in search, is a rich heiress, and, though young, her life is one of continued sorrow and trouble; for every gallant courts her for her wealth and beauty, but no gallant upon whom she smiles has ever been allowed to live to wed her. They have been slain either in fair fight or by treachery, and he, in whose breast you saw me plunge my dagger, was only one of a score who have shared a similar fate."

Arthur winced slightly as he thought of the cold-blooded scene; but he made no remark, and D'Anville continued—

"But other eyes, save those of chivalrous knights, were anxiously longing to gaze upon her treasure. Priests and bishops laboured hard to get her in their power, and even the king would have done so had he dared; but the most avaricious of all was the cardinal whom you saw at the banquet. He strove hard to discover the place where she is at present secreted, in the hope of inducing her to take the veil, and pour her immense wealth into his saintly coffers."

"But has this aught to do with your story?"

"All. Listen. The king invited the cardinal to a grand boar hunt in his largest forest, and I and several other favourites were allowed to accompany them, and his reverence, who was not the best of horsemen, was mounted on one of the king's most fiery steeds, and more than once I expected to see him thrown from his saddle.

"Yet the cardinal contrived to keep his place at the king's right hand, turning the discourse, whenever it was possible, on church matters, and the cause of his visit to the court, which, though it was the most that occupied the king's thoughts, was the last matter upon which he wished to discourse.

"Henry, having listened to him with attention, yet without having returned any answer which could tend to prolong the conversation, signed to me, who rode at no great dis-lance, to come up on the other side of his horse.

"'We came hither for sport and exercise,' said he, "but the reverend father here would have us hold a council of state.'

"'I hope your highness will excuse my assistance,' said I; 'I am born to fight the battles of our country, and have heart and hand for them, but I have no head for her councils.'

"My Lord Cardinal hath a head turned for nothing else,' said the king; 'he hath confessed our Prince Edward at the castle gate, and he hath communicated to us his whole shrift. Said you not the *whole?*" he continued, with an emphasis on the word, and a glance at the cardinal, which shot from betwixt his long dark eye-lashes, as a dagger gleams when it leaves the scabbard.

"The cardinal trembled, as, endeavouring to reply to the king's jest, he said, "That though his order was obliged to conceal the secrets of their penitents in general, there was no secret confession, which could not be melted at his majesty's breath.'

"'And as his eminence,' said the king, 'is ready to communicate the secrets of others to us, he naturally expects that we should be equally communicative to him; he very reasonably desires to know if the Lady Agnes be actually in our territories. But supposing they were with us, what say you, D'Anville, to our cousin's peremptory demand?'

"'I will answer you, my liege, if you will tell me in sincerity whether you want war or peace,' replied I with frankness.

"I was expecting some sharp answer, when the king, either by accident or design, pricked the flank of the cardinal's spirited steed with his lance, and the animal began at once to plunge and rear in such a manner as to baffle all the churchman's skill in horsemanship to quiet him, and whilst I and the king were laughing inwardly at the cardinal's fears, the terrified steed made a desperate effort to dislodge his rider, and then bounded off through the forest at a fearful speed.

"'Thou art a scandalous fellow, D'Anville,' said the king to me, 'to speak thus of holy matters. But to the devil with the discourse, for the boar is unharboured. Lay on the dogs, in the name of the holy Saint Hubert! Ha! ha! tra-la-la-lira-la!'

"And without another word the king galloped forward, leaving me to enjoy the scene occasioned by the sight of the churchman's flying robes.

"The violet-coloured gown of the cardinal, which he used as a riding-dress (having changed his long robes before he left the castle), his scarlet stockings, and scarlet hat, with the long strings hanging down, together with his utter helplessness, gave infinite zest to his exhibition of horsemanship.

"The horse, having taken matters entirely into his own hand, flew rather than galloped up a long green avenue, overtook the pack in hard pursuit of the boar, and then, having overturned one or two yeomen prickers, who little expected to be charged in the rear, animated by the clamours and threats of the huntsmen, carried the terrified cardinal past the formidable animal itself, which was rushing on at a speedy trot, furious and embossed with the foam which he churned around his tusks.

"The unshriven rogue, on beholding himself so near the boar, set up a dreadful cry for help, which produced such an effect on his horse, that the animal interrupted its headlong career by suddenly springing to one side; so that the cardinal, who had long been expecting it, was hurled to the ground, and the blast of the king's horn rang in his ear as his majesty passed him.

"After all the chase had passed him, a single cavalier, who seemed rather to be a spectator than a partaker of the sport, rode up with one or two attendants, and expressed no small surprise to find the cardinal there upon foot, without a horse or attendants, and in such a plight as plainly showed the nature of the accident which had there placed him, whilst I dashed through the thicket and tried to follow the king.

"By keeping my eye on the foot-tracks of the huge beast, I soon found that most of the knights who had passed on before me on swifter steeds had taken a false track, but I still kept on in the right one, and soon heard the baying of the dogs.

"But fortune was against me on that day; in leaping my horse over a fallen tree he fell, and I could not come up with the king, who was mounted on a good horse, and followed close on the hounds, so that when the boar turned at bay in a marshy piece of ground, there was no one near him but Henry himself.

"His majesty showed all the bravery and expertness of an experienced huntsman; for, unheeding the danger, he rode up to the tremendous animal, which was defending itself with fury against the dogs, and struck him with his boar-spear; yet as the horse shyed from the boar, the blow was not so effectual as either to kill or disable him.

"No effort could prevail on the horse to charge a second time; so that the king, dismounting, advanced on foot against the furious animal, holding in his hand the short spear he invariably carried.

"The boar instantly quitted the dogs to rush on his human enemy, while the king, taking his station, and posting himself firmly, presented the sword, with the purpose of aiming it at the boar's throat, or rather chest, within the collar-bone; in which case, the weight of the beast, and the impetuosity of his career, would have served to accelerate his own destruction. But, owing to the wetness of the ground, the king's foot slipped, just as this delicate and perilous manœuvre ought to have been accomplished, and the point of the lance encountering the cuirass of bristles, on the outside of the creature's shoulder, glanced off without making any impression, and Henry fell flat on the ground.

"This was so far fortunate for the monarch, because the animal, owing to the king's fall, missed his blow in his turn, and only rent with his tusk the king's short hunting-cloak, instead of ripping up his thigh. But as, after running a little a-head in the fury of his course, the boar turned to repeat his attack on the king in the moment when he was rising, the life of Henry was in imminent danger, when Daverill Duke, who had been thrown out in the chase by the slowness of his horse, but who, nevertheless, had luckily distinguished and followed the blast of the king's horn, rode up, and transfixed the animal with his spear.

"The king, who had by this time recovered his feet, came in turn to Daverill's assistance, and cut the animal's throat with his sword. Before speaking a word to Daverill, he measured the huge creature not only by paces, but even by feet—then wiped the sweat from his brow, and the blood from his hands—then took off his hunting cap, hung it on a bush and shook hands with Daverill Duke, whom he swore to befriend to the utmost of his power.

"This scene I watched through an opening in the bushes, and from that day I swore to be revenged ; for the king lost all faith in me, and I was cast out. But, see you yonder?—there is a damsel."

"Ha ! ha !" laughed the knight ; " ride on ; let us overtake her."

CHAPTER CXLIII.

ROBIN HOOD IS WOUNDED.

The horses' hoofs aloud did ring,
As down the road they sped ;
A cry that startled Robin's ears,
Caused him to turn his head.

WHEN Robin was again left to himself, he fell into the same gloomy abstraction, at intervals pacing the floor with hurried strides, and muttering wild and incoherent sentences to himself.

The hounds that lay crouched in a corner looked at him in wonder and alarm ; this strange conduct of their master was entirely new to them, for they missed his cheerful voice and his warm caressing hand.

Presently the outlaw chief paused in his walk, and blew a low note on his horn.

A page answered his summons, and having received a few hasty orders, departed hastily to obey them.

Soon after, Robin Hood left the stronghold with a heavy bag of silver, and took his way to the hovels of the poor, oppressed peasantry, who had visited him in numbers that morning, to ask alms of him, and he alleviated their distress with unsparing hand.

Having accomplished his errand of mercy, he was about to return home, when his attention was attracted to the figure of a man crouching in a suspicious manner beneath the bushes that lined the path he had to travel.

"St. Herman !" muttered the outlaw, as at a glance he discovered the fellow to be armed. "This accounts for my dream ; some treachery is afoot."

"But I'll unearth the knave !" he added, fiercely ; and with a few rapid strides he made to the place where the man had crept closer into concealment. Robin walked boldly to the spot, and thrust his arm into the foliage to clutch whoever it might be ; but he nearly paid for this rash act with his life, for a man whom he instantly recognised as Stukely, sprang from the bush and aimed a powerful blow at his head with a drawn sword.

Sudden as was the attack, however, Robin Hood's presence of mind was equal to the emergency. He raised the staff that he carried in his left hand and dashed aside the murderous blade just in time to save his life.

"Caitiff !" he thundered, as he started back and prepared for the renewed attack. "Take that for thy villany," and he hurled a crushing blow at Stukely that would have split his head had the blow taken effect.

But Stukely was well skilled in the use of the sword, and he parried the blow, returning it with such vigour as to almost cut through the oaken stave that was opposed to his short, broad blade.

"Now, who is the caitiff ?" cried Stukely, pressing hard upon him. Yield thee, outlaw as thou art, or by the rood, I will slay you with as little mercy as you slay the king's deer."

Robin Hood gave a defiant laugh ; but made no reply. He saw that his staff was of little use against the heavy two-edged sword, therefore he watched narrowly for a chance to draw his own stout weapon. The opportunity at length presented itself, and Robin instantly seized it, and then the fight began in earnest.

For some minutes the contest was carried on with undisturbed fury, until a troop of four horsemen swept along the road that crossed the narrow lane.

The thunder of the horses' heavy hoofs disturbed the combatants, and caused them both to cease and gaze curiously in the direction of the sound.

At that moment a shriek for help, uttered in a female voice, assailed their ears, and Robin Hood, forgetful of the opportunity he was giving to his opponent, started at full speed towards the road.

"By heavens, 'twas Marian's voice !" he ejaculated, as he ran, and, in his excitement and eagerness to gain a view of the road, he stumbled and fell.

At the same moment he experienced a

ROBIN HOOD,

AND THE OUTLAWS OF SHERWOOD FOREST.

THE CAPTIVES.

sharp, stinging pain in his arm, and he discovered that Stukely had followed and wounded him.

Like lightning he sprang to his feet, and faced his foe, and, with one desperate thrust, he pierced his adversary through the body.

Without waiting to see what injury he had done, he darted down the road after the horsemen, who were just visible through the cloud of dust thrown up by the clattering hoofs of the goaded steeds.

For nearly a mile he sped over the ground with the swiftness of a deer, and then the horsemen were hidden from his view by a turn in the road.

Still on he went, heedless of the pain of his wound, until, weak and faint, he fell on the road, and went off into a swoon.

When he came to, he found himself laying on a grassy bank, surrounded by a party of miners who were going to their toil.

One of them, a lad, was bathing his brow with water, and the only man of the party was binding up the wound of his arm, from which, it was evident, a deal of blood had flowed.

"Bob Bland," were the first words Robin uttered, "thanks for your kindness. How came I here?"

"Marry, I know not, good sir," the man replied, "unless you were wounded by those ruffians who passed us on the road."

ROBIN HOOD,

"Ah! saw you them?" ejaculated the outlaw, as a faint recollection of the horsemen dawned on his mind. "By Saint Mary, did you have time to notice them?"

"Marry I did not, good Robin," replied Bob Bland; "they passed us so swiftly, but I saw they had with them a female who cried loudly for help."

Robin was about to question the men further, but a sudden faintness again coming over him, he fell back on the sward like one dead.

Bob Bland became alarmed at this, and he held a conference with his younger companions as to the course to pursue, and they decided on conveying him to the nearest cottage, which chanced to be that of the miller's.

Grace met them at the door, and seeing the helpless state of Robin, she quickly prepared a couch for him, and then rewarded the man with a silver piece for his pains and trouble.

"Nay, good lady," said the honest miner; "thinkest thou I need payment for this small return of the kindness good Robin Hood hath shown to me? Did he not assist me when my leg was broken? and did he not help me when I was unable to pay the rent for my widowed mother?"

"Name it not, Robert. Take this, it will purchase something for thee and the boys."

"By our Lady, 'tis a shame to rob ye," replied the man, as she thrust the coin in his hand, "but as denial gives you offence, I will e'en take it, and pray heaven that dear Robin may soon get over this."

The little party left in glee, and when Grace returned to the house she found Robin Hood making an exertion to rise from the couch.

The effort was too much for him, however, and he sank back on the pillow, whilst Grace procured a stoup of wine and contrived to pour a little between his compressed lips.

This revived him sufficiently to make inquiries after the miller and his son Much, and he learnt that the miller had that morning started to town with a load of flour, and that Much had seized his cap and staff and started off hurriedly a few minutes before Robin had been brought in; but where he had gone, or what caused his haste, she could not explain.

This news caused Robin so much uneasiness and excitement, that Grace began to fear a fever would set in, so she at once sent a message to Sherwood for assistance to convey him home.

Friar Tuck and Little John, with a party of some half-dozen sturdy foresters, soon obeyed the summons; and, the friar having examined the wound of the outlaw's arm, he soon gave them a specimen of his leech craft.

Having bound up the wound and administered a draught to the sick man, the friar had him removed to an inner room, where he took upon himself the duty of nurse, and soon had the satisfaction of seeing his patient fall asleep.

We must now explain the cause of the hurried departure of Much, the miller's son, and the reason he did not acquaint Grace with the strange circumstances of the case.

Much, in performing his duty as chief woodward, had to see that the pickets were at their different posts, and being in the vicinity of the mill, he just stepped in to have a word with Grace and rest himself.

Whilst Grace was busied in drawing a jug of beer, Much stood at the door gazing at some distant object that had attracted his attention, which was a cloud of dust rising above the bushes that lined the road.

As it drew near, and then swept by the path that led to the mill, he heard the shrill cry of Marian for help.

Then — as Grace had described it — he rushed into the cottage, seized his cap and staff, and dashed off in pursuit.

Following the cloud of dust with his eye, he at once had good cause to suspect that Marian was the victim of some treacherous design, for the horsemen came suddenly to view on a rise of the road, and he saw the horses turn into another road that wound round the outskirts of the town.

The very idea of overtaking them on foot, by following the road they were traversing, was madness in itself; but the brave youth hoped to gain upon them, and keep on their track by taking a near cut across the fields, which would lessen the distance by about two miles and a half.

But in this even he was deceived.

Long before he reached the point where he hoped to meet them, they had passed, and a slight shower of rain had laid the dust, so that he could only follow their track by the footmarks of the horses.

But to one experienced as he was in following the chase, this was a task of little difficulty.

He could mark the track of a hunted deer across the grassy glade, and, therefore, it was easy for him to follow the hoof tracks on the damp road.

But as he began to tire, and wished to get up to the fugitives quickly, he began to look about him for any stray animal that he might press into his service.

As fortune would have it, he espied a horse grazing in a field.

The poor beast was lean and emaciated, and bore traces of having been overworked; but as the halter was still on its neck, the forester, without further hesitation, mounted it bare-backed, and urged it at its utmost speed along the road, reached the next village, and, having gleaned sufficient information to assure him that he was on the right path, he proceeded on his way.

But the animal he rode was not fitted for so much exertion.

As he was trying to force it up a steep incline, from the summit of which he hoped to get a good view of the road before him, the jaded beast staggered and fell.

In the fall, one of its legs got broken, and Much, to end its sufferings, drew his knife and put an end to its existence.

Leaving the carcase on the roadside, he proceeded on foot.

On reaching the brow of the steep, Much found to his surprise that he had gained greatly on the party he was pursuing.

He calculated that, if the beast had held up one hour longer, he would have overtaken the party, for they were resting and refreshing their horses on the banks of a stream.

With a feeling of mingled pleasure and vexation, he again set forward, clutching his staff firmly in his hand as he went, and muttering vows of vengeance on the abductors of his cousin.

CHAPTER CXLIV.

MUCH, THE MILLER'S SON, HAS A STRANGE ADVENTURE.

The stream was up, the ford was deep,
    Yet he plunged boldly in;
And Much would surely have lost his life,
    Had he not learned to swim.

THE golden rays of an early sun was just tingeing the leaves of the tall trees and gilding the glassy surface of a broad stream, as a youth, dusty and travel stained, leaned upon his staff on the river's bank, gazing at a tall battlemented tower that just reared its head sufficiently above the dense foliage to render it visible.

On the opposite bank, the side of which stood the castle, two men loitered, and amused themselves in watching the youth who appeared to be the object of their discourse.

But suddenly the youth aroused himself from his listless apathy and descended the rugged bank to the water's edge. The younger of the two loiterers remarked to his companion—

"It is our man ; the carl that insulted us at the fair and disturbed us when we were partaking of a social cup. If he attempts to cross the ford, he is a lost man ; the water is up, and the ford impassable."

"Let him make that discovery himself, gossip," said the elder personage ; "it may, perchance, save a rope, and break a proverb."

"An' I judge him rightly," said the other, "he is a bigger knave than fool, and will not make the attempt ; but hark ! sir—he halloos to know whether the water is deep."

"Nothing like experience in this world," answered the other; "let him try."

The young man, in the meanwhile, receiving no hint to the contrary, and taking the silence of those to whom he applied as an encouragement to proceed, entered the stream without further hesitation than the delay necessary to take off his buskins.

The elder person, at the same moment, discovered his friend's error, and hallooed to him to beware, adding in a lower tone to his companion, " A malison on thee, gossip, you have made another mistake. This is not the rogue we wot of."

But the intimation to the youth came too late. He either did not hear or could not profit by it, being already in the deep stream.

To one less alert, and practised in the exercise of swimming, death had been certain, for the brook was both deep and strong.

" By Saint Anne ! but he is a proper youth," said the elder man. " Run, gossip, and help your blunder by giving him aid, if thou canst. He belongs to thine own troop —if old saws speak truth, water will not drown him."

Indeed, the young traveller swam so strongly, and buffeted the waves so well ; that, notwithstanding the strength of the current, he was carried but a little way down from the ordinary landing place.

By this time the younger of the two strangers was hurrying down to the shore to render assistance, while the other followed him at a graver pace, saying to himself as he approached, " I knew water would never drown that young fellow. By my halidame he is ashore, and grasps his pole. If I make not the more haste, he will beat my gossip for the only charitable action which I ever saw him perform in his life."

There was some reason to augur such a conclusion of the adventure, for the bold forester, had already accosted the younger Samaritan, who was hastening to his assistance, with these ireful words. " Discourteous dog ! why did you not answer when I called to know if the passage was fit to be attempted ? May the foul fiend catch me, but I will teach you the respect due to strangers on the next occasion."

This was accompanied with a significant flourish with his pole, holding it in the middle, brandishing the two ends in every direction, like the sails of a windmill in motion. His opponent, seeing himself thus menaced, laid hand upon his sword, for he was one of those who on all occasions are more ready for action than for speech ; but his more considerate comrade, who came up, commanded him to forbear, and turning to the young man, accused him in turn of precipitation in plunging into the swollen ford, and of intemperate violence in quarrelling with a man who was hastening to his assistance.

The young man, on hearing himself thus reproved by a man of advanced age and soldierly appearance, immediately lowered his weapon, and said he would be sorry if he had done them injustice ; but in reality, it appeared to him as if they had suffered him to put his life in peril for want of a word of timely warning, which could be the part neither of honest men nor of good Christians, far less of respectable soldiers such as they seemed to be.

"Fair son," said the elder person, "you seem, from your accent and complexion, a stranger ; and you should recollect your dialect is not so easily comprehended by us as perhaps it may be uttered by you."

"Well, father," answered the youth, "I do not care much about the ducking I have had, and I will readily forgive your being partly the cause, providing you will direct me to some place where I can have my clothes dried, for it is my only suit, and I must keep it somewhat decent."

"For whom do you take us, fair son ?" said the elder stranger, in answer to this question.

"Good men and true," replied the youth, who was no other than our friend Much, the miller's son, not wishing to offend them, "and, if I opine rightly, men of no mean condition," he added.

"Thou hast guessed rightly, my son," replied the elder, pleased with his remark. "As to your accommodation, we will try to serve you. But I must first know who you are, and whither you are going ; for in these times the roads are filled with travellers on foot and horseback, who have anything in their head but honesty and the fear of God."

Much cast another keen and penetrating glance on him who spoke and on his silent companion, as if doubtful whether they, on their part, merited the confidence they demanded, and the result of his observation was as follows.

The elder of the two, from his half military attire, he took to be a mercenary knight of small pretensions, or a leader of a band of robbers ; and the younger, he judged, was a soldier, somewhat above the common rank, and this made the miller's son very cautious of his speech.

"My history is brief," he replied to a query put by the elder. "I have been brought up simply as a poor woodman ; but wishing for a somewhat active life, I have wandered here by chance, and seeing yonder castle, I crossed the stream, thinking there might be a vacancy in the garrison, and that I might enlist under the banner of "——

"Its noble occupant, Sir Gustave Malcolm, as fine a knight as ever carried armour. Well, my lad, I will do all that lays in my power to aid you in your wish ; but as you require a dry suit, and doubtless have a vacancy in your stomach, we will first pay a visit to the village inn, and then we will quietly talk matters over."

"Ay, and gladly will I listen to aught thou hast to tell me, concerning the castle we have named, and pleased will I be to pay a visit within its walls."

"My son tells of one that is little versed in these matters ; think you the drawbridge is lowered, and the gates of the castle thrown open to the visit of every curious knave ? No, no ; the Baron de Leslie, who owns this noble pile, has left it in charge of his trusty follower Malcolm, who is too keen to let every curious eye pry into his secrets."

"Zounds !" replied Much, trying to sound the fellow, for he had every reason to believe that the party he had so scrupulously followed had entered the castle, and that his cousin was either a prisoner within its walls, or concealed thereabouts. "It bodes no good, when a baron has such secrets to keep. For my part, I have always been brought up in the free life of the woods ; and no traveller ever knocked at the door of our humble cot, without gaining admittance."

His companion looked round with an alarmed gaze, and said, "Hush, hush, Sir Varlet with the Velvet Pouch ! for I forgot to tell you that one great danger of these precincts is, that the very leaves of the trees are like so many ears, which carry all which is spoken to the knight's own cabinet."

"I care little for that," said Much. "I bear a Saxon tongue in my head, bold enough to speak my mind to his face—God bless him!—and for the ears you talk of, if I could see them growing on a human head, I would crop them out of it with my wood-knife."

While Much and his new acquaintance thus spoke they came in sight of the whole front of the castle, and they stood to take a view of the massive pile that extended, or rather arose, though by a very gentle elevation, an open esplanade, clear of trees and bushes of every description, excepting one gigantic and half-withered old oak.

This space was left open, according to the rules of fortification in all ages, in order that an enemy might not approach the walls under cover, or unobserved from the battlements, and beyond it arose the castle itself.

There were three external walls, battlemented and turreted from space to space, and at each angle, the second inclosure rising higher than the first, and being built so as to command it in case it was won by the enemy ; and being again, in the same manner, commanded by the third and innermost barrier.

Around the external wall, as the man informed his young companion (for as they stood lower than the foundation of the wall, he could not see it), was sunk a ditch of about twenty feet in depth, supplied with water by a dam-head on the river, and in front of the second inclosure, he said, there ran another fosse, and a third, both of the same unusual dimensions, was led between the second and the innermost inclosure.

The verge, both of the outer and inner circuit of this triple moat, was strongly fenced with palisades of iron, serving the purpose of what are called *chevaux-de-frise* in modern fortification, the top of each pale being divided into a cluster of sharp spikes, which seemed to render any attempt to climb over an act of self-destruction.

From within the innermost inclosure arose the castle itself, containing buildings of different periods, crowded around, and united with the ancient and grim-looking donjon-keep, which was older than any of them, and which rose, like a black Ethiopian giant, high into the air.

The other buildings seemed scarcely better adapted for the purposes of comfort, for what windows they had opened to an internal court-yard.

This formidable place had but one entrance, at least Much saw none along the spacious front, except where, in the centre of the first and outward boundary, arose two strong towers, the usual defences of a gateway; and they could observe their ordinary accompaniments, portcullis and drawbridge—of which the first was lowered, and the last raised.

Similar entrance towers were visible on the second and third bounding wall, but not in the same line with those on the outward circuit; because the passage did not cut right through the whole three inclosures at the same point, but, on the contrary, those who entered had to proceed nearly thirty yards betwixt the first and second wall, exposed, if their purpose was hostile, to missiles from both; and again, when the second boundary was passed, they must make a second digression from the straight line, in order to attain the portal of the third and innermost inclosure; so that before gaining the outer court, which ran along the front of the building, two narrow and dangerous defiles were to be traversed, under a flanking discharge of artillery, and three gates, defended in the strongest manner known to the age, were to be successively forced.

To enhance his surprise, his companion told him that the environs of the castle, except the single winding path by which the portal might be safely approached, were—like the thickets through which they had passed—surrounded with every species of hidden pit-fall, snare, and gin, to entrap the wretch who should venture thither without a guide; that upon the walls were constructed certain cradles of iron, called swallows' nests, from which the sentinels, who were regularly posted there, could take deliberate aim at any who should attempt to enter without the proper signal or pass-word of the day; and that the archers of the guard performed that duty day and night, for which they received high pay and much honour and profit, at the hands of the baron.

"And now, tell me, young man," he continued, "did you ever see so strong a fortress, and do you think there are men bold enough to storm it?"

His informant little knew what was passing in Much's mind as he eyed the place, the sight of which interested him so much that he had forgotten, in the eagerness of his curiosity, the wetness of his dress.

His eye glanced, and his colour mounted to his cheek, like that of a daring man who meditates an honourable action, as he replied—

"It is a strong castle, and strongly guarded, but there is no impossibility to brave men."

"Are there any in your country who could do such a feat?" said the elder, rather scornfully.

"I will not affirm that," answered the youth, "but there are thousands that, in a good cause, would attempt as bold a deed."

"Umph!" said the senior. "Perhaps you are yourself such a gallant?"

"I should sin if I were to boast where there is no danger," answered the forester; "but my father has done as bold an act, and I trust I am no coward."

"Well," said his companion, smiling, "you might meet your match, and your kindred withal in the attempt, for the archers stand sentinels on yonder walls."

"I trow me, there is not one amongst them could draw to the ear with bold Robin Hood," remarked Much, carelessly.

His companion again smiled, and turning his back on the castle, which, he observed, they had approached a little too near, he led the way again into the wood by a more broad and beaten path than they had yet trodden.

"This," he said, "leads us to the village, where you, as a stranger, will find reasonable and honest accommodation."

"I thank you, kind master, for your information, but my stay will be so short here, that so I fail not in a morsel of meat, and a drink of something better than water, my necessities will be amply satisfied."

CHAPTER CXLV.

ROBIN HOOD AND LITTLE JOHN START ON THEIR JOURNEY.

"Come hither, lass," the miller cried,
　"And tell me of my son;
Who kens which way, what road he took—
　Thou art the only one."

* 　 * 　 * 　 * 　 * 　 *

Then Robin mounted on his horse,
　The henchman by his side,
And queried of every one he met,
　As 'long the road he hied.

THE wound our hero had received from the sword of Stukely, though a bad one, was not dangerous, and the skill of the friar soon displayed itself by causing it to heal rapidly, and his careful nursing soon restored the patient's health.

With Stukely, fortune dealt more harshly. A party of foresters, who went in search of him, found his dead body crouched under a bush whither he had managed to crawl, and it was discovered that the outlaw's sword had passed through his body, causing a speedy death.

Friar Tuck, in his zeal for the recovery of the chief, would not permit him to be removed. Therefore, all transactions of a business nature were carried on at the mill, and a party of citizens waited upon Robin

Hood to counsel with him as to the best mode of dealing with the high sheriff, who had again commenced to oppress them sorely.

Robin Hood was in no mood to give them advice at that time on such a subject. His whole mind was wrapped in thoughts entirely foreign to such a subject: he could not rest night nor day for thinking of his Marian, and he longed anxiously for the time when his strength would permit him to seek out her vile persecutors, and punish them in manner befitting to their crime.

He, therefore, advised the people to bear for a time submissively with their oppression, and to wait with patience the hour when it would be most suitable for them to retaliate.

The miller seconded him in this for more reasons than one.

He had not only lost his son, Much, but his niece, Marian, also, and he looked upon their restoration as the most important subject to discuss.

"Now, Grace," he said, one evening on returning from a fruitless search to gain information of his son's whereabouts, "thou art the only one, lass, that can tell me aught of Much's departure; so speak, lass, and tell me which way he hied. Was it northward, think ye? Come, tax thy brain a little."

"Gramercy! I wot not, or I would tell you, good father," said Grace, bursting into tears. "An' I knew he would have been absent so long, I would have watched him. Saint Mary protect him wherever he be, say I!"

"And I, too, lass," replied the miller, dashing a tear from his eye with the back of his brawny hand. "I would give a whole week's grinding of the mill to know what has befallen him."

"Fash not thyself, good father," said Robin Hood, who chanced to hear him; "to-morrow, ill or well, I will go in search of him. I have half a guess of the road he has taken."

"By the mass, good master, you forget that you are still too weak to attempt such a perilous journey; for, should you chance to come to blows, I would not answer for thy life."

"Cease thy bickerings and idle forebodings, Friar Tuck," said Robin, glancing reprovingly at the speaker. "Like the owl, thou art always croaking and professing thou canst see into the darkness of the future. Avaunt, I say, or by the blood I have lost, I swear I will try my skill first upon thee, and give thee a sound thrashing for thy kind nursing."

Friar Tuck said no more.

He knew that to argue with Robin Hood in his present mood would be fruitless, and, upon reflection, he considered he had done well in persuading the outlaw chief to rest quiet so long a time as he had.

Next morning Robin mounted his noble steed, and, accompanied by his stout henchman, Little John, he started on his journey northward, for he had a suspicion that Marian was in the power of one of the treacherous knights, and that it was intended that she should be borne away in company of the Lady Agnes to the distant shores of Brittany.

With this conviction, he took the road, followed by the mailed horsemen, and ere night set in, he gathered sufficient on the way to assure him that his conviction was right.

His chief informant was a travelling musician, who gained a scanty living by attending the fairs and merry-makings, enlivening the hearts of the rustics with the notes of his pipe, and who chanced to drop in at the tavern where the foresters had halted to partake of refreshments and bait their steeds.

When the man had told his story, and received his reward, Robin again set forward, and, watching a favourable opportunity, he and Little John assumed the disguise they had purposely brought with them, and boldly entered the next town.

CHAPTER CXLVI.

MUCH'S INTERVIEW WITH THE ARCHER.

His hauberk made of purest steel,
    Did dazzle keen and bright;
Much scarce believed his sight was real,
    He was astounded quite.

A massive chain of solid gold
    The soldier's neck did grace,
He held it up to Much's view,
    And shook it in his face.

THE Miller's son was so much taken up with what he had seen that he had quite forgotten the stranger who walked beside him, until he tapped him on the shoulder and said—

"Come on, my son, I owe you a breakfast which I had almost forgotten, for the wetting which my mistake procured you. It is the penance of my offence towards you."

"In truth," said the light hearted forester, "I had forgot wetting, offence, and penance and all. I have walked my clothes dry, or nearly so, and I will not refuse your offer in kindness, for my dinner yesterday was a light one, and supper I had none. And I see no reason why I should not accept your courtesy."

In the meanwhile, they descended a narrow lane, overshadowed by tall elms, at the bottom of which a gate-way admitted them into the court-yard of an inn of unusual magnitude, calculated for the accommodation of the nobles and suitors.

The repast which the stranger called for was such as to excite not only the appetite but the astonishment of the miller's son, especially as he knew that soldiers seldom carried a heavy purse ; but when his friend desired him to fall to, he did so vigorously.

The soldier eyed him narrowly and with something akin to delight, and Much, seeing that he was observed, complimented the meal.

"Eat thy fill, lad, I begrudge it not," said the old man ; "but I was about to say, since you like your present meal so well, that the archers of the guard eat as good a one or a better every day."

"No wonder," said Much ; "for if they are stuck up on the ramparts all night they must needs have a curious appetite in the morning."

"And plenty to gratify it upon," said the soldier. "They need not, like the Normans, choose a bare back that they may have a full belly ; they dress like counts, and feast like abbots."

"It is well for them," said Much.

"And wherefore will you not take service here, young man ? The knight might, I dare say, have you placed on the file when there should a vacancy occur. And, hark in your ear, I myself have some little interest, and might be of some use to you. You can ride, I presume, as well as draw the bow ?"

"Our race are as good horsemen as ever put a plated shoe into a steel stirrup ; and I know not but that I could ride as well, bare-backed, on the wildest steed as any of your men-at-arms."

"Ha, ha !" said the soldier, rising, and trying to imitate a laugh.

As he spoke, he took a large purse from his bosom, made of the fur of the sea-otter, and streamed a shower of small silver pieces into the goblet, until the cup, which was but a small one, was more than half full.

"You have reason to be more thankful, young man," said he, "both to your patron, Saint Quentin, and to St. Dunstan, than you seemed to be but now. I would advise you to bestow alms in their name Remain in this hostelry until you see the captain of the guard, Bolero, who will be relieved from guard in the afternoon. I will cause him to be acquainted that he may find you here, for I have business in the castle."

Much would have said something to have excused himself from accepting the profuse liberality of his new friend ; but the soldier, bending his dark brows, and erecting his stooping figure into an attitude of more dignity than he had yet seen him assume, said, in a tone of authority—

"No reply, young man, but do what you are commanded."

With these words, he left the apartment, making a sign to the forester to remain seated, and not to follow him.

Much sat for some hours buried in deep thought, wondering first who the stranger could be, and feeling certain that he was something more than a common soldier, and, secondly, wondering within himself whether he had hit upon the right spot where his cousin was concealed, and, thirdly, whether it was ever possible that he could gain admittance to the castle.

While he was thinking thus a heavy footstep disturbed him, and a soldier, whom the host announced as the captain of the guard, entered.

Each eyed the other curiously, as Bolero seated himself on the opposite side of the table to that on which Much was seated, and the forester had a good opportunity of taking the dimensions of the soldier's portly form.

He was upwards of six feet high, strong, robust, and hard-favoured in countenance, and bore a deep a scar upon his left cheek, which rendered his features ghastly.

On his head he wore a green cap with a feather, which was slouched over his massive forehead, and around his neck he wore a long gold chain with enormous links.

The archer's gorget, arm-pieces, and gauntlets, were of the finest steel, curiously inlaid with silver, and his hauberk, or shirt of mail, was as clear and bright as the frost-work of a winter morning upon fern or briar.

He wore a loose surcoat, or cassock, of rich blue velvet, open at the sides like that of a herald, with a large white cross of embroidered silver bisecting it both before and behind—his knees and legs were protected by hose of mail and shoes of steel—a broad strong poniard hung by his right side — the bauldrick for his two-handed sword, richly embroidered, hung upon his left shoulder ; but, for convenience, he at present carried in his hand that unwieldy weapon, which the rules of his service forbade him to lay aside.

Much, accustomed even as he was to arms and weapons of war, could not help admiring the stalwart soldier and his complete equipment, and he began to reckon the chance he would stand in an engagement with so formidable an opponent.

The man-at-arms seemed to have an inkling of his thoughts, and gave a smile as he said—

"Well, my lad, what brings thee to these parts ? I have heard that you have a dash of spirit, and wish to become a soldier, and also that you have some skill in archery and the likes. Say, is it so ?"

"Quotha! it is ; but first I should like to have an insight into the life and manners of the brave fellows who are to become my companions," said Much. "There might be that in it which would not savour with my haste ; in truth, I have never had an opportunity of seeing within the walls of so strong a castle."

"By my halidame ! you shall then, though in doing so I may incur the baron's anger ; but Bolero is no coward as you shall find, and he will show you not only the interior of the fortress, but the armoury and the guard-room where my band of daring archers wile away the time, and toast their sweethearts in as good wine as ever graced the lips of King Henry himself, but I warrant me thou hast no great treasure to bear thy charges."

"Only a few pieces of silver," said the forester : "for to you, Sir Stranger, I must make a free confession."

"Alas !" replied Bolero, "that is hard. Now, though I am never a hoarder of my pay, because it doth ill to bear a charge about one in these perilous times, yet I always have (and I would advise you to follow my example) some odd gold chain or bracelet, or carcanet, that serves for the ornament of my person, and can at need spare a superfluous link or two for any immediate purpose."

"But you may ask," he added, " how you are to come by such toys as this—(he shook his chain with complacent triumph). They hang not on every bush ; they grow not in the fields like the daffodils, with whose stalks children make knights' collars. What then ? You may get such where I got this, in the service of the good baron, where there is always wealth to be found, if a man has but the heart to seek it, at the risk of a little life or so."

"But how am I to gain service under the good baron ? I have heard that he is absent from the fortress, and that he has left it in charge of a knight."

"And you have heard aright ; but I have power sufficient to urge matters for thee, on thy promise that what you see and hear you will not divulge. There are visitors at the castle, and our master wishes such news to be kept within bounds."

"Marry ! my tongue is sealed at any moment, though curiosity might prompt me to inquire the visitors' names, for it is amusing to me to hear of such."

"Give ear, then," said the soldier, lowering his voice. "One of them is the Duke d'Anville, and the other is his cousin, Sir Arthur of Bretagne, a gallant knight forsooth, who is about to visit his native land."

The archer took up his goblet and drained it to the dregs, eyeing his companion over the top of the huge cup to see what impression his words had made upon him.

Much observed this, though he appeared to take no notice, and as the man-at-arms had become so far communicative, he remarked, in well-feigned surprise—

"Saint Quentin ! Thy story loses its interest in the telling on't. I had hoped to hear of some gallant exploit having been done either in love or war. Marry ! 'tis but a dry tale after all, and thy cavaliers are no more than simple travellers."

"By the mass, as our good priest would say," exclaimed the man, "thou art a plucky youth, and thine ideas vault higher than I had imagined. 'Tis passing strange that one who has led a sedentary life in the woods should have a taste so refined and romantic."

"Ah ! good sir, you know not the life we lead in the merry green woods," said Much, with mock deference. " We never see knight or noble there, unless he be on some mission of honour or gallantry ; therefore, we dream of such things as would never find room in your mind ; but I long to enter the castle, and then perchance it may renew my chivalrous ideas, which your last few words have banished.

CHAPTER CXLVII.

ROBIN HOOD'S TIMELY ARRIVAL SAVES THE LIFE
OF THE MILLER'S SON.

But soon this act of rashness Much sorely did repent.
The soldiers gathered round him with direful intent :
No mercy would they give him—that he could plainly see :
They vowed that they would hang him to revenged be.

FOR some time after the soldier had taken his departure, the daring forester sat in moody silence, wondering within himself what turn matters would take, and longing for the time to come when the archer was to admit him within the gates of the strongly fortified castle.

Now that he felt certain his cousin was either within the battlemented walls, or was a prisoner in some part of the town, he was prepared to run the risk of any danger ; and though it seemed strange that the stranger he had first met should interest himself so much in his favour, yet he did not evince the least sign of fear.

Feeling assured from the reserved manner of the host that nothing was to be gained from him, and not wishing to muddle himself with too much of the wine, the miller's son wandered out into the road to survey the place and examine more fully the outward strength of the castle.

He had not proceeded far, however, when, on a mound by the roadside, he beheld a massive oak backed by a row of chestnut trees.

Beside them stood three or four peasants, motionless, with their eyes turned upwards, and fixed apparently upon some object amongst the branches of the tree next to them.

His youthful and impulsive nature aroused his curiosity at once.

The forester hastened his pace, and ran lightly up the rising ground, in time to witness the ghastly spectacle which attracted the notice of these gazers, which was nothing less than the body of a man, convulsed by the last agony, suspended on one of the branches.

"Why do you not cut him down ?" said the bold forester, whose hand was as ready to assist affliction as to maintain his own honour when he deemed it assailed.

One of the peasants, turning on him an eye from which fear had banished all expres-

ROBIN HOOD,
AND THE OUTLAWS OF SHERWOOD FOREST.

THE MEETING IN THE VILLAGE.

sion but its own, and a face as pale as clay, pointed to a mark cut upon the bark of the tree, bearing the rude resemblance of a dagger, which was a sign that the tree had been desecrated by the priests, and this led the outlaw to believe that the man had been hung merely to satisfy their desires.

Much sprung lightly up into the tree, drew his knife, and, calling to those below to receive the body on their hands, cut the rope asunder in less than a minute after he had perceived the exigency.

But his humanity was ill seconded by the bystanders.

So far from rendering him any assistance, they seemed terrified at the audacity of his action, and took to flight with one consent, as if they feared their merely looking on might have been construed into accession to his daring deed.

The body, unsupported from beneath, fell heavily to earth in such a manner that Much, who presently afterwards jumped down, had the mortification to see that the last sparks of life were extinguished.

He gave not up his charitable purpose, however, without farther efforts.

He freed the wretched man's neck from the fatal noose, undid the doublet, and threw water on the face.

While he was thus humanely engaged, a wild clamour of tongues arose around him; and he had scarcely time to observe that he was surrounded by several men and women of a singular appearance, when he found himself roughly seized by both arms, while a naked knife, at the same moment, was offered to his throat.

"Vile slave!" said a man in a passionate tone, "are you robbing him you have murdered? But we have you, and you shall abuy it."

Knives were drawn on every side of him as these words were spoken, and the grim and distorted countenances which glared on him were like those of wolves rushing on their prey.

Still the young forester's courage and presence of mind bore him out.

"What mean ye, my masters?" he said, "If that be your friend's body, I have just now cut him down, in pure charity, and you will do better to try to recover his life, than to misuse an innocent stranger to whom he owes his chance of escape."

The women had by this time taken possession of the dead body, and continued the attempts to recover animation which Much had been making use of, though with the like bad success; so that, desisting from their fruitless efforts, they seemed to abandon themselves to despair.

The forester on seeing how matters stood, was about to withdraw himself from a neighbourhood so perilous, when a galloping of horses was heard, and the men, who had raised by this time the body of their comrade upon their shoulders, were at once charged by a party of soldiers.

This sudden apparition changed the measured wailing of the mourners into irregular shrieks of terror. The body was thrown to the ground in an instant, and those who were around it showed the utmost and most dexterous activity in escaping, under the bellies as it were of the horses, and from the point of the lances which were levelled at them, with exclamations of "Down with the accursed heathen thieves—take and kill—bind them like beasts—spear them like wolves!"

These cries were accompanied with corresponding acts of violence; but such was the alertness of the fugitives, the ground being rendered unfavourable to the horsemen by thickets and bushes, that only two were struck down and made prisoners. Much, whom fortune seemed at this period to have chosen for the butt of her shafts, was at the same time seized by the soldiers, and his arms, in spite of his remonstrances, bound down with a cord, those who apprehended him showing a readiness and dispatch in the operation, which proved them to be no novices in such matters.

Looking anxiously to the leader of the horsemen, from whom he expected to get his liberty, Much saw that in his manner which dispelled his hopes and alarmed him.

But he had no time for reflection.

"Bell and Griffith's," said the officer to two of his band, "these same trees stand here quite convenient. I will teach these misbelieving, thieving sorcerers to interfere with the king's justice, when it has visited any of their accursed race. Dismount, and do your office briskly."

They were in an instant on foot, and Much observed that they had each at the crupper and pommel of his saddle, a coil or two of ropes, which they hastily undid, and showed that, in fact, each coil formed a halter, with the fatal noose adjusted, ready for execution.

The blood ran cold in Much's veins, when he saw three cords selected, and perceived that it was purposed to put one around his own neck.

He called on the officer loudly for justice. The officer whom Much thus addressed, scarce deigned to look at him while he was speaking.

He barely turned to one or two of the peasants who were now come forward, either to volunteer their evidence against the prisoners, or out of curiosity, and said gruffly—

"Was yonder young fellow with the vagabonds?"

"That he was, sir, an' it please ye. He was the very first blasphemously to cut down the rascal whom his majesty's justice most deservedly hung up."

"I'll swear by God and St. Martin to have seen him with their gang," said another.

"Nay, but, father," said a boy, "yonder knave was black, and this youth is fair; yonder one had short curled hair, and this hath long fair locks."

"Ay, child," said the peasant, "and yonder one had a green coat and this a grey jerkin. But we know that they can change their complexions as easily as their jerkins, so that I am still minded he was the same."

"It is enough that you have seen him intermeddle with the course of the king's justice by attempting to recover an executed traitor," said the officer; "these fellows have been stealing the king's deer, and this churl has endeavoured to assist them; string them up."

He made a sign with his left hand to the executioners; then, with a smile of triumphant malice, touched with his forefinger his right arm, which hung suspended in a scarf, disabled probably by the blow which Much had dealt him in the fray.

Much had now time to examine the men who were to perform the kindly office upon him.

Griffiths was a tall, thin, ghastly man, with a peculiar gravity of visage, and a large rosary round his neck, the use of which he was accustomed piously to offer to those sufferers on whom he did his duty. He had one or two Latin texts continually in his mouth, on the nothingness and vanity of human life ; and, had it been regular to have enjoyed such a plurality, he might have held the office of confessor in commendam with that of executioner.

Bell, on the contrary, was a joyous-looking, round, active, little fellow, who rolled about in execution of his duty as if it were the most diverting occupation in the world. He seemed to have a sort of fond affection for his victims, and always spoke of them in kindly and affectionate terms.

He endeavoured to inspire them with a philosophical or religious regard to futurity, and seldom failed to refresh them with a jest or two, and gave them a fair sample of his abilities on the occasion by slapping Much upon the shoulder, and calling out—

"Courage, my fair son ! since you must begin the dance, let the ball open gaily, for all the rebecs are in tune," twitching the halter at the same time to give point to his joke, and rendering his meaning plainer by gently urging him forward to the fatal tree, and bidding him be of good courage, for it would be over in a moment.

In this fatal predicament, the youth cast a distracted look around him.

Not till now did he thoroughly understand the awkward predicament in which he stood ; for his arms, being bound, prevented him making even one bold stroke for freedom.

Presently a voice was heard calling on the executioners to desist, and on looking round Much discovered to his surprise the outlaw chief dressed in the costume of a Norman archer or cross-bow man.

"By Saint Andrew ! they shall make at you through me," said the Archer, and unsheathed his sword.

"Cut my bonds, friend," said Much, making it appear that they were strangers, " and I will do something for myself."

This was done with a touch of the archer's weapon ; and the liberated captive, springing suddenly on one of the guard, wrested from him a halberd with which he was armed.

"And now," he said, "come on, if you dare."

The two officers whispered together.

"Ride thou after the captain," said Bell, "and I will detain them here if I can. Soldiers of the guard ! stand to your arms !"

The man mounted his horse and left the field, and the other men in attendance drew together so hastily at the command of Bell that they suffered the other two prisoners to make their escape during the confusion.

CHAPTER CXLVIII.

FORTUNE AGAIN TAKES A FAVOURABLE TURN.

Then up spoke bold Bolero,
" Release him with all speed;
He is one of my archers,
And a kinsman, too, indeed."

FORTUNATELY the soldiers that formed the provost guard were fellows of little pluck, and were only accustomed to hanging criminals, or in arresting those who failed to pay the tithes levied upon them by the good father of a neighbouring monastery, or it might have gone hard with the foresters in so unequal a match.

As it was they looked upon the form of bold Robin Hood, and from the manner in which he delivered his speech they fancied him something above what his present costume made him appear to be.

They gained heart, however, when their leader re-appeared, and demanded of Robin Hood by what authority he interfered.

"An' it please, mine own," replied the outlaw, fiercely, "I am determined to see justice done by the youth. What hath he done, pray ?"

Robin winked at Much, and the miller's son, taking the hint, replied—

"I will tell you the truth as if I were at confession. I saw a man struggling on the tree, and I went to cut him down out of mere humanity. I thought neither of his guilt nor his innocence, and had no idea of offending our father the abbot."

"Zounds !" ejaculated Robin, in feigned anger. "What a murrain had you to do with the dead body, then ? You'll see them hanging in the rear of this gentleman like acorns on every tree, and you will have enough to do in this country if you go a gleaning after the hangman. However, I will not quit your cause if I can help it. Hark ye, master, you see this is entirely a mistake. You should have some compassion on so young a traveller ; he has not been accustomed to see such active proceedings as yours and your master's."

"Marry, we will teach him, then," said the provost leader. "Stand aside, Sir Archer. Let the work proceed !"

"Not till you have proved yourself a better hand at the sword than I," said Robin, coldly, placing his hand on his sword hilt as he spoke.

"We are strong enough to beat the proud caitiff twice over, if it be your pleasure," said one of these soldiers to the leader.

But that cautious official made a sign to

him to remain quiet, and addressed the archer with great civility.

"Surely, sir, this interference is a great insult to the king, and it is no act of justice to me, who am in lawful possession of my criminal. Neither is it a well-meant kindness to the youth himself, seeing that fifty opportunities of hanging him may occur, without his being found in so happy a state of preparation as he was before your ill-advised interference."

At this moment a tall, giant form stepped forward, and demanded the prisoner's immediate release.

"How so? What now, Master Bolero? What game scents the wind, that you take so much interest in this fellow?"

"'Tis enough. I have said release him," replied the man, whom Much recognised as the captain of the bowmen.

"Marry! but this pleaseth me. 'Tis indeed wondrous strange when Bolero, the chief bowman of the castle, opposes the execution of a criminal."

"I deny that I do so," answered Bolero. "Saint Martin! there is, I think, some difference between the execution of a criminal, and the slaughter of one of my own band."

"Your man may be a criminal as well as another," said the outwitted captain, "and every stranger even is amenable to the laws."

"Yes, but we have privileges, we archers," said Bolero; "have we not?"

The leader was too exasperated to reply, and at that instant a party of Bolero's own men appeared over the brow of the slope.

Bolero turned to his men and addressed them thus:—

"What say you, comrades, to this? Our younker has fallen into the claws of these vultures, who want to turn him into a crow's nest. Will you stick by him or no? Say the word; remember he is one of us."

"But no archer of the guard, I think," retorted Bell, thrusting his sallow face forward.

The archers looked on each other in some uncertainty.

"Stand to yet, cousin," whispered Cunningham, one of the archers to Bolero. "Say he is engaged with us."

"Saint Martin! you say well, fair kinsman," answered Bolero; and, raising his voice, swore that he had that day enrolled his kinsman as one of his own retinue.

This declaration was a decisive argument, though the provost leader had a doubt whether Bolero and the prisoner were anything akin.

"It is well, gentlemen," said the provost captain, who was aware of the baron's nervous apprehension of disaffection creeping in among his guards, "you know, as you say, your privileges, and it is not my duty to have brawls with the guards, if it is to be avoided. But I will report this matter for the baron's own decision; and I would have you to be aware, that in doing so, I act

more mildly than perhaps my duty warrants me."

So saying, he put his troop into motion, while the archers remaining on the spot held a hasty consultation what was next to be done.

CHAPTER CXLIX

THE DISCOVERY AND LOSS OF THE BURIED TREASURE.

"I was there, I vow," the priest he said,
"The fact none can deny.
And this imprint of Tuck's great foot,
I see with half an eye."

THE absence of Robin Hood was a source of comfort to De Lois, and a terrible discomfiture to the people, for the sheriff, taking advantage of the opportunity offered, used his power to the utmost in oppressing those who came within his jurisdiction.

In the meantime the good father of the chapel, whom Stukely had held a conversation with, concerning his brother-in-law, failed not to keep his promise, he visited sister Lydia and obtained her consent to remove the body.

This was accordingly done at night, by a brace of ruffians, or resurrectionists, who were kept by the monks for the especial performance of such work.

They felt no repugnance at having to perform such a task, for they were accustomed to such; it being their duty to unclose the graves of the rich, and procure the treasure which the monks purposely ordered should be buried with them.

The night was dark and favourable for such work, and the two men set off with spade and lantern, to perform their task.

But they were little prepared for the surprise that awaited them, and when they came upon the buried treasure, they were seized with a feeling tantamount to fear, and without waiting for the body, they hurried back to acquaint the good friar with the news.

The saintly man, though surprised at the news, did not give any outward signs of it, but in an angry tone rebuked the men for leaving the open grave unprotected.

Drawing his hood over his head, and taking a crucifix in his hand, he accompanied them in person back to the forest, calculating in his mind as he went along the probable extent of the treasure, and planning in his mind how he should secretly convey it to his sanctum, unknown to the rest of the brethren, but when he got there, a sad disappointment awaited him, and all his cherished hopes fled.

The grave was still open, and there laid the chest, but the treasure, of which, there was unmistakable signs had been removed, and the body of the hermit filled its place.

The priest gave vent to his anger in no

measured terms on making this discovery, and when he saw the trace of a sandal in the newly removed earth, he heaped his curses freely on the wearer's head, and gave the two dumb-stricken men a fair share also.

"May the curse of the Virgin rest on his unhallowed soul," he muttered with an intensity of passion. "'Tis the well-known foot of that rascal Friar Tuck, I know it well. I cannot be deceived in the make of his sandal, and these deep indentures are the foot-marks of some of that villanous band, who have gone away loaded with spoil."

With this uncomfortable reflection he was obliged to satisfy himself, and the men by his order raised the chest on their shoulders, and bore the corpse of the hermit to the chapel.

Now the treasure was gone, and there was nothing to be gained by his cherishing the secret, the good father recounted to his brethren the sad loss, and reminded Sister Lydia of the knight's vow to have vengeance on Robin Hood.

This served as a twofold incentive for their vengeance, and that night in the chapel, before the altar, each one of them was bound by an oath to take the life of Robin Hood, or any of his men who might chance to fall within range of their power.

CHAPTER CL.

THE MILLER'S SON GAINS AN ENTRY TO THE CASTLE.

The watchful sentries vigilant did guard the gate so strong,
And at the breast of Much they held their pikes both bright and long.
Then Bolero explained the cause why he had brought him there,
And to the knight they led him, and soon settled the affair.

WHILST the archers arranged their plans Robin Hood stood aloof, but sufficiently near to understand what passed, and he thus learnt the course they were about to take with Much, the miller's son.

After arguing for some time amongst themselves, it was decided that they should take him with them to the castle; and as he was young and strong, and just such an one as they wanted, to fill up a vacancy on the muster roll, they started towards the castle.

At their approach, the wicket was opened, the drawbridge fell, and one by one they entered, but when Much appeared, the sentinals crossed their pikes, and commanded him to stand, while bows were bent and arbalists pointed at him from the walls.

Bolero, who stood by his side, gave the necessary explanations, and Much, after some hesitation and delay, was escorted under a strong guard to the knight's own apartment.

The knight was seated with two other personages clad in armour, holding a strong argument on some important point, and he expressed his anger at being disturbed; but after exchanging a few words with Bolero he ordered Much to be taken to the keep where the head warder was to enroll him on the list, and the armourer was to supply him with such things as he might require.

This was accordingly done, and the captain of the guard gazed with a look of mingled pride and admiration on the noble form of the newly made archer, whose compact and well-knit form showed off his equipage to such advantage.

Bolero next led him to the guard-room, and introduced him to the men who were to be his future companions.

This gave Much a good opportunity to form an idea of the strength of the garrison, and also to get an insight into the characters of the men who formed it.

Thus far matters had progressed well in his favour, and while he was seated wondering what movement he must choose next, the trumpet sounded to arms.

The clash of armour that followed the hoarse note awoke Much from his reverie, and on a signal given, the guards were put into motion by Bolero, who assumed the command, and were marched to the inner courtyard, from which, after undergoing inspection, they were led to an open space, without the walls, on the left wing of the castle.

Here butts were erected, and preparations made for exercising with the broadsword, arbalist and longbow, in all of which Much did not fail to show his skill.

A large concourse of the peasants had gathered to see the performance, and one amongst them, a tall fellow miserably clad in the garb of a fisherman, stepped from the crowd and picking up an arrow that fell near, carried it to the young archer, who began to cause some stir in displaying his wonderful skill.

"Thanks, good fellow," said Much, as he took the shaft, and in order to show himself off before the others, he rewarded the man with a coin for his trouble.

The man took it, at the same time grasping Much by the hand, and a look that spoke a volume of words passed between them.

The man had given him the foresters' grip, and Much at once saw through the man's disguise, and discovered him to be Little John.

*   *   *   *   *

That night the watchful sentinels paced their dreary posts upon the walls and battlemented towers, awaiting anxiously the time for them to be relieved, and Much, who could not sleep, listened eagerly for the heavy tramp of the captain to come and summons these off guard to fall in and relieve their companions, when he was startled at hearing a light foot creep into the room, and carefully approach him.

"Rise, lad," whispered the well-known

voice of Bolero; "Much, I have great business for thee to do."

Much was on his feet in an instant, and without further speech, Bolero led him from the room, through several gloomy passages, and conducted him into a small chamber, where Cunningham was seated very comfortably partaking of wine.

His steel cap was laid on the table, and this enabled Much to get a look at his features, which he immediately recognised as those of the stranger who had taken him to the tavern, and had so liberally supplied him with money.

He pushed the goblet to Much, and bade him be seated, an example which Bolero followed, and then they began to converse on matters which the forester pretended to take little interest in, but which in fact he listened to with great eagerness.

From their conversation, which was in a manner guarded from him, the miller's son learnt that two ladies occupied the north tower, and that preparations were being made to convey them to a distant land, and that a vessel was actually expected to arrive the next day to receive them.

It was then explained to Much that he would have to relieve the sentry over the tower, and also that if he chose, he could form one of the body guards that were to accompany the ladies, and a party of knights on their voyage.

This was exactly what Much wished, but he was in a manner perplexed how he was to acquaint Robin with the matter, but he made up his mind to get a glimpse at the prisoners if it were possible, and assure himself of who they were, and then act accordingly.

When the hour arrived, Bolero told him to prepare to relieve guard, and led him partly through private passages exposed to the open air, but chiefly through a maze of stairs, vaults, and galleries, communicating with each other by secret doors, and at unexpected points, into a large and spacious latticed gallery, which, from its breadth, might have been almost termed a hall hung with tapestry more ancient than beautiful.

"You will keep watch here," said Bolero, in a low whisper as if the hard delineations of monarchs and warriors around could have been offended at the elevation of his voice, or as if he fancied each coat of mail that graced the walls, or stood on pedestals, were occupied by a human figure.

"You are permitted to stand still while you list, but on no account to sit down, or quit your weapon. You are not to sing aloud, or whistle, upon any account; but you may, if you list, mutter some of the church's prayers, or what you list that has no offence in it, in a low voice. Farewell, and keep good watch."

"Good watch!" thought the youthful soldier as his guide stole away from him with that noiseless gliding step which was peculiar to him, and vanished through a side-door

behind the arras. "Good watch! but upon whom, and against whom?—for what, save bats or rats, are there here to contend with, unless these grim old representatives of humanity should start into life for the disturbance of my guard? Well, it is my duty, I suppose, and I must perform it."

With the vigorous purpose of discharging his duty, even to the very rigour, he tried to while away the time with some of the pious hymns which he had learned of Friar Tuck.

Having wearied himself with this, he began to walk his post with hasty steps, wondering in his mind where the ladies chamber could be and in a vexed and melancholy mood.

There are, however, charms in sweet sounds which can lull to rest even the natural feelings of impatience, by which Much was now visited.

At the opposite extremities of the long hall or gallery were two large doors ornamented with heavy architraves, probably opening into different suites of apartments, to which the gallery served as a medium of mutual communication.

As the sentinel directed his solitary walk betwixt these two entrances, which formed the boundary of his duty, he was startled by a strain of music, which was suddenly waked near one of those doors, and which, at least in his imagination, was a combination of the same lute and voice by which he had been enchanted in bygone days.

All the dreams of the morning, so much weakened by the agitating circumstances which he had since undergone, again arose more vivid from their slumber, and, planted on the spot where his ear could most conveniently drink in the sounds, he leant upon his arbalist and listened.

Fully convinced that it was his cousin Marian's voice he heard, he felt half inclined to dash open the doors and make himself known, and then, if discovered by the captain of the guard, to strike out boldly in his own and her defence.

But these thoughts were banished by a rough grasp laid upon his weapon, and a harsh voice, which exclaimed, close to his ear, "Ha! Sir Archer, methinks you keep sleepy ward here!"

The voice was the tuneless, yet impressive and ironical tone of the knight, and Much, suddenly recalled to himself, saw, with shame and fear, that he had, in his reverie, permitted Malcolm himself—entering probably by some secret door, and gliding along by the wall, or behind the tapestry—to approach him so nearly, as almost to master his weapon.

The first impulse of his surprise was to free his arbalist by a violent exertion, which made the knight stagger backward into the hall. His next apprehension was, that, in obeying the animal instinct, as it may be termed, which prompts a brave man to resist an attempt to disarm him, might prove the ruin not only of himself, but also of his cousin; he stammered out some excuse, which, weak as it was, served to appease the knight's anger.

The noise of the disturbance had evidently reached the ears of the ladies; for the music ceased, and the knight evinced some uneasiness as he glanced at the doors and muttered to Bolero, who at that instant appeared—

"Marry! this will not do. By my halidame! this soldier you have recommended me is no more than a love-sick swain, who has a keener ear for a lady's lute than the ring of a knight's battleaxe against his foeman's steel. Heed him well, and let him look to himself; or, by the relics of Saint Anthony, he shall suffer the punishment he so richly earns!"

Bolero cast a reproving look at Much; and then, bowing to the knight, said, "My lord, it shall not occur again; I will, as thou say'st, heed him well."

It was a relief to the forester, when the knight turned towards him and, in a modulated voice, said—

"Look ye, lad; Bolero has recommended ye to me as a lad of strict honesty and integrity; and, as you have discovered that there are females in the castle, and I bear thee no enmity for thy lack of duty, I will charge thee with a duty which thou must fulfil to the very letter."

"Holy Mother forbid that I should neglect to serve you faithfully," replied Much, calmly surveying the sinister features of the knight. "Command me as you please; I am your servant."

"I will be frank with thee, then," said the knight. "I have taken especial favour to one of the ladies; and, for reasons of my own, I have sworn that she leaves not the castle in company either of the Duke D'Anville or the knight, Sir Arthur, while I have power to hinder it, or even have one stout arm as your own to send a bolt in my defence. Follow me."

The knight took Much, for whom he seemed to have taken a special favour, through the side-door by which he had himself entered; saying, as he showed it him, "He who would thrive here must know the private wickets and concealed staircases."

After several turns and passages, the knight entered a small vaulted room, where a table was prepared for dinner with three covers. The whole furniture and arrangements of the room were plain almost to meanness.

A beauffet, or folding and moveable cupboard, held a few pieces of gold and silver plate, and was the only article in the chamber which had in the slightest degree the appearance of comfort.

Behind this cupboard, and completely hidden by it, was the post assigned to Much.

Having instructed him how to act if the required signal was given, he left him.

Much had not long to wait in suspense however, for the door opened, and three mailed figures entered and took their seats at the table.

Much was compelled to be a silent listener to a discourse that not only brought the blush to his cheek, but fired his heart with indignation.

Marian, his cousin, was the chief subject of their dispute.

The knights soon got to hot words concerning her, each of them vowing their determination to have her, even should it have to be decided at the sword's point.

D'Anville, who had remained quiet till now, interfered at this juncture.

"Sir Knights," he said, "I opine, were my cousin the Baron de Leslie here, he would not brook such language. Desist, Malcolm, or by the god of war I will draw upon ye!"

This speech was the signal for a *melée*.

"Let's draw, then, archer!" shouted Malcolm, "and if you fail, use your knife. What, ho! there. Bolero to the rescue!"

Much drew as he was desired, and let fly the bolt; but, owing to the men closing suddenly together, the bolt shot under Sir Arthur's arm and entered Malcolm's chest.

CHAPTER CLI.

ROBIN HOOD AND LITTLE JOHN GAIN THE BATTLEMENTS.

Bold Robin Hood and Little John did use both
    strength and skill,
But noways daunted were they till their promise did
    fulfil.
They crossed the slimy waters, and climbed the
    sturdy walls,
While Much was under strong arrest within the
    castle halls.

At the very moment when the tragical affair was being enacted in the castle, a scene no less exciting was passing without the walls.

It was a moonlight night, but dark, heavy clouds at intervals shaded the moon's rays, and a strong wind swept round the massive building, and visited the battlements in fearful gusts, so that the sentinels had to keep a watchful eye in case Bolero might creep in upon them unawares, as he often did, and reward them for their negligence with a sound drilling.

But in spite of all their precaution, they did not observe two figures creep from the shelter of the woods while the moon was obscured, and glide silently but swiftly up to the very walls, bearing between them a huge bark of timber, and a long coil of knotted thongs.

When they reached the edge of the moat, the moon again shone forth, but they had thrown themselves down in the long grass, and thus evaded the eager glances of the bowmen as they took their searching survey, and when the moon was again clouded, the figures rose to their feet, and slipped the log silently into the sluggish water of the pool.

"Body-o'-mine! good master," said one of the men, "one would almost venture to walk across to yon buttress. Marry, there is more mud than water in the moat, if I rightly opine."

"Ay, John," replied the other, who was Robin Hood; "but that only adds to the danger. If a fellow once got into this slough, he might as well try to fly as swim. Gramercy, and its smell is not the most savoury."

"Bladebone of St. Hubert! no; and we have not improved its smell by disturbing it. But we have not come here to judge its merits, so let us make good use of our time."

Whilst this half muttered conversation was going on, Robin had slid down the bank, and into the inky slime, and, placing the timber under his arms, used his hands as paddles to propel the log across.

This was a task not only requiring patience but time, and as soon as he was near enough, he took a crook, like a shepherd's, only sharper hooked, and with this he drew himself to a portion of the abutment which was decayed, and soon gained a footing on it.

Little John, who held the thong, one end of which was fast to the log, hauled it back to his side, and trusted his long body on the frail raft, whilst Robin, who held the end of another portion of the line, then drew him across.

Having secured the raft, Robin undid another coil, and fastening the end to his belt, climbed up the abutment by means of his crook, which he hooked firmly in the chinks, between the stones, and following it up with his feet and hands.

In this manner he ascended midway between the moat and the battlement, when, on glancing upwards, he saw the bright steel cap of a sentinel looking over the wall immediately above him.

Robin placed himself as flat as he could, for he knew that from his position the man could not hit him, unless he dropped something upon him, and, in spite of the danger of his situation, he could not help indulging in a quiet grin, as he listened to the man's angry ejaculations.

One downward glance assured him that Little John was safe from observation, and as he had proceeded so far, and was prepared to meet with danger, he made up his mind to go forward, as his retreat would be equally as dangerous.

"Hist!" said Robin, in reply to the soldier's challenge. "Who art thou, Bolero or Cunningham?"

"Marry! you will soon know," replied the man. "I am neither, but honest Jock Lockland; and if you do not want me to throw a missile on your head, you will tell me who you are, and how you came there."

"'Adzooks, Jock!" said Robin, familiarly, "this is no time to speak to a man when he is hanging on by the eyelids; wait till I reach the top, and then your own eyes shall convince you who and what I am, and the reason I have undertaken this hazardous job for our good knight, Sir Malcolm."

At the mention of the knight's name, the soldier's ire cooled; but his curiosity was heightened. He could not imagine what important duty had necessitated so much risk; and, moreover, he was anxious to learn, so he let the daring outlaw proceed without further questioning.

Robin shielded his face as much as possible from the light, and only glanced upwards sufficiently to serve his purpose, and catch an occasional glimpse of the man; and his head was as busy in planning a means to rid himself of his troublesome interference as his hands were in assisting him to climb.

In the meantime the soldier was not idle.

He was wondering what excuse he could invent for his negligence in not detecting Robin Hood before he had ascended so far, and have seen where he started from, for it was a perfect mystery to him, as there was not such a thing even as a loophole in that part of the wall Robin had chosen.

"Thanks to the Virgin!" said Robin, as his crook hitched the top stone; "by all the saints in the calendar, and every bead on our good Father's rosary, I have had a tight job; and even now, if I do not unfortunately make a slip, I am doubtful whether Sir Gustave Malcolm will give me more than a soldier's reward—that is, a jug of sour beer and a promise of promotion."

"Many would think thou deservest something better," replied the man; "but let me assist ye, and then perchance I may do a little in the way of lightening thy task with the sour beer."

"Boddikins, thou art welcome to it all!" said Robin, as he felt the strong grasp fixed firmly on his shoulders; "by my halidame, you are the best fellow I have met in my journey upwards, so take that for your reward!"

As Robin spoke, the man assisted him, wet as he was, to reach the battlement. As soon as the outlaw found himself safe, he dealt the man a sharp blow on the head with his crook, and then bound and gagged him with the cord.

There was still enough to reach to Little John, which the outlaw found by feeling it angrily jerked; for Little John, on feeling it drawn up so swiftly, and losing so much at once, was afraid he was going to take the whole of it.

Robin fastened the end securely, and then gave the signal for Little John to ascend, which the tall forester did with more agility than grace, and soon stood on the battlement beside his master.

"Now, what think ye of it?" asked Robin of him when he thought he had sufficiently recovered breath. "Canst remember what yon fellow said to thee?"

ROBIN HOOD,

AND THE OUTLAWS OF SHERWOOD FOREST.

"Marry, and I do; but I little thought of seeing a place like this, and for the life of me I cannot see how we are to act."

"Saint Herman! that is easy enough, as long as we are not interfered with. But we must be brisk, or all the labour we have admirably used will be thrown away. Quick! throw yourself into that fellow's harness, and see how it fits."

Little John was not long in doing this.

The man was not many inches shorter than himself, and was much less in figure, so that the forester managed pretty well to squeeze himself into the archer's attire.

This accomplished, the soldier's half-dead body was drawn into concealment, and Robin looked around to see what should be his next act.

He was not long in deciding.

At the father end of the rampart, where was a small turret, another sentinel stood,

and he was leaning against the wall which shielded him from the wind, evidently asleep or buried in deep thought.

Robin clutched his crook, for Little John had appropriated the soldier's arms to his own use, and crouching low he crept along the wall until within arm's length of the man, who, unconscious of danger, little dreamt of an enemy lurking so near, and dealt him such another blow with his staff as he had given his comrade.

The man fell prostrate, with a groan, and Robin was upon him in a moment, bound him securely, and stripped him as he had done the other.

He had barely time to complete his arrangements, when the clank of a mailed heel caught his ear, and the form of Bolero stepped on to the battlements, and walked towards him.

As Robin's back was to the moon, he

had a full view of the archer's features as he approached, and he could see that he was excited, and his countenance heated and flushed.

Robin Hood gave him the customary salute, and was surprised to hear him address himself to him in a tone of familiarity.

"Danton," said the captain of the guard, "a sorry job has come to pass through Cunningham introducing that fellow. He is a stout youth, but, by my patron saint, he has commenced business in a wrong way, and what is more, as I have taken him under my protection and avowed him my kinsman, I am partly answerable for his misdeeds."

"'Adzooks!" exclaimed Robin, in well-feigned alarm, "what hath the lad been up to. Gramercy! Hath he been caught napping on his first night's watch. Saint Quentin! it is a bad sign for a beginning."

"You are right," said Bolero, meditatively: "but were this all I would not care."

"All!" ejaculated Robin.

"Ay, all. He has done even worse, even to the wounding, if not taking the life, of our good knight."

"Sir Gustave Malcolm?"

"Yes; he sent a bolt through him, as he says, in mistake. But I have seen sufficient of his skill in archery to know that he did it wilfully or negligently; but he'll suffer for his act, even if it falls to my own hand to hang him; and serve him well right, say I. Curse him!"

"And what hast done with him now?" asked Robin Hood, in no way pleased at hearing of Much's downfall."

"Sent him to keep company with the rats in the lowest dungeon. What else could we do? Had the baron not been absent he would have given him a dance from the beam above the gate-house; but, as it is, I have no fear but that he'll get there soon enough."

Robin felt half-inclined to knock the captain down, and he had, in fact, great difficulty to keep himself from doing so.

But prudence and second thought restrained him; and when Bolero had gone, he paced the rampart with hurried strides, and wondered in his mind how he could save the life of the gallant youth.

Then, when he had fairly puzzled his brain and racked his mind to no purpose, he held a council with Little John, and he assisted him greatly with his advice.

CHAPTER CLII.

MUCH, THE MILLER'S SON, IS MADE PRISONER.

"A curse upon the foul fiend!" D'Anville then did cry.
"Behind yon screen," he, pointing, said, "the traitor he doth lie.
Come hither, caitiffs, every one forward, the cur to seize.
And if he doth resistance make, do with him as you please."

WHEN the fatal bolt struck the knight, Much scarcely knew whether to feel vexed or pleased, as it rid him of one enemy; but what occurred after caused him some uneasiness, as it bid fair for ruining all his plans.

As Bolero and the guards rushed in, D'Anville shouted, pointing to the beauffet,

"Yonder is concealed a traitor. See here what his hand hath done. Hunt the knave out as you would a cur, and spike him as you would a boar."

"See you here!" he added, raising his voice. "See you here, this is his work. He has practised his treachery on our own good friend, the noble Malcolm. To the dungeon with him! Away! away!"

The soldiers gazed angrily at the newly enlisted archer, for they already conceived a certain amount of jealousy towards him, owing to his beating them at the butts, and, besides, they looked upon his presence so near the knight's person as an omen greatly against themselves.

A better opportunity to wreak their vengeance they could not have had than the present, and they would have slain their rival on the spot, had it not been for Bolero.

He ordered them to fall back, and then gave orders for Much to be heavily ironed, and placed in a dungeon for the present.

It was a wretched cell, and greatly exceeded in misery the expectations he had formed as he travelled thither through the gloomy and loathsome passages that formed a labyrinth beneath the castle.

It was a small vault, with a lofty arched roof, and a small loophole close to the top on one side, to admit air and light, and in the wall was a massive iron ring, to which the miller's son was securely chained.

This sudden change of fortune wrought a terrible effect upon the prisoner, and when the door of the dungeon was closed, and the rusty bolts shot into their sockets, he threw himself upon the bare stone bench, and heaved a deep-drawn sigh.

Then it was he had leisure to reflect on his folly, for he attributed his accident to his own fault, and his brain whirled with the myriad of thoughts that crowded upon him.

It was not for his own fate that he cared so much; but he regretted that he had not been able to communicate with Robin Hood, for he was utterly ignorant that he was so near him.

Robin Hood and his brave follower were not idle in the meantime.

They knew that if they did not take some measures before the morning that daylight would betray them, and, therefore, they were bound to be expedient.

When the patrol had gone its round, Robin crept from his post, and cautiously left the ramparts by the steps Bolero had descended, and, after groping his way along a passage in the darkness, and descended a winding staircase, he found himself in a dimly-lighted chamber.

At the farther end he could hear a voice speaking in a subdued tone, and, through the gloom, he distinguished the figures of two men.

Towards these he softly crept, and ensconced himself behind a pillar, from which position he could hear their conversation, and then he learnt sufficient to guide him in his acts.

"But why this hurry, Sir Arthur?" said a voice whom Robin easily recognised as Bolero's. "Will you not stay and see whether the wound is mortal?"

"In faith I cannot. The vessel is expected in port to-morrow. We have to prepare for a long journey, and, what is worse, the ladies do not care to be hurried."

"But if the wound of our good knight, Sir Gustave Malcolm, turns out mortal, how am I to report it to my lord, the baron, on his return?"

"You have simply to tell him how it occurred. You have the traitor safely caged, and, now I bethink me, there is a kinswoman of Sir Gustave's who professes much skill in leechcraft, at least so I have heard Malcolm often boast. It is not a long journey to Kirkless, why not despatch a messenger for her at once?"

"Marry and I will, but if you depart at dawn, as you say, what escort will you need?"

"D'Anville has fifty stout men in this castle; they will do. But I have forgotten —only a score accompanies us on the voyage. Well, a score of trusty fellows and our own two trusty swords will suffice. We have no cause to fear molestation in these parts, so go, Bolero. Send off the messenger, and give the men a hint to get ready."

"Pardon, Sir Knight," said Bolero, hesitating, "but the duke has not given me any authority to prepare his men."

"Fool! Is not my word sufficient?" thundered the knight, darting at him an angry glance. "Get thee to, minion, and lack no speed in doing my bidding, and let everything be in readiness at my call. In the meantime, I will see D'Anville."

Robin Hood had to bite his lip to conceal his rage; and as each of the speakers departed by different doors, he crept back to the battlements, where Little John anxiously awaited him.

"What news, good master mine?" eagerly asked the bold forester.

"Such as demands our immediate action. They leave the castle at dawn, with a score of men-at-arms. The party is strong for us to attack, and "——

"Body o' mine, say not so. A shaft or two amongst them would"——

"Probably kill those we have the least wish to harm," interrupted Robin. "No, no, an open attack will not do. Besides, there is our friend Much to look after. I will leave you to see to him, and I myself will either rescue Marian or perish."

Little John would fain have questioned him more closely, but Robin gave him a hearty grasp of the hand, and bade him God speed; then, seizing the thong by which

Little John had ascended, he flung himself over the wall and began the dangerous descent.

CHAPTER CLIII.
D'ANVILLE AND THE KNIGHT FORM THEIR PLANS.

We must away before the dawn
To create no surprise;
We dare not wait till open morn—
'Twill fill the peasants' eyes.

"Hush! Sir Gustave is worse," said D'Anville, as Sir Arthur entered the chamber where he sat. "The wound, I fear, is fatal; and if so, De Leslie may suspect us of treachery."

"Just so. I have thought the same; and to prevent any unpleasantness—though 'tis certain that one, if not both of us, owe our lives to the fellow's awkwardness—I am determined to start on our journey at once."

"By the mass, 'tis as well. There is no one now to dispute our right to possess the females, and once in Brittany, we shall have nought to fear from the king."

"Saint Dunstan! no; but if we stay here, and it gets wind that we are about to quit the country with the rich heiress, the king will be down upon us, or, what is worse, the officious Edward; and then, again, there is a little to fear from the outlaw, Robin Hood."

"Ay, indeed. I had quite forgotten him; but as it is as well we leave here as secretly as possible, I vote that we start before daylight reveals us to the prying eyes of the peasants."

With this D'Anville strode from the room, and repaired to that part of the castle where the garrison was kept, and ordered his men to fall in.

Having selected a score of the most stalwart of his party, who he thought he could rely upon most in case of need, he put them in charge of his favourite leader, and ordered them to horse at once.

The others he ordered back to his brother, from whose castle in the north they had only come on the previous day, and then he went to prepare Marian and the Lady Agnes for their journey.

D'Anville had arranged his plans well, providing matters had been as he anticipated, for he little expected Robin to be on his track.

He had visited a monk who pretended to be an astrologer on the previous day, and the wise man, for a considerate sum, ventured to predict that there would be bloodshed before he got clear of the land, and as this had been fulfilled in what had since passed, D'Anville considered there was nothing more to fear, and set his mind entirely at rest on that point.

Previous to the accident to the knight, D'Anville had been troubled in his mind concerning what the magician said, for he feared some treachery might have been meditated by the master of the French vessel;

and in that case he would have needed all his men; otherwise, he did not care to make too great a show, as he did not want to leave too clear a track behind, and it might so happen that the ship might not be able to sail at once.

One hour before daybreak the drawbridge was lowered, and the cavalcade passed out in silence.

CHAPTER CLIV.

ROBIN HOOD DISGUISES HIMSELF AS A FISHERMAN.

Anchors and planks thou shalt not want,
    Masts and ropes that are so long.
And if you thus do furnish me,
    Said Robin, nothing shall go wrong.*

"A MERRY greeting, good fellows all!" said Robin, as he strode into an inn where a party of fishermen were quaffing a foaming tankard, previous to starting on their voyage, "and to you, dame," he added to the woman, who was gazing in astonishment at his ruddy face and stalwart figure, which looked anything but suited to the coarse canvas garb in which it was encased.

"And a greeting to ye, my good fellow, whoever thou beest, for I opine you have not long taken to the craft. Thy very gait would belie ye, did ye say so."

"By our Lady, you have a shrewd guess of my condition; and to be frank with ye, I have come here purposely to try my luck."

"Good fellow, I can engage with thee, then. Here are my bonny lads waiting to put off; but the carl of a boy is not to be found. I can warrant thee a sturdy bark, and a stout anchor in time of need to boot."

"Then more I do not want," said Robin; "and, when I have quaffed a tankard to thee, my jolly companions, I will embark at once."

They plucked up anchor, and away did sayle
    More of a day, then two or three;
When others cast in their baited hooks,
    The bare lines into the sea cast he.

"A malison on the knave, and a curse on the day that brought him among us!" said the master of the boat. "Not one penny will he earn, and yet will he expect a share; but"——

Robin checked him suddenly.

"See you yonder ship?" he said.

"Marry do I, and a Frenchman withal. These robbers will not spare of us one man!"

And he made a movement as he spoke to seize the helm; but Robin caught him by the shoulder, and then, to the fisherman's astonishment, he found that Robin Hood (whose real name he did not know) was armed with a bow and a quiver of arrows.

He drew back in alarm as one of the barbed points was pointed at his breast, and

Robin demanded, in a firm voice, that the prow be pointed in a direct line for the French vessel—an order that was reluctantly obeyed; but, as Robin held their lives, as it were, in his hand, there was not one dared to question his authority.

As the vessel drew near, Robin fixed his back against the mast, and taking steady aim at the man who steered the French vessel, he pinned him to the ship's side, and then let fly a shower of arrows at the men crowded on the raised part forward; and the fisherman, on seeing this, took courage and steered his boat clear of the Frenchman, upon whose deck Robin was strewing both soldiers and sailors, bleeding and wounded, as fast as they appeared from below.

His quick eye had already singled out D'Anville, who he fastened to the mainmast with an arrow through his shoulder; and then, as Sir Arthur rushed up from below, and shouted to the few remaining soldiers to leap aboard the boat and put an end to their indomitable enemy, a cloth-yard shaft pierced his throat, and the men crouched in terror beneath the bulwarks.

Fortunately for the fisherman, not one of D'Anville's men was possessed of a crossbow, and such things as the ship carried for defence had been stowed down below, as the captain deemed that the presence of the soldiers was sufficient protection.

As Robin's arrows were getting spent, he now thought it time to call a parley, and the only two soldiers who were not wounded gladly yielded to his request, and entered with the rest of the sailors into the boats, leaving Robin and the fisherman in possession of the French ship.

The fisherman had no cause to repent of their voyage, for the ship was well loaded with treasure, which he portioned to the men, and gave his share to the dame,* reserving to himself his dearest treasure—his beloved Marian.

CHAPTER CLV.

THE PLOT TO OVERTHROW ROBIN HOOD.

Therefore the king called a council of state
    To know what was to be done
For to quell their pride, or else, he replied,
    The land would be overrun.

THIS daring act of Robin Hood's greatly incensed the king against him, for the news had flown on the wings of the wind to the Court, though it must be acknowledged that in that short time it had undergone a serious transformation.

Henry's short-sightedness would not allow him to see this, he only heard the continual whispering of his favourite courtiers, who failed not to dingle in his ears the account which had reached them, that Robin Hood had actually the audacity to attack a

---

* From three old black letter copies in the possession of Anthony A. Wood, another in the British Museum, and a third in a private collection.

* It is supposed that his share was given to the building of almshouses.

vessel in the British waters, and take therefrom, by force, the proud heiress, the Lady Agnes, for the favour of whose smile, the noblest knight and the proudest baron was ready to pick a quarrel with his most esteemed friend.

He therefore called a council of his nobles, and it was agreed that the bold outlaw and his merry band should be totally exterminated, and then the king, selecting one of the most importunate nobles, Louis de Brabant, said to him—

> Go you from hence to bold Robin Hood,
> And bid him, without more ado,
> Surrender himself, or else, the proud elf
> Shall suffer, and all of his crew.

The fawning noble bowed, and made a quick selection of his men, all of whom were picked archers, and well armed and armoured, and the cavalcade set off without delay to the forest of Sherwood.

Robin Hood was totally unaware of what was passing, and he was, in fact, preparing his men for a sortie on Nottingham Castle, when a loud blast of a horn gave token of danger.

Thinking that De Lois had had the audacity to come out and face him, Robin Hood sounded his horn to assemble his men, and then went to give a cheering word to Maid Marian and the Lady Agnes, previous to his arming himself.

He had scarcely buckled on his sword, and adjusted his baldric, when the blast of another horn woke the stillness of the greenwood, and Will Scarlett came running up and out of breath.

"So ho! what news bear you in such haste?" said Robin. "Has the sheriff dared to set his foot again on our green sward? By my halidame! he shall rue it if he has. What say you, Friar Tuck? for I hear you have gotten your name up, during my absence, for thy skill in witchcraft and sorcery."

"By the mass! I cannot venture to say till I have heard this gossip's tale. One would think he had seen the king, which is as rare a sight as any about these parts, by the way he runs."

"I have seen as good," said Will Scarlett, as soon as he recovered breath sufficiently to speak; "four hundred of the king's best archers are now within the forest."

"Let them come. What have we to fear? If they mean fighting, we are prepared; if they are peaceable, they are welcome."

"Ay, to this," said Little John, whirling his staff over his head. "I will e'en get my buckler and get ready to give them a bout."

"And I, too," said Much, who returned at that moment from drilling a party of the foresters who were to be under his command in assaulting the castle.

"I have other work for thee," said Robin Hood, turning to the miller's son. "Take with thee half a score of men, and guard the stronghold. We will go meet these churls and demand their errand; you stay behind and see to Agnes and your cousin."

The miller's son did not much relish the post assigned him.

His young blood was up, and he felt eager for the fray.

George-a-Green, too, was in the cue for fighting, and he viewed with silent pleasure the prospect of engaging with the king's men, even though they mustered such a number.

Of them all Robin Hood was the most moody.

A fearful presentiment of some coming evil hung upon him, and, though his heart was as fearless and bold as ever, yet he did not walk with the firm step as was his wont.

Something seemed to whisper in his ear, "Beware of treachery."

Who was he to suspect?

His men still bore the same fearless look and he could read in the looks of each a determination to fight and conquer, or fall in his defence.

The only one amongst them who looked at all dissatisfied was Much.

He, we have explained, was vexed at having to stay behind, and not take an active part in the fight.

The cause of this was that he shared in Robin Hood's presentiment.

And there were others who viewed the coming fray with unfavourable eyes as well as Much.

They were Will Gammell and Friar Tuck, for they calculated that they would have a hard fight, and a poor chance of victory, if Geoffrey de Lois had got wind of the king's men coming, and joined his force to theirs.

But the jolly friar soon found a solace for his cares.

He strengthened his courage with sundry stoups of wine, and then clutched his quarterstaff to take his share in the fray.

It was on a rising slope in the open glade, about midway between the stronghold and the outer edge of the forest, that the two chiefs met.

"Lois de Brabant doffed his casque as he caught sight of the formidable outlaw whose doings had been so often recounted to him, but of whom he knew nothing more than by hearsay, and he at once communicated to him his mission.

"Surrender, do you say? Was that the king's word?" vociferated Robin Hood, after listening patiently to his words. "Never! Go back, and give your master this message."

Lois frowned angrily at the outlaw's reply.

"Sirrah!" said the offended noble, "I cannot brook this insult. My orders are to take you dead or alive, and I have sworn not to return until I am able to fulfil my oath."

"You have had my answer," said Robin Hood, folding his arms carelessly and gazing fixedly in the cheek of the chafing noble. "Robin Hood never answers twice—not even to the whine of his own faithful hound, much less to the bark of a foreign cur."

This answer raised the noble's anger to its highest pitch, and sent the hot blood mantling in his face ; and he would have drawn his sword and answered the insult only Robin's keen glance held him in a kind of awe.

So potent was the spell that held him that it was some moments ere he could find words to reply, and when he did, he said—

"Look ye here, proud outlaw, you have miscalculated on the strength I have at my command—four hundred picked men of the king's best Kentish bowmen ; every arrow will go true to its mark, and, what is more, four hundred swords yielded by as many stout and powerful arms at a word from me will glitter in the sunlight."

"I care not. Let them stand forth!" said Robin Hood.

Lois de Brabant, thrown off his guard, ordered his men to advance from the thicket, and at that instant a shower of shafts from the opposite trees brought one-sixth of their number to the ground.

The two chiefs had drawn aside out of line of the shafts, and were engaged hand to hand, foot to foot, with sword and buckler, where the ring of steel and showers of sparks that fell around them proclaimed how desperately they fought.

For nearly an hour they fought thus, most part of which time Robin's sword was broken, and then the gallant outlaw gave his foe a mortal wound.

Up to this moment the archers on both sides had been carrying on a kind of forest warfare, keeping each other at long range. But now a shout arose ; there was a commotion amongst the foresters, and Robin, on rushing up to ascertain the cause, discovered that his men were totally hemmed in by the sheriff, who, having been apprised of Lois arrival, hastened to his assistance with two hundred men.

Whilst the foresters were engaged De Lois carefully inserted his men between them and the outlaws' stronghold, cutting their retreat in that quarter completely off, and by harassing them in the rear, gave the Kentish archers an opportunity to close in on them on the other side.

But the brave little band, though they stuck together well, got routed from their position, and their enemies, who even now mustered three to one, backed them, inch by inch, to the borders of the forest, where Robin Hood received a blow that stretched him senseless.

Little John raised his beloved chief in his arms and fled with him ; but, being himself wearied, he had much difficulty in carrying him, though he managed to reach Kirkless Priory before he succumbed to his own weakness.

Little John craved of the superioress to take Robin in and see to his wants, which she readily consented to do ; but the giant would not have left him had he noticed the malignant smile on the features of the woman, as she ordered him to be taken to her own apartment.

Little John returned to the forest, but the strife was at an end.

The band was entirely routed, and the stronghold was in flames.

As he afterwards learned, Much had fired it, at the last moment, with his own hands, and, with a few of his men, had carried off all the treasure, and Marian and the Lady Agnes.

Having learnt this sad news, the forester returned to inquire after the health of his beloved master.

But they would not admit him to the priory ; and, having been satisfied that he was fast recovering, he sat himself down on the grass to ponder over their sad misfortune, and wait Robin Hood's recovery.

*   *   *   *   *

When Robin awoke to consciousness, he found that a vein had been opened in his arm, that the blood was flowing fast, and that he was bleeding quickly to death ; and he made an effort to stay the crimson tide, but could not, and when he essayed to reach the door, he thrice stumbled through weakness.

But when, by dint of exertion, he did reach it, he found it locked, and then a presentiment of foul play entered his mind ; and, bethinking himself of his horn, he blew three feeble blasts.

Little John heard them, however, and considering his master was in danger, he broke his way into the priory, dashed down every obstacle that stood in his way, and at last found bold Robin stretched on a couch, weak and faint, and at the point of death.

Little John was so overcome at the sight, and the story Robin told him, that he shed tears, and then implored of Robin Hood to let him be revenged by burning the priory to the ground, and taking summary justice on the prioress.

"Let me die," he said, "as I have lived, an honest and an injured man. Never yet have I raised my hand but in a just cause, and when I am dead, let there be not one stain or blot on my character for them to reproach me with."

He was now growing so weak that he could scarcely speak, and he muttered in Little John's ear a message for his loved Marian ; then asked the giant for his bow, that he might take his last shot and point out the spot where he would be laid.

The arrow fell near to St. Anne's Well, the favourite trysting place where Robin Hood and Maid Marian used to meet, and the brave outlaw smiled faintly as he noted the spot, and fell back exhausted with the effort.

Little John interred him according to his wish, and laid the bow and arrow by his side, and then, overcome with grief, and despairing of ever again seeing Maid Marian, the bold forester left that part of the country, and he was the last that was seen of the Outlaws of Sherwood Forest.

THE END.